RHYTHM
OF WAR

BY BRANDON SANDERSON

THE STORMLIGHT ARCHIVE

The Way of Kings
Words of Radiance
Edgedancer
Oathbringer
Rhythm of War

THE MISTBORN SAGA

The Final Empire
The Well of Ascension
The Hero of Ages
The Alloy of Law
Shadows of Self
The Bands of Mourning
Misborn: Secret History

LEGION

Legion
Legion: Skin Deep
Legion: Lies of the Beholder

COLLECTIONS

Legion: The Many Lives of Stephen
Leeds
Arcanum Unbounded: The Cosmere
Collection
Legion and the Emperor's Soul

ALCATRAZ VS THE EVIL LIBRARIANS

Alcatraz vs the Evil Librarians
The Scrivener's Bones
The Knights of Crystallia
The Shattered Lens
The Dark Talent

THE RECKONERS

Steelheart
Mitosis
Firefight
Calamity

SKYWARD

Skyward
Starsight

Elantris
Warbreaker
The Rithmatist
Snapshot

GRAPHIC NOVELS

White Sand
Dark One

BRANDON SANDERSON

RHYTHM OF WAR

Book Four of
THE STORMLIGHT ARCHIVE

GOLLANCZ

LONDON

First published in Great Britain in 2020 by Gollancz
an imprint of The Orion Publishing Group Ltd
Carmelite House, 50 Victoria Embankment
London EC4Y 0DZ

An Hachette UK Company

3 5 7 9 10 8 6 4

A CIP catalogue record for this book is
available from the British Library.

ISBN (Hardback) 978 0 575 09338 6
ISBN (Export Trade Paperback) 978 0 575 09339 3
ISBN (eBook) 978 0 575 09340 9

Printed in Great Britain by Clays Ltd, Elcograf S.p.A

MIX
Paper from
responsible sources
FSC® C104740

www.gollancz.co.uk

For Isaac Stewart,
Who paints my imagination.

PREFACE AND ACKNOWLEDGMENTS

I am proud to present to you *Rhythm of War*, Book Four of the Stormlight Archive. It's been ten years now since I began this series, and it has been an increasingly satisfying experience to see the story grow and fulfill the vision I've had for it all these years. In particular, one scene at the end of this book is among the very first I ever imagined for the series, over twenty years ago!

We are approaching the last book of this sequence of the Stormlight Archive. (I imagine the series as two sets of five books, with two major arcs.) Thank you for sticking with me all these years! My goal is to keep delivering these in a timely manner. And as always, deadlines for this one were tight, and a lot of people put in a lot of hours to bring it to pass. This list will be a little long, but each and every one of them deserves to be commended for their efforts.

At Tor Books, my primary editor on this novel was Devi Pillai, and she was tireless, punctual, and a wonderful advocate for the Stormlight Archive. This is my first Cosmere book that wasn't done with my longtime editor Moshe Feder, who still deserves a great deal of thanks for shepherding this series during its early years. But I want to give a special thanks to Devi for helping make this transition smooth and easy.

As always, thanks go to Tom Doherty, who gave me my first chance in publishing. Devi and Tom's team at Tor who worked on this book with us include Rachel Bass, Peter Lutjen, Rafal Gibek, and Heather Saunders.

At Gollancz, my UK publisher, I want to give special thanks to Gillian Redfearn who provides editorial support through the entire process, and who also works very hard to make the books look great.

Our copyeditor was the always-great Terry McGarry, and joining us for the first time as a line editor was Kristina Kugler. I've wanted to work with Kristina for a long time on a Cosmere book, and she did an excellent job with this one.

For the audio book, Steve Wagner was our producer. And returning to the series are the excellent Michael Kramer and Kate Reading, the best audio narrators in the world. They have my hearty thanks for continuing to humor us by taking on these fifty-plus-hour beasts of an epic fantasy series.

My primary agent for this book was JABberwocky Literary Agency, with Joshua Bilmes at the helm. Assisting him were Susan Velazquez, Karen Bourne, and Valentina Sainato. Our UK agent is John Berlyne at the Zeno Literary Agency. I continue to be grateful for their work and advocacy on my behalf.

At my own company, Dragonsteel Entertainment, we have my wonderful wife Emily Sanderson as our manager. The Ineffable Peter Ahlstrom is our vice president and editorial director, and Isaac Stewart is our Art Director. Normally I do something silly with his name, but considering that this book is dedicated to him, I figured I'd let him off this time. Isaac not only is the one who creates our beautiful maps, but is the person who introduced me to my wife. (On a blind date, no less.) So if you ever get a chance to meet him, have him sign your copy of this book, and be sure to swap stories with him about your favorite LEGO sets.

Also at Dragonsteel Entertainment are Karen Ahlstrom, our continuity editor, and Kara Stewart, our warehouse manager and CFO. Adam Horne is my in-house publicist, personal assistant, and all around "I can do that" guy who gets things done. Our other store employees include Kathleen Dorsey Sanderson, Emily "Mem" Grange, Lex Willhite, and Michael Bateman. They're the ones who get you your T-shirts, posters, and signed books. Their assistants, the "mini minions" of our team, include: Jacob, Hazel, Isabel, Matthew, Audrey, Tori, and Joe. Additionally, thanks to all those who volunteer, especially to the always awesome Christi Jacobson.

The artists who contributed to *Rhythm of War* braved not only pandemic and tragedy during the completion of the art, some even braved literal storms to deliver it. I'm in awe of their talent and commitment, and to all of them I not only give my heartfelt thanks, but I also wish them peace through the turbulent times they've faced.

One of the highlights of my career is getting to work with Michael Whelan. I'm humbled that he is so supportive of the books that he sets aside personal projects for a time to create the beautiful paintings he's done for the series. I would have been grateful for just one of his cover illustrations, so I feel incredibly lucky that he continues to work his magic for *Rhythm of War*, producing what I think is the best Stormlight cover so far. It's without a doubt a masterpiece, and I am in awe of it.

In *Oathbringer*, we printed portraits of the Heralds on the front and back U.S. endpapers, and we continue that tradition here. Early in the writing process for this book, we commissioned the remaining six Heralds, knowing that two of them would have to be saved for a future book. Each artist stepped up to the task and provided masterpieces. Donato's Herald Talenelat is careworn yet triumphant, and I'm thrilled to have his beautiful vision of this character. Miranda Meeks is no stranger to the Stormlight Archive—we love getting to work with her any chance we have—and her Herald Battah is regal and mysterious. Karla Ortiz, whose work I've been a fan of for some time, has given us glorious and nigh-on-perfect visions of Heralds Chanaranach and Nalan. Lastly, Magali Villeneuve's Heralds Pailiah and Kelek are stunning and wonderful. Howard Lyon collaborated with her to paint amazing oil versions of these last two, which will eventually be displayed with the others.

Dan dos Santos is a living legend and a good friend. He brings his signature style to the fashion plates in this volume, tackling the difficult challenge of portraying the singers as alien but also in a way that readers can identify with them emotionally. I think he's done a fantastic job walking that line.

Ben McSweeney joined the Dragonsteel team full time this year, and the book showcases some of his best art. Shallan's spren pages especially continue to help fill out the visual aesthetic of Roshar. I love how Ben's piece detailing Urithiru's atrium helps convey the immensity of the city; special thanks here to Alex Schneider, who consulted on some of the architectural layout.

A great big thanks to Kelley Harris, a core member of our Stormlight team who always brings Navani's notebook pages to life with an impeccable design sense that reminds me of Alphonse Mucha's product designs from the early twentieth century.

Additionally, many artists and others helped behind the scenes on this book and deserve a huge thank-you: Miranda Meeks, Howard Lyon, Shawn Boyles, Cori Boyles, Jacob, Isabel, Rachel, Sophie, and Hayley Lazo.

We had a few very important subject experts help us with this book. Shad "Shadiversity" Brooks was our primary historical martial arts consultant. Carl Fisk also lent us some of his expertise in this area—though if I got something wrong, it's not their fault. It's almost assuredly something I either didn't show them or time, or forgot to change.

Our expert on Dissociative Identity Disorder was Britt Martin. I truly appreciate her willing to give me raw feedback on how to get better at how I represent mental illness in these books. She was our secret Knight Radiant for this novel, always there urging me forward.

Special thanks go to four of the beta readers in particular, for their detailed feedback on a certain aspect of sexuality: Paige Phillips, Alyx Hoge, Blue, and First Last. The book is better off with your contribution.

Our writing group on this book was Kaylynn ZoBell, Kathleen Dorsey Sanderson, Eric James Stone, Darci Stone, Alan Layton, Ben "can you please just spell my name right for once, Brandon" Olzedixploxipllentivar, Ethan Skarstedt, Karen Ahlstrom, Peter Ahlstrom, Emily Sanderson, and Howard Tayler. And a better group of merry men/women you will not find. They read huge chunks of this book each week, and dealt with me making constant and enormous changes, in order to help me get the novel into shape.

Our expert team of beta readers this time included Brian T. Hill, Jessica Ashcraft, Sumejja Muratagić-Tadić, Joshua "Jofwu" Harkey, Kellyn Neumann, Jory "Jor the Bouncer" Phillips (Congrats, Jory!), Drew McCaffrey, Lauren McCaffrey, Liliana Klein, Evgeni "Argent" Kirilov, Darci Cole, Brandon Cole, Joe Deardeuff, Austin Hussey, Eliyahu Berelowitz Levin, Megan Kanne, Alyx Hoge, Trae Cooper, Deana Covel Whitney, Richard Fife, Christina Goodman, Bob Kluttz, Oren Meiron, Paige Vest, Becca Reppert, Ben Reppert, Ted Herman, Ian McNatt, Kalyani Poluri, Rahul Pantula, Gary Singer, Lingting "Botanica" Xu, Ross Newberry, David Behrens, Tim Challener, Matthew Wiens, Giulia Costantini, Alice Arneson, Paige Phillips, Ravi Persaud, Bao Pham, Aubree Pham, Adam Hussey, Nikki Ramsay, Joel D. Phillips, Zenef Mark Lindberg, Tyler Patrick, Marnie Peterson, Lyndsey Luther, Mi'chelle Walker, Josh Walker, Jayden King, Eric Lake, and Chris Kluwe.

Our special beta reader comment coordinator was Peter Orullian, an excellent author in his own right.

Our gamma readers included many of the beta readers, plus Chris McGrath, João Menezes Morais, Brian Magnant, David Fallon, Rob West, Shivam Bhatt, Todd Singer, Jessie Bell, Jeff Tucker, Jesse Salomon, Shannon Nelson, James Anderson, Frankie Jerome, Zoe Larsen, Linnea Lindstrom, Aaron Ford, Poonam Desai, Ram Shoham, Jennifer Neal, Glen Vogelaar, Taylor Cole, Heather Clinger, Donita Orders, Rachel Little, Suzanne Musin, William "aberdasher," Christopher Cottingham, Kurt Manwaring, Chris Macy, Jacob Hunsaker, Aaron Biggs, Amit Shteinheart, Kendra Wilson, Sam Baskin, and Alex Rasmussen.

I know a lot of you reading this would like to join the beta or gamma reader team—but know that it's not quite as sweet a gig as you might imagine. These folks have to read the book often under a great time crunch, and they have to experience it in an unfinished form. In a lot of ways, they're giving up the chance to experience the book in its best form, getting an inferior experience, so they can make the book better for the rest of you. I appreciate their tireless work, and their feedback. This book is much better for their efforts.

That was a huge list, I know. It gets bigger in each book! But I sincerely appreciate every one of them. As I often say, my name goes on the cover, but these novels really are a group effort, using the talents and knowledge of a great array of dedicated people.

Because of them, you can now experience *Rhythm of War*, Book Four of the Stormlight Archive. May you enjoy the journey.

CONTENTS

ILLUSTRATIONS

NOTE: *Many illustrations, titles included, contain spoilers for material that comes before them in the book. Look ahead at your own risk.*

BOOK

FOUR

⬥

RHYTHM OF WAR

Roshar

Endless Ocean

Rall Elorim

RESH

Kasitor

IRI

RIRA

Kurth

Resh

Eila

The Misted Mountains

BABATHARNAM

Panatham

MARABETH

The Purela

SHINOVAR

GULAY

Fu No

DESH

AZIR

Aimian Sea

ALM

UEZIER

Azimir

Urithiru

AIMIA

The Va

LIAFOR

Yeddaw

TASHIKK

EMUL

CRE

Steen

Sesemalex Dar

TUKAR

MARA

Icewater

N

LEEWARD

STORMWARD

S

SOUTHERN DEPTHS

STEAMWATER OCEAN

ISLES

ARAK

SUML

...Sea

NORTHGRIP

HERDAZ

MOURN'S VAULT

AKAK

u Parat

ELANAR

JAH KEVED

VARIKEV

KHOLINAR

ALETHKAR

SHULIN

UNCLAIMED HILLS

VALATH

Horneater Peaks

BAVLAND

RATHALAS

DAWN'S SHADOW

SILNASEN

VEDENAR

DUMADARI

TRIAX

KARANAK

Shattered Plains

Tarat Sea

KHARBRANTH

FROSTLANDS

NEW NATANAN

Longbrow's Straits

THAYLEN CITY

KLNA

THAYLENAH

The Shallow Crypts

OCEAN of ORIGINS

FOR HIS ROYAL MAJESTY KING GAVILAR KHOLIN, BY HIS ROYAL HIGH CARTOGRAPHER, ISASIK SHULIN 1167

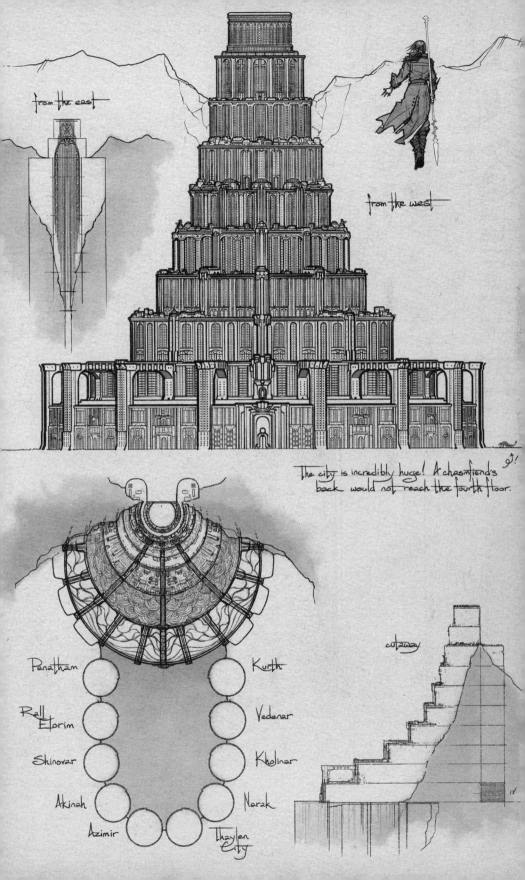

from the east

from the west

The city is incredibly huge! A chasmfiend's back would not reach the fourth floor.

cutaway

Panatham

Rall Elorim

Shinovar

Akinah

Azimir

Kurth

Vedenar

Kholinar

Narak

Thaylen City

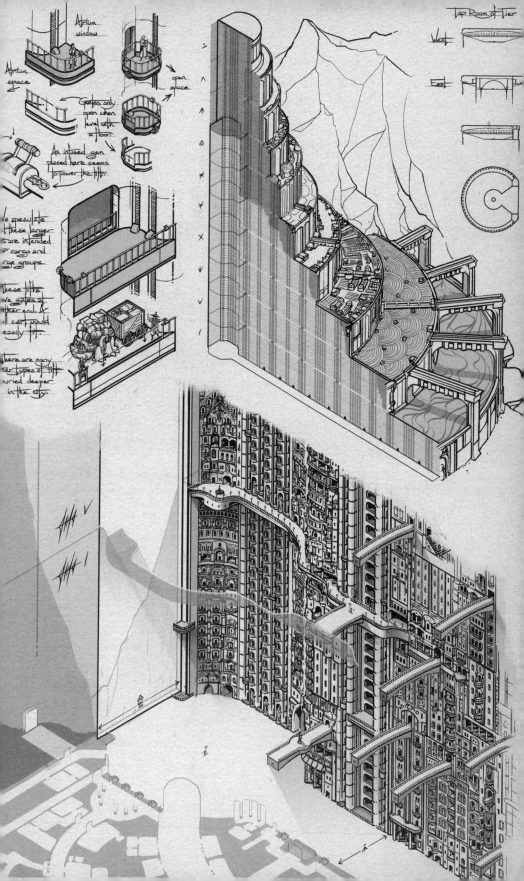

Atrium
window

Atrium
space

open
space

Gates only
open when
level of lift
= floor.

An infused gem
placed here seems
to power the lift.

We speculate
these larger
ones are intended
for cargo and
large groups.

These lifts
have gates at
their end. A
full cart would
easily fit.

There are many
other types of lift
buried deeper
in the city.

West

East

PROLOGUE

TO PRETEND

SEVEN YEARS AGO

Of course the Parshendi wanted to play their drums.

Of course Gavilar had told them they could.

And of *course* he hadn't thought to warn Navani.

"Have you seen the size of those instruments?" Maratham said, running her hands through her black hair. "Where will we put them? And we're already at capacity after your husband invited all the foreign dignitaries. We can't—"

"We'll set up a more exclusive feast in the upper ballroom," Navani said, maintaining a calm demeanor, "and put the drums there, with the king's table."

Everyone else in the kitchens was close to panicking, assistant cooks running one direction or another, pots banging, anticipationspren shooting up from the ground like streamers. Gavilar had invited not only the highprinces, but their relatives. And every highlord in the city. *And* he wanted a double-sized Beggar's Feast. And now . . . drums?

"We've already put everyone to work in the lower feast hall!" Maratham cried. "I don't have the staff to set up—"

"There are twice as many soldiers as usual loitering around the palace tonight," Navani said. "We'll have *them* help you set up." Posting extra guards, making a show of force? Gavilar could always be counted on to do *that*.

For everything else, he had Navani.

"Could work, yes," Maratham said. "Good to put the louts to work rather than having them underfoot. We have two main feasts, then? All right. Deep breaths." The short palace organizer scuttled away, narrowly avoiding an apprentice cook carrying a large bowl of steaming shellfish.

Navani stepped aside to let the cook pass. The man nodded in thanks; the staff had long since stopped being nervous when she entered the kitchens. She'd made it clear to them that doing their jobs efficiently was recognition enough.

Despite the underlying tension, they seemed to have things well in hand now—though there had been a scare earlier when they'd found worms in three barrels of grain. Thankfully, Brightlord Amaram had stores for his men, and Navani had been able to pry them out of his grip. For now, with the extra cooks they'd borrowed from the monastery, they might actually be able to feed all the people Gavilar had invited.

I'll have to give instructions on who is to be seated in which feast room, she thought, slipping out of the kitchens and into the palace gardens. *And leave some extra space in both. Who knows who else might show up with an invitation?*

She hiked up through the gardens toward the side doors of the palace. She'd be less in the way—and wouldn't have to dodge servants—if she took this path. As she walked, she scanned to make certain all the lanterns were in place. Though the sun hadn't yet set, she wanted the Kholinar palace to shine brightly tonight.

Wait. Was that Aesudan—her daughter-in-law, Elhokar's wife—standing near the fountains? She was supposed to be greeting guests inside. The slender woman wore her long hair in a bun lit by a gemstone of each shade. All those colors were gaudy together—Navani preferred a few simple stones themed to one color—but it did make Aesudan stand out as she chatted with two elderly ardents.

Storms bright and brash . . . that was *Rushur Kris,* the artist and master artifabrian. When had *he* arrived? Who had invited him? He was holding a small box with a flower painted on it. Could that be . . . one of his new fabrials?

Navani felt drawn toward the group, all other thoughts fleeing her mind. How had he made the heating fabrial, making the temperature vary? She'd seen drawings, but to talk to the master artist himself . . .

Aesudan saw Navani and smiled brightly. The joy seemed genuine, which was unusual—at least when directed at Navani. She tried not to take Aesudan's general sourness toward her as a personal affront; it was the prerogative of every woman to feel threatened by her mother-in-law. Particularly when the girl was so obviously lacking in talents.

Navani smiled at her in turn, trying to enter the conversation and get a better look at that box. Aesudan, however, took Navani by the arm.

"Mother! I had completely forgotten about our appointment. I'm so fickle sometimes. Terribly sorry, Ardent Kris, but I must make a hasty exit."

Aesudan tugged Navani—forcefully—back through the gardens toward the kitchens. "Thank *Kelek* you showed up, Mother. That man is the most dreadful bore."

"Bore?" Navani said, twisting to gaze over her shoulder. "He was talking about . . ."

"Gemstones. And other gemstones. And spren and boxes of spren, and *storms*! You'd think he would understand. I have *important* people to meet. The wives of highprinces, the best generals in the land, all come to gawk at the wild parshmen. Then I get stuck in the gardens talking to *ardents*? Your son abandoned me there, I'll have you know. When I find that man . . ."

Navani extricated herself from Aesudan's grip. "Someone should entertain those ardents. Why are they here?"

"Don't ask me," Aesudan said. "Gavilar wanted them for something, but he made Elhokar entertain them. Poor manners, that is. Honestly!"

Gavilar had invited one of the world's most prominent artifabrians to visit Kholinar, and he hadn't bothered to *tell* Navani? Emotion stirred deep inside her, a fury she kept carefully penned and locked away. That man. That *storming* man. How . . . how could he . . .

Angerspren, like boiling blood, began to well up in a small pool at her feet. *Calm, Navani,* the rational side of her mind said. *Maybe he intends to introduce the ardent to you as a gift.* She banished the anger with effort.

"Brightness!" a voice called from the kitchens. "Brightness Navani! Oh, please! We have a problem."

"Aesudan," Navani said, her eyes still on the ardent, who was now slowly walking toward the monastery. "Could you help the kitchens with whatever they need? I'd like to . . ."

But Aesudan was already hurrying off toward another group in the gardens, one attended by several powerful highlord generals. Navani took a deep breath and shoved down another stab of frustration. Aesudan claimed to care about propriety and manners, but she'd insert herself into a conversation between men without bringing her husband along as an excuse.

"Brightness!" the cook called again, waving to her.

Navani took one last look at the ardent, then set her jaw and hurried to the kitchens, careful not to catch her skirt on the ornamental shalebark. "What now?"

"Wine," the cook said. "We're out of both the Clavendah and the Ruby Bench."

"How?" she said. "We have reserves. . . ." She shared a glance with the cook, and the answer was evident. Dalinar had found their wine store again. He'd grown quite ingenious at secretly draining the barrels for himself and his friends. She wished he'd dedicate half as much attention to the kingdom's needs.

"I have a private store," Navani said, pulling her notebook from her pocket. She gripped it in her safehand through her sleeve as she scribbled a note. "I keep it in the monastery with Sister Talanah. Show her this and she'll give you access."

"Thank you, Brightness," the cook said, taking the note. Before the man was out the door, Navani spotted the house steward—a white-bearded man with too many rings on his fingers—hovering in the stairwell to the palace proper. He was fidgeting with the rings on his left hand. Bother.

"What is it?" she asked, striding over.

"Highlord Rine Hatham has arrived, and is asking about his audience with the king. You remember, His Majesty promised to talk with Rine tonight about—"

"About the border dispute and the misdrawn maps, yes," Navani said, sighing. "And where is my husband?"

"Unclear, Brightness," the steward said. "He was last seen with Brightlord Amaram and some of those . . . uncommon figures."

That was the term the palace staff used for Gavilar's new friends, the ones who seemed to arrive without warning or announcement, and who rarely gave their names.

Navani ground her teeth, thinking through the places Gavilar might have gone. He would be angry if she interrupted him. Well, good. He should be seeing to his guests, rather than assuming she'd handle everything and everyone.

Unfortunately, at the moment she . . . well, she would have to handle everything and everyone.

She let the anxious steward lead her up to the grand entryway, where guests were being entertained with music, drink, and poetry while the feast was prepared. Others were escorted by master-servants to view the Parshendi, the night's true novelty. It wasn't every day the king of Alethkar signed a treaty with a group of mysterious parshmen who could talk.

She extended her apologies to Highlord Rine for Gavilar's absence, offering to review the maps herself. After that, she was stopped by a line of impatient men and women brought to the palace by the promise of an audience with the king.

Navani assured the lighteyes their concerns were being heard. She promised to look into injustices. She soothed the crumpled feelings of those who thought a personal invitation from the king meant they'd actually get to *see* him—a rare privilege these days, unless you were one of the "uncommon figures."

Guests were still showing up, of course. Ones who weren't on the updated list an annoyed Gavilar had provided for her earlier that day.

Vev's golden keys! Navani forcibly painted on an amicable face for the guests. She smiled, she laughed, she waved. Using the reminders and lists she kept in her notebook, she asked after families, new births, and favorite axehounds. She inquired about trade situations, took notes on which lighteyes seemed to be avoiding others. In short, she acted like a queen.

It was emotionally taxing work, but it was her duty. Perhaps someday she'd be able to spend her days tinkering with fabrials and pretending she was a scholar. Today, she'd do her job—though a part of her felt like an impostor. However prestigious her ancient lineage might be, her anxiety whispered that she was really just a backwater country girl wearing someone else's clothing.

Those insecurities had grown stronger lately. *Calm. Calm.* There was no room for that sort of thinking. She rounded the room, pleased to note that Aesudan had found Elhokar and was chatting with him for once—rather than other men. Elhokar did look happy presiding over the pre-feast in his father's absence. Adolin and Renarin were there in stiff uniforms— the former delighting a small group of young women, the latter appearing gangly and awkward as he stood by his brother.

And . . . there was Dalinar. Standing tall. Somehow taller than any man in the room. He wasn't drunk yet, and people orbited him like they might a fire on a cold night—needing to be close, but fearing the true heat of his presence. Those haunted eyes of his, simmering with passion.

Storms alight. She excused herself and made a brief exit up the steps to where she wouldn't feel so warm. It was a bad idea to leave; they were lacking a king, and questions were bound to arise if the queen vanished too. Yet surely everyone could get on without her for a short time. Besides, up here she could check one of Gavilar's hiding places.

She wound her way through the dungeonlike hallways, passing Parshendi carrying drums nearby, speaking a language she did not understand. Why couldn't this place have a little more natural light up here, a few more windows? She'd brought the matter up with Gavilar, but he liked it this way. It gave him more places to hide.

There, she thought, stopping at an intersection. *Voices.*

". . . Being able to bring them back and forth from Braize doesn't mean anything," one said. "It's too close to be a relevant distance."

"It was impossible only a few short years ago," said a deep, powerful voice. Gavilar. "This *is* proof. The Connection is not severed, and the box allows for travel. Not yet as far as you'd like, but we must start the journey somewhere."

Navani peered around the corner. She could see a door at the end of the short hallway ahead, cracked open, letting the voices leak out. Yes, Gavilar was having a meeting right where she'd expected: in *her* study. It was a cozy little room with a nice window, tucked away in the corner of the second floor. A place she rarely had time to visit, but where people were unlikely to search for Gavilar.

She inched up to peek in through the cracked door. Gavilar Kholin had a presence big enough to fill a room all by himself. He wore a beard, but instead of being unfashionable on him, it was . . . classic. Like a painting come to life, a representation of old Alethkar. Some had thought he might start a trend, but few were able to pull off the look.

Beyond that, there was an air of . . . distortion around Gavilar. Nothing supernatural or nonsensical. It was just that . . . well, you accepted that Gavilar could do whatever he wanted, in defiance of any tradition or logic. For him, it would work out. It always did.

The king was speaking with two men that Navani vaguely recognized. A tall Makabaki man with a birthmark on his cheek and a shorter Vorin man with a round face and a small nose. They'd been called ambassadors from the West, but no kingdom had been given for their home.

The Makabaki one leaned against the bookcase, his arms folded, his face completely expressionless. The Vorin man wrung his hands, reminding Navani of the palace steward, though this man seemed much younger. Somewhere . . . in his twenties? Maybe his thirties? No, he could be older.

On the table between Gavilar and the men lay a group of spheres and gemstones. Navani's breath caught as she saw them. They were arrayed in a variety of colors and brightness, but several seemed strangely off. They glowed with an inverse of light, as if they were little pits of violet darkness, sucking in the color around them.

She'd never seen anything like them before, but gemstones with spren trapped inside could have all kinds of odd appearances and effects. Those . . . they must be meant for fabrials. What was Gavilar doing with spheres, strange light, and distinguished artifabrians? And why wouldn't he talk to her about—

Gavilar suddenly stood up straight and glanced toward the doorway, though Navani hadn't made any sound. Their eyes met. So she pushed open the door as if she had been on her way in. She wasn't spying; she was queen of this palace. She could go where she wished, *particularly* her own study.

"Husband," she said. "There are guests missing you at the gathering. You seem to have lost track of time."

"Gentlemen," Gavilar said to the two ambassadors, "I will need to excuse myself."

The nervous Vorin man ran his hand through his wispy hair. "I want to know more of the project, Gavilar. Plus, you need to know that another of us is here tonight. I spotted her handiwork earlier."

"I have a meeting shortly with Meridas and the others," Gavilar said. "They should have more information for me. We can speak again after that."

"No," the Makabaki man said, his voice sharp. "I doubt we shall."

"There's more here, Nale!" the Vorin man said, though he followed as his friend left. "This is important! I want out. This is the only way. . . ."

"What was that about?" Navani asked as Gavilar closed the door. "Those are no ambassadors. Who are they really?"

Gavilar did not answer. With deliberate motions, he began plucking the spheres off the table and placing them into a pouch.

Navani darted forward and snatched one. "What are these? How did you get spheres that glow like this? Does this have to do with the artifabrians you've invited here?" She looked to him, waiting for some kind of answer, some explanation.

Instead, he held out his hand for her sphere. "This does not concern you, Navani. Return to the feast."

She closed her hand around the sphere. "So I can continue to cover for you? Did you promise Highlord Rine you'd mediate his dispute *tonight* of all times? Do you know how many people are expecting you? And did you say you have *another* meeting to go to now, before the feast begins? Are you simply going to ignore our guests?"

"Do you know," he said softly, "how *tired* I grow of your constant questions, woman?"

"Perhaps try answering one or two, then. It'd be a novel experience, treating your wife like a human being—rather than like a machine built to count the days of the week for you."

He wagged his hand, demanding the sphere.

Instinctively she gripped it tighter. "Why? *Why* do you continue to shut me out? Please, just tell me."

"I deal in secrets you could not handle, Navani. If you knew the scope of what I've begun . . ."

She frowned. The scope of what? He'd already conquered Alethkar. He'd united the highprinces. Was this about how he had turned his eyes toward the Unclaimed Hills? Surely settling a patch of wildlands—populated by nothing more than the odd tribe of parshmen—was nothing compared to what he'd already accomplished.

He took her hand, forced apart her fingers, and removed the sphere. She didn't fight him; he would not react well. He had never used his strength against her, not in that way, but there had been words. Comments. Threats.

He took the strange transfixing sphere and stashed it in the pouch with the others. He pulled the pouch tight with a taut snap of finality, then tucked it into his pocket.

"You're punishing me, aren't you?" Navani demanded. "You know my love of fabrials. You taunt me *specifically* because you know it will hurt."

"Perhaps," Gavilar said, "you will learn to consider before you speak, Navani. Perhaps you will learn the dangerous price of rumors."

This again? she thought. "*Nothing* happened, Gavilar."

"Do you think I care?" Gavilar said. "Do you think the court cares? To them, lies are as good as facts."

That was true, she realized. Gavilar *didn't* care if she'd been unfaithful to him—and she hadn't. But the things she'd said had started rumors, difficult to smother.

All Gavilar cared about was his legacy. He wanted to be known as a great king, a great leader. That drive had always pushed him, but it was growing into something else lately. He kept asking: Would he be remembered as Alethkar's greatest king? Could he compete with his ancestors, men such as the Sunmaker?

If a king's court thought he couldn't control his own wife, wouldn't that stain his legacy? What good was a kingdom if Gavilar knew that his wife secretly loved his brother? In this, Navani represented a chip in the marble of his all-important legacy.

"Speak to your daughter," Gavilar said, turning toward the door. "I believe I have managed to soothe Amaram's pride. He might take her back, and her time is running out. Few other suitors will consider her; I'll likely need to pay half the kingdom to get rid of the girl if she denies Meridas again."

Navani sniffed. "*You* speak to her. If what you want is so important, maybe you could do it *yourself* for once. Besides, I don't care for Amaram. Jasnah can do better."

He froze, then looked back and spoke in a low, quiet voice. "Jasnah *will* marry Amaram, as I have instructed her. She will put aside this fancy of becoming famous by denying the church. Her arrogance stains the reputation of the entire family."

Navani stepped forward and let her voice grow as cold as his. "You realize that girl still loves you, Gavilar. They all do. Elhokar, Dalinar, the boys . . . they *worship* you. Are you sure you want to reveal to them what you truly are? *They* are your legacy. Treat them with care. They will define how you are remembered."

"Greatness will define me, Navani. No mediocre effort by someone like

Dalinar or my son could undermine that—and I personally doubt Elhokar could rise to even mediocre."

"And what about me?" she said. "I could write your history. Your life. Whatever you think you've done, whatever you think you've accomplished . . . that's ephemeral, Gavilar. *Words on the page* define men to future generations. You spurn me, but I have a grip on what you cherish most. Push me too far, and I *will* start squeezing."

He didn't respond with shouts or rage, but the cold void in his eyes could have consumed kingdoms and left only blackness. He raised his hand to her chin and gently cupped it, a mockery of a once-passionate gesture.

It was more painful than a slap.

"You know why I don't involve you, Navani?" he said softly. "Do you think you can take the truth?"

"Try for once. It would be refreshing."

"You aren't worthy, Navani. You claim to be a scholar, but where are your discoveries? You study light, but you are its opposite. A thing that destroys light. You spend your time wallowing in the muck of the kitchens and obsessing about whether or not some insignificant lighteyes recognizes the right lines on a map.

"These are not the actions of greatness. You are no scholar. You merely like being near them. You are no artifabrian. You are merely a woman who likes trinkets. You have no fame, accomplishment, or capacity of your own. Everything distinctive about you came from someone else. You have no power—you merely like to marry men who have it."

"How dare you—"

"Deny it, Navani," he snapped. "*Deny* that you loved one brother, but married the other. You pretended to adore a man you detested—all because you knew he would be king."

She recoiled from him, pulling out of his grip and turning her head to the side. She closed her eyes and felt tears on her cheeks. It was more complicated than he implied, as she had loved both of them—and Dalinar's intensity had frightened her, so Gavilar had seemed the safer choice.

But there was a truth to Gavilar's accusation. She could lie to herself and say she'd seriously considered Dalinar, but they'd all known she'd eventually choose Gavilar. And she had. He was the more influential of the two.

"You went where the money and power would be greatest," Gavilar said. "Like any common whore. Write whatever you want about me. Say it, shout it, proclaim it. I will outlive your accusations, and my legacy *will* persist. I have discovered the entrance to the realm of gods and legends, and once I join them, my kingdom will never end. *I* will never end."

He left then, closing the door behind him with a quiet click. Even in an argument he controlled the situation.

Trembling, Navani fumbled her way to a seat by the desk, which boiled over with angerspren. And shamespren, which fluttered around her like white and red petals.

Fury made her shake. Fury at him. At herself for not fighting back. At the world, because she knew what he said was at least partially true.

No. Don't let his lies become your truth. Fight it. Teeth gritted, she opened her eyes and began rummaging in her desk for some oil paint and paper.

She began painting, taking care with each calligraphic line. Pride—as if proof to him—compelled her to be meticulous and perfect. The act usually soothed her. The way that neat, orderly lines became words, the way that paint and paper transformed into meaning.

In the end, she had one of the finest glyphwards she'd ever created. It read, simply, *Death. Gift. Death.* She'd drawn each glyph in the shapes of Gavilar's tower or sword heraldry.

The prayer burned eagerly in the lamp flame, flaring bright—and as it did, her catharsis turned to shame. What was she doing? Praying for her husband's death? The shamespren returned in a burst.

How had it come to this? Their arguments grew worse and worse. She *knew* he was not this man, the one he showed her lately. He wasn't like this when he spoke to Dalinar, or to Sadeas, or even—usually—to Jasnah.

Gavilar was better than this. She suspected he knew it too. Tomorrow she would receive flowers. No apology to accompany them, but a gift, usually a bracelet.

Yes, he knew he should be something more. But . . . somehow she brought out the monster in him. And he somehow brought out the weakness in her. She slammed her safehand palm against the table, rubbing her forehead with her other hand.

Storms. It seemed not so long ago that they'd sat conspiring together about the kingdom they would forge. Now they barely spoke without reaching for their sharpest knives—stabbing them right into the most painful spots with an accuracy gained only through longtime familiarity.

She composed herself with effort, redoing her makeup, touching up her hair. She might be the things he said, but *he* was no more than a backwater thug with too much luck and a knack for fooling good men into following him.

If a man like that could pretend to be a king, she could pretend to be a queen. At any rate, they had a kingdom.

At least one of them should try to run it.

⋅⋅⋅

Navani didn't hear of the assassination until it had been accomplished.

At the feast, they'd been the model of perfect royalty, cordial to one another, leading their respective meals. Then Gavilar had left, fleeing as soon as he could find an excuse. At least he'd waited until the dining was finished.

Navani had gone down to bid farewell to the guests. She had implied that Gavilar wasn't *deliberately* snubbing anyone. He was merely exhausted from his extensive touring. Yes, she was certain he'd be holding audience soon. They'd love to visit once the next storm passed. . . .

On and on she went, until each smile made her face feel as if it would crack. She was relieved when a messenger girl came running for her. She stepped away from the departing guests, expecting to hear that an expensive vase had shattered, or that Dalinar was snoring at his table.

Instead, the messenger girl brought Navani over to the palace steward, his face a mask of grief. Eyes reddened, hands shaking, the aged man reached out for her and took her arm—as if for stability. Tears ran down his face, getting caught in his wispy beard.

Seeing his emotion, she realized she rarely thought of the man by his name, rarely thought of him as a person. She'd often treated him like a fixture of the palace, much as one might the statues out front. Much as Gavilar treated her.

"Gereh," she said, taking his hand, embarrassed. "What happened? Are you well? Have we been working you too hard without—"

"The king," the elderly man choked out. "Oh, Brightness, they've taken our king! Those parshmen. Those *barbarians*. Those . . . those *monsters*."

Her immediate suspicion was that Gavilar had found some way to escape the palace, and everyone thought he'd been kidnapped. *That man . . .* she thought, imagining him out in the city with his uncommon visitors, discussing secrets in a dark room.

Gereh held to her tighter. "Brightness, they've *killed* him. King Gavilar is dead."

"Impossible," she said. "He's the most powerful man in the land, perhaps the world. Surrounded by Shardbearers. You are mistaken, Gereh. He's . . ."

He's as enduring as the storms. But of course that wasn't true—it was merely what he wished people to think. *I will never end. . . .* When he said things like that, it was hard to disbelieve him.

She had to see the body before the truth started to seep in at last, chilling her like a winter rain. Gavilar, broken and bloody, lay on a table in the larder—with guards forcibly turning aside the frightened house staff when they asked for explanations.

Navani stood over him. Even with the blood in his beard, the shattered Shardplate, his lack of breath and the gaping wounds in his flesh . . . even then she wondered if it was a trick. What lay before her was an impossibility. Gavilar Kholin couldn't simply *die* like other men.

She had them show her the fallen balcony, where Gavilar had been found lifeless after dropping from above. Jasnah had witnessed it, they said. The normally unflappable girl sat in the corner, her fisted safehand to her mouth as she cried.

Only then did the shockspren begin to appear around Navani, like triangles of breaking light. Only then did she believe.

Gavilar Kholin was dead.

Sadeas pulled Navani aside and, with genuine sorrow, explained his role in the events. She listened in a numb sense of disconnect. She had been so busy, she hadn't realized that most of the Parshendi had left the palace in secret—fleeing into the darkness moments before their minion attacked. Their leaders had stayed behind to cover up the withdrawal.

In a trance, Navani walked back to the larder and the cold husk of Gavilar Kholin. His discarded shell. From the looks of the attending servants and surgeons, they anticipated grief from her. Wailing perhaps. Certainly there were painspren appearing in droves in the room, even a few rare anguishspren, like teeth growing from the walls.

She felt something *akin* to those emotions. Sorrow? No, not exactly. Regret. If he truly was dead, then . . . that was it. Their last real conversation had been another argument. There was no going back. Always before, she'd been able to tell herself that they'd reconcile. That they'd hunt through the thorns and find a path to return to what they'd been. If not loving, then at least aligned.

Now that would never be. It was over. He was dead, she was a widow, and . . . storms, she'd *prayed* for this. That knowledge stabbed her straight through. She had to hope the Almighty hadn't listened to her foolish pleas written in a moment of fury. Although a part of her had grown to hate Gavilar, she didn't truly want him dead. Did she?

No. No, this was not how it should have ended. And so she felt another emotion. Pity.

Lying there, blood pooling on the tabletop around him, Gavilar Kholin's corpse seemed the ultimate insult to his grand plans. He thought he was eternal, did he? He thought to reach for some grand vision, too important to share with her? Well, the Father of Storms and the Mother of the World ignored the desires of men, no matter how grand.

What she *didn't* feel was grief. His death was meaningful, but it didn't mean anything to *her*. Other than perhaps a way for her children to never have to learn what he'd become.

I will be the better person, Gavilar, she thought, closing his eyes. *For what you once were, I'll let the world pretend. I'll give you your legacy.*

Then she paused. His Shardplate—well, the Plate he was wearing—had broken near the waist. She reached her fingers into his pocket and brushed hogshide leather. She eased out the pouch of spheres he'd been showing off earlier, but found it empty.

Storms. Where had he put them?

Someone in the room coughed, and she became suddenly cognizant of how it looked for her to be rifling through his pockets. Navani took the spheres from her hair, put them into the pouch, then folded it into his hand before resting her forehead on his broken chest. That would appear as if she were returning gifts to him, symbolizing her light becoming his as he died.

Then, with his blood on her face, she stood up and made a show of composing herself. Over the next hours, organizing the chaos of a city turned upside down, she worried she'd get a reputation for callousness. Instead, people seemed to find her sturdiness comforting.

The king was gone, but the kingdom lived on. Gavilar had left this life as he'd lived it: with grand drama that afterward required Navani to pick up the pieces.

PART
ONE

Burdens

KALADIN • SHALLAN • NAVANI •
VENLI • LIRIN

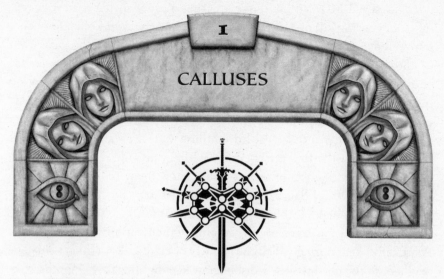

I

CALLUSES

First, you must get a spren to approach.

The type of gemstone is relevant; some spren are naturally more intrigued by certain gemstones. In addition, it is essential to calm the spren with something it knows and loves. A good fire for a flamespren, for example, is a must.

—Lecture on fabrial mechanics presented by Navani Kholin to the coalition of monarchs, Urithiru, Jesevan, 1175

Lirin was impressed at how calm he felt as he checked the child's gums for scurvy. Years of training as a surgeon served him well today. Breathing exercises—intended to keep his hands steady—worked as well during espionage as they did during surgery.

"Here," he said to the child's mother, digging a small carved carapace chit from his pocket. "Show this to the woman at the dining pavilion. She'll get some juice for your son. Make certain he drinks it all, each morning."

"Very thank you," the woman said in a thick Herdazian accent. She gathered her son close, then looked to Lirin with haunted eyes. "If . . . if child . . . found . . ."

"I will make certain you're notified if we hear of your other children," Lirin promised. "I'm sorry for your loss."

She nodded, wiped her cheeks, and carried the child to the watchpost outside of town. Here, a group of armed parshmen lifted her hood and compared her face to drawings sent by the Fused. Hesina, Lirin's wife, stood nearby to read the descriptions as required.

Behind them, the morning fog obscured Hearthstone. It seemed to be a group of dark, shadowy lumps. Like tumors. Lirin could barely make out tarps stretched between buildings, offering meager shelter for the many refugees pouring out of Herdaz. Entire streets were closed off, and phantom sounds—plates clinking, people talking—rose through the fog.

Those shanties would never last a storm, of course, but they could be quickly torn down and stowed. There simply wasn't enough housing otherwise. People could pack into stormshelters for a few hours, but couldn't live like that.

He turned and glanced at the line of those waiting for admittance today. It vanished into the fog, attended by swirling insectile hungerspren and exhaustionspren like jets of dust. Storms. How many more people could the town hold? The villages closer to the border must be filled to capacity, if so many were making their way this far inward.

It had been over a year since the coming of the Everstorm and the fall of Alethkar. A year during which the country of Herdaz—Alethkar's smaller neighbor to the northwest—had somehow kept fighting. Two months ago, the enemy had finally decided to crush the kingdom for good. Refugee numbers had increased soon after. As usual, the soldiers fought while the common people—their fields trampled—starved and were forced out of their homes.

Hearthstone did what it could. Aric and the other men—once guards at Roshone's manor, now forbidden weapons—organized the line and kept anyone from sneaking into town before Lirin saw them. He had persuaded Brightness Abiajan that it was essential he inspect each individual. She worried about plague; he just wanted to intercept those who might need treatment.

Her soldiers moved down the line, alert. Parshmen carrying swords. Learning to read, insisting they be called "singers." A year after their awakening, Lirin still found the notions odd. But really, what was it to him? In some ways, little had changed. The same old conflicts consumed the parshmen as easily as they had the Alethi brightlords. People who got a taste of power wanted more, then sought it with the sword. Ordinary people bled, and Lirin was left to stitch them up.

He returned to his work. Lirin had at least a hundred more refugees to see today. Hiding somewhere among them was a man who had authored much of this suffering. He was the reason Lirin was so nervous today. The next person in line was not him, however, but was instead a ragged Alethi man who had lost an arm in battle. Lirin inspected the refugee's wound, but it was a few months old at this point, and there was nothing Lirin could do about the extensive scarring.

Lirin moved his finger back and forth before the man's face, watching his eyes track it. *Shock*, Lirin thought. "Have you suffered recent wounds you're not telling me about?"

"No wounds," the man whispered. "But brigands . . . they took my wife, good surgeon. Took her . . . left me tied to a tree. Just walked off laughing . . ."

Bother. Mental shock wasn't something Lirin could cut out with a scalpel. "Once you enter the town," he said, "look for tent fourteen. Tell the women there I sent you."

The man nodded dully, his stare hollow. Had he registered the words? Memorizing the man's features—greying hair with a cowlick in the back, three large moles on the upper left cheek, and of course the missing arm— Lirin made a note to check that tent for him tonight. Assistants there watched refugees who might turn suicidal. It was, with so many to care for, the best Lirin could manage.

"On with you," Lirin said, gently pushing the man toward the town. "Tent fourteen. Don't forget. I'm sorry for your loss."

The man walked off.

"You say it so easily, surgeon," a voice said from behind.

Lirin spun, then immediately bowed in respect. Abiajan, the new citylady, was a parshwoman with stark white skin and fine red marbling on her cheeks.

"Brightness," Lirin said. "What was that?"

"You told that man you were sorry for his loss," Abiajan said. "You say it so readily to each of them—but you seem to have the compassion of a stone. Do you feel nothing for these people?"

"I feel, Brightness," Lirin said, "but I must be careful not to be over-whelmed by their pain. It's one of the first rules of becoming a surgeon."

"Curious." The parshwoman raised her safehand, which was shrouded in the sleeve of a havah. "Do you remember setting my arm when I was a child?"

"I do." Abiajan had returned—with a new name and a new commission from the Fused—after fleeing with the others following the Everstorm. She had brought many parshmen with her, all from this region, but of those from Hearthstone only Abiajan had returned. She remained closed-lipped about what she had experienced in the intervening months.

"Such a curious memory," she said. "That life feels like a dream now. I remember pain. Confusion. A stern figure bringing me more pain— though I now recognize you were seeking to heal me. So much trouble to go through for a slave child."

"I have never cared who I heal, Brightness. Slave or king."

"I'm sure the fact that Wistiow had paid good money for me had noth-ing to do with it." She narrowed her eyes at Lirin, and when she next spoke there was a cadence to her words, as if she were speaking the words to a song. "Did you feel for me, the poor confused slave child whose mind had been stolen from her? Did you weep for us, surgeon, and the life we led?"

"A surgeon must not weep," Lirin said softly. "A surgeon cannot *afford* to weep."

"Like a stone," she said again, then shook her head. "Have you seen any plaguespren on these refugees? If those spren get into the city, it could kill everyone."

"Disease isn't caused by spren," Lirin said. "It is spread by contaminated water, improper sanitation, or sometimes by the breath of those who bear it."

"Superstition," she said.

"The wisdom of the Heralds," Lirin replied. "We should be careful." Fragments of old manuscripts—translations of translations of translations— mentioned quick-spreading diseases that had killed tens of thousands. Such things hadn't been recorded in any modern texts he'd been read, but he *had* heard rumors of something strange to the west—a new plague, they were calling it. Details were sparse.

Abiajan moved on without further comment. Her attendants—a group of elevated parshmen and parshwomen—joined her. Though their clothing was of Alethi cut and fashion, the colors were lighter, more muted. The Fused had explained that singers in the past eschewed bright colors, pre- ferring to highlight their skin patterns instead.

Lirin sensed a search for identity in the way Abiajan and the other parsh- men acted. Their accents, their dress, their mannerisms—they were all distinctly Alethi. But they grew transfixed whenever the Fused spoke of their ancestors, and they sought ways to emulate those long-dead parshmen.

Lirin turned to the next group of refugees—a complete family for once. Though he should have been happy, he couldn't help wondering how dif- ficult it was going to be to feed five children and parents who were all flagging from poor nutrition.

As he sent them on, a familiar figure moved along the line toward him, shooing away hungerspren. Laral wore a simple servant's dress now, with a gloved hand instead of a sleeve, and she carried a water bucket to the waiting refugees. Laral didn't walk like a servant though. There was a cer- tain . . . determination about the young woman that no forced subservi- ence could smother. The end of the world seemed roughly as bothersome to her as a poor harvest once had.

She paused by Lirin and offered him a drink—taken from her waterskin and poured into a fresh cup as he insisted, rather than ladled straight from the bucket.

"He's three down," Laral whispered as Lirin sipped.

Lirin grunted.

"Shorter than I expected him to be," Laral noted. "He's supposed to be a great general, leader of the Herdazian resistance. He looks more like a
traveling merchant."

"Genius comes in all shapes, Laral," Lirin said, waving for her to refill his cup to give an excuse for them to keep talking.

"Still . . ." she said, then fell silent as Durnash passed by, a tall parshman with marbled black and red skin, a sword on his back. Once he was well on his way, she continued softly, "I'm honestly surprised at you, Lirin. Not once have you suggested we turn in this hidden general."

"He'd be executed," Lirin said.

"You think of him as a criminal though, don't you?"

"He bears a terrible responsibility; he perpetuated a war against an overwhelming enemy force. He threw away the lives of his men in a hopeless battle."

"Some would call that heroism."

"Heroism is a myth you tell idealistic young people—specifically when you want them to go bleed for you. It got one of my sons killed and another taken from me. You can keep your heroism and return to me the lives of those wasted on foolish conflicts."

At least it seemed to almost be over. Now that the resistance in Herdaz had finally collapsed, hopefully the refugee flood would slow.

Laral watched him with pale green eyes. She was a keen one. How he wished life had gone in another direction, that old Wistiow had held on a few more years. Lirin might call this woman daughter, and might have both Tien and Kaladin beside him now, working as surgeons.

"I won't turn in the Herdazian general," Lirin said. "Stop looking at me like that. I hate war, but I won't condemn your hero."

"And your son will come fetch him soon?"

"We've sent Kal word. That should be enough. Make sure your husband is ready with his distraction."

She nodded and moved on to offer water to the parshman guards at the town entrance. Lirin got through the next few refugees quickly, then reached a group of cloaked figures. He calmed himself with the quick breathing exercise his master had taught him in the surgery room all those years ago. Although his insides were a storm, Lirin's hands didn't shake as he waved forward the cloaked figures.

"I will need to do an examination," Lirin said softly, "so it doesn't seem unusual when I pull you out of the line."

"Begin with me," said the shortest of the men. The other four shifted their positions, placing themselves carefully around him.

"Don't look so much like you're guarding him, you sodden fools," Lirin hissed. "Here, sit down on the ground. Maybe you'll seem less like a gang of thugs that way."

They did as requested, and Lirin pulled over his stool beside the apparent leader. He bore a thin, silvered mustache on his upper lip, and was perhaps in his fifties. His sun-leathered skin was darker than most Herdaz-ians'; he could almost have passed for Azish. His eyes were a deep dark brown.

"You're him?" Lirin whispered as he put his ear to the man's chest to check his heartbeat.

"I am," the man said.

Dieno enne Calah. Dieno "the Mink" in Old Herdazian. Hesina had explained that *enne* was an honorific that implied greatness.

One might have expected the Mink—as Laral apparently had—to be a brutal warrior forged on the same anvil as men like Dalinar Kholin or Meridas Amaram. Lirin, however, knew that killers came in all kinds of packages. The Mink might be short and missing a tooth, but there was a power to his lean build, and Lirin spotted not a few scars in his examina-tion. Those around the wrists, in fact . . . those were the scars manacles made on the skin of slaves.

"Thank you," Dieno whispered, "for offering us refuge."

"It wasn't my choice," Lirin said.

"Still, you ensure that the resistance will escape to live on. Heralds bless you, surgeon."

Lirin dug out a bandage, then began wrapping a wound on the man's arm that hadn't been seen to properly. "The Heralds bless us with a quick end to this conflict."

"Yes, with the invaders sent running all the way back to Damnation from which they were spawned."

Lirin continued his work.

"You . . . disagree, surgeon?"

"Your resistance has failed, General," Lirin said, pulling the bandage tight. "Your kingdom has fallen like my own. Further conflict will only leave more men dead."

"Surely you don't intend to obey these monsters."

"I obey the person who holds the sword to my neck, General," Lirin said. "Same as I always have."

He finished his work, then gave the general's four companions cursory examinations. No women. How would the general read messages sent to him?

Lirin made a show of discovering a wound on one man's leg, and—with a little coaching—the man limped on it properly, then let out a painful howl. A poke of a needle made painspren claw up from the ground, shaped like little orange hands.

"That will need surgery," Lirin said loudly. "Or you might lose the leg. No, no complaints. We're going to see to that right away."

He had Aric fetch a litter. Positioning the other four soldiers—the general included—as bearers for that litter gave Lirin an excuse to pull them all out of line.

Now they just needed the distraction. It came in the form of Toralin Roshone: Laral's husband, former citylord. He stumbled out of the fog-shrouded town, wobbling and walking unsteadily.

Lirin waved to the Mink and his soldiers, slowly leading them toward the inspection post. "You aren't armed, are you?" he hissed under his breath.

"We left obvious weapons behind," the Mink replied, "but it will be my face—and not our arms—that betrays us."

"We've prepared for that." *Pray to the Almighty it works.*

As Lirin drew near, he could better make out Roshone. The former citylord's cheeks hung in deflated jowls, still reflecting the weight he'd lost following his son's death seven years ago. Roshone had been ordered to shave his beard, perhaps because he'd been fond of it, and he no longer wore his proud warrior's takama. That had been replaced by the kneepads and short trousers of a crem scraper.

He carried a stool under one arm and muttered in a slurred voice, his wooden peg of a foot scraping stone as he walked. Lirin honestly couldn't tell if Roshone had gotten drunk for the display, or if he was faking. The man drew attention either way. The parshmen manning the inspection post nudged one another, and one hummed to an upbeat rhythm—something they often did when amused.

Roshone picked a building nearby and set down his stool, then—to the delight of the watching parshmen—tried stepping up on it, but missed and stumbled, teetering on his peg, nearly falling.

They loved watching him. Every one of these newly born singers had been owned by one wealthy lighteyes or another. Watching a former citylord reduced to a stumbling drunk who spent his days doing the most menial of jobs? To them it was more captivating than any storyteller's performance.

Lirin stepped up to the guard post. "This one needs immediate surgery," he said, gesturing to the man in the litter. "If I don't get to him now, he might lose a limb. My wife will have the rest of the refugees sit and wait for my return."

Of the three parshmen assigned as inspectors, only Dor bothered to check the "wounded" man's face against the drawings. The Mink was top of the list of dangerous refugees, but Dor didn't spare a glance for the litter bearers. Lirin had noticed the oddity a few days earlier: when he used refugees from the line as labor, the inspectors often fixated solely on the person in the litter.

He'd hoped that with Roshone to provide entertainment, the parshmen would be even more lax. Still, Lirin felt himself sweating as Dor hesitated on one of the pictures. Lirin's letter—returned with the scout who had arrived begging for asylum—had warned the Mink to bring only low-level guards who wouldn't be on the lists. Could it—

The other two parshmen laughed at Roshone, who was trying—despite his drunkenness—to reach the roof of the building and scrape away the crem buildup there. Dor turned and joined them, absently waving Lirin forward.

Lirin shared a brief glance with his wife, who waited nearby. It was a good thing none of the parshmen were facing her, because she was pale as a Shin woman. Lirin probably didn't look much better, but he held in his sigh of relief as he led the Mink and his soldiers forward. He could sequester them in the surgery room, away from the public eye until—

"Everyone stop what you're doing!" a female voice shouted from behind. "Prepare to give deference!"

Lirin felt an immediate urge to bolt. He almost did, but the soldiers simply kept walking at a regular pace. Yes. Pretend that you hadn't heard.

"You, surgeon!" the voice shouted at him. It was Abiajan. Reluctantly Lirin halted, excuses running through his mind. Would she believe he hadn't recognized the Mink? Lirin was already in rough winds with the citylady after insisting on treating Jeber's wounds after the fool had gotten himself strung up and whipped.

Lirin turned around, trying hard to calm his nerves. Abiajan hurried up, and although singers didn't blush, she was clearly flustered. When she spoke, her words had adopted a staccato cadence. "Attend me. We have a visitor."

It took Lirin a moment to process the words. She wasn't demanding an explanation. This was about . . . something else?

"What's wrong, Brightness?" he asked.

Nearby, the Mink and his soldiers stopped, but Lirin could see their arms shifting beneath their cloaks. They'd said they'd left behind "obvious" weapons. Almighty help him, if this turned bloody . . .

"Nothing's wrong," Abiajan said, speaking quickly. "We've been blessed. *Attend me.*" She looked to Dor and the inspectors. "Pass the word. Nobody is to enter or leave the town until I give word otherwise."

"Brightness," Lirin said, gesturing toward the man in the litter. "This man's wound may not appear dire, but I'm certain that if I don't tend to it immediately, he—"

"It will wait." She pointed to the Mink and his men. "You five, wait. Everyone just *wait.* All right. Wait and . . . and you, surgeon, come with me."

She strode away, expecting Lirin to follow. He met the Mink's eyes and nodded for him to wait, then hurried after the citylady. What could have put her so out of sorts? She'd been practicing a regal air, but had now abandoned it completely.

Lirin crossed the field outside of town, walking alongside the line of refugees, and soon found his answer. A hulking figure easily seven feet tall emerged from the fog, accompanied by a small squad of parshmen with weapons. The dreadful creature had a beard and long hair the color of dried blood, and it seemed to meld with his simple wrap of clothing—as if he wore his hair itself for a covering. He had a pure black skin coloring, with lines of marbled red under his eyes.

Most importantly, he had a jagged carapace unlike any Lirin had seen, with a strange pair of carapace fins—or horns—rising above his ears.

The creature's eyes glowed a soft red. One of the Fused. Here in Hearthstone.

It had been months since Lirin had seen one—and that had been only in passing as a small group had stopped on the way to the battlefront in Herdaz. That group had soared through the air in breezy robes, bearing long spears. They had evoked an ethereal beauty, but the carapace on this creature looked far more wicked—like something one might *expect* to have come from Damnation.

The Fused spoke in a rhythmic language to a smaller figure at his side, a warform parshwoman. *Singer,* Lirin told himself. *Not parshwoman. Use the right term even in your head, so you don't slip when speaking.*

The warform stepped forward to translate for the Fused. From what Lirin had heard, even those Fused who spoke Alethi often used interpreters, as if speaking human tongues were beneath them.

"You," the interpreter said to Lirin, "are the surgeon? You've been inspecting the people today?"

"Yes," Lirin said.

The Fused replied, and again the interpreter translated. "We are searching for a spy. He might be hidden among these refugees."

Lirin felt his mouth go dry. The thing standing above him was a nightmare that should have *remained* a legend, a demon whispered of around the midnight fire. When Lirin tried to speak, the words wouldn't come out, and he had to cough to clear his throat.

At a barked order from the Fused, the soldiers with him spread out to the waiting line. The refugees backed away, and several tried to run, but the parshmen—though small beside the Fused—were warforms, with powerful strength and terrible speed. They caught runners while others began searching through the line, throwing back hoods and inspecting faces.

Don't look behind you at the Mink, Lirin. Don't seem nervous.

"We . . ." Lirin said. "We inspect each person, comparing them to the drawings given us. I promise you. We've been watchful! No need to terrorize these poor refugees."

The interpreter didn't translate Lirin's words for the Fused, but the creature spoke immediately in its own language.

"The one we seek is not on those lists," the interpreter said. "He is a young man, a spy of the most dangerous kind. He would be fit and strong compared to these refugees, though he might have feigned weakness."

"That . . . that could describe any number of people," Lirin said. Could he be in luck? Could this be a coincidence? It might not be about the Mink at all. Lirin felt a moment of hope, like sunlight peeking through stormclouds.

"You would remember this man," the interpreter continued. "Tall for a human, with wavy black hair worn to the shoulders. Clean shaven, he has a slave's brand on his forehead. Including the glyph *shash*."

Slave's brand.

Shash. Dangerous.

Oh no . . .

Nearby, one of the Fused's soldiers threw back the hood of another cloaked refugee—revealing a face that should have been intimately familiar to Lirin. Yet the harsh man Kaladin had become looked like a crude drawing of the sensitive youth Lirin remembered.

Kaladin immediately burst alight with power. Death had come to visit Hearthstone today, despite Lirin's every effort.

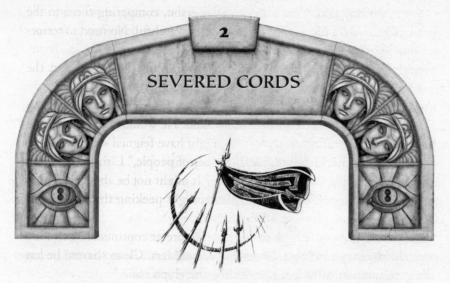

2

SEVERED CORDS

Next, let the spren inspect your trap. The gemstone must not be fully infused, but also cannot be fully dun. Experiments have concluded that seventy percent of maximum Stormlight capacity works best.

If you have done your work correctly, the spren will become fascinated by its soon-to-be prison. It will dance around the stone, peek at it, float around it.

—Lecture on fabrial mechanics presented by Navani Kholin to the coalition of monarchs, Urithiru, Jesevan, 1175

I told you we'd been spotted," Syl said as Kaladin flared with Stormlight.

Kaladin grunted in reply. Syl formed into a majestic silvery spear as he swept his hand outward—the weapon's appearance forcing back the singers who had been searching for him. Kaladin pointedly avoided looking at his father, to not betray their relationship. Besides, he knew what he would see. Disappointment.

So, nothing new.

Refugees scrambled away in a panic, but the Fused no longer cared about them. The hulking figure turned toward Kaladin, arms folded, and smiled.

I told you, Syl said in Kaladin's mind. *I'm going to keep reminding you until you acknowledge how intelligent I am.*

"This is a new variety," Kaladin said, keeping his spear leveled at the Fused. "You ever seen one of these before?"

No. Seems uglier than most though.

Over the last year, new varieties of Fused had been appearing on the battlefields in a trickle. Kaladin was most familiar with the ones who could fly like Windrunners. Those were called the *shanay-im*, they'd learned; it roughly meant "Those Ones of the Heavens."

Other Fused could not fly; as with the Radiants, each type had their own set of powers. Jasnah posited there would be ten varieties, though Dalinar—offering no explanation of why he knew this—said there would be only nine.

This variety marked the seventh Kaladin had fought. And, winds willing, the seventh he would kill. Kaladin raised his spear to challenge the Fused to single combat, an action that always worked with the Heavenly Ones. This Fused, however, waved for his companions to strike at Kaladin from all sides.

Kaladin responded by Lashing himself upward. As he darted into the sky, Syl automatically lengthened her shape into a long lance ideal for striking at ground objects from the air. Stormlight churned inside Kaladin, daring him to move, to act, to *fight*. But he needed to be careful. There were civilians in the area, including several very dear to him.

"Let's see if we can draw them away," Kaladin said. He Lashed himself downward at an angle so he swooped backward toward the ground. Unfortunately, the fog kept Kaladin from going too far or too high, lest he lose sight of his enemies.

Be careful, Syl said. *We don't know what kinds of powers this new Fused might—*

The fog-shrouded figure in the near distance collapsed suddenly, and something shot out of the body—a small line of red-violet light like a spren. That line of light darted to Kaladin in the blink of an eye, then it *expanded* to re-form the shape of the Fused with a sound like stretching leather mixed with grinding stone.

The Fused appeared in the air right in front of Kaladin. Before Kaladin could react, the Fused had grabbed him by the throat with one hand and by the front of the uniform with another.

Syl yelped, fuzzing to mist—her lance form was far too unwieldy for such a close-quarters fight. The weight of the enormous Fused, with his stony carapace and thick muscles, dragged Kaladin out of the air and slammed him against the ground, flat on his back.

The Fused's constricting fingers cut off Kaladin's airflow, but with Stormlight raging inside him, Kaladin didn't need to breathe. Still, he grabbed the Fused's hands to pry them free. Stormfather! The creature was *strong*. Moving his fingers was like trying to bend steel. Shrugging off the initial panic of being yanked out of the air, Kaladin gathered his wits and summoned Syl as a dagger. He sliced the Fused's right hand, then his left, leaving the fingers dead.

Those would heal—the Fused, like Radiants, used Light to repair their wounds. But with the creature's fingers dead, Kaladin kicked free with a grunt. He Lashed himself upward again, soaring into the air. Before he could catch his breath, however, a red-violet light streaked through the fog below, looping about itself and zipping up behind Kaladin.

A viselike arm grabbed him in an arm triangle from behind. A second later, a piercing pain stabbed Kaladin between the shoulders as the Fused knifed him in the neck.

Kaladin screamed and felt his limbs go numb as his spinal cord was severed. His Stormlight rushed to heal the wound, but this Fused was plainly experienced at fighting Surgebinders, because he continued to plunge the knife into Kaladin's neck time and time again, keeping him from recovering.

"Kaladin!" Syl said, flitting around him. "Kaladin! What should I do?" She formed into a shield in his hand, but his limp fingers dropped her, and she returned to her spren form.

The Fused's moves were expert, precise as he hung on from behind—he didn't seem to be able to fly when in humanoid shape, only as a ribbon of light. Kaladin felt hot breath on his cheek as the creature stabbed again and again. The part of Kaladin trained by his father considered the wound analytically. Severing of the spine. Repeated infliction of full paralysis. A clever way of dealing with an enemy who could heal. Kaladin's Stormlight would run out quickly at this rate.

The soldier in Kaladin worked more by instinct than deliberate thought, and noticed—despite spinning in the air, grappled by a terrible enemy—that he regained a single moment of mobility before each new stab. So as the tingling feeling rushed through his body, Kaladin bent forward, then *slammed* his head back into that of the Fused.

A flash of pain and white light disrupted Kaladin's sight. He twisted as he felt the Fused's grip slacken, then drop. The creature seized Kaladin by his coat, hanging on—a mere shadow to Kaladin's swimming vision. That was enough. Kaladin swept his hand at the thing's neck, Syl forming as a side sword. Cut through the gemheart, the head, or the neck with a Blade, and—great powers notwithstanding—the Fused would die.

Kaladin's vision recovered enough to let him see a violet-red light burst from the chest of the Fused. He left a body behind each time his soul—or whatever—became a ribbon of red light. Kaladin's Blade sliced the body's head clean off, but the light had already escaped.

Stormwinds. This thing seemed more spren than singer. The discarded body tumbled through the fog, and Kaladin followed it down, his wounds fully healing. He breathed in a second pouch of spheres as he landed beside the fallen corpse. Could he even kill this being? A Shardblade could cut spren, but that didn't kill them. They re-formed eventually.

Sweat poured down Kaladin's face, his heart thundering inside him. Though Stormlight urged him to move, he stilled himself and watched the fog, searching for signs of the Fused. They'd gotten far enough from the city that he couldn't see anyone else. Just shadowed hills. Empty.

Storms. That was close. As close to death as he'd come in a long, long while. Made all the more alarming by how quickly and unexpectedly the Fused had taken him. There was a danger to feeling like he owned the winds and the sky, to knowing he could heal quickly.

Kaladin turned around slowly, feeling the breeze on his skin. Carefully, he walked over to the lump that remained of the Fused. The corpse—or whatever it was—looked dried out and fragile, the colors faded, like the shell of a snail long dead. The flesh had turned into some kind of stone, porous and light. Kaladin picked up the decapitated head and pressed his thumb into the face, which crumbled like ash. The rest of the body followed on its own a few moments later, then even the carapace disintegrated.

A line of violet-red light came streaking in from the side. Kaladin immediately launched himself upward, narrowly avoiding the grasp of the Fused that formed from the light beneath him. The creature, however, immediately dropped the new body and shot upward after Kaladin as a light. This time Kaladin dodged a little too slowly, and the creature—forming from the light—seized him by the leg.

The Fused heaved upward, using his powerful upper-body strength to climb Kaladin's uniform. By the time the Sylblade formed in Kaladin's hands, the Fused had him in a powerful grip—legs wrapped around his torso, left hand grabbing Kaladin's sword hand and holding it out to the side while he shoved his right forearm into Kaladin's throat. That forced his head up, making it difficult to see the Fused, let alone get leverage against him.

He didn't need leverage, however. Grappling with a Windrunner was a dangerous prospect, for whatever Kaladin could touch, he could Lash. He poured Light into his enemy to Lash the creature away. The Light resisted, as it did when applied to Fused, but Kaladin had enough to push through the resistance.

Kaladin Lashed himself in the other direction, and it soon felt like enormous hands were pulling the two of them apart. The Fused grunted, then said something in his own language. Kaladin dropped the Sylblade and focused on trying to push the enemy away. The Fused was glowing with Stormlight now; it rose off him like luminescent smoke.

Finally the enemy's grip slipped, then he shot away from Kaladin like an arrow from a Shardbow. A fraction of a second later, that relentless red-violet light darted from the chest and headed straight for Kaladin yet again.

Kaladin narrowly avoided it, Lashing himself downward as the Fused formed and reached for him. After missing, the Fused fell through the mists, vanishing. Again Kaladin found himself low on Stormlight, his heart racing. He breathed in his third—of four—pouch of spheres. They'd learned to start wearing those sewn into the inside of their uniforms. Fused knew to try to cut away a Radiant's sphere reserve.

"Wow," Syl said, hovering up beside Kaladin, naturally taking a position where she could watch behind him. "He's good, isn't he?"

"It's more than that," Kaladin said, scanning the featureless fog. "He's attacking with a different strategy than most. I haven't done a lot of grappling."

Wrestling wasn't often seen on the battlefield. At least not a disciplined one. Kaladin was practiced with formations, and was growing more confident with swordplay, but it had been years since he'd trained on how to escape a headlock.

"Where is he?" Syl asked.

"I don't know," Kaladin said. "But we don't have to beat him. We only need to stay out of his grasp long enough for the others to arrive."

It took a few minutes of watching before Syl cried out. "There!" she said, forming a ribbon of light pointing the way toward what she'd seen.

Kaladin didn't wait for further explanation. He Lashed himself away through the fog. The Fused appeared, but grasped empty air as Kaladin dodged. The creature's body fell as the line of light ejected again, but Kaladin began an erratic zigzag pattern, evading the Fused twice more.

This creature used Voidlight to form new bodies somehow. Each one looked identical, with hair as a kind of clothing. He wasn't being reborn each time—he was teleporting, but using the ribbon of light to transfer between locations. They'd met Fused that could fly, and others that had powers like Lightweavers. Perhaps this was the variety whose powers mirrored, in a way, the traveling abilities of Elsecallers.

After the creature materialized the third time, he again briefly gave up the chase. *He can teleport only three times before he needs to rest,* Kaladin guessed. *He attacked in a burst of three each time. So after that, his powers need to regenerate? Or . . . no, he probably needs to go somewhere and fetch more Voidlight.*

Indeed, a few minutes later, the red-violet light returned. Kaladin Lashed himself directly away from the light, picking up speed. Air became a roar around him, and by the fifth Lashing, he was fast enough that the red light couldn't keep up, and dwindled behind.

Not quite so dangerous if you can't reach me, are you? Kaladin thought. The Fused evidently came to the same conclusion, the ribbon of light diving downward through the fog.

Unfortunately, the Fused probably knew Kaladin intended to return to Hearthstone. So, instead of continuing, Kaladin flew down as well. He came to rest on a hilltop overgrown with lumpish rockbuds, their vines spilling out liberally in the humidity.

The Fused stood at the bottom of the hill, looking up. Yes . . . that dark brown wrap he wore *was* hair, from the top of his head, wound long and tight around his body. He broke a carapace spur off his arm—a sharp and jagged weapon—and pointed it toward Kaladin. He had probably used one of those as a dagger when attacking Kaladin's back.

Both spur and hair seemed to imply he couldn't take objects with him when teleporting—so he couldn't keep Voidlight spheres on his person, but had to retreat to refill.

Syl formed as a spear. "I'm ready," Kaladin called. "Come at me."

"So you can run?" the Fused called in Alethi, his voice rough, like stones grinding together. "Watch for me from the corner of your eye, Windrunner. We'll meet again soon." He became a ribbon of red light—leaving another crumbling corpse as he disappeared into the fog.

Kaladin sat down and let out a long breath, Stormlight puffing in front of him and mingling with the fog. That fog would burn away as the sun rose higher, but for now it still blanketed the land, making it feel eerie and forlorn. Like he had accidentally stepped into a dream.

Kaladin was hit with a sudden wave of exhaustion. The dull sense of Stormlight running out, mixed with the usual deflation after a battle. And something more. Something increasingly common these days.

His spear vanished and Syl reappeared, standing in the air in front of him. She'd taken to wearing a stylish dress, ankle-length and sleek, instead of the filmy girlish one. When he'd asked, she'd explained that Adolin had been advising her. Her long, blue-white hair faded to mist, and she didn't wear a safehand sleeve. Why would she? She wasn't human, let alone Vorin.

"Well," she said, hands on hips, "we showed him."

"He almost killed me twice."

"I didn't say *what* we showed him." She turned around, keeping watch in case this was a trick. "You all right?"

"Yeah," Kaladin said.

"You look tired."

"You always say that."

"Because you always look tired, dummy."

He climbed to his feet. "I'll be fine once I get moving."

"You—"

"We are *not* going to argue about this again. I'm fine."

Indeed, he felt better when he got up and drew in a little more Stormlight. So what if the sleepless nights had returned? He'd survived on less sleep before. The slave Kaladin had been would have laughed himself silly to hear that this new Kaladin—lighteyed Shardbearer, a man who enjoyed luxurious housing and warm meals—was upset about a little lost sleep.

"Come on," he said. "If we were spotted on our way here—"

"If?"

"—*because* we were spotted, they'll send more than just one Fused. Heavenly Ones will come for me, and that means the mission is in jeopardy. Let's get back to the town."

She waited expectantly, her arms folded.

"Fine," Kaladin said. "You were right."

"And you should listen to me more."

"And I should listen to you more."

"And therefore you should get more sleep."

"Would that it were so easy," Kaladin said, rising into the air. "Come on."

⁘

Veil was growing increasingly upset that nobody had kidnapped her.

She strolled through the warcamp market, in full disguise, idling by shops. She'd spent more than a *month* wearing a fake face out here, making exactly the right comments to exactly the right people. And still no kidnapping. She hadn't even been mugged. What was the world coming to?

I could punch us in the face, Radiant noted, *if it would make you feel better.*

Levity, from Radiant? Veil smiled as she pretended to browse a fruit stand. If Radiant was cracking jokes, they really were getting desperate. Usually Radiant was as funny as . . . as . . .

Usually Radiant is as lighthearted as a chasmfiend, Shallan offered, bleeding to the front of their personality. *One with a particularly large emerald inside . . .*

Yes, that. Veil smiled at the warmth that came from Shallan, and even Radiant, who was coming to enjoy humor. This last year, the three of them had settled into a comfortable balance. They weren't as separate as they'd been, and swapped personas easily.

Things seemed to be going so well. That made Veil worry, of course. Were they going too well?

Never mind that, for now. She moved on from the fruit stand. She'd spent this month in the warcamps wearing the face of a woman named Chanasha: a lowborn lighteyed merchant who had found modest success hiring out her chull teams to caravans crossing the Shattered Plains. They'd bribed the real woman to lend her face to Veil, and she now resided in a secure location.

Veil turned a corner and strolled down another street. The Sadeas warcamp was much as she remembered it from her days living in these camps—though it was somehow even rougher. The road needed a good scraping; rockbud polyps caused nearby wagons to rattle and bump as they passed. Most of the stalls had a guard prominently stationed near the goods. This wasn't the sort of place where you trusted the local soldiers to police for you.

She passed more than a few luckmerches, selling glyphwards or other charms against the dangerous times. Stormwardens trying to sell lists of coming storms and their dates. She ignored these and moved on to a specific shop, one that carried sturdy boots and hiking shoes. That was what sold well in the warcamps these days. Many customers were travelers passing through. A quick survey of the other merchants would tell the same story. Rations that would keep for a long trip. Repair shops for wagons or carts. And, of course, anything that wasn't reputable enough to have a place at Urithiru.

There were also numerous slave pens. Nearly as many as there were brothels. Once the bulk of the civilians moved to Urithiru, all ten warcamps quickly became a seedy stopover for caravans.

At Radiant's prompting, Veil covertly checked over her shoulder for Adolin's soldiers. They were well out of sight. Good. She did spot Pattern watching from a wall nearby, ready to report to Adolin if needed.

All was in place, and their intelligence indicated her kidnapping *should* happen today. Maybe she needed to prod a little more.

The shoe merchant finally approached her—a stout fellow who had a beard striped with white. With that contrast, Shallan had an urge to draw him, so Veil stepped back and let Shallan emerge to take a Memory of him for her collection.

"Is there anything that interests you, Brightness?" he asked.

Veil emerged again. "How quickly could you get a hundred pairs of these?" she asked, tapping one of the shoes with a reed Chanasha always carried in her pocket.

"A hundred pairs?" the man asked, perking up. "Not long, Brightness. Four days, if my next shipment arrives on time."

"Excellent," she said. "I have a special contact with old Kholin at his silly tower, and can unload a large number if you can get them to me. I'll need a bulk discount, of course."

"Bulk discount?" the man said.

She swiped her reed in the air. "Yes, naturally. If you want to use my contacts to sell to Urithiru, I'll need to have the very best deal."

He rubbed at that beard of his. "You're . . . Chanasha Hasareh, aren't you? I've heard of you."

"Good. You'll know I don't play games." She leaned in and poked him in the chest with her reed. "I've got a way past old Kholin's tariffs, if we move quickly. Four days. Any way you can make it three?"

"Perhaps," he said. "But I am a law-abiding man, Brightness. Why . . . it would be illegal to avoid tariffs."

"Illegal only if we accept that Kholin has authority to *demand* these tariffs. Last I checked, he wasn't our king. He can claim whatever he wants, but now that the storms have changed, the Heralds are going to show up and put him in his place. Mark my words."

Nice work, Radiant thought. *That was well handled.*

Veil tapped the reed on the boots. "A hundred pairs. Three days. I'll send a scribe to haggle details before the end of the day. Deal?"

"Deal."

Chanasha wasn't the smiling type, so Veil didn't favor this merchant with one. She tucked her reed into her sleeve and gave him a curt nod before continuing through the market.

You don't think it was too blatant? Veil asked. *That last part about Dalinar not being king felt over the top.*

Radiant wasn't certain—subtlety wasn't her strong suit—but Shallan approved. They needed to push harder, or she'd never get kidnapped. Even lingering near a dark alleyway—one she knew her marks frequented—drew no attention.

Stifling a sigh, Veil made her way to a winehouse near the market. She'd been coming here for weeks now, and the owners knew her well. Intelligence said they, like the shoe merchant, belonged to the Sons of Honor, the group Veil was hunting.

The serving girl brought Veil inside out of the cool weather to a small, out-of-the-way corner with its own table. Here she could drink in solitude and go over accounts.

Accounts. Blah. She dug them out of her satchel and set them out on the table. The lengths they went to in the name of staying in character. They had to perfectly maintain the illusion, as the real Chanasha never let a day go by without reconciling her accounts. She seemed to find it *relaxing.*

Fortunately, they had Shallan to handle this part; she had some practice with Sebarial's accounts. Veil relaxed, letting Shallan take over. And actually, this wasn't *so* bad. She did doodles along the sides of the margins as she worked, even if it wasn't *quite* in character. Veil acted like it was imperative that they keep absolutely in character at all times, but Shallan knew they needed to relax a little, now and then.

We could relax by visiting the gambling dens . . . Veil thought.

Part of the reason they had to be so diligent was because these warcamps were a tempting playground for Veil. Gambling without concern for Vorin propriety? Bars that would serve whatever you wanted, no questions asked? The warcamps were a wonderful little storm away from Dalinar Kholin's perfect seat of honesty.

Urithiru was too full of Windrunners, men and women who would fall over themselves to make sure you didn't bruise your elbow on a misplaced table. This place, though. Veil could get to like this place. So, maybe it *was* better that they stayed strictly in character.

Shallan tried to focus on the accounts. She could do these numbers; she'd first trained on accounting when doing her father's ledgers. That had begun before she . . .

Before she . . .

It might be time, Veil whispered. *To remember, once and for all. Everything.*

No, it was not.

But . . .

Shallan retreated immediately. *No, we can't think of that. Take control.*

Veil sat back in the seat as her wine arrived. Fine. She took a long drink and tried to pretend to be doing ledgers. Honestly, she couldn't feel anger at Shallan. She channeled it instead toward Ialai Sadeas. That woman couldn't be content with running a little fiefdom here, making a profit off the caravans and keeping to herself. Oh no. She had to plan storming treason.

And so Veil tried to do ledgers *and* pretend she liked it. She took another long drink. A short time later her brain started to feel fuzzy, and she almost drew in Stormlight to burn off the effect—but stopped. She hadn't ordered anything particularly intoxicating. So if she was getting light-headed . . .

She looked up, her eyes growing unfocused. They'd drugged the wine! *Finally,* she thought before slumping over in her seat.

※

"I don't understand how hard it can be," Syl was saying as she and Kaladin drew close to Hearthstone. "You humans sleep *literally* every day. You've been practicing it all your lives."

"You'd think that, wouldn't you," Kaladin said, landing with a light step right outside town.

"Obviously I would, since I just said so," she replied, sitting on his shoulder, watching behind them. Her words were lighthearted, but he sensed in her the same tension he felt, like the air itself was stretched and pulled tight.

Watch for me from the corner of your eye, Windrunner. He felt a phantom pain from his neck, where the Fused had plunged his dagger into Kaladin's spine over and over.

"Even babies can sleep," Syl said. "Only *you* could make something so simple into something extremely difficult."

"Yeah?" Kaladin asked. "And can you do it?"

"Lie down. Pretend to be dead for a while. Get up. Easy. Oh, and since it's you, I'll add the mandatory last step: complain."

Kaladin strode toward the town. Syl would expect a response, but he didn't feel like giving one. Not out of annoyance, but more . . . a kind of general fatigue.

"Kaladin?" she asked.

He'd felt a disconnect these last months. These last years . . . it was as if life for everyone continued, but Kaladin was separate from them, incapable of interacting. Like he was a painting hanging in a hallway, watching life stream past.

"Fine," Syl said. "I'll do your part." Her image fuzzed, and she became a perfect replica of Kaladin, sitting on his own shoulder. "Well well," she said in a growling, low-pitched voice. "Grumble grumble. Get in line, men. Storming rain, ruining otherwise terrible weather. Also, I'm banning toes."

"Toes?"

"People keep tripping!" she continued. "I can't have you all hurting yourselves. So, no toes from now on. Next week we'll try not having feet. Now, go off and get some food. Tomorrow we're going to get up before dawn to practice scowling at one another."

"I'm not *that* bad," Kaladin said, but couldn't help smiling. "Also, your Kaladin voice sounds more like Teft."

She transformed back and sat primly—clearly pleased with herself. And he had to admit he felt more upbeat. *Storms,* he thought. *Where would I be if I hadn't found her?*

The answer was obvious. He'd be dead at the bottom of a chasm, having leaped into the darkness.

As they approached Hearthstone, they found a scene of relative order. The refugees had been returned to a line, and the warform singers who had come with the Fused waited near Kaladin's father and the new citylady, their weapons sheathed. Everyone seemed to understand that their next steps would depend greatly upon the results of Kaladin's duel.

He strode up and seized the air in front of him, the Sylspear forming as a majestic silver weapon. The singers drew their weapons, mostly swords.

"You can fight a Radiant all on your own, if you'd like," Kaladin said. "Alternatively, if you don't feel like dying today, you can gather the singers in this town and retreat a half hour's walk to the east. There's a storm-shelter out that way for people from the outer farms; I'm sure Abiajan can lead you to it. Stay inside until sunset."

The six soldiers rushed him.

Kaladin sighed, drawing in a few more spheres' worth of his Stormlight. The skirmish took about thirty seconds, and left one of the singers dead with her eyes burned out while the others retreated, their weapons shorn in half.

Some would have seen bravery in this attack. For much of Alethi history, common soldiers had been encouraged to throw themselves at Shard-bearers. Generals taught that the slightest chance of earning a Shard was worth the incredible risk.

That was stupid enough, but Kaladin wouldn't drop a Shard when killed. He was Radiant, and these soldiers knew it. From what he'd seen, the attitudes of the singer soldiers depended greatly upon the Fused they served. The fact that these had thrown their lives away so wantonly did not speak highly of their master.

Fortunately, the remaining five listened to Abiajan and the other Hearthstone singers who—with some effort—persuaded them that despite fighting bravely, they were now defeated. A short time later, they all went trudging out through the quickly vanishing fog.

Kaladin checked the sky again. *Should be close now*, he thought as he walked over to the checkpoint where his mother waited, a patterned ker-chief over her shoulder-length unbraided hair. She gave Kaladin a side hug, holding little Oroden—who reached out his hands for Kaladin to take him.

"You're getting tall!" he said to the boy.

"Gagadin!" the child said, then waved in the air, trying to catch Syl—who always chose to appear to Kaladin's family. She did her usual trick, changing into the shapes of various animals and pouncing around in the air for the child.

"So," Kaladin's mother said, "how is Lyn?"

"Does that *always* have to be your first question?"

"Mother's prerogative," Hesina said. "So?"

"She broke up with him," Syl said, shaped as a tiny glowing axehound. The words seemed odd coming from its mouth. "Right after our last visit."

"Oh, Kaladin," his mother said, pulling him into another side hug. "How's he taking it?"

"He sulked for a good two weeks," Syl said, "but I think he's mostly over it."

"He's *right here*," Kaladin said.

"And he doesn't ever answer questions about his personal life," Hesina said. "Forcing his poor mother to turn to other, more divine sources."

"See," Syl said, now prancing around as a cremling. "*She* knows how to treat me. With the *dignity* and *respect* I deserve."

"Has he been disrespecting you again, Syl?"

"It's been *at least* a day since he mentioned how great I am."

"It's demonstrably unfair that I have to deal with both of you at once," Kaladin said. "Did that Herdazian general make it to town?"

Hesina gestured toward a nearby building nestled between two homes, one of the wooden sheds for farming equipment. It didn't appear terribly sturdy; some of the boards had been warped and blown loose by a recent storm.

"I hid them in there once the fighting started," Hesina explained.

Kaladin handed Oroden to her, then started toward the shed. "Grab Laral and gather the townspeople. Something big is coming today, and I don't want them to panic."

"Explain what you mean by 'big,' son."

"You'll see," he said.

"Are you going to go talk to your father?"

Kaladin hesitated, then glanced across the foggy field toward the refugees. Townspeople had started to drift out of their homes to see what all the ruckus was about. He couldn't spot his father. "Where did he go?"

"To check whether that parshman you sliced is actually dead."

"Of course he did," Kaladin said with a sigh. "I'll deal with Lirin later."

Inside the shed, several very touchy Herdazians pulled daggers on him as he opened the door. In response, he sucked in a little Stormlight, causing wisps of luminescent smoke to rise from his exposed skin.

"By the Three Gods," whispered one of them, a tall fellow with a ponytail. "It's true. You've returned."

The reaction disturbed Kaladin. This man, as a freedom fighter in Herdaz, *should* have seen Radiants before now. In a perfect world, Dalinar's coalition armies would have been supporting the Herdazian freedom effort for months now.

Only, everyone had given up on Herdaz. The little country had seemed close to collapse, and Dalinar's armies had been licking their wounds from the Battle of Thaylen Field. Then reports had trickled in of a resistance in Herdaz fighting back. Each report sounded like the Herdazians were nearly finished, and so resources were allocated to more winnable fronts. But each time, Herdaz stood strong, relentlessly harrying the enemy. Odium's armies lost tens of thousands fighting in that small, strategically unimportant country.

Though Herdaz had eventually fallen, the blood toll exacted on the enemy had been remarkably high.

"Which of you is the Mink?" Kaladin asked, glowing Stormlight puffing out of his mouth as he spoke.

The tall fellow gestured to the rear of the shed, to where a shadowed figure—shrouded in his cloak—had settled against the wall. Kaladin couldn't make out his face beneath the hood.

"I'm honored to meet the legend himself," Kaladin said, stepping forward. "I've been told to extend you an official invitation to join the coalition army. We will do what we can for your country, but for now Brightlord Dalinar Kholin and Queen Jasnah Kholin are both very eager to meet the man who held against the enemy for so long."

The Mink didn't move. He remained seated, his head bowed. Finally, one of his men moved over and shook the man's shoulder.

The cloak shifted and the body fell limp, exposing rolls of tarps assembled to appear like the figure of a person wearing the cloak. A dummy? What in the Stormfather's unknown name?

The soldiers seemed equally surprised, though the tall one merely sighed and gave Kaladin a resigned look. "He does this sometimes, Brightlord."

"Does what? Turns into rags?"

"He sneaks away," the man explained. "He likes to see if he can do it without us noticing."

One of the other men cursed in Herdazian as he searched behind nearby barrels, eventually uncovering one of the loose boards. It opened into the shadowed alley between buildings.

"We'll find him in town somewhere, I'm sure," the man told Kaladin. "Give us a few minutes to hunt for him."

"One would think he'd avoid playing games," Kaladin said, "considering the dangerous situation."

"You . . . don't know our gancho, Brightlord," the man said. "This is *exactly* how he treats dangerous situations."

"He is no like being caught," another said, shaking his head. "When in danger, he is to vanish."

"And abandon his men?" Kaladin asked, aghast.

"You don't survive like the Mink has without learning to wiggle out of situations others could never escape," the tall Herdazian said. "If we were in danger, he'd try to come back for us. If he couldn't . . . well, we're his guards. Any of us would give our lives so he could escape."

"Is no like he needs us a lot," another said. "The Ganlos Riera herself couldn't catch him!"

"Well, locate him if you can, and pass along my message," Kaladin said.

"We need to be out of this town quickly. I have reason to suspect a larger force of Fused is on its way here."

The Herdazians saluted him, though that wasn't necessary for a member of another country's military. People did odd things around Radiants.

"Well done!" Syl said as he left the shed. "You barely scowled when they called you Brightlord."

"I am what I am," Kaladin said, hiking out past his mother, who was now conferring with Laral and Brightlord Roshone. Kaladin spotted his father organizing some of Roshone's former soldiers, who were trying to corral the refugees. Judging by the smaller line, a few seemed to have run off.

Lirin spotted Kaladin approaching, and his lips tightened. The surgeon was a shorter man—Kaladin got his height from his mother. Lirin stepped away from the group and wiped the sweat from his face and balding head with a handkerchief, then took off his spectacles, polishing them quietly as Kaladin stepped up.

"Father," Kaladin said.

"I had hoped," Lirin said softly, "that our message would inspire you to approach *covertly*."

"I tried," Kaladin said. "But the Fused have set up posts all through the land, watching the sky. The fog unexpectedly cleared up near one of those, and I was exposed. I'd hoped they hadn't seen me, but . . ." He shrugged.

Lirin put his spectacles back on, and both men knew what he was thinking. Lirin had warned that if Kaladin kept visiting, he would bring death to Hearthstone. Today it had come to the singer who had attacked him. Lirin had covered the corpse with a shroud.

"I'm a soldier, Father," Kaladin said. "I fight for these people."

"Any idiot with hands can hold a spear. I trained *your* hands for something better."

"I—" Kaladin stopped himself and took a long, deep breath. He heard a distinctive thumping sound in the distance. *Finally.*

"We can discuss this later," Kaladin said. "Go pack up any supplies you want to take. Quickly. We need to leave."

"Leave?" Lirin said. "I've told you already. The townspeople need me. I'm not going to abandon them."

"I know," Kaladin said, waving toward the sky.

"What are you . . ." Lirin trailed off as an enormous dark shadow emerged from the fog, a vehicle of incredible size flying slowly through the air. To either side, two dozen Windrunners—glowing bright with Stormlight—soared in formation.

It wasn't a ship so much as a gigantic floating platform. Awespren formed around Lirin anyway, like rings of blue smoke. Well, the first time Kaladin had seen Navani make the platform float, he'd gaped too.

It passed in front of the sun, casting Kaladin and his father into shade.

"You've made it quite clear," Kaladin said, "that you and Mother won't abandon the people of Hearthstone. So I arranged to bring them with us."

3

THE FOURTH BRIDGE

The final step in capturing spren is the most tricky, as you must remove the Stormlight from the gemstone. The specific techniques employed by each artifabrian guild are closely guarded secrets, entrusted only to their most senior members.

The easiest method would be to use a larkin—a type of cremling that feasts on Stormlight. That would be wonderful and convenient if the creatures weren't now almost entirely extinct. The wars in Aimia were in part over these seemingly innocent little creatures.

—Lecture on fabrial mechanics presented by Navani Kholin to the coalition of monarchs, Urithiru, Jesevan, 1175

Navani Kholin leaned out over the side of the flying platform and looked down hundreds of feet to the stones below. It said a lot about where she'd been living that she kept being surprised by how *fertile* Alethkar was. Rockbuds clustered on every surface, except where they'd been cleared for living or farming. Entire fields of wild grasses waved green in the wind, bobbing with lifespren. Trees formed bulwarks against the storms, with interlocking branches as tight as a phalanx.

Here—as opposed to the Shattered Plains or Urithiru—things *grew*. It was the home of her childhood, but now it felt almost alien.

"I *do* wish you wouldn't crane like that, Brightness," said Velat. The middle-aged scholar wore tight braids against the wind. She *did* try to mother everyone around her.

Navani, naturally, leaned out farther. One would think that during more than fifty years of life, she would have found a way to rise above her natural impetuous streak. Instead she'd rather alarmingly found her way to enough power to simply do as she chose.

Below, her flying platform made a satisfyingly geometric shadow on the stones. Townspeople clustered together, gawking upward as Kaladin and the other Windrunners backed them off to provide room for the landing.

"Brightlord Dalinar," Velat said, "can you talk sense into her, please? She's going to drop right off, I swear it."

"It's *Navani's* ship, Velat," Dalinar said from behind, his voice as steady as steel, as immutable as mathematics. She loved his voice. "I think she'd have me thrown off if I tried to prevent her from enjoying this moment."

"Can't she enjoy it from the *center* of the platform? Perhaps nicely tethered to the deck? With two ropes?"

Navani grinned as the wind tugged at her loose hair. She held the rail with her freehand. "This area is clear of people now. Send the order—a steady descent to the ground."

She'd started this design using old chasm-spanning bridges as a model. After all, this wasn't a warship, but a transport intended to move large groups of people. The end construction was little more than a large wooden rectangle: over a hundred feet long, sixty feet wide, and around forty feet thick to support three decks.

They had built high walls and a roof on the rear portion of the upper deck. The front third was exposed to the air, with a railing around the sides. For most of the trip, Navani's engineers had maintained their command post in the sheltered portion. But with the need for delicate maneuvers today, they'd moved the tables out and bolted them to the deck in the right front corner of the platform.

Right front, she thought. *Should we be using nautical terms instead? But this isn't the ocean. We're flying.*

Flying. It had *worked.* Not just in maneuvers and tests on the Shattered Plains, but on a real mission, flying hundreds of miles.

Behind her, over a dozen ardent engineers tended the open-air command station. Ka—a scribe from one of the Windrunner squads—sent the order to Urithiru via spanreed. When in motion, they couldn't write full instructions—spanreeds had trouble with that. But they could send flashes of light that could be interpreted.

In Urithiru, another group of engineers worked the complex mechanisms that kept this ship in the air. In fact, it used the very same technology that powered spanreeds. When one of them moved, the other moved in concert with it. Well, halves of a gemstone could also be paired so that when one was lowered, the other half—no matter where it was—would rise into the air.

Force was transferred: if the distant half was underneath something heavy, you'd have trouble lowering yours. Unfortunately, there was some additional decay; the farther apart the two halves were, the more resistance you felt in moving them. But if you could move a pen, why not a guard tower? Why not a carriage? Why not an *entire ship*?

So it was that hundreds of men and chulls worked a system of pulleys connected to a wide lattice of gemstones at Urithiru. When they let their lattice down along the side of the plateau outside the tower, Navani's ship rose up into the sky.

Another lattice, secured on the Shattered Plains and connected to chulls, could then be used to make the ship move forward or backward. The real advancement had come as they'd learned to use aluminum to isolate motion along a plane, and even change the vectors of force. The end result was chulls that could pull for a while, then be turned around—the gemstones temporarily disjoined—to march back the other direction, as all the while the airship continued in a straight line.

Alternating between those two lattices—one to control altitude and a second to control horizontal movement—let Navani's ship *soar*.

Her ship. *Her* ship. She wished she could share it with Elhokar. Though most people remembered her son only as the man who had struggled to replace Gavilar as king, she'd known him as the curious, inquisitive boy who had adored her drawings. He had always enjoyed heights. How he'd have loved the view from this deck . . .

Work on this vessel had helped sustain her during the months following his death. Of course, it hadn't been her math that had finally made this ship a reality. They'd learned about the interactions between conjoined fabrials and aluminum during the expedition to Aimia. This wasn't the direct result of her engineering schematics either; the ship was a fair bit more mundane in appearance than her original fanciful designs.

Navani merely guided people smarter than she was. So maybe she didn't deserve to grin like a child as she watched it work. She did anyway.

Deciding upon a name had taken her months of deliberation. In the end, however, she'd taken inspiration from the bridges that had inspired her. In specific, the one that had—so many months ago—rescued Dalinar and Adolin from certain death, something she hoped this vessel would do for many others in similarly dire situations.

And so, the world's first air transport had been named the *Fourth Bridge*. With the permission of Highmarshal Kaladin's old team, she'd embedded their old bridge in the center of the deck as a symbol.

Navani stepped away from the ledge and walked to the command station. She heard Velat sigh in relief—the cartographer had tethered herself to the deck with a rope. Navani would have preferred to bring Isasik, but he was off on one of his mapping expeditions, this time to the eastern part of the Shattered Plains.

Still, she had a full complement of scientists and engineers. White-bearded Falilar was reviewing schematics with Rushu while a host of assistants and scribes ran this way and that, checking structural integrity or measuring Stormlight levels in the gemstones. At this point, there wasn't a whole lot for Navani to do other than stand around and look important. She smiled, recalling Dalinar saying something similar about battlefield generals once the plan was in motion.

The *Fourth Bridge* set down, and the front doors of the bottom level opened to accept passengers. A dozen Edgedancers flowed out toward the town. Glowing with Stormlight, they moved with a strange gait—alternating pushing off with one foot while sliding on the other. They could glide across wood or stone as if it were ice, and gracefully leaped over stones.

The last Edgedancer in the group—a lanky girl who seemed to have grown an entire foot in the last year—missed her jump though, and tripped over a large rock the others had dodged. Navani covered a smile. Being Radiant did not, unfortunately, make one immune to the awkwardness of puberty.

The Edgedancers would usher the townspeople onto the transport and heal those who were wounded or sick. Windrunners darted through the sky to watch for potential problems.

Rather than bother the engineers or soldiers, Navani drifted over to Kmakl, the Thaylen prince consort. Fen's aging husband was a navy man, and Navani had thought he might enjoy joining them on the *Fourth Bridge*'s first mission. He gave her a respectful bow, his eyebrows and long mustaches drooping alongside his face.

"You must think us very disorganized, Admiral," Navani said to him in Thaylen. "No captain's cabin and barely a handful of bolted-down desks for a command station."

"She is an odd ship, to be sure," the elderly sailor replied. "But majestic in her own way. I was listening to your scholars talk, and they were guessing the ship made about five knots on average."

Navani nodded. This mission had begun as an extended endurance test—indeed, Navani hadn't been on the voyage when it had begun. The *Fourth Bridge* had spent weeks flying out over the Steamwater Ocean, taking refuge from storms in laits and coastal coves. During that time, the ship's only crew had been her engineers and a handful of sailors.

Then the request had come from Kaladin. Would they like to try a more rigorous stress test by stealing an entire town out of Alethkar—rescuing an infamous Herdazian general in the process? Dalinar had made the decision, and the *Fourth Bridge* had changed course toward Alethkar.

Windrunners had delivered the command staff—Navani included—and Radiants to the vessel earlier today.

"Five knots," Navani said. "Not particularly fast, compared to your best ships."

"Pardon, Brightness," he said. "But this is essentially a giant barge—and for that five knots is impressive, even ignoring the fact that it is *flying*." He shook his head. "This ship is faster than an army marching at double time—yet it brings your troops in fresh *and* provides its own mobile high ground for archery support."

Navani couldn't refrain from beaming with pride. "There are still a lot of kinks to work out," she said. "The fans on the rear barely increased speed. We're going to need something better. The manpower involved is enormous."

"If you say so," he said. The elderly man adopted a distant expression, turning and staring out toward the horizon.

"Admiral?" Navani asked. "Are you all right?"

"I'm simply imagining the end of an era. The livelihood I've known, the way of the oceans and the navy . . ."

"We'll continue to need navies," Navani said. "This air transport is merely an additional tool."

"Perhaps, perhaps. But for a moment, imagine a fleet of ordinary ships suffering an attack from one of *these* up above. It wouldn't need trained archers. The flying sailors could drop stones and sink a fleet in minutes. . . ." He glanced to her. "My dear, if these things become ubiquitous, it won't only be navies that are rendered obsolete. I can't decide if I'm glad to be old enough to wish my world a fond farewell, or if I envy the young lads who get to explore this new world."

Navani found herself at a loss for words. She wanted to offer encouragement, but the past that Kmakl regarded with such fondness was . . . well, like waves in water. Gone now, absorbed by the ocean of time. It was the future that excited her.

Kmakl seemed to sense her hesitance, as he smiled. "Don't mind the ramblings of a grouchy old sailor. Look, the Bondsmith wishes your attention. Go and guide us toward a new horizon, Brightness. That is where we'll find success against these invaders."

She gave Kmakl a fond pat on the arm, then hastened off toward Dalinar. He stood near the front center of the deck, and Highmarshal Kaladin was striding toward him accompanied by a bespectacled man. This must be the Windrunner's father—though it took some imagination on her part to see the resemblance. Kaladin was tall, and Lirin was short. The younger man had that unruly hair falling in a natural curl. Lirin, on the other hand, was balding, with the rest of his hair kept very short.

However, as she stepped up beside Dalinar, she caught Lirin's eyes—and the familial connection became more obvious. That same quiet intensity, that same faintly judgmental gaze that seemed to know too much about you. In that moment she saw two men with the same soul, for all their physical differences.

"Sir," Kaladin said to Dalinar. "My father, the surgeon."

Dalinar nodded his head. "Lirin Stormblessed. It is my honor."

". . . Stormblessed?" Lirin asked. He didn't bow, which Navani found undiplomatic, considering whom he was meeting.

"I assumed you would take your son's house name," Dalinar said.

Lirin glanced at his son, who evidently hadn't told him about his elevation. But he said nothing more, instead turning to give her airship a proper nod of respect.

"This is a magnificent creation," Lirin said. "Do you think it could quickly deliver a mobile hospital, staffed with surgeons, to a battlefield? The lives that could be saved that way . . ."

"An ingenious application," Dalinar said. "Though Edgedancers generally do that job now."

"Oh. Right." Lirin adjusted his spectacles, then finally seemed to find a little respect for Dalinar. "I appreciate what you're doing here, Brightlord Kholin, but can you say how long my people will be trapped on this vehicle?"

"It will be a several-week flight to reach the Shattered Plains," Dalinar said. "But we'll be delivering supplies, blankets, and other items of comfort during the trip. You'll be performing an important function, helping us learn how to better equip these transports. Plus we'll be denying the enemy an important population center and farming community."

Lirin nodded, thoughtful.

"Why don't you inspect the accommodations?" Dalinar offered. "The holds aren't luxurious, but there's space enough for hundreds."

Lirin accepted the dismissal—though he again didn't bow or offer respect as he strode away.

Kaladin hung back. "I apologize for my father, sir. He doesn't deal well with surprises."

"It's all right," Dalinar said. "I can only imagine what these people have been through lately."

"It might not be over quite yet, sir. I was spotted while scouting earlier today. One of the Fused—a variety I've never seen before—came to Hearthstone hunting me. I ran him off, but I have no doubt we'll soon encounter more resistance."

Dalinar tried to remain stoic, but Navani could see his disappointment in the downturn of his lips. "Very well," he said. "I'd hoped the fog might cover us, but that was plainly too convenient. Go alert the other Windrunners, and I'll send word for the Edgedancers to hasten the evacuation."

Kaladin nodded. "I'm running low on Light, sir."

Navani slipped her notebook from her pocket as Dalinar raised his hand and pressed it against Kaladin's chest. There was a faint . . . warping to the air around them, and for a moment she thought she could see into Shadesmar. Another realm, filled with beads of glass and candle flames floating in place of people's souls. She thought, for the briefest moment, she heard a *tone* in the distance. A pure note vibrating through her.

It was gone in a moment, but she wrote her impressions anyway. Dalinar's powers were related to the composition of Stormlight, the three realms, and—ultimately—the very nature of deity. There were secrets here to unlock.

Kaladin's Light was renewed, wisps of it steaming off his skin, visible even in daylight. The spheres he carried would be renewed as well. Somehow Dalinar reached between realms to touch the Almighty's own power, an ability once reserved solely for storms and the things that lived in them.

Appearing invigorated, the young Windrunner stepped across the deck. He knelt and rested his hand on the rectangular patch of wood that stood out from the rest—not newly cut, but dinged and marked from arrows. His old bridge had been embedded to be flush with the rest of the deck. The Bridge Four Windrunners all enacted this same wordless ritual when they left the airship. It took only a moment, then Kaladin launched into the air.

Navani finished her notes, covering a smile as she found Dalinar reading over her shoulder. That was still a decidedly odd experience, for all that she tried to encourage him.

"I've already let Jasnah make notes on what I do," Dalinar said. "Yet each time, you pull out this notebook. What are you looking for, gemheart?"

"I'm not sure yet," she said. "Something is odd about the nature of Urithiru, and I think Bondsmiths might be related to the tower, at least from what we read about the old Radiants." She flipped to another page and showed him some schematics she'd drawn. The tower city of Urithiru had an enormous gemstone construction at its heart—a crystal pillar, a fabrial unlike any she'd ever seen. She was increasingly certain the tower had once been powered by that pillar, as this flying ship was powered by the gemstones her engineers had embedded within the hull. But the tower was broken, barely functioning.

"I tried infusing that pillar," Dalinar said. "It didn't work." He could infuse Stormlight into ordinary spheres, but those tower gemstones had

resisted.

"We must be approaching the problem in the wrong way. I can't help thinking if I knew more about Stormlight, the solution would be simple."

She shook her head. The *Fourth Bridge* was an extraordinary accomplishment, but she worried she was failing in a greater task. Urithiru was high in the mountains, where it was too cold to grow plants—yet the tower had numerous fields. People had not only survived up in that harsh environment, they had *thrived*.

How? She knew the tower had once been occupied by a powerful spren named the Sibling. A spren on the level of the Nightwatcher or the Stormfather—and capable of making a Bondsmith. She had to assume the spren, or perhaps something about its relationship with a human, had allowed the tower to function. Unfortunately, the Sibling had died during the Recreance. She wasn't certain what level of "dead" that meant. Was the Sibling dead like the souls of Shardblades that still walked around? Some spren she interviewed said the Sibling was "slumbering," but they treated that as final.

The answers weren't clear, and that left Navani struggling to try to understand. She studied Dalinar and his bond with the Stormfather, hoping it would offer some further clue.

"So," an accented voice said from behind them, "the Alethi really have learned to fly. I should have believed the stories. Only your kind are stubborn enough to bully nature herself."

Navani started, though she was slower to respond than Dalinar, who spun—hand on his side sword—and immediately stepped between Navani and the strange voice. She had to peek around him to see the man who had spoken.

He was a short fellow, missing a tooth, with a flat nose and a jovial expression. His worn cloak and ragged trousers marked him as a refugee. He stood next to Navani's engineer station, where he'd picked up the map that charted the *Fourth Bridge*'s course.

Velat, standing at the center of the desks, yelped when she saw him, then reached over to snatch the paper away.

"Refugees are to gather belowdecks," Navani said, pointing the way back to the steps.

"Good for them," the Herdazian man said. "Your flying boy says you've got a place for me here. Don't know what I think of serving an Alethi. I've spent most of my life trying to stay away from them." He eyed Dalinar. "You specifically, Blackthorn. No offense."

Ah, Navani thought. She'd heard that the Mink wasn't what people expected. She revised her assessment, then glanced toward the Cobalt Guardsmen who were belatedly rushing up from the sides of the ship. They appeared chagrined, but Navani waved them off. She'd ask some pointed questions later about why they'd been so lax as to let this man sneak up the steps to the command station.

"I find wisdom in men who knew to avoid the person I once was," Dalinar said to the Mink. "But this is a new era, with new enemies. Our past squabbles are of no concern now."

"Squabbles?" the man asked. "So that's the Alethi word for them. Yes, yes. My mastery of your language, you see, is lacking. I'd been mistakenly referring to your actions as 'raping and burning my people.'"

He pulled something from his pocket. Another of Velat's maps. He glanced over his shoulder—to check that she wasn't watching—then unrolled it and cocked his head, inspecting it.

"What remains of my army is secluded in four separate hollows between here and Herdaz," he said. "I have only a few hundred left. Use your flying machine to rescue them, and we'll talk. Alethi bloodlust has cost me many loved ones over the years, but I'd be a fool not to admit the value in pointing it—like the proverbial sword's blade—at *someone else*."

"It will be done," Dalinar said.

Navani didn't miss that—despite claiming earlier that the *Fourth Bridge* was her ship—he agreed to fly it per the Mink's request without so much as consulting her. She tried not to let things like that bother her. It wasn't that her husband didn't respect her—he'd proven on numerous occasions that he did. Dalinar Kholin was simply accustomed to being the most important—and generally most capable—person around. That led a man to surge forward like an advancing stormwall, making decisions as the need arose.

Still, it irked her more than she'd ever admit out loud.

The first of the real refugees began to arrive down below, herded gently by the Edgedancers. Navani focused on the problem at hand: making certain each person was settled and comfortable in the most economical and orderly way possible. She'd drawn up a plan. Unfortunately, the welcome was interrupted as Lyn—a Windrunner woman with long dark hair worn in a braid—slammed down onto the deck.

"Incoming Fused, sir," she reported to Dalinar. "Three full flights of them."

"Kaladin was right, then," he said. "Hopefully we can drive them away. Storms help us if they decide to harry the ship all the way to the Shattered Plains."

That was Navani's worst fear—that flying enemies would be able to strike at and even disable the transport. She had precautions in place to try to prevent that, and it looked like she'd get to witness their initial test firsthand.

4

ARCHITECTS OF THE FUTURE

To draw Stormlight out of a gemstone, I use the Arnist Method. Several large empty gemstones are brought close to the infused one while the spren is inspecting it. Stormlight is slowly absorbed from a small gemstone by a very large gemstone of the same type—and several together can draw the Light out quickly. The method's limitation is, of course, the fact that you need not merely acquire one gemstone for your fabrial, but several larger ones to withdraw the Stormlight.

Other methods must exist, as proven by the extremely large gemstone fabrials created by the Vriztl Guild out of Thaylenah. If Her Majesty would please repeat my request to the guild, this secret is of vital importance to the war effort.

—Lecture on fabrial mechanics presented by Navani Kholin to the coalition of monarchs, Urithiru, Jesevan, 1175

W hen they awoke, Radiant immediately took charge and assessed the situation. She had a sack over her head, so nobody saw her disorientation, and she was careful not to move and warn her captors. Shallan had fortunately attached her Lightweaving in such a way that it would keep up their illusory face even while they were unconscious.

Radiant didn't appear to be bound, though she was being carried over someone's shoulder. He smelled of chulls. Or maybe it was the sack.

Her body had activated her powers, healed her, and let her wake sooner than she would have otherwise. Radiant didn't like sneaking about or pretending, but she trusted that Veil and Shallan knew what they were doing. She instead did her part: judging the danger of the current situation.

She seemed to be fine, though uncomfortable. Her head kept bouncing into the man's back, pressing the sack against her face with each step. Deep down, she felt satisfaction from Veil. They'd nearly given up on this mission. It was nice to know that all their work hadn't been in vain.

Now, where were they taking her? That had proven one of the biggest mysteries: where the Sons of Honor held their little meetings. Shallan's team had managed to get one person into the group months ago, but he hadn't been important enough to be given the information they needed. A lighteyes had been required.

They suspected Ialai had taken over the cult, now that Amaram was dead. Her faction was planning to seize the Oathgate at the center of the Shattered Plains. Unfortunately, Radiant didn't have proof of these facts, and she would *not* move against Ialai without solid proof. Dalinar agreed with her, particularly after what Adolin had done to Ialai's husband.

Too bad he didn't find a way to finish off the pair of them, Veil thought.

That would not have been right, Radiant thought back. *Ialai was no threat to him then.*

Shallan didn't agree, and naturally Veil didn't either, so Radiant let the matter drop. Hopefully Pattern was still following at a distance as instructed. Once the group stopped and began initiating Radiant, the spren would fetch Adolin and the soldiers in case she needed extraction.

Eventually her captors halted, and rough hands hauled her off the shoulder. She closed her eyes and forced herself to remain limp as they set her on the ground. Wet and slimy rock, someplace cool. The sack came off, and she smelled something pungent. When she didn't stir fast enough, someone dumped water on her head.

It was time for Veil to take over. She gasped "awake," shoving aside her first instinct, which was to grab a knife and make short work of whoever had drenched her. Veil wiped her eyes with her safehand sleeve, and found herself someplace dank and humid. Plants on the stone walls had pulled in at the ruckus, and the sky was a distant crack high in the air. Lifespren bobbed around many thick plants and vines.

She was in one of the chasms. Kelek's breath! How had they carried her down into the *chasms* without anyone seeing?

A group of people in black robes stood around her, each holding a brightly shining diamond broam in one palm. She blinked at the sharp light. Their hoods looked a fair bit more comfortable than her sack. Each robe was embroidered with the Double Eye of the Almighty, and Shallan had a fleeting thought, wondering at the seamstress they'd hired to do all this work. What had they told her? "Yes, we want twenty identi-

cal, mysterious robes, sewn with ancient arcane symbols. They're for . . .
parties."

Forcing herself to stay in character, Veil gazed up with wonder and confusion, then shied back against the chasm wall, startling a cremling with
dark purple colorings.

A figure at the front spoke first, his voice deep and resonant. "Chanasha
Hasareh, you have a fine and reputable name. After the legacy of Chanaranach'Elin, Herald of the Common Man. Do you truly wish for their
return?"

"I . . ." Veil raised her hand before the light of the spheres. "What is
this? What is happening?" *And which one of you is Ialai Sadeas?*

"We are the Sons of Honor," another figure said. Female this time, but
not Ialai. "It is our sworn and sacred duty to usher in the return of the
Heralds, the return of storms, and the return of our god—the Almighty."

"I . . ." Veil licked her lips. "I don't understand."

"You will," the first voice said. "We've been watching you, and we find
your passion to be worthy. You wish to oust the false king, the Blackthorn,
and see the kingdom rightfully returned to the highprinces? You wish the
justice of the Almighty to fall upon the wicked?"

"Of course," Veil said.

"Excellent," the woman said. "Our faith in you is well placed." Veil was
pretty sure that was Ulina, a member of Ialai's inner circle. She'd initially
been an unimportant lighteyed scribe, but was rapidly climbing the social
ladder in the new power dynamic of the warcamps.

Unfortunately, if Ulina was here, Ialai probably was not. The high-
princess often sent Ulina to do things she did not wish to do herself.
That indicated Veil had failed in at least one of her goals: she hadn't made
"Chanasha" seem important enough to deserve special attention.

"We guided the return of the Radiants," the man said. "Have you wondered why they appeared? Why all of this—the Everstorm, the awakening
of the parshmen—is happening? *We* orchestrated it. *We* are the grand
architects of the future of Roshar."

Pattern would have enjoyed that lie. Veil found it wanting. A good lie,
the delicious kind, hinted at hidden grandeur or further secrets. This was
instead the lie of a drunken has-been at the bar, trying to drum up enough
pity to get a free drink. It was more pathetic than interesting.

Mraize had explained about this group and their efforts to bring back
the Heralds—who had actually never been gone. Gavilar had led them
along, used their resources—and their hearts—to further his own goals.
During that time, they'd briefly been important movers in the world.

Much of that glory had faded when the old king had fallen, and Amaram
had squandered the rest of it. These scattered remnants weren't architects

of the future. They were a loose end, and even Radiant agreed that this task—given them by both Dalinar and secretly Mraize—was worthy. It was time to end the Sons of Honor once and for all.

Veil looked up at the cultists, walking a careful line between appearing cautious and fawning. "The Radiants. You're Radiant?"

"We are something greater," the man said. "But before we say more, you must be initiated."

"I welcome any chance to serve," Veil said, "but . . . this is quite sudden. How can I be sure you're not agents of the false king seeking to trap people like me?"

"All will be made clear in time," the woman said.

"And if I insist on proof?" Veil said.

The figures glanced at one another. Veil got the feeling they hadn't encountered much resistance during their previous recruitments.

"We serve the *rightful* queen of Alethkar," the woman finally said.

"Ialai?" Veil breathed. "Is she here?"

"Initiation first," the man said, gesturing to two others. They approached Veil—including a tall one whose robes came down only to midcalf. He was notably rough as he grabbed her by the arms and hauled her upward, then repositioned her on her knees.

Remember that one, she thought as the other figure removed a glowing device from a black sack. The fabrial was set with two bright garnets, and had a series of intricate wire loops.

Shallan was particularly proud of that design. And although Veil had initially found it showy, she now recognized that was good for this group. They seemed to trust it implicitly as they held it up to her and pressed some buttons. The garnets went dark, and the figure proclaimed, "She bears no illusions."

Selling them that device had been delicious fun. Wearing the guise of a mystic, Veil had used the device to "expose" one of her Lightweavers in a carefully planned scheme. Afterward Veil had charged them double what Shallan had wanted—and the extravagant price had seemed only to make the Sons believe in its power more. Almighty bless them.

"Your initiation!" the man said. "Swear to seek to restore the Heralds, the church, and the Almighty."

"I swear it," Veil said.

"Swear to serve the Sons of Honor and uphold their sacred work."

"I swear it."

"Swear to the true queen of Alethkar, Ialai Sadeas."

"I swear it."

"Swear you do not serve the false spren who bow before Dalinar Kholin."

"I swear it."

"See," the woman said, looking to one of her companions. "If she'd been a Radiant, she couldn't have sworn a false oath."

Oh, you sweet soft breeze, Veil thought. *Bless you for being so naive. We're not all Bondsmiths or their ilk.* The Windrunners or Skybreakers might have had trouble being so glib with a broken promise, but Shallan's order was *founded* on the idea that all people lied, especially to themselves.

She couldn't break an oath to her spren without consequences. But this group of human debris? She wouldn't think twice about it—though Radiant *did* express some discontent.

"Rise, Daughter of Honor," the man said. "Now, we must replace your hood and return you. But fear not; one of us will soon contact you with further instructions and training."

"Wait," Veil said. "Queen Ialai. I need to see her to prove to myself whom I'm serving."

"Perhaps you will earn this privilege," the woman said, sounding smug. "Serve us well, and eventually you will receive greater rewards."

Great. Veil braced herself for what that meant: *more* time in these war-camps pretending to be a fussy lighteyed woman, carefully worming her way up through the ranks. It sounded dreadful.

Unfortunately, Dalinar was genuinely concerned about Ialai's growing influence. This little cult here might be gaudy and overacted, but it would be unwise to let a martial presence grow unchecked. They couldn't risk another incident like Amaram's betrayal, which had cost thousands of lives.

Besides, Mraize considered Ialai to be dangerous. That was recommendation enough for Veil to see the woman brought down. So she'd have to keep working on this—and they'd therefore also have to find more ways to sneak Adolin out to spend time with Shallan. The girl wilted if not given proper loving attention.

For her sake, Veil tried again. "I don't know if waiting is wise," she said to the others as the tall man prepared to replace her sack. "You should know, I have connections to Dalinar Kholin's inner circle. I can feed you information about his plans, if I'm properly incentivized."

"There will be time for that," the woman said. "Later."

"Don't you want to know what he's planning?"

"We already know," the man said, chuckling. "We have a source far closer to him than you."

Wait.

Wait.

Shallan came alert. They had someone near Dalinar? Perhaps they were lying, but . . . could she risk that?

We need to do something, she thought. If Ialai had an operative in Dalinar's inner circle, it could be life-threatening. They didn't have time for Veil to slowly infiltrate her way to the top. They needed to know who this informant was *now*.

Veil stepped back, letting Shallan take over. Radiant could fight, and Veil could lie. But when they needed a problem solved quickly, it was Shallan's turn.

"Wait," Shallan said, standing up and pushing aside the man's hands as he tried to shove the sack over her head. "I'm not who you think I am."

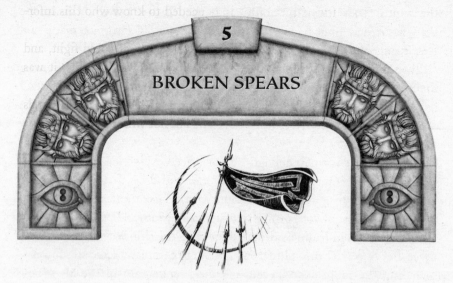

5

BROKEN SPEARS

If the Stormlight in a gemstone is withdrawn quickly enough, a nearby spren can be sucked into the gemstone. This is caused by a similar effect to a pressure differential, created by the sudden withdrawal of Stormlight, though the science of the two phenomena are not identical.

You will be left with a captured spren, to be manipulated as you see fit.

—Lecture on fabrial mechanics presented by Navani Kholin to the coalition of monarchs, Urithiru, Jesevan, 1175

The Windrunners rose around Kaladin in a defensive spread. They hung in the air like no skyeel ever could: motionless, equidistant.

Below, refugees stopped—despite the chaos of the evacuation—to stare up through the awespren at the sentinels in blue. There was something natural about the way Windrunners swooped and banked, but it was another matter altogether to be confronted by the surreal sight of a squad of soldiers hanging in the sky as if on wires.

The fog had mostly burned away, giving Kaladin a good view of the Heavenly Ones as they advanced in the distance. The enemy wore solid-colored battle garb, muted save for the occasional bright crimson. They wore robes that trailed behind them several feet, even in battle. Those would be impractical to walk in, but why walk when they could fly?

They'd learned much about the Fused from the Herald Ash. Each of those Heavenly Ones was an ancient entity; ordinary singers had been sacrificed, giving up their bodies and lives to host a Fused soul. Each approaching enemy carried a long lance, and Kaladin envied the way they moved with the winds. They did it naturally, as if they hadn't merely claimed the sky—as he had—but had instead been *born* to it. Their grace made him feel like a stone tossed briefly into the air.

Three flights would mean fifty-four members. Would Leshwi be among them? He hoped she would, as they needed a rematch. He wasn't certain he'd be able to recognize her, as she'd died last time. He couldn't claim credit; Rock's daughter Cord had done the deed with a well-placed arrow from her Shardbow.

"Three flights is small enough we don't need everyone," Kaladin called to the others. "Squires beneath rank CP4, you drop to the ground and guard the civilians—don't pick a fight with a Fused unless they come at you first. The rest of you, primary engagement protocol."

The newer Windrunners dropped down to the ship with obvious reluctance, but they were disciplined enough not to complain. Like all squires—including the more experienced ones he'd let remain in the air—these hadn't bonded their own spren, and therefore relied on having a nearby full Windrunner knight for their powers.

Kaladin had some three hundred Windrunners at this point—though only around fifty full knights. Almost all of the surviving original members of Bridge Four had bonded a spren by now, as had many of the second wave—those who had joined him soon after he had moved to Dalinar's camp. Even some of the third wave—those who had joined the Windrunners after moving to Urithiru—had found a spren to bond.

There, unfortunately, progress stopped. Kaladin had lines of men and women ready to advance and say the oaths, but there weren't willing honorspren to be found. At this point, there was only a single one he knew of who was willing, but didn't have a bond.

But that was another problem for another time.

Lopen and Drehy moved up beside him, floating slowly, brilliant Shardspears forming in their waiting hands. Kaladin reached overhead and seized his own spear as it formed from mist, then thrust it forward. His Windrunners broke apart, flying out to meet the approaching Heavenly Ones.

Kaladin waited. If Leshwi was among this force, she'd spot him. Ahead, the first of the Heavenly Ones met Windrunners, proffering spears in challenge. Each gesture was an offer of one-on-one combat. His soldiers accepted, instead of ganging up on the enemy. The layman might have found that odd, but Kaladin had learned to use the ways of the Heavenly Ones and their ancient—some might say archaic—methods of fighting.

The paired Windrunners and Fused broke off to engage in contests of skill.

The resulting confrontation looked like two streams of water crashing into one another, then spraying to the sides. In moments, all of the Windrunners were engaged, leaving behind a handful of Fused.

In small-scale skirmishes, the Heavenly Ones preferred to wait for opportunities to fight one-on-one, instead of doubling up on enemies. It wasn't always so—Kaladin had twice been forced to fight multiples at once—but the more Kaladin fought these creatures, the more he respected their ways. He hadn't expected to find honor among the enemy.

As he scanned the unengaged Fused, his eyes focused on one in particular. A tall femalen with a stark red, black, and white skin pattern, marbled like the turbulent mixing of three shades of paint. Though her features were different, the pattern seemed much the same. Plus there was something about the way she held herself, and the way she wore her long crimson and black hair.

She saw him and smiled, then held out her spear. Yes, this was Leshwi. A leader among the Fused—high enough that the others deferred to her, but not so high that she stayed behind during fights. A status similar to Kaladin's own. He held out his spear.

She darted upward, and Kaladin swooped to follow. As he did, an explosion of light expanded below. For a brief moment Kaladin glimpsed Shadesmar, and he soared in a black sky marked by strange clouds flowing like a roadway.

A wave of power surged through the battlefield, causing Windrunners to burst alight. Dalinar had fully opened a perpendicularity, becoming a reservoir of Stormlight that would instantly renew any Radiant who drew near. It was a powerful edge, and one of the reasons they continued to risk bringing the Bondsmith on missions.

Stormlight raged inside Kaladin as he flew after Leshwi. She trailed white and red cloth behind her, slightly longer than the others' garments; it flowed in a swooping, fluid response to her actions as she turned and curved around, leveling her spear at Kaladin and diving toward him.

Fully trained Windrunners had several important advantages in these battles. They had much greater potential speed than the Heavenly Ones, and they had access to Shardweapons. One might have thought these advantages insurmountable, but the Heavenly Ones were ancient, practiced, and cunning. They had trained for *millennia* with their powers, and they could fly forever without running out of Voidlight. They only drained it to heal, and—he'd heard—to perform the occasional rare Lashing.

And, of course, the Fused had a singular terrible edge over Kaladin's people: They were immortal. Kill them, and they'd be reborn in the next Everstorm. They could afford a recklessness that Kaladin could not. As he and Leshwi clashed—spears slamming together, each grunting as they tried to slide their weapon around and stab the other—Kaladin was forced to pull away first.

Leshwi's spear was lined with a silvery metal that resisted Shardblade cuts. More importantly, it was set with a gemstone at its base. If the weapon struck Kaladin, that gemstone would suck away Kaladin's Stormlight and render him unable to heal—a potentially deadly tool against a Radiant, even one infused by Dalinar's perpendicularity.

As soon as Kaladin broke away, Leshwi dove deeper, trailing fluttering cloth. He followed, Lashing himself downward and plummeting through the battlefield. A beautiful chaos, each pair dancing their own individual contest. Leyten zipped past directly overhead, chasing a Heavenly One dressed in grey-blue. Skar shot beneath Kaladin, nearly colliding with Kara as she scored a hit on her opponent.

Orange singer blood sprayed in the air, individual drops splashing Kaladin on the forehead, other drops chasing him as he swooped toward the ground. Kara didn't have a Blade yet; she would have said the Third Ideal by now, he was certain. If only she had a spren.

Kaladin pulled up near the ground, skimming the stone by inches, orange blood raining down around him. Ahead, Leshwi dodged through a crowd of screaming refugees.

Kaladin followed, darting between Leven the cobbler and his wife. Their horrified screams, however, made him slow. He couldn't risk colliding with bystanders. He flew up to the side, then pulled to a stop in the air, watching, anticipating.

Nearby, Lopen skimmed past. "You all right, gancho?" he called to Kaladin.

"I'm fine," Kaladin said.

"I can fight her if you want a breather!"

Leshwi emerged on the other side, and Kaladin ignored Lopen, zipping after. He and Leshwi brushed the outer buildings of the town, rattling stormshutters. He discarded his spear, and Syl appeared near his head as a ribbon of light. He controlled his general direction with Lashings, using his hands, arms, and the contours of his body to govern fine motions. This much air rushing around him gave him the ability to sculpt his trajectory, almost as if he were swimming.

He increased his speed with another Lashing, but Leshwi dodged down through the crowds again. Her recklessness almost cost her as she buzzed a group under the protection of Godeke the Edgedancer. He was a hair too slow, and his Shardblade only sliced off the end of her trailing robes.

She turned away from the people after that, though she stayed near the ground. The Heavenly One couldn't go as fast as a Windrunner, and so she focused on sudden turns or weaving around obstacles—requiring Kaladin to moderate his speed and remain unable to press one of his strongest advantages.

He followed, the chase thrilling him in part *because* of how well Leshwi flew. She turned again, this time coursing in close to the *Fourth Bridge*. She slowed as they skimmed along the side of the enormous vehicle, and she peered at the wooden construction keenly.

She's intrigued by the airship, Kaladin thought, following. *She likely wants to gather as much information about it as she can.* In Jasnah's interviews with the two Heralds—who had lived thousands of years—it had come out that they too were amazed by this creation. As incredible as it seemed, modern artifabrians had discovered things that even the Heralds hadn't known.

Kaladin broke off the chase for a moment, instead soaring over the top of the large ship. He spotted Rock standing at the side of the vehicle with his son, delivering water to the refugees. When Rock saw Kaladin gesturing, the large Horneater snatched a spear from a pile placed there and Lashed it into the air. It shot up to Kaladin, who grabbed it, then Lashed himself after Leshwi.

He got on her tail again as she rose in a wild loop. She often tried to wear him down—leading him in intricate chases—before coming in to fight at close quarters.

Syl, flying beside Kaladin, eyed the spear Rock had thrown. Despite the wind rushing in his ears, Kaladin heard her dismissive sniff. Well, she couldn't be infused with Stormlight. Trying to push it into her was like trying to fill an already brimming cup with more water.

The next few turns strained Kaladin's abilities to their fullest as Leshwi dove and dodged through the battlefield. Most of the others were engaged directly in duels, fighting with spear or Blade. Some led one another on chases, but none were as intricate as the weaving Kaladin was required to do.

His focus narrowed. The other combatants became nothing more than obstacles in the air. His entire being, the fullness of his attention, fixated on chasing that figure ahead of him. The roaring air seemed to fade, and Syl shot ahead of him, leaving a trail of light—a beacon for Kaladin to follow.

Windspren darted from the sky and fell in beside him as he curved in a gut-wrenching turn, spinning as Leshwi arrowed between Skar and another Fused. Kaladin followed, sliding directly through the space between the two spears—narrowly avoiding being stabbed—then Lashed himself around to follow Leshwi. Sweating, he gritted his teeth against the force of the turn.

Leshwi glanced back at him, then dove. She was going to make another pass at the *Fourth Bridge*.

Now, Kaladin thought, pouring Light into his weapon as he dove after Leshwi. It tried to pull out of his hand, but he held it back even as he thrust it forward. As Leshwi neared the ground, he finally let go of the spear, launching it toward her.

She, unfortunately, glanced behind at just the right moment, allowing her to narrowly dodge the spear. It crashed to the ground, splintering, the head smashed up into the shaft. Recovering, Leshwi pulled upward in a stunning move, soaring past Kaladin, who—in the moment—lost concentration and nearly collided with the ground.

He landed roughly, catching himself on the stone—hard enough that he'd have broken bones without Stormlight—then cursed and looked upward. Leshwi disappeared into the fight, leaving him behind with an exultant swirling maneuver in the sky. She seemed to revel in losing him when she could.

Kaladin groaned, shaking his hand where he'd hit the ground. His Stormlight healed the sprain in moments, but it still hurt in a phantom way, like the echoing of a loud noise in one's mind after it left one's ears.

Syl appeared in the air before him in the shape of a young woman, hands on her hips. "And don't you dare return!" she shouted up at the departing Fused. "Or we'll . . . um . . . come up with a better insult than this one!" She glanced at Kaladin. "Right?"

"You could have caught her," Kaladin said, "if you'd been flying on your own without me."

"Without you, I'd be as dumb as a rock. And without me you'd fly like one. I think we're better off not worrying about what we could do without the other." She folded her arms. "Besides, what would I do if I caught her? *Glare* at her? I need you for the stabby-stabby part."

He grunted, climbing to his feet. A moment later, a Radiant with a white beard hovered down nearby. It was odd how much difference a small change in perspective could make. Teft had always seemed . . . rumpled. Beard a little ragged, skin a little rough, mood a lot of both.

But hovering in the sky, the glow of Stormlight making his beard shine, he seemed divine. Like a wise god from one of Rock's stories.

"Kaladin, lad?" Teft asked. "You all right?"

"Fine."

"You sure?"

"I'm *fine*. How's the battlefield?"

"Mostly quick engagements," Teft said. "No casualties so far, thank Kelek."

"They're more interested in inspecting the *Fourth Bridge* than they are in killing us," Kaladin said.

"Ah, that makes sense," Teft said. "Shall we try to stop them?"

"No. Navani's fabrials are hidden in the hold. A few flybys won't tell the enemy anything."

Kaladin surveyed the town, then studied the battlefield in the air. Rapid clashes, with the Heavenly Ones generally backing away quickly. "They aren't committed to a full assault; they're testing our defenses and surveying the flying machine. Spread the word. Have our Windrunners lead the enemy in chases; have them fight defensively. Minimize our casualties."

Teft saluted as another group of townspeople was led up into the ship. Roshone ushered them on, and the old blowhard looked *concerned* for the people under his care. Perhaps he'd been taking acting lessons with the Lightweavers.

Atop the ship, Dalinar glowed with a near impenetrable light. Though it wasn't the enormous pillar of radiance he'd created the first time he'd done this, today's beacon was still powerful enough that it was difficult to look directly at it.

In the past, the Fused had focused their attacks on Dalinar. Today they buzzed the ship—but didn't try to strike at the Bondsmith. They were afraid of him for reasons nobody yet understood, and only committed to a full assault on him if they had overwhelming numbers and ground support.

"I'll pass the word," Teft told Kaladin, but seemed hesitant about him. "You *sure* you're well, lad?"

"I'd be better if you'd stop asking."

"Right, then." Teft shot into the sky.

Kaladin dusted himself off, eyeing Syl. First Lopen, then Teft, acting like he was fragile. Had Syl told the others to keep watch over him? Just because he was feeling a tad tired lately?

Well, he didn't have time for that nonsense. A Heavenly One was approaching, red clothing fluttering, spear proffered toward him. It wasn't Leshwi, but Kaladin was happy to accept the challenge. He needed to be up and flying again.

.:.

The cultists froze, staring at Shallan through the eyeholes in their hoods. The chasm fell silent, save for the noises of scuttling cremlings. Even the tall man with the sack didn't move, though that wasn't as surprising. He'd be waiting for her to take the lead.

I'm not who you think I am, Shallan had said, implying she was going to make some startling revelation.

Now she had to think of one.

I'm really curious to see where this goes . . . Radiant thought at her.

"I am no simple tradeswoman," Shallan said. "You obviously don't trust me yet—and I'm guessing you've seen the oddities about my lifestyle. You want an explanation, don't you?"

The two lead cultists glanced at one another.

"Of course," the woman said. "Yes, you should not have tried to hide things from us."

Remember Adolin, Radiant thought. *Making a disturbance could be tactically dangerous.*

She'd told Pattern and Adolin—who might be watching by now—that if she was in distress, she'd create a distraction so they could attack. They'd try to take the cultists captive, but it could lose them the chance to capture Ialai.

Hopefully they'd see she wasn't in distress, but was instead prying information out of these people.

"Did you ever wonder why I disappear from the warcamps sometimes?" Shallan asked. "And why I have far more money than I should? I have a second business, a hidden one. With the help of agents at Urithiru, I've been copying schematics the Kholin artifabrians have been developing."

"Schematics?" the woman said. "Like what?"

"Surely you've heard news of the enormous flying platform that left Narak a few weeks ago. I have the plans. I know *exactly* how it was done. I've sold smaller fabrial schematics to Natan buyers, but nothing on this level. I've been searching for a buyer of enough means to purchase this secret."

"Selling military secrets?" the male cultist said. "To other kingdoms? That is treason!"

Says the man wearing a silly hood and trying to depose the Kholin monarchy, Veil thought. *These people . . .*

"It's only treason if you accept Dalinar's family as rightful rulers," Shallan said to him. "I do not. But if we can truly help House Sadeas assert itself . . . These secrets could be worth thousands of broams. I would share them with Queen Sadeas."

"We will take them to her," the woman said.

Radiant affixed her with a calculated stare, level and calm. A leader's stare, one Shallan had sketched a dozen times over as she watched Dalinar interact with people. The stare of one in power, who didn't need to say it.

You will not take this from me, the stare said. *If you want favor for having been involved in this revelation, you'll do it by assisting me—not by taking it for yourself.*

"I'm certain that someday this might—" the man began.

"Show me," the woman said, interrupting him.

Hooked, Veil thought. *Nice work, you two.*

"I've got some of the plans in my satchel," Shallan said.

"We searched the satchel," the woman said, waving to a nearby cultist to produce the bag. "There were no plans."

"You think I'd be foolish enough to leave them where they could be discovered?" Shallan said, taking the satchel. She dug inside and covertly took a quick breath of Light as she pulled out a small notebook. She flipped to a rear page, then took out a charcoal pencil. Before the others could crowd around, she breathed out carefully, snapping a Lightweaving in place. Fortunately, she'd been asked to help with the schematics—Shallan had real trouble creating a Lightweaving of something she hadn't previously drawn.

By the time the lead cultists had positioned themselves to peer over her shoulder, she had the Lightweaving in place. As she carefully rubbed her charcoal across the page, it seemed to reveal a hidden schematic.

Your turn, Shallan said as Veil took over.

"You trace the schematic on a piece of paper above this one," Veil explained, "and press very hard. That leaves an indentation in the page. A light brush of charcoal reveals it. This isn't the entire thing, naturally; I keep it as proof for potential buyers."

Shallan felt a little stab of pride at the complicated illusion. It appeared exactly as she wanted it to, making a complicated series of lines and notations appear magically on the page as she did the rubbing.

"I can't make any sense of that," the man complained.

The woman, however, leaned closer. "Replace her sack," the woman said. "We'll bring the matter to the queen. This might be interesting enough for her to grant an audience."

Veil steeled herself as a cultist snatched away her notebook, probably to try applying charcoal to the other pages, which would of course do nothing. The tall man pulled the sack over her head, but as he did so he leaned close.

"What now?" he whispered to Veil. "This feels like trouble."

Don't break character, Red, she thought, bowing her head. She needed to get to Ialai and discover if the woman really did have a spy in Dalinar's court. That meant taking a few risks.

Red was the first one they'd embedded into the Sons of Honor, but his persona—that of a darkeyed workman—hadn't been important enough to get any real access. Hopefully, together they could—

Shouts rose nearby in the chasm. Veil spun, blinded by the sack. Storms alight. What was that?

"We've been followed," the male leader of the conspirators said. "To arms! Those are Kholin troops!"

Damnation, Veil thought. *Radiant was right.*

Adolin, seeing her sack replaced, had decided it was time to take this group captive and cut their losses.

⸭

Kaladin traded blows with his enemy, landing one hit, then another. As he came back around, the Heavenly One thrust down with his lance. But Kaladin had drilled spearplay until he could practically fight in his sleep. Hovering in the air, surging with Stormlight, his body knew what to do and deflected the thrust.

Kaladin made his own lunge, scoring another hit. As they danced, they rotated around one another. Much of Kaladin's formal training had been with spear and shield, intended for formation tactics, but he'd always loved the longspear, wielded two-handed. There was a power to it, a control. He could move the weapon so much more deftly this way.

This Heavenly One wasn't as good as Leshwi. Kaladin scored yet another slice along the enemy's arm. The Shardspear did no physical damage other than greying the flesh around where the cut would have been. It soon healed, but each healing came more slowly. The enemy's Voidlight was running out.

The enemy started humming one of the Fused songs, gritting his teeth as he tried to spear Kaladin. They saw Kaladin as a challenge, a test. Leshwi always got to fight Kaladin first, but if he disengaged or defeated her, another was always waiting. A part of him wondered if this was why he was so tired lately. Even little skirmishes were a slog, never giving him a break.

A deeper part of him knew that wasn't the reason at all.

His enemy prepared to strike, and Kaladin reached with his off hand for one of his belt knives, then whipped it into the air. The Fused overreacted and fumbled his defense. That let Kaladin score a spear hit along the thigh. Defeating a Fused was a test in endurance. Cut them enough, and they slowed. Cut them more, and they stopped healing entirely.

His opponent's humming grew louder, and Kaladin sensed the wounds weren't healing any longer. Time to go for the kill. He dodged a strike— then changed Syl into a hammer, which he swung down on the enemy's weapon, smashing it. The powerful blow threw the Heavenly One completely off balance.

Kaladin dropped the hammer and thrust his hands forward; Syl was instantly a spear, steady in his grip. His aim was true, and he speared the enemy right through the arm. The Fused grunted as Kaladin whipped the spear out by reflex, then spun it around and leveled it at the enemy's neck.

The Fused met his eyes, then licked his lips, waiting. The creature began to slowly drop from the sky, his Light expended, his powers failing.

Killing him does no good, Kaladin thought. *He'll simply be reborn*. Still, that was one Fused out of combat for a few days at least.

He's out anyway, he thought as the creature's arm flopped down at his side, useless and dead from the Shardspear cut. *What good is another death?*

Kaladin lowered his spear, then gestured to the side. "Go," he said. Some of them understood Alethi.

The Fused hummed a different tone, then raised his broken spear to Kaladin—holding it in his off hand. The Heavenly One dropped the weapon toward the rocks below. The creature bowed his head to Kaladin, then drifted away.

Now, where had—

A ribbon of red light streaked in from the side.

Kaladin immediately Lashed himself backward and spun, weapon out. He hadn't realized he'd been dedicating a part of his energy to watching for that red light.

It darted away from him now that he'd noticed it. Kaladin tried to follow it with his eyes, but couldn't keep track of it as it maneuvered among the homes below.

Kaladin breathed out. The fog was all but gone, letting him scan the entirety of Hearthstone—a little cluster of homes bleeding people toward the *Fourth Bridge* in a steady stream. The citylord's manor stood on the hilltop at the far edge of town, overlooking them all. It had once seemed so large and imposing to Kaladin.

"Did you see that light?" he asked Syl.

Yes. That was the Fused from before. When she was a spear, her words came directly into his mind.

"My quick reaction scared it away," Kaladin said.

"Kal?" a feminine voice called. Lyn came swooping in, wearing a brilliant blue Alethi uniform, Stormlight puffing from her lips as she spoke. She wore her long dark hair in a tight braid, and carried a functional—but ordinary—lance under her arm. "You all right?"

"I'm fine," he said.

"You sure?" she said. "You seem distracted. I don't want anyone stabbing you in the back."

"Now you care?" he snapped.

"Of course I do," she said. "Not wanting us to be more doesn't mean I stopped caring."

He glanced at her, then had to turn away because he could see genuine concern in her face. Their relationship hadn't been right. He knew that as well as she did, and the pain he felt wasn't for the end of that. Not specifically.

It was simply one more thing weighing him down. One more loss.

"I'm *fine*," he said, then glanced to the side as he felt the power from Dalinar end. Was something wrong?

No, the time had merely passed. Dalinar generally didn't keep his perpendicularity open for entire battles, but instead used it periodically to recharge spheres and Radiants. Holding it open was taxing for him.

"Run a message to the other Windrunners in the air," Kaladin said to Lyn. "Tell them I spotted that new Fused, the one I told them about earlier. He moved toward me as a ribbon of red light—like a windspren, but the wrong color. He can fly incredibly quickly, and could strike at one of us up here."

"Will do . . ." she said. "If you're sure you don't need any help . . ."

Kaladin pointedly ignored that comment and dropped toward the ship. He wanted to make sure Dalinar was being watched, in case the strange new Fused came after him.

Syl landed on his shoulder and rode downward with her hands primly on her knees.

"The others keep checking on me," Kaladin said to her, "like I'm some delicate piece of glasswork ready to fall off the shelf at any moment and break. Is that your doing?"

"What? That your team is considerate enough to watch out for one another? That would be *your* fault, I'd say."

He landed on the deck of the ship, then turned his head and looked straight at her.

"I didn't say anything to them," she told him. "I know how anxious the nightmares make you. It would be worse if I told anyone about them."

Great. He hadn't liked the idea of her talking to the others, but at least it would have explained why everyone was acting so strangely. He crossed over to Dalinar, who was speaking with Roshone, who had come up from below.

"The town's new leaders keep prisoners in the manor's stormcellar, Brightlord," Roshone was saying, pointing at his former dwelling. "There are currently only two people there, but it would be a crime to abandon them."

"Agreed," Dalinar said. "I'll send one of the Edgedancers to free them."

"I will accompany them," Roshone said, "with your permission. I know the layout of the building."

Kaladin sniffed. "Look at him," he whispered to Syl, "acting like some hero now that Dalinar is around to impress."

Syl reached up and flicked Kaladin on the ear, and he felt a surprisingly sharp pain, like a jolt of power.

"Hey!" he said.

"Stop being a stumer."

"I'm not being a . . . What's a stumer?"

"I don't know," Syl admitted. "It's a word I heard Lift using. Regardless, I'm pretty sure *you're* being one right now."

Kaladin glanced at Roshone, who headed toward the manor with Godeke. "Fine," Kaladin said. "He has maybe improved. A little."

Roshone was the same petty lighteyes he'd always been. But during this last year, Kaladin had seen another side to the former citylord. He seemed to legitimately care. As if realizing, only now, his responsibility.

He'd still gotten Tien killed. For that, Kaladin didn't think he could ever forgive Roshone. At the same time, Kaladin didn't intend to forgive *himself* for that loss either. So at least Roshone was in good company.

Rock and Dabbid were helping the refugees, so Kaladin told them he'd seen the strange Fused again. Rock nodded, understanding immediately. He waved to his older children—including Cord, who carried Amaram's old Shardbow strapped to her back and wore the full set of Shardplate she'd found in Aimia.

Together they moved in a not-so-subtle way over near Dalinar, keeping a watch on the sky for red lines of light. Kaladin glanced upward as one of the Heavenly Ones shot past, chased by Sigzil.

"That's Leshwi," Kaladin said, launching into the air.

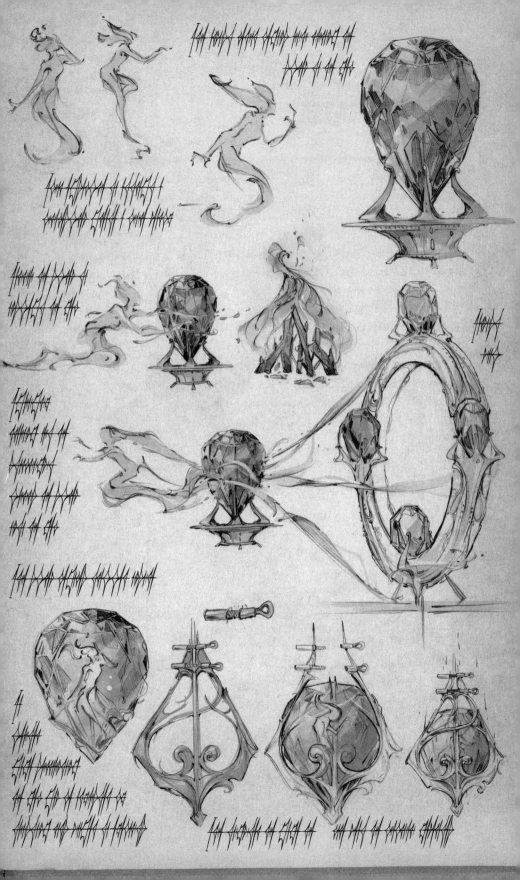

6

A LOOSE THREAD

With a captured spren, you may begin designing a proper fabrial. It is a closely guarded secret of artifabrians that spren, when trapped, respond to different types of metals in different ways. A wire housing for the fabrial, called a "cage," is essential to controlling the device.

—Lecture on fabrial mechanics presented by Navani Kholin
to the coalition of monarchs, Urithiru, Jesevan, 1175

Radiant backed up, the sack on her head. She pressed her fingers against the cool stone of the wall as the shouting continued. Yes, that was Adolin's voice. As she'd feared, he'd come to rescue her.

Radiant considered pulling off the hood, summoning her Shardblade, and demanding the conspirators surrender. However, she acknowledged what Veil and Shallan wanted. They needed to meet Ialai face-to-face.

A scraping sounded nearby. Radiant turned toward it. Rock on rock. And . . . some sort of mechanism turning?

She strode blindly toward the sound. "Bring me," she shouted. "Don't leave me to them!"

"Fine," Ulina said from somewhere nearby. "You two, grab her. You, guard the doorway from inside. Try to jam the mechanism closed. Quickly!"

Rough hands grabbed Radiant by the shoulders and pulled her along, steering her into what sounded—from the echoing footsteps—like a tunnel. Stone ground on stone behind them, cutting off the noise of the skirmish in the chasm. At least she knew how the cultists were getting in and out of the chasms. Radiant stumbled and purposefully fell to her knees so she could put her hands on the ground. Smooth, cut rock. Done with a Shardblade, she suspected.

The others forced her to her feet and pushed her up an incline. They didn't remove the sack, even when she protested that it wasn't necessary.

Well, a tunnel made sense. This warcamp had been occupied by Sadeas and Ialai for years before everyone else moved to Urithiru. They would have wanted a secret escape route from their warcamp, particularly during the early years on the Plains when everyone—Adolin said—had been so certain the princedoms would shatter apart and start fighting one another.

The tunnel eventually reached another door, and this one opened into what sounded like a small room. A cellar perhaps? Those weren't common on the Shattered Plains—too easy to flood—but the richer lighteyes had them for chilling wine.

The conspirators muttered to themselves about what to do. Four people. Judging by the sounds of rustling cloth, they were removing their robes. Probably had ordinary clothing underneath. Red wasn't here; he'd have squeezed her arm to let her know. So she was alone.

The others eventually hauled her up some steps and then outside; she felt wind on her hands and warm sunlight on her skin. She pretended to be pliable and easy to move, though she waited—ready to attack—in case this was some kind of ruse, and she was assaulted.

They led her through the streets quickly, the hood still on. Shallan took over, as she had an incredible—likely supernatural—ability to sense and memorize direction. She mapped their path in her head. Sneaky little cremlings; they led her in a large double loop, ending at a location near where they'd emerged from the cellar.

The hike up had taken only a few minutes, so they had to be near the eastern edge of the warcamp. Perhaps the fortress there? That would put her near the old Sadeas lumberyards, where Kaladin had spent months building Bridge Four from the broken remnants of the men delivered there to die. She wondered if anyone in the area had found it odd that they were leading around a woman with a sack on her head. Judging by how upset they seemed as they finally pulled her into a building, they weren't thinking very clearly. They forced her down into a chair, then left, boots thumping on wood.

She soon heard them arguing in a nearby room. Carefully, Veil reached up and removed her hood. The cultist left guarding her—a tall man with a scar on his chin—didn't demand she replace it. She was sitting in a stiff wooden chair right inside the door of a stone room with a large circular rug. The rug didn't do much to liven the otherwise bare chamber. These warcamp buildings were so fortresslike: few windows, little ornamentation.

Shallan had always viewed Sadeas as a blowhard. A fortress like this—and the escape tunnel she'd traveled through—made Veil revise that assessment. She sifted through Shallan's memories, and what *Veil* saw in the man was pure craftiness.

Shallan didn't have many memories of Ialai, but Veil knew enough to be careful. Highprince Thanadal had started this new "kingdom" at the warcamps. But soon after Ialai had set up here, Thanadal had been found dead, supposedly knifed by a prostitute. Vamah—the other highprince who hadn't supported Dalinar—had fled the warcamps in the night. He seemed to believe Ialai's lie that Dalinar had ordered the assassination.

That left Ialai Sadeas the one true remaining power here in the warcamps. She had an army, had co-opted the Sons of Honor, and was demanding tariffs from arriving trade caravans. This woman remained a thorn, a reminder of the old Alethkar full of squabbling lighteyes always eyeing one another's lands.

Veil listened as best she could to the arguments coming from the next room; the conspirators seemed frustrated that they'd lost so many in the strike. They seemed frantic, and worried that it was "all falling apart."

At last, the door swung open and three people stormed out. Veil recognized Ulina, the woman she'd suspected earlier from her voice. They were followed by a lighteyed soldier in Sadeas colors.

The guard gestured for Veil to enter, so she rose and carefully poked her head into the room. It was larger than the antechamber, with very narrow windows. Despite the attempt to soften it with a rug, couches, and pillows, it still felt like a fortress. A place for lighteyes to hole up in during storms or to fall back to if attacked.

Ialai Sadeas sat at a table on the far side of the room, shrouded in shadows, away from the windows and the glowing sphere lamps on the walls. Near to her sat a large hutch with a roll top covering its front.

All right, Veil thought, walking forward. *We've found her. Have we decided what we're going to do with her?*

She knew Radiant's vote: get her to say something incriminating, then bring her in. Veil, however, hadn't pushed this mission solely to gather evidence for Dalinar. She hadn't even done it because the Ghostbloods saw Ialai as a threat. Veil had done it because this woman stubbornly continued to jeopardize everything Shallan loved.

Dalinar and Jasnah needed to keep their eyes on the real prize: reclaiming Alethkar. And so, Veil had determined to snip this particular loose thread. Adolin had killed Highprince Sadeas in a moment of honest passion. Veil had come to finish the job he'd begun.

Today Veil intended to assassinate Ialai Sadeas.

.•.

The hardest thing in the world for Kaladin to do was nothing. It was excruciating to watch one of his soldiers fight for his life against a skilled, dangerous opponent—and do nothing to help.

Leshwi was a being of incredible age, the spirit of a singer long dead turned into something more akin to a spren—a force of nature. Sigzil was a capable fighter, but far from the order's best. His true talents lay in his understanding of numbers, his knowledge of other cultures, and his ability to remain focused and practical in situations where others lost their heads.

He was quickly forced onto the defensive. Leshwi loomed over him— thrusting down with her spear—then swung around and stabbed from the side. She expertly flowed from one attack to the next, forcing Sigzil to keep spinning around, barely deflecting or dodging her strikes.

Kaladin Lashed himself forward, fingers tight on his spear. It was vital his team keep to the Heavenly Ones' sense of honor. So long as the enemy agreed to one-on-one combat, his soldiers were never in danger of being overwhelmed and wiped out.

The forces on the ground might mercilessly brutalize one another, but up here—in the skies—they'd found mutual respect. The respect of combatants who *would* kill one another, but as part of a contest, not a slaughter. Break that unspoken rule, gang up on Leshwi now, and that precarious balance would end.

Leshwi shot forward and speared Sigzil in the chest. Her weapon impaled him straight through, bursting from the back of his blue uniform, slick with blood. He struggled, gasping, Stormlight leaking from his mouth. Leshwi hummed a loud tone, and the gemstone on her spear began to glow, sucking Stormlight from her prey.

Kaladin groaned, the deaths of so many he'd failed flashing before him. Tien? Nalma? *Elhokar?*

He was again in that terrible nightmare at the Kholinar palace, where his friends killed one another. Screams and lights and pain and blood all swirled around one image: a man Kaladin was sworn to protect, lying on the floor.

Moash's spear straight through him.

"*No!*" Kaladin shouted. He couldn't simply watch. He *couldn't.* He Lashed himself forward, but Leshwi met his eyes. He paused.

She yanked her spear from Sigzil's chest right before his Stormlight went out. Sigzil sagged in the air, and Kaladin grabbed him, holding him as he blinked in a daze, clutching his silvery Shardspear.

"Drop your weapon," Kaladin said to him, "and bow to her."

"What? Sir?" Sigzil frowned as his wound healed.

"Drop your spear," Kaladin said, "and bow to her."

Sigzil, looking confused, did as he requested. Leshwi nodded to him in turn.

"Go back to the ship," Kaladin said, "and sit out the rest of this battle. Stay with the squires."

"Um, yes, sir," Sigzil said. He floated off, poking at the bloody hole in his jacket.

Leshwi glanced to the side. A short distance away—hanging in the air with no weapon—was the Heavenly One that Kaladin had defeated earlier.

Leshwi shouldn't care that Kaladin had spared the creature. It had been a foolish gesture toward a being who could be reborn with each new storm. Then again, Leshwi probably knew that if Sigzil were killed, a new Radiant could be raised up using his spren. It wasn't exactly the same—in fact, in terms of Kaladin's relief, there was a *huge* difference.

At any rate, as Leshwi raised her spear to him, he was glad to accept the challenge.

⁘

In the middle deck of the *Fourth Bridge,* Navani counted off another family and pointed them toward a clearly marked and numbered section of the hold. The ardents there were quick to provide comfort to the worried family. Wide-eyed children clutching blankets settled in, several of them sniffling. Parents arranged sacks with the clothing and other possessions they'd hastily packed.

"Some few are refusing to leave," Ardent Falilar said quietly to Navani. He fretted at his pure white beard as he looked over the list of names. "They'd rather continue living in oppression than abandon their homeland."

"How many?" she asked.

"Not many. Fifteen people. Otherwise the evacuation is going faster than I'd estimated. The refugees, obviously, were already prepared to move—and most of the normal townspeople had already been forced into close quarters with their neighbors to give parshmen their dwellings."

"Then what are you so worried about?" Navani asked, making a notation on her list. Nearby, Renarin had stepped up to the family with the sniffling children. He summoned a small globe of light, then began bouncing it between his hands. Such a simple thing, but the children who saw it grew wide-eyed, forgetting their fear.

The ball of light was bright blue. Part of Navani felt it should be red—to reveal the true nature of the spren that hid inside Renarin. A Voidspren. Or at least an ordinary spren corrupted to the enemy's side. None of them knew what to do about that fact, least of all Renarin. As with most Radiants, he hadn't known what he was doing when he began. Now that he'd formed the bond, it was too late to turn back.

Renarin claimed the spren was trustworthy, but something was odd about his powers. They had managed to recruit several standard Truthwatchers—and they could create illusions like Shallan. Renarin couldn't do that. He could only summon lights, and they did strange, unnatural things sometimes. . . .

"So many things could still go wrong!" Falilar said, drawing Navani's attention back to the moment. "What if we underestimated the weight this many people will add? What if the strain cracks gemstones faster than we'd planned? The fans barely worked at all. It's not a disaster, Brightness, but there's *so much to worry about*."

He tugged at his beard again. It was a wonder he had any hairs left at this point.

Navani patted his arm fondly—if Falilar didn't have something to worry about, he'd go mad. "Do a visual inspection of the gemstones. Then double-check your calculations."

"Triple-check, you mean?" he said. "Yes, I suppose. Keep myself busy. Stop worrying." He reached for his beard, then pointedly shoved his hand in the pocket of his ardent robes.

Navani passed her checklist to another ardent, then climbed the steps to the top deck. Dalinar said he'd reopen the perpendicularity soon, and she wanted to be there—her pencil poised—when he did.

Down below, the townspeople kept clustering and looking up at the strange battle overhead. All this gawking was *really* going to throw off the orderly boarding plan she'd commissioned. Next time she'd have the ardents draw up a second plan that indicated how long it might take if a battle were occurring.

Well, at least only the Heavenly Ones were here. They tended to ignore civilians, considering them little more than battlefield obstacles. Other groups of Fused were far more . . . brutal.

The command station was mostly empty now, all of her ardents having been recruited to comfort and guide the boarding townspeople. Only Rushu remained, absently watching the flying Windrunners with her notebook open.

Bother. The pretty young ardent was *supposed* to be cataloguing the town's food supplies. Rushu was brilliant, but like a sphere, she tended to shine in all directions unless carefully focused.

"Brightness," Rushu said as Navani walked up. "Did you see that? The Fused over there—the one now fighting Highmarshal Kaladin—she let one of the Windrunners go after stabbing him."

"I'm sure she was merely distracted by Kaladin's arrival," Navani said, glancing toward Dalinar, who stood directly ahead.

The large Horneater bridgeman had taken a position near Dalinar and was looking over some sacks of supplies that Rushu had apparently forgotten about. Navani didn't miss that his daughter—the Shardbearer—was standing very close as well. Kaladin had been promoted beyond being a simple bodyguard, but he did tend to keep an eye out for Dalinar regardless. Almighty bless him for it.

"Brightness," Rushu said, "I *swear* there is something odd about this battle. Too many of the Windrunners are idling about, not fighting."

"Reserves, Rushu," Navani said. "Come, let my husband worry about tactics. We have another duty."

Rushu sighed, but did as asked, tucking her notebook under her arm and accompanying Navani. Dalinar stood with his hands clasped behind his back, watching the fighting. As Navani had hoped, he relaxed his posture, then brought his hands to the sides—as if gripping some unseen fabric.

He pulled his hands together, and the perpendicularity opened as a burst of light. Gloryspren, like golden spheres, began to spiral around him. Navani got a better glimpse of Shadesmar this time. And again she heard that *tone*. That was new, wasn't it? Though she didn't consider herself talented at drawing—at least not compared to a master like Shallan—she sketched what she saw, trying to capture an image of that place with the strange sun over a sea of beads. She could visit it in person if she wished, using the Oathgates—but something felt different about these visions.

"What did you see?" she asked Rushu.

"I didn't see anything, Brightness," Rushu said. "But . . . I felt something. Like a pulse, a powerful *thump*. For a moment I felt as if I were falling into eternity. . . ."

"Write that down," Navani said. "Capture it."

"Very well," Rushu said, opening her notebook again. She glanced up as Kaladin skimmed the deck overhead, dangerously close, following one of the Fused.

"Focus, Rushu," Navani said.

"If you wish depictions or descriptions of Shadesmar," Rushu said, "Queen Jasnah has released journals of her travels there."

"I'm well aware," Navani said, still drawing. "And I've read the journals." The ones Jasnah would give her, anyway. Storming woman.

"Then why do you need my depiction of it?" Rushu asked.

"We're looking for something else," Navani said, glancing at Dalinar—then shielding her watering eyes. She blinked, then waved for Rushu to follow her to withdraw back to the nearby command post. "There's someplace beyond Shadesmar, a place where Dalinar gets this power. Once long ago, the tower was maintained by a Bondsmith like my husband—and from what the spren have said, I conclude that the tower got *its* power from that place beyond Shadesmar as well."

"You're still worrying about that, Brightness?" Rushu pursed her lips. "It's not your fault we haven't decoded the tower's secrets. It's a puzzle one woman—or an army of women—can't be expected to unlock after only a year."

Navani winced. Was she truly that transparent? "This is about more than the tower, Rushu," Navani said. "Everyone is praising the effectiveness of this ship. Brightlord Kmakl is imagining entire fleets of airships blotting out the sun. Dalinar speaks of moving tens of thousands of troops in an assault on Kholinar. I don't think either of them realistically understands how much *work* goes into keeping this one ship in the air."

"Hundreds of laborers in Urithiru turning winches to raise and lower the ship," Rushu said, with a nod. "Dozens of chulls used to move it laterally. Thousands of fabrials to facilitate both—all needing to be perpetually reinfused. Careful synchronization via a half dozen spanreeds to coordinate maneuvers. Yes, it is highly improbable we could field more than two or three of these vessels."

"Unless," Navani said, stabbing her finger at her notes, "we discover how the ancients made the tower work. If we knew that secret, Rushu, we would not only be able to restore Urithiru—we might be able to power these airships. We might be able to create fabrials beyond what anyone has ever imagined."

Rushu cocked her head. "Neat," she said. "I'll write down my thoughts."

"That's all? Just . . . 'neat'?"

"I like big ideas, Brightness. Keeps my job from getting boring." She glanced to the side. "But I still think it's odd how many Windrunners are standing around."

"Rushu," Navani said, rubbing her forehead. "Do try to focus."

"Well, I do try. I simply fail. Like that fellow over there? What's he doing? Not guarding the ship. Not helping with the refugees. Shouldn't he be fighting?"

"He's probably a scout," Navani said. She followed Rushu's gaze past the edge of the ship, toward the fertile stone fields. "Obviously he . . ."

Navani trailed off as she picked out the man in question standing atop a hill—distinctly separated from the battle. Navani could see why Rushu would think him a Windrunner. He wore a uniform after the exact cut of Bridge Four. In fact, Rushu—who paid attention to the oddest things, but never seemed to notice important details—might have once seen this man in their ranks. He'd often been at Kaladin's side during the early months of Bridge Four's transition into Dalinar's army.

Rushu missed the fact that this man's uniform was black, that he wore no patch on his shoulder. That his narrow face and lean figure would mark him as a man interdicted. A traitor.

Moash. The man who had killed Navani's son.

He seemed to meet her eyes, despite the distance. He then burst alight with Stormlight and dropped out of view behind the hill.

Navani stood there, frozen with shock. Then she gasped, heat washing over her as if she'd suddenly stepped into burning sunlight. He was here. That *murderer* was here!

She scrambled over to one of the Windrunner squires on the deck. "Go!" she shouted at him, pointing. "Warn the others. Moash, the traitor, is here!"

⁘

Kaladin again chased Leshwi through a chaotic battlefield. The flight gave him the chance to quickly survey how his soldiers were doing, and what he saw was encouraging.

Many of them had pushed back their opponents. The bulk of the Heavenly Ones were hovering in a wide perimeter, pulling away from fights. Kaladin suspected they'd realized there was little to discover by looking at the outside of the ship.

The Heavenly Ones, unsupported by ground troops or other Fused, didn't seem to want to fully commit. Only a few contests continued, and Kaladin's was the most furious. Indeed, he had to turn his full attention to the chase, lest he lose Leshwi.

Kaladin found himself grinning as he followed her through a wide loop, weaving and dodging around other combatants. When he'd begun training, he'd have thought maneuvers like this turn impossible. To perform the feat, he had to constantly dismiss and renew his Lashings, each at a different angle in a loop—doing so without conscious thought—all while sculpting his motion with the rushing wind to avoid obstacles.

He could now execute such a maneuver. If not easily, at least regularly. It left him wondering what else Windrunners could do with enough training.

Leshwi seemed to want to buzz past every other combatant on the battlefield, forcing Kaladin to constantly reorient. A test. She wanted to push him, see how good he truly was.

Let me get close, and I'll show you *how good I am,* he thought, cutting out of the loop and flying down to intercept her. That put him close enough to strike with his spear.

She deflected, then darted to the side. He Lashed himself after her, and the two of them shot through the air parallel to the ground, curling around one another while each tried to get in a hit. The wind was a huge factor, tugging at his spear. At these speeds, it was like dueling in a highstorm.

They quickly left the town and the main battle. Kaladin had Syl re-form as a sword—but Leshwi was prepared for his lunge. She slid her spear through her hands and gripped it near the head, then dove in and struck at his neck, throwing off his next attack.

Kaladin took a slice on the neck—but not enough for her to siphon away his Stormlight. He pulled away farther, still flying parallel to her, the wind making his hair whip and twist. He didn't want to end up isolated, so he curved back toward the main battlefield.

Leshwi followed. Apparently she'd determined he could keep up with her, and now wanted to spar. Their loop took them toward the manor, coming in from the north side.

This land was so familiar to Kaladin. He'd played on these hills with Tien. He first touched a spear—well, a length of wood he pretended was a spear—right over there. . . .

Stay focused, he thought. *This is a time for fighting, not reminiscing.*

Only . . . this wasn't some random battlefield off in the Unclaimed Hills. For the first time in his life, he *knew* the terrain. Better than anyone else in this battle.

He smiled, then came in close to Leshwi for a clash, slowing and nudging them to the east. He allowed a slice along his arm, then pulled away as if in shock. He shot toward the ground, leveling off and darting among the hills, Leshwi following.

There, he thought. *That one.*

He ducked around the side of a hill, pulling his water flask off his belt. Here, on the leeward side of the hill, the rock had been carved away into a cavern for storing equipment. And as it had always been when he was young, the door was slightly ajar and crusted over with the cocoons of lurgs: little creatures that spent days hiding inside their coverings, waiting for rain to wake them up.

Kaladin sprayed water from his canteen across the door, then dropped the canteen and ducked around the next hill over, falling still near the ground. He heard Leshwi come in behind him. She slowed—evidenced by the sound of rustling cloth. She'd have found the discarded canteen.

Kaladin peeked around and spotted her hovering between the hills, maybe two feet off the ground, her long clothing dragging on the stone. She slowly turned in a circle, trying to locate him.

The lurgs started dropping from their cocoons, thinking rain had come. They began hopping around, causing the door to creak. Leshwi immediately spun and leveled her lance toward them.

Kaladin launched toward her. She nearly reacted in time, but this close to the ground her long lance was a hindrance. Leshwi had to twist it around and grab it closer to the head before striking, which gave Kaladin the chance to ram a newly shortened Sylspear toward her chest.

He caught her in the shoulder, making her gasp in pain. She ducked his follow-up slash, but again had trouble maneuvering her lance as he slashed her in the leg.

For a moment, the struggle was everything. Leshwi dropped her lance and pulled a short sword from her belt, then came in closer than Kaladin had expected, knocking aside his spear and trying to grab him by the arm. Her greyed flesh healed slowly enough that he was able to ram his shoulder into her wound, making her grunt. When she tried to slide the sword into his neck, he deflected it with a Sylbuckler that appeared on his arm.

Leshwi feinted toward him to make him pull back, then snatched her lance and streaked toward the sky. Kaladin followed, his spear materializing before him—and was on her before she could pick up enough speed to dodge. She was forced to defend by sweeping his attacks away, growing more and more reckless. Until Kaladin saw his moment and made the Sylspear vanish in his hands right as she blocked.

Then—while Leshwi was reacting to the failed block—he stabbed forward, the spear forming as he did so, and slammed it straight into—

Pain.

Leshwi had brought her spear around to strike precisely as he did. Her weapon hit him in the shoulder, mirroring where he'd struck her opposite shoulder. He felt his Stormlight draining away, leeched into the spear; it felt as if his very soul was being drawn out. He held on, sucking in all the remaining Light from the recharged spheres in his pouches—then forced his spear deeper into her wound until tears leaked from the corners of her eyes.

Leshwi smiled. He grinned back, a full-toothed grin, even while she was draining away his life.

He yanked away almost at the same moment she did. She immediately put her free hand to her wound, and Kaladin shivered. Frost crackled on his uniform as a great deal of Stormlight rushed to fill the wound. That had cost him. He was dangerously low, and Dalinar had taken another break from his perpendicularity.

Leshwi eyed him as they hovered. Then Kaladin heard the screaming.

He started, turning toward the sounds. People yelling for help? Yes, the citylord's manor was on fire—plumes of smoke rising through broken windows. What was going on? Kaladin had been so focused on his duel, he hadn't seen.

Keeping one eye on Leshwi, he scanned the region. Most of the people had made it to the ship, and the other Windrunners were withdrawing. The Edgedancers had already boarded, but there was a small group of people standing in front of the burning manor.

One of them stood a good foot or two taller than the others. A hulking form of red and black with dangerous carapace and long hair the color of dried blood. The Fused from earlier, the one that could become a red line of light. He had gathered the soldiers Kaladin had sent away. Several were accosting townspeople, slamming them to the ground, threatening them with weapons and causing them to scream in pain and panic.

Kaladin felt a burning anger. This Fused went after the civilians?

He heard an angry-sounding hum beside him. Leshwi had drifted near—closer than he should have let her get—but she didn't strike. She watched the Fused and his soldiers below, and the sound of her angry humming intensified.

She looked to him, then nodded toward the Fused and the unfortunate people. He understood the gesture immediately. *Go. Stop him.*

Kaladin moved forward, then paused and held up his spear before Leshwi. Then he dropped it. Though Syl vanished to mist almost immediately, he hoped Leshwi would understand.

Indeed, she smiled, then—her off hand still pressed to her wound—she held out her own spear and pointed the tip downward. *A draw*, the gesture seemed to say.

She nodded again toward the manor. Kaladin needed no further encouragement. He shot toward the terrified people.

7

THE RAREST VINTAGE

The two metals of primary significance are zinc and brass, which allow you to control expression strength. Zinc wires touching the gemstone will cause the spren inside to more strongly manifest, while brass will cause the spren to withdraw and its power to dim.

Remember that a gemstone must be properly infused following the spren's capture. Drilled holes in the gemstone are ideal for proper use of the cage wires, so long as you don't crack the structure and risk releasing the spren.

—Lecture on fabrial mechanics presented by Navani Kholin
to the coalition of monarchs, Urithiru, Jesevan, 1175

Veil stepped up to Ialai Sadeas. She'd heard of this woman's craftiness, her competence. Veil was therefore surprised to find the woman looking so . . . weathered.

Ialai Sadeas was a woman of moderate height. While she'd never been renowned as a great beauty, she seemed to have withered since Shallan had last seen her. Though she wore a dress of the sharpest and most recent fashion—embroidered along the sides—it seemed to hang on her like a cloak on a tavern's wall peg. Her cheeks were sunken and hollow, and she held an empty wine cup in her hand.

"So, you've finally come for me," she said.

Veil hesitated. What did that mean?

Strike now, Veil thought. *Summon the Blade; burn those self-satisfied eyes out of her skull.*

But she wouldn't act on her will alone. They had a balance, an important one. The Three never did what only one of them wanted, not in regard to a decision this important. And so, she held back. Radiant didn't want to kill Ialai. She was too honorable. But what of Shallan?

Not yet, Shallan thought. *Talk to her first. Find out what she knows.*

Therefore, Veil bowed—staying in character. "My queen."

Ialai snapped her fingers, and the guard retreated with the last of the cultists, closing the door behind him. She wasn't the frightened type, Ialai Sadeas—though Veil did notice a door on the far wall of the room, behind Ialai, as a potential exit.

Ialai sat back in her chair, letting Veil hold the bow. "I do not intend to be queen," she eventually said. "That is a lie that some of my more . . . overeager followers perpetuate."

"Who then do you support for the throne? Surely not the usurper Dalinar, or the niece he has appointed unlawfully."

Ialai watched Veil, who slowly stood from the bow. "In the past," Ialai said, "I have supported the heir—Elhokar's son, Gavilar's grandson, the rightful king."

"He is only a boy, not yet six."

"Then urgent action must be taken," Ialai said, "to rescue him from the clutches of his aunt and great-uncle, the rats who have deposed him. To support me is *not* to upset the lineage, but to work for a better, stable, and *correct* Alethi union."

Clever. Under such a guise, Ialai could pretend to be a humble patriot. But . . . why did she look so haunted? A wreckage of her former self? She'd been hit hard by Sadeas's death and the traitorous turn of Amaram's army. Had those events encouraged a downward spiral? Most importantly, who was the spy this woman had close to Dalinar?

Ialai stood up, letting her wine cup roll off the table and shatter on the floor. She walked past Veil to the nearby hutch and rolled up the front, revealing a dozen or more carafes of wine, each a different color.

While Ialai was surveying these, Veil held her hand to the side and began summoning her Shardblade. Not to strike, but because Pattern was with Adolin. The act of summoning should give Pattern an indication of her direction. She stopped almost immediately, preventing the sword from coalescing.

Adolin would want to come find her. Unfortunately, striking against Ialai's fortress would be more dangerous than jumping a group of conspirators in the chasm. Dalinar had no authority here, and though the Lightweaving Shallan had stuck to Adolin would keep him from being recognized, Veil wasn't certain he could risk moving in the open.

"Do you favor wines?" Ialai asked her.

"I'm not particularly thirsty, Brightness," Veil said.

"Join me anyway."

Veil stepped up beside her, looking at the array of wines. "This is quite a collection."

"Yes," Ialai said, selecting one, a clear—probably a grain alcohol. Left uninfused, the color gave no indication of flavoring or potency. "I requisition samples of the vintages that pass through the warcamps. It is one of the few luxuries these Heralds-forsaken stormlands can offer."

She poured a small cup, and Veil could immediately tell she'd been wrong. It didn't have the sharp, immediately overpowering sensation of something like a Horneater vintage. Instead there was a fruity scent mixed with the faint stench of alcohol. Curious.

Ialai offered it to Veil first, who accepted the cup and took a drink. It tasted sharply sweet, like a dessert wine. How had they made it clear? Most fruit wines had natural coloring.

"No fear of poison?" Ialai asked.

"Why should I fear poison, Brightness?"

"This was prepared for me, and there are many who would see me dead. Remaining in my proximity can be dangerous."

"Like the attack in the chasm earlier?"

"It is not the first such strike," she said, though Veil knew of no others that Dalinar had ordered. "Strange, how easily my enemies strike at me in quiet, dark chasms. Yet it has taken them so long to attack me in my chambers." She looked right at Veil.

Damnation. She knew what Veil had come here to do.

Ialai drank deeply. "What do you think of the wine?"

"It was nice."

"That's all?" Ialai held up her cup, inspecting the last few drops. "It's sweet, fermented from a fruit, not a grain. It reminds me of visits to Gavilar's wineries. I would guess it an Alethi vintage, rescued before the kingdom fell, made from simberries. The flesh of the fruit is clear, and they took great care to remove the rinds. Revealing what was truly inside."

Yes, she *did* suspect. After a moment of decision, Shallan emerged. If it was to be wordplay, then she should be the one in control.

Ialai selected another carafe, this time a pale orange. "How is it," she said, "that you have access to such important documents as Navani's schematics? She can be extremely secretive with her projects—not because she fears someone stealing them, but because she relishes a dramatic reveal."

"I cannot give away my sources," Shallan said. "Surely you understand the importance of protecting the identities of those who serve you." She pretended to think. "Though I can perhaps share a name, if I were to get one in return—someone you have close to the king. A way for both of us to have further access to the Kholin inner circle."

A little clumsy, Veil noted. *You sure you want control right now?*

Ialai smiled, then handed Shallan a small cup of the orange. She took it—and found it bland and flavorless.

"Well?" Ialai asked, sipping her own cup.

"It is weak," Shallan said. "Powerless. Yet I taste a hint of something wrong. A touch of sourness. An . . . annoyance that should be exterminated from the vintage."

"And yet," Ialai said, "it looks so good. A proper orange, to be enjoyed by children—and those who act like them. Perfect for people who want to maintain appearances before others. Then the sourness. That's what this vintage *truly* is, isn't it? Awful, no matter how it may appear."

"To what end?" Shallan asked. "What good does it do to package an inferior wine with such a fine label?"

"It might fool some, for a time," Ialai said. "Allow the winemaker to gain quick and easy ground over his competition. But he'll eventually be revealed as a fraud, and his creation will be discarded in favor of a truly *strong* or *noble* vintage."

"You make bold claims," Shallan said. "One hopes the winemaker doesn't hear. He might be irate."

"Let him be. We both know what he is."

As Ialai moved to serve a third cup, Shallan began to summon her Shardblade again—giving Pattern another hint to indicate her direction.

Bring it all the way, Veil thought. *Strike.*

Is this who we want to be with our powers? Radiant thought. *If we start down this path, where will it lead us?*

Could they really serve Dalinar Kholin by acting against his explicit orders? He didn't want this. He probably should, but he didn't.

"Ah, here," Ialai said. "Perfect." She held up a deep blue. This time she didn't offer it to Shallan first, but took a sip. "A wonderful vintage, but the last of its kind. Every other bottle destroyed in a fire. After today, even this bit will be gone."

"You seem so resigned," Shallan said. "The Ialai Sadeas I've heard about would scour entire kingdoms looking for another bottle of the vintage she so loves. Never surrendering."

"That Ialai wasn't nearly so tired," she said, her hand drooping—as if the weight of the cup of wine was somehow too great. "I've fought so long. And now I'm alone . . . sometimes it seems the very shadows work against me." Ialai selected a carafe of Horneater white—Shallan could smell it as soon as the top was off—and held it out. "I believe this is yours. Invisible. Deadly."

Shallan didn't take the drink.

"Get on with it," Ialai said. "You killed Thanadal when he tried to deal. So I can't try that. You hunted Vamah and murdered him after he fled, and there's little chance of me surviving the same. I thought I might be safe if I hunkered down for a time. Yet here you are."

Invisible. Deadly. Sweet wisdom of Battah . . .

Shallan had been engaging in this entire conversation assuming that Ialai knew her for an operative of Dalinar. That wasn't the case at all. Ialai saw her as an operative of Mraize, of the *Ghostbloods.*

"*You* killed Thanadal," Shallan said.

Ialai laughed. "He told you that, did he? So they lie to their own?"

Mraize hadn't specifically told her Ialai had killed Thanadal. But he'd clearly implied it.

Veil gritted her teeth, frustrated. She'd come here of her own volition. Yes, Mraize was always hinting to her what he and the Ghostbloods wanted. But Veil did *not* serve him. She had undertaken this mission for . . . the good of Alethkar. And Adolin. And . . .

"Go on," Ialai said. "Do it."

Veil thrust her hand to the side, summoning her Shardblade. Ialai dropped the carafe of Horneater white, jumping despite herself. Though fearspren boiled up from the ground, Ialai merely closed her eyes.

Oh! a perky voice said in Veil's mind. *We were almost here anyway, Veil! What are we doing?*

"Did they at least tell you why they decided we need to die?" Ialai asked. "Why they hated Gavilar? Amaram? Me and Thanadal, once we knew the secrets? What it is about the Sons of Honor that frightens them?"

Veil hesitated.

You found her! Pattern said in her mind. *Do you have evidence, like Dalinar wanted?*

"They'll send you after Restares next," Ialai said. "But they'll watch you. In case you rise high enough, learn enough to threaten them. Have you asked yourself what they want? What they expect to *get* out of the end of the world?"

"Power," Veil said.

"Ah, nebulous 'power.' No, it is more specific than that. Most of the Sons of Honor simply wanted their gods back, but Gavilar saw more. He saw entire worlds. . . ."

"Tell me more," Veil said.

Shouts sounded outside the room. Veil glanced at the door in time to see a brilliant Shardblade slice through the lock. Adolin, wearing the false face she'd given him, kicked open the door a moment later.

People flooded in around him—soldiers and five of Shallan's Lightweaver agents.

"Once I'm dead," Ialai hissed, "don't let them search my rooms before you do. Look for the rarest vintage. It is . . . exotic."

"Don't give me riddles," the Three said. "Give me answers. What *are* the Ghostbloods trying to do?"

Ialai closed her eyes. "*Do it.*"

Instead, the Three dismissed her Blade. *I vote against killing her,* Veil thought. Killing her would mean she had been manipulated by Mraize. She *hated* that idea.

"You're not dying today," the Three said. "I have more questions for you."

Ialai kept her eyes closed. "I won't get to answer. They won't let me."

Shallan emerged, calming her nerves as several soldiers rushed up to surround Ialai. Veil and Radiant settled back, both pleased at this outcome. They were their *own* person. They did not belong to Mraize.

She shook her head and trotted over to Adolin, then dismissed his illusory face with a touch. She needed to see him as himself.

"Which one are you?" he asked quietly, giving her a pouch of infused spheres.

"Shallan," she said, putting the pouch into her satchel, which a soldier had fetched for her from beside the wall. She glanced over her shoulder as the soldiers bound Ialai, and again Shallan was struck by how *deflated* the woman looked.

Adolin pulled Shallan close. "Did she confess to you?"

"She danced around it," Shallan said, "but I think I can make a case to Dalinar that what she said constitutes treason. She wants to depose Jasnah and put Elhokar's son on the throne."

"Gavinor is way too young."

"And she'd be guiding him," Shallan said. "Which is why she's a traitor—she wants the power."

But . . . Ialai had spoken like that plan was in the past, as if she were now fighting only for survival. Had the Ghostbloods truly killed Highprinces Thanadal and Vamah?

"Well," Adolin said, "with her in custody, perhaps we can get her armies to stand down. We can't afford a war with our own right now."

"Ishnah," Shallan called, drawing the attention of one of her agents. The short Alethi woman hastened over. She'd been with Shallan for over a year now, and—along with Vathah, leader of the deserters that Shallan had recruited—was one of those she trusted most.

"Yeah, Brightness?" Ishnah asked.

"Take Vathah and Beryl. Go with those soldiers and make certain they don't let Ialai speak to anyone. Gag her if you have to. She has a way of getting inside people's heads."

"Consider it done," Ishnah said. "You want to put the illusion on her first?"

The contingency plan for extraction was simple: They'd use Light-weaving to make themselves into House Sadeas guards, and Ialai into someone lowborn. They'd march her out the gates with ease, capturing the highprincess right out from underneath the watchful eyes of her guards.

"Yes," Shallan said, waving the soldiers to bring the woman over. Ialai walked with her eyes closed, still maintaining her fatalistic air. Shallan took Ialai by the arm, then breathed out and let the Lightweaving surround her, changing the woman to look like one of the sketches Shallan had done recently—a kitchen woman with rosy cheeks and a wide smile.

Ialai didn't deserve such a kindly face, nor did she deserve such a light treatment. Shallan felt an unexpected spike of disgust at touching Ialai; this creature and her husband had plotted and executed a terrible plan to betray Dalinar. Even after the move to Urithiru, Ialai had worked to undermine him at every opportunity. If this woman had gotten her way, Adolin would have died before Shallan met him. And now they were just going to take her in to play more games?

Shallan let go, hand going to her satchel. Radiant was the one who emerged, however. She grabbed Ialai by her arm and towed her over to Adolin's soldiers, handing her off.

"Take her out with the others," Adolin said.

"You got the rest of the conspirators?" Shallan asked, walking back to him.

"They tried to escape out the side door as we burst in, but I think we managed to round them all up."

Ishnah and the soldiers—Adolin's men, hand-picked from among his finest—led the disguised and bound Ialai out the door. The highprincess sagged in their grip.

Adolin watched her go, a frown on his lips.

"You're thinking," Shallan said, "that we shouldn't have ever let her leave Urithiru. That it'd be easier if we'd ended her, and the threat she represented, before it went this far."

"I'm thinking," Adolin said, "that maybe we don't want to travel that road."

"Maybe we started already. Back when you . . ."

Adolin drew his lips to a line. "I don't have any answers right now," he eventually said. "I don't know if I ever did. But we should ransack this place quickly. Father might want more proof than your word, and it would be awfully helpful if we could present him with incriminating journals or letters."

Shallan nodded, waving over Gaz and Red. She would have them search the place.

And what of what Ialai had said? *Look for the rarest vintage.* . . . Shallan eyed the wines set out on the counter of the hutch. Why speak in riddles? *Adolin and the others were coming in,* Shallan thought. *She didn't want them to understand.* Storms, the woman had grown paranoid. But why trust Shallan?

I won't get to answer. They won't let me. . . .

"Adolin," she said. "Something is wrong with this. With Ialai, with me being here, with—"

She cut herself off as shouts sounded in the antechamber. Shallan scrambled out, feeling a sense of dread. She found Ialai Sadeas lying on the floor, foam coming from the mouth of her fake face. The soldiers watched with horror.

The highprincess stared up with lifeless eyes. Dead.

⁂

Kaladin flew through the smoke billowing up over the manor. He soared down toward where the townspeople were being threatened by the strange Fused and his soldiers. That was Waber, the manor's gardener, being held against the ground with a boot to his face.

This is obviously a trap, Syl said in Kaladin's mind. *That Fused knows exactly what to do in order to draw the attention of a Windrunner: attack innocents.*

She was right. Kaladin forced himself to drop carefully a short distance away. The Fused had torn a hole in the wall around a side entrance of the manor. Though flames licked the upper floors of the structure, the room beyond the hole was dark, not yet afire. At least not completely.

As soon as Kaladin landed, the singers released Waber and the others, then retreated through the broken hole in the stone wall. *Five soldiers,* Kaladin noted. *Three with swords, two with spears.*

The Fused carried one captive as he strode into the building; thin, with a gaunt face, the captive was bleeding from a slash along his stomach. Godeke the Edgedancer. His Stormlight had apparently run out. Storms send he was still alive. The Fused wanted to use him as bait, so the chances seemed good.

Kaladin strode toward the broken wall. "You want to fight me, Fused? Come on. Let's have at it."

The creature, shadowed inside the building, growled something in his own rhythmic language. One of the soldiers translated. "I will fight you inside where you cannot fly away, little Windrunner. Come, face me."

I don't like this, Syl said.

"Agreed," Kaladin whispered. "Be ready to go get help."

He Lashed himself upward slightly, enough to make him lighter on his feet, then inched into the burning building. This large room had once been the dining chamber, where Kaladin's father had eaten with Roshone and talked of thieves and compromises. The ceiling was burned in patches, the fire consuming it from above. Flamespren danced along the wood with a frantic delight.

The hulking Fused stood directly ahead, two soldiers at each side. They moved forward to flank Kaladin. Where was the fifth soldier? There, near an overturned table, fiddling with something that glowed a deep violet-black. Voidlight? Wait . . . was that a *fabrial*? The light dimmed suddenly.

Kaladin's powers vanished.

He felt it as a strange *smothering* sensation, as if something heavy had been placed on top of his mind. His full weight came upon him again, his Lashing canceled.

Syl gasped and her spear puffed away as she became a spren—and when Kaladin tried to resummon his Blade, nothing happened.

Immediately, Kaladin stepped backward to try to escape the range of the strange fabrial. But the soldiers quickly rushed to surround him, cutting off his retreat. Kaladin's assumption that he could beat them easily had relied on his Shardspear and his powers.

Storms! Kaladin strained to create a Lashing. Stormlight still raged inside him, and kept him from needing to breathe the acrid smoke, but something was suppressing his other abilities.

The Fused laughed and spoke in Alethi. "Radiants! You rely too much on your powers. Without them, what are you? A peasant child with no *real* training in the art of warfare or—"

Kaladin slammed himself against the soldier to his right.

The sudden motion caused the singer to cry out and fall backward. Kaladin yanked the spear from the man's hand, then—in a fluid motion—whipped it into a two-handed lunge, impaling a second soldier.

The two soldiers on his left recovered and leaped for him. Kaladin felt the wind encircle him as he spun between the two of them, catching one sword—aimed low—with the butt of his spear as he caught the second one—aimed high—right behind the spear's head. Metal met wood with a familiar *thunk,* and Kaladin finished his spin, throwing off both weapons.

He gutted one man, then tripped him—sending him stumbling to the ground in front of his ally. These soldiers were trained well, but hadn't seen much actual combat yet—as evidenced by how the remaining singer froze when he saw his friends dying.

Kaladin kept moving, almost without thought, spearing the fourth soldier in the neck. *There,* Kaladin thought as the expected ribbon of red light came darting toward him. *He will go for my back again.*

Kaladin dropped his spear, pulled a throwing knife off his belt, and turned. He rammed the knife into the air right before the Fused appeared—slamming the small blade into the creature's neck, angled between two pieces of carapace.

The Fused let out an *urk* of shock and pain, his eyes wide.

Fire made wood snap overhead, and burning cinders dropped down as the enormous Fused toppled forward like a felled tree, the floorboards shaking with the impact. Blessedly, no red ribbon of light rose from him this time.

"That's a relief," Syl said, landing on Kaladin's shoulder. "I guess if you catch him before he teleports, you really can kill him."

"At least until the Everstorm rebirths him," Kaladin said, checking the singers he'd killed. Other than the one dying slowly from the gut wound, he'd left only two alive—the one he'd shoved, and the fifth one, across the room, who had activated the fabrial.

The former had scrambled out the gaping hole in the wall to escape. The latter had left the fabrial and was inching to the side, his sword out, eyes wide.

The man was trying to reach Godeke—perhaps to use him as a hostage. In the fray, the wounded Edgedancer had fallen to the ground beside the husk after the Fused had teleported to Kaladin. Godeke was now moving—but not under his own power. A small, gangly figure had the Edgedancer by one leg and was slowly dragging him away from the fight. Kaladin hadn't seen Lift sneak into the room—but then again, she often showed up where one did not expect her.

"Take him out the hole, Lift," Kaladin said, stepping toward the last singer. "Are your powers suppressed too?"

"Yeah," she said. "What'd they do to us?"

"I'm extremely curious about this too," Syl said, zipping over to the device on the floor, a gemstone covered in metal pieces and resting on tripod legs. "That is a *very* strange fabrial."

Kaladin pointed his spear at the last singer, who—hesitantly—dropped his sword and raised his hands. He had a jagged skin pattern of red and black.

"What is that fabrial?" Kaladin asked.

"I . . . I . . ." The soldier swallowed. "I don't know. I was told to twist the gemstone at the base to activate it."

"That's Voidlight powering it," Syl said. "I've never seen anything like it."

Kaladin glanced at the smoke pooling on the ceiling. "Lift?" he said.

"On it," she said, scrambling over to the device while Kaladin kept the soldier guarded. A moment later, Kaladin's powers returned. He sighed in relief, though that made Stormlight puff before him. Nearby, Godeke gasped, unconsciously breathing in Stormlight, and his wound started to heal.

Strengthened by the Light, Kaladin grabbed the soldier and lifted him up, infusing him enough to make him hang in the air. "I told you to leave the city," Kaladin growled softly. "I'm memorizing your face, your pattern, your *stench*. If I see you again, ever, I will send you hurtling upward with so much Stormlight that you will have a long, *long* time to think during the fall back down. Understood?"

The singer nodded, humming a conciliatory sound. Kaladin shoved him, recovering his Stormlight and making the man fall to the ground. He scrambled away out the hole.

"There was another human in here," Lift said. "An old lighteyed man in beggar's clothing. I was watching from outside the building, and saw the man come in here with Godeke. A short time later, that Fused broke through the wall, carrying Godeke—but I didn't spot the other man."

Roshone. The former citylord had told Dalinar he was going to search the manor's stormcellar to free imprisoned townspeople. Though he wasn't proud of it, Kaladin hesitated—but when Syl looked at him, he gritted his teeth and nodded.

So long as it is right . . . he thought.

"I'll find him," Kaladin said. "Make sure Godeke recovers, then get that fabrial to Brightness Navani. She's going to find it very interesting."

⁙

Shallan removed the illusion, revealing Ialai's face, spittle dripping from her lips. One of Adolin's men checked her pulse, confirming it.

She *was* dead.

"Damnation!" Adolin said, standing helpless above the body. "What happened?"

We didn't do this, Veil thought. *We decided not to kill her, right?*

I . . . Shallan's mind began to fuzz, everything feeling blurry. Had she done this? She'd wanted to. But she hadn't, had she? She was . . . was more in control than that.

I didn't do it, Shallan thought. She was reasonably certain.

So what happened? Radiant asked.

"She must have taken poison," said Vathah, leaning down. "Blackbane."

Even after many months as Shallan's squire and then agent, the former deserter didn't look like he belonged with Adolin's soldiers. Vathah was too rough. Not sloppy, but unlike Adolin's men, he didn't care much for the spit and polish. He showed his disdain by leaving his jacket undone, his hair messy.

"I've seen someone die like that before, Brightness," he explained. "Back in Sadeas's army, an officer was smuggling and selling supplies. When he finally got found out, he poisoned himself rather than be taken."

"I didn't see her do it," Ishnah said, sheepish. "I'm sorry."

"Nale's nuts," muttered one of Adolin's soldiers. "This is going to look bad, isn't it? This is exactly what the Blackthorn *didn't* want. Another Sadeas corpse on our hands."

Adolin drew in a long deep breath. "We have enough evidence to have seen her hanged; my father will simply have to accept that. We'll bring troops to the warcamps to make certain her soldiers don't get rowdy. Storms. This mess should have been cleaned up months ago."

He pointed at several soldiers. "Check the other conspirators for poison, and gag them all. Shallan will disguise the body like a rug or something so we can get it out. Gen and Natem, search Ialai's things in the next room to see if you can find any useful evidence."

"No!" Shallan said.

Adolin froze, glancing at her.

"I'll search through Ialai's things in the next room. I know what to watch for, and your soldiers don't. You handle the captives and search the rest of the building."

"Good idea," Adolin said. He rubbed his brow, but then—perhaps seeing the little anxietyspren that appeared near her, like a twisting black cross—smiled. "Don't worry. Every mission has a few hitches."

She nodded, more to put him at ease than to indicate her real feelings. As the soldiers moved to follow his orders, she knelt by Ialai's body.

Ishnah joined her. "Brightness? Do you need something?"

"She didn't eat poison, did she?" Shallan asked softly.

"Can't be certain," Ishnah said. "I know a little about blackbane though. . . ." She blushed. "Well, I know a lot. My gang would use it on rivals. It's tough to make, because you need to dry the leaves out, then make a gum out of them to get it to full potency. Anyway, eating it isn't the best. If you can get it into the blood though, it kills quickly. . . ." She trailed off, frowning—perhaps realizing as Shallan had that Ialai had died very quickly.

Shallan knew of blackbane herself. She'd studied up on poisons recently. *Would I be able to spot a pinprick?* Shallan thought, kneeling beside the corpse.

Either way, she suspected Ialai had been right: The Ghostbloods hadn't trusted Shallan to kill her, and they'd sent a second knife to see the job done. That would mean they had an operative among Adolin's guards or Shallan's own agents. The idea made Shallan's stomach twist.

And this person was separate from the spy Ialai supposedly had among Dalinar's elite? Storms. It was tying Shallan's mind in knots. "Look the body over," Shallan whispered to Ishnah. "See if you can find evidence if this was self-inflicted, or if someone else killed her."

"Yes, Brightness."

Shallan quickly walked back into the room with the wine hutch. Gaz and Red were already working to gather Ialai's things. Storms, could she trust these two?

In any case, Ialai's prediction had proven correct. And it was possible that this room held secrets Mraize didn't want Shallan to find.

8

SURRENDER

A bronze cage can create a warning fabrial, alerting one to objects or entities nearby. Heliodors are being used for this currently, and there is some good reasoning for this—but other gemstones should be viable.

—Lecture on fabrial mechanics presented by Navani Kholin
to the coalition of monarchs, Urithiru, Jesevan, 1175

K aladin crossed the burning room, haunted by that moment when he'd suddenly lost his powers. The experience left him rattled. The truth was, he *had* come to rely upon his abilities. Like you relied on a good spear, battle-tested and sharp. There was little worse than having your weapon fail you in battle.

"We're going to have to watch for those fabrials," Kaladin said. "I don't like the idea of our powers being subject to removal by the enemy." He glanced at Syl, who sat on his shoulder. "Have you experienced anything like that before?"

She shook her head. "Not that I remember. It made me feel . . . faded. As if I wasn't quite here."

He shied away from rooms consumed by the blaze, full of primal shadows and lights, bright orange and red, deep and angry colors. If the citylords had been content with a normal house, this could never have happened. But no, they needed to be set apart, own a home full of delicate wood instead of sturdy stone. The hungry flames seemed excited as they played with the dying manor. There was a *glee* to the sounds of the fire: its roars and hisses. Flamespren ran up the wall alongside him, leaving tracks of black on the wood.

Ahead, the kitchen was fully engulfed. He didn't mind the heat so far—his Stormlight healed burns before they had a chance to more than itch. As long as he stayed away from the heart of the fire, he should be all right.

Unfortunately, that might prove impossible.

"Where's the cellar?" Syl asked from his shoulder.

Kaladin pointed through the kitchen inferno toward a doorway—barely visible as a shadow.

"Great," Syl said. "You going to run for it?"

Kaladin nodded, not daring to lose his Stormlight by speaking. He braced himself, then dashed into the room, flames and smoke curling around him. A forlorn groaning sound from above indicated that the ceiling was close to giving in.

A quick Lashing upward let Kaladin leap the burning kitchen counter. He landed on the other side and slammed his shoulder into the charred door to the cellar, breaking through with a loud crash, bits of flame and soot spraying before him.

He entered a dark tunnel sloping downward, cut directly into the rock of the hillside. As he moved away from the inferno behind, Syl giggled.

"What?" he asked.

"Your backside's on fire," she said.

Damnation. He batted at the back of his coat. Well, after getting stabbed by Leshwi, this uniform was ruined anyway. He was going to have to listen to Leyten complain about how often Kaladin went through them. The Windrunner quartermaster seemed convinced that Kaladin let himself get hit solely to make it difficult to keep uniforms in supply.

He started through the dark stone tunnel, counting on his Stormlight to provide illumination. Soon after entering, he crossed a metal grate covering a deep pit: the watercatch, to divert rainwater that flooded the tunnel. A stormcellar like this was where lighteyed families retreated during highstorms.

He'd have dismissed potential flooding as another problem with living in a wooden home, but even stone houses occasionally got damaged during storms. He didn't blame anyone for wanting to put several feet of rock between them and the raging winds. He had played down here with Laral as a child, and it seemed smaller to him now. He remembered a deep, endless tunnel. But soon after he passed the watercatch, he saw the lit cellar room ahead.

As Kaladin stepped into the underground room, he found two prisoners manacled to the far wall, slumped in place, their heads bowed. He didn't recognize one of them—perhaps he was a refugee—but the other was Jeber, father to a couple of the boys Kaladin had known as a youth.

"Jeber," Kaladin said, hurrying forward. "Have you seen Roshone? He . . ."

Kaladin trailed off as he noticed that neither person was moving. He knelt, feeling a growing dread as he got a better glimpse of Jeber's lean face. It was perfectly normal, save for the pale cast—and the two burned-out pits, like charcoal, in place of the eyes. He'd been killed with a Shardblade.

"Kaladin!" Syl said. "Behind you!"

He spun, thrusting out his hand and summoning his Blade. The rough-hewn room sloped back to the left of the doorway, making a small alcove that Kaladin hadn't been able to see when first entering. There, standing quietly, was a tall man with a hawkish face, brown hair flecked with black. Moash wore a sharp black uniform cut after the Alethi style, and held Brightlord Roshone in front of him with a knife to the man's neck. The former citylord was crying silently, Moash's other hand covering his mouth, fearspren undulating on the ground.

Moash jerked the knife in a quick, efficient slice, opening Roshone's throat and spilling his lifeblood across the front of his ragged clothing.

Roshone fell to the stone. Kaladin shouted, scrambling to help, but the surgeon within him shook his head. A slit throat? That wasn't the kind of wound a surgeon could heal.

Move on to someone you can help, his father seemed to say. *This one is dead.*

Storms! Was it too late to fetch Lift or Godeke? They could . . . They could . . .

Roshone thrashed weakly on the ground before a helpless Kaladin. Then the man who had terrorized Kaladin's family—the man who had consigned Tien to death—simply . . . faded away in a pool of his own blood.

Kaladin glared up at Moash, who silently returned his knife to its belt sheath. "You came to save him, didn't you, Kal?" Moash asked. "One of your worst enemies? Instead of finding vengeance and peace, you run to rescue him."

Kaladin roared, leaping to his feet. Roshone's death sent Kaladin back to that moment in the palace at Kholinar. A spear through Elhokar's chest. And Moash . . . giving a Bridge Four salute as if he in *any way* deserved to claim that privilege.

Kaladin raised his Sylspear toward Moash, but the tall man merely looked at him—his eyes now a dark brown, but lacking any emotion or *life* whatsoever. Moash didn't summon his Shardblade.

"Fight me!" Kaladin shouted at him. "Let's do this!"

"No," Moash said, holding his hands up to the sides. "I surrender."

⁘

Shallan forced herself to stare through the doorway at Ialai's body as

Ishnah inspected it.

Shallan's eyes wanted to glide off the body, look anywhere else, think anything else. Confronting difficult things was a problem for her, but part of finding her balance—three personas, each of them distinctly useful—had come when she'd accepted her pain. Even if she didn't deserve it.

The balance was working. She was *functioning*.

But are we getting better? Veil asked. *Or merely hovering in place?*

I'll accept not getting worse, Shallan thought.

For how long? Veil asked. *A year now of standing in the wind, not sliding backward, but not progressing. You need to start remembering eventually. The difficult things . . .*

No. Not that. Not yet. She had work to do. She turned away from the body, focusing on the problems at hand. Did the Ghostbloods have spies among Shallan's inner circle? She found the idea not only plausible, but likely.

Adolin might be willing to call today's mission a success, and Shallan could accept that successfully infiltrating the Sons of Honor had at least proven that she could plan and execute a mission. But she couldn't help feeling she'd been played by Mraize, despite Veil's best efforts.

"Nothing in here except some empty wine bottles," Red said, opening drawers and cabinets on the hutch. "Wait! I think I found Gaz's sense of humor." He held up something small between two fingers. "Nope. Just a withered old piece of fruit."

Gaz had found a small bedchamber at the rear of the room, through the door that Veil had noticed. "If you *do* find my sense of humor, kill it," he called from inside. "That will be more merciful than forcing it to deal with your jokes, Red."

"Brightness Shallan thinks they're funny. Right?"

"Anything that annoys Gaz is funny, Red," she said.

"Well, I annoy myself!" Gaz called. He stuck out his head, fully bearded, now with two working eyes—having regrown the missing one after he'd finally learned to draw in Stormlight a few months ago. "So I must be the most hilarious storming man on the planet. What are we searching for, Shallan?"

"Papers, documents, notebooks," she said. "Letters. Any kind of writing."

The two continued their inspection. They would find anything obvious, but Ialai had indicated there was something unusual to be discovered, something hidden. Something that Mraize wouldn't want Shallan to have. She stepped through the room, then whirled a little on one heel and looked up. How had Veil missed the fine scrollwork paint near the ceiling, ringing the room? And the rug in the center might have been monochrome, but it was thick and well maintained. She kicked off her shoes and stockings and walked across it, feeling the luxurious threads under her toes. The room was understated, yes, but not *bleak*.

Secrets. Where were the secrets? Pattern hummed on her skirt as she stepped over to the hutch and inspected the wines. Ialai had mentioned a rare vintage. These wines were the clue.

Nothing to do but try them. Shallan had suffered far worse tests in the course of her duties. Red gave her a cocked eyebrow as she began pouring and tasting a little of each.

Despite Ialai's lengthy rumination on the wines, most of them tasted distinctly ordinary to Shallan. She wasn't an expert though; she favored anything that tasted good and got her drunk.

Thinking of that, she took in a little Stormlight and burned away the effects of the alcohol. Now wasn't the time for a muddy head. Though most of the wines were ordinary, she did land on one she couldn't place. It was a sweet wine, deep red, bloody in color. It didn't taste like anything she'd had before. Fruity, yet robust, and perhaps a little bit . . . heavy. Was that the right word?

"I've got some letters here," Gaz said from the bedroom. "There are also some books that seem like she handwrote them."

"Gather it all," Shallan said. "We'll sort it out later. I need to go ask Adolin something."

She carried the carafe out to him. Several guards watched the door, and it didn't seem anyone in the warcamp had noticed the attack. At least, no one had come knocking.

Shallan pointedly ignored—then forced herself to look at—the body again. Adolin stepped over to meet her, speaking softly. "We should get going. A couple of the guards escaped. We might want to write for some Windrunners to meet us for quicker extraction. And . . . what happened to your shoes?"

Shallan glanced at her bare feet, which poked out from under her dress. "They were impeding my ability to think."

"Your . . ." Adolin ran a hand through his delightfully messy hair, blond speckled with black. "Love, you're deliciously weird sometimes."

"The rest of the time, I'm just tastelessly weird." She held up the carafe. "Drink. It's for science."

He frowned, but tried a sip, then grimaced.

"What is it?" she asked.

"Shin 'wine.' They have no idea how to ferment a proper alcohol. They make it all out of the same strange little berry."

"Exotic indeed . . ." Shallan said. "We can't leave quite yet. Pattern and I have a secret to tease out."

"Mmm . . ." Pattern said from her skirt. "I wish I had shoes to take off so my brain would work right." He paused. "Actually, I don't think I *have* a brain."

"We'll be back in a second," she said, returning to the room with the wine hutch. Red had joined Gaz in the extremely tiny bedchamber. There were no windows, with barely enough room to stand. It held a mattress with no frame and a trunk that apparently stored the notes and letters Gaz had gathered.

Ialai would expect those to be found. There might be secrets in them, but not what Shallan hunted. *Ialai moved here after her palace burned down. She slept in a closet and refused to leave this fortress. And still Mraize got not one, but* two *people in to kill her.*

Shin wine. Was that the clue? Something about the hutch? She glanced it over, then got out her sketchpad.

"Pattern," she said, "search the room for patterns."

Pattern hummed and moved off her skirt—rippling the floor as he moved across it, as if he were somehow inside the stone, making the surface bulge. As he began searching, she did a sketch of the hutch.

There was something about committing an object to memory, then freezing it into a drawing, that let her see better. She could judge the spaces between the drawers, the thickness of the wood—and she soon knew there was no room in the hutch for hidden compartments.

She shooed away a couple of creationspren, then stood. Patterns, patterns, patterns. She scanned the carpet, then the painted designs on the upper trim of the room. Shinovar. Was the Shin wine truly important, or had she mistaken the clue?

"Shallan," Pattern said from across the room. "A pattern."

Shallan hurried to where he dimpled the rock of the wall, near the far northwest corner. Kneeling, she found that the stones *did* have a faint pattern to them. Carvings that—worn by time—she could barely feel beneath her fingers.

"This building," she said, "it's not new. At least part of it was already standing when the Alethi arrived at the warcamps. They built the structure on an already-set foundation. What are the markings? I can barely make them out."

"Mmm. Ten items in a pattern, repeating," he said.

This one feels a little like a glyph. . . . she thought. These warcamps dated back to the shadowdays, when the Epoch Kingdoms had stood. Ten kingdoms of humankind. Ten glyphs? She wasn't certain she could interpret ancient glyphs—even Jasnah might have had trouble with that—but maybe she didn't have to.

"These stones run around the base of the wall," Shallan said. "Let's see if any of the other carvings are easier to make out."

A few of the stones were indeed better preserved. They each bore a glyph—and what appeared to be a small map in the shape of one of the old kingdoms. Most were indistinct blobs, but the crescent shape of Shinovar's mountains stood out.

Shin wine. A map with the Shinovar mountains. "Find every block with this shape on it," she told Pattern.

He did so, every tenth block. She moved along to each one until, on the third try, the stone wiggled. "Here," she said. "In the corner. I think this is right."

"Mmm . . ." he said. "A few degrees off, so technically acute."

She carefully slid the stone out. Inside, like the mythical gemstone cache from a bedtime tale, she found a small notebook. She glanced up and checked whether Gaz and Red were still in the other room. They were.

Damnation, she has me distrusting my own agents, Shallan thought, slipping the notebook into her safepouch and replacing the stone. Maybe Ialai's only plan had been to sow chaos, distrust. But . . . Shallan couldn't entirely accept that theory, not with how haunted Ialai had seemed. It wasn't hard to believe the Ghostbloods had been hunting her; Mraize had infiltrated Amaram and Ialai's inner circle a year ago, but hadn't gone with them when they'd fled Urithiru.

Though Shallan itched to peek through the notebook, Gaz and Red emerged with a pillowcase full of notes and letters. "If there's anything more in there," Gaz said, thumbing over his shoulder, "we can't find it."

"It will have to do," Shallan said as Adolin waved her to join him. "Let's get out of here."

◆◆

Kaladin hesitated, spear held toward Moash's throat. He could end the man. *Should* end the man. Why did he hesitate?

Moash . . . had been his friend. They'd spent hours by the fire, talking about their lives. Kaladin had opened his heart to this man, in ways he hadn't to most of the others. He'd told Moash, like Teft and Rock, of Tien. Of Roshone. Of his fears.

Moash wasn't just a friend though. He was beyond that a member of Bridge Four. Kaladin had sworn to the storms and the heavens above—if anyone was there watching—that he'd protect those men.

Kaladin had failed Moash. As soundly as he'd failed Dunny, Mart, and Jaks. And of them all, losing Moash hurt the most. Because in those callous eyes, Kaladin saw himself.

"You bastard," Kaladin hissed.

"You deny that I was justified?" Moash kicked at Roshone's body. "You know what he did. You know what he cost me."

"You killed Elhokar for that crime!"

"Because he deserved it, like this one did." Moash shook his head. "I did this for you too, Kal. You would let your brother's soul cry into the storms, unavenged?"

"Don't you *dare* speak of Tien!" Kaladin shouted. He felt himself slipping, losing control. It happened whenever he thought of Moash, of King Elhokar dying, of failing the people of Kholinar and the men of the Wall Guard.

"You claim justice?" Kaladin demanded, waving toward the corpses chained to the wall. "What about Jeber and that other man. You killed them for *justice*?"

"For mercy," Moash said. "Better a quick death than to leave them to die, forgotten."

"You could have set them free!" Kaladin's hands were sweaty on his weapon, and his mind . . . his mind wouldn't think straight. His Stormlight was running low, almost out.

Kaladin, Syl said. *Let's leave.*

"We have to deal with him," Kaladin whispered. "I have to . . . have to . . ."

What? Kill Moash while he stood defenseless? This was a man Kaladin was supposed to *protect*. To save . . .

"They're going to die, you know," Moash said softly.

"Shut up."

"Everyone you love, everyone you think you can protect. They're all going to die anyway. There's nothing you can do about it."

"I said shut up!" Kaladin shouted.

Moash stepped toward the spear, dropping his hands to his sides as he took a second step.

Kaladin, strangely, felt himself shying away. He'd been so tired lately, and while he tried to ignore it—tried to keep going—his fatigue seemed a sudden weight. Kaladin had used a lot of his Stormlight fighting, then getting through the fire.

It ran out right then, and he deflated. The numbness he'd been shoving down this entire battle flooded into him. The exhaustion.

Beyond Moash, the distant fire crackled and snapped. Far off, a loud crashing crunch echoed through the tunnel: the kitchen ceiling finally collapsing. Bits of burning wood tumbled down the tunnel, the embers fading to darkness.

"Do you remember the chasm, Kal?" Moash whispered. "In the rain that night? Standing there, looking down into the darkness, and knowing it was your sole release? You knew it then. You try to pretend you've forgotten. But you *know*. As sure as the storms will come. As sure as every lighteyes will lie. There is only one answer. One path. One result."

"No . . ." Kaladin whispered.

"I've found the better way," Moash said. "I feel no guilt. I've given it away, and in so doing became the person I could always have become—if I hadn't been restrained."

"You've become a monster."

"I can take away the pain, Kal. Isn't that what you want? An end to your suffering?"

Kaladin felt like he was in a trance. Frozen, as he'd been when he watched . . . watched Elhokar die. A disconnect that had festered inside him ever since.

No, it had been growing for *longer*. A seed that made him incapable of fighting, of deciding—paralyzing him while his friends died.

His spear slipped from his fingers. Syl was talking, but . . . but he couldn't hear her. Her voice was a distant breeze. . . .

"There's a simple path to freedom," Moash said, reaching out and putting his hand on Kaladin's shoulder. A comforting, familiar gesture. "You are my dearest friend, Kal. I want you to stop hurting. I want you to be free."

"No . . ."

"The answer is to stop existing, Kal. You've always known it, haven't you?"

Kaladin blinked away tears, and the deepest part of him—the little boy who hated the rain and the darkness—withdrew into his soul and curled up. Because . . . he did want to stop hurting.

He wanted it *so badly*.

"I need one thing from you," Moash said. "I *need* you to admit that I'm right. I need you to *see*. As they keep dying, *remember*. As you fail them, and the pain consumes you, remember *there is a way out*. Step back up to that cliff and jump into the darkness."

Syl was screaming, but it was only wind. A distant wind . . .

"But I won't fight *you*, Kal," Moash whispered. "There is no fight to be won. We lost the moment we were born into this cursed life of suffering. The sole victory left to us is to *choose* to end it. I found my way. There is one open to you."

Oh, Stormfather, Kaladin thought. *Oh, Almighty.*

I just . . . I just want to stop failing the people I love. . . .

Light exploded into the room.

Clean and white, like the light of the brightest diamond. The light of the sun. A brilliant, concentrated *purity*.

Moash growled, spinning around, shading his eyes against the source of the light—which came from the doorway. The figure behind it wasn't visible as anything more than a shadow.

Moash shied away from the light—but a version of him, transparent and filmy, broke off and stepped *toward* the light instead. Like an after-image. In it, Kaladin saw the same Moash—but somehow standing taller, wearing a brilliant blue uniform. This one raised a hand, confident, and although Kaladin couldn't see them, he knew people gathered behind this Moash. Protected. Safe.

The image of Moash burst alight as a Shardspear formed in his hands.

"No!" the real Moash screamed. "No! Take it! Take my pain!" He stumbled away to the side of the room, furious, a Shardblade—the Blade of the Assassin in White—forming in his hands. He swung at the empty air. Finally he lowered his head—shadowing his face with his elbow—and shoved past the figure in the light and rushed back up the tunnel.

Kaladin knelt, bathed in that warm light. Yes, warmth. Kaladin felt *warm*. Surely . . . if there truly was a deity . . . it watched him from within that light.

The light faded, and a spindly young man with black and blond hair rushed forward to grab Kaladin.

"Sir!" Renarin asked. "Kaladin, sir? Are you all right? Are you out of Stormlight?"

"I . . ." Kaladin shook his head. "What . . ."

"Come on," Renarin said, getting under his arm to help lift him. "The Fused have retreated. The ship is ready to leave!"

Kaladin nodded, numb, and let Renarin help him stand.

9

CONTRADICTIONS

A pewter cage will cause the spren of your fabrial to express its attribute in force—a flamespren, for example, will create heat. We call these augmenters. They tend to use Stormlight more quickly than other fabrials.

—Lecture on fabrial mechanics presented by Navani Kholin to the coalition of monarchs, Urithiru, Jesevan, 1175

By the time Kaladin started to come to himself, the *Fourth Bridge* had already begun lifting into the air. He stood near the railing, watching Hearthstone—now abandoned—shrinking beneath them. From this distance, the houses resembled a group of discarded crab shells, shed as the creature grew. Their function served, they were now scattered refuse.

Once, he'd imagined returning to this place triumphant. Instead, that return had eventually brought the town's end. It surprised him how little it hurt, knowing he'd probably visited his birthplace for the last time.

Well, it hadn't been home to him in years. Instinctively, he searched out the soldiers of Bridge Four. They were mingled among the other Windrunners and squires on the upper deck, crowding around, talking about something Kaladin couldn't make out.

The group was so big now. Hundreds of Windrunners—far too many to function as the tight-knit group he'd formed in Sadeas's army. A groan escaped his lips, and he blamed it on his fatigue.

He settled down on the deck and put his back to the railing. One of the ardents brought him a cup of something warm, which he took gratefully—

until he realized the drinks were distributed to the townspeople and refugees, not the other soldiers. Did he look so bad?

Yes, he thought, glancing down at his bloodied and burned uniform. He vaguely remembered stumbling up to the ship with Renarin's help, then barking at the flood of Windrunners who came to fawn over him. They kept offering him Stormlight, but he had plenty. It surged in his veins now, but for once the extra energy it lent seemed . . . wan. Faded.

Stop, he thought forcibly. *You've held yourself together in rougher winds than this, Kaladin. Breathe deeply. It will pass. It always does.*

He sipped his drink, which turned out to be broth. He welcomed its warmth, especially as the ship gained elevation. Many of the townspeople gathered near the sides, awespren bursting around them. Kaladin forced out a smile as he closed his eyes and leaned his head back, trying to recapture the wondrous feeling of taking to the air those first few times.

Instead, he found himself reliving other darker times. When Tien had died, and when he'd failed Elhokar. Foolish though it was, the second one hurt almost as much as the first. He hadn't particularly *liked* the king. Yet somehow, seeing Elhokar die as he nearly spoke the first Radiant Ideal . . .

Kaladin opened his eyes as Syl flew up in the form of a miniature *Fourth Bridge*. She often took the shape of natural things, but this one seemed extra odd. It didn't belong in the sky. One might argue that Kaladin didn't either.

She re-formed into the shape of a young woman, wearing her more stately dress, and landed at eye level. She waved toward the gathered Windrunners. "They're congratulating Laran," Syl explained. "She spoke the Third Ideal while we were in that burning building."

Kaladin grunted. "Good for her."

"Are you going to congratulate her?"

"Later," Kaladin said. "Don't want to force my way through the crowd." He sighed, pressing his head back against the railing again.

Why didn't I kill him? he thought. *I'll kill parshmen and Fused for existing, but when I face Moash, I lock up? Why?*

He felt so stupid. How had he been so easy to manipulate? Why hadn't he simply rammed his spear into Moash's too-confident face and saved the world a whole ton of hassle? At the least it would have shut the man up. Stopped the words that dripped from his mouth like sludge . . .

They're going to die . . . Everyone you love, everyone you think you can protect. They're all going to die anyway. There's nothing you can do about it. I can take away the pain. . . .

Kaladin forced his eyes open and found Syl standing before him wearing her more usual dress—the flowing, girlish one that faded to mist around her knees. She seemed smaller than normal.

"I don't know what to do," she said softly. "To help you."

He glanced down.

"The darkness in you is better some times, worse others," she said. "But lately . . . it's grown into something different. You seem so *tired*."

"I just need some good rest," Kaladin said. "You think I'm bad now? You should've seen me after Hav made me hike at double time across . . . across . . ."

He turned away. Lying to himself was one thing. Lying to Syl was harder.

"Moash did something to me," he said. "Put me into some kind of trance."

"I don't think he did, Kaladin," she whispered. "How did he know about the Honor Chasm? And what you nearly did there?"

"I told him a lot of things, back during better days. In Dalinar's army, before Urithiru. Before . . ."

Why couldn't he remember *those* times, the warm times? Sitting at the fire with real friends?

Real friends including a man who had *just* tried to persuade him to go kill himself.

"Kaladin," Syl said, "it's getting worse. This . . . distance to your expression, this fatigue. It happens whenever you run out of Stormlight. As if . . . you can only keep going while it's in you."

He squeezed his eyes shut.

"You freeze whenever you hear reports of lost Windrunners."

When he heard of his soldiers dying, he always imagined running bridges again. He heard the screams, felt the arrows in the air. . . .

"Please," she whispered. "Tell me what to do. I can't understand this about you. I've tried *so* hard. I can't seem to make sense of how you feel or why you feel that way."

"If you ever do figure it out," he said, "explain it to me, will you?"

Why couldn't he simply shrug off what Moash had said? Why couldn't he stand up tall? Stride toward the sun like the hero everyone pretended he was?

He opened his eyes and took a sip of his broth, but it had gone cold. He forced it down anyway. Soldiers couldn't afford to be picky about nourishment.

Before long, a figure broke from the crowd of Windrunners and ambled toward him. Teft's uniform fit neatly and his beard was trimmed, but he seemed like an old stone now that he wasn't glowing anymore. The type of mossy stone you found sitting at the base of a hill, marked by rain and the winds of time; it left you wondering what it had seen in its many days.

Teft started to sit next to Kaladin.

"I don't want to talk," Kaladin snapped. "I'm fine. You don't need to—"

"Oh, shut up, Kal," Teft said, sighing as he settled down. He was in his early fifties, but sometimes acted like a grandfather some twenty years older. "In a minute here, you're going to go congratulate that girl for saying her Third Ideal. It was rough on her, like it is on most of us. She needs to see your approval."

A protest died on Kaladin's lips. Yes, he was highmarshal now. But the truth was, every officer worth his chips knew there was a time to shut your mouth and do what your sergeant told you. Even if he wasn't your sergeant anymore; even if there wasn't a squad anymore.

Teft looked up at the sky. "So, the bastard is still alive, is he?"

"We had a confirmed sighting of him two months ago, at that battle on the Veden border," Kaladin said.

"Aye, two months ago," Teft said. "But I figured someone on their side would have killed him by now. Have to assume they can't stand him either."

"They gave him an Honorblade," Kaladin said. "If they can't stand him, they have an odd way of showing it."

"What did he say?"

"That you were all going to die," Kaladin said.

"Ha? Empty threats? He's gone crazy, that one has."

"Yeah," Kaladin said. "Crazy."

It wasn't a threat though, Kaladin thought. *I* am *going to lose everyone eventually. That's how it works. That's how it always works. . . .*

"I'll tell the others he's sniffing around," Teft said. "He might try to attack some of us in the future." Teft eyed him. "Renarin said he found you kneeling there. No weapon in hand. Like you'd frozen in battle."

Teft left the sentence dangling, implying a little more. *Like you'd frozen in battle. Again.* It hadn't happened that often. Only this time, and that time in Kholinar. And the time when Lopen had nearly died a few months back. And . . . well, a few others.

"Let's go talk to Laran," Kaladin said, standing up.

"Lad . . ."

"You told me I had to do this, Teft," Kaladin said. "You can storming let me get to it."

Teft fell in behind him as Kaladin went and did his duty. He let them see him stand tall, let them be reassured he was still the brilliant leader they all knew. He had Laran summon her new Blade for him, and he congratulated her spren. They had few enough honorspren that he tried to always acknowledge them.

Afterward, as he'd hoped, Dalinar requested Windrunners to fly him, Navani, and a few of the others to the Shattered Plains. Many of the

Radiants would stay behind to guard the *Fourth Bridge* as it made its longer voyage, but the command staff was needed for other duties.

After seeing to his parents—who of course decided to stay with the townspeople—Kaladin took off. At least with the wind rushing around them during flight, Teft couldn't ask any more questions.

∴

Navani both loved and detested contradictions.

On one hand, contradictions in nature or science were testaments to the logical, reasonable order of all things. When a hundred items indicated a pattern, then one *broke* that pattern, it showcased how remarkable the pattern was in the first place. Deviation highlighted natural variety.

On the other hand, that deviant stood out. Like a fraction on a page of integers. A seven within a sequence of otherwise sublime multiples of two. Contradictions whispered that her knowledge was incomplete.

Or—worse—that maybe there *was* no sequence. Maybe everything was random chaos, and she pretended the world made sense for her own peace of mind.

Navani flipped through her notes. Her featureless round chamber was too small to stand up in. It had a table—bolted to the floor—and a single chair. She could touch the walls to both sides simultaneously by stretching out her arms.

A goblet to hold spheres was affixed to the table and fastened shut at the top. She'd brought only diamonds for light, naturally. She couldn't stand when her light was made up of a hundred different colors and sizes of gems.

She stretched her legs forward under the table, sighing. Hours spent in this room made her long to get up and go for a walk. That wasn't a possibility, so instead she laid out the offending pages on her desk.

Jasnah enjoyed finding inconsistencies in data. Navani's daughter seemed to thrive on contradictions, little deviations in witness testimony, questions raised by a historical account's biased recollections. Jasnah picked carefully at such threads, pulling at them to discover new insights and secrets.

Jasnah loved secrets. Navani was more wary of them. Secrets had turned Gavilar into . . . whatever it was he'd been at the end. Even today, the greed of artifabrians across the world prevented the greater society from learning, growing, and creating—all in the name of preserving trade secrets.

How many secrets had the ancient Radiants preserved for centuries, only to lose them in death—forcing Navani to have to discover everything anew? She reached down beside her chair and picked up the fabrial Kaladin and Lift had discovered.

She had no idea what to make of the thing. A collection of four garnets?

No spren appeared to be trapped in any of them. She didn't recognize the metal of its cage, the cut of its gemstones. . . . Studying the thing was like trying to understand a foreign language. How had it suppressed the Radiants' abilities? Was this related to the gemstones embedded in the weapons of the enemy soldiers, the ones that drained away Stormlight? So many storming secrets.

She held up a sketch of the gemstone pillar at the heart of Urithiru. *It is the same,* she thought, turning the fabrial in her hand, then comparing it to a similar-looking construction of garnets in the picture. The ones in the pillar were enormous, but the cut, the arrangement of stones, the *feel* was the same.

Why would the tower have a device to suppress the powers of Radiants? It was their home.

Could it be the opposite? she thought, putting down the alien fabrial and making a note in the margins of the drawing. *A way to suppress the abilities of the Fused?*

So much about the tower still didn't make any sense. She had a Bondsmith in Dalinar. Shouldn't he and the Stormfather be able to mimic whatever the long-dead tower spren had done to power the pillar and the tower?

She held up a second picture, this one of a more familiar device—a construction of three gemstones connected by chains, meant to be worn on the back of the hand. A Soulcaster.

Soulcasters had long bothered Navani. They were the proverbial flaw in the system, the fabrial that didn't make sense. Navani wasn't a scholar herself, but she had a strong working knowledge of fabrials. They produced certain effects, mostly amplifying, locating, or attracting specific elements or emotions—always tied to the type of spren trapped inside. The effects were so logical that theoretical fabrials had been correctly predicted years before their successful construction.

A technological masterpiece like the *Fourth Bridge* was no more than a collection of smaller, simpler devices intertwined. Pair one set of gemstones, and you had a spanreed. Interwork hundreds, and you could make a ship fly. Assuming you'd discovered how to isolate planes of motion and reapply force vectors through conjoined fabrials. But even these discoveries had been more small tweaks than revolutionary changes.

Each step built on the previous ones in logical ways. It made perfect sense, once you understood the fundamentals. But Soulcasters . . . they broke all the rules. For centuries, everyone had explained them as holy objects. Created by the Almighty and granted to men in an act of charity. They weren't *supposed* to make sense, because they weren't technological, but divine.

But was that really true? Or could she, with study, eventually discover their secrets? For years, they'd assumed no spren were trapped in Soulcasting devices. But with the Oathgates, Navani could travel into Shadesmar—and everything in the Physical Realm reflected there. Human beings manifested as floating candle flames. Spren manifested as larger, or more complete versions of what was seen in the Physical Realm.

Soulcasters manifested as small unresponsive spren, hovering with their eyes closed. So the Soulcasters *did* have a captured spren. A Radiant spren, judging by their shape. Intelligent, rather than the more animal-like spren captured to power normal fabrials.

These spren were held captive in Shadesmar, and made to power Soulcasters. *Is this the same, perhaps?* Navani thought, holding up the gemstone device Kaladin had discovered. There had to be a connection. And perhaps a connection to the tower? The secret to making it function?

Navani shuffled through pages in her notebook, looking at the multitude of schematics she'd drawn during the last year. She'd been able to piece together many of the tower's mechanics. Though they were—like Soulcasters—created by somehow trapping spren in Shadesmar. Their functions, however, were similar to the ones designed by modern artifabrians.

The moving lifts? A combination of conjoined fabrials and a hidden waterwheel that dipped into an underground river, which flowed from melting snow in the peaks. The city's wells constantly replenished with fresh water? A clever manipulation of attractor fabrials, powered by ancient gemstones exposed to the air and the storms far beneath the tower.

Indeed, the more she studied Urithiru, the more she saw the ancients using simple fabrial technology to create their marvels. Modern artifabrians had exceeded such constructs; her engineers had repaired, refitted, and streamlined the lifts, making them function at several times their original speed. They'd enhanced the wells and pipes, which could now draw water farther up the tower into long-abandoned waterways.

She'd learned so much in the last year. She'd almost started to feel she could deduce it all—answer the questions pertaining to time and to creation itself.

Then she remembered Soulcasters. Their armies ate and remained mobile because of Soulcasters. Urithiru depended on extra food from Soulcasters. The Soulcaster cache discovered in Aimia earlier in the year had brought an incredible boon to the coalition armies. They were among the most coveted, important devices in modern history.

And she didn't know how they worked.

Navani sighed, snapping her notebook shut. Her little room trembled as she did so, and she frowned, leaning to the side and opening a small hatch in the wall. She looked out through the glass at an incongruous sight—a group of people flying in the air alongside her. The Windrunners held a loose formation, facing into the wind—which Navani had pointed out was a little ridiculous. Why not fly the other way? You didn't need to see where you were going.

They'd claimed that flying feet-first felt silly, and had refused, no matter how much sense it made. They did seem to sculpt the air around themselves and prevent their faces from being buffeted by the worst of the winds. Dalinar, however, had no such protection. He flew in the line—kept aloft by a Windrunner—and wore a face mask with goggles to keep his proud nose from freezing right off.

Navani opted for a more comfortable conveyance. Her "room" was a person-size wooden sphere with long tapering points at either end to help with airflow. The simple vehicle was infused by a Windrunner, then Lashed into the sky. This way, Navani could ride in comfort and get some studying done during extended travel.

Dalinar claimed that he liked the feeling of the wind in his face, but Navani suspected that he found her vehicle too close to an airborne version of a palanquin. A woman's vehicle. One might assume that—in deciding to learn how to read—Dalinar would no longer worry about what was traditionally considered masculine or feminine. But the male ego could be as complicated as the most intricate fabrial.

She smiled at his mask and three layers of coats. Nearby, lithe scouts in blue flitted one way or another. Dalinar looked like a chull that had found itself among a flock of skyeels and was doing its best to pretend to fit in.

She loved that chull. Loved his stubbornness, the concern he took for every decision. The way he thought with intense passion. You never got half of Dalinar Kholin. When he put his mind to something, you got the whole man—and had to simply pray to the Almighty that you could handle him.

She checked her clock. A trip like this, all the way from Alethkar to the Shattered Plains, still took close to six hours—and that was with a triple Lashing, using Dalinar's power to provide Stormlight.

Thankfully, they were nearing the end, and she saw the Shattered Plains approaching ahead. Her engineers had been busy; over the last year they'd constructed sturdy permanent bridges connecting many of the relevant plateaus. They desperately needed to be able to farm this region to supply Urithiru—and that meant dealing with Ialai Sadeas and her rebels. Hopefully Navani would soon hear good news from the Lightweavers and their mission to—

Navani cocked her head, noticing something odd. The wall beside her reflected a faint shade of red, blinking on and off. Like the light of a spanreed.

Her immediate thought was panic. Had she somehow activated the strange fabrial? If the powers of the Windrunners vanished, she'd drop from the air like a stone. Her heart leapt, and her breath caught.

She didn't start plummeting. And . . . the light *wasn't* coming from the strange fabrial. She leaned back, then peeked under her table. There, stuck to the bottom with some wax, was a tiny ruby. No, *half* a ruby. *Part of a spanreed,* she thought, picking it free with her fingernail.

She held it up between her fingers and studied the steady pulsing light. Yes, this was a spanreed ruby—when inserted into a spanreed, it would connect her to someone with the other half, allowing them to communicate. It had clearly been stuck here for her to find. But who would do it so sneakily?

The Windrunners began lowering her vehicle down near the center of the Shattered Plains, and she found herself increasingly excited by the blinking light. A spanreed wouldn't work if she was in a moving vehicle, but as they landed, she dug one of her own reeds from her supplies. She had the new ruby affixed and a piece of paper in place before anyone had time to check on her.

She turned the ruby, eager to see what the unknown figure wanted to say to her.

You must stop what you are doing, the pen wrote out, using a cramped, nearly illegible version of the Alethi women's script. *Immediately.* It waited for a response.

What a strange message. Navani turned the ruby and wrote her response, which would be copied for whoever had the other side of the ruby. *I'm not sure what you mean,* she wrote. *Who are you? I don't believe I'm doing anything that needs to be halted. Perhaps you don't know the identity of the person you are writing to. Has this spanreed been misplaced?*

Navani set the spanreed into position for a response, then turned the ruby. When she removed her hand, the pen remained in position on the paper, upright. Then it started moving on its own, worked by the unseen person on the other end.

I know who you are, it wrote. *You are the monster Navani Kholin. You have caused more pain than any living person.*

She cocked her head. What on Roshar?

I couldn't watch any longer, the pen continued. *I had to stop you.*

Was it a madwoman who wrote with the other reed? The ruby started blinking, indicating they wanted a response.

All right, Navani wrote. *Why don't you tell me* what *it is you want me to stop? Also, you have neglected to give me your name.*

The response came quickly, written as if by a fervent hand.

You capture spren. You imprison them. Hundreds of them. You must stop. Stop, or there will be consequences.

Spren? Fabrials? This woman couldn't *seriously* be concerned about such a simple thing, could she? What was next? Complaining about chulls that pull carts?

I have spoken with intelligent spren, Navani wrote, *such as those bonded to the Radiants. They agree that the spren we use for our fabrials are not people, but are as unthinking as animals. They may not like the idea of what we do, but they don't think it monstrous. Even the honorspren accept it.*

The honorspren cannot be trusted, the pen wrote. *Not anymore. You must stop creating this new kind of fabrial. I will make you stop. This is your warning.*

The pen halted, and try though she might, Navani couldn't get any further responses from the mysterious woman or ardent who had written to her.

⁙

The Windrunners at Urithiru had been called to one of the battlefronts for air support, and Kaladin was still busy with his little enterprise in Alethkar. So in the end, Shallan and her team had to travel to Narak the hard way. Fortunately, the "hard way" wasn't too bad these days. With permanent bridges and a direct path maintained by soldiers, a journey that had once taken days had been reduced to a few hours.

At the first main fortified plateau where Dalinar kept standing troops to watch the warcamps, Shallan and Adolin were able to deliver up the prisoners—with instructions for them to be brought to Narak for questioning. Adolin and Shallan requisitioned a carriage, and left the rest of the troops to make their way back more slowly.

Shallan passed the time looking out the carriage window, listening to the clopping of the horses and watching the fractured landscape of plateaus and chasms. Once this had all been so difficult to traverse. Now she did it in a plush carriage, and considered *that* inconvenient compared to being flown about by a Windrunner. How would it be once Navani got her flying devices working efficiently? Would flying by Windrunner be the inconvenience then?

Adolin scooted over beside her, and she felt his warmth. She closed her eyes and melted into him, breathing him in—as if she could feel his soul brushing against her own.

"Hey," he said. "It's not so bad. Really. Father knew this plan might come to fighting. If Ialai had been willing to quietly rule in the warcamps, we'd have left her alone. But we couldn't ignore someone sitting in our backyard raising an army to depose us."

Shallan nodded.

"That's not what you're worried about, is it?" Adolin asked.

"No. Not completely." She turned and pressed her face into his chest.

He'd removed his jacket, and the shirt beneath reminded her of when he came to their rooms after sparring. He always wanted to bathe immediately, and she . . . well, she rarely let him. Not until she was done with him, at least.

They rode in silence for some time, with Shallan snuggled against him. "You never push," she eventually said. "Though you know I keep secrets from you."

"You'll tell me eventually."

She gripped his shirt tight between her fingers. "It bothers you though, doesn't it?"

He didn't reply at first, which was different from his normal cheery assurances. "Yeah," he finally said. "How could it not? I trust you, Shallan. But sometimes . . . I wonder if I can trust all *three* of you. Veil especially."

"She's trying to protect me in her own way," Shallan said.

"And if she does something you or I wouldn't want her to? Gets . . . physical with someone?"

"*That's* not a worry," Shallan said. "I promise, and she will too if you ask her. We have an understanding. I'm not worried about you and me, Adolin."

"What *are* you worried about, then?"

She pulled closer, and couldn't help imagining it. What he would do if he knew the *real* her. If he knew all the things she'd *actually* done.

It wasn't just about him. What if Pattern knew? Dalinar? Her agents?

They would leave, and her life would become a wasteland. She'd be alone, as she deserved. Because of the truths she hid, her entire life was a lie. Shallan, the one they all knew best, was the fakest mask of them all.

No, Radiant said. *You can face it. You can fight it. You imagine only the worst possible outcome.*

But it's possible, isn't it? Shallan asked. *It's possible that they would leave me if they knew.*

Radiant had no reply. And deep within Shallan, something else stirred. Formless. She had told herself that she would never create a new persona, and she *wouldn't*. Formless wasn't real.

But the possibility of it frightened Veil. And anything that frightened Veil *terrified* Shallan.

"I will explain someday," Shallan said softly to Adolin. "I promise. When I'm ready."

He squeezed her arm in reply. She didn't deserve him—his goodness, his love. That was the trap she'd found herself in. The more he trusted her, the worse she felt. And she didn't know how to get out. She *couldn't get out.*

Please, she whispered. *Save me.*

Veil reluctantly emerged. She sat up, not pulling against Adolin any longer—and he seemed to understand, shifting his position in the seat. He had an uncanny ability to tell which of her was in control.

"We're trying to help," Veil said to him. "And we think that this year has been good for Shallan, overall. But right now, it's probably better if we discuss another topic."

"Sure," Adolin said. "Can we talk about the fact that Ialai was more frightened of capture than death?"

"She . . . didn't kill herself, Adolin," Veil said. "We are reasonably certain she died from a pinprick of poison."

He sat up straight. "So you're saying someone in our team did it? One of my soldiers or one of your agents?" He paused. "Or . . . did you do it, Veil?"

"I didn't," Veil said. "But would it have been so bad if I had? We both know she needed to die."

"She was a defenseless woman!"

"And it's *that* different from what you did to Sadeas?"

"He was a soldier," Adolin said. "That's what makes it different." He glanced out the window. "Maybe. Father thinks I did something terrible. But . . . I was *right*, Veil. I'm not going to let someone hide behind social propriety while threatening my family. I *won't* let them use my honor against me. And . . . Stonefalls. I say things like that, and . . ."

"And it doesn't sound so different from killing Ialai," Veil said. "Regardless, I didn't kill her."

Shallan, having had a short breather, started to reemerge. Veil retreated, letting Shallan lean up against Adolin. He, though tense at first, let her do so.

She rested her head on his chest, listening to his heartbeat. His life. Pulsing within him like the thunder of a captive storm. Pattern seemed to sense the way that pulse calmed her, for he began humming from where he hung on the roof.

She would tell Adolin everything, eventually. She'd told him some already. About her father, and her mother, and her life in Jah Keved. But not the deepest things, the things she didn't even remember herself. How could she tell him things that were clouded in her own memory?

She also hadn't told him about the Ghostbloods. She wasn't certain she could share that secret, but could . . . could she try? Begin, at least? At Veil and Radiant's prompting, she searched for a way. After all, Dalinar kept saying that the next step was the most important one.

"There's something you need to know," she said. "Before you came in, Ialai implied that if I took her captive, she *would* be killed. She knew the blow was coming—that's why I was suspicious of her death. She also said she didn't kill Thanadal. That it was another group called the Ghostbloods. She thought the Ghostbloods would send someone for her—which was why she was certain she'd die."

"We've been hunting them. Ialai was leading them."

"No, dear, she was leading the Sons of Honor. The Ghostbloods are a different group."

He scratched his head. "Are they the ones your . . . brother Helaran belonged to? The one that attacked Amaram, right? And Kaladin killed Helaran without knowing who he was?"

"Those were the Skybreakers. They're not so secret any longer. They joined with the enemy—"

"Right. Radiants on the other team." Those likely made sense to him, as he'd taken battlefield reports on them. The shadowy groups moving at night, on the other hand, were something he couldn't fight directly. Dealing with them was to be her job.

She dug in her pocket as the carriage rolled over a particularly robust series of bumps. This path hadn't been graded or leveled, and though the carriage driver did his best to miss the larger rockbuds, there was only so much he could do.

"The Ghostbloods," Shallan said, "are the people who tried to kill Jasnah—and me by extension—by sinking our ship."

"So they're on Odium's side," Adolin said.

"It's more complicated than that. Honestly, I'm not *sure* what they want, besides secrets. They were trying to get to Urithiru before Jasnah, but we beat them to it." *Led them to it* might have been more accurate. "I'm not at all sure what they want those secrets for."

"Power," Adolin said.

That response—the same one she'd given to Ialai—now seemed so simplistic. Mraize, and his inscrutable master Iyatil, were deliberate, precise people. Perhaps they were merely seeking to glean leverage or wealth from the chaos of the end of the world. Shallan realized she would be disappointed to discover that their plans were so pedestrian. Any corpse robber on a battlefield could exploit the misfortune of others.

Mraize was a hunter. He didn't wait for opportunities. He went out and *made* them.

"What's that?" Adolin asked, nodding to the book in her hand.

"Before she died," Shallan said. "Ialai gave me a hint that led me to search the room and find this."

"That's why you didn't want the guards to do it," he said. "Because one of them might be a spy or assassin. Storms."

"You might want to reassign your soldiers to boring, out-of-the-way posts for a season."

"These are some of my best men!" Adolin complained. "Highly decorated! They just pulled off an extremely dangerous covert operation."

"So give them a rest at some quiet post," Shallan said. "Until we figure this out. I'll watch my agents. If I discover it's one of them, you can bring the men back."

He sulked at the suggestion; he hated the idea of punishing a group of good men because one of them might be a spy. Adolin might claim he was different from his father, but in fact they were two shades of the same paint. Often, two similar colors clashed worse than wildly different ones would.

Shallan kicked the bag of notes and letters that Gaz had gathered, resting at their feet. "We'll give that to your father's scribes, but I'll look through this book personally."

"What's in it?" Adolin asked, leaning to the side so he could see—but there were no pictures.

"I haven't read the entire thing," Shallan said. "It seems to be Ialai's attempts to piece together what the Ghostbloods are planning. Like this page—a list of terms or names her spies had heard. She was trying to define what they were." Shallan moved her finger down the page. "Nalathis. Scadarial. Tal Dain. Do you recognize any of those?"

"They sound like nonsense to me. Nalathis might have something to do with Nalan, the Skybreaker Herald."

Ialai had noticed the same connection, but indicated these names might be places—ones she could not find in any atlas. Perhaps they were like Feverstone Keep, the place Dalinar had seen in his visions. Somewhere that had disappeared so long ago, no one remembered the name anymore.

Circled several times on one page at the end of the list was the word "Thaidakar" with the note, *He leads them. But who is he? The name seems a title, much like Mraize. But neither are in a language I know.*

Shallan was pretty sure she'd heard Mraize use the name Thaidakar before.

"So, this is our new mission?" Adolin asked. "We find out what these Ghostblood people are up to, and we stop them." He took the palm-size notebook from her and flipped through the pages. "Maybe we should give this to Jasnah."

"We will," she said. "Eventually."

"All right." He gave it back, then put his arm around her and pulled her close. "But promise me that you—and I mean all of you—will avoid doing anything crazy until you talk to me."

"Dear," she said, "considering who you're talking to, *anything* I am prone to try will be—by definition—crazy."

He smiled at that, but gave her another comforting hug. She settled into the nook between his arm and chest, though he was too muscly to make a good pillow. She continued reading, but it wasn't until an hour or so later that she realized—despite dancing around the topic with him—she hadn't revealed she was a *member* of the Ghostbloods.

They were likely to put Shallan in the middle of whatever they were up to. So far—despite telling herself she was spying on them—she'd basically achieved every goal they'd asked of her. That meant a crisis was coming. The inflection point, past which she could not continue down this duplicitous path. Keeping secrets from Adolin was eating at her from the inside. Fueling Formless, pushing it toward a reality.

She needed a way out. To leave the Ghostbloods, break ties. Otherwise they'd get inside her head. And it was *way* too crowded in there already.

I didn't kill Ialai though, Shallan thought. *I was close to it, but I didn't. So I'm not theirs entirely.*

Mraize would want to speak to her about the mission, and about some other things she'd been doing for him, so she could bet on him visiting her soon. Maybe when he did, she would finally find the strength to break with the Ghostbloods.

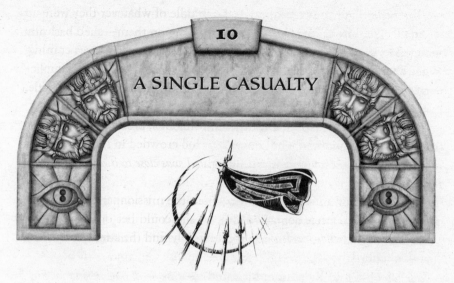

10

A SINGLE CASUALTY

A tin cage will cause the fabrial to diminish nearby attributes. A painrial, for example, can numb pain. Note that advanced designs of cages can use both steel and iron as well, changing the fabrial's polarity depending on which metals are pushed to touch the gemstone.

—Lecture on fabrial mechanics presented by Navani Kholin to the coalition of monarchs, Urithiru, Jesevan, 1175

Kaladin was feeling quite a bit better as they neared the Shattered Plains. A few hours' flying through open sky and sunlight always left him feeling refreshed. Right now, the man who had crumpled before Moash in that burning building seemed an entirely different person.

Syl flew up beside him as a ribbon of light. Kaladin's Windrunners were Lashing Dalinar and the others; all Kaladin had to do was fly at the head of them all and look confident.

I've spoken to Yunfah again, Syl said in his mind. *He's here on the Plains. I think he wants to talk to you.*

"Tell him to come up and see me, then," Kaladin said. His voice was lost to the rushing wind, but Syl would catch it anyway.

She flitted off, followed by a few windspren. From this distance, Kaladin could almost make out the pattern to the Shattered Plains. So he gave a hand signal and reduced to a single Lashing.

A short time later, two blue-white ribbons of light came zipping up toward him. He could somehow tell Syl from the other one. There was a specific shade to her, as familiar to him as his own face.

The other light resolved into the shape of a tiny old man reclining on a small cloud as he flew beside Kaladin. The spren, Yunfah, had been bonded to Vratim, a Windrunner who had died a few months ago. At first, when they'd begun losing Radiants in battle, Kaladin had worried it would cause him to lose the spren as well. Syl, after all, had gone comatose many centuries ago when she'd lost her first Radiant.

Others, however, handled it differently. The majority, though grieved, seemed to want another bond soon—as it helped them move past the pain of loss. Kaladin didn't pretend to understand spren psychology, but Yunfah had seemed to deal with the death of his Radiant well. Treating it as a battlefield loss of an ally, rather than the destruction of part of his own soul. Indeed, Yunfah appeared willing to bond another.

So far, he hadn't—and for reasons Kaladin couldn't understand. And as far as Kaladin knew, he was the sole free honorspren among them.

He says, Syl told Kaladin in his mind, *that he's still considering picking a new knight. He's narrowed it down to five possibilities.*

"Is Rlain one of them?"

Yunfah stood up on his cloud, his long beard whipping in the wind—though he had no real substance. Kaladin could read anger in his posture before Syl gave him the reply. She was acting as intermediary since the sound of the rushing wind was fairly loud, even at a single Lashing.

No, Syl said. *He is angry at your repeated suggestion he bond one of the enemies.*

"He won't find a potential Windrunner more capable or earnest."

He's acting mad, Syl said. *But I do think he'll agree if you push him. He respects you, and honorspren like hierarchy. The ones who have joined us did so against the will of the general body of their peers; they'll be looking for someone to be in charge.*

All right then. "As your highmarshal and superior officer," Kaladin said, "I forbid you to bond anyone else unless you try to work with Rlain first."

The elderly spren shook his fist at Kaladin.

"You have two choices, Yunfah," Kaladin said, not waiting for Syl. "Obey me, or throw away all the work you've done to adapt to this realm. You need a bond or your mind will fade. I'm tired of waiting on your indecisiveness."

The spren glared at him.

"Will you follow orders?"

The spren spoke.

He asks how long you'll give him, Syl explained.

"Ten days," Kaladin said. "And that is generous."

Yunfah said something, then sped away, becoming a ribbon of light. Syl pulled up alongside Kaladin's head.

He said "fine" before leaving, she said. *I have little doubt he'll at least consider*

Rlain now. Yunfah doesn't want to go back to Shadesmar; he likes this realm too much.

Kaladin nodded, and felt uplifted by the result. If this worked out, Rlain would be thrilled.

Followed by the others, Kaladin swooped down toward Narak, their outpost at the center of the Shattered Plains. Navani's engineers were turning the entire plateau from ruins into a fortified base. A wall to the east—easily six feet wide at its foot—was being built, low and squat, against the storms. A thinner wall wrapped the rest of the plateau, and lightning rods helped protect from the Everstorm.

Kaladin alighted on top of the wall and surveyed the fort. The engineers had scraped away most of the old Parshendi buildings, preserving only the most ancient of the ruins for study. Supply dumps, barracks, and storm cisterns rose around them now. With the wall going right up to the chasm, and with collapsible bridges outside, this isolated plateau was quickly becoming impregnable from ordinary ground assault.

"Imagine if the Parshendi had known modern fortification techniques," Kaladin said to Syl as she blew past in the shape of tumbling leaves. "A few strategic forts set up like this across the Plains, and we'd *never* have broken them out."

"As I recall," she replied, "we didn't so much break them out as purposely fall into their trap and hope it wouldn't hurt too much."

Nearby, the other Windrunners lowered Dalinar, some of the Edgedancers, and Navani's wooden travel vehicle. That had been a good idea, although it was a little harder to keep the larger object in the air. The thing had four fins on it, like an arrow. They'd started with two wings—which Navani had thought would make the vehicle fly better, but which had made it pull upward uncontrollably once a Windrunner Lashed it.

He hopped down from his perch. Syl whirled in a long arc around the old pillar at this edge of the plateau. Tall, with steps along the outside, it had become a perfect scout nest. Rlain said it had been used in Parshendi ceremonies, but he hadn't known its original purpose. Much of these ruins—the remnants of a once-grand city that had stood during the shadowdays—baffled them.

Perhaps the two Heralds could explain the pillar. Had they walked here? Unfortunately—considering that one of them was full-on delusional and the other dabbled in it now and then—he wasn't certain they'd be useful in this.

He wanted to get to Urithiru as quickly as possible. Before people had a chance to start talking to him again, trying—with forced laughs—to cheer him up. He walked over to Dalinar, who was taking a report from the battalionlord who commanded Narak. Oddly, Navani hadn't emerged from her vehicle yet. Perhaps she was lost in her research.

"Permission to take the first group back, sir," Kaladin said. "I want to go clean up."

"A moment, Highmarshal," Dalinar said to Kaladin, scanning the written report. The battalionlord, a gruff fellow with an Oldblood tattoo, looked away pointedly.

Though Dalinar had never said he'd moved to written reports specifically to make his officers confront the idea of a man reading, Kaladin could see the showmanship in the way he held up the sheet and nodded to himself as he read.

"What happened to Brightness Ialai is regrettable," Dalinar said. "See that her decision to take her own life is published. I authorize a full occupation of the warcamps. See it done."

"Yes, Your Majesty," the battalionlord said. Dalinar was a king now, officially recognized by the coalition of monarchs as ruler of Urithiru—a station separate from Jasnah's queenship over Alethkar. In acknowledgment of this, Dalinar had officially renounced any idea of being a "highking" over any other monarch.

Dalinar handed the sheet to the battalionlord, then nodded to Kaladin. They walked off from the others, then a little further, to a section of the base between two Soulcast grain shelters. The king didn't speak at first, but Kaladin knew this trick. It was an old disciplinary tactic—you left silence hanging in the air. That made your man begin explaining himself first. Well, Kaladin didn't bite.

Dalinar studied him, taking note of his burned and bloodied uniform. Finally, he spoke. "I have multiple reports of you and your soldiers letting enemy Fused go once you've wounded them."

Kaladin relaxed immediately. That was what Dalinar wanted to talk about?

"I think we're starting to reach a kind of understanding with them, sir," Kaladin said. "The Heavenly Ones fight with honor. I let one of them go today. In turn, their leader—Leshwi—released one of my men instead of killing him."

"This isn't a game, son," Dalinar said. "This isn't about who gets first blood. We're literally fighting for the existence of our people."

"I know," Kaladin said quickly. "But this can serve us. You've noticed already how they'll hold back and attack us one-on-one, so long as we play by their rules. Considering how many more Heavenly Ones there are than Windrunners, I think we want to encourage this kind of encounter. Killing them is barely an inconvenience, as they'll be reborn. But each of ours they kill requires training an entirely new Windrunner. Getting back wounded for wounded favors us."

"You never did want to fight the parshmen," Dalinar said. "Even when you first joined my army, you didn't want to be sent against the Parshendi."

"I didn't like the idea of killing people who showed us honor, sir."

"Does it strike you as odd to find it among them?" Dalinar asked. "The Almighty—Honor himself—was our god. The one their god killed."

"I used to think it odd. But sir, wasn't Honor *their* god before he was ours?"

That was one of the revelations that had shaken the foundation of the Radiants—both ancient and new. Though many of the orders had accepted the truth as an oddity and moved on, many Windrunners had not. Nor had Dalinar; Kaladin could see the way he winced whenever the idea was discussed.

This world had belonged to the singers with Honor as their god. Until humans had arrived, bringing Odium.

"All of this highlights a bigger problem," Dalinar said. "This war is increasingly being fought in the skies. Navani's flying transport will only escalate the situation. We *need* more honorspren and Windrunners."

Kaladin looked to where Syl hung in the air beside him. Dalinar fixed his gaze on her a moment later, so she must have decided to reveal herself to him.

"I'm sorry," she said softly. "My relatives can be . . . difficult."

"They have to see that we're fighting for the survival of Roshar as much as for the survival of the Alethi," Dalinar said. "We can't do that without their help."

"To my cousins, *you* are dangerous," Syl said. "As dangerous as the singers. The betrayal of the Knights Radiant killed so many of them. . . ."

"The other spren have begun coming around," Kaladin said. "They see it."

"Honorspren are more . . . rigid," she said. "Most of them at least." She shrugged and looked to the side, as if ashamed. Human gestures from her were so common these days that Kaladin barely paused to notice them.

"We need to do something," Dalinar said. "It's been eight months without a new honorspren coming to us." He eyed Kaladin. "But that's a problem I suppose I'll continue to contemplate. For now, I'm worried about the way the Heavenly Ones and the Windrunners are interacting. It smacks of neither of you giving this your all—and I can't have soldiers on the battlefield that I worry won't be able to fight when the pressure mounts."

Kaladin felt cold as he met Dalinar's eyes. So. This conversation *was* about Kaladin after all. What had happened to him.

Again.

"Kaladin," Dalinar said. "You're one of the best soldiers I've ever had the privilege of leading. You fight with passion and dedication. You single-handedly built up what has become the most important wing of my military—and did all this while living through the worst nightmare I could imagine. You are an inspiration to everyone who meets you."

"Thank you, sir."

Dalinar nodded, then put his hand on Kaladin's shoulder. "It's time that I relieved you of duty, son. I'm sorry."

A jolt went through Kaladin. Like the shock of being stabbed—or the feeling of suddenly coming awake in an unfamiliar place, frightened by a sudden noise. A visceral clenching of the stomach. A sudden racing of the heart. Every piece of you alert, looking for the fight.

"No," he whispered. "Sir, I know how it seems."

"How does it seem?" Dalinar asked. "Diagnose yourself, Kaladin. Tell me what you see."

Kaladin closed his eyes. *No.*

Dalinar gripped his shoulder tighter. "I'm no surgeon, but I can tell you what *I* see. A soldier who has been on the front lines for far, far too long. A man who has survived so many horrors, he now finds himself staring at nothing, his mind going numb so he doesn't have to remember. I see a soldier who can't sleep, who snaps at those who love him. He's a soldier who pretends he can still function. But he can't. He knows it."

Kaladin knocked Dalinar's hand away, snapping open his eyes. "You can't do this. *I* built the Windrunners. They're *my* team. You can't take that from me."

"I will because I have to," Dalinar said. "Kaladin, if you were anyone else, I'd have pulled you from active duty months ago. But you're you, and I kept telling myself we needed every Windrunner."

"That's true!"

"We need every *functional* Windrunner. I'm sorry. There was a point where if I'd removed you from command, it would have destroyed the momentum of the entire team. We're safely past that now. You will still be with us . . . but you won't be going on any more missions."

A growling sound escaped Kaladin's throat, one a piece of him refused to believe he was making. He sucked in Stormlight.

He would *not* be beaten down again. He would *not* let some lighteyed blowhard take everything from him again. "I can't believe this!" Kaladin said, angerspren pooling underneath him. "You were supposed to be *different*. You—"

"Why?" Dalinar asked, standing calmly.

"Why *what*?" Kaladin snapped.

"Why am I different?"

"Because you don't throw us away!" Kaladin shouted. "Because you . . . Because . . ."

Because you care about your men.

Kaladin deflated. He suddenly felt small. A child standing before a stern parent. He wavered, putting his back to the nearest building. Syl hung beside him, looking concerned, confused. She didn't speak up to contradict Dalinar. Why didn't she stick up for Kaladin?

He glanced to the side. He'd brought most of what had been Bridge Four with him; the Windrunners he'd left to protect the airship had once been Bridge Thirteen and their squires.

So he saw a lot of friendly faces standing in the distant Narak courtyard. Rock and Teft. Renarin. Sigzil, Lyn, Lopen. Leyten and Peet, Skar and Drehy. Laran, newly forged as a full Radiant. None had yet spoken the Fourth Ideal. He liked to think that it was as hard for them as it was for him, and none had yet cracked it. But . . . but could they be restraining themselves because of him? Out of some misguided respect?

He turned back to Dalinar. "What if I'm not there?" he pled. One final complaint. "What if something happens when they're out fighting? What if one of them dies because *I couldn't protect them?*"

"Kaladin," Dalinar said softly, "what if something happens because you *are* with them? What if one of them dies because they expect your help, but you freeze again?"

Kaladin breathed in sharply. He turned aside and squeezed his eyes shut, feeling tears leak out. What if . . .

Storms, Dalinar was right.

He was *right.*

"I . . ." he whispered. What were the Words?

You couldn't say the Words, he thought. *You needed to. A year ago, when Dalinar could have died. You needed to speak the Words. You crumpled instead.*

Kaladin would never say them, would he? He was finished at the Third Ideal. Other spren had said . . . said that many Radiants never spoke the later oaths.

Kaladin took a deep breath and forced his eyes open. "What . . . what do I do now?"

"You aren't being demoted," Dalinar said firmly. "I want you training, teaching, and helping us fight this war. Don't be ashamed, son. You fought *well.* You survived things no man should have to. That sort of experience leaves scars, same as any wound. It's all right to admit to them."

Kaladin brushed his fingers at his forehead and the scars he still bore. Unhealed, despite all of his powers, years after he'd been branded.

Dalinar cleared his throat, seeming uncomfortable. Perhaps, upon remembering Kaladin's wound, he thought the mention of scars to be in poor taste. It wasn't. The metaphor was particularly sound.

"Can . . . can I keep my oaths without fighting?" Kaladin asked. "I need to protect."

"There are many ways to protect," Dalinar said. "Not all Radiants went into battle in the old days. I myself have found many ways to serve this war without swinging a Blade on the front lines."

Kaladin looked to Syl, who nodded. Yes, he could keep his oaths this way.

"You won't be the first celebrated soldier who has moved to a support position after seeing one too many friends die," Dalinar said to Kaladin. "God Beyond willing, we'll persuade the honorspren to work with us—and then we'll need to train flocks of new Windrunners. You'll be of great use overseeing Radiant training either way."

"I just won't be anywhere I can cause harm," Kaladin whispered. "Because I'm broken."

Dalinar took him by the shoulder once more, then raised his other hand, holding up a finger, as if to force Kaladin to focus on it.

"This," Dalinar said, "is what war does to all of us. It chews us up and spits us out mangled. There's no dishonor in taking a step away to recover. No more than there's dishonor in giving yourself time to heal from a stab wound."

"So I'll come back to the battle?" Kaladin asked. "I'll take a leave, then return?"

"If we feel it's right for you to do so. Yes, that's possible."

Possible, Kaladin thought. *But not likely.* Dalinar had probably seen more men succumb to battle fatigue than Kaladin had—but in all his years of fighting, Kaladin had never seen someone recover. It didn't seem the kind of thing you got over.

If only he'd been stronger. Why hadn't he said the Words?

"We'll find a way to make this a smooth, natural transition," Dalinar promised him. "We can introduce it to the others in whatever way you'd like. That said, we're also not going to delay. This isn't a request, Kaladin. It's an order. From now on, you stay out of battle."

"Yes, sir," Kaladin said.

Dalinar squeezed his shoulder. "You're not valuable to me because of how many enemies you can kill. It's because you're man enough to understand, and to say words like those." He nodded, letting go. "This is *not* a disciplinary action, Kaladin. I'll have new orders for you tomorrow. You can trust that I *will* put you to work. We will explain to everyone else that it's a promotion."

Kaladin forced out a smile, and that seemed to relieve Dalinar. Had to keep on a good face. Had to look strong.

Don't let him know.

"Sir," Kaladin said. "I'm not sure I'll be able to take a post training other Radiants. Being with the Windrunners, sending them off to die without me . . . well, sir, it would rip me apart. I don't think I could see them fly, and not join them."

"I hadn't considered that." Dalinar frowned. "If you'd rather request another duty, I will allow it. Perhaps in logistics or battle planning? Or maybe as an ambassador to Thaylenah or Azir. Your reputation would put you in high esteem there. At any rate, I won't have someone like you sitting around growing crem. You're too valuable."

Sure. Of course. Take from me the one thing that matters, then tell me I'm valuable. We both know I'm nothing.

Kaladin fought against those thoughts, and forced out another smile. "I'll think about it, sir. I might need time to decide what I want, though."

"Very well," Dalinar said. "You have ten days. Before then, I want you to report to me your decision."

Kaladin nodded. He put on another smile, which had the intended effect of convincing Dalinar not to worry. The man walked over to the other Windrunners.

Kaladin looked away, feeling his stomach twist. His friends laughed and joked with one another, in high spirits. So far as they knew, the Windrunners hadn't lost any members today.

They didn't know the truth—that they'd taken a single profound casualty. His name had been Kaladin Stormblessed.

This folio page, produced in occupied Kholinar, depicts a warform male and a nimbleform female. These versions of traditional Alethi clothing show the singers embracing novel fashions and blending them with Alethi sensibilities.

11

PASSION
AND COURAGE

An iron cage will create an attractor—a fabrial that draws specific elements to itself. A properly created smoke fabrial, for example, can gather the smoke of a fire and hold it close.

New discoveries lead us to believe it is possible to create a repeller fabrial, but we don't yet know the metal to use to achieve this feat.

—Lecture on fabrial mechanics presented by Navani Kholin
to the coalition of monarchs, Urithiru, Jesevan, 1175

Quickly, up the stairs!" Venli shouted the words to the Rhythm of Command. "The lady returns!"

The servants scrambled up the tower steps. They didn't need Venli to order them about, but it was expected of her, and she'd gotten very good at playing the role. She didn't whip them as some might—most of the *shanay-im* disliked such physical punishments, fortunately—but she did grab Vod out of line and straighten his shirt and sash. He hummed to Appreciation in thanks as she shoved him after the rest.

Last in line, Venli grabbed her scepter and hurried up the steps. The others ahead of her wore workform or nimbleform, so she towered over them in envoyform.

There were a variety of different levels a person could have in the singer culture. Normal people—simply called singers, or common singers—had ordinary forms such as workform or warform. Then there were forms of power, like Venli's envoyform. This was a level higher in authority and strength, and required taking a Voidspren into your gemheart. That influenced your mind, changed how you perceived the world. These singers were called Regals.

Further up the hierarchy were the Fused. Ancient souls put into a modern body, which extinguished the soul of the host completely. And above them? Mysterious creatures like the thunderclasts and the Unmade. Souls more like spren than people. Venli still didn't know much about them.

Serving one of the Fused was difficult enough. She hurried up the steps, which wound dizzily around the spire. This wasn't a proper fortification; it was no more than a column of stone with wooden steps—basically a staircase into the sky. The design reminded her of the tall stone pillar in Narak.

At the top of the spire, she entered a room that gave her vertigo. Open on two sides, the room looked out over the grand city of Kholinar—and there were no railings to prevent a careless worker from toppling a hundred feet to the city streets below. Though the footing was sound, it felt unstable, like a tower of blocks with a too-large capstone, awaiting the inevitable child's foot.

The storms should have destroyed these tower rooms on first blow. But the Fused had overseen their construction, and so far only one in the line of twenty had been felled by a highstorm and needed to be rebuilt. That one had caused heavy damage to the homes below, of course—but there was little use seeking logic in the ways of the Fused.

Venli stepped to the front of the group of servants, sweating from the protracted climb. Her form of power was slender and tall, with long orange-red hairstrands and delicate carapace along the cheeks and in ridges on the backs of the hands. Not armor; more like ornamentation. It wasn't a fighting form, more intended to inspire awe—and give her powers to translate text and languages.

Though she was a Regal, she held a secret deep within her gemheart, a friend who protected her from the Voidspren's influence. Her Radiant spren—Timbre—buzzed softly, comforting her.

Venli scanned the horizon and finally picked out figures approaching as dots in the sky. Though Venli had rushed the others, none would complain. You didn't question a Regal—and besides, they'd rather be shouted at by Venli than suffer punishment from a Fused. Leshwi was fair, but that did not mean her anger was tame.

Soon the *shanay-im*—Those Ones of the Heavens—came streaking into the city. Only the most important of them merited tower rooms like this one, and so the majority swooped down toward more conventional housing in the city proper. Leshwi, however, was among Odium's elite. She wasn't the most powerful, but was lofty compared even to most Fused.

Part of Leshwi's favor had to do with her prowess in battle, but Venli suspected an equal measure came because she'd maintained her sanity over the centuries. The same could not be said for many, though the Heavenly Ones had fared better than other kinds of Fused. The nine varieties were called "brands" in their own language, a word evoking the heat of a branding iron, though Venli had seen no such mark on their skin.

Leshwi slowed as she approached, her traveling garb—bright white and red this time—rippling in the wind. It trailed a good thirty feet below and behind her, and she wore her hair loose. She reached her hands to the sides as she landed, and servants immediately came forward to un-hook clasps and remove the longer parts of the train. Others brought water and fruit, bowing as they held the bowls toward her.

Leshwi waited for her garments to be unhooked before taking refresh-ment. She glanced at Venli, but made no sound, so Venli remained where she was—standing tall, holding her scepter. She had long since overcome her initial fears that she'd be found out for the fraud she was.

Once the long train was removed, other servants helped Leshwi out of the robes. A few servants averted their eyes from the sight of her flowing undergarments—but Leshwi didn't care about mortal feelings of propriety. She didn't so much as hum a note of Embarrassment, though in this incar-nation, the body that had been offered to her was malen.

Indeed, after drinking and being wrapped in her robes of luxury, she sat down to be seen by the barber, who shaved her face after the manner of humans. She hated whiskers, even if the ones she grew when inhabiting a malen body were soft and faint. The Fused exerted some measure of will upon their forms—skin patterns persisted, for example, and some grew carapace in individual patterns. Knowing that, you could easily distinguish the same Fused across multiple incarnations.

Of course, Venli had the advantage of her ability to look into Shadesmar—which immediately told her if someone was Fused, Regal, or ordinary singer. She tried very hard not to use that ability except in the most secret of loca-tions. It would be a disaster of incredible proportions if anyone figured out that Venli—Last Listener, envoyform Regal, Voice of Lady Leshwi—was a Knight Radiant.

Sound thrummed through her. Timbre could read her thoughts—and Venli could read the little spren's words and intents through the pulsing of her rhythms. In this case, Timbre wanted Venli to acknowledge she was *not* a Knight Radiant. Not yet, as she'd only said the First Ideal. She had work to do if she wanted to progress.

She acknowledged this quietly; she grew uncomfortable if Timbre pulsed when a Fused was near. There was no telling what might give her away.

Considering that, she pointedly did *not* look at Dul and Mazish among the servants. At least not until they brought the new recruit forward—a young femalen in workform, bright lines of red marbling her otherwise black skin. Venli hummed to Indifference, pretending to inspect the newcomer—whose name was Shumin—though they'd met several times in secret.

Finally, Venli stepped up to Leshwi, who was still being shaved. Venli waited to be acknowledged—a sign given her when Leshwi hummed to Satisfaction.

"This one," Venli said, waving to Shumin, "has been determined worthy of service. Your stormsetter needs a new assistant." The stormsetter made certain Leshwi's possessions in the High Chamber were packed before each storm, then reset afterward.

Leshwi hummed. Though it was a short beat done to Craving, it meant so much more to Venli. The longer she'd held envoyform, the more remarkable its abilities had become. She could not only speak all languages, she instinctively understood what her mistress said to her through simple humming. In fact, the experience was eerily familiar to the way she understood Timbre—yet she was certain that ability wasn't related to her form.

Regardless, as Leshwi's Voice, Venli's duty was to express the lady's desires to others.

"The lady wishes to know," Venli said to Derision, "if this newcomer can embrace the height of the chamber."

She pointed, and Shumin stepped nervously to the edge of the room, beside the drop-off. The chamber was large enough that, standing among the lady's furniture at the center, one might be able to ignore how high they were.

Venli strode over and joined Shumin. Here at the edge, there was no pretending or denying. With your toes to the rim, feeling the wind press you from behind as if to shove you off into the sky above the sunlit streets . . . Venli was not particularly afraid of heights, but part of her wanted to run to the center of the room and hug the floor. People were not meant to be this high. This was the domain of stormclouds and thunder, not singers.

Shumin quaked, drawing some fearspren, but she stood firm. She stared outward, however, and did not look down.

"Passion," Venli said softly, to Determination—one of the old rhythms. The pure rhythms of Roshar. "Remember that with the Fused, your Passion will do you credit. To hold this post, you must match fear with determination."

It was the great contradiction of serving the Fused. They did not want simpering children who were too quick to obey, but they *also* expected exactness in service. They wanted only the strongest of wills among their followers—but wished to control and dominate them.

Shumin hummed to the Rhythm of Winds, then looked down at the city. Venli made her stand an uncomfortable minute, then hummed and turned, walking back. Shumin followed with hasty steps, sweating visibly.

"She seems timid," Leshwi said to Venli, speaking in their ancient language.

"We are all timid when we begin," Venli replied. "She will serve well. How can one sing with Passion if never given a chance to learn the proper songs?"

Leshwi took the towel from her barber and wiped her face, then selected a fruit from the bowl offered nearby. She inspected it for flaws. "You are compassionate to them, despite your attempts to appear stiff and stern. I can see the truth in you, Venli, Last Listener."

If that were so, Venli thought, *I would undoubtedly be dead by now.*

"I favor compassion," Leshwi said, "so long as it does not override worthier Passions." She began eating her fruit, giving instruction in a quick hum.

"You are accepted," Venli said to Shumin. "Serve with devotion, and you will be taught to speak the words of the gods and sing the rhythms of lost peoples."

Shumin hummed her pleasure, backing away to join the others. Venli caught the eye of Dul, the stormsetter, and he nodded before fetching the next item of business.

"If I may," Venli said, turning to Leshwi. "Did you kill him on this excursion?"

There was no need to explain "him." Leshwi was fascinated by the Windrunners, and in particular their leader—the young man who had forged a group of Radiants without the guidance of god or Herald.

Leshwi finished her fruit before giving a reply. "He was there," Leshwi said. "And so was his spren, though she did not appear to me. We fought. No conclusion. Though I fear I might not have a chance to face him again."

Venli hummed to Craving, to indicate her curiosity.

"He killed Lezian, the Pursuer."

"I do not know that name," Venli said. With that title, the creature must be one of the Fused. As beings thousands of years old, each one had a lore and history long enough to fill books. It angered them that no one knew them individually this time around.

Indeed, Leshwi spoke to Derision when she replied, "You will. He is newly reawakened, but always worms his way into the stories and minds of mortals. He takes great pride in it."

And the rest of you don't? Venli kept the comment in. Leshwi appreciated Passion—but wry comments were entirely different.

"Is there other business for me?" Leshwi asked.

"One other matter," Venli said, gesturing as Dul arrived with a very frightened woman in tow. A human woman, thin and somewhat scrawny, with long curling eyebrows. She was dressed in the humble clothing of a worker. "You asked me to find a tailor who could experiment with new designs. This one was of that profession once."

"A human," Leshwi said. "Curious."

"You wished for the best," Venli said. "Our people are learning to excel in many areas, but mastering some professions requires much longer than the year we've had. If you wish for an expert tailor, you will need a human."

Leshwi stood, then rose into the air, her robes of luxury—gold and stark black—trailing beneath her. She hummed a message to Venli.

"The great lady wishes to know your name," Venli said.

"Yokska, great one," said the cowering woman.

"You were a tailor?" Venli said, Voicing for Leshwi.

"Yes, once I dressed princes and lighteyes. I know . . . I know the most current of fashions."

"Your fashions and clothing will not suit a Fused," Venli Voiced. "The designs will be unfamiliar to you."

"I . . . I live to serve . . ." Yokska said.

Venli glanced at Leshwi and knew immediately from the lady's hummed tone that this servant would be rejected. Was it the woman's mannerisms? Too cowering? Perhaps she didn't look presentable enough—though Venli had decided against dressing Yokska well, as that could offend the Fused.

"A human will not do," Leshwi said. "To elevate this one would be to say our people are not good enough. In any case, tell her to stand up and meet my eyes. So many of these are cremlings."

"Can they be blamed? Other Fused beat humans who meet their eyes."

Leshwi hummed to Fury, and Venli met the tone with her own. At this, Leshwi smiled. "It is a problem among my kind," Leshwi admitted. "The nine brands do not present uniform expectations of the humans. But still, this one cannot be my tailor. Already there are comments and questions about the raising of a human to the title of He Who Quiets. I would not heap up fuel for those seeking to prove we are soft. Save your hidden compassion for your own, Voice. But perhaps allow this one to teach a singer wearing artform, so they may learn her skill."

Venli bowed her head, humming to Subservience. She would have been pleased regardless of the outcome—this was mostly a test to see what her lady thought of the humans. Leshwi spoke so often of the Windrunners, Venli was curious whether she would sympathize with a human of lower station.

"My tasks are done," Leshwi said. "I will meditate. Empty the High Chamber and see that the new servant is properly trained." She rose through a hole in the roof, seeking the clouds.

Venli thumped her scepter against the wooden floor, and the other servants began to disperse down the steps. Several helped the human woman.

Venli made Shumin wait. Once everyone was safely on their way, she led the newcomer down the long winding steps to her own room: the guardhouse that one needed to pass through to reach the steps. Venli's position was, quite literally, the gate one needed to pass in order to approach Leshwi.

Dul waited beside the hatch that closed off access to the steps above. Shumin made as if to speak, but Venli quieted her, waiting until Dul closed the hatch and the window shades. Mazish returned from checking outside, then closed the door behind her. Dul and Mazish were married. Not once-mates, as the listeners would have called it, but married. They had insisted after having their minds restored; they'd been mates while enslaved by the humans, and had adopted Alethi ways.

Venli had a great deal of work to do. She needed to counteract the indoctrination of the Fused *and* help the singers cast off the traditions of those who had enslaved them. But a cremling did not shed its shell until it had grown too large for it; she hoped her guidance would eventually encourage them to shed—of their own choice—the burdens of both Fused and human society.

"You may speak now," Venli said to Shumin. Venli changed her rhythm to that of Confidence—one of the old rhythms. The true rhythms, uncorrupted by the touch of Odium.

"Stormfather!" Shumin said, turning to Dul and Mazish. "That was difficult. You didn't tell me she was going to practically dangle me off the edge!"

"We warned you it would be hard," Dul said to Reprimand.

"Well, I think I did pretty well otherwise," Shumin said, looking to Venli. "Right? Brightness, what did you think?"

The change in the femalen's attitude made Venli sick. She was so . . . human. From her curses to her way of gesturing when she spoke. But then, those who were most loyal to the Fused were unlikely to join Venli. She would work with what she had.

"I worry you were overly timid," Venli said. "The Fused do not want weakness, and neither do I. Our organization is formed from those who are strong enough to resist, and eventually break free of, all chains."

"I'm ready," Shumin said. "When do we attack the Fused? Each storm I worry I'll be next, and that one of the waiting Fused souls will boot my mind out and take over."

It didn't work that way. Venli had witnessed the transformation; she'd nearly been taken herself. Accepting the soul of a Fused into your body had an element of agency to it.

Agency, however, was difficult to define. If you took a Regal form, Odium got inside your mind. New forms with their new rhythms altered your mannerisms, your way of seeing the world. Even common singers were carefully indoctrinated, constantly told that sacrificing themselves was a great privilege.

This, in the end, was what made Venli decide she needed to try to rebuild her people. The Fused and the humans . . . there was an equivalency to them. Both sought to take away the minds of common folk. Both were interested solely in the convenience of a useful body, without the accompanying "burden" of a personality, desires, and dreams.

Venli was determined not to do the same. She would accept those who came to her. If she wanted them to change, she would show them a better way. It was Timbre's suggestion. Volition. Agency. Cardinal tenets of whatever it was she was becoming.

Strange sentiments for one who had once—with a grin on her face— brought death and enslavement to her people. But so be it. She nodded to her friends, who backed away to watch the doors. Venli gestured for Shumin to sit down with her at the small table by the wall, away from the windows.

Before she spoke, Venli checked for spies. She drew a bit of Voidlight from a sphere in her pocket. She could use either of the two types of Light: the strange Voidlight Odium provided, or the old Stormlight of Honor. From what Timbre said, this was new—whatever Venli was doing, it hadn't been done before.

Eshonai would have been excited by that idea, so Venli tried to take strength from memories of her sister. Using that Light, she peeked into Shadesmar: the Cognitive Realm. Timbre pulsed to Concern. They'd tested Venli's other power—the ability to mold stone—only once, and it had drawn secretspren. A kind of specialized spren that flew through the city, watching for signs of Knights Radiant using their powers.

She had escaped those secretspren without revealing herself, but it had been close. As long as the secretspren were near, Venli could not practice the full extent of her abilities. Fortunately, this power—the one that let her peek into Shadesmar—did not draw the same attention.

With it, she saw a world overlapping the physical one. The second world was made up of an ocean of beads, a strange sun set too far back in a black sky, and hovering lights. One for every soul. The souls of Fused were dark flames that pulsed like a beating heart. With care, she'd also learned to judge which spren a common singer had bonded to provide their form.

Some Voidspren could hide from the eyes of all except those they wanted to see them—but none could hide from Venli, who could see their traces in Shadesmar. She made certain none were nearby, and that Shumin was not one of the *mavset-im,* Fused who could imitate the shapes of others. Even other Fused seemed wary of the *mavset-im,* Those Ones of Masks.

Shumin's soul was as Venli expected: a common singer soul bonded to a small gravitationspren to take workform.

Venli stopped using her powers. She knew she could travel to that strange world if she wished—but Timbre warned that the place was dangerous for mortals, and it was difficult to return once fully there. Today, looking was enough.

"You must know what we are," Venli said to Shumin. "And what we are not. We do not seek to overthrow the Fused."

"But—"

"We are *not* a rebellion," Venli said. "We are a group of objectors who do not like the choices we've been offered. Fused oppression or human tyranny? The god of hatred or the supposedly honorable god who abandoned us to slavery? We accept neither. We are the listeners. We will cast off everything—including our very forms if we must—to find freedom.

"Once we have enough members, we will leave the city and travel someplace where no one will bother us. We will remain neutral in the conflicts between humans and Fused. Our only goal is to find a place where we can thrive on our own. Our society. Our government. Our rules."

"But . . ." Shumin said. "They're not simply going to let us walk away, right? What safe place is there away from everyone else?"

They were good questions. Venli hummed to Annoyance—at herself, not at Shumin. When her ancestors had first broken away in an ultimate act of bravery and sacrifice, it had been at the *end* of the wars between humans and singers. The listeners were able to escape in the confusion, a loose thread no one thought to tie up.

This was different. She knew it was.

She leaned forward. "We have two current plans. The first is to find sympathetic Fused and convince them we deserve this privilege. They respect Passion and courage."

"Yeah, sure, but . . ." Shumin shrugged in a human way. So casual. "There's a *big* difference between respecting Passion and letting someone curse you out. The Fused seem pretty intolerant of people *truly* disagreeing with them."

"You're making a mistake," Venli said to Reprimand. "You assume the Fused are all of a single mind."

"They're the immortal servants of a terrible god."

"And they're still *people.* Each with different hearts, thoughts, and goals. I retain hope that some of them will see what we're planning as worthy."

It was a frail hope, Venli admitted to herself. Timbre pulsed within her, agreeing. Leshwi though . . . the high lady seemed to respect her enemies. She could be brutal, she could be unforgiving, but she could also be thoughtful.

Leshwi said the conquest of Roshar was being undertaken on behalf of the common singer people. Perhaps using similar language, Venli could present her plan for a new listener homeland.

Unfortunately, she feared that the Fused had fought their wars so long that—despite paying lip service to giving the world back to the singers—they no longer saw freedom as the goal. To many of them, the war was for vengeance: the destruction of their enemies, finally proving which side was *right*. So if Leshwi—who was among both the most sane and the most empathetic of Fused—could not be persuaded, then that left only one option. To run and hide. Venli's ancestors had shown that courage. She was uncertain, when being honest with herself, whether she had the same moral strength.

Shumin idly played with her hair rather than humming to an emotion as a listener would have. Was that hair-twisting a sign she was bored, perhaps the human way of humming to Skepticism?

"If we must run," Venli said, "we are not without resources."

"Forgive me if I'm hesitant, Brightness," Shumin said. "They summoned rock monsters that were taller than the storming *city wall*. They have Regals and Fused. I think our sole hope is to get the entire city to turn against them."

"We have a Regal as well," Venli said, gesturing to herself. "There is a Voidspren in my gemheart, Shumin, but I have learned to *contain* and *imprison* it. It gives me powers, such as the ability to look into Shadesmar and see if any spren are nearby spying on us."

"Regal powers . . ." Shumin said, glancing to the others in the room. "And . . . I could have them too? Without surrendering my will to Odium?"

"Possibly," Venli said. "Once I have perfected the process so others can use it."

Timbre pulsed inside her, disapproving. The little spren wanted Venli to tell the full truth—that she was Radiant. However, the time wasn't right. Venli wanted to be certain she could offer others what she had before exposing what she was. She needed to be certain other spren like Timbre were willing, and she needed to prepare her friends for the path.

"Long ago," Venli explained to Shumin, "the singers were allies of the spren. Then humans came, and the wars started. The events of those days are lost to all but the Fused—in the end, however, we know the spren chose humans.

"Eventually, the humans betrayed them. Killed them. Some spren have chosen to give humans a second chance, but others . . . Well, I have been contacted by a spren who represents an entire people in Shadesmar. They realize that perhaps *we* deserve a second chance more than humans do."

"What does that mean?" Shumin asked.

"That we will not be completely without allies, once we make our move," Venli said. "Our ultimate goal is to find a place where we can escape other people's rules and their laws. A place where we can be what we wish and cast off the roles forced upon us."

"I'm in," Shumin said. "That sounds like a *storming* delight, Brightness. Maybe . . . maybe if we have forms of power that *aren't* granted by Odium, the enemy *will* leave us alone."

Either that or Odium would see that his minions scoured Venli and her faction from the planet.

Timbre pulsed, saying no great work could be accomplished without risk. Venli hated when she said things like that. It reminded her exactly how dangerous her current actions were. She drew in a little Light to check Shadesmar again. She saw nothing spying on her, so—

A dark, pulsing flame was moving down from above.

Leshwi.

Venli leaped to her feet, her chair slamming to the ground. Dul and Mazish noticed her urgency and stood upright, searching around, trying to decide what to do.

"Open the shades!" Venli said. "Quickly! So she doesn't see anything odd!"

They slammed the windows open right as the hatch rattled. Lady Leshwi—brilliant in her outfit of gold and black—entered, skimming above the steps. She almost *never* came down here. What was going on?

Timbre trembled inside Venli. They'd been discovered. It had to mean they'd—

"Gather yourself, Last Listener," Leshwi said to the Rhythm of Agony. "Something is happening. Something dangerous. I fear the war is about to take a distinctly different turn."

12

A WAY TO HELP

One of my pleas is for artifabrians to stop shrouding fabrial techniques with so much mystery. Many decoy metals are used in cages, and wires are often plated to look like a different metal, with the express intent of confusing those who might try to learn the process through personal study. This might enrich the artifabrian, but it impoverishes us all.

—Lecture on fabrial mechanics presented by Navani Kholin to the coalition of monarchs, Urithiru, Jesevan, 1175

As they arrived at Urithiru, Kaladin wanted nothing more than to vanish. To go someplace where he wouldn't have to listen to everyone laughing. There were a hundred of them together, mostly squires of the various Windrunners who had once been his team.

Kaladin didn't have many squires left—none, unless you counted Dabbid and Rlain. Rock didn't have a spren either, but he . . . had moved on to something else. Kaladin wasn't sure what it was, but he didn't call himself a squire.

Rlain would soon have a spren, and would finally be able to move on too. Dabbid had gone on the mission today to help Renarin deliver water and supplies to the townspeople. He'd never recovered from his battle shock, however, and didn't have Radiant powers. He wasn't so much a squire as someone Kaladin and the others looked after.

The rest had all ascended to at least the Second Ideal. That made them more than a squire, but not yet a full Radiant—having bonded a spren, but not yet having earned a Blade. They were all so jovial as they walked together across the Oathgate plateau, and Kaladin didn't begrudge them their mirth. They were dear to him, and he wanted them to laugh.

Yet at the moment, he couldn't imagine anything more painful than the way they all tried to cheer him up. They sensed his mood, though he hadn't spoken to them regarding his . . . relegation? His retirement?

Storms. It made him sick to think about it.

As they walked, Lopen told him a particularly bad joke. Skar asked him for a sparring session—which was his way of offering help. Normally Kaladin would have agreed. But today . . . sparring would remind him of what he'd lost.

Sigzil, showing admirable restraint, told him that battle reports could wait until tomorrow. Storms. How bad did he look? Kaladin did his best to deflect them all, pasting on a smile so wide it felt like it cracked his skin.

Rock kept his distance, carefully ignoring Kaladin. Rock generally did have a better sense of his true mood than most. And Rock could see Syl, who—fretful as she buzzed around Kaladin—eventually zipped off. She caught a current nearby, flying into the air. She found flight as reassuring as he did.

I need to be careful not to let this break her, he thought. *Keep up a strong front for her, for all of them. They shouldn't have to be in pain because of how I feel.* He could do this gracefully. He could fight this one last battle.

They crossed the open field of stone before the tower city. Kaladin *almost* managed to keep walking without staring up at the tower. He nearly didn't feel a shock of dissociation at its immensity. He spent only a split second in disbelief that something so grand could exist. Yes, these days the tower was practically mundane.

"Hey," Leyten said as they reached the tower entrance. "Rock! Got any stew for us maybe? For old times' sake?"

Kaladin turned. The word "stew" pierced the cloud.

"Ah, coming up to the beautifully thin air makes you suddenly think straight!" Rock said. "You remember the glories of good cooking! But . . . this thing cannot be today. I have appointment."

"It's not with the surgeons, is it?" Kara called. "Because I don't think they can do anything about your breath, Rock!"

"Ha!" Rock said, then bellowed a laugh, going so far as to wipe a tear from his eye. Kara grinned, but then Rock held out his hand. "No no, you think I am laughing at what you *said*? Airsick! I'm laughing because you thought *that* to be funny joke, Kara. Ha! *Ha!*"

Kaladin smiled. A real smile, for a moment.

Then they started to break apart into small clusters, usually a Knight with their squad of squires. His friends all had their own teams now. Even Teft was pulled away by one of the groups, though his squires had been in

Bridge Thirteen—and they had stayed behind to guard the ship. In fact, many of them had become Radiants themselves. Kaladin wasn't certain how many squires Teft had left.

Could Kaladin do as Dalinar wanted? Could he stand being high-marshal of the Windrunners without going into the field? Being a part of their lives, but not being able to help them, fight alongside them?

No. A clean break would be better.

A few groups invited him to go with them, but he found himself turning them down. He stood tall, like a commander should, and gave them *the nod*. The captain's nod that said, "You run along, soldier. I have important things to be about, and cannot be bothered with frivolity."

Nobody pushed him, though he wished that one of them would. But these days, they had their own lives. Many had families; all had duties. Those who had served with him in the early days still wore their Bridge Four patches with pride, but Bridge Four was something they *used* to belong to. A legendary team already passed into myth.

Kaladin kept his back straight, his chin high, as he left them and strode through the now-familiar corridors of the tower city. Lined with entrancing patterns of different shades of strata, the tower had sphere lanterns lining most major hallways—locked, of course, but changed regularly. The place was starting to feel truly lived in. He passed families, workers, and refugees. People of all walks, as varied as a goblet full of spheres.

They saluted him, or stepped aside for him, or—in the case of many children—waved to him. The highmarshal. Kaladin Stormblessed. He kept on the proper face all the way to his rooms, and was proud of himself for it.

Then he stepped inside and found an empty nothingness.

His were the quarters of a highlord, supposedly luxurious and spacious. He had little furniture though, and that left it feeling hollow. Dark, the sole light coming from the balcony.

Every honor he'd been given seemed to highlight how vacant his life really was. Titles couldn't fill a room with life. Still, he turned and closed the door with a firm push.

Only then did he break. He didn't make it to the chair. He sank down with his back to the wall beside the door. He tried to unbutton his coat, but ended up bending forward with his knuckles pressing his forehead, digging into his skin as he hyperventilated, gasping in deep breaths of air while he trembled and shook. Exhaustionspren like jets of dust gleefully congregated around him. And agonyspren, like upside-down faces carved from stone, twisted and faded in and out.

He couldn't cry. Nothing came out. He wanted to cry, because at least that would be a release. Instead he huddled, knuckles pressing against the scars in his forehead, wishing he could shrivel away. Like the eyes of a person struck by a Shardblade.

In moments like this—alone and huddled on the floor of a dark room, tormented by agonyspren—Moash's words found him. The truth of them became undeniable. Out in the garish sunlight, it was easy to pretend that everything was all right. In here, Kaladin could see clearly.

You're just going to keep hurting. . . .

His entire life had been a futile effort to stop a storm by yelling at it. The storm didn't care.

They're all going to die. There's nothing you can do about it.

You could never build anything that lasted, so why try? Everything decayed and fell apart. Nothing was permanent. Not even love.

Only one way out . . .

A knock came at his door. Kaladin ignored the sound until it became insistent. Storms. They were going to barge in, weren't they? Suddenly panicked that anyone should find him like this, Kaladin stood up and straightened his coat. He took a deep breath, and the agonyspren faded.

Adolin pushed his way in, a treasonous Syl on his shoulder. That was where she had gone? To fetch Adolin storming Kholin?

The young man wore a uniform of Kholin blue, but not a regulation one. He'd taken to having embellishments added, regardless of what his father thought. While it was sturdy—a little stiff, starched to maintain neat lines—its sleeves were embroidered to match his boots. The cut left the coat longer than most—a bit like Kaladin's own captain's coat, but more trendy.

Somehow Adolin wore the uniform, when the uniform had always worn Kaladin. To Kaladin, the uniform was a tool. To Adolin it was a part of an ensemble. How did he get his hair—blond, peppered black—so perfectly messy? It was both casual and deliberate at the same time.

He was smiling, of course. Storming man.

"You *are* here!" Adolin said. "Rock said he thought you were heading for your room."

"Because I wanted to be *alone*," Kaladin said.

"You spend too many evenings alone, bridgeboy," Adolin said, glancing at the nearby exhaustionspren, then grabbing Kaladin by the arm—something few other people would have dared.

"I like being by myself," Kaladin said.

"Great. Sounds awful. Today, you're coming with me. No more excuses. I let you blow me away last week *and* the week before."

"Maybe," Kaladin snapped, "I just don't want to be *around* you, Adolin."

The highprince hesitated, then leaned forward, narrowing his eyes and putting his face up close to Kaladin's. Syl still sat on Adolin's shoulder, her arms folded—without even the decency to look ashamed when Kaladin glared at her.

"Tell me honestly," Adolin said. "With an oath, Kaladin. Tell me that you should be left alone tonight. Swear it to me."

Adolin held his gaze. Kaladin tried to form the words, and felt of the ten fools when he couldn't get them out.

He definitely *shouldn't* be alone right now.

"Storm you," Kaladin said.

"Ha," Adolin said, tugging him by the arm. "Come on, Brightlord Master Highmarshal Stormface. Change your coat to one that doesn't smell like smoke, then come with me. You don't have to smile. You don't have to talk. But if you're going to be miserable, you might as well do it with friends."

Kaladin extracted his arm from Adolin's grip, but didn't resist further. He grabbed new clothes—tossing aside the ones he'd been fighting in. He did, however, shoot Syl another glare as she flew over to him.

"Adolin?" Kaladin said as he changed. "Your first thought was to get *Adolin*?"

"I needed someone you couldn't intimidate," she replied. "That list at best includes three people. And the queen was likely to transform you into a crystal goblet or something."

Kaladin sighed and walked out to join Adolin, lest the highprince think he was dallying. Syl eyed Kaladin as she walked in the air alongside him, keeping up with him despite her dainty steps.

"Thank you," Kaladin said softly, turning his eyes forward.

⁜

Adolin made good on his promise. He didn't force Kaladin to say much. Together they made their way to the Ten Rings, a section of the tower's central market where the merchants had agreed to lay their shops out according to Navani's plan. In exchange they got a deal on taxes and knew guard patrols would be frequent and courteous.

Rows of wooden storefronts here made neat, orderly streets. The shops were of similar sizes and dimensions, with storage and housing on top. The place felt quaint, an island of order contrasting the more organic, chaotic feeling of the rest of the Breakaway market—where after a year, many people still used tents instead of permanent structures.

Admittedly, it did feel strange to have rows of permanent structures built in the middle of a several-stories-high interior room. The oddest part to Kaladin was that the most upscale shops—catering to the richest of the lighteyed families—had refused Navani's invitation exactly as the seedier shops had. Neither wanted to agree to her oversight. The rich shops were all outside the market, in a series of rooms along a hallway nearby.

The upshot was that while the Ten Rings wasn't terribly upscale, it *was* reputable—two concepts that weren't necessarily the same thing. Adolin's favorite winehouse was called Jez's Duty. He'd forced Kaladin to join him there on more than one occasion, and so the interior was familiar. Themed after a stormshelter—though no such thing was needed here in the tower—it had fabrial clocks on the walls that listed when a storm was happening in Alethkar, and held a daily vigil for the kingdom. An ardent even visited and burned glyphwards.

Barring that, it could be a raucous place—more of a tavern than a winehouse. Adolin had a reserved booth at the rear. It was a mark of pride that the highprince frequented this location rather than more upscale winehouses.

That was the sort of thing Adolin did. Nobody bowed when he entered; instead they cheered and raised cups. Adolin Kholin wasn't some distant brightlord or general who sat in his keep and pronounced edicts, tyrannical or wise. He was the type of general who drank with his men and learned the names of every soldier.

Dalinar disapproved. In most cases Kaladin would have as well. But . . . this was Adolin. He'd have gone mad if he'd been forced to remain aloof. It went against every traditional Alethi protocol of leadership, but Adolin made it work. So who was Kaladin to judge?

As Adolin went to greet people, Kaladin made his way around the perimeter of the room, noting the larger-than-usual crowd. Was that Rock over there with his family, drinking mugs of Horneater mudbeer?

He said he had an appointment tonight, Kaladin remembered. Indeed, some kind of celebration seemed to be going on. A few other Windrunners and Radiants he knew were in attendance, though not many. Mostly it seemed to be common folk. Perhaps a higher than normal percentage of soldiers.

Syl took off to begin poking through the room, looking at each table. Though he'd once seen her fascination as childlike, he'd evolved on that idea. She was just curious, desirous to learn. If that was childlike, then everyone needed more of it.

She was fascinated by human beings. In a room like this one, Kaladin would often find her standing on a crowded table—unseen by the occupants—head cocked as she tried to imitate the mannerisms or expressions of one person or another.

Adolin's booth was occupied by a young woman with long dark hair wearing trousers and a buttoned shirt, her long white coat hung on the peg nearby. She had her hat on, the wide-brimmed one with the peaked front.

"Veil," Kaladin said, sliding into the booth. "We going to have you all night, or will Shallan show up?"

"Probably just me," Veil said, tipping back her cup to reach the last of her drink. "Shallan had a busy day, and we're on Shattered Plains time, not Urithiru time. She wants a rest."

It must be nice, Kaladin thought, *to be able to retreat and become someone else when you get tired.*

It was sometimes difficult to treat Shallan's personas as three distinct people, but it was what she seemed to prefer. Fortunately, she tended to change her hair color to give the rest of them cues. Black for Veil, and she'd started using blonde for Radiant.

A young barmaid came by, refilling Veil's cup with something deep red.

"And you?" the serving girl asked Kaladin.

"Orange," he said softly. "Chilled, if you have it."

"Orange?" the girl said. "A man like you can stomach something stronger. It's a party! We've got a nice yellow infused with peca, an Azish fruit. I'll—"

"Hey," Veil said, putting her boots on the table with a thump. "The man said orange."

"I just thought—"

"Bring him what he asked for. That's all you need to think about."

Flustered, the girl scampered off. Kaladin nodded to Veil in thanks, though he wished people wouldn't stick up for him quite so zealously. He could speak for himself. As long as Dalinar followed the strictest interpretation of the Codes of War, so would Kaladin. And barring that . . . well, his friends knew. When Kaladin was in one of his moods, alcohol—for all that it seemed it would help him forget his pain—always made the darkness worse. He could use Stormlight to burn off the effects, but once he had a drink or two in him, he often . . . didn't want to. Or felt he didn't deserve to. Same difference.

"So," Veil said. "I hear your mission went well? An entire town stolen right out from underneath their storming noses? The Mink himself rescued? Heads will roll in Kholinar when Odium hears about this."

"I doubt he cares much about one town," Kaladin said. "And they don't know we got the Mink."

"Regardless," Veil said, lifting her cup to him.

"And you?" Kaladin asked.

She leaned forward, taking her boots off the table. "You should have seen it. Ialai was basically a skeleton, withered away. We'd defeated her before we arrived. But it sure was satisfying to bring her down."

"I'm sure."

"Pity someone murdered her," Veil said. "I'd have enjoyed watching her squirm before Dalinar."

"Murdered her?" Kaladin said. "What?"

"Yeah, someone offed her. One of our people, unfortunately. They must have been bribed by someone who wanted to see her dead. That's a secret, by the way. We're telling everyone she killed herself."

Kaladin glanced around.

"Nobody will hear in here," Veil said. "Our booth is isolated."

"Still. Don't discuss military secrets in public."

Veil rolled her eyes, but then she shook her head, and her hair blended to blonde and she sat up straighter. "Do get a full report from Dalinar later, Kaladin. There are oddities about the event that trouble me."

"I . . ." Kaladin said. "We'll see. You share Veil's opinion that Shallan is fine? She merely needs a rest?"

"She is well enough," Radiant said. "We've found a balance. A year now, without any new personas forming. Except . . ."

Kaladin raised an eyebrow.

"There are some, half-formed," Radiant said, turning away. "They wait, to see if the Three really *can* work. Or if it could crumble, letting them out. They aren't real. Not as real as I am. And yet. And yet . . ." She met Kaladin's eyes. "Shallan wouldn't wish me to share that much. But as her friend, you should know."

"I'm not sure if I can help," Kaladin said. "I can barely keep a handle on my own problems these days."

"You being here helps," Radiant said.

Did it? When Kaladin was in moods like this, he felt that he would bring only darkness to those around him. Why would they want to be with him? *He* wouldn't want to be with him. But he supposed this was the sort of thing Radiant had to say; it was what made her distinct from the others.

She smiled as Adolin returned, then shook her head, hair bleeding to black. She leaned back, relaxed. How nice it must be to transform into Veil, with her laid-back attitude.

As Adolin was settling down, the barmaid returned with Kaladin's drink. "If you decide you want to try that yellow . . ." she said to Kaladin.

"Thanks, Mel," Adolin said quickly. "But he doesn't need anything to drink today."

The barmaid gave him a radiant smile—married man or not, they still treated him that way—and floated off, seeming encouraged by the fact that the highprince had spoken to her. Although he'd basically given her a reprimand.

"How's the groom?" Veil asked, getting out her dagger and balancing it on the end of her fingertip.

"Befuddled," Adolin said.

"Groom?" Kaladin asked.

"Wedding party?" Adolin said, waving toward the room of festive people. "For Jor?"

"Who?" Kaladin asked.

"Kaladin," Adolin said, "we've been coming to this place for eight months."

"Don't bother, Adolin," Veil said. "Kaladin doesn't notice people unless they've pulled a weapon on him."

"He notices," Adolin said. "He cares. But Kaladin's a soldier—and he thinks like one. Right, bridgeboy?"

"I have no idea what you mean," Kaladin grumbled, sipping his drink.

"You've learned to worry about your squad," Adolin said. "And to cut out extraneous information. I'll bet Kaladin could tell you the age, eye color, and favorite food of everyone serving beneath him. But he's not going to bother with remembering the names of the bar staff. Father's the same way."

"Well," Veil said, "this is real fun and everything, but shouldn't we be moving on to a more important topic?"

"Such as?" Adolin asked.

"Such as who we're going to fix Kaladin up with next."

Kaladin about spat out his drink. "He doesn't *need* fixing up with *anyone.*"

"That's not what Syl says," Veil replied.

"Syl used to think human children came out through the nose in a particularly violent sneeze," Kaladin said. "She is *not* an authority on this topic."

"Mmm," their table said, vibrating with a soft buzzing sound. "How *do* they come out? I've always wondered."

Kaladin started, only now realizing that Pattern dimpled part of the wooden tabletop. Pattern didn't go about invisibly as Syl did, but somehow infused the material of objects nearby. If you focused on him now, you'd see a section of the tabletop that seemed to be carved into a circular pattern—one that somehow moved and flowed, like ripples in a cistern.

"I'll explain babies later, Pattern," Veil said. "It's more complicated than you're probably imagining. Wait . . . no. Ask *Shallan* to explain. She'll *love* that."

"Mmm," the table said. "She changes colors. Like a sunset. Or an infected wound. Mmm."

Adolin relaxed, resting his arm along the back of the bar seat—but not putting it around Veil. The two of them had a weird relationship when Shallan was wearing Radiant or Veil. At least they seemed to have mostly gotten over the part where they acted like lovesick fools all the time.

"The ladies have a point, bridgeboy," Adolin said to him. "You *have* been extra sulky since Lyn broke up with you."

"This isn't about that."

"Still, a fling couldn't hurt, right?" Veil said. She nodded her chin toward one of the passing barmaids, a tall young woman with unusually light hair. "What about Hem over there? She's tall."

"Great. Tall," Kaladin said. "Because we both measure roughly the same in inches, we're *sure* to get along. Think of all the tall-person topics of conversation we could engage in. Like . . . Hmm . . ."

"Oh, don't be sour," Veil said, smacking him on the shoulder. "You didn't even glance at her. She's cute. Look at those *legs*. Back me up, Adolin."

"She's attractive," he said. "But that blouse is terrible on her. I need to tell Marni that the house uniforms here are dreadful. They should at *least* have two different shades to match different skin tones."

"What about Ka's sister," Veil said to Kaladin. "You've met her, right? She's smart. You like smart girls."

"Is there really anyone who doesn't like smart girls?" Kaladin said.

"Me," Veil said, raising her hand. "Give me dumb ones, please. They're *so* easy to impress."

"Smart girls . . ." Adolin said, rubbing his chin. "It's too bad Skar snatched up Ristina. They'd have been a good match."

"Adolin," Veil said, "Ristina is like three feet tall."

"So?" Adolin said. "You heard Kaladin. He doesn't care about height."

"Yeah, well, most women do. You've got to find someone who *matches* him. Too bad he screwed up his chance with Lyn."

"I didn't . . ." Kaladin protested.

"What about her," Adolin said, pointing as someone new entered the tavern. A couple of lighteyed women in havahs, though they probably weren't of high rank if they were visiting a winehouse frequented by darkeyes. Then again, Adolin was here. And things like nahn and rank had been . . . strangely less divisive this last year, under Jasnah's rule.

One of the two newcomers was a younger woman with a luscious figure, accentuated by the tight havah. She had dark skin and red lips, clearly brightened with lip paint.

"Dakhnah," Adolin said. "She's the daughter of one of Father's generals, Kal. She *loves* talking strategy—she's acted as scribe in his war meetings since she was fourteen. I can introduce you."

"Please don't," Kaladin said.

"Dakhnah . . ." Veil said. "You courted her, didn't you?"

"Yeah. How'd you know?"

"Adolin dear, swing a Herdazian in a crowded room, and you'll hit six women you courted." She narrowed her eyes at the newcomer. "Those aren't real, are they? She pads, right?"

Adolin shook his head.

"*Seriously?*" Veil said. "Stormfather. To get mine that big I'd have to eat six chulls. How do they feel?"

"You're making assumptions," Adolin said.

She glared at him, then poked him in the shoulder. "Come on."

He turned eyes toward the ceiling and pointedly took a drink, though he smiled as she poked him again. "This is not a topic for gentlemen to discuss," he said with an airy tone.

"I'm neither gentle nor a man," Veil said. "I'm your wife."

"You're *not* my wife."

"I share a body with your wife. Close enough."

"You two," Kaladin said, "have the *strangest* relationship."

Adolin gave him a slow nod that seemed to say, *You have no idea.* Veil downed the rest of her drink, then upended the empty cup. "Where's that storming barmaid?"

"You sure you haven't had enough?" Adolin asked.

"Am I sitting up straight?"

"A vague approximation."

"There's your answer," she said—sliding out of the booth by moving over him in a maneuver that involved a lot of her touching a lot of him—then went picking through the crowd for the barmaid.

"She's in rare form today," Kaladin noted.

"Veil has been cooped up for a month, pretending to be that woman in the warcamps," he replied. "And Radiant stressed greatly about their mission. The few times we managed to meet, Shallan was practically crawling up the walls with tension. This is her way of letting loose."

Well, if it worked for them . . . "Is Ialai Sadeas really dead?"

"Unfortunately. Father already has armies moving to the warcamps. Initial reports say her men have offered articles of surrender; they must have known this was coming. . . ." He shrugged. "Still makes me feel like I failed."

"You had to do something. That group was getting too powerful, too dangerous, to leave alone."

"I know. But I hate the idea of fighting our own. We're supposed to be moving on to better things. Greater things."

Says the man who killed Sadeas, Kaladin thought. That wasn't common knowledge yet, so he didn't speak it out loud in case someone was listening.

Their conversation lapsed. Kaladin played with his cup, wishing for a refill, though he wasn't about to go fighting through the crowd to find one. People were taking turns cheering for Jor—and as the groom himself passed by, Kaladin realized he did recognize the man. He was the house bouncer, an affable fellow. Syl was riding on his shoulder.

Veil's quest ran long. Kaladin thought he spotted her over at one corner, playing a game of breakneck for chips. He was surprised there was anyone left in the city who would still play against Veil.

Eventually, Adolin scooted a little closer. He had his own drink, an intoxicating violet—but he'd barely made his way through half the cup. He no longer strictly followed the Codes, but he seemed to have found his own balance.

"So," Adolin said, "what's going on? This *is* more than just what happened with Lyn."

"I thought you said I didn't have to talk."

"You don't." Adolin took a sip, waiting.

Kaladin stared at the table. Shallan often carved parts of it, so the wood here was etched with small but intricate art projects—many of them half finished. He ran his finger across one that depicted an axehound and a man who looked remarkably like Adolin.

"Your father relieved me of active duty today," Kaladin said. "He thinks I'm . . . I'm not fit to see battle any longer."

Adolin let out a long exhalation. "That storming man . . ."

"He's right, Adolin," Kaladin said. "Remember how you had to pull me out of the palace last year."

"Everyone gets overwhelmed in a fight sometimes," Adolin said. "I've gotten disoriented before, even in Shardplate."

"This is worse. And more frequent. I'm a surgeon, Adolin. I've trained to spot problems like these, so I *know* he's right. I've known for months."

"Very well," Adolin said. He nodded curtly. "So it is. What are we going to do about it? How do you get better?"

"You don't. Dabbid, the guy in my crew? The one who doesn't talk? Battle shock, like mine. He's been like that since I recruited him."

Adolin fell silent. Kaladin could see him sort through potential responses. Adolin was many things, but "hard to read" would never be one of them.

Fortunately, he didn't make any of the expected comments. No simple affirmations, no encouragement for Kaladin to cheer up or soldier on. The two of them sat quietly in the loud room for a long pause. Then eventually, Adolin spoke. "My father can be wrong, you know."

Kaladin shrugged.

"He's human," Adolin said. "Half the city thinks he's some kind of Herald reborn, but he's only a man. He's been wrong before. *Terribly* wrong."

Dalinar killed Adolin's mother, Kaladin thought. That news *was* out, spread wide. The city had all either read, listened to, or been told about Dalinar's strange autobiography. Handwritten by the Blackthorn himself, it wasn't quite finished, but drafts had been shared. In it Dalinar confessed to many things, including the accidental killing of his wife.

"I'm not a surgeon," Adolin said. "And I'm not half the general my father is. But I don't think you need to be removed from combat, at least not permanently. You need something else."

"Which is?"

"Wish I knew. There should be a way to help you. A way to make it so you can think straight."

"I wish it were that easy," Kaladin said. "But why do you care? What does it matter?"

"You're my only bridgeboy," Adolin said with a grin. "Where would I get another? They've all started flying away." The grin faded. "Besides. If we can find a way to help you, then maybe . . . maybe we can find a way to help her." His gazed drifted across the room, toward Veil.

"She's fine," Kaladin said. "She's found a balance. You've heard her explain how she thinks she's fine now."

"Like how you tell everyone *you're* fine?" Adolin met his eyes. "This isn't right, how she is. It hurts her. Over this last year I've seen her struggling, and I've seen hints that she's sliding—if more slowly now—toward worse depths. She needs help, the kind I don't know if I can give her."

Their table hummed. "You are right," Pattern said. "She hides it, but things are still wrong."

"What does your surgeon's knowledge say, Kal?" Adolin said. "What do I do?"

"I don't know," Kaladin said. "We are trained in dealing with physical ailments, not in what to do when someone is sick in the mind, other than send them to the ardents."

"Seems wrong."

"Yeah, it does." Kaladin frowned. He wasn't totally certain what the ardents did with mentally ill patients.

"Should I talk to them?" Pattern asked. "Ardents, for help?"

"Maybe," Kaladin said. "Wit might know some way to help too. He seems to know about all kinds of things like this."

"Surely you can give some advice, Kal," Adolin said.

"Let her know you care," Kaladin said. "Listen to her. Be encouraging, but don't try to force her to be happy. And don't let her be alone, if you're worried about her. . . ."

He trailed off, then shot Adolin a glare.

Adolin smirked. This hadn't just been about Shallan. Damnation. Had he let *Adolin* outsmart him? Maybe he *should* get something stronger to drink.

"I'm worried about you both," Adolin said. "I'm going to find a way to help. Somehow."

"You're a storming fool," Kaladin said. "We need to get you a spren. Why hasn't an order picked you up yet?"

Adolin shrugged. "I'm not a good fit, I guess."

"It's that sword of yours," Kaladin said. "Shardbearers do better if they drop any old Shards. You need to get rid of yours."

"I'm not 'getting rid' of Maya."

"I know you're attached to the sword," Kaladin said. "But you'd have something better, if you became Radiant. Think about how it would feel to—"

"I'm *not* getting *rid* of Maya," Adolin said. "Leave it, bridgeboy." The finality in his voice surprised Kaladin, but before he could push further, Jor showed up to introduce his new bride, Kryst, to Adolin.

And, mark Kaladin as the fourth fool if Adolin didn't immediately pull out a *gift* for the pair. Adolin hadn't merely shown up at his favorite wine-house on the night of a wedding party, he'd come ready with a present.

Veil eventually tired of her game and found her way back, more than a little tipsy. When Adolin joked about it, she made a wisecrack about being lucky she was Veil, "because Shallan *really* can't hold her alcohol."

As the evening progressed, Syl returned to proclaim she wanted to take up gambling. Kaladin felt increasingly glad for what Adolin had done. Not because Kaladin felt better; he was still miserable. Yet the misery did lessen around others, and it required Kaladin to keep up a semblance. To pretend. It might be a front, but he'd found that sometimes the front worked even on himself.

The balance lasted for a good two hours, until—as the wedding party started to wane—Rock stepped up. He must have spoken to Adolin and Veil earlier, as they slipped out of the booth as soon as they noticed him, leaving Rock and Kaladin to speak in private.

The look on Rock's face made Kaladin's stomach churn. So, the time had arrived, had it? Of *course* it would happen today, of all days.

"Lowlander," Rock said. "My captain."

"Do we have to do this today, Rock?" Kaladin said. "I'm not at my best."

"Is what you said before," Rock said. "And before that."

Kaladin braced himself, but nodded.

"I have waited, as you asked, though these Shards from Amaram for my people gather dust in their box," Rock said, his large hands pressed to the tabletop. "Was good suggestion. My family was tired from travel. Best to spend time, let them know my friends. And Cord, she wanted to train.

Ha! She says Horneater traditions *and* Alethi traditions to be foolish. First Shardbearer among my people was not *nuatoma*, but young woman."

"It could have been you, Rock," Kaladin said. "Either with those Shards you won, or as a Radiant with your own spren. We need you. *I* need you."

"You have had me. Now, *I* need me. It is time to return, my *ula'makai*. My captain."

"You just said your traditions were foolish."

"To my daughter." Rock pointed to his heart. "Not to me, Kaladin. I lifted the bow."

"You saved my life."

"I made that choice because you are worth that sacrifice." He reached across the table and rested his hand on Kaladin's shoulder. "But it is *no* sacrifice unless I now go, as is right, to seek justice from my people. I would leave with your blessing. But I will leave either way."

"Alone?"

"Ha! I would not have anyone to talk to! Song will go with me, and younger children. Cord and Gift, they wish to stay. Gift should not fight, but I fear he will. It is his choice. As this is my choice."

"Moash is out there, Rock. He might attack you. If you won't fight . . . your family could be in danger."

This gave Rock pause, then he grinned. "Skar and Drehy both said they wanted to see my Peaks. Perhaps I will let them help fly my family, so we do not have to walk all across stupid lowlands. Then we will have protection, yes?"

Kaladin nodded. It was the best he could do—send an escort. Rock seemed to wait for something . . . and Kaladin realized it might be an offer to go with them. To see the Horneater Peaks that Rock had so often bragged about. The large cook never could get his stories straight. Was the place a frigid wasteland or a lush and warm paradise?

In any case . . . maybe Kaladin *could* go. Maybe he could fly off to adventure. Take Rock to his home, then stay—or simply run away, find a battle somewhere. Dalinar couldn't stop him.

No. Kaladin dismissed the thought immediately. Fleeing would be the action of a child. Plus, he couldn't go with Rock. Not merely because of the temptation to flee, but because he doubted he could hold back if Rock gave himself up to justice. The Horneater had been deliberately quiet about what punishment his people might impose as a consequence for his actions, but Kaladin found their entire tradition of birth-order-based roles in life stupid. If Kaladin went, it would be to undermine his friend's decision.

"I give my blessing, Rock," Kaladin said. "Both to you going, and to any who wish a short leave to accompany you. A Windrunner honor guard—

you deserve that and more. And if you do encounter Moash . . ."

"Ha," Rock said, standing. "He should try to come for me. That will let me get close enough to put hands on his neck and squeeze."

"You don't fight."

"That? Is not fighting. Is exterminating. Even cook can kill rat he finds in his grain." He grinned, and Kaladin knew him well enough to realize it was a joke.

Rock held out his arms for an embrace. "Come. Give me farewell."

Feeling like he was in a trance, Kaladin stood. "Will you return? If you can, after?"

Rock shook his head. "This thing I have done here with all of you, he is the end. When we meet again, I suspect it shall not be in this world. This life."

Kaladin embraced his friend. One final, *crushing* Horneater hug. When they pulled apart, Rock was crying, but smiling. "You gave me back my life," he said. "Thank you for that, Kaladin, bridgeleader. Do not be sad that now I choose to *live* that life."

"You go to imprisonment or worse."

"I go to the gods," Rock said. He held up his finger. "There is one who lives here. One *afah'liki*. He is powerful god, but tricky. You should not have lost his flute."

"I . . . don't think Wit is a god, Rock."

He tapped Kaladin's head. "Airsick as always." He grinned, bowing in a sweeping, deferential way Kaladin had never seen from him before.

Following that, Rock retreated to meet Song at the door, and left. Forever.

Kaladin slumped into his seat. At least he wouldn't be around to see Kaladin removed from his post. Rock could safely spend the rest of his days—short or long—pretending that his captain, his *ula'makai*, had remained strong all his days.

13

ANOTHER HUNT

Advanced fabrials are created using several different techniques. Conjoined fabrials require a careful division of the gemstone— and the spren inside. If performed correctly, the two halves will continue to behave as a single gemstone.

Note that rubies and flamespren are traditional for this purpose— as they have proven the easiest to divide, and the quickest in response times. Other types of spren do not split as evenly, as easily, or at all.

—Lecture on fabrial mechanics presented by Navani Kholin
to the coalition of monarchs, Urithiru, Jesevan, 1175

T he morning after the wedding party, Shallan had to deal with Veil's alcohol abuse. Again. Her head throbbed, and much of the late night was a blur in her mind. Storming woman.

Fortunately, with some Stormlight and some herbs for headaches, she was feeling better by the time she finished meetings with her accountants and ministers. She was wife to a highprince, and though their lands in Alethkar were under enemy control, she and Adolin had a tenth of Urithiru to tend.

Considering Shallan's Radiant duties, they'd put several trustworthy women in control of finances—their husbands overseeing police and guards. The meeting mostly involved Radiant dispensing a few decisions and Shallan auditing the accounts. She'd have more work to do in the future, but for now things were in hand. Adolin said she was supposed to be taking some time off following the mission anyway.

He was using that time to go ride horses. Once the scribes withdrew from her audience chamber, Shallan found herself alone—and for the first time in weeks, she didn't have a role to play. She went through her letters and spanreed communications for a while, and eventually froze on a certain one that had arrived a day before she returned.

The deal is set and arranged. The spren will come.

She held this one for a moment, then burned it. Feeling a chill, she decided she didn't want to be alone in her room any longer—so went to visit her brothers.

Their quarters weren't far from hers. Jushu was the only one there when she arrived, but he let her in and chatted with her about her mission. Then, as usually happened when she visited, Shallan found her way to the room's hearth to draw. It felt . . . natural. Visiting her brothers didn't necessarily mean talking to them the entire time.

She nestled in the blankets beside the hearth, and for a blessed few minutes could imagine she was home in Jah Keved. In her fantasy, a fire crackled in the hearth. Nearby, her stepmother and her father chatted together with some visiting ardents—men and women of the church, which meant her father was being well-behaved.

Shallan was allowed her sketchbook, as Father loved to show off her skill. Eyes closed, she drew the hearth—each brick engraved in her mind from the many times she'd drawn here. Good days. Warm days.

"Hey, what're you drawing?" Jushu asked. "Is it the hearth from home?"

She smiled, and though the real Jushu had spoken, she incorporated him into her mental image. One of her four older brothers—because in this memory, she still had four. Jushu and Wikim were twins, though Jushu laughed more than Wikim did. Wikim was thoughtful. And Balat, he would sit in the chair nearby, pretending to be confident. Helaran was back, and Balat always puffed up when the eldest Davar brother was around.

She opened her eyes and glanced at the little creationspren gathering around her, imitating mundane things. Her mother's teakettle. The fireplace poker. Objects from her home in Jah Keved, not objects here—somehow they responded to her imaginings. One in particular made her feel cold. A necklace chain slinking across the ground.

In truth, those days at home had been terrible times. Times of tears, and screams, and a life unraveling. It was also the last time she could remember her entire family together.

Except . . . no, that wasn't the entire family. This memory had happened after . . . after Shallan had killed her mother.

Confront it! she thought at herself, angry. *Don't ignore it!* Pattern moved across the floor of the room here in Urithiru, spinning among the dancing creationspren.

She'd been only eleven years old. Seven years ago now—and if that timeline was correct, she must have begun seeing Pattern as a young child.

Long before Jasnah had first encountered *her* spren. Shallan didn't remember her first experiences with Pattern. Other than the distinct image of summoning her Shardblade to protect herself as a child, she had excised all such memories.

No, they're here, Veil thought. *Deep within, Shallan.*

She couldn't see those memories; didn't *want* to see them. As she shied away from them, something dark shifted inside her, growing stronger. Formless. Shallan didn't want to be the person who had done those things. That . . . that person could not . . . not be loved. . . .

She gripped her pencil in tight fingers, the drawing half-finished in her lap. She'd buckled down and forced herself to read studies on other people with fragmented personas. She'd found only a handful of mentions in medical texts, though the accounts implied people like her were treated as freaks even by the ardents. Oddities to be locked away in the darkness for their own good, studied by academics who found the cases "novel in their bizarre nature" and "giving insight to the addled mind of the psychotic." It was clear that going to such experts with her problems was not an option.

Memory loss was apparently common to these cases, but the rest of what Shallan experienced seemed distinctly different. Importantly, she wasn't experiencing continued memory loss. So maybe she was fine. She'd stabilized.

Everything was getting better. Surely it was.

"Storms," Jushu said. "Shallan, that's some . . . some weird stuff you've drawn."

She focused on the sketch—which she'd drawn poorly, since her eyes had been closed. It took her a second to notice that in the fireplace back home, she'd drawn burning souls. One might have mistaken them for flamespren, but for the fact that they looked so similar to her and her three brothers. . . .

She snapped the sketchbook closed. She wasn't back in Jah Keved. The hearth before her now had no flames; it was a depression with a heating fabrial resting in it, set into the wall of a Urithiru room.

She had to live in the present. Jushu was no longer the plump, readily smiling boy from her memories. He was an overweight man with a full beard who had to be watched almost constantly, lest he steal something and try to pawn it for gambling money. They'd *twice* caught him trying to remove the heating fabrial.

The way he smiled at her was a lie. Or maybe he was simply trying the best he could to remain upbeat. Almighty knew she understood that.

"Nothing to say?" he asked. "No quip? You almost never make wisecracks anymore."

"You aren't around enough for me to make sport of," she said. "And no one else is quite as inspiring in their incompetence."

He smiled, but winced, and Shallan immediately felt ashamed. The joke was too accurate. She couldn't act like when they'd been kids; then, their father had been a great unifying enemy, making their gallows humor a way to cope.

She worried about them drifting apart. So she visited, almost defiantly.

Jushu rose to get some food, and Shallan wanted to try another joke. She let him go instead. With a sigh, she rummaged in her satchel and brought out Ialai's little notebook. She was piecing some of its meanings together. For instance, Ialai's spies had caught members of the Ghostbloods talking about a new route through the Sea of Lost Lights. That was the place she and the others had traveled in Shadesmar a year back. Indeed, an entire three pages were filled with locations from the mysterious world of the spren.

I saw a map, Ialai had written, *in the things of the Ghostblood we captured— and should have thought to copy it, for it was lost in the fire. Here is what I remember.*

Shallan made some notes at the bottom of Ialai's crude map. Whatever skills in politics the woman had possessed, they had been offset by a dearth of artistic ability. But perhaps Shallan could find some actual maps of Shadesmar and compare?

The door opened, admitting Balat and a friend returning from their duties as guardsmen, though Shallan's back was to the group. From the quiet voices, Eylita—Balat's wife—had met them somewhere in the hallway, and was laughing at something Balat said. Over the last year, Shallan had grown surprisingly fond of the young woman. As a child, Shallan remembered being jealous of anyone who might take her brothers away—but as an adult, she saw better. Eylita was kind and genuine. And it took a special person to love a member of the Davar family.

Shallan continued her study of the book, listening with half an ear as Balat and Eylita chatted with their friend. Eylita had encouraged Balat to find an occupation, though Shallan wasn't certain becoming a guardsman was the best match for him. Balat had a tendency to enjoy the pain of other creatures a little too much.

Balat, Eylita, and his friend made their way to the other room, where a cooling fabrial kept some meats and curries chilled for meals. Their life was growing so convenient, and it could be even more so. Shallan's elevation to wife of a highprince could have awarded this home dozens of servants.

Her brothers, however, had grown distrustful of servants—and they had grown accustomed to living without in the lean days. Besides, these fabrials did the work of a dozen people. No need for someone to chop or carry wood, no need for a fresh trip to the tower kitchens each day. Almost, Shallan feared, Navani's artifabrians would make them all lazy.

As if having servants hasn't already made most lighteyes lazy, Shallan thought. *Focus. Why are the Ghostbloods so interested in Shadesmar? Veil, any thoughts?*

Veil frowned, absently turned around to put her back to the wall, then tucked her foot through the strap of her satchel to prevent it from being pulled away. When she became Veil, the colors in the room . . . muted. The colors didn't change, but her perception shifted. Shallan would have described those strata lines as rust colored, but to Veil they were just red.

Veil kept one eye on the door to the balcony. Balat, Eylita, and Jushu had all moved out there, and were joking with that other guardsman. Laughterspren moved in front of the door. Who was this friend? Shallan hadn't bothered to check.

Sorry, Shallan thought. *I was distracted.*

Veil studied the words in the notebook, picking out the relevant pieces. Maps, names of places, discussions of the cost of moving items through Shadesmar. Shallan's first mission for the Ghostbloods—back when Veil had been no more than a drawing in a notebook—had been to spy on Amaram, who had been trying to work out how to find Urithiru and the Oathgates.

The Oathgates—though primarily used to quickly move troops and supplies—had another function. They had the ability to send people back and forth into Shadesmar, a usage that Dalinar's scholars and Radiants had slowly managed to unlock during the past year. Was that what Mraize had wanted?

Veil saw the pieces of something grand in Mraize's moves: find the Oathgates, attempt to secure unfettered—perhaps exclusive—access to Shadesmar. Along the way, try to remove rivals, like Jasnah. Then recruit a Radiant who could look into Shadesmar. Finally, attack other factions who were trying to discover the secrets.

She would have to . . . Wait. That voice.

Veil's head jolted up. The guard her brothers were talking to. *Damnation.* Veil snapped the book closed and tucked it in the pocket of her dress, then stood and had Shallan make her hair red again, though Veil kept control.

She peeked out onto the balcony to check, but she already knew she'd find Mraize there.

He stood tall, with his peculiarly scarred face, wearing a gold and black uniform like Balat. Those were colors of the Sebarial Princedom—the house Shallan had chosen to align with before marrying into the Kholins. She'd once seen Mraize in a similar uniform, serving Ialai and her house a year ago.

Mraize didn't fit the uniform. Not that it was poorly tailored, he was simply . . . wrong in it. He was at once too lofty and too *jagged* a person for the job. Predatory, where a guardsman should be obedient—yet also refined, when being a guardsman was one of the more lowly jobs for a lighteyes.

He saw her, of course. Mraize always watched the doors; she'd learned the trick from him. He didn't break character, laughing at what Balat said, but he didn't fake nearly as well as Shallan could. He couldn't keep the haughty tone from his laugh, or the bite from his grin. He didn't reside in the character; he wore it as a costume.

Veil folded her arms and lounged by the doorway. A cold breeze blew in off the mountains, making her shiver. Mraize and the boys pretended not to be cold, though their breath puffed in front of them and coldspren grew like spikes on the balcony railing. Odd, how in this tower it could feel so much warmer inside, even if you left the door open. Indeed, Eylita soon made an excuse and went in, passing Veil with a smile and a wave, which Shallan returned.

Veil kept her attention on Mraize. He clearly wanted her to see him interacting with her brothers. He rarely used overt threats, but this *was* a warning. He had been the one to bring the young men here safely, a reward for her services rendered. What he had given her, he could remove. As a guardsman, he'd train each day with the sword near Balat. Accidents happened. Shallan panicked slightly at this discovery, but Veil could play this game, even if the pieces were people she loved.

We need to be ready to make a move, Radiant thought, *to put our brothers where they will be safe.*

Veil agreed. Did such a place exist? Or instead should she gather a few pieces of her own to use? She needed information—about the Ghostbloods, and about Mraize himself. Despite their time working together, she knew next to nothing about the man.

She was curious to see how Mraize would create an opportunity for the two of them to speak together alone. It would be strange if he—supposedly a lowly lighteyed soldier—were to request time with Shallan.

After a short conversation, Mraize said, "I do admire your view here, Balat! I wish I merited a balcony room. Look at those mountains! Next time I walk the gardens below, I'll glance up and see if I can find you. Regardless, for now I should be returning to my quarters."

He pretended to see Shallan there for the first time, and hastily bowed to her. It was a fair effort, but overdone. She nodded to him as he retreated through their rooms and left. He'd want to meet her in the gardens, but she didn't intend to rush off to do his bidding.

"Balat," she said. "That man. Have you known him long?"

"Hm? What was that, small one?" Balat turned toward her. During their first months together, talking to him had felt so awkward. Balat expected her to be the same timid girl who had left searching for Jasnah. Being with them had made Shallan realize how different she'd become in their months apart.

It had been a fight, strangely, not to backslide when around these three. It wasn't that she wanted to be the younger, timid version of herself. But it *was* familiar in ways these new versions of her were not.

"That man," Veil said. "What's his name?"

"We call him Gobby," Balat said. "He's old to be in training, but with the call out for new soldiers, lots of people who haven't really held a sword before are joining up."

"Is he good?" Veil asked.

"Gobby? Nah. He's fine, I mean, but makes a lot of mistakes. Almost chopped a man's arm off by accident last week! Captain Talanan laid into him for that one, I'll tell you!" He chuckled, but Veil's unamused face made him trail off.

She became Shallan and smiled belatedly, but her brothers left to go eat. She watched them chatting together and felt something stir inside her: regret. They'd found an equilibrium as a family, but she wasn't certain she'd ever get used to being the adult in the room when they were together.

It made her want to go bother Adolin. She thought she could pick him out below, riding Dalinar's horse on the field they'd dedicated to the animals. But she wouldn't interrupt him—spending time with the Ryshadium was one of the purest joys of Adolin's life.

Best to go attend Mraize, as he wanted.

◆◆

"Garden" was too grand a term by far for the small field beneath the windows to her brothers' quarters. Yes, some of the Alethi gardeners had begun growing shalebark ridges or other ornamental plants here—but the cold weather stunted growth. The result, even with the occasional use of a heating fabrial, was little more than a network of colored mounds on the ground, not the gorgeous cultivated walls of a true garden. She picked out only two small lifespren.

Mraize was a dark pillar on the far side, surveying the frosted mountain peaks. Veil didn't try to sneak up on him; she knew he'd sense her coming.

He seemed to be able to do that no matter how little sound she made. It was a trick she'd been trying to replicate.

Instead she stepped up beside him. She'd fetched her hat and coat, the latter buttoned against the cold, but she'd covered that and her face with the illusion of a guard in Sebarial's army. In case someone saw the two of them meeting.

"You," Mraize said without looking at her, "are to be commended again, little knife. The Sons of Honor are basically defunct. The few remaining members have fled into hiding, separately. With Dalinar's soldiers 're-storing order' in the warcamps, there is little chance of the infestation restarting."

"One of your operatives killed Ialai," Veil said, trying to pick out what Mraize was looking at. He was staring intently, tracking something out there. She saw only snow and slopes.

"Yes," Mraize said.

"I don't like the idea of someone watching over my shoulder," Veil said. "It says you don't trust me."

"*Should* I trust you three? I'm under the impression that at least part of you isn't . . . fully committed."

She finally picked out what Mraize was watching: a small dot of color soaring through one of the canyons. His pet chicken, the green one. Mraize whistled sharply, and the sound echoed below. The creature turned in their direction.

"You must decide," Mraize said to her, "how long you are going to continue this flirtation, Veil. You tease us. Are you a Ghostblood or not? You enjoy the benefits of our organization, but refuse to get the tattoo."

"Why would I want something that could reveal me?"

"Because of the commitment it represents. Because of the permanence." He eyed her, noting her illusion. "Of course, with your powers nothing is permanent, is it? You deal exclusively in the ephemeral."

He held up his arm as the chicken returned, fluttering its wings as it landed, its talons clutching his coat. The chicken was one of the strangest varieties Veil had ever seen, with that large hooked beak and those bright green feathers. It carried something in its mouth, a small furry creature. It could have been a rat, but the look was wrong.

"What is that?" Veil asked. "What did it catch?"

"A mole," Mraize said.

"A what?"

"Like a rat, but different. You know the word, 'mole'? An informant? Comes from these creatures, which live in Shinovar and dig into places they're not wanted. They've made their way across Azir over the centuries, then into the mountains."

"Whatever," Veil said.

The scarred man eyed her, a hint of a smile on his lips. "Shallan will find this interesting, Veil. Do you not want to ask, for her sake? An invasive species from Shinovar, slowly making a home in the mountains? Where Rosharan creatures cannot live. They lack the fur, the adaptations, you see."

Shallan emerged as he said it, so she took a Memory. She needed to draw the little beast. How *did* it survive in this cold? Surely there wasn't anything to eat up here.

"A hunter knows the advantages his prey relies upon to hide and to thrive," Mraize said. "Shallan understands this; she seeks to understand the world. You should not dismiss this kind of knowledge so quickly, Veil. It has applications you may not anticipate, but which will serve you both well."

Damnation. Shallan hated talking with him. She found herself wanting to nod, to agree with him, to *learn* from him. Radiant whispered truth: Shallan had lived her childhood with a father who had been paternal in all the wrong ways and none of the right ones. In Mraize, a part of her saw a substitute. Strong, confident, and—most importantly—willing to offer praise.

His chicken held its prey with one foot, eating almost like a person did with their hands. The thing was so strange, so alien. It stood upright, like no other beast Shallan had studied. When it chirped at Mraize, it sounded almost like it was talking, and she swore she could occasionally make out words. It was like a tiny parody of a person.

She glanced away from the brutal display of the feasting chicken, though Mraize watched the creature with an air of approval.

"I can't join the Ghostbloods fully," she said, "unless I know what it is you're trying to accomplish. I don't know your motivations. How can I align with you until I do?"

"Surely you can guess," Mraize said. "It's about power, obviously."

She frowned. So . . . was it really that simple? Had she imagined depths to this man that weren't there?

Mraize continued to hold his chicken on one arm, fishing in his pocket with the other hand. He took out a diamond broam, then handed it to her, wrapping her fingers around it. Her fist shone from within.

"Power," Mraize said. "Portable, easily contained, renewable. You hold the energy of a storm in your hand, Veil. That raw energy, plucked from the heart of the raging tempest. It is tamed—not only a safe source of light, but of power that those with . . . particular interests and abilities can access."

"Sure," Veil said, emerging again. "At the same time it's practically worthless—because anyone can get it. The gemstones are the valuable part."

"That's small thinking," Mraize said. "The stones are but containers. No more valuable than a cup. Important, yes, if you wish to carry liquid across the dry expanse. But the value comes solely from what it contains."

"What kind of 'dry expanse' would you cross?" Veil asked. "I mean, you can always simply wait for a storm."

"Locked into your conditioned way of thinking," Mraize said, shaking his head. "I thought you'd be able to see bigger, to dream bigger. Tell me, when you traveled Shadesmar, how valuable was a little Stormlight?"

"Very," she said. "So . . . this is about bringing Stormlight to Shadesmar? What do the spren have that you want?"

"That, little knife, is the wrong question."

Blast. Veil felt her temper rising. Hadn't she proven herself? How *dare* he treat her as if she were some lowly apprentice.

Fortunately, they had Radiant to guide them here. She learned lessons Veil refused to. Radiant didn't mind being treated like an apprentice; Radiant liked learning. She had Shallan bleed their hair to blonde, though they were still wearing a man's face, and folded her hands behind her back, standing up straighter.

Ask a better question. "Nalathis," Radiant said. "Scadarial. What are they?"

"Nalthis. Scadrial." He spoke the words with a different accent. "*Where* are they. That's an excellent question, Radiant. Suffice it to say they are places in Shadesmar where our Stormlight—so easily captured and transported—would be a valuable commodity."

Curious. She knew so little of Shadesmar, but the spren had vast cities—and she knew Stormlight was prized there. "That's why you wanted to get to Urithiru before Jasnah. You knew the Oathgates would offer easy access to Shadesmar. You want to control commerce, travel, to these other places."

"Excellent," Mraize said. "Trade to Roshar through Shadesmar has been historically difficult, as there is only one stable access point—one controlled by the Horneaters, who have been unpleasant to deal with. Yet Roshar has something that so many other peoples in the cosmere want: free, portable, easy-to-access power."

"There has to be more," Radiant said. "What is the catch? The problem with the system? You wouldn't be telling me this if there weren't a problem."

He glanced at her. "Excellent observation, Radiant. I find it unfortunate we don't normally get along."

"We would get along much better if you were more straightforward with people," Radiant said. "Your type turns my stomach."

"What?" Mraize asked. "Me? A simple guardsman?"

"One who has a reputation for being clumsy—for nearly *killing* other guardsmen. If you harm Shallan's brothers, Mraize . . ."

"We don't harm our own," Mraize said.

So remain one of us, that indicated. Radiant hated his games, though Veil delighted in them. For now, however, Radiant remained in control. She was making progress.

"The catch?" she asked, holding up the broam. "The problem?"

"This power is something we call Investiture," Mraize said. "Investiture manifests in many forms, tied to many places and many different gods. It is *bound* to a specific land—making it very difficult to transport. It resists. Try to carry this too far, and you'd find it increasingly difficult to move, as it became increasingly heavy.

"The same limitation restrains people who are *themselves* heavily Invested. Radiants, spren—anyone *Connected* to Roshar is bound by these laws, and cannot travel farther than Ashyn or Braize. You are imprisoned here, Radiant."

"A prison as large as three planets," Radiant said. "Forgive me if I don't feel confined."

Veil, however, was hiding. Things like this daunted her—such large-scale ideas and problems. Shallan though . . . Shallan wanted to soar, learn, discover. And to find that she was restricted in that discovery, even if she'd never known about the restriction, *did* bother her.

Mraize took the broam back. "This gemstone cannot go where it is needed. A more perfect gemstone could contain the Light long enough to go offworld, but there is still the Connection problem. This little flaw has caused untold trouble. And the one who unlocks the secret would have untold power. *Literal* power, Radiant. The power to change worlds . . ."

"So you want to unravel the secret," Radiant said.

"I already have," Mraize said, making a fist. "Though putting the plan into motion will be difficult. I have a job for you."

"We don't want another job," Radiant said. "It is time for this association to be finished."

"Are you certain? Are all *three* of you certain?"

Radiant drew her lips to a line, but she knew the truth. No, they were not certain. Reluctantly, she let Shallan emerge, hair bleeding to its natural auburn-red.

"I have news for you," Shallan said. "Sja-anat contacted me while I was away. She agreed to your terms, and is sending one of her spren to the tower, where it will investigate your members for a possible bond."

"Those weren't the terms," he said. "She was to promise me a spren to bond."

"Considering where we started last year," Shallan said, "you should take what you can get. It's been difficult to contact her lately; I think she's worried about how people are treating Renarin."

"No," Mraize said. "Odium watches. We must be careful. I will . . . accept these terms. Have you any other reports?"

"Ialai's agents have a spy close to Dalinar," Shallan said. "So the Sons of Honor might not be completely stamped out yet."

"An interesting line of reasoning," Mraize said, "but you're wrong. The Sons of Honor don't have an agent close to Dalinar. They simply managed to intercept some communications from one of *our* agents who is close to Dalinar."

Ah . . . That explained a few things. Ialai didn't have the reach to get close to Dalinar, but if she'd found a way to intercept intelligence from the Ghostbloods, the result would be the same.

Mraize didn't lie to her, as far as she'd been able to determine. So . . .

"I don't need to worry about two spies then," Shallan said. "Only the one you have watching me, the one who killed Ialai. It's one of Adolin's guards, isn't it?"

"Don't be silly. We have no interest in men such as that. They offer us nothing."

"Who, then?"

"I cannot betray this secret," Mraize said. "Let's just say that Lightweavers fascinate me, and leave it at that. And you should not fear if I did keep someone close to you. Such a person could be an . . . aid in times of need. Iyatil did the same for me."

Shallan fumed. He all but promised the Ghostblood spy was among her Lightweavers, which did make sense. Mraize would want someone who could watch Shallan in places a soldier might not be able to reach. One of the deserters then? Or Ishnah? One of the newer squires? The idea made her sick.

"Iyatil has reported to Master Thaidakar," Mraize said, "and he has accepted—after some initial anger—that we will not be able to control the Oathgates. I explained that there at least is a calming wind in this, like the riddens of a storm. With Dalinar controlling the Oathgates, he can prosecute the war against Odium."

"And that helps your cause?"

"We have no interest in seeing the enemy rule this world, Shallan. Master Thaidakar wishes only to secure a method for gathering and transporting Stormlight." Mraize held his broam up again. Like a miniature sun beside the real one.

"Why attack the Sons of Honor though?" Shallan asked. "At first I understood—they were trying to find Urithiru before us. But now? What threat was Ialai?"

"Now *that* is a brilliant question," Mraize said, and she couldn't suppress a thrill from Veil at being praised by him. "The secret has to do with Gavilar. The old king. What was he doing?"

"The same old question," Shallan said. "I spent weeks researching his life under Jasnah's tutelage. She seemed to think he was after Shardblades."

"His aspirations were not nearly so lowly as that," Mraize said. "He recruited others, promising them a return to the old glories and powers. Some, like Amaram, listened because of these promises—but for the same reason were as easily lured by the enemy. Others were manipulated through their religious ideals. But Gavilar . . . what did *he* truly want?"

"I don't know. Do you?"

"Immortality, in part. He thought he could become like the Heralds. In his quest, he discovered a secret. He had Voidlight before the Everstorm—he carried it from Braize, the place you call Damnation. He was testing the movement of Light between worlds. And one close to him might have answers. At any rate, we couldn't risk Ialai or the Sons of Honor recovering these secrets."

Mraize's chicken finished its meal. Though it had picked at and eaten the flesh, in the end it swallowed the rest of the corpse whole. Then it fluffed its feathers and hunkered down. Shallan didn't have a lot of experience with the creature, but it seemed to dislike the cold.

So odd, how Mraize flaunted it. But she supposed that was part of who he was—he was never content blending in. Most would probably consider keeping strange exotic animals a quirk. Shallan couldn't help but see more to it. Mraize collected trophies—she'd seen many odd things in his possession.

She blinked and took another Memory of the chicken on his arm, receiving a scratch at its neck.

"There is so much out there, little knife," Mraize said. "Things that will rock your understanding, expand your perspective, and make into pebbles what once seemed mountains. The things you could know, Shallan. The people you could collect in your notebook, the sights you could see . . ."

"Tell me," she said, finding an unexpected hunger within. "Let me see them. Let me know them."

"These things require effort and experience," Mraize said. "I could not simply be told of them, and neither can you. I have given you enough for now. To go further, you must *hunt* the secrets. *Earn* them."

She narrowed her eyes at him. "All right. What do you want this time?"

He grinned in his predatory way.

"You always make me *want* to do the things you ask," Shallan said. "You tempt me not just with rewards, but with the secrets—or the dangers—themselves. You knew I'd be intrigued by what Amaram was studying. You knew I'd want to stop Ialai because of the threat she presented to Adolin. I always end up doing what you want. So what is it this time? What are you going to make me do?"

"You become a hunter in truth. I have known from the beginning your potential." He looked to her, light violet eyes lingering on her still-red hair. "There is a man. Restares. You know the name?"

"I've heard of him. He was connected to the Sons of Honor?" Though she might have heard the name before getting Ialai's book, it was written several times in there. The woman had been trying to contact him.

"He was their leader, at one point," Mraize said. "Perhaps their founder, though we aren't certain. Either way, he was involved from the beginning—and he knew the extent of what Gavilar was doing. Restares is perhaps the only living person who did."

"Great. You want me to find him?"

"Oh, we know where he is," Mraize said. "He has asked for—and been granted—asylum in a city no other Ghostblood has been able to enter."

"A place you can't enter?" Shallan asked. "Where is security *that* tight?"

"The fortress named Lasting Integrity," Mraize said. "Home and capital city of the honorspren in Shadesmar."

Shallan let out a long whistle of appreciation. The chicken, curiously, mimicked it.

"This is your mission," Mraize said. "Find your way to Lasting Integrity. Get in, then find Restares. There should be no more than a handful of humans in the city; in fact, he might be the only one. We don't know."

"How am I supposed to accomplish *that*?"

"You are resourceful," Mraize said. "You and yours have connections to the spren that no other Ghostblood has been able to manage so far." His eyes flickered to Pattern, who sat on her coat, silent as usual when others were talking. "You will find a way."

"Assuming I am able to do this," Shallan said, "what should I do with the man? I'm not going to kill him."

"Don't be so hasty," Mraize said. "When you find him, you'll know what to do."

"I doubt that."

"Oh, you will. And once you successfully return from this mission, your reward will be—as always—something for which you hunger. Answers. All of them."

She frowned.

"We will hold nothing back," Mraize said. "Everything we know becomes yours after this."

Shallan folded her arms, weighing her desires. For well over a year now, she'd told herself that she only continued with the Ghostbloods to find out their secrets. But Veil *liked* being part of them. The thrill of the intrigue. Even the suspense of potentially being found out.

Shallan, however, had always been seeking answers. Real secrets. Surely even Jasnah couldn't be *too* angry with Shallan. She was infiltrating them, seeking to find their answers. Once Shallan learned everything the Ghostbloods had been hiding, she could go to Jasnah. What good would it do to pull out when the ultimate prize was so close?

I sense another reason you're doing this, Shallan, Radiant thought at her. *What is it? What aren't you sharing with us?*

"Aren't you afraid?" Shallan asked Mraize, ignoring Radiant. "If I know your secrets, you'll no longer have power to keep stringing me along. You won't be able to keep bribing me."

"If you do this, little knife," he said, "you won't *need* to be bribed any longer. Once you complete the mission with Restares and return, you may ask me any questions, and I will answer with what I know. About the world. About the Radiants. About other places. About you, and your past . . ."

He thought to tease that last one. But at it, Shallan shuddered, trembling deep inside. Formless grew stronger each time she thought about that.

"After getting your answers," Mraize continued, "if you decide you no longer desire our association, you may leave us as Radiant wishes. She is weak, but everyone has weakness within them. If you succumb to yours, then so be it."

She folded her arms, considering.

"I'm being sincere," Mraize said. "I cannot promise you will be safe if you leave; other members of the organization do not like you. I do promise that I will not hunt you or yours, nor will my *babsk*. We will discourage others."

"An easy promise," Shallan said, "because you are certain I will never leave the Ghostbloods."

"Find a reason to visit the honorspren," Mraize said. "Then we shall talk." He lifted his arm and threw the bird off toward another hunt.

Shallan gave no promise, but as she walked away, she knew he had her. They'd been hooked as soundly as any fish. For in Mraize's mind were answers. About the nature of the world and its politics, but more beyond. About Shallan. The Davar house steward had belonged to the Ghostbloods. It was possible Shallan's father had as well. Mraize had never been willing to speak of that, but she had to think they'd been grooming her—and her family—for over a decade.

He knew the truth about Shallan's past. There were holes in her childhood memories. If they did what he asked, Mraize would fill them.

And maybe then, at long last, Veil could force Shallan to become complete.

All gemstones leak Stormlight at a slow rate—but so long as the crystal structure remains mostly intact, the spren cannot escape. Managing this leakage is important, as many fabrials also lose Stormlight through operation. All of this is tied up in the intricacies of the art. As is understanding one last vital kind of spren: logicspren.

—Lecture on fabrial mechanics presented by Navani Kholin to the coalition of monarchs, Urithiru, Jesevan, 1175

T he palace at Kholinar had undergone a dramatic transformation. To a new form, so to speak. Here, more than any other place in the city, Venli felt she could look into the past and see the history of her people.

Gone was the ornate, but boring human fortress. In its place stood a grand construction that used many of the original foundations and walls, but expanded upon them in a unique design. Instead of boxy lines, it contained grand arcs, with large ridges sweeping down from the sides like curved blades. These multiplied toward the top, the ridges rising to points.

The result was a curved conical shape, the peak resembling a crown. The architecture had a distinctly organic feel, enhanced by walls grown over with shalebark to give a rough, uneven texture. The palace vaguely resembled a plant: bulging at the base, with gentle blades sweeping up to the cap.

Venli approached, attuned to Tension. The last twenty hours had been a chaotic jumble as she'd accompanied Leshwi through the city, meeting with other Fused, looking for information. Venli didn't completely understand why it had set Leshwi off, but a new group of Fused spirits had awakened and come for bodies.

That wasn't unexpected. Some of the Fused on Braize slumbered, or . . . hibernated? Meditated? They were coming aware in groups, and joining the battle. But several in particular had Leshwi worried. Perhaps terrified. After a day of chaos spent investigating with Leshwi, Venli had awakened to thunder early in the morning. The Everstorm.

Right after it, she'd received word. A conclave of the most important singers had been called to the palace. As Voice, Venli was expected to arrive quickly—and on her own, for Leshwi would take the entrance provided for the *shanay-im* above.

Venli tried to calm herself as she walked by focusing on the beautiful palace structure. She wished she could have lived in a time when this architecture was commonplace. She imagined entire cities made of these transfixing arcs, one part dangerous, one part beautiful. Like the natural world.

We did this, she thought. *When Eshonai first returned from the human lands, she spoke to Awe about the grand creations of the humans. But we did things like this too. We had cities. We had art. We had culture.*

The rebuilding of the palace had been overseen and accomplished by several Fused of a tall, limber variety called *fannahn-im,* Those Ones of Alteration. Though all Fused were trained as warriors, many had other skills. Some were engineers, scientists, architects. She thought perhaps they'd all once been soldiers before being granted immortality, but the time they'd had to grow since was expansive.

What would it be like to live so many lives? Such wisdom, and such capacity! Seeing such things awakened emotions within her. Not just Awe, but Craving. Were new Fused being made? Could someone like her aspire to this immortality?

Timbre pulsed a warning inside her, and Venli forcibly resisted those instincts. It was not easy. Perhaps as a Surgebinder, she *should* have been naturally selfless. Naturally noble. Like Eshonai.

Venli was neither. A part of her still longed for the path she'd once imagined—blessed by the Fused for opening the way to their Return, heaped with honors for being the first among her people to listen to the Voidspren. Bringer of the Everstorm. Should she not have become a queen for these actions?

Timbre pulsed another warning, comforting this time. Odium would never give her these honors—Venli had been deceived. Her lusts had led to great pain and destruction. She needed a way to balance her heritage and her goals. She was determined to escape the rule of the Fused, but that did not mean she wanted to abandon singer culture. Indeed, the more she discovered about the singers of old, the more she wanted to know.

She reached the top of the steps and passed by two of the *fannahn-im*, the Altered Ones, with limber, seven-foot-tall bodies and piles of hair that sprouted only from the very tops of their heads, tumbling down around the carapace that covered the rest of their skulls. These two had not been among those who had built the palace, for they sat with vacant stares. Timbre pulsed to the Rhythm of the Lost. Gone. Like so many of the Fused, their minds had been claimed by the infinite cycle of death and rebirth.

Perhaps there was a reason not to envy their immortality.

The inner entryway of the palace had been rebuilt with sweeping staircases. Walls had been removed, and dozens of rooms had been combined. In the large chambers, they didn't shut the windows during storms; they simply rolled up the carpets.

Venli climbed all the way to the fifth floor, entering a pinnacle room added by the Fused architects. Large and cylindrical, it was the center of the crown shape. This place was the home of the Nine: leaders of the Fused.

Other Voices were gathering. There were some thirty of them—she'd been led to believe that there would be as many as a hundred, once all the Fused were awake. This room wouldn't hold that many Voices, even if they lined up shoulder-to-shoulder. As it was, it was growing crowded as each Voice found their place before their master.

Leshwi hovered a few feet off the ground near the other Heavenly Ones, and Venli hastened over. She looked up, and Leshwi nodded, so Venli thumped the butt of her staff on the stones, indicating her master was ready.

The Nine were already there, of course. They couldn't leave. They'd been entombed in stone.

Nine pillars adorned the center of the chamber, rising in a circle. The stones had been Soulcast into shape—with people *inside* them. The Nine lived here, permanently melded into the pillars. Again there was an organic feel to the construction, as if the pillars had grown there like trees around the Nine.

The pillars twisted and tapered, shrinking and growing into the chests of the Nine but leaving their heads and the tops of their carapaced shoulders bare. Most had at least one arm free.

The Nine faced inward, their backs to the room. The bizarre entombment was discomforting, alien. Nauseating. It lent the Nine an air of permanence to accent their ageless nature. The pillars seemed to say, "These are older than the stones. They have lived here long enough for the rock to grow over them, like crem reclaiming the ruins of a fallen city."

Venli couldn't help but be impressed by their dedication; being locked into motionlessness like this had to be agonizing. The Nine did not eat, subsisting on Odium's Light alone. Surely this entombment wasn't good for their sanity.

Though . . . if they really *did* want to leave their imprisonment, they could simply have themselves killed. A Fused could also will their spirit from their body, freeing it to seek another host. Indeed, the humans had tried imprisoning Fused as a method of defeating them, but had found it to be futile.

So the Nine could leave, if they wanted. In that light, these tombs were a flagrant, wasteful act—the ultimate price for this show was paid not by the Nine, but by the poor singers they had killed to give themselves bodies.

The Nine must have counted the knocking of the staffs on the ground, for they raised their heads in unison once the final high lord was in place. Venli glanced at Leshwi, who was humming softly to Agony—the new rhythm that was a counterpart to Anxiety.

"What is happening?" Venli whispered to Craving. "What does this have to do with the new Fused who have awakened?"

"Watch," Leshwi whispered. "But take care. Remember, what power I have outside is a mere candle's light in here."

Leshwi was, for a high lady, low ranked. A field commander, but still merely a soldier. She was both the very crust of the unimportant and the very dregs of the important. She was always careful in walking that line.

The Nine hummed together, then began singing in unison, a song and rhythm Venli had never heard. It sent chills through her, particularly when she realized she couldn't understand the lyrics. She felt near to comprehending—it was *almost* within reach—but her powers seemed to shy back from this song. As though . . . if she *could* understand, her mind would not be able to handle the meaning.

She was fairly certain what this indicated. Odium, the god of the singers, was watching this conclave. She knew his touch, his stench. He was forbidding any of the Voices from interpreting this song.

It died down, and silence claimed the chamber. "We would hear a report," one of the Nine said at last—Venli had trouble telling who spoke, since they were all facing one another. "A firsthand account of what was seen at the recent clash in northern Avendla."

Avendla was their name for Alethkar; Venli's powers instantly knew the meaning of the word. Land of the Second Advance. Her abilities stopped there, however, and she couldn't answer the more interesting question. Why was it called that?

Leshwi hummed, so Venli stepped forward and cracked her scepter against the floor twice, then bowed, head down.

Leshwi rose behind her, clothing rustling. "I will have Zandiel provide sketches. The large human ship flew of its own power, using no gemstones we could see—though certainly they were embedded somewhere inside."

"It flew by Lashings," one of the Nine said. "The work of Windrunners."

"No," Leshwi said. "It did not have that appearance or that feel. This was a device, a machine. Created by their artifabrians."

The Nine sang together, and their alien song made Timbre—deep within Venli—pulse nervously.

"We were away far too long," one of the Nine said. "It has let the humans fester like an infection, gaining strength. They create devices we have never known."

"We are behind them, not ahead," another said. "It is a dangerous position from which to fight."

"No," said a third. "They have made great strides in understanding the prisons of spren, but they know little about the bond, the power of oaths, the nature of the tones of the world. They are cremlings building a nest beneath the shadow of a great temple. They take pride in what they have done, but cannot grasp the beauties around them."

"Still," said the first. "Still. *We* could not have crafted the flying device they have."

"Why would we? We have the *shanay-im*."

Venli remained bowed, hand on her staff. Holding the pose exactly grew uncomfortable, but she would never complain. She was as close to important events as a mortal could get, and she was certain she could use the knowledge to some advantage. The Nine spoke for the ears of those listening. They could have conversed quietly, but these meetings were about the spectacle.

"Leshwi," one of the Nine said. "What of the suppressor we sent to be tested? Did it work?"

"It worked," Leshwi said, "but it was also lost. The humans captured it. I fear this will lead them to further explorations and discoveries."

"This was poorly handled," said one of the Fused.

"I take no responsibility for this error," Leshwi said. "You must speak to the Pursuer to find record of the mistake."

Each spoke with formal tones and rhythms. Venli had the impression that the Nine knew how these answers would play out.

"Lezian!" the Nine called together. "You will—"

"Oh, dispense with the pageantry," a loud voice said. A tall Fused emerged from the shadows on the far side of the room.

Leshwi lowered down, and Venli straightened and stepped back into line before her master. That gave her a good view of this new Fused, which was of a variety that Venli had never seen. Enormous, with jagged carapace and deep red hair, the being wore only a simple black wrap for clothing. Or . . . was his hair the clothing? It seemed to meld with the wrap.

Fascinating. *Nex-im,* Those Ones of Husks, the ninth brand of Fused. She had heard them spoken of; supposedly very few existed. Was this the recently awakened Fused who had Leshwi so concerned?

"Lezian, the Pursuer," said one of the Nine. "You were entrusted with a delicate device, a suppressor of Stormlight abilities. You were told to test it. Where is this device?"

"I *tested* it," Lezian snapped, showing little of the formality or respect others gave the Nine. "It didn't work."

"You are certain of this?" the Nine asked. "Was the man Invested when he attacked you?"

"You think *I* could be defeated by a common human?" the Pursuer demanded. "This Windrunner must be of the Fourth Ideal—something I was led to believe had not yet happened. Perhaps our reconnaissance teams have lost their edge, during the long time spent between Returns."

Behind Venli, Leshwi hummed sharply to Conceit. She did not like that implication.

"Regardless," the Pursuer said, "I was killed. The Windrunner is more dangerous than any of us were led to believe. I must pursue him now, as is my right by tradition. I will leave immediately."

Curious, Venli thought. If he'd fought Stormblessed, then he could not be the newly awakened one that Leshwi feared. The Pursuer stood with arms crossed as the Nine began to sing to one another again, softer than before. In the past, such deliberations had taken several minutes. Many of the other Fused began conferring quietly as they waited.

Venli leaned back, whispering, "Who is he, Lady?"

"A hero," Leshwi responded to Withdrawal. "And a fool. Millennia ago, Lezian was the first Fused to be killed by a human. To avoid the shame of such death, upon returning to life, Lezian ignored all orders and rational arguments—and went into battle seeking *only* the man who had killed him.

"He was successful, and his tradition was born. Any time he is killed, Lezian ignores everything else until he has claimed the life of the one who killed him. Seven thousand years, and he's never failed. Now the others— even those chosen as the Nine—encourage his quests."

"I thought in the past, you were exiled to Braize once you died? How could he return to hunt the one who had killed him?"

Much of this was still confusing to Venli. For thousands of years, the humans and the singers had fought many rounds of an eternal war. Each new wave of attacks had involved what was called a Return, when the Fused would descend to Roshar. The humans called these Desolations.

There was something special about the way the human Heralds interacted that could lock the Fused on Braize, the land called Damnation by the humans. Only once the Fused broke the Heralds through torture—sending them back to Roshar—could a Return be initiated. This cycle had played out for millennia, until the Last Desolation, where something had changed. Something to do with a single Herald and an unbreakable will.

"You mistake the cycle, simplify it," Leshwi said softly. "We were only locked on Braize once the Heralds died and joined us there. Until then, there would often be years or even decades of rebirths during a Return—during which time the Heralds would train humans to fight. Once they were confident that humans could continue to stand, the Heralds would give themselves to Braize to activate the Isolation. The Heralds would need to die for this to work."

"But . . . they didn't die the last time?" Venli said. "They remained, but you were still locked away."

"Yes . . ." Leshwi said. "They somehow found a way to shift the Oathpact to depend on a single member." She nodded toward the Pursuer. "Regardless, before an Isolation began, that one always managed to find and kill any humans who had bested him. As soon as the Isolation was begun, he'd kill himself, so he'd never return to Braize permanently after having died by human hand.

"As I said, the others encourage his tradition. He is allowed to act outside command structures, given leeway to Pursue. When he is not hunting one who killed him, he seeks to fight the strongest of the enemy Radiants."

"That sounds like a worthy Passion," Venli said, picking her words carefully.

"Yes, it does *sound* like one," Leshwi said to Derision. "Perhaps it would be, in someone less reckless. Lezian has endangered our plans, undermined strategies, and ruined more missions than I can count. And he's growing worse. As all of us are, I suppose . . ."

"He was killed by the Windrunner hero?" Venli asked. "The one they call Stormblessed?"

"Yes, yesterday. And the Radiant's powers were suppressed at the time, no matter what Lezian said. Stormblessed is not yet of the Fourth Ideal. I would know. This is doubly a shame on the Pursuer. He grows careless, overly confident. These Radiants are new to their powers, but that does not make them less worthy."

"You like them," Venli said, cautiously broaching the topic. "The Windrunners."

Leshwi was silent for a moment. "Yes," she said. "They and their spren would make excellent servants, should we be able to subdue them."

So she *was* open to new ideas, new ways of thinking. Perhaps she *would* react favorably to the idea of a new nation of listeners.

"Announce me, Voice," Leshwi said.

"Now?" Venli said, shocked out of her contemplations. "While the Nine are conferring?"

Leshwi hummed to Command, so Venli scrambled to obey, stepping forward and slamming the butt of her staff against the floor, then bowing.

The Nine interrupted their song, and the one who spoke said the words to Destruction. "What is this, Leshwi?"

"I have more to say," Leshwi proclaimed to Command. "The Pursuer is losing control. He approaches the state where his mind and intentions cannot be trusted. He was defeated by a common human. It is time for special privileges to be revoked."

Lezian spun toward her, shouting to Destruction, "How *dare* you!"

"You are low to make such a declaration, Leshwi," one of the Nine said. "This is both above and beneath you, at once."

"I speak my Passion," she said. "The man who killed the Pursuer has killed me. I claim prior privilege to the life of Stormblessed. The Pursuer must, in this case, wait upon my pleasure."

"You know my tradition!" he shouted at Leshwi.

"Traditions can be broken."

The tall Fused stomped toward her, and Venli had to forcibly hold herself in place, bowing—though she was allowed to look up and watch. This Pursuer was enormous, intimidating. He was also nearly out of control, a storm at its height—so angry she couldn't make out the rhythm to his shouted words.

"I will hunt you!" he shouted. "You cannot deny me my vows! My tradition *cannot* be broken!"

Leshwi continued to hover in place unperturbed, and Venli saw an ulterior motive in the conflict. Yes, the Nine were humming to Derision. In losing his temper, the Pursuer proved his Passion—a good thing to them—but also risked proving he was going crazy. Leshwi had purposefully goaded him.

"We accept Leshwi's prior claim on this man," the Nine said. "Pursuer, you will not hunt this human until Leshwi has a chance to battle him again."

"This undermines my entire existence!" the Pursuer said, pointing at Leshwi. "She seeks to destroy my legacy out of spite!"

"Then you should hope she loses their next conflict," one of the Nine said. "Leshwi, you may hunt this Windrunner. But know that if a battle comes and he must be removed, another may be granted the task."

"This is understood and accepted," Leshwi said.

None of them realize she's trying to protect that Windrunner, Venli thought. *Maybe she doesn't realize it herself.* There were schisms among the Fused, cracks much larger than any would admit. What could be done to take advantage of them?

Timbre pulsed inside her, but in this case Venli was certain her ambition was well placed. To lack it would be to simply go along with whatever she was told. That was not freedom. Freedom, if she was to seek it, would require ambition—in the right place.

The Pursuer, still raging to no particular rhythm, stomped out of the conclave chamber. Leshwi settled down behind Venli, humming softly to Exultation.

"Do not praise yourself overly much, Leshwi," one of the Nine called. "Do not forget your low station in this room. We have our own reasons for denying the Pursuer."

Leshwi bowed her head as the Nine returned to their private conversation.

"You could be more," Venli whispered, returning to her place beside Leshwi. "These are not as clever as you are, Lady. Why do you let them continue to treat you so poorly?"

"I have chosen my station carefully," Leshwi snapped. "Do not challenge me on this, Voice. It is not your place."

"I apologize," Venli said to Agony. "My Passion outstripped my wisdom."

"That was not Passion, but curiosity." Leshwi narrowed her eyes. "Be alert. This matter was not the reason the conclave was called. The danger I've been fearing is yet to come."

That made Venli stand up straighter, on her guard. Eventually the Nine stopped singing, but they did not address the leaders of the Fused. Instead the hall fell silent. Moments stretched to minutes. What was happening?

A figure darkened the doorway of the chamber, backlit by sunlight. It was a tall femalen, of the *fannahn-im*—the builders who had created the palace—with a tall topknot of hair and carapace like a helmet otherwise covering her head. She wore a luxurious robe and was willowy, with a narrow figure and long arms, fingers fully twice the length of Venli's.

Leshwi hissed. "Gods, no. Not her."

"What?" Venli asked as the room flooded with whispers from the others. "Who is she?"

"I thought her mad," Leshwi said to Agony. "How . . ."

The tall Fused walked into the room and did a slow, careful loop around the perimeter, perhaps to make certain she was seen by everyone. Then she did something Venli had never seen anyone do—no matter how high. She walked into the center of the Nine and looked them in the eyes.

"What does it mean, Lady?" Venli asked.

"She was one of the Nine for many centuries," Leshwi said. "Until she decided it was too . . . hampering upon her ambitions. After the last Return, and her madness, she was to remain asleep. . . . Why . . ."

"Raboniel, Lady of Wishes," one of the Nine said. "You have brought us a proposal. Please speak it."

"It is obvious," Raboniel said, "that the humans have been allowed too much time to grow. They run rampant across Roshar. They have steel weapons and advanced military tactics. They outstrip our own knowledge in areas.

"The one thing they do not yet have is mastery over their powers. There are few among them of the Fourth Ideal—perhaps only one individual—and they do not have full access to the tower, now that the Sibling is dead. We must strike *now*. We must seize the tower from them."

Leshwi moved forward, not waiting for Venli to announce her. "This was tried! We attempted to seize the tower, and failed!"

"That?" Raboniel said. "That was a stalling tactic intended to isolate the Bondsmith. The strike could never have succeeded. I was not involved."

"You forget your place *again*, Leshwi," one of the Nine said. "This makes us wonder if *you* are the one who is losing her mind."

Leshwi retreated to her spot, and Venli felt the eyes of the other thirty Fused and their Voices on her, shaming her as they hummed.

"You have nearly perfected the suppression fabrials," Raboniel said. "Do not forget, it is technology *I* discovered from the tower itself thousands of years ago. I have a plan to use it in a more dramatic way. As the Sibling is essentially a deadeye, I should be able to turn the tower's defenses against its owners."

A Voice across the room stepped forward and thumped his staff, announcing Uriam the Defiant. "Pardon," Uriam said to Craving. "But are you implying that you can suppress the powers of the Radiants *inside* their own *tower*?"

"Yes," Raboniel said. "The device preventing us from attacking them there can be inverted. We will need to lure the Elsecaller and the Bondsmith away. Their oaths may be advanced enough to push through the suppression, much as the Unmade have done at the tower in the past. With them gone, I can lead a force into Urithiru and seize it from within—and the Radiants will be unable to resist."

The Nine started singing to one another privately, giving everyone else time for conversations. Venli looked to her mistress. Leshwi rarely spent these moments talking to the other high Fused; she was beneath most of them, after all.

"I don't understand," Venli whispered.

"Raboniel is a scholar," Leshwi said. "But not the kind you would wish to work beneath. We used to call her Lady of Pains, until she decided she didn't like the title." Her expression grew distant. "She has always been fascinated by the tower and the connection between Radiants. Their oaths, their spren. Their Surges.

"During the last Return, she developed a disease intended to kill all humans on the planet. Near the end, it was discovered that the disease would likely kill many singers as well. She released it anyway . . . only to find, to all of our fortunes, that it did not work as expected. Fewer than one in ten humans were killed, and one in a hundred singers."

"That's *terrible*!" Venli said.

"Extinction is the natural escalation of this war," Leshwi whispered. "If you forget why you are fighting, then victory itself becomes the goal. The longer we fight, the more detached we become. Both from our own minds, and from our original Passions." She hummed softly to Abashment.

"Explain your plan, Raboniel," one of the Nine said, loudly enough to cut through conversations.

"I will lead a team into the tower," Raboniel said, "then secure control of the Sibling's heart. Using my natural talents, and the gifts of Odium, I will corrupt that heart, and turn the tower to our needs. The humans will fall; their powers will not work, but ours will. From there I suspect that—with a little time—I can learn much studying the gemstones at the Sibling's heart. Perhaps enough to create new weapons against the Radiants and the humans."

One of the Heavenly Ones, a malen named Jeshishin, came forward as his Voice rapped the floor. "As Leshwi said, we *did* strike at the tower a year ago. True, that attempt was not meant to be a permanent seizure, but we *were* rebuffed. I would know the specifics of what we will do this time to ensure victory."

"We will use the king who has given himself to us," Raboniel said. "He has delivered intelligence about guard patterns. We don't need to take the entire tower at first—we simply need to get to the heart and use my knowledge to turn the defenses to our advantage."

"The heart is the most well-guarded location!" Jeshishin said.

Raboniel spoke to Conceit. "Then it is fortunate that we have an agent in their inner circle, is it not?"

Jeshishin floated back, his Voice returning to his place.

"What is her true game?" Leshwi whispered to Craving. "Raboniel has never *really* been interested in the war or its tactics. This must be about something more. She wants the opportunity to experiment upon the Sibling. . . ."

"This *is* dangerous," one of the Nine loudly said to the room. "The humans are suspicious of Taravangian already. He reports that he is watched at all times. If we use his intelligence in this way, there is little doubt he will be compromised entirely."

"Let him be compromised!" Raboniel said. "What good is a weapon if you don't swing it? Why have you delayed? The humans are untrained, their powers fledgling, their understanding laughable. I find it *embarrassing* to awaken and find you struggling against these pitiful shadows of our once-mighty enemies.

"Without the tower, their coalition will disintegrate, as they will be unable to deliver support through the Oathgates. We will gain great advantage through the use of those same portals. In addition, this endeavor will give me the opportunity to test some . . . theories I have developed while slumbering these last millennia. I am increasingly certain I have discovered a path that will lead to an end to the war."

Leshwi hissed out slowly, and Venli felt cold. It seemed that whatever Raboniel thought would end the war would involve techniques best left untouched.

The rest of the room, however, appeared impressed. They whispered to Subservience, indicating consent to the idea. Even the *Nine* started humming to the rhythm. The Fused put on a strong Passionate show, but there was a *fatigue* to these ancient souls. It underpinned their other Passions, like the true color of a dyed cloth. Wash it, leave it out in the storms long enough, and the core shone through.

These creatures were fraying, surrendering their minds—their will and very individuality offered up to Odium on the altar of eternal war. Perhaps the humans were new to their abilities, untested, but the Fused were old axes, chipped and weathered. They would take great risks, after so many rebirths, to be finished at last.

"What of Stormblessed?" a voice called out, thickly accented, from the recesses of the grand chamber.

Venli found herself humming to Abashment as she searched the room. Who had spoken so brashly without first ordering their Voice to step forward? She found him sitting on a raised ledge up above, in shadow, right as her mind connected the accent to the lack of decorum.

Vyre. The human, once called Moash. He dressed like a soldier, with perfectly trimmed hair, a sharp uniform cut after human tailoring. He was an oddity. Why did the Nine continue to suffer him? Not only that, why had they given him an *Honorblade*, one of the most precious relics on Roshar?

He draped one leg off the ledge. Held in his lap, his sword reflected sunlight as the tip moved. "He'll stop you," Vyre said. "You should have a plan for dealing with him."

"Ah, the human," Raboniel said, looking at Vyre on his ledge. "I've heard of you. Such an interesting specimen. Odium favors you."

"He takes my pain," Vyre said. "And leaves me to achieve my potential. You did not answer my question. What of Stormblessed?"

"I'm not afraid of a Windrunner, no matter how . . . mythical his reputation may be growing," Raboniel said. "We will focus our attention on the Bondsmith and the Elsecaller. *They* are more dangerous than any simple soldier."

"Well," Vyre said, pulling the tip of his sword back into the shadows, "I'm sure you know your business, Fused."

The Nine, as always, suffered the strange human. His position had been chosen by Odium. Leshwi seemed to think highly of him—of course, he'd once killed her, and that was a sure way to gain her respect.

"Your proposal is bold, Raboniel," one of the Nine said. "And decisive. We have long been without your guidance in this Return, and we welcome your Passion. We will move forward as you request. Prepare a team for your infiltration of the tower, and we shall contact the human Taravangian with instructions. He can divert the Bondsmith and Elsecaller."

Raboniel sang loudly to Satisfaction, a stately and decisive sound. Venli was reasonably certain this entire meeting had been for show—the Nine had not stopped to debate the plan. They'd known what Raboniel would suggest, and had already worked out the details.

The other Fused waited respectfully as Raboniel—her victorious proposal elevating her further in their eyes—walked toward the exit. Only one of the Fused moved. Leshwi.

"Come," she said, floating after Raboniel.

Venli hurried, joining Leshwi as she intercepted the tall femalen just outside the doors. Raboniel looked over Leshwi, humming to Derision as the two emerged into sunlight on the balcony rooftop around the chamber. The stairwell down was to the right.

"Why did you seek to block my proposal, Leshwi?" Raboniel asked. "Have you begun to feel the effects of madness?"

"I am not mad, but afraid," Leshwi said to Abashment—and Venli started at the words. Lady Leshwi, *afraid?* "Do you truly think you can *end* the war?"

"I'm certain of it," Raboniel said to Derision. "I have had a long time to ponder on the discoveries made before the end of the false Return." She reached into the pocket of her robe and removed a gemstone glowing with Stormlight, a shifting spren captured inside. A fabrial like the humans created.

"They imprisoned some of the Unmade in these, Leshwi," Raboniel said. "How close do you think they are to discovering they could do the same for us? Can you imagine it? Forever imprisoned in a gemstone, locked away, able to think but unable to ever break free?"

Leshwi hummed to Panic, a pained rhythm with unfinished measures and chopped-up beats.

"One way or another," Raboniel said, "this is the final Return. The humans will soon discover how to imprison us. If not, well, the best of us who remain are but a few steps from madness. We *must* find a solution to this war."

"You are newly Returned," Leshwi said. "You have no servants or staff. Your undertaking will require both." She gestured to the side, to Venli. "I have gathered a staff of faithful and highly capable singers. I would lend them to you for this enterprise, and would attend you myself, as an apology for my objections."

"You do always have the best servants," Raboniel said, eyeing Venli. "This one is the Last Listener, is she not? Once Voice of Odium himself? How did you collect her?"

Timbre pulsed inside Venli—she was annoyed by the term "collect," and Venli felt the same. She bowed her head and hummed to Subservience to keep from revealing her true feelings.

"She was cast off by Odium," Leshwi said. "I have found her an excellent Voice."

"The daughter of traitors," Raboniel said, but to Craving—she was curious about Venli. "Then a traitor to her own kind. I will take her, and those you send, as my servants during the infiltration. You may join us as well. Serve, and perhaps I will forgive your crass objections. There were certainly others thinking the same; you gave opportunity for refutation."

Raboniel strode away, though as she reached the steps, Venli spotted someone waiting for her in the shadows below. The hulking figure of the Pursuer, who had been dismissed earlier. He bowed to Raboniel, who hesitated at the top of the stairwell. Their exchange was not audible to Venli.

"He's begging for a chance to go with her," Leshwi whispered. "Raboniel will have jurisdiction during this infiltration—and can authorize him to continue his hunt. He will try *anything* to justify another chance at that Windrunner. I fear he will ignore the Nine, particularly if Raboniel approves of him." She looked to Venli. "You must gather our people and attend her. You will not need to fight; that will be done by others. You will serve her as you have me, and report to me in secret."

"Mistress?" Venli asked. She lowered her voice. "So you *don't* trust her."

"Of course not," Leshwi said. "Last time, her recklessness nearly cost us everything. The Nine favor her boldness; they feel the weight of time. Yet boldness can be one step from foolishness. So *we* must prevent a catastrophe. This land is for the ordinary singers to inherit. I will not leave it desolate simply to prove we can murder better than our enemies."

Venli swelled at that. Timbre surged inside her, pulsing, encouraging her.

"Mistress," she whispered, "do you think there . . . could be a way to re-form *my* people? Find a land away from both Fused and humans? To be on our own again, as we were?"

Leshwi hummed to Reprimand, glancing toward the chamber with the other Fused. None had left yet. They wouldn't want to be seen rushing after Raboniel—and Venli realized, in a moment of understanding, why Leshwi preferred to remain lowly among them. Her lack of standing gave her freedom to do things others considered beneath them.

"Do not speak of such things," Leshwi hissed. "Others already mistrust you for what your ancestors did. You wish to rule yourselves? I commend that—but the time is not right. Help us defeat the humans, and then we Fused will fade into time and leave this world to you. *That* is how to achieve your independence, Venli."

"Yes, mistress," she said to Subservience. She didn't feel it, and Timbre pulsed her own frustration.

Venli had felt Odium's hand directly. He would not leave this people alone, and she suspected the other Fused—tired though they might be— would not abandon ruling the world. Too many of them enjoyed the luxury of their positions. Victory for them was no path to independence for Venli and her people.

Leshwi soared off, leaving Venli to walk down the steps. As she did, she caught sight of Raboniel and the Pursuer speaking conspiratorially in the dim reaches of the third floor. Storms, what was Venli getting pulled into now?

Timbre pulsed inside her.

"Opportunity?" Venli said. "What kind of opportunity?"

Timbre pulsed again.

"I thought you hated the human Radiants," Venli whispered. "Who cares if we're going to find them at the tower?"

Timbre pulsed decisively. She had a point. Perhaps the humans *could* train Venli. Maybe she could capture one of their Radiants and make them teach her.

At any rate, she needed to prepare her staff to leave the city. Her recruitment efforts would have to be put on hold. Like it or not, she was going to be at the forefront of another invasion of the human lands.

15

THE LIGHT
AND THE MUSIC

*Logicspren react curiously to imprisonment. Unlike other spren,
they do not manifest some attribute—you cannot use them to
make heat, or to warn of nearby danger, or conjoin gemstones. For
years, artifabrians considered them useless—indeed, experimenting with them was uncommon, since logicspren are rare and difficult to capture.*

*A breakthrough has come in discovering that logicspren will
vary the light they radiate based on certain stimuli. For example, if
you make the Light leak from the gemstone at a controlled rate, the
spren will alternate dimming and brightening in a regular pattern.
This has led to fabrial clocks.*

*When the gemstone is tapped with certain metals, the light will
also change states from bright to dim. This is leading to some very
interesting and complex mechanisms.*

—Lecture on fabrial mechanics presented by Navani Kholin
to the coalition of monarchs, Urithiru, Jesevan, 1175

I n the weeks following the assault on Hearthstone, Kaladin's anxiety
began to subside, and he pushed through the worst of the darkness.
He always emerged on the other side. Why was that so difficult to
remember while in the middle of it?

He'd been given time to decide what to do after his "retirement," so
he didn't rush the decision, and didn't tell anyone other than Adolin. He
wanted to find the best way to introduce the idea to his Windrunners—
and if he could, make his decision first. Better to bring them a clear plan.

He found himself understanding Dalinar's order more and more as the days passed. At least Kaladin didn't have to keep pretending he wasn't exhausted. He did delay his decision though. So Dalinar eventually gave him a gentle—but firm—nudge. Kaladin could have a little more time to decide his path, but they needed to start promoting other Windrunners to take over his duties.

So it was that ten days after the mission to Hearthstone, Kaladin stood in front of the army's command staff and listened to Dalinar announce that Kaladin's role in the army was "evolving."

Kaladin found the experience humiliating. Everyone applauded his heroism even as he was forced out. Kaladin announced that Sigzil—with whom he'd conferred earlier in the day—would take over daily administration of the Windrunners, overseeing things like supplies and recruitment. He'd be named to the rank of companylord. Skar, when he returned from leave at the Horneater Peaks, would be named company second, and would oversee and lead active Windrunner missions.

A short time later, Kaladin was allowed to go—fortunately, there was no forced "party" for him. He retreated down a long dark hallway in Urithiru, relieved that he didn't feel nearly as bad as he had worried he would. He wasn't a danger to himself today.

Now he just had to find new purpose in life. Storms, that scared him—having nothing to do reminded him of being a bridgeman. When he wasn't on bridge runs, those days had stretched. Full of blank space that numbed the mind, a strange mental anesthetic. His life was far better now. He wasn't so lost in self-pity that he couldn't notice or acknowledge that. Still, he found the similarity uncomfortable.

Syl hovered in front of him in the Urithiru hallway, taking the form of a fanciful ship—only with sails on the *bottom*. "What is *that*?" Kaladin asked her.

"I don't know," she said, sailing past him. "Navani was drawing it during a meeting a few weeks ago. I think she got mixed up. Maybe she hasn't seen boats before?"

"I sincerely doubt that's the case," Kaladin said, looking down the hallway. Nothing to do.

No, he thought. *You can't pretend you have nothing to do because you're scared. Find a new purpose.*

He took a deep breath, then strode forward. He could at least *act* confident. Hav's first rule of leadership, drilled into Kaladin on his first day as a squadleader. Once you make a decision, commit to it.

"Where are we going?" Syl asked, transforming into a ribbon of light to catch up to him.

"Sparring grounds."

"Going to try some training to take your mind off things?"

"No," Kaladin said. "I'm going to—against my better judgment—seek wisdom there."

"Many of the ardents who train there seem pretty wise to me," she said. "After all, they shave their heads."

"They . . ." Kaladin frowned. "Syl, what does that have to do with being wise?"

"Hair is gross. It seems smart to shave it off."

"*You* have hair."

"I do not; I just have me. Think about it, Kaladin. Everything else that comes out of your body you dispose of quickly and quietly—but this strange stuff oozes out of little holes in your head, and you let it *sit* there? Gross."

"Not all of us have the luxury of being fragments of divinity."

"Actually, *everything* is a fragment of divinities. We're relatives that way." She zipped in closer to him. "You humans are merely the weird relatives that live out in the stormshelter; the ones we try not to let visitors know about."

Kaladin could smell the sparring grounds before he arrived—the mingled familiar scents of sweat and sword oil. Syl shot to the left, making a loop of the room as Kaladin hurried past shouting pairs of men engaged in bouts of all types. He made his way to the rear wall where the swordmasters congregated.

He'd always found martial ardents to be a strange bunch. Ordinary ardents made more sense: they joined the church for scholarly reasons, or because of family pressure, or because they were devout and wanted to serve the Almighty. Most martial ardents had different pasts. Many had once been soldiers, then given themselves over to the church. Not to serve, but to escape. He'd never really understood what might lead someone to walk that path. Not until recently.

As he walked among the training soldiers, he was reminded why he'd stopped coming. Bowing, murmurs of "Stormblessed," people making way for him. That was fine in the hallways, when he passed people who didn't know him. But the ones who trained here were his brothers—and in some few cases sisters—in arms. They should know he didn't need such attention.

He reached the swordmasters—but unfortunately, the man he sought wasn't among them. Master Lahar explained that Zahel was on laundry detail, which surprised Kaladin. Though he knew all ardents took turns on service detail, he wouldn't have thought a swordmaster would be sent to wash clothing.

As he left the sparring chamber, Syl came soaring back to him, wearing the shape of an arrow in flight. "Did I hear you asking for *Zahel*?" she asked.

"You did. Why?"

"It's just that . . . there are several swordmasters, Kaladin. A few of them are actually *useful*. So why would you want to talk to Zahel?"

He wasn't certain he could explain. One of the other swordmasters—or likely any of the ardents who frequented the sparring grounds—could indeed answer his questions. But they, like the others, regarded Kaladin with an air of respect and awe. He wanted to talk to someone who would be completely honest with him.

He made his way out to the edge of the tower. Here, open to the sky, various tiered discs of stone projected from the base of the structure like enormous fronds. Over the last year, a number of these had been turned into pastures for chulls, lobberbeasts, or horses. Others were hung with lines for drying wash. Kaladin started toward the drying wash, but paused—then decided to make a short detour.

Navani and her scholars claimed that these outer plates around the tower had once been fields. How could that ever have been the case? The air up here was cold, and though Rock seemed to find it invigorating, Kaladin could tell it lacked something. He grew winded more quickly, and if he exerted himself, he sometimes felt light-headed in ways he never did at normal elevations.

Highstorms hit here infrequently. Nine out of ten didn't get high enough—passing as an angry expanse below, rumbling their discontent with flashes of lightning. Without the storms, there simply wasn't enough water for crops, let alone proper hillsides for planting polyps.

Still, at Navani's urging, the last six months had involved a unique project. For years the Alethi had fought the Parshendi over gemhearts on the Shattered Plains. It had been a bloody affair built upon the corpses of bridgemen whose bodies—more than their tools—spanned the gaps between plateaus. It shocked Kaladin that so many involved in this slaughter had missed asking a specific and poignant question:

Why had the Parshendi wanted gemstones?

To the Alethi, gemstones were not merely wealth, but power. With a Soulcaster, emeralds meant food—highly portable sources of nutrition that could travel with an army. The Alethi military had used the advantage of mobile forces without long supply lines to ravage across Roshar during the reigns of a half dozen interchangeable kings.

The Parshendi hadn't possessed Soulcasters though. Rlain had confirmed this fact. And then he'd given humankind a gift.

Kaladin walked down a set of stone steps to where a group of farmers worked a test field. The flat stone had been spread with seed paste—and that had grown rockbuds. Water was brought from a nearby pump, and Kaladin passed bearers lugging bucket after bucket to dump on the polyps and simulate a rainstorm.

Their best farmers had explained it wouldn't work. You could simulate the highstorm minerals the plants needed to form shells, but the cold air would stifle growth. Rlain had agreed this was true . . . unless you had an edge.

Unless you grew the plants by the light of gemstones.

The common field before Kaladin was adorned with a most uncommon sight: enormous emeralds harvested from the hearts of chasmfiends, ensconced within short iron lampposts that were in turn bolted to the stone ground. The emeralds were so large, and so full of Stormlight, that looking at one left spots on Kaladin's vision, though it was in full daylight.

Beside each lantern sat an ardent with a drum, softly banging a specific rhythm. This was the secret. People would have noticed if gemstone light made plants grow—but the mixture of the light and the music changed something. Lifespren—little green motes that bobbed in the air—spun around the drummers. The spren glowed brighter than usual, as if the Light of the gemstones was *infusing* them. And they'd move off to the plants, spinning around them.

This drained the Light, like using a fabrial did. Indeed, the gemstones would periodically crack, as also happened to fabrials. Somehow, the mixture of spren, music, and Light created a kind of organic machine that sustained plants via Stormlight.

Rlain, wearing his Bridge Four uniform, walked among the stations, checking the rhythms for accuracy. He usually wore warform these days, though he'd confessed to Kaladin that he disliked how it made him seem more like the invaders, with their wicked carapace armor. That made some humans distrust him. But workform made people treat him like a parshman. He hated that even more.

Though to be honest, it *was* odd to see Rlain—with his black and red marbled skin—giving direction to Alethi. It was reminiscent of what was happening in Alethkar, with the invasion. Rlain didn't like it when people made those kinds of comparisons, and Kaladin tried not to think that way.

Regardless, Rlain seemed to have found purpose in this work. Enough purpose that Kaladin almost left him and continued on his previous task. But no—the days where Kaladin could directly look out for the men and women of Bridge Four were coming to an end. He wanted to see them cared for.

He jogged through the field. While any one of these head-size rockbuds would have been considered too small to be worth much in Hearthstone, they were at least big enough that there would be grain inside. The technique was helping.

"Rlain," Kaladin called. "Rlain!"

"Sir?" the listener asked, turning and smiling. He hummed a peppy tune as he jogged over. "How was the meeting?"

Kaladin hesitated. Should he say it? Or wait? "It had some interesting developments. Promotions for Skar and Sigzil." Kaladin scanned the field. "But someone can fill you in on that later. For now, these crops are looking good."

"The spren don't come as readily for humans as they did for the listeners," he said, surveying the field. "You cannot hear the rhythms. And I can't get humans to sing the pure tones of Roshar. A few are getting closer though. I'm encouraged." He shook his head. "Anyway, what was it you wanted, sir?"

"I found you an honorspren."

Kaladin was accustomed to seeing an unreadable, stoic expression on Rlain's marbled face. That melted away like sand before a storm as Rlain adopted a wide, face-splitting grin. He grabbed Kaladin by the shoulders, his eyes dancing—and when he hummed, the exultant rhythm to it *almost* made Kaladin feel he could sense something beyond. A sound as bombastic as sunlight, as joyful as a child's laughter.

"An honorspren?" Rlain said. "Who is willing to bond with a listener? Truly?"

"Vratim's old spren, Yunfah. He was delaying choosing someone new, so Syl and I gave him an ultimatum: Choose you or leave. This morning, he came to me and agreed to try to bond with you."

Rlain's humming softened.

"It was a gamble," Kaladin said. "Since I didn't want to drive him away. But we finally got him to agree. He'll keep his word; but be careful. I get the sense he'll take any chance he can to wiggle out of the deal."

Rlain squeezed Kaladin on the shoulder and nodded to him, a sign of obvious respect. Which made the next words he spoke so odd. "Thank you, sir. Please tell the spren he can seek elsewhere. I won't be requiring his bond."

He let go, but Kaladin caught his arm.

"Rlain?" Kaladin said. "What are you saying? Syl and I worked hard to find you a spren."

"I appreciate that, sir."

"I know you feel left out. I know how hard it is to see the others fly while you walk. This is your chance."

"Would *you* take a spren who was forced into the deal, Kaladin?" Rlain asked.

"Considering the circumstances, I'd take what I could get."

"The circumstances . . ." Rlain said, holding up his hand, inspecting the pattern of his skin. "Did I ever tell you, sir, how I ended up in a bridge crew?"

Kaladin shook his head slowly.

"I answered a question," Rlain said. "My owner was a mid-dahn lighteyes—nobody you'd know. An overseer among Sadeas's quartermasters. He called out to his wife for help as he was trying to add figures in his head, and—not thinking—I gave him the answer." Rlain hummed a soft rhythm, mocking in tone. "A stupid mistake. I'd been embedded among the Alethi for years, but I grew careless.

"Over the next few days, my owner watched me. I thought I'd given myself away. But no . . . he didn't suspect I was a spy. He just thought I was too smart. A clever parshman frightened him. So he offered me up to the bridge crews." Rlain glanced back at Kaladin. "Wouldn't want a parshman like that breeding, now would we? Who knows what kind of trouble they would make if they started thinking for themselves?"

"I'm not trying to tell you that you shouldn't think, Rlain," Kaladin said. "I'm trying to help."

"I know you are, sir. But I have no interest in taking 'what I can get.' And I don't think you should force a spren into a bond. It will make for a bad precedent, sir." He hummed a different rhythm. "You all name me a squire, but I can't draw Stormlight like the rest. There's a wedge between me and the Stormfather, I think. Strange. I expected prejudice from humans, but not from him. . . . Anyway, I will wait for a spren who will bond me for who I am—and the honor *I* represent." He gave Kaladin a Bridge Four salute, tapping his wrists together, then turned to continue teaching songs to farmers.

Kaladin trailed away toward the washing grounds. He could see the man's point, but to pass up this chance? Maybe the only way to get what Rlain wanted—respect from a spren—was to start with one who was skeptical. And Kaladin hadn't *forced* Yunfah. Kaladin had given an order. Sometimes, soldiers had to serve in positions they didn't want.

Kaladin hated feeling he'd somehow done something shameful, despite his best intentions. Couldn't Rlain accept the work he'd put into this effort, then do what he asked?

Or maybe, another part of him thought, *you could do what you promised him—and listen for once.*

Kaladin entered the washing field, passing lines of women standing at troughs as if in formation, warring with an unending horde of stained shirts and uniform coats. He trailed around the ancient pump, which bled water into the troughs, and through a rippling field of sheets hung on lines like pale white banners.

He found Zahel at the edge of the plateau. This section of the field overlooked a steep drop-off. In the near distance, Kaladin could see Navani's large construction hanging from the plateau—the device used to raise and lower the *Fourth Bridge*.

It seemed like falling from here would leave one to fall for eternity. Though he knew the mountain must slope down there somewhere, clouds often obscured the drop. He preferred to think of Urithiru as if it were floating, separated from the rest of the world and the agonies it suffered.

Here, at the outermost of the drying lines, Zahel was carefully hanging up a series of brightly colored scarves. Which lighteyes had pressed him into laundering those? They seemed the sort of frivolous neckpieces the more lavish among the elite used to accent their finery.

In contrast to the fine silk, Zahel was like the pelt of some freshly killed mink. His breechtree cotton robe was old and worn, his beard untamed— like a patch of grass growing freely in a nook sheltered from the wind— and he wore a rope for a belt.

Zahel was everything Kaladin's instincts told him to avoid. One learned to evaluate soldiers by the way they kept their uniforms. A neatly pressed coat would not win you a battle—but the man who took care to polish his buttons was often also the man who could hold a formation with precision. Soldiers with scraggly beards and ripped clothing tended to be the type who spent their evenings in drink rather than caring for their equipment.

During the years of the Sadeas/Dalinar divide in the warcamps, these distinctions had become so stark they'd practically been banners. In the face of that, the way Zahel kept himself seemed deliberate. The swordmaster was among the best duelists Kaladin had ever seen, and possessed a wisdom distinct from any other ardent's or scholar's. The only explanation was that Zahel dressed this way on purpose to give a misleading air. Zahel was a masterpiece painting intentionally hung in a splintered frame.

Kaladin halted a respectful distance away. Zahel didn't look at him, but the strange ardent always seemed to know when someone was approaching. He had a surreal awareness of his surroundings. Syl took off toward him, and Kaladin carefully watched Zahel's reaction.

He can *see her*, Kaladin decided as Zahel carefully hung another scarf. He arranged himself so he could watch Syl from the corner of his eye. Other than Rock and Cord, Kaladin had never met a person who could see invisible spren. Did Zahel have Horneater blood? The ability was rare even among Rock's kind—though he had said that occasionally a distant Horneater relative was born with it.

"Well?" Zahel finally asked. "Why have you come to bother me today, Stormblessed?"

"I need some advice."

"Find something strong to drink," Zahel said. "It can be better than Stormlight. Both will get you killed, but at least alcohol does it slowly."

Kaladin walked up beside Zahel. The fluttering scarves reminded him of a spren in flight. Syl, perhaps recognizing the same, turned to a similar shape.

"I'm being forced into retirement," Kaladin said softly.

"Congratulations," Zahel said. "Take the pension. Let all this become someone else's problem."

"I've been told I can choose my place moving forward, so long as I'm not on the front lines. I thought . . ." He looked to Zahel, who smiled, wrinkles forming at the sides of his eyes. Odd, how the man's skin could seem smooth as a child's one moment, then furrow like a grandfather's the next.

"You think you belong among us?" Zahel said. "The worn-out soldiers of the world? The men with souls so thin, they shiver in a stiff breeze?"

"That's what I've become," Kaladin said. "I know why most of them left the battlefield, Zahel. But not you. Why did you join the ardents?"

"Because I learned that conflict would find men no matter how hard I tried," he said. "I no longer wanted a part in trying to stop them."

"But you couldn't give up the sword," Kaladin said.

"Oh, I gave it up. I let go. Best mistake I ever made." He eyed Kaladin, sizing him up. "You didn't answer my question. You think you belong among the swordmasters?"

"Dalinar offered to let me train new Radiants," Kaladin said. "I don't think I could stand that—seeing them fly off to battle without me. But I thought maybe I could train regular soldiers again. That might not hurt as much."

"And you *think* you *belong* with us?"

"I . . . Yes."

"Prove it," Zahel said, snapping a few scarves off the line. "Land a strike on me."

"What? Here? *Now?*"

Zahel carefully wound one of the scarves around his arm. He had no weapons that Kaladin could see, though that ragged tan robe might conceal a knife or two.

"Hand-to-hand?" Kaladin asked.

"No, use the sword," Zahel said. "You want to join the swordmasters? Show me how you use one."

"I didn't say . . ." Kaladin glanced toward the clothing line, where Syl sat in the shape of a young woman. She shrugged, so Kaladin summoned her as a Blade—long and thin, elegant. Not like the oversized slab of a sword Dalinar had once wielded.

"Dull the edge, chull-brain," Zahel said. "My soul might be worn thin, but I'd prefer it remain in one piece. No powers on your part either. I want to see you fight, not fly."

Kaladin dulled Syl's Blade with a mental command. The edge fuzzed to mist, then re-formed unsharpened.

"Um," Kaladin said. "How do we start the—"

Zahel whipped a sheet off the line and tossed it toward Kaladin. It billowed, fanning outward, and Kaladin stepped forward, using his sword to knock the cloth from the air. Zahel had vanished among the undulating rows of sheets.

Carefully, Kaladin entered the rows. The cloths billowed outward in the wind, but then fluttered down, reminiscent of the plants he'd often passed in the chasms. Living things that moved and flowed with the unseen tides of the blowing wind.

Zahel emerged from another row, pulling a sheet off and whipping it out. Kaladin grunted, stepping away as he swiped at the cloth. That was the man's strategy, Kaladin realized. Keep Kaladin focused on the cloth.

Kaladin ignored the sheet and lunged toward Zahel. He was proud of that strike; Adolin's instruction with the sword seemed almost as natural to him now as his old spear training. The lunge missed, but the form was excellent.

Zahel, moving with remarkable spryness, dodged back among the rows of sheets. Kaladin leaped after him, but again managed to lose his quarry. Kaladin turned about, searching the seemingly endless rows of fluttering white sheets. Like dancing flames, pure white.

"Why do you fight, Kaladin Stormblessed?" Zahel's phantom voice called from somewhere nearby.

Kaladin spun, sword out. "I fight for Alethkar."

"Ha! You ask me to sponsor you as a swordmaster, then immediately lie to me?"

"I didn't ask . . ." Kaladin took a deep breath. "I wear Dalinar's colors proudly."

"You fight *for* him, not *because* of him," Zahel called. "Why do you fight?"

Kaladin crept in the direction he thought the sound came from. "I fight to protect my men."

"Closer," Zahel said. "But your men are now as safe as they could ever be. They can care for themselves. So why do you keep fighting?"

"Maybe I don't think they're safe," Kaladin said. "Maybe I . . ."

". . . don't think they can care for themselves?" Zahel asked. "You and old Dalinar. Hens from the same nest."

A face and figure formed in a nearby sheet, puffing toward Kaladin as if someone were walking through on the other side. He struck immediately, driving his sword through the sheet. It ripped—the point was still sharp enough for that—but didn't strike anyone beyond.

Syl momentarily became sharp—changing before he could ask—as he swiped to cut the sheet in two. It writhed in the wind, severed down the center.

Zahel came in from Kaladin's other side, and Kaladin barely turned in time, swinging his Blade. Zahel deflected the strike with his arm, which he'd wrapped with cloth. In his other hand he carried a long scarf that he whipped forward, catching Kaladin's off hand and wrapping it with shocking tightness, like a coiling whip.

Zahel pulled, yanking Kaladin off balance. Kaladin maintained his feet, barely, and lunged with a one-handed strike. Zahel again deflected the strike with his cloth-wrapped arm. That sort of tactic would never have worked against a real Shardblade, but it could be surprisingly effective against ordinary swords. New recruits were often surprised at how well a nice thick cloth could stop a blade.

Zahel still had Kaladin's off hand wrapped in the scarf, which he heaved, spinning Kaladin around. Damnation. Kaladin managed to maneuver his Blade and slice the cloth in half—Syl becoming sharp for a moment—then he leaped backward and tried to regain his footing.

Zahel strode calmly to the side, whipping his scarf with a solid *crack*, then spinning it around like a mace. Kaladin didn't see any Stormlight coming off the ardent, and he had no reason to believe the man could Surgebind . . . but the way the cloth had gripped Kaladin's arm had been uncanny.

Zahel stretched the scarf in his hands—it was longer than Kaladin had expected. "Do you believe in the Almighty, boy?"

"Why does that matter?"

"You ask why faith is relevant when you're considering joining the ardents—to become a *religious advisor*?"

"I want to be a teacher of the sword and spear," Kaladin said. "What does that have to do with the Almighty?"

"All right, then. You ask why God is relevant when you're considering teaching men to kill?"

Kaladin inched carefully forward, his Blade held before him. "I don't know what I believe. Navani still follows the Almighty. She burns glyphwards every morning. Dalinar says that the Almighty is dead, but he also claims there's another true God somewhere in a place beyond Shadesmar. Jasnah says that a being having vast powers doesn't make them God, and concludes—from the way the world works—that an omnipotent, loving deity cannot exist."

"I didn't ask what they believe. I asked what you believe."

"I'm not confident *anyone* knows the answers. I figure I'll let the people who care argue about it, and I'll keep my head down and focus on my life right now."

Zahel nodded to him, as if that answer was acceptable. He waved Kaladin forward. Trying to keep his sword form in mind—he'd trained mostly on Smokestance—Kaladin tested forward. He feinted twice, then lunged.

Zahel's hands became a blur as he pushed the sword to the side with his stretched-out scarf, then twisted his hands around, neatly wrapping the scarf around the sword. That gave him leverage to push the sword farther away as he stepped into Kaladin's lunge and slid his makeshift wrapping along the length of the Blade, coming in close.

Here, he somehow twisted his cloths around to wrap Kaladin's *wrists* as well. Kaladin tried a head-butt, but Zahel stepped into the move and raised one side of the scarf—letting Kaladin's head go underneath it. With a twirl and a twist, Zahel completely tied Kaladin in the scarf. How long was that thing?

The exchange left Kaladin with not only his hands tied tightly, but a scarf now holding his arms pinned to his sides, Zahel standing behind him. Kaladin couldn't see what Zahel did next, but it involved sending a loop of scarf up over Kaladin's head and around his neck. Zahel pulled tight, choking off Kaladin's air.

I think we're losing, Syl said. *To a guy wielding something he found in Adolin's sock drawer.*

Kaladin grunted, but a part of him was excited. Frustrating as Zahel could be, he was an excellent fighter—and he tested Kaladin in ways he'd never seen before. That was the sort of training he needed in order to beat the Fused.

As Zahel tried to choke him, Kaladin forced himself to remain calm. He changed Syl into a small dagger. A twist of the wrist cut the scarf, which unraveled the entire trap, leaving Kaladin free to spin and slash with his again-dulled knife.

The ardent blocked the knife with his cloth-wrapped arm. He immediately caught Kaladin's wrist with his other hand, so Kaladin dismissed Syl and summoned her again with his off hand—swinging to make Zahel dodge back.

Zahel snatched a sheet off the fluttering lines, twisting it and wrapping it into a tight length, like a cord.

Kaladin rubbed his neck. "I think . . . I think I *have* seen this style before. You fight like Azure does."

"*She* fights like *me*, boy."

"She's hunting for you, I think."

"So Adolin has said. The fool woman will have to get through Cultivation's Perpendicularity first, so I won't hold my Breaths waiting for her to arrive." He waved for Kaladin to come at him again.

Kaladin slipped a throwing knife from his belt, then fell into a sword-and-knife stance. He waved for Zahel to come at him instead. The swordmaster smiled, then threw his sheet at Kaladin. It puffed out, spreading wide as if going for an embrace. By the time Kaladin had cut it down, Zahel was gone, ducking out into the rippling cloth forest.

Kaladin dismissed Syl, then waved toward the ground. She nodded and dived to look under the sheets, searching for Zahel. She pointed in a direction for Kaladin, then dodged between two sheets as a ribbon of light.

Kaladin followed carefully. He thought he caught a glimpse of Zahel through the sheets, a shadow across the cloth.

"Do *you* believe?" Kaladin asked as he advanced. "In God, or the Almighty or whatever?"

"I don't have to believe," the voice drifted back. "I know gods exist. I simply hate them."

Kaladin dodged between a pair of sheets. In that moment, sheets began *ripping* free of the lines. They sprang for Kaladin, six at once, and he swore he could see the outlines of faces and figures in them. He summoned Syl and—keeping his head—ignored the unnerving sight and found Zahel.

Kaladin lunged. Zahel—moving with almost supernatural poise—raised two fingers and pressed them to the moving Blade, turning the point aside exactly enough that it missed.

The wind swirled around Kaladin as he stepped into the rippling sheets. They flowed against him—insubstantial—but then entangled his legs. He tripped with a curse, falling to the hard stone.

A second later Zahel had Kaladin's own knife in hand, pressed to his forehead. Kaladin felt the point right among his scars.

"You cheated," Kaladin said. "You're doing something with those sheets and that cloth."

"I couldn't cheat," Zahel said. "This wasn't about winning or losing, boy. It was for me to see how you fought. I can tell more about a man when the odds are against him."

Zahel stood and dropped the knife with a clang. Kaladin recovered it, sitting up, and glanced at the fallen sheets. They lay on the ground—normal cloths, occasionally shifting in the breeze. In fact, another man might have dismissed their motions as a trick of the wind.

But Kaladin knew the wind. That had *not* been the wind.

"You can't join the ardents," Zahel said to him, kneeling and touching one of the cloths with his finger, then lifting it and pinning it onto the drying line. He did the same for the others, each in turn.

"Why can't I?" Kaladin asked. He wasn't certain Zahel had the authority to forbid him, but he also wasn't certain he wanted to take this path if Zahel—the one ardent he felt true respect for—was opposed. "Do you make everyone who wants to retire to the ardentia fight you for the privilege?"

"It *wasn't* a fight about winning or losing," Zahel said. "You're not unwelcome because you lost; you're unwelcome because you don't belong with us." He whipped a sheet in the air, then pinned it in place. "You love the fight, Kaladin. Not with the Thrill that Dalinar once felt, or even with the anticipation of a dandy going to a duel.

"You love it because it's part of you. It's your mistress, your passion, your lifeblood. You'd find the daily training unsatisfying. You'd thirst for something more. You'd eventually turn and leave, and that would put you in a worse position than if you'd never started."

He tossed his scarf at Kaladin's feet. Though it must have been a different scarf, for the one he'd started with had been bright red, and this one was dull grey.

"Return when you hate the fight," Zahel said. "*Truly* hate it." He walked off between the sheets.

Kaladin picked up the fallen scarf, then glanced at Syl, who descended through the air near him on an invisible set of steps. She shrugged.

Kaladin gripped the cloth, then strode around the sheets. The swordmaster had moved to sit at the rim of the plateau, legs over the edge, staring out across the nearby mountain range. Kaladin dropped the scarf on a pile of others—each of which was now grey.

"What are you?" Kaladin asked. "Are you like Wit?" There had always been something about Zahel, something too knowing. Something distinct, set apart, different from the others.

"No," Zahel said. "I don't think there's anyone else quite like Hoid. I knew him by the name Dust when I was younger. I think he must have a thousand different names among a thousand different peoples."

"And you?" Kaladin settled down on the stone beside Zahel. "How many names do you have?"

"A few," Zahel said. "More than I normally share." He leaned forward, elbows on thighs. Wind blew at the hem of his robe, dangling over a drop of thousands of feet. "You want to know what I am? Well, I'm a lot of things. Tired, mostly. But I'm also a Type Two Invested entity. Used to call myself a Type One, but I had to throw the whole scale out, once I learned more. That's the trouble with science. It's never done. Always upending itself. Ruining perfect systems for the little inconvenience of them being wrong."

"I . . ." Kaladin swallowed. "I don't know what any of that meant, but thanks for replying. Wit never gives me answers. At least not straight ones."

"That's because Wit is an asshole," Zahel said. He fished in his robe's pocket and pulled something out—a small stone in the shape of a curling shell. "Ever seen one of these?"

"Soulcast?" Kaladin asked, taking the small shell. It was surprisingly heavy. He turned it around, admiring the way it curled.

"Similar. That's a creature that died long, long ago. It settled into the mud, and slowly—over thousands upon thousands of years—minerals infused its body, replacing it axon by axon with stone. Eventually the entire thing was transformed."

"So . . . natural Soulcasting. Over time."

"A long time. A *mind-numbingly* long time. The place I come from, it didn't have any of these. It's too new. Your world might have some hidden deep, but I doubt it. That stone you hold is *old*. Older than Wit, or your Heralds, or the gods themselves."

Kaladin held it up, then—out of habit—used a few drops of water from his canteen to reveal its hidden colors and shades.

"My soul," Zahel said, "is like that fossil. Every part of my soul has been replaced with something new, though it happened in a flash for me. The soul I have now resembles the one I was born with, but it's something else entirely."

"I don't understand."

"I'm not surprised." Zahel thought for a moment. "Imagine it this way. You know how you can make an imprint in crem, then let it dry, and fill the imprint with wax to create a copy of your original object? Well, that happened to my soul. When I died, I was drenched in power. So when my soul escaped, it left a duplicate. A kind of . . . fossil of a soul."

Kaladin hesitated. "You . . . died?"

Zahel nodded. "Happened to your friend too. Up in the prison? The one with . . . that sword."

"Szeth. Not my friend."

"The Heralds too," Zahel said. "When they died, they left an imprint behind. Power that remembered being them. You see, the power *wants* to be alive." He gestured with his chin toward Syl, flying down beneath them as a ribbon of light. "She's what I now call a Type One Invested entity. I decided that had to be the proper way to refer to them. Power that came alive on its own."

"You *can* see her!" Kaladin said.

"See? No. Sense?" Zahel shrugged. "Cut off a bit of divinity and leave it alone. Eventually it comes alive. And if you let a man die with too Invested a soul—or Invest him right as he's dying—he'll leave behind a shadow you can nail back onto a body. His own, if you're feeling charitable. Once done, you have this." Zahel waved to himself. "Type Two Invested entity. Dead man walking."

What a . . . strange conversation. Kaladin frowned, trying to figure out why Zahel was telling him this. *I suppose I did ask. So . . . Wait.* Maybe there was another reason.

"The Fused?" Kaladin asked. "That's what they are?"

"Yeah," he said. "Most of us stop aging when it happens, gaining a kind of immortality."

"Is there a . . . way to kill something like you? Permanently?"

"Lots of ways. For the weaker ones, just kill the body again, make sure no one Invests the soul with more strength, and they'll slip away in a few minutes. For stronger ones . . . well, you might be able to starve them. A lot of Type Twos feed on power. Keeps them going.

"These enemies of yours though, I think they're too strong for that. They've lasted thousands of years already, and seem Connected to Odium to feed directly on his power. You'll have to find a way to disrupt their souls. You can't just rip them apart; you need a weapon so strong, it *unravels* the soul." He squinted, looking off into the distance. "I know through sorry experience those kinds of weapons are very dangerous to make, and never seem to work right."

"There's another way," Kaladin said. "We could convince the Fused to stop fighting. Instead of killing them, we could find a way to live with them."

"Grand ideals," Zahel said. "Optimism. Yeah, you'd make a terrible swordmaster. Be wary of those Fused, kid. The longer one of us exists, the more like a spren we become. Consumed by a singular purpose, our minds bound and chained by our Intent. We're spren masquerading as men. That's why she takes our memories. She knows we aren't the actual people who died, but something else given a corpse to inhabit. . . ."

"She?" Kaladin asked.

Zahel didn't respond, though when Kaladin handed back the stone shell, Zahel took it. As Kaladin hiked off, the swordmaster cradled it to his chest, staring out toward the endless horizon.

16

AN UNKNOWN SONG

*My final point of the evening is a discussion of Fused weapons.
The Fused use a variety of fabrial devices to fight Radiants. It is
obvious from how quickly they've fabricated and employed these
countermeasures that they have used these in the past.*

—Lecture on fabrial mechanics presented by Navani Kholin
to the coalition of monarchs, Urithiru, Jesevan, 1175

Navani held up the dark sphere, closing one eye to inspect it
closely. It *was* different from Voidlight. She held up a Voidlight
sphere for comparison, a diamond infused with the strange
Light gathered during the Everstorm.

They still didn't know how the enemy infused spheres with Voidlight;
all they owned were stolen from the singers. Fortunately, Voidlight leaked
far more slowly than Stormlight did. She probably had a few more days
before this one went dun.

The Voidlight sphere had a strange glow to it. A distinctive purple-
on-black, which Rushu described as a hyperviolet—a color she claimed
existed in theory, though Navani didn't know how a *color* could be theoretical. Regardless, this was a purple-on-black, coexisting in such a way that
both shades simultaneously occupied the same space.

The strange sphere that Szeth had provided seemed exactly the same
at first glance. Purple upon black, an impossible color. Like the ordinary
Voidlight sphere, its blackness expanded, making the surrounding air dim.

But there was an added effect with this sphere, one she hadn't noticed
right away. It *warped* the air around it. Looking at the sphere for too long

was a distinctively disorienting sensation. It evoked a *wrongness* that she couldn't define.

Gavilar had possessed Voidlight spheres—she remembered seeing them—and that fact was befuddling enough. How had her husband obtained Voidlight *years* before the arrival of the Everstorm? But this other black sphere. What on Roshar was *it?*

"Assassin," Navani said. "Look at me."

Szeth, the Assassin in White, looked up from within his cell. Sixteen days had passed since Navani and Dalinar had returned from testing the *Fourth Bridge* in battle. Sixteen days spent catching up on mundane work in the tower, like overseeing planned expansions of the market and dealing with sanitation problems. Only now did she have a large chunk of time to dedicate to Voidlight and the nature of the tower.

The strange individual who had contacted her via spanreed had not spoken to her again. Navani had decided not to worry about them—she didn't even know if they were sane. She had plenty else to worry about, such as the man sitting in the prison cell in front of her.

Szeth cradled his strange Shardblade in his lap, the one that leaked black smoke when unsheathed. When challenged about letting the prisoner remain armed, Dalinar had replied, "I believe the safest place to keep the thing is in his possession."

Navani questioned that wisdom. In her opinion, they should sink the strange Blade in the ocean, like they'd done with the gemstone that contained the Thrill. Szeth did not seem stable enough to be trusted with a Shard, particularly not one so dangerous as this. In fact, she wished the assassin had been executed as he deserved.

Dalinar disagreed, and so they'd decided together to leave Szeth alive. Today, the Shin man sat on the floor of his stone cell, eyes closed, wearing white clothing by his own request. He had been given what few amenities he asked for. A razor for shaving, a single blanket, a chance to bathe each day.

And light. A great deal of light. Dozens of spheres to illuminate his small stone cell and banish all traces of shadow.

They'd fitted the front of the room with bars, though those wouldn't keep the assassin contained should he decide to escape. That Shardblade could reduce objects to smoke simply by nicking them.

"Tell me again," Navani said to him, "of the night you killed my husband."

"I was instructed by the Parshendi to execute him," Szeth said softly.

"Were you curious why they'd kill a man on the very night they were signing a peace treaty with him?"

"I thought I was Truthless," Szeth said. "That status required that I do as my master commanded. Without question." His voice bore only the faintest hint of an accent.

"Your master is now Dalinar."

"Yes. I have . . . found a better way. Throughout my Truthless existence, I followed the way of the Oathstone. I would obey anyone who held that stone. Now, I have realized I was never Truthless. I have sworn to an Ideal instead: the Blackthorn. Whatever he wishes, I will make reality."

"What if Dalinar dies?"

"I . . . will seek another Ideal, I suppose. I had not considered it."

"How could you not think of that?"

"I simply did not."

Storms, this is dangerous, Navani thought. Dalinar could speak of redemption and mending broken spirits, but this creature was a fire burning unchecked, ready to escape the hearth and consume any fuel it could find. Szeth had murdered kings and highprinces—over a dozen rulers all across Roshar. Yes, much of that blame fell on Taravangian, but Szeth was the tool employed to cause such destruction.

"You didn't finish your story," Navani said. "The night you killed Gavilar. Tell me again what happened. The part with this sphere."

"We fell," Szeth whispered, opening his eyes. "Gavilar was injured by the impact, his body fatally broken. In that moment he treated me not as an enemy, but as the last living man he would ever see. He made a request. A holy request, the last words of the dying.

"He spoke a few names, which I do not remember, asking if those men had sent me. When I assured him they had not, he was relieved. I think he feared the sphere falling into their hands, so he gave it to me. He trusted his own murderer more than those who surrounded him."

Including me, Navani thought. Storms, she'd assumed she was *over* her anger and frustration with Gavilar, but there it was, twisting around itself in the pit of her stomach, causing angerspren to rise beneath her feet.

"He told me a message to give his brother," Szeth continued, his eyes flickering toward the pooling angerspren. "I wrote the words, as it was the best I could do to fulfill that dying request. I took the sphere and hid it. Until you asked me if I'd found anything on his body, whereupon I recovered it."

This he'd done only a month ago because Navani had thought to ask the question. Otherwise he would simply have gone on without saying a word of this sphere—as if his mind were too childlike or stressed to realize he should speak up.

Navani shivered. She was in favor of comforting the sick of mind—once they were carefully contained, and things like *evil talking Shardblades* were removed from their possession. She had a list of facts she'd collected from him about that Blade, and she thought maybe it was an Honorblade that had been corrupted somehow. It had been given to Szeth by one of the Heralds, after all. She found it difficult to study, however, because being around Szeth made her feel sick.

At least the sword's spren had stopped speaking into the minds of those who passed by the prison. It had taken three demands from Dalinar to get Szeth to finally restrain the thing.

"You're certain this is the exact sphere he gave you," Navani said.

"It is."

"And he said nothing about it to you?"

"I have answered this question."

"And you will answer it again. Until I'm certain you haven't 'forgotten' any more details."

Szeth sighed softly. "He did not speak of the sphere. He was dying; he could barely force out his last words. I am not certain they are prophetic, as the voices of the dying sometimes are in my land. I followed them anyway."

She turned to go. She had more questions, but she had to budget her time with the assassin. Each moment near him made her feel physically ill; even now her stomach was beginning to churn, and she feared losing her breakfast.

"Do you hate me?" Szeth asked from behind, calm, almost emotionless. *Too* calm, *too* emotionless for words spoken to a widow at his hand.

"Yes," Navani said.

"Good," Szeth said, the word echoing in the small chamber. "Good. Thank you."

Shivering and nauseous, Navani fled his presence.

⁂

Less than an hour later, she stepped out onto the Cloudwalk, a garden balcony set at the base of the eighth tier of the tower. Urithiru was nearly two hundred floors tall, ten tiers of eighteen floors each—and so the eighth tier was near the top, at a dizzying height.

Most of the tower was built up against the mountains, with chunks of the structure embedded fully into the stone. It was only here, near the top, that the tower fully peeked up above the surrounding stone. The Cloudwalk rounded almost the entire perimeter of the tier, an open stone pathway with a sure railing on one side.

It sported some of the best views Urithiru had to offer. Navani had often come here during their early months in the tower, but news of the spectacular views had spread. When once she'd been able to walk the entire Cloudwalk without encountering another soul, today she was met by the sight

of tens of people strolling up here.

She forced herself to see it as a victory, not an encroachment. Part of their vision for this tower was a city where the different peoples of Roshar intermixed. With the Oathgates providing direct access to cities around the continent, Urithiru could grow to be cosmopolitan in ways that Kholinar could never have dreamed.

As she walked, she saw not only the uniforms of seven different princedoms, but people wearing the patterns of three different Makabaki local governments. Thaylen merchants, Emuli soldiers, and Natan tradesmen were represented. There were even a few Aimians, remnants of the humans who had escaped Aimia, the men with their beards bound in cords.

Most of the world was embroiled in war, but Urithiru stood apart. A place of calm serenity above the storms. Soldiers came here when rotated off active duty. Tradesmen brought their wares, enduring wartime tariffs to avoid the cost of trying to deliver goods across battle lines. Scholars came to let their minds spark against those working to solve the problems of a new era. Urithiru was truly something great.

She wished Elhokar had lived to see how wonderful it was becoming. Best she could do was see that his son grew up to appreciate it. So, Navani opened her arms as she reached the meeting point. The nursemaid set Gavinor down, and he rushed over, jumping into Navani's embrace.

She hung to him tightly, appreciating the progress they'd made. When Gavinor had finally been recovered, he'd been so frightened and timid he had cringed when Navani tried to hug him. That trauma, now a year past, was finally fading from the boy. He was often solemn—too solemn for a boy of five—but at least with her, he'd learned to laugh again.

"Gram!" he said. "Gram, I rode a horse!"

"All on your own?" she asked, lifting him.

"Adolin helped me!" he said. "But it was a big horse, and I *wasn't* scared, even when it started walking! Look! Look!" He pointed, and she lifted him up as they peered toward the fields far below. It was too far to make out details, but that didn't stop little Gav from explaining to her—at length—the different colors of horses he'd seen.

She gave him an encouraging smile. His excitement was not only infectious, it was relieving. During his first few months in the tower, he'd hardly spoken. Now, his willingness to do more than barely go near the horses—which fascinated him, but also terrified him—was a huge improvement.

She held Gav, warm despite the chill air, as he talked. The child was still far too small for his age, and the doctors weren't certain if something strange had been done to him during his time in Kholinar. Navani was furious at Aesudan for all that had happened there—but equally furious at herself. How much was *Navani* to blame for leaving the woman alone to invite in one of the Unmade?

You couldn't have known, Navani told herself. *You can't be to blame for everything.* She'd tried to overcome those feelings—and the equally irrational ones that whispered she shared blame for Elhokar's death. If she'd stopped him from going on that fool's mission . . .

No. No, she would hold Gav, she would hurt, but she would move forward. She pointedly thought on her wonderful moments holding Elhokar as a little boy, *not* fixating on the idea of that little boy dying to a traitor's spear.

"Gram?" Gav asked as they looked out over the mountains. "I want Grampa to teach me the sword."

"Oh, I'm certain he can get to that eventually," Navani said, then pointed. "See that cloud! It's so huge!"

"Other boys my age learn the sword," Gav said, his voice growing softer. "Don't they?"

They did. In Alethkar, families—particularly lighteyed ones—would go to war together. The Azish thought it unnatural, but to the Alethi it was the way of things. Children as young as ten would learn to serve as officers' aides, and boys would often be given a training sword as soon as they could walk.

"You don't need to worry about that," Navani said to him.

"If I have a sword," Gav said, "nobody will be able to hurt me. I'll be able to find the man who killed my father. And I could kill him."

Navani felt a chill unrelated to the cold air. On one hand, it was a *very* Alethi thing to say. It broke her heart regardless. She hugged Gav tight. "Don't worry about it."

"Will you talk to Grampa, please?"

She sighed. "I'll ask him."

Gav nodded, smiling. Her time with him was short, unfortunately. She had a meeting with Dalinar and Jasnah in under an hour, and she needed to check with some scientists up here on the Cloudwalk first. So, she eventually turned Gav back over to the nursemaid. Then she wiped her eyes, feeling silly at crying over something so trivial, and hurried on her way.

It was just that . . . Elhokar had been learning so much. During these last years, she'd seen him growing into something great—a better man than Gavilar, worthy of the kingship. A mother should never have to grieve for her children. Should never have to think of her poor little boy, lying alone and dead on the floor of an abandoned palace . . .

She forced herself forward, nodding to those soldiers who chose to bow or—oddly—salute her, hands to shoulders with the knuckles out. Soldiers these days. She supposed with some of their commanders learning to read and some of their sisters joining the Radiants, life could get confusing.

She eventually reached the research station set up at the far end of the Cloudwalk. The head scientist in charge of atmospheric measurements was an ardent with a particularly long neck. With his bald head and the sagging skin under his chin, Brother Benneh resembled nothing so much as an eel who had put on robes and grown a pair of arms through sheer determination. But he was a happy fellow, and he spryly bounced over to her with his notebooks.

"Brightness!" he said, pointedly ignoring Elthebar the stormwarden, who was taking his own measurements from the nearby instruments. "Look here, look here!"

Benneh pointed out the historical barometer readings he'd recorded in his notebook. "Here, here," he said, tapping the barometer—which was set up on a scientific table with thermometers, some plants, a sundial, and a small astrolabe. That was in addition to the various astrological nonsenses the stormwardens had erected.

"It *rises*," Benneh said, almost breathless, "ahead of a storm."

"Wait. The barometer *rises* ahead of a storm?"

"Yes."

"That's . . . backward, isn't it?"

"Yes indeed, indeed. And see, the temperature readings before a storm rise slightly too. You wondered how much colder it was up here on the Cloudwalk than it was below near the fields. Brightness, it's *warmer*."

She frowned, then glanced toward the promenading people. No sign of their breath in front of their faces. It felt colder up here—she herself had noted that—but could that be because she expected it to be? Besides, she always left the interior of the tower to come out; it was impossible not to compare it to the warmth inside instead of the temperature below.

"How cold is it right now?" she asked. "Down below?"

"I asked via spanreed. Measurements are conclusive. At least five degrees colder on the plateau."

Five degrees? Storms. "Heat in front of a storm and a rise in pressure," Navani said. "It defies our understanding, but has anyone done readings like this from such an elevation? Perhaps what is natural near sea level is inverted up here."

"Yes, yes," the ardent said. "I could perhaps see that, but look at these books. They contradict such a theory. Measurements taken from various Horneater trading expeditions . . . Let me find them . . ."

He started digging through papers, though she didn't need them. She had a suspicion of what was happening. Why would pressure and temperature rise before a storm? Because the structure was bracing itself. The tower could adapt to the storms. More proof; the data was growing as mountainous as these peaks. The tower could regulate temperature, pressure, humidity. If Urithiru could be made fully functional, life up here would improve dramatically.

But how to fix it, when the spren that had lived here was supposedly dead? She was so absorbed by the problem, she nearly missed the bowing. Her subconscious initially assumed the bows were for her, but too many people were involved. And they were going too low.

She turned to find Dalinar passing by, Taravangian at his side. People backed out of the way before the two kings, and Navani felt like a fool. She'd known they were meeting this afternoon, and this was one of their favorite places to promenade. Others found it encouraging to see the two kings together, but Navani did not miss the gap between them. She knew things others did not. For instance, Dalinar no longer met his former friend beside the hearth to chat for hours. And Taravangian no longer attended private meetings of Dalinar's inner circle.

They hadn't been able—nor were they yet willing—to excise Taravangian from the coalition of monarchs. His crimes, though terrible, were no more bloody than Dalinar's own. The fact that Taravangian had sent Szeth against the Azish emperors had certainly strained relations and increased tensions within the coalition. But for now, they all agreed that the servants of Odium were a far more pressing enemy.

Taravangian, however, would never again be a man to trust. At least Dalinar's terrible actions had been part of an official act of war.

Though . . . she had to admit some moral high ground *had* been lost upon the early circulations of Dalinar's memoir. The Kholin troops—once so proud, they'd bordered on imperious—walked with slightly slumped shoulders, their heads no longer held quite as high. Everyone had known about the atrocities of the Kholin unification war. They'd heard of the Blackthorn's fearsome reputation, and of cities burned and pillaged.

So long as Dalinar had been willing to pretend his actions had been noble, the kingdom could pretend along with him. Now the Alethi had to face the truth long tucked away behind justifications and political spin. No army, no matter how clean its reputation, walked away from war untainted. And no leader, no matter how noble, could help but sink into the crem when he stepped into the game of conquest.

She spent a little longer going over readings with Benneh, then checked on the royal astronomers, who were erecting a new set of telescopes made with the highest-quality lenses out of Thaylenah. They were certain they'd be able to get some spectacular views from up here once the telescopes were calibrated. Navani asked the women a few questions as they worked, but left when she felt she was becoming a bother. A true patron of the sciences knew when she was hindering instead of helping.

As she turned to leave, however, Navani paused—then dug Szeth's strange Voidlight sphere from her pocket. "Talnah?" she asked one of the engineers. "You were a jeweler, weren't you? Before taking up lens work?"

"Still am, some seasons," the short woman replied. "I put in a few hours at the mint last week, checking sphere weights."

"What do you think of this?" Navani said, holding up the sphere.

Talnah tucked a strand of hair behind her ear and took the sphere, holding it up in a gloved hand. "What is this? Voidlight?" She searched in her jacket pocket and pulled out a jeweler's loupe, then pressed it to her eye.

"We're not sure," Navani said.

"Stormfather," the woman said. "That's a nice diamond. Hey, Nem! Have a look."

Another of the engineers came over and accepted the sphere and loupe, whistling softly. "I have a higher magnification in my bag over there," she said, waving, and an assistant engineer helpfully fetched a larger magnifying device, one you could look through with both eyes.

"What is it?" Navani asked. "What do you see?"

"Practically flawless," Nem said, clamping the sphere in some small grips. "This wasn't grown as a gemheart, I can tell you that. The structure would never align so perfectly. This sphere is worth thousands, Brightness. It will probably hold Stormlight for months without leaking any out. Maybe years. Longer, for Voidlight."

"It was left in a cave for over six years," Navani said. "And was glowing—or whatever you call that blackness—the same when it was retrieved."

"Quite strange indeed," Talnah said. "What an odd sphere, Brightness. That must be Voidlight, but it feels wrong. I mean, it's black-violet like others I've seen, but . . ."

"The air warps around it," Navani said.

"Yeah!" Talnah said. "That's it. How strange. Can we keep it to study it?"

Navani hesitated. She'd planned to do her own tests on the sphere, but she had to see to the needs of the tower and work on new iterations of her flying machine. To be honest, she'd been planning to run tests on this sphere ever since she'd received it—but there was never enough time.

"Yes, please do," Navani said. "Run some standard Stormlight measuring tests for luminosity and the like, then see if you can move the Light to other gemstones. If you can, try to use it to power various fabrials."

"Voidlight doesn't work on fabrials," Nem said, frowning. "But you're right—maybe this *isn't* Voidlight. It certainly does look strange. . . ."

Navani made them promise to keep the sphere hidden and to reveal the results of their tests only to her. She gave them leave to requisition several real Voidlight spheres, captured in battle, to use in comparisons. Then she left the strange sphere with them, feeling agitated. Not because she didn't trust the two—they dealt with extremely expensive and delicate equipment, and had proven reliable. But the piece of Navani hoping to study this sphere herself was disappointed.

Unfortunately, this was work for scholars. Not her. She left it in their capable hands, and moved on. She was therefore the first to arrive in the small windowless chamber near the top of the tower where Jasnah and Dalinar held their private meetings. These top floors were small enough to control entirely, with guard posts to regulate access.

Too often down below, rooms and hallways felt oppressive. As if something was watching. Openings in walls—running as air ducts through the rooms—often led in bizarre patterns barely mapped by the children they'd sent to crawl through them. You could never be completely certain that someone wasn't listening at an opening nearby, eavesdropping on private conversations.

Up here though, the floors often had a dozen or fewer rooms—all carefully mapped and tested for acoustics. Most had windows, which made them feel inviting. She felt lighter even in a windowless stone chamber like this one, so long as her mind knew open sky was right beyond the wall.

As she waited, Navani puttered in her notebooks, theorizing about Gavilar's dark sphere. She flipped to a testimonial she'd transcribed from Rlain, the listener member of Bridge Four. He swore that Gavilar had given his general, Eshonai, a Voidlight sphere years before the coming of the Everstorm. When Navani showed him this second sphere, his reaction had been curious.

I don't know what that is, Brightness, he'd said. *But it feels* painful. *Voidlight is dangerously inviting, like if I touched it, my body would drink it in eagerly. That thing . . . is different. It has a song I've never heard, and it vibrates wrong against my soul.*

She flipped to another page and wrote some thoughts. What would happen if they tried to grow plants by the dark light of this sphere? Dared she let a Radiant try to suck out its strange energy?

She was writing along these lines when Adolin and Shallan arrived with the Mink. They'd periodically been entertaining him these last few weeks, showing him around the tower, dividing out space for his troops once they arrived with the Fourth Bridge in the next few days. The short Herdazian didn't wear a uniform, merely some common trousers and a buttoned shirt cut after simple Herdazian styles, with suspenders and a loose coat. How odd. Didn't he know he wasn't a refugee any longer?

". . . think you could teach me?" Shallan was saying. Red hair and no hat. "I *really* want to know how you got out of those cuffs."

"There's an art to it," the general said. "It's more than practice; it's about instinct. Each set of confines is a puzzle to be solved, and your reward?

Going where you shouldn't. Being what you shouldn't. Brightness, it is not a particularly seemly hobby for a well-connected young woman."

"Trust me," she said, "I am *anything* but well-connected. I keep finding pieces of myself lying around, forgotten. . . ."

She led the Mink over to the other door to point out the guard post beyond. Adolin gave Navani a hug, then took the seat next to her.

"She's fascinated by him," he whispered to Navani. "I should have guessed she would be."

"What's that clothing he's wearing?" Navani whispered.

"I know, I know." Adolin grimaced. "I offered him my tailors, said we'd get him a Herdazian uniform. He said, 'There is no Herdaz anymore. Besides, a man in uniform can't go the places I like to go.' I don't know what to make of him."

Across the small room, the Mink glanced at one of the stone air vents, nodding as Shallan explained the room's security.

"He's plotting how to sneak away," Adolin said with a sigh, putting his feet up on the table. "He lost us *five* times today. I can't decide if he's paranoid, crazy, or merely has a cruel sense of humor." He leaned toward Navani. "I suspect it wouldn't have been that bad if Shallan hadn't been so impressed the first time. He does like to show off."

Navani eyed Adolin's new gold-trimmed boots. They were the third pair she'd seen him wearing this week.

Dalinar arrived, depositing two bodyguards outside the front door. He kept trying to get Navani to accept some guards of her own, and she always agreed—when she had equipment she needed carried. And honestly, Dalinar couldn't complain. How often had he ditched his own guards?

The room had been set up with a few chairs and only one small table, the one Adolin had his boots on. That boy. He never leaned back in his chair or put his feet up when he was wearing ordinary shoes.

Dalinar passed by, rapping the boots with his knuckles. "Decorum," he said. "Discipline. Dedication."

"Detail, duel, dessert . . ." Adolin glanced at his father. "Oh, sorry. I thought we were saying random words that start with the same sound."

Dalinar glowered at Shallan.

"What?" she said.

"He was never like this before you arrived," Dalinar said.

"Stormfather help us," Shallan said lightly, sitting beside her husband and laying a protective hand upon his knee. "A Kholin has learned to *relax* once in a while? Surely the moons will stop orbiting and the sun will come crashing down."

Neither Shallan nor Dalinar would admit to squabbling over Adolin—indeed, Navani suspected Dalinar would insist he approved of the marriage.

But he'd also never needed to give up one of his children to the influence of an outsider. Navani felt Dalinar blamed Shallan too much for the changes in the boy. Shallan wasn't pushing him to be something he was not; more, he finally felt free enough to explore an identity that wasn't tied to being the Blackthorn's son.

Adolin was highprince now. He should have the opportunity to define what that meant for him.

For his part, Adolin just laughed. "Shallan, you're *really* complaining that someone is too intense? You? Even your jokes sometimes feel like a competition."

She glanced to him, then—instead of being provoked—seemed to relax. Adolin had that effect on people.

"Of course they are," she said. "My life is a constant struggle against boredom. If I relax my guard, you'll find me knitting or something dreadful like that."

The Mink watched the exchange with a smile. "Ah . . . reminds me of my own son and his wife."

"I should hope," Dalinar said, "they are a little less frivolous."

"They're dead, in the war," the Mink said softly.

"I'm sorry," Dalinar said. "The Everstorm and Odium have cost us all much."

"Not that war, Blackthorn." The Mink gave him a look laden with implication. Then he turned toward Navani. "The highprince mentioned maps for me to inspect? He said they'd be waiting, but I don't see any in here, nor a table of proper size to roll them out upon. Should we fetch them? I'm very curious to see your troop layouts against the Voidbringers."

"We don't use the term 'Voidbringers' anymore," Dalinar said. "It has proven to be . . . imprecise. We call our enemies the singers. As for the map, it's right here." He looked to Shallan, who nodded, taking in a breath of Stormlight from the spheres in her satchel. Navani hurried to prepare her notebook.

Together, Shallan and Dalinar summoned the map.

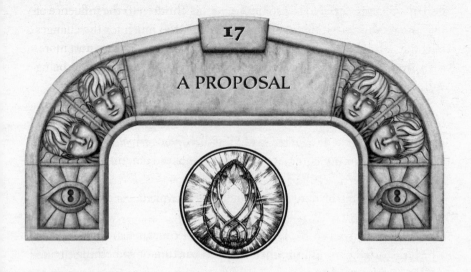

A PROPOSAL

The simplest Fused weapon against us isn't truly a fabrial, but instead a metal that is extremely light and can withstand the blows of a Shardblade. This metal resists being Soulcast as well; it interferes with a great number of Radiant powers.

Fortunately, the Fused seem unable to create it in great quantities—for they equip only themselves, and not their average soldiers, with these wonders.

—Lecture on fabrial mechanics presented by Navani Kholin
to the coalition of monarchs, Urithiru, Jesevan, 1175

Navani had seen Shallan and Dalinar summon the map dozens of times, but—as with Dalinar's ability to recharge spheres—she felt there was more to be learned by careful examination.

First Shallan breathed out, and her Stormlight expanded outward in a disc. Dalinar breathed out his own Light, which melded with Shallan's, spiraling across the surface like a whirlpool. The two planes of luminescent smoke spun outward, flat and round, filling the room at about waist height.

Somehow Shallan's Lightweaving mixed with Dalinar's Connection to the land to create this magnificent representation of Roshar. The Stormfather implied that Dalinar—as a Bondsmith—could do similar marvels with other orders, but so far their experiments had been fruitless.

The map's sudden appearance caused the Mink to scramble away. He was at the door in a fraction of a second, standing with it cracked, ready to flee. He *was* a paranoid type, wasn't he?

Navani focused on the map, her pen poised. Could she sense anything?

Perhaps Shadesmar? No . . . something else. The sensation of flight, soaring above a tempestuous ocean, free. Dreamlike. The Light seemed to become solid, snapping into the shape of a map of the continent as if seen from high above. Fully rendered in color, it showed mountains and valleys in exacting topographical detail, all to scale.

The Mink's eyes went wide, and awespren burst above him like a ring of smoke. Navani understood that emotion. Watching the Radiants work was like experiencing the intensity of the sun or the majesty of a mountain. Yes, it was becoming commonplace to her, but she doubted it would ever become *common*.

The Mink shut the door with a click, then stepped over to reach a hand into the illusion. A small portion of it wavered and swirled into misty Stormlight. He cocked his head, then walked into the center of the map, which distorted around him, then snapped back into focus after he stilled.

"By Kalak's mighty breath," the Mink said, leaning over to inspect a miniature mountain. "This is incredible."

"The combined powers of a Lightweaver and a Bondsmith," Dalinar said. "It is not a picture of the world as it exists at this moment, unfortunately. We update the map every few days when the highstorm blows through. This limits our ability to count enemy troop numbers, since they tend to move inside for the storm."

"The map gets *that* detailed?" the Mink asked. "You can see individuals?"

Dalinar waved, and a portion of the map expanded. The far perimeters vanished as this specific section became more and more detailed, focusing in on Azimir. The Azish capital expanded from a dot to a full-sized city, then stopped at its best magnification: a scale where buildings were the size of spheres and people were specks.

Dalinar zoomed the map back out to full size and glanced to Shallan. She nodded, and numbers began to hover in the air above portions of the map—swirling and made from Stormlight, marked by glyphs that men could read.

"These are our best estimates of troop numbers," Dalinar said. "Singer counts in gold, our troop counts—which of course are more accurate—in the color of the appropriate army. Divided by glyph, you'll find foot soldiers, heavy infantry, archers, and what few cavalry we can likely field in each area."

The Mink walked through the map and Navani tracked him with her eyes, more interested in him than the numbers. The Mink took his time, inspecting each region of Roshar and its troop concentrations.

As he was thus surveying, the door opened. Navani's daughter—Her Majesty Queen Jasnah Kholin of Alethkar—had arrived. She had four guards; Jasnah never went about alone, though she was more capable with her powers than any other Radiant. She deposited the guards outside the door and entered with only one man shadowing her: the Queen's Wit, tall and lanky, with jet-black hair and an angular face.

It was the same Wit who had served Elhokar, so Navani had known this man for a few years. Yet he was . . . different now. Navani often noted him and Jasnah whispering in conspiratorial tones during meetings. He treated Navani—and, well, everyone—as if he knew them intimately. There was a mystery about this Wit that Navani had never noticed during Elhokar's reign. Perhaps he molded himself to the monarch he served.

He stayed in step right behind Jasnah, silvery-sheathed sword on his hip, his lips drawn ever so slightly to a smile. The type that made you think he must be considering a joke about you that no one had the decency to say to your face.

"I see we have our map," Jasnah said. "And our new general."

"Indeed," said the Mink, who was reading the troop numbers over Azir.

"Thoughts?" Jasnah asked, ever practical.

The Mink continued his inspection. Navani tried to guess what conclusions he'd draw. The war was happening on two main fronts. In Makabak—the region encompassing Azir and the many small kingdoms surrounding it—coalition forces continued to battle the singers over a specific region, the kingdom of Emul. The drawn-out conflicts were only the newest in a series of wars that had left the kingdom—once proud—war-torn and broken.

So far, neither side had an advantage. Azish armies, with the help of Alethi strategists, had recaptured some ground in northern Emul. However, they didn't dare advance too far, as the wildcard of the region might come into play if they reached the south. Nestled behind Odium's forces was the army of Tezim, the god-priest. A man they now knew was Ishar, the ancient Herald gone mad.

Tezim had been quiet lately, unfortunately. Dalinar had hoped he would rage against the rear lines of the singers, forcing them to fight pressed between two armies. As it stood, the brutal fighting in Emul continued at a standstill. The coalition could easily resupply its lines through the Oathgate to the north and Thaylen shipping to the south. The enemy had vast numbers of former parshmen and access to larger numbers of irregulars—Fused, in this case.

The Mink took in the details of this battlefront, studying the shipping and navy numbers with interest. "You control the entire Southern Depths?" he asked.

"The enemy has a navy, stolen from Thaylenah," Jasnah said. "We have only the ships that we've managed to build since then, and the ones that escaped that fate. So our continued dominance is not assured. But following a singular victory by Fen's navy four months ago, the enemy retreated their ships into Iriali waters to the far northwest. Currently, they seem content to control the northern seas while we control the south."

The Mink nodded and moved to the east, inspecting the second of the war's two battlefronts: the line between Alethkar and Jah Keved. Here, Navani's captured homeland made a secure staging base for the enemy, who fought the coalition forces led by Taravangian and Dalinar.

Fighting on this front had mostly been skirmishes along the border. The Fused had so far refused to be caught in any traditional large-scale battles—and much of the border between Alethkar and Jah Keved was difficult terrain, making it easy for roving bands on both sides to raid and then vanish.

Dalinar felt that the coalition would soon need to make a large offensive. Navani agreed. The protracted nature of this war gave the advantage to the enemy. The coalition's Radiant numbers were increasing slowly now, particularly with the honorspren withholding their support. However, the enemy singers—once untrained—were growing into better troops by the day, and more and more Fused were appearing. Dalinar wanted to push into Alethkar and seize the capital.

The Mink trailed through the illusory mountains along the Alethi border. So far, other than raids, Dalinar had focused on seizing control of the southwestern corner of Alethkar—the part that touched the Tarat Sea—to reinforce the coalition's naval superiority in the south. The close proximity of Jah Keved—and the Oathgate in Vedenar—allowed them to field troops here with quick resupply.

It was the sole part of Alethkar they'd reclaimed so far. And it was a long, long way from the capital of Kholinar. Something had to be done. Each day their homeland remained in the enemy's hands was another day for the people there to be beaten down, controlled. Another day for the enemy to further entrench, feeding its armies on the sweat of Alethi farmers.

It was a deep, unyielding kind of pain, thinking of Alethkar and knowing they were essentially a people in exile here in Urithiru. They'd lost their nation, and Dalinar—she knew—blamed himself. He thought if he'd been able to quash the squabbling highprinces and finish the war at the Shattered Plains, Alethkar would not have fallen.

"Yes . . ." the Mink said, squinting at the numbers of Alethi troops near the ocean in southern Alethkar, then glancing back at the Veden armies manning the border. "Yes. Tell me, why do you show me this? This intelligence is precious. You trust me quickly."

"We don't have much choice," Jasnah said, causing him to turn toward her. "Have you followed the recent histories of Alethkar and Jah Keved, General?"

"I have had my own troubles," he said, "but yes. Civil war in both countries."

"Ours was *not* a civil war," Dalinar said.

That was debatable. The rivalry with Sadeas, the contest on the Shattered Plains, the eventual turning of Amaram . . .

"Regardless of what you term it," Jasnah said, "the last few years have been painful for our two kingdoms. Jah Keved lost practically its entire royal family—and most of its best generals—following the assassination of their king. We didn't fare much better. Our command staff has been gutted several times over."

"We are spread thin," Dalinar said. "Many of our best field generals are needed in Azir. When I heard we had a chance to rescue the man who single-handedly held off the singer invasion for a year . . ."

Dalinar strode into the middle of the illusion, and it treated him differently—in subtle ways—from others. The color swirled near him, but the threads of Stormlight reached out, connecting to him. Like the arms of petitioners reaching toward their king.

"I want to know what you see," Dalinar said, sweeping his hand over the map. "I want your analysis on what we're doing. I want your help. In exchange, we will use our forces to recover Herdaz. Help me retake Alethkar, and I will spare no effort in seeing your people freed."

"Having the Blackthorn on my side *would* be novel," the Mink said. "Before I make any promises though, tell me why you have so many troops stationed here, here, and here." He pointed at several fortifications on the southern border of Alethkar, near the ocean.

"We need to hold the ports," Dalinar said.

"Hmm. Yes, I assume that excuse works for the others in your coalition?"

Dalinar drew his lips to a line, glancing at Jasnah. Behind her, Wit raised both eyebrows and leaned against the far wall. He was uncharacteristically quiet in meetings—but one could read entire strings of mockery in his expressions.

"The enemy concentrations are here, across the river," the Mink said, pointing. "If you were truly concerned only with them, you'd fortify directly opposite to prevent a strike when the river runs dry between storms. You don't. Curious. Of course, you'd be exposed from behind. It's almost like you don't trust the one watching your back. . . ."

The much shorter man met Dalinar's gaze and left the words hanging in the air. Wit coughed into his hand.

"I believe Taravangian is working for the enemy," Dalinar said, with a sigh. "One year ago, someone let enemy troops in to attack Urithiru, and—despite excuses and deflections that have convinced the others—I am certain Taravangian's Radiant was the one who did it."

"Dangerous," the Mink said, "fighting in a war where your strongest ally is also your greatest fear. And Radiants, serving the other side? How could this be?"

"They wouldn't be the only ones, unfortunately," Jasnah said. "We've lost one entire order, the Skybreakers, to the enemy—and they have been harrying Azir, requiring us to keep dedicating forces in that region. The Dustbringers continue to flirt with rebellion, often ignoring Dalinar's orders."

"Troubling," the Mink said. He walked up along the border of Alethkar, passing Jasnah. "You amass here as well. You want to push into your homeland, don't you? You seek to recapture Kholinar."

"Delaying will lose us the war," Navani said. "The enemy grows in strength each day."

"I agree with this assessment," the Mink said. "But attacking Alethkar?"

"We want to make a large, powerful offensive," Dalinar explained. "We are trying to persuade the other monarchs to see how vital it is."

"Ah . . ." the Mink said. "Yes, and an outside general—approaching this fresh—would be persuasive to them, wouldn't he?"

"That's the hope," Dalinar said.

"Yet you couldn't help trying to predispose me, eh?" the Mink said. "You wanted to show this to me early, get me on your side first. Not risk any surprises?"

"We've had . . . enough surprises dropped on us in meetings of the monarchs," Navani said.

"I suppose I can't blame you," the Mink said. "Nope. No blame. But a question remains. What do you want from me, you Kholins? Would you prefer a reinforcement of what you already want to believe, or do you seek the truth?"

"I always want the truth," Dalinar said. "And if you know anything of my niece, you'll know she has no qualms stating the truth as she sees it. Regardless of the consequences."

"Yes," the Mink said, looking at Jasnah. "I know of your reputation, Your Majesty. As for the Blackthorn . . . I would not have believed you two years ago." The Mink lifted his finger. "Then my niece read to me your book. The whole thing, yes. We got a copy, which was difficult, and I listened with much interest. I do not trust the Blackthorn, but perhaps I can trust the man who would write the words you did."

He studied Dalinar, as if weighing him. Then the Mink turned and strode across the map. "I can perhaps help you escape this mess. You must not attack Alethkar."

"But—" Dalinar began.

"I agree you need to make an offensive," the Mink said. "However, if

Taravangian is not trustworthy, an expedition into Alethkar now would expose your forces to catastrophe. Even without the danger of betrayal, the enemy is too strong in the area. I've spent time fighting them; I can tell you that their footing is sure in your country. We won't push them out easily, and we certainly can't do it while prosecuting a two-front war."

The Mink stopped in Azir, then pointed toward the fighting in Emul. "Here, you have the enemy pinned between you and a rival force. They're using those Skybreakers to distract you from how exposed they are here. Your enemy is landlocked, with serious supply troubles, isolated from its allies in Iri and Alethkar. You want a big offensive that has a chance to *work*? Reclaim Emul, push the Voidbringers—the singers—out of Makabak.

"You need to consolidate, focus on where the enemy is weakest. You do *not* need to smash your armies into the most fortified enemy position in a reckless attempt to satisfy your wounded Alethi pride. That is the truth."

Navani looked at Dalinar, hating the way the words made him deflate, his shoulders slouching. He wanted so badly to free his homeland.

She was not the tactical genius Dalinar was. She would not have objected if he'd insisted that freeing Alethkar was the correct move. But the way he turned—bowing his head as the Mink spoke—told her he knew the Mink was right.

Perhaps Dalinar had known it already. Perhaps he'd needed to hear it from someone else.

"Let us get you more detailed reports," Jasnah said. "So you can see if the facts support your instincts, Mink."

"Yes, that would be wise," the Mink said. "Many a locked room reveals a hidden path to escape, after all."

"Adolin, if you would, please?" Jasnah asked. "Yes, and you, Shallan. See our guest to the military briefing chambers and give him access to our scribes and any maps from our archive vault. Teshav should be able to provide exact numbers and recent battle data. Study with care, Mink. We meet with the monarchs in a few weeks' time to discuss our next big offensive, and I would have a plan ready."

The Mink bowed to her and retreated with Adolin and Shallan. As soon as he was gone—the map collapsing as Shallan left—Jasnah changed subtly. Her face became less of a mask. She didn't walk with a queenly gait as she strode over and settled down at the room's small table. This was the woman taking off her crown, now that she was with only family.

Family and Wit, Navani thought as the lanky man, dressed all in black, walked over to fetch some wine. She couldn't tell if the rumors about those two were true or not, and hadn't felt comfortable asking. Strange, that a mother should feel so unwilling to chat with her daughter about intimate matters. But . . . well, that was Jasnah.

"I was worried about this," Dalinar said, taking a seat opposite Jasnah at the table. "I need to persuade him that the battle *must* push toward Alethkar."

"Uncle," Jasnah said, "are you going to be stubborn about this?"

"Maybe," he said.

"He saw it almost immediately," Jasnah said. "Taravangian must know we don't trust him. We *can't* strike into Alethkar right now. It hurts me as much as it does you, but . . ."

"I know," Dalinar said, as Navani sat next to him and put her hand on his shoulder. "But I have this *terrible* feeling, Jasnah. It whispers that there *is* no way to win this war. Not against an immortal enemy. I worry about losing, but I worry *more* about something else. What do we do if we force them out of Azir, and they agree to cease hostilities? Would we give up Alethkar, if it meant ending the war?"

"I don't know," Jasnah said. "That seems to be putting our chulls to work before we've bought them. We don't know if such a compromise as you suggest is possible."

"It wouldn't be," Wit said.

Navani frowned, glancing toward the man, who sipped his wine. He walked over and absently handed Jasnah a cup, his beak of a nose hidden in his own cup as he tipped it back.

"Wit?" Dalinar asked. "Is this one of your jokes?"

"Odium is a punch line, Dalinar, but not to any joke you've been told." Wit sat with them at the table, not asking permission. He always acted as if dining with kings and queens was his natural state. "Odium will not compromise. He will not settle for anything other than our complete submission, perhaps destruction."

Dalinar frowned, then glanced to Navani. She shrugged. Wit often spoke like that, as if he knew things he shouldn't. They couldn't tell whether he was pretending or serious—but pressing him usually merely got you ridiculed.

Dalinar wisely remained silent, contemplating the offered tidbit.

"A strong offensive in Emul," Jasnah said thoughtfully. "There might be a gemheart at the center of this monster, Dalinar. A stable Makabak would strengthen our coalition. A clear, powerful victory would raise morale and energize our allies."

"A valid point," Dalinar said, with a grunt.

"There is more," Jasnah said. "A reason to want Azir and the surrounding countries secured in the months moving forward."

"What more?" Dalinar asked. "What are you talking about?"

Jasnah looked to Wit, who nodded, rising. "I'll fetch them. Don't belittle anyone while I'm gone, Brightness. You'll make me feel obsolete." He slipped out the door.

"He will bring the Heralds," Jasnah said. "Until he returns, perhaps we can discuss the proposal I showed you before you left for Hearthstone, Uncle."

Oh dear, Navani thought. *Here we go. . . .* Jasnah had been pushing toward a singular law for Alethkar. A dangerous one.

Dalinar stood up and began to pace. Not a good sign. "This isn't the time, Jasnah. We can't create social upheaval on this scale during such a terrible moment in our history."

"Says the man," Jasnah said, "who wrote a *book* earlier this year. Upending centuries of established gender norms."

Dalinar winced.

"Mother," Jasnah said to Navani, "I thought you said you'd talk to him."

"There wasn't a convenient opportunity," Navani said. "And . . . to be honest, I share his concerns."

"I forbid this," Dalinar said. "You can't simply *free every Alethi slave.* It would cause mass chaos."

"I wasn't aware," Jasnah said, "that you could *forbid* the queen from taking action."

"You called it a proposal," Dalinar said.

"Because I am not finished with the wording yet," Jasnah replied. "I intend to propose it to the highprinces soon and gauge their reactions. I will deal with their concerns as best I can before I make it law. Whether or not I *will* make it law, however, is not a matter I intend to debate."

Dalinar continued to pace. "I cannot see reason in this, Jasnah. The chaos this will cause . . ."

"Our lives are already in chaos," Jasnah said. "This is *precisely* the time to make sweeping changes, when people are already adjusting to a new way of life. The historical data supports this idea."

"But *why?*" Dalinar asked. "You're always so pragmatic. This seems the opposite."

"I seek the line of action that does the most possible good for the most people. This *is* in keeping with my moral philosophy."

Dalinar stopped pacing and rubbed his forehead instead. He looked to Navani as if to say, *Can you do anything?*

"What did you think would happen?" Navani asked. "Putting her on the throne?"

"I thought she'd keep the lighteyes in check," he said. "And figured she wouldn't be bullied by their schemes."

"That is *exactly* what I'm doing," Jasnah said. "Though I apologize for needing to count you in the group, Uncle. It is good for you to oppose me. Feel free to do so visibly. Too many saw Elhokar bending knee to you, and that nasty business with a 'highking' still lingers as a distasteful scent. By showing we are not united in this, we strengthen my position, proving I am no pawn of the Blackthorn."

"I wish you'd slow down," Dalinar said. "I'm not completely opposed to the *theory* of what you're doing. It shows compassion. But . . ."

"If we slow down," Jasnah said, "the past catches up to us. History is like that, always gobbling up the present." She smiled fondly at Dalinar. "I respect and admire your strength, Uncle. I always have. Once in a while though, I *do* think you need to be reminded that not everyone sees the world the way you do."

"It would be better for us all if they did," he grumbled. "I wish the world would stop making a mess of itself every time I turn the other direction."

He got something to drink from the pitcher of wine. Orange, naturally.

"Would this include the ardents, daughter?" Navani asked.

"They're slaves, aren't they?"

"Technically, yes. But in this, some might say you're pursuing a vendetta against the church," Navani said.

"By freeing the ardents from being owned?" Jasnah asked, amused. "Well, I suppose some *will* say that. They'll see an attack in anything I do. Contrastingly, this is for their good. In freeing the ardents, I risk letting the church become a political power in the world again."

"And . . . that doesn't worry you?" Navani asked. Sometimes sorting out this woman's motivations—which she claimed were always very straightforward—was like trying to read the Dawnchant.

"Of course it worries me," Jasnah said. "However, I'd prefer ardents actively participating in politics, as opposed to the behind-the-scenes smoke screen they use now. This will give them more opportunity for power, yes, but also expose their actions to increased public scrutiny."

Jasnah tapped the table with a nail on her freehand. She wore her safehand in a sleeve, eminently proper, though Navani knew Jasnah thought little of social constructs. She followed them anyway. Immaculate makeup. Hair in braids. A beautiful, regal havah.

"This *will* be for the good of Alethkar in the long run," Jasnah said. "Economically and morally. Uncle Dalinar's objections are valuable. I will listen, figure out how to respond to such challenges. . . ."

She trailed off as Wit returned, bringing two individuals with him. One was a beautiful young woman with long black hair, Makabaki in ethnicity, though her eyes and some of her features looked Shin. The other was a tall stoic man, also Makabaki. He was strong, powerful of build, and had a certain regality about him—at least until you saw the distant expression in his eyes and heard him whispering to himself. He needed to be led into the room by the woman, as if he were simple of mind.

One could not have known from a glance that these two were ancient beings older than recorded history. Shalash and Talenelat, Heralds, immortals born to dozens of lives, worshipped as gods by many religions—and as demigods in Navani's own. Sadly, they were both insane. The woman could at least function. The man . . . Navani had never heard anything from him other than mumbles.

Wit treated them with a reverence Navani did not expect from him. He closed the door behind them, then gestured quietly for them to sit at the table. Shalash—Ash, as she preferred to be called—led Talenelat to the seat, but remained standing after he sat.

Navani felt distinctly uncomfortable in their presence. For her entire life, she'd burned glyphwards speaking of these two, praying to the Almighty for their help. She used them in her vows, thought of them in her daily worship. Jasnah had abandoned her faith, and Dalinar . . . she wasn't certain what he believed anymore. It was complicated.

But Navani held to her hope for the Heralds and the Almighty. Hope that they had plans mere mortals could not understand. Seeing these two in such a state . . . it rocked her to the very core. Surely this *was* part of what the Almighty wanted to happen. Surely there *was* a reason for everything. Right?

"Two gods," Wit said, "delivered as requested."

"Ash," Jasnah said. "During our last interview, you were telling me what you knew of my uncle's abilities. The powers of a Bondsmith."

"I told you," the woman snapped, "that I don't know anything." Considering how gently she treated Taln, one might not have expected such terse language from her. Navani, unfortunately, had come to accept it as normal.

"What you told me was useful," Jasnah said. "Kindly repeat it."

Dalinar walked over, curious. Jasnah held weekly meetings with the Heralds, trying to pry every bit of historical knowledge from their minds. She'd claimed the meetings were mostly fruitless, but Navani knew to hang on to the word "mostly" when coming from Jasnah. She could hide a great deal in the spaces between those letters.

Ash sighed loudly, pacing. Not in thought as Dalinar had, but in a way reminiscent of a caged animal. "I didn't know anything of what the Bondsmiths did. That was always Ishar's purview. My father would occasionally discuss matters of deep Realmatic Theory with him—but I didn't care for it. Why should I? Ishar had it in hand."

"He forged the Oathpact," Jasnah said. "The . . . binding that made you immortal and trapped the Voidbringers in another realm of reality."

"Braize isn't another realm of reality," Ash said. "It's a planet. You can see it in the sky, along with Ashyn—the Tranquiline Halls, you call it. But yeah, the Oathpact. He did that. We all simply went along with it." She shrugged.

Jasnah nodded, showing no sign of annoyance. "But the Oathpact no longer functions?"

"It's broken," Ash said. "Done, shattered, upended. They killed my father a year ago. Permanently, somehow. We all felt it." She looked directly at Navani, as if having seen the reverence in her eyes. The next words came with a sneer. "We can do *nothing* for you now. There is no more Oathpact."

"And do you think Dalinar," Jasnah asked, "as a Bondsmith, could repair or replicate it somehow? Sealing the enemy away?"

"Who knows?" Ash said. "It doesn't work the same for you all as it did for us, when we had our swords. You're limited, but sometimes you do things we couldn't. At any rate, I never knew much about it."

"But there are some who know, aren't there?" Jasnah said. "A group of people who have practice with Surgebinding? Who experimented with it, who know about Dalinar's powers?"

"Yeah," Ash said.

"The Shin," Navani said, understanding Jasnah's point. "They hold the Honorblades. Szeth says they trained with them, knew their abilities. . . ."

"Scouts sent to Shinovar vanish," Dalinar said. "Windrunner flybys prompt storms of arrows. They don't want anything to do with us."

"For now," Jasnah said, looking at Ash. "Right?"

"They are . . . unpredictable," the Herald said. "I eventually left them behind. They tried to kill me, but that I could take. It was when they started to worship me . . ." Ash crossed her arms, pulling them tight. "They had legends . . . prophecies about the coming of this Return. I didn't believe it would ever happen. Didn't want to believe."

"We need a stable region in Makabak, Uncle," Jasnah said. "Because eventually, we're going to have to deal with the Shin. And at the very least, we will want to find out what they know about Bondsmiths from centuries of holding an Honorblade and experimenting with powers like yours."

Dalinar turned to Navani. She nodded. There was something here. If they could find a way to seal the Fused away again . . . well, that could mean the end of the war.

"You make an interesting point," Dalinar said.

"Excellent," Jasnah said. "If we do bring a large offensive into Emul, then I will attend personally and join the war effort there."

". . . You will?" Dalinar said. "And how . . . involved do you intend to be in the prosecution of the war?"

"As involved as seems appropriate."

He sighed, and Navani knew what he was thinking. If Jasnah tried to join in wartime planning and strategy too forcefully, the highprinces wouldn't like it. But Dalinar couldn't complain, not after what he'd done.

"We'll deal with that if it becomes a problem, I suppose." The Blackthorn turned toward the Herald. "Ash, tell me more of what you know about the Shin—specifically the ones among them who might know more about my powers."

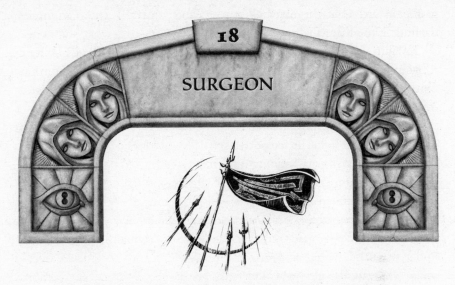

18

SURGEON

The Fused have a second metal I find fascinating—a metal that conducts Stormlight. The implications for this in the creation of fabrials are astounding. The Fused use this metal in conjunction with a rudimentary fabrial—a simple gemstone, but without a spren trapped inside.

How they pull Stormlight out of a Radiant and into this sphere remains baffling. My scholars think they must be employing an Investiture differential. If a gemstone is full of Stormlight—or, I assume, Voidlight—and that Light is removed quickly, it creates a pressure differential (or a kind of vacuum) in the gemstone.

This remains merely a theory.

—Lecture on fabrial mechanics presented by Navani Kholin
to the coalition of monarchs, Urithiru, Jesevan, 1175

Kaladin stood on the edge of an Oathgate platform, overlooking the mountains. That frigid landscape of snow was an otherworldly sight. Before Urithiru, he'd seen snow on only a handful of occasions, in small patches at sunrise. Here the snow was thick and deep, pristine and pure white.

Is Rock looking at a similar landscape right now? Kaladin wondered. Rock's family, Skar, and Drehy had left nearly four weeks ago. They'd sent word a single time via spanreed, soon after their departure, noting that they'd arrived.

He worried about Rock, and knew he'd never *stop* worrying. The details of the trip though . . . well, those weren't Kaladin's problems any longer. They were Sigzil's. In a perfect world, Teft would have become companylord—but the older Windrunner had given Kaladin a tongue-lashing at the mere suggestion.

Kaladin sighed and walked over to the Oathgate's control building at the center of the plateau. Here, a scribe nodded to him. She had confirmed with the Oathgate on the Shattered Plains that it was safe to initiate a transfer.

He did so, using the Sylblade in the lock on the wall of the small building. In a flash of light, he teleported to the Shattered Plains—and seconds later he was soaring via Lashing into the sky.

The Windrunners weren't making a fuss about him "stepping back." They likely assumed he'd be moving on to become a strategic or logistics general. It happened to most battlefield commanders eventually. He hadn't yet told them he planned to do something else—though he had to decide today what that would be. Dalinar still wanted him to become an ambassador. But could Kaladin really spend his days in political negotiations? No, he'd be as awkward as a horse in a uniform standing in a ballroom and trying not to step on women's dresses.

The idea was silly. But what *would* he do?

He reached a good height, then soared in an invigorating loop, Lashing without conscious thought. His powers were becoming as intuitive as wiggling his fingers. Syl zipped alongside him, laughing as she met a couple of windspren.

I'll miss this, he thought, then immediately felt foolish. He wasn't dying. He was retiring. He would still fly. To pretend otherwise was self-pity. Facing this change with dignity was difficult, but he *would* do it.

He spotted something in the distance, and soared toward it. Navani's flying platform was finally reaching the Plains. The front of the top deck was packed with faces, gawking at the landscape.

Kaladin alighted on the deck, returning the salutes from the Windrunners left to guard the ship. "I'm sorry the trip took so long," he told the gathering refugees. "At least it's given us plenty of time to get things ready for you."

◆◆

"We've begun organizing the tower by neighborhoods," Kaladin said an hour later as he led his parents through Urithiru's deep hallways. He held aloft a large sapphire for light. "It's difficult to keep a sense of community in here, with so many hallways looking alike. You can get turned around easily, start to feel like you're living in a pit."

Lirin and Hesina followed, entranced by the multicolored strata in the walls, the high ceilings, the general majesty of an enormous tower carved completely from stone.

"We originally organized the tower by princedom," Kaladin continued. "Each of the Alethi highprinces was assigned a section of a given floor. Navani didn't like how that turned out; we weren't using as much of the rim of the tower—with its natural light—as she wanted. It often meant crowding large numbers of people into vast rooms that clearly hadn't been designed as living spaces, since the highprinces wanted to keep their people close."

He ducked under a strange outcropping of stone in the hallway. Urithiru had numerous such oddities; this one was round, a stone tube crossing the center of the hallway. Perhaps it was ventilation? Why had it been put right where people walked?

Many other features of the tower defied logic. Hallways dead-ended. Rooms were discovered with no way in save tiny holes to peek through. Small shafts were discovered plummeting down thirty or more stories. One might have called the arrangement mad, but even at its most baffling, hints of design—such as crystal veins running along the corners of rooms, or places where strata wove to form patterns reminiscent of glyphs set into the wall—made Kaladin think this place was purposeful and not haphazard. These oddities had been built for reasons they couldn't yet fathom.

His parents ducked under the obstruction. They'd left Kaladin's brother with Laral's children and their governess. She seemed to be recovering from the loss of her husband, though Kaladin thought he knew her well enough to see through the front. She truly seemed to have *cared* for the old blowhard, as had her children, a solemn pair of twins far too withdrawn for their young age.

Under Jasnah's new inheritance laws, Laral would gain the title of city-lady, so she'd gone to be formally greeted by Jasnah. While the rest of the people received an orientation to the tower via Navani's scribes, Kaladin wanted to show his parents where the people of Hearthstone would be housed.

"You're quiet," Kaladin said to them. "I suppose this place can be stunning at first. I know I felt that way. Navani keeps saying we don't know the half of what it can do."

"It is spectacular," his mother said. "Though I'm a little *more* stunned to hear you referring to Brightness Navani Kholin by her first name. Isn't she queen of this tower?"

Kaladin shrugged. "I've grown more informal with them as I've gotten to know them."

"He's lying," Syl said in a conspiratorial tone from where she sat on

Hesina's shoulder. "He's *always* talked like that. Kaladin called King Elhokar by his name for *ages* before becoming a Radiant."

"Disrespectful of lighteyed authority," Hesina said, "and generally inclined to do whatever he wants, regardless of social class or traditions. Where in Roshar did he get it?" She glanced at Kaladin's father, who stood by the wall inspecting the lines of strata.

"I can't possibly imagine," Lirin said. "Bring that light closer, son. Look here, Hesina. These strata are *green*. That can't be natural."

"Dear," she said, "the fact that the wall is part of a tower roughly the size of a mountain didn't clue you in to the fact that this place isn't natural?"

"It must have been Soulcast in this shape," Lirin said, tapping the stone. "Is that jade?"

Kaladin's mother leaned in to inspect the green vein. "Iron," she said. "Makes the stone turn that shade."

"Iron?" Syl said. "Iron is grey though, isn't it?"

"Yes," Lirin said. "It should be copper that makes the rock green, shouldn't it?"

"You'd think that, wouldn't you?" Hesina said. "I'm pretty sure that's not how it works. In any case, maybe we should let Kal show us on to the prepared rooms. He's obviously excited."

"How can you tell?" Syl asked. "I don't think he *ever* gets excited. Not even when I tell him I have a fun surprise for him."

"Your surprises," Kaladin said, "are never fun."

"I put a rat in his boot," Syl whispered. "It took me *forever*. I can't lift something so heavy, so I had to lead it with food."

"Why in the Stormfather's name," Lirin said, "would you put a *rat* in his *boot*?"

"Because it *fit so well*!" Syl said. "How can you not see how great the idea was?"

"Lirin surgically removed his sense of humor," Hesina said.

"Got good money for it on the open market too," Lirin said.

Hesina leaned in close to Syl. "He replaced it with a clock, which he uses to monitor exactly how much time everyone else wastes with their silly emotions."

Syl looked at her, smiling hesitantly—and Kaladin could tell she wasn't quite certain it was a joke. When Hesina nodded encouragingly, Syl let out a genuine laugh.

"Now, let's not get ridiculous," Lirin said. "I don't need a clock to monitor how much time everyone wastes. It's evident that number is nearly a hundred percent."

Kaladin leaned against the wall, feeling a familiar peace at their banter.

Once, having them close again would have been nearly everything he wanted. Watching Lirin obsess. Hearing Hesina trying to get him to pay attention to the people around him. The fond way Lirin took the jokes, playing into them by being comically stern.

It reminded Kaladin of days spent at the dinner table, or gathering medicinal herbs from the cultivated patches outside of town. He cherished those pastoral memories. Part of him wished he could simply be their little boy again—wished they didn't have to intersect with his current life, where they would undoubtedly start hearing of the things he'd endured and done. The things that eventually had broken him.

He turned and continued down the hallway. A steady light ahead told him they were approaching the outer wall. Molten sunlight, open and inviting. The cold Stormlight sphere in his hand represented power, but a secretive, angry sort. Inspect gem light, and you could see it shifting, storming, trying to break free. Sunlight represented something more free, more open.

Kaladin entered a new hallway, where the strata lines on the walls turned downward in a fanning pattern—like lapping waves. Sunlight poured in through doorways on the right.

Kaladin pointed as his parents caught up to him. "Each of these rooms on the right leads to a large balcony, extending all along the rim here. Laral will get that corner room, which is the largest, with a private balcony. I thought we'd reserve the ten here in the center and make them a meeting area. The rooms are connected, and some of the other neighborhoods have made their balcony section a large common space."

He continued forward, passing the rooms—which contained stacks of blankets, planks for making furniture, and sacks of grain. "We can put chairs in there and have a communal kitchen," he said. "It's easier than trying to find a way for everyone to cook on their own. Firewood—from the rockbud farms on the Plains—needs to be carted in through the Oathgate, so it's on a strict ration. There's a functioning well on this level not too far away though, so you won't lack for water.

"I'm not sure yet what everyone's duties will be. As you probably noticed flying in, Dalinar has started large-scale farming operations out on the Shattered Plains. That might require relocation, but we also might be able to get things growing up here. That's part of how I persuaded Dalinar to let me fetch everyone from Hearthstone—we have a lot of soldiers, but surprisingly few people who know their way around a lavis field during worming season."

"And those rooms?" Hesina asked, pointing down an inward hallway lined with openings.

"Each is big enough for a family," Kaladin said. "Those don't have any natural light, I'm afraid, but there are two hundred of them—enough for everyone. I'm sorry I had to put you all the way up here on the sixth floor. That's going to mean either waiting for lifts, or taking the stairs. It's the only way I could find you a spot with balcony rooms. It's still pretty low I guess—I feel bad for whoever has to eventually start living up in those high floors."

"It's wonderful," Hesina said.

Kaladin waited for Lirin to say something, but he simply walked into one of the balcony rooms. He passed the supplies and stepped out onto the large balcony, glancing upward.

He doesn't like it, Kaladin thought. Of course Lirin would find something to complain about, even after being handed enviable quarters in the mythical city of the Epoch Kingdoms.

Kaladin joined him, following his father's gaze as Lirin turned and tried to look up at the tower, though the balcony above got in the way.

"What's at the top?" Lirin asked.

"Meeting rooms for the Radiants," Kaladin said. "There's nothing on the very top—just a flat roof. The view is great though. I'll show it to you sometime."

"Enough chatting!" Syl said. "Come on. Follow me!" She zipped off Hesina's shoulder and darted through the rooms. When the humans didn't immediately follow, she flew over, whirled around Hesina's head, then shot back out. "Come *on.*"

They followed, Kaladin trailing his parents as Syl led them through the several balcony rooms he imagined becoming a large meeting area, with a wonderful view out over the mountains. A little chilly, but a large fabrial hearth acting as the communal oven would help greatly.

At the other end of the connected balcony chambers was a large suite of six rooms, with their own washrooms and a private balcony. It was the mirror of Laral's at the other end. These two seemed to have been built for officers and their families, so Kaladin had reserved it for a special purpose.

Syl led them through a front room, down a hallway past two closed doors, and into a main sitting room. "We spent *all week* getting it ready!" she said, darting around this chamber. The far wall had a set of stone shelves full of books. He'd spent a large chunk of his monthly stipend to acquire them. As a youth, he'd often felt bad for how few books his mother had.

"I didn't know there were so many books in the world," Syl said. "Won't they use up all the words? Seems like eventually you'd say everything that could be said!" She zipped over to a smaller side room. "There's a space for the baby here, and *I* picked out the toys, because Kaladin would probably have bought him a spear or something dumb. Oh! And over here!"

She whirled past them, into the hallway again. Kaladin's parents followed, and he shadowed them. At Syl's prompting, Lirin opened one of the doors in the hallway, revealing a fully stocked surgery room. Exam table. A glistening set of the finest instruments, including equipment Kaladin's father had never been able to afford: scalpels, a device for listening to a patient's heartbeat, a magnificent fabrial clock, a fabrial heating plate for boiling bandages or cleansing surgical tools.

Kaladin's father stepped into the room, while Hesina stood in the doorway, hand to her mouth in amazement, a shockspren—like shattering pieces of yellow light—adorning her. Lirin picked up several of the tools, one at a time, then began inspecting the various jars of ointment, powder, and medication Kaladin had stocked on the shelf.

"I ordered in the best from Taravangian's physicians," Kaladin said. "You'll need to have Mother read to you about some of these newer medications—they're discovering some remarkable things at the hospitals in Kharbranth. They say they've found a way to infect people with a weak, easily overcome version of a disease—which leaves them immune for life to more harsh variants."

Lirin seemed . . . solemn. More than normal. Despite Hesina's jokes, Lirin did laugh—he had emotions. Kaladin had seen them from him frequently. To have him respond to all of this with such quietude . . .

He hates it, Kaladin thought. *What did I do wrong?*

Oddly, Lirin sat and slumped in one of the nearby seats. "It is very nice, son," he said softly. "But I don't see the use of it anymore."

"What?" Kaladin asked. "Why?"

"Because of what those Radiants can do," Lirin said. "I saw them *healing* with a touch! A simple gesture from an Edgedancer can seal cuts, even regrow limbs. This is wonderful, son, but . . . but I don't see a use for surgeons any longer."

Hesina leaned in to Kaladin. "He's been moping about this the whole trip," she whispered.

"I'm *not* moping," Lirin said. "To be sad about such a major revolution in healing would be not only callous, but selfish as well. It's just . . ." Lirin took a deep breath. "I guess I'll need to find something else to do."

Storms. Kaladin knew that *exact* emotion. That loss. That worry. That sudden feeling of becoming a burden.

"Father," Kaladin said, "we have fewer than *fifty* Edgedancers—and just three Truthwatchers. Those are the only orders that can heal."

Lirin looked up, cocking his head.

"We brought over a dozen with us to save Hearthstone," Kaladin said, "because Dalinar wanted to be certain our new flying platform didn't fall to the enemy. Most of the time those Edgedancers are serving on the battlefront, healing soldiers. The few on duty in Urithiru can be used for only the most dire of wounds.

"Plus their powers have limitations. They can't do anything for old wounds, for example. We have a large clinic in the market staffed by ordinary surgeons, and it's busy all hours of the day. You're not obsolete. Trust me, you're going to be very, very useful here."

Lirin regarded the room again, seeing it with new eyes. He grinned, then—possibly thinking he shouldn't take joy in the idea that people would still need surgeons—stood up. "Well then! I suppose I *should* familiarize myself with this new equipment. Medications that can *prevent* diseases, you say? What an intriguing concept."

Kaladin's mother gave him an embrace, then went into the other room to look over the books. Kaladin finally let himself relax, settling into a chair in the surgery room.

Syl landed on his shoulder and took the form of a young woman in a full havah, with her hair pinned up in the Alethi fashion. She folded her arms and glared up at him expectantly.

"What?" he asked.

"You going to tell them?" she said. "Or do I have to?"

"Now's not the time."

"Why not?"

He failed to come up with a good reason. She kept bullying him with her frustratingly insistent spren stare—she didn't blink unless she pointedly decided to, so he'd never met anyone else who could glare quite like Syl. Once she'd even enlarged her eyes to disturbing proportions to deliver a particularly important point.

Eventually Kaladin stood, causing her to streak off as a ribbon of light. "Father," he said. "You need to know something."

Lirin turned from his study of the medications, and Hesina peeked her head into the room, curious.

"I'm going to be leaving the military," Kaladin said. "I need a break from the fighting, and Dalinar commanded it. So I thought maybe I would take the room beside Oroden's. I . . . might need to find something different to do with my life."

Hesina raised her hand to her lips again. Lirin stopped dead, going pale, as if he'd seen a Voidbringer. Then his face burst with the widest grin Kaladin had ever seen on him. He strode over and seized Kaladin by the arms.

"That's what this is about, isn't it?" Lirin said. "The surgery room, the supplies, that talk of the clinic. You've realized it. You *finally* understand that I've been right. You're going to become a surgeon like we always dreamed!"

"I . . ."

That was the answer, of course. The one Kaladin had been purposely avoiding. He'd considered the ardents, he'd considered the generals, and he'd considered running away.

The answer was in the face of his father, a face that a part of Kaladin dreaded. Deep down, Kaladin had known there was only one place he could go once the spear was taken from him.

"Yes," Kaladin said. "You're right. You've always been right, Father. I guess . . . it's time to continue my training."

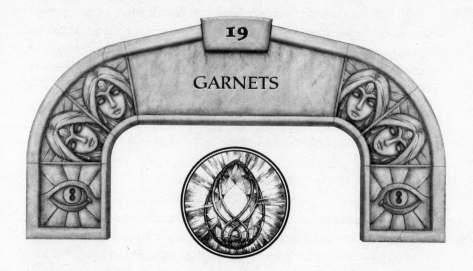

*The world becomes an increasingly dangerous place, and so I come
to the crux of my argument. We cannot afford to keep secrets from
one another any longer. The Thaylen artifabrians have private
techniques relating to how they remove Stormlight from gems
and create fabrials around extremely large stones.*

*I beg the coalition and the good people of Thaylenah to
acknowledge our collective need. I have taken the first step by
opening my research to all scholars.*

I pray you will see the wisdom in doing the same.

—Lecture on fabrial mechanics presented by Navani Kholin
to the coalition of monarchs, Urithiru, Jesevan, 1175

I'm sorry, Brightness," Rushu said, holding up several schematics as they
walked around the crystalline pillar deep within Urithiru. "Weeks of
study, and I can't find any other matches."

Navani sighed, pausing beside a particular section of the pillar. Four
garnets stood out, the same construction used in the suppression fabrial.
The layouts were too precise, too exact, to be a coincidence.

It had seemed like a breakthrough, and she'd set Rushu and the others
comparing all other known fabrials to the pillar, searching for any that
seemed similar. That once-promising lead, unfortunately, had reached another dead end.

"There's another problem," Rushu said.

"Only one?" When the young ardent frowned, Navani waved for her to
continue. "What is it?"

"We inspected the suppression fabrial in Shadesmar, as you asked," Rushu said. "Your theory is correct, it manifests a spren in Shadesmar as Soulcasters do. But on this side, there is no sign of that spren in the gemstones."

"What's the problem, then?" Navani asked. "My theory is correct."

"Brightness, the spren that runs the suppression device . . . has been corrupted, very similar to . . ."

"To Renarin's spren," Navani said.

"Indeed. The spren refused to talk to us, but didn't seem as insensate as the ones in Soulcasters. This reinforces your theory that ancient fabrials—things like the pumps, the Oathgates, and the Soulcasters—somehow imprisoned their spren in the Cognitive Realm. When we pressed it, the spren closed its eyes pointedly. It seems to be working with the enemy deliberately, which raises questions about your nephew's spren. Dare we trust it?"

"We have no reason to assume that one spren serving the enemy means all of its type do," Navani said. "We should assume they each have individual loyalties, like humans."

She had to admit, however, that Renarin's spren made her uncomfortable. Seeing the future? Well, she had already tied her mind in knots thinking about Glys. Instead, she tried to focus on the nature of this fabrial's spren.

You capture spren, the strange person had said to her via spanreed. *You imprison them. Hundreds of them. You are a monster. You must stop.*

Weeks had passed without a quiver from the spanreed. Was it possible this person knew how to create fabrials the old way, which appeared to use *sapient* spren, locking them in the Cognitive Realm? Perhaps this method was preferable and more humane. The magnificent spren that controlled the Oathgates didn't seem to begrudge their attachment to the devices, for example, and were fully capable of interacting.

"For now, study this," Navani said to Rushu, tapping her knuckles against the majestic gemstone pillar. "See if you can find a way to activate this specific group of garnets. In the past, the tower was protected from the Fused. Old writings agree on this fact. This part of the pillar must be why."

"Yes . . ." Rushu said. "A fine theory, and a fine suggestion. If we focus on this one piece of the pillar, which we know is a distinct fabrial, maybe we can activate it."

"Also try resetting the suppression fabrial we stole. It smothered *Kaladin's* abilities, but let the Fused use *their* powers. There might be a way to reverse the device's effects."

Rushu nodded in her absentminded way. Navani continued to stare up at the pillar, which sparkled with the light of a thousand facets. What was she missing? Why couldn't she activate it?

She handed the schematic to Rushu and began walking from the room. "We haven't been giving enough thought to the tower's security," she said. "Clearly the ancients were worried about incursions by the Fused—and we experienced one already."

"The Oathgates are under constant guard now," Rushu said, hurrying to keep up. "And authentication by two different orders of Radiants is required for activation. It seems unlikely the enemy could do what they did before."

"Yes, but what if they came in another way?" The spren she'd interviewed claimed that the Masked Ones—Fused with Lightweaving powers— couldn't enter the tower. Its ancient protections had some lingering effects, like the changes in pressure or the warmth. Indeed, this seemed proven, as while Masked Ones sometimes slipped into human camps, they had never come to Urithiru.

At least so far as Navani could tell. Perhaps they'd just been very careful. "The enemy," Navani said to Rushu, "has abilities we can only guess at—and the powers we do know about are dangerous enough. Masked Ones could be among us and we'd never know it. You or I could be one of them right now."

"That . . . is a highly disturbing thought, Brightness," Rushu said. "What could we possibly do? Other than fixing the tower's defenses."

"Gather a team of our best abstract thinkers. Assign them the task of creating protocols to identify hidden Fused."

"Understood," Rushu said. "Dali would be perfect for that. Oh, and Sebasinar, and . . ." She slowed, pulling out her notebook, oblivious to how she was standing in the middle of the corridor, forcing people to step around her.

Navani smiled fondly, but left Rushu to her task, instead turning right and entering one of the ancient "library" rooms. When first studying the tower, they'd found dozens of gemstones in this room, all encoded with short messages from the ancient Knights Radiant.

Over the months, the room had transformed from a dedicated study of those gemstones into a laboratory where Navani had organized her finest engineers. She had been around enough intelligent people to know they worked best in an encouraging environment where study and discovery were rewarded.

Inside this room, concentrationspren moved like ripples in the sky, and a few logicspren—like little stormclouds—hovered in the air. Engineers worked on dozens of projects: some practical designs, others more fanciful.

As soon as she stepped in, an excited young engineer scrambled up. "Brightness!" he said. "It's working!"

"That's wonderful," she said, struggling to remember his name. Young, bald, barely a beard to speak of. What project had he been on?

He grabbed her by the arm and towed her to the side, ignoring propriety. She didn't mind. It was a mark of pride to her that so many of the engineers forgot she was anything other than the person who funded their projects.

She spotted Falilar at the worktable, and that jogged her memory. The young ardent was his nephew, Tomor, a darkeyed youth who wanted to follow his uncle's path of scholarship. She'd assigned the two one of her more serious designs, a set of new lifts that worked on the same principle as the flying platform.

"Brightness," Falilar said, bowing to her. "The design requires a great deal more tweaking. I fear it's going to require too much manpower to be efficient."

"But it's working?" Navani said.

"Yes!" Tomor said, bringing her a device shaped like a jewelry box, around six inches square, with a handle on one side. The handle—like the one you might use to pull open a drawer—held a trigger for the index finger on the inside. A button on the top was the box's only other feature, except for a set of straps that she took for a wrist brace.

Navani accepted the box and peeked in through the access panel. There were two separate fabrial constructions inside. One she recognized for a simple conjoining ruby, like those used in spanreeds. The other was more experimental, a practical application of the designs she'd given Tomor and Falilar: a device for redirecting force, and for quickly engaging or disengaging alignment with the conjoined fabrial.

It wasn't exactly the same method that kept the *Fourth Bridge* flying. It was more a cousin to that technology.

"We decided to make the prototype an individual device," Falilar said, "as you wanted something portable."

"Here!" Tomor said. "Let me get the workers ready!" He scrambled over to a couple of soldiers at the side of the room, assigned to run errands for the engineers. Tomor got them into position holding a rope, like they were about to engage in a tug-of-war—only instead of a rival team on the other end, their rope was attached to a different fabrial box on the floor.

"Go ahead, Brightness!" Tomor said. "Point your box to the side, then conjoin the rubies!"

Navani strapped the device to her wrist, then swung her arm around, pointing it to the side. Right now, the rubies weren't conjoined, allowing the box to move freely. Once she pressed the button, however, the device snapped into conjoinment with the second box, the one on the floor attached to the rope.

Next, she pulled the trigger with her index finger. This made the ruby flash brightly for the soldiers, who began pulling their rope. They moved their box along the floor, and the force was transferred across the space to Navani. And she was yanked—by the box and handle strapped to her wrist—steadily across the room.

It was a common application of conjoined fabrials. The big difference here was not in the fact that force was being transferred, but the *direction* of the transfer. The men were pulling the box backward along the wall, moving steadily eastward. Navani was being pulled forward along the axis where she'd pointed her arm—a random direction south by southwest.

She flashed the light to warn the soldiers, then disjoined the fabrials, so she stopped skidding. The men were ready for this, and prepared as she pointed her hand in a different direction. When she conjoined again and flashed the ruby for the men, they began pulling—and she moved that way instead.

"It's working wonderfully," Navani said, skidding on her heels. "The ability to redirect the force in any direction—on the fly—is going to have huge practical applications."

"Yes, Brightness," Falilar said, walking beside her, "I agree—but the manpower issue *is* a serious one. It already requires the work of hundreds to keep the *Fourth Bridge* in the air and moving. How many more can we spare?"

Fortunately, that was the exact problem Navani had been trying to solve. *This* is *working*, she thought with excitement, turning off the fabrial, then having the men pull her in a third direction. Making the *Fourth Bridge* rise into the air had not been terribly difficult—the truly hard part had been getting it to move laterally after raising it into the air.

The secret to making the *Fourth Bridge* fly—and to making this hand-held device work—involved a rare metal called aluminum. It was what the Fused used for weapons that could block Shardblades, but the metal didn't just interfere with Shardblades—it interfered with *all kinds* of Stormlight mechanics. Interactions with it during the expedition into Aimia earlier in the year had led Navani to order experiments, and Falilar himself had made the breakthrough.

The trick was to use a specific fabrial cage, made from aluminum, around the conjoined rubies. The details were complicated, but with the proper caging, an artifabrian could make a conjoined ruby *ignore* motion made by the other along specific vectors or planes. So, in application, the *Fourth Bridge* could use two different dummy ships to move. One to go up and down, the other to go laterally.

The complexities of that excited Navani and her engineers, and had led to the new device she now wore. She could move her arm in any direction she wanted, conjoin the fabrial, then direct force through it in a specific direction.

Momentum and energy were conserved per natural conjoined fabrial mechanics. Her scientists had tested this a hundred different ways, and some applications quickly drained the fabrial—but they'd known about those from ancient experiments. Still, there were thoughts whirring in her head. There were ways they could use this to directly translate *Stormlight* energy into *mechanical* energy.

And she'd been thinking of other ways to replace the manpower needs. . . .

"Brightness?" Falilar said. "You seem concerned. I'm sorry if the device has more problems than you expected. It's an early iteration."

"Falilar, you worry too much," Navani said. "The device is amazing."

"But . . . the manpower problem . . ."

Navani smiled. "Come with me."

∴

A short time later, Navani led Falilar into a section of the twentieth floor of the tower. Here she had another team working—though this one was made up of more laborers and fewer engineers. They'd located a strange shaft, one of many odd features of the tower. This one plummeted through the tower past its basements, eventually connecting to a cavern deep beneath.

Though the original purpose of it baffled their surveyors and scientists, Navani had a plan for the shaft. It had involved setting up several steel weights here, each as heavy as three men, suspended on ropes.

She nodded to the workers as they bowed, several holding up sphere lanterns for her and the ardents as they stepped up to the deep hole, which was a good six feet across. Navani peered over the side, and Falilar joined her, gripping the railing with nervous fingers.

"How far down does it go?" he asked.

"Far past the basement," Navani said, holding up the box he had constructed. "Let's say that, instead of men pulling a rope, we bolted the other half of this fabrial to one of these weights. Then we could connect the device's trigger to these pulleys at the top—so that the trigger dropped the weight."

"You'd get your arm pulled off!" Falilar said. "You'd be yanked hard in whatever direction you've pointed the device."

"Resistance on the pulley line could modulate the initial force," Navani said. "Maybe we could make it so the strength of the trigger pull determines how fast the line is let out—and how fast you are propelled."

"A clever application," Falilar said, wiping his brow as he glanced at the dark shaft. "It doesn't do anything about the manpower issue though. Someone has to get those weights back up here."

"Captain?" Navani asked the soldier leading the crew on this floor.

"The windmills have been set up as requested," the man said—he was missing an arm, the right sleeve of his uniform sewn up. Dalinar was always on the lookout for ways to keep his wounded officers involved in the important work of the war effort. "I'm told they're rated for storms, though of course no device can be perfectly protected in a highstorm."

"What's this?" Falilar asked.

"Windmills inside steel casings," Navani said, "with gemstones on the blades—each one conjoined with a ruby on the pulley system up above. The storm blows, and these five weights are ratcheted to the top, potential energy stored for later use."

"Ah . . ." Falilar said. "Brightness, I see. . . ."

"Every few days," Navani said, "the storms gift us an enormous outpouring of kinetic strength. Winds that level forests; lightning as bright as the sun." She patted one of the ropes with the weights. "We simply need to find a way to store that energy. *This* could power a fleet of ships. Enough pulleys, weights, and windmills . . . and we could fly an air force around the world, all using the harnessed energy of the highstorms."

"How . . ." Falilar said, his eyes alight. "How do we make this happen, Brightness? What can I do?"

"Testing," she said, "and iterations. We need systems that can withstand the strain of repeated use. We need more flexibility, more streamlining. Your device here. Can you install a switching mechanism so we can move between fabrials on these five weights? A lift that could go up five times before needing to be recharged is far more useful than one that can go up only once."

"Yes . . ." he said. "And we could use the weight of people traveling back down to help recharge some of the weights. . . . Do you want us to make true lifts, or continue with the personal lift device, as Tomor designed? He's excited by the idea. . . ."

"Do both," Navani suggested. "Let him continue on the single-person device, but suggest he shape it like a crossbow you point somewhere, rather than a box with a handle. Make it look interesting, and people will be more interested. One of the tricks of fabrial science."

"Yes . . . I see, Brightness."

She checked the clock she wore in the fabrial housing on her left arm. Storms. It was almost time for the meeting of monarchs. It wouldn't do for her to be late after the number of times she'd chided Dalinar for ignoring his clock.

"See where your imagination takes you," she repeated to Falilar. "You've spent years building bridges to span chasms. Let's learn how to span the sky."

"It will be done," he said, taking the box. "This is genius, Brightness. Truly."

She smiled. They liked to say that, and she appreciated the sentiment. The truth was, she merely knew how to harness the genius of others—as she was hoping to harness the storm.

⁙

She arrived at the meeting with time to spare, fortunately. It was held in a chamber near the top of the tower, where Dalinar had made each monarch carry their own seat months ago.

She remembered the tension of those initial meetings, each member speaking carefully—anxiously, as if a whitespine slumbered nearby. These days, the room was loud and full of chatter. She knew most of the ministers and functionaries by name, and asked after their families. She caught sight of Dalinar chatting amiably with Queen Fen and Kmakl.

It was remarkable. In another time, a united coalition of Alethi, Veden, Thaylen, and Azish forces would have been the most incredible thing to have happened in generations. Unfortunately, it was only possible in response to greater marvels—and threats.

Still, she couldn't help feeling optimistic as she chatted. Right up until she turned around and came face-to-face with Taravangian.

The kindly-looking old man had regrown his wispy beard and mustache— of a style that was reminiscent of old scholars from ancient paintings. One might easily imagine this robed figure as some guru sitting in a shrine, pontificating about the nature of storms and the souls of men.

"Ah, Brightness," he said. "I have yet to congratulate you on the success of your flying ship. I am eager to see the schematics once you feel comfortable sharing them."

Navani nodded. Gone was the feigned innocence, the pretended stupidity, that Taravangian had maintained for so long. A lesser man might have persisted stubbornly in his lies. To his credit, once the Assassin in White had joined Dalinar, Taravangian had dropped the act and immediately slipped into a new role: that of a political genius.

"How go the troubles at home, Taravangian?" Navani asked.

"We have reached agreements," Taravangian said. "As I suspect you already know, Brightness. I have chosen my new heir from Veden stock, ratified by the highprinces, and made provisions for Kharbranth to go to my daughter. For now, the Vedens see the truth: We cannot squabble over details during an invasion."

"That is well," she said, trying—and failing—to keep the coldness from her voice. "A pity we don't have access to the military minds of the Veden elite, not to mention their best young soldiers. All sent to their graves in a pointless civil war mere months before the coming of the Everstorm."

"Do you think, Brightness," Taravangian said, "that the Veden king would have accepted Dalinar's proposals of unification? Do you *really* think that old Hanavanar—the paranoid man who spent years playing his own highprinces against one another—would *ever* have joined this coalition? His death might well have been the best thing that ever happened to Alethkar. Think on that, Brightness, before your accusations set the room aflame."

He was correct, unfortunately. It *was* unlikely the late king of Jah Keved would ever have listened to Dalinar—the Vedens had deep-seated grudges with the Blackthorn. The coalition's early days had depended greatly upon the fact that Taravangian had joined it, bringing the might of a broken— but still formidable—Jah Keved.

"It might be easier to accept your goodwill, Your Majesty," Navani said, "if you hadn't tried to undermine my husband by revealing sensitive information to the coalition."

Taravangian stepped close, and a part of Navani panicked. This man *terrified* her, she realized. Her instincts toward him were the same she might have toward an enemy soldier with a sword. Yet at the end of the day, a single man with a sword was no threat to kingdoms. *This* man had fooled the smartest people in the world. He had conned his way into Dalinar's inner circle. He had played them for fools, all while seizing the throne of Jah Keved. And everyone had *praised* him.

That was true danger.

She forced herself not to shy away as he leaned in close; he didn't seem to intend the maneuver to be threatening. He was shorter than she was, and had no physical presence with which to impose. Instead he spoke softly. "*Everything* I've done was in the name of protecting humankind. Every *step* I've taken, every *ploy* I've devised, every *pain* I've suffered. It was all done to protect our future.

"I *could* point out that your own husbands—both of them—committed crimes that far outweigh mine. I ordered the murder of a handful of tyrants, but I burned no cities. Yes, the lighteyes of Jah Keved turned on one another once their king was dead, but I did *not* force them. Those deaths are not my burden.

"All of this is immaterial, however. Because I *would* have burned villages to prevent what was coming. I *would* have sent the Vedens into chaos. No matter the cost, I would have paid it. Know this. If humankind survives the new storm, it *will* be because of the actions I took. I stand by them."

He stepped back, leaving her trembling. Something about his intensity, the confidence of his words, left her speechless.

"I truly am impressed by your discoveries," he said. "We all benefit from what you've accomplished. Perhaps in future years few will think to thank you, but I do so now." He bowed to her, then walked over to take his seat, a lonely man who no longer brought attendants with him to these meetings.

Dangerous, a part of her thought again. And incredible. Yes, most men would have denied the accusations. Taravangian had leaned into them, taken ownership of them.

If mankind was truly fighting for its very survival, could any of them turn away the aid of the man who had expertly seized the throne of a kingdom far more powerful than his lowly city-state? She doubted Dalinar would have thought twice about Taravangian—even with the assassinations exposed—if not for one difficult question.

Was Taravangian working for the enemy? They risked the future of the world itself on the answer.

Navani found her seat as Noura—the head Azish vizier—called the meeting to order. She generally led the meetings these days; everyone responded well to her calm air of wisdom. The primary order of business was to discuss Dalinar's proposal for making a large offensive into Emul, crushing the enemy troops there up against the god-priest of Tukar. Noura had him stand up to outline the proposal, though Jasnah's scribes had sent detailed explanations to everyone in advance.

Navani let her mind wander, her thoughts circling around the phantom spanreed author. *You must stop making this new kind of fabrial. . . .* Perhaps they meant the ones using aluminum?

Soon enough Dalinar finished his proposal, opening the floor to discussion by the other monarchs. As expected, the young Azish Prime Aqasix was the first to respond. Yanagawn was looking more and more like an emperor each day, as the rest of his body was growing into the lanky height puberty had given him. He stood up, speaking for himself in the meeting—something he preferred to do, despite Azish custom.

"We were delighted to receive this proposal, Dalinar," the Prime said in excellent Alethi. He'd likely prepared this speech ahead of time, so he wouldn't make mistakes. "And we thank Her Majesty Jasnah Kholin for her thorough written explanations of its merits. As you can likely guess, we needed no persuasion to accept this plan."

He gestured toward the Emuli prime, a man living—as most of the Alethi did—in exile. The coalition had promised him a restored Emul in the past, but had so far been unable to deliver.

"The union of Makabaki states has discussed already, and we support this proposal wholeheartedly," Yanagawn said. "It is bold and decisive. We will lend it our every resource."

No surprise there, Navani thought. *But Taravangian will oppose it.* The old schemer had always pushed them to invest more heavily into the fight on his borders. The Mink had been clear in his final report; he feared Taravangian's actions were a ploy to get Dalinar to overextend into Alethkar. Additionally, Taravangian had historically taken the role of the more cautious, conservative one in the council, and as such, had good reason to oppose committing to Emul.

The wildcard would be Queen Fen and the Thaylens. She wore a bright patterned skirt today, decidedly *not* of Vorin fashion, and the white ringlets of her eyebrows bounced as she looked from Jasnah to Dalinar, thoughtful. Most of the room seemed to be able to read how this would play out. Taravangian disagreeing, Azir supporting. So how would Fen—

"If I may speak," Taravangian said, standing. "I would like to applaud this bold and wonderful proposal. Jah Keved and Kharbranth support it wholeheartedly. I have asked my generals how we might best lend our aid, and we can deliver twenty thousand troops to march immediately through the Oathgates for deployment into Emul."

What? Navani thought. He *supported* the proposal?

Storms. What had they missed? Why would he be so willing to pull troops away from his border now, after a year of insisting he couldn't spare even a handful? He'd always used the ubiquity of his medical support to cloud his miserly troop deployments.

Had he realized Dalinar wasn't going to give an opportunity for betrayal? Was this something else?

"We are grateful for your support, Taravangian," Yanagawn said. "Dalinar, that is two for your proposal. Three with you, and four, assuming your niece is already persuaded. The only one we await is Her Majesty." He turned to Fen.

"Her Majesty," Fen said, "is storming baffled. When's the last time the lot of us all *agreed* on something?"

"We all vote favor for lunching break," Yanagawn said, smiling and deviating from his script. "Usually."

"Well, *that's* the truth." Fen leaned back in her seat. "You surprised me with this one, Dalinar. I knew you were tacking toward some goal, but I thought for *sure* you would insist on trying to recapture your homeland. This general you recovered, he changed your mind, didn't he?"

Dalinar nodded. "He would like me to move that Herdaz be granted a seat on our council."

"Herdaz is no more," Fen said. "But I suppose the same could be said for Alethkar. I suggest that if his help proves useful in Emul, we grant such a request. For now, how do we proceed? I suspect an attack into Emul will provoke the enemy navy to finally come out and engage us, so I'll need to plan for a blockade. Tukar has a long coast; that's going to be a challenge.

Stormblessed, I suppose we can count on Windrunner patrols to help warn us of . . ."

Fen trailed off, twisting around toward the small group of Radiants at the side of the room. Each Radiant order usually sent at least one representative. Taravangian's Dustbringer was there as usual, and Lift was likely somewhere, judging from the state of the snack table—though a few other Edgedancers were sitting at the rear as well.

Normally Kaladin would be there, leaning against the wall, looming like a stormcloud. No longer. Instead Sigzil stepped forward, newly minted as companylord. It was an interesting move, elevating a foreigner—but it was a freedom Dalinar gained by no longer being directly tied to Alethkar. In this tower, ethnicity was secondary to Radiant bonds.

Sigzil didn't have the presence of his highmarshal; he always seemed too . . . fiddly to Navani. He cleared his throat, sounding uncomfortable in his new role. "You will have Windrunner support, Your Majesty. The enemy air troops might not want to fly in from Iri or Alethkar, as both routes would require them to traverse our lands. The Heavenly Ones might try to loop around and come in from the ocean. Plus, they've been employing Skybreakers frequently in the region—so we'll need to contend with them."

"Good," Fen said. "Where's Stormblessed?"

"Leave of absence, Your Majesty. He was wounded recently."

"What kind of wound can bring down a Windrunner?" Fen snapped. "Don't you regrow body parts?"

"Um, yes, Your Majesty. The highmarshal is recovering from a different kind of wound."

She grunted, looking over at Dalinar. "Well, the guilds of Thaylenah agree to this plan. If we retake Emul and Tukar, it will give us absolute dominance of the Southern Depths. You couldn't ask for a better staging platform for eventually recovering Alethkar. You're wise, Blackthorn, to delay striking for your homeland in favor of the tactically sound move."

"It was a difficult decision, Fen," Navani said. "One we made only after exploring every other option." *And Taravangian agreeing to it has me worried.*

"It highlights another problem though," Fen said. "We need more Windrunners. Kmakl has been raving about your flying fortress—I'll have you know, I haven't seen him this smitten since our first days courting. But the enemy has both Fused and Skybreakers, and you can't protect a ship like that without air support. Stormfather help us if enemies in the air catch one of our ocean fleets unprotected."

"We've been working on a solution," Dalinar promised. "It is a . . . difficult problem. Spren can be even more stubborn than men."

"Makes sense," Fen said. "I've never met a wind or current that would change course because I shouted at them."

Someone cleared their throat, and Navani was surprised to see Sigzil stepping forward again. "I've been speaking with my spren, Your Majesty, and I might be able to offer a potential solution to this problem. I believe we should send an envoy to the honorspren."

Navani leaned forward in her seat. "What kind of envoy?"

"The honorspren can be a . . . touchy group," Sigzil explained. "Many are not as carefree as our initial interactions with them led us to believe. Among spren, they are some of the closest in spirit and intent to the god Honor. While obviously individuals will vary in personality, there is a general feeling of discontent—well, insult—among them regarding humans."

Sigzil surveyed the crowd, and could plainly see that many of them weren't following him. He took a deep breath. "Here, let me say it this way. Pretend there was a kingdom you wanted to be our ally in this war. Except we betrayed them a few generations ago in a similar alliance. Would we be surprised that they refused to help us now?"

Navani found herself nodding.

"So, you're saying we need to repair relations," Fen said, "for something that happened thousands of years ago?"

"Your Majesty," Sigzil said, "with respect, the Recreance is ancient history to us—but to the spren it was only a few generations ago. The honorspren are upset; they feel their trust was betrayed. In their eyes, we never addressed what we did to them. For lack of a better term, their *honor* was offended."

Dalinar leaned forward in his seat. "Soldier, you're saying they want us to go to them begging? If Odium claims this land, they'll suffer as much as we will!"

"I know that, sir," Sigzil said. "You don't have to persuade me. But again, think of a nation your ancestors offended, but whose resources you now need. Wouldn't you at least send an envoy with an official apology?" He shrugged. "I can't promise it will work, but my advice is that we try."

Navani nodded again. She'd usually ignored this man because he acted so much like . . . well, a scribe. The kind of nitpicky person who often created more work for others. She now recognized that was unfair. She had found wisdom in the efforts of scholars others thought to be too focused on details.

It's because he's a man, she thought. *And a soldier, not an ardent.* He didn't act like the other Windrunners, so she'd dismissed him. *Not a good look, Navani,* she thought at herself. *For one who claims to be a patron of the thoughtful.*

"This man speaks wisdom," she said to the others. "We *have* been presumptuous in regards to the spren."

"Can we send you, Radiant?" Fen asked Sigzil. "You seem to understand their mindset."

Sigzil grimaced. "That might be a bad idea. We Windrunners . . . we're acting in defiance of honorspren law. We'd make the worst envoys, because of . . . well, they don't much like Kaladin, to be honest. If one of us showed up at their fortress, they might try to arrest us.

"My advice is to send a small but important contingent of other Radiants. Specifically, Radiants who have bonded spren whose relatives approve of what we're doing. They can make arguments on our behalf."

"That rules me out," Jasnah said. "The other inkspren are generally opposed to what Ivory did in bonding with me." She glanced to Renarin, who sat at the rear of the room, behind his brother. He glanced up in a panic, his puzzle box frozen in his hands. "We probably," Jasnah continued, "don't want to send Renarin either. Considering his . . . special circumstances."

"An Edgedancer, then?" Dalinar said. "The cultivationspren have generally embraced our new order of Radiants. I believe some of those who bonded Radiants are regarded highly in Shadesmar."

True to Navani's earlier guess, Lift emerged from underneath the table—though she hit her head climbing out, then glared at the table. The Reshi girl—well, teen—barely fit in spaces like that any longer, and seemed able to hit her elbows on every piece of furniture she passed.

"I'll go," Lift said, then yawned. "I'm getting bored here."

"Perhaps . . . someone older," Dalinar said.

"Nah," Lift said. "You need them all. They're all *good* at the Edgedancing part. 'Sides, Wyndle is famous on the other side on account of him figuring out how chairs work. I didn't believe it at first, 'cuz I never heard of him before he started bothering me. It's true though. Spren are weird, so they like weird things, like silly little vine people."

The room fell silent, and Navani suspected that everyone was thinking along the same lines. They couldn't send *Lift* to lead an envoy representing them. She was enthusiastic, yes, but . . . she was also . . . well . . . Lift.

"You are excellent with healing," Dalinar said to her, "among the best of your order. We need you here, and besides, we should send someone with practice as a diplomat."

"I could give it a try, sir," said Godeke, a shorter Edgedancer who had once been an ardent. "I have some experience with these matters."

"Excellent," Dalinar said.

"Adolin and I should lead this envoy," Shallan said. She seemed reluctant as she stood up. "Cryptics and honorspren don't get along fantastically, but I'm a good choice regardless. Who better to represent us than a highprince and his Radiant wife?"

"An excellent suggestion," Dalinar said. "We can send one of the Truthwatchers—other than Renarin—and one Stoneward. With Godeke, that would give us four different Radiants and their spren, plus my own son. Radiant Sigzil, would that satisfy the honorspren?"

He cocked his head, listening to something none of the rest of them could hear. "She thinks so, sir. It's a good start, at least. She says to send gifts, and to ask for help. Honorspren have a difficult time turning away people in need. Apologize for the past, promise to do better, and explain how dire our situation is. That might work." He paused. "It also wouldn't hurt if the Stormfather were to speak on our behalf, sir."

"I'll see if that can be arranged," Dalinar said. "He can be difficult." He turned to Shallan and Adolin. "You are both willing to lead this expedition? Shadesmar is dangerous."

"It's really not that bad," Adolin said. "Assuming we're not being chased the entire time, I think it might be fun."

There's something there, Navani thought, reading the boy's excitement. *He's wanted to get back into Shadesmar for months now.* But what of Shallan? She settled down in her seat, and while she nodded to Dalinar at his question, she seemed . . . reserved. Navani would have expected her to be excited as well; Shallan loved going new and strange places.

Dalinar took their agreement, and the general lack of objections from the monarchs, as enough. It was set. An expedition into Shadesmar and a large military push into Emul—both plans unanimously agreed upon.

Navani wasn't certain what to think about how easily it had happened. It was nice to make headway; yet in her experience, a fair breeze one day was the herald of a tempest to come.

⁘

She didn't get a chance to voice her concerns until much later in the night, when she managed to pull away from dinner with Fen and Kmakl. She tried to make time for the monarchs individually when she could, as Dalinar was so often off inspecting troops on one front line or the other.

He didn't intentionally ignore social responsibilities as Gavilar had done at the end—in Dalinar's case, he simply didn't *notice*. And with him, that was generally fine. People liked seeing him think like a soldier, and spoke with fondness—rather than insult—about his occasional social missteps. He was, despite having grown calmer over the years, still the Blackthorn. It would be wrong if he didn't sometimes eat his dessert with his fingers or unthinkingly call someone "soldier" instead of using their royal title.

Regardless, Navani took care to make certain everyone knew that they were appreciated. It was left mostly unsaid, but no one *truly* knew what Dalinar's relationship was with the coalition. Merely another monarch, or something more? He controlled the Oathgates, and almost all the Radiants looked to him as their superior officer.

Beyond that, many who had broken off from mainstream Vorinism were treating his autobiography as a religious text. Dalinar wasn't highking in name, just monarch of Urithiru, but the other monarchs stepped delicately—still wondering if this coalition would eventually become an empire beneath the Blackthorn.

Navani soothed worries, made oblique promises, and generally tried to keep everyone pointed in the right direction. It was exhausting work, so when she finally trailed into their rooms, she was glad to see that Dalinar had their heating fabrial warming the place with a toasty red light. He had unalon tea for her on the heating plate—very thoughtful, as he never brewed it for himself, finding it too sweet.

She fetched a cup, then found him on the couch nearest the fabrial, staring at its light. His jacket was off, draped across a nearby chair, and he'd dismissed the servants—as he usually did, and often too frequently. She'd need to let them know—again—that he wasn't offended by something they'd done. He merely liked to be alone.

Fortunately, he'd made it clear that being alone didn't include being away from her. He had a strange definition of the word sometimes. Indeed, he immediately made space for her as she sat down, letting her melt into the crook of his arm before the warm hearth. She undid the button on her safehand sleeve and gripped the warm cup in both hands. She'd grown comfortable with a glove these last few years, and found it increasingly annoying to have to wear something more formal to meetings.

For a time, she simply enjoyed the warmth. Three sources of it. The first the warmth of the fabrial, the second the warmth of the tea, and the third the warmth of him against her back. The most welcome of them all. He rested his hand along her upper arm and would occasionally rub with one finger—as if wanting to constantly remind himself that she was there with him.

"I used to think these fabrials were terrible," he eventually said, "replacing the life of a fire with something so . . . cold. Warm, yes, but *cold*. Strange, how quickly I've come to enjoy them. No need to keep piling on logs. No worry about the flue clogging and smoke boiling out. It's amazing how much removing a few background worries can free the mind."

"To think about Taravangian?" she guessed. "And how he supported the war proposal instead of objecting?"

"You know me too well."

"I'm worried too," she said, sipping her tea. "He was far too quick to offer troops. We'll have to take them, you know. After spending months complaining he was withholding his armies, we can't turn them away now."

"What is he planning?" Dalinar asked. "This is where I'm most likely to fail everyone, Navani. Sadeas outmaneuvered me, and I fear Taravangian is more crafty in every respect. When I tried to make initial moves to cut him out of the coalition, he'd already worked on the others to undermine any such attempt. He's playing me, and doing it deftly, right beneath my nose."

"You don't have to face him alone," Navani said. "This isn't only upon you."

"I know," Dalinar said, his eyes seeming to glow as he stared at the bright ruby in the hearth. "I won't ever suffer that feeling again, Navani. That moment of standing on the Shattered Plains watching Sadeas retreat. Of knowing that my faith in someone—my stupid naivety—had doomed the lives of thousands of men. I *won't* be Taravangian's pawn."

She reached up and cupped his chin in her hand. "You suffered betrayal by Sadeas because you saw the man as he *should* have been, if he'd risen above his own pettiness. Don't lose that faith, Dalinar. It's part of what makes you the man you have become."

"Taravangian is confident, Navani. If he's working with the enemy, there's a reason for it. He always has a reason."

"Wealth, renown. Vengeance maybe."

"No," Dalinar said. "No, not him." He closed his eyes. "When I . . . when I burned the Rift, I did it in anger. Children and innocents died because of my fury. I know that feeling; I could spot it. If Taravangian killed a child, he'd do it not for vengeance. Not for fury. Not for wealth or renown. But because he *sincerely* thought the child's death was necessary."

"He would call it good, then?"

"No. He would acknowledge it as evil, would say it stains his soul. He says . . . that's the point of having a monarch. A man to wallow in blood, to be stained by it and *destroyed* by it, so that others might not suffer."

He opened his eyes and raised his hand to hold hers. "It's similar, in a way, to how the ancient Radiants saw themselves. In the visions they said . . . they were the watchers at the rim. They trained in deadly arts to protect others from needing to do so. The same philosophy, less tarnished. He's so close to being right, Navani. If I could only get through to him . . ."

"I worry that instead he'll change *you*, Dalinar," she said. "Don't listen too closely to what he says."

He nodded, and seemed to take that to heart. She rested her head against his chest, listening to his heartbeat.

"I want you to stay here," he said, "in the tower. Jasnah wants to deploy with us into Emul; she's eager to prove she can lead in battle. With an offensive so large, I'll be needed in person as well. Taravangian knows that; he must be planning a trap for us. Someone needs to be here in the tower, safe—to pull the rest of us out if something goes wrong."

Someone to lead the Alethi, in case Jasnah and I are killed in Taravangian's trap, he left unsaid.

She didn't object. Yes, an Alethi woman would normally go to war to scribe for her husband. Yes, he was defying this in part because he wanted her safe. He was a little overprotective.

She forgave him this. They *would* need a member of the royal family to stay in reserve, and besides, she was increasingly certain that the best thing *she* could do to help would involve unraveling the mysteries of this tower.

"If you're going to leave me," she said, "then you'd best treat me well in the days leading up to your departure. So I remember you fondly and know that you love me."

"Is there ever a question of that?"

She pulled back, then lightly ran her finger along his jaw. "A woman needs constant reminders. She needs to know that she has his heart, even when she cannot have his company."

"You have my heart always."

"And tonight specifically?"

"And tonight," he said, "specifically." He leaned forward to kiss her, pulling her tight with those formidable arms of his. In this she encountered a fourth warmth to the night, more powerful than all the rest.

THE END OF

Part One

INTERLUDES

SYLPHRENA • SJA-ANAT • TARAVANGIAN

SYLPHRENA

Sylphrena felt the energy of the approaching highstorm like one might hear the sound of a distant musician walking ever closer. Calling out with friendly music.

She zipped through the halls of Urithiru. She was invisible to almost everyone but those she chose—and today she chose the children. They never seemed suspicious of her. They always smiled when they saw her. They also rarely acted too respectful. Despite what she told Kaladin, she didn't *always* want people to treat her like a little deity.

Unfortunately, this early, there weren't a lot of people—children or not—out in the tower. Kaladin was still asleep, but she liked that he slept a little better now.

She heard noises from a particular doorway, so she went that direction, darting into the room to find Rock's daughter cooking. The others called her Cord, but her real name—Hualinam'lunanaki'akilu—was much prettier. It was a poem about a wedding band.

Cord deserved such a pretty name. She looked so *different* from the Alethi. More solid, a person who wouldn't be blown over by a storm, as if she were made of bronze—a shade subtly reflected by her skin tone. And that beautiful red hair was different from Shallan's. Cord's was more rusty, darker and deeper; she wore it in a tail, tied with a ribbon.

She saw Syl, of course; she had inherited her father's blessing of being able to see all spren. She paused, head bowed, and touched one shoulder, then the other, then her forehead. She separated out the next slices of tuber she cut and set them in a neat pile on the counter: an offering for Syl. That was silly, since Syl didn't eat. She turned into a tuber anyway and rolled around on the counter to say thanks.

That music though. The *storm*. She could hardly contain herself. It was coming!

She rolled off the counter and zipped over to examine Cord's Shardplate stacked neatly in the corner. The young Horneater woman was never without it. She was the first of her people in . . . well, a very, very long time to have a Shard.

It was pretty. Maybe Syl should have hated it, as she did Shardblades, but she didn't. It was kind of a corpse—well, lots of corpses—but not as offensive. The difference, she supposed, was attitude. She could sense contentment, not pain, from the Plate.

Cord began making noise with her pot, and Syl found herself darting that direction to watch what was being dumped into the water. Sometimes Syl felt like she had two brains. One was the responsible brain; it had driven her to defy the other honorspren and her father in seeking out Kaladin and forming a Radiant bond. This was the brain that she *wanted* to control her. It cared about important things: people, the fate of the world, figuring out what it truly meant to be of Honor.

She had a different brain too. The brain that was fascinated by the world—the brain that acted like it belonged to a small child. A loud noise? Better go see what caused it! Music on the horizon? Dart back and forth, eager with anticipation! A strange cremling on the wall? Mimic its shape and crawl along to see what it feels like!

Thoughts bombarded her. What did it feel like to be a tuber being cut? How long had it taken Rock and Song to come up with Cord's name? Should Syl have a name that was a poem? Maybe they had a name for her among the Horneaters. Did they have names for every spren, or just important ones?

On and on and on. She could deal with it. She always had. It wasn't an honorspren thing though. The others weren't like her, except maybe Rua.

Puffs of steam rose from the cook pot, and Syl became the same shape: a puff of steam rising toward the ceiling. When that got boring—it took only a few seconds—she soared up into the air to listen to the music. The storm wasn't near enough yet. She wouldn't be able to see it.

Still, she zipped out onto the balcony and flitted along the outside of the tower, searching for Kaladin's room.

The tower was dead. She barely remembered the place from before, when she'd bonded her old wonderful knight. He'd spent most of his life traveling to little villages, using her as a Shardblade to cut cisterns or aqueducts for the people. She remembered coming to Urithiru with him once . . . and the tower had been bright with lights. . . . A strange kind of light . . .

She stopped in the air, realizing she'd flown up seventeen stories. *Silly spren. Don't let the child be in charge.* She darted down and found Kaladin's window, then squeezed through the shutters, which had just enough space between them for her to enter.

In the dark room beyond, he slept. She didn't need to come look to know that. She'd have felt if he'd woken. But . . .

He has two brains too, she thought. *A light brain and a dark brain.* She wished she could understand him. He needed help. Maybe this new duty would be all he needed. She so profoundly hoped that it would. But she worried it wouldn't be enough.

He needed *her* help, and she couldn't give it. She couldn't understand.

The storm! The storm was here.

She slipped back outside, though the responsible brain managed to keep her attention. Kaladin. She needed to help *Kaladin.* Perhaps he would be satisfied as a surgeon, and it would be good for him to not have to kill anymore. However, there was a reason he'd had difficulties as a surgeon in the past. He would continue to have the dark brain. This wasn't a solution. She needed a *solution.*

She kept hold of that idea, not letting it evaporate like steam above a cauldron. She held to it even as the stormwall hit, washing around the base of the tower from the east. Hundreds of windspren flew before it in a multitude of shapes. She joined them, laughing and becoming like them. She loved her little cousins for their joy, their simple excitement.

As always, small thoughts bombarded her as she flew between them, waving, smiling, changing shapes repeatedly from one moment to the next. Honorspren—all of the intelligent spren—were something new to Roshar. Well, new as in ten-thousand-years-old new. So . . . new*er.*

How had the first honorspren—or cultivationspren, or inkspren, or peakspren, or any of the other intelligent ones—been created? Had they been shaped from raw Investiture by Honor himself? Had they grown out of these, their cousins? She felt so much kinship with them, though they were clearly different. Not as smart. Could she help them become smart?

These were heavy thoughts when she just wanted to soar. The music, the cataclysm of the storm was . . . strangely peaceful. She often had trouble in a room full of talking people, whether they were humans or spren. She would be intrigued by every conversation, her attention diverted constantly.

One might have thought the storm would be the same way, but it wasn't loudness that bothered her—it was a *diversity* of loudness*es*. The storm was a single voice. A majestic, powerful voice singing a song with its own harmonies. In here she could simply enjoy the song and relax, renewed.

She sang with the thunder. She danced with the lightning. She became debris and let herself be pushed along. She zipped into the inmost, darkest part of the storm, and she became its heartbeat. Light-thunder. Light-thunder. Light-thunder.

Then blackness took her. A fuller blackness than the absence of light. It was the split moment that her father could create. Time was a funny thing. It was always flowing along in the background like a river, but bring too much power to bear, and it warped. It slowed; it wanted to pause and take a look. Anytime too much power—too much Investiture, too much *self*—congregated, realms became porous and time behaved oddly.

He didn't need to make a face in the sky for her as he did for mortals. She could feel his attention like the sun's own heat.

CHILD. REBELLIOUS CHILD. YOU HAVE COME TO ME WISHING.

"I want to understand him," Syl said, revealing the thought she'd been holding—protecting—and sheltering. "Will you make me feel the darkness he does, so I can understand it? I can *help* him better if I *know* him better."

YOU GIVE TOO MUCH OF YOURSELF TO THAT HUMAN.

"Isn't that why we exist?"

NO. YOU HAVE ALWAYS MISUNDERSTOOD THIS. YOU DO NOT EXIST FOR THEM. YOU EXIST FOR YOU. YOU EXIST TO CHOOSE.

"And do *you* exist for *you*, Father?" she demanded, standing in blackness—insisting on holding her human form. She stared up at the deep eternity. "You never make choices. You merely blow as you always do."

I AM BUT THE STORM. YOU ARE MORE.

"You avoid responsibility," she said. "You claim you do only what a storm must, but then act like I'm somehow wrong for doing what I feel I must! You tell me I can make choices, then berate me when I make ones you do not like."

YOU REFUSE TO ADMIT THAT YOU ARE MORE THAN AN APPENDAGE TO A HUMAN. SPREN ONCE LET THEMSELVES BECOME CONSUMED BY THE NEEDS OF THE RADIANTS, AND THAT KILLED THEM. NOW, MANY OF MY CHILDREN HAVE FOLLOWED YOUR FOOLISH PATH, AND ARE IN GREAT DANGER.

THIS IS OUR WORLD. IT BELONGS TO THE SPREN.

"It belongs to everyone," Syl said. "Spren, humans, even the singers. So we need to figure out how to live together."

THE ENEMY WILL NOT ALLOW IT.

"The enemy is going to be defeated by Dalinar Kholin," Syl said. "And so we need to have his champion ready."

YOU ARE SO CERTAIN THAT YOUR HUMAN IS THE CHAMPION, the Stormfather said. I DO NOT THINK THE WORLD WILL BEND TO YOUR WISHES.

"Regardless, I need to understand him so I can help him," Syl said. "Not because I'm going to be consumed by his desires, but because this is what I *want* to do. So I ask again. Will you make me capable of feeling what he does?"

I cannot do this thing, the Stormfather said. Your wishes are not evil, Sylphrena, but they are dangerous.

"You cannot? Or you will not?"

I have the power, but not the ability.

The time between ended abruptly, dumping her back into the storm. Windspren spiraled around her, laughing and calling, mimicking the words, "You cannot, you cannot, you cannot!" Insufferable things. As bad as she was sometimes.

Syl kept hold of the idea, cradling it, then let herself be otherwise distracted by the storm. She danced for its entire passing, though she couldn't leave with it. She needed to stay within a few miles of Kaladin, or her Connection to the Physical Realm would start to fade and her mind would weaken.

She enjoyed this time, an hour passing in moments. When the riddens finally approached, she stopped in eager anticipation, overjoyed. Up here in the mountains, the end of the storm made *snow*. By now, the storm had dropped all its crem-laced water, so the snow was white and pure. Each snowflake was so magnificent! She wished she could talk to objects like Shallan did, and hear each one's story.

She fell with the flakes, imitating them—and creating patterns unique to her. She *could* be herself, not only live for some human. The thing was, Kaladin wasn't just *some* human. She'd picked him deliberately out of millions and millions. Her job was to help him. As powerful a duty as the Stormfather's duty to drop water and crem to give life to Roshar.

She soared back toward Urithiru, weaving between snowbanks, then shooting upward. This section to the west of the tower included deep valleys and frosted peaks. She dove through the former and crested the latter before looping around in circles outside the magnificent tower.

She eventually reached the Bondsmith's balcony. Dalinar was always awake for highstorms, regardless of the hour. She landed on his balcony, where he stood in the cold. The rock at his feet was slick with water; today the highstorm had been high enough to cover the lower stories of the tower. She'd never seen it get to the top, but she hoped it would someday. That would be different!

She made herself visible to Dalinar, but he didn't jump as humans sometimes did when she appeared. She didn't understand why they did that—weren't they used to spren fading in and out all the time around them? Humans were like storms, magnets for all kinds of spren.

They seemed to find her more disturbing than a gloryspren. She supposed she'd take that as a compliment.

"Did you enjoy your storm, Ancient Daughter?" Dalinar asked.

"I enjoyed *our* storm," she said. "Though Kaladin slept through the entire thing, the big lug."

"Good. He needs more rest."

She took a step toward Dalinar. "Thank you for what you did. In forcing him to change. He was stuck, doing what he felt he had to, but getting darker all the time."

"Every soldier reaches a point where he has to set down the sword. Part of a commander's job is to watch for the signs."

"He's different, isn't he?" Syl said. "Worse, because his own mind fights against him."

"Different, yes," Dalinar said, leaning on the railing next to her. "But who is to say what is worse or better? We each have our own Voidbringers to slay, Brightness Sylphrena. No man can judge another man's heart or trials, for no man can truly know them."

"I want to try," she said. "The Stormfather implied there was a way. Can you make me understand Kaladin's emotions? Can you make me *feel* what he's going through?"

"I have no idea how to accomplish something like that," Dalinar said.

"He and I have a bond," she said. "You should be able to use your powers to enhance that bond, strengthen it."

Dalinar clasped his hands on the stonework before him. He didn't object to her request—he wasn't the type to reject any idea out of hand.

"What do you know of my powers?" Dalinar asked her.

"Your abilities are what made the original Oathpact," she said. "And they existed—and were named—long before the Knights Radiant were founded. A Bondsmith Connected the Heralds to Braize, made them immortal, and locked our enemies away. A Bondsmith bound other Surges and brought humans to Roshar, fleeing their dying world. A Bondsmith created—or at least discovered—the Nahel bond: the ability of spren and humans to join together into something better. You Connect things, Dalinar. Realms. Ideas. People."

He surveyed the frosted landscape, freshly painted with snow. She thought she knew his answer already, from the way he took a breath and set his jaw before speaking.

"Even if I could do this," he said, "it would not be right."

She became a small pile of leaves, disintegrating and stirring in the wind. "Then I'll never be able to help him."

"You can help without knowing exactly what he's feeling. You can be available for him to lean on."

"I try. Sometimes he doesn't seem to want even me."

"That's likely when he needs you most. We can never know another man's heart, Brightness Sylphrena, but we all know what it is to live and have pain. That is the advice I'd have given to another. I do not know if it applies to you."

Syl looked upward, along the tower's pointing finger, raised toward the sky. "I . . . had another knight once. We came here to the tower, when *it* was alive—though I don't fully remember what that meant. I lost memories during the . . . pain."

"What pain?" Dalinar asked. "What pain does a spren feel?"

"He died. My knight, Relador. He went to fight, despite his age. He shouldn't have, and when he was killed, it hurt. I felt alone. So alone that I started to drift . . ."

Dalinar nodded. "I suspect that Kaladin feels something similar, though from what I've been told about his ailment, it doesn't have a specific cause. He will sometimes start to . . . drift, as you put it."

"The dark brain," she said.

"An apt designation."

Maybe I can already *understand Kaladin,* she thought. *I had a dark brain of my own, for a while.*

She had to remember what that had been like. She realized that her responsible brain *and* her child's brain aligned in trying hard to forget that part of her life. But Syl was in control, not either of those brains. And maybe, if she remembered how she'd felt during those old dark days, she could help Kaladin with his current dark days.

"Thank you," she said to Dalinar as a group of windspren passed. She regarded them, and for once didn't particularly feel like giving chase. "I think you have helped."

Sja-anat had been named Taker of Secrets long ago by a scholar no one remembered. She liked the name. It implied action. She didn't simply hear secrets; she took them. She made them hers.

And she kept them.

From the other Unmade.

From the Fused.

From Odium himself.

She flowed through the Kholinar palace, existing between the Physical and Cognitive Realms. Like many of the Unmade, she belonged to neither one fully. Odium trapped them in a halfway existence. Some would manifest in various forms if they resided too long in one place, or if they were pulled through by strong emotions.

Not her.

Sometimes Fused, or even common singers, would notice her. They'd grow stiff, look over their shoulders. They'd glimpse a shadow, a brief darkness, quickly missed. Actually *seeing* her required reflected light.

It was similar in Shadesmar. She experienced that realm at the same time as she experienced the Physical Realm, though both were shadowy to her. She dreamed that somewhere a place existed that was completely right for her and her children.

For now, she would live here.

She flowed up steps in one realm, but barely moved in the other. Space was not entirely equal between the realms—it wasn't that she had a foot in each realm; more, she was like two entities that shared a mind. In Shadesmar, she floated above the ocean of beads, her essence rippling. In the Physical Realm, she passed among singers who worked in the palace.

Sja-anat did not consider herself the most clever of the Unmade.

Certainly she was one of the more intelligent, but that was not the same. Some of the Unmade—such as Nergaoul, sometimes called the Thrill—were practically mindless, more like emotion spren. Others—such as Ba-Ado-Mishram, who had granted forms to the singers during the False Desolation—were crafty and conniving.

Sja-anat was a little like both. During the long millennia before this Return, she'd mostly slumbered. Without her bond to Odium she had trouble thinking. The Everstorm appearing in Shadesmar—long before it had emerged into the Physical Realm—had revitalized her. Had let her begin planning again. But she *knew* she was not as smart as Odium was. She could keep only a few secrets from him, and she had to choose carefully, clouding them behind other secrets that she gave away.

You sacrificed some of your children so others could live. It was a law of nature. Humans didn't understand it. But she did. She . . .

He was coming.

God of passion.

God of hatred.

God of all adopted spren.

Sja-anat flowed into the hallway of the palace and met with two of her children, touched windspren. Humans called them "corrupted," but she hated this term. She did not corrupt. She Enlightened them, showing them that a different path was possible. Did not the humans revere Transformation—the ability of all beings to become someone new, someone better—as a core ideal of their religion? Yet they grew angry when she let spren change?

Her children darted away to do her bidding, then one of her greater children manifested. A glowing and shimmering light, constantly changing. One of her most precious creations.

I will go, Mother, he said. *To the tower, to this man Mraize, as you have promised.*

Odium will see you, she replied. *Odium will try to unmake you.*

I know. But Odium must be distracted from you, as we discussed. I must find my own way, my own bond.

Go then, she said. *But do not bond this human because of what I said. I merely promised to send a child to investigate options. There are other possibilities there. Choose for yourself, not because I desire it.*

Thank you, Mother, he said. *Thank you for my eyes.*

He left, following the others. Sja-anat regretted that the smaller two—the Enlightened windspren—were essentially distractions. Odium would see them for certain.

Protect some children.

Sacrifice others.

A choice only a god could make.

A god like Sja-anat.

She rose up, taking the form of a woman of streaming black smoke with pure white eyes. Shadows and mist, Odium's pure essence. If he were to know the deepest secret parts of her soul, he would not be surprised. For she *had* come from him. Unmade by his hand.

But as with all children, she had become more.

His presence came upon her like the sun piercing the clouds. Powerful, vibrant, smothering. Some Fused in the hallway noticed it and looked around, though the common singers weren't attuned enough to hear Odium's song—like a rhythm but more resonant. One of the three pure tones of Roshar.

She didn't fully understand the laws that bound him. They were ancient, and related to compacts between the Shards, the high gods of the cosmere. Odium wasn't simply the mind that controlled the power: the Vessel. Nor was he merely that power alone: the Shard. He was both, and at times it seemed the power had desires that were counter to the purposes of the Vessel.

Sja-anat, a voice—infused with the tone of Odium—said to her. *What are these spren you have sent away?*

"Those that do your bidding," she whispered, prostrating herself by pooling down onto the floor. "Those that watch. Those that hear."

Have you been speaking to the humans again? To . . . corrupt them with lies?

That was the fabrication she and Odium played at currently. She pretended that she had contacted the Radiant Shallan, and a few others, working on his behalf—anticipating his desires. He pretended he didn't know she had done it *against* his will.

Both knew she wanted more freedom than he would allow. Both knew that she wanted to be a god unto herself. But he didn't know for certain she was taking actions to undermine him, like when she'd saved Shallan and her companions from death in Kholinar a year ago. She had played that off as accidental, and he couldn't prove otherwise.

If Odium caught her in a verifiable lie, he would unmake her again. Steal her memory. Rip her to pieces. But in so doing, he would lose a useful tool.

Hence the game.

Where have you sent them? he asked.

"To the tower, Lord. To watch the humans, as we've discussed. We must prepare for the Bondsmith's next move."

I will prepare, he said. *You focus too much on the tower.*

"I am eager for the invasion," she said. "I will very much like to see my cousin again. Perhaps they can be awakened? Persuaded?"

Odium had likely planned to send her on this mission, but her eagerness now gave him pause. He would follow her children and see that they were indeed going to the tower; that would reinforce his decision. The one she hoped he would make right now . . .

You will not go to the tower, Odium said. He hated how she referred to the Sibling—the slumbering child of Honor and Cultivation—as her cousin. *But we are about to make a ploy with the betrayal of the man Taravangian. You will watch him.*

"I would be of much more use in the tower," she said. "Better that I—"

You question? Do not question.

"I will not question." However, she felt a surging to the power that moved within him. The mind did not like being questioned, but the power . . . It *liked* questions. It *liked* arguments. It *was* passion.

There was a weakness here. In the division between the Vessel and the Shard.

"I will go wherever you demand," she said, "my god."

Very well. He moved on to speak with the Nine. And Sja-anat planned her next steps. She had to pretend to sulk. Had to try to find a way out of going to Emul. She had to hope that she wasn't successful.

Odium suspected that she'd helped the Radiant Shallan. He was watching to see that she didn't contact other Radiants. So she wouldn't. Once he'd found her windspren, and unmade them to lose their minds and memories, he would hopefully be content—and not see the other child she'd sent.

And Sja-anat herself? She *would* go with Taravangian and watch him as asked. And she would stay close.

For Taravangian was a weapon.

INTO THE FIRE

Taravangian had long suspected he would not get a funeral. The Diagram hadn't indicated this specifically—but it hadn't said otherwise. Besides, the farther they progressed, the less accurate the Diagram became.

He had chosen this path, however, and knew it was not the sort that led to a peaceful death surrounded by family. This was the sort of path that led into the dark forest, full of perils. His goal had never been to emerge from the other side unscathed; it had always been to simply accomplish his goal before he was killed.

And he had. His city, his family, his people—they would be safe. He had made a deal with the enemy that ensured Kharbranth would survive the coming destruction. That had always been his end. That *alone*.

To tell himself otherwise was both foolish and dangerous.

So it was that he arrived at this day: the day he sent his friends away. He'd had a fire built in his hearth, here in his rooms at Urithiru. A real hearth, with real wood, dancing with flamespren. His pyre.

His friends gathered for the farewell. Recently they'd been spending more and more time away at Kharbranth, in order to make their eventual departure less suspicious. He'd made it seem as if they were needed to help rule that city now that Taravangian was focused on Jah Keved.

But today . . . today they were all here. One last time. Adrotagia, of course, kept her composure as he hugged her. She'd always been the stronger one. Though Taravangian was moderately intelligent today, he was still overcome with emotion as they pulled apart.

"Give my best to Savrahalidem and my grandchildren," Taravangian said. "If they ask, tell them that I lost myself at the end and became insensate."

"Won't that hurt Savri more?" Adrotagia asked. "To know that her father is trapped among enemies, senile and confused?"

"No, that is not my girl," he said. "You don't know her as I do. Tell her I was singing when you last saw me. That will comfort her." He squeezed Adrotagia's wrists as she held to his. How lucky was he, to have had a friend for . . . storms, *seventy-three years*?

"It shall be done, Vargo," she said. "And the Diagram?"

He'd promised her a final confirmation. Taravangian released her wrists, then walked to the window, passing Mrall—the enormous bodyguard was crying, bless him.

Later today, Taravangian would leave for Azir with Dalinar and Jasnah. Soon afterward, Taravangian's armies—acting on Odium's orders—would betray their allies and switch sides. It was a death sentence for Taravangian, who would be left surrounded by his enemies. He was bringing an army just the right size to put Dalinar and the other monarchs at ease: large enough to convince them Taravangian was committed, but small enough to leave them certain they could capture him in the event of a betrayal.

It was a calculated move on Odium's part. What powerful monarch would leave himself so vulnerable?

Feeling tired, Taravangian rested his weathered hands upon the stone windowsill of his tower room. He'd asked for a room where he could look southward, to where this had all begun with a request to the Nightwatcher. He now suspected that his boon had been chosen by someone more grand than that ancient spren.

"The Diagram," Taravangian said, "has served its purpose. We have protected Kharbranth. We have fulfilled the Diagram.

"Both the book *and* the organization we named after it were merely tools. It is time to disband. Dismantle our secret hospitals; release our soldiers to the city guard. If there are any middling members you think know too much, give them a time-consuming 'secret' quest far from civilization. Danlan should be among the first of this group.

"As for Delgo, Malata, and the others too useful to waste, I think they will accept the truth. We have achieved our goal. Kharbranth will be safe." He peered down at his aged hands. Wrinkles like scars for each life he'd taken. "Tell them . . . there is nothing more pitiful than a tool that has outlived its usefulness. We will not simply invent something new for our organization to do. We must allow that which has served its purpose to die."

"That is all fine," Mrall said, stepping forward, folding his arms and acting as if he hadn't been crying a moment before. "But you are still our king. We won't leave you."

"We will," Adrotagia said softly.

"But—"

"Vargo has the Blackthorn's suspicion," Adrotagia said. "He will not be allowed to leave, not now. And if he *did* go, he would be hunted once the betrayal happens. We, on the other hand, can slip away—and then be ignored. Without him, Kharbranth will be safe."

"This was always the intent, Mrall," Taravangian said, still staring out over the mountains. "I am the spire that draws the lightning. I am the bearer of our sins. Kharbranth can distance itself from me once our armies in Jah Keved turn against the Alethi. The Veden highprinces are eager and bloodthirsty; each has promises from the Fused. They will perpetuate the fight, believing that they will be favored once Odium's forces win."

"You're being *thrown away!*" Mrall said. "After all you've done, Odium casts you aside? At least go to Jah Keved."

Naturally, Mrall didn't see. That was fine. These details weren't in the Diagram—they were in uncharted territory now.

"I am a diversion," Taravangian explained. "I *must* go with the expeditionary force into Emul. Then, when Jah Keved turns, the Blackthorn will be so focused on me and the immediate threat to his soldiers that he will miss whatever Odium will be attempting in the meantime."

"It can't be important enough to risk you," Mrall said.

Taravangian had his suspicions. Perhaps Odium's ploy would be worth the cost, perhaps not. It didn't matter. At the god's orders, Taravangian had spent a year preparing Jah Keved to switch sides, promoting the people Odium wanted in place, moving troops into position. Now that he was done, Taravangian was useless. Worse, he was a potential weakness.

And so, Taravangian would be given to the Alethi for execution, and his corpse would be burned without a proper funeral. The Alethi gave no honors to traitors.

Acknowledging his fate hurt. Like a spear right through his gut. Odd, how much that should bother him. He'd be dead, so what did he care about a funeral?

He turned from the window and gave Mrall a firm handshake—then an unexpected hug. He gave another to short, trustworthy Maben—the servant woman who had watched over him all this time. She handed him a small bundle of his favorite jams, all the way from Shinovar. Those were increasingly rare, now that trade into the strange country had cut off. The Diagram indicated it was likely one or more of the Unmade had set up there.

"Too often," Taravangian said to Maben, "those who write history focus on the generals and the scholars, to the detriment of the quiet workers who see everything done. The salvation of our people is as much your victory as mine." He bowed and kissed her hand.

Finally he turned to Dukar, the stormwarden who administered Taravangian's intelligence tests each morning. His robe was as extravagant—and silly—as always. But the man's loyalty remained solid as he held up his pack of tests.

"I should stay with you, sire," he said as the nearby hearth sparked, the logs shifting. "You will still need someone to test you each day."

"The tests are no longer relevant, Dukar," Taravangian said gently. He held up a finger. "If you stay, you will be executed—or perhaps tortured to get information out of me. While I promised to do whatever was necessary to save our people, I will not go *one step* further. Not a *single* death more than needed. So, my final act as your king is to *command* you to leave."

Dukar bowed. "My king. My eternal king."

Taravangian looked back to Adrotagia and unfolded a piece of paper from his pocket. "For my daughter," he said. "She will be queen of Kharbranth when this is through. Be certain she disavows me. This is the reason I've kept her clean. Guide her well, and do not trust Dova. Having met more of the other Heralds, I'm certain Battah is not as stable as she seems."

Adrotagia took his hand one last time, then patted him on the head as she'd done to annoy him in their childhood, once she had started growing taller than he. He smiled, then watched as the group slowly left—bowing one at a time.

They closed the door, and he was alone. He took his copy of the Diagram, bound in leather. Despite years of hoping, he'd never been given another day like that one where he'd created this book. But that one day had been enough.

Was it? a part of him whispered. *You saved a single city.*

The best he could do. To hope for more was dangerous.

He walked to the hearth and watched the dancing flamespren before dropping his copy of the Diagram into the fire.

PART
TWO

Our Calling

SHALLAN • ADOLIN • KALADIN •
NAVANI • VENLI

Nohadon's
Stairways

Urithiru
in the Physical
Realm X

Add to wish
list: ride one
of these.

Basin of the Veiled Sun

Something X
weird here.
Will report
in person.

Perpetual
Sobriety

Just a
lighthouse
with a couple of
grouchy attendants
and their bratty
kids. The quiche,
however, was
exceptional.

Also
perpetually
boring.

Azimir
Oathgate

Ageless
Beauty

Abiding
Light

Must've
been named
a thousand
years ago.

THE EMPYREAN GULF

Justice
Untarnished

Reliqq's
Channel

THE RADIANT DEPTHS

Path of Adolin and Shallan's Voyage

The Oathbound Spires

This place is
literally called
"Nameless."

THE ASTRAL BANKS

X

Little more
than a rest stop
with acceptable
snack choices.

Lasting
Integrity

X

There's a
strange storm
brewing on the
horizon here. I
don't like it.

Brilliance
Eternal

To the
Expanse of
Vibrance

To the
Nexus of
Imagination

Are you ever going to return the last map? Then again, I've had that other
thing of yours so long I've engraved my initials on it. I suppose we're even now.

Dear Wanderer,

   I did receive your latest communication. Please forgive formality on my part, as we have not met in person. I feel new to this role, despite my years holding it. You will admit to my relative youth, I think.

R adiant marched through a chamber deep beneath Urithiru, listening to the crashing sound of the waterworks and worrying about the mission Shallan had agreed to undertake. Volunteering to visit the honorspren? Traveling into Shadesmar?

That positioned them to do as Mraize had tasked them. Again.

Radiant did not like Mraize, and she certainly didn't trust him. However, she would keep to the agreement: the will of two should be respected. Veil wished to participate in the Ghostbloods wholeheartedly. Shallan wanted to work with them long enough to find out what they knew. So Radiant would not go to Dalinar and Jasnah. The compact meant harmony, and harmony meant the ability to function.

Mraize wants something out of this Restares person, Veil thought. *I can feel it. We need to find out what that secret is, then use it. We can't do that from here.*

A valid enough point. Radiant clasped her hands behind her back and continued her walk along the edge of the vast reservoir as her Lightweavers trained nearby. She had chosen to wear her vakama, the traditional Veden warrior's clothing. It was similar to the Alethi takama, but the skirt was pleated instead of straight. She wore a loose matching coat with a tight vest and shirt beneath.

The bright clothing featured vibrant blues embroidered over reds with gold woven between, and it had trim on the skirt. She'd noticed the Alethi doing double takes—both for the variegated colors, and because she wore what was traditionally a man's outfit. But a warrior was who she was, and Jah Keved was her heritage. She would convey both.

The room echoed with a low roar. Openings high in the walls on the other side of the reservoir let streams gush down and crash into the basin. The noise was distant enough to not disturb conversation, and the longer she practiced here, the more comforting she found the sound of rushing water. It was a natural thing, but contained, restrained. It seemed to represent humankind's mastery over the elements.

So we must master ourselves, Radiant thought—and Veil approved. Radiant was careful not to think poorly of Veil. Though their methods differed, they both existed to protect and help Shallan. Radiant respected Veil's efforts there. She had accomplished things Radiant could not.

Indeed, perhaps Veil could have been persuaded to talk to Dalinar and Jasnah. But Shallan . . . the idea frightened Shallan.

That deep wound had surprised Radiant as it began to emerge this last year. Radiant was pleased with the improvement they'd made in working together, but this wound was impeding further progress. It seemed similar to what often happened with strength training. You eventually reached a plateau—and sometimes getting to new heights required more pain first.

They'd get through this. It might seem like regression, but Radiant was certain this last knot of agony was the final answer. The final truth. Shallan was *terrified* that the ones she loved would turn on her when they found out the extent of her crimes. But she *needed* to confront her truths.

Radiant would do what she could to help ease that burden. Today, that meant helping prepare for the mission into Shadesmar. Veil could fulfill Mraize's demand and find this Restares person. Radiant would instead make certain the official side of their journey—speaking to the honorspren and pleading for them to join the war—was handled competently.

She turned and inspected her Lightweavers. She brought them to this chamber under the tower because they didn't like to train in the standard sparring halls. Though Radiant would have preferred them to associate with other soldiers, she had reluctantly agreed to find them a more private place. Their powers were . . . unusual, and could be distracting.

Nearby, Beryl and Darcira—two of her newer Lightweavers—changed faces as they fought. Diversions, to put their opponent off guard. Curiously, when wearing new faces, both women attacked more recklessly. Many Lightweavers, when offered a part to play, threw themselves into it wholeheartedly.

It didn't seem they had the same mental crisis as Shallan, fortunately. They just liked acting, and sometimes took it too far. If given a helmet, they'd stand up and shout orders like a battle commander. Wearing the right face they'd argue politics, stand in front of a crowd, even lob insults at the mighty. But catch either of these two women alone, wearing her own face? They'd speak in muted voices and avoid crowds, seeking to curl up quietly and read.

"Beryl, Darcira," Radiant said, interrupting the women. "I like how you are learning to control your powers—but today's task is to practice the sword. Try to watch your footwork more than your transformations. Darcira, when you wear a male face, you always lose your stance."

"Guess I feel more aggressive," Darcira said, shrugging as her Lightweaving puffed away, revealing her normal features.

"You must control the face rather than let it control you," Radiant said. Inside she felt Shallan forming a wisecrack—the Three had their own trouble with that idea. "When you're fighting, and you intend to distract someone, don't let that distract *you* as well."

"But Radiant," Beryl said, waving toward her side sword, "why do we even *have* to learn to fight? We're spies. If we have to pick up our swords, haven't we already lost?"

"There may be times when you will need to pretend to be a soldier. In that case, using the sword could be part of your disguise. But yes, fighting is our last resort. I would have it be a *viable* last resort—if you need to break disguise and abandon your cover, I want you to survive and return to us."

The young woman thought on that. She was a few years older than Shallan, but a few years younger than how Radiant saw herself. Beryl claimed to have forgotten her real name, she'd lived so many different lives. Veil had found her after hearing rumors of a prostitute working in the warcamps whose face changed to match that of people her clients most loved.

A hard life, but not an uncommon story for the Lightweavers. Half of Radiant's band of twenty included the deserters Shallan had first recruited. Those men might not have forgotten their former lives, but there were certainly parts in the middle they'd rather not discuss.

Beryl and Darcira took Radiant's tips—which were really Adolin's tips, drilled into her brain over many nights practicing—and returned to their sparring.

"I couldn't spot her Cryptic," Radiant said as she walked away to inspect the others.

"Mmm?" Pattern said, riding on her back, right below her collar. "Pattern? She usually rides on the inside of Beryl's shirt, near her skin. Pattern doesn't like to be seen."

"I'd prefer if you used the Cryptic's other name," Radiant said. "It's confusing, otherwise." After being pressured, each of the other Cryptics had picked individual names for the humans to use.

"I don't understand why," he said. "Our names are already all different. I am Pattern. She is Pattern. Gaz has Pattern."

"Those . . . are the same words, Pattern."

"But they're not," he said. "Mmm. I could write the numbers for you."

"Humans can't speak equations as intonations," Radiant said.

Like most of Shallan's team, Beryl and Darcira already had their own spren—though they had yet to earn their swords. That meant they weren't squires according to the Windrunner definition. Cryptics weren't as uptight as honorspren, and didn't wait as long to start bonds. Everyone in her team had one at this point, and newcomers got them quickly.

So her team had begun using their own terminology. Shallan was the Master Lightweaver. The others were Agent Lightweavers. If someone new joined, they were called a squire during the short time before they acquired a spren. Together, they'd begun calling themselves the Unseen Court. Both Veil and Shallan loved the title . . . though Radiant had noticed more than a few eye rolls from Windrunners when it was mentioned.

She completed her round of the room, the walking portion of which was shaped like a crescent. She looked over her twenty agents, and started deliberating on the true question at hand: Which ones should she take with her into Shadesmar?

She and Adolin had agreed that the team should be small. Shallan and Adolin, along with three Radiants: Godeke the Edgedancer, Zu the Stoneward, and the Truthwatcher woman who preferred to be called by her nickname, the Stump. They'd bring some of Adolin's soldiers as grooms and guards—and he'd choose men who *hadn't* been on the mission to the warcamps, just in case.

In addition they wanted three Lightweaver agents to Soulcast food, water, and other materials. It was a practical decision, and would also give some of Shallan's people experience with Shadesmar. Radiant approved, but she had to deal with one discomforting problem.

Did the Ghostbloods really have a spy among her agents? Veil emerged at this contemplation, and took control. She had to prepare for the possibility that one of the other Lightweavers might betray her if brought on this mission. *There must be a spy*, she thought, *and it will be someone who was on the mission to the warcamps. Because whoever they are, they killed Ialai.*

Shallan agreed with this. Though Radiant, for some odd reason, seemed uncertain at that logic.

Well, Veil needed to figure out who the most likely candidates were—then make certain they went on the mission to Shadesmar.

What? Radiant thought. *No, if we suspect them of being a spy, we should keep them far away.*

No, Veil replied. *We keep them close. To better manipulate and watch them.*

That would be reckless.

And what would you rather have, Radiant? Veil asked. *An enemy you can see, watch, and maybe fight—or one you leave off somewhere, doing who knows what?*

That was more of a valid point. Veil surrendered control to Shallan, who knew the team the best. And as she strolled through the room—her hair bleeding to red—she found herself planning. How did she identify which agents were most likely to be a spy?

She started by walking over to where Ishnah was sparring. The short woman's straight black hair framed a face accented by bright red lip paint, and she wore an Alethi havah with a gloved hand instead of a sleeve. Ishnah was one of those who had earned her Blade. By Windrunner terms, she should be off gathering her own squires and making her own team—they seemed to assume everyone would want to follow their command structure. The Unseen Court, however, didn't care for Windrunner methods.

Instead, the Unseen Court would remain together. A balanced team, with roughly equal men and women, as all but one of her new recruits over the year had been female. Indeed, Shallan felt the Court was complete. Beryl had been with them for nearly three months now, and Shallan hadn't felt a need to recruit anyone else. She wanted a tight-knit group. Hopefully other groups of Lightweavers would come to join the Radiants—but they would form their own teams.

Ishnah had once wanted to join the Ghostbloods. Could the woman have found her way to Mraize? Would she have agreed to watch Shallan? It was possible, making Ishnah a prime suspect. That hurt Shallan to consider, to the point that she forced Radiant to take over again.

What of Vathah? Radiant glanced toward him. The brutish former deserter was the most naturally talented Lightweaver. He often used his powers without recognizing it—even now as he sparred with Red, he'd made himself appear taller and more muscular. He had joined her under protest, and never *quite* seemed tamed by modern society. How much of a bribe would it take to coax him to spy on her?

We're going to have to be careful, Radiant, Shallan said from within. *The Court could tear itself apart thinking like this.*

Somehow Radiant had to distrust them all while encouraging them to trust one another.

"Ishnah," Radiant said, "what do you think of the mission we've been given?"

Ishnah dismissed her Shardblade and walked over. "Going into the dark, Brightness? That place offers opportunities. The ones who master it will get ahead quickly."

It was a pragmatic but ambitious attitude. Ishnah always saw opportunities. Her Cryptic tended to ride about on the ornament on the end of the central hairspike she used to keep her braids in place. Much smaller than Pattern, this one constantly made new designs on the surface of the pale white sphere.

"Adolin and I have decided to bring a small group," Radiant said. "The honorspren need to be met with a coalition of spren and Radiants, not an overwhelming group of Cryptics—particularly considering they don't much care for them."

"From what I've heard," Ishnah replied, "the honorspren don't much like anyone."

"This is true," Radiant said. "But Syl has told me that while they don't trust Cryptics, honorspren don't hate them like they do inkspren or highspren. I have decided to bring three Lightweavers along with me."

"Can I have one of the slots?" Ishnah said. "I want to see more of the spren world."

Mraize's spy would volunteer for the mission, Veil noted.

"I will consider it," Radiant said. "If you were going to take two others, who would they be?"

"Not sure," Ishnah said. "The more experienced would be more useful, but the newer recruits could learn a lot—and we don't expect this mission to be dangerous. I guess I'd ask around and see who wanted to go."

"A wise suggestion," Radiant said.

And a clear way to begin hunting the spy. Inside, Shallan squirmed again. She *hated* thinking about one of her friends being a traitor.

Well, Radiant hoped it wasn't Ishnah. The woman had survived the fall of Kholinar with admirable grit. She'd stared one of the worst disasters in modern history in the face and had not only weathered it, but had helped Kaladin's squires rescue the crown prince. She would be a great advantage on this mission, but Radiant wasn't certain—despite what Veil said—that they wanted to bring suspicious ones along.

She made another quick circuit of her people, joined by Ishnah, and gauged their eagerness to go on the mission. Most were ambivalent. They wanted to prove themselves, but stories of Shadesmar disturbed them. In the end, she had a short list of the most eager. Ishnah, naturally. Vathah and Beryl, the former prostitute, and Stargyle, the male recruit she'd picked up before Beryl. A tall fellow who was talented at seeing into Shadesmar.

These four were already among the most suspicious, Veil thought. *Ishnah, who knows about the Ghostbloods. Vathah, who is always so quiet, so dark, hard to read. Beryl and Stargyle, our newest recruits—and therefore least known to me and the others.*

All had been on the mission to the warcamps. So, did she bring three of these four as Veil wanted, or leave them behind as Radiant wanted? Little as she wanted it right now, Shallan took control at the urging of the other two. She had to make the deciding vote.

Strong. With Veil and Radiant supporting her, she found she *could* face this. She made her decision—she'd leave these four behind, and pick others who hadn't been on the mission to the Shattered Plains.

She started toward Ishnah to break the news to her, but felt something like nausea. A twisting of her insides. She hunched over, then tried to suppress it, embarrassed to so suddenly lose control. But then, appearing foolish in front of the others was a small price to pay for an opportunity. And really, if it made them underestimate her, then what harm was done? Veil could use that; she could use most anything.

Veil cleared her throat and took a few deep breaths.

"You all right, Brightness?" Ishnah asked, walking up.

"Fine," Veil said. "I've made my decision; you'll be joining me in Shadesmar. Would you kindly go tell Vathah and Stargyle that I'd like them to join us as well? I'll do as you suggested—one more practiced Lightweaver for the resource they offer, one newer agent to learn from the experience."

"Great," Ishnah said. "That puts Red in charge during our absence, I suppose? And I assume you could come up with some Lightweaving exercises everyone else can perform while we're gone."

"Perfect," Veil said.

Ishnah grinned as she hurried off. Yes, she *did* feel suspicious. And if Veil had chosen wrong? Well, she suspected the true spy would somehow end up on the mission anyway. Mraize would make certain of it.

The compact, Shallan thought. *Veil . . . we agreed . . .*

But this was *important.* Veil *had* to find out which one of them was the spy. She *couldn't* let them stay behind and fester.

We don't even know if there is a spy, Radiant said. *We can't take too much of what Mraize says as truth.*

Well, they would see. Leaving your suspected spy *behind,* so they could run amok unwatched? They would poison her friends against her. Besides, once she unmasked the actual spy, Veil could use this knowledge against Mraize.

She braced herself for anger from Radiant at breaking the compact. It did set a dangerous precedent, didn't it?

This is important to you, I see, Radiant thought. She felt strangely quiet. *I change my vote, then. I agree to bring them with us.*

Veil found this odd. Was Radiant well? Just in case, Veil kept control. She stood tall, trying to appear puffed up like Radiant always acted—as if she wanted to be bigger than she was, some hulking monster in armor.

Veil held full control all through the rest of the day. She almost let go—Shallan was *pounding* at her from the inside, and that kind of mental doublethink could really wear a woman down. However, Veil needed to see to the rest of the preparations. The mission would be leaving in mere days.

Only when Veil stepped into her rooms—late into the evening—did she begin to relax her grip. However, on the floor inside the room she found a green feather. Mraize?

It was a sign. Veil scanned the room, and her eyes landed on a dresser near the door to the bedroom. A green cloth peeked from one of the drawers.

Holding an amethyst mark for light, she eased the drawer open. Inside she found a metal cube roughly the size of a person's head. The note on it was in one of Mraize's ciphers.

"Mmm . . ." Pattern said from where he dimpled the skirt of her vakama. "What is it, Veil?"

Damnation. She'd hoped to be able to fool Pattern into thinking she was Shallan, but of course he saw through her.

"A note." She showed it to him, holding the light near the text. "Can you break the cipher, or do I have to go dig out the notebook Mraize gave us?"

"I memorized the patterns. It reads, 'Spanreeds do not work between realms, but this will. Be *very* careful with it. It has a value beyond that of some kingdoms. Do not open it, or you risk destroying it. Once on your mission and in a secluded place, hold the cube and call my name. I will speak to you through it. Good hunting, little knife.'"

Curious. She immediately glimpsed into Shadesmar, and found a sphere of light on the other side, glowing with a strange mother-of-pearl coloring. There was power inside the cube, but no Stormlight. Her attention back to the Physical Realm, she shook it and knocked on the sides. It seemed hollow, but she couldn't find the slightest crack in it.

Storms. How was she going to hide *this* from Adolin? Well, she'd have to find a way. She would make another trip into Shadesmar, but not by accident. Veil would go on her terms—and she would not spend this trip running.

This time, *she* was the hunter.

THE SEETHING KNOT

I have been fascinated to discover how much you've accomplished on Scadrial without me noticing your presence. How is it that you hide from Shards so well?

Choosing an outfit for the day was a lot like fighting a duel. In both, instincts—rather than conscious decisions—were the key to victory. Adolin didn't often fret about what to wear; nor did he plan each strike of the sword. He went with what felt right.

The real trick in both cases was making the effort to *build* your instincts. You couldn't parry a thrust with muscle memory if you hadn't spent years practicing those maneuvers. And you couldn't rely on your gut in fashion choices if you hadn't already spent hours studying the folios.

That said, once in a while your instincts locked up. Even he sometimes hesitated in a duel, uncertain. And similarly, some days he simply *couldn't* decide upon the right jacket.

Adolin stood in his underclothing as he held up the first jacket. Traditional: Kholin blue with white cuffs. Bold white embroidery, with his glyphs—the tall tower and a stylized version of his Blade—on the back. It made him easy to see in battle. It was also boring.

He glanced at the trendy yellow jacket on his bed. He'd ordered that tailored after the fashions he'd seen in Kholinar. It didn't fully button closed, and it had silver embroidery up the sides and covering the pocket and cuffs. Storms, it was bold. Daring. A bright *yellow* outfit? Most men couldn't ever have pulled it off.

Adolin could. Walk into a feast wearing something like this, and you would *own* everyone's attention. Look confident, and at the next feast half the men would be trying to imitate you.

He wasn't going to a feast though. He was starting out on an important mission into Shadesmar. He began rifling through his bureau again.

Shallan strolled in as he tossed three more jackets onto the bed. She wore Veil's clothing—trousers, long loose jacket, a buttoned shirt. At his suggestion she'd replaced the white trousers and jacket with a more practical tan and blue ensemble. White wouldn't travel well; she wanted something more rugged, something that wouldn't show the dirt. Blue and tan matched her white hat, though he'd added a leather band around the base of the crown.

Clothing notwithstanding, she wasn't Veil today—not with the red hair. Plus, he could usually tell by the way she looked at him. It had been three days since she'd chosen her members for the team, but it was only today that they were finally ready to leave.

Shallan leaned against the door, folding her arms and surveying his work. "You know," she said, "a girl could get jealous over how much attention you give a choice like this."

"Jealous?" Adolin said. "Of jackets?"

"Of the one you're wearing them for."

"I doubt you have anything to worry about from a group of stuffy old honorspren."

"I don't have anything to worry about regardless," Shallan said. "But you're *not* fussing today because of the honorspren. We won't meet them for a few weeks at best."

"I'm not fussing. I'm *strategizing.*" He tossed another jacket onto the bed. *No. Too outdated.* "Don't give me that look. Are we ready?"

"Pattern's run off to say goodbye to Wit for some reason," she said. "Said it was very important—but I suspect that he's misunderstood some joke Wit made. Other than waiting on him, everything is ready. We just need you."

Supplies were gathered, transportation secured, and traveling companions chosen. Adolin had packed for the trip quickly and efficiently, and his trunks were already loaded. Those choices had been easy. But today's jacket . . .

"So . . ." Shallan said. "Shall I tell them *two* more hours or *three*?"

"I'll be down in fifteen minutes," he promised, checking the fabrial clock set in the leather bracer Aunt Navani had given him. Then he eyed Shallan. "Maybe thirty."

"I'll tell them an hour," Shallan said, with a grin. She trailed out, tossing her satchel over her shoulder.

Adolin put his hands on his hips and surveyed his options. None of them were right. What was he looking for?

Wait. Of course.

He emerged from his room a few minutes later wearing a uniform he hadn't put on in years. It was Kholin blue, still a military outfit, but cut for a more relaxed fit. Though not specifically trendy, it had a more stylized set of glyphs on the back and thicker cuffs and collar than a standard uniform.

Many would have simply assumed it to be an ordinary Kholin uniform. Adolin had designed it himself four years earlier. He'd wanted to create something that would look sharp while satisfying his father's requirements to be in uniform. The project had excited him for weeks; it had been his first—and only—real attempt at clothing design.

The first day he'd worn it, Dalinar had chewed him out. So it had gone into the trunk, tucked away. Forgotten.

Father probably still wouldn't approve, but these days Dalinar didn't approve of Adolin in general. So what was the harm? He replaced his arm bracer, strapped on his side sword, and entered the hallway. Then he hesitated.

Shallan *had* given him an hour, and there was something else Adolin wanted to check off his list before leaving. So he turned the other direction and climbed the steps toward the sixth floor.

．•．

Adolin was surprised to find a line at the clinic. The sixth floor wasn't particularly well populated, but news had apparently spread. None of the waiting patients seemed too unfortunate—children cradling scrapes, with hovering parents nearby. A line of women with coughs or aches. Anything serious would warrant the attention of an Edgedancer or a Truthwatcher.

Some bowed to Adolin as he slipped into the front room, where Kaladin's mother was greeting each patient and recording their symptoms. She smiled at Adolin, holding up two fingers, and waved him down the hallway beyond.

Adolin went that direction. The first room he passed had the door cracked, revealing Kaladin's father seeing a young man. A town girl stood next to him, reading aloud the notes Lirin's wife had taken.

The second room along the hallway was a similar—but empty—exam room. Adolin slipped in, and Kaladin entered a few minutes later, drying his hands on a cloth. It was odd to see him in simple brown trousers and a white buttoned shirt—in fact, had Adolin *ever* seen Kaladin out of uniform? Honestly . . . Adolin had assumed the man slept in the thing. Yet here he was, with sleeves rolled up to his elbows, his shoulder-length hair pulled back into a tail.

Kaladin stopped when he saw Adolin. "You can go to your brother for healing, Adolin. I have real patients that need help."

Adolin ignored the comment and glanced out into the hallway, looking toward the waiting room. "You're a popular fellow, bridgeboy."

"I'm convinced half of them are here to get a peek at me," Kaladin said, with a sigh. He tied on a white surgeon's apron. "I fear my notoriety could overshadow the clinic's purpose."

Adolin chuckled. "Be careful. Now that I've vacated the position, you're Alethkar's most eligible bachelor. Shardbearer, Radiant, Landed, and *single*? I wouldn't be surprised to hear that half the young ladies in the kingdom are suddenly coming down with headaches. . . ." He trailed off as he noticed Kaladin's frown.

"It's already happened, hasn't it!" Adolin said, pointing.

"I . . . had wondered why so many lighteyed women suddenly needed medication," he said. "I'd thought that maybe their personal surgeons had been recruited into the war. . . ." He glanced at Adolin, then blushed.

"You can be deliciously naive sometimes, Kal," Adolin said. "You need to use this angle. Work it."

"That would betray the ethics of the surgeon-patient relationship," Kaladin said, closing the door—preventing Adolin from counting the suspiciously well-dressed young women in the waiting room. "Have you come to torment me, or is there an actual purpose behind this visit?"

"I just wanted to check on you," Adolin said. "See how retirement is going."

Kaladin shrugged. He walked over to begin arranging the medications and bandages on the shelf, where sphere lanterns glowed with a pure white light.

Syl winked into existence beside Adolin's head, forming from luminous mist, as if she were a Shardblade. "This *is* good for him," she said, leaning in. "He's actually *relaxing* for once."

"There aren't many serious cases," Kaladin said, his back to them. "It can be grueling with so many people in line, but . . . it isn't as tense as I worried it would be."

"It's working," Syl continued, landing on Adolin's shoulder. "His parents are always around, so he's almost never alone. He still has nightmares, but I think he's getting more sleep."

Adolin watched Kaladin fold bandages, then noticed how Kaladin glanced at the surgery knives laid out in a row. He shouldn't keep them out like that, should he?

Adolin made a sudden motion, standing up straight from where he'd been leaning against the door, his feet scraping the stone. Kaladin immediately reached for the knives, then glanced back, and—seeing nothing was wrong—relaxed.

Adolin walked over and put his hand on Kaladin's shoulder. "Hey," he said. "It chases us all. Including me, Kal." He fished in his pocket, then brought out a metal disc about an inch across. He held it toward Kaladin. "I dropped by to give you this."

"What is it?" Kaladin asked, taking the disc. One side was engraved with a picture of a divine figure in robes, while the other side bore the same figure in battle gear. Both were surrounded by strange foreign glyphs. It had been coated with some colored enamel at one point, but that had mostly worn off.

"Zahel gave it to me when I finished my training with him," Adolin said. "Says it's from his homeland—they use these things as money. Weird, eh?"

"Why don't they use spheres?"

"Maybe they don't have enough gemstones? He's from somewhere to the west. He doesn't look like a foreigner though, so I'm guessing it must be Bavland."

"This side might be a Herald," Kaladin said, squinting at the strange glyphs. "What does it say?"

"'War is the last option of the state that has failed,'" Adolin said, tapping the side with the divine robed figure. He pushed it to spin it in Kaladin's fingers, showing the other side. "'But it is better than having no options.'"

"Huh," Kaladin said.

"Zahel told me," Adolin said, "that he always considered himself a coward for training soldiers. He said that if he truly believed in stopping war, he'd walk away from the sword completely. Then he gave me the disc, and I knew he understood. In a perfect world, no one would *have* to train for battle. We don't live in a perfect world."

"How does this relate to me?" Kaladin asked.

"Well, there's no shame in you taking time away from the sword. Maybe permanently. All the same, I know you enjoy it."

"I shouldn't enjoy killing," Kaladin said softly. "I shouldn't even enjoy the fight. I should hate it like my father does."

"You can hate killing and enjoy the contest," Adolin said. "Plus there are practical reasons to keep your skills up. Take these months to relax. When I return though, let's find a chance to spar together again, all right? I want you to see what I see in duels. It's not about hurting others. It's about being your best."

"I . . . don't know if I can ever think like you do," Kaladin said. He wrapped his fist around the metal disc. "But thank you. I'll keep the offer in mind."

Adolin clapped him on the shoulder, then glanced toward Syl. "I need to be off into Shadesmar. Any last tips for me?"

"Be careful, Adolin," she said, flitting up into the air. "My kind aren't like highspren—we don't look to laws, but to morality, as our guide."

"That's good, isn't it?" Adolin said.

"It is . . . unless you happen to disagree with their interpretation of morality. My kind can be very difficult to persuade with logic, because for us . . . well, what we *feel* can often be more important to us than what we *think*. We're spren of honor, but remember, honor is—even to us—what humans and spren define it to be. Particularly with our god dead."

Adolin nodded. "Right, then. Kal, don't let anyone burn the tower down while I'm away."

"You should have been the surgeon, Adolin," Kaladin said. "Not me. You care about people."

"Don't be silly," Adolin said, pulling open the door as he gestured at Kaladin's work clothing. "I could *never* dress like that." He left Kaladin with a wink.

∴

Adolin strode out the front gate of Urithiru's imposing tower and entered the chill air of the plateau. He was a full six minutes early. Handy, the way Aunt Navani's device let him time himself—if everyone had clocks, he'd spend way less time waiting around at winehouses for his friends to arrive.

The broad plain in front of him—too smooth to be natural—stretched like a roadway toward the mountain peaks in the distance. Ten perfectly circular platforms rose from the sides of the plateau, with ramps leading up to each. These Oathgates were portals to places around the world. Currently only four functioned: the ones to the Shattered Plains, Thaylenah, Jah Keved, and Azir.

A group had gathered on the platform leading to the Shattered Plains, but they wouldn't travel to that destination. This was just the gate where Adolin's team would enter Shadesmar. His breath puffing before him, Adolin jogged over to the ramp, where his armorers were packing his Shardplate in its traveling chest, cushioned with straw. Though the stuff was as hard as stone, they always took the utmost care with it. There was a certain reverence due to a Shard.

"It's not going to make the transfer, Brightlord," one armorer warned him. "When you go to Shadesmar, it will be left behind on the platform. It's been tested on several suits already."

"My armor might act differently," Adolin said. "I want to be sure. If it does fail to make the trip, send it along with Father and his expeditionary force. He'll lend it to Fisk, to complement his Blade."

The armorers saluted. Nearby, a few other stragglers were hurrying up the slope to the Oathgate—including Shallan's newest agent, a tall Alethi woman with excellent taste in dresses. She carried a pack over her shoulder, but . . . she wasn't going on the trip, was she?

"Beryl?" Adolin called to her as she passed. "Wasn't Stargyle chosen to make this journey?"

"Oh, Brightlord!" the darkeyed woman said. "Stargyle's wife has come down with a sickness. He wants to stay with her, so we decided I should go instead."

Huh. He nodded absently as the woman hurried up the slope. Shallan had seemed very particular about whom she wanted to bring. Hopefully this hadn't upset her plans.

Well, nothing to do about it. He stepped over to a tall black horse standing at the ready. Gallant was surrounded by Adolin's grooms, who were preparing to strap equipment to the horse's back—including Adolin's weapons and his trunk of clothing. The horse should have been loaded already. Adolin stepped up to the Ryshadium and stared into his watery blue eyes—which, if he looked closely, had a faint swirl of rainbow colors to them.

The horse glanced at the pack straps the porters were affixing onto his back; they required stools to get high enough.

"What?" Adolin asked.

The horse blew out, then glared at the straps again.

"You think because we're royalty, we're above doing a little labor?" Adolin pointed at the horse, meeting his eyes. "It's like Father always says. Never be unwilling to do something you might ask another to do for you." He reached into his pocket and pulled out a palafruit. "Here."

The horse turned away.

"Fine," Adolin said. "I'll have them saddle up one of the common horses instead. Leave you behind."

Gallant turned back to him, glaring. Then, reluctantly, the horse ate the palafruit and spat out the pit. Adolin rubbed him on the muzzle, then patted his neck. Nearby one of the grooms watched, baffled, until one of the others nudged him.

"I talk to my sword too," Adolin told them. "Funny thing is, she eventually talked back. Never be afraid to show a little respect to those you depend upon, friends."

The two grooms scuttled away as two workmen hitched Adolin's armor boxes into place on one side of the horse.

"Thank you," Adolin said to Gallant. "For being with me. I know you'd rather be with Father."

The horse blew out, then reached his muzzle into Adolin's hand. Ryshadium chose their riders; they were not broken or trained. They accepted you, or they did not—and it was very rare for one to allow two riders.

Father loved his horse, he really did. But he was so busy with meetings these days, and Gallant seemed so forlorn. Abandoned, just a little. And well . . . Adolin had his own loss he was dealing with. So it had seemed a natural pairing, one that over the months had become more and more strong.

The grooms finished with the armor trunks, and then hooked Adolin's clothing trunk on the other side. That wasn't nearly as heavy as the Plate, so to weight that side roughly equal, a worker approached with a long box. Adolin stopped him, wanting to do one last check. He knelt to undo the latches and peeked inside.

"Storms," a voice said. "Pardon, Brightlord, but how many swords do you need?"

Adolin grinned up at Godeke the Edgedancer, who was leading his horse nearby. The slender man wore his hair cropped short, though he wasn't technically an ardent any longer, and so didn't need to shave it. Beyond him, Zu—the team's Stoneward—was lifting her pack onto her back. The golden-haired woman continually complained about the cold, and huddled in a coat several sizes too large.

"Well," Adolin said to Godeke, "you can never have too many swords. Besides, no Shardblades can enter Shadesmar, so a man must be prepared."

"You're wearing a sword."

"This?" Adolin said, patting his side sword. "Oh sure, this is better than nothing, but I'd hate to be caught with just it and no buckler. Besides, I've trained to duel mostly on longswords and greatswords." He pulled his greatsword out of his arms box; the long weapon was intended to be used two-handed. It wasn't as long as some Shardblades, of course, nor as wide.

"I don't . . . know how much dueling you'll be doing, Brightlord."

"Obviously," Adolin said. "That's why I need these others." He handed it to the groom. "Fix its scabbard to Gallant's left shoulder, its guard in line with the saddle." To Godeke, he continued, "See here, a hand-and-a-half sword for use with or without my shield. A nice swordstaff for horseback—I can screw in this piece to make it longer . . ."

"I see."

"Here, this is an Emuli kusu," Adolin said, holding up the long curved sword. "Great for slicing and cutting, especially when doing ride-by charges. Easier to withdraw the blade and better against someone unarmored. And here, I need this Veden house sword if we end up fighting against mail. . . ."

"I should be—"

"Don't forget Shardbearers," Adolin said, hefting a warhammer. It looked small, almost like a workman's hammer with a longer handle—so tiny compared to the massive Shardbearers' hammers wielded by men in Plate. He didn't want to make Gallant haul one of *those* on their trip. "Need this if I end up being forced to crack some Plate—the swords will simply break, except maybe the house sword. Might be able to get that through a crack, once the armor is weakened."

"I really—"

"And here, see this one?" He pulled out a unique triangular weapon, gripped at the base with a kind of handle instead of a true hilt. "Thaylen gtet. I've always wanted to train with one of these. Figured I might get some practice in."

Godeke waved to someone farther up the ramp, then hastily said farewell before hiking off, tugging his horse after him. Adolin grinned, then had the workers hang a few more weapons from the horse's saddle. Gallant tapped his hooves with what seemed to be satisfaction, happier to be outfitted with proper weapons and not just luggage. The workers affixed the box with the rest in place.

"You seem almost pleased," Zu said, strolling over in her oversized coat. "To not be able to use Shardblades, I mean."

Adolin hadn't spoken to the woman much; he hadn't realized how good her Alethi was. Apparently her people had turned her out when her powers had first manifested several years ago—they hadn't realized she was a Radiant, and had thought her cursed by some strange god whose name Adolin hadn't recognized.

The Iriali fought for the enemy now, but Dalinar didn't turn away anyone who came asking for asylum—particularly if they'd said Radiant oaths.

"Well," Adolin said, "I wouldn't say *happy*. A Shardblade is the superior weapon. No amount of specialization for the situation can make up for the ability to slice through your opponent's weapons, armor, even body as if they were water. I love wielding mine in duels; there's just a part of me that regrets that it makes other weapons obsolete."

"I disagree," Zu said, summoning her Blade. "Why would you ever regret the existence of one of these?" It appeared in her hand upon her command, forming from mist. She preferred a slender Blade, even longer than his father's, with a wicked curve to it.

Adolin stood up, breathing heat into his hands as Merit began leading the pack animals up the ramp onto the Oathgate platform. Adolin glanced at Gallant; the horse clopped off to follow, needing no bridle or rope to guide him.

Zu waved her sword overhead slowly in a kind of kata that caught the sun. It transformed in her hands, becoming smaller and shorter—like his side sword—then became straight, with a tip for thrusting. The fact that living Shardblades could change shapes explained a lot to Adolin.

The ancient Shardblades—the dead ones that most Shardbearers used—were locked, apparently into the last shape they'd held. Most were massive things, not clunky—a Shardblade could never be clunky—but also not particularly well suited to most battlefield actions. They were light, yes, but the size could be unwieldy nonetheless.

Modern Radiants preferred functional weapons when actually fighting. However, when they wanted to show off, they created something majestic and otherworldly—something that was less about practicality and more about awe. That indicated most Shardblades, his own included, had practical forms—but had been abandoned in their more showy styles.

"I didn't mean to imply there's not art to a Shardblade," Adolin told Zu. "I truly love Shardblade duels. I just love finding the best weapon for the job. And when that answer isn't always the same sword, it's more satisfying."

"You should become a Radiant," she said. "Then your sword would always be the right weapon for the job."

"As if it were that easy," Adolin said. "Just become a Radiant."

His equipment seen to, Adolin did a quick head count. Six of his soldiers were coming as guards and workers—darkeyed men specifically chosen because they had good heads on their shoulders. Adolin didn't pick the best duelists; he chose men who could cook and do laundry in the field. Most importantly, he needed men who wouldn't balk at oddities.

Felt was the best of them, an older foreign man, one of Dalinar's friends from the early days. He was steady and reliable, and had training as a scout. Merit was a groom, and Urad was an excellent hunter, should they need to forage. Adolin wasn't certain how useful that would be in Shadesmar, but best to be prepared.

Felt's wife, Malli, worked in the quartermaster's office, and was along to act as a scribe. No actual servants, though Shallan's three Lightweavers did odd jobs for her.

That left the three full Radiants. Godeke and Zu he'd already checked on. Asking around, Adolin found that their final Radiant—a Tashikki woman—had returned to the tower to check on something. So he idled near the ramp, waiting until he saw her crossing the plateau.

The woman had to be in her seventies, with dark brown furrowed skin and silver hair. She was slender, but not frail. Adolin suspected from her firm step that she relied on Stormlight to strengthen her. Though he'd seen her wearing a Tashikki wrap in the tower before, today she wore rugged traveling clothing and a shawl over her hair, with a pack slung over one shoulder. As she approached, Adolin reached to help her carry it, but she tightened her fingers.

She didn't speak much Alethi, but most of the spren were able to speak several human languages. He wasn't certain if it was an aspect of their nature, or if they simply lived so long that they ended up picking up multiple languages.

Either way, the spren could translate if necessary, and Adolin really did want to bring a Truthwatcher. They had once been well-regarded by the honorspren. Though the woman's name was Arshqqam, everyone called her the Stump—a nickname that Lift had spread, he believed. Arshqqam had mentioned she was fond of the name, and the way she strode—unbowed by age, insisting on carrying her own things—gave him an inkling of where the moniker had come from.

With her arrival, the entire expedition was accounted for. A half dozen pack animals weren't many for fifteen people. Normally he'd have expected that many animals for just the food, plus some wagons carrying stormbarrels that could be chained down to catch rainwater. Fortunately, this group had Shallan's Lightweavers to provide food and water through Soulcasting.

As Adolin crossed the platform, he passed the queen standing—as always—with Wit at her shoulder. She, Dalinar, and Taravangian were the only monarchs at the tower today, and they'd all come to see off the expedition. Jasnah was supervising Ishnah and Vathah, two of Shallan's agents, determining for herself if they were capable.

Adolin lingered as Vathah knelt beside a large block of obsidian. The glassy stone had been mined in Shadesmar and brought through for the test. Vathah's hand sank into the block, and then the structure of the obsidian changed—in the blink of an eye, the rock transformed into grain. Kind of. What Vathah made was a large square lump of hardened lavis pulp, not individual seeds like some advanced Soulcasters could make. They could cut off chunks, cook it to mush. It wasn't tasty, but it was hearty and healthy.

Do they know? Adolin wondered. *How much Jasnah sees them as tools?* For centuries the Alethi Soulcasting devices—limited though they were—had given his kingdom an unparalleled edge in battle. Now, Lightweavers were Soulcasting and didn't seem to suffer the same ill effects as users of the devices.

Adolin could see deeper motives in the months Jasnah had spent training Shallan and her agents. Though Shallan wanted her team to become spies, Jasnah seemed to see their powers of illusion as a distant second to their ability to feed armies.

Hopefully the cache of Soulcasting devices found in Aimia would relieve some of that pressure. Shallan watched from the near distance, sitting on a supply box, her expression unreadable. Though by far the most talented at illusions among her people, Shallan's own abilities in Soulcasting had proven . . . erratic. Adolin had peeked in on her sessions to see only occasional lumps of grain. Other times, she accidentally created twisted things: flames, sometimes pools of blood, once a translucent crystal.

Jasnah had finally, after eight months of work, officially released Shallan from her wardship. And Shallan truly had earned that release. She'd gone to lessons, memorized the works of scholars, and acted as the perfect ward. Though mastery of Soulcasting eluded her, she had improved over the year.

Jasnah dismissed the two agents, who hastened to join the others. Adolin found himself growing anxious as everyone gathered around the small building at the center of the platform. Not that he had any reason. It was just that it had been months since he'd last visited Shadesmar.

Dalinar stepped up to the group and waited for everyone to quiet. He would want to speak, of course. Adolin's father could turn anything into an excuse for an inspirational speech.

"I commend your bravery," Dalinar said to the gathered people. "Know that you go representing not only me, but the entire coalition. With you go the hopes of millions.

"The realm you traverse will be alien and at times hostile. Do not forget that it once held allies, and their fortresses welcomed men with open arms. Your task is to rekindle those ancient alliances, as we have re-formed the ancient bond between nations. Know that you take with you my utmost confidence."

Not bad, Adolin thought. *At least it was short.* Adolin's six men cheered as expected. The Radiants applauded politely, which generally wasn't the response that one of Dalinar's rousing speeches received. He continued to treat them like soldiers, though most of the Radiants here today had never been in the military. Shallan was a country lighteyes and scholar turned spy; the Stump had run an orphanage; Godeke had been an ardent. So far as Adolin knew, Zu was the only one who had held anything resembling a weapon before saying her oaths.

Jasnah said a few words, and so did Taravangian. Adolin listened with half an ear, wondering if Taravangian found it odd that the expedition wasn't taking any Dustbringers. No one had spoken the reason, but it was obvious to Adolin. The Dustbringers didn't serve Dalinar, at least not loyally enough for his taste.

At the end of the speeches, the members of the expedition began squeezing into the small control building, leading the horses in as well. There might be some way to bring everyone on the platform into Shadesmar, but so far they'd been limited to people standing in the small control building.

Adolin waved for Shallan to go in first without him. Jasnah, Taravangian, and Wit began to retreat across the platform with their attendants. Soon, Adolin and Dalinar stood facing one another, alone outside the building.

A snort broke the air. Gallant had lingered, refusing the grooms who tried to coax him into the building with fruit. Dalinar broke his stern posture and patted the horse on the neck. "Thank you," he said to Adolin, "for caring for him these last months. I don't get much time for riding these days."

"We both know how busy you are, Father."

"That's a new uniform," Dalinar said to him. "Better than some you've been wearing lately."

"That's amusing," Adolin said. "Four years ago when I last wore this, you called it disgraceful."

Dalinar stiffened, lowering his hand from Gallant's neck. Then he clasped his hands behind his back and stood tall. So storming tall. Sometimes Adolin's father was more like a Soulcast statue than a person.

"I guess . . . we've both become more lax over the years," Dalinar said.

"I think I've stayed the same person," Adolin said. "I'm just more willing to let you be disappointed by that person."

"Son," Dalinar said, "I'm *not* disappointed in you."

"Aren't you? Can you say that truthfully, with an oath?"

Dalinar fell silent. "I merely want you to be the best man you can be," he finally said. "A better man than I was at your age. I know *that's* the person you really are. And I want you to represent me well. Is that such a terrible thing?"

"I don't represent you anymore, Father. I'm a highprince. I represent myself. Is *that* such a terrible thing?"

Dalinar sighed. "Don't go down this road, son. Do not let my failings drive you to rebel against what you know is right, merely because it's what I wish of you."

"I'm not—" Adolin made fists, trying to squeeze out his frustration. "I'm *not* simply rebelling, Father. I'm not fourteen anymore."

"No. When you were fourteen you looked up to me for some reason." Dalinar glanced after the departing figures, growing small on the platform. "You see Taravangian out there? Do you know how he sees the world? Any cost, any price, is worth paying if what you want to achieve is—in the end—worthy.

"Follow him, and you'll be able to justify anything. Lying to your soldiers? Necessary, to get them to do their work. Gathering wealth? You need it to further your important goals. Killing innocents? All to forge a stronger nation." He eyed Adolin. "Murdering a man in a back alley, then lying about it? Well, the world is better off without him. In fact, there are a lot of people this world could do without. Let's start removing them quietly. . . ."

Maybe I murdered Sadeas, Adolin thought. *But at least I never killed anyone innocent. At least I didn't burn my own wife to death.*

There it was. The seething knot deep inside him, the one Adolin didn't dare touch lest it burn him. He knew Dalinar had been a different man then. A man not in his right mind, betrayed, consumed by the power of one of the Unmade. Besides, Dalinar hadn't killed Adolin's mother on purpose.

One could know these things without feeling them. And this. Wasn't. Something. You. *Forgave.*

Adolin shoved that furious knot down and didn't let it rule him, ignoring the angerspren at his feet. He said nothing to his father. He didn't trust the anger, the frustration, and—yes—the shame churning within. If he opened his mouth, one of the three might come out, but he couldn't say which.

"You either believe as Taravangian does," Dalinar said, "or you accept the better path: that your actions define you more than your intentions. That your goals *and* the journey used to attain them must align. I'm trying to stop you before you do some things you will truly, sincerely regret."

"And if I think the actions I've taken *are* worthy?" Adolin said.

"Then perhaps we need to consider that my training of you in your youth was faulty. That is not surprising. I was not exactly the best of examples."

It's about you again, Adolin thought. *I can't have an opinion or make choices—I'm only acting like this because of your influence.*

Kelek, Jezerezeh, and Heralds above! Adolin loved his father. Even now, with everything he'd learned about what Dalinar had done. Even with . . . that event. He *loved his father.* He loved that Dalinar tried so hard, and he *had* become someone far better than he'd once been.

But *Damnation.* This last year, Adolin had begun to realize how difficult it could be to live around the man.

"Maybe," Adolin said, calming himself with effort. "Maybe—incredible though it may seem—there are more than *two* choices in life. I'm not you, but that doesn't mean I'm Taravangian. Maybe I'm my own brand of wrong."

Dalinar rested his hand on Adolin's shoulder. It should have been comforting, but Adolin couldn't help but see it as a way to control the conversation. To put himself in the position of father, and Adolin squarely into his role as whining child.

"Son," Dalinar said, "I believe in you. Go, succeed on this mission.

Convince the honorspren that we're worthy of them. Prove to them that we have men waiting to take up the oaths and soar."

Adolin glanced at his father's hand on his shoulder, then met the man's eyes. There was something in those words . . .

"You want me to become one of them, don't you?" Adolin said. "Part of the purpose of this trip, in your eyes, is for me to become a Radiant!"

"Your brother is worthy," Dalinar said, "and your father—against his best efforts—has proven worthy. I'm sure you will prove yourself too."

As if I didn't have enough burdens.

Complaints died on Adolin's lips—complaints that there were likely thousands of worthy people in the world and not all of them would be chosen. Complaints that he was fine with his life and didn't need to live up to some spren's ideals.

Instead, Adolin simply bowed his head and nodded. Dalinar won the argument. The Blackthorn was unaccustomed to anything else. It wasn't that Adolin agreed, but more that he didn't know what to think, and that was the real problem. He couldn't stand up to his father with maybes.

Dalinar clapped him on the shoulder with his other hand and wished him farewell. Adolin walked Gallant into the chamber—highprince, leader of the expedition, and somehow still a little boy.

It was crowded inside with the horses. These circular control buildings had a rotating inner wall, along with murals on the floor indicating various locations. Normally in order to initiate a swap, a Radiant used their Shard-blade as a key to rotate the inner wall to the proper point.

Today, Shallan did something different. At a nod from him, she summoned her Shardblade and fit it into the keyhole on the wall. Then she kept pushing, her sword melting out like a silvery puddle on the wall, the hilt flowing like liquid around her hand.

She lifted her hand upward, moving the entire locking mechanism straight up. In a flash, they were thrown into Shadesmar.

The porcelain masks sometimes catch the light and sparkle, almost translucently. When a mistspren speaks, its mask's lips do not move, neither does the mask's expression change.

Many of the mistspren I encountered worked aboard the mandra ships, and their clothing and gear reflected that occupation.

Mistspren can determine how they appear in Shadesmar.

They usually choose a shape like a person, but they don't have to.

They appear in the Physical Realm like the light reflected onto a surface from a sunbeam passing through a crystal, regardless of whether a surface or light exists when they appear.

*I have reached out to the others as you requested, and have received
a variety of responses.*

Over the last week, Adolin had tasked his soldiers with making the transfer to Shadesmar several times. He'd even sent the horses in and out to make certain they wouldn't panic. So most everyone was ready for what they saw. Nevertheless, they all—Adolin included—fell silent, struck by the incredible sights.

The sky was black as midnight, only without stars. The sun seemed too distant, too frail, to properly light the place, though he wasn't in darkness. He could easily see the small platform around them, which was the size of the control room. The sunlight illuminated the landscape, but strangely didn't light the sky.

The control room hadn't come with them. Instead, two enormous spren stood in the air nearby: the attendants of this gateway, thirty or forty feet tall, one marble white and the other onyx.

Adolin raised a hand toward them as he stepped across the platform. "Thank you, Ancient Ones!" he called.

"It is done as the Stormfather requires," the marble one replied, voice booming. "Our parent, the Sibling, has died. We will obey him instead."

Long ago, a mysterious spren named the Sibling had lived in Urithiru. It was now dead. Or sleeping. Or maybe that was the same thing. Spren answers about the Sibling contradicted one another. In any case, before dying, the Sibling had commanded these sentries to stop allowing people into Shadesmar.

Many of the gatekeepers maintained this rule. However, a few had listened to the Stormfather's request. They said that in the absence of other Bondsmiths, Dalinar and the Stormfather were worthy of obedience—even in contradiction of ancient orders.

That was fortunate, for while Shallan could slip into Shadesmar using her powers, she couldn't take anyone with her—and she couldn't return on her own. Even Jasnah, whose powers supposedly allowed it, had trouble bringing herself back from Shadesmar.

This platform was one of ten set upon tall pillars here, rising in a pattern similar to the one the Oathgates made in front of Urithiru. Adolin could see the other sentries hanging above them.

Each pillar had a long spiraling ramp around it, leading down to the bead ocean far below. But the tower itself was far more majestic than any other sight. Adolin turned around, gazing up at the shimmering mountain of light and colors. The mother-of-pearl radiance didn't exactly mimic the shape of the tower, but had a more crystalline feel to it. Except it wasn't physical, but light. Radiant, resplendent, and brilliant.

The tower was the same color the sky turned in Shadesmar when a high-storm was passing over Roshar. And the place was positively *swarming* with emotion spren on this side. They soared through it in great swarms, taking a variety of shapes—most distant enough that Adolin saw them only as small bits of color, though he knew they had strange shapes here. More organic, more beastly. They flew, crawled, and climbed across and through the tower's shimmering light, making it look like a hive. It wasn't until coming here that Adolin had realized just how many spren the humans of Urithiru attracted.

Some of those could be dangerous on this side, but they'd been told the nature of the tower offered protection from that. Spren here were glutted on emotions, and were calmer.

Everyone took a few minutes to absorb the stunning vista—the mountain of iridescent colors, the sentinels, the spren, and the long drop to the ocean below. Adolin finally tore his eyes away to do a quick recount of their numbers, as the Radiants had been joined by their personal spren.

Pattern stood near Shallan; he was a tall figure in too-stiff robes with a changing symbol for a head. Adolin felt he could tell Pattern from the other Cryptics. There was a spring to Pattern's step; he bounced when the other three Cryptics glided. Their symbols were also slightly . . . different.

Adolin cocked his head, trying to decide why he should think that, as the symbols were always changing, never repeating that he could see. Yet the speed at which they changed, and the general *feel* of each one, was distinct.

Zu—the closest Radiant to Adolin—leaped up and grabbed her tall spren in a hug. "Ha!" said the golden-haired Stoneward. "You're a mountain on this side, Ua'pam!"

Her spren's skin appeared as if it were made of cracked rock, and it was glowing from within as if molten. Otherwise, he had generally humanlike features. Ua'pam wore fur-lined clothing on this side, like one might expect from one who lived high in the mountains. Adolin wasn't certain how all that worked. Did spren get cold?

Godeke was an Edgedancer, so his spren was a cultivationspren, a type Adolin had seen many times before: shaped roughly like a short woman, she was composed entirely of vines. Those vines wound tightly together into a face that had two crystals for eyes. Crystal hands, incredibly fine and delicate, emerged from the sleeves of her robe, and she had an aloof air as she looked around.

The last spren was the oddest to Adolin. She seemed to be made entirely from mist, all save for the face, which hovered on the front of the head in the shape of a porcelain mask. That mask had a kind of twinkling reflection to it, always catching the light—in fact, he could have sworn that from some perspectives it was made of translucent crystal. The spren seemed to be female, or at least had a feminine figure and voice.

This would be the spren of Arshqqam, the Truthwatcher. The spren wore a vest and trousers, both of which somehow floated and encapsulated the body made entirely of white fog. Her hands ended in gloves. Was it mist inside there, moving her fingers?

"Do you like staring at me, human?" she asked with a delicate voice that tinkled like cracking glass. The mask's lips didn't move when she spoke. "We mistspren can choose our forms, you know. We usually choose a shape like a person, but we don't need to. You seem so fascinated. Do you think me pretty, or do you think me a monster?"

"I . . ." Adolin said.

"Answer not," Zu's peakspren—Ua'pam—said with a grinding voice. "You. Tease not."

"I'm not teasing," she replied. "Merely questioning. I like to know how minds think."

"A worthy enough goal," Adolin said, searching around again. All of the Radiant spren were there, but where was *she*?

Shallan caught his eyes and nodded toward the ramp down, so he hurried over, stopping at the top as he found a final spren sitting there waiting. She was another cultivationspren, with cordlike vines making up her face. But her vines were a dull brown and they pulled tighter— giving her features a sunken-in cast.

Maya still wore the same dull brown rags. However, he saw hints of what they'd once been. Not robes as Godeke's spren wore. This had been a uniform.

Her most unnerving feature was her scratched-out eyes. It seemed as if someone had taken a knife to her face, except she hadn't bled or been scarred by the cuts. She'd been *erased*. Ripped apart. Removed from existence. When she looked at Adolin, she seemed like a painting that had been vandalized.

She sat huddled on the ramp. She didn't speak; she never did—except one time over a year ago when she'd told him her name. She was his Shard-blade. And, he hoped, his friend.

"Mayalaran," he said, holding out his hand toward her.

She regarded the hand, then cocked her head. As if it were some strange alien object for which she could determine no use. Adolin moved down the ramp and lightly took her hand, then put it into his. The coiled cords of her skin had a firm, smooth texture. Like a good hogshide hilt.

"Come on," he said. "Let me introduce the others."

He tugged on her hand and she followed, standing up and wordlessly joining him on the top of the platform.

"That's Shallan," Adolin said, pointing. "My wife. You remember her and Pattern, right? There's Godeke—he was once an ardent. Arshqqam is our Truthwatcher; she used to take care of orphans. And Zu, she's . . ." Adolin hesitated. "Zu, what did you used to do?"

"Make trouble, mostly," the Iriali woman said. She pulled off her thick coat, letting out a deep sigh. Underneath she wore a tight wrap around her upper torso, a little like a warrior's sarashi. She had bronze skin that seemed metallic to Adolin, and her hair wasn't like his own blond—it was too golden. Though his mother had been from Rira, near Iri, the two peoples were distinct.

"Come on, Ua'pam!" she said. "Let's see what's at the bottom of this ramp!"

"Be careful," the peakspren said as Zu put her coat over her shoulder and strolled to the side of the ramp.

"Well," Adolin said to Maya, "that's Zu. Those other six are Shallan's Lightweavers and their spren. Here, meet my soldiers. . . ."

As he pulled Maya over to introduce her to Felt, the mistspren walked over beside him. "There is no use talking to a deadeye," the creature said with unmoving lips. "Do you not understand this? What about you makes you wish to talk to something that cannot understand you?"

"She understands," Adolin said.

"You think that she does. This is curious."

Adolin ignored the odd spren, instead introducing Maya to his team. He'd told them to expect her, so they each bowed respectfully and didn't stare at her strange eyes *too* much. Ledder even complimented her appearance as a Blade, saying he'd always admired her beauty.

Maya took it all with her characteristic mute solemnity. She didn't cock her head; she simply stood by Adolin, looking at whoever was speaking.

She *did* understand. He'd felt her emotions through the sword; in fact, he felt like he'd *always* been able to sense her encouraging him.

Shallan came over and took him by the arm. "We should be moving on," she said. "See if the ship has arrived."

"Right, right," he said. "Here, watch Maya a moment. I need to check on Gallant."

He hurried over to the horse, and by the time he arrived he already knew to expect some bad news. Humans in the Physical Realm were represented here as lights like floating candle flames. A group of them gathered near the horse and were interacting with some shimmering, glowing blue colors.

To be certain, Adolin checked Gallant's armor trunks. The Shardplate hadn't made the trip. Adolin had hoped . . . well, it meant his armor wasn't different from any of the others. It couldn't be brought into Shadesmar. The lights on the other side were his armorers collecting the Plate, which would have dropped to the platform on the other side.

"Ah well," he said, unhooking the now-empty armor trunks. "Let's get these off you."

Gallant blew out in a way that Adolin chose to interpret as sympathetic. Adolin redistributed the weight, then checked the weapons in Gallant's sheaths—including the massive greatsword that had *almost* the bulk of a Shardblade.

They started walking toward the ramp, but Adolin paused, cocking his head. When Gallant moved, he trailed a faint shadow of light. It was almost imperceptible. When the horse shook his head from side to side, there was a distinct impression of an afterimage the shape of the head, but glowing.

"Didn't expect *you* to be different here," Adolin said to the horse.

Gallant blew out again. His version of a shrug. Then he nibbled at Adolin's coat pocket.

Adolin chuckled and dug out the other fruit he'd hidden there—wrapped in a handkerchief, naturally. Wouldn't do to stain his coat. He gave it to the horse with a pat on the neck. "Well, at least you won't need to haul that Plate around."

It made Adolin feel exposed. No Blade, no Plate, and the Radiants would be limited—for while they brought plenty of infused gemstones, they couldn't renew them.

He called for the group to begin carefully making its way down the ramp. With the railing, it wasn't too dangerous—but the walk was a long one. Urithiru was high in the mountains, and they needed to hike down to sea level. Strangely, Shallan told him they'd done measurements, and the path wasn't nearly as long as it would be in the Physical Realm. Space wasn't a one-to-one correlation in Shadesmar. Things seemed more compressed here, specifically in the vertical dimension. Isasik the mapmaker thought the place was incredible for reasons Adolin hadn't been able to grasp, despite having it explained to him three times.

At any rate, the hike would take several hours. They started out, and Shallan joined him, watching Maya walk with Gallant ahead.

Adolin put his arm around his wife. "Do you think she was happy to see me? I hope she enjoys being around us. It has to be better than simply walking around on this side, haunting wherever I happen to be going."

"I'm sure she's happy," Shallan said.

"You don't . . . think I'm crazy, do you? To treat her as I do?"

"I find it endearing," Shallan said.

"Even if you tease me about it?"

"That's how you know." She smiled and stopped him, then went up on her tiptoes to kiss him. "I like the outfit too. You chose well."

"Thanks, I . . ." Adolin trailed off as someone else put their arm around him, then around Shallan. Adolin twisted his head to find Pattern standing behind them, giving both of them a hug. His clothing was stiff, like it was made out of glass, and his collar pressed uncomfortably against Adolin's ear.

"Mmm . . ." Pattern said. "I like having arms. If Maya does not speak, and you want to hear someone speak, I am very good at talking. I can say words about many kinds of things."

"Um, thanks?" Adolin said.

"You are welcome. Should we not walk? On our feet? The ones I now have again? I do like my feet. They are befittingly perambulatory." He held up his leg, and showed bare feet beneath his robe. Curious. Adolin had always assumed they didn't have feet. Pattern moved off, humming delightedly to himself.

⁘

An hour later, Adolin could still see Urithiru shimmering above. A bonfire of colors and light, though oddly it didn't cast shadows. Many sources of light in Shadesmar didn't. And those that did sometimes cast them in the *wrong* direction.

They ate field rations, continuing steadily downward in a spiral around the enormous pillar. Eventually he was able to pick out the ocean below. In Shadesmar, land and sea were reversed—so here, the continent was manifest as a vast ocean of beads. They'd find ground where rivers ran after highstorms or at the edges of the continent, where the oceans began in the real world.

All things in Roshar manifested in Shadesmar. Most objects became beads, while living people and animals became little flames of light like the ones he'd seen above. They passed some of those as they walked, hovering off in the distance. Adolin assumed those were the guards who watched over the complex of tunnels and caverns beneath Urithiru. Indeed, there were more lights than he'd expected; Aunt Navani must have gotten her wish to have the caverns better guarded.

Eventually those vanished above, and he was left with only the endless view of the ocean. It bent his mind to think about those beads. The *souls* of all the objects that made up the physical world. Churning and mixing together, forming waves and surging tides, each composed of small beads no wider than his index finger.

He passed the time trying to get to know the members of his team. Zu liked to run off ahead, her spren often advising caution—and as often ignored. Zu had worked as a guide in the Reshi Isles for years, after fleeing there to find a place where people wouldn't, as she put it, "keep making rules about how I should live." She'd been glad to come on the mission and get away from the tower, which she considered stuffy.

She admitted to some brief combat experience. Her spren didn't speak much, and often in short sentences when he did, but Adolin liked the defensive implications of having a spren that was literally made of stone.

As she ran off again to scout ahead, Adolin fell into line beside Godeke. The Edgedancer kept staring at the sky, grinning like a child with a new sword. "The works of the Almighty are wondrous," he said. "To think, this beauty was always here with us. Look, are those a new kind of spren?"

He pointed at some that drifted by in the air—they resembled chickens, with flapping wings and bulbous bodies.

"I think those are gloryspren," Adolin said. "Emotion spren are like this world's animals. They get pulled through to our side when they sense some kind of strong emotion, and we see them in distorted ways."

"Amazing," Godeke said. "Thank you for bringing me on this trip, Brightlord. Archinal has told me of this place at length, but I never thought I'd experience it. I will burn prayers of thanks tonight . . . if we have a fire, that is. I'm still not sure how all this works!"

"You . . . continue to follow the Almighty then?" Adolin asked. "Vorinism and all that? Despite finding out that the Heralds betrayed us?"

"The Heralds are not God, but His servants," Godeke said. "Storms know, I've failed Him more than once myself." He adopted a distant expression. "I don't think we can blame them for eventually wearing out. Rather, I think about how remarkable it is that they worked for so long to keep us safe."

"And the fact that they confirmed the death of the Almighty?"

"The death of *Honor*," Godeke said. "One aspect of the Almighty." He smiled. "It's all right, Brightlord. I can understand someone questioning now, of all times. Remember though, the church taught that we are *all* aspects of the Almighty—that He lives in us. As He lived in the being called Honor, who was tasked with protecting men.

"The Almighty cannot die. People can die. Heralds can die. Even Honor could die. But Honor, people, and Heralds will all live again—transformed, Soulcast through His power." Godeke glanced back at his packhorse, which his spren was riding. Stuffed into the saddlebags and peeking out were several books. "I'm still learning. We all are. The *Book of Endless Pages* cannot be filled . . . though your father made a very nice addition to the text."

"You're okay with a man writing then?" Adolin said, frowning.

"Your father is not simply a man, Adolin," Godeke said.

"He—"

"Your father is a *holy* man. As I was, before taking up this new role." Godeke shook his head. "All my life I lived with a deformity—and then in an instant I was transformed and healed. I became what I'd always seen myself as being. Your father has undergone a more vibrant transformation. He is as divine as any ardent.

"And . . . I must admit some of what he says makes sense. How can it be forbidden for a person to see the holy words of the Almighty, solely because that person is male? Makes me wonder whether we've misinterpreted all along. Whether we've been selfish, wanting to keep all this for ourselves.

"I don't accept the conclusions your father came to—but I'm glad people are talking about the church rather than merely going about their lives, assuming the ardents will take care of everything. Many people only thought of religion when it was time for one of their Elevations." He grinned as another group of gloryspren sailed past. "I cannot *wait* to write of this to the others of my devotary. When they hear what wonders the Almighty has created here . . ."

Adolin wasn't certain it all made sense as Godeke explained, but at the same time it was nice to hear someone being so positive. He left Godeke to his excitement, and went to chat with Arshqqam, translated by her spren. She felt much as he had on his first time in Shadesmar. Overwhelmed.

"I used to think my life made sense," the woman said through the spren. "I used to think I knew how it would end. I didn't want to leave Tashikk. There my life was hard, but it was clear."

"Why *did* you leave, then?"

She studied him with a piercing gaze, unwavering. "How could I stay? I still don't know why *I* was chosen. A woman at the end of her life? But if a child could answer the call, then I certainly could find no excuse."

The child she referenced was Lift—who had recruited this woman, along with several others, over the past year. The teen seemed to have a knack for locating others who were manifesting powers.

"What do you think of her?" Adolin asked. "Lift? She acts strange sometimes, even for a Radiant."

Arshqqam grimaced, lips drawn to a distasteful line. "She is what I needed, though I knew it not. And I would not have you tell her of my fondness for her, please. She needs a firm hand."

That was fondness?

"Stump," Arshqqam said through her spren, seeming wistful. "That is what the children called me. A nickname. The only other person who ever gave me a term of endearment was my father. The children see me as a person, when so many others have trouble. So the Stump I am. A glorious title, to come from children."

What an odd woman. But there was a calm solidity to her, and Adolin was glad to have her along. Once the conversation fell off, Adolin moved to walk with Shallan. They again went over the plans that Jasnah had drawn up for them. Working with the support of the collected monarchs, she'd left Adolin what seemed like an entire book's worth of instructions. Fortunately, he felt he could execute them. He might not be able to grasp why the shape of Shadesmar was so fascinating to a mapmaker, but acting as a dignitary and an emissary? He'd been trained for this role since his youth.

The basic plan was to present the honorspren with gifts along with written requests to begin relations. Nothing too pushy. An essay written by Jasnah, another written by Dalinar with Queen Fen's advisement, and a third from the Azish imperial court. Adolin was to request admittance to the honorspren fortress, stay a few days to get them used to the idea of talking to humans, then leave with a promise that they'd speak more in the future.

Some of the Windrunner spren thought this would be enough, but Syl—in a rare appearance when Kaladin wasn't around—had come to him the day before.

"I worry that this isn't going to work, Adolin," she'd said. "I don't think they'll even let you in. They aren't like honorspren used to be. They're afraid and they're angry. I'm glad you want to try, but . . . be prepared for disappointment. And don't let them try to blame you for what Radiants did before."

Ua'pam spotted the ship first. He waved to Adolin, then pointed over the side of the railing toward the rolling beads that were now only a hundred or so feet below. There, docked at the small patch of ground at the base of the pillar, was a flat ship. A barge. The front portion had a small raised deck, from which to steer its flying mandras.

There was no sign of cabins or a hold—far less luxurious than the vessels they'd taken the last time. Of course, he wouldn't care to repeat much about that particular experience. He'd gladly take a barge if it meant a peaceful voyage instead.

"My cousin," Ua'pam said, pointing to a figure on the barge waving a light. "Like him!"

"I'll try."

"You will!" Ua'pam said.

"Another peakspren?" Adolin asked, squinting.

"Yes!"

"We saw some of those on our last trip," Adolin said. "They left us stranded at Celebrant."

"Kasiden peakspren, from the east? They are fools! Forget them."

"You have . . . different nationalities?"

"Obviously! Silly man. You will learn." The creature clapped Adolin on the back with a firm strength. Though his stone hand was warm to the touch, it wasn't hot like Adolin might have expected from the glowing light coming from the cracks.

They made the last few rotations around the column before—at long last—arriving at sea level. There was a little stone building built up against the pillar underneath the ramp here, though scouts sent into Shadesmar had reported it empty.

Adolin sent two men to search it anyway, then walked forward to meet Ua'pam's cousin. He was bald, like other peakspren Adolin had met— though they tended to have more cracks on the head than on other parts of the body. He wore a hat not unlike the one Veil favored. He replaced that after bowing to them.

"Welcome, human prince!" he said with an affable voice. "You will present payment!"

Adolin held up a small bag of glowing spheres. "How long do you think it will take to get to the southern bank?"

"Two weeks, perhaps," he said, waving for Adolin's men to lead the horses onto the long barge, which was around forty feet wide and a hundred feet long. A few other peakspren worked on board, moving boxes to make room for the newcomers. "Easy sailing lately. Few ships. You will be happy and relaxed!"

"Few ships?"

"Fused to the east," the peakspren captain said, pointing. "Strange things in Shinovar. Honorspren acting uppity. Nobody wants to travel."

They'd tried to find a spren captain who would sail them straight to

Lasting Integrity, the honorspren stronghold. Unfortunately, their options were limited—and all the spren they'd spoken to refused. They said that the honorspren didn't like ships to sail too close.

Most agreed that the safest path for Adolin's group was to sail almost directly south until they hit land. From there, they could caravan southwest—along the Tukari coastline in the real world—until they reached Lasting Integrity.

Adolin walked Gallant aboard, then set to unhooking the animal's burdens. It wasn't long before everyone was settled and looking happy to be done with the hike. He'd thought that going downhill the entire way would make it easy, but his calves ached and his knees hurt from the unnatural motion of stepping constantly on a slope.

He'd noticed some of the Radiants using Stormlight to keep their energy up, but he hadn't complained. Though their Stormlight resources couldn't be renewed, the smaller spheres would start running out even before the ocean trip was over. The real reserves—the ones they needed to preserve—were all larger gemstones that would keep their Light much longer.

Ua'pam joined his cousin in unhooking the ropes from the dock and helping the crew prepare the barge for sailing. This included harnessing up four very large mandras—long flying spren with several sets of filmy, undulating wings—that had been hovering about lazily on leashes.

As soon as the mandras were hooked to the vessel, it rose a little higher in the beads. With that they were off—Adolin's soldiers making camp on the barge deck, where they began arranging boxes to form walls and using tarps to make a kind of shelter. The barge didn't move quickly, but there was a relaxing rhythm to the way it rolled over the beads. The previous ships had cut through them with great crashes. Here the sound of the beads was more peaceful, a quiet clicking.

Adolin helped Shallan settle her things, including several trunks full of supplies—and she gracefully refrained from joking about how many more trunks Adolin had brought than her. It didn't seem the boat would be moving quickly enough to require them to lash things down, so once her trunks were piled, he brushed his hands off—then paused, noticing his wife. She knelt in front of one of the trunks, which she'd opened to inspect. Her eyes were wide.

"What?" he asked.

She shook her head. "Nothing. Just some of my paints spilling. That's going to be a mess to clean." She shut the lid with a sigh, shaking her head as he offered to help. "No, I can do it."

Well, Adolin didn't want to rest while his men were working. So he walked over to Gallant, who deserved a brushing after carting Adolin's things down that ramp.

He set to work, enjoying the familiar motions of the grooming. Gallant kept glancing at Adolin's luggage, where he'd hidden some fruit.

"Not yet," Adolin said.

The horse blew out in annoyance, then looked at Adolin's brush.

"Yes," Adolin replied. "I brought all three. You think I'd bring seven different swords but forget your brushes?"

The horse made a kind of clicking sound with his mouth, something Sureblood had never done. Adolin wasn't certain how to interpret it. Mirth?

"I'll give you the fruit," Adolin promised, continuing to brush, "but only after . . ."

He trailed off as he noticed Maya standing nearby. He'd settled her near the others earlier, but she'd apparently decided not to stay there.

Adolin continued brushing. She watched for a time. Then she tentatively held out her palm. Adolin handed her the brush and she stared at it. She seemed so baffled that he figured he must have misunderstood what she wanted.

Then she started brushing the horse as he had. From the top down the side, with the same exact motion Adolin had used.

Adolin chuckled. "You have to brush more than one section, Maya, or he'll get annoyed."

He showed her, brushing along Gallant's flank in the direction of the hair growth. Long, slow, careful strokes. She soon got the hang of it, and Adolin stepped back to get a drink. He found two of the peakspren sailors watching him.

"Your deadeye," one said, scratching at his stone head with a sound of rock on rock. "I've never seen one trained so well."

"She's not trained," Adolin said. "She wanted to help, so I showed her how."

One sailor looked to the other, then shook his head. They said something in a language Adolin didn't understand, but they seemed unnerved by Maya, giving her a wide berth as they continued about their duties.

Adolin sipped from his canteen, watching as the pillar retreated. He could barely make out the glow of the tower city far above, dwindling as they moved.

I'll do my part, Father, Adolin thought. *I'll give them your letters, but I'll do more. I'll find a way to persuade them to help us. And I'll do it my way.*

The trick, of course, was to discover what his way was in the first place.

⁘

Shallan knelt before her trunk as everyone else unpacked and Adolin brushed his horse. She tried not to panic. She failed. So she settled for *seeming* like she wasn't panicking.

While packing her things, she'd taken a Memory of Mraize's communication cube, packed away in her trunk. With her uncanny abilities, she could picture it precisely where she'd placed it. She'd wanted to be extra careful, but she hadn't thought the Memory would be relevant so quickly.

Because the cube had been moved. Not just shifted in among her things; it had been picked up and rotated. The face that *had* been up when she'd packed had a few faint scratches on it. That face was now to the side. An imperceptible difference; someone without her abilities would never have noticed.

Someone had moved the cube. Somehow, between packing and arriving on the barge, someone had *rifled through her things* and *used the cube*.

She could come to only one conclusion. The spy was indeed on this mission—and they were using this very device to report to Mraize.

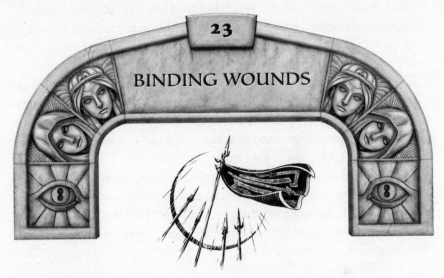

23

BINDING WOUNDS

Much as you indicate, there is a division among the other Shards I would not have anticipated.

Kaladin pulled the bandage snug on the boy's ankle. "Next time, Adin," he said, "take the steps *one at a time.*"

The youth nodded solemnly. He was perhaps twelve or thirteen. "One at a time. Until I get my spren."

"Oh? Your spren?"

"I'm gonna be a Windrunner," the boy said. "Then I'll *float* down steps."

"That's what it means to be a Radiant, is it?" Kaladin asked, standing. "Floating."

"That, and you can stick your friends to the walls if they argue with you," he said. "A Windrunner told me."

"Let me guess. Short fellow. Herdazian. Big smile?"

"Yup."

"Well, until then," Kaladin said, "I need you to keep your weight off that foot." He looked to the father, standing nearby, his trousers marked with potter's crem. "That means a crutch if he has to walk somewhere. Come back and see me in a week; his progress will let us know for certain it didn't fracture."

The father helped his son with a thankful murmur. As they left, Kaladin dutifully washed his hands in the exam room's basin. He'd picked up his father's mannerisms in that regard. Wisdom of the Heralds, it was said. He'd met some of those Heralds now, and they didn't seem so wise to him, but whatever.

It felt strange to be wearing a white surgeon's apron. Lirin had always wanted one of these; he'd said white clothing made people calm. The traveling butchers or barbers—men who often did surgery or tooth work in small towns—tended to be dirty and bloody. Seeing a surgeon wearing white instantly proclaimed, "This isn't that sort of place."

He sent Hawin—the town girl who was reading for him today—to fetch the next patient. He dried his hands. Then, standing in the center of the small exam room, he released a long breath.

"Are you happy?" Syl asked, flitting into the room from the one next door, where she'd been watching his father work.

"I'm not sure," Kaladin said. "I worry about the rest of them out there, going into battle without me. But it's good to do something, Syl. Something that helps, but doesn't wring me out like an old washrag."

Near the end of his time as a Windrunner, he'd found even simple sparring to be emotionally taxing. Daily activities, like assigning duties, had required so much effort that they'd left him with a pounding headache. He couldn't explain why.

This work—rememorizing medical texts, seeing patients, dealing with difficult parents or lighteyes—should have been worse. It wasn't. Busy, but not overwhelmed, Kaladin never saw anyone who was hurt too badly—those went for Regrowth. So while there was tension to his work, there wasn't *immediacy*.

Was he happy?

He wasn't sad.

For now, he'd accept "not sad."

Hawin led in the next patient, then excused herself to run to the privy. This patient was an older man with a patchwork beard and a friendly face. Kaladin recognized him; Mil never *had* been able to grow that beard out like he wanted. While the clinic drew mostly from the people who had lived in Hearthstone, his little town had sprouted significantly in the last few years. Most of the refugees hadn't been Herdazian, but Alethi from villages closer to the border. So while Kaladin felt he *should* know all of his patients, many were strangers.

It was good to see Mil again. He'd always been less mean to Kaladin's family than some others. The old man was complaining of persistent headaches. And indeed, the same painspren from earlier in the day wiggled back up from the floor. After ruling out the easy causes—dehydration, lack of sleep—Kaladin had him describe where the pain generally originated from, and whether the headaches affected his vision.

"Hawin," Kaladin said, "read me the list of migraine prodromes please. You'll find them at the divider between head and neck . . ." He trailed off, remembering his reader had left.

A moment later though, a different voice said, "Um, prodromes. Right . . . Uh, just a sec."

He looked toward the reading desk to find Syl laboriously lifting pages and flipping them over. She didn't have much strength in the Physical Realm, but ignoring gravity—walking up into the air to tow the page by its corner—helped, and the book wasn't far from the appropriate page.

She found it and landed on the large tome, kneeling to read the words one at a time. "Neck stiffness," she said. "Um . . . conster . . . cons—"

"Constipation," Kaladin said.

She giggled, then kept reading. "Mood changes, cravings, thirst, um, I think that says frequent need to pee. Storms. Stuff goes out of you, and it's bad. Stuff *doesn't* go out of you and it's bad. How do you live like this?"

He ignored that, chatting with Mil about his pains. He suggested visiting the Edgedancers for Regrowth—but Mil's pains had been around for months, so it was unlikely that they could do anything.

Fortunately, there were medicines that could help, and—with Jasnah capable of Soulcasting a wide range of substances—they had access to rare medications. Though Kaladin and the queen didn't often see eye to eye, it said a great deal about her that she was willing to take time to make medicine.

Kaladin gave Mil a requisition chit to get some from the medical quartermaster, and told him to spend a month recording each and every headache, with signs he'd noticed of it coming on. It wasn't much, but Mil grinned ear to ear. Often people just wanted to know they weren't fools or weaklings for coming in. They wanted to know their pains were real, and that there was something—even something small—they could do about the problem. Simple affirmation could be worth more than medication.

He waved farewell to Mil, grateful that—despite several lifetimes' worth of tragedy squeezed into the years between then and now—much of his surgeon's training remained. He walked over to Syl, who had settled down with her legs over the side of the book. Today she was wearing something akin to what his mother often wore: an unassuming skirt and a buttoned blouse, faintly Thaylen in style.

"So," he said, "when did you learn to read?"

"Last week."

"You learned to read in a *week*."

"It's not as hard as it seemed at first. I figured you'd need someone to read for you, as a surgeon. I think I might be able to become surgery tools too. I mean, not a scalpel since, you know, I don't actually cut flesh. But your father was using a little hammer the other day . . ."

"For testing reflexes," Kaladin said. "It's best with a cloth wrap on the front, or rubber. Can you become things other than metal? I'd love to not have to share the stethoscope with Father." Another expensive tool that Taravangian's surgeons had provided for them upon request.

"I don't know," she said. "I feel like . . . I feel like there is a lot to explore with our powers, Kaladin. Things that in the past maybe they didn't have the time or resources to think about. Because they were always fighting."

He nodded, thoughtful. Syl got a far-off look in her eyes, and when she noticed him watching, she plastered a smile on her face. That struck him as fake; she seemed to be trying a little too hard today. Or maybe he was projecting.

He stretched, then stepped out and peeked into the waiting room. Only a handful of people remained today. So Kaladin had time for a short break.

He walked along the hallway into the family room, which had a door out onto the communal balcony. As he'd hoped when they'd come here, that wide balcony now served as a general-purpose meeting place for the people of Hearthstone, like a town square. Laundry flapped on lines to one side. Children ran and played. People sat and chatted.

Kaladin trailed out to the edge of the balcony. Below he could see Dalinar's armies gathering for the trip to Azir. He forced himself to look and to acknowledge he wasn't going with them.

A figure in blue streaked by, soaring through the air. Leyten must have seen Kaladin, because a short time later a larger group of Windrunners hovered up near the balcony. Most everyone stopped their activities, children running to the balcony's edge.

As one, the Windrunners saluted. The Bridge Four salute; though most had never been in Bridge Four and didn't use the salute to one another, they always gave it to him and other members of the original Windrunners.

He returned the Bridge Four salute to them all, tapping his wrists together.

The fifty-odd Windrunners turned and streaked back down. Below, light flashed in a circle around the Oathgate, making an entire battalion of troops vanish. They'd learned that how much Stormlight was expended for a transfer depended on the Radiant operating the device—the more experienced the Radiant, the less Stormlight required. Jasnah was probably operating today; she could do things with her powers that were well beyond the rest of them. Though she didn't show it off, she'd plainly sworn the Fourth Ideal. The one Kaladin would never reach.

"They're all going away," Syl said softly, landing on his shoulder.

"Not all of them," Kaladin said. "Around twenty will stay to guard the tower."

"But none of our friends."

It was true. All the former members of Bridge Four were going with

Dalinar. Maybe Rlain would stay behind, and work on the fields? Though he often chose to go with the Windrunner support staff, to help out there, with Dabbid and a few squire hopefuls.

Watching them all fly off, it was impossible not to feel so very alone.

Remember the peace you have felt this last week, Kaladin thought. *Don't be sorry for yourself. Be excited for the new path forward you're making.*

The thoughts didn't work; it still hurt to see them all leave. Hurt to know Shallan and Adolin had gone off to Shadesmar without him. He had his parents and his new brother, and he appreciated that. But the men and women of Bridge Four had become equally important to him.

That part of his life was over. Best not to dwell on it. Kaladin returned to the exam room. Hawin was waiting, so he sent her for the next patient.

He settled into a rhythm, seeing patients, occasionally sticking his head into the next exam room to ask his father for advice on a diagnosis or remedy. He dealt with an unusual number of coughs. Apparently there was something moving through the tower—a sickness that left people with mucus in their lungs and an overall feeling of aches. He'd never encountered anything like it. His father had been tracking it though, and said that Kharbranthian surgeons reported it wasn't deadly. A plague from the West that, when all was said and done, didn't live up to its reputation. The sickness barely attracted any plaguespren—though there didn't seem to be many around the tower to attract, so that would be part of it.

He recommended lots of rest, fluids, and handwashing. The day stretched long, and the patients slowed to a trickle. One woman stood out to him. She was a refugee, and while getting treated for her coughs, she asked if Kaladin had seen her uncle. She'd heard of someone matching his description arriving in Hearthstone immediately before the evacuation.

Kaladin had her wait and went looking for his father. Lirin's exam room was empty, but Hesina's voice rose from the waiting room, so Kaladin walked out to ask her about the refugee's uncle.

Right before he arrived, Kaladin heard a familiar voice that made him freeze in place.

"—always been like this," the gruff voice said. "Been clean for . . . what, six months now? Storm me. Six months. That's something. Can't stand the battle though, not any longer. It's gotten inside me, see. Itches at my brain."

Kaladin burst into the waiting room to find Teft chatting with his mother. The older man was out of uniform, wearing common trousers and shirt, his grey beard trimmed. Not as short as an ardent's beard, but not distinctively long either. There was no sign of his spren, Phendorana, though she generally preferred to hide from sight.

"Teft?" Kaladin said. "You were mobilized. Why aren't you with every-one else?"

"Can't go," Teft said. "Too much wrong with my brain. Went and spoke to the Blackthorn, and he said it would be a good idea for me to step down."

"You . . . Teft, you're doing better. You have no reason to step down from duty."

Teft shrugged. "Felt like it was time. Got a bit of a cough too. And an ache in my knee, even when there aren't storms. War's for young kids, not old dried-up pieces of bark."

Hesina cocked her head, seeming confused—but Syl landed on Kaladin's shoulder and gasped at seeing Teft, then clapped excitedly.

"Rock is gone," Teft said, "and Moash . . . Moash is worse than gone. Sigzil needs to lead the rest of them, without me being baggage to bother him. You and I were the start of this though. Figure we ought to stick together."

"Teft," Kaladin said softer, stepping forward. "You can't follow me here."

Teft lifted his chin, defiant.

"I order you to go back to duty," Kaladin said.

"Oh? Orders? You ain't got knots on your shoulder now, lad. You can't order me to do anything." He sat down in a waiting room chair, folding his arms. "I feel sick. Not right in the head. Nobody can argue *that* ain't so."

Kaladin looked to his mother, feeling helpless.

She shrugged. "You shouldn't force someone into war, Kaladin. Not unless you want to be like Amaram."

"You're taking Teft's side?" Kaladin asked.

"Lad," Teft said softly, "you ain't the only one with a mind full of horrors. You ain't the only one whose hands shake now and then, thinking of it all. I need a rest too. That's Kelek's own truth."

He was exaggerating. Kaladin knew he was. The man—while prone to addictive and self-destructive behavior—was *not* battle shocked. That wasn't something you could easily prove, however. Especially when the man in question was as obstinate as Teft.

Teft unfolded his arms, then folded them again, as if to make the gesture more firmly. His clothing was neat and clean, but there was always something a little frayed about Teft. You got the sense that the uniform never quite fit him, as if Teft was half a size between standard measurements.

That said, he was—to his core—a military man. If there was one thing a good sergeant knew, it was to never let your officer go into an unknown situation alone. Who knew what trouble a lighteyes would get into without his common sense tagging along? Teft took ideas like that to heart. And Kaladin knew, meeting Teft's eyes, that the man was *never* going to budge.

"Fine," Kaladin said.

Teft leaped to his feet, gave Kaladin's mother a little salute, then fell into step behind Kaladin as they walked toward the exam room.

"So, what are we doing?" Teft asked.

"You said you wanted a diagnosis," Kaladin said, stopping outside the door.

"Nah. Know I'm crazy already. You going to poke at me until I snap? Skip that part. What are we doing today? Binding wounds?"

Kaladin gave him a level stare. Teft just stared back, stubborn as a storm. Well, Kaladin *had* trained them all as surgeon's assistants, with knowledge of basic field medicine. He could do worse than Teft as an aide.

It didn't seem like he had a choice either way. That should have frustrated him. Instead he found himself feeling warm. They weren't *all* gone.

"Thank you, Teft," he whispered. "You shouldn't have given up so much. But . . . thank you."

Teft nodded.

"There is a refugee woman here looking for her uncle," Kaladin said. "Shall we see if we can track him down for her?"

I doubt it's truly possible to capture the shapes of these patterns in a drawing. They are constantly in motion, lines that flow and twist according to some unknown principle.

There is a subtle variety of unique forms in the shape of their robes.

The body appears to be made of glassy solid planes that casually fold and split into new angles as they move.

In so many ways, Cryptics are more abstract than other spren.

They have such bony hands, and yet I am nearly certain they do not have bones.

Some appear to have hands chiseled from obsidian, while others appear carved from white marble.

Cryptics have feet, but they aren't often visible below the long robes.

I've never seen a Cryptic running. I expect they would look very silly.

24

FULL OF AWE

Endowment at least responded to my overtures, though I have not been able to locate Invention again following our initial contact.

R adiant did not want to be in control at the moment.

As the second day of their voyage dawned—or, well, *occurred*, since the sun didn't move in Shadesmar—Shallan retreated entirely. Spending the last day feigning an upbeat attitude had left her exhausted. Unfortunately, after Veil's stunt in seizing control a few days back—violating the compact—neither wanted *her* to be in charge.

So it rested on Radiant to rise, do her exercises, and then try to figure out something to do with her day. Adolin's soldiers busied themselves tidying the camp space on the barge, then doing the multitude of other things—like sharpening weapons or oiling armor—that military men used to pass the time. Zu was chatting with the other peakspren, Arshqqam was reading, and Adolin was caring for his swords.

Radiant set Beryl and Ishnah to recording observations about Shadesmar, and assigned Vathah to see if the peakspren sailors needed any help.

And what to do with herself? *Find the spy,* Shallan whispered deep inside. *We need to find out which one is the spy.*

I am ill-equipped for espionage, Radiant thought. She walked the perimeter of the deck, observing the Radiant spren. Four different varieties, each unique. *Perhaps you can do drawings for now, until we decide to let Veil finish her punishment. Finding the spy isn't something we need to do immediately, after all.*

But Shallan didn't emerge. Sometimes this was how it was; they couldn't always choose which of them would be in control. But Shallan's growing tension . . . that was worrisome.

You're still troubled by how Veil violated our compact, aren't you? Radiant asked.

We're supposed to be getting better, not worse, Shallan thought.

Everyone makes mistakes. Everyone slips.

Not you, Shallan thought. *You have never seized control like that.*

Radiant felt an immediate stab of guilt. But there was nothing to be done about that; best to move forward. Radiant took a seat on the deck near the railing, then flipped through Ialai's book as she listened to the churning beads.

Together, the Three had figured out most everything in the book. The place names were locations beyond the various expanses in Shadesmar—worlds beyond the edge of the map. Pattern had confirmed this by chatting with a few other spren who had met travelers from these places.

Another section of the book contained Ialai's conjectures and information about the leader of the Ghostbloods, the mysterious Thaidakar. Whoever this was, Radiant thought—from the context of what was written—that he must be someone from one of those far-off worlds.

There was a final clue in the book, one that Radiant found most curious. Ialai had discovered that the Ghostbloods were obsessed with a specific spren named Ba-Ado-Mishram. That was a name from myth, one of the Unmade. It had been this spren who had taken over for Odium following the Final Desolation; she had granted the singers forms of power.

By capturing Ba-Ado-Mishram—locking her in a gemstone—humankind had stolen the minds of the singers in ancient times. They knew this from the brief—but poignant—messages left by the ancient Radiants before they abandoned Urithiru. By cross-referencing those with musings in Ialai's book, Radiant began to get a picture of what had happened so many centuries ago.

She was increasingly certain Mraize was hunting the gemstone that held Ba-Ado-Mishram. He'd likely thought he would find it at Urithiru; but if it had been there, then the Midnight Mother—who had controlled the place for centuries—surely would have found it and rescued her ally.

He also wants to transport Stormlight offworld, Shallan thought, emerging. *I believe he was honest in that point. So perhaps these two are related? Perhaps Ba-Ado-Mishram can help him in this quest?*

You'd do better at connecting these ideas than I will, Radiant thought to her. *Why don't you take control?*

Is that what this is? Shallan demanded. *You're trying to trick me? Go find the spy.*

It is not my area of expertise, Shallan.

Fine, she thought. *It's time to let Veil out then. I vote to end her punishment.*

Radiant subsided, and Veil surprisingly found herself in control. It had been four days now since she'd taken over and invited the three most questionable Lightweavers to join the expedition.

She leaped to her feet, looking around the barge. It felt good to be in charge again, particularly in this place of mystery and secrets. Shadesmar. The bead ocean, a black sky, strange spren, and infinite questions to investigate. It was . . .

It was the perfect place for Shallan.

Find the spy, Shallan said.

Veil hesitated, then sat back down and pointedly dug through Shallan's satchel. She got out a charcoal pencil and flipped to an empty page, then began to draw.

What are you doing? Shallan demanded. *You're a terrible artist.*

"I know," Veil whispered. "And you hate watching me try." She made a crude attempt at drawing Ua'pam, the peakspren, as he thumped past. The result was cringeworthy.

Why? Shallan asked.

"I'm sorry," Veil said, "for violating the compact. I needed to get those three on the mission so I could watch them. But I should have persuaded you two first."

So go investigate.

"Radiant is right," Veil said. "That can wait." It was painful for her to admit, but something was more important. She continued her terrible drawing.

We're not going to let you retreat and hide, Radiant thought—and Veil could feel her relief in discovering the two of them agreed on this. *Something is wrong, Shallan. Something bigger than what Veil did. Something that's affecting all of us, making us erratic.*

"I used to think you kept secrets from Adolin because you were like me and enjoyed the thrill of being part of the Ghostbloods," Veil said. "I was wrong. There's something more, isn't there? Why do you keep lying? What is going on?"

I . . . Shallan said. *I . . .*

The dark thing stirred inside her. Formless, the personality that could be. The dark thing that represented Shallan's fears, compounded.

Veil had her flaws. She was a drunkard and had trouble with scope and perspective. She represented a whole host of attributes Shallan wanted, but knew she *shouldn't.*

Yet at her core, Veil had a singular purpose: She'd been created to protect Shallan. And she would send herself to Damnation before she let that Formless thing take her place.

She gripped her pencil and started drawing Adolin. Really, *really* poorly.

I don't care, Shallan thought.

Veil gave him a unibrow.

Veil . . .

Veil drew him with crossed eyes.

That's going too far.

Veil put him in an ugly coat. And *cut-off, knee-length trousers.*

"Fine!" Shallan said, ripping the page out of the sketchbook and wadding it up. "You win. Insufferable woman." She settled back against the barge's railing and took a deep breath. Then, as the other two insisted, she let herself relax.

It really . . . really was all right. Yes, someone had used the communication cube to call Mraize. Yes, someone had invaded her things. Yes, one of her friends was undoubtedly a spy. But she *could* handle the problem. She *could* get through this.

But they had two weeks of travel ahead of them. So today, she could relax. Because she was on a barge full of spren, and they were all so *fascinating.* Storms, how had she let herself retreat at a time like this? And for Veil to give up so willingly . . .

I'm sorry, Veil thought. *I'll do better. And we can work on the spy another time.*

Right, then. Shallan pointedly ripped up the sketch of Adolin and stuffed the pieces in her satchel, then gripped her charcoal pencil and allowed herself to just *draw.*

⁘

Adolin found her five hours later, still sitting on the deck, her back to the railing, sketching furiously. He'd brought her food—warm curry and lavis, from the smell of it. That would be some of the last "real" food they'd have for a while. A part of her acknowledged the way the scents made her stomach growl. But for the moment, she remained mesmerized as she worked on her sketches of the peakspren.

It felt so good to let go and draw. To not worry about a mission, or her own psychosis, or even about Adolin. To become so wrapped up in the art that nothing else mattered. There was an *infinite* sensation to creation, as if time smeared like paint on a canvas. Mutable. Changeable.

When she finally drifted out of it to the scent of sweet curry and the sight of Adolin smiling as he sat down beside her, she felt *worlds* better. More whole. More herself than she'd been in months.

"Thanks," she said, handing him the sketchbook and taking the food. She leaned against him as she began to eat, watching Arshqqam and her mistspren pass—Shallan needed to do a sketch of that strange spren at some point.

"Have you made any progress on that book of Ialai's?" Adolin asked.

"I've figured out nearly the entire thing," Shallan said. "It's filled with conjectures, though, and not much substance. The Ghostbloods seem to be searching for Ba-Ado-Mishram, one of the Unmade. But I can't determine for certain what they intend to do once they find her."

Adolin grunted. "And the spy? Among our numbers?"

"Still working on it," she said. "But I'd rather not talk about that today. I need some time to mull it over." She took another bite, feeling his chest against her back. "You're tense, Adolin. Aren't we supposed to be able to relax, this part of the trip?"

"I'm worried about the mission."

"Because of what Syl said? About the honorspren being unlikely to listen?"

He nodded.

"If they turn us away, they turn us away," she said. "But you can't blame yourself for things that haven't happened yet. Storms, who knows what will change between now and the time we arrive."

"I suppose," he said.

She took a spoonful of lavis and felt the individual grains with her tongue, plump and saturated with sweet curry making a mush in her mouth— gross, but wonderful. Pattern always talked about how strange humans were, surviving off the things they destroyed.

"When I left my homeland," she said to Adolin, "I thought I knew what I was heading into. But I had no idea what would happen to me. Where I'd end up."

"You had a pretty good idea," Adolin said. "You set out to be Jasnah's ward, and you managed it."

"I set out to rob her," Shallan said softly. She felt Adolin shift, looking toward her. "My family was impoverished, threatened by creditors, my father dead. We thought maybe I could rob that heretic Alethi woman, steal her Soulcaster—then we could use it to become rich again."

She braced herself for the criticism. The shock.

Instead, Adolin laughed. Bless him, he *laughed.* "Shallan, that is the most ridiculous thing I've ever heard!"

"Isn't it though?" she said, twisting and grinning at him.

"Robbing Jasnah."

"Yes."

"Robbing *Jasnah.*"

"I know!"

He eyed her, then his grin broadened. "She's never mentioned this, so I bet you did it, didn't you? At least, you fooled her for a little while?"

Storms, I love this man, she thought. For his humor, his brightness, his genuine goodness. With that smile, brighter than the cold Shadesmar sun, she became *Shallan*. Deeply and fully.

"I totally did," she whispered to him. "I swapped it for a fake one, and *almost* escaped. Except, you know, *she's Jasnah*."

"Yes, the big flaw in your plan. You'd probably have managed it against a normal person."

"Well, the Soulcaster was always a dummy, so I was doomed from the start. Even if it had been real . . . I had this overinflated idea of how great a thief I could be. It's funny to remember I had those same silly inclinations before Veil."

"Shallan," he said. "You don't need to feel insecure any longer. The mission in the warcamps? You executed that *perfectly*."

"Until someone else executed Ialai. Perfectly." She looked at him, then smiled. "Don't worry. I don't struggle with feelings of insecurity any longer."

"Good."

"I'd say I'm pretty good at them."

"Shallan . . ."

She grinned again, letting him know she was feeling all right despite the comment. He stared into her eyes, then grinned himself. And somehow she knew what was coming.

"Well, I'd say you're a pretty good thief . . ." he began.

"Oh, don't you dare."

". . . because you stole my heart."

She groaned, leaning her head back. "You dared."

"What? You're the only one who can make bad jokes?"

"My jokes are *not* bad. They're *incredible*. And they take a *ton* of work to create *on the spot* for the *exact perfect* situation."

"A ton of work. To create on the spot. As if you don't prepare them ahead of time?"

"Never."

"Yeah? I've noticed you often seem to have one ready when you meet someone."

"Well, of course. That kind of joke is a great greeting. They're supposed to be *hi*larious."

He frowned.

"As in," she added, "not *goodbye*larious."

He stared at her. Then he went a little cross-eyed.

Ha! Veil thought. *HA!*

"Oh dear," Shallan said. "Did I break you?"

"But . . . 'hilarious' doesn't start with a 'hi' sound. . . . It doesn't make sense. . . ."

"It was a *stealth* joke," Shallan said. "Hiding in plain sight, like a Light-weaver. That's what makes it genius."

"Genius? Shallan, that was awful."

"You're full of awe," she said. "Got it." She smiled and snuggled against him, relaxing as she set down her bowl and took her sketchbook from him. She would finish her meal after she drew a little more. The moment demanded it.

Adolin put his arm around her and watched, then whistled softly. "Those sketches are really good, Shallan. Even for you. Have you done any others?"

Feeling warm, she turned the page to show off the cultivationspren she'd drawn. "I'd like to find both male and female subjects for each variety of spren. There might not be time for it on this trip, but it occurred to me that no one, at least not in the modern era, has ever done a natural history of the Radiant spren."

"This is wonderful," he said. "And thank you. For helping me relax. You're right—I can't know what is coming. The entire situation could change by the time we reach the honorspren. I'll try to remember that." He wrapped his arm loosely around her, the skin of his hand brushing her face. "Anything I can help you with?"

"Help me get the clothing correct?" she asked, turning back to the peak-spren page. "I feel like this garment pinned to the shoulder isn't hanging right in the picture. . . ."

They moved on to light topics. A piece of Shallan felt like she should be doing something more important, but Veil whispered a promise. They'd worry about the spy on the next day. Work on something else for a while. Then approach the problem fresh.

You told Adolin about robbing Jasnah, Radiant said. *Well done. It wasn't so bad, was it?*

No. It hadn't been. But that was the least of her crimes. Others were darker, hidden deeply—so deeply she honestly couldn't remember them. And didn't want to.

Eventually, the strange mistspren drifted near. The creature's free-form shape seemed like it would be difficult to capture in a sketch. Like steam, somehow trapped into a humanoid shape, contained by clothing and that strange mask.

She flipped to a new page and began drawing, but the spren—who had introduced herself as Dreaming-though-Awake—peeked at the sketchbook.

"Oh," she said. "It is just me?"

"What did you expect?" Adolin asked.

"She mentioned the Unmade earlier," Dreaming-though-Awake said. "I thought she might be drawing them."

Shallan paused, lifting her pencil. "Do you know anything of the Unmade?"

"Hardly anything," the spren said. "What do you want to know?"

"What happened to Ba-Ado-Mishram?" Shallan asked, eager. "What was she like? How did she Connect to the singers, and how did trapping her cause them to become parshmen?"

"Excellent questions," the spren said.

"And . . ." Adolin prompted.

"I told you, I know hardly anything," she replied. "I find the questions fascinating. What you wonder tells me so much." She began to move off.

"Seriously?" Shallan said. "You don't know *anything* about Ba-Ado-Mishram."

"I was not alive when she was free," the spren said. "If you wish to know more, ask the Heralds. I have heard several were there for her binding. Nalan. Kelek. Find them; ask them." She walked off, more drifting than stepping, though she did have legs and feet.

"That one makes me uncomfortable," Adolin said.

"Yeah," Shallan said, setting aside the sketchbook and picking up her bowl of food—now cold, but still tasty. "But that's comforting, in a way. Spren *should* be alien, *should* have their own ways of thinking and talking. I like that Dreaming-though-Awake is a little weird."

"You simply like the company," Adolin said.

She smiled, but the words the spren had said lingered with her. *Heralds were there. And the Heralds were a major focus of the Sons of Honor—whose leader Mraize has sent me to hunt.*

It was all connected. She had to figure out how to unravel it all. *Without* unraveling herself.

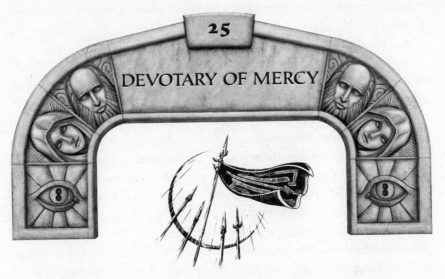

25

DEVOTARY OF MERCY

Whimsy was not terribly useful, and Mercy worries me. I do think that Valor is reasonable, and suggest you approach her again. It has been too long, in her estimation, since your last conversation.

I'm sorry, Brightlord," the ardent said as she walked through the room, picking up cushions from the floor and stacking them in her arms. "I do know the man you're searching for, but he's not here anymore."

"You discharged him?" Kaladin asked, walking at her side.

"No, Brightlord. Not exactly." She handed the stack of cushions to him, clearly expecting him to hold them as she walked to the next row and began gathering those.

Kaladin followed, balancing the stack of pillows. He and Teft were still trying to track down the refugee woman's missing uncle. His name was Noril, and Kaladin's father remembered the man. Not surprising, considering Lirin's near-superhuman ability to recall people and faces.

Noril, who had lost an arm sometime in the past, had arrived in Hearthstone on the same day Kaladin had brought the flying ship. Noril had displayed signs of severe shock, so Lirin had taken extra care of him, making sure the man was on the airship for the flight to Urithiru.

After the ship arrived, things got chaotic. Overwhelmed by the number of refugees and their ailments, Lirin had sent Noril to the ardents. So, that was where Kaladin and Teft had come today. It felt odd to be spending so much time personally looking for one man when there were many patients to see. Coming here wasn't particularly effective triage.

Unfortunately, that was a part of being a surgeon that Kaladin had never mastered. Giving up on one to save two others? Sure, it was great in principle. But doing it *hurt*.

Kaladin walked alongside the ardent while Teft leaned against the wall near the entrance to the room. It was otherwise empty, though some kind of training or teaching had plainly been going on earlier, judging by the rows of cushions.

"If you didn't let Noril go," Kaladin said, "what happened to him?"

"We sent him on," the ardent explained. She was holding so many cushions, he couldn't see her through them. "My devotary cares for physical ailments. We help rehabilitate those who have lost limbs, eyes, or their hearing in battle. He had only one arm, yes, but his wounds ran deeper."

There were three cushions left on the floor, and when she tried to bend to pick them up, her stack teetered. So Kaladin held out his hand for her stack. Then he held out his other hand as well.

"You can't carry them all," she said. "Let's . . ."

She trailed off as she saw what Kaladin had done. The stack he'd originally been holding—now Lashed upward just enough—remained floating in the air beside him.

"Oh," she said, then inspected him more closely. "Oh! You're Brightlord Stormblessed!"

Kaladin nudged the floating stack of cushions so they lazily floated over toward the far wall—where other unused cushions were piled—then took her stack.

The ardent quickly grabbed the last three, blushing as she walked him over to the wall. "I had no idea who you were! I'm sorry, Radiant."

"It's fine," Kaladin said. "Don't make anything of it, please." As if being lighteyed wasn't bad enough.

"Well, the man you want," she said, "we couldn't help him. We . . . did try to keep him rather than sending him on. We knew he was in bad shape, after all. But . . ."

"Bad shape?" Kaladin asked.

"Oh yes," she said. "Last week we caught him trying to hang himself. The surgeon who sent him here warned us to watch for it, fortunately, so we saved him. Then we sent him on to the Devotary of Mercy. They care for those who . . . have trouble with their minds."

"You knew he might be a danger to himself," Teft said, walking up, "and you didn't send him there immediately?"

"We . . . no," she said. "We didn't."

"Irresponsible," Teft said.

"My father knew and sent him here first," Kaladin reminded Teft. "I'm sure the ardents did what they could."

"Go to level four, Brightlord," she said. "Right near the center, along Northbeam and not quite to the Aladar Princedom."

He set down the last of the cushions and nodded to Teft, and the two of them began the hike. Everything in Urithiru was a hike, especially on the lower floors.

Shallan always knew her way around just by the strata on the walls, which waved in colorful lines as different layers of rock had been cut through to make the tunnel. Kaladin considered himself good with directions, but he had to use the painted lines on the floor to get anywhere.

"Still can't believe how much of this place hasn't been explored," Teft said as they walked.

"I suspect by now most of it *has* been explored," Kaladin said. "Brightness Navani's teams have mapped all the lower levels, and done walk-throughs of all the upper ones."

"Walk-throughs, yes," Teft said, eyeing a dark corridor. "But explored? You might walk the woods every day and never see one out of a hundred things in there watching you."

As they struck inward, they saw fewer people. The lit areas—lined with Stormlight lanterns locked tight and bolted to the walls—dwindled behind, and they needed handheld spheres for light. There was a certain eeriness to these inner sections of the tower. Most everyone lived and worked on the rim. The only times they would strike inward would be to visit the atrium or one of the first-floor markets. He'd noted people taking long walks all the way around the rim to one of the lit corridors rather than cutting through the darker center. Storms, he'd found himself doing the same thing.

There was still space on the rim of the fifth and sixth floors, so why had this monastery chosen such an inward section? He was glad when they eventually reached a section of hallway that had permanent lanterns again. Paint on the floor indicated they were approaching Aladar's princedom. A right turn at a large intersection with glyphs on the floor led them to the monastery—marked by a large wooden door blocking the way forward, painted with a glyphpair in the shape of the Vorin sword, indicating a religious building.

"Building" was, of course, a stretch. Generally for a small complex like this, people would find an area with a grouping of different-sized rooms and hallways and divide them off with a few doors at key entry points. Someone was monitoring the door, for it swung open as they approached, revealing a younger male ardent.

"Brightlord," the man said, bowing. He squinted at Teft, trying to pick out his eye color. Then he bowed again. "Brightlord."

Teft grumbled at that. These days, after being Radiant for as long as they had, their eyes rarely faded anymore. And there was no stopping him from complaining about being a lighteyes. Unlike Kaladin, who had gotten over it ages ago.

"If you have come to commission prayers or burn glyphwards, I would direct you toward the Devotary of Kelek, a little farther outward from here," the ardent said, polishing a pair of spectacles and squinting at Kaladin. "We don't take prayer commissions here."

"Pardon," Kaladin said. "But we're not wanting prayers. Did you receive a patient recently who was missing an arm? His family is looking for him, and we're helping track him down."

"Can't reveal patient information," the man said in a bored tone, putting on his spectacles—then cursing softly and pulling them off again and rubbing them on his shirt, trying to get a spot he'd apparently missed. "I'd need the authorization of at least a highlord of the third dahn. Otherwise, speak to Sister Yara for normal visitation requests. I have a form somewhere for your wife to fill out."

Teft glanced at Kaladin.

"You do it," Kaladin said. "Syl's out for her morning flight, and she'll snap at me if I call her back early."

Teft sighed and reached his hands out, making a silvery Shardspear appear. The Stormlight in the three nearest lanterns went out, streaming into him, setting his eyes aglow. A luminescent mist began to rise from his skin. Even his beard seemed to shine, and his clothing—once so pedestrian—rippled as he rose into the air about a foot.

The ardent stopped polishing his spectacles. He squinted at Teft, as if forgetting what was in his hands. "Oh. Brightlord Radiant," he said, then bowed reverently first to Teft, then to Kaladin—though the man didn't seem to recognize Kaladin. "Brightlord Radiant. I will see to your request."

Kaladin didn't much care for the reverence people showed them. People who had once spat after hearing someone speak of the "Lost Radiants" had turned around quickly when their highprince and their queen had each become one. It made Kaladin wonder how quickly these people might turn on them, if reverence suddenly became unfashionable.

That said, there *were* perks. Particularly with the ardents, who had quickly pointed out that Vorinism had always been closely aligned with the Knights Radiant. This one let them in now, absently tucking his spectacles in his robe's breast pocket. He led them to a records room, stacked with ledgers and paper, and asked one of the ardents inside to watch the door while he saw to their "esteemed guests." There wasn't much enthusiasm in his tone, but he didn't seem the enthusiastic type.

"One arm . . ." the ardent said, searching a ledger near the door.

"Name is Noril," Teft said. "Doesn't seem he'd have any reason to go by a false one."

"He's here, Brightlord," the ardent said, leaning in close and pointing at words on the page. He patted at his robe's lower pockets, as if searching for his spectacles. "He told us he has no living relatives though. Maybe it's a different person. Ah, and he's on watch for suicide, Brightlords. One unsuccessful attempt. A profoundly disturbed man."

"Show us to him," Kaladin said.

The ardent finally found his spectacles, but just started wiping them again. He led the way out of the records room and down a dark corridor lit by infrequently placed lanterns.

Kaladin followed, raising a sphere to give the place more light. As if it weren't bad enough to be trapped deep in the tower, away from light and wind. Did they have to make it so dim as well? He couldn't help but be reminded of his days in prison, following that time he'd helped Adolin in the arena. Kaladin had been locked up on dozens of occasions, but that one had felt the worst. Sitting in there fuming, stewing, festering. Feeling that the winds and the open sky had been stolen from him . . .

Dark times. Ones he'd rather not remember.

They passed door after door alongside the corridor, each marked by a numeric glyph. He saw not a few gloomspren around. The doors had small windows in them, but Kaladin assumed the dark cells beyond were unused—at least until he heard a voice muttering from one of them. At that, he stopped and held up his sphere, looking in. A woman sat in the featureless cell, her back to a bare wall, rocking back and forth as she muttered something unintelligible.

"How many of these rooms have people in them?" Kaladin asked.

"Hm? Oh, most of them," the ardent said. "We're a little understaffed, to be honest, Brightlord. We took in patients from most all the princedoms when we consolidated here. If you could bring the matter to the queen's attention . . ."

"You lock them in here?" Teft demanded. "In the *dark*?"

"Many of the mentally deficient react poorly to overstimulation," the ardent said. "We work hard to give them quiet, calm places to live, free of bright lights."

"How do you know?" Kaladin asked, striding after the ardent.

"The therapy is prescribed by some of the best thinkers among the ardentia."

"But how do you *know*?" Kaladin said. "Do any of them get better? Have you tried multiple theories and compared them? Have you tested different cures or remedies on different patient populations?"

"There are no cures for mental ailments, Brightlord," the ardent said. "Even the Edgedancers can't do anything for them, unless their state is related to a recent brain trauma." He stopped beside a specific door scratched with the glyph for twenty-nine. "With all due respect, Brightlord, you should leave medical issues to those trained in them." He rapped on the door with his knuckles. "This is him."

"Open the door," Kaladin said.

"Brightlord, he might be dangerous."

"Has he ever attacked anyone?" Kaladin asked. "Has he hurt anyone other than himself?"

"No," the ardent said, "but the insane can be unpredictable. You could be harmed."

"Lad," Teft said, "you could stick us with a hundred swords, and we'd just complain that our outfits got ruined. Open the storming door."

"Oh. Um, all right." He fished in his pocket, came out with his spectacles, then fished in the other one until he found a ring of keys. He held the keys close to his nose one by one to see the glyphs on them, then finally unlocked the door.

Kaladin stepped in, his sapphire broam revealing a figure who lay huddled on the floor by the wall. There was some straw for a bed beside the other wall, but the man wasn't using it.

"Can't give him blankets or sheets," the ardent explained, peeking in. "Might try to strangle himself."

"Noril?" Kaladin asked, hesitant. "Noril, are you awake?"

The man didn't say anything, though he did stir. Kaladin stepped closer, noting the sewn-up sleeve. The man was missing his entire left arm. The room didn't smell too bad, all things considered, so at least the ardents kept him clean. The clothing was barely shorts and a thin shirt.

"Noril," Kaladin said, kneeling. "Your niece, Cressa, is looking for you. You aren't alone. You have family."

"Tell her I'm dead," the man whispered. "Please."

"She's worried about you," Kaladin said.

The man grunted, continuing to lie on the floor, facing the wall. *Storms. I know that feeling,* Kaladin thought. *I've been there.* He looked around the silent chamber cut off from the sunlight and wind.

This was so, so wrong.

"Can you stand?" he asked Noril. "I won't force you to go talk to her. I merely want to take you somewhere else."

Noril didn't reply.

Kaladin leaned closer. "I know how you feel. Dark, like there's never been light in the world. Like everything in you is a void, and you wish you could just feel something. *Anything.* Pain would at least tell you you're alive. Instead you feel nothing. And you wonder, how can a man breathe, but already be dead?"

Noril turned his head, looking at Kaladin and blinking eyes red from lack of sleep. He wore a rough beard, unkempt.

"Come with me and talk," Kaladin said. "That's all you have to do. Afterward, if you want me to tell your niece that you're dead, I will. You can come back here and rot. But if you don't come now, I'm going to keep annoying you. I'm good at it. Trust me; I learned from the best."

Kaladin stood up and offered a hand. Noril took it and let Kaladin haul him to his feet. They walked toward the door.

"What is this?" the ardent said. "You can't let him out. He's in our charge! We have to care for . . ."

He trailed off as Kaladin fixed him with a stare. Storms. *Anyone* would turn suicidal if kept in here too long.

"Lad," Teft said, pulling the ardent gently out of the way, "I wouldn't confront Brightlord Stormblessed right now. Not if you value keeping all your bits attached to you."

Kaladin led Noril out of the monastery and straight toward the rim of the tower. Teft joined him, and the ardent—Kaladin hadn't asked his name—trailed along behind. He didn't go running for help, fortunately, but he clearly wasn't willing to let them just leave with a patient either.

Noril walked quietly, and Kaladin let him adjust to the idea of being out of his cell.

"Kelek's breath," Teft muttered to Kaladin. "I was too harsh on that lady ardent. I chewed her out for keeping Noril instead of sending him to the experts—but if *that's* what the experts were going to do, I see why she'd hesitate."

Kaladin nodded. Soon after, Syl came zipping through the corridor. "*There* you are," she said.

"Honorspren can feel where their knight is," Kaladin said. "So you don't need to act surprised at finding me."

Syl gave an exaggerated eye roll, and he swore she made her eyes bigger for emphasis.

"What are we doing?" she said, landing on his shoulder and sitting primly with her legs crossed and her hands on her knees. "Actually, I don't care. I need to tell you something. Aladar's axehounds had *puppies*. I had no idea how much I needed to see puppies until I flew by them this morning. They are the *grossest* things on the planet, Kaladin. They're somehow so gross that they're cute. So cute I could have died! Except I can't, because I'm an eternal sliver of God himself, and we have standards about things like that."

"Well, glad you're feeling better."

"Yeah," she said. "Me too." She pointed toward Noril. "You found him, I see. Taking him to his niece?"

"Not yet," Kaladin said.

He led Noril past a large corridor where people flowed in both directions. Across that, at long last, they stepped onto a balcony. A larger communal one, like the one by his clinic.

Noril stopped in the archway, his eyes watering as he looked up at the sky. Teft took him by the arm and led him out a little farther, to where some chairs were set beside the railing, overlooking the mountains.

Kaladin stepped up to the railing, and didn't say anything at first.

Noril finally spoke. "Is she all right? My niece?"

"She's worried about you," Kaladin said, turning and settling into one of the seats. "My father—the surgeon you met in Hearthstone—says that you had a rough time of things before he met you."

The man nodded, his stare hollow. He'd lost his family in a brutal way, Lirin had said, while being unable to help.

"For some of us," Kaladin said, "it piles up bit by little bit. Until we realize we're drowning. I thought I had it bad, but I suppose I wouldn't trade places with you. Getting hit all at once like that . . ."

Noril shrugged.

"Nightmares?" Teft asked.

"Yeah," he said. "I can't remember the details. Maybe that's some mercy from the Almighty." He took a deep breath, tipping his head back to see the sky. "I don't deserve mercy. I don't deserve anything."

"You just want to stop existing," Kaladin said. "You don't want to actually kill yourself, not on most days. But you figure it sure would be convenient if you weren't around anymore."

"Better for everyone to not have to deal with me," Noril said.

Syl landed again on Kaladin's shoulder and leaned forward, watching Noril with an intense expression.

"It wouldn't be, you know," Kaladin said. "Better for everyone, if you vanished. Your niece loves you. Your return would make her life better."

"I can't feel that way," Noril said.

"I know. That's why you need someone to tell it to you. You *need* someone to talk to, Noril, when the darkness is strong. Someone to remind you the world hasn't always been this way; that it won't always be this way."

"How do you . . . know this?" Noril asked.

"I've felt it," Kaladin said. "Feel it most days."

Noril turned toward Teft.

"A man can't hate himself because of what he's done or not done," Teft said. "I used to. Still try to sometimes, but I keep reminding myself that's the easy path. It isn't what they would have wanted of me, you know?"

"Yeah," Noril said, sitting back. He still had that haunted cast to his eyes, but he at least seemed to be breathing more deeply. "Thank you. For bringing me out of that place. For talking to me."

Kaladin glanced at the ardent, who hovered behind them. Teft kept Noril talking—not about anything important, just where he was from. Apparently he'd lost his arm years ago, in a different event than when he'd lost his family.

The more he talked, the better he seemed to feel. Not cured, by any means. But better.

Kaladin rose and approached the ardent, who had settled down on a stone bench that was part of the balcony. The man had put on his spectacles, and was staring at Noril.

"He's talking," the ardent said. "We haven't been able to get more than a grunt out of him."

"That's not surprising," Kaladin said. "When you're like him, it's hard to feel like doing anything—even talking. Storms . . . when it's bad for me, I think I want *anything* but someone to talk to. I'm wrong though. While you can't force it, having someone to talk to usually helps. You should be letting him meet with others who feel like he does."

"That's not in the book of treatments," the ardent said. "It says we should keep lunatics away from each other. Talking together would make them feed off one another's melancholy."

"I could see that happening," Kaladin said. "But do you really know for certain? Have you tried it?"

"No," the ardent said. Seeming embarrassed, he glanced away from Kaladin. "I know you're angry at us, Brightlord. But we do what we can. Most people, they want to ignore men like him. They shove them off to the ardents. You might think us callous, but we're the only ones who care. Who try."

"I don't think you're callous," Kaladin said. "I think you're simply approaching this wrong. In surgery, we know that a man in shock should be repositioned so that his feet are up, his head down. But someone who has a wound to the back or neck should *never* be moved, not until we determine the extent of the damage. Different ailments, different wounds, can require severely different treatments. Tell me, what treatments do you give a person with melancholia?"

"We . . ." The ardent swallowed. "Keep them away from anything that might aggravate or disturb them. Keep them clean. Let them be in peace."

"And someone with aggressive tendencies?" Kaladin asked.

"The same," the ardent admitted.

"Battle shock? Seeing hallucinations?"

"You know my answer already, Brightlord."

"Someone needs to do better for these people," Kaladin said. "Someone needs to talk to them, try different treatments, see what *they* think works. What *actually* helps." Storms, he sounded like his father. "We need to study their responses, use an empirical approach to treatment instead of just assuming someone who has suffered mental trauma is permanently broken."

"That all sounds great, Brightlord," the ardent said. "But do you realize how much of a fight it would be to change the minds of the head ardents? Do you realize how much money and time it would cost to do what you're suggesting? We don't have the resources for that."

He looked to Noril, who had tipped his head back, his eyes closed, feeling the sunlight on his skin. Syl had landed on the chair beside him and was studying him as one might a grand painting.

Kaladin felt a stirring deep within him. He'd worried that working with his father wouldn't be truly fulfilling. He'd worried that he wouldn't be able to protect people, as his oaths drove him to do. That he would make an inferior surgeon.

But if there was one thing he understood that most ardents and surgeons—even his father—did not, it was this.

"Release this man to my care," Kaladin said. "And warn your superiors I will be coming for others. The ardents can complain all the way to Brightness Navani if they want. They'll get the same answer from her that I'm giving you now: We're going to try something new."

The deaths of both Devotion and Dominion trouble me greatly, as I had not realized this immense power we held was something that could be broken in such a way. On my world, the power always gathered and sought a new Vessel.

The fourth day of the trip, Shallan was truly enjoying herself. The closest they'd come to danger was when they'd spotted a pair of Fused soaring past in the distance three days ago. The humans had quickly scrambled into their hiding place—the tarp stretched between two piles of goods at the rear of the barge—but they needn't have worried. The Fused hadn't deviated in the barge's direction.

Other than that one event, she'd been able to spend her time in carefree drawing. Except, of course, when the Cryptics found her.

They loved to watch her draw. Currently, all four of them—Pattern, plus the three bonded to her agents—surrounded her. As a group, they hummed and buzzed and bounced up and down, watching as she tried to sketch Ua'pam standing on the high deck of the barge.

She'd grown accustomed to Pattern's presence. She was fond of it, in fact—she enjoyed the way he'd hum when he heard something he knew was untrue, or the way he'd pipe up with questions about the most mundane of human activities. But when all four crowded around, Shallan's serenity started building toward panic instead.

She'd almost forgotten how frightened she'd been when his strange symbol-headed figure had begun appearing in her drawings. She remembered now, though. Fleeing through the hallways of Kharbranth, her sanity unraveling as she sketched the hallway behind her, filled with Cryptics. She'd been peeking into Shadesmar. Her unconscious mind had begun to perceive spren as they appeared in the Cognitive Realm.

The same tension twisted her insides now, making her pencil lines sharp and stark. She tried to suppress the feeling. There was no reason for her to feel like she needed to run, scramble, *scream*.

Her lines were too dark, too rigid, to properly capture the Memory of Ua'pam standing with one foot up on the railing, looking like an explorer setting out for adventure. She tried to make herself relax, drawing a fanciful image of sunlight streaming around him. That, however, made the four Cryptics start humming in excitement.

"Could you all step back and give me more room?" Shallan asked the creatures.

They didn't cock their heads like humans might have, but she could sense confusion in the way their patterns sped up. Then, as if one, all four took *exactly* one step backward. They then proceeded to lean in even closer.

Shallan sighed, and as she kept drawing, she got Ua'pam's arm wrong. Spren were hard, because they didn't quite have human proportions. The Cryptics started humming with excitement.

"That's *not* a lie!" Shallan said, reaching for her eraser. "It's a mistake, you nitwits."

"Mmmm . . ." Ornament said. Beryl's Cryptic had a fine pattern, delicate like lace, and a squeaky voice. "Nitwit! I am a nitwit. Mmmm."

"A nitwit is a stupid person or spren," Pattern explained. "But she said it in an endearing way!"

"Stupidly endearing!" Mosaic said. She was Vathah's Cryptic, and her pattern had sharp lines to it. She often included rapid fast sections that waved like the women's script. "Contradiction! Wonderful and blessed contradiction of nonsense and human complication to be alive!"

Motif, Ishnah's Cryptic, simply made a bunch of clicking noises in rapid succession. His Alethi was not good, so he preferred to speak in the Cryptic language. The others began rapidly clicking to one another, and in the overlapping cacophony, she lost track of Pattern. For a moment they were all just a clump of alien creatures, huddled together with their patterns almost touching. The nearby sound of beads slapping against one another seemed the chatter of hundreds of Cryptics. Thousands of them. Watching her. Always watching her . . .

Radiant came to her rescue. Radiant, who had trained to ignore the chaos of battle, with its distracting sounds and constant yelling. When she took over, she brought with her a *stability*. She couldn't draw, so she tucked away the pad. She excused herself from the Cryptics and made her way to the stern of the barge, where she watched the rolling beads until Shallan recovered and emerged.

"Thank you," she said as Radiant withdrew.

Shallan listened to the peaceful rolling of the beads, endlessly surging. Perhaps it wasn't just the Cryptics that were bothering her. And after several days on the barge spent drawing, it was time to dive into the problem of finding the spy. She took a deep breath, and submitted to Veil.

No, Veil said.

. . . No?

You said we could look for the spy today, Shallan said.

We are. You. With my help.

Is this, Shallan asked, *penance because you broke the compact?*

In a way. I want to coach you through a little espionage.

I don't need to know it, she thought. *I have you.*

Humor me, kid. I need this.

Shallan sighed, but agreed. They couldn't share skills, as evidenced by Veil's drawing abilities. She knew espionage, Radiant could use a sword, and Shallan had their Lightweaving ability. And their sense of humor.

Oh please, Radiant thought.

"So how do we start?" Shallan asked.

We need to test each of the three subjects, Veil said, *and plant a—*

Wait, Radiant thought. *Shouldn't we first make absolutely certain the communication device couldn't have been moved another way? If we're using that as evidence that the spy is along on this mission?*

Shallan ground her teeth. Veil sighed softly.

But both agreed that Radiant was, unfortunately, correct. So Shallan strolled to the large tent they'd set up on the deck of the barge, using boxes and tarps. It was more like a large cave. While they didn't need shelter from the elements in Shadesmar, it made them feel comfortable.

Shallan ducked inside and went to the nook, made from boxes, that she shared with Adolin. She'd left the trunk unguarded—after all, she *did* want to catch the person doing this. She didn't want to hover about the place and make it obvious what she knew.

For now, she unlocked the trunk and checked on the device. It hadn't been moved again, so far as she could tell. But she didn't trust the trunk's lock. Tyn had been able to pick most locks—and beyond that, in the Physical Realm at least, spren could slip through openings like a keyhole. She'd seen Syl do it, not to mention Pattern.

She closed the trunk and—checking to make sure no one could see her around the corner in the box-walled nook—she tipped the trunk to one side, then the other. When she looked inside, the device had barely moved. She had it packed tightly enough between books and art materials that it couldn't have flipped on its own.

Satisfied? she asked.

Yes, Radiant said. *It couldn't have shifted faces without being removed from the trunk.*

Agreed, Veil said.

And we *didn't do it, right?* Radiant asked pointedly.

It was a discomforting question. They weren't *always* aware of what one of them did when another was in control. Often these days they worked together, giving up control by conscious choice, helping one another. But there were worse days. Shallan couldn't remember all the things Veil had done during that day she'd seized control, for example.

I didn't move it, Veil said. *I promise.*

I didn't either, Radiant said.

"Nor did I," Shallan whispered. And she knew it to be true. None of the Three had moved it, though she worried about Formless. Could part of her mind be betraying her? She didn't think that piece was even aware, or real, yet.

It wasn't us, Veil said. *I know this, Shallan. You have to trust it.*

She did. And that was what had disturbed her so much upon seeing the device moved. It was concrete proof that someone among her staff was lying to her.

All right, Veil said. *I've gone over the places the trunk was out of our sight . . . and it's not good. There were a ton of opportunities when it was alone back in Urithiru. We're not going to get anywhere trying to discover who had access to it, particularly not from this barge.*

"I still wish you'd do this part yourself," Shallan whispered to her.

Tough. Go back out, and we'll get started.

As she strode out, however, Pattern intercepted her. He walked up, his fingers laced before him. "Mmm . . ." he said. "I am sorry for earlier. For their overexcitement. The others do not have as much experience with humans."

"They have their Radiants," Shallan noted.

"Yes. That is not humans. That is one human each."

"You only have me."

"No! Before you, I studied humans. I talked about them much. I am very famous."

"Famous?"

"*Very* famous." His pattern sped up. "Cryptics do not often go into the cities of other spren. We are not liked. I went. I watched humans in Shadesmar, as we had planned to find humans to bond again. The other Cryptics were impressed by my bravery."

"Yes, very brave," Shallan said. "We humans are known to bite."

"Ha ha. Yes, bite. And break your oaths and murder your spren. Ha ha."

Shallan winced. True, those were the actions of *other* Radiants. Not Radiants from her generation. At least none of the noble ones, like Kaladin or Dalinar.

Nearby, in the center of the deck, the other three Cryptics were chatting with their heads together in a huddle.

"Do you think it strange," Shallan asked, "that Cryptics would end up with the Lightweavers, the order of Radiants with the most artists? You, who cannot lie—and who are basically walking numerical equations?"

"We *can* lie," Pattern said. "We are simply bad at it in general. It is not odd to end up with you. We like you in the way that a person likes new foods or new places. Besides, art is math."

"No it's not," Shallan said, offended. "Art and math are basically *opposites*."

"Mmm. No. All things are math. Art especially is math. You are math."

"If so, I'm the type with a misplaced number hidden so deep in the equation, I can never find it—but always calculate out wrong." She left Pattern then, strolling across the deck of the barge, passing several peakspren with molten light shining out through the cracks in their skin. High overhead, clouds had formed—the familiar ones of this place that pointed toward the distant sun like a roadway.

Those clouds didn't seem to move according to ordinary weather patterns, but appeared and disappeared as the barge moved. Was it something to do with the angle at which they were being seen?

All right, Veil, she thought. *What do we do?*

There are several ways to uncover a spy, Veil thought. *We're in a fortunate position, since we know they communicated directly with Mraize recently—and will likely do so again. We also have three specific suspects, a manageable number.*

We're going to try two different methods of finding the spy. The first is to catch them in a lie or a past misdeed, then push them until they grow uncomfortable and admit to us more than they intended. Everyone has a guilty conscience about something.

"Radiant doesn't," Shallan noted.

Don't be so sure, Veil replied. *But if this method doesn't work, we'll try something else—something that takes longer, but is more likely to work. We will find a way to feed each suspect a different tidbit of false information: a tidbit they will in turn feed to Mraize. Depending on which piece of information is leaked, we'll know who did the leaking, and identify our spy.*

That's quite clever, Radiant noted.

Well, it's more standard than clever, Veil admitted. *This is a time-tested method, and our biggest problem in using it is that I'm certain Mraize is aware of it. So we're going to have to be very subtle—and it might not work, as it requires Mraize to not only be told this information, but to not be suspicious of it, and to relate it back to us.*

Fortunately, we have a long trip ahead of us, and so if neither of these methods works, we can try something else. Point is, today, trying this will be good practice for Shallan.

"I don't need practice," she whispered. "I have you."

But Veil was being stubborn, so Shallan wandered across the deck to where Ishnah was helping Ua'pam and Unativi—his cousin, who ran the barge—as they manifested goods.

This was how almost everything—from clothing to building supplies—was created in Shadesmar. Spren didn't quarry stone or spin threads; they took the souls of objects from the physical world, then "manifested" them. The term referred to making the object's bead on this side instead reflect its physical nature.

Ua'pam held up a bead, inspecting it. Shallan could sense the souls of things by touching beads, though Veil had more trouble, and Radiant couldn't do it at all. Spren also varied in skill in this area, and true ability to manifest was somewhat rare.

Ua'pam pressed the bead against the deck, then held up a diamond chip—shining with Stormlight—in his other hand. He drew in the Light much as a Radiant would, breathing it into his lungs. She'd heard that this would invigorate spren, making them feel alert and awake—they could feed on Light, even if they didn't need it to survive. Today, Ua'pam immediately used this Stormlight to manifest the bead.

The hand with the soul pressed against the deck began to glow, then something blossomed underneath it. He stood up as an ornate wooden table emerged beneath his hand, growing like a plant at a highly accelerated speed.

"So fine!" his cousin—Unativi—said, clapping his hands. It sounded like rocks striking one another. "We are lucky! A grand table."

Ua'pam, shoulders slumping from exhaustion, nodded and dropped the drained sphere to the side for Ishnah to catch. Spren didn't care much for the value of most gemstones; it was the Light that interested them. The bead that had been the table's soul had vanished, replaced by the object. Interestingly, so far as Veil knew, the real table in the physical world would be unaffected by this process.

Shallan focused her attention on Ishnah, who was now trying to sketch the transformation process. Shallan had told the former thief to practice her art skills so she could better imitate lighteyed women.

"You are surprised by how nice this table is," Ishnah said to Unativi. She reached out to touch the table. "You didn't know what would be created before this moment?"

"No," Unativi said. "Understand. I find furniture. I know it is furniture. But how nice?" The peakspren spread his hands in a display of ignorance.

"We must work more today," Ua'pam explained. "Stormlight in gems runs out, but manifestations last long. Many months without reinfusion, if done by one with skill." He slapped the table. "I have skill."

"So you make as much cargo as you can," Ishnah said, gesturing to the many chairs, tables, and other articles of furniture surrounding them, "before the Stormlight we gave you runs out. Then you can sell what you created."

"Yes!" Unativi said. "Also, cousin will do the hard work. He is better."

"You have skill," Ua'pam said.

"You have more." Unativi shook his head. "Skill I need. Instead you go chasing humans. Losing your mind. Going to *fight*?"

"Odium comes," Ua'pam said, softly. "Odium will come here. We must fight."

"We can run."

"We cannot."

The two stared at one another, and Shallan took some mental notes to add to her natural history. Too often humans—even some spren—regarded all spren as basically the same in personality and temperament. That was wrong. They might not be as fractured as the many nations of men, but they were not a monoculture.

Keep focused, Veil thought. *The book you want to write is exciting, but we should make some progress on the spy today before getting distracted again.*

Each of the three Lightweavers was suspicious in their own way, Beryl most so currently. That said, Ishnah *had* worked with actual thieves in the past, and she was the only agent who had come to Shallan instead of needing to be recruited. Ishnah had wiggled her way into being Shallan's right-hand woman, and was the most skilled member of her Unseen Court.

The most damning fact was Ishnah's previous fascination with the Ghostbloods. Thinking of her as a traitor made Shallan's insides squirm, but she forced herself to confront the problem, Radiant cheering her on.

Shallan joined Ishnah as the two peakspren returned to their work. "You look overwhelmed," Shallan noted to Ishnah. "Are you well?"

"I've seen into this place, Brightness. . . ." Ishnah closed her notebook and looked across the rolling beads. "When I Soulcast, it's there. I see the souls of objects, hear their thoughts. I've dreamed of this world, but being here is different. Do you ever . . . feel something? Below, in the ocean?"

"Yes," Shallan admitted. She leaned against the railing. Ishnah mimicked her posture.

Now, Veil said. *Try steering the conversation in a way that implies you know something secret, something she should be ashamed about.*

Steering conversations was, fortunately, comfortable for Shallan. She was good with words. Better than Veil in many cases.

"There are currents to this world, Ishnah," Shallan said. "They move unseen. They can tow you under suddenly, abruptly, when you thought you were swimming along perfectly safe."

"I'm . . . not sure what you mean by that, Brightness."

"I think you do."

Ishnah immediately glanced away.

Aha! Veil thought. *We're on to something already.*

Too easy, Radiant thought. *Don't judge so quickly.*

"We all lie, Ishnah," Shallan continued. "Especially to ourselves. It's part of what makes us Lightweavers. The purpose of the Ideals, however, is to make us learn to live for truth. We have to be something better, *become* something better, to be worthy of our spren."

Ishnah didn't respond, instead staring at the ocean beads passing beneath.

Give it time, Veil suggested. *Don't be in a rush to fill the silence.*

Shallan obeyed, and the silence quickly became uncomfortable. She could see Ishnah shifting, not meeting her eyes. Yes, she felt guilty about something.

Now, push.

"Say it, Ishnah," Shallan said. "It's time to tell me."

"I . . . I didn't know what they'd do with the money, Brightness," Ishnah finally said. "I didn't mean for it . . . I mean, I was only trying to help."

Money? Radiant thought.

Drat, Veil thought. *We caught the wrong fish.*

Shallan gave the conversation even more uncomfortable silence. People hated it, and would often do anything to banish it.

"How did you know?" Ishnah asked.

"I have my ways."

"I should have guessed I couldn't keep it quiet," Ishnah said. She seemed younger all of a sudden, fidgeting as she spoke. She was older than Shallan, but not by that much. Old enough to be seen as a full adult. Young enough to not believe it yet.

"My old friends in the underground came to me," Ishnah said. "They were hard up, you know? We acted so tough, but that's the way you *have* to act. Pretend you're important, pretend you're dangerous, all while you're actually scraping crem to get by.

"So, I started giving them some of my stipend, ostensibly to help them pull themselves up and out of that life." She put her hand to her forehead. "Stormfather, I'm an idiot. Even *I* can hear how naive that sounds, saying it out loud. I should have known they just saw an opportunity in me.

Everyone's a mark. 'Ishnah got a good break, eh? What about the rest of us?' Of course they'd use it to set up another racket."

I feel embarrassed, Veil thought. *How did I miss hearing about this?*

"Well," Shallan said out loud, "I'm glad to hear that you aren't *intentionally* funding a criminal enterprise."

"Maybe we can clean it up quietly? It's not as bad as you might have heard. Or . . . well, I guess I'm not a good one to judge that. They bought up some gambling dens, started a protection scheme in one of the lower-end markets. My money bought them some enforcers, and . . . I know they started using my name as proof they had authority." She sighed. "How much does the queen know?"

"I'm honestly not sure," Shallan said. "I haven't told her."

"If it means anything, I cut them off last month, once I learned what they were doing."

Let's push a little harder, Veil decided. *Mention Mraize, imply he was involved. See if she lets anything slip.*

"When did Mraize get involved?" Shallan asked.

Ishnah cocked her head, scrunching up her brow. "Who?"

"The Ghostbloods, Ishnah."

The shorter woman grew pale, and her hand genuinely seemed to be trembling as she put it back on the railing. "Stormfather! Did I . . . Did they . . ."

"They've contacted you, I know."

"If they have, I didn't know it was them!" Ishnah said, shaken. She slumped against the railing. "What happened? Was it that man that Den threatened? Was he . . . Storms, Brightness. I've made a mess of this."

Shallan remained in place, hands clasped, trying to determine if it was an act. She couldn't persuade herself that it was; Ishnah appeared legitimately shocked by the implication that the Ghostbloods might have noticed her friends' little scheme. She even caught sight of a shamespren, swimming through the beads toward them. Those were rare out here, as they were passing mountains in the Physical Realm, where no one lived.

If she's lying, she's good enough to fool me, Veil said.

"I thought I'd escaped the underworld," Ishnah whispered. "I came to you, thinking you were someone powerful. Power was all I wanted . . . but then I saw something more. A way to be *free.* Everyone else lives such normal lives out in the light. No threads yanking toward the darkness. They seem *happy.* I suppose it was too much to assume I'd be able to really get away and belong in the light. . . ."

Storms. Shallan settled down and put her freehand on Ishnah's shoulder, ashamed at having caused such pain in her friend.

That is a silly emotion, Veil thought. *If Ishnah wants out, we've done her a favor by exposing this.*

And how would we feel? Shallan asked. *If someone forced us to expose all our flaws, all our lies, and hung them in the open like an unfinished painting?*

"We'll deal with this when we return, Ishnah," Shallan said. "And I promise, I will help you clear it up. You've made a misstep, but we all make those as we seek our truths. You do belong in the light. You're there now. Stay there with me."

"I will," Ishnah said.

"For now, if you hear any mention of the Ghostbloods, come directly to me."

"Of course, Brightness. Thank you. For not giving up on me completely, I mean."

Well done, Veil thought. *Let's slip in a tidbit that might get fed to Mraize, if she reports to him.*

I sincerely doubt she's the spy, Veil, Radiant said. *You yourself indicated she couldn't fool you.*

I didn't indicate that at all, Veil said. *I said if she's the spy, she's a better actor than I am. Which would make her extremely dangerous. Shallan, find some bit of information to feed her that is distinct and interesting enough to be worth reporting, but something she's unlikely to talk about to the other members of the team.*

That felt like a tall order. But Veil wasn't willing to offer any more advice, so Shallan soldiered forward.

"Hey," she said to Ishnah. "Just focus on helping with the mission. I like that you're taking notes on manifesting. Those will be useful."

She nodded. "Is there anything else you want me to do?"

Shallan considered it, tapping her finger against the deck. "Keep your eyes open for spren that look odd," she said softly. "You remember Sja-anat?"

"Yes," Ishnah said. Shallan had shared about the Unmade with her and a few others.

"I think I saw a corrupted windspren flying past earlier. I can't be certain, so keep it to yourself. I don't want to alarm anyone. But if you're going to be sitting back here watching the manifesting, maybe keep an eye out? And if you see an odd spren, let me know. All right?"

"I will. Thank you, Brightness. For your trust."

Shallan squeezed Ishnah's arm encouragingly, then wandered away. *How was that?* she asked.

Not bad, Veil said. *Your warning will keep her from talking about it to the other Lightweavers—but corrupted spren are also something Mraize is distinctly interested in. So if she reports to him, she is likely to feed him the information. If you can find a way to tell the others you saw a* different *kind of corrupted spren, we'll have planted just the right seed.*

I don't think it's going to work, Radiant said. *The idea is a clever one, but I can't see her reporting on such a minor detail to Mraize.*

You'd be surprised, Veil replied. *People are always eager to prove how important their mission is, and actively search for interesting things to report. Keep going, Shallan. You're doing very well.*

Feeling bolstered, she went to find Beryl. After the previous conversation, Ishnah now seemed the least likely to be the spy. And, Ishnah *had* been helpful in identifying Ialai's method of death. Besides, Mraize would know she had wanted to join the Ghostbloods—and would recognize that she'd draw suspicion.

It was probably one of the other two. And Beryl was the obvious choice. Shallan hadn't failed to notice the way Stargyle had dropped out of the mission at the last minute, with Beryl joining the team instead—a clear sign. But perhaps *too* obvious?

Beryl was on Soulcasting duty today. Yesterday they'd stopped by a small strip of land—representing a river in the Physical Realm—and used pickaxes to cut out some chunks of obsidian ground. Shallan had quickly understood why the spren of this realm didn't use obsidian for anything other than the occasional weapon; the rock was hard to work with, shattering like glass when struck.

While it wouldn't make a good building material, they'd had success Soulcasting it into food. The stone here was eager to be something else, and could easily be persuaded to change. Today, Beryl knelt beside a stone they'd cut, and was practicing turning it into food.

Shallan lingered nearby, taking in Beryl's tall Alethi figure, with luscious dark hair and a perfectly tan skin tone. She reminded Veil of Jasnah, only more relaxed.

She uses Lightweaving to enhance her appearance, Veil noted. *Probably does it by instinct.*

Today, Beryl wore a long skirt rather than a true havah, along with a sleeveless top and a pair of silk gloves that went up to her elbows. She had removed her freehand glove, and now reached out with delicate, supple fingers to caress the chunk of obsidian. She adopted an expression of concentration, and the chunk transformed to lavis grain in the blink of an eye. The clump of lavis held the shape of the obsidian for a moment, then collapsed, spreading out on the cloth underneath.

"Brightness?" Beryl asked, glancing up from her work. She was dark-eyed, like many camp followers, though that didn't really matter anymore. Importantly, she had not yet earned her Blade. "Am I doing something wrong?"

Beryl had learned Lightweaving on her own away from the structure and order of the Radiants. She was an unknown factor, a Surgebinding savant who had come with her own spren already bonded.

Shallan knelt and made a show of picking up a handful of grain and inspecting it. "You're not doing anything wrong at all. This is good work. Most of us have trouble making individual grains."

"Oh! It helps to have a seed," she said, pulling some from her pocket. "*Literal* seeds, in this case." She grinned, holding them up. "If you have something to *show* the obsidian's soul, you intrigue it enough to want to transform."

"That's not how Jasnah does it," Veil said.

"Yeah, Vathah told me. But my way works better for him too. Queen Jasnah doesn't know everything, right?" She smiled brightly. "Or maybe it's different for our order. It's not her fault if she doesn't know how Lightweavers work."

Storms, Veil thought. *I always forget how downright* sunny *Beryl can be.*

Shallan folded her arms, thinking back to her own troubles with Soulcasting. Could it be that all along, the problem hadn't been her, but Jasnah's training method? They'd assumed two orders using the same power would be analogous. The Skybreakers and the Windrunners seemed to fly the same way, after all.

Then again, the way that Lightweaving worked for Truthwatchers seemed different—even if one disregarded whatever Renarin was. So maybe?

Focus, Veil thought. *Try nudging her to be uncomfortable, find out if she's hiding something.*

Shallan opened her mouth to make a comment like she had to Ishnah. Something else entirely came out.

"Are you actually happy?" Shallan asked.

"Brightness?" Beryl asked, still sitting on a box next to some chunks of obsidian. "Happy?"

"There's a lightness about you," Shallan said. "Is it real, or are you hiding the pain?"

"I think we all hide pain to an extent," Beryl said. "But I don't think I'm in particular agony."

"And your past?" Shallan asked. "It doesn't haunt you?"

"I won't pretend my life was easy. The profession isn't an easy one, and the women who find their way to it often have their problems magnified. There are ways to keep it from chewing you up, however. To make it your choice, done in your way." She grimaced. "Or at least ways to tell yourself that . . ."

Shallan nodded, and heard a humming behind her. Pattern—her

Pattern—had wandered over, and was inspecting Beryl's Soulcasting handiwork.

"By the end," Beryl continued, "I had a lot of control over the men who came to me. I liked becoming the woman they wanted. It wasn't until you came searching for me, though, that I realized the truth." She looked straight at Shallan. "That I *could* walk away if I wanted to. Nothing was keeping me there. Not any longer. I could have left months earlier. Odd, isn't it?"

"That's how it always is," Veil said.

"Pardon, Brightness, but it's not. A lot of the women are worse off than me. They couldn't simply leave; it was the moss for some, threats for others. Some of us though . . ." She looked at her hand and let the seeds drop into the pile. "We talk about transformation. The Almighty's greatest blessing to humans: the ability to change. Sometimes we need a seed too, eh?"

Shallan shuffled, looking to the side as Vathah walked by with one of the peakspren sailors. Maybe she should go talk to him, see if he was the spy.

You're uncomfortable around Beryl, Radiant thought. *Is it because she seems to have a greater handle on her life, when you assume she should be worse at it?*

Feelings, feelings, Veil said. *Blah blah blah. Shallan, stay on topic, please.*

Shallan found her mind spiraling around her past. The things *she* had done. The things she was still hiding from, wearing this face that she *pretended* was her own. That she *pretended* she deserved. Shallan could be happy, but that happiness was built on lies.

Would it not be better to accept what she *really* was? Become the person she *deserved* to be? Formless—who had been hiding deep inside these last few days—stirred. She'd thought him forgotten, but he had been waiting. Watching . . .

"Help," Shallan whispered.

"Brightness?" Beryl asked.

Radiant stood up straight, no longer lounging. "You are to be commended for your diligence, Beryl. You say that this method of Soulcasting has helped Vathah. Have you shown it to any of the others yet?"

"No, not yet. I—"

"I would like you to approach Ishnah and train her in it. Report to me the results of the experiment."

"I will!" Beryl said. "Um, you seem different. Did you . . . become one of the others?"

"I have merely realized I have a great deal yet to do today," Radiant said. That caused Pattern to hum. "Continue your efforts."

She moved to leave, then pretended to reconsider and stepped back, speaking softly. "We need to be careful. I saw a gloryspren earlier that appeared odd. I think that Sja-anat, the corrupter of spren, is watching us. Report to me if you see any odd gloryspren, but stay very quiet about this to the others. I do not wish to inspire a panic."

Beryl nodded.

That's a little straightforward and blunt, Radiant, Veil said. *The goal is to not act suspicious.*

I do as I can, Radiant thought. *And I am not suited to subterfuge.*

Liar, Veil said. *Shallan? Kid, you all right?*

But Shallan had pulled into a knot within Radiant.

It was the conversation that set her off . . . Veil said. *Something about it. About leaving your old life, and finding a new one?*

Shallan whimpered.

I see . . . Veil said, retreating as well.

Great. She'd lost both of them. Well, Radiant's job was to see that things got done. She walked after Vathah; Pattern stayed behind with Beryl, watching her work.

Vathah was carrying a large pole that was at least thirty feet long. What was he up to? Regardless, in Radiant's estimation, Vathah was suspicious in an entirely different way from the other two. Vathah had always been the most dark of the former deserters. And she understood why. Following something, believing in something, then abandoning it? Leaving your companions-in-arms? It was a horrifying thought.

She usually let the others deal with him. A lot of the other deserters she'd come to understand. Gaz had run from gambling debts, and Isom from a cruel captain in Sadeas's army who constantly beat him.

But Vathah . . . his true past was still a mystery. He was cruel and possibly corrupt; he had returned with Shallan only because the circumstances had been right. Shallan liked to think she'd changed the deserters—shown them the nobler side of their personalities.

While she might be correct about the others, Radiant wasn't certain about Vathah. If he had deserted once, he was capable of it again. And storms, he didn't look *at all* like he belonged with the rest of the Court. Even cleaned up and wearing work clothing, Vathah looked rough. Like he'd recently gotten out of bed—after collapsing into it drunk. He was never properly shaved, but also never ended up with a full beard.

Vathah climbed the few steps up to the prow of the barge, the section where the mandras were harnessed. Radiant marched up after him. A female peakspren sailor instructed Vathah to heft the long pole so that the tip went high in the air and the bottom end slipped through a ring at the front of the barge. Once he'd done so, Vathah began lowering the pole slowly, hand over hand. The butt of the pole passed between the mandra harness lines to hit the beads beneath.

They're measuring depth, Radiant thought. *He's doing sailor jobs, like yesterday.* Strange.

"Hold it steady," the peakspren said to Vathah. "Brace it against the prow of the barge. Yes. Keep going."

Vathah continued lowering the pole. The current of the beads below was clearly stronger than a current of water would be, and it pressed the pole backward. The rings on the front of the ship were there to keep the force of the beads from pulling the pole out of his hands.

"Keep going," the peakspren said. "Slower though!"

Vathah grunted, continuing to lower the depth gauge. "They use weighted strings in my world."

"Wouldn't work here."

"I just bumped something," he said. "Yeah, that's the bottom. Huh. Not as far down as I thought it would be."

"We've entered the shallows," the peakspren said, helping him raise the pole. "Skirting to the west of the great trench we call the Radiant Depths."

Vathah got the pole up and walked to stow it along the railing. Then the spren tossed him a brush. Vathah nodded and walked toward the water station. The metal device fed on Stormlight to somehow make water.

"What is this task?" Radiant asked, following after him.

"Deck needs to be scrubbed," he said. "They don't wash them here as often as they do on ships back home—guess they don't need to, without ocean water spilling up on everything. Planks don't need tar to keep them waterproof either."

"You were a sailor?" Radiant asked, surprised.

"I've done a lot of jobs." He filled up a bucket, then picked a section of the deck and went to work, kneeling and scrubbing at the wood.

"I'm impressed," Radiant said. "I had not thought you would be one to volunteer for work, Vathah."

"It needs to be done."

"It is good to work the body, but I find myself objecting to that statement. The peakspren seem to have continued for a while without the deck being washed." She folded her arms, then shrugged and moved to get a brush herself.

As she returned, Vathah glanced at her with a dark expression. "Did you simply come to taunt me, Radiant? Or is there a point?"

"I suppose it's easy to tell me apart from the others, isn't it?"

"Veil would never have decided to help," he said, continuing to brush. "She'd have mocked me for doing extra work. Shallan would be off somewhere drawing or reading. So, here we are."

"Indeed," Radiant said, kneeling and scrubbing alongside him. "You are

an observant man, Vathah."

"Observant enough to know you want something from me. What is it?"

"I'm merely curious," she said. "The Vathah *I* know would have avoided work and found a place to relax."

"Relaxing isn't relaxing," he said. "Sit around too much, and you start sitting around even more." He kept brushing. "Go across the planks, rather than up and down them, so you don't wear grooves. Yeah, like that. This *does* need to be done. The sailors used to scrub the wood every month, but they haven't had as much help lately. Something about Reachers not being around? What are Reachers, anyway?"

"They're a specific bronze-skinned kind of spren," Radiant said. "They were sailors on our previous voyage."

"Well, they aren't around as much to hire these days, I guess," Vathah said.

"Did the others say why?"

"I didn't ask," Vathah said.

"How odd," Radiant said. Now, how could she get to the topic of a corrupted spren? She considered, and began to regard this as a silly exercise. Why not *ask* him if he was the spy. If she was firm enough, he'd admit to his wrongdoing.

She opened her mouth to do just that, but had enough common sense to stop herself. This was . . . not a good idea, was it? Having her do espionage?

No, Shallan thought, emerging with a sigh. *I guess it isn't.*

"Hey," Shallan said to Vathah as they scrubbed. "You know we're a family, right? The Court, the group of us? You don't have to always go off alone and punish yourself."

"Not punishing myself," he growled. "Just wanted to be busy. And away from questions. Everyone asks too many questions when they get bored."

"You don't have to answer them," she said. "Really, Vathah. You're one of us, and we accept you. As you are."

He glanced at her, then sat back on his knees, dripping brush in hand. Shallan did likewise, noting that she'd scuffed her trousers. Radiant was always too eager to throw herself into labor, never worrying about her clothing.

"Shallan," he said.

She nodded.

Vathah returned to his work and didn't speak as he continued to scrub. Unlike Ishnah, he was perfectly willing to let silence hang. It was harder for Shallan, but she did. For a time the only sound was that of bristles on wood.

"Does it work?" Vathah finally asked. "These three faces you put on? Does it actually help you somehow?"

"It does," Shallan said. "It really does. Most of the time, at least."

"Can't decide if I envy you or not," Vathah replied. "I'd like to be able to pretend. Something broke in me, you know? A long time ago. Used to be a good soldier. Used to care. But then you see what you've done—legitimately *see* it—and realize everything you fought for was a sham. What do polished buttons matter when you've got a child's blood on your boots?" He scrubbed harder at a spot on the deck. "Figure if I learn to Lightweave well enough, maybe I'll turn into someone else . . ."

That stabbed her straight through.

Strength, Shallan, Radiant thought. *Strength before weakness.*

"Wouldn't that be a blessing?" Vathah continued. "To become someone else? Someone new?"

"You can do that without Lightweaving," Shallan said.

"Can I?" Vathah asked. "Can *you*?"

"I . . ."

"We've got a blessing in this power," he continued. "Lets us turn into other people."

"It's not a blessing," Shallan whispered. "It's survival."

"Feels worse in this place," Vathah said, eyeing the sky. "I always feel like something is watching me."

"Yeah," Shallan said. "The other day, I caught a spren swimming alongside the boat, watching me. One of those fearspren, the long eel-like ones on this side."

"What color was it?" Vathah asked. "Was it . . . hers?"

"Yeah," Shallan whispered. "I didn't tell the others. Didn't want them worried."

"Smart," Vathah said. "Well, Sja-anat is something else for me to worry about. I'll have to double-check every storming spren now."

"Let me know if you see anything," Shallan said. "But don't trouble the others, not yet. Not until we know for certain what she wants."

Vathah nodded.

Nice work, Veil thought at her, emerging from her contemplation. *That was smooth, Shallan. We'll think of ways to push him for secrets he might be hiding later. For now, this was a good day's work.*

I hate that I'm back to acting like an apprentice, Shallan thought back. *You learned all this from Tyn. Why do we need to learn it again?*

We learned it, Veil thought, *but we never tried it out. Remember, we . . . are new to this, despite what we might . . . might pretend.*

It was hard for Veil to acknowledge that she didn't actually have years of experience. Hard for her to admit that she was an alter—a part of Shallan's personality, manifesting as a distinct person. But it was a good reminder.

One that Radiant often brought up. They *were* learning, and they *weren't* experts. Not yet.

Still, Shallan did know a few things about people. Though Veil wanted to move on, Shallan knelt beside Vathah. "Hey," she said. "Whatever you did, it's behind you. We accept you, Vathah. The Unseen Court is a family."

"A family," he said with a grunt. "Never had one of those before."

"I knew it," she said softly.

"What? That I was lonely?"

"No," she said solemnly, "that you were the child of a couple of particularly ugly rocks."

He glared at her.

"You know," she said, "since you have no family. Must be rocks. It makes sense."

"Really? We were having a moment."

She smiled, putting her hand on his shoulder. "It's okay, Vathah. I appreciate your sediment." She got up to go.

"Hey," Vathah said as she walked away.

She glanced back at him.

"Thanks for smiling."

She nodded before continuing on her way.

What you said applies to us too, Radiant thought. *That what we did in the past doesn't matter.*

I suppose, Shallan thought.

You don't mean that, Veil accused her. *You think what you did was worse. You're always willing to give others more charity than you extend yourself.*

Shallan didn't respond.

I'm figuring it out, Shallan, Veil said. *Why you keep working with Mraize. Why you won't tell Adolin. What this is all about. It has to do with what you said earlier. When—*

"Not now," Shallan said.

But—

In response, Shallan retreated and Radiant found herself in control. And no amount of prodding would bring Shallan back.

27

BANNERS

That said, the most worrying thing I discovered in this was the wound upon the Spiritual Realm where Ambition, Mercy, and Odium clashed—and Ambition was destroyed. The effects on the planet Threnody have been . . . disturbing.

N avani had always found war banners to be curious things. The wind was crisp and cold on Urithiru's outer platform today, and it made the banners—brilliant Kholin blue, with Dalinar's glyphpair emblazoned on them—crack with the sound of breaking sticks. They seemed alive up there on their poles, writhing like captive skyeels among the windspren.

Today, the banners waved above waiting battalions. A thousand men at a time stood for their turn at the Oathgate, where Radiants transferred them to Azir. With a flash—a ring of light rising around the plateau— both men and banners were off, sent hundreds of miles in a heartbeat.

Navani appreciated the aesthetic nature of banners—the way they marked divisions, battalions, companies. At the same time, there was a strange incongruity to them. It was essential to keep your men organized and engaged on the battlefield. Dalinar said far more battles were lost by improper discipline than by lack of bravery.

But the banners also acted like enormous arrows, pointing the way to the most important men on the field. Banners were *targets*. Bold proclamations that *here* was where you'd find someone to kill. They were symbols of an organized army, helmed by men and women who knew the best way to end you—if only you'd do them the favor of wandering in their direction.

"You look preoccupied," Dalinar said as he stepped over, trailed by an honor guard of ten men.

"I'm thinking about symbols and why we use them," Navani said. "Trying *not* to think about you leaving again."

He reached down to cup her cheek. Who had known those hands could be so tender? She placed her hand alongside his face. His skin always felt rough. She swore she'd touched his cheek right after he'd shaved, and still found it ragged like sandpaper.

The honor guard stood tall and tried to ignore Dalinar and Navani. Even this little sign of affection wasn't particularly Alethi. That was what they told themselves, anyway. The stoic warriors. Not ruined by emotion. That was *their* banner, never mind that for centuries one of the Unmade had driven their lust for battle to a frenzy. Never mind that they were human like any others. They had emotions; they displayed them. They merely pretended to ignore them. In the same way you might tactfully ignore a man who accidentally went about with his trousers undone.

"Watch him, Dalinar," Navani whispered. "He will try something."

"I know," Dalinar said. Taravangian was walking up the slope onto the platform for the next transfer. Through some careful finagling, his honor guard was Alethi—and Dalinar planned to station the man's armies away from the command post on another part of the Azish front, with extra soldiers in between to protect his flank from a potential double cross.

It was an unfortunately obvious move. Taravangian would realize he was being kept hostage, after a fashion, to ensure the loyalty of his troops.

As an extra protection, a singular secret weapon hid among Dalinar's servants. Szeth, wearing the face of a common soldier, had been assigned to guard Dalinar. Navani couldn't spot him, so the disguise—maintained by one of Shallan's Lightweavers—was working. Though the sheath to his strange sword had required some physical decorations and disguises, as a Lightweaving wouldn't stick to it. So she thought she could pick him out as the one with the oversized weapon at his waist.

Another Lightweaver had created an illusion of Szeth in his jail cell. If Taravangian had people reporting on Szeth, they'd indicate he was safely locked up. They wouldn't know he was instead staying very close to Dalinar. Though she hated the idea, Navani had to admit that Szeth *had* remained in prison all these months, without a single incident. He seemed obedient to Dalinar without question. And *if* Szeth could be trusted, there was likely no better guard.

Almighty send that the cure was not worse than the disease. Beyond that, Navani couldn't help wondering if even in all this, they were being manipulated by Taravangian. Surely he couldn't *want* them to surround him with enemy troops. Surely she misread the clever turn of the old man's lips, the knowing look in his eyes.

But now it was time for Dalinar to leave. So, Navani carefully tucked away her anxiety and embraced him. He plainly wasn't thrilled to get a hug in front of his soldiers, but he didn't say anything. After that, the two of them went to meet the governess who had brought little Gav, with his trunks of things. The young boy—trying hard not to look too eager—saluted Dalinar.

"It is a big duty," Dalinar told him, "going to war for the first time. Are you ready?"

"I am, sir!" the child said. "I'll fight well!"

"You *won't* be fighting," Dalinar said. "And neither will I. We'll be handling strategy."

"I'm good at that!" Gav said. Then he gave Navani a hug.

The governess led him toward the Oathgate building. Navani watched with worry. "He's young to be going."

"I know," Dalinar said. "But I owe him this. He feels terrified to be left behind again in a palace while . . ." He left it unsaid.

Navani knew there was more. Things Dalinar had said about how he'd been angry when younger, and had prevented Adolin and Renarin from spending time with him when they wanted to. Well, the child should be safe. And he really did deserve more time with Dalinar.

She held his hand for a season, then let him go. He tramped up the slope toward the Oathgate as a half dozen anxious scribes scurried over to ask him questions.

Navani composed herself, then went to say farewell to her daughter, who would also be going on the expeditionary force. She spotted the queen arriving via palanquin. Curiously, Jasnah—who often took extra care not to seem weak—almost always used a palanquin these days. And Taravangian, who truly needed one, refused the distinctive treatment.

Taravangian seemed weaker while walking—while Jasnah seemed stronger when carried. More confident, in control. *Which is exactly how each of them wishes to appear,* Navani thought as the porters lowered Jasnah's palanquin and she emerged. Though her havah, her hair, and her makeup were immaculate, Jasnah wore little in the way of ornamentation. She wanted to be seen as regal—but not excessive.

"No Wit?" Navani asked.

"He promised to meet me in Azir," Jasnah said. "He vanishes sometimes, and won't grace my questions with answers. Not even mocking ones."

"There is something odd about that one, Jasnah."

"You have no idea, Mother."

The two of them stood facing one another, until finally Jasnah reached forward. What followed was the most awkward hug Navani had ever been part of, both of them making the proper motions, but unenthusiastic at the same time.

Jasnah pulled back. She *was* regal. Technically they were both of a similar rank, yet there had always been something about Jasnah. Dalinar was a big rock of a man that you wanted to prod until you found out what kind of crystals were inside. Jasnah . . . well, Jasnah was just . . . unknowable.

"Storms," Jasnah said under her breath. "Mother, are we really so awkward that we embrace like teenagers meeting a boy for the first time?"

"I don't want to ruin your image," Navani said.

"A woman can hug her mother, can't she? My reputation won't come crashing down because I showed affection." Still, she didn't lean in for another. Instead she took Navani's hand. "I apologize. I haven't had much time for family lately. I always told myself that when I finished my travels, I'd work diligently to be available to you all. I recognize that family relations need attendant time to . . ." Jasnah took a deep breath, then pressed her safehand against her forehead. "I sound like a historical treatise, not a person, don't I?"

"You have a lot of pressure on you, dear," Navani said.

"Pressure that I asked for and welcome," Jasnah said. "The quickest changes in history often happen during times of strife, and these are important moments. But *you're* important too. To me. Thank you. For always being you, despite the rise of kingdoms and the fall of peoples. I don't think you can understand how much your constant strength means to me."

What an unusual exchange. Yet Navani found herself smiling. She squeezed Jasnah's hand, and that moment together—seeing through the mask—became more precious than a hundred awkward embraces.

"Watch little Gav for me," Navani said. "I don't know what I think of him going with Dalinar."

"Boys younger than him go on campaign."

"To locations not so near the battlefront," Navani said. It was a fine distinction that many of their allies misunderstood. But these days, with Fused who could fly, *anywhere* could become a battlefront.

"I'll make sure he keeps well away from the fighting," Jasnah promised.

Navani nodded. "Your uncle feels that he failed Adolin and Renarin as children by spending so long in the field, and so little of it with them when they were young. He intends to make up for it now. I don't dislike the sentiment, but . . . just keep an eye on them both for me, please."

Jasnah retreated to her palanquin, and Navani stepped back. The banners continued to applaud as Dalinar's best soldiers arranged themselves with him, the queen, and Taravangian. Though the chill air sliced through her shawl, Navani was determined to stay and watch until she had word via spanreed that they'd arrived in Azir.

As she waited, Sebarial wandered past. The portly, bearded man had taken to wearing clothing that was more appropriate to his overall look: something reminiscent of a Thaylen merchant's clothing, with trousers and a vest under a long Alethi officer's coat, meant to be left unbuttoned. Navani wasn't certain if Palona was to credit for the transformation, or if Adolin had finally gotten to the highprince—but it was a marked improvement on the takama ensemble Sebarial had once favored.

Most of the highprinces were out in the field on Dalinar's orders. It was Alethi tradition: being a leader was essentially the same as being a general. If a king went to war, highprinces would go with him. That was so ingrained in them that it was hard to remember that other cultures—like both the Azish and the Thaylens—did it differently.

Not many of the original highprinces remained. They'd been forced to replace Vamah, Thanadal, and—most recently—Sadeas with distant scions loyal to Dalinar and Jasnah. But building a reputation and a princedom in exile was a difficult task. Roion's son struggled for precisely that reason.

They had three they could count on. Aladar, Sebarial, and Hatham. Bethab and his wife had fallen into line, which left Ruthar the lone holdout of hostility—the last remnant of Sadeas's faction against Dalinar. Navani picked out the man with his retinue preparing to leave with Dalinar's force.

Ruthar would present a problem, but if Navani were to guess, Jasnah would find a way to deal with him soon. Her daughter hated loose ends. Hopefully whatever Jasnah did wouldn't be *too* dramatic.

Sebarial was staying behind to help administer the tower. And he offered his own set of difficulties. "So," he said to Navani. "We taking bets on how long it takes Taravangian to knife us in the back?"

"Hush," Navani said.

"Thing is," Sebarial said, "I kind of respect the old goof. If I manage to live as long as him, I can imagine throwing up my hands and trying to take over the world. I mean . . . at that point, what do you have to lose?"

"Your integrity."

"Integrity doesn't stop men from killing, Brightness," Sebarial said. "It just makes them use different justifications."

"Glib, but meaningless," Navani said. "Do you *really* want to draw a moral equivalency between wholesale conquest and resisting the Voidbringer invasion? Do you *genuinely* believe that a man of integrity is the same as a murderer?"

He chuckled. "You have me there, Brightness. You seem to have discovered my one great weakness: actually listening to anything I say. You might be the only person in all of Roshar who takes me seriously."

Light rose in a ring around the Oathgate platform, swirling into the air.

A scribe stood nearby at her workstation, waiting for spanreed confirmation of the army's arrival.

"I'm not the *only* one who takes you seriously, Turinad," Navani told Sebarial. "There's at least one more."

"If she took me seriously, Brightness, I'd be a married man." He sighed. "I can't decide if she thinks me unworthy of her, or if somehow she's decided a highprince shouldn't marry someone of her station. When I try to get it out of her, the response is never clear."

"Could be neither option," Navani said.

"If that's the case, I'm at a complete loss."

The scribe changed the flag outside her workstation. Green for a successful transfer, with a red flag underneath, meaning people were still leaving the other platform and it wasn't ready for another transfer yet.

Another use for banners, Navani thought. They could at times be more effective than a spanreed. You could look down from the twentieth floor and see a flag much more quickly than you could write out a question and receive a response.

Reputations were banners also. Jasnah had crafted a distinctive persona. People halfway around the world knew about her. Dalinar had done the same thing. Not as deliberately, but with equal effect.

But what banner did Navani want to fly? She turned with Sebarial and walked toward the tower. She'd originally come to the Shattered Plains to chase something new. A different life, one that she wanted rather than one she thought she *should* want. Yet here she found herself doing the same things as before. Running a kingdom for a man who was too grand to be contained by simple day-to-day tasks.

The love she felt for this man was different, true. Deeper. And there was certainly a fulfilling satisfaction to bringing order to the chaos of a newly born kingdom like Urithiru. It presented unique challenges both logistical and political.

Was it selfish to want something more? This was what she seemed to be good at doing, and it was where the Almighty had placed her. She was one of the most powerful women in the world. Why would she think she deserved more?

Together with Sebarial, she entered the tower by its broad front gates. The temperature change was immediate, though with these broad gates standing open all day, the inner foyer should have been as cold as the plateau outside.

"You want me to return to the warcamps, I assume?" Sebarial asked. "I still have some interests working in the area."

"Yes. By the time my husband returns, I want those camps fully under our control again."

"You know," Sebarial said, "some wouldn't trust me with such a duty. My vices align well with the delights offered by the region."

"We'll see. Of course, if you *fail* to bring order to the warcamps, then I'll need to impose martial law. Tragic, wouldn't you say? Closing down all of those entrepreneurs? Destroying the single place that is under Alethi rule, but which also offers an escape from the strict oversight of the Radiants?

"If only someone with precisely the right mindset would watch the warcamps and make sure they become safe for travelers, and that the nearby lumber operations are proceeding without interruption. Someone who could see the need for law, while also understanding that it's not a *terrible* thing to be a little more relaxed. To let good Alethi citizens live their lives safely—but without being under my husband's direct glare."

Sebarial laughed. "How much do you suppose I can pocket before Dalinar would find my thieving too blatant?"

"Stay under five percent," Navani said.

"Four and nine-tenths it is," Sebarial said, bowing to her. "I'll be practically respectable, Brightness. Perhaps Palona will finally see that I *can* be useful, if given the proper motivation."

"Turi?" Navani said.

"Yes, Brightness?" he asked, rising from the flowery bow.

"If a man takes nothing in his life seriously, it makes a woman wonder. What is *she*? Another joke? Another whim?"

"Surely she knows her value to me, Brightness."

"Surely there is no problem in making it clear." Navani patted him on the arm. "It is difficult not to question your value to someone who seems to value nothing. Sincerity might not come easily for you, but when she finds it in you, she'll value it even more for the scarcity."

"Yes . . . All right. Thank you."

He waddled off, and Navani watched him go with genuine fondness. That was incredible, considering her former opinion of the man. But he'd stood with them, whether through intent or accident, when most others had refused. Beyond that, she'd found he *could* be trusted to get things done.

Like everyone, deep down he wanted to be useful. Humans were orderly beings. They liked to see lots of straight lines, if only so—in some cases—they could be the one drawing curves. And if a tool seemed broken at first glance, perhaps you were simply applying it to the wrong task.

Once in the tower, Navani took a palanquin inward, attended by Brightness Anesa, who brought various reports for Navani to inspect. Navani passed over the sanitation figures, instead reading up on water distribution through the tower, as well as reports of foot traffic in the stairwells.

There were more random fights and arguments in Urithiru than there had been in Dalinar's warcamp. Part of that was the diverse population, but she suspected that keeping everyone in relatively tight confines was a culprit as well. Dalinar wanted to post more guard patrols, but if she could divert traffic flow to keep people from jostling one another . . .

She had some ideas mapped out by the time her palanquin reached the atrium at the far eastern edge of the tower. She stepped out into one of the city's most dynamic locations: a place where a vast corridor stretched tens and tens of floors upward, almost to the roof. While lifts ran up and down the large artery that led inward to the atrium—and there were a multitude more stairwells—this was the sole place one could catch a lift all the way to the top floor.

Stretching along the eastern wall was an enormous window, hundreds of feet tall. The tiers of Urithiru weren't full circles—most were closer to half-circles, with the flat side aligned here at the atrium. So you could look all the way up, or stare out toward the Origin.

As one of the brighter sections of the tower, and with its many lifts, the area bustled with traffic. That made it all the more remarkable that the atrium—of all places—had hidden an architectural mystery. Navani crossed the circular chamber to the far wall, just to the left side of the window. A few days back, one of her scribes had noted an oddity here: a small division in the rock, too straight to be a crack.

With Dalinar's permission, a Stoneward had been called in to shape the rock into an opening—they could make stone soft to their touch. Navani's morning report had indicated she should come see the results, but this was the first time she'd been able to pull away. Badali, a Stoneward, guarded the door. He was an affable older man with a powdery beard and smiling eyes. He bowed to her as she stepped through his newly made door.

Falilar, the engineer, was already inside measuring what they'd discovered: a large room hidden entirely in the stone.

"Brightness," Brightness Anesa said, walking alongside her. "What was the purpose of *sealing off* an entire room like this?"

Navani shook her head. This wasn't the only room they'd found in the tower with apparently no entrances. This one was particularly significant though, for it had a large picture window along the rear wall, which let in the sunlight.

Standing in front of that window was an odd structure: a tall stone model of the tower. She'd read about it in the report, but as she approached, she was still surprised by its intricacy. The thing was a good fifteen feet tall, and was divided in two—the halves pulled apart—to give a cross section of the tower. At this scale, floors weren't even an inch tall, but everything she saw about them was reproduced in intricate detail. At least, as much as was allowed at that scale.

Falilar joined her beside it, holding a notebook full of figures. "What do you make of it, Brightness?"

"I have no idea," she said. "Why put this here, but then seal it off?" She bent over, noting that the crystal pillar room—along with the two library rooms nearby—was represented in the model.

Falilar used a small reed to point. "See here? This room itself is reproduced, with a tiny representation of this very model. But there is an open door leading in, where there wasn't one in the real tower."

"So the rooms were sealed off before the Radiants left?"

"Or," Falilar said, "they could open and close some other way. When the tower was abandoned, some were already closed, others open."

"That would explain a lot." They'd found so many rooms with actual doors—or, the remnants of ones rotted away—that she hadn't considered that there might be other mechanisms on undiscovered rooms. A clearly biased approach. She glanced at the wall they'd come in through. "Did that Stoneward discover any mechanism for such an opening?"

"There was a gemstone embedded in the stone," Falilar said. "I had him get it out for us to inspect. I intend to have him see if perhaps the rock was somehow intended to slide open to the sides there. If so, it would be a remarkable mechanism."

Navani made a mental note to have one of the Windrunners fly out to do a close inspection of the mountains that Urithiru was built into. Perhaps windows like this one would reveal other hidden rooms, with equally mysterious contents.

"I'll do a thorough inspection of this model," Falilar said. "It might yield secrets."

"Thank you. I, unfortunately, have some sanitation reports to read."

"If you get a chance, stop by the library and talk to my nephew," Falilar said. "He's made some improvements on his device."

Navani nodded and started back toward her palanquin, trusting Falilar to send her whatever he discovered. As she was climbing into the palanquin, she saw Isabi—one of her younger scholars—rush into the room, holding a blinking red light.

The mysterious spanreed. The one she'd received weeks ago from the unknown person who was so angry about fabrials. It was the first time they had tried to contact her since that day.

Sanitation reports would wait.

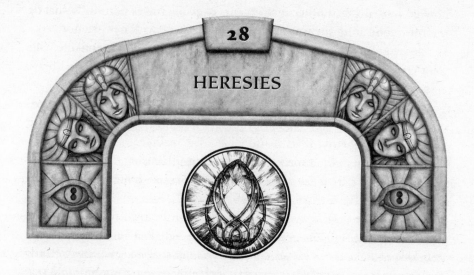

Other Shards I cannot identify, and are hidden to me. I fear that their influence encroaches upon my world, yet I am locked into a strange inability because of the opposed powers I hold.

Hold it steady!" Falilar said. It had been years since Navani had seen the old white-bearded engineer this animated. "Put it here on the table. Isabi, you have the scale, yes? Hurry, hurry. Set it up like we practiced!"

The small swarm of ardents and scholars fussed around Navani, settling the spanreed into its board and preparing standard violet ink. They'd carried it out and set it up in a guard post near the perimeter of the tower. Kalami stood next to Navani, her arms folded. Hair streaked with grey, the scribe had an increasingly worrisome leanness to her these days.

"I'm not sure about this, Brightness," she said as the engineer and his assistants set up their instruments. "I worry that whoever is on the other side of that spanreed, they'll learn more about us than we do about them."

Falilar wiped his shaved head with a handkerchief, then gestured for Navani to sit at the table.

"Noted," Navani said to Kalami, settling down. "We ready?"

"Yes, Brightness," Falilar said. "Judging by the weight of your pen once the conversation is engaged, we should be able to tell how far away the other pen is."

Spanreeds had a certain decay to them. The farther apart they were, the heavier the pens became after activation. In most cases, this was a slight—almost imperceptible—difference. Today, the spanreed board, with pen attached, had been placed on Falilar's most precise scale. The pen was hooked by strings to other instruments as well. Navani carefully turned the ruby, indicating she was ready to communicate with her phantom correspondent. The six scholars and ardents, Kalami included, seemed to hold their collective breath.

The pen started writing. *Why have you ignored my instructions?*

Falilar gestured animatedly to the others, who began taking measurements—adding tiny weights to the balance and reading the tension in the pull of the string.

She left them to their measurements, instead focusing on the conversation. *I'm not sure what exactly you expected of me,* she wrote. *Please, explain further.*

You must stop your experiments with fabrials, the reed wrote. *I made it explicitly clear that you needed to stop. You have not. You have only increased your heresies. What is this you do, putting fabrials in a pit and connecting them to the blowing of the storms? Do you make a weapon of the spren you have trapped? Do you kill? Humans always kill.*

"Heresies?" Kalami noted as the engineers worked. "Whoever it is seems to have a theological opposition to our actions."

"She references humans as a singer might," Navani said, tapping the paper. "Either she's one of them, or she wants us to think she is."

"Brightness," Falilar said, "this can't be correct. The decay is almost nonexistent."

"So they're near to us," Navani said.

"Extremely near," Falilar said. "Inside the tower. If we could figure out a way to make more precise scales . . . Regardless, a second measurement would help me with possible triangulation."

Navani nodded. *Why do you call this a heresy?* Navani wrote. *The church sees no moral problem with fabrials. No more than they have a problem with hitching a chull to a cart.*

A chull hitched to a cart is not confined to a tiny space, the reply came, the pen moving furiously, animatedly. *Spren are meant to be free. By capturing them, you trap nature itself. Can a storm survive if placed in a prison? Can a flower bloom with no sunlight? This is what you do. Your religion is incomplete.*

Let me think on this, Navani wrote. *I will need a few minutes to speak with my theological advisor.*

Each moment you wait is a moment of pain brought to the spren you dominate, the pen wrote. *I will not suffer it for much longer.*

Please wait, Navani wrote. *I will use another spanreed for a moment, to talk to my theological advisor, but then will respond to you soon.*

No response came, but the pen continued to hover—the phantom was waiting.

"All right," she said. "Let's get the second measurement."

The engineers moved with a flurry of activity, disjoining the spanreed so the link between the two pens was temporarily broken. They gathered the equipment and started running.

Navani and Kalami hurried into the palanquin waiting for them outside the room. A group of six men hefted it and charged after the engineers and scribes as the entire group rushed through the tower. They eventually burst out onto the plateau in front of Urithiru. You couldn't tell the direction of a second spanreed, not directly, even from the decay.

However, because you could measure the decay—and therefore judge distance—you could triangulate from multiple measurements and get a rough idea of location. The team set up out here, on the plateau, among the coldspren.

By the time she climbed free of the palanquin, Falilar and his team had the spanreed ready on the stone ground. Navani knelt and reengaged the device.

They waited, Falilar dabbing at his head with his handkerchief, Kalami kneeling beside the paper and whispering, "Come on." Falilar's little apprentice—Isabi, daughter to one of the Windrunners—seemed ready to burst as she held her breath.

The pen engaged, then wrote, *Why did you move? What are you doing?*

I have spoken to my ardents, Navani wrote as the engineers again began taking measurements. *They agree that our knowledge must be flawed. Can you explain how you know that this is evil? How is it you know what our ardents do not?*

"How does she know we moved?" Kalami asked.

"She has a spy watching us," Navani said. "Probably the same person who hid the spanreed ruby for me to find."

The person on the other end didn't reply.

I have many duties, Navani wrote. *You interrupted me on my way to an important meeting. I have a few more minutes now to talk. Please. Tell us how you know what we don't.*

The truth is evident to me, the pen wrote.

It is not obvious to us, Navani wrote.

Because you are human, it replied. *Humans cannot be trusted. You do not know how to keep promises, and promises are what make the world function. We make the world function. You must release your captive spren. You must you must.*

"Ash's mask . . ." Kalami said. "It's a spren, isn't it?"

"Yes," Navani said.

"I have measurements," Falilar said. "It *is* coming from the tower. I should be able to pin it down to a specific region. I must say, Brightness, you don't seem surprised by any of this."

"I had my suspicions," Navani said. "We found one ancient spren hiding in the tower. Is it such a stretch to assume a second has done the same?"

"Another of the Unmade?" Kalami asked.

Navani tapped her finger against the spanreed paper, thinking. "I doubt it," she said. "A spren who wishes to free its kind? A liberationspren? Has anyone heard of such a thing?"

The scholars collectively shook their heads. Navani reached to write further to the phantom, but the spanreed shut off, dropping to the paper, no longer actively conjoined.

"So . . . what do we do?" Kalami asked. "Another of those *things* could be watching us from the darkness. Planning more murders."

"It's not the same," Navani said. "There's something here. . . ." *We make the world function.*

As they gathered up their things, a plan began budding in Navani's mind. A touch reckless, particularly since she didn't want to explain it to the others where the spren might be able to hear.

She went ahead with the idea anyway. As they were walking to the tower proper, Navani stumbled and—trying to make it appear as accidental as possible—dropped the spanreed while walking. She cried out as she clumsily kicked it across the stone plateau—right over the edge. She rushed over, but it had already vanished, tumbling to the rocks thousands of feet below.

"The spanreed!" Falilar said. "Oh, Brightness!"

"Damnation," she said. "That's terrible."

Kalami eyed her, walking up. Navani smothered a smile.

"Falilar," Navani said. "Gather a team to see if they can recover that. I need to take better care."

"Yes, Brightness," he said.

Of course if they *did* find it, the team would have discreet directions to break the ruby as if from the fall. And of course they would be instructed to speak loudly of the tragedy of it among her scholars in the tower.

Navani had a budding suspicion as to the identity of this spren who had contacted her. She wanted to make sure that it, and its agent, heard of the lost spanreed.

Let's see what you do now, Navani thought, strolling back into the tower.

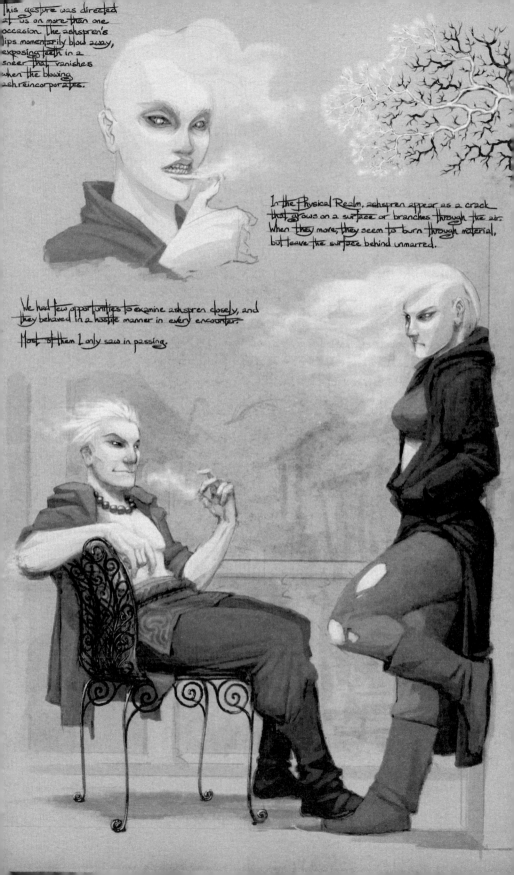

This gesture was directed at us on more than one occasion. The ashspren's lips momentarily blow away, exposing teeth in a sneer that vanishes when the blowing ashreincorporates.

In the Physical Realm, ashspren appear as a crack that grows on a surface or branches through the air. When they move, they seem to burn through material, but leave the surface behind unmarred.

We had few opportunities to examine ashspren closely, and they behaved in a hostile manner in every encounter.

Most of them I only saw in passing.

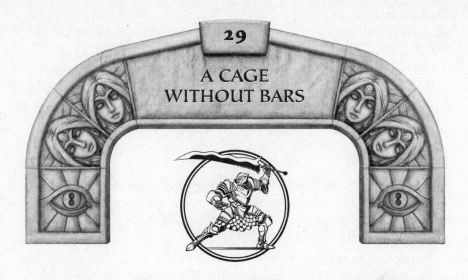

29
A CAGE WITHOUT BARS

I have begun searching for a pathway out of this conundrum by seeking the ideal person to act on my behalf. Someone who embodies both Preservation and Ruin. A . . . sword, you might say, who can both protect and kill.

Adolin glanced up as he heard the call from the watchpost at the front of the barge. Land sighted.

Finally, he thought, giving Gallant a firm pat on the neck. The animal nickered in anticipation.

"Trust me," he said to the Ryshadium, "I'm as happy to land as you are." Adolin had always been fond of traveling—feeling the open breeze on your face, the welcoming sky overhead. Who knew what exotic tastes and fashions you'd find at your destination? Taking a ship, though, was excruciating. No space to run, no good sparring grounds. A ship was a cage without bars.

He left Gallant and rushed up to the barge's prow. A dark strip of obsidian broke the sea ahead, with quiet lights shimmering above. Not souls, but actual candles in the windows of small structures. In Shadesmar, spren could manifest the beads that represented the soul of a fire—and in so doing, create flames that provided light, but very little heat.

Others gathered at the sides of the barge, and Godeke joined Adolin on the small upper deck. The lanky Edgedancer seemed as eager as Adolin to be off the boat; Adolin had seen Godeke pacing more than once these last few days.

Unfortunately, the responsible side of Adolin—drilled into him over years with his father—made him call for caution. "We don't know the situation in this town yet," he said to the others. "Last time I was in Shadesmar, the first town we entered ended up being held by the Fused. We should send some of the Lightweavers in, wearing disguises, to scout."

"You will not find danger here," Ua'pam promised, rubbing his knuckles together in a curious gesture, making a sound like two rocks grinding. "These are free lands. Neither honorspren nor Fused control this outpost."

"Still," Adolin said, looking to the others. "Humans, under the tarp until we've done some basic scouting."

Grumbling, they gathered their horses and moved into the large "room" under the tarps. Shallan was resting here already; most of them had opted to place their bedrolls here, where the tall boxes of cargo had been stacked to make various nooks and cubbies.

Adolin nudged her. "Shallan? You all right?"

The dark lump that was his wife stirred. "Might have had a little too much to drink last night."

Adolin smiled. The trip had been genuinely relaxing, save for his worry about their destination. It had been good to spend time with Shallan—and he had enjoyed even the appearances of Veil and Radiant. The latter made an excellent sparring partner, and the former knew a seemingly infinite number of card games. Some of which were good Vorin games, and others . . . well, they had too much randomness for propriety, but were more fun than Adolin had expected.

It had culminated with Shallan pulling out an excellent Thaylen violet, Kdisln vintage, last night. As usual, she'd had a few more cups than Adolin. Shallan had a strange relationship with drink, one that varied based on her persona. But since she could burn off the effects using Stormlight, she theoretically could never be drunk unless she wanted to be. It baffled him why she would sometimes go to sleep like she did, risking the morning hangover.

"I want someone to scout the town before we go in," Adolin said. "You want me to send—"

"I'll go," she said, climbing out of her bedroll. "Give me a few minutes."

True to her word, she was ready a short time later, wearing a Lightweaving that made her look like a cultivationspren. She took Vathah in a similar disguise, and the two of them disembarked with Ua'pam and his cousin to walk through the town.

The rest of them waited under the tarp. Godeke fished in his pockets and brought out a few spheres. His personal money seemed to mostly have been chips—which had gone dun by this point. They'd seen a highstorm several times—storms manifested here as shimmering lights in the sky— but the spheres hadn't been recharged.

"Even the broam I brought is starting to fade," Godeke noted, holding up the amethyst to give light to the darkness under the tarp. "The larger gemstones we brought probably won't last until we reach the fortress, Brightlord."

Adolin nodded. They'd gone over the Stormlight budget a dozen times leading up to leaving. No matter how they'd been able to spin it, there wasn't a way to reach Lasting Integrity with any Stormlight remaining. So the gifts they'd brought were things Syl said would be appreciated: newly written books, puzzles made of iron that could engage the mind for hours, and some weapons.

There was one way they might have brought Stormlight that lasted longer. The Thaylens owned gemstones that were—because of their near-perfect structures—capable of retaining Stormlight over long time periods. The best of those had been used a year ago to capture one of the Unmade, and Jasnah wanted the others for experiments.

Jasnah had mentioned something else about these near-flawless gemstones that troubled her. She found it odd that the gemstones in circulation as spheres were always so flawed that they lost Light quickly. She said that they should vary, and more perfect ones should be found on occasion—but that wasn't the case.

Why was she concerned by that? He pondered the question as he waited for Shallan, and tried to trace Jasnah's thoughts. What if someone had been in the know, while everyone else thought gemstones were all basically the same? If you knew the supreme value of gemstones that could hold Stormlight over long trips through Shadesmar, you could spend years gathering them.

He frowned, considering it. Finally, he glanced at Godeke, who was holding up one of his fading broams.

"When you're free to go into the city," Adolin told him, "take most of our remaining Stormlight and do as we discussed. Trade it for supplies to use on the next leg of our trip—then spend the remainder to load up the barge."

Ua'pam's cousin would wait at the town to guard their supplies. Adolin's group only needed to carry enough to get to and from Lasting Integrity.

Assuming everything went well with Shallan's investigation of the town. As they waited, Adolin found himself feeling increasingly anxious. He felt like something was going to drop on him. Had the trip here been *too* easy?

He passed the time checking on his soldiers and scribe. As they were in good spirits, Adolin checked on Maya. She sat in a little nook at the rear of the room, and Adolin had to pull out a gemstone—a thick sapphire, big as his thumb—to get enough light to see her.

Maya stared at it. Her eyes had been scratched out by the events of the Recreance, but she could still see. She'd been blinded without going blind, killed without dying. The ways of spren were strange.

"Hey," he said, crouching down. "We'll soon be able to go ashore."

She didn't respond, as usual—though as one of the peakspren passed outside the tarp awning, she snapped her head to stare in that direction.

"Anxious too, eh?" Adolin said. "We both need to calm down. Here." He moved to where his things had been stored and took out his longsword, then fell into a stance. The ceiling of the tarp was a good foot over his head, and most everyone had clustered on the other side, near Godeke and the spheres. So he had some space for a basic kata.

Each day, Maya joined him in his morning stretching routines, where he did a centering kata that Zahel had taught him years ago. Would she follow a different kata, if he showed it to her? A longsword was a bad imitation of a Shardblade, but it was the closest he had.

He placed his sapphire on the top of his closed sword trunk for light, then fell into a slow, careful kata meant to teach thrusting practice. Nothing flashy, no stupid twirls or spins of the blade. A basic exercise, but one he'd done hundreds of times with his Shardblade on the practice grounds. This particular portion imitated hallway fighting, where you couldn't swing too high or too far to the sides, lest you hit stone. So it was perfect for this enclosed space.

Maya watched him, her head cocked.

"You know this one," he told her. "Remember? Hallway fighting. Practice with thrusts and controlled swings?"

He started over, but slower. One motion flowing into the other. Step, good two-handed grip, lunge forward with a thrust, then reset while turning the other direction. Back and forth, a rhythm, a song without music. A fight without an opponent.

Maya hesitantly stood up, so he paused. She walked over to him, inspecting his sword with her head still cocked. The fine intertwining vines of her face looked like sinew, a human face with the skin removed. She traced the length of the sword with her gaze.

Adolin reset again. Maya carefully did the same beside him—and her form was perfect. Even Zahel on his worst day wouldn't have found reason to reset her stance. Adolin slowly moved through the kata, and she followed—holding nothing but empty air, but moving in lockstep with him as he thrust, then reset, then turned.

Conversation on the other side of the enclosure died off, spren and soldiers alike watching. Soon they faded from Adolin's attention. It was just him, the sword, and Maya. The relaxing repetition made his tension melt away. Katas were about more than training; they were a way to focus.

That was something every young swordsman needed to learn, whether he intended to fight in duels or lead a battlefield charge. Adolin felt sorry for those who had never known the centering peace of training; it could turn aside even the mightiest of storms.

After some time—Adolin didn't notice how much—Shallan ducked under the tarp. She'd dismissed her Lightweaving, so plainly didn't consider them to be in any danger. Ua'pam, however, stared at Maya, the cracks in his skin pouring a molten light over the deck and the bottom of the tarp.

Adolin finally stopped, Maya pausing beside him. As he relaxed and wiped his brow, she settled back down in her little cubby.

Ua'pam walked up to him, scratching at his head in a distinctly human gesture. "Another kata?" he asked. "This is more than simple training. Truly, you must tell me. *How* have you done this? Each day, your training of her proves more remarkable."

Adolin shrugged, snatching a towel as Felt tossed it to him. "She remembers the times we've sparred together as man and Blade."

"She's a deadeye," Ua'pam said. "She was killed thousands of years ago. She doesn't think. The trauma of her Radiant betraying her broke her mind."

"Yeah, well, maybe it's wearing off."

"We are spren. We are eternal. Our deaths do not merely 'wear off.'"

Adolin tossed the towel back to Felt. "And spren were never going to bond humans again—yet here you are, Zu's companion spren. Words like 'eternal' and 'forever' aren't as definitive as you all pretend."

"You don't know what you're saying," Ua'pam said.

"And that might just be why Maya and I are able to do things you think impossible." Adolin glanced at Shallan. "We're good to go into town?"

"No hints of Fused activity," she said. "Lots of caravans come through here—some are even camped outside the town—and humans aren't unusual in them. The spren at this waystop won't consider us odd. We merely need to tell everyone we're traders."

"Right then," Adolin said. "Let's all get off this boat and stretch our legs. Stay together in groups though, and don't make trouble."

⁘

Shallan continued to have a hangover. Her brain pounded, incessant, angry. A kind of "How could you?" accusation. She worried that now that they had reached land, she might attract painspren—which could be dangerous.

This is your fault, Veil, Radiant thought at her. *How could you let us go to sleep without burning off the wine?*

I wasn't thinking straight, Veil thought. *That's* kind of *the point of drinking. . . .*

She can't use Stormlight very well, Shallan thought. *Don't blame her.* At least the pain was fading. When she'd taken in Stormlight to put on her illusory face, it had healed some of the agony. Stormlight was precious, however, and she'd used only what she needed to get her illusion going.

She probably could spare a little more.

No, Radiant thought. *We should suffer, as our punishment for abusing drink.*

It's not Shallan's fault, Veil complained. *She shouldn't have to hurt because of what I did.*

I had more than a few cups myself, Shallan thought. *So let's drop this.*

The others—eager to get out and see the town—broke up into teams, though Adolin waited for her. They walked onto the simple stone dock and into the town—though "town" was a generous term for it. She'd been able to walk through all four streets in under half an hour.

Still, although small, the place presented a shocking variety of spren, most of them coming from the five or six caravans that were camped here at the moment. Even from her perspective now, she was able to spot six different varieties. She'd taken some Memories to continue her natural history—and intended to go back out and get a few more.

Plus, some of those caravans had humans in them. Who were they? How had they found their way to this side? Were they from other lands, like Azure? She longed to get back out and do closer inspections.

Except . . . Veil said. *You know.*

She did. This might be a chance to—after two weeks of travel—finally have some time alone. Indeed, Unativi's sailors were drawing lots to determine who had to stay on the barge to guard it. Perhaps . . .

"Go on ahead," Veil said, pulling her hat on—from where it had been hanging behind her neck by its laces—so Adolin knew who she was. "I've had a chance to stretch my legs; I think I'll rest a little more."

"You should drink less," Adolin said.

She poked him on the shoulder. "You should stop sounding like your father."

"Low blow, Veil," he said with a wince. "But point taken. Watch our things."

He went and got Maya, who followed when he asked. He likely thought she needed to get some exercise or something. He was a little strange about that spren.

I think the way he cares for her is sweet, Shallan thought.

Maybe it was. But it was strange too. Veil sauntered over to Unativi. "You can all go, if you want," she said to the group of peakspren. "I'm going to stay behind anyway, so I can watch the barge."

Unativi studied her, the light of his molten interior growing brighter through the cracks in his skin. "You stay? Why?"

She shrugged. "I've had a chance already today. You can all go; the boat doesn't need more than one guard. It's not like there's any danger here, right?"

"If there were," Unativi said, "you are Radiant. Better at facing it than a peakspren!" He turned to his sailors, who seemed eager. A couple of weeks on the same barge could make anyone bored of the scenery, including sailors.

Soon, Veil was blessedly alone. So far this trip, she'd been alone only when using the chamber pot in the draped-off section beneath the tarp. Even *that* had been situated far too near everyone else for comfort. She—

"Mmmmm . . ."

She spun and found that of course Pattern was still there. Watching her. "Going to contact Mraize, Veil?" he asked with a peppy voice. "Mmm . . ."

Yes, she was. All three were in agreement that they needed to talk to him, but it was uncomfortable how easily Pattern recognized this.

"Stay here," she said to him, "and make certain nobody interrupts me."

"Oh. I can't listen?" His pattern slowed, seeming to almost *wilt*. "I like Mraize. He is very strange. Ha ha."

"It would be better if someone were to watch out for me," Veil said. Then she sighed. "Though it might be good for you to listen to Mraize too. You might spot something untrue that he says."

"I do not think he says things that are fully untrue," Pattern said. "Which makes his lies the best. Mmm. But I cannot tell automatically if something is a lie. I can simply appreciate them better than most, once I realize what they are."

Well, in Veil's experience, he was more expert at noticing subterfuge than many humans. She waved for him to join her under the awning, still happy to be *mostly* alone.

Part of her worried about that emotion. She'd lived a double life for basically the entire time she'd known Adolin—and it put a strain on Shallan. Worse, lying to herself was so ingrained it was becoming second nature.

This is a problem, Shallan, Veil thought as she made her way back to her trunk.

I'm getting better, Shallan retorted. *No new personas in over a year now.*

And Formless? Radiant demanded.

Formless isn't real. Not yet, Shallan thought. *We're close to getting out of the Ghostbloods. One more mission, and we're done. And Formless won't manifest.*

Veil had her suspicions. And she had to admit, she was a big part of the problem herself. Shallan idealized how Veil was able to live so relaxed, without worrying about her past or the things she'd done. Indeed, Shallan conflated this attitude with the life the Ghostbloods lived. A life she was beginning to envy . . .

Get answers, Shallan thought. *Stop thinking about this. We need to contact Mraize before time runs out.*

Veil sighed, but positioned Pattern near the open front of the tarp enclosure. He would be able to hear the conversation with Mraize, but could warn her if someone came onto the barge. Then she unlocked her trunk of personal effects.

Here she paused. Then she let Shallan take over for a few moments. Long enough to be certain.

Yes, Shallan thought. *It has been moved again.*

They'd checked it every day since that first time, and this was only the second time it had been moved. The night she'd gotten drunk. Inside, Radiant groaned in annoyance.

Sorry, Veil thought, taking over. *But we can't watch it all the time. Besides, we* want *the spy to feel comfortable using it, right? So that we have more chances to catch them?*

Regardless, she couldn't deny it felt creepy to know someone had snuck in and somehow used the cube while she was snoring a few feet away. She lifted the cube and inspected it. Other than having been set so a different face was up, nothing about it seemed different.

How did she activate it? Mraize had said to use his name. "I need to speak to Mraize. Um, that's actually his title rather than his name. . . ."

The cube's corners began to shine from a bright light inside, as if the metal were thinner there.

"I know him," the cube said, making Veil start.

"You can talk!" she said.

It didn't reply. She frowned, looking closely at the seams—the glow shimmered and changed. A short time later a strong voice came from inside, making the cube quiver in her hands.

"Little knife," Mraize said. "I've been waiting."

⁘

Adolin kept to his own rules, and didn't wander off alone. He and Maya stuck close to his soldiers and scribe, who walked the small town in a tight cluster, laughing too loudly as they chatted—as if trying to prove they were absolutely *not* nervous to be in such a strange location.

Normally he would have joined in to put them at ease, but he found himself weighed down by the seriousness of the task ahead of him. His worries were resurfacing, now that the voyage was over. He needed to prove he could bring the honorspren to the coalition. After failing at Kholinar, he just . . . he *needed* to do this. Not for his father. For the coalition. For the war. For his homeland.

He tried to focus on the next step, which involved getting supplies at this waystop. It was basically a market, meant to cater to caravans and merchant ships. Like in Celebrant—the other spren city he'd visited—most of the buildings were made up of a mishmash of types of stone, speckled a variety of colors. Manifested building materials. Real rock and metal were far more valuable here, as they had to be transported in through a portal like the Oathgates.

There was no cohesive sense of architecture to the buildings. Azish influences were most common, but spren took what they could get, and so ended up with a patchwork of designs and styles. Most of the spren running the shops appeared to be cultivationspren. They called out offers in Azish or Alethi, offering fresh water or food supplies they knew humans might want.

Browsing the goods were spren of all varieties. Of those, he found the ashspren the most transfixing. They looked like people, but their flesh would crumble off at times, exposing bone. As he passed one, she snapped her fingers, making all the ash of her hand blow away and vanish—then it quickly grew back. He even spotted a couple of highspren, like tears in reality in the shape of people. He gave them a wide berth, though they seemed to be just another pair of merchants.

Spren clothing was as eclectic as their building materials. He passed one peakspren wearing a Veden uniform coat over a Tashikki wrap, of all things. It should have been garish—and certainly Adolin would never have worn any of it together—but he didn't find himself bothered. They'd taken human clothing and made it their own; why should they follow the trends of kingdoms in another world?

In that way, there was something fresh and interesting about the fashion here. Like the work of a talented but untrained artist. They came up with combinations that no member of Adolin's culture could ever have dared imagine.

Though, he thought, passing a tall willowy spren of a type he didn't recognize, *someone ought to tell that one what a protective cup is used for on our side. . . .*

His soldiers stopped to browse a weapon shop, though he'd warned them that they shouldn't rely on manifested weapons. Still, it was difficult not to stare at the sheer variety of swords on display. In the Physical Realm a masterwork sword was an expensive purchase—and it often surprised people how valuable even an everyday side sword could be. Here though, manifesting a sword took roughly the same amount of Stormlight as manifesting a brick, so you could find them in barrels or stacked in piles outside shops.

This bizarre economy would certainly fascinate Shallan. He'd heard they kept near-perfect gemstones in spren banks, storing vast amounts of Stormlight for future use. And of course, having so many humans nearby had attracted small emotion spren, Shadesmar's equivalent of animals. Gloryspren darted overhead, and fearspren huddled in alleyways looking like large, multi-legged eels with long, globby antennae.

A long flying spren with mustaches and a graceful body landed on the top of a building, then leaped off, ejecting an explosion of tiny crystalline shards that floated down and vanished. Was that a passionspren? He'd have to tell Shallan.

He turned toward the distant barge, where Shallan remained. Maya dutifully stopped beside him, but just stared straight ahead with her scratched-out eyes.

"I wonder why she stayed behind," Adolin said. "It's odd for her to want to rest when there's so much to see."

Maya didn't respond. That didn't prevent him from talking to her. She had a . . . relaxing air about her.

"Veil probably is in control," Adolin said. "She's worried about our things being stolen, I bet. Shallan says the other two exist to protect her or help her, and I see that. I want to understand. I don't want to be like the others, who whisper about her being crazy and laugh."

He looked to Maya, who looked back.

"It's silly of me to be jealous of the time Veil controls her, isn't it?" Adolin said. "Shallan created Veil as a tool. It's just . . . I don't know if I'm doing this right. I don't know how to be supportive."

He wasn't good with relationships. He never had been. He could admit that to himself now. He'd been in dozens, and they'd all fallen apart—so he had all kinds of experience doing this *wrong*, but very little doing it *right*.

He wanted to do it right. He loved Shallan, in part because of her eccentricities. She felt alive in a different way from everyone else—she was also somehow more authentic. She was stuffed full of personas and covered in illusions. Yet incredibly, she felt more *real* because of them.

Adolin lingered, not wanting to get ahead of the others, and wished he could shove his hands in his pockets. Unfortunately, this uniform's pockets were sewn shut. The trousers looked better that way.

He knew why he was feeling so off. Seeing another spren settlement reminded him of the last time they'd come to Shadesmar. When he'd been forced to leave Elhokar dead in his palace, the city fallen. Worse, Adolin had accidentally abandoned his troops to face the invasion while he ended up in Shadesmar.

He wasn't one to stew and brood . . . but storms, if there was a man who deserved his place in Damnation, it was the general who left his men to die.

Adolin was drawn out of his brooding as he realized Maya was staring to the side, focused on something. That was odd enough, as she didn't often pay much attention to her surroundings. But when he drew closer, he saw what had transfixed her. It was another deadeye.

This deadeye was a Cryptic who stood beside a storefront. Cryptics didn't have eyes, but there was no mistaking that the creature had suffered Maya's fate: the pattern had halted completely, the normally graceful lines twisted and turned in jagged directions, like broken fingers. The same odd scraping marred its center.

Maya released a kind of low whine from deep in her throat.

"I'm sorry," Adolin said. "I know it's distressing. Let's move on quickly."

She took his arm as he tried to walk off, which shocked him. It seemed to surprise her too, as she looked down at her hands holding his arm, then cocked her head. She held on and turned toward the deadeye Cryptic, pulling him. It was as if she wanted to say something.

His men were still shopping, so Adolin turned in the direction Maya wanted, heading toward the store with the deadeye. Like most he'd seen here in Shadesmar, the shop was open-sided—an awning in front of a small building where the shopkeepers probably lived. There weren't storms to worry about here, so structures tended to have open-air designs that left Adolin feeling exposed.

The shopkeeper was an inkspren. Adolin had heard that there were fewer of them than there were of other varieties, and they kept to themselves. The creature was jet black, even reflective, like he was made out of stone—but with an oil-on-water shimmer of color when the light hit him right. He sold books, which he kept carefully on shelves, not in stacks and piles like many other shops.

"You are Alethi," he said, inspecting Adolin. He spoke with a sharp nasal accent. "And you are male. You have no need for books. This is."

"I wanted to ask after your deadeye," Adolin said, nodding to the Cryptic.

"A friend she was," the shopkeeper said, his voice terse.

"Back when there were Radiants."

"No. A sooner time that was. My partner in business, once." He frowned. "Do you know something of this, human? The danger that is?"

"What danger?"

"New deadeyes," the shopkeeper said, shaking his head. "Radiants should not have started again. Do you know that this thing is? In your kingdom it began, did it not?"

"I don't know of any Radiants betraying their oaths," Adolin said. "You're sure about this?"

The inkspren waved to his friend. "She was my partner for many centuries. She left ten years ago to join others hunting for Radiants. Last year I found her like this, sitting alone on an island far to the east. She insisted on coming out this direction—at least, she walked this way incessantly. So I set up shop here."

"You're *sure*," Adolin said. "That she was afflicted like this *recently*."

"My memory is not flawed," the inkspren said. "This is what you do, killing spren. You should feel ashamed." He looked at Maya. "Is this another you killed?"

"Of course not," Adolin said. "I . . ." He trailed off, not wanting to say too much. He'd instructed everyone to be circumspect.

But . . . a new deadeye? That seemed impossible. Maybe . . . maybe some young new Surgebinder out in the backwaters of Bavland could have been left without support or friends, and had broken their oaths. It wasn't too outlandish; the more they learned, the more they realized that Kaladin, Jasnah, and Shallan hadn't been unique in forming new Radiant bonds these last few years. A general revolution had been happening all across Roshar, with spren sensing the coming of the Everstorm, and some returning to bond with humans.

He got nothing but more frosty accusations from the inkspren, so he returned to the street—and Maya let him. Had she somehow known this deadeye was strange? Was that why she'd wanted him to go in and talk to the shopkeeper?

He moved to join his men, but stopped as he saw Godeke and his spren hastening up the street. The former ardent had a graceful way about him as he arrived and fluidly bowed. "Brightlord, I think you'll want to see this."

"What? It's not another deadeye spren, is it?"

"No," Godeke said. "It's the humans."

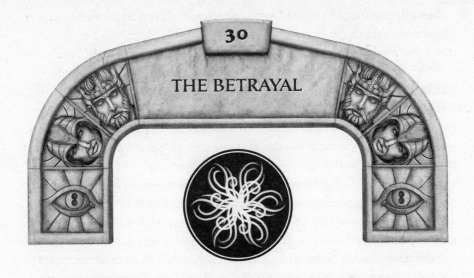

*But this does not get to the core of your letter. I have encouraged
those who would speak to me to heed your warnings, but all seem
content to ignore Odium for the time being. In their opinion, he is
no threat as long as he remains confined in the Rosharan system.*

Light shimmered in the strange cube, seeping through at the corners as Mraize spoke. Veil watched, and suddenly felt disjointed—
trapped between two moments.

This experience . . . she'd *done* this before. She'd been here, kneeling
on the ground, holding a cube that glowed from the corners. *Exactly like
this.*

She reached to the top of the cube, feeling the smooth metal, and expected it to be dimpled. She cocked her head, inspecting her fingers as she
lifted them up and rubbed them against her thumb. This was wrong. . . .
She glanced over her shoulder, and saw the enclosure beneath the tarp.

She was on a mission into Shadesmar. Why should she expect to see
gardens behind her? Her father's gardens?

Veil faded into Shallan. These memories . . . these were something lost to
her. From the years leading up to her . . . her mother's death. That twisted,
knotted, overgrown time in her brain, hidden behind carefully cultivated
flower beds. When she sorted through her memories, it didn't *feel* like anything was missing. Yet she knew from other clues that there were holes.

Remember, Veil thought. *Remember.*

She'd trained with Pattern as a child. She'd spoken oaths. She'd summoned a Shardblade and struck down her own mother, frantic to survive.
And—she looked back at the cube—she'd held one of *these*?

She gripped the cube tightly, becoming hyperfocused on Mraize's voice. She couldn't think about the past. She *couldn't*. Unfortunately, the sounds coming out of the cube seemed garbled to her. Her mind fixated on each syllable alone, and she couldn't understand the Alethi as a language—it was instead a jumble of sounds.

She shook herself, and the barge seemed to *lurch* beneath her. She gasped, forcing Veil to take over, and Mraize's words started to make sense.

". . . have been careful," Mraize was saying, "not to attract attention in this communication?"

"I . . ." Veil said. "Of course I did this in secret. You know me better than that." What had he been saying before? She'd missed it entirely.

"It is always good," he said, "to reinforce the behavior you want, little knife. In people as in axehounds. Your report?"

"We have landed," she said, "and the others went out to explore a small dockside town here on the coast. We have several weeks' further travel via caravan, hopefully as uneventful as these, before reaching the fortress."

"Have you learned anything of interest about your fellow Radiants?"

"Nothing I'd report to you, Mraize," Veil said. "Mostly I wanted to make sure this cube of yours worked." She considered. "What happens again if I pry the thing open?"

"You will immediately destroy the spren that lives inside," Mraize said.

"You can't kill spren."

"I didn't say kill."

She held up the cube. Light escaped from the corners—had the cube opened a little? "Perhaps I do have a tidbit for you," she said. "Something I might be willing to trade for information about this cube."

"That is not your mission, nor our arrangement, little knife," Mraize said—sounding amused. "The hound does not withhold affection to get her feast. She performs first, and then receives her reward."

"You tell me to be the hunter, not the prey," Veil said. "Yet snap at me when I show initiative?"

"Initiative is wonderful, and your possession of it is commendable. However, our organization survives based on principles of hierarchy. A group of hunters working together could turn upon one another far too easily.

"And so, I respect my *babsk,* and you respect me. We do not strike against our own, and we do not negotiate upward. To do otherwise is to invite anarchy. So continue to hunt, but do not think to hold hostage your results. Now, is there anything else to report on the mission that might be relevant?"

He didn't press her further on information about the other Radiants; so in essence, he conceded that point. She hadn't been assigned to report on them, and he knew he had no right to press for that information.

Note this fact, Veil thought. *There is wiggle room in this arrangement, despite what he implies.*

"There have been some odd spren watching us," Veil noted. "I only catch glimpses of them, but they seem the wrong color. As if they'd been corrupted."

"Curious," Mraize said. "Sja-anat extends her influence. I am still waiting for the spren she promised would bond me."

"She promised to send a spren," Veil said. "Not that the spren would choose you. Do not blame Shallan if you fail to secure what you want."

"And yet, Sja-anat spies on you during this trip. These spren you see? What can you tell me about them?"

"They're all the same variety, and they stay far away or obscured somehow. None of the others on our trip have seen them, though I've warned my team to watch for them."

"Sja-anat is important, little hunter," Mraize said. "We must bind her to us. A spren of Odium willing to betray him? An ancient creature with equally ancient knowledge? I give you this secondary mission. Watch for these spren closely, and make contact if you can."

"I will," Veil said. "Is there news of the tower or of Dalinar's invasion?"

"Oh, things here are subject to their usual flares of activity and surprise," Mraize said. "Nothing unexpected for those who have been paying attention. I will let you know if anything here requires your involvement."

Veil nodded, feeling distracted as the sensation of holding the cube overcame her once more. She forced Shallan to take control again, to see the shadows of reflections of memories. She breathed in and out, trying to force herself to remain strong. To not run.

Should she ask Mraize whether he knew anything of her past, and whether she'd ever communicated this way before? He'd be unlikely to answer, but that wasn't why she hesitated.

I don't want to know, she thought. Instead she said, "I will contact you once we have traveled a distance on the caravan."

"Very well," Mraize said. "Again, I must emphasize: Watch for any signs of these corrupted gloryspren. I worry that Sja-anat is playing us both, and I do not like the feeling."

Shallan almost dropped the cube in surprise. She intentionally hadn't mentioned the specific variety of spren. Yet he called them gloryspren.

HA! Veil thought.

Oh, storms, Radiant thought. *Veil's plan worked. She's going to be insufferable now.*

Insufferable? I'm incredible. *Mraize has fallen into a common trap—that of being so clever, you start forgetting your fundamentals. Always question your*

information.

"Understood," Shallan forced herself to say. "I will keep diligent watch." The glow in the cube faded. She carefully set it back in the chest, then took another Memory of it there before locking the lid.

Word had gotten to Mraize, and the false tidbit—that she'd seen a gloryspren watching her—had revealed the truth.

Beryl was the spy.

⁘

The humans that Godeke had found were an unexpected lot. They didn't appear to be soldiers, but common workers with brown skin and black hair, both male and female. You found some Vorin people with that skin tone, but more likely you'd find it in midlands. Marat, Tukar, the Reshi Isles.

They wore simple clothing of a cut Adolin thought he recognized as being from southeastern Makabak. It had colors similar to Azish patterns, but the cloth was thicker and coarser, the outfits more enveloping, with braided tassels that hung low from the waist.

Yes, he thought. *They look like they're from Marat, or maybe Tukar.*

Multiple caravans had made camps outside town, and all the others had spren occupants. As Adolin and Godeke had passed, those had waved or gestured in friendly ways. One had even called out to Archinal—Godeke's spren—recognizing her.

This human camp, by contrast, was an unwelcoming place. While the spren camps had manifested fires, this one was dark, lit by neither flame nor Stormlight. The human caravan had brought no pack animals, but the people had piled their things in the center of camp while some of their number slept. The rest of them, mostly men with cudgels resting on shoulders, watched the perimeter.

"Who are they?" Adolin asked softly, watching from beside the wall of a small shop. The landscape outside the town was relatively barren, an open field of obsidian with some small crystalline plants growing in clusters, bobbing with lifespren—which were larger on this side.

"Traders from another land perhaps?" Archinal said. The short cultivationspren wrung her hands. "Oh, it *does* happen, and more and more these days. People come in caravans seeking to trade. They like your wines, human brightlord. And many have heard tales of your weapons, and I've known several to ask to trade for one! As if a Shardblade would be available for purchase."

"Other lands," Adolin said, rubbing his chin. "Maybe some other traders you met are from far away, but these are wearing Marati or Tukari clothing. They seem like locals to me—but if that's the case, I'm left wondering how they got here. We only recently learned how to cross into Shadesmar, and it requires the aid of a Radiant. How did a trading caravan from our world slip through into here?"

"That's why I fetched you," Godeke said. "Something feels off about the whole group."

"They could still be foreigners," Archinal said. "They could be wearing manifested clothing they traded for while here. Oh! You mustn't assume that what you see here relates to what you know from your life, human highprince."

"We could ask them, right?" Godeke said. "See if they'll talk to us?"

The two exchanged a look, and then Adolin shrugged. Why not? He walked out, joined by Godeke and his spren, Maya trailing along behind.

He was noticed immediately by the caravaneers. One pointed, and a small group rushed up. The lighting of this place—with that distant sun, but strangely omnipresent illumination—played tricks on Adolin's eyes. The shadows stretched the wrong way, and distance was harder to judge. So Adolin was accustomed to things feeling off.

Even with that considered, the way these people seemed to be constantly wreathed in shadow . . . it was unnerving. As they stepped up, he felt like he could see only hints of features, and no matter which way they turned, the pits of their faces—the eye sockets, the lines along their noses—were always dark. He saw occasional glimpses of their eyes.

They spoke to him in a language he didn't know.

"Do you speak Alethi?" he asked. "Or Veden?"

"*Gthlebn* Thaylen?" Godeke asked.

"Alethi?" one of the men said. "Go away, Alethi."

Yes, that *was* a Tukari accent. "We just want to chat," Adolin said. "We haven't seen other humans here. We thought it would be nice to talk to others."

"Go away," the man repeated. "We not talk."

Adolin glanced past him, to where some of the humans had moved to fish among their goods. Though the people he spoke with carried cudgels, he caught a glint of reflected light among the others. They were carrying real weapons, but didn't want to hold them openly.

"Fine," Adolin said. "Suit yourselves."

He and the others retreated to the town. The Tukari watched them all the way.

"Those *were* Tukari," Godeke said.

"Yeah," Adolin said. "Their country is led by a man claiming to be a god—who is actually a Herald. Father is planning to push the singer army in Emul down to crush them against those zealots. A hammer-and-anvil advance."

Were these strange travelers somehow connected to that business in Tukar? Or was it a coincidence?

Adolin met up with his soldiers, and they walked back toward the barge. They'd want to get on with unloading their supplies and making camp. Archinal had been to the honorspren stronghold before, and was confident she could lead them there. It shouldn't be difficult; if they simply followed the coast to the west, they'd eventually end up at the place.

As they approached the barge, however, Adolin slowed. A figure was speaking to Unativi in front of the barge—a figure of white, tinted blue. Tall, distinguished. Adolin was accustomed to seeing this spren in a sharp uniform, not a buttoned shirt and trousers, but it *was* the same person.

"Is that an honorspren?" Godeke asked.

"Yes," Adolin said, continuing forward. "That's Notum. The captain of the ship we sailed on last time we were in Shadesmar."

It seemed his confrontation with the honorspren might happen sooner than he'd planned.

⁂

Shallan finished sketching by the light of gemstones, still sitting underneath the canopy. The locked chest beside her held the strange communications device, now re-created in her sketches.

She'd attracted a few spren out of the ocean. Creationspren, which here were little swirling shapes of changing colors of light. They evoked different impressions, often faces. But they were small, and easy to treat like spren in the Physical Realm. She shooed them away as Pattern sat down beside her.

"Mmmm . . ." he said. "You have drawn the same cube four times, Shallan. Are you well?"

"No," she said, "but this isn't a sign of that." She flipped through her sketchbook. "Someone has been moving this cube. Between times I get it out."

Pattern's pattern slowed to almost a crawl. "You are certain?"

"Yes," she said, showing him the sketches. "There's a scratch on this side near the corner, and that face was up yesterday—but it's to the side today."

"Mmmm . . ." he said. "That is a very fine detail. One nobody else would have noticed."

"Yeah," she said. Her drawings were eerily accurate. Supernaturally so, even. "Beryl is the spy. I have evidence of this, and I know she's been contacting Mraize with the cube. I'm extremely curious how she activated it without drawing attention. Did you see her doing it?"

"No," he said. "I did not."

"Well, it's a relief to know who it is," Shallan said—and was surprised to find that it was. She could accept this, the traitor being the new girl. Shallan had begun to retreat at the idea of it being Vathah or Ishnah.

Beryl. She could accept it being Beryl. That hurt—being betrayed would always hurt—but it could have been worse.

Damnation, Veil thought.

What? Shallan thought. *What's wrong?*

Does this feel too easy? Veil asked. *Too convenient?*

Veil, Radiant thought. *You went to all this trouble to seed the information and find the spy. Now you're questioning?*

I just mentioned fundamentals, Veil replied. *We need to question every bit of information, and ask ourselves if we're being fed it. I need to think about this more.*

Shallan sighed, then shook her head. If Veil hadn't gotten them drunk, then maybe they'd have caught Beryl. She started sketching again, the cube one more time—but this time adding dimples to the top. Did she remember? Did she want to remember?

"Shallan?" Pattern said. "Mmm . . . Something is wrong, isn't it? Something more than there being a spy among us?"

"I don't know," she said, rubbing her forehead. The remnants of her earlier hangover throbbed in the back of her mind. "Do . . . you remember me ever using a cube like this one when I was younger?"

"Mmm. No?"

"I did," Shallan said. "I don't know how, but I did. I can't make sense of my own memories though."

"Perhaps . . . I can help you? Remember?"

She stared at the sketchbook.

"Shallan," Pattern said. "I'm worried about you. Mmm. You say you're getting better, but I worry. Adolin agrees, though I don't think he sees what I do."

"What do you see?" she asked softly.

"Something else looking out of your eyes, sometimes. Something new. It comes out when . . . when I try to talk about your past. So I'm afraid to do it. Sometimes you tease that you want me to say more. Then those other eyes *see me.*"

"There's another truth," Shallan whispered. "Another . . ."

"Another . . ."

She squeezed her eyes shut. *Veil, take over.*

But—

Veil found herself in control again, and heard voices drifting in from outside the barge. Adolin, strong and confident. Veil didn't love him like Shallan did, but she knew right then that they needed to be near him. *Shallan* needed to be near him.

No, Shallan thought from deep within. *No. He'll hate me. He'll hate . . . what I did. . . .*

Veil went to be near him anyway. But she couldn't find it in herself to tell him of Shallan's fears—she would not risk pain she wasn't certain Shallan could handle. She couldn't risk giving more meat to Formless, and so remained silent.

⁘

"So it *is* you," Notum said to Adolin. "You did not learn from your last excursion into this land? You *had* to return?"

Notum appeared as an Alethi man, sturdy and tall, with close-cropped hair and a militaristic attitude. He had a beard a little like that of a Horn-eater, with prominent sideburns running down his cheeks, but with an additional thin mustache. It, along with his simple clothing, was all part of him. Though some spren wore manifested clothing, honorspren created it from their own substance.

Notum's face was impassive, but his words dripped with condescension. Why wasn't he wearing his captain's uniform? Was he on leave? His ship certainly wasn't anywhere nearby.

The spren—as extremely formal as Adolin remembered him being—clasped his hands behind his back to wait for a reply, reminding Adolin of his father. Adolin waved for his soldiers to stay back, though Maya stuck by his side as he stepped closer to Notum. The honorspren gave her barely a glance; they tended to ignore deadeyes.

"I've been sent on a diplomatic mission, Notum," Adolin said, "to visit Lasting Integrity. I'm representing the new orders of Radiants and my father, the king of Urithiru. Our monarchs have sent letters of introduction. We hope to forge a new alliance."

The honorspren opened his eyes wide and drew in a sharp breath—something spren only did for effect, as they didn't normally breathe.

"What?" Adolin said. "It's *that* surprising?"

"It wouldn't be polite for me to interrupt," Notum said. "Please continue your insane rant."

"We merely want to enter a dialogue," Adolin said. "Regularize diplomatic relations between the human world and the spren one. It's a perfectly reasonable request."

The street nearby emptied as spren gave a wide berth to the honorspren. They'd glance at him and veer in another direction. He wasn't liked here. His presence was suffered, but not enjoyed.

"Let me posit a similar situation for you," he said to Adolin. "A criminal, on the run, has stolen a precious memento from the king—his beloved goblet, perhaps. A memory of his lost wife. Would it be *reasonable* for this thief to stroll up to the palace one day and try to *normalize* relations between him and the king? Would that instead not be idiocy?"

"We took nothing from the honorspren."

"Save the Stormfather's most precious daughter."

"Syl made that choice," Adolin said. "Even the Stormfather has acknowledged that. Besides, if she's so precious, maybe you all could *listen* to her once in a while." Maya growled softly at this comment, which drew both Adolin and Notum to glance at her. Sounds from a deadeye were always an oddity.

"The Stormfather," Notum said, "won't be much help to you. Now that he's agreed to be bound, the honorspren no longer revere him as they once did. They think he must have been wounded by the death of Honor, and that wound is now manifesting as irrational behavior. So yes, he no longer commands the return of the Ancient Daughter. But do not think that will make the honorspren welcome you."

"As soon as someone they respect tells them something reasonable, they cast him aside?" Adolin asked. "Spren are supposed to be better than men."

"I wish that were so," Notum said, his voice quieter. "Prince Adolin. I am not an unreasonable person. You know this. I seek only to do my duty, the best I can. Still, I can tell you *exactly* what will happen if you approach Lasting Integrity. You will be turned away. Even friends of the honorspren are not allowed into the fortress currently, and you are anything but a friend.

"To many there, you are a criminal. Your *entire race* is one of criminals. It isn't about the Ancient Daughter so much as it is about what you did to us." Notum nodded his chin toward Maya.

"Again, *we* did *nothing* to them," Adolin said, keeping his tone calm through sheer force of will. "Maya and the others were killed thousands of years ago."

"Not even a single lifetime to many spren," Notum said. "We have long memories, Prince Adolin. Perhaps you would not be blamed, save for the fact that your people have returned to those oaths. You have not learned from the past, and are restarting the abomination, bonding spren and risking their lives."

"These Radiants won't do what those of the past did," Adolin said. "Look, for thousands of years before the Recreance, spren and humans got along. Will we let one event wipe that all out?"

"One event?" Notum said. "One event that caused *eight* genocides, Prince Adolin. Pause and think on that. Nearly every honorspren was bound, and those were *all killed*. Can you imagine the betrayal? The pain of being murdered by the person you trusted with your life? Your very soul? Men die, and their souls travel to the Spiritual Realm to meld with deity. But what of us?"

He waved to Maya, standing in her rags, eyes scratched away. "We are left," Notum said, "to wander Shadesmar as dead souls, unable to think or talk. Our bodies are used, screaming, as weapons by the descendants of the ones who killed us. It was not a simple mistake that led us to this state, but a coordinated and calculated betrayal of oaths.

"Your people are criminals. The sole reason there was no swift retribution was because you killed every spren who could have acted against you. Do *not* go to Lasting Integrity. They will not accept letters from your kings and queens. They will not even speak to you."

Notum turned and stalked toward a small caravan set up outside. Judging by the organized layout—and the two uniformed Reachers guarding the perimeter—Adolin guessed it was Notum's own caravan.

"Captain," Adolin called after him. "Perhaps my task is doomed as you say. However, I can't help but think that it would be helped if we had someone vouch for my intentions. Perhaps a respected honorspren, a ship's captain and military man. Someone who understands the urgency of our mission."

Notum froze, then turned on his heel, his head cocked. "Ship's captain? You didn't see my clothing?"

"You're . . . on leave?"

"I was removed from duty," Notum said, "for letting the Ancient Daughter go after capturing her. I spent five months in prison, and when I was released I was demoted to the lowest rank an honorspren can hold. I've been assigned to spend two centuries patrolling the empty land between here and Lasting Integrity, traveling back and forth endlessly. I am not allowed to set foot in Lasting Integrity. I can see it, but not enter."

"Until when?" Adolin asked. "Until . . . your patrol is done?"

"Until never, Prince Adolin. I am exiled." He looked up at the sky, where shimmering lights revealed a highstorm beginning to pass in the Physical Realm. "I knew what I was doing, what I was tempting, when I let you go. At least tell me, did you save him? The Bondsmith?"

Adolin swallowed, his mouth having gone dry. Exiled for eternity? Because he had done the right thing? Adolin had known not to expect the honorspren of Lasting Integrity to be like Syl was, but he'd been expecting to be able to speak with people such as Notum. Tough, strict, but ultimately fair-minded people capable of listening to reason.

But if they had treated Notum—who had seemed the ultimate embodiment of propriety and honor—in such a terrible way . . . Stormwinds.

Notum was still waiting for an answer. He'd let Syl and the rest of them go because Kaladin had insisted they needed to rescue Dalinar. Adolin wanted to offer some kind of quick assurance that Notum's sacrifice had been vital . . . but the words wouldn't come out. This spren deserved honesty.

"*He* saved *us*, Notum," Adolin said. "My father didn't ultimately end up needing our help—though I think that Shallan and Kaladin helped turn the battle when we arrived."

Notum nodded. "I am marching along this road toward Lasting Integrity, but will be forced to turn back when I draw near. Perhaps we will meet again along the path, human prince, and I can dissuade you from this course." He continued on.

Ua'pam and Zu were already on the barge, and they'd apparently arranged for Adolin's party to set up in one of the several camps established outside town. So Adolin joined the others as they unloaded their gear—helping with the horses, then moving his weapons—all the while lost in thought.

Adolin had been useless in that battle at Thaylen City. The world was about gods and Radiants now, not handsome young lighteyes who fancied themselves skilled with the sword. Best thing he could do was accept that, then find a different way to be useful.

He *would* find a way to get the honorspren to listen to him. Somehow.

31

DAUGHTER OF TRAITORS

I do not share their attitude. If you can, as you suppose, maintain Odium's prison for now, it would give us necessary time to plan. This is a threat beyond the capacity of one Shard to face.

Even weeks after first meeting one, Venli caught herself staring at the new brand of Fused.

These ones—called the *makay-im*, or "Those Ones of the Depths"—had access to one of her same Surges: the ability to turn stone into a liquid.

The Deepest Ones had smooth skin, no hair, and barely any carapace—just shells over their heads and genitals. This put their vibrant patterns on display across the full lengths of their sinuous bodies. Long-legged and long-armed, they reminded Venli of her current form, which was tall without reaching the unnatural willowy level of Raboniel and the builders like her.

The *makay-im* wore open-fronted robes, if they wore anything at all. They stayed aloof from the rest of the strike team as they moved through the frozen mountain passes. After weeks of traveling together, Venli still hadn't been addressed directly by one of the Deepest Ones—though the pace Raboniel set left little time for chitchat.

These mountains, as far as Venli could tell, weren't claimed by any particular kingdom. The isolated valleys were too inaccessible from the outside. Her team had been dropped in by Heavenly Ones several weeks before, then left to travel the rest of the way to Urithiru on foot.

The human fortress lay somewhere in here—presumed hidden and un-assailable. Windrunner patrols made it impossible to fly in too close, but Raboniel felt that a small group of ground troops—moving carefully at night or during storms—would be able to approach the lower tunnels to the tower unseen.

So it was that Venli joined the rest of the group in moving out from the shadow of tree cover, crossing the stone ground. As on other days, Raboniel set a characteristically difficult pace, though Venli knew she wouldn't start to feel tired until they'd been going for a few hours.

The ancient scholar had changed from stately robes into travel leathers suitable for battle, her topknot of pure red-orange hairstrands spilling down around her otherwise carapace-covered skull. She urged the group forward, increasingly eager. They were nearing the tower; only a few days now.

This highland valley was mostly barren, supporting just the most rugged of rockbuds and the occasional clump of squat trees, their branches interwoven to create a storm-resistant snarl. Though leaves on these trees would retract before storms, the branches remained firm and interlocked. There wasn't a single lifespren in sight, though coldspren lined the ground, pointing toward the sky.

As one might expect, there were more rockbuds on the leeward slopes, but blasted scars of black ground and burned patches showed that when the Everstorm came through, it did not temper its fury. The heights seemed to suffer more lightning strikes than the lowlands did.

She hiked more quickly to pass the soldiers and position herself next to the Deepest Ones. She liked watching them, because they *melded* with the stone, even as they moved. The bright azure light of Honor's Moon revealed thirty figures, some in rippling robes, *sliding* across the ground while standing. It wasn't quite like the *shetel-im*, the Flowing Ones, who could slide across any surface as if it were slick. This was something different. The Deepest Ones stood with their feet sunken *into* the ground up past their ankles.

They moved like nothing Venli had ever seen. Like sticks in a current following a powerful highstorm, as if the stone were pushing them along while they stood perfectly still. Their eyes glowed red—like those of all Fused and Regals—but theirs seemed a more sinister, dark shade.

"They interest you, I've noticed," a voice said from Venli's side.

She jumped, and turned to find Raboniel walking alongside her. Venli attuned Anxiety, and Timbre thrummed within her, worried. Had she been paying too much attention? Would it be seen as suspicious? She lowered her head and hummed to Agony. Already she worried this mission risked exposing her bond.

"No need to be ashamed," Raboniel said to Conceit. "Curiosity is welcome in singers. It is a worthy Passion, Last Listener."

Venli held Anxiety as she walked—at a swift hike—beneath Raboniel's gaze. She intended to serve this Fused well, as Leshwi had asked. Of the staff, only Venli was Regal, so only she could make this difficult trip. So far, she had served the femalen in quiet capacities: setting out her bedroll at night, fetching water for her to drink. She hadn't been given many other duties, and had barely been addressed. She'd begun to think that serving Raboniel would be—if not easy—at least uneventful. Why was she now drawing the femalen's attention?

"You are such an odd choice by Leshwi," Raboniel said. "When I discovered just *who* had been given as my new Voice . . . To so many, you are merely the child of traitors. Yet Leshwi gave you honor. Named you Last Listener."

"She was kind, Ancient One."

"She thinks highly of you," Raboniel said. "Fused are not kind; they reward competence and Passion. Even if one is the daughter of traitors. I should have expected Leshwi's Voice to be someone . . . irregular. She is among the most clever and capable of the Heavenly Ones."

"She . . . might dispute that, Ancient One."

"Yes, I realize how much work she does to make others underestimate her." Raboniel said it to Satisfaction. "She is dangerous, and that is good." She looked to Venli and blinked her red eyes once, humming softly to Satisfaction.

Timbre thrummed within Venli. Raboniel knew too much. She'd plainly discerned that Venli was a spy for Leshwi. But how much more had Raboniel figured out? Surely she didn't know the full truth.

"Tell me," Raboniel said. "What about the Deepest Ones interests you so? Why do you spend hours staring at them?"

"I find their powers fascinating," Venli said—best not to lie until she had to.

"Nine brands of Fused," Raboniel said. "Nine Surges. You know of the Surges?"

"The innate forces by which all life, all *reality*, are connected. Gravitation. Transportation. Transformation. But . . . I thought there were ten?"

"That is human talk," Raboniel said to Derision. "They claim a tenth, of Honor alone. Adhesion is not a true Surge, but a lie that was presented to us as one. True Surges are of both Honor *and* Cultivation—Cultivation for life, Honor to make the Surge into natural law. Things must fall to the ground, so they created Surges to make it happen."

"And the Surge of these ones?" Venli asked, gesturing toward the Deepest Ones.

"Cohesion," Raboniel said. "The Surge of Axial Connection—the Surge that binds the smallest pieces of all objects to one another. The Surge that holds us together. The *makay-im* can meld their essence into the essences of other things, intermingling their axi. All things are mostly emptiness, though we cannot see that it is so. A stone, like a mind, exists to be filled by thought and Investiture."

Venli hummed to Craving. Answers. Finally, *answers*. She didn't know what half of any of this meant, but to have one of the Fused answer so easily . . . It excited her, though Timbre thrummed to Caution.

"The Radiants each have two Surges," Venli said. "The Fused each have one. So are the Radiants more powerful?"

"Powerful? Is it better to have more abilities, or to have one ability handled expertly? We of the Fused know our Surge with an intimacy a Radiant will never know. Humans. They were not created for this world, these Surges, or the storms. Light leaks from humans like water through fingers. They get flares of great power, but cannot *hold* what they have.

"One of the Fused can contain Light and bask in it indefinitely. Even a Regal such as you knows this power in a lesser way—most don't know it, but you contain a small amount of Voidlight in your gemheart. You can't use it actively, of course, but you might have felt it enflaming your emotions.

"As for Fused, our dominance over our Surge is eternal. Where humans visit, we reign." She gestured toward the Deepest Ones. "Can any Radiant claim to know the stones as these do, melding with rock, mixing their very axi? Radiants are so outwardly focused. They change the world, but ignore themselves. Yes, a Radiant can cast a stone into the sky, but the *shanay-im* can soar without worry of ever dropping."

Venli hummed to Craving, though she wasn't certain she agreed. Although she had been timid about using her Radiant powers in Kholinar, they excited her. Timbre said that she would be able to move stone, shape it.

She glanced at the Deepest Ones, who moved so quietly, so smoothly. Next to them, Venli's own hiking gait—and that of the five hundred stormform soldiers marching behind—felt awkward. And she did feel envy at the way they flowed. So . . . *why* was it that the powers manifested differently in Radiants than they did in Fused?

She attuned Annoyance as she considered what Raboniel had said. Each answer seemed to give rise to a dozen new questions, but Venli knew that the Fused—even one that was in an accommodating mood like Raboniel—would not suffer questions forever. So, Venli settled on one last thing to ask.

"If Surges are from Honor and Cultivation," she said, "then why do we serve Odium?"

"A dangerous question," Raboniel said to Derision. "You truly are the daughter of traitors, aren't you?"

"I—"

"Don't cover up your ambition, child," Raboniel said, leading Venli past a line of snarled shrubs, with little furry creatures scampering underneath in the night. "I like it in my servants. Still, there is a certain silliness to your question. Which would you rather worship? A god of plants? Or a god of emotions?" She waved to the southeast. "Cultivation hides in these mountains somewhere. She is everywhere, but she is also here. Alive, but frightened. She knows. She is not a god of *people,* but of *creatures.*

"And Honor? A god of laws? Again, which would you prefer? A god who knows only how to make a rock fall to the ground? Or a god who knows us, understands us, *feels* as we do? Yes, Surges are bound by Honor. Yet as you can see, his death did not change the world in any appreciable manner. His power binds all things together, but this alone is not worthy of worship. Odium . . . Passion . . . *he* will grant rewards."

Venli hummed to Craving.

"You want more, don't you?" Raboniel said. "Only one with pure ambition would stand where you do now. Serve well, and you may find the blessings available to the worthy. True knowledge. True life."

Venli continued to hum, though her internal rhythm was something far more uncertain. The Rhythm of the Lost. She didn't know what to make of Raboniel. Many Fused were some variety of unhinged: vengeful, destructive, conceited.

Listening to this creature's careful, insightful offers, Venli found herself afraid. This creature was far more dangerous than any she'd encountered before.

Raboniel left, striding forward alongside the silent drifting figures of the Deepest Ones. Venli continued walking, and was surprised when Rothan worked his way up beside her. He was head of Lady Leshwi's soldiers—not part of Venli's staff, but analogous to her in authority. He, like most of Leshwi's soldiers, had been given to Raboniel for this incursion.

The soldiers of the Pursuer had also joined them—and they were a group Venli knew by their fearsome reputation. They'd been harsh to the humans of Kholinar, but were among the strongest and proudest singer troops, with distinctive uniforms always worn with pride. Now those intermingled with Leshwi's carefully trained and calmer troops, forming a powerful strike force with both strength and discipline.

Venli hadn't interacted much with Rothan or the other soldiers, but she had nothing against him. Other than the fact that other Regals made her worried, as they held Voidspren in their gemhearts. With each step, his powerful figure seemed to crackle with energy. Sparks occasionally flashed across his deep red eyes. She remembered that feeling, holding stormform. The form she'd used when she'd led her people to their doom.

"You should not bother the Fused, Venli," Rothan said to Derision, looking toward Raboniel. "Most are not as lenient as Leshwi. Take care. I would not see you fall. You are useful to us."

"I . . . hadn't noticed that you cared," she said.

"Leshwi values you," he said. "Therefore, so do the rest of us." He left her with that simple warning as he retreated. Rothan didn't often want answers or even engagement. He simply stood tall, spoke his mind, then expected to be understood.

He would be a good one to have on my side, Venli thought. But no, too dangerous. Far too dangerous. She couldn't afford to think about recruitment right now. She had to focus on staying alive. For, as grueling as this hike through the mountains had been, she knew a more dangerous part was coming.

Within the week, they would arrive at Urithiru. And then the real test would come.

Unfortunately, as proven by my own situation, the combination of Shards is not always a path to greater power.

Adolin joined Zu atop the obsidian outcropping. The golden-haired Stoneward still wore her traditional clothing, a wrap around the chest and loose, flowing trousers. She claimed she'd picked up scouting skills as a guide in the Reshi Isles, but he thought she moved with too much stealth for that.

"There," she said, pointing. "They *are* still following."

Adolin raised the spyglass, sighting where she pointed. Indeed, he could make out the Tukari caravan in the distance. Those strange humans had been following them—never more than a few hours' march behind—since they'd left the port town weeks earlier.

"Damnation," Adolin said. "So they didn't turn at the crossroads after all." The terrain had grown uneven since this morning, full of crags and outcroppings, and it had been more difficult to spot their tail.

"Wanna go confront them?" Zu asked, grinning.

"Two on twenty?"

"One of those two can shape stone at her will and make clothing into weapons."

"I don't dare waste what Stormlight remains," Adolin said.

"It will run out soon anyway," she said. "Might as well give it a last hurrah! A new experience for the One."

From below, Ua'pam called up, "Do not encourage her! She *will* do this foolish thing!"

Zu grinned at Adolin, then winked, as if her bravado were partially just to unnerve her spren. Even after weeks traveling with her, Adolin didn't know what to make of the strange Stoneward. She lightly leaped off the outcropping and slid down the smooth obsidian, graceful as an Edgedancer. Below, she slapped Ua'pam on the shoulder and the two of them wandered toward camp.

He was tempted to do as Zu said, if only because their Stormlight *was* running out. They'd been in Shadesmar almost thirty days at this point, long enough that their spheres had all run out weeks ago. Though they'd spent much of their Stormlight at the caravan stop, they'd retained a few larger gemstones lent them by the Thaylens, capable of holding Light longer even than others the same size. Those were starting to dim, unfortunately. And once gems started to dim, they went dun quickly.

Adolin took another long look at the Tukari, then shook his head. They didn't *seem* like they were trying to catch up to Adolin's group; they didn't push fast or move during the nights. The latter would have been easy, as "night" in Shadesmar wasn't a strict time set by the movement of the sun. Those humans could easily have done a double march and overtaken his team.

He'd already sent a runner to ask Notum about them; his smaller patrol was marching a little ahead of Adolin's group. The honorspren had said that it wasn't illegal for those Tukari to use the road, but to report to him if they did anything expressly threatening.

Adolin tucked away the spyglass and returned to meet with the others, who were preparing to break camp. He'd learned from his father that a commander was best seen doing things, so he inspected the work, set the forward and rear guard for the day, and checked on Maya—who had been traveling on Gallant's back.

The large midnight stallion had taken to her—he wouldn't let just anyone ride him—and seemed to recognize that she was injured somehow. Gallant stepped extra carefully, moving gently so Maya wouldn't be knocked from her seat. And Adolin was *not* simply imagining it, no matter what the others thought.

He got everyone moving, then sought out Shallan.

⋄⋄

The last few weeks, Shallan had been of two minds—well, three, technically—on how to use the information that Beryl was a spy. As the caravan started out for the day, she stuck close to Beryl, ostensibly to help her with Lightweaving.

"I still need to find my focus, Brightness," Beryl said, keeping pace easily with her long Alethi legs. It was almost criminal how luxurious her dark hair was, despite there being little water for bathing. "I have tried drawing as you suggest, but I'm not any good at it."

"You used Lightweaving with men in the warcamps," Shallan said. "And I've seen you use it in sparring."

"Yes, but I can't change anything but my own appearance!" she said. "I *know* I can do more. I've seen the rest of you."

"It's limited for most of us at the start," Shallan said, nodding toward Vathah, who was walking alongside the Cryptics. "The first time I caught *him* Lightweaving, he didn't believe he'd actually done it. It seems to surprise him each time he makes it happen."

"I've tried his way," Beryl said with a grimace. "He acts like the person or thing he's trying to be, and then his Lightweaving takes over. If he wants to make an illusion of a large rock, he says he *thinks* like a rock. How does that even work?" She gave Shallan a weak smile. "I don't mean to complain, Brightness. I'm sure I merely have to keep trying. It will come to me as it did the others, right?"

"It will, I promise," Shallan said. "I was frustrated like you at the start, unable to control it. But you *can* do this."

Beryl nodded eagerly.

Inside, Veil was marveling. *She's an extremely good actor. I couldn't spot any sign of a tell. I swear, either she hides her true emotions marvelously, or we have the wrong woman.*

Veil's surety of that had been growing and building during the trip. Shallan didn't want to accept it, but it was hard to continue pretending at this point.

Perhaps we should speak with Ornament again, Radiant thought. *I feel if we chat with her enough, she will let something slip.*

They'd been trying that too, but . . . Veil thought they were hitting a dead end there. If Beryl's spren knew about her treason, then the Cryptic wasn't letting on.

It twisted Shallan about to consider this all might be for nothing. She *wanted* the spy to be Beryl. And they had a pretty damning confirmation, didn't they?

Well, Veil thought, *let's assume the worst. That the real spy is extremely careful and skilled. Is it too much of a stretch to wonder if they discovered, by speaking to the others, that we'd seeded a bit of misinformation? Mraize is clever. He could have purposely fed us a line to put suspicion on Beryl.*

What was the point of the inquiry, then? Shallan thought, frustrated. *Why go to all that trouble if we were just going to doubt the results?*

Because I doubt everything, Veil said. *It's information, but not conclusive.*

I agree, Radiant thought. *We have had time to investigate Beryl, and have uncovered nothing. To proceed further, we must find proof. Hard proof. We cannot erroneously condemn someone who might be innocent.*

Storms, Veil thought. *You sound like a law officer, Radiant.*

I'm agreeing with you!

Yeah, but you hurt my cause when you're so stiff. Couldn't you relax now and then?

Shallan put her hands to her head, feeling . . . unsettled. She could remember a time not so long ago when her personas hadn't held arguments inside her head. They'd mostly remained isolated; she would shift without noticing. Was it healthier now that they worked together, even if they argued? Or was it more dangerous, since the conflict was so difficult? Either way, she was growing exhausted of the struggle today.

So, reluctantly, Veil took over. And for now she stuck close to Beryl, trying to catch her in a lie. Unfortunately, a short time later, Adolin came tromping up. Like an axehound looking for something to chase. However, even Veil had to admit that with his floppy hair and his can-do attitude, Adolin had a way of making you feel better.

"Hey," he said to Veil. "You have a moment?"

"I suppose," Veil said. "I'm Veil right now, by the way."

"Well, maybe you will have a useful perspective on this," he said, walking her off from the others to speak in private. "The more I think about it, the more I worry we should change how we approach the honorspren. Notum was *convinced* the honorspren wouldn't talk to us. Worse than Syl."

"Change our approach? How? You mean not give them the letters and gifts?"

"I don't think they'll take either. I worry we'll then be turned away immediately."

"That would be aggravating," Veil admitted. She hadn't forgotten her real duty—that of getting into the fortress and locating Restares, leader of the Sons of Honor. Even Radiant was eager to find this man, to discover what secrets he held that Mraize wanted so badly. Finding the spy was important, but this mission superseded it.

"What if there's a better way than delivering Father's and Jasnah's letters?" Adolin said. "What if we offered to give the honorspren as much Stormlight as they could take, delivered by my father, if they'd only send a representative back with us? What if we asked to exchange emissaries, and promised to build their representative a fantastic palace in Shadesmar near the Oathgate? We can bring tons of rock in from our side that is extremely valuable here."

"Hmmm," Veil said. "Adolin, they're like an entire *race* of spren who act like Radiant does—and they see us as criminals. If we worry they won't even accept some letters and books, wouldn't it be dangerous to offer extremely valuable gifts? They might see those as bribes, or as admissions of our guilt."

"Maybe," he said, then punched one fist into the palm of his other hand a few times.

"I agree with Veil, Brightlord," Radiant said. "I would be highly suspicious of valuable gifts, if I were them. It is not a payoff they want, but isolation."

"All right then," Adolin said. "An entirely different idea. We beg. Abjectly. We bow down and say that without them we're doomed. If the spren are anything like Windrunners, then maybe they won't be able to say no."

Radiant considered. "Perhaps. *I* would find that more appealing than bribes, I suppose."

"I wouldn't," Veil said. "But I guess I'm the wrong person to ask. Because at seeing you beg, I'd figure that I was correct to stay out of the conflict—because it's unwinnable."

"Damnation," Adolin said. "I hadn't thought about that."

"Let me consider," Radiant said. "I am Radiant again, by the way."

Adolin nodded.

"This is a difficult challenge, Adolin," Radiant finally said. "And I agree with your worries. We have exactly one chance to present ourselves properly to the honorspren. They are a hostile group—indeed, one that has *self-selected* toward hostility. We can surmise that the spren most willing to listen to our arguments have already joined the Knights Radiant.

"Your ploy of acting weak and begging for help is a promising idea. I wonder, however, if appealing to the honorspren's rational side would be a better plan."

"The way the honorspren insist on turning away from all of humankind is emotional though, right?" Adolin said. "They were hurt in the past. They are afraid of that pain."

"One might call that rational. If your entire species had essentially been wiped out by fraternization with humans, would you not—logically—be wary of reengaging in that same fraternization?"

"But how's it going to go for them if Odium wins?" Adolin asked. "He hates Honor. Well, I guess he hates everything. It's kind of in the name. . . . Anyway, will they spend the rest of their existences inside their little bunker? Will they eventually bow before him? Decide to fight only once everyone else is dead or subjugated?"

Radiant smiled. "I can feel your determination, Brightlord. That passion is admirable. The things you said to me could be good arguments to make to the honorspren."

"Those are the ones my father makes in his letter," Adolin said. "That's basically what Syl said before abandoning them and going to find Kaladin. I can't help thinking that the arguments Father and Jasnah have made are the ones the honorspren will be prepared for, bracing themselves. . . ."

He got a far-off look, then glanced behind him. Radiant frowned, trying to figure out what he was searching for. The line of people? His Ryshadium, clopping along with the deadeye on its back? The glittering obsidian hills overgrown with crystalline plants?

"You have had a thought?" Radiant asked.

"Kind of," Adolin said. "I . . . realized that they'll be ready for *anything* we can bring. I mean, these creatures have been alive for thousands of years—and have spent all of that time angry at us. I can't possibly think of an argument they haven't already considered. I doubt Father, or even Jasnah, could do so."

"A reasonable assumption," Radiant said, nodding as they walked. "However, if they are anticipating all arguments, then perhaps the sole hope we have is the skill of the one arguing. Brightness Jasnah can be *quite* persuasive. I suggest, upon reflection, that we continue with the tactic of offering the letters."

"Either that or we could surprise the honorspren."

"How?" Radiant said. "You pointed out they've had thousands of years to consider these arguments."

Adolin shook his head, his expression still distant. "Look," he eventually said, "could I speak to Shallan?"

"Shallan is exhausted at the moment," Radiant said. "She asks that I handle this conversation. Why do you ask?"

"I just feel more comfortable with her, Radiant." He glanced at Radiant. "Is . . . something wrong with Shallan? I thought everything was going better during the boat ride, but these last few weeks . . . I don't know, she feels different. Off."

He noticed! Shallan thought in a panic.

He noticed, Veil thought with relief.

"She has been retreating more and more these days," Radiant said. "She claims to be tired. But . . . there is something going on with us. I can try to make her emerge."

"Please."

She tried. She sincerely did. In the end though, she grimaced. "I'm sorry. Shallan is tired. Maybe scared. Veil can explain, perhaps."

"So . . . can I talk to her?"

"You already are," Veil said, sighing. "Adolin, look. This is really complicated. It's wrapped up in Shallan's past, and the pain she felt as a child. Pain that I was created specifically to help her overcome."

"I can help. I can understand."

"*I* barely understand, Adolin," Veil said. "And I'm living in her head." She took a deep breath, forcing herself to see him as Shallan did. She loved Adolin. She'd chosen Adolin. The least Veil could do was try to explain.

"All right," she said. "Pretend you're her, and you experienced some things that were so traumatic that you don't want to believe they happened to you. So you pretend they happened to someone else. Someone different."

"That's you?" Adolin said.

"Not exactly," Veil said. "This is hard to put into words. Radiant and I are coping mechanisms that, for the most part, work. But something deeper has started to manifest.

"Shallan is worried that the person you see in her is a lie. That the person you *love* is a lie. And it's not only you. Pattern, Dalinar, Jasnah, Navani—she worries that they all don't know the *real* her.

"Because of things that happened to her—and more, some of the things she was forced to do—she's beginning to think that 'Shallan' is the fake one, the false identity. That there is a monster deep inside that is her real self. She fears it's inevitable that the truth will come out, and everyone will leave her when it does."

Adolin nodded, his brow knit. "She couldn't have told me that, could she?"

"No." Indeed, in saying those things, she'd made Shallan retreat into a little knot of fear. Right next to Formless.

"You can say things she can't," Adolin said. "And that's why we need you, isn't it?"

"Yes."

"I think I do understand, a little bit." He met her eyes. "Thank you, Veil. Sincerely. I'll find a way to help. I promise."

Huh. She believed him. How interesting. "I was wrong about you," she said. "For what it's worth, I'm glad I was outvoted."

"If she's listening," he said, "make sure she knows that I don't care what she did. And tell her I know she's strong enough to deal with this on her own, but she should know she doesn't have to anymore. Deal with it on her own, that is."

I wasn't ever alone, part of her whispered. *I had Pattern. Even in the dark days of our childhood, we had him. Although we don't remember.*

So Adolin was wrong, but he was also right. They *didn't* have to do this alone. If only they could persuade Shallan of that fact.

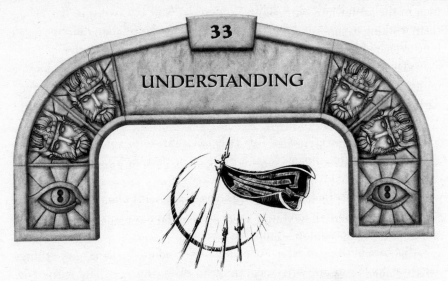

*We must assume that Odium has realized this, and is seeking a sin-
gular, terrible goal: the destruction—and somehow Splintering or
otherwise making impotent—of all Shards other than him.*

There was more than one way to protect.

Kaladin had always known this, but he hadn't *felt* it. Feeling and
knowing seemed to be the same to his father, but not to Kaladin.
Listening to descriptions from books was never good enough for him. He
had to try something to understand it.

He threw himself into this new challenge: finding a way to help Noril
and the others in the sanitarium. At his father's recommendation—then
insistence—Kaladin took it slowly, confining his initial efforts to men who
shared similar symptoms. Battle fatigue, nightmares, persistent melancholy, suicidal tendencies.

Lirin was correct, of course. Kaladin had complained that the ardents
were treating all mental disorders the same; he couldn't swoop in and treat
each and every person in the entire sanitarium at once. First he needed to
prove that he could make a difference for these few.

He still didn't know how his father balanced work and emotion. Lirin
genuinely seemed to care for his patients, but he could also turn it off. Stop
thinking about the ones he couldn't help. Such as the dozens of people
trapped in the darkness of the sanitarium, locked away from the sun, moan-
ing to themselves or—in one severe case—writing gibberish all over her
room using her own feces.

Temporarily excused from seeing ordinary patients, Kaladin located six men in the sanitarium with similar symptoms. He released them and got them working to support each other. He developed a plan, and showed them how to share in ways that would help.

Today they sat in seats on the balcony outside his clinic. Warmed by mugs of tea, they talked. About their lives. The people they'd lost. The darkness.

It *was* helping. You didn't need a surgeon or ardent to lead the discussion; they could do it themselves. Two of the six were mostly quiet, but even they grunted along when others talked about their problems.

"Remarkable," Kaladin's mother said, taking notes as she stood with Kaladin to the side. "How did you know? Previous documentation indicated that they would feed each other's melancholy, driving one another to destructive behavior. But these are having the *opposite* experience."

"The squad is stronger than the individual," Kaladin said. "You simply need to get them pointed in the right direction. Get them to lift the bridge together . . ."

His mother frowned, glancing up at him.

"The ardents' stories about inmates feeding each other's despair," Kaladin said. "They probably came from inmates who were situated next to one another in the sanitariums. In dark places, where their gloom could run rampant . . . Yes, there I could see them driving each other closer toward death. It happens sometimes to . . . to slaves. In a hopeless situation, it's easy to convince one another to give up."

His mother rested her hand on his arm, and her face looked so sad he had to turn away. He didn't like to talk to her about his past, the years between then and now. During those years she'd lost her loving boy, Kal. That child was dead, long ago buried in crem. At least by the time he'd found her again, Kaladin had become the man he was now. Broken, but mostly reforged as a Radiant.

She didn't need to know about those darkest months. They would bring her nothing but pain.

"Anyway," Kaladin said, nodding toward the group of men, "I suspected after talking to Noril that this would help. It changes something to be able to speak to others about your pain. It helps to have others who *actually* understand."

"I understand," his mother said. "Your father understands."

He was glad she thought that, wrong though she was. They were sympathetic, but they didn't *understand*. Better that they didn't.

For the men chatting together softly, the change was in being shown sunlight again. In being reminded that the darkness *did* pass. But perhaps most important, the change was in not merely knowing that you weren't alone—but in *feeling* it. Realizing that no matter how isolated you thought you were, no matter how often your brain told you terrible things, there *were* others who understood.

It wouldn't fix everything. But it was a start.

To combine powers would change and distort who Odium is. So instead of absorbing others, he destroys them. Since we are all essentially infinite, he needs no more power. Destroying and Splintering the other Shards would leave Odium as the sole god, unchanged and uncorrupted by other influences.

I like none of these proposals," the Stump said, with her spren interpreting for her.

She leaned forward to warm her gnarled hands—out of habit most likely, as this manifested fire gave very little heat. It could be packed up and carried in your pocket. All you had to do was grab the bead. It was more like a painting of a fire that flickered and crackled like the real thing.

Veil sat with Shallan's sketchbook open, her back to a large chunk of obsidian, pretending to draw as Adolin held counsel with the Radiants. So far, despite doing the *worst* job sketching, she hadn't been able to coax Shallan out.

"None of them?" Adolin asked. He stood tall, wearing a black uniform embroidered with silver around the cuffs. The polished buttons perfectly matched the silver of the sheathed side sword he wore on his hip.

He was striking—brilliant, even, as he stood before the fire in a sharply tailored uniform. The fire was cold somehow, though it should have been warm. And he was warm somehow, when a stiff black uniform should have made him seem cold.

Arshqqam, though coming from a very different background, was not timid about speaking her mind to him. Veil liked the old Truthwatcher.

Too many people refused to look past a person's age. To them this woman—as exemplified by her nickname—would be defined by how old she was.

Veil saw more. The way Arshqqam kept her silver hair carefully braided. The engraved ring she wore on her right hand was her only jewelry, and it bore no valuable gemstone, just some milky white quartz. She argued with Adolin—one of the most powerful men in the world—as easily as she might have argued with a water bearer. There was so much to this woman, and yet they barely knew her.

Don't you want to draw that, Shallan? Veil thought. *Don't you want to come out and do a better job than I am?*

Instead, she felt a deep resentment from Shallan. For the things Veil had said to Adolin. The pain they threatened.

The pain of a past best left forgotten.

"Brightlord," the Stump said to Adolin through her spren, "I understand why you are concerned. Dreaming-though-Awake has read the letters Dalinar and Jasnah sent, then told me the contents. If the honorspren are truly as antagonistic as they seem, then I doubt they will listen to these written pleas. Dreaming-though-Awake says that honorspren can be quite passionate, and would likely respond better to a personal plea.

"However, the arguments you've offered tonight aren't strong enough. Claiming that unless they agree, you're going to go to the inkspren? They know how badly we need Windrunners, and they undoubtedly know the inkspren are being even *more* difficult to recruit. Trying to play upon their guilty consciences to provoke them to help? I don't think they *do* feel guilty. That's the problem."

"I agree," Godeke said. The solemn Edgedancer clasped his hands before him, seated on an overturned rations box, his squared beard a reminder of his ardent past. "We can't guilt them into agreeing, Brightlord. Nor can we win them over with threats. We must present our request: that we are in need, and we sincerely wish them to reconsider their lack of support."

"Zu?" Adolin asked the final Radiant.

The golden-haired woman leaned back and shrugged. "I'm not one for politics. I'll tell them they're being storming stupid if they think they can ride this."

"Your people are trying to ride it," Godeke said.

"My people are storming stupid," Zu said, shrugging again.

Behind them, the soldiers packed up camp. It was morning—though that didn't mean much in Shadesmar—and they were now one day away from Lasting Integrity. It was late in the mission to still be uncertain, and Adolin's worry was making Veil nervous. If their delegation got turned away, she'd have to find a way to sneak in and locate Restares alone.

Adolin looked down, seeming to wilt. He'd spent a good long time coming up with these plans, and Veil had helped him with some. Unfortunately, he hadn't shown much confidence in the ideas, and the reactions of the others were further confirmation.

Radiant emerged as Veil searched for a way to bolster his confidence. Unfortunately, Radiant couldn't think of anything useful—though she did spot someone else sitting by the campfire. "Beryl," Radiant found herself saying. "What do you think?"

The stately woman was the only one of Shallan's agents at the campfire meeting; the other two were preparing breakfast. She looked up sharply from where she'd been sitting behind the others.

"I . . . I really don't know," she said, glancing back at her feet and blushing as everyone turned toward her.

"You're a knight," Radiant said. "At least one in training. This is our mission as much as it is that of Highprince Adolin. You should have an opinion. Should we present the letters, or should we attempt something more dramatic?"

"It's . . . so outside my realm of experience, Brightness. Please."

It's not her, Veil thought. *It simply can't be.*

"I'll work on these ideas some more," Adolin said. "Beryl, thank you."

"Highprince Adolin," Arshqqam said. "There is something none of these proposals do properly that I think you should consider. How can you appeal to their *honor*? Are they not spren of this attribute? I suspect any success we have will relate to that."

Adolin nodded slowly, and Radiant cocked her head. Jasnah's proposal tried to do as the Stump said, but Shallan had sensed something off about the arguments.

Honor, Radiant thought. *Yes. Jasnah thinks like a scholar, but not a soldier.* There was something wrong about her lofty words and sweeping conclusions.

Honor. How to appeal to the honor of these spren?

Adolin dismissed everyone to get breakfast. He walked over to take another report from the soldier he had keeping watch over that strange band of Tukari humans, who continued keeping pace behind them.

Beryl stood up, wearing a flowing dress—not a traditional havah, but something of an older classical style that covered both her hands in voluminous sleeves. She walked up to Radiant, who still sat with her back to the rock.

Radiant quickly snapped closed the sketchbook; it wouldn't do for someone to see how terrible Veil's drawings were.

"Why did you ask me to come to this meeting, Brightness?" Beryl asked.

"You have to get used to playing a role in important events. I want you to gain experience with the politics of our current problem. Besides, you asked to come on this mission when Stargyle proved unavailable."

"I wanted to see Shadesmar," she said. "But Brightness, I've barely had time to get used to the idea of being a Lightweaver. I'm no politician." She folded her arms, and suddenly looked cold as she glanced at the rest of the camp. "I don't belong here, do I? I'm not ready."

Radiant tapped the top of Shallan's sketchpad with her pencil, trying to judge whether this woman was lying. But this was Veil's area of expertise. She'd spent over a decade being a spy.

Be careful, Shallan thought. *Remember that decade of experience is imagined.*

True. It was hard to remember.

Yeah . . . Veil thought. *My empty past . . . being nothing back then . . . unnerves me.*

Radiant didn't miss noting Shallan's interjection. That was the most they'd gotten out of her in a few days.

"Beryl," Radiant said, "I want you to practice being around important people. You don't need to solve Adolin's problems; you just need experience giving your opinion in a place where it's safe for you to fail."

"Yes, Brightness," she said, relaxing visibly. "Thank you, Brightness." She bowed and ducked away to go help with breakfast.

I am not the expert, Radiant thought. *But I increasingly agree with Veil's skepticism.*

Shallan, lurking deep inside, started to budge. It would be painful to acknowledge that one of her friends, instead of Beryl, might actually be the spy. But it was better than insisting on believing the lie. No matter how expert they were at that particular trick.

Adolin walked over. Radiant tucked her sketchbook under her arm as she stood up, noting the frown on Adolin's lips.

"The Tukari are still back there?" she guessed.

He nodded. "They turn away any messenger I send, but they're obviously following us."

"We could outrun them," Radiant said. "It would involve putting the Stump and Maya on horseback, then pushing hard to reach the stronghold."

"Perhaps," he said. "I kind of need another day to come up with something. . . ." He handed her a small bar of crushed lavis held together with sugar.

A ration bar? She took it with a frown.

"I thought we'd take a walk," he said. "While the others eat breakfast. It feels strange to say this, but I feel like we haven't had any time together since the boat ride."

Radiant nodded. Fine with her, though she gave way to Veil—who enjoyed conversation more. She tucked her sketchbook into her satchel and slung it over her arm. She wore her rugged travel clothing, with the darker coat and a nice solid pair of boots. Ones that fit her far better than the pair Shallan had stolen from Kaladin.

Adolin waved to his men, then pointed. They waved back, and he started out of camp with Veil following. They didn't get far before a glowing figure approached, riding on something incredible.

Veil had grown accustomed to the wonders of this place. The way glory-spren would sail overhead in formations, or the way that their evening conversation last night had drawn a large joyspren—which manifested here as a spinning cyclone of color.

Every now and then though, something came along that shocked away even Veil's deliberate cynicism. Notum's grand white steed was *almost* a horse, though it was more graceful and supple, with long legs and a neck that bent in a way no physical spine could manage. It had large eyes but seemingly no mouth, and its hair waved in a phantom wind, like long glowing ribbons. Shallan thought she had never in her life seen something so graceful. She didn't *deserve* to see something so divine. As if merely by gazing at it, she sullied it with the cares of a world that it should never touch.

Notum pulled up, controlling the grand spren with a simple bridle of twisted threads. "Human prince," he said to Adolin, "it is here where I must turn another way. I am forbidden to approach Lasting Integrity. I'll patrol along to the south, instead of continuing west."

They'd invited the honorspren to join them, since his patrol had been going along the coast nearby. He'd refused every invitation.

"I wish you the best then, Notum," Adolin said. "It was good to see you again. Thanks for your advice."

"I would prefer you take that advice. I assume you have not reconsidered your imprudent quest?"

"I've reconsidered plenty," Adolin said. "I'm still going to try it though."

"As you wish," Notum said, then saluted. "If I don't see you after you're turned away, give my best to the Ancient Daughter. It is . . . well that she is not trapped in the stronghold. It would not suit her."

The honorspren turned to go.

"Notum," Adolin called. "That spren you ride. It's strikingly similar to a horse."

"Is that odd?" he asked.

"Most spren appear nothing like creatures from our world."

Notum smiled, a rare expression on the spren's face, then gestured to himself. "Do we not?"

"The humanoid ones, yes," Adolin said. "I've never seen one in the shape of a horse."

"Not all spren were imagined by men, Adolin Kholin," Notum called to him. "Farewell."

As he turned and rode his graceful animal away, Shallan nearly emerged to sketch the thing.

"Storms," Adolin said. "He's so cold, and he's one of the spren who seem to *like* us. I'm not feeling good about this entire mission."

"Maybe I can sneak in," Veil said. "If they do turn us away."

"What would that accomplish?" Adolin asked.

"I could see if all the honorspren feel the same way, perhaps. Or if there are a few tyrants in charge who refuse to listen to reason."

"That doesn't feel like the way spren work, Veil. I have a terrible feeling this is going to go all wrong. And I'll have come all this way, only to need to slink back to Father and tell him I failed. Again."

"Through no fault of your own, Adolin."

"Father talks about the importance of the journey, Veil, but he's always been equally focused on results. He's always able to get them himself, so it baffles him why everyone else always seems so incompetent."

Adolin had an unrealistic view of Dalinar. The Blackthorn had an enviable reputation, yes, but he'd clearly suffered his own failures—not the least of which had been letting his brother be assassinated. He'd certainly done less to help in *that* attack than Adolin had in trying to get Elhokar out of Kholinar as it fell.

Arguing was, of course, useless. Adolin should know his father's failings better than anyone. He wasn't going to suddenly recognize them because Veil said something now.

"Any luck getting Shallan to come out?" he asked her.

"I got a thought from her a little earlier," Veil said. "But other than that . . . no. I even did a sketch of you. A terrible one, I'll note. I particularly liked the buck teeth."

Adolin grunted. And together they continued their walk. He led the way through a hollow in the obsidian, where the strange rock mimicked a rolling wave. The constant sound of clacking beads became a quiet hum as they moved farther from the shore, and Shallan stirred again. The landscape here was so *interesting*.

Plants grew like frost here, coating much of the obsidian—and they crackled wherever she and Adolin stepped, breaking and tinkling to dust. Larger plants grew like cones, with spirals of color in their translucent skin, as if crafted by a master glassblower. She touched one, expecting it to be fragile like many other Shadesmar plants, but it was sturdy and thick.

Tiny spren watched them from beneath the leaves of small clumping trees. Jagged lightning branches made of something that wasn't quite glass—for it was too rough to the touch—sprouted silvery leaves that felt metallic and cold. The spren hopped from one branch to another, little more than shadows of swirling smoke with large eyes.

And they move a little like smoke too, Shallan thought. *Curling in the vectors of heat above a fire, alive like the soul of a flame long extinguished remembering its former light . . .*

Veil normally reviled such poetic nonsense, but sometimes she could see the world as Shallan did. And it became a brighter place. As they passed a larger stand of the trees, Adolin reached down to take her hand and help her up onto a ridge. Touching her freehand to his skin made something spark.

His touch is a flame never extinguished. Bright and alive, and the only smoke is in his eyes . . .

They walked along the ridge, and she could pick out the camp below, where the others were packing up their things. Was anyone lingering near her trunk?

Thinking of that almost pushed Shallan away to hide again. Veil, however, had a thought. They needed to leave the device unguarded in a non-suspicious way, then catch who used it. Out here in the caravan, rather than cooped up on the barge, she should be able to make the opportunity extremely appealing. She could perhaps pretend to get drunk. As she had the evening before the last time she knew for certain the spy had moved the device.

"I saw you in there, Shallan," Adolin said, gripping her hand as they stood on the ridge. "Just now. I'm sure of it."

Veil glanced away. Feeling like she was intruding.

He squeezed her hand. "I know it's still you, Shallan. That they're all you. I'm worried though. We're worried. Veil says you feel like you need to hide from me. But you don't. I won't leave, no matter what you've done."

"Shallan is weak," Shallan whispered. "She needs Veil to protect her."

"Was Shallan too weak to save her brothers?" Adolin asked. "To protect her family against her own parents?"

She squeezed her eyes closed.

He pulled her closer. "I don't know the perfect words, Shallan. I just want you to know that I'm here, and I'm trying." Then he gestured, leading her farther along the ridge.

"Where are we going?" she asked. "This isn't some casual stroll, is it?"

"Ua'pam has walked this caravan route before," Adolin replied. "He mentioned the view up along here is gorgeous."

Veil narrowed her eyes, but really, was she going to be suspicious of *Adolin*? She forced her attention back to the spy problem as she followed him, but storms, he was right. The view up here was breathtaking. The endless sea of beads reflected distant sunlight from a million different spheres. They caught the light, and for a moment she thought the entire ocean had caught fire.

Her hand twitched on the strap of her satchel, to reach for her sketchbook, but she remained firm and left it alone. Instead she walked with Adolin to the end of the ridge where the obsidian rose in a low spire, overgrown with a type of delicate plant. Flowering blooms that looked almost fungal, though they glowed with their own inner light, red like molten rock.

I should sketch those. . . .

Then, overhead, the strange Shadesmar clouds began to churn. She gasped as something *emerged* from them high above: an incredible beast with an ashen carapace and a long neck. It resembled a greatshell, faintly echoing the sinuous look of a chasmfiend, but flew somehow on enormous insect wings—seven sets of them. It trailed clouds behind it, emerging as if from a shroud of dust. Others clung to its chin, giving it a beard made of clouds.

She stared as it passed directly overhead, and she noticed sparkling lights along its wings and legs. They glowed beneath its skin or shell—like they were points on a constellation, marking its joints and outline.

"Ash's brush of endless paint . . ." Shallan said. "Adolin, it's a starspren. That's a *starspren*!"

He grinned, taking in its majesty.

"Holy halls!" Shallan said, scrambling to get out her sketchbook. "I have to draw it. Hold this." She handed him her satchel and pulled out the sketchbook and charcoal. She could take a Memory—she took several as it passed—but she wanted to capture the moment, the grace, the *majesty*.

"You knew," she said, sitting to better brace the sketchbook.

"Ua'pam told me," Adolin said. "There are certain places where you can see them emerge. From other angles they're invisible. This place is . . . a little weird."

"A little? Adolin dear, I'm *a little* weird. This place is downright bizarre."

"Wonderful, isn't it?"

Shallan grinned, getting down some sweeping lines of the thing as it landed on a different section of clouds above. A few creationspren peeked out of her satchel, little swirling bits of color. When had those hidden in there?

Storms . . . she felt as if she could see the starspren's every detail, though it was distant. As it reclined on the cloud, it leaned over—as if looking straight at her. Then it threw its head back, arching its neck, and held the position.

"Storms!" she said. "It's *posing*. Vainglorious spren monster. Here, hand me that smaller charcoal pencil. I need to do some detail."

He handed it to her, then settled on the ground beside her. "It's good to see you drawing."

"You knew what this would do to me," she said. "You deliberately put me in a position where I'd *have* to start sketching. And here I was thinking how ingenuous you are."

"I only wanted to see you enjoy yourself," he said. "You've been so serious these last few weeks."

She sketched by instinct, absorbing the sight and bleeding it out on the paper. It wasn't a completely automatic process, but it did leave her mind free.

What she found, with barely any effort, left her feeling embarrassed. "I'm sorry," she said. "I just . . . I'm dealing with some difficult things."

He nodded and didn't push her. Wonderful man.

"Veil is really coming around to you lately," she noted. "And Radiant always liked you."

"That's great," he said. "I still worry you've been . . . odd these last few weeks. And uncommonly unlike yourself."

"Veil is part of my self, Adolin. So is Radiant. We have a balance."

"Are you sure that's the right word?"

She didn't particularly want to argue. She'd been Veil more lately because there was more for Veil to do. In Urithiru, she was Shallan or Radiant a much larger portion of the time.

Nevertheless, it was good to . . . let go. Maybe she *ought* to break out the last of the wine and force some relaxation into their stomach. The way Adolin had been pacing so much, he could probably use a nice diverting evening in her arms.

"I feel like he's watching me," Adolin said, gazing up at the majestic starspren.

"That's because it is," Shallan said. "Spren notice when they're being watched. Recent scholarly reports indicate spren will *change* based on direct individual perception. Like, you can be in another room and think about the spren, and it will respond."

"Now *that's* bizarre," Adolin said.

"And somehow normal at the same time," Shallan said.

"Like you?" Adolin said.

She glanced at him and caught a grin on his face, then found herself smiling in return. "Like every person, I think. We're all strangely normal. Or normally strange."

"Not my father."

"Oh, *especially* your father. Do you think it's *normal* for a person to look as if their parentage involved an anvil and an uncommonly stern storm-cloud?"

"So . . . what are you saying about me?"

"That you take after your mother, obviously." She drew a bold stroke, finishing off her sketch. She sprayed lacquer on it, then set it aside and started another one immediately. This was *not* a one-sketch experience.

As soon as she put charcoal to paper, however, she found herself drawing Adolin as he stared up at the sky.

"How in the world," she said, "did I get lucky enough to grab you, Adolin Kholin? Someone *should* have snatched you up years ago."

He grinned. "They tried. I ruined it quite spectacularly each time."

"At least *your* first crush didn't try to kill you."

"I recall you saying he tried to *avoid* killing you, but failed. Something about jam."

"Mmm . . ." she said. "I'm sick enough of rations, I'd probably eat some jam on Thaylen bread even if it *was* poisoned."

"My first crush didn't try to kill me," Adolin said, "but I probably could have died of embarrassment from the interaction."

She leaned forward immediately, opening her eyes wide. "Oooh . . ."

He glanced at her, then blushed. "Storms. I *really* shouldn't have said anything."

"Can't stop now," she said, poking him in the side with her foot. "Go on. Talk."

"I'd rather not."

"Tough." She poked him again. "I can keep going. I'm a storming Knight Radiant. I have *legendary* endurance for annoying people. If I have to use up every last gemstone on this fight, I'll—"

"Ow," he said. "Look, it's not even that good a story. There was this girl, Idani, a cousin to the Khal boys. She was . . . uncommonly well put together for a fourteen-year-old. She was a bit older than I was, and let's just say she understood the world better than I did."

Shallan cocked her head. "What?"

"Well, she kept talking about how she loved swords. And how I was supposed to have a great sword. And how she wanted to see me wield my sword. And . . ."

"And what?"

"I bought her a sword," he said, shrugging. "As a gift."

"Oh Adolin."

"I was *fourteen*!" he said. "What fourteen-year-old understands innuendo? I thought she actually wanted a sword!"

"What is a girl going to do with a sword? A real one, mind you. This conversation could *quickly* get off track. . . ."

"I don't know!" he said. "I figured she thought they were nifty. Who doesn't think they're nifty?" He rubbed his side, where Shallan had been poking him. "It was a *really* nifty sword, too. Classic antique ulius, the style used in lighteyed challenges of honor during the Sunmaker's reign. Had a little nick in it from the Velinar/Gulastis duel."

"I assume you told poor Idani about all this, at length?"

"I went on for like an hour," Adolin admitted. "She finally grew bored and drifted off. Didn't even take her storming gift." He glanced at Shallan, then grinned. "I got to keep the sword though. Still have it."

"Did you ever figure it out? What she was saying?"

"Eventually," he said. "But by then . . . things had changed."

She cocked her head, pausing in her sketch.

"I overheard her making fun of Renarin to her friends," Adolin said. "She said some . . . nasty things. That ruined something in me. She was gorgeous, Shallan. At the time, my little mind figured she must be the most divine thing that ever walked the land.

"Then I heard her saying those things. I don't think I'd ever realized, until that moment, that a person could be beautiful and ugly at the same time. When you're a teenage boy, you want the beautiful people to be truly beautiful. It's hard to see otherwise, stupid as it sounds. I guess I owe her for that."

"It's a lesson a lot of people never learn, Adolin."

"I suppose. Thing is, there's more to it. She was newly moved into the city, and was desperate to find a place. So her joking about Renarin was crass, yes, but she was trying so hard to find acceptance. I don't see an evil child in her now. The others were unkind to Renarin, and she figured she could bond by doing likewise."

"Doesn't excuse that kind of behavior."

"You used to think he was weird too," Adolin noted.

"Maybe," Shallan said, as it was uncomfortably true. "But I came around, and I never gossiped about him. It merely took you showing me that while he was weird, it was the good kind. As an expert on weird, I'm uniquely qualified to know." She returned to her sketch of Adolin, focusing on his eyes. There was so much in his eyes.

"I don't excuse the things Idani said," Adolin said. "I simply feel it's important to recognize that she might have had reasons. We all have reasons why we fail to live up to what we should be. . . ."

Shallan froze, pencil hovering above the sketchbook page. So. That was what he was about. "You don't have to live up to what your father wants you to be, Adolin."

"No one ever accomplished anything by being content with who they were, Shallan," Adolin said. "We accomplish great things by reaching toward who we *could* become."

"As long as it's what *you* want to become. Not what someone else thinks you *should* become."

He continued staring at the sky, stretched out, somehow making it seem comfortable to be lying with his head on a rock. Wonderfully messy hair, blond peppered black, impeccable uniform. And that face in between. Not messy, not impeccable, just . . . him.

"It wasn't long ago," Adolin said, "that all I wanted was for everyone to respect my father again. We thought he was aging, losing his senses. I wanted everyone else to see him as I did. How did I lose that, Shallan? I mean, I'm proud of him. He's becoming someone who deserves love, and not merely respect.

"But storms, these days I can't stand to be *around* him. He's become everything I wanted him to be, and that transformation shoved us apart."

"It wasn't what you found out he'd done? To . . . her?"

"That's part of it," Adolin admitted. "It hurts. I love him, but can't yet forgive him. I think I will, with time. There's more though. Straining our relationship. He has this misguided notion that I've always been better than him.

"To Father, I'm some pristine remnant of my mother—this noble little statue who got all of her goodness and none of his coarseness. He doesn't want me to be me, or even him. He wants me to be this imagined perfect child who was born better than he ever could be."

"And that makes you not a person," Shallan said, nodding. "It erases your ability to make choices or mistakes. Because you're perfect. You were born to be perfect. So you can never earn anything on your own."

He reached over, putting his hand on her knee, and met her gaze—almost teary-eyed. Because she understood. And storms, she did. She rested her hand on his, then pulled him closer. Feeling his breath on her neck as he drew close. She kissed him then, and as she did, she caught a glimpse of the sky. The majestic spren had started to fade into the cloud—perhaps feeling ignored now that her attention was on someone else.

Well, it wasn't the spren's fault.

It simply couldn't compete.

THE STRENGTH
OF A SOLDIER

*You say that the power itself must be treated as separate in our
minds from the Vessel who controls it.*

Adolin walked a little easier, knowing he could get through to
Shallan. So, after returning from seeing the starspren, he gave
Ua'pam a thumbs-up. It had been an excellent suggestion, and
the alone time had been exactly what they needed.

Shallan gave him a fond hug and a squeeze of the arms before hurrying off to gather her things. It made sense, he supposed, that she'd been
nervous lately. A spy had infiltrated their quest here. Perhaps he hadn't
devoted enough thought to that particular problem.

That was Shallan's area of expertise though. Illusions, lies, art, and
fiction. Politics was supposed to be his. He'd been raised as second in
line for the throne—eventually third, following little Gav's birth. Though
Adolin had turned down that very throne when it had been offered to him,
he should make a competent emissary to a foreign nation.

Appeal to their honor, he thought, remembering Arshqqam's suggestion.

He sought out Gallant and took him from the grooms to load the horse's
burden himself: the swords in their sheaths, the box of other weapons, then
the trunk of clothing on the opposite side. He stared into Gallant's blue
eyes. Adolin often felt he could see some kind of light deep within them.

"Must be nice," Adolin said, patting the horse, "to not have to worry
about things like politics or relationships."

The horse snorted in a way that Adolin thought was distinctly dismissive. Well, perhaps there was more to complicate a horse's life than a man
could ever see.

Malli, Felt's wife, led Maya over. Adolin had asked the scribe to look after Maya while he went on his walk. He gestured toward the Ryshadium. "Shall we?"

It was hard to get any kind of acknowledgment out of Maya, but he did prefer to ask. Indeed, he thought he got a nod out of her. He took it as permission, so he helped her up onto the horse. The first few times getting her mounted had been a difficult process, involving stepping on some boxes and pulling her awkwardly into the saddle. Now she knew what to do, though—and only needed a hand over the saddle to help her into place.

Maya was heavier than she appeared, made of thick cords that were tight and dense, like muscle. Still, even at the start, it had been worth the effort to get her into the seat. It made traveling easier, as she would sit placidly on the horse and follow the rest of them. Plus, Adolin admitted that he felt better with Gallant watching over her. The Ryshadium understood. You took special care of a soldier who had left part of herself on the battlefield.

They started out for the day, Adolin leading the column, though Godeke and his spren were scouting ahead. The solemn Edgedancer didn't have any Stormlight—they'd used the last of it the previous night, making food stores for the trip home—but Godeke had practice scouting as part of his Radiant training.

Adolin spent the early part of the hike trying to settle on a final strategy for approaching the honorspren. The others were right; the ideas he'd presented were unlikely to work. So, he'd start with the letters. Could he develop a backup plan though?

Nothing came to him, and by midday he'd lost any sense of calm or satisfaction he'd gained from the morning with Shallan. With effort, he kept himself from snapping when Felt came up from the rear guard. The foreign scout had been a stable, valuable part of the mission so far. Felt might not be quite as spry as he'd once been, but he seemed to have a sixth sense for traveling in unknown places.

"Brightlord," the man said, wearing a floppy old hat. He'd inherited that when Bashin had retired from service, and he now wore it as a memento. While not regulation, it was the kind of thing you let a man like Felt get away with. "The humans just broke and turned away toward the south. Looks like they've given up on following us."

"Really?" Adolin asked. "Now, of all times?"

"Yeah. Feels strange to me, though I can't exactly pinpoint why."

Adolin gave the call for a break and a snack. Merit approached to unload Gallant to give him a rest, and Adolin followed Felt to the rear of the small column. Here they climbed up a small outcropping of obsidian—fragile glass plants crackling and shattering underfoot, lifespren dodging away—where they could use spyglasses to observe the Tukari.

The strange group of humans was now far enough away that he could barely make them out in the dim Shadesmar landscape. They had indeed turned southward.

"Why would they chase us all this way," Adolin said, "then give up now?"

"Maybe they *weren't* chasing us. They could have simply been going this direction anyway; that would explain why they were always careful to stay away from us and not catch up."

A valid point—in fact, if the humans hadn't seemed so unusual to him upon their first meeting, Adolin probably would have assumed this all along. He hadn't thought it odd that Notum was traveling this same way. Why should he have worried so much about these humans?

There is *something odd about them,* he thought. *The way they hovered so close, the way they watched us . . .*

Adolin studied them through the spyglass, though at this distance he could make out little more than the shadows of figures carrying torches. "Well, they do appear to be leaving," he said to Felt, handing back the spyglass. "Keep watch while we eat, just in case."

Adolin was halfway back to the front of the column when the truth struck him.

⁂

Veil closed the top of the trunk with the communication cube, then locked it. She couldn't always rely on the spy to return the cube in a different orientation after moving it, so—using a trick she'd learned from Tyn long ago—she'd started dusting it with a faint bit of powder.

It hadn't been disturbed all this trip, so far as she could tell. She needed to find a way to use it as bait, leaving it alone in a tempting way. Pondering that, she walked over and took a bowl of mush from Ishnah. Veil braced herself to eat the terrible Soulcast stuff. She should force Radiant to take over for meals. Soldiers were accustomed to eating terrible rations in the field, right? Radiant would see it as an honor to eat this slop. It would build character, and—

Adolin dashed past.

Radiant dropped the cup and leaped to her feet. That was the posture of a man running toward a fight. She took off after him, reflexively trying to summon her Shardblade—which of course didn't work. Not here in Shadesmar.

Adolin scrambled up to the top of the outcropping where Felt was still watching their rear. Radiant started climbing, and was joined by two of Adolin's other soldiers. The rest of the Radiants and agents—even Zu the

Stoneward, who always seemed so eager and excitable—just stood looking back with confused expressions.

At the top of the outcropping, she found Adolin peering through a spyglass, tense and alert.

"What?" Radiant asked.

"They weren't following *us*," he said. "Leave a spren or two to watch the camp, then bring everyone else after me! Be ready for a fight."

With that, he leaped off the outcropping. His boots slapped stone below—storms, he *did* remember he wasn't in Shardplate, didn't he? Adolin took off running toward the distant Tukari caravan, hand on the sheathed sword at his belt, holding it in place.

Radiant stood stunned. Was Adolin going to walk all the way to—

The sound of cracking stone thundered from behind. Radiant jumped, searching the nearby formations for some kind of avalanche. Only then did she realize it was the sound of hooves striking obsidian at high speed as Gallant galloped past. A panicked Maya clung to his mane with a two-fisted grip—but his supplies appeared to have been unloaded.

Barely breaking stride, Adolin grabbed the dangling reins as Gallant pulled up beside him. Adolin did an odd running hop, then hoisted himself into the saddle behind Maya, a maneuver that a part of Radiant's brain refused to believe was possible.

"Rusts," Felt said, lowering his spyglass. "How did the beast know? Did anyone hear Highprince Adolin whistle for it?"

The other soldiers shook their heads.

"Let's move!" Radiant said. "Get the packhorses and send outriders to follow him. I'll have Pattern watch our things. Everyone else get ready to march!"

She had them all going in what she considered an impressively short amount of time. Three soldiers on horses went chasing after Adolin, but they were far slower than the Ryshadium. Something that large shouldn't be so *fast*.

She marched double-time beside Godeke and Zu, and they outpaced the Stump and some of the spren. However, while Radiant's training with Adolin over the last twelve months meant she wasn't soft, she also hadn't done any forced marches.

She'd come to rely on Stormlight. With it, she could have run at a full dash without tiring. Godeke could have slid out ahead of them, moving on the stone like it was ice. They didn't have any Stormlight left, so they followed as best they could. What was it that Adolin had said? The strange humans hadn't been following Adolin's party? So who *had* they been following?

It clicked almost immediately. The humans had skirted close, always in sight, seeming like they wanted to overtake the group—but never daring. They'd turned away today, heading south.

The same direction Notum had gone.

⁘

Riding behind Maya as she clung to Gallant's neck wasn't particularly comfortable for Adolin. Fortunately, the Ryshadium didn't need much direction from him.

Adolin leaned low—gripping the reins, feeling the rhythm of Gallant's hooves pounding the obsidian ground. The Tukari humans had likely planned to jump Notum soon after his patrol left the port town, but had held off once Adolin's group started going the same way. They'd likely worried Adolin's team would come to Notum's defense.

They'd stayed close, never daring to attack. Until at last Notum had turned south while Adolin continued west.

Gallant was sweating heavily by the time they approached the humans' caravan. They'd left some people behind with supplies and sent a larger group after Notum, bearing torches. Adolin ignored the ones guarding the supplies. He leaned lower, one hand around Maya's waist, hoping he was wrong. Hoping this was all about nothing.

Adolin's worry mounted as he drew closer. Harsh torchlight. Figures shouting.

"When we get there," Adolin said to the horse, "stay out of the fight."

Gallant snorted his disagreement.

"I'll need you to get me out," Adolin said, "and you'll need to catch your breath to do that."

Ryshadium were far more than the average warhorse, with speed that seemed to defy their grand size. That said, they weren't built for long gallops.

And Adolin wasn't built for fighting a large group on his own. The others would be far behind. So what was Adolin's plan? If Notum really was in trouble, Adolin couldn't very well face ten or more people without his Plate.

He drew close, picking out men in thick, patterned Tukari clothing holding aloft torches and swords—short one-handed cutlasses with a steep curve to them. Chopping weapons, common sidearms. Only two of the enemy had shields, and there was no armor to speak of, though he did spot a few spears that he'd need to keep in mind.

They'd stopped in a large circle, surrounding something at their center. Adolin gritted his teeth and guided Gallant with his knees to charge in close so he could survey better. Spren had been . . . cagey about whether they could be killed in Shadesmar. He'd seen them carry weapons, and during his earlier trip, Notum's sailors had admitted that spren could be cut and would feel pain. "Killing" them involved hurting them so much that their minds broke and they became something akin to a deadeye.

Stormfather! Adolin caught enough as he rode by; his worst fears were true. In the center of the group, a glowing figure lay huddled on the ground, bound in ropes. Over a dozen animated Tukari were repeatedly stabbing him with spears and swords. Notum's attendants—a group of three Reachers—had been bound and set in a row. Perhaps they would be next to suffer torture.

The assailants didn't appear to have bows, fortunately, so Gallant made it past them without incident. In fact, Adolin was increasingly certain from their postures and lack of discipline that this was more a mob than a force of soldiers. Why would they attack an honorspren? How had they even gotten into Shadesmar in the first place?

Adolin reined in once they were a safe distance away. He'd hoped to draw some of the Tukari away after him, but they remained clustered, a good twenty men with torches, spears, swords. After briefly glancing at Adolin, they returned to stabbing at Notum.

Storms. How long could a spren last under such treatment?

Adolin checked for help—spotting several figures on horseback approaching in the distance—but it would be precious minutes before they were close enough. Jeopardize the mission, or go save Notum on his own?

Jeopardize it how? he thought. *You barely know what you're doing here. The others can deliver some letters.*

You're nothing but a uniform and sword, Adolin. Use them.

He swung off Gallant. "If this goes poorly, get Maya to the others," he told the horse. "I'm going to stall those men."

Gallant blew out again. He was accustomed to riding into combat with Dalinar.

"No," Adolin said. "You'll get hurt."

Maya grabbed his shoulder with a tense hand. She'd spent the ride holding tightly to Gallant's mane, and he sensed terror from her—perhaps at moving so quickly. He looked to her scratched-out expression, feeling her grip on his uniform shoulder.

"If I draw those men off, Maya," he said, "can you get to Notum and cut him free? You could use one of the swords in the saddle sheaths."

Her reply was a low growl, half a whine, and a tightening of her grip on his shoulder.

"It's all right," he said, prying her fingers free. "It's not your fault. Stay here. Stay safe."

Adolin took a deep breath and heaved his greatsword from its scabbard on Gallant's shoulder. His swordstaff was back at camp, in the box of weapons—along with his shield and helm. So his best option against this rabble was the weapon with the best reach.

He hefted the massive sword. It was thinner than a Shardblade, but as long as many—and heavier. Many swordsmen he knew looked down on them as inferior to Shardblades, but you could use many of the same sword forms—and there was something *solid* about a greatsword that Adolin had always liked.

He strode across the black obsidian ground and started shouting. "Hey!" he said, holding the sword out to the side with both hands. "Hey!"

That got their attention. The dark figures moved away from Notum, a huddled form of soft white and blue.

Right, then, Adolin thought. *Stall for time.* He didn't have to defeat all twenty men here; he only had to last long enough for his soldiers to arrive and help even the odds.

Unfortunately, even if these Tukari weren't battle-trained, he was at a severe disadvantage. As a young man—his head full of stories of Shard-bearers defeating entire companies on their own—he'd assumed he could easily take on two or three opponents at once in a bout. He'd been sorely disabused of this notion. Yes, one man could stand against many with proper training—but it was never preferable. It was too easy to get sur-rounded, too easy to take a strike from behind while you were engaging someone else.

Unless your enemy didn't know what they were doing. Unless they were frightened. Unless you could keep them from pressing their advantage. He wouldn't win here because he outdueled anyone.

He'd win because his opponents lost.

"Hey, let's talk!" Adolin said. "You've got an honorspren there. How much do you want for him?"

They responded in Tukari, and as before—when he'd approached them in the camp—their postures were immediately hostile. They advanced on him with their weapons out, bearded faces and thick hair accenting their dark expressions. Adolin caught anticipationspren, like enormous lurgs, hovering around the outside of the battlefield. Even heard a painspren howl in the distance.

"Don't suppose you'd agree to fighting one at a time," Adolin said. "A set of friendly duels? I'll go easy on you, I promise."

They drew closer and closer, just a few feet away now. One spearman was out in front of the others. Spears would be most dangerous; Adolin would have reach against the ones with cutlasses.

"I guess not," he said with a sigh.

Then he launched himself forward, greatsword in a firm two-handed grip. He batted away the first man's spear thrust, then came in with a wide powerful swing and took off the man's head.

That was harder to do than people sometimes thought—even the sharpest blade could get caught in muscle or on the spine. Angle was everything, that and follow-through.

Ignoring the gore of the strike, Adolin moved into Flamestance. Fast. Brutal. The other Tukari came at him, and Adolin rounded them to the side, trying to keep out of the point of their haphazard formation. His quick motions kept them off balance as they scrambled to try to surround him.

Training, fortunately, was on Adolin's side. He knew how to keep moving, putting as many of them in front of him as possible. Untrained soldiers would move in packs, letting you get around them and keep them from your back. And they shied away as he made great sweeps with his sword, more warding blows than actual attacks.

As he dodged around the side, some of them glanced the other way as a soldier at the rear barked an order. That cost them. Adolin crashed into the pack's flank, slamming the greatsword into one man's side, then ripping it free with a heave and slashing across another's throat with the backswing. He gutted one more with a lunge—another spearman, his primary goal for this offensive.

The men shouted and scattered away in a panic, the man he'd speared through screaming and stumbling. Even those accustomed to battle could be intimidated by the casual brutality of a greatsword at work. Adolin managed to catch one final Tukari, who wasn't quick enough to get away. Adolin connected with a large sweep into the man's arm.

The Tukari howled, dropping his weapon, and Adolin kicked him while yanking at the sword—which had gotten caught in the bone. Adolin pulled it free with effort and a spray of blood, then did a full-body spin and swept outward, making the others leap away in fear. This wasn't the delicate beautiful dance of a duel—this wasn't what he loved. This was butchery. Fortunately, he had some good role models in that realm.

His best allies were speed and intimidation. As he'd hoped, these men responded poorly to losing several of their number in such a swift, terrible strike. They shied away instead of pressing their numerical advantage. They cried out in shock, anger, and fear as he engaged the next man—isolating this foe in a line between Adolin and the others, so they wouldn't have a clear rush at him. Adolin struck in rapid succession to batter away the man's shield, then cut him down with a strike at the collarbone.

Not the cleanest kill, that, but the blood on Adolin's uniform and face must have made him fearsome—for the Tukari scrambled even farther back, shouting in their language. Now, unfortunately, came the bad part.

Adolin tried to keep them frightened by advancing on the nearest man, but they refused to engage him—and kept trying to surround him.

When you were alone in the open, simply keeping from being surrounded was a chore. He had to dedicate all his attention to dancing backward, using sweeps to ward away foes, looking for an opening—but constantly wary of letting anyone get behind him. He could do that, so long as he didn't get tired—but they'd wear him down eventually, and he'd slow.

He tried another ploy, moving to Stonestance, a warding posture, trying to conserve energy. So long as they were circling him, afraid of him like they might fear a hissing skyeel, it gave more time for the others to arrive.

This allowed him to move in close to Notum, who was groaning, his body pierced in a dozen places with wounds that bled a fine, white-blue mist. Unfortunately, his bonds were tight—and even if he could get free, Adolin doubted he'd be able to run for safety in his condition.

Keep stalling, Adolin thought, but the enemy was closing in again. He'd brutalized them quickly and efficiently at first—but it was still fourteen on one, and they seemed to realize he was doomed. They pulled tighter around him, forcing him to keep moving and trying to watch all of them at once.

There was one man left with a shield, and he shouted orders. Four came running, two from the left, two from the right. That leader must have had some combat experience—for he didn't send everyone at once, as a chaotic jumble would have favored Adolin. Better to have the others wait until he was engaged, then come in and overwhelm him.

With a soft curse, Adolin engaged the first pair swiftly, his sole hope being to fell those two, then get at the two behind. Unfortunately, these front two fought defensively, raising their swords and refusing to fully engage him. He was forced to spin and sweep at the two on the other side—then try to come back and keep the front two from taking him.

He managed to land a blow, but as he was engaged in keeping from being surrounded, the leader sent others at him—just running. Storms. He had to dodge to the side to prevent himself from getting knocked over, and while he cut down two that came running, the resulting chaos was just what he'd feared. They managed to surround him as he was so distracted trying to keep from getting knocked down.

In the jumble, he ended up getting pressed by two men with swords, who forced in so close as he came out of a spin that he had to half-sword his greatsword. That let him get a precision strike at the throat of one of the enemies, but left his back open. He heard the boots on stone, and while Adolin tried to spin in time, he was too late. The man's off-center spear thrust took Adolin on his right side, near the stomach.

Adolin grunted at the pain, but managed to get his sword in and batter the spearman away. Damnation. He'd taken exactly the kind of hit he'd feared—an unseen spear while he was overwhelmed. His own blood began to stain his uniform; the end had begun. They didn't have to defeat him in some spectacular duel; they merely had to cut him a few times and let blood loss drop him.

But if I can just hold on . . .

The howl of a painspren echoed in the distance. Adolin fought off his nearest foes, intimidating them backward with a roar and several grand sweeps. However, the leader sent in four fresh swordsmen. They'd have done better if they all had spears, but it gave scant advantage to Adolin, as he had to fight wildly—with callous sweeps—to try to keep them all away. Adolin was proud that, as one attacker stumbled, he was able to strike at the man's exposed thigh and send him screaming to the ground.

The cries of their wounded friend frightened the others for a brief moment, until their captain shouted them back into place. Maybe if Adolin could get at that man, a figure wearing a blue-on-yellow-patterned overcoat . . .

Adolin tried, but two men stepped in to defend the leader. Boots on stone behind made Adolin spin, block, then spin again. All around him, others danced in a strange motion, moving unexpectedly. Adolin was tiring, and it was getting harder and harder to keep them all on one side of him.

Plus, they were untrained—which could be dangerous. Untrained soldiers were far more aggressive, not realizing that they were likely to just leave you both dead with those kinds of tactics. Adolin couldn't watch them all, let alone fight them all, and he felt his own doom as he leaped away from an attack—and his back connected with someone behind him. They had gotten in that close? He braced himself for the blade that would follow.

Instead he heard a low growl.

Startled, Adolin glanced over his shoulder to find that the figure he'd run into had put *her* back to *his*. Maya had his shortsword out of its sheath, but she held it like a baton, her arm outstretched, sword straight up. Not an effective stance—plus, when the enemy drew close, she didn't swing at them, but merely growled.

"You shouldn't have come," Adolin said, warm blood from his wound leaking down his side and leg. He didn't dare try to stanch it, or he'd leave his hand slippery for the fight. "But thank you."

She growled in return. Gallant approached to the left, completely disobeying orders, but two of the enemy who still had spears noticed and began forcing him away. The remaining Tukari moved around Adolin and Maya, predatory, circling. They seemed concerned about this new arrival, though Adolin wasn't certain how long that hesitance would last. They'd soon realize she wasn't much of a threat.

Unless . . .

"Maya!" Adolin said, resetting his stance with arms overhead, holding the sword in a distinctive manner. The way Zahel had taught him to do his morning kata.

She glanced at him, and though he couldn't read her scratched-out eyes, something changed in her posture. She seemed to understand. She'd done this kata with Adolin every morning out here, and before that he'd done it with her as his sword countless times.

Blessedly, she moved into the same form, now holding the sword in a proper grip, her stance powerful.

"Go," he said. He began the kata, and she did likewise. It wasn't meant for actual fighting, but it looked impressive, sweeping with glistening blades.

The Tukari leader glanced toward the approaching horses bearing Adolin's soldiers, then barked a command. His men pressed closer to Adolin, though they seemed terrified of Maya. And who wouldn't be? A deadeye, *fighting*? A couple were distracted by Gallant, who came in snorting.

Most importantly, Adolin's biggest disadvantage had been mitigated. He didn't have to watch his back. Even wounded, warm blood staining his side, Adolin felt his confidence surge. Three men came at him, and Adolin stood firm. No. He would not be pushed around.

Never underestimate the strength of a soldier trained to stand fast.

He roared at the men, swinging his greatsword before them, breaking their charge as they pulled up short. Yes, a crowd could overwhelm one, and sword skill could only hold them back so long. But training was about more than learning to swing a weapon. It was about confidence.

Never underestimate the simple intimidating force of a man who won't back down.

The first came at Adolin with a sword, but hadn't been caring for his weapon. The handguard had come off, so Adolin hacked the man's fingers as they wrapped the hilt of the weapon, dropping them. A foolish mistake; a good swordmaster *always* taught you to watch your hands. As this man screamed, the other two came in, and Adolin did a full-bodied lunge, stretching out the greatsword with a reach that obviously surprised the men as Adolin speared right through the stomach of one from a full body-length away. Adolin reset, stepping forward and spinning, putting all his weight and momentum into the strike that hit the second man. And another head went flying.

Movement at his side showed two others approaching, but as Adolin returned to his stance and put his back to Maya, they—they scrambled away. With their friends dying on the ground before them, these men had had enough. Trembling, they ran away yelling, joined by their friend who had lost his fingers, cradling his bloody hand.

The Tukari leader himself came in with one bodyguard as others began to scatter. Adolin didn't retreat a single step as he met the bodyguard, sidestepping his lunge.

Never underestimate the worth of being willing to hold.

Your.

GROUND.

He shouldered aside the stumbling bodyguard, then swept out and nearly managed to take the leader's head—the man dodged just in time, escaping with a gash in his shoulder instead. Thundering sounds made it seem like Adolin's soldiers were close, though it was only Gallant, brilliantly stomping loudly and letting out a scream.

Together, it was too much for the men. Adolin didn't win.

But the Tukari lost, running toward their supply dump and the safety of the numbers they'd left behind. The leader finally joined them.

When Felt and the others arrived a few minutes later, they found a bloodied Adolin propping up Notum—dazed, but alive—surrounded by the corpses of what had once been overwhelming odds against him.

Among the Radiant spren, the honorspren civilization appears to be the most humanlike in its organization, ranks, and hierarchy. They are also the spren most devastated by the Recreance, having rebuilt only a fraction of their former numbers. Countless deadeye honorspren wander the floors of the bead seas.

The substance of their forms is made up of a softly glowing light, yet their hair, skin, and clothing all feel physical as real as a human's.

Their clothing is composed of the same light as their bodies. The fashions range from military uniforms to loose, flowing robes. The style of clothing seems to correlate in some respects with their personal beliefs, even more so than a human's might.

They wear very real steel swords

They most often appear in the Physical Realm as miniature versions of their Shadesmar selves, made from the same blue-white light, though they may wear any shape they wish and will change their forms on a whim. Often they mimic windspren, appearing as ribbons of light that ride unseen currents.

I find this difficult to do on an intrinsic level, as although I am nei-
ther Ruin nor Preservation, they make up me.

"I cannot fathom this," Notum said, staring ahead. He didn't blink. "I just cannot *fathom* this."

Radiant had noticed that quirk in numerous spren in this world; they forgot to blink when they were distracted or overwhelmed. She shooed away the shockspren who were clustering around the spren, practically trying to climb in his lap. It was so strange for all the spren here to have physical forms; they sometimes had to be pushed away with a weapon.

Adolin's soldiers stood in a cluster on a nearby rise, spyglasses to their eyes, keeping a cautious watch on the enemy caravan. It was—fortunately— withdrawing. Shallan's agents were circumspectly going through the pockets of the dead, searching for clues to their origins. She spotted Vathah depositing some spheres into his own pouch, and was going to shout at him, but Veil persuaded her to hold her tongue. What else were they going to do? Leave the money?

The spheres, as expected, were dun. There was no Stormlight here. Though Godeke had inspected Adolin's side wound and given a good prognosis, she would rather see him healed. Sepsis could claim any wound, but especially gut wounds.

In addition, Radiant suspected Notum could use a little Stormlight. Though his wounds had stopped "bleeding," his glow had dampened noticeably, and his cheery blue-white coloring had become a dull brown-white.

He spoke in a daze. "Why . . . why would they do this? Humans have never . . . attacked spren. What would be the point, the use, the purpose? There is no honor in this!"

His Reacher companions had been released from their bonds as well. In Radiant's experience, the bronze-colored spren tended to be quiet. These three—one male, two female, wearing simple uniforms—gave no response. They seemed as baffled as Notum.

"We need to take you to Lasting Integrity," Adolin said, sitting on a rock nearby as Godeke bound his wound.

"No," Notum said. "No, I am exiled."

"You're wounded, and we can't guarantee those humans won't return the moment we leave you," Adolin said. "Exile or not, you're coming with us."

Notum glanced from Adolin to Radiant, then looked down. "Your honor does you credit, Prince Adolin, but you must realize my presence in your party will do you harm. I was exiled precisely because I showed you leniency in the past. If I arrive with you now, whatever the reason, it will be seen as conspiracy between us."

"We'll deal with that then," Adolin said, wincing as Godeke pulled his bandage tight. "Kelek knows, it's probably not going to matter—since they're likely to turn us away regardless."

"I wish that were not true, but it is," Notum said.

Radiant joined her agents. Ishnah was speaking softly to Beryl, who sat on the ground nearby, picking through some of the loot. Beryl had thrown up several times upon first encountering the corpses, and she still seemed pallid from the sight, though her tan skin tone made that difficult to read.

"Make sure you check the insides of rings, the backs of necklaces," Ishnah was saying. "Sometimes there are inscriptions with names."

Beryl nodded. She kept glancing at the bloodied cloth they'd put over a dead Tukari man's neck stump. She put her hand to her lips, pointedly turning away.

All right, Shallan admitted, *if she's the Ghostblood, she's an* incredible *actor. I agree with Veil. We need to rethink our conclusion there.*

Adolin stood up. "Let's get moving," he said to the others. "I want more space between us and the rest of those Tukari."

It took a little time to get Notum up on one of the horses, during which Godeke—oddly—began moving among the fallen, inspecting their faces.

"Godeke?" Shallan asked.

"They're going to be left out here to rot," Godeke said quietly. "Those others won't come back for them."

"They tried to kill Notum," Adolin said. "And me."

"I realize this," Godeke said. "But we don't know their story. These could be soldiers following orders. They could be confused, mistaking the honorspren for enemies. They could have motives we can't even guess. I want to remember them. In case no one else does."

Edgedancers. Shallan shook her head, then checked on Adolin herself. She poked at his bloodied side. "That's another uniform you've ruined."

"Cold water and a soak in salt can get the blood out," he said. "And I brought my sewing kit. Bet I can have it presentable with a little work."

"Still," she said, resting her head against his chest—careful not to touch the wound. "You need to be careful. We don't have any Stormlight left to heal ourselves."

"So . . . basically it's how it's been for most of my life?" Adolin said. He rested his hand on her back. "Maybe I did get carried away, Shallan. But it was good to find something I could *do*. Successfully, I mean. These days it's not common that I find a place where I'm useful."

"Adolin . . ." She pulled away and studied his face. He was smiling, but his tone wasn't joking.

"Sorry," he said. "That sounded a lot like self-pity, didn't it? I'm just tired. Come on, we really should get going."

That wasn't the end of the discussion—she'd press him on it later—but for now it was probably best to do as he said. They left the corpses and trudged across the open field of obsidian toward their camp. About half-way back, they met the Cryptics—save Pattern—and the Stump with her spren, hiking slowly.

Arshqqam took in the sight, then nodded in satisfaction and turned to start hiking back. Fortunately, Notum *did* seem to be looking better already.

"Your deadeye," he said, moving up beside Adolin. "How did you train her to fight for you like that?"

Shallan glanced at Maya, who was riding on Adolin's Ryshadium. Shallan hadn't seen it, but she'd heard. The dead spren had picked up a sword and fought beside Adolin.

"I didn't train her, Notum," Adolin said. "She chose to help me."

"Deadeyes can't make choices," Notum said. "They don't have the presence of mind for it. I know this personally. My own father is a deadeye, cared for in the fortress now."

"Revise what you know, Notum," Adolin said. "Maybe something changed once Radiants started returning. Or maybe some deadeyes are more responsive than others."

"It simply . . . it doesn't make sense . . ." Notum said, but abandoned the argument.

At their camp, a perky Pattern was happily waving to them. Shallan smiled at that. No matter what else happened, she could count on Pattern to be his same awkward—yet encouraging—self.

Adolin didn't give them time to rest. He ordered the horses watered, but supplies packed up so they could march straight for Lasting Integrity. Radiant took over from Shallan again as he gave the commands, and she immediately recognized the wisdom in them. Despite Adolin's brilliant show of swordplay, their group was quite exposed. Without Stormlight, most of the Radiants barely counted as warriors. Adolin was wounded, and Notum struggled to remain upright. If the Tukari regrouped and decided to charge them . . . Well, best to remove the option and push—difficult as it would be—to reach the honorspren stronghold before the day was done.

Veil checked with Vathah and Ishnah about the corpses they'd searched. The pilfering had been quick, and their findings slim. A few cloth bracelets had patterns Ishnah said she thought were Tukari clan writing.

After that Radiant checked with Pattern, but nothing unusual had happened while they were gone. Finally, as their supplies were being loaded onto the packhorses, Shallan took over and moved to check on Mraize's communication cube out of habit. Shallan unlocked the trunk and popped it open, then gave a quick glance inside. She didn't expect . . .

The powder had been disturbed.

Suppressing her immediate shock, Shallan took a Memory, then shut the trunk and clicked the lock closed. She moved by rote, letting one of the soldiers load it on a horse. Then she stood there, stunned. The powder had been brushed faintly by fingers; she could visualize it *distinctly*. It had been returned in the right orientation, but Veil's trick with the powder revealed the truth.

How . . . She'd checked it earlier. Just before they'd all run off after Adolin. But then she'd left the camp under the watch of . . .

Of Pattern.

"Mmmm . . ." he said, making Shallan jump as she noticed him standing right behind her. "An eventful day with humans! Your lives are always so exciting. Mmm . . ."

"Pattern," Veil said, "nothing happened here while we were gone. You are sure?"

"Yes, very sure. Ha ha. You had excitement, and I was bored. It is irony! Ha ha."

Veil, this can't . . . this can't be possible, Shallan thought. *We can't be suspicious of* Pattern *of all people. It . . . I can't . . .*

Yet hadn't *he* been standing nearby when she'd mentioned the secret to Beryl that had made its way to Mraize? And she'd told him about the orientation issue with the cube, so it was no wonder that this time—in using it—the spy had returned it exactly the right way.

Radiant wasn't convinced. And . . . it was ridiculous, wasn't it? To think Pattern could be spying on her for the Ghostbloods? He loved lies, but she doubted he could manage one himself. At least not one that would fool Veil.

Shallan took over, and tried to put the idea out of her mind as they began walking. But it wouldn't leave her alone. Veil and even Radiant began to wonder. He'd had opportunity. He knew about the communication cube, and had been watching over it the night she'd been drunk.

Shallan's father had belonged to the Ghostbloods; her family had been involved with them all the way back in her youth. Perhaps in her childhood, during those shadowy days she'd forgotten? Could the conspiracy go back that far?

Her association with Pattern stretched back to that time, for certain. She'd used him as a Blade to kill her mother. Shallan had suppressed many of those memories, but this fact was indisputable. Pattern and she had begun to bond nearly a decade ago.

Could Pattern have been working with them all along? Feeding them information about her progress? Leading her to contact them when she'd first come to the warcamps?

The implications of that shook her to the core. If her spren was a spy . . . could she trust anything?

Could she even keep going? This revelation was far, far worse than discovering Vathah or Ishnah had been the spy. This . . . this made her tremble. Made her legs weak.

Shallan, Radiant thought. *Be strong. We don't know all the facts yet.*

No. No, she couldn't be strong. Not in the face of this.

She crawled away, deep within, and started whimpering like a child. Something *was* odd about Pattern, about his interactions with her all along. The way he covered up what happened in the past. The timeline of her past . . . disregarding the holes in it . . . didn't quite work. It never had worked. . . .

Strength, Shallan, Veil thought.

Take over, Shallan thought. *You can face this. It's why you were created.*

Try to keep going, Veil thought, refusing to take over. *Just keep walking. You* can *do this.*

So Shallan reluctantly maintained control. When Adolin called a brief break two hours later, Shallan forced herself to make a quick sketch of the communication cube in its trunk. The Memory was perfect, and the details did not lie. The powder *had* been scuffed with finger marks. It was a very, very thin coating, almost invisible. But her Lightweaver ability allowed her to memorize such details.

Shallan tried hard to ignore the problem, instead focusing on their surroundings, which had grown more uneven and rocky. The glass trees here were beautiful, like they were molten liquid, and made sweeping curls reminiscent of crashing waves. Yes, focus on those. That beauty.

She was particularly thrilled when she spotted what had to be Lasting

Integrity: a large fortress on a bleak outcrop of obsidian jutting out into the bead ocean. Imperious—with high walls crafted of some uniformly blue stone—the large boxy fortress was positioned perfectly to defend a natural bay to the north. You even had to cross a bridge to reach the place. Honorspren, it was clear, did not take fortification lightly.

Shallan wanted to draw it. She could lose herself in the picture and not have to confront other facts. But then Pattern walked up beside her, and she instead whimpered and retreated again.

Veil at last took control. For Shallan's own good.

"We are almost arrived!" Pattern said, his pattern rotating in an intensely excited manner.

Veil needed proof, so she chose her words deliberately. "I've been thinking a lot about your early days with Shallan. It seems possible that the Ghostbloods were watching her when she was a child. If we can discover facts to confirm this, it might help us figure out how to beat them."

"Mm. That makes sense, I suppose!" he said. "I don't remember much though."

"You were together once, in the garden, with Shallan," Veil said—fabricating a complete lie. "I can see her memories. Shallan saw Balat speaking to someone who looked, in hindsight, like she might have been wearing a mask. Do you suppose *he* might be the spy?"

"Oh!" Pattern said. "Your brother? Working with the Ghostbloods? Hmmm . . . That would be painful for you! But maybe it makes sense. Mraize always *does* seem to know too much about your brothers and where they are."

"Do you remember that day in Shallan's past?" Veil pushed. "Anything about it?"

"In the garden, with Balat meeting someone wearing a mask . . ." Pattern said.

"An important moment," Veil said. "You were there. I can remember you being with Shallan."

"Um . . . Yes!" he said. "I remember now. Ha ha. Yes, that happened. Balat and a mysterious figure. You have made my memory start to return, Veil! We were together then. And maybe Balat *is* a spy. My my. That is very naughty of him."

From deep inside, Shallan whimpered again. But Veil, Veil had been *created* to soldier through moments like this. She ignored the profound sickening feeling. Pattern was lying to her.

Pattern was *lying*.

Veil couldn't take anything for granted any longer. She couldn't assume *anyone* was trustworthy. She had to be careful, redouble her defenses, and keep Shallan safe.

"Veil?" Pattern asked. "Are you well? Did I say something wrong?"

"I'm merely thinking," Veil said. "Have you seen any strange spren watching us?"

"The corrupted gloryspren?" he asked. "Like you said to watch out for? No, I have not. Mmm . . ."

She saw something ahead, a small group of riders glowing a faint blue-white. The honorspren had seen them approaching, and had sent a contingent to engage them.

Adolin halted the column, dismounting and telling his soldiers to water the horses and settle everyone. Then he stepped forward, still wearing the bloodied uniform, his side bandaged.

Veil moved to follow. "Keep your eyes—or whatever it is you have—open," she said to Pattern as he ambled along beside her. "These are dangerous times, Pattern. We have to always be on the watch. Careful, lest we be taken advantage of . . ."

"Yes, truly."

Shallan grew very small, very quiet. *It's all right,* Veil thought. *I'll figure it out. I'll find a way to keep you safe. I promise.*

⁘

Adolin stopped in front of his caravan, Shallan at his side. The pain medication he'd taken was working, and he felt only a small ache from his gut wound. And the march here—during which he'd admitted he needed to ride, letting him rest—had helped with his light-headedness.

He still required sleep and time to recover. This wound wouldn't be debilitating, unless it started to rot. But he also wouldn't be in fighting shape for weeks at least.

For now, he kept a strong front. He had Notum stay back, though he was certain the three approaching honorspren had seen him. They rode on those same graceful not-horses that Notum had been riding earlier. His had run off in a panic when he'd been attacked, and they hadn't been able to locate it.

These newcomers wore sharp field uniforms after an unfamiliar style—long sweeping coats that trailed almost to the knees, with high collars. They wore crowns on their heads, and carried long swords at their sides, slim and beautiful. The swords were the only things they wore that weren't made of their own substance—coats, crowns, shirts, all were simply created by the honorspren.

A woman at the front had the highest collar of the three. She wore her hair up, tight save for one small tail of it pouring out the back. That, like the uniforms, was a fashion style unfamiliar to Adolin.

She pulled her not-horse to a halt about five paces from him. "Human," she said. "You've been recognized by our scouts. Are you Adolin Kholin, as we have surmised?"

"Your intelligence is good," he said to her, hand resting on his sheathed sword. "I've come by order of the Bondsmith, my father, to visit your lands and deliver a message on his behalf. I bring with me Knights Radiant of four different orders, all of whom work in concert against the rising Everstorm. Proof that men and spren once again need their bonds of old."

"Lasting Integrity is not accepting visitors or emissaries, regardless of their pedigree," the woman said, her tone sharp, each word a barked order. "You are to leave. We are not interested in bonds with murderers and traitors."

Adolin took out the letters he'd been given, proffering them. He waited, sweating, hoping. One of the honorspren urged its mount forward, then took the letters.

Adolin felt a wave of relief as the honorspren returned to the other two. "Those letters explain our position," Adolin said. "My father hopes that we can forge a new—"

He was interrupted as the spren deliberately ripped the letters in half. "We will not accept," the woman said, "a contract from you."

"It's not a contract!" Adolin said, stepping forward, ignoring a spike of pain from his side. "They're just letters! At least read them!"

"By reading these, we imply there is an argument you could make to persuade us," the woman said as the other honorspren further shredded the letters. "You will withdraw from these lands and take with you the traitor Notum. Inform him that we now know his complicities run deeper than anticipated. His exile is complete."

Adolin gritted his teeth. "He was attacked," he said. "Nearly killed before we could get there! The world is changing. Barricading yourselves in your fortress won't stop the change, but it might leave you completely without allies when you finally realize you need to do something!"

The honorspren unsheathed her sword and pointed it at him. "This is our realm. Our sovereign land. So you will leave as ordered. Humans never respect that, never accept that spren can *own* anything. We are possessions to you."

"I don't—"

"You will *leave*," she said. "We reject your offer! We reject your bonds!"

Adolin took a deep breath, each of his arguments dying like shriveled plants starved for rainwater. Until only one dangerous possibility remained. A plan he had barely dared consider, let alone suggest to the others.

When he spoke, it was with the same brashness—but the same sense of instinctive *rightness*—that had led him to attack Sadeas. "You mistake me!" he snapped at the honorspren. "I didn't come to offer you bonds with Radiants."

"What, then?" she demanded.

"I've come," Adolin said, "to face your judgment. You've named us murderers, traitors. I reject this, and vow to prove it. Take me, as a representative of the Kholin house and the new government of Urithiru. I am a highprince of Alethkar and the son of the Bondsmith. I will stand in the place of those humans whom you say betrayed you. You wish to reject *us* because of what *they* did? Prove, through judgment, that *I* deserve this treatment."

The lead honorspren fell silent, then she leaned to the side and whispered quickly to her companions. They seemed equally baffled. Behind, Shallan took Adolin by the arm on his good side, her face concerned.

He stood firm. Not because he was confident, but because he was angry. They wanted to call him a traitor? They wanted to blame *him* for what had been done to Maya? Well, they were honorspren. He suspected they wouldn't be able to resist a chance to formally defend their honor—as they saw it.

"You would stand trial?" the honorspren said at last. "For your ancestors?"

"I will stand trial for myself. In turning me away, you insult my sense of dignity, my integrity. You say I am not worthy, when you do not know me?"

"We know humans," one said.

"I reject that argument. Honor demands you let me speak for myself, if you are going to punish me. Where is the trial? Where is the chance for me to speak? Where is your *honor*?"

This provoked a reaction at last. The three began looking at one another.

"You are honorspren, are you not?" Adolin said. "You believe in justice? In fairness? Let's see if you can uphold those ideals while blaming *me* for what was done in the past. Let me speak for myself. Then *prove* that I, Adolin Kholin, deserve to be turned away."

Finally the leader sat up straight in her saddle. "Very well. We cannot reject a demand for judgment. Come with us. Know that if you enter Lasting Integrity, there is little chance of you ever leaving."

"We shall see," Adolin said, then turned and waved to beckon the others.

"No," the honorspren said. "Just you."

"My party has traveled far," Adolin said, "and they include representatives of—"

"You may bring two others," the honorspren said. "And that deadeye. You have bound her corpse, haven't you, human? You're not one of these new Radiants? Or have you already killed your spren?"

"I'm not a Radiant," Adolin said. "But yes, Maya is my Blade."

"Then we must be certain you are not mistreating her," the honorspren said. "We care for all deadeyes. Bring her, and two others. Decide quickly."

Adolin ground his teeth. "Allow me to confer."

As he and Shallan returned to the others, she seized him by the arm. "What are you doing?" she demanded. "You can't stand trial for what a bunch of people did thousands of years ago."

"I will if it gets us in those gates," Adolin said. "Do we have a choice?"

"Yes," she said. "We could turn back."

And face my father, having failed him again?

The others gathered around him. Adolin explained what was happening, the Stump's spren translating for her.

"I don't like this," Zu said, shaking her head, her golden hair shimmering. "I don't like splitting us up."

"The first step to completing this mission is getting the honorspren to talk to me," Adolin said. "If they turn us away here, we're done. If I can get through those gates, I can maybe start a conversation."

"They're not going to listen to you, Brightlord," Godeke said. "They're going to arrest you."

"If it gets me in, I don't particularly care. We'll send a small group back immediately to tell my father what I've done. The rest can camp out here for a few days, care for Notum, and wait for word from me. We have a few weeks until supplies make it necessary for you to return; we'll decide what to do then."

The others offered a few more token objections. Shallan—actually, she seemed like Veil right now—merely listened as Adolin persuaded the others. She plainly knew he would take her in with him, as well as her spren. It seemed the natural choice.

A short time later he approached the honorspren—leading Gallant, with Maya on his back—along with Veil, Pattern, and their trunks of clothing on pack animals. The honorspren spun about, then led them to the front of the fortress. There, they conferred with a few others who stood guard outside the walls.

Then the gates opened. Adolin strode in, accompanied by Veil, Pattern, and Maya. He grunted at the pain from his wounded side as a group of glowing blue-white figures immediately seized him and slapped his wrists in chains. The gates swung shut behind them with a booming sound.

So be it. He was *not* going to return to his father empty-handed. He would *not* abandon his mission.

No matter the cost.

37

SILENCE
FROM THE DEAD

Regardless, I will try to do as you suggest. However, you seem more afraid of the Vessel. I warn you that this is a flaw in your understanding.

Weeks after destroying the spanreed, Navani still hadn't made headway discovering the nature of the spren who had contacted them. Their triangulation of the spanreed had led them to a strange dark location on the fourth floor of the tower, near a monastery. The measurements hadn't been precise enough to tell them exactly where, and searches had revealed nothing.

Nevertheless, Navani had plenty of other things to occupy her. Running a kingdom—even one consisting of a single enormous city—was a wearying task.

She rarely got a break from the demands of merchants, lighteyes, ardents, and the thousands of others who needed her attention. Whenever she did, she retreated to the basement of the tower, where she could peek in on the efforts of her scholars. Today she could spare only an hour—but she wanted to make the most of it.

As soon as she entered, Tomor—the young relative of Falilar—ran over and intercepted her, carrying a strange device. "Brightness!" he said, with a quick bow. "You're here! See, it's finally done!"

Tomor held up a device that resembled a leather glove. *He was working on that lifting fabrial,* she remembered. *I told him to connect it to those weights in the deep shaft.* She was still excited by that prospect: the idea of using the power of the storms to wind up weights, then activate them with a fabrial to raise a lift.

This lifting fabrial was only a small part of that larger, more important device. Navani took the fabrial from him, hesitant. "You . . . made it into a glove?"

"Yes, like you asked!" Tomor said.

"I didn't ask for a glove," Navani said. "I wanted the device to be more portable and elegant."

"Like . . . a glove?" he said.

"It's intended to be mounted to a lift, Ardent Tomor," Navani said. "I don't see how this shape enhances its function."

"But with this, you don't *need* a lift!" he explained with enthusiasm. "Look, here, put it on!"

He nodded eagerly as Navani fit the device over her hand and wrist, then had Tomor tie the straps to brace it up to her elbow. Made of stiff leather, it was almost more a gauntlet than a glove. The gemstones were hidden in a compartment at the side, affixed with metal caging that could be covered over with another piece of leather.

"See, see!" Tomor said. "You can conjoin different fabrials with this dial on the side of the index finger. You can move it with your thumb, allowing single-handed manipulation! By making a fist, you can slow the unwinding of the weight! Open palm, you go at maximum speed. Closed fist, you stop!"

"Maximum speed . . ." It registered what he was saying. He expected people to rise through the central shaft of the tower being *pulled by their hand*. It was a wildly imaginative application of what she'd wanted—and also a *terrible* design.

"Tomor," Navani said, trying to find a way to explain without dampening his enthusiasm. "Don't you think this might be a little dangerous? We should be designing lifts."

"But we already have fabrials for that!" he said. "Think of the flexibility this would allow Brightlord Dalinar. Wearing this gauntlet, he could go *zip* all the way to the top without needing to wait for a lift! Walking outside the tower, and don't want to go all the way to the central shaft to catch a lift? No problem. *Zip!* All the way up high."

She tried to imagine Dalinar dangling in the sky after going "zip" because he activated this insane device, and couldn't help smiling. If her husband wanted, he could have a Windrunner fly him up—but he never did. As efficient as that sounded, it really wasn't worth the hassle and inconvenience, rather than simply riding a lift like everyone else.

"It's a wonderfully creative design, Tomor," she said. "I sometimes miss the flexibility of a young mind—it truly does lead one to explore paths that we, in our aged wisdom, never think to notice. You've done well here."

He beamed. Now, if she could get him to do what she'd *actually* asked—

"Try it!" he said.

Try it. *Oh dear.* She glanced at his animated smile, and didn't miss Kristir—the head scholar on duty today—passing behind, hiding her own smile with a stack of papers as she walked. The other scholars in the room pretended to be busy amid their logicspren, but Navani could feel their eyes.

"I assume," she said to Tomor, "you've tested this yourself."

"Yes!" he said. "I've been doing it in here for days!"

Well, at least it was probably safe. Navani gave him a polite smile, then inspected the controls. Yes . . . so this fabrial held several separate rubies, each attached to a distant weight. You pointed the glove in the direction you wanted to go—presumably up, but it could move you laterally as well—then conjoined one of the rubies. Then you unhooked the weight with a different control, and the glove pulled you along—using the force of the falling weight.

She took a deep breath, then raised her hand in the air.

"Be sure to make a fist first!" Tomor said.

She did so, then conjoined the device. The glove locked into place. She released one of the distant weights, then carefully relaxed her fist, and the distant weight slowly moved down.

Navani went up. Pulled somewhat uncomfortably by her arm, she rose several feet into the air. Tomor let out a whoop, and a number of the watching scribes applauded.

Navani tightened her fist, halting her ascent. She floated there, dangling by her arm roughly four feet in the air, her fist nearly touching the ceiling.

"See!" Tomor said. "See!"

"And . . . exactly how does one get *down*, Tomor?" she asked.

"Um . . ." He ran to the side and grabbed a large stepstool by the wall. "I've been using this. . . ."

He placed it for her, and—thankfully—she was allowed to deactivate the device. She dropped a few inches onto the stepstool to further applause. Now they were just baiting her.

Still, Tomor was sincere. And maybe there *could* be some use for this device. If someone needed to reach a flying ship that had already taken off, for example.

"I like it," she told Tomor. "It's a little hard on the shoulder though. I wonder if it would be better as some kind of belt, instead of a glove."

"A belt . . ." he said, eyes opening wide. "A *flying belt.*"

"Well, a levitating belt," Navani said, unstrapping the device. "Our fabrials still have the problem that they can only move in one direction at a time."

"Yes, but with *two* belts," he said, "you could fly up high, then shoot off into the distance!"

"Only until the weight hits the bottom of the shaft and you stop moving," Navani said. "Unless we want to use an entire chull rig with dozens of attendants to keep you going, like we do with the *Fourth Bridge*."

"Hmm," Tomor said. "So many knots to untangle . . ."

"I also suggest," Navani said before he could get distracted by the belt idea, "changing the method of speeding up and slowing down. It is more natural to open your fist when surprised, I think, so that should halt the device. Make it so that there is a bar—like a throttle for opening a pressure valve—across the hand. Squeeze it to get speed."

"Right, right . . ." He sat and began sketching. "I'll keep it as a gauntlet for now, and iterate . . . And maybe the dial on the finger is too easy to shift by accident. Perhaps we give up single-handed manipulation in favor of more specific control. . . ."

Navani left him and walked over to Kristir. She was short of stature, but not of personality, and bore a smile on her rosy cheeks. Navani leaned in to whisper, "You enjoyed that, didn't you?"

"We've had a pool going on whether you would actually try it out, Brightness," Kristir whispered. "I won seven clearmarks." She grinned. "You want me to point him back at making a lift, like he was supposed to be doing?"

"No," Navani said. "Encourage him to keep going in this direction. I'd like to see what he comes up with."

"Understood—though it would help us all immeasurably if you could break the altitude/lateral movement exclusivity problem for us."

"It will take a better mind than mine to do that, Kristir," Navani said. "Put our best mathematicians on it—but not Rushu. I have her thinking about how to protect the tower from—"

A shout came from outside the room. Navani turned and strode toward the door—but was stopped by a young soldier with his hand out toward her. He waved for the room's guards to check the noise first. "Sorry, Brightness," he said. "The Blackthorn would have my spheres if I let anything happen to you."

"I'm pretty sure I know what this is, Lieutenant," she said, but folded her arms and waited. The gathered scholars in the room behind her murmured in concerned tones. Navani peeked out into the hallway, where a couple of soldiers—men she'd assigned to Kalami's investigation—were holding a struggling figure, surrounded by fearspren. Hopefully this wasn't a false alarm.

"What is it?" the lieutenant asked as one of his guards jogged over.

"Not sure," he said. "Those men say they're working at Brightness Navani's request."

"I apologize, Brightness," the lieutenant said, stepping back. He let her pass, though his soldiers maintained close proximity to her as she stepped into the hallway.

The man they'd captured was a wiry fellow, Alethi, but with skin on the paler side. He searched about, wild-eyed, struggling but not saying anything.

The bait had been her workstation, which she'd set up unoccupied across the hall, in the room used mostly for storing books and as a quiet reading nook. Her station there had been a tempting prospect, easy to reach from the door, and mostly ignored this last week.

Chananar—one of the soldiers she'd had secretly watching the workstation—stepped over to her and proffered half of a small ruby, illuminated faintly by the light of the spren trapped inside. A spanreed fabrial. The phantom spren in the tower had taken the bait. It had heard that she'd lost the previous spanreed, and had decided to send a replacement.

Navani plucked the ruby from the soldier's hands and approached the captive. He looked around wildly, though he'd stopped struggling. "Who gave this to you?" Navani asked, holding the ruby before him. "Who told you to hide it among my things?"

He just stared at her and didn't speak.

"Did you hide the other one too?" Navani asked. "The one in my traveling sphere? Speak, man. You're in some serious trouble—but I will be lenient if you cooperate."

The man trembled, but said nothing. The ruby started flashing in Navani's fingers, indicating the phantom spren wished to talk with her. It might be a distraction, but in any case, she wanted to be in the presence of a Lightweaver when she replied this time—they had the ability to see spren in Shadesmar even when they were invisible to others.

"Bring him," she said to the soldiers. "We're going to my audience chamber for a proper interrogation. Isabi, please write to Kalami and have her meet me there."

The young ward—who was among the increasingly large crowd of gawking scholars—hurried off. Navani gestured for the soldiers to tow the captive away, then moved to follow, but one of the other soldiers approached her.

"Brightness," he whispered. "I think I recognize that fellow. He's with the Radiants."

"A squire?" Navani asked, surprised.

"More a servant, Brightness. He was there helping with meals when I tried out for the Windrunners last month."

Well, that would explain how he'd gotten into her traveling sphere to place the first gemstone—the Windrunners often practiced with it, training to keep the device in the air. Was she wrong about her phantom spren correspondent? Was it possible they were an honorspren? Many of those *did* have a somewhat antagonistic relationship with the current Knights Radiant. She tucked the blinking gemstone away in her glove's wrist pouch. *You can wait,* she thought to the phantom spren. *I'm in control of this conversation now.*

Unfortunately, as she was leaving, Navani noticed Isabi taking a message from one of her spanreeds and looking anxious. Navani stepped over to the girl's table, mentally preparing herself. What would it be this time? More tariff complaints from the Thaylens?

She leaned in, reading over Isabi's shoulder, and got to the words "explosion" and "dead" before she snapped alert and realized this was *not* what she'd been expecting.

.•.

The Everstorm didn't arrive like a highstorm.

Honor's storm would come as a violent tempest, with a crashing stormwall full of wind and fury. It was an abrupt scream, a battle cry, an intense moment of exultation.

Odium's storm came as a slow, inevitable crescendo. Clouds boiled from one another, ever expanding, creeping forward until they smothered the sunlight. Like a single spark that grows to consume a forest. The Everstorm was a trance of extended passion—an experience, not an event.

Venli couldn't say which she preferred. The highstorm was violent, but somehow trustworthy. It had proved the listeners for generations, granting safe forms, fulfilling the Rider's ancient promise to her people. Allegiances might have changed, but that couldn't separate the souls of her people from the storm that—in the ancient songs—was said to have given them birth.

Yet she couldn't help but feel a *thrill* at the arrival of the Everstorm, with its vivid red lightning and its persistent energy. She hated Odium for what he'd done to her people, and for the constant lure he—even now—could place in her mind. Voidlight, the emotions it stoked, and the beauty of crossing the landscape by the light of crackling red fire upon the sky . . .

Beneath those irregular eyes of an angry deity, Venli joined the others in a quick jog. Their several-week journey was at an end, their food stores exhausted. They'd spent this last day hiding in a forest, waiting for the Everstorm. As it arrived, the mountain landscape took on a nightmare cast.

The company of five hundred scrambled up the final incline.

Flash.

A glimpse of gnarled trees casting long, terrible shadows.

Flash.

Rubble and broken stone on the slope ahead. Stones doused in fire-red light.

Flash.

Skin with vibrant patterns and wicked carapace, loping alongside her.

Each burst of lightning seemed to catch a moment frozen in time. Venli ran near the front, and though her form wasn't as athletic as some, she held her own as the strike force reached the top of the slope.

Here they were confronted by a cliff face, more sheer than a normal mountain should have allowed. They were far, far below the tower. From this angle, she couldn't see the city. Perhaps it was above the black clouds. If so . . . storms. Until this moment, she hadn't been able to fully conceive of something inhabitable being built so far up.

One of the Deepest Ones glided toward Venli and Raboniel, her feet sunken in rock. She moved with an unnatural grace, as if her bones weren't completely solid. This was the scout Raboniel had sent ahead this morning to search for a proper incursion point.

"Come," she said to Command.

Venli followed, joining Raboniel, Rothan, three Deepest Ones, and a soldier she didn't know. Raboniel didn't forbid Venli, and none of the others seemed to care that she was there. They made their way around the side of the mountain, passing a pile of what looked like rotting grain and some broken wood boxes. Did humans travel this way?

No, she realized. *This must have fallen from above. Perhaps a shipment of food, coming via Oathgate to the city.*

"Here," the Deepest One said, bringing out a Stormlight sphere to light a particular patch of rock. She then sank her hand into the stone as if it were liquid. Or . . . no, that wasn't exactly correct. When the Deepest One put her hand into the ground, she didn't displace anything, and the stone seemed to meld to her skin.

"The ancient protections have not been maintained," the scout said. "I can feel that the ralkalest has fallen from the walls of the tunnel below. How could they allow this oversight?"

"These new Radiants know nothing," another Deepest One said to Craving. "Raboniel, Lady of Wishes, you are correct in pushing to strike now. Yours is wisdom that the Nine do not share. They have been too timid."

Venli did not miss the Fused using Raboniel's title. All of them had similar formal names; the Deepest One using Raboniel's here—to the Rhythm of Craving—conveyed respect.

"The Nine," Raboniel said, "are taking care to not lose our footing in this world. We have waited thousands of years for this chance; they do not wish to trip by running too fast."

She said it, however, to Satisfaction. Her words were respectful, but the tone of the rhythm was clear. She appreciated the compliment, and she agreed.

The other Fused with them hummed to Subservience, something Venli almost *never* heard from their kind.

"The Sibling sleeps," the scout said. "Just as the Midnight Mother felt. Perhaps the Sibling has truly *died*. Permanently made into an unthinking creature."

"No," said another. "The Sibling lives."

Venli started. The one she'd mistaken for a soldier earlier, in the dark, was something more. A Fused malen with rippling patterns that shifted and changed on his skin. That was the mark of the *mavset-im,* Those Ones of Masks. The Masked Ones, illusionists, had the power to change how they appeared.

"My form is disrupted," the Masked One said. "The ralkalest might have fallen from the wall, but that is a mere physical barrier. The tower's spiritual protections are at least partially in effect—and as we determined months ago, the *mavset-im* cannot bear our many images while near Urithiru."

"This is as we anticipated," Raboniel said. "And we do not need your mask to proceed. As long as the Deepest Ones can move through the tunnels, our mission is viable. Go. We will meet you at the southwest opening."

The Deepest Ones dropped their robes, exposing naked skin and carapace-covered privates. Then they slid into the rock, sinking as if into a dark ocean up to their necks. Then, eyes closed, they vanished beneath the stone.

◆◆

"I feel blind," Lirin explained as Kaladin sat with him. Today Hesina was taking Kaladin's patients—the ones with battle shock—to see the tower stables. She insisted that taking care of animals would help, though Kaladin couldn't fathom how being around those beasts could help anyone's mood. Still, several of the patients had expressed eagerness at the idea of going riding.

"Blind?" Kaladin asked.

"I've had seven textbooks on sanity read to me over the last week," Lirin said. "I hadn't realized how *little* most of them would say. Mostly the same few quotes repeated over and over, traced to fewer sources. I can't believe that we have spent so long knowing so little, documenting nothing!"

"It's not so odd," Kaladin said, building a tower of blocks for his little brother to knock down. "Surgeons are looked at with suspicion even in some of the larger cities. Half the population thinks mental illness is caused by staying out in storms, or by taunting deathspren, or some nonsense."

Lirin rested a hand on the charts on his lap. Oroden laughed, walking among the blocks and kicking them.

"I spent my entire life trying to help," Lirin said softly. "And I thought that the best way to help lunatics was to send them to the ardents. Storms, I did it a few times. Lakin's son, remember? I assumed they'd be specialists. . . ."

"Nobody knows anything," Kaladin said. "Because they don't *want* to know. People like me scare them."

"Don't include yourself in that group, son," Lirin said, adjusting his spectacles as he held up a medical chart written in glyphs. His father read glyphs *far* better than Kaladin had ever known. Lirin used them like a stormwarden.

"Why shouldn't I?" Kaladin asked, stacking blocks again.

"You're not . . ." Lirin lowered the chart.

"Insane?" Kaladin asked. "That's the problem, isn't it? We don't see them as our brothers, sisters, children. They make us feel helpless. We are afraid because we can't bind a broken mind the way we do a broken finger."

"So we pretend we've done the best we can by sending them away," Lirin said. "Or we tell ourselves they're not *really* hurt. Since we can't see their wounds. You're right, son. Thank you for challenging me." He picked up another of his pages of notes, scribbled on in glyphs. Pictures, not letters, so it wasn't actual writing.

Storms. This was wrong. Doctors couldn't read about diagnoses on their own. Ardents were forced to take in patient after patient just so everyone else could breathe a little easier. Many people believed that seeing a surgeon was unnatural—that if the Almighty wanted them to heal, he'd see it done. The Edgedancers, ironically, were reinforcing that opinion.

"We need a medical revolution," Kaladin said, starting another tower. Oroden stood hopping up and down, barely able to contain himself as it was built. "We need to change *everything*."

"Change is hard, son," Lirin said. "And little men like us don't often get heard. . . ." He trailed off, perhaps realizing that excuse didn't work any longer. Not when his son was one of the most powerful men alive—despite his retirement.

Kaladin *could* change things. He could get doctors some kind of religious appointment, so they could learn to read without feeling like they were breaking social mores. Everyone was saying it was okay for Dalinar because he was a Bondsmith, after all.

Kaladin *could* change the way people thought about those afflicted by battle shock or melancholia. Lirin's textbooks listed no recommended medication other than sedatives. But no proper tests or research had been done to determine other options. There was so much here. So much to do. And as Kaladin thought about it, stacking block after block, it occurred to him that he was starting to see his oaths in a new way. He thought about that monastery with the sanitarium, and realized something chilling.

I could have ended up in there, Kaladin thought. The patients surrendered to the ardents, those were the ones who came from homes and cities where people cared enough to try something, even if it was the wrong thing. There was a chance that if he hadn't gone to war, he'd have found his way to one of those dark, terrible rooms.

A low rumble shook him out of his reverie. Was that thunder outside? He stood up and glanced out the window. Dark clouds blanketed the horizon. The Everstorm. Right, he'd heard there would be one today. Up here it was easy to lose track.

Oroden dashed forward, smashing through the blocks. Kaladin smiled, then heard the outer door of the clinic open and shut. Teft marched into the room a moment later. "Kal, he ain't at his quarters, and they say he ain't come in for days."

"What?" Kaladin asked. "When was the last time anyone saw him?"

"Three days ago."

Three *days?*

"Who is this?" Lirin asked.

"Friend of ours," Teft said. "Named Dabbid."

"The nonverbal?" Lirin asked. "Badly battle shocked?"

"I thought maybe he'd do well meeting with the men I'm treating," Kaladin said.

"Maybe," Lirin said, "you shouldn't have left someone that troubled without supervision."

"He does fine on his own," Kaladin said. "He's not an invalid. He just doesn't talk." Or . . . well, that might be understating it.

"Let's check with Rlain," Teft said. "Dabbid goes to help in the fields sometimes."

Kaladin had been delighted to find that Rlain had chosen to remain at the tower instead of going with the army. He thought his work in the fields was more useful than running water and things for the Windrunners, and Kaladin honestly couldn't blame him. Being with your friends, watching them fly, but not being able to do so yourself . . . that had to be even worse than what Kaladin had been experiencing lately.

I should have gone to him more, Kaladin thought. *Been a better friend.* He thought he finally understood what Rlain must be feeling.

He stood up and nodded to Teft, who was again rubbing his forehead. "You all right?" Kaladin asked.

"Fine," Teft said.

"Cravings?" Kaladin guessed.

Teft shrugged. "Thought I'd gotten past the headaches a few months ago. Guess they're back."

∴

Venli smashed the human soldier's skull against the stone wall, and the bone cracked with a sickening sound—like a wooden shell breaking. In a flash of red lightning from one of the stormforms, she saw the soldier's eyes cross, dilating. But he clung to her, his knife scraping her carapace, so—driven by the Rhythm of Panic—she slammed his head against the ground.

This time he fell still. She crouched above him, breathing heavily, then suddenly felt as if she *couldn't* breathe. She gasped, hoarse, and pulled her hands away. For a moment, the only sound she could hear was her rhythm.

The dying man twitched on the ground. She barely felt where he'd cut her along the side of her head. Within her, Timbre thrummed the Rhythm of the Lost.

I didn't mean to . . . Venli thought. *I* . . .

Sound suddenly returned to Venli. She started, looking around. In the heat of the moment, her own struggle had consumed all of her attention. Now, the intense fighting at the mouth of the cavern overwhelmed her. She cringed, trying to make sense of it all.

"The spanreed!" someone shouted to the Rhythm of Command. "Don't let them—"

Raboniel suddenly dashed through the center of the frenetic scramble. The others were all limbs and shadows, but she was somehow haloed by the crimson light of the Everstorm behind. Raboniel stepped directly into a spear strike—though when the weapon rammed into her, it immediately transformed to dust.

She sidestepped the soldier and approached a human woman at the side of the cavern. The woman was fumbling with a glowing ruby. Raboniel's thin blade—shorter than a sword, but narrow and pointed like a spike—rammed up through the human woman's chin. Raboniel yanked her blade free, then turned back toward the soldier, who had pulled out his side knife. She breathed out toward him, and something black left her lips—something that sent the man stumbling away, clawing at his face.

Raboniel plucked the spanreed from the dead woman's hands, then casually wiped her blade on a handkerchief. She saw Venli kneeling nearby. "Your first kill, child?" the Fused asked to Ridicule.

"Y . . . yes, Ancient One."

"I thought your kind fought the humans for years on the Shattered Plains."

"I was a scholar, Ancient One. I did not go into battle."

"Do not let them bring you to the ground," Raboniel said. "As a Regal—even in envoyform—you are stronger than most humans; use that. And carry a knife, for Ado's sake."

"I . . . Yes, Ancient One. I didn't see him coming at me, I mean . . . I thought . . ."

That she could remain aloof, as she'd always done with the listeners. Even during the battle at Narak, where they'd lost so many, she hadn't been directly involved in the fighting. She hadn't lost her mind to the spren that inhabited her; she'd told herself it was because she was so strong. In truth, she had *already* been selfish and ambitious.

Timbre pulsed comfortingly, but Venli couldn't accept the sentiment. She bore the humans no love—they had murdered thousands of her people. But Venli herself had doomed many listeners.

She didn't want to kill anyone. Not anymore. She climbed to her feet, shaken. Nearby, the last few human soldiers were subdued and killed as the Everstorm crashed outside, pouring red light in through the mouth of the cavern. Venli turned away from the deaths, then felt embarrassed. What had she expected, in coming on this mission? What did she hope to accomplish here? Make contact with the Radiants while actively *invading* their base? Look for allies as a massacre occurred?

No. Neither. She was just trying to stay dry during the storm. Raboniel got out a Stormlight sphere as a group of their Deepest One scouts finally emerged from the rock, sliding up out of the floor like spirits.

"How?" Raboniel asked. "You said you'd cleared the guards at this entrance."

"We did," a scout said to Agony. "This was a patrol that came to check on them, it seems. We did not hear them on the stones until it was too late."

"We assumed they were all up higher," another said. "We are sorry."

"Sorrow is meaningless," Raboniel said. "And bad assumptions are the last failing of many dead. We will not have another chance at this. Ever. Make *certain* the rest of the way is clear."

They hummed again to Agony, then melted into the rock floor of the cavern. The soldiers formed up, and Raboniel strode inward, not waiting to see if anyone followed.

The group left the rumbling sound of the storm behind and started upward. Though they'd begun midway up through the caverns at an entrance in a highland valley, it would take hours to reach the tower itself. Tense hours, hoping that there wouldn't be any more mistakes or missed human patrols. Hoping that silence from the dead wouldn't be noticed.

Venli walked, disquieted, uncertain which was worse: the feeling of primal terror that had stabbed her when she'd heard the human behind her, or the haunting feeling of watching the light fade from his eyes.

38

RHYTHM
OF THE TERRORS

*You have not felt what I have. You have not known what I have.
You rejected that chance—and wisely, I think.*

Accompanied by several of her scholars and an entire host of soldiers, Navani arrived at the scene of the explosion. It was less damaging than she'd feared when reading that initial spanreed report: only two dead, and the explosion had destroyed the contents of only a single room in the tower.

It was still deeply troubling. The two dead were Nem and Talnah, the lensmakers, astronomers, and gemstone experts. The destroyed room was their shared laboratory. Thousands of broams' worth of equipment ruined. And one invaluable sphere.

Szeth's sphere. The Voidlight one that Gavilar had considered most important out of all his strange spheres. As Navani stood in the hallway outside the destroyed room—smelling smoke, hearing the weeping of the cleaning woman who had first rushed to help at the sound of the detonation—she had a sinking feeling.

She had caused this somehow by asking those two women to study the sphere. Now she'd likely lost it *and* the lives of two expert scholars. Storms. What had happened?

The guards wanted a scholar to inspect the room for other possible dangers before letting Navani enter. She probably could have ordered them aside, but they were just doing their best to keep her safe. So she let Rushu go in first. Navani doubted that anything dangerous could have survived what seemed to be complete destruction—but then again, she'd never known a fabrial or sphere to *explode*.

Rushu slipped out a short time later and nodded for her to enter. Navani stepped in, her shoes grinding against broken glass as she surveyed the wreckage. Smoldering wood marked the remnants of tables. The bodies were under several bloody sheets. Not two sheets: five. For two corpses. Storms.

Navani picked through carefully, avoiding larger bits of broken glass. The smoke was nearly overpowering. Civilized people used spheres for light, and she rarely kept a hearth burning these days. Smoke was a dangerous scent.

If anything was salvageable in the mess, Navani didn't spot it. And of course there was no sign of the strange sphere.

Rushu stepped up beside Navani. "I . . . had dinner scheduled with Talnah later this week . . ." she whispered. "We were . . . were going to talk about weather readings. . . ."

Navani steeled herself. "I need you to do something for me, Rushu," she said. "Catalogue everything in this room. Don't let the soldiers move a single bit of glass. Remove the bodies, see them properly cared for, but otherwise leave this room pristine. Then go through every inch of it. Save every scrap of paper. Every broken lens or cracked beaker."

"If you wish, Brightness," Rushu said. "But . . . if I might ask . . . why? What do you hope to find?"

"Have you ever known a fabrial accident to cause an explosion like this?" Navani asked.

Rushu pursed her lips and thought for a moment. "No."

"I have some details on what they might have been working on. I'll explain them to you later. For now, secure this area. And Rushu, please don't get distracted."

The ardent glanced again toward the shrouded corpses. "I doubt that will be a problem this time, Brightness."

Navani nodded and moved out, walking toward where the prisoner was being kept—the voiceless man who had delivered the ruby. She also sent for a few Radiants to see if they could identify him for certain. She didn't know if this explosion was tied to the mysterious communications she'd been getting—but things had certainly been off about the tower lately. And she had grown tired of wanting answers.

⋰

By the time the second hour had passed—judged by the Rhythm of Peace—Venli's legs were aching, her breathing ragged from the hike. As a Radiant, she *could* have used Stormlight to strengthen her. But that would have been far too dangerous.

She would have to be satisfied with the strength her Regal form gave her. Certainly she was better off than an average singer would have been. The rest of the force, however—in stormform—was stronger than she was, and Raboniel kept an aggressive pace.

Each moment became excruciating, and Venli focused only on taking the next step. Yet Raboniel kept pushing. No breaks. No rests. Onward, ever upward.

Timbre thrummed inside her, helping with a comforting rhythm. Venli used that to keep herself moving, putting one leaden foot in front of the other. After what seemed like an eternity, light shimmered in the tunnel ahead. She tried to smother the spark of hope that gave her. The last twenty times, the light had been only a sphere lantern set into an intersection, placed by the humans to help navigate.

Raboniel called a halt. Venli leaned against the side of the tunnel, breathing deeply but as softly as she could. And the wall . . . the wall was straighter than the ones below. This was of worked stone. And shadows moved in the light ahead.

They were here. *Finally.* The tunnel had come up beneath the city of Urithiru, and would now emerge into the basement chambers. Squinting, Venli made out the source of light—a large wooden door up ahead, glowing at the edges. And . . . there were lumps on the ground. Guards who had been killed silently by the Deepest Ones.

Other than the light around the door, the only illumination came from the red-ember eyes of the people around her. The sign that a person's soul had been mingled with that of a Voidspren. Her own eyes glowed as well, lying on her behalf. She had a Voidspren too; Timbre simply held it captive.

Some of the nearby eyes sank, then vanished as the Deepest Ones slid into the stone. The rest of them waited in agonizing silence. This was the point where their invasion was most likely to be thwarted. Deepest Ones worked well as surprise troops, but—from planning meetings she'd attended—she knew they didn't have the skill or strength to challenge Radiants in direct battle. So if Radiants could be gathered to defend the crystalline heart of the tower, they could rebuff this attack.

Venli waited, tense, sweat from the climb dripping down her cheeks and from her chin.

The door ahead rattled. Then opened.

A Deepest One scout stood beyond. As soon as Raboniel started moving, Venli shoved forward, staying at the front of the crowd as they passed into the basement chamber.

It was a horrific scene. The bodies on the ground included a few soldiers, but were mostly human scholars—women in dresses or priests in their robes. A couple were still alive, held to the ground by arms that reached up out of the stone. Most of those who were dead had been away from the walls, and it seemed Deepest Ones had dropped from the ceiling to grapple them. It had all been accomplished without a single human crying out.

Venli shuddered, imagining being pulled to the floor while other arms reached up to grab your mouth and neck. The living humans struggled with wide eyes. Some of those phantom hands had long knifelike carapace fingernails. One at a time, they slit the throats of the captives.

Venli looked away, sick to her stomach. She had to walk through blood to follow Raboniel toward the center of the room—and the monolith of crystal that stood here. The wide pillar was made of a thousand different gems. Other than the tunnel they had emerged from, only one exit led from this circular chamber: a larger, well-lit corridor with tile murals on the walls and ceiling.

"I hope your slumber is peaceful, Sibling," Raboniel said, resting a hand upon the imposing pillar. "You shall not awake, at least not as yourself."

Voidlight—glowing violet on black—surged along Raboniel's arm. She'd said she would need time to accomplish her task: corrupting the pillar and fully activating the tower's defenses, but in a way that muted Radiants, not Fused.

Please, Venli thought to the Rhythm of the Lost, *let it happen without more killing.*

⁘

"Can't believe how dead this place is," Teft said as they passed through the winehouse.

"I'd guess a lot of the patrons were soldiers," Kaladin said, gesturing toward Adolin's corner booth. It felt strange to visit without him and Shallan. In fact, it felt strange to be going out *anywhere* without those two.

Kaladin tried to remember the last time he'd gone out for fun without Adolin forcing him. Skar's wedding? Yes, Lyn had made him go right before their breakup. That had been the last time he'd gone out with Bridge Four.

Blood of my fathers, he thought, sliding into the booth. *I really have been withdrawing from them. From everyone.* Except Adolin, who wouldn't stand for it. Half the reason Kaladin had begun courting Lyn was due to Adolin and Syl conspiring against him. Storming man. Storming spren. Bless them both. Though the relationship hadn't worked out, he could now see that they'd both grown because of it.

Teft went to fetch drinks. Orange for both of them. As Kaladin settled into the seat, he noted some of the scratched-in sketches Shallan had done with a knife on the tabletop. One was a rather unflattering picture of him in oversized boots.

When Teft returned, Kaladin eagerly took a long drink from his mug. Teft just stared at his. "What happens if I get some red?"

"Tonight? Probably nothing. But you'll get it next time."

"And then I'll get some violet," Teft said. "Then something clear. Then . . ." He sighed, then took a sip of the orange. "This is storming unfair, you realize."

Kaladin held out his cup. Teft clicked his against it.

"To unfairness," Kaladin said.

"Storming straight," Teft said, then downed his entire mug at once in an impressive display.

Syl darted in a short time later. The place wasn't busy, but there were some people about. Relaxing into their seats, complaining jovial complaints, laughing ornery laughs, all of it lubricated by a little alcohol.

That stopped when Rlain stepped in behind Syl. Kaladin winced at how obvious it was. The people of the tower knew about Rlain—he was nearly as famous as Kaladin—but . . . well, Kaladin heard what they said about him. The "savage" that Dalinar had somehow "tamed."

Many treated Rlain like some dark unknown quantity that should be locked away. Others, ostensibly more charitable, spoke of Rlain as some noble warrior, a mystical representative of a lost people. Both groups shared a similar problem. They saw only their own strange ideal of what he *should* be. A controversy, a curiosity, or a symbol. Not who he was.

Though Rlain seemed not to notice the way the winehouse grew quiet, Kaladin knew that was a front. The listener always noticed. Still, he crossed the room with a ready smile—he often exaggerated his facial expressions around humans, to try to put them at ease.

"Teft," he said, taking a seat. He looked to Kaladin. "Sir."

"Just Kaladin now," Kaladin replied as Syl flew up to settle onto his shoulder.

"You might not be in command anymore," Rlain said with a slight cadence to his words, "but you're still the captain of Bridge Four."

"What did you think all that time, Rlain?" Teft asked. "Carrying bridges against your own kind?"

"Didn't think a ton at first," Rlain said, trying to flag down a passing server. She jumped, then quickly moved in the other direction to tug on the arm of a more experienced server. Rlain sighed, then turned back to Teft. "I was in Damnation, same as the rest of you. I wasn't thinking about spying; I was thinking about surviving. Or about how to get a message to Eshonai—she was our general."

His demeanor changed, as did his tone, the cadence to his words becoming slower. "The first time I almost died," he said, "I realized that the archers would have no idea—from a distance—who I was. They couldn't see my pattern. It had been discussed what we'd do if the humans ever started using parshmen for runs, and we'd decided we had to drop them, same as humans. Then there I was, staring at my friends, knowing they would do their best to kill me. . . ."

"That's terrible," Syl said, causing Teft and Rlain to glance at her. Apparently she'd decided to let them see her. "That's so terrible. . . ."

"It was war," Rlain said.

"Is that an excuse?" she asked.

"An explanation," Teft said.

"One used to explain too much," Syl said, wrapping her arms around herself and growing smaller than usual. "It's war, you say. Nothing to be done about it. You act like it's as inevitable as the sun and storms. But it's not. You don't *have* to kill each other."

Kaladin shared a glance with Teft and Rlain, the latter humming to a mournful cadence. She wasn't wrong. Most everyone would agree. Unfortunately, when you got down to the bloody details, it wasn't so simple.

It was the same problem Kaladin had always had with his father. Lirin said you couldn't fight without perpetuating the system, eventually causing the common people to suffer more than if you'd refused. Kaladin found fault in that reasoning, but hadn't been able to explain it to Lirin. And so he doubted he could explain it to a piece of divinity—a literal embodiment of hope and honor.

He could just do his best to change what he could. That started with himself. "Rlain," Kaladin said. "I don't think I've ever apologized for what we did in desecrating the bodies of the fallen listeners to make armor."

"No," Rlain said. "I don't think you ever did, sir."

"I apologize now. For the pain we caused you. I don't know if there was anything else we could have done, but . . ."

"The sentiment means a lot to me, Kal," Rlain said. "It does." They sat in silence for a short time.

"So . . ." Teft eventually said. "Dabbid."

"I saw him yesterday," Rlain said. "He stopped by the fields, but didn't do much work. Wandered around a bit, helped when I asked him to run an errand. Then he faded away."

"And you couldn't find him today?" Teft asked.

"No, but the tower is a big place." Rlain turned around, glancing toward something Kaladin couldn't see. "Bad day to get lost though . . ."

"What do you mean?" Teft asked, frowning.

"The Everstorm?" Rlain said. "Right. You can't hear the rhythms. You can't feel when it passes."

Kaladin had forgotten again. Storms, being up here in the tower felt like being blind. Losing a sense you'd always had—in this case the ability to glance at the sky and know if a storm was happening.

Teft grunted, finally getting one of the servers to come over so he could order some red for Rlain.

"How worried should we be about Dabbid?" Rlain asked.

"I don't know," Kaladin said. "Lopen always looked after him. I want Dabbid to join the program Teft and I are setting up. To help people like him. Like *us*."

"You think it will get him talking?" Rlain asked.

"At any rate, I think listening to the others could help him."

"Don't take this wrong, sir," Rlain said. "But . . . has it helped you?"

"Well, I don't know that . . ." Kaladin looked down at the table. Had it? Had talking to Noril helped?

"He's been avoiding joining in," Teft said.

"I haven't," Kaladin snapped. "I've been busy."

Teft gave him a flat stare. Storming sergeants. They always heard the things you weren't saying.

"I need to get the program up and running first," Kaladin said. "Find all the men who've been tucked away in dark rooms, and get them help. Then I can rest."

"Pardon, sir," Rlain said, "but don't you need it as much as they do? Maybe it would be restful to participate."

Kaladin turned away, and found Syl—on his shoulder—glaring as hard as Teft. She'd even given herself a little Bridge Four uniform . . . and was he wrong, or was it more *blue* than the rest of her body? As their bond deepened and she entered this realm more strongly, the variety, detail, and hues of her forms were improving.

Maybe they were right. Maybe he should take part more in the meetings with the battle-shocked men. He just wasn't sure he deserved to divert resources or time from them. Kaladin still had a family. He had support. He wasn't locked away in darkness. How could he worry about himself when others needed him?

His friends weren't going to relent on this, he could tell. All three of them, bullying him together. "Fine," Kaladin said. "I'll join the next meeting. I was thinking about it anyway."

They acted like he was avoiding getting help. But he'd stepped down as Dalinar demanded. He'd started working as a surgeon. And he had to admit it *was* helping. Being with his family, talking to his parents, knowing he was wanted and needed . . . that helped more.

This project though, finding those who were like him, alleviating their suffering . . . that would help the most. *Strength before weakness.* He was coming to understand that part of his first oath. He had discovered weakness in himself, but that wasn't something to be ashamed of. Because of that weakness, he could help in ways nobody else could.

Syl glowed a little brighter on his shoulder as he acknowledged that, and he felt a warmth within. His own darkness hadn't gone away, of course. He continued to have nightmares. And the other day when a soldier had handed Kaladin his spear, it had . . . Well, it had made him panic. That reaction reminded him of how he'd refused to hold a spear when first training Bridge Four in the chasms.

His illness stretched all the way back to before that time. He'd never treated it—he'd merely kept heaping on the stress, the pain, the problems.

If this went well, maybe he *wouldn't* ever have to pick up the spear again. And maybe he'd be fine with that. He smiled at Rlain. "It *has* been helping," he said. "I think . . . I think I might be putting myself back together, for the first time in my life."

⁂

Venli could see the exact moment when the tower broke. Raboniel stood, her hands on the pillar, glowing fiercely with Voidlight. The pillar, in turn, began glowing with its own light: a vivid white, tinged faintly green-blue. This light that seemed to transcend the type of gemstones in the pillar. The tower was resisting.

An alarm sounded from the corridor; the invasion had been noticed. Raboniel didn't move, though Venli pulled back against the wall—trying not to step on corpses—as a hundred stormforms pushed out into the corridor.

Shouting humans, clashes of metal, *cracks* of sound. Any moment now, the Radiants would arrive and shear through the Regals and Deepest Ones like a flash of lightning on a dark night. Still Raboniel worked, calmly humming to a rhythm that Venli did not know.

Then finally it happened: the Voidlight moved from *Raboniel* into the *pillar*. It infused a small section of the majestic construction, crawling into an embedded grouping of garnets.

Raboniel stumbled away and Venli managed to dash over and catch her, keeping her from tumbling to the ground. Raboniel sagged, her eyes drooping, and Venli held her tight, attuned to the Rhythm of the Terrors.

Cries continued in the hallway outside.

"Is it done?" Venli asked softly.

Raboniel nodded, then righted herself and spoke to the rest of the singers gathered in the tunnel leading to the caverns. "The tower is not fully corrupted, but I have achieved my initial goal. The tower's defenses have been activated and inverted to our favor. The Radiants will be unable to fight. Go. Give the signal to the *shanay-im*. Seize the city."

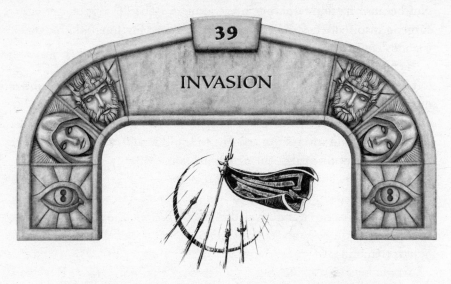

39

INVASION

However, though you think not as a mortal, you are their kin. The power of Odium's Shard is more dangerous than the mind behind it. Particularly since any Investiture seems to gain a will of its own when not controlled.

Teft dropped limp, as if he'd suddenly lost motor functions, his head thumping against the table and his arm flopping to the side, pushing his empty mug off it to crash to the floor.

Kaladin felt a striking moment of disorientation. A feeling of oppression on his mind, like a dark force trying to smother him. He gasped, then gritted his teeth. Not now. He would *not* let his treasonous mind overwhelm him now! His friend was in trouble.

Kaladin pushed through the melancholy and was on Teft in a second, loosening the man's collar, pressing fingers to his carotid artery. *Good pulse,* Kaladin thought. *No arrhythmia I can sense, and no obvious signs of abrasion on the body.* He pulled back an eyelid with his thumb. *Dilated eyes. Trembling, shaking, sightless.*

"Storms!" Rlain said, scrambling out of the booth and standing up. People from nearby tables leaped up in shock, then began crowding to see what was happening, shockspren like breaking triangles appearing around them.

"Kaladin?" Rlain asked. "What's wrong with him?"

Kaladin felt it again, the oppressive sense of gloom and darkness. It felt more *external* than normal, but he'd learned—these last few months—that his battle shock could take many forms. He was getting to where he could confront it. But *later.* Not *now.*

"Have the people stand back," Kaladin said to Rlain, his voice calm.

Not because he felt calm, but because of his father's training. A calm surgeon inspired trust. "Give us some air. He's breathing and his pulse is good."

"Is he going to be all right?" Rlain held out his hands to get the people to back away. His voice had fallen into a thick Parshendi accent—which in this case meant a heavy rhythm as if he were singing.

Kaladin held Teft's hand, watching for signs of epileptic motion. "I think it might be a seizure," Kaladin said, feeling inside Teft's mouth. "Some firemoss addicts have them during withdrawal."

"He hasn't touched the stuff in months."

So he says, Kaladin thought. Teft had lied before. He had tells, though, and he usually came clean to Kaladin. *He's not clamping his jaw. No danger to his tongue.* Still best to keep him facing sideways, in case of vomit. And he *was* trembling, the muscles of his arms spasming faintly.

"Might be a kind of aftereffect," Kaladin said. "Some addicts feel them for years." Not seizures though. "If it's not that, then . . ."

"What?" Rlain asked as the winehouse owner pushed through the crowd to see what was happening.

"Stroke," Kaladin said, making the decision. He got underneath Teft and rolled his limp form up onto his shoulders, then stood with a grunt. "There isn't much I can do here, but we have some anticoagulants at the clinic. If it is a stroke, those sometimes help."

Rlain moved to take one of Teft's arms. "The Edgedancers maybe? They have that clinic in the market nearby."

Kaladin felt stupid. Of course. That was a far better option. He nodded.

"I'll help you carry," Rlain said.

"I can Lash him," Kaladin said, reaching for Stormlight. The Light oddly resisted for a moment, then streamed into him from the spheres in his pocket. He came alive with power. It churned in his veins, urging him to use it. To act. To run.

"I'll make a hole," Rlain said. He shoved his way through the crowd, opening up a path for Kaladin.

Kaladin commanded the Light into Teft, to Lash him upward in order to make him lighter.

And it didn't work.

∴∴

"Yes, I recognize him," Red said.

Navani nodded in thanks, encouraging the tall Lightweaver to continue. He wore darkeyed worker's clothing—brown trousers, a buttoned shirt with the sleeves rolled to the elbows, and some bright suspenders. Thaylen sailor fashion had been making its mark on Urithiru.

She was holding her interrogation on the fifth floor, not far from where the laboratory had been destroyed. She'd ordered the prisoner placed in an adjoining small room, accompanied by several guards.

Red had been the first to respond among the Radiants she'd sent for. "His name's Dabbid," Red explained, peeking into the room with the prisoner. "Doesn't talk. I don't think he's right in the head. Well, pardon, most Windrunners ain't right in the head. They act like some kind of cult to Stormblessed, Brightness, pardon that, but they do that. This one's extra odd though. I think he was one of the old ones, from Bridge Four. Gaz could tell you. He's got a history with them."

"Do you see a spren?" Navani asked.

Red's eyes unfocused, and he seemed to be staring into the distance. He had light violet eyes now, though he'd been a darkeyes before joining the Lightweavers. Like others of his order, he could peer into Shadesmar.

"Don't think so," he said.

"That's not a terribly encouraging answer, Radiant."

"This tower makes things hard," he said. "In Shadesmar, this place glows like Nomon's own backside. That interferes. But I'm pretty sure I'd be able to see an honorspren. Same for one of the other Radiant spren."

She peeked into the interrogation room. This Windrunner—or whatever he was—sat at a small table, legs in chains, watched over by two of Navani's soldiers. When he glanced at Navani, he had that same wild cast as before. His hands were free, so he raised them toward her. One of the soldiers reached to stop him, but wasn't fast enough to prevent the captive from tapping his wrists together.

The Windrunner salute. He made the gesture again and again as the soldiers tried to settle him.

"Leave him alone," Navani said, stepping into the room.

The soldiers backed off, and the young man continued tapping his wrists together, frantic. Then he pointed at the wall. What? Was he actually mute?

He pointed more fervently. Navani turned. No, he wasn't pointing at the wall, but at the sphere in the lantern hanging there, lighting the room. Next, he made a writing motion, frantic.

I think he wants me to contact the spren, she thought.

He'd been delivering a new ruby when they'd caught him. Navani fished it out of her glove, and the prisoner grew more animated, pointing at it.

"Kalami?" Navani said into the other room.

The scribe poked her head in, and Navani handed her the ruby. The woman took it and retreated to set up the spanreed equipment.

"Red says you don't speak," Navani said to the man.

He looked down. Then he shook his head.

"Perhaps you should reconsider," Navani said. "Do you realize the trouble you're in? It's a spren that has been talking to you, is that right?"

The man hung his head farther. Then he nodded.

"You realize it could be one of the Unmade," Navani said. "A Voidspren. The enemy."

The man looked up sharply. Then he shook his head.

"Brightness!" Kalami shouted from the other room. "Brightness, you need to see this!"

Frowning, Navani strode into the larger chamber outside the interrogation room where Kalami—along with several of her wards—had set up the spanreed. It was scribbling on its own as Navani glanced at the text.

Fool human. We are under attack. The enemy is already inside the tower. Quickly! You must do exactly as I say, or we are all doomed.

It stopped writing, and Navani seized the pen, turned the ruby, and wrote back.

Who are you? she demanded.

I am the Sibling, the pen wrote in a quick script. *I am the spren of this tower The enemy They are They are doing something to me This is bad You need to infuse—*

Red the Lightweaver—who had been standing near the door—suddenly collapsed to the floor.

⁂

The failure of his powers was so unexpected that Kaladin stumbled. He'd started to take a step, fully anticipating Teft's limp body would grow lighter. When it didn't, he was thrown off balance.

He tried again, focusing. Again nothing.

Storms, Kaladin thought. Something was deeply wrong with him. The last time something like this had happened, he'd been dangerously close to violating his oaths and killing Syl.

"Syl?" he asked, scanning the room. She'd been flying around over near the bar, hadn't she? "Syl!"

No response.

"Phendorana?" Kaladin asked, naming Teft's honorspren. "This would be a great time to show yourself to me!"

Nothing. The winehouse had grown quiet, many of them staring at Kaladin as he steamed with Stormlight.

"Kal?" Rlain called from the doorway.

Kaladin shifted Teft on his shoulders, then strode after Rlain. Stormlight didn't seem to give one much additional raw strength, but it did steady the limbs, repairing the muscles if they began to tear beneath strain. So he could bear Teft at a brisk jog, even without Lashing him. He gripped the body in a secure medic's carry—a skill he'd learned on the battlefield.

"Something's wrong," Kaladin said to Rlain as they reached the door. "More than whatever happened to Teft."

"I know," Rlain said. "I didn't notice it at first, but the rhythms are going *crazy*. I can faintly hear new ones in the distance. I don't much like them. They sound like the rhythms I hear during an Everstorm."

"Is that one still blowing outside?"

"It just ended," Rlain said.

Together they took the most direct route toward the Edgedancer clinic at the center of the market. Unfortunately, a number of people had crowded here, and that slowed Kaladin and Rlain's progress.

They eventually shoved through to the front, calls of "Brightlord Storm-blessed" making people turn around. At the center of the mess though, they found something horrifying: two Edgedancers lying on the ground. An ordinary non-Radiant nurse was yelling at people to give them space.

Kaladin left Teft with Rlain and scrambled over to kneel before one of the unconscious Radiants, a vaguely familiar Edgedancer woman, short, with dyed hair. "What happened?" he asked the nurse, who seemed to recognize Kaladin immediately.

"They both suddenly dropped, Brightlord! I'm afraid Lorain hit her head; there's bleeding. I evacuated the clinic immediately, in case the unconsciousness was caused by leaking dazewater."

"Quick thinking," Kaladin said. The Edgedancers seemed more deeply unconscious than Teft. No quivering eyes. No muscle spasms.

"Have you ever seen anything like it?" the nurse asked.

"Something similar just happened to my friend. Another Radiant."

"Not you though?"

I always live, Kaladin thought, a bitter thought echoing from long ago. *So I can keep suffering.*

He pushed that aside. "The best thing I can think of to do is go to my father. He's the most experienced surgeon I know. Treat these for shock and bandage that head wound. I'll send you word if I discover anything."

The nurse nodded and Kaladin left her, helping Rlain lift Teft as they pushed through the crowd.

"Why don't you Lash him again?" Rlain said.

"I can't. My Lashings don't seem to work."

"What, just on Teft?" Rlain asked. "Or at all?"

Storms, *that* was a stupid thing to have not checked. Kaladin set down Teft's legs and took his sphere pouch from his pocket, kneeling as he tried to infuse the ground.

It didn't work. He frowned, then tried a different Lashing—the type that made things stick to other objects. Not a gravitational Lashing, but a Full Lashing. The one Lopen loved to use to stick people to walls.

That Full Lashing worked. When he touched his boot to that patch of stone, it stuck in place. He reclaimed the Light without any problems. So . . . Adhesion worked but Gravitation didn't?

"I have no idea what is going on," Kaladin said to Rlain.

"This can't be a coincidence," Rlain said. "You losing some of your powers? Three Radiants all fainting? People don't have strokes in *groups*, do they?"

"No," Kaladin said as the two of them began jogging, carrying Teft between them. "There's more, Rlain. I feel something pressing against my mind. I thought it was my illness. But if you say you can hear something odd . . ."

What did it mean? Was this . . . this like the fabrial the Fused had used on him in Hearthstone? It felt eerily similar in many ways.

They headed toward the grand staircase. It was wide and tall, and led up the first ten floors. It would be a faster climb than using the lifts. However, as they neared the steps, a scream echoed from one of the nearby tunnels.

Kaladin and Rlain froze at the intersection. Sphere lanterns lined the tunnels here, and the strata spiraled, making it seem as if—in looking down a tunnel—you were looking at the inside of a nut threaded for a screw. An agitated group was forming at the other side.

"I'll check," Rlain said. "You keep going with Teft?"

Kaladin nodded, not wanting to speak and waste Stormlight. He took Teft toward the steps as Rlain jogged off. The people Kaladin passed didn't seem to sense anything wrong; they only looked curiously at Kaladin and his burden. Some saluted, others bowed, but Radiants were common enough in these halls that most simply stepped aside.

He was halfway up the first flight of the grand staircase when Rlain came running up at a sprint. People gave way for him, even made superstitious gestures when they saw him.

"Thank the storms I can wear warform around you people now," he said, reaching Kaladin. He was puffing from the run, but didn't seem exhausted. "I'd hate to try to make that run in dullform. Someone found a Stoneward unconscious in the hallway. Something *is* striking at the Radiants specifically. One of the Unmade?"

"It feels like that fabrial I found in Hearthstone," Kaladin said. "But it's obviously on a much grander scale, and more powerful, if it's knocking out Radiants. The one I faced must have been some kind of prototype."

"What do we do?"

"My mother has my spanreed to Dalinar's scribes, so the clinic is probably still our best course for now."

The other flights passed in a flash, though Rlain had drawn three different exhaustionspren—like jets of dust—by the time they reached the sixth floor. He waved Kaladin ahead. They'd meet up at the clinic.

Kaladin sucked in another breath of Stormlight and redoubled his efforts, dashing through the hallway, Teft across his shoulders. He shoved past the people waiting outside the clinic—that was another oddity, since it was after hours—and pushed through the door.

The waiting room was lit with spheres and crowded with worried people. When Kaladin's mother saw him, she immediately began clearing room for him to pass.

"Lirin!" she shouted. "Another one!"

Kaladin jogged down the hall to the first exam room, where a Radiant—in an Aladar uniform—lay on the exam table. He recognized her. Another Stoneward.

Lirin looked up from examining her pupils. "Sudden unconsciousness?" he asked.

"I thought it might be a stroke at first," Kaladin said, carefully unslinging Teft and settling him on the floor. A quick check told Kaladin that his friend was still breathing, and his heartbeat was still regular, though his face was spasming. As if he was dreaming.

"We found others too," Kaladin said. "Different orders. All unconscious."

"I have two of this one's squires in the other room," Lirin said, nodding to the prone Stoneward. "Her friends and family hauled her up here in a big mess. I don't know what it's going to take to get people not to move an injured person. Fortunately, this doesn't seem to be a neck injury."

"It's striking only Radiants," Kaladin said.

"Not you though?"

"*Something's* happening to me," Kaladin said, feeling exhaustion hit him now that his Stormlight was running out. "My powers are inhibited and . . ."

He trailed off as he felt something new tugging on him. New, but familiar at the same time.

Syl? he thought, throwing himself to his feet, sweat spraying from his skin. "Syl!" he shouted.

"Son, a surgeon must be calm during—"

"Storm off with the lectures for once, Father!" Kaladin shouted. "*Syl!*"

. . . *here* . . . He felt her voice. He tried to concentrate on that feeling, and he sensed something tugging on his soul. It was as if . . . as if someone was using his mind like a proffered arm to help them climb out of a pit.

Syl exploded into sight in front of him in the shape of a small woman, growling softly, her teeth clenched.

"Are you all right?" he asked.

"I don't know! I was in the winehouse, and then . . . Teft! What's wrong?"

"We don't know," Kaladin said. "Do you see Phendorana?"

"No. Not anywhere. My mind feels cloudy. Is this what it feels like to be sleepy? I think I'm *sleepy*." She scrunched up her face. "I hate it."

Rlain arrived, huffing, trailed by Kaladin's mother, who peeked around him, appearing worried.

"Kal," Rlain said. "I passed people in the hall who were shouting warnings. There are Fused in the tower. It's another raid."

"Why haven't we heard about this via spanreed?" Kaladin asked.

"They don't work," his mother said. "We tried to write to Brightness Navani the moment these Radiants arrived. You activate the reed, but nothing happens. It just falls over."

Kaladin felt cold. He pushed past Rlain and walked down the hall to the living room of his family's quarters. It had a window out into the evening sky. The sun had set, though fading sunlight painted the sky, so he could see the hundreds of flying figures—trailing long clothing and infused with Voidlight—descending upon the tower.

"You were wrong, Rlain," Kaladin said. "It's not a raid. This is an invasion."

⁘

Several of the women clustered around Red, who was breathing, but unconscious. Navani let the others deal with the Lightweaver. She reread the lines the phantom spren had written.

The Sibling. The third Bondsmith spren. Not dead after all, not even asleep. But why spend over a year saying nothing? Why let everyone think you were dead?

Navani picked up the pen, which had fallen to the paper. Twisting the gemstone did nothing; the fabrial was lifeless.

The enemy, the Sibling had written. *They are doing something to me. . . .*

Navani rushed to her spanreed satchel, which was usually watched by one of her scribes' wards. It had leather sheaths for each reed, positioned in a row so that the ruby was visible through a slit in the leather. A dozen of her most important spanreeds.

None of them were blinking. Indeed, the two she pulled out gave no response when she twisted the rubies. They were as dead as the one on the table. She glanced at Red lying on the floor. Kalami was checking his eyes; she was an officer's daughter, and had been taught field medicine. She'd already sent one of the girls to run for an Edgedancer.

An attack. With no spanreeds to communicate? Storms, it would be chaos.

Navani stood up. If it was going to be chaos, then someone had to fight it. "Soldiers, I need you in here! Spanreeds aren't working. Who is the fastest runner among you?"

The scribes gaped at her, and all three of her soldiers—the ones who had been watching the captive in the other chamber—stepped in. The men looked at one another, then one of the soldiers raised his hand. "I'm probably fastest, Brightness."

"All right," Navani said, dashing to the table and pulling out a sheet of paper. "I need you to run to the first floor—use the stairs, not the lifts—and get to the scouting office near the second sector. You know it, the place where we're organizing the mapping of the Plains? Good. Have them mobilize every runner they have.

"They are to send someone to each of the tower's seven garrisons with a copy of this message. Every remaining runner, and all the scribes in the office, are to meet me on the second floor at the maps room. It's the largest secure place I can think of right now."

"Um, yes, Brightness."

"Warn them to move quickly!" Navani said. "I have reason to believe that a dangerous attack is coming." She scribbled some instructions on the paper—commanding the seven garrisons to deploy according to one of the predefined plans, then adding her current authentication phrase. She ripped off the paper and thrust it at the soldier, who took off at a dash.

Then she wrote it again and sent it with her second-fastest man—telling him to use a different route. Once he was off, she sent the last soldier to the Windrunners. There should be about twenty of them—four full knights and their squires—remaining in the tower.

"But Brightness," the guard said, taking the note she handed him, "you'll be unguarded."

"I'll manage," she said. "Go!"

He hesitated, perhaps trying to determine if Dalinar would be angrier at him for abandoning Navani or for disobeying her. Finally he dashed away.

Storms, she thought, looking at the fallen Red. *What if they can do to other Radiants what they did to Red? How did they pick him out?* She got a sick feeling in her stomach, a premonition. What if whatever had happened to him hadn't been targeted, but was instead a side effect of whatever was happening to the spanreeds?

"Gather our things," she said to the scribes. "We're moving to the map room."

"Red—" Kalami began.

"We have to leave him. Leave a note saying where we went."

She stepped into the smaller room. The prisoner, Dabbid, had pulled off his chair, and was now huddled on the floor. The manacles on his legs clanked as he shifted.

"The spren of the tower spoke to you," Navani said to him. "It had you place the spanreed gem for me. How did you know what to do?"

The man only looked at the floor.

"Listen to me," Navani said—keeping her distance just in case, but also trying to make her voice sound calm, reassuring. "I'm not angry at you; I understand why you did what you did, but something terrible is happening, and spanreeds aren't working. I *need* to know how to contact the spren."

The man stared at her, wide eyed. Storms, she wasn't sure he was capable of understanding. Something was clearly wrong with him.

The man moved, the chains clanking, and Navani jumped despite herself. He didn't move toward her though. He shifted and stood, then reached out to touch the wall. He rested his hand against the stone there, which was marked by strata lines. And . . . and a vein of crystal?

Navani moved closer. Yes, running through the strata was a fine garnet vein. She'd noted similar veins; in some rooms they were nearly invisible, perfectly mimicking the waving strata. In others they stood out starkly, straight and bold, running from floor to ceiling.

"The spren of the tower," Navani said. "She talked to you through these veins of garnet?"

The captive nodded.

"Thank you," Navani said.

He tapped his wrists together. *Bridge Four.*

Navani tossed him the key to his manacles. "We're going to the map room on the second floor. We must move quickly. Join us, if you wish."

She hurried back to the others. There was a vein of garnet in the map room. She'd see what she could do with it once she arrived.

⁙

Kaladin stared at his surgery knives.

Syl couldn't form a Shardblade. Something was wrong with his powers; he wasn't certain that Stormlight would even heal him any longer. However, that wasn't what made him stop and stare at the knives.

Six little pieces of steel in a row. The scalpel of a surgeon was a very different thing from a soldier's knife. A surgeon's knife could be a subtle thing, meant to cause as *little* harm as possible. A delicate contradiction. Like Kaladin himself.

He reached out to touch one of them, and his hand didn't shake as he'd feared it would. The knife—glowing in the spherelight as if it were aflame—was cold to his touch. A part of him had expected it to be angry, but this tool didn't care how he used it. It had been designed to heal, but could kill as efficiently. Like Kaladin himself.

Outside the surgery room, people screamed amid writhing fearspren. The Fused were landing on the balconies of this level, and the cries of the terrified echoed through the halls of Urithiru. Kaladin had sent Rlain to hide in the living quarters of the clinic—he didn't know how the Fused would react to finding a listener here, wearing an Alethi uniform.

Kaladin delayed. He should go hide too. Wait it out. That was what his father wanted.

Instead, Kaladin's fingers wrapped around the knife, and he turned toward the screams. He was needed. Life before death. This was what he *did*.

Yet as he walked toward the door, he found himself laden by a terrible weight. His feet were as if in chains, and his clothing could have been made of lead. He reached the doorway, and found himself panting in a cold sweat.

It had been going so well.

He felt so tired all of a sudden. Why couldn't he just rest for a little while?

No. He had to march out there and fight. He was Kaladin Stormblessed. They were depending on him. They needed him. He'd had a short leave. But now . . . now he needed to . . .

What if one of them dies because they were expecting your help, but you've frozen up again. What if they died like Tien? What if he froze like when Elhokar died? What if . . .

What if . . .

"Kaladin?"

Syl's voice shook him awake. He found himself sitting beside the surgery room doorway, his back up against the wall, clutching the knife in front of him and trembling.

"Kaladin?" Syl asked again. She stepped forward on the floor. "I went to warn Queen Navani, as you asked. But I couldn't get too far away from you, for some reason. I found some messengers though, and they said that they had orders from the queen—so she seems to know about the invasion already."

He nodded.

"Kaladin, they're *everywhere*," Syl said. "The messenger said a big force came up from the caverns and took the heart pillar room. The enemy has the Oathgates running. They're bringing in troops, and . . . Kaladin, what's wrong with you?"

"Cold sweats," he muttered. "Emotional detachment. Insensibility, accompanied by hyper-recall of traumatic moments." Someone shouted out on the balcony and he jumped, brandishing the knife. "Severe anxiety . . ."

Footsteps in the hallway made Kaladin grip the knife harder in a sweaty hand. No Fused appeared, however. It was just his father carrying a bloodred sphere for light. He halted upon seeing Kaladin, then moved with exaggerated calmness, smiling in a friendly way. Storms. If his father put on that face, things really *were* bad.

"Put down the knife, son," Lirin said softly. "It's all right. You aren't needed."

"I'm well, Father," Kaladin said. "I just . . . wasn't quite ready to take up the fight so soon. That's it."

"Put down the knife and we'll plan."

"I need to resist."

"Resist what?" Lirin said. "Together Laral, your mother, and I got our people into their rooms. The invading parshmen aren't here to kill; nobody was hurt except for that fool Jam, who found a spear somehow."

"Has the queen surrendered?" Kaladin asked.

Lirin didn't reply, though his eyes were still on the knife.

"No," Syl said. "At least, she was sending out orders. But Kaladin . . . they can't fight for long. There are Fused among the enemy, and Regals, and . . . and almost every Shardbearer is out in the field. Every Surgebinder in the tower has been knocked unconscious."

Kaladin took his father by the arm. "There's one left," he said, then hauled himself to his feet.

"Kal!" Lirin said, anger peeking through his calm surgeon's mask. "Don't be a fool. There's no point in playing the hero."

"I'm not playing anything," Kaladin said. "This is who I am."

"So you'll go fight, like this?" Lirin demanded. "Overwhelmed by diaphoresis and hand tremors, barely able to stay on your feet!"

Kaladin gritted his teeth and started along the hall toward the front door of the clinic. Syl landed on his shoulder, but didn't insist he stop.

"You said that Jam had a spear," Kaladin said. "Do you know what happened to it?"

"Storms, son, *listen to me*," Lirin said, grabbing him from behind. "There is *no battle* for you here! The tower has fallen. You go out there, and you throw away any advantage you had. Storms, you won't only get yourself killed—you'll get *us* killed."

Kaladin stopped in place.

"That's right," his father said. "What do you think they'll do to the family of the Radiant who attacked them? You'd probably kill a few before you died. Stormfather knows, you're good at breaking things. Then they'll come and string me up. Do you want to see that happen to me? To your mother? To your *baby brother?*"

"Storm you," Kaladin whispered. Lirin didn't care about saving himself; he was not so selfish as that. But he was a surgeon. He knew the vital spots in which to stick a knife.

Shouts came from deeper within Urithiru—the voices of singers, with rhythms. They'd landed Fused here on the sixth floor, but others were boiling up from below.

Kelek's breath . . . Dalinar had taken the reserves to the battle in Emul. There were seven garrisons left in the tower, but each was severely undermanned, populated mostly with those men who were off rotation, enjoying leave. Five thousand men, max. Everyone had assumed the large numbers of Radiants would be able to prevent another raid on the tower. . . .

Kaladin sagged against the wall. "We . . . we need to find a way to contact Dalinar and Jasnah. The spanreeds aren't working?"

"None of them," Lirin said. "No fabrials at all."

"How are they using the Oathgates?" Kaladin asked, settling down on the floor of the hallway.

"Maybe it's the Skybreakers," Syl said. "But . . . I don't know, Kaladin. Something is *very* wrong with our bond. When I flew down just one floor, I found myself growing distant. Forgetful. Normally I can go miles away before that happens."

"We can plan," Lirin said. "We can think of some way to contact the Blackthorn. There are other ways to fight, son."

"Perhaps," Kaladin said. He met his father's eyes. "But you would say anything to keep me from going out there, wouldn't you?"

Lirin held his eyes and said nothing.

I'm really not *in any shape to go to battle,* Kaladin thought. *And . . . and if they have the Oathgates . . .*

Lirin calmly took the knife from Kaladin's hands. He let it go. His father helped him to his feet and led him to the back rooms, where a village girl was with Oroden, keeping him quiet with toys. Kaladin's mother entered a short time later, hairs escaping her bun and blood on her skirt. Not hers. Probably Jam's.

She went to hug Lirin while Kaladin sat staring at the floor. Urithiru might continue to fight, but he knew that it had lost the battle long ago.

Like Kaladin himself.

40

IN FOR ALL

My instincts say that the power of Odium is not being controlled well. The Vessel will be adapted to the power's will. And after this long, if Odium is still seeking to destroy, then it is because of the power.

By the time Navani neared the map room, the area was already a bustle of activity. The runners had done their jobs, and she found checkpoints in place in the hallways, attended by guards, with anticipationspren streaming overhead. The soldiers at each one waved her through with visible relief.

The map room was lit by a large number of diamond spheres. A smattering of officers in Kholin blue stood with some functionaries. Roion—the youngest highprince, and the only one in the tower currently—had gathered them around the tables. Here, maps of the lower levels had been unrolled and weighted at the corners.

Captains mostly, she thought, reading the shoulder knots of her command staff. *One battalionlord.* Men who had been here on leave. Various runners, both male and female, hovered at the perimeters of the chamber.

"Do we have word of Commander Lyon?" Navani asked as she strode in. "We'd best have the head of the Tower Guard here."

"He's fallen unconscious, Brightness," said one of the men. "He had a spren choose him last month. . . ."

"Storms," Navani said, stepping up to the table as several men made room for her. "It's true then? Every Radiant in the tower?"

"As far as we can tell, Brightness," one of the men said.

"There are enemy troops on every floor, Brightness," said an older man, the battalionlord. "Stormform Regals, mostly. Pouring in through the basement. But there are Heavenly Ones landing on balconies all up and down the lower levels."

"Damnation," she muttered. The enemy had the library rooms then. And the pillar. Was that where the Sibling resided?

She glanced at the battalionlord again. A lean, balding man with close-cropped hair, a thick neck despite his age, and a powerfully intense stare. He . . .

She did a double take. Darkeyed? Dalinar had made good on his decision to begin promoting based on merit, not eye shade, but there still weren't many darkeyed officers. Strangely, some darkeyes seemed to consider the change as unnatural as some of the more high-minded lighteyes did.

"Your name, Battalionlord?" she asked.

"Teofil," he said. "Ninth Kholin Division, infantry. We just came in off the lines in southern Alethkar. I put my men at the stairwell here." He pointed at the map. "But . . . Brightness, they got the drop on us, and there aren't many of our troops in the tower. First floor was halfway overrun by the time we mobilized."

"We can't fight Fused," said another man, young and nervous, his hand shaking as he pointed at a map of the sixth floor. "They're trapping us from both above and below. There's no way to hold them. They heal when cut, and they can strike from above. Without Radiants, we're *doomed*. There's no—"

"Calm down," Navani said. "Brightlord Teofil is right to have . . ." Navani paused. He was a darkeyes, not a brightlord. What did you call a battalionlord who wasn't a lighteyes? "Er, Battalionlord Teofil is correct. We need to plug the stairwells. The *shanay-im*'s ability to fly won't matter in such tight quarters. With proper barricades, it won't even matter that they can heal. We can try to hold the second through fifth floors."

"Brightness," another man said. "We can try—but there are *dozens* of stairwells, and not a lot of materials for barricades."

"Then we'd best start small," she said. "Have all our troops retreat to this level; we'll try to hold the second and third floors."

"And if they just fly down the outside and come in the windows on this floor?" the nervous young man asked.

"We barricade ourselves in here tight," Navani said. "Storms. The Soul-casters—"

"—don't work, like the other fabrials."

Damnation. "We have garrison stores?" she asked, hopeful.

"I've sent men to recover them," Teofil said, pointing at a map of the
third floor. "Dumps are here and here."

"With those, we can hold for weeks," Navani said. "Plenty of time for my husband to return with our forces."

The officers looked at one another. Her scribes, clustered near the doorway, stood quietly. After her furious rush to get here—often pushing through confused crowds—it felt unnerving to be in such silence. She almost felt as if the entire tower were bearing down on top of her.

"Brightness," Teofil said. "They pushed straight for the plateau outside. They have the Oathgates—and are working them somehow, though other fabrials aren't functioning. Singers will soon flood this tower. But disregarding that, I don't think barricades would be a prudent strategy.

"Yes, I plugged the stairwells to slow them, but they have stormforms, and I have reports of Fused who can move through stone. They'll blast and burn away what we put in front of them. If you want us to hold, we'll hold as long as we can—but I want to make certain you understand the situation fully. In case you want to consider a different plan."

Halls above. She pressed her hands against the table, forcing order upon her thoughts. *Don't feel like you need to decide everything,* she told herself. *You're not a general.*

"Advice?" she asked.

"Surrender is distasteful," Teofil said, "but might be our best option. My soldiers are brave, and I vouch for them—but they cannot stand for long against Regals and Fused. Can you think of any way to restore the Radiants?"

She eyed the maps. "I suspect whatever the enemy did to the Radiants has to do with a specific construction of garnets in the crystal pillar. If we can retake that room, I might be able to reverse all this. I can't guarantee anything, but it's my best guess and probably our best hope."

"That would mean reclaiming part of the first floor," Teofil said. "We'd have to push down the stairs into the basement . . ."

Nearby, other officers shuffled and muttered at that idea. Teofil met Navani's eyes and nodded. He didn't advise standing in a hopeless fight against a superior enemy. But if she could offer a chance of success, even with a difficult gamble, that was different.

"That will be bloody," a soldier said. "We'll have to advance on the position of enemy Surgebinders."

"And if we fail, we'll have given up most of our ground," said another man. "This is basically an in-for-all maneuver. Either we seize the basement, or . . . that's it."

Navani looked over the maps again, determined to think this through, though each minute she debated would make their task that much more difficult.

Teofil is right, she decided. *This tower is too porous to hold for long against an enemy with powers.* Trying to hold these center rooms wouldn't work. The enemy would be electrocuting men in large batches, breaking formations, terrifying her troops.

She had to strike before everyone in the tower started feeling like that frightened captain. Before the enemy momentum grew too large to overcome.

They had one hope. Move now.

"Do it," she ordered. "Throw everything we have into recovering that pillar in the basement."

Again the room fell silent. Then Teofil barked, "You heard the queen! Shuanor, Gavri, grab your men from the upper floors! Withdraw, leaving only a harrying force to cover the retreat. Radathavian, you command that. Withdraw slowly, making those Heavenly Ones bleed as they have to advance on you. Fused might heal, but they still hurt.

"The rest of you, pull your men to the foot of the grand staircase. We'll muster there, then make our push! We will carve a hole to the basement steps, then fight down and clear a path for the queen. By the blood of our fathers!"

They scrambled into motion, the various lesser officers calling for runners to deliver orders. Navani didn't miss their delayed response. They'd moved only after hearing the command from Teofil. These soldiers would fall over themselves to do her bidding when it came to peacetime requests, but during a fight . . .

Navani glanced at Teofil, who leaned in next to her and spoke in a soft voice. "Pardon them, Brightness," he said. "They likely don't much like following a woman's orders. Masculine arts and all that."

"And you?" she asked.

"I figure the Blackthorn has studied every military text known to man," he said. "And we could do worse for a general than the person who likely read 'em to him. Particularly if she's willing to listen to a little sense. That's more than I can say for some highlords I've followed."

"Thank you," she said.

"What we needed most was for someone to make the decision," he said. "Before you came, they were all balking at doing what I wanted. Storming fools. Almost anyone worth his Stormlight is on the front lines somewhere, Brightness."

He glanced at the others as they sent runners with orders. Then he spoke even softer to Navani. "We've got some solid troops mixed among them here, but many of these are Roion's men. Best I could tell, there was a single Shardbearer in the tower who wasn't a Radiant. Tshadr, a Thaylen man.

"His rooms were on the fourth floor. I sent a runner, but she returned just before you arrived. Those Heavenly Ones went straight for him, Brightness. Must have known *exactly* where his quarters were. The enemy has his Plate now; may the Almighty accept his soul to the eternal battlefield."

Navani breathed out. Taravangian must have told the enemy where to find the Shardbearer.

"There might be one other Shard we could take," Teofil said, gesturing toward a spot on the third-floor map. "A black Blade. Speaks to people when they come close . . ."

"The assassin in that cell is a Lightweaving," Navani whispered. "We sent the real man with my husband in secret, and he took the sword with him."

"Damnation," Teofil muttered.

"What are our chances, Battalionlord?" she asked. "Our *actual* chances, in your estimation?"

"Brightness," he said, "I've tried fielding regular troops against Regals. It doesn't go well—and it will be worse here. Normally these close quarters would benefit us fighting defensively. But in corridors we're limited to small clashes of squads. And if *their* squads can throw lightning . . ."

"I came to the same conclusion," she said. "Do you think this order of mine foolish?"

He slowly shook his head. "Brightness, if there's a *chance* to turn this tide right now, I think we need to take it. We lose the tower, and . . . well, it will be a disaster for the war. If there is even a possibility you can wake the Radiants, I'll risk everyone we have on that chance."

"Try this push, then," she said. "But if it doesn't work . . . I need to know how the enemy is treating the people on the upper floors as we withdraw the troops. Think you can have a scout find that out for me?"

He nodded, and she read understanding in his expression. Fused usually occupied rather than destroyed. Honestly, they generally treated the cities they took better than her fellow Alethi might have during a squabble between highprinces.

As much as she hated it, surrender *was* an option. As long as she was sure the enemy wasn't intending to make a slaughter of this attack.

They'd tried something like this once before, but then it had been only a raid—intended to slow down the Alethi reinforcements and to steal the Honorblade. She had a worse feeling about today's attack. They seemed to know about the Sibling—and how to disrupt the tower's defenses.

"I'm going to try something with the tower's fabrials," Navani said. "It might help us. Take command, see our plan put into action. Bring me anything of significance before you make a decision, please. Assuming you're still willing to take orders from a woman."

"Brightness," he said, "before my promotion, I spent years taking orders from every fuzz-faced teenage lieutenant who decided to make a name for himself on the Shattered Plains. Trust me when I say I consider *this* to be an honor."

He saluted her, then turned and began barking further orders. As he did, Navani noted the Bridge Four man named Dabbid slinking into the room. People didn't give him much more than a quick glance. The way he walked, with his eyes down, cringing when someone brushed past, was reminiscent of a servant, or . . . well, of how parshmen used to be. Invisible, to an extent.

It was good to know he had arrived in case what she was about to try didn't work. Navani walked up to the vein of crystal on the wall. It was more obvious in this room—a line of red garnet slicing the wall in half, interrupting the natural pattern of the strata. Navani rested her hand against it.

"I know you can hear, Sibling," Navani said softly. "Dabbid told me you could—but it was clear to me anyway. You knew where to place those rubies, and you knew when I'd lost one. You've been listening in on us the entire time, haven't you? Spying? How else would you know that I'm the one who leads the fabrial scholars in the tower?"

As she finished speaking, she noted something: a small twinkle of light, like a starspren, moving up through the line of crystal. She forced herself to keep her fingers in place as it touched her skin.

I can hear you, a voice said in her mind—quiet, like a whisper. She couldn't tell if it was male or female. It seemed pitched between the two. *Though I do not see all that you assume I do. Regardless, Dabbid should not have spoken of this.*

"Be glad he did," Navani whispered. "I want to help."

You are a slaver, the Sibling said.

"Am I better than a Fused?"

The Sibling didn't respond at first. *I'm not sure,* they said. *I have avoided your kind. You were supposed to think I was dead. Everyone was supposed to think I was dead.*

"I'm glad you're not. You said you were the soul of the tower. Can you restore its functions?"

No, the voice said. *I really was asleep. Until . . . a Bondsmith. I felt a Bondsmith. But the tower is not functional, and I have not the Light to restart it.*

"If that is true, then how have they done what they have to the Radiants?"

I . . . They have corrupted me. A little part of me. They used their Light to activate defenses I could not.

"Is what they did related to that construction of garnets in your crystal pillar?"

You know too much, the Sibling said. *It makes me uncomfortable. You know and do things that weren't possible before.*

"They were possible, they simply weren't known," Navani said. "That is the nature of science."

What you do is dangerous and evil, the Sibling said. *Those ancient Radiants gave up their oaths because they worried they had too much power—and you have gone far beyond them.*

"I am willing to listen to you," Navani said. "Willing to change. But if the Fused take the tower, corrupt it . . ."

The . . . Lady of Pains is here, the Sibling said, voice growing softer. More frightened? It sounded like a child's voice, Navani decided.

"I don't know who that is," Navani said.

She is bad. Terrible. Few Fused are as . . . frightening to me as she is. She's trying to change me. So far, she changed only the portion of me that suppresses Surgebinding, reversing it so it affects Radiants instead of Fused. But she intends to go further. Much further.

"Is there a way to rescue our Radiants other than recovering the pillar?"

No, the Sibling said. *Get to the pillar, and we could reverse the effects. But otherwise . . . no. Those highly Invested might not be as strongly affected. Unmade, for example, were sometimes able to push through my suppression. Radiants of the high oaths might be able to access their powers. And Honor's Truest Surge, the Surge of Binding and Oaths, could still work.*

"What can I do to help?" Navani said. "We're mounting an assault to try to recapture the pillar heart. Is there something else I could try? Earlier you told me I needed to infuse something—but were cut off before you could finish."

The Lady of Pains is returning, the Sibling said. *I think . . . I think she's going to change me. My mind might alter. I might not care.*

"Do you care now?" Navani asked, urgent.

Yes. The voice seemed very small.

"Tell me what to do."

Long ago, before I banished men from these halls, my last Bondsmith made me something. A method of protecting me from the dangers I saw in men. He thought it would help me trust again. It did not. But it might stop the Fused from corrupting me further.

"Please," Navani said. "Let me help. *Please.*"

You cannot be trusted.

"Let me show you that I can."

I . . . You will need Stormlight, Navani Kholin. A great deal of Stormlight.

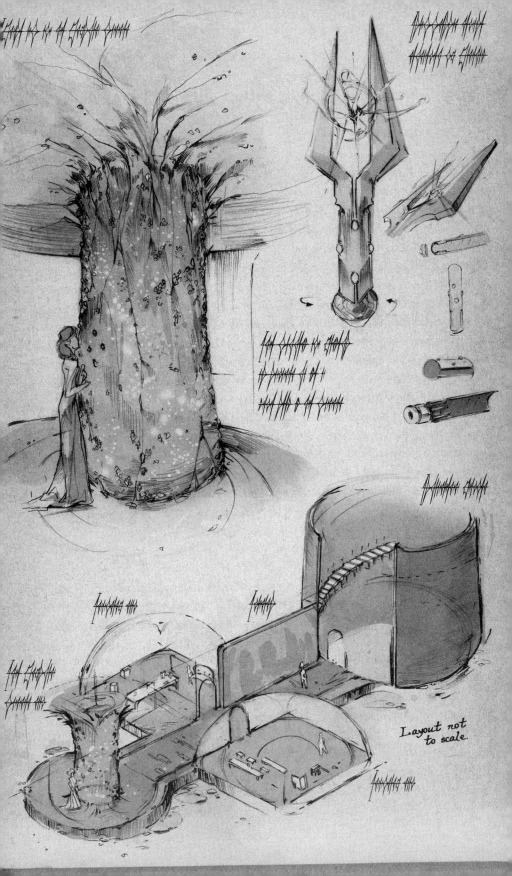

Layout not to scale.

41

THE MOST DANGEROUS

Of course, I admit this is a small quibble. A difference of semantics more than anything.

Venli wasn't required to fight unless she was attacked. A part of her wanted to go up above and look for Leshwi, who would have arrived by now with the other Heavenly Ones. But no, that was foolish. Even if being near Leshwi would help make sense of all this. Leshwi seemed to see so much more clearly than other Fused.

Regardless, as their troops marched up the steps to assault the first floors of the tower city, Venli stayed with Raboniel in the basement. The Lady of Wishes didn't seem terribly nervous about the invasion. She strolled along the wide hallway here, inspecting its murals. Venli stayed at her side as directed, and realized the reason she'd been brought along. Raboniel wanted a servant at hand.

"Does this strike you as a particularly *human* form of decoration, Last Listener?" Raboniel asked her, speaking to Craving as she stood with her hands before her, fingertips touching the large mural, this portion of which depicted Cultivation in the shape of a tree.

"I . . . I don't know humans well enough to say, Ancient One."

Sounds echoed from the stairwell at the opposite end of this hallway from the pillar room. Screams. Calls of horror. Clashes of weapon against weapon. By now the *shanay-im* would have arrived by air, delivering some of the most terrible and capable Fused to the sixth floor.

"To me it seems obvious," Raboniel said. "Humans never use what is around them to its fullest. They always impose their will far too strongly. Though the shells of beasts and the colors of stone would offer striking variety for creating complex murals, the humans ignored natural materials. Instead they painted each square, then affixed it to this wall.

"One of the singers of old, creating a similar work of art, would have divided the bits of shell into a spectrum of colors. They would have asked themself what kind of mural would naturally be suggested by the pieces they had obtained. Their mural would have used no paint, and would have lasted millennia longer than this one. See how the colors here fade."

A hulking form darkened the other end of the hallway, near the stairwell. The Pursuer looked like a dark scar of black and red upon the light stone. As he moved forward, Venli found herself trembling. Surely this was the most dangerous Fused in all the army.

"I have your leave," the Pursuer said to Raboniel, "to find this Windrunner and kill him?"

"Him alone," Raboniel said. "If he is here. There's a good chance one of his skill went with the others to Azir."

"If he is not here, he will return to try to liberate the tower," the Pursuer said. "It is in his nature." He turned, looking upward through the stone. "The Radiants we capture are dangerous. They have skill beyond what we anticipated, considering the newness of their bonds. We should behead them, each and every one."

"No," Raboniel said. "I will need them. Your orders are the same as what I told the others: Kill only those who resist. Gather the fallen Radiants for me. On my orders, you are to show . . . restraint."

The Pursuer hummed—loudly and forcefully—to Craving. "You, who were once banished for recklessly endangering our kind in your attempts to exterminate humankind? *You*, Lady of Wishes, ask for *restraint*?"

Raboniel smiled and hummed softly another rhythm that Venli had never heard. Something brand new. Something incredible. Dark, dangerous, predatory, and beautiful. It implied destruction, but a quiet and deadly destruction.

Odium had granted this femalen her *own rhythms*.

No, Venli thought, *the Pursuer is not the most dangerous of them*.

"I care not for a single battle," Raboniel said. "We *will* end this war, Pursuer. Forever. We have spent far, far too long in an endless cycle. I will break it—and once I am finished in this tower, there will be no turning back, *ever*. You will help in this, and you will start by collecting the fallen Radiants and delivering them to me."

"I may kill the one, when I find him?" he repeated. "You relieve the Nine's prohibition upon me?"

"Yes," Raboniel said. "You may claim your prize and keep your custom, Pursuer. I take responsibility for this order."

He hummed to Destruction and stalked off.

"If Stormblessed is here in the tower, he'll be helpless when you find him, Pursuer!" Venli called. "You would murder an enemy who cannot resist you?"

"Tradition is more important than honor, foolish one," the Pursuer called back to Derision. "I must kill those who have killed me. I have *always* killed those who have killed me."

He transformed into a ribbon of red light, leaving behind a lifeless husk, and shot out into the stairwell so he could fly to the upper levels.

Timbre pulsed uncertainly in Venli's chest. Yes . . . she was right. The Pursuer *did* have a madness to him. It wasn't as obvious as in the other Fused—the ones who would grin and refuse to speak, their eyes seeming to stare without seeing. It was there nonetheless. Perhaps this Pursuer had lived so long that his traditions had taken control of his reason. He was like a spren, existing more than living.

Timbre pulsed at that. She didn't think *she* existed without living, and Venli was forced to apologize. Still, she worried that all the Fused were like him. Maybe not mad—maybe that was the wrong word for it, and disrespectful to people who were themselves mad. The Fused instead seemed more like people who had lived so long thinking one way that they had come to accept their opinions as the natural state of things.

Venli had been like that once.

"So telling," Raboniel said to Thoughtfulness, still regarding the murals. "Humans take as their own everything they see. Yet they do not understand that by holding so tightly, they cause the very thing they desired to crumble. They truly are children of Honor."

Raboniel turned from the mural and strolled farther down the hallway, approaching an intersection where doors opened on either side. These led into chambers with tables, bookshelves, stacks of paper. Venli followed Raboniel into one of them, then hurried—at a wave of her fingers, a gesture Venli's translation powers interpreted—to fetch a cup of wine from the station at the side of the room.

Venli passed huddled scholars and monks, sitting on the floor by the wall beneath the watchful eyes of a few Regal stormforms. The poor humans were surrounded by fearspren, though Venli had to remind herself that no human could ever be *completely* trusted. They didn't have forms. A human might wear the robes of their priesthood, but could secretly have trained as a warrior. It was part of what made humans so duplicitous. No rhythms to hum to, just facial features easy to fake. No forms to indicate their duty. Just clothing that could be changed as easily as a lie required it.

Timbre pulsed.

Well, of course I'm different, Venli thought. Even if she *did* lie by humming the wrong rhythms at times. And wear a form that didn't express the spren she truly followed.

Timbre pulsed in satisfaction.

Don't make this harder than it already is, Venli thought, hastening to Raboniel. *I'm not here to help the humans. I can barely help my own kind.*

She delivered Raboniel's wine as the tall Fused was inspecting a contraption of metal and gemstones. A human fabrial delivered by one of the Deepest Ones.

"What should we make of this?" the Deepest One asked to Craving. "I have never seen its like before. How can the humans have discovered things we never knew about?"

"They have always been clever," Raboniel said to Derision. "We merely left them alone too long this time. Go and interrogate the scholars. I would find out who leads their studies here."

The Fused glanced upward.

"The conquest will happen easily," Raboniel said to Conceit. "By now, the *shanay-im* have used Vyre to activate the Oathgate, bringing our troops. Let us stay focused while they work."

"Yes, Lady of Wishes," the Deepest One said, gliding off.

Raboniel absently took the cup from Venli's hands. She turned the fabrial over in her hand, and hummed softly to . . . to *Subservience?*

She's impressed, Venli realized. *And she's keeping most of the scholars alive—along with the Radiants. She wants something from this tower.*

"You don't care about the conquest," Venli guessed, speaking to Craving. "You aren't here to further the war or to dominate the humans. You're here because of these things. The fabrials humans are creating."

Raboniel hummed to Command. "Yes, Leshwi *does* pick the best, doesn't she?" She held out the fabrial, letting the light catch it. "Do you know what the humans *gain* by being so forceful? By reaching to seize before they are ready? Yes, their works crumble. Yes, their nations collapse from within. Yes, they end up squabbling, and fighting, and killing one another.

"But in the moment, they are the sprinter who outpaces the steady runner. In the moment, they create *wonders.* One cannot fault their audacity. Their *imagination.* Surely you've noticed that the Fused have a problem. We think along the same old, familiar pathways. We don't create because we assume we've already created what we need to. We are immortal, and so think nothing can ever surprise us—and that makes us complacent."

Venli hummed to Abashment, realizing she'd been thinking that same thing.

"That is the reason this war is eternal," Raboniel said. "They cannot hold or exploit that which they create, but we cannot stretch far enough to come up with anything new. If we truly want an end, it will take a partnership."

"I do not think the Alethi will partner with you," Venli said. "Like the Iriali have."

"They can be guided," Raboniel said. She glanced at Venli, then smiled again, humming her new rhythm. Her individual dangerous rhythm. "If there is one thing I can guarantee you about humankind, Last Listener, it is this: Provide them with a sword, and they *will* find a way to impale themselves upon it."

⁜

The stench of burned flesh assaulted Navani as she entered the ground floor of Urithiru. She hoped that most of the civilians had been able to flee to the upper floors, for what she saw now seemed nothing short of Damnation itself. The large foyer in front of the grand staircase was empty save for a few scattered corpses. Burned. Human.

The thick, pungent scent made her want to retch.

Red lights flashed in the near hallways, and cracks of thunder echoed off the stone. Loud, sharp, and unnatural. One shouldn't be able to hear thunder in these hallways, buried beneath a million tons of stone and a ten-minute walk to the perimeter.

Between the peals of thunder, Navani was certain she heard distant moans and cries. Her kingdom had become a war zone. What scout reports she received spoke of fragmented squads of soldiers desperately holding out before nightmares moving in quick roving bands. They thought the singers were securing points of strategic value, but their information was too disjointed to get a full picture of the enemy's plans.

Storms . . . they'd become so dependent on spanreeds. It felt downright *primitive* to lack knowledge of enemy movements. Navani moved through the foyer, urging her band of scholars, ardents, and engineers to follow. They balked, remaining in a cluster on the wide steps. She glanced back and saw many staring in horror at the burned corpses on the ground.

Right. Few of her current attendants had ever been subjected to *real* battlefields. They had worked the warcamps, had designed bridges and flying platforms, but they weren't the types who saw corpses in anything other than a sanitized funeral service.

Navani remembered being like that. Before Gavilar. He'd always promised that a unified Alethkar would be a wonderful blessing to all the people of the land. With him around, it always *had* been easier to rationalize the price in blood.

Regardless of their feelings, they had to keep moving. They'd given Battalionlord Teofil an hour to gather his assault force and send some initial sallies to clear the landing. During that time Navani had gathered as much

Stormlight as she could. Her attendants carried the spheres and gemstones in large bags.

The wait had let Navani send for two specific women. They stood near the center of the huddle of attendants: Thaylen scholars from Queen Fen's court who were visiting the tower to listen to Navani's lectures. They'd come to her command post willingly, probably believing that Navani had sent for them because she wanted to protect them during the invasion. Their panicked glances now showed they were beginning to question those assumptions.

A soldier stood guarding the way through a particular hallway. Navani hurried in that direction, leaving her attendants behind for now. She entered a large open hall that in times past they'd used as a meeting place. Some five hundred soldiers crowded the corners and a couple of side corridors. Not fully out of sight, but obscured enough for their purpose. Other than the numerous crossbowmen among them, the items of most interest were two large metal pillars on wheels.

Teofil noticed her and stepped over. "Brightness," he said. "I'd be more comfortable if you waited closer to the steps."

"Objection noted," Navani said. "How does it look?"

"I've gathered our best veterans," he said. "This will be bloody work, but I think we have a chance. The enemy is relying on the Regals to seize the ground floor. I keep reminding the men that as frightening as the enemy powers are, the ones using them have only a year of training."

The human advantage had so far been their experience. Parshmen newly awakened from their lives of slavery were no replacement for battle-hardened troops. This advantage was slowly being worn away as enemy troops gained more and more practical combat experience.

An exhausted messenger dashed into the room from the hallway directly across from Navani—the hallway leading toward the steps to the basement. The messenger nodded to Teofil before moving to the side and putting her hands on her knees, breathing in deep gasps.

Teofil gestured for Navani to retreat, and she moved to the mouth of the corridor. She didn't retreat farther than that, so Teofil stoically walked over and handed her some wax and pointed at his ears. Then he fell into position, sword out, with one group of soldiers.

A controlled retreat was difficult enough, but what they were trying here—a fake rout leading to an ambush—was even trickier. You had to bait the enemy into thinking you were fleeing, and that involved turning your backs on them. A trickle of human soldiers soon came running into the room, and their panic seemed real to Navani. It probably was. The line between a feint and a true collapse of morale was thin as a sheet of paper.

The trickle of soldiers became a flood. Fleeing men, chased by flashes of light and thunder that made Navani hastily stuff her ears with the wax. She spared a moment of grief for the slowest of the fleeing soldiers, who sold this ruse with their lives, dying in a bright flash of lightning.

The chasing Regals soon charged into the room: wicked-looking singers with pointed carapace and glowing red eyes. Teofil waited longer than Navani would have to give the order to loose—he wanted as many Regals in the room as possible. The pause was long enough that the first of the enemies had time to stop, then raise arms crackling with electric energy.

Navani braced herself as they released flashes of light toward the waiting soldiers. Those flashes, however, struck the carefully placed metal pillars, which drew the lightning like tall trees might in an open field.

Teofil gave the order with a raised piece of red cloth—though Navani barely saw it, as she was blinking blinded eyes. Crossbows loosed in wave after deadly wave, cutting down the Regals—who didn't have the same power to heal themselves that the Fused possessed.

"Hoist those lightning rods!" Teofil shouted, his voice sounding muted to her ears. "Move, men! Stay away from blood on the ground. We push for the basement!"

As quickly as that, the "rout" reversed, and human troops piled into the hallway to chase the remaining Regals. Teofil left her with a salute. He set out on a near-impossible task: to push down a long stairwell into the basement, harried by Regals and Fused. If Navani wasn't able to get to him after he reached the pillar, he was to destroy the construction of garnets that suppressed Radiant powers. The Sibling indicated this would be effective at restoring the Radiants.

In the meantime, Navani's job was to activate the Sibling's fail-safe. She hurried to collect her scribes, hoping they wouldn't balk too much at climbing over the corpses.

◆◆

Kaladin ducked into a room, carrying an armful of blankets. He didn't recognize the young family inside—father, mother, two toddlers—so they had to be refugees who had fled to Hearthstone.

The young family had done much to make this small, windowless room their own. Both walls were covered in Herdazian sand paintings, and the floor was painted in a large and intricate glyph.

Kaladin didn't like the way they cringed as he entered, the children whimpering. *If you don't want people to cringe when they see you,* he thought, *act less like a ruffian and more like a surgeon.* He never had possessed his father's gentle grace, that unassuming way that wasn't weak, but also rarely seemed threatening.

"Sorry," Kaladin said, shutting the door behind him. "I know you were expecting my father. You wanted blankets?"

"Yes," the wife said, rising and taking them from him. "Thank you. It cold."

"I know," Kaladin said. "Something's wrong with the tower, so heating fabrials aren't working."

The man said something in Herdazian. Syl, sitting on Kaladin's shoulder, whispered the interpretation—but the woman translated right afterward anyway.

"Dark ones in the corridors," the woman said. "They . . . are staying?"

"We don't know yet," Kaladin said. "For now, it's best to remain in your rooms. Here, I brought water and some rations. Soulcast, I'm afraid. We'll send someone around tomorrow to gather chamber pots, if it comes to that."

He slung his pack onto his shoulder after getting out the food and water. Then he slipped back out into the corridor. He had three more rooms to visit before meeting up with his father. "What time is it?" he asked Syl.

"Late," she said. "A few hours to dawn."

Kaladin had been working to deliver blankets and water for a good hour or so. He knew that fighting was still going on far below, that Navani was holding out. The enemy, however, had quickly secured this floor, leaving guards and pushing downward to press against the Alethi defenders.

So while the tower wasn't yet lost, Kaladin's floor felt quiet. Syl turned around and lifted into the air, shimmering and becoming formless like a cloud. "I keep seeing things, Kaladin. Streaks of red. Voidspren I think, patrolling the halls."

"You can see them even if they're invisible to humans, right?"

She nodded. "But they can see me too. My cognitive aspect."

A part of him wanted to ask further. Why, for instance, could Rock always see her? Was he somehow part spren? Lift seemed to be able to do it too, though she wouldn't speak about it. So was she part Horneater? The other Edgedancers didn't have the ability.

The questions wouldn't form on his lips. He was distracted, and honestly he was exhausted. He let the thoughts slip away as he moved to the next room on his list. These ones would probably be extra frightened, having not heard anything since—

"Kaladin," Syl hissed.

He stopped immediately, then looked up, noting a stormform Regal walking down the hallway with a sphere lantern in one hand, a sword on his hip. "You there," he said, speaking with a rhythm, but otherwise no hint of an accent. "Why are you out of your rooms?"

"I'm a surgeon," Kaladin said. "I was told by one of the Fused that I could check on our people. I'm delivering food and water."

The singer sized him up, then waved for him to open his pack and show what was inside. Kaladin obliged, and didn't look toward Syl, who was doing her windspren act—flitting about and pretending she didn't belong with a Radiant—just in case.

The singer inspected the rations, then studied Kaladin.

Looking at my arms, my chest, Kaladin thought. *Wondering why a surgeon is built like a soldier.* At least his brands were covered by his long hair.

"Return to your rooms," the man said.

"The others will be frightened," Kaladin said. "You could have hysterical people on your hands—chaos that would interfere with your troops."

"And how often did you check on the parshmen of your village, when they were frightened?" the singer asked. "When they were forced into dark rooms, locked away and ignored? Did you spare any concern for *them*, surgeon?"

Kaladin bit off a response. This wasn't the kind of taunt where the speaker wanted an answer. Instead he looked down.

The singer, in turn, stepped forward and snapped his hand at Kaladin to strike him. Kaladin moved without thinking, raising his hand to catch the singer's wrist before it connected. He felt a small *jolt* of something when he touched the carapace-backed hand.

The singer grinned. "A surgeon, you say?"

"You've never heard of a battlefield medic?" Kaladin said. "I've trained with the men, so I can handle myself. But you can ask anyone in this town if I'm the surgeon's son, and they'll confirm it."

The singer shoved at Kaladin's hand, trying to throw him off balance, but Kaladin's stance was solid. He met the red eyes, and saw the smile in them. The eagerness. This creature wanted a fight. Likely he was angry he'd been posted to something as boring as patrolling halls on what was to have been a daring and dangerous mission. He'd love nothing more than to have an excuse for a little excitement.

Kaladin's grip tightened on the man's hand. His heartbeat sped up, and he found himself reaching for the Stormlight at his belt. Draw in a breath, suck it in, end this farce. Enemies were invading the tower, and he was *delivering blankets*?

He held those red eyes with his own. He heard his heart thundering. Then he forced himself to look away and let the singer shove him into the wall, then trip him with a sweep to his legs. The creature loomed over him, and Kaladin kept his eyes down. You learned to do that, when you were a slave.

The creature snorted and stomped away without another word, leaving Kaladin. He felt tense, alert, like he often did before a battle—his fatigue washed away. He wanted to act.

Instead he continued on his way, delivering comfort to the people of Hearthstone.

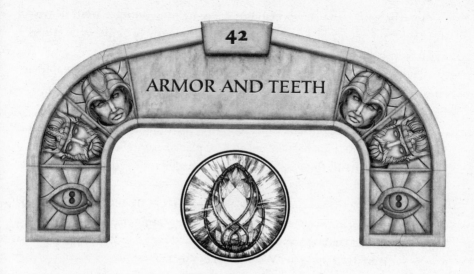

42

ARMOR AND TEETH

In truth, it would be a combination of a Vessel's craftiness and the power's Intent that we should fear most.

Navani and her timid attendants soon left the broad hallway scattered with corpses and entered a series of corridors with darkened lanterns on the walls. The broken latches bespoke thieves with crowbars getting at the spheres inside. For some people, no nightmare was terrible enough—no war bloody enough—to discourage some creative personal enrichment.

The sounds of screams and echoes of thunder faded. Navani felt as if she were entering the mythical centerbeat—the heart of a highstorm spoken of by some poor wanderers trapped within its winds. A moment when for reasons inexplicable, the wind stopped and all became still.

She eventually reached the place where the Sibling had told her to go—a specific intersection among these twisting corridors. Though no part of the first level went completely unused, this area was among the least trafficked. The corridors here made a maze of frustrating design, and they used the small rooms for various storage dumps.

"Now what?" asked Elthebar, the stormwarden. Navani wasn't particularly happy to have the tall man along; he looked silly with his pointed beard and his mysterious robes. But he'd been in the map room with them, and forbidding him hadn't seemed right when she needed every mind she could get.

"Search this area," Navani said to the others. "See if you can find a vein of garnet on the walls. It might be small and hidden among the changing colors of the strata."

They did as she requested. Dabbid, the mute bridgeman, started searching the floor instead of the walls—working with his sphere enclosed entirely in his hand so it gave almost no light.

"Cover up your spheres and lanterns," Navani said to the others. The command drew expressions that ranged between confused and horrified, but Navani led the way, closing the shield on her lantern.

The others obeyed one at a time, plunging the room into darkness. Light from a distant corridor flashed red in a sequence—only with no thunder. A few people's hands glowed softly from the spheres inside, backlighting veins and bones.

"There," Navani said, picking out a faint twinkling on the floor near one of the walls. They clustered around it, investigating the spark of garnet light in a hidden vein of crystal.

"What is it?" Isabi asked. "What kind of spren?"

The light started moving through the vein, across the floor, then down the corridor. Navani ignored the questions, following the spark until it moved up a wall. Here it followed the curving strata into a specific room, rounding the stone and slipping through the gap between door and doorway.

Venan had keys, fortunately. Inside, they had to step over rolled rugs to find the spark of light at the rear. Navani brushed her fingers against it and found a small bulge in the wall.

A gemstone, she realized. *Connected to the line of crystal. It's embedded in here so deeply, it's difficult to see.* Seemed to be a topaz. Hadn't there been a similar gemstone embedded into the wall of that room where they'd found the model of the tower?

Infuse the topaz, the Sibling's voice said in her mind. *You can do this without Radiants? I have seen you perform such marvels.*

"I need several small topazes," Navani said to her scholars. "No larger than three kivs each."

Her team scrambled; they kept gemstones of all sizes on hand for their experiments, and one soon brought forth a small case of infused topazes. Navani instructed her and several others to take the gemstones in tweezers and present them to the topaz set into the wall.

An infused gemstone touched to an uninfused one could be made to lend some of its Stormlight—assuming they were the same variety, and the uninfused gemstone was much larger than the infused ones. It worked a little like a pressure differential. A large empty vessel would take Stormlight from small full vessels.

It was a slow process, especially when the gemstone you wanted to infuse was relatively small—limiting the potential size differential. She moved up next to Ulvlk and Vrandl, the two Thaylen scholars. Both were artifabrians of a very secretive guild.

"Almighty send we can make this work in time," Navani said as thunder echoed behind them.

"So that is why you brought us," Vrandl said. She was a short woman who preferred havahs to traditional Thaylen dress. She wore her eyebrows in tight curls. "The tower is invaded, your men are dying, and you see an opportunity to pry trade secrets from our fingers?"

"The world is ending," Navani countered, "and our greatest advantage—this tower, with its ability to instantly move troops from one end of Roshar to the other—is threatened. Is this *really* the time to hoard trade secrets, Brightness?"

The two women didn't reply.

"You'd watch it burn?" Navani said, feeling exhausted—and snappish. "You'd *actually* let Urithiru fall rather than share what you know? If we lose the Oathgates permanently, that's *it* for the war. That's *it* for your homeland."

Again they remained silent.

"Fine," Navani said. "I hope when you die—knowing your homeland is doomed, your families enslaved, your queen executed—you feel satisfied knowing that at least you maintained a slight market advantage."

Navani pushed to the front of the group, where her scholars were coaxing Stormlight into the wall gem bit by bit. Often a fabrial needed to fill a certain percentage before it activated—but the more this one drew in Stormlight, the slower the drain would occur.

Footsteps scraped the stone behind her, and Navani turned to see Ulvlk—junior of the two Thaylen scholars—standing behind her. "We use sound," she whispered. "If you can make the gemstone vibrate at a certain frequency, it will draw in Stormlight regardless of the size of gems placed next to it."

"Frequency . . ." Navani said. "How did you discover this?"

"Traditions," she whispered. "Passed down for centuries."

"Create a vibration . . ." Navani said. "You use drilled holes? No . . . that would require Stormlight to be already infused. Tuning forks?"

"Yes," Ulvlk explained. "We touch the tuning fork against the full gemstone, making it vibrate, then can lead a line of Stormlight out to the empty one. After that, it will siphon, like liquid."

"Do you have the equipment here, now?" Navani asked.

"I . . ."

"Of course you do," Navani said. "When I sent runners to fetch you, you thought I was going to evacuate you. You'd have grabbed anything of value in your rooms."

The young Thaylen woman fished in her pocket, pulling out a metal tuning fork.

"You will be expelled from the guild!" Vrandl snapped from behind, angerspren pooling beneath her. "This is a ploy!"

"It's no ploy," Navani assured the nervous young woman. "Honestly, we were close to a breakthrough using the weapons the Fused have—which are able to drain Stormlight out of a person. All you've done here is potentially save this tower from invaders."

Navani tried the method, hitting the tuning fork, then touching one of the infused gemstones. Indeed, as she pulled it away from the stone and toward the gemstone on the wall, it trailed a small stream of Stormlight. Like how Light behaved when a Radiant was sucking it in.

That did the trick, infusing the wall gemstone in seconds. The Sibling had explained what was coming, but Navani still jumped when—upon being infused—the fabrial made the entire wall *shake*.

It parted at the center; it had been a hidden door all along—locked by a fabrial that in the old days probably only a Radiant could have activated. They quickly uncovered their lanterns and spheres, revealing a small circular chamber with a pedestal in the center. Set into that was a large sapphire, uninfused.

"Quickly," Navani said to the others, "let's get to work."

⁘

Kaladin slung his pack over his shoulder, then slipped out of the room of another frightened family. This one, like those before, had asked him for news, for information, for promises. Was it going to be all right? Would the other Radiants rise as he had? When would the Bondsmith return?

He wished he had answers. He felt so blind. He'd grown accustomed to being in the thick of everything important—privy to not only the plans of important people, but their worries and their fears as well.

He followed Syl, who darted into the hallway. The hour was late, and Kaladin had to fight off a bout of grogginess, despite the shakes and thumps in the stone. Distant explosions from far below, so powerful they had to be the acts of Regals or Fused. Somewhere in the tower, men fought. But up here on the sixth floor, they cowered. The place dripped with the silence of a thousand frightened people.

He reached an intersection, fighting off his fatigue. He was supposed to get back to the clinic and meet up with his father, but Syl was flitting around another way—she clearly wanted his attention. They had decided to keep her distant from him in case a Voidspren noticed her.

He followed her down the left fork, through a doorway that led out onto the large, patio-like balcony near his quarters. Though many of these balconies were being used as community spots, this one was empty tonight—save for one figure standing near the edge. The carapace jutting out through holes in the uniform made Rlain distinctive, even in silhouette.

"Hey," Kaladin said, stepping up to him. Syl settled on the banister, glowing softly. Kaladin found it eerie to stare out in the darkness of night, overlooking an endless landscape of mountains and clouds—shimmering green from the final moon.

"More troops," Rlain said, nodding toward the plateau below—where another formation of singers was moving toward the tower's front gates. "They march like human armies, not like listener warpairs."

"I thought you were going to stay hidden in the clinic."

"This will be an occupation, Kal," Rlain said, voice tinged by a mournful rhythm. "We won't be recovering Urithiru tonight—or anytime soon. So where does that leave me?"

"You're not one of them."

"Am I one of you?"

"You'll always be a member of Bridge Four."

"That's not what I meant." Rlain turned toward him, green moonlight shining against his carapace and skin. "If I try to hide among the humans, I will be courting disaster. Assuming I could somehow stay out of sight, *someone* is going to reveal me to the Fused. *Someone* will think I'm a spy for the enemy, and after that . . . well, it's going to be very difficult to explain why I didn't walk out and embrace their occupation."

Kaladin wanted to object. But storms, he was worried about a similar thing happening to him. One mention that he'd been a Radiant—that the surgeon's son was Kaladin Stormblessed, Windrunner—and . . . well, who knew what would happen?

"So what do you do?" Syl asked from the railing.

"Go to them," Rlain said. "Pretend I'm not a listener, just an ordinary parshman who never managed to escape—and didn't know what I should do. It might work. Either that, or maybe I can hide among them, pretend I've always been with them. Merely another face in their forces."

"And if they take you out into the Everstorm?" Kaladin asked. "Demand you take a Regal form—or worse, give yourself up to the soul of a Fused?"

"Then I'll have to find a way to escape, won't I?" Rlain said. "This has been coming, Kal. I think I've always known I would have to face them. I could make a home here if I wanted. I know that, and I'll always be grateful to you and the others for making a place for me.

"At the same time, I can't ignore what was done to my people at the hands of human empires. I won't be fully comfortable here. Not while I wonder if there are other listeners out there who survived the

Everstorm. Not while I wonder if there's more I could be doing to stop the disaster."

Kaladin took a deep breath, though part of him was tearing inside. "Another farewell then."

"A temporary one, I hope," Rlain said. Then, looking somewhat awkward, he held out his hands and gave Kaladin an embrace. Rlain had never seemed fond of that human custom, but Kaladin was glad for the gesture.

"Thank you," Rlain said, pulling back. "For trusting me to make this decision."

"That's what you said you wanted, all those months ago," Kaladin said. "When I promised I'd listen."

"To be trusted and acknowledged," Rlain said.

"I keep my oaths, Rlain. Especially to friends."

"I'm not going to join them, Kal. I am a spy. That is my training—as best my kind could offer. I'll find a way to help from the inside. Remember that the first people Odium destroyed when he returned were not human, but listener."

"Bridge Four," Kaladin said.

"Life before death," Rlain returned. Then he slipped away toward the interior of the tower.

Syl remained seated on the banister. Kaladin leaned against the stone, waiting for a cheerful line from Syl. When others tried to console him with laughs, it often struck him as false, unnecessary. But from her . . . well, she helped pull him out of the deep waters.

"They're all going to leave, aren't they?" she whispered instead. "Moash, Rock, now Rlain . . . every one of them. They're going to leave. Or . . . or worse . . ." She looked at Kaladin, uncharacteristically solemn. "They'll all go away, and then there will be nothingness."

"Syl," Kaladin said. "You shouldn't say things like that."

"It's true though," she said. "Isn't it?"

"I won't leave you."

"Like you almost did?" she said softly. "My old knight . . . he didn't want to leave. . . . It's not his fault. He was mortal though. Everyone dies. Except me."

"Syl?" Kaladin said. "What's wrong? Is whatever they did to the tower affecting you?"

She was silent for a time, staring out over the green clouds. "Yes, of course," she said. "I'm sorry. That's not what you needed, is it? I can be perky. I can be happy. See?" She launched into the air, becoming a line of light that zipped around his head.

"I didn't mean—" Kaladin said.

"Don't be such a worrier," she cut in. "Can't you take a joke these days, Kaladin? Come on. We need to get back to the clinic."

She zipped off, and—confused, worried, but most of all just exhausted—he followed.

∴

Navani watched as her people worked, infusing the gemstone at the center of the small chamber. They had borrowed a second tuning fork from the Thaylen scholars, doubling their speed.

Such a simple tool. She and Rushu had theorized for hours about the process the Thaylen artifabrians were using—guessing everything from hidden Radiants to intricate machinery that mimicked water osmosis methods, which followed similar scientific principles to Light infusion. In the end, their actual method was far, far humbler.

Wasn't that often how it turned out? Science seemed easy in retrospect. Why hadn't the ancients figured out you could intentionally trap a spren in a gemstone? Why hadn't they discovered that a split gemstone would be paired? Add a little aluminum for the cage, and you could do incredible things. With this knowledge, people four thousand years ago could have had flying ships as easily as Navani's people.

True, the hundreds of tiny leaps that led to advances were not as intuitive as they seemed. Regardless, it left Navani wondering. What wonders could she create if she knew the next few leaps that would appear simple to her descendants? What marvelous creations did she brush past each day, lying in pieces, waiting to be combined?

More thunder sounded; she hoped that the continued noise was a good sign for Teofil and his men. *Move faster,* she willed the Stormlight. Unfortunately, something was odd about this gemstone. Though the new Thaylen method did indeed transfer Stormlight quickly, the strange fabrial seemed to be drinking far too much in. They'd emptied most of the spheres they'd brought, and still the sapphire barely glowed. They seemed to be injecting Light not just into the gemstone, but into the entire network of gemstones and crystal veins.

Was it actually a fabrial? Navani didn't recognize the cage, though it did have metal wire running around it. And why did it have a glass globe, the size of her fist, set off to the side in its own nook and attached to the gemstone by wires?

As her scholars worked, emptying one gemstone after the other, Navani brushed the back of her freehand fingers against a vein of garnet in the wall.

You must move quickly, the Sibling said in her mind.

"We are going as fast as we can," Navani whispered. "Are my soldiers still alive?"

I cannot see them, the Sibling said. *My vision is limited, in ways that are confusing to me, as it was not always so. But I think the soldiers you sent are close. I can hear shouts nearby the crystal heart of the tower.*

Navani closed her eyes, hoping the Almighty would accept a whispered prayer, as she had no glyphward to burn.

Hurry, the Sibling said. *Hurry.*

She glanced toward the pile of gemstones. Fortunately, the Thaylen method could move Stormlight between different types of polestone. "We are trying. Do you know why spren prefer different kinds of gemstones?"

Because they are different, the Sibling said. *Why do humans prefer one kind of food to another?*

"Yet foods dyed different colors—but with the same taste—are often equally acceptable to us." Navani nodded to a small pile of emeralds. "Many gemstones are identical, at least by their structure. We think they might even have the same basic chemical composition."

Color is like flavor to spren, the Sibling said. *It is part of the soul of a thing.* Curious.

You must move quickly, the Sibling repeated. *The Lady of Pains has the Surge of Transformation and dangerous knowledge. She will infuse my entire heart—the pillar—in the proper order, using her Voidlight. In so doing, she would corrupt me and leave me . . . leave me as one of the Unmade. . . .*

"And what we do here will defend you?" Navani whispered.

Yes. It will erect a barrier, preventing anyone—human, Unmade, or singer— from reaching me.

"That would stop Teofil too," Navani said. "From breaking the construction that is blocking our Radiants."

Teofil is doomed, the Sibling said. *You must hurry. Navani, they have activated the Oathgate again. Fresh enemy troops have arrived.*

"How are they working it? They have Skybreakers, but they should be as limited as our Radiants, right?"

They brought a human with one of the Honorblades.

Moash. The murderer. Navani felt her anger rising. There was, unfortunately, little more she could do.

Quickly. Please. Quickly . . . The Sibling seemed to hesitate. *Wait. Something has happened. The Lady of Pains has stopped.*

⁘

Venli witnessed the last push of the human soldiers. She stood at the base of the steps—which were of an odd sort. The stairwell up to the ground floor was a large column of open space. Steps wound around the outside wall of the cylinder. They looked so narrow and uncertain, hanging as they did with a cavity of open space up the center.

It was pure madness to attempt to fight down such steep and uncertain footing while harried by Fused and Regals. Yet the humans made a valiant run of it. They locked shields and moved together with a precision that Venli's sister had always admired. While listeners would fight as warpairs, in tune with one another and the rhythms of Roshar, humans seemed to have their own kind of symbiosis—forged from hours upon hours spent training.

A canopy of shields protected against Heavenly Ones, who hovered about the formation, trying to stab with their lances—but indoors, they didn't have proper room to maneuver. Before beginning their assault, the humans had poured barrels of water into the breach here—and it had rained upon the stormform Regals below. Their powers reacted poorly around water, something Venli had always found somewhat ironic.

The descent was so dramatic that Venli sent for Raboniel, interrupting the Fused's work with the pillar. Raboniel marched out and looked up with shock at how close the humans were.

"Quickly," she snapped at the nearby stormforms. "Up those steps! Engage the soldiers directly!"

They obeyed, but with their powers dampened by the water, they were no match for the troops. The humans stabbed them dead or forced them off the sides of the steps, pushing ever downward, rounding the circular wall, grimly stepping over the bodies of their fallen comrades and maintaining a front line that was three men wide.

"Amazing," Raboniel whispered. The humans fought like a great-shelled beast—a winding, relentless chasmfiend, all armor and teeth.

Raboniel waved for the rest of the Deepest Ones to join the fight—but even these proved ineffective. They had disrupted the formation a few times early on, shoving their hands out of walls to push men, or reaching out from the side to grab ankles. These soldiers, however, quickly adapted. The men closest to the wall now marched with swords out, watching for Deepest Ones. More than one disembodied arm dropped to the ground near Venli, joining the fallen men and Regals who had lost their footing.

Standing there beside an increasingly angry Raboniel, Venli thought the humans might make it. Led by a grizzled older soldier—and reduced from hundreds to just fifty—they barreled stubbornly onward. Venli found herself cheering them silently, Timbre exulting to the Rhythm of Hope. She cared little for the humans as a whole, but it was impossible to watch such a display of tenacity without being impressed.

This was why her people had dwindled, nearly vanished, during their years at war with the humans. It wasn't entirely the human access to Shards, or their incredible resources. It was the way they, individually weaker than any listener, worked together. They had no forms, but compensated with training, sacrificing individuality until they were practically spren—having become so good at a single thing, they could never change to another purpose.

They rounded the next loop, only twenty feet from the ground, while Raboniel began shouting for more Deepest Ones. Then a red line of light zipped down from above. The Pursuer had arrived.

He materialized in the very center of the formation of humans, swinging out with arms bearing sharpened carapace. The formation shattered as the men frantically tried to reorient to this new foe—but of course the Pursuer zipped back into the air. He left behind a dummy, a fake carapace version of himself. The humans began stabbing it repeatedly as the real Pursuer appeared with a crash among another segment of the line.

As quickly as that, the tide changed.

The Heavenly Ones found holes in the shield wall to begin stabbing individual humans. The Deepest Ones used the confusion to grab sword arms or trip soldiers. A small group of humans, led by the older veteran, tried to surge forward and dash the rest of the way—but the Regals near Venli had toweled dry, and they managed to unleash a collective bolt of lightning that destroyed the steps in a wide gap right in front of the men.

The human leader, and the men closest to him, dropped with the rubble to die. The rest began a frantic attempt at retreat. It ended quickly.

Raboniel changed her rhythm to one of Relief, then strode back into the mural-lined corridor toward the pillar. Unwilling to watch the final slaughter, Venli turned and scurried alongside her. The sounds of bodies falling—the din of armor against stone—chased them all the way.

⁂

It is done, the Sibling whispered to Navani. *Your men have fallen.*

"Are you certain?" Navani asked. "What do you see?"

I used to be able to watch the entire tower. Now . . . I see just patches. A small portion of the sixth floor. A room on the fourth floor, with a cage in it. The place nearest the Lady of Pains. She returns. She will kill me now.

The large gemstone her people had been working on—finally primed with Stormlight—began glowing brightly. The light inside it started to shift and dance, furious. Then it drained away, vanishing.

Navani felt a spike of alarm, until the Sibling spoke into her mind. *It worked. Melishi . . . I have hated you . . . but now I bless you. It worked. I am safe, for now.*

Navani let out a relieved breath.

If they reach the gemstone you just infused, the Sibling said, *they could corrupt me through it. You will need to destroy it.*

"Will that break the shield?" Navani forced out.

No. It will weaken the shield, but that is better than the alternative. You cannot defend this place. Your soldiers on the steps have fallen.

She breathed out, and would remember to burn a prayer for the fallen when she could. But if Teofil had been killed . . . then the tower was captured. Navani's only course was to surrender. She would have to hope that the barrier would last long enough either for Dalinar to reach them, or for Navani to find a way to free the Radiants.

Assuming she wasn't killed. The Fused did not often slaughter indiscriminately, but there *were* reports of them executing high-ranking lighteyes. That depended on the Fused who led the individual forces, and how much the people resisted.

"Shatter that sapphire," she said to her scholars. "Destroy the entire fabrial, cage included, and that glass globe. Send people to both the map room and the information vault to burn our maps of the tower. The rest of you, join me. We must find a way to deliver a formal surrender without being killed before we can make our intentions known."

⋄⋅⋄

Raboniel approached the pillar again with some eagerness. Venli stood nearby as the Fused reached up to touch a specific set of gemstones that were embedded in the construction, then began infusing those with Voidlight.

As soon as she'd begun, though, she hesitated. "Something curious is happening here. There is *Stormlight* in the system. That shouldn't be possible; the Sibling cannot create it."

"I thought that Stormlight was what the Radiants, and their fabrials, always used," Venli said.

"The tower is something else." She glanced at Venli, noting her confusion—and unlike many Fused, she chose to explain. "The Sibling—the tower, Urithiru—is the child of Honor and Cultivation, created to fight Odium. The place runs on the *Sibling's* Light, a mixture of the essences of its parents. Stormlight alone shouldn't be able to work the tower's core systems. Stormlight, to the Sibling, is incomplete. Like a key missing several of its teeth."

"And with Voidlight, you're using a key . . . with no teeth?" Venli asked.

"I'm not using a key at all. I'm breaking the lock." Raboniel put her hands on the pillar, infusing another specific gemstone. "The Sibling is insensate, completely unaware that we are here. That I can determine. I can corrupt them, awaken them to serve us. Just as I expected. But also, there *is* Stormlight. I feel it, a large amount. Perhaps . . . it's simply the power they're using to work the pumps, or the lifts. Not true parts of the Sibling; systems added later, attached to the construction. Those could take Storm-light alone. . . ."

Raboniel stopped and stepped back, humming to Craving—a rhythm to indicate confusion or a question. And then a wave of blue light began to expand from the pillar. She stumbled away, and Venli joined her, dashing out into the corridor—where the blue light stopped and seemed to *solidify*, blocking the way.

Raboniel stepped forward and rested a hand on it. "Solid," she said. "And powered by Stormlight, judging by the tone . . ."

Venli anticipated anger. This shield, whatever it was, clearly thwarted whatever the Lady of Wishes was doing. Instead she seemed *fascinated*.

"Remarkable, truly remarkable," Raboniel said, tapping the shield with her knife. It clicked like glass when touched. "This is incredible."

"Does it ruin our plans?" Venli asked.

"Absolutely."

"And . . . you don't mind?"

"Of course not. This is going to be so *interesting* to crack open. I was right. The answers, the way to end the war, *must* be here."

A shimmer of red lightning moved across the ground up the hallway. Venli had seen this before—a spren like lightning running along a surface. Indeed, it materialized into the shape of a small human—not a singer, but a *human*, with odd eyes and hair that waved in an unseen wind.

Ulim. The first Voidspren she'd ever met, all those years ago. "Lady of Wishes," he said, performing a flowery bow. "We have located the Black-thorn's wife, queen of this tower."

"Oh?" Raboniel asked. "Where was she hiding?"

"A Deepest One—the Caller of Springs—found her near a strange fab-rial that is now unfortunately destroyed. The Caller summoned a force and captured Queen Blackthorn, who has come peacefully. She is now asking to speak with whomever was leading our assault. Shall I have her killed?"

"Don't be wasteful, Ulim," Raboniel said. "The Blackthorn's wife will make a very useful pawn. I would have thought better of you."

"Normally I would be *nothing* but eager for a new toy," Ulim said. "But this woman is dangerous and crafty. Reports say she's the one who created the flying machine that raided Alethkar last month."

"Then we *certainly* won't kill her," Raboniel said.

"She could be seen as a symbol to the people of this tower . . ." Ulim said. Then the small spren cocked his head, looking at the shield covering the doorway. "What's that?"

"You only just noticed it?" Venli asked.

Ulim glanced at her, then turned away, pretending to ignore her. What did he think of Venli now, all these years later? He'd made such promises to her. Was he embarrassed that she'd lived, knowing what a liar he was?

"It is a puzzle," Raboniel said. "Come. I would meet this queen of the tower."

.•.

Navani composed herself, standing with hands clasped before her, surrounded by singer soldiers. Though the effects of fatigue made her want to droop, she kept her head high. She wished she had chosen a formal havah today, instead of this simple work dress with a gloved hand, but that couldn't be helped. A queen was a queen, regardless of what she wore. She kept her expression calm, though she wasn't certain whether she was awaiting imprisonment or death.

They had immediately separated her from the others, naturally, and had taken her arm sheath with its fabrials. She wished she could burn a prayer to the Almighty that her scholars would be kept safe. The only reason *to* surrender was to protect them and the others of the tower. In this, the Fused had been wise. They'd made it clear time and time again that they didn't slaughter populations who surrendered. You always knew you had an out. All you had to do was submit.

It was the same lesson that Gavilar and Navani herself had taught many, many years ago. Cities that had joined the unified Alethkar had prospered. Of course, with Gavilar and Dalinar involved, there had always been an explicit addition to that lesson. *Fail* to submit, and you would be sent the Blackthorn.

With those memories haunting her, it was difficult to evoke any sense of outrage as the enemy soldiers led her down the steps. How could Navani feel outrage at having done to her what she'd willingly done to others? It was the enormous flaw in Gavilar's reasoning. If their strength justified their rule of Alethkar, then what happened when someone stronger came along? It was a system that ensured there would always be war, a constant clash for rule.

She was able to use such high-minded philosophical thoughts to distract her up until she saw the first bodies. They lay slumped against the wall, in the crook of the steps, men in Roion uniforms. Men with too-young faces, slaughtered as they'd tried to push for the crystal pillar.

Men she'd sent to their deaths. Navani steeled herself, but had to walk through their blood to proceed. Vorin teachings abhorred gambling, and Navani had often been proud that she avoided such games of chance. Yet she gambled with lives, didn't she?

The blood was pervasive, dribbling down steps, threatening to make her slip. One of her captors placed a strong hand under her arm, as they marched her around and around, passing breaks in the wooden railing where the fighting had grown intense.

At the bottom she found a pile of corpses, including some in Kholin uniforms. Poor Teofil and his men. It seemed they'd almost made it, judging by the fact that a Heavenly One had to fly Navani over a break in the steps where a few last corpses slumped—bespeaking their final moments.

Thank you, Teofil, she thought. *And all of you.* If the tower had a chance, it came because these men had bought her time. Even if they hadn't reached the pillar, they had done something remarkable. She would remember that sacrifice.

At the base of the steps, she was marched through the hallway with the murals. As she walked, she found herself proud of how much of a fight they'd put up. Not only Teofil and the soldiers, but the entire tower. Yes, it had taken less than half a day for the Fused to conquer all of Urithiru, but considering Navani's lack of Radiants and Shards, it was remarkable to have lasted that long.

She felt particularly satisfied with their efforts when she saw the glowing blue light at the end of the hallway, blocking off the way to the pillar room. Odd, that she should feel most a queen in the moments before the position was taken from her.

The soldiers steered her into the larger of the two library rooms, where a tall femalen Fused stood in light armor, looking over papers from one of the many stacks in the room. Navani's most precious engineering and design secrets. The Fused had a strange hairstyle, with carapace covering nearly her entire head, save for a topknot-style bundle of thick orange singer hair. The way the guards presented Navani made it clear that this was the leader.

The Fused continued to read, barely acknowledging Navani.

"I am ready to discuss terms of surrender," Navani finally said.

A lithe Regal stepped to the femalen's side. "Raboniel, Lady of Wishes, is not to be directly addressed by—"

She was interrupted by the Fused saying something. Whatever it was, the Regal didn't seem to have expected it, for when she spoke again her voice cadence had changed markedly.

"The Lady says, 'She comes to me as a queen, though she will leave without the title. For now she may speak when she wishes, as befitting her rank.'"

"Then let me offer surrender," Navani said. "My soldiers have been instructed to turn in their arms, should you approach with the proper sign given—proof that we've reached an accord."

"I will require your Radiants," the Fused—Raboniel—said through her interpreter. "You will release a proclamation: Anyone harboring a Radiant is subject to harsh punishment. We will search the tower to bring all of them under our care. Your soldiers and officers will be disarmed but spared.

"Your people may continue living in the tower under our laws. All lighteyes—including you—will be made of equal status to darkeyes. You are humans, nothing more, nothing less. The will of a singer must be obeyed immediately, and humans may not carry weapons. Otherwise, I am content to let them continue their occupations—and even engage in trade, a privilege not extended to most humans in Alethkar."

"I can't give up the Knights Radiant to execution," Navani said.

"Then we will kill them all as they lie unconscious," the Fused said. "And once finished, we will approach you with less lenient terms of surrender. Conversely, we can make an accommodation now, and perhaps your Radiants will live. I cannot promise I won't change my mind, but I don't intend to execute them. We simply need to be certain they are properly restrained."

"They're unconscious. How much more restraint do they need?"

Raboniel didn't reply. She flipped through the pages.

"I agree to these terms," Navani said. "The tower is yours. If your people approach my men with a white flag bearing a circle painted black, they will surrender."

Several Regals went running with the news, and Navani wished them the wind's own speed. "What have you done with my scholars? And the soldiers down here in these rooms?"

"Some are dead," Raboniel said through the interpreter. "But not many."

Navani closed her eyes. Some? Which of her friends had been killed in this incursion? Was she foolhardy, for resisting as long as she had?

No. Not if it bought us time to put the shield up. She knew very little about the Sibling and this tower, but at least now she had a chance. Only by working with the enemy, pretending to be docile and controlled, would she find opportunity to restore the Radiants.

"You drew these?" Raboniel asked through her interpreter, turning around the pages. They were indeed some of Navani's sketches—more airships, of a more practical design, now that they better understood the mechanics of flight. They were signed by her seal.

"Yes," Navani said.

The Fused read through them further. Then, remarkably, she spoke in Alethi—heavily accented, but understandable. "Is it common for human queens of this era to be engineers?"

This startled her attendant Regal, who seemed to not have known this Lady of Wishes could speak Alethi. Or perhaps she was surprised to hear one so high speak to a human.

"I have unusual hobbies," Navani said.

Raboniel folded the sheet of paper and finally met Navani's eyes. "They are remarkable. I would like to hire you."

". . . Hire me?" Navani asked, taken aback.

"You are no longer a queen, but you are obviously a talented engineer. I am told the scholars of this tower respect you. So, I would hire you to work on fabrial projects for me. I assure you, being in my employ will be a far more rewarding job than carrying water or washing clothing."

What game is this? Navani thought. Surely this Fused didn't *actually* expect Navani to design fabrials for the enemy?

"Carrying water or washing clothing is fine work," Navani said. "I've done both before in my life. Neither will involve giving secrets to an enemy who, I'm afraid, will inevitably use them to kill and conquer my people."

"True," Raboniel said. "You are not prideful. I respect that. But consider my offer before rejecting it. If you are close to me, you would have a much easier time tracking what I'm doing, spying on my projects. You will also have greater opportunity to sneak information out to your husband, in hope of an eventual rescue. I know many things about Stormlight and Voidlight that you do not. Pay attention, and I suspect you'd learn more from me than you'd give up."

Navani felt her mouth go dry, searching the Fused's red eyes, glowing faintly from her corrupted soul. Storms. Raboniel said it all so calmly. This creature was ancient, thousands of years old. What secrets must her mind hold. . . .

Careful, Navani thought to herself. *If she's thousands of years old, she has had thousands of years to practice manipulating people.*

"I will consider the offer," Navani said.

"Refer to me as 'Ancient One' or 'Lady of Wishes,'" Raboniel said, "as you no longer have the rank to ignore my title. I will put you with your scholars. Discuss it together, then inform me of your decision."

The soldiers led Navani away. And just like that, she had lost another throne.

*Regardless, please make yourself known to me when you travel my
lands. It is distressing that you think you need to move in the shadows.*

By the time they heard confirmation that the queen had surrendered, sunlight was beginning to stream through the windows of
the clinic. Kaladin and his family had spent the entire night seeing
patients. Twenty hours, a full day, without sleep.

Even the exhaustionspren near Kaladin seemed tired, swirling slowly,
lethargic. The messenger woman sat down at their table in the clinic, bleary
eyed and wearing a disheveled uniform, as she accepted a cup of cold tea
from Kaladin's father.

"The queen attempted a final push to restore the Radiants," the woman
said. "I don't know what that entailed—only that the soldiers involved are
dead now. I've been running messages to the neighborhoods on the sixth
floor. But yes, in answer to your question, I've seen Queen Navani and the
head of the Fused army together. She confirmed the surrender to me. We
are to live under singer law, and not resist."

"Stormwinds," Kaladin whispered. "I never realized how blind I'd feel
without spanreeds." It had taken hours for any sort of factual information
to filter up to the sixth floor.

"So we're supposed to go right back to living under their rule?" Kaladin's
mother said from her seat at the table.

"It wasn't so bad," Lirin said. "The highlords won't like it, but it won't
matter much for the rest of us."

"Fabrials don't work," Hesina said. "We can't heat our rooms, not to mention our food. The water pumps will have halted. This tower won't remain livable for long."

"The Fused use their powers," Lirin replied. "Maybe if we infuse the fabrials with Voidlight, they'll work."

"Pardon, Brightlord," the scout said, "but that . . . feels wrong for many reasons."

Kaladin had started rummaging in the cupboard for something to eat, so he didn't see his father's reaction at being called "Brightlord." He could guess though. It was an odd situation anyway, considering that Lirin's eyes hadn't changed, he'd simply been adopted into Kaladin's house. Rank was becoming a jumbled mess these days.

"Kaladin, son," Hesina said, "why don't you go lie down?"

"Why?" he said, getting out a stack of flatbread, then counting how many pieces they had.

"You've been prowling about like a caged animal," she said.

"No I haven't."

"Son . . ." she said, in a calm—but infuriatingly wise—voice.

He set down the bread and felt at his brow, which was cold from sweat. He took a deep breath, then turned around to face them, his father leaning against the wall, his mother at the table with the messenger woman. She had white and grey hair, but was young enough that it seemed premature, and had a pair of white gloves tucked into her belt. An Alethi master-servant doing double duty as a messenger.

"You're all taking this too calmly," Kaladin said, tossing up his hands. "Don't you realize what this means? They control the tower. They control the Oathgates. That is *it*. The war is over."

"Brightlord Dalinar still has the bulk of the Radiants with him," Alili, the messenger, said. "And our armies were mostly deployed around the world."

"And now they're all isolated!" Kaladin said. "We can't fight a war on multiple fronts without the Oathgates. And what if the enemy can repeat whatever they did here? What if they start making Radiant powers go away on every battlefield?"

That quieted her. Kaladin tried to imagine what the war would be like without Windrunners or Edgedancers. Already, the battlefields were starting to look very little like the ones he'd known during his days as a spearman. Fewer large-scale formations maneuvering against other blocks of men. Those were too easy to disrupt from above, or by other types of Fused.

Men spent their days in protected camps, making only sudden surges to claim ground and shove away the enemy. Battles stretched on for months, instead of occurring in decisive engagements. Nobody quite knew how to fight a war like this—well, nobody on *their* side, at least.

"I keep waiting," Kaladin said, wiping his brow again, "for the thunder to hit. The lightning struck last night. We saw the flash, and need to brace ourselves for the shock wave. . . ."

"Brightlord," Alili said, "pardon, but . . . maybe you could help the other Radiants? To do whatever you did?"

"What did I do?"

"That's what I'm asking," she said. "Again, pardon, but Brightlord Stormblessed . . . you're the sole Radiant I've seen in the tower who is still standing. Whatever the enemy did, it knocked out all the others. Every *single* one. Except you."

He thought of Teft, lying on the slab in the other room. They'd spooned broth into his mouth, and he had taken it, stirring and muttering softly between mouthfuls.

The long night weighed on Kaladin. He *did* need rest. Probably should have taken it hours ago. But he worried about his patients, the men suffering from battle shock. Before all this had happened, he'd gotten them rooms on the fourth floor, among the men who had lost arms or legs in the war, and who now did work maintaining gear for other soldiers.

Kaladin's patients had been making real progress. He could imagine exactly how they felt now though, living through another horror as the battle—so frequently a source of nightmares to them—found them again. They must be beside themselves.

Not just them, Kaladin thought, wiping his brow again with his hand.

The messenger woman rose and stretched, then bowed and moved on her way to continue delivering the news. Before she reached the front door, however, Syl zipped in from underneath it, twirled around in a few circles, then zipped back out.

"Enemy soldier," Kaladin said under his breath to his parents, "coming this way."

Indeed, as the messenger left, a singer wearing a sleek Regal form peeked in to check on Kaladin and his parents. The singer lingered only a short time before turning away. There weren't enough of them yet to guard each and every home. Kaladin suspected that as more and more singers moved into the tower, he and his family wouldn't be able to speak as openly as they'd been doing so far this morning.

"We should get some sleep," Lirin said to Kaladin.

"The other townspeople—" Kaladin began.

"Laral and I will visit them," Hesina said, rising. "I got some sleep earlier."

"But—"

"Son," Lirin said. "If the Radiants are in comas, that means no Edgedancers—and no Regrowth. You and I need sleep, because we're going to become *very* busy men over the next few days. There's an entire tower full of frightened people, and likely as not a few hotheaded soldiers will take it upon themselves to make trouble despite the queen's orders. They're all going to need two rested surgeons."

Hesina gave her husband a fond touch on the cheek with her safehand, then a kiss. She pulled a handkerchief from her pocket and gave it to Kaladin as he found himself yet again wiping his brow. Then she left to go visit Laral—who had seen the messenger before them and already knew the situation.

Kaladin reluctantly joined his father and walked down the long hallway past the patient rooms toward the family's living quarters.

"What if I'm one of those hotheads?" Kaladin asked. "What if *I* can't live with this?"

Lirin stopped in the hallway. "I thought we'd discussed this already, son."

"You think I can ignore the fact that the enemy has conquered my home?" Kaladin said. "You think you can just turn me into a good, well-behaved slave like—"

"Like me?" Lirin asked with a sigh. His eyes flicked up, likely noting the brands on Kaladin's forehead, mostly covered by his hair. "What would have happened, son, if instead of trying so hard to escape all those years, you'd instead proven yourself to your masters? What if you'd shown them you could heal instead of kill? How much misery would you have saved the world if you'd used your talents instead of your fists?"

"You're telling me to be a good slave and do what I'm told."

"I'm telling you to *think*!" his father snapped. "I'm telling you that if you want to change the world, you have to stop being part of the problem!" Lirin calmed himself with obvious difficulty, making fists and breathing in deeply. "Son, think about what all those years spent fighting did to you. How they broke you."

Kaladin looked away, not trusting himself to answer.

"Now," Lirin said, "think about these last few weeks. How good it felt to be helping for once."

"There is more than one way to help."

"And your nightmares?" Lirin asked. "The cold sweats? The times where your mind numbs? Was that caused by *my* kind of help, or *your* kind? Son, our mandate is to find those who are hurt, then see them cared for. We can do that even if the enemy has conquered us."

In a way, Kaladin could understand what his father said. "Your words make sense up here," Kaladin said, tapping his head. "But not down here." He slapped his breast.

"That's always been your problem, son. Letting your heart override your head."

"My head can't be trusted sometimes," Kaladin said. "Can you blame me? Besides, isn't the entire reason we became surgeons *because* of the heart? Because we care?"

"We need both heart and mind," Lirin said. "The heart might provide the purpose, but the head provides the method, the path. Passion is nothing without a plan. *Wanting* something doesn't make it happen.

"I can acknowledge—*have* to acknowledge—that you accomplished great things serving Dalinar Kholin. But with the Radiants down and most of the king's surgeons on the battlefield, *we* are what stands between the people of this tower and deathspren. You acknowledge that you don't think right sometimes? Then trust *me*. Trust *my thoughts*."

Kaladin grimaced, but nodded. It was true that his thoughts had proven—time after time—that they couldn't be trusted. Besides, what did he think he was going to do? Fight a war against the invaders all by himself? After Navani had surrendered?

Before retiring, they checked on the unconscious people in the patient rooms. The Stoneward was completely out cold, less responsive than Teft, though Lirin was able to get her to take soup by spooning it to her lips. Kaladin studied her—checking her eyes, her heart rate, her temperature. Then he moved over to Teft. The bearded Windrunner shifted, his eyes closed, and when Kaladin put broth to his lips he took it far more eagerly. His hands twitched, and though Kaladin couldn't make out anything he was saying, he kept muttering under his breath.

He's a Windrunner, of the same oath as me, Kaladin thought. *I'm awake when the others fell. Teft is close to being awake.* Was there a connection?

Whatever fabrial the enemy was using to do this, perhaps it didn't work as well on Windrunners. He needed to see the other Radiants and compare them. There had been around two dozen other Windrunners in the tower. His status as a surgeon should let him visit them and check their vitals.

Storms. His father was correct. Kaladin could accomplish far more by backing down than he could by fighting.

Syl came zipping into the room a short time later. Lirin noticed her too, so she'd made herself visible to him.

"Syl," Kaladin said, "will you check again to see if you can spot Teft's spren? He seems like he's coming closer to waking, so she might be becoming more visible."

"No time," Syl said, turning into the shape of a young woman with a sword strapped to her waist, wearing a scout's uniform. She halted in the air, standing as if on an invisible platform. "They're coming."

"Another Regal coming to check in on us?" Kaladin said.

"Worse," Syl said. "A group of soldiers, led by a different Regal, is searching each residence, methodically heading this direction. They're hunting for something."

"Or some*one*," Kaladin said. "They've heard that Stormblessed is awake."

"Don't jump to conclusions, son," Lirin said. "If they were searching for you specifically, they'd have come straight here. I'll go see what this is about. If they *are* looking for you, escape out the window and we'll decide what to do later."

Kaladin withdrew into the family room, which had doors to their bedrooms—including the small closet where little Oroden was sleeping in his crib. Kaladin didn't go to his bedroom though. He cracked the door into the hallway, and was able to hear voices when his father opened the door at the far front of the clinic. Unfortunately, he couldn't hear what they were saying. He nodded to Syl, who risked zipping out to get closer and overhear.

Before she could return, the voices drew nearer. Kaladin made out the Regal by the rhythm of his speech.

". . . don't care if you're a surgeon, darkeyes," the soldier said. "I have the queen's sealed writ here, and its instructions supersede what you might have been told by messengers. All Radiants are to be taken into custody."

"These are my patients," Lirin said. "They were entrusted to my care. Please; they're no danger to you like this."

"Your queen accepted these terms," the Regal replied. "Complain to her."

Kaladin peeked out the door into the hallway. A Regal led five ordinary warform singers. Their larger figures appeared cramped in the stone corridor as they walked to the two patient rooms. So they *weren't* after him, not specifically. They were searching for fallen Radiants.

Indeed, the Regal gestured his attendants toward the first exam room. Two moved out soon after, carrying the fallen Stoneward between them. They shoved Lirin aside as they carted her off down the hallway.

Syl came zipping back to Kaladin, agitated as she moved into the room with him. "They don't seem to know about you. Only that the surgeon has a couple of fallen Radiants."

Kaladin nodded, though he'd grown tense.

"I can care for these far better than you can," Lirin said. "Removing them like this could be dangerous to their health, even deadly."

"Why would we care?" the Regal said, both tone and rhythm sounding amused. Two of his soldiers took the Stoneward's squires, one each, and hauled them out of the second exam room. "I think we should throw them all off the tower and rid ourselves of a huge problem. The Fused want us to collect them though. Guess they want to have the fun of killing these themselves."

He's posturing, Kaladin thought. *The Fused wouldn't go to the effort of taking the Radiants captive only to kill them.* Would they?

Did it matter?

They were going to take Teft.

The Regal moved into the first exam room, and Kaladin's father followed, making more objections. Kaladin stood with one hand on the wall, one hand on the door, breathing deeply. Wind surged through the window behind, brushing past him, bearing with it two twisting windspren that moved as lines of light.

A hundred objections held him. His father's arguments. His soul in fragments. The knowledge that he was probably too tired to be making decisions. The fact that the queen had decided it was best to end hostilities.

So many reasons to stay where he was. But one reason to move.

They were going to take Teft.

Kaladin pulled open the door and stepped into the hallway, feeling the inevitable shift of a boulder perched on the top of a slope. Just. Beginning. To tip.

"Kaladin . . ." Syl said, landing on his shoulder.

"It was a nice dream, wasn't it, Syl?" he asked. "That we could escape? Find peace at long last?"

"Such a wonderful dream," she whispered.

"You ready for this?" he asked.

She nodded, and he stepped into the doorway of the exam room. Two enemy soldiers remained in the room: one warform and the stormform Regal. The Regal had helped get Teft up onto the regular soldier's shoulders.

Lirin looked straight at Kaladin, then shook his head urgently, his eyes going wide.

"You will put him down," Kaladin said to the singers. "And leave quietly. Send one of the Fused to get him, if they're so insistent."

The two froze, and the Regal sized him up. "Go back to bed, boy," he eventually said. "You don't want to try my patience today."

Lirin dashed forward, trying to push Kaladin out of the room. With a quick pivot to the side, Kaladin sent his father tumbling into the hall—and hopefully out of danger. He stepped back into the doorway.

"Why not go for reinforcements?" Kaladin said to the two singers. Almost more a plea than a request. "Don't press this issue right now."

The Regal gestured for his companion to set Teft back onto the exam table, and for a moment Kaladin thought they might actually do what he said. Then the Regal unhooked the axe from its sheath at his side.

"No!" Lirin said from behind. "Don't do this!"

In response, Kaladin drew in a breath of Stormlight. His body came alight with the inner storm, and wisps of luminescent smoke began to curl from his skin.

That gave the two singers pause, until the warform pointed. "That's *him*, Brightlord! The one the Pursuer is searching for! He matches the description exactly!"

The Regal grinned. "You're going to make me very rich, human." Dark red lightning crackled across his skin. The warform shied away, hitting the counter and causing surgery implements to clink against one another.

Lirin grabbed Kaladin from behind.

Kaladin stood quietly on that precipice. Balanced.

The Regal leaped forward, swinging his axe.

And Kaladin stepped off the edge.

He shook free of his father's grip and shoved him backward with one hand, then caught the Regal's arm with his other before the axe could fall. Kaladin braced himself for the *jolt* of energy that shot through him at touching a stormform—he'd fought these before. It stunned him for a moment nonetheless, so he wasn't ready to guard as the Regal cuffed him across the face, ripping his cheek with the barbed carapace on the back of his hand.

Stormlight would heal that. Kaladin got his other hand up, preventing another punch while continuing to hold back the axe. The two struggled for a moment, then Kaladin managed to get the advantage, tipping their center of balance forward so he could twist and ram his shoulder into the Regal.

Storms it hurt. That carapace was no joke. Still, the maneuver put his opponent momentarily off balance, so Kaladin was able to control the fight, spinning his enemy around and slamming the creature's hand into the corner of an exam table. A resounding *snap* split the air, and the carapace on the hand cracked.

The Regal hissed in pain and dropped the axe. But then he pivoted hard and rammed his side into Kaladin's chest, shoving him against the counter. Kaladin's father was shouting, but the warform—instead of helping—remained by the opposite wall. He didn't seem eager to attack a Radiant.

Without Stormlight, Kaladin wouldn't have been able to withstand the constant jolts of energy from the stormform's touch. As it was, he was able to hold on—not letting the enemy force him back too much—until the Regal tried another punch. At the windup, Kaladin hooked his leg around the foot of his opponent, then sent them both to the ground.

He landed with a grunt and tried to roll into position to choke his opponent unconscious. If the fight ended without bloodshed, perhaps his father would forgive him.

Unfortunately, Kaladin hadn't done a lot of wrestling. He knew enough to keep himself from being pinned easily, but the Regal was stronger than he was, and that carapace kept jabbing in surprising places and interfering with his holds. The Regal leveraged his superior weight and strength, twisting Kaladin around with a grunt. Then—with Kaladin pinned beneath him—the creature began pummeling him in the face with his good fist, the one that hadn't cracked.

Kaladin breathed in a gasp of Stormlight, draining the spheres on the counter. He brought his fist up and slammed it into the back of the hand that had cracked earlier. His enemy flinched, and Kaladin was able to kick free, throwing the Regal off—though both slammed into the counters in the tight confines as he did so.

Kaladin scrambled to find his feet so he could attack his enemy from above—but the Regal began to glow red. The hairs on Kaladin's arms stood up, and he had a fraction of a second to duck to the side as a flash of light—and an earsplitting *crack*—filled the room.

He hit the ground, blinded and deafened, the sharp scent of a lightning strike filling his nostrils. Strange and distinctive, it was a scent he associated with rainfall. Kaladin didn't think he'd been struck directly—stormforms had trouble aiming their lightning—but it took a moment for Kaladin's Stormlight to heal his ears and restore his vision.

A shadow moved over him, swinging its axe down. Kaladin twisted to the side just in time. The axe clanged against the ground.

I'm sorry, Father, Kaladin thought, reaching for the scalpel in his boot. As the axe fell again, Kaladin let it bite him in the left shoulder, praying his Stormlight would hold. He rammed the scalpel into the side of the Regal's knee, directly between bits of carapace.

The Regal screamed and stumbled. Kaladin's shoulder hurt like Damnation, but he pushed through the pain and leaped to his feet. His Stormlight ran out as he rushed his enemy, toppling them again—but this time Kaladin fell with more care and dropped on top of the Regal. With the momentum of the fall, he rammed his scalpel into the creature's neck, right above its carapace gorget.

The knife wasn't intended for battle, but it *was* sharpened to exactness. Kaladin twisted it and swiftly cut the carotid artery, then threw himself up.

He stumbled back against the counter, covered in sweat, panting, his hearing not fully healed from the blast. The Regal thrashed on the floor, and orange blood . . . Well, Kaladin turned away. Some sights were sickening even for a surgeon.

Even for a soldier, he corrected. *You're no surgeon.*

He looked across the room at the singer who huddled beside the far wall. He'd watched, stunned, and hadn't intervened.

"Haven't been in many fights, have you?" Kaladin asked, hoarse.

The singer jumped, his eyes wide. He was in warform, so he appeared fearsome, but his expression told another story. That of a person who wanted to be anywhere else, a person horrified by the brutality of the fight.

Storms . . . He hadn't considered that singers might feel battle shock too.

"Go," Kaladin said, then winced as the dying Regal's leg thumped against the wall with a frantic, panicked sound. Bleeding out always seemed to happen too quickly to your friends, and not quickly enough to those you killed.

The singer stared at him, haunted, and Kaladin realized the malen might also have been deafened by the lightning. Kaladin pointed, mouthing the word. "Go!"

The singer scrambled away, leaving wet orange footprints from the dying singer's blood. Kaladin pulled himself over to the opposite counter, where a few spheres still glowed. He drew those in and healed the rest of his wounds. He should have kept another pouch on him. This had been coming.

He searched out the doorway, and found his father on the floor where Kaladin had shoved him, lit by morning light coming in through the distant window.

"You all right?" Kaladin asked him. "Did that blast hurt you?"

Lirin stood up, staring past Kaladin. Into the room, square at the dying Regal. In the other room, Oroden had started crying. Then Lirin, overcoming his shock, scrambled into the room to try to help the dying singer.

Father is fine, Kaladin thought. The thunder of stormform lightning blasts—at least those made by a single individual—wasn't as bad as that of real lightning. As long as you were sheltered, as his father had been, you wouldn't suffer permanent hearing loss.

Kaladin tiredly glanced to Syl, who sat on the counter with her hands in her lap. Her eyes were closed, her head turned away from the dying Regal as Lirin tried to stanch the blood flow. Kaladin had killed dozens, perhaps hundreds of them during this war—though he'd tried to focus his attention on the Fused. He'd told himself that those fights were more meaningful, but the truth was that he hated killing common soldiers. They never seemed to have much of a chance against him.

Yet each Fused he killed meant something even worse. A noncombatant would be sacrificed to give that Fused new life, so each one of *them* Kaladin killed meant taking the life of some housewife or craftsman.

He moved over to Teft, Kaladin's glowing body illuminating the man, unconscious on the table. Kaladin spared a momentary worry for the Stoneward who had been taken. Could he somehow rescue her too?

Don't be a fool, Kaladin. You barely saved Teft. In fact, you might not have saved him yet. Deal with the current problems before creating new ones.

Nearby, Lirin gave up, lowering his head and slumping in place as he knelt before the body. It had stopped moving, finally.

"We'll need to hide," Kaladin said to his father. "I'll fetch Mother." He surveyed his bloody clothing. "Perhaps you should do that, actually."

"How *dare* you!" Lirin whispered, his voice hoarse.

Kaladin hesitated, shocked.

"How dare you kill in this place!" Lirin shouted, turning on Kaladin, angerspren pooling at his feet. "My sanctuary. The place where we heal! What is *wrong* with you?"

"They were going to take Teft," Kaladin said. "Kill him."

"You don't know that!" Lirin said. He stared at his bloodied hands. "You . . . You just . . ." He took a deep breath. "The Fused are probably gathering the Radiants to keep them in one location, and watch to see that none of them wake up!"

"*You* don't know *that*," Kaladin said. "I wasn't going to let them take him. He's my friend."

"Is that it, or did you just want an excuse?" Lirin's hands trembled as he tried to wipe the blood onto his trousers. When he looked back at Kaladin, something seemed to have broken in him, tears on his cheeks. Storms, he seemed *exhausted*.

"Heralds above . . ." Lirin whispered. "They really *did* kill my boy, didn't they? What have they done to you?"

Kaladin's smidgen of Stormlight ran out. Damnation, he was so *tired*. "I've tried to tell you. Your boy died years ago."

Lirin stared at the floor, wet with blood. "Go. They'll come for you now."

"You need to go into hiding with me," Kaladin said. "They'll know you're my—"

"We're not going anywhere with you," Lirin snapped.

"Don't play the sixth fool, Father," Kaladin said. "You can't let them take you after this."

"I can and will!" Lirin shouted, standing up. "Because *I* will take responsibility for what I've done! *I* will work within whatever confines I must in order to protect people! *I* have taken oaths not to harm!" He grimaced, sickened. "Oh, Almighty. You murdered a man inside my home."

"It wasn't murder," Kaladin said.

Lirin didn't respond.

"It *wasn't* murder."

Lirin sank to the floor. "Just . . . go," he said, his voice growing soft again. The grief in it, the disappointment, was far worse than the anger had been. "I will . . . find a way to get the rest of us out of this. That singer saw me trying to make you stop. They won't harm a surgeon who didn't fight. But you, they'll kill."

Kaladin hesitated. Could he really leave them here?

"Storms . . ." Lirin whispered. "Storms, my son has become a monster. . . ."

Kaladin steeled himself, then slipped into the back room and recovered an extra pouch of spheres he kept there. Then he returned to the exam room, trying—and failing—to avoid the blood. He lifted Teft with a grunt, putting him in a medic's carry across his back.

"I've taken oaths too, Father," he said. "I'm sorry I'm not the man you wanted me to be. But if I *were* a monster, I would never have let that other soldier go."

He left, running for the uninhabited center of the sixth floor as shouts in the singer tongue began to sound behind him.

THE END OF

Part Two

İNTERLUDES

VYRE • LIFT • TARAVANGIAN

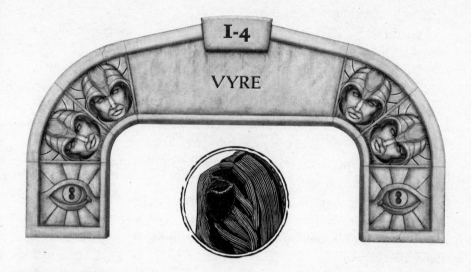

VYRE

Vyre was unchained.

Moash, the man he'd once been, had lived his entire life chained up and never known it. Oh, he'd recognized the bonds the lighteyes used on him. He'd experienced their tyranny both directly and indirectly—most painfully in the deaths of those he loved, left locked away in their dungeons.

But he hadn't recognized the truer chains. The ones that bound his soul, constraining him to mere mortality, when he could always have been so much more.

Vyre threw his Shardblade with a wide, overhand throw. Sunlight flashed along the spinning blade as it soared across the quarry and then *clanged* against a large rock before bouncing free, tearing a gash in the ground, then finally coming to a rest wedged in the stone.

"I . . . still don't understand what you're doing, Vyre," Khen said to Confusion. Warform suited her. It always had. "That weapon was not meant to be thrown."

They worked together in the quarry—which had been created by mining through the crem many feet down to reach marble—outside of Kholinar. As usual, his small band of singers went where he did, and started working—quietly—as he did. Moments earlier, Vyre had been cutting stones out with this Blade.

Now, his attention had turned inward. Toward chains, and bindings, and prisons unseen. He gestured, and the distant Shardblade vanished to mist. Yet it took him ten heartbeats to summon it again.

"I saw Prince Adolin throw his Blade," Vyre said. "Three months ago, on the battlefield in northern Jah Keved. He is no Radiant, yet his Blade responds to him as if he were one. . . ."

"Maybe it was just a lucky throw."

Vyre threw his Blade again. It clanged uselessly off his target. He narrowed his eyes, then dismissed it into a puff of mist.

"No," Vyre said. "He must be able to change the balance to allow for this maneuver. And it returned to him faster than ten heartbeats, even accounting for the accelerated pulse of battle."

Vyre waited until the weapon appeared in his grip. This was an ancient weapon, one of the mighty Honorblades. Yet it was inferior. It couldn't change shape, and cost far more Stormlight to use, often crusting his clothing with frost when he used it too quickly.

He didn't feel anger at his Blade's inferiority. Or humiliation. The lack of those emotions let him consider the situation clearly, fueling his curiosity, his determination. This was what it was like to be unchained. To be freed from captivity.

To never again feel guilt.

He strode through the quarry. A thousand clinks of metal on stone surrounded him, like the dancing feet of cremlings. An overcast sky and a calm wind chilled his skin as he picked a new section of the quarry in which to work. He began slicing at the wall to cut free another large block of the precious marble.

"Vyre," Khen said. To Determination. Curious. What did she want that made her so afraid? "I . . . I am leaving."

"Very well," Vyre said, working.

"You're . . . not angry?"

"I can't be angry," he said, truthfully. "Nor can I feel disappointment."

After all these months together, she still didn't understand—because she rushed to explain, worried he'd be upset, despite what he'd said. "I don't want to go on these raids and fight anymore, Vyre. I feel like I woke up to life, and then immediately started killing. I want to see what it is like to live. Really *live*. With my own mind, my own Passions."

"Very well," Vyre said.

She hummed to Reconciliation.

"You are chained, Khen," Vyre explained. "You haven't given your negative emotions to him. Your insecurities. Your fears. Your pain. I was like you for many years." He narrowed his eyes, turning and looking to the west. Toward *him*. "Then I took the chains off and saw what I could truly become."

She hummed to . . . was that Curiosity? Yes, he thought it was.

"What?" Vyre asked.

"You say you're unburdened, Vyre," she said. "That you don't care anymore. But you keep hunting him. The Windrunner."

At the mention of Kaladin, Moash felt a hint of old, painful emotions—

though Odium quickly sucked them away. "Kaladin is a friend," Moash said. "It is important to me that he find his freedom. Go your way, Khen. If you become unchained in the future, seek me out. You are a capable warrior, and I would fight beside you again."

Vyre heaved a rock onto his right shoulder and began hauling it out of the quarry. The others remained in place, working.

Vyre enjoyed hauling rocks. Simple work was best to pass the time. It reminded him of days spent walking with caravans. Except this was better, because it tired out his body, but left him capable of thinking on his curious state. His new state.

Large stone settled on his shoulder, he hiked steadily up the path toward Kholinar. The marble was heavy, but not so much that he needed Stormlight or supernatural help. That would defeat the purpose. For a time, he walked, happy with his status. And he thought about Kaladin.

Poor Kaladin. There *was* freedom available for his old friend. Two freedoms, in fact. But he doubted Kaladin would ever accept the same freedom as Vyre, so he offered the other one. The sweet peace of nonexistence.

Khen was correct in questioning Vyre. So many things that had once been important didn't bother him any longer, so why did Kaladin tease at him, draw his attention? Why did Kaladin always make the old emotions churn again, if briefly?

There was one chain still holding to him, Vyre admitted. That of his friend. *I have to be right*, Vyre thought. *And he has to be wrong.* Kaladin *had* to acknowledge that Vyre was right. Until he did . . .

Until he did, that last chain would remain.

Vyre eventually reached Kholinar and passed through the gates. The city had well and truly settled into its new existence. The peoples intermixed, though singers were properly given deference. They were models of behavior the humans needed to learn to follow. When disputes happened, the singers *forced* men to be fair to one another. After all, when the parents came home, it was their duty to remove privileges if they found a mess. Humankind had been given millennia to prove they could self-govern properly, and they had failed.

People stared at him. He wasn't wearing his uniform, and he'd covered his Bridge Four shoulder tattoo with elbow-length sleeves. He was not distinctive. Yet he was. For they knew him; they whispered of him. Vyre. He Who Quiets.

He who hauls rocks.

Vyre soon reached a building site near the District of Colors. Here, workers were constructing special housing for some of the Deepest Ones. Each brand of Fused had its particularities. These liked to have homes without floors, so they could touch the natural stone ground with their unshod feet.

They could move through other materials too, so long as they were solid, but they liked the feeling of uncut stone underfoot, stretching to the heart of Roshar. So Vyre's marble would be used for the walls.

Vyre hadn't been asked to help with this job. If negative emotions could rule him, he suspected he'd have been annoyed at their neglect. Hard labor in the city? Not telling him was like hiding sweets from a child. Fortunately, he'd found out about it a few days ago, and had started cutting his own rocks and hauling them.

Vyre set his block of marble down by the masons' station, where they were honing them. Then he helped unload a cart that had pulled in from the other quarry, full to the brim.

One stone at a time. Heave, haul, drop. It was excellent work. Difficult, grueling. He was so lost in the effort that when the chull carts were all empty, he dusted his hands off—and was surprised to find himself virtually alone. When had the masons and other workers left? It wasn't yet midday.

"Where is everyone?" he asked the chull keeper, who was quickly gathering his beasts to take them to their pen.

"Everstorm tonight, Brightlord. We were given a half day off, in celebration."

"I'm not a brightlord," Vyre said, checking the sky—though, as he now recalled, the storm wouldn't arrive for many more hours. But it was likely approaching Urithiru right now. The armies were preparing to attack. Well, he'd been told to stay back from that fight, so he looked at the chull keeper. "How much more stone do you need?"

"Well, um, Bright . . . er, Lord Silencer? Sir? Um. Yes, we need about double what we have now. There's a pile at the second quarry, but we have chulls and carts to—"

"We shouldn't let the chulls have all the fun," Vyre said, turning and walking along the road toward the city gates.

Before Vyre reached the gates, however, he was taken into a vision. He materialized on a vast field of golden light. Odium was there, a hundred feet tall, seated on a throne. In the guise of a mighty Fused, majestic like a king *should* be.

Vyre walked closer and knelt. "You can take me without a storm now, Lord?"

Our Connection grows stronger, Odium said. I haven't needed a storm to bring you into a vision for months now, Vyre. I usually do it for tradition's sake.

That made sense. Vyre waited for further instructions.

I've noticed you walking freely about in storms on previous days, Vyre, Odium said, his voice like thunder. You have given me

YOUR WORST EMOTIONS, BUT YOU SHOULD MAINTAIN A SENSE OF SELF-PRESERVATION. FEAR OF MY MAJESTY. WHY ARE YOU NOT WARY OF THE LIGHTNING?

"You won't strike me down," Vyre said.

HOW DO YOU KNOW THIS?

"I haven't finished what I'm supposed to do," Vyre said. "I still have a truth to prove."

INTERESTING, Odium said. YOU RESPOND TO MY GIFT IN SUCH AN ODD WAY. YOU ARE BECOMING SOMETHING I HAVE NEVER BEFORE CREATED, VYRE.

"Some people say I've become your avatar," Vyre said. "That you act through me, control me."

Odium laughed. AS IF I WOULD GIVE SUCH POWER TO A MORTAL. NO, VYRE, YOU ARE UNIQUELY YOURSELF. SO INTERESTING.

"I am unchained."

AND YET, YOU THINK SO OFTEN OF KALADIN.

"I am . . . mostly unchained."

Odium leaned forward, lightning crackling across his carapaced body. I NEED YOU AT URITHIRU. WE CANNOT MAKE THE OATHGATES WORK, AND SO I NEED YOU TO TRANSPORT THE GROUND FORCES. I SUSPECT YOUR SWORD WILL STILL FUNCTION.

"I will go right away," Vyre said. "But I thought you didn't want me there."

I WORRY ABOUT THE EFFECT YOUR FRIEND HAS ON YOU. THE WIND-RUNNER.

"You needn't worry. Those emotions belong to you now."

INDEED. Odium leaned closer. YOUR FRIEND IS A PROBLEM TO ME—A BIGGER PROBLEM THAN I HAD ASSUMED. I HAVE FORESEEN THAT HE WILL CONTINUE TO BE ONE.

That was not surprising. Kaladin was a problem to many.

HE HAS LEFT THE BATTLE, WHICH I HADN'T THOUGHT HIM CAPABLE OF DOING, Odium said. STRANGELY, THIS WILL MAKE HIM FAR MORE DANGEROUS IN THE FUTURE. UNLESS WE ACT. BUT I CANNOT STRIKE HIM DOWN DIRECTLY. NOT UNLESS HE PUTS HIMSELF INTO MY HANDS.

"Kaladin can't be killed," Vyre said. He knew it, sure as he knew the sun was hot, and that it circled Roshar forever.

NOT EVEN BY YOU?

"Especially not by me."

I DO NOT THINK THAT IS TRUE, VYRE, THOUGH I UNDERSTAND WHY YOU THINK IT SO. I FEEL YOUR PASSIONS, AS THEY ARE MINE. I UNDERSTAND YOU.

Vyre remained kneeling.

I WOULD CLAIM THIS ONE, AS I HAVE CLAIMED YOU, Odium said.

And Vyre would see him dead first. A mercy.

CAN YOU THINK OF A WAY TO HURT HIM? Odium asked. DRIVE HIM TOWARD ME?

"Isolate him. Take away his friends."

HE WILL SOON BE ALONE.

"Then make him afraid. Make him dread. Break him."

HOW?

Vyre looked up, across the endless field of golden stone. "How do you bring me here?"

THIS IS NOT A PLACE, BUT A WARPING OF THE REALMS. A VISION.

"Could you show me anything?"

YES.

"Could you show *him* anything?"

I HAVEN'T THE CONNECTION TO HIM. Odium considered, humming softly to a rhythm. I SEE A WAY. THERE ARE HOLES IN HIS SOUL. SOMEONE COULD GET IN. SOMEONE WHO KNOWS HIM, SOMEONE CONNECTED TO HIM. SOMEONE WHO FEELS AS HE DOES.

"I will do it."

PERHAPS. YOU COULD INFLUENCE HIM IN SMALL WAYS ONLY. PERHAPS EACH NIGHT, WHEN HE SLUMBERS . . . HE THINKS OF YOU STILL, AND THERE IS MORE. A CONNECTION BECAUSE OF YOUR PAST, YOUR SHARED DREAMS. ANY BOND SUCH AS THAT CAN BE MANIPULATED.

WILL THIS BE ENOUGH? IF WE SHOW HIM VISIONS, WILL THAT BREAK HIM?

"It will be a start. I can bring him to the brink. Get him to step up to the ledge."

THEN WHAT?

"Then we find a way to make him jump," Moash said softly.

Cultivationspren seem to be composed of living vines that interweave in subtle patterns, like finely woven cloth whose weave is nearly invisible to human eyes.

They often act as traders and merchants in Shadesmar, and as such they maintain relations with almost every group of spren, even those who are normally hostile to each other.

Their hands, eyes, and teeth appear to be made of perfect crystal, clear yet filled with reflections of light. Their hands are as flexible and mobile as flesh, but their teeth appear firm as bone.

In the Physical Realm, they most often appear as a rippling river of vines and crystals that sprout, weave, and shatter into dust within moments as they move sinuously across a surface.

Sometimes they appear with an expressive, humanlike face that resembles the one they bear in the Cognitive Realm.

I-5

LIFT

A s Lift hung from the ceiling—dangling precariously from a rope with one hand, reaching out with the other toward the basket— she was forced to acknowledge that stealing food just didn't give her the same thrill it once had.

She continued to pretend because she didn't want her life to change. She *hated* change. Stealing people's food was basically her *thing*. She'd been doing it for years, and she *did* get a thrill when she saw their starvin' faces. They'd turn away, then when they looked back, their chouta wrap would be gone. Or they'd lift the cover on their meal, and find the plate empty. After that came the most sublime moment of cross-eyed panic and confusion.

But then they'd smile and look to see where she was. They didn't *see* her, of course. She was way too good at hidin'. But they'd look, and they seemed *fond*.

You weren't supposed to be fond when someone stole from you. Ruined the entire experience.

Then there was this. She stretched a little farther, fingers brushing the basket. . . .

There. She snatched the handle.

She stuffed the handle between her teeth, scuttled up the rope, then vanished into the hidden labyrinth of small tunnels that latticed the ceilings and walls of Urithiru. Up here Wyndle waited, coiled up on himself and making a face out of vines and crystal.

"Oh!" he said. "A full basket! Let's see what he left you this time!"

"Ain't nobody leaving me nothin'," Lift snapped. "I stole it, unfair and square. Also hush. Someone might hear."

"They *can't* hear me, mistress. I am—"

"I can hear you. So hush, whineyspren." She crept down the tunnel. There was an Everstorm going on right now, and she wanted to be safe at her nest. The things felt creepy in ways that the other Radiants didn't seem to notice. And even though everything seemed normal in the tower, she couldn't help noticing the strange sensation that everything was *wrong*.

She felt that every time though. So today, she just pushed the basket ahead of her as she crawled through the small tunnel. The next intersection was a tight squeeze, but she could make herself slick with Stormlight, so she got through.

Two turns and a straight crawl later, they entered a small intersection where she'd left a sphere for light. The roof of the tunnel was a little higher here, letting her settle with her back against the stone wall so she could inspect her prize.

Wyndle came in on the ceiling, taking the shape of a growing vine that crept across the stone. He formed a face again right above her as she rifled through the basket. Flatbread . . . some curry . . . sugared mashed beans . . . a little jar of jam with a cute face drawn on top above the Horn-eater symbol for "love."

Lift glanced up at the ceiling and the blinking vine face hanging from it. "Fine," she admitted. "*Maybe* he left it out for me."

"Maybe?"

"Starvin' stupid Horneater boy," Lift grumbled, slathering jam on the flatbread. "His dad knew how to make it appear like an accident, leavin' stuff out so I could take it. Let me stormin' pretend."

She stuffed the bread into her mouth. Damnation. It was *good*. Only made the experience more humiliating.

"I don't see the problem, mistress," Wyndle said.

"That's 'cuz you're a dummyspren," she said, then stuffed the rest of the flatbread into her mouth, talking around it. "Dodnoif lifhf anyfunf inftor lif."

"I do *too* like fun in my life!" he said. "Last month, with the help of some human children, I displayed the most *beautiful* art installation of chairs. The other cultivationspren thought it quite majestic. They complimented the stools in particular."

Lift sighed, leaning back, slumping there. Too annoyed to even make a good stool joke. She wasn't really angry. Wasn't really sad. Just . . . blarglegorf. Supremely blarglegorf.

Storms. The wrap she wore underneath her shirt was itchy today. "Come on," she said, grabbing the basket and sphere, then moving on through the tower's innards.

"Is it really so bad?" Wyndle said, following. "Gift likes you. That is why he leaves things out for you."

"I'm not supposed to be liked," Lift snapped. "I'm a shadow. A dangerous and unknown shadow, moving mysteriously from place to place, never seen. Always feared."

"A . . . shadow."

"Yes, a starvin' shadow, all right?" She had to squeeze through the *next* tunnel too. Stupid, stupid, *stupid*. "This tower, it's like a big ol' corpse. And I'm like blood, sneaking around through its veins."

"Why would a corpse have blood in its veins?"

"Fine. It's not dead. It's sleepin' and we are its stormin' blood. All right?"

"I should think," Wyndle said, "these air vents are much more like intestines. So the allegory would make you more akin to . . . um . . . well, feces I guess."

"Wyndle?" she said, pulling through.

"Yes, mistress?"

"Maybe stop tryin' to help with my deevy metaphors."

"Yes, all right."

"Storming lamespren," she muttered, finally reaching a section of larger air vents. She *did* like this tower. There were a lot of places to hide and to explore. Up here in this network of stone ventilation shafts, she found the occasional mink or other scavenger, but it was actually *her* domain. The adults were too big, and the other children too frightened. Plus she could glow—when properly fed—and her awesomeness could get her through tight squeezes.

A year ago, there hadn't been *nearly* as many of those as there were now. *Stupid, stupid, stupid.*

They eventually reached her nest, a large opening where four tall ventilation shafts met. Here she'd piled up blankets, food stores, and some treasures. One of Dalinar's knives she was absolutely *sure* he hadn't wanted her to steal. Some interesting shells. An old flute that Wyndle said looked strange.

They were near a well where she could get all the water she wanted—but far enough away from people that she could talk freely. Her previous nest had let her listen in on the echoes of people nearby—but they'd also been able to hear her.

She'd heard them talking about the echoing. The spirit of the tower, they'd called her. That had been nifty at first, but then they'd started leaving stuff out for her, like she was the stormin' Nightwatcher. And she'd started feeling guilty. You can't be taking stuff from people who don't have much. That was the first rule of not being a total-and-utter-useless-piece-of-chull-dung.

She munched on more of the "stolen" food from her basket, then sighed and got up. She stepped up to a side wall, putting her back to the stone. "Come on," she said. "Do it."

Wyndle moved up the wall. As always, he left a trail of vines behind him. They would crumble and decay soon after, but could be used to mark something for a short time. He moved across the wall atop her head, then she turned around and marked the line with a more permanent one out of chalk.

"That's almost a full *inch* since last time," she said.

"I'm sorry, mistress."

She flopped down in her nest of blankets, wanting to curl up and cry. "I'll stop eating," she said. "That'll stunt my growth."

"You?" Wyndle said. "Stop *eating*."

Storming spren. She pulled off her shirt, redid the wrap tighter—although it pinched her skin—then replaced her shirt. After that, she lay and stared up at the marks on the wall, which showed the progress of her height over the last year.

"Mistress," Wyndle said, curling up like an eel and raising a vine head beside her. He was getting better at making faces, and this one was one of her favorites—it had vines that looked like little mustaches. "Don't you think it's time you told me what *exactly* it was you asked the Nightwatcher?"

"Doesn't matter," she said. "It was all lies. The boon. The promises. Lies, lies, *lies*."

"I have met the Nightwatcher," Wyndle said. "She does not . . . think the same way the rest of us do. Cultivation created her to be apart, separated from humankind, un-Connected. Mortal perception of the Nightwatcher does not influence her like it does other spren. Mother wanted a daughter whose shape and personality would grow organically.

"This makes the Nightwatcher less . . . well, human . . . than a spren like me. Still, I don't believe her capable of lying. It isn't something she could conceive of, I believe."

"She's not the liar," Lift said, closing her eyes. Storms. She'd made the wrap too tight. She could barely breathe. "It's the other one. The one with a dress like leaves, merging into the underbrush. Hair like twigs. Skin the color of deep brown stone."

"So you did see Cultivation herself. Both you *and* Dalinar . . . Mother has been intervening far more than we assumed, but behind a cloud of subterfuge. She uses tales of the Old Magic to distract, and to make it less obvious the specific ones she is drawing to her. . . ."

Lift shrugged.

"I had suspected it was true. Your . . . situation is unique. Why, seeing into the Cognitive Realm—even a little—is an uncommon feature in a human! And turning food into Light. Why . . . if Mother is involved . . . perhaps this isn't Stormlight you use at all. Hmm . . . You realize how special you are, Lift."

"I didn't want to be special."

"Says the girl who was comparing herself so dramatically to a shadow earlier."

"I just wanted what I asked for."

"Which was?" Wyndle asked.

"Not important now."

"I rather think it is."

"I asked not to change," Lift whispered, opening her eyes. "I said, when everything else is going wrong, I want to be the same. I want to stay me. Not become someone else."

"Those are the exact words?" Wyndle asked.

"Best I can remember."

"Hmm . . ." Wyndle said, snuggling down into his vines. "I believe that is too vague."

"I wasn't! I told her. Make me so I don't grow up."

"That is *not* what you said, mistress. And if I might be so bold—having spent a *great* deal of time around you—you are *not* an easy person to understand."

"I asked not to change! So why am I *changing*?"

"You're still you. Merely a bigger version."

She squeezed her eyes shut again.

"Mistress," Wyndle said. "Lift. Will you tell me why this bothers you so much? Everyone grows. Everyone changes."

"But I'm . . . I'm her little girl."

"Whose little girl?" he asked gently. "Your mother's?"

Lift nodded. Stupid. It sounded stupid and *she* was stupid. Mother was dead. That was that.

Why hadn't she said the correct words? Why hadn't Cultivation just *understood*? Cultivation was supposed to be some sort of starvin' god. It was *her fault* if a little girl came and begged for a promise, and the god *deliberately* misinterpreted and . . .

And Lift liked who she was. Who she had been. She wouldn't be the same when she got older.

Crawl through dark tunnels? Sure. Fight against Fused? Eh, why not.

But feel your own body changing you into someone else, and not be able to stop it?

Every human being lived with a terrible terror, and they all ignored it. Their own bodies mutated, and elongated, and started bleeding, and became all wrong. Nobody talked about it? Nobody was *scared* of it? What was wrong with them?

The last time things felt right, Lift thought, *I was with her. Before she got sick. And I was her little girl.*

If she saw me now, she wouldn't recognize me.

A few strange spren, like faces mocking her, faded in nearby. Wyndle slowly wrapped his vines around her. Gentle, like an embrace. Though others could barely feel the touch of their spren, Wyndle felt solid to her. He wasn't warm. But . . . it *was* comforting when he rested his vine head on her shoulder. For once he didn't ruin the sentiment by saying something dumb.

And then he perked up in a suspicious-like way.

Lift wiped her eyes. "What?" she demanded.

"I don't know," Wyndle said. "Something just happened. In the tower. I feel . . . a darkness resting on me like a blanket. I think I felt the tower stir."

"You said the tower's spren was dead."

"Dead spren can stir, Lift," Wyndle said. "Something is wrong. Something is *very* wrong."

Lift grabbed a large piece of flatbread and stuffed it in her mouth. Then she scurried through the tunnels, Wyndle following. She tried to use Stormlight to make her body slick to get through a particularly tight squeeze, but it didn't work. She frowned, tried again, then finally forced herself through without it.

What on Roshar?

She came out above an empty room at the perimeter of the tower. She dropped from the opening in the ceiling, then trotted to the window. It was nearing evening, and the Everstorm had passed. Nothing *looked* wrong about the tower from her vantage; just an average day up in the mountains.

"Something's wrong with my powers," she whispered as Wyndle lowered himself from the top of the windowsill. "I couldn't become awesome."

"Look, down there."

Some people had gathered on the Oathgate platform to the Shattered Plains. Several figures who seemed to have fallen to the ground. Blue uniforms.

"Windrunners," she said, squinting. "Somethin's wrong with them. Maybe they broke the Oathgates?"

"Maybe."

Lift searched out across the snowy landscape, trying to listen. Listen. The Sleepless had told her, *Always listen.*

She heard screams. But not human ones.

"There," she said, pointing. "What's that?"

A bright red *something* was flying through the air in a desperate loop— being chased by something else that was green. Faster, more dangerous. The two collided in midair, and when the red something tore away, it dropped feathers in the sky.

Chickens. Flying chickens. She didn't need to be told to instinctively understand that the green one was the predator, while the red one was prey. It gave a few beleaguered flaps toward the tower, seeming barely able to stay in the air.

"Come on," Lift said, swinging out the window. "I need handholds."

"Oh, mistress!" Wyndle said, moving onto the outside of the tower. He wove back and forth to make a ladder of vines clinging to the stone, which she climbed. "We are *far* too high up for this! What if I drop!"

"You're a stormin' spren. You'd be fine."

"We don't know that!" he said. "I could fall hundreds of feet!"

"Cowardspren."

"Wisdomspren, if anything!" he said, but kept weaving as she scrambled upward.

The red chicken barely dodged another attack in the sky before darting in toward a balcony above and vanishing from her sight. The green chicken rounded, and she got a good look at it. Wicked talons, a sharp knifelike beak. She'd always thought chickens looked silly, but this one was different.

She reached the balcony and found the red one on the floor, bleeding from one wing, trying weakly to right itself. It was bigger than she'd thought, at least a foot tall, with a vivid red body and head. It had bright blue wings that went red at the ends, like fire. It chirped weakly as it saw her.

She perched on the rim of the balcony and turned to see the green one coming in. "Wyndle, I need you," she said, holding her hand to the side to make him into a weapon. Not a sword. She hated those things. A rod she could swing at the nightmare chicken.

Nothing happened.

"I can't become a weapon, mistress!" Wyndle cried. "I don't know why! It's something about the wrongness in the tower!"

Fine. She didn't need a weapon anyway. The green chicken came swooping toward her, claws extended. It seemed to expect her to flinch. So she didn't. She took the hit directly in the face and grabbed the chicken as it tried to rake her with its claws.

Then she bit it. Right on the wing.

Its startled scream seemed more confused than pained, but it tore out of her grip and fluttered away, crying as if it thought Lift wasn't playing fair.

She spat out a feather as Stormlight healed the cuts to her face. Well, at least that part of her abilities was still working. She hopped down and scooped up the wounded red-feathered chicken. It gave her a timid bite on the arm, and she glared at it.

"You ain't in any position to complain," she said, then tried to heal it.

She pressed her Light into the body, and it *resisted*. The healing didn't work either. Damnation.

The chicken calmed as she hurried into the room beyond, where a young lighteyed man had been walking to the balcony to see what the fuss was.

"Sorry," Lift said. "Important Radiant business." As he leaped back, startled, she snatched a limafruit off his table, then hurried out into the hallway beyond.

Let's see . . . fifth floor . . .

She found her way to one of the ventilation openings, and Wyndle made a ladder for her to climb up—the red chicken under her arm complaining softly about the treatment. Inside, safely around a few corners, she put the chicken on the floor, then pressed her hand to it again.

She pushed harder. When she'd tried to become awesome earlier, nothing had happened. But when she'd tried to heal, she'd felt something different—a resistance. So this time she pushed it, growling softly until . . . it worked. Stormlight left her, and the chicken's wing healed. Her powers didn't regrow the lost feathers, but in a moment the thing had rolled over and was picking at the bare skin on its side with a tentative beak. Finally, it looked at her and released a confused squawk.

"It's kind of what I do," she said, and shrugged. "I'm 'posed to listen too. Damnation take me if I can figure out how that applies to chickens though."

The chicken squawked. She tried to summon her awesomeness, but that power didn't merely resist. It seemed to not *exist*. As she tried again, she heard something odd. People shouting?

"Wyndle?" she asked.

He moved away as a vine. People could sometimes notice the remnants of those vines when they disintegrated, but he himself was invisible.

The chicken began walking away down the tunnel. It had a funny stride, like it was indignant about being forced to use its feet.

Lift hurried forward and blocked it off. "Where do you think you're going?"

It squawked insistently, then squeezed past her.

"At least wait for Wyndle," she said, blocking it off again. It let out a more threatening squawk, but soon Wyndle returned.

"Radiants are dropping unconscious!" he said. "Oh, mistress. This seems very bad!"

The chicken, uncaring, pushed past her and continued along the tunnel. Together she and Wyndle followed, the spren growing increasingly worried—particularly after the bird fluttered down into a corridor, then stared at the ground and chirped in an annoyed way.

It turned toward her, plaintive.

"You need to go down lower," she said, "but you don't know how? What are you following?"

It squawked.

"Mistress," Wyndle said, "chickens are *not* intelligent. Talking to one would make me question *your* intelligence, if I hadn't seen you talk to cremlings sometimes."

"Never can tell if one of those is reporting back to someone or not," she muttered, then climbed down and picked up the chicken. It seemed to have trouble flying without all its feathers, so she carried it as they used the stairs to descend several levels, following the chicken's body language. It would stretch out its head, then cock it, looking at the floor with one eye. When they got to the second level, it leveled out its head, staring insistently along a corridor, and made a kind of hooting noise.

Something distant rumbled from one of the corridors behind them. Lift spun, and Wyndle whimpered.

"That was thunder," she said. "There are stormforms in the tower."

"Oh, mistress!" Wyndle cried. "We should do something! Like hide! Or run away and *then* hide!"

Instead she followed the chicken's gaze. She was supposed to listen. It was one of her stormin' oaths, or something. She hurried through a side passage as the chicken started to squawk louder.

"Mistress?" Wyndle said. "Why are we . . ."

He trailed off as they stumbled across the corpse.

It was an old Alethi man in robes. He'd been killed with some kind of knife wound to the chest, and lay—his eyes open—on the ground. Blood on his lips.

She turned away. She never had gotten used to this sort of thing.

The chicken let out an angry screech, fluttering out of her hands to the man. Then—in perhaps the most heart-wrenching thing she'd ever seen—it began to nuzzle the corpse and chirp softly. It climbed into the crook of his dead arm and pushed its head against his side, chirping again, more worried this time.

"I'm sorry," Lift said, squatting down. "How did you know he was here?"

It chirped.

"You could feel him, couldn't you?" she asked. "Or . . . you could feel where he'd been. You're no ordinary chicken. Are you a *Voidbringer* chicken?"

"Why," Wyndle said, "do you insist on using that word? It's horribly inaccurate."

"Shut it, Voidbringer," she muttered at him. She reached over and carefully picked up the chicken, who had begun to let out pained chirps almost like words. Eerily similar to them, in fact.

"Who was he?" she asked. "Wyndle, do you recognize him?"

"I believe I've seen him before. A minor Alethi functionary, though his eyes are different now. Curious. Look at his fingers—tan skin with bands of lighter skin. He was wearing jewelry once."

Yes . . . thinking about it, she thought she recognized him. One of the old people in the tower. Retired, once an important official in the palace. She'd gone and talked to him because nobody paid attention to old people. They smelled.

"Robbed," she said. Back-alley killings still happened in this tower, though the Kholins tried to make the place safe. "I'll remember you. I promise. I—"

Something moved in the darkness nearby. A kind of scraping sound, like . . . feathers. Lift went alert and stood, holding out a sphere for light. It had come from farther down the corridor, where her light didn't reach.

Something flowed from that darkness. A man, tall with scarred features. He wore an Alethi uniform, but she swore she'd never seen him before. She would recognize a man this dangerous. Those eyes seemed to be part of the darkness—deep in shadow as he stepped into the light.

On his shoulder sat the green chicken from before, its wicked claws gripping a patch of leather affixed to the uniform.

"Little Radiant," the man said. "I'll admit, I've always wanted an excuse to hunt you."

She clutched her red chicken and started running.

The man behind her laughed. As if he'd been given the grandest of gifts.

I-6

A BOON AND A CURSE

Taravangian's solitude was painful today. As was increasingly common, he wasn't particularly smart.

Smart Taravangian hated company. Smart Taravangian forgot the point of being around other people. Smart Taravangian was terrifying, but he would gladly have been that version of himself today. He would have welcomed the emotional anesthesia.

He sat alone in a stormwagon, hands in his lap, surrounded by swirling brown exhaustionspren. The Everstorm was nearing its end. He was now to give the order for his men to betray the coalition. If Taravangian's guesses were right, it also meant Odium had launched an attack on Urithiru.

Taravangian did not give the order yet. Odium had said he would come to confirm, and so far he hadn't. Perhaps . . . perhaps Taravangian's service wouldn't be needed today. Perhaps the plan had changed.

Weak, frail hopes for a weak, frail man.

He so wished he could be smart. When had he last been intelligent? Not brilliant—he'd given up on feeling that way again—but merely smart? The last time had been . . . storms, over a year ago. When he'd planned how to destroy Dalinar.

That attempt had failed. Dalinar had refused to be broken. Smart Taravangian, for all his capacities, had proven insufficient.

Smart Taravangian came up with the plan that forced Odium to make a deal, he thought. *That is enough.*

And yet . . . and yet he wavered. Smart Taravangian *had* failed. Besides, he hadn't *just* been made intelligent. He'd been given a boon and a curse. Intelligence on one side. Compassion on the other. When smart, he assumed the compassion was the curse. But was it really? Or was the curse that he could never have both at once?

He stood up in the wagon, and withstood the moment of dizziness that took him each time he stood these days: blackness creeping at the edges of his vision, like deathspren eager to claim him. He thought perhaps it was his heart, though he had not asked for a surgeon. Best not to trouble someone who could be helping wounded soldiers.

He breathed out in short breaths, listening to the soft cracks of the Everstorm outside. The thunder was ebbing. Almost at the end.

He shuffled the short distance to his trunk. Here, Taravangian forced himself to kneel. Storms, when had *kneeling* become so painful? His bones ground against one another like a pestle against its bowl.

Trying not to focus on the painspren, he fumbled at the lock's combination with trembling fingers, then unhooked the lid. He undid the trunk's lining on the top, reached to the secret compartment and flipped a hidden latch. That disengaged the small ink vial he'd rigged to spill and ruin the contents of the compartment if it was tampered with.

Only then could he feel around inside and locate the pages. He pulled them out with a tentative hand. A year ago, during his most recent bout of intelligence, he'd created this. A few pages from the Diagram, cut out and rearranged, with some scribbled notes. He'd burned his copy of the book itself, but had kept this excised section.

Exhausted, he crawled to his chair and struggled into the seat. Wheezing, he cradled the old sheets from the Diagram, then tried to shoo away the exhaustionspren.

When he'd created this little section, he hadn't been as smart as he'd been on that singular day—now seven years gone—when he'd created the Diagram. On that day, he'd been a god. On the day when he'd created this fragment a year ago, he'd considered himself a prophet to that god.

So what was he now? A priest? A humble follower? A fool? In a way, it felt a betrayal to think in religious terms. This was not the act of gods, but men.

No. A god made you what you are.

He held up the pages and read through them, squinting without his reading spectacles. The cramped handwriting listed instructions, spliced together with original pieces of the Diagram. Most of it detailed the ploy to unseat Dalinar by the careful reveal of secrets—a plan designed to bring the poor man to his knees, to turn the coalition against him. In the end, that ploy had only galvanized the Blackthorn—and increased his suspicion of Taravangian. Before that day, they had been friends.

Taravangian turned this page over in his fingers, trying to understand the strange creature he became when intelligent. A being unburdened by empathy, capable of seeing straight to the heart of matters. Yet also a being who couldn't understand the *context* of his efforts. He would work to preserve a people at the same time he casually ordered the deaths of children.

Smart Taravangian knew the *how* but not the *why*.

Dumb Taravangian didn't make connections, didn't remember things quickly, couldn't compute in his head. In this document—intended to demoralize, defame, and destroy a man he dearly respected—dumb Taravangian found pain. He was weeping by the time he finished reading it, and the exhaustionspren had been replaced by the white petals of shamespren.

All this, he thought, *to save a handful of people?* He'd preserved Kharbranth by selling out the rest of humankind. He was certain Odium could not be defeated. And so, saving a remnant was the only logical path.

Right now, that seemed pathetic. Smart Taravangian considered himself so brilliant, so masterful, but *this* was the best he could do?

It was a dangerous line of thought. And pointless. Hadn't he told off Mrall for making this very argument? They had to focus on what they could do. Smart Taravangian understood that, and had accomplished it.

Dumb Taravangian instead wept for all the people he had failed. All the people who would die when Odium scoured the world of humankind.

Taravangian looked back at the notes, and today saw something new in them. A small comment about a specific person. *Why specifically can't the Diagram see Renarin Kholin?* the notes read. *Why is he invisible?*

Smart Taravangian had moved on quickly from this question. Why waste time on something minor that you couldn't solve? Dumb Taravangian lingered on it, remembering a later time when he'd been visited by Odium. Odium had shown Taravangian something, and Renarin . . . Renarin Kholin had appeared as a chain of blacked-out futures, unseeable.

The wagon began to grow lighter around Taravangian. He cursed under his breath, quickly folding the papers together and hiding them in the pocket of his robes. In an instant, the stormwagon melted away—walls vanishing before a brilliant golden light. The floor changed, and Taravangian found himself sitting in his chair on a brilliant field, the ground made as if from solid gold.

A figure stood in front of him, a twenty-foot-tall human bearing a scepter. His features were Shin, and his hair and beard were completely gold, as if he were Iriali. Odium's robes were more ornate than last time, red and gold, with a sword tied at the waist.

It was a presentation meant to stun and awe, and Taravangian couldn't help but gasp. It was so *gorgeous.* He forced himself out of his seat, falling again on painful knees, bowing his head but unable to tear his eyes away from the magnificent display.

"I prefer you when you are like this, Taravangian," Odium said with a powerful voice. "You may not think as quickly, but you do understand more quickly."

"My lord," Taravangian said. "Is it time?"

"Yes," Odium said. "You are to send the orders."

"It will be done."

"Will they obey, Taravangian? You ask them to turn against their allies. To side with the enemy."

"The Alethi *are* their enemies, Lord," Taravangian said. "The Vedens have hated their neighbors for centuries. Plus their new leaders—installed by your own hand—are hungry for power. They believe you will reward them."

They had not obtained promises. A god could be bound, but only by oaths. These foolish men believed that they'd be rewarded above the others, but Taravangian knew their entire country was doomed. Every human in those lands would eventually be destroyed.

They were oblivious of this fate, and Taravangian was confident they would do as they were told and attack their former allies. He had spent a year preparing them, promoting the right men at Odium's command, subtly indicating to all who followed him that the war was a problem for Alethkar and Azir, not for Jah Keved. That the enemy would never come for *them*.

He looked up to find the god inspecting him with a curious expression. "Do you not fear death, Taravangian?" Odium asked. "You know you are doomed."

"I . . ." Taravangian trembled. He tried not to think about it too much, particularly when he was stupid. Because yes, he did fear death. He feared it terribly. He hoped that beyond death there was nothing. Oblivion.

For if anything else awaited *him*, it would not be pleasant.

"I do fear it," he whispered.

"So honest, this version of you," Odium said. He walked around Taravangian, who continued to kneel. "I much prefer it, yes. There is a straightforwardness to your Passion."

"Could you not spare them?" Taravangian asked, tears in his eyes. "The people of Jah Keved, the Iriali, those who come to you willingly. Why waste their lives?"

"Oh, I will not waste them, Taravangian," Odium said. "Their lives will be spent as they expect—in war, in glory, in blood. I will give them exactly what they've been asking for. They don't know it, but they beg me for death in their requests for power. Only you have begged me for peace."

He looked to Taravangian. "Kharbranth will remain an eye of calm in the storm to come. Do not let the others concern you. They will fight in the war they've been promised since birth, and though it will consume and destroy them, they *will* enjoy it. I shall make certain of that fact. Even if they will not be led in this glory by the one who should have been their king . . ."

As the god mused, Taravangian noticed something—a light emanating from Odium. It pulsed, making his skin transparent, glowing from within. There was a . . . sickly feel to it somehow. Indeed, Odium stopped and seemed to concentrate, making the light retreat before continuing.

I have failed in many ways, but you failed too, Taravangian thought at the god. The "one who should have been their king" was in reference to Dalinar. Odium had been planning for something for many years, a war far greater—even—than the one that now consumed Roshar. Some strange battle for the heavens.

He had wanted Dalinar for this war, but had failed to secure him. Odium still intended to use all of humankind as his frontline troops, once he won Roshar. He would throw their lives away, turn them into slaves focused on fueling his war for the heavens. He would use their blood to preserve the singers, which Odium saw as more valuable troops.

Merely considering all this horrified Taravangian. It was even worse than the quick and swift destruction he'd been imagining. This would be a drawn-out nightmare of slavery, blood, and death. Yet one thought comforted him. One that smart Taravangian would have discarded as sentimental.

You expected Dalinar to turn, Taravangian thought. *You wanted him for your champion. You failed. So in the end, you were no smarter than I was. And for all your boasting that you can see the future, you do not know everything.*

Taravangian had seen the god's plans once. Could he . . . could he make it happen again?

No. He didn't dare plot. He wasn't smart. He was . . . he was only a man.

But . . . who better to stand up for men everywhere? In a moment of impassioned boldness, Taravangian reached into his pocket and took out the piece of the Diagram he'd worked on. He held it close, as if for comfort.

Odium took the bait. He strode over and snatched it from Taravangian's fingers.

"What is this?" Odium asked. "Ah . . . another piece of your Diagram, is it? Edited, I see. You think yourself so smart, do you."

"No," Taravangian whispered, hoarse. "I know nothing."

"As well you should acknowledge it," Odium said, then held the papers up before himself and shredded them in a flash of light. "This is nothing. You are nothing."

Taravangian cried out, grabbing one of the pieces as it fluttered.

Odium waved. And for a second time, Taravangian was given a glimpse of the god's plans. Hundreds of thousands of panes of writing, hovering as if on invisible glass. This was what Odium had shown him a year ago; it was intended to impress Taravangian with how thorough and extensive

Odium's planning was. And Taravangian had managed to tempt him into showing it off, like a prized stallion.

Storms . . . Odium could be tricked. By *dumb* Taravangian.

Taravangian glanced around, trying to find the black portion he'd seen before. Yes, there it was, the corrupted writing, a section of plans ruined by Renarin Kholin.

The implications of that seemed profound now. Odium wasn't able to see Renarin's future. No one could.

The scar had expanded. Taravangian turned away quickly, not wanting to draw Odium's ire. Yet right before looking away, Taravangian saw something half-consumed in the black scar.

His own name. Why? What did it mean?

I'm close to Renarin, Taravangian realized. *Everyone close to the boy has their future clouded. Perhaps that was why Odium was wrong about Dalinar.*

Taravangian felt a surge of hope.

Odium couldn't see Taravangian's future right now.

Taravangian bowed his head and bit his lip, squeezing his eyes closed, hoping the tears at the corners of his eyes would be mistaken for tears of awe or fear.

"Resplendent, isn't it?" Odium asked. "I've wondered why she would give you a taste of what we can do. In some ways, you're the only one I can talk to. The only one who understands, if in a limited way, the burden I bear."

You could have simply come and given me the order today, then left, Taravangian thought. *You talk instead. You're lonely. You want to show off. You're . . . human.*

"I will miss you," Odium said. "I'm pleased that you made me promise to keep the humans of Kharbranth alive. They will remind me of you."

If Odium could be lonely, if he could boast, if he could be tricked . . . he could be afraid. Taravangian might be dumb, but when dumb, he understood emotion.

Odium had incredible power; that was clear. He *was* a god, in power. But in mind? In mind he was a *man*. What did Odium fear? He *would* have fears, wouldn't he? Taravangian opened his eyes and scanned through the many hovering panes of description. Many were in languages he couldn't read, but Odium used glyphs for names.

Taravangian looked for a knot of tight writing. He looked for letters that evoked terror—the terror of a genius. He found them, understanding them without being able to read them, in a knot near the black scar. Words written in cramped letters, circling a name being consumed by the scar. A simple, terrifying name.

Szeth. The Assassin in White.

Trembling, Taravangian turned away. Odium began ranting again, but Taravangian missed what the creature said.

Szeth.

The sword.

Odium *feared the sword.*

Except . . . Szeth was at Urithiru. Why was his name being consumed by the scar that represented Renarin? It didn't make any sense. Could Taravangian have misunderstood?

It took him a painfully long time to see the obvious answer. Szeth was here, in the army, near Dalinar. Who was in turn near Renarin. Dalinar must have brought Szeth in secret.

"You cannot conceive how long I've planned for this," Odium was saying—though the light was building within him again, his skin like thin paper. He seemed . . . not weak—a being who could spawn storms and destroy entire nations would never be weak. But vulnerable.

Odium had bet so much upon Dalinar being his champion. Now that was in chaos. The god bragged about his plans, but Taravangian knew firsthand that you could plan and plan and plan, but if one man's choices didn't align to your will, it didn't matter. A thousand wrong plans were no more useful than a single wrong one.

"Don't be too pained, Taravangian," Odium said. "Dalinar won't kill you immediately. He'll seek to understand; it has become his way. Poor fool. The old Blackthorn would have immediately murdered you, but this weaker version won't be able to help himself. He'll need to talk to you before he orders your execution."

You're doing the same, Taravangian thought, a dangerous plan budding in his mind. *You should have killed me.*

Out loud he said, "So be it. I have accomplished my goal."

"So you have," Odium said. "So you have. Go, my son. Make good on your part of our compact, and earn salvation for those you love."

The golden expanse faded, depositing Taravangian on the floor of his stormwagon. He opened his hand, finding the fragment of the Diagram in it. But . . . the other pieces were gone. They had vanished when the vision ended. That stunned him, for it implied that he had truly been in another place. That he'd taken the papers there with him, but only this one piece remained when he returned.

He stared at the fragment for a long time, then forced himself into his seat. He took a moment to recover before digging into his satchel. He brought out the spanreed board, oriented it, and positioned the pen. When he finally got a response, he wrote out two simple words.

Do it.

He had to go through with the betrayal, of course. He needed to keep his agreement; he *had* to protect Kharbranth. That came before any other plots or plans. And any other such plots would *have* to be executed in such a way that Odium either did not know what he'd done, or couldn't act against him to remove Kharbranth's protections.

It took less than fifteen minutes for Dalinar's soldiers to arrive and break into his wagon, shattering the door and storming in with weapons drawn. Yes, they'd been waiting for this betrayal. Odium had his distraction. They'd need to dedicate weeks of frantic work to be certain the Veden armies didn't gain too much of an advantage—and Dalinar would be occupied here, fighting off Taravangian's soldiers.

Taravangian groaned as the soldiers seized his spanreeds, a scribe among them reading the two words he'd sent.

They didn't harm him. Odium was probably right. Taravangian likely had a few weeks before his execution. He found that he hurt less, felt less tired, as they bound and gagged him. It was painful, yes, but he could suffer a little pain. For he knew something powerful. A quiet, furtive secret as dangerous as the Diagram had been.

Taravangian had decided not to give up.

PART
THREE

Songs of Home

KALADIN • NAVANI • DALINAR •
VENLI • ESHONAI • JASNAH • RENARIN

44

TINDER WAITING
FOR THE SPARK

I find this format most comfortable, as it is how I've collaborated in the past. I have never done it in this way, and with this kind of partner.

—From *Rhythm of War*, page 1

Kaladin jogged through the dark tunnels of Urithiru, Teft across his shoulders, feeling as if he could *hear* his life crumbling under-foot with each step. A phantom cracking, like glass shattering.

Each painful step took him farther from his family, farther from peace. Farther into the darkness. He'd made his decision. He would *not* leave his friend to the whims of enemy captivity. But though he'd finally thought to take off his bloodied shoes—and now carried them with the laces looped around his neck—he still felt as if he were leaving stained tracks behind him.

Storms. What did he think he could accomplish by himself? He was effectively disobeying the queen's order to surrender.

He tried his best to banish such thoughts and keep moving. He would have time later to ruminate on what he'd done. For now, he needed to find a safe place to hide. The tower was no longer home, but an enemy fortress.

Syl zipped out in front of him, checking each intersection before he arrived. Stormlight kept him moving, but he worried what would happen when it ran out. Would his strength fail him? Would he collapse in the center of the corridor?

Why hadn't he collected more spheres from his parents or Laral before leaving? He hadn't even thought to take the stormform's axe. That left him unarmed, save for a *scalpel*. He was too used to having Syl as his Shard-spear, but if she couldn't transform—

No, he thought to himself. *No thoughts. Thoughts are dangerous. Just move.*

He pushed forward, relying on Syl, who sped toward a stairwell. The easiest way to lose themselves would be to find a hiding place on the unin-habited floors, perhaps somewhere on eleven or twelve. He took the stairs two at a time, propelled by the pulsing Light in his veins. His glow was enough to see by. Teft began muttering quietly, perhaps responding to the jostling.

They reached the seventh floor, then started straight up toward the eighth. Here, Syl led him farther inward. Try as he might to ignore them, Kaladin continued to hear the echoes of his failure. His father's shouts. His own tears . . .

He'd been so close. So *close.*

He lost track of their location in the endless tunnels. The floor here wasn't painted to give directions, so he trusted in Syl. She zipped ahead to an intersection, spun around in a circle a few times, then shot to the right. He kept pace with her, though he was feeling Teft's weight more and more.

"Just a second," he whispered to her at the next intersection, then rested against the wall—Teft still weighing heavily on his shoulders—and fished a chip from his pouch. The small topaz was barely enough to see by, but he needed it as the Stormlight he was holding finally gave out. And he didn't have many spheres left.

He grunted under the weight of his friend, then pushed himself to stand up straight, clinging tightly to Teft with both hands while gripping the sphere between two fingers. He nodded to Syl, then continued after her, pleased that his strength was holding. He could manage Teft without Light. Despite Kaladin's last few weeks spent as a surgeon, his body was still that of a soldier.

"We should go higher," Syl said, floating alongside his head as a ribbon of light. "Can you manage?"

"Get us to floor ten at least," Kaladin said.

"I'll have to take us up stairwells as I see them. I don't really know this section of the tower. . . ."

He let himself sink into an old familiar mindset as they continued. Teft's weight across his shoulders wasn't that different from carrying a bridge. It brought him back to those days. Running bridges. Eating stew.

Watching his friends die . . . feeling terror anew each day . . .

Those memories offered no comfort. But the rhythm of steps, carrying a burden, working his body on an extended march . . . it was at least familiar.

He followed Syl up one set of steps, then another. Then across another long tunnel, the strata here waving vigorously like ripples in a churning pond. Kaladin kept moving.

Until suddenly he came alert.

He couldn't pinpoint what alarmed him, but he moved on instinct to immediately cover his sphere and duck into a side passage. He stepped into a nook and knelt to slide Teft off his shoulders. He pressed his hand against the unconscious man's mouth to silence his mumbling.

Syl darted over a moment later. He could see her in the darkness, but she didn't illuminate things around her. He shoved his other hand in his pocket, tightly holding the sphere so it couldn't give off any betraying illumination.

"What?" Syl asked.

Kaladin shook his head. He didn't know, but didn't want to speak. He huddled there—hoping Teft wouldn't mutter or shift too loudly—his own heartbeat thumping in his ears.

Then, faint red light crept into the hallway he'd left. Syl immediately zipped to hide her light behind Kaladin's dark form.

The light approached, revealing a single ruby along with a pair of glowing red eyes. Those illuminated a terrible face. Pure black, with hints of marbled red under the eyes. Long dark hair, which appeared woven into his simple wrap of clothing. It was the creature Kaladin had fought in Hearthstone, the one he'd killed in the burning room of the mansion. Though the Fused had been reborn into a new body, Kaladin knew from the skin patterns that it was the same individual. Come for revenge.

The Fused didn't seem to spot Kaladin hiding in the darkness, though he did pause at the intersection for an extended period of time. He moved on, thankfully, going deeper along the path Kaladin had been taking.

Storms . . . Kaladin had defeated the thing last time without any Stormlight, but he had done so by playing on its arrogance. Kaladin doubted it would let him get such an easy kill again.

Those singers in the clinic . . . one of them mentioned that a Fused was looking for me. They called him the Pursuer. This thing . . . it had come to the tower *specifically* to find Kaladin.

"Follow it," he mouthed, turning to Syl, counting on her to understand his meaning. "I'll find someplace more secluded to hide."

She wove her line of light into a brief luminescent representation of a *kejeh* glyph—meaning "affirmative"—then zipped after the Pursuer. She couldn't get too far from Kaladin anymore, but she should be able to follow for a while. Hopefully she could do so circumspectly, as some of the Fused could see spren.

Kaladin hauled Teft back up onto his shoulders, then struck out into the darkness, barely allowing himself any light. There was always something oppressive about being deep in the tower, feeling so far away from the sky and the wind—but it was worse in the darkness. He could all too easily imagine himself trapped in here without spheres, left to wander forever in a tomb of stone.

He wove through a few more turns, hoping to find a stairwell up to another floor. Unfortunately, Teft started muttering again. Gritting his teeth, Kaladin ducked into the first room he found—a place with a narrow doorway. Here he set Teft down, then tried to stifle his noises.

Syl darted into the room a moment later, which made Kaladin jump.

"He's coming," she hissed. "He went only a short distance down the wrong hallway before he stopped, inspected the ground, then doubled back. I don't think he saw me. I followed long enough to see him stop at the place where you hid a bit ago. He found a little smear of blood on the wall there. I hurried ahead of him, but he knows you're nearby."

Storms. Kaladin glanced at his bloody clothing, then at Teft—who was muttering despite Kaladin's attempts to quiet him.

"We need to lead the Pursuer away," Kaladin whispered. "Be ready to distract him."

She made another affirmative signal. Kaladin left his friend as a restless lump in the darkness, then backtracked a little. He pulled up near an intersection, gripping his scalpel. He allowed no light other than Syl's, his few remaining infused spheres tucked away in his black pouch.

He took a few deep breaths, then mouthed his plan to Syl. She sailed farther away through the black corridor, leaving Kaladin in total darkness.

He'd never been able to find the pure emptiness of mind that some soldiers claimed to adopt in battle. He wasn't certain he'd ever want something like that. However, he did compose himself, making his breathing shallow, and came fully alert, listening.

Loose, relaxed, but ready to come alight. Like tinder waiting for the spark. He was ready to breathe in his last spheres of Stormlight, but wouldn't until the last moment.

Footsteps scraped the corridor to Kaladin's right, and the walls slowly bled with red light. Kaladin held his breath, ready, his back to the wall.

The Pursuer froze just before reaching the intersection, and Kaladin knew the creature had spotted Syl, who would have zipped past in the distance. A heartbeat later, scraping noises announced the Pursuer dropping his body as a husk—and a red ribbon of light rushed after Syl. The distraction had worked. Syl would lead him away.

As far as they knew, the Fused couldn't harm spren naturally—the only way to do so was with a Shardblade. Even that was temporary; cut spren with a Shardblade, even rip them to pieces, and they eventually re-formed in the Cognitive Realm. Experiments had proven that the only way to keep them divided was to store separate halves in gemstones.

Kaladin gave it ten heartbeats, then brought out a small sphere for light and dashed into the corridor—sparing a brief glance at the Pursuer's discarded body—before running for the room where he'd put Teft.

It was amazing what a jolt of energy came from being so close to a fight. He heaved Teft on his shoulders without trouble, then was jogging away in moments—almost as if he were infused with Stormlight again. Using the light of the sphere, he soon found a stairwell. He almost rushed up it, but a faint light from above made him stop fast.

Voices speaking to rhythms echoed from above. And from below, he realized. He left that stairwell, but two hallways over he saw distant lights and shadows. He pulled into a side corridor, sweating in streams, fearspren—like globs of goo—writhing up through the stone beneath him.

He knew this feeling. Scurrying through the darkness. People with lights searching in a pattern, hunting him. Breathing heavily, he hauled Teft through a different side passage, but soon spotted lights in that direction as well.

The enemy was forming a noose, slowly tightening around his position. That knowledge sent him into flashbacks of the night when he'd failed Nalma and the others. A night when, like so many other times, he'd survived when everyone else had died. Kaladin wasn't a runaway slave anymore, but the sensation was the same.

"Kaladin!" Syl said, zipping up to him. "I was leading him toward the edge of the level, but we ran into some regular soldiers and he turned back. He seemed to figure out I was trying to distract him."

"There are multiple squads up here," Kaladin said, pulling into the darkness. "Maybe a full company. Storms. The Pursuer must have repurposed the entire force sent to go through homes on the sixth floor."

He was shocked at the speed with which they'd set up the trap. He had to admit that was likely the result of him letting a soldier run and tell the others.

Well, he doubted the enemy had found the time to appropriate one of Navani's maps of this level. They couldn't have managed to place people in every hallway or stairwell. The net closing around him *had* to have gaps.

He began searching. Down a side corridor, he found shadowy figures approaching. And in the next stairwell. They were relentless, and everywhere. Plus, he didn't know this area any better than they did. He twisted around through a group of corridors until he reached a dead end. A quick search of the nearby rooms showed no other exits, and he looked over his shoulder, hearing voices calling to one another. They spoke Azish, he thought—and to the rhythms.

Feeling a sense of growing dread, he set Teft down, counted his few spheres, and took out his scalpel once more. Right. He'd . . . he'd need to take a weapon from the first soldier he killed. A spear, hopefully. Something with reach if he was going to survive a fight in these corridors.

Syl landed on his shoulder and took the shape of a young woman, seated with her hands in her lap.

"We have to try to punch through," Kaladin whispered. "There's a chance they'll send only a couple men this direction. We kill them, then slip out of the noose and run."

She nodded.

It didn't sound like a "couple men" though. And he was reasonably certain he caught a harsher, louder voice among them. The Pursuer was still tracking him, possibly by the faint marks of blood smeared on the walls or floor.

Kaladin pulled Teft into one of the rooms, then positioned himself in the doorway to wait. Not calm, but prepared. He gripped his scalpel in a reverse grip—a hacking grip—for ramming into the space between carapace and neck. Standing there, he felt the weight of it all pressing down on him. The darkness, both inside and out. The fatigue. The dread. Gloomspren like tattered pieces of cloth faded in, as if banners attached to the walls.

"Kaladin," Syl said softly, "could we surrender?"

"That Fused isn't here to take me captive, Syl," he said.

"If you die I'll be alone again."

"We've slipped out of tighter problems than this. . . ." He trailed off as he glanced at her, sitting on his shoulder, seeming far smaller than usual. He couldn't force the rest of the words out. He couldn't lie.

Light began to illuminate the corridor, coming toward him.

Kaladin gripped his knife more tightly. A part of him seemed to have always known it would come to this. Alone in the darkness, standing with his back to the wall, facing overwhelming numbers. A glorious way to die, but Kaladin didn't want glory. He'd given up on that foolish dream as a child.

"Kaladin!" Syl said. "What's that? On the floor?"

A faint violet light had appeared in the crook of the rightmost corner. Almost invisible, even in the darkness. Frowning, Kaladin left his post by the door, inspecting the light. There was a garnet vein in the stone here, and a small portion of it was glowing. As he tried to figure out why, the glow moved—running along the crystal vein. He followed it to the doorway, then watched it cross the hallway to the room on the other side.

He hesitated only briefly before putting away his weapon and hauling Teft onto his shoulders once again. He stumbled across the hallway outside—

and one of the approaching people said something in Azish. It sounded hesitant, as if they hadn't caught more than a glimpse of him.

Storms. What was he doing? Chasing phantom lights, like starspren in the sky? In this small chamber, the light moved across the floor and up the wall, revealing what appeared to be a gemstone embedded deeply in the stone.

"A fabrial?" Syl said. "Infuse it!"

Kaladin breathed in some of his Stormlight, then glanced over his shoulder. Voices outside, and shadows. Rather than hold his Stormlight for that fight, however, he did as Syl told him—pressing the Light into the gemstone. He had maybe two or three chips' worth left after that. He was practically defenseless.

The wall split down the center. He gaped as the stones *moved*, but with a silence that defied explanation. They cracked open just wide enough to admit a person. Carrying Teft, he entered a hidden corridor. Behind him, the doorway smoothly slid shut, and the light in the gemstone went out.

Kaladin held his breath as he heard voices in the room behind. Then he pressed his ear against the wall, listening. He couldn't make out much—an argument that seemed to involve the Pursuer. Kaladin worried they had spotted the door closing, but he heard no scraping or pounding. They would spot the spren he'd drawn though, and would know he was close.

Kaladin needed to keep moving. The little violet light on the floor twinkled and moved, so he lugged Teft after it through another series of corridors. Eventually they reached a hidden stairwell that—blessedly—was undefended.

He climbed that, though each footfall was slower than the one before it and exhaustionspren hounded him. He kept moving somehow, as the light led him to the eleventh floor, and then into another dark room. The oppressive silence told him he'd reached a portion of the tower the enemy wasn't searching. He wanted to collapse, but the light pulsed insistently on the wall—and Syl encouraged him to look.

Another embedded gemstone, barely visible. He used the last of his Stormlight to infuse it, and slipped through the door that opened. In absolute darkness, Kaladin set Teft down, feeling the door closing behind.

He didn't have the strength to inspect his surroundings. He instead slid to the cold stone floor, trembling.

There, he finally let himself drift to sleep.

45

A BOLD HEART, A KEEN AND CRAFTY MIND

NINE YEARS AGO

Eshonai had been told that mapping the world removed its mystery. Some of the other listeners insisted the wilderness should be left uncharted—the domain of the spren and the greatshells—and that by trying to confine it to paper, she risked stealing its secrets.

She found this to be flat-out ridiculous. She attuned Awe as she entered the forest, the trees bobbing with lifespren, bright green balls with white spines poking out. Closer to the Shattered Plains, most everything was flat, grown over by only the occasional rockbud. Yet here, not so far away, plants thrived in abundance.

Her people made frequent trips to the forest to get lumber and mushrooms. However, they always took the exact same route. Up the river a day's walk inward, gather there, then return. This time she'd insisted on leaving the party—much to their concern. She'd promised to meet them again at their normal camp, after scouting the outer perimeter of the forest all the way around.

After hiking around the trees for several days, she'd encountered the river on the other side. Now she could cut back through the heart of the forest and reach her family's camp from that direction. She'd bear with her a new map that revealed exactly how large the forest was, at least on one side.

She started along the stream, attuned to Joy, accompanied by swimming riverspren. Everyone had been so worried about her being out in the storms alone. Well, she had been out in storms a dozen times in her life, and had survived with no trouble. Plus, she'd been able to move in among the trees for shelter.

Her family and friends were concerned nonetheless. They spent their lives living in a very small region, dreaming of the day they could conquer one of the ten ancient cities at the perimeter of the Shattered Plains. Such a small-minded goal. Why not strike out, see what else there was to the world?

But no. Only one possible goal existed: win one of the cities. Seek shelter behind crumbling walls, ignoring the barrier the woods provided. Eshonai considered it proof that nature was stronger than the creations of listeners. This forest had likely stood when the ancient cities had been new. Yet this forest still thrived, and those were ruins.

You couldn't steal the secrets from something so strong just by exploring it. You could merely learn.

She settled down near a rock and unrolled her map, made from precious paper. Her mother was one of the few among all the families who knew the Song of Making Paper, and with her help, Eshonai had perfected the process. She used a pen and ink to sketch the path of the river as it entered the forest, then dabbed the ink until it was dry before rerolling the map.

Though she was confident, Resolve attuned, the others' complaints had been particularly bothersome lately.

We know where the forest is and how to reach it. Why map its size? What will that help?

The river flows this direction. Everyone knows where to find it. Why bother putting it on paper?

Too many of her family wanted to pretend the world was smaller than it was. Eshonai was convinced that was why they continued to squabble with the other listener families. If the world consisted only of the land around the ten cities, then fighting over that land made sense.

But their ancestors hadn't fought one another. Their ancestors had turned their faces to the storm and marched away, abandoning their very gods in the name of freedom. Eshonai would use that freedom. Instead of sitting by the fire and complaining, she would experience the beauties Cultivation offered. And she would ask the best question of them all.

What will I discover next?

Eshonai continued walking, judging the river's course. She used her own methods of counting the distance, then rechecked her work by surveying sights from multiple angles. The river continued flowing for days once a storm passed. How? When all other water had drained away or been lapped up, why did this river keep going? Where did it start?

Rivers and their carapace-covered spren excited her. Rivers were markers, guideposts, roadways. You could never get lost if you knew where the river was. She stopped for lunch near one of the bends, and discovered a type of cremling that was *green*, like the trees. She'd never seen one that shade before. She'd have to tell Venli.

"Stealing nature's secrets," Eshonai said to Annoyance. "What is a secret but a surprise to be discovered?"

Finishing her steamed haspers, she put out her fire and scattered the flamespren before continuing on her way. By her guess, it would take her a day and a half to reach her family. Then, if she left them again and rounded the *other* side of the forest, she'd have a finished picture of how it looked.

There was so much to see, so much to know, so much to *do*. And she was going to discover it all. She was going to . . .

What was that?

She frowned, halting in her tracks. The river wasn't strong now; it would likely slow to a trickle by tomorrow. Over its gurgling, she heard shouts in the distance. Had the others come to find her? She hurried forward, attuning Excitement. Perhaps they were growing more willing to explore.

It wasn't until she was almost to the sounds that she realized something was very wrong with them. They were flat, no hint of a rhythm. As if they were made by the dead.

A moment later she rounded a bend and found herself confronted by something more wondrous—and more terrible—than she'd ever dared imagine.

Humans.

⁘

"'. . . dullform dread, with the mind most lost,'" Venli quoted. "'The lowest, and one not bright. To find this form, one need banish the cost. It finds you and brings you to blight.'"

She drew in a deep breath and sat back in their tent, proud. All ninety-one stanzas, recited *perfectly*.

Her mother, Jaxlim, nodded as she worked the loom. "That was one of your better recitations," she said to Praise. "A little more practice, and we can move to the next song."

"But . . . I got it right."

"You mixed up the seventh and fifteenth stanzas," her mother said.

"The order doesn't matter."

"You also forgot the nineteenth."

"No I didn't," Venli said, counting them in her head. Workform? ". . . Did I?"

"You did," her mother said. "But you needn't be embarrassed. You are doing fine."

Fine? Venli had spent *years* memorizing the songs, while Eshonai barely did anything useful. Venli was better than *fine*. She was *excellent*.

Except . . . she'd forgotten an entire stanza? She looked at her mother, who was humming softly as she worked the loom.

"The nineteenth stanza isn't that important," Venli said. "Nobody is going to forget how to become a worker. And dullform. Why do we have a stanza about that? Nobody would *willingly* choose it."

"We need to remember the past," her mother said to the Rhythm of the Lost. "We need to remember what we passed through to get here. We need to take care not to forget ourselves."

Venli attuned Annoyance. And then, Jaxlim began to sing to the rhythms in a beautiful voice. There was something amazing about her mother's voice. It wasn't powerful or bold, but it was like a knife—thin, sharp, almost liquid. It cut Venli to the soul, and Awe replaced her Annoyance.

No, Venli wasn't perfect. Not yet. But her mother was.

Jaxlim sang on, and Venli watched, transfixed, feeling ashamed of her earlier petulance. It was just so hard sometimes. Sitting in here day after day, memorizing while Eshonai played. The two of them were nearly adults, only a year off for Eshonai and a little more than two for Venli. They were supposed to be responsible.

Her mother eventually trailed off, after the tenth stanza.

"Thank you," Venli said.

"For singing something you've heard a thousand times?"

"For reminding me," Venli said to Praise, "of what I am practicing to become."

Her mother attuned Joy and continued working. Venli strolled to the doorway of the tent and peered out, where family members worked at various activities, like chopping wood and felling trees. Her people were the First-Rhythm family, and had a noble heritage. They were thousands strong, but it had been many years since they'd controlled a city.

They kept talking of winning one back soon. Of how they'd strike out of the forest and attack before a storm, claiming their rightful seat. It was an excellent and worthy goal, yet Venli found herself dissatisfied as she watched warriors making arrows and sharpening ancient metal spears. Was this really what life amounted to? Fighting back and forth over the same ten cities?

Surely there was more for them. Surely there was more for *her*. She had come to love the songs, but she wanted to use them. Find the secrets they promised. Would Roshar create someone like Venli, only to have her sit in a hogshide tent and memorize words until she could pass them on, then die?

No. She had to have some kind of destiny. Something grand. "Eshonai thinks we should draw pictures to represent the verses of the songs," Venli said. "Make stacks of papers full of pictures, so we won't forget."

"Your sister has a wisdom to her at times," her mother said.

Venli attuned Betrayal. "She shouldn't be off away from the family so much, being selfish with her time. She should be learning the songs like me. It's her duty too, as your daughter."

"Yes, you are correct," Jaxlim said. "But Eshonai has a bold heart. She merely needs to learn that her family is more important than counting the number of hills outside the camp."

"I have a bold heart!" Venli said.

"You have a keen and crafty mind," her mother said. "Like your mother. Do not dismiss your own talents because you envy those of another."

"Envy? Her?"

Venli's mother continued weaving. She wasn't required to do such work—her position as keeper of songs was lofty, perhaps the most important in the family. Yet her mother always sought to keep busy. She said working her hands kept her body strong, while going over songs worked her mind.

Venli attuned Anxiety, then Confidence, then Anxiety again. She walked to her mother and sat on the stool next to her. Jaxlim projected Confidence, even when doing something as simple as weaving. Her complex skin pattern of wavy red and black lines was among the most beautiful in the camp—like true marbled stone. Eshonai took after their mother's colorings.

Venli, of course, took after her father—primarily white and red, her own pattern more like swirls. In truth, Venli's pattern had all three shades. Many people claimed they couldn't see the small patches of black at her neck, but she could pick them out. Having all three colors was very, very rare.

"Mother," she said to Excitement, "I think I've discovered something."

"And what would that be?"

"I've been experimenting with different spren again. Taking them into the storms."

"You were cautioned about this."

"You didn't forbid me, so I continued. Should we only ever do as we are told?"

"Many say we need no more than workform and mateform," her mother said to Consideration. "They say that courting other forms is to take steps toward forms of power."

"What do *you* say?" Venli asked.

"You are always so concerned for my opinions. Most children, when they reach your age, start to defy and ignore their parents."

"Most children don't have you as a mother."

"Flattery?" Jaxlim said to Amusement.

"Not . . . entirely," Venli said. She attuned Resignation. "Mother, I want to use what I've learned. I have a head full of songs about forms. How can I *help* wanting to try to discover them? For the good of our people."

Jaxlim finally stopped her weaving. She turned on her stool and scooted closer to Venli, taking her hands. She hummed, then sang softly to Praise—just a melody, no words. Venli closed her eyes and let the song wash over her, and thought she could feel her mother's skin vibrating. Feel her soul.

Venli had done this as long as she could remember. Relying on her, and her songs. Ever since her father had left, seeking the eastern sea.

"You make me proud, Venli," Jaxlim said. "You've done well these last few years, memorizing after Eshonai gave up. I encourage you to seek to improve yourself, but remember, you must not become distracted. I need you. *We* need you."

Venli nodded, then hummed the same rhythm, attuning Praise to be in sync with her mother. She felt love, warmth, acceptance from those fingers. And knew whatever else happened, her mother would be there to guide her. Steady her. With a song that pierced even storms.

Her mother returned to her weaving, and Venli began to recite again. She went through the entire thing, and this time did *not* miss a stanza.

When she was done, she waited, taking a drink of water and hoping for her mother's praise. Instead, Jaxlim gave her something better. "Tell me," she said, "of these experiments with spren you've been doing."

"I'm trying to find *warform*!" Venli said to Anticipation. "I've been staying near the edge of the shelter during storms, and trying to attract the right spren. It is difficult, as most spren flee from me once the winds pick up.

"However, this last time I feel I was close. A painspren is the key. They're always around during storms. If I can keep one close to me, I think I can adopt the form."

If she managed it, she'd become the first listener to hold warform in many generations. Ever since the humans and the singers of old destroyed one another in their final battle. This was something she could bring her people, something that would be remembered!

"Let's go speak with the Five," Jaxlim said, standing up from beside the loom.

"Wait," Venli said, taking her arm and attuning Tension. "You are going to tell them what I said? About warform?"

"Naturally. If you are going to continue on this path, we will want their blessing."

"Maybe I should practice more," Venli said. "Before we tell anyone."

Jaxlim hummed to Reprimand. "This is like your refusal to perform the songs in public. You are afraid of exposing yourself to failure again, Venli."

"No," she said. "No, of course not. Mother, I just think this would be better if I knew for certain it worked. Before causing trouble."

Why *wouldn't* someone want to be certain before inviting ridicule by failing? That did *not* make Venli a coward. She'd adopt a new form when nobody else had. That was *bold*. She wanted to control the circumstances, that was all.

"Come with me," Jaxlim said to Peace. "The others have been discussing this—I approached them after you asked me before. I hinted to the elders that I thought adopting new forms might be possible, and I believe they are willing to try."

"Really?" Venli asked.

"Yes. Come. They will celebrate your initiative. That is too rare for us, in this form. It is far better than dullform, but it *does* affect our minds. We need other forms, despite what some may say."

Venli felt herself attuning Excitement as she followed her mother out of the tent. If she *did* obtain warform, would it open her mind? Make her even more bold? Quiet the fears and worries she often felt? She hungered for accomplishments. Hungered to make their world better, less dull, more *vibrant*. Hungered to be the one who carried her people to greatness. Out of the crem and toward the skies.

The Five were gathered around the firepit amid the trees, discussing offensive tactics for the upcoming battle. That mostly equated to which boasts to make, and which warriors to let cast their spears first.

Jaxlim stepped up to the elders and sang a full song to Excitement. A rare delivery from the keeper of songs, and each stanza made Venli stand taller.

Once the song was finished, Jaxlim explained what Venli had told her. Indeed, the elders were interested. They realized that new forms were worth the risk. Confident that she would not be rejected, Venli stepped forward and attuned Victory.

As she began, however, something sounded outside of town. The warning drums? The Five hastened to grab their weapons—ancient axes, spears, and swords, each one precious and passed down for generations, for the listeners had no means of creating new metal weapons.

But what could this be? No other family would attack them out here in the wilderness. It hadn't happened in generations, since the Pure-Song family had raided the Fourth-Movement family in an attempt to steal their weapons. The Pure-Songers had been thoroughly shunned for that action.

Venli stayed back as the elders left. She didn't wish to be involved in a skirmish—if indeed that was happening. She was an apprentice keeper of songs, and was far too valuable to risk in battle. Hopefully whatever this was, it would be over soon and she could return to basking in the respect of the elders.

So it was that she was one of the last to hear about Eshonai's incredible discovery. Among the last to learn that their world had forever been changed. And among the last to learn that her grand announcement had been utterly overshadowed by the actions of her reckless sister.

46

THE WEIGHT
OF THE TOWER

*I approach this project with an equal mixture of trepidation and
hope. And I know not which should rule.*

—From *Rhythm of War*, page 1

Raboniel denied Navani servants. The Fused apparently thought it
would be a hardship for Navani to live without them. So Navani
allowed herself a small moment of pride when she stepped out
of her rooms on the first full day of Urithiru's occupation. Her hair was
clean and braided, her simple havah pressed and neat, her makeup done.
Washing in cold water hadn't been pleasant, but the fabrials weren't
working, so it wasn't as if she could expect warm water even if she had
servants.

Navani was led down to the library rooms in the basement of Urithiru.
Raboniel sat at Navani's own desk, going through her notes. Upon arriving, Navani bowed precisely, just low enough to indicate obedience—but
not low enough to imply subservience.

The Fused pushed back the chair and leaned an elbow on the desktop,
then made a shooing motion with a hummed sound to dismiss the guards.

"What is your decision?" the Fused asked.

"I will organize my scholars, Ancient One," Navani said, "and continue
their research under your observation."

"The wiser choice, and the more dangerous one, Navani Kholin." Raboniel
hummed a different tone. "I do not find the schematics for your flying
machine in these notes."

Navani made a show of debating it, but she'd already considered this
issue. The secrets of the flying platform would be impossible to keep; too

many of Navani's scholars knew them. Beyond that, many of the new style of conjoined fabrials—which allowed lateral motion while maintaining elevation—were already in use around the tower. Though fabrials didn't work, Raboniel's people could surely discern their operation.

After a long debate with herself, she'd come to the conclusion that she needed to give up this secret. Her best hope in escaping the current predicament was to appear to be willing to work with Raboniel, while also stalling.

"I intentionally don't keep priority schematics anywhere but in my own head," Navani lied. "Instead I explain each piece I need built to my scholars as I need them. Given time, I can draw for you the mechanism that makes the machine work."

Raboniel hummed to a rhythm, but Navani couldn't tell what it represented. However, Raboniel seemed skeptical as she stood and waved for Navani to sit down. She placed a reed in Navani's hands and folded her arms to wait.

Well, fine. Navani began drawing with quick, efficient lines. She made a diagram of a conjoined fabrial, with a quick explanation of how it worked, then she drew the expanded vision of hundreds of them embedded into the flying machine.

"Yes," Raboniel said as Navani sketched the last portions, "but how do you make it move laterally? Surely with this construction, you could raise a machine high in the air—but it would have to remain there, in one place. You don't expect me to believe that you have a ground machine moving in exact coordination to the one in the sky."

"You understand more about fabrials than I assumed, Lady of Wishes."

Raboniel hummed a rhythm. "I am a quick learner." She gestured to the notes on Navani's desk. "In the past, my kind found it difficult to persuade spren to manifest themselves in the Physical Realm as devices. It seems Voidspren are not as naturally . . . self-sacrificing as those of Honor or Cultivation."

Navani blinked as the implications of that sank in. Suddenly a dozen loose threads in her mind tied together, forming a tapestry. An *explanation*. That was why the fabrials of the tower—the pumps, the climbing mechanisms—didn't have gemstones with captive spren. Storms . . . that was the answer to Soulcasting devices.

Awespren burst around her in a ring of blue smoke. Soulcasters didn't *hold* spren because they *were* spren. Manifesting in the Physical Realm like Shardblades. Spren became metal on this side. Somehow the ancient spren had been coaxed into manifesting as Soulcasters instead of Blades?

"You didn't know, I see," Raboniel said, pulling a chair over for herself. Even sitting, she was a foot taller than Navani. She made such an odd image: a carapace-armored figure, as if prepared for war, picking through notes. "Odd that you should have made so many advances that we never dreamed of in epochs past, yet you've forgotten the far simpler method your ancestors used."

"We . . . we didn't have access to spren who would talk to us," Navani explained. "Vev's golden keys . . . this . . . I can't believe we didn't see it. The implications . . ."

"Lateral movement?" Raboniel asked.

Feeling almost in a daze, Navani sketched out the answer. "We learned to isolate planes for conjoined fabrials," she explained. "You have to use this construction of aluminum wires, rigged to touch the gemstone. That maintains vertical position, but allows the gemstone to be moved horizontally."

"Fascinating," Raboniel said. "Ralkalest—you call it aluminum in your language—interfering with the Connection. That's quite ingenious. It must have taken a great deal of testing to get the correct configuration."

"Over a year's worth," Navani admitted. "After the initial possibility was theorized. We have a problem that we can't move vertically and laterally at the same time—the fabrials that move us upward and downward are finicky, and we have been touching aluminum to them only after locking them into place."

"That's inconvenient."

"Yes," Navani said, "but we've found a system where we stop, then do our vertical motions. It can be a pain, since spanreeds are very difficult to make work in moving vehicles."

"It seems there should be a way to use this knowledge to make spanreeds that can be used while moving," Raboniel said, inspecting Navani's sketch.

"That was my thought as well," Navani said. "I put a small team on it, but we've been mostly occupied by other matters. Your weapons against our Radiants still confuse me."

Raboniel hummed to a quick and dismissive rhythm. "Ancient technology, barely functional," she said. "We can suck the Stormlight from a Radiant, yes—so long as they remain hanging there impaled by one of our weapons. This method does nothing to prevent the spren from bonding a new Radiant. I should like it if your spren were easier to capture in gemstones."

"I'll pass the request along," Navani said.

Raboniel hummed to a different rhythm, then smiled. It was difficult not to see the expression as predatory on her marbled face, with its lean danger. Yet there was also something tempting about the efficiency of this interaction. A few minutes of exchange, and Navani knew secrets she'd been trying to crack for decades.

"This is how we end the war, Navani," Raboniel said, standing. "With information. Shared."

"And this ends the war how?"

"By showing everyone that our lives will all be improved by working together."

"With the singers ruling."

"Of course," Raboniel said. "You are obviously a keen scholar, Navani Kholin. If you could improve the lives of your people manyfold, is that not worth abandoning self-governance? Look what we've done in mere minutes by sharing our knowledge."

Shared only because of your threats, Navani thought, careful not to show that on her face. This wasn't some free exchange. *It doesn't matter what you tell me, Raboniel. You can reveal any secret you desire—because I'm in your power. You can just kill me once you have everything you want.*

She smiled at Raboniel, however. "I would like to check on my scholars, Lady of Wishes, to see how they're being treated, and find out the extent of our . . . losses." That made one point clear, Navani hoped. Some of her friends had been murdered. She was not simply going to forget about that.

Raboniel hummed, gesturing for Navani to join her. This was going to require a delicate balance, with both of them trying to play one another. Navani had to be explicitly careful not to let herself be taken in by Raboniel. That was one advantage Navani had over her scholars. She might never be worthy to join them, but she did have more experience with the real world of politics.

Raboniel and Navani entered the second of the two library rooms— the one with more desks and chairs. Navani's best—ardents and scholars alike—sat on the floor, heads bowed. They'd plainly been made to sleep here, judging by the spread-out blankets.

A few looked up to see her, and she noted with relief that Rushu and Falilar were both unharmed. She did a quick count, immediately picking out the notable exceptions. She stepped over to Falilar, squatting down and asking, "Neshan? Inabar?"

"Killed, Brightness," he said softly. "They were in the crystal pillar room, along with both of Neshan's wards, Ardent Vevanara, and a handful of unfortunate soldiers."

Navani winced. "Pass the word," she whispered. "For the time being, we are going to cooperate with the occupation." She stopped by Rushu next. "I am glad you are well."

The ardent—who had obviously been crying—nodded. "I was on my way down here to gather some scribes to help catalogue the destruction up in that room, when . . . this happened. Brightness, do you think it's related?"

In the chaos, Navani had nearly forgotten the strange explosion. "Did you by chance find any infused spheres in the wreckage?" *Specifically, a strange Voidlight one?*

"No, Brightness," Rushu said. "You saw the place. It was in shambles. But I did darken it to see if anything glowed, and saw nothing. Not a hint of Stormlight, or even Voidlight."

As Navani had feared. Whatever that explosion had been, it had to be tied to the strange sphere—and that sphere was likely now gone.

Navani stood and walked back to Raboniel. "You didn't need to kill my scholars during your attack. They were no threat to you."

Raboniel hummed to a quick-paced rhythm. "You will not be warned again, Navani. You will use my title when addressing me. I do not want to see you harmed, but there are proprieties thousands of years old that you *will* follow."

"I . . . understand, Lady of Wishes. I think putting my remaining people to work immediately would be good for morale. What would you like us to do?"

"To ease the transition," Raboniel said, "have them continue whatever they were doing before my arrival."

"Many were working on fabrials, which will no longer function."

"Have them do design sketches then," Raboniel said. "And write about the experiments they'd done before the occupation. I can see that their new theories get tested."

Did that mean there was a way to get fabrials working in the tower? "As you wish."

Then she got to work on the real problem: planning how she was going to get them out of this mess.

◆◆

Kaladin was awakened by rain. He blinked, feeling mist on his face and seeing a jagged sky lit by spears of lightning frozen in place—not fading, just hanging there, framed by black clouds in a constant boil.

He stared at the strange sight, then rolled to his side, half submerged in a puddle of frigid water. Was this Hearthstone? The warcamps? No . . . neither?

He groaned, forcing himself to his feet. He didn't appear to be wounded, but his head was pounding. No weapons. He felt naked without a spear. Gusts of rain blew around him, the falling water moving in sheets—and he swore he could see the outlines of figures in the rainfall. As if it were making momentary shapes as it fell.

The landscape was dark, evoking distant crags. He started through the water, surprised to see no spren around—not even rainspren. He thought he saw light atop a hill, so he started up the incline, careful not to lose his footing on the slick rock. A part of him wondered why he could see. The frozen jagged lightning bolts didn't give off much illumination. Hadn't he been in a place like this once? With omnipresent light, but a black sky?

He stopped and stared upward, rain scouring his face. This was all . . . all wrong. This wasn't real . . . was it?

Motion.

Kaladin spun. A short figure moved down the hill toward him, emerging from the darkness. It seemed composed entirely of swirling grey mist with no features, though it wielded a spear. Kaladin caught the weapon with a quick turn of his hand, then twisted and pushed back in a classic disarming move.

This phantom attacker wasn't terribly skilled, and Kaladin easily stole the weapon. Instinct took command, and he spun the spear and rammed it through the figure's neck. As the short figure dropped, two more appeared as if from nothing, both wielding spears of their own.

Kaladin blocked one strike and threw the attacker off with a calculated shove, then spun and dropped the other one with a sweep to the legs. He stabbed that figure with a quick thrust to the neck, then easily rammed his spear into the stomach of the other one as it stood up. Blood ran down the spear's shaft onto Kaladin's fingers.

He yanked the spear free as the smoky figure dropped. It felt good to hold a spear. To be able to fight without worries. Without anything weighing him down other than the rainwater on his uniform. Fighting used to be simple. Before . . .

Before . . .

The swirling mist evaporated off the fallen figures and he found three young messenger boys in Amaram's colors, killed by Kaladin's spear. Three corpses, including his brother.

"No!" Kaladin screamed, ragged and hateful. "How dare you show me this? It didn't happen that way! I was there!"

He turned away from the corpses, looking toward the sky. "I didn't kill him! I just failed him. I . . . I just . . ."

He stumbled away from the dead boys and dropped his spear, hands to his head. He felt the scars on his forehead. They seemed deeper, like chasms cutting through his skull.

Shash. Dangerous.

Thunder rumbled overhead and he stumbled downhill, unable to banish the sight of Tien dead and bleeding on the hillside. What kind of terrible vision was this?

"You saved us so we could die," a voice said from the darkness.

He knew that voice. Kaladin spun, splashing in the rainwater, searching for the source. He was on the Shattered Plains now. In the rain he saw the *suggestions* of people. Figures made by the falling drops, but somehow empty.

The figures began attacking each other, and he heard the thunder of war. Men shouting, weapons clashing, boots on stone. It surrounded him, overwhelmed him, until—in a flash—he emerged into an enormous battle, the suggested shapes becoming real. Men in blue fighting against other men in blue.

"Stop fighting!" Kaladin shouted at them. "You're killing your own! They're all our soldiers!"

They didn't seem to hear him. Blood flowed beneath his feet instead of rainwater, sprays and gushes melding as spearmen climbed eagerly over the bodies of the fallen to continue killing one another. Kaladin grabbed one spearman and pushed him away from another, then seized a third and pulled him back—only to find that it was Lopen.

"Lopen!" Kaladin said. "Listen to me! Stop fighting!"

Lopen bared his teeth in a terrible grin, then knocked Kaladin aside before launching himself at yet another figure—Rock, who had stumbled on a corpse. Lopen killed him with a spear through the gut, but then Teft killed Lopen from behind. Bisig stabbed Teft, and Kaladin didn't see who brought him down. He was too horrified.

Sigzil dropped nearby with a hole in his side, and Kaladin caught him.

"Why?" Sigzil asked, blood dribbling from his lips. "Why didn't you let us sleep?"

"This isn't real. This can't be real."

"You should have let us die on the Shattered Plains."

"I wanted to protect you!" Kaladin shouted. "I *had* to protect you!"

"You cursed us . . ."

Kaladin dropped the dying body and stumbled away. He ducked his head, his mind cloudy, and started running. A part of him knew this horror wasn't real, but he could still hear the screaming. Accusing him. *Why did you do this, Kaladin? Why have you killed us?*

He pressed his hands to his ears, so intent on escaping the carnage that he nearly ran straight into a chasm. He pulled up, teetering on the edge. He stumbled, then looked to his left. The warcamps were there, up a short slope.

He'd been here. He remembered this place, this storm, lightly raining. This chasm. Where he'd nearly died.

"You saved us," a voice said, "so we could suffer."

Moash. He stood on the edge of the chasm near Kaladin. The man turned, and Kaladin saw his eyes—black pits. "People think you were merciful to us. But we both know the truth, don't we? You did it for you. Not us. If you were truly merciful, you'd have given us easy deaths."

"No," Kaladin said. "No!"

"The void awaits, Kal," Moash said. "The emptiness. It lets you do anything—even kill a king—without regret. One step. You'll never have to feel pain again."

Moash took a step and dropped into the chasm. Kaladin fell to his knees on the edge, rain streaming around him. He stared down in horror.

Then started awake someplace cold. Immediately, a hundred pains coursed through his joints and muscles, each demanding his attention like a screaming child. He groaned and opened his eyes, but there was only darkness.

I'm in the tower, he thought, remembering the events of the previous day. *Storms. The place is controlled by the Fused. I barely got away.*

The nightmares seemed to be getting worse. Or they'd always been this bad, but he didn't remember. He lay there, breathing deeply, sweating as if from exertion—and remembered the sight of his friends dying. Remembered Moash stepping into that darkness and vanishing.

Sleeping was supposed to refresh you, but Kaladin felt more tired than when he'd collapsed. He groaned and put his back to the wall, forcing himself to sit up. Then he felt around in a sudden panic. In his addled state, a part of him thought for sure he'd find Teft dead on the floor.

He let out a sigh of relief as he located his friend lying nearby, still breathing. The man had wet himself, unfortunately—he'd grow dehydrated quickly if Kaladin didn't do something, and the potential for rotspren was high if Kaladin didn't get him cleaned up and properly situated with a bedpan.

Storms. The weight of what Kaladin had done hung above him, nearly as oppressive as the weight of the tower. He was alone, lost in the darkness, without Stormlight or anything to drink—let alone proper weapons. He needed to take care of not only himself, but a man in a coma.

What had he been thinking? He didn't believe the nightmare—but he couldn't completely banish its echoes either. Why? Why couldn't he have let go? Why did he keep fighting? Was it really for them?

Or was it because he was selfish? Because *he* couldn't let go and admit defeat?

"Syl?" he asked in the darkness. When she didn't answer him, he called again, his voice trembling. "Syl, where are you?"

No reply. He felt around his enclosure, and realized he had no idea how to get out. He'd entombed himself and Teft here in this too-thick darkness. To die slow deaths alone . . .

Then a pinprick of light appeared. Syl, blessedly, entered the enclosure. She couldn't pass through walls—Radiant spren had enough substance in the Physical Realm that they were impeded by most materials. Instead she appeared to have come in through some sort of vent high in the wall.

Her appearance brought with it a measure of his sanity. He released a shuddering breath as she flitted down and landed on his outstretched palm.

"I found a way out," she said, taking the shape of a soldier wearing a scout's uniform. "I don't think you'd be able to get through it though. Even a child would be cramped.

"I looked around, though I couldn't go too far. Guards are posted at many stairwells, but they don't seem to be searching for you. These floors are big enough that I think they've realized finding one man in here is virtually impossible."

"That's some good news, I guess," Kaladin said. "Do you have any idea what that light was that led me in here?"

"I . . . have a theory," Syl said. "A long time ago, before things went poorly between spren and humans, there were three Bondsmiths. One for the Stormfather. One for the Nightwatcher. And one other. For a spren called the Sibling. A spren who remained in this tower, hidden, and did not appear to humans. They were supposed to have died long ago."

"Huh," Kaladin said, feeling at the door that had opened to let him in. "What were they like?"

"I don't know," Syl said, moving to his shoulder. "We've talked to Brightness Navani about this, answering her questions, and the other Radiant spren didn't know more than I just said. Remember, many of the spren who knew about the old days died—and the Sibling was always secretive. I don't know what kind of spren they were, or why they could create a Bondsmith. If they are alive though, I don't know why so much in the tower doesn't work."

"Well, this wall worked," Kaladin said, finding the gemstone in the wall. The gem was dark now, but it was also much more prominent on this side. He could easily have missed it from the other direction. How many other rooms had such gemstones embedded in the wall, hiding secret doors?

He touched the gemstone. Despite the fact that he didn't have any more Stormlight, light appeared deep inside it. A white light that twinkled like a star. It expanded into a small burst of Stormlight, and the door silently split open again.

Kaladin let out a long breath and felt a little of his panic wash away. He wouldn't die in the darkness. Once the gemstone was charged, it worked like any other fabrial, continuing to function so long as it had remaining Stormlight.

He looked to Syl. "Think you can find your way back here to Teft if we leave and do some scouting?"

"I should be able to memorize our path."

"Great," Kaladin said. "Because we need supplies." He couldn't afford to think about the long term yet. Those daunting questions—what he was going to do about the tower, the dozens of Radiants in enemy captivity, his family—would need to wait. First he needed water, food, Stormlight, and—most importantly—a better weapon.

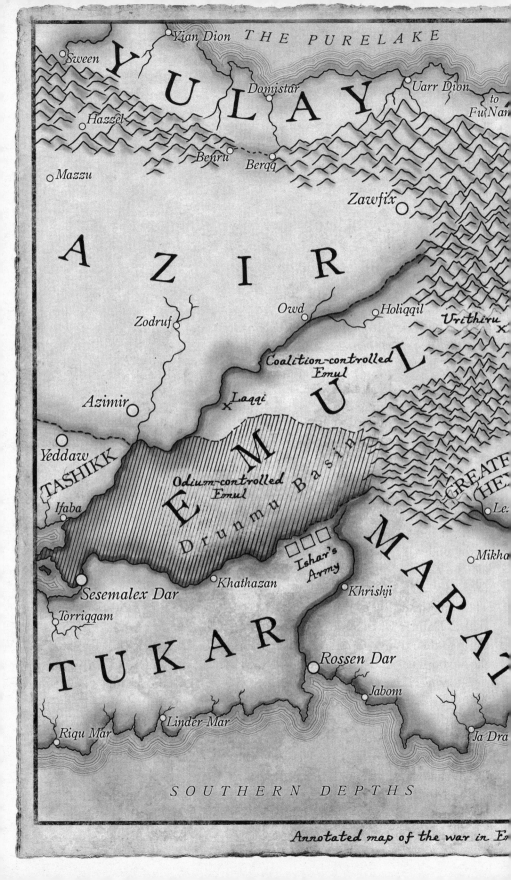

THE PURELAKE

Yian Dion

Sween

Domistar

Uarr Dion

to
Fu Nan

Hazzel

Benru   Berqq

Mazzu

Zawfix

A Z I R

Owd

Holiqqil

Urithiru
x

Zodruf

Coalition-controlled
Emul

Azimir

x Laqqi

E M U L

Yeddaw

Odium-controlled
Emul

Drunmu Basin

GREATS
HE

TASHIKK

Ifaba

Le

MARA

Mikha

Ishar's
Army

Sesemalex Dar

Khathazan

Khrishji

Torriqqam

T U K A R

Rossen Dar

Jabom

Linder Mar

Riqu Mar

Ja Dra

SOUTHERN DEPTHS

Annotated map of the war in En

A CAGE
FORGED OF SPIRITS

*I approach this project with inspiration renewed; the answers are
all that should matter.*

—From *Rhythm of War*, page 1 undertext

The wood lurched under Dalinar's feet, and he grabbed a railing to
steady himself. "Skybreakers!" he shouted. "Trying to get at the
fabrial housings!"

Two figures in blue leaped off the deck nearby, bursting with Light
as the platform continued to shake. Two wouldn't be able to handle this.
Storm it, where was—

Sigzil and his force of ten Windrunners came swooping back, striking
at the underside of the flying platform. It wasn't truly a flying machine
like the *Fourth Bridge*, but these platforms were nevertheless an excellent
vantage for viewing a battlefield. Assuming they didn't get attacked.

Dalinar held firm to the railing, glancing at the Mink—who was tethered to Dalinar with a rope. The shorter man was grinning wildly as he
clung to the railing. Fortunately, the platform soon stopped lurching and
the Skybreakers scattered, trailed by figures in blue with spears.

Fewer Heavenly Ones than I'd have expected, Dalinar noted as the wind
ruffled his hair. He picked out only four of the flying Fused watching
the battlefield from above and occasionally delivering instructions to the
ground troops. They didn't engage. *They're leaning on the Skybreakers for this
battle*. Perhaps the bulk of the Heavenly Ones were with the main enemy
forces, stationed several days' march away.

The Mink leaned out over the side of the platform, trying to get a
view directly beneath—where Radiants were clashing. He didn't seem

at all bothered by the three-hundred-yard drop to the ground. For a man who always seemed so paranoid, he could certainly be cavalier regarding danger.

Beneath them, the battle lines held formation. Dalinar's troops, augmented by ranks of Azish, fought Taravangian's treasonous forces—who had tried to strike inward to rescue their king. The Vedens were accompanied by a small number of Fused and some singer troops, a small enough force to have moved in close without detection before the betrayal.

On Dalinar's platform, some fifty archers re-formed their ranks following the chaos of the sudden Skybreaker attack. In moments, they were sending a hail of arrows on the Vedens.

"They'll break soon," the Mink said softly, surveying the battlefield. "Their line is bowing. Those Azish fight well. Better than I thought they would."

"They have excellent discipline," Dalinar agreed. "They simply needed proper direction." Any given Azish soldier was no match for an Alethi, but after witnessing their discipline this last year, Dalinar was grateful he'd never had to face their infantry in battle. The vast blocks of Azish pikes were less mobile than the Alethi equivalent, but were impeccably coordinated.

They were a tremendous addition to an Alethi system, which had far more flexibility and a variety of specialized troops. Using Azish blocks like wedges, and Alethi tactics, they'd been able to stand against the enemy despite their natural advantages, like carapace armor and stronger builds.

And the Veden traitors? Well, the Mink was right. The enemy line was beginning to bow and crack. They had no cavalry, and the Mink made a quiet order to one of the waiting scribes, who transferred it. Dalinar guessed—correctly—he'd ordered a harrying strike of light riders along the left flank. Those filled the Veden back rows with arrows, distracting them to further stress the wavering lines.

"I do have to admit," the Mink said to Dalinar as they watched, bowstrings snapping behind them, "this is an excellent way to oversee a battlefield."

"And you were worried about there being no escape."

"Rather," the Mink said, looking toward the ground below, "I was worried about all avenues of escape being interrupted by an unfortunate collision with the ground. Still don't know the wisdom of putting us both up here; seems like we should be on separate platforms, so that if one falls, the other can continue to lead our forces."

"You mistake my purpose, Dieno," Dalinar said, tugging on the rope that bound them. "My job in this battle isn't to command if you are killed. It's to get you out *before* you are killed."

One of Jasnah's escape boats waited on the other side, in Shadesmar. In an emergency, Dalinar could get himself and the Mink through the perpendicularity. They'd drop a short distance—but not nearly as far as they would on this side—into a padded ship with mandras hooked in place.

The Mink, unsurprisingly, didn't like that escape route. He couldn't control it. In truth, Dalinar wasn't a hundred percent comfortable with it himself—he didn't fully trust his powers yet. His mastery over them was tenuous.

He opened the perpendicularity as the Windrunners approached for more Stormlight. He managed to open it only a sliver, renewing those nearby, but preventing the Skybreakers from partaking. They retreated; Skybreakers couldn't match Windrunners who were being constantly renewed, and were usually deployed on battlefields where Dalinar was not present.

As the Mink took casualty reports—which included two Windrunner squires, unfortunately—a young scribe stepped up to Dalinar with a sheaf of papers and a blinking spanreed. "Word from Urithiru, Brightlord," she said. "You wanted to know as soon as we heard something, and we have."

Dalinar felt a huge weight slide off his shoulders. "Finally! What is happening?"

"Trouble with the tower fabrials," the scribe reported. "Brightness Navani says that some kind of strange defensive aura has been deployed, preventing Radiants from using their powers. It also interferes with fabrials. She had to send a scouting team out along the ridge into the mountains before they were able to deliver her message.

"Everyone is safe, and she's working on the problem. That is why the Oathgates have stopped working, however. She begs for your patience, and asks if anything strange has happened here."

"Tell her about Taravangian's betrayal," Dalinar said, "but report that I'm safe, as is our family. We are fighting the traitors, and should soon win the day."

She nodded and went to send the message. The Mink stepped closer; he'd either overheard, or had received a similar report.

"They're trying to confuse and distract us during the betrayal," he said. "Heaping attacks on multiple fronts."

"Another ploy to negate the Oathgates," Dalinar agreed. "That device they used on Highmarshal Kaladin must have been some sort of test. They've knocked out Urithiru for a while to isolate us."

The Mink leaned out, squinting at the armies below. "Something about this smells wrong, Blackthorn. If this was merely a ploy to isolate the fighting in Azir and Emul, they've made a tactical mistake. Their forces in this part of the land are exposed, and we have the upper hand. They wouldn't go through so much effort to block us from the Oathgates unless it were *truly* cutting off our escape route. Which it won't because we're not going to need one."

"You think this is a distraction from something else?"

The Mink nodded slowly. Far below, the cavalry did another sweep. The line of the traitors buckled further.

"I'll tell the others to watch out," Dalinar said, "and send scouts to investigate Urithiru. I agree, something about this is off."

"Make certain the armies we're going to fight in Emul haven't been secretly reinforced. That could be terrible for us—the only true disaster I can envision here is Azimir being besieged, and unable to be resupplied via the Oathgates. Having seen that city, I'd hate to be trapped there."

"Agreed," Dalinar said.

The Mink leaned out further, precariously, as he watched the battlefield below. It was hard to hear—muffled clangs, shouts from far away. Men moved like lifespren.

But Dalinar could smell the sweat. Could hear the roar. Could *feel* himself standing among the struggling, screaming, dying bodies and *dominating* with Blade in hand. Once you'd tasted the near invincibility of wearing Plate and wading in among mortals, it was a . . . difficult flavor to forget.

"You miss it," the Mink said, eyeing him.

"Yes," Dalinar admitted.

"They could use you on the ground."

"Down there, I'd be merely another sword. I can do more in other positions."

"Pardon, Blackthorn, but you were *never* merely another sword." The Mink crossed his arms, leaning against the wooden railing. "You keep saying you're more use elsewhere, and I suppose you make a pretty good storm for renewing spheres. But I can sense you stepping away. What are you planning?"

That was the question. He sensed there was so much more for him to do. Greater things. Important things. The tasks of a Bondsmith. But getting to them, figuring them out . . .

"They're breaking," the Mink said, standing up straight. "You want to let them go, or pin them and crush them?"

"What do you think?" Dalinar asked.

"I hate fighting men who feel they have no way out," the Mink said.

"We can't afford to let them reinforce the enemy to the south," Dalinar said. That would be their true battlefield, once this skirmish was over. The war for Emul. "Keep pressing them until they surrender."

The Mink began giving the orders. From below, drums washed over the battlefield: the frantic attempts by enemy commanders to maintain discipline as the lines disintegrated. He could almost hear their shouted, panic-tinged cries. Desperation in the air.

The Mink is right, Dalinar thought. *They made a real effort here to strike at us—but something is wrong. We're missing a piece of the enemy's plan.*

As he was watching, a nondescript soldier stepped up beside him. Dalinar had brought only a handful of bodyguards today: three men from the Cobalt Guard, and a single Shardbearer. Cord, the Horneater woman, who had taken it upon herself to join his guards for reasons he didn't quite understand.

He also held a hidden weapon—the man who stood beside him, so ordinary in his Alethi uniform, holding a sheathed sword that was admittedly longer than regulation. Szeth, the Assassin in White, wearing a false face. He didn't speak, though the complex Lightweaving he wore would disguise his voice. He simply watched, his eyes narrowed. What did he see in this battlefield? What had caught his attention?

Szeth suddenly grabbed Dalinar by the front of his uniform and towed him to the side. Dalinar barely had time to shout in surprise as a glowing figure rose up beside the archer platform, radiant with Stormlight and bearing a silvery Blade. Szeth stepped between Dalinar and the Skybreaker, hand going to his sword. But Dalinar caught him by the arm, preventing him from drawing it. Once that weapon came out, dangerous things happened. They would want to be absolutely certain it was needed before unleashing it.

The figure was familiar to Dalinar. Dark brown skin, with a birthmark on his cheek. Nalan—called Nale. Herald and leader of the Skybreakers. He had shaved his head recently, and held out his Blade in a defiant— perhaps challenging—posture as he addressed Dalinar.

"Bondsmith," Nale said, "your war is unjust. You must submit to the laws of the—"

An arrow slammed into his face, dead center, interrupting him. Dalinar glanced back, then stopped Cord, who was drawing her Shardbow again. "Wait. I'd hear him."

Nale, with a suffering expression, pulled the arrow free and dropped it, letting his Stormlight heal him. Could this man be killed? Ash said the enemy had somehow killed Jezrien—but before, when Heralds died, their souls had returned to Damnation to await torture.

Nale didn't continue his diatribe. He lightly stepped up onto the railing of the platform, then dropped to the deck. He tossed his Blade away, letting it vanish to mist in midair.

"How are you a Bondsmith?" Nale asked Dalinar. "You should not exist, Blackthorn. Your cause is not righteous. You should be denied the true Surges of Honor."

"Perhaps it is a sign that *you* are wrong, Nalan," Dalinar said. "Perhaps our cause *is* righteous."

"No," Nale said. "Other Radiants can lie to themselves and their spren. So-called honorspren prove that morality is shaped by their perceptions. You should be different. Honor should not allow this bonding."

"Honor is dead," Dalinar said.

"And yet," Nale said, "Honor still should prevent this. Prevent *you*." He looked Dalinar up and down. "No Shardblade. Fair enough."

He launched forward, reaching for Dalinar. Szeth was upon him in a moment, but hesitated to draw his strange Blade. Nale moved with a skyeel's grace, twisting Szeth about and slamming him to the deck of the wooden platform. The Herald slapped aside Szeth's sheathed sword, punching him in the crook of the elbow and making him drop his weapon. Nale casually reached up and caught the arrow launched from Cord's Shardbow mere feet away—an inhuman feat.

Dalinar pressed his hands together, reaching beyond reality for the perpendicularity. Nale leaped over Szeth toward Dalinar as the others on the platform shouted, trying to react to the attack.

No, the Stormfather said to Dalinar. *Touch him.*

Dalinar hesitated—the power of the perpendicularity at his fingertips—then reached out and pressed his hand to Nale's chest as the Herald reached for him.

Flash.

Dalinar saw Nale stepping away from a discarded Blade rammed into the stone.

Flash.

Nale cradling a child in one arm, his Blade out as dark forces crawled across a ridge nearby.

Flash.

Nale standing with a group of scholars and unrolling a large writ, filled with writing. "The law cannot be moral," Nale said to them. "But *you* can be moral as you create laws. Ever must you protect the weakest, those most likely to be taken advantage of. Institute a right of movement, so that a family who feels their lord is unrighteous can leave his area. Then tie a lord's authority to the people who follow him."

Flash.

Nale kneeling before a highspren.

Flash.

Nale fighting on a battlefield.

Flash.

Another fight.

Flash.

Another fight.

The visions came faster and faster; Dalinar could no longer distinguish one from another. Until

Flash.

Nale clasping hands with a bearded Alethi man, regal and wise. Dalinar knew this was Jezerezeh, though he couldn't say how.

"I will take this charge," Nale said softly. "With honor."

"Do not consider it an honor," Jezerezeh said. "A duty, yes, but not an honor."

"I understand. Though I had not expected you would come to an enemy with this offer."

"An enemy, yes," Jezerezeh said. "But an enemy who was correct all along, making me the villain, not you. We will fix what we've broken. Ishar and I agreed. There is no person we would welcome more eagerly into this pact than you. You are the single most honorable man I have ever had the privilege of opposing."

"I wish that were true," Nale said. "But I will serve as best I can."

The vision faded and Nale lurched away from Dalinar, gasping, his eyes wide. He left a line of light stretching between him and Dalinar.

Bondsmith, the Stormfather said in Dalinar's mind. *You forged a brief Connection with him. What did you see?*

"His past, I think," Dalinar whispered. "And now . . ."

Nale scratched at his head, and Dalinar saw a skeletal figure overlapping him. Like the echo of light that followed Szeth, only worn, dim. Dalinar stepped forward, walking among his stunned bodyguards, noting eight lines of light extending from Nale into the distance.

"I see the Oathpact, I think," Dalinar said. "The thing that bound them together and made them capable of holding the enemy in Damnation."

A cage, forged of their spirits, the Stormfather said in his mind. *It was broken. Even before Jezrien's death, they shattered it by what they did long ago.*

"No, only one line of it is completely broken. The rest are there, but weak, impotent." Dalinar pointed to one line, bright and powerful. "Except one. Still vibrant."

Nale looked up at him, then ripped free of the line of light Connecting him to Dalinar and threw himself off the platform. The Herald burst alight and shot away as—belatedly—a few Windrunners came to Dalinar's aid.

You wield the power of gods, Dalinar, the Stormfather said. *I once thought I knew the extent of your abilities. I have abandoned that ignorant supposition.*

"Could I reforge it?" Dalinar asked. "Could I remake the Oathpact, and bind the Fused away again?"

I do not know. It may be possible, but I have no idea how. Or if it would be wise. The Heralds suffer for what they did.

"I saw that in him," Dalinar said, watching as Nale vanished in the distance. "He is burdened with a terrible pain that warps how he sees reality. An insanity unlike the ones that afflict ordinary men—an insanity that has to do with his worn soul . . ."

Szeth recovered his sword, seeming ashamed he'd been so easily bested. Dalinar did not fault him, nor the others, who insisted that he and the Mink retreat from the battlefield, now that the rout of Taravangian's troops was fully in progress.

Dalinar let the Windrunners spirit him away. All the while, he was lost in thought.

He needed to understand his powers. His duty was no longer to stand with a sword held high, shouting orders on the battlefield. He instead needed to find a way to use his abilities to solve this war. Reforge the Oathpact, or barring that, find another solution—one that included binding Odium once and for all.

48

SCENT OF DEATH, SCENT OF LIFE

NINE YEARS AGO

There was more than one way to explore. It turned out you could do it from the center of your own tent, if a group of living relics walked out of the forest and came to visit.

The humans thrilled Eshonai. They *hadn't* been destroyed after all. And their ways were so strange. They spoke without rhythm, and couldn't hear the songs of Roshar. They made carapace out of metal and tied it to themselves. Though she first assumed they had lost their forms, she soon realized that they had only a *single* form, and could never change. They had to deal with the passions of mateform *all the time*.

More intriguing, they brought with them a tribe of dullform creatures who also had no songs. They had skin patterns like the listeners, but didn't talk, let alone sing. Eshonai found them fascinating and disturbing. Where had the humans found such strange individuals?

The humans made camp across the river in the forest, and at first the Five let only a few listeners come to meet them. They worried about frightening away the strange humans if the entire family came to bother them.

Eshonai thought this foolish. The humans wouldn't grow frightened. They knew ancient things. Methods of forging metal and of writing sounds on paper. Things that the listeners had forgotten during the long sleep, the time they'd spent wearing dullform, memorizing songs by sheer force of will.

Eshonai, Klade, and a few others joined a few human scholars, trying to decipher one another's tongues. Preserved in the songs, fortunately, were human phrases. Perhaps her past with the songs was what helped Eshonai learn faster than the others. Or maybe it was her stubbornness. She spent evenings sitting with the humans, making them repeat sounds over and over late into the night by the light of their brilliant glowing gemstones.

That was another thing. Human gemstones glowed far more brightly than listener ones. It had to do with the way the gemstones were cut and shaped. Each day with the humans taught her something new.

Once the language barrier began to fall, the humans asked if they could be taken out onto the Shattered Plains. So it was that Eshonai led the way, though she kept them far from the ten ancient cities and the other listener families, for now.

Using one of Eshonai's maps, they approached from the north and walked along the chasms until they reached an ancient listener bridge. The rift in the stone smelled of wet rotting plants. Pungent, but not unpleasant. Where plants rotted, others often soon grew, and the scent of death was the same as the scent of life.

The humans followed gingerly across the bridge of wood and rope, the guards going first—wearing their buffed metal carapace breastplates and caps. They seemed to expect the bridge to collapse at any moment.

Once across, Eshonai stepped up onto a boulder and took a deep breath, feeling the winds. Overhead, a few windspren swirled in the sky. Once the guards had crossed, some of the others started over as well. Everyone had wanted to come see the Plains where the monsters of the chasms lived.

One of the attendants was a curious woman who was the surgeon's assistant. She climbed up onto the rock beside Eshonai, though her clothing—which enveloped her from neck to ankles and covered up her left hand for some reason—wasn't particularly good for exploring. It was nice to see that there were some things that the listeners had figured out that the humans hadn't.

"What do you see?" she asked Eshonai in the human tongue. "When you look at the spren?"

Eshonai hummed to Consideration. What did she mean? "I see spren," Eshonai said, speaking slowly and deliberately, as her accent was sometimes bad.

"Yes, what do they look like?"

"Long white lines," Eshonai said, pointing at the windspren. "Holes. Small holes? Is there a word?"

"Pinpricks, perhaps."

"Pinpricks in sky," Eshonai said. "And tails, long, very long."

"Curious," the woman said. She wore a lot of rings on her right hand, though Eshonai couldn't tell why. It seemed like they would get caught on things. "It *is* different."

"Different?" Eshonai said. "We see different?"

"Yes," the woman said. "You seem to see the reality of the spren, or closer to it. Tell me. We have stories, among the humans, of windspren that act like people. Taking different shapes, playing tricks. Have you ever seen one like that?"

Eshonai went over the words in her mind. She *thought* she understood some of it. "Spren like people? Act like people?"

"Yes."

"I have seen this," she said.

"Excellent. And windspren that talk? That call you by name? Have you met any like this?"

"What?" Eshonai said, attuning Amusement. "Spren talking? No. It seems . . . not real? Fake, but a story?"

" 'Fanciful' is perhaps the word you want."

"Fanciful," Eshonai said, examining the sounds in her mind. Yes, there was more than one way to explore.

The king and his brother finally crossed onto the plateau. "King" was not a new word to her, as it was mentioned in the songs. There had been debate among the listeners whether they should have a monarch. It seemed to Eshonai that until they managed to stop squabbling and became a single unified people, the discussion was silly.

The king's brother was a brutish man who seemed like a slightly different breed from everyone else. He was the first she'd met, along with a group of human scouts, back in the forest. This human wasn't simply larger than most of the others, he walked with a different step. His face was harder. If a human could ever be said to have a form, this man was warform.

The king himself though . . . he was proof that humans didn't have forms. He was so erratic. Sometimes loud and angry, other times quiet and dismissive. Listeners had different emotions too, of course. It was just that this man seemed to defy explanation. Perhaps the fact that the humans spoke with no rhythms made her more surprised when they acted with such passion. He was also the only male in the group who wore a beard. Why was that?

"Guide," the king said, walking up to her. "Is this where the hunts happen?"

"Sometimes," she said. "Depends. It is season, so maybe they come. Maybe not."

The king nodded absently. He had taken little interest in her or any of the listeners. His scouts and scholars, however, seemed as fascinated by Eshonai as she was with them. So she tended to spend time with them.

"What kinds of greatshells can live here?" the brother asked. "There doesn't seem to be space for them, with all these cracks in the ground. Are they like whitespines? Jumping from place to place?"

"Whitespine?" she said, not knowing the word.

The woman with the rings brought out a book with a drawing in it for her.

Eshonai shook her head. "No, not that. They are . . ." How to explain the monsters of the chasms? "They are great. And large. And powerful. They . . . these lands are theirs."

"And do your people worship them?" one of the scholars asked.

"Worship?"

"Reverence. Respect."

"Yes." Who wouldn't respect a beast so mighty?

"Their gods, Brightlord," said the scribe to the king. "As I suspected, they worship these beasts. We must take care with future hunts."

Eshonai hummed to Anxiety, to indicate she was confused—but they didn't recognize this. They had to say everything with words.

"Here," the king said, pointing. "This plateau seems a good enough place for a break."

The human attendants began unpacking their things—tents made of a marvelous tough cloth, and a variety of foods. They enjoyed their lunches, these humans. Their traveling luxury was so opulent, it made Eshonai wonder what their *homes* were like.

Once they left, she intended to see. If they'd made it here without a properly durable form such as workform, then they must not have come that far. She attuned Amusement. After all these years with no contact, she likely would have found her way to their home on her own, given a few more months.

Eshonai kept busy by helping erect the tents. She wanted to figure out the pieces. She was fairly certain she could carve poles like the ones used for holding up the roof. But the cloth was lighter, smoother, than what the listeners could create. One of the workers was having trouble with a knot, so Eshonai took out her knife to cut it free.

"What is that?" a voice said from behind her. "Do you mind showing me that knife?"

It was the woman with the rings. Eshonai had thought she might be once-mates with the king, considering how often she spoke with him. But apparently there was no relation.

Eshonai glanced down, realizing that she'd brought out her good hunting knife. It was one of the weapons her ancestors had salvaged from the ruins at the center of the Plains, with beautiful metal that had lines in it, and a carved hilt of majestic detail.

She shrugged and showed it to the woman. The strange woman, in turn, waved urgently to the king. He left the shade and stepped over, taking the knife and narrowing his eyes as he studied it.

"Where did you get this?" he asked Eshonai.

"It is old," she said, not wanting to say too much. "Handed down. Generations."

"Lasting back to the False Desolation, perhaps?" the woman asked the king. "Could they really have weapons two thousand years old?"

The listener Shardblades were far more marvelous, but Eshonai didn't speak of those. Her family didn't own any anyway.

"I would like to know," the king said, "how you—"

He was interrupted by a trumping in the near distance. Eshonai spun, attuning Tension. "Monster of Chasms," she said. "Get soldiers! I did not think one would come close."

"We can handle a . . ." the king began, but trailed off, and his eyes became wide. An awespren approached—a floating blue ball of a creature that expanded with great enthusiasm.

Eshonai turned and saw a distant shadow emerging from a chasm. Sleek yet strong, powerful yet graceful. The beast walked on numerous legs, and didn't bestow the humans with a glance. They were to it as it was to the sun—indeed, it turned upward at the light to bask. Gorgeous and mighty, as if the Rhythm of Awe had been given life.

"Blood of my fathers . . ." the king's brother said, stepping up. "How big *is* that thing?"

"Bigger than any we have in Alethkar," the king said. "You'd have to make your way to the Herdazian coast to come across a greatshell so large. But those live in the waters."

"These live in chasms," Eshonai whispered. "It doesn't seem angry, which is our fortune."

"It might be far enough away that it hasn't noticed us," the king's brother said.

"It noticed us," Eshonai said. "It simply doesn't care."

Others gathered around, and the king hushed them. Finally, the chasmfiend turned and looked them over. Then it slunk down into the chasm, trailed by a few shimmering chasmspren, like arrows in flight.

"Storms," the king's brother said. "You mean at any time, standing on these plateaus, one of *those* might be right below? Prowling about?"

"How can they live in those chasms?" one of the women asked. "What do they eat?"

It was a more solemn and quick group that returned to their lunch. They were eager to finish and leave, but none of them said it, and none hummed to Anxiety.

Of them all, only the king seemed unperturbed. While the others busied themselves, he continued studying Eshonai's knife, which he hadn't returned to her.

"You truly kept these for thousands of years?" he asked.

"No," she admitted. "We found them. Not my parents. Their parents' parents. In the ruins."

"Ruins, you say?" he looked up sharply. "What ruins? Those cities the other guide mentioned?"

Eshonai cursed Klade softly for having mentioned the ten cities. Deciding not to clarify that she meant the ruins at the center of the Plains, she attuned Anxiety. The way he inspected her made her feel like she was a map that had been drawn wrong. "My people built cities," she said. "Old parents of my people."

"You don't say . . ." he said. "Very curious. You remember those days then? You have records of them?"

"We have songs," she said. "Many songs. Important songs. They talk of the forms we bore. The wars we fought. How we left the . . . I don't know the word . . . the ones of old. Who ruled us. When the Neshua Kadal were fighting, with spren as companions, and had . . . had things . . . they could do . . ."

"Radiants?" he said, his voice growing softer. "Your people have stories about the *Knights Radiant*?"

"Yes, maybe?" she said. "I can't words, yet. Of this."

"Curious, curious."

As she'd expected, the humans decided to return to the forest soon after their meal. They were frightened—all but the king. He spent the entire trip asking about the songs. She had plainly been mistaken when she'd assumed he didn't care much about the listeners.

For from that moment on, he seemed very, *very* interested. He had his scholars interrogate them about songs, lore, and whether they knew of any other ruins. When the humans finally left for their lands several days later, King Gavilar gave Eshonai's people a gift: several crates of modern weapons, made of fine steel. They were no replacement for the ancient weapons, but not all of her people had those. No family had enough to outfit all their warriors.

All Gavilar wanted in exchange was a promise: that when he returned in the near future, he wanted to find Eshonai's people housed in one of the cities at the edge of the Plains. At that time, he said, he hoped to be able to hear from the keepers of songs in person.

49

SOUL OF DISCOVERY

In my fevered state, I worry I'm unable to focus on what is important.

—From *Rhythm of War,* page 3

Navani set to work organizing her scholars under the careful supervision of a large number of singer guards.

The situation left Navani with a delicate problem. She didn't want to give away more than was absolutely necessary. But if she failed to make progress, Raboniel would eventually notice and take action.

For now, Navani set the scholars to doing some busywork. The singers kept her people enclosed in a single one of the two library rooms, so Navani had the wards and younger ardents begin cleaning the room. They gathered up old projects and boxes of notes, then carried them out to stack in the hallway. They needed to make space.

She assigned the more experienced scholars to do revision work: going back over projects and either checking calculations or drawing new sketches. Ardents brought out fresh ledgers to go over figures, while Rushu unrolled large schematics and set several younger women to measuring each and every line. This would take up several days, perhaps longer—and it was also quite a natural thing to do. Navani frequently ordered recalculations after an interruption. It restored the scholars to a proper mindset, and they sometimes found legitimate errors.

Soon enough, she had an orderly room full of calming sounds. Papers shuffling, pens writing, people quietly discussing. No creationspren or logicspren, as often attended exciting work. Hopefully the singers in the room wouldn't realize that was odd.

Those singers were always underfoot, lingering close enough to overhear what Navani told her people. She'd grown accustomed to a clean workspace—giving her people enough freedom to innovate, but also enough careful corralling to keep them innovating in the proper direction. All of these guards undermined that effort, and Navani often caught her scholars glancing up and staring at some armed brute standing nearby.

At least most were merely common soldiers. Only one Fused—other than Raboniel—stayed near the scholars, and she wasn't one of those unnerving ones who could meld with the rock. No, this was a Fused of Raboniel's same type, a tall Fused with a topknot and a long face marbled white and red. The femalen sat on the floor, watching them, her eyes glazed over.

Navani kept covert watch over this Fused during the morning work. She had been told that many Fused were unhinged, and this one seemed to fit that description. She often stared off into nothingness, then giggled to herself. She would let her head flop from one side to the other. Why would Raboniel put this one here to watch them? Were there possibly so few sane Fused left that there was no other choice?

Navani leaned against the wall, touching her palms to the stone—where a vein of garnet ran almost imperceptibly along one line of strata—and pretended to watch as several young women carried boxes of papers out into the hallway.

You didn't talk to me last night, the Sibling said.

"I was being watched," Navani said under her breath. "They didn't let me stay in my own rooms, but took me to a smaller one. We'll need to talk here. You can hear me if I speak very softly like this?"

Yes.

"Can you see what Raboniel is doing?"

She had some workers set up a desk near the shield, where she is doing tests upon it to see if she can get through.

"Can she?"

I don't know. This is the first time it has been deployed. But she doesn't seem to realize you were the one who activated it. She explained to several others that she must have triggered some unknown fail-safe left by the ancient Radiants. She thinks that I must be dead after all this time, since the tower doesn't work.

"Curious," Navani said. "Why would she think that?"

The Midnight Mother told her. That Unmade who infected me for so many years, the one your Radiants frightened away? I remained hidden from her all that time, never fighting back, and so she thinks I died.

"All that time?" Navani asked. "How long?"

Centuries.

"Wasn't that hard?"

No. Why? Centuries mean nothing to me. I do not age.

"Other spren act like time has meaning."

Radiant spren, yes. Radiant spren put on a show, pretending as if they are male or female, malen or femalen, when they are neither. They think like humans because they want to be like humans.

I do not pretend. I am not human. I do not need to care about time. I do not need to look like you. I do not need to beg for your attention.

Navani cocked an eyebrow at that, considering that the Sibling *had* needed to beg for her help. She held her tongue. How to best use this advantage? What was the path to freedom? Navani liked to think that she could see patterns, that she could make order from chaos. There *was* a way out of this mess. She had to believe that.

Treat it like any other problem, Navani thought to herself. *Approach it systematically, breaking it down into manageable pieces.*

Last night, she'd decided on a few general courses of action. First, she had to maintain the ground she'd already obtained. That meant making certain the Sibling's shield remained in place.

Second, she had to get word to Dalinar and those on the outside, apprising them of what had happened.

Third, Navani needed to figure out what the enemy had done to negate Radiant powers. According to the Sibling, it involved a corruption of ancient tower protections. Navani needed to deactivate it.

Finally, she needed to turn that power upon the invaders. Barring that, she needed to use the awakened Radiants to mount a counterattack.

Standing here, trapped in the basement and constantly watched, those seemed impossible tasks. But her scholars had made a ship fly. She could do this, with their help.

Navani counted off the singer guards as they strolled through the room, looking over the shoulders of working scholars. One stopped the girls carrying out notes and checked through the boxes. That one Fused—the one who kept moving her head from one side to the other, humming a loud rhythm—was watching Navani at the moment. Navani tried not to let that unnerve her, and turned her head so her lips wouldn't be visible, then continued talking under her breath.

"Let's assume," she said, "that Raboniel is smart enough to figure out what those ancient Radiants did in creating this shield for you. What would be the best way for her to go about circumventing it?"

The Sibling didn't respond, and Navani began to worry. "Has something happened? Are you well?"

I am fine, the Sibling said. *But we are not friends, human. You are a slaver. I do not trust you.*

"You've trusted me so far."

Out of necessity. I am safe now.

"And for how long will you be safe? You're saying there is *no* way for Raboniel to get through?"

The Sibling didn't respond.

"Fine," Navani said. "But I can't plan a way to help you if I don't know your weaknesses. You'll be alone, subject to whatever Raboniel decides to do."

. . . I hate humans, the Sibling eventually said. *Humans twist what is said and always make themselves out to be right.*

How long until you demand that I bond a human, give up my freedom, and risk my life? I'm sure you'll have wonderful explanations as to why I should absolutely do that.

This time Navani was the one who remained silent. The Sibling could create another Bondsmith, and considering how useful Dalinar's powers were to the war effort, Navani would be foolish not to seize the opportunity. So she *would* need to find a way to make the Sibling bond a human again. She'd have to find someone completely unthreatening. Someone who didn't work with fabrials, someone who wasn't a politician. Someone the Sibling would like.

For now, Navani didn't prod. The Sibling clearly had some strange ways, but their interactions so far had been quite human, despite what they claimed. And Navani would expect a human to . . .

The shield we created is something Raboniel might have heard about, the Sibling said at last. *Therefore, she might understand how to circumvent it.*

"Tell me more," Navani said.

The shield is an extrapolation of the Surge of Soulcasting. It solidifies the air in a region by persuading it that it is glass. For the shield to be maintained, the system needs to be fed by external sources of Stormlight. Raboniel might realize this—especially if she researches the remnants of the node you used to activate the shield.

There are other nodes like that one, with crystals connected directly to my heart. There were four. You destroyed one. If she finds one of the other three, she could use it to corrupt me from the outside.

"So we need to find them first," Navani said, "and destroy them."

No. NO! That will weaken the shield, then destroy it. We need to defend them. Breaking one was bad enough. Do not think because I gave you permission once, you can continue to do this. Humans always break things.

Navani took a deep breath. She had to speak very carefully. "I won't break any of them unless it's absolutely necessary. Let's talk about something else. How did you contact me earlier? Can you work a spanreed?"

I hate the things. But using one was necessary.

"Yes, but how? Do you have hands somewhere?"

Just helpers. There is an insane woman, locked in a monastery, who I contacted. Those isolated, those with permeable souls, respond better to spren sometimes. This one, however, only wrote down everything I said—never responding. I had Dabbid bring her a spanreed, and I communicated through her.

Drat. That didn't seem particularly useful, at least now that spanreeds weren't working. "How is it that the enemy knocked the Radiants unconscious?" Navani asked.

It is an aspect of Ur, the Tower, the Sibling said. *A defense set up to prevent the Fused—and the Unmade, depending on circumstances—from entering it.*

"I encountered a fabrial designed to do the same—one I think must have been modeled after part of the crystal pillar. I don't mean to be rude, but did you not consider activating this defense when they attacked?"

The Sibling fell silent for a time, and Navani wondered if she had pushed the spren too far. Fortunately they spoke again, softly. *I have . . . been wounded. Thousands of years ago, something happened that changed the singers. It hurt me too.*

Navani covered her shock. "You're speaking of the binding of that Unmade, which made the singers lose their forms?"

Yes. That terrible act touched the souls of all who belong to Roshar. Spren too.

"How have no spren mentioned this?"

I don't know. But I lost the rhythm of my Light that day. The tower stopped working. My father, Honor, should have been able to help me, but he was losing his mind. And he soon died . . .

There was enough sorrow in the Sibling's voice that Navani didn't push them for answers. This changed everything.

When that Fused touched me, the Sibling continued, *she corrupted part of me to the tone of Odium. This wouldn't have been possible, once—but it is now. She fills my system with his Light, ruining me. Corrupting me.*

"So . . ." Navani said. "If we could find a way to destroy the Voidlight inside you, or somehow recover the rhythm you lost, you could reactivate the tower to our defense?"

I suppose. It doesn't seem possible. I feel . . . like we're doomed.

The mood shift seemed familiarly human. Indeed, Navani felt a little of the same. She rested her head against the wall, closing her eyes.

Break it down into little pieces, she reminded herself. *Protect the Sibling long enough to figure out the other problems. That's your first task.*

You didn't fill out a map all at once. You did it one line at a time. That was the soul of discovery.

But . . . the Sibling said.

"But?" Navani said, opening her eyes. "But what?"

But we might not need to wake up any Radiants. There are two in the tower who are still awake.

Again Navani nearly broke her calm facade. Why hadn't the Sibling mentioned this immediately? "How?"

One makes sense to me, the Sibling said. *She is awake because she was created oddly, to use Light differently from others. She was made by my mother for this purpose. But I have lost track of her, and I do not know where she is. A young woman. Edgedancer.*

"Lift," Navani said. That one always *had* been strange. "You can't see her anymore?"

No. I think one reason I can see parts of the tower has to do with Radiants, who are Connected to me. I caught glimmers of this Edgedancer girl for a while, but she vanished yesterday. She was in a cage, and I suspect they surrounded her with ralkalest.

But there is one other. A man. He must be of the Fourth Ideal, but he has no armor. So . . . maybe of the Third, but close to the Fourth? Perhaps it is something about his closeness to my father—and his closeness to the Surge of Adhesion—that keeps him conscious. His power is that of bonds. This man is a Windrunner, but no longer wears a uniform.

Kaladin. "Can you contact him?"

⁘

Kaladin's first goal was Stormlight. Fortunately, he knew exactly where to find some infused spheres. Workers frequently erected gemstone lanterns in busier corridors, pushing away the darkness and making the interior more welcoming and comfortable. One such project had been happening on the sixth floor, far enough from his family's clinic that he felt it wasn't too dangerous to try approaching.

He started by feeling his way through the darkened hallways near his hiding place on the eleventh floor. Together with Syl, he made a mental map of the area, then inched to the perimeter. Kaladin felt like he was leaving a slaver's cage when he saw that first glimmer of sunlight in the distance, and had to keep himself from running all-out to reach it.

Slow, steady, careful. He let Syl explore on ahead. She snuck up to the balcony, then peeked out. Kaladin crouched in the darkness waiting, watching, listening. Finally she darted back and made a swirl in the air, the signal that she hadn't seen anything suspicious.

He emerged into the light. He tried to memorize the strata here in this outermost hallway, then glanced over his shoulder back into the bowels of the eleventh floor. That corridor was basically a straight shot to his hiding place. His stupid brain imagined forgetting the way and leaving Teft to die, wasting away, perhaps waking at the end. Alone, trapped, terrified . . .

Kaladin shook his head, then inched out into a balcony room where he could survey the exterior of the tower. They hadn't seen a single guard while walking here. Glancing out, he didn't see a single Heavenly One flying. What was happening? Had they *retreated* for some reason?

No. He still felt the oppressive dullness, the sign of whatever they'd done to suppress the Radiants. Kaladin leaned out farther. On the plateaus, he saw figures in blue uniforms guarding the Oathgates in their usual locations. He felt a spike of relief, and even disbelief. Had it *all* been some terrible nightmare?

"Kaladin!" Syl hissed. "Someone's coming."

The two of them pressed their backs to the nearby wall as a group of figures passed through the hallway outside. They were speaking to the rhythms, in Azish. Singer guards—Kaladin caught a glimpse of them carrying spears. He almost jumped them, but restrained himself. There would be an easier and less blatant way of getting a proper weapon.

The enemy was clearly still in control. And as he considered it, the truth occurred to him.

"They're making the outside of the tower look like nothing has happened," he whispered to Syl after the patrol had passed. "They know Dalinar will send Windrunners to scout the tower once communication fails, so the enemy is trying to pretend the place hasn't been conquered. Those are either Fused illusions, or human sympathizers—perhaps the remnants of Amaram's army—wearing stolen uniforms."

"And Windrunners won't be able to get close enough to discover the truth, lest their powers fail," Syl said.

"That part will be suspicious," Kaladin said. "The enemy can't keep this going for long."

The two moved to a nearby stairwell. It didn't seem to be guarded, but he sent Syl ahead to check anyway. Then they started down, finding the tenth, ninth, and eighth floors relatively unguarded. There was simply too much space up here to watch it all. Though they did spot one other patrol at the tower's perimeter, it was easy going until they reached the seventh floor. Here, leading down to the more populated sixth floor, they found guards at the bottom of the first five stairwells they tried.

They had to move inward and find a small out-of-the-way stairwell that Syl remembered. Reaching it meant entering the darkness again. To Kaladin, sunlight was as vital as food or water. Leaving it was agony, but he did it.

And as hoped, the smaller stairwell was unguarded. They emerged onto the sixth floor in quiet darkness. It seemed most of the tower's human population was still confined to quarters. The enemy was working on how to rule this place, which should leave Kaladin with an opening. With that in mind, he sent Syl on a task.

She zipped out toward the balcony rooms, leaving him crouched in the stairwell, armed with his scalpel. Kaladin shivered, wishing he had a coat or jacket. It felt colder now than it ever had in the tower. Whatever the enemy had done to stop the Radiants had also interfered with the tower's other functions. That made him worry about the people.

Syl eventually returned. "Your family is confined to quarters like everyone else," she said softly. "But there are actual guards at their door. I didn't dare try to talk to your father or mother, but I saw them together through the window. They look healthy, if frightened."

Kaladin nodded. That was the best he could have hoped for, he supposed. Hopefully his father had talked his way out of trouble, as he'd said. Together, Kaladin and Syl snuck inward to the hallway where the lanterns were being installed. The workers had left a pile of lanterns here, along with tools for drilling their mountings into the rock.

They hadn't left gemstones in the equipment piles, and the lanterns in this particular corridor were empty. But in the next corridor over, the lanterns had been fitted with amethysts—midsized gemstones for light, a little larger than a broam. That meant a lot of Stormlight, if he could get it out.

"What do you think?" Kaladin asked Syl. "Grab a crowbar and snap them quickly, then run for it?"

"Seems like that would make a lot of noise," she said, landing on one of the lanterns.

"I could just steal the Stormlight and infuse the spheres I've been carrying. I wish I could get some of these gemstones though. I need a better reserve."

"We could try to find the lampkeeper and get her keys," Syl said.

"The one assigned to this floor is a lighteyed woman who lives somewhere on the third floor, I think. Lopen tried to get her to go to dinner with him."

"Of course he did," Syl said. "But . . . as I think about it, trying to find her seems like it would be difficult and dangerous."

"Agreed."

She stood on the top of the glowing lantern, then flitted around to the side, becoming a ribbon of light, and zipped in through the lantern's small keyhole. Although she couldn't pass through solid objects, squeezing through a crack or hole usually served well enough.

Her ribbon wound around inside the lantern. These were sturdy iron devices built to resist break-ins. They had glass sides, but those were reinforced with a lattice of metal. A key would unlock one of the faces, letting you swing it open and access the inside. The other faces of the lantern could be unlatched from the inside, and could open as well.

Syl flew over to one of these latches and formed into a person again. Theoretically, if you didn't have a key, you could break the glass and use a wire to manually turn the inside latches to open one of the faces. But the device had been designed to make this difficult, with thick glass and that iron webbing behind.

Syl tried pushing on the latch, but it was too heavy for her. She put her hands on her hips, glaring at it. "Try a Lashing," Syl called, her voice echoing against the glass, louder than her tiny form would have suggested.

"Lashings don't work," Kaladin said softly, keeping an eye down the corridor for guard patrols.

"Gravitational Lashings don't work," Syl said. "The other ones do though, right?"

Windrunners had three varieties of Lashings. Most commonly he used the gravitational Lashing, where you infused an object or person and changed the direction gravity pulled them. But there were two others. He'd tested a Full Lashing while carrying Teft to the clinic during the invasion. That Lashing allowed you to infuse an object with Light and command it to stick to anything that touched it. He'd used it during his early days as a bridgeman to stick rocks to a chasm wall.

The last Lashing was the most strange and arcane of the three. The Reverse Lashing made something *attract* other objects. It was like a hybrid of the other two. You infused a surface, then commanded it to pull on specific items. They were drawn to it. As if . . . as if the object you infused had become the *source* of gravity. As a bridgeman, Kaladin had unknowingly used this Lashing to pull arrows through the air to his bridge, making them swerve to miss his friends.

"What you call 'Lashings,'" Syl said to him, "are really two Surges working together. Gravitation and Adhesion, combined in different ways. You say Gravitation Lashings don't work, and Adhesion ones do. What about a Reverse Lashing?"

"Haven't tried," Kaladin admitted. He stepped to the side and drew the Stormlight out of a different lantern. He felt the energy, the power, in his veins—something he'd been yearning for. He smiled and stepped back, alight with power.

"Try making the glass attract the latch," Syl said, gesturing. "If you can get the latch to move toward you, it will pop out and unlock."

He touched the side of the lantern housing. During the last year, he'd practiced his Lashings. Sigzil had monitored, making him do experiments, as usual. They'd found that a Reverse Lashing required a command—or at least a visualization of what you wanted. As he infused the glass, he tried to imagine the Stormlight attracting things.

No, not things. The latch specifically.

The Stormlight resisted. As with the basic gravitational Lashing, he could feel the power, but something blocked it. However, the blockage was weaker here. He concentrated, pushing harder, and—like a floodgate opening—the Light suddenly burst from him. A Reverse Lashing didn't glow as brightly as it should, considering the Stormlight. It was kind of inverted, in a way. But Kaladin's actions were followed by a faint *click*.

The power had attracted the latch, which—pulled by that unseen force—had popped free of its housing. Eager, Kaladin slipped the front of the lantern open, then plucked the gemstone out and slipped it into his pocket.

Syl zipped out. "We need more practice on these, Kaladin. You don't use them as instinctively as the other two."

He nodded, thoughtful, and reclaimed the Stormlight he'd pressed into the lantern housing. Then the two of them moved furtively along the corridor, dropping it into darkness with each gemstone stolen.

"Reverse Lashings take effort," Kaladin told Syl softly. "It makes me wonder though, if I could somehow make basic gravitational Lashings function." He'd come to rely on those in a fight—the ability to leap into the air, to send his opponent flying off. Even the simple ability to make himself lighter so he flowed more easily through the battle.

He finished off the last of the lanterns, satisfied with the healthy pocketful of Stormlight. A fortune by Hearthstone terms, though he'd started to grow accustomed to having that much on hand. With these gemstones secured in a dark pouch so his pocket wouldn't glow, the two of them set off on their next task. Supplies.

They kept to the inner part of the floor this time, where they'd be able to see a patrol coming by the light it carried. Kaladin led Syl down some steps, as he had a good idea of where to get food and water.

As he'd hoped, the monastery in the middle of the fourth floor wasn't a high priority to guard. He found a pair of singers in uniform occupying one watchpost along the way, but was able to sneak down a side corridor and find a completely unguarded door.

Kaladin and Syl entered, then crept through a corridor lined with cells. He still thought of them that way, even though the ardents here insisted they weren't a prison. Of course, the rooms the ardents *themselves* stayed in were properly lit, furnished, and downright homey. Kaladin found one of these by the light under the door, checked the glyph painted on the wood, then slipped in.

He startled the ardent inside, the same man he'd met during his earlier visit to this place. Kuno, Kaladin had learned his name was. The ardent had been reading, but scrambled—and failed—to pull his spectacles down onto his eyes as Kaladin crossed the room in a rush and made a shushing gesture.

"Are there other guards?" Kaladin whispered. "I saw two at the front gate."

"N-no, Brightlord," Kuno said, spectacles dangling loosely from his fingers. "I . . . How? How are you here?"

"By the grace of god or luck. I haven't decided which. I need supplies. Rations, jugs of water. Medical supplies if you have any."

The man stuttered, then leaned close, ignoring the spectacles in his hand as he squinted at Kaladin. "By the Almighty. It really *is* you. Storm-blessed . . ."

"Do you have the things I need?"

"Yes, yes," Kuno said, rising and running his hand across his shaved head, then led the way out of the room.

"You were right," Syl said from Kaladin's shoulder as he followed. "They probably secured all the guard posts, clinics, and barracks. But an out-of-the way sanitarium . . ."

Kuno took them to a little storeroom. Inside, Kaladin was able to find almost everything he needed. A hospital robe and bedpan for Teft. Various other articles of clothing. A sponge and washbasin, even a large syringe for feeding someone unconscious.

Kaladin packed these into a sack along with bandages, fathom bark for pain, and some antiseptic. Some dried rations followed, mostly Soulcast, but they'd do. He tied four wooden jugs of water to a rope he could sling around his neck, then noticed a bucket with some cleaning supplies in it. He picked out four brushes with thick bristles and sturdy wooden handles, used for scrubbing floors.

"Need to . . . wash some floors, Radiant?" the ardent said.

"No, but I can't fly anymore, so I need these," Kaladin said, stuffing them in his bag. "You don't have any broth, do you?"

"Not handy," Kuno said.

"Pity. What about a weapon?"

"A weapon? Why would you need one? You have your Blade."

"Doesn't work right now," Kaladin said.

"Well, we don't keep weapons here, Brightlord," Kuno said, wiping his face, which was dripping with sweat. "Storms. You mean . . . you're going to fight them?"

"Resist them, at least." Kaladin put the rope with the jugs around his neck, then stood with some effort and settled the weight so the cord didn't bite *too* harshly. "Don't tell anyone about me. I don't want you getting taken in for questioning. I will need more supplies."

"You . . . you're going to return? Do this . . . regularly?" The man pulled his spectacles off and wiped his face again.

Kaladin reached out and put his hand on the man's shoulder. "If we lose the tower, we lose the war. I'm not in any shape to fight. I'm going to do it anyway. I don't need you to lift a spear, but if you could get me some broth and refill my water jugs every couple of days . . ."

The man nodded. "All right. I can . . . I can do that."

"Good man," Kaladin said. "As I said, keep this quiet. I don't want the general public getting it into their heads that they should pick up a spear and start fighting against Fused. If there's a way out of this mess, it will involve me either getting word to Dalinar or somehow waking the other Radiants."

He drew in a little Stormlight. He would need it to help him carry all this, and seeing the glow gave the ardent an obvious boost of confidence.

"Life before death," Kaladin said to him.

"Life before death, Radiant," Kuno said.

Kaladin picked up his sacks and started out into the darkness. It was slow going, but he eventually arrived on the eleventh floor. Here he oriented himself while Syl poked around to see if she could remember the way. They needn't have worried—a small spark of light appeared in a vein of garnet on the floor.

They followed the light to the room where they had left Teft. The door opened easily, without needing more Stormlight. Inside, Kaladin set down his supplies, checked on his friend, then started a better inventory of what he'd grabbed. The garnet light sparkled on the floor beside him, and he brushed the crystal vein with his fingers.

A voice immediately popped into his head.

Highmarshal? Is it true? Are you awake and functioning?

Kaladin started. It was the queen's voice.

⁘

Brightness Navani? Kaladin's voice said in Navani's head. *I am awake. Basically functioning. My powers are . . . acting strange. I don't know why I'm not comatose like the others.*

Navani drew in a long, deep breath. The Sibling had watched him sneak to the fourth floor, then raid a monastery for supplies. While he'd been returning, Navani had done several circuits of her room—talking to her scholars and giving them encouragement—to not draw suspicion. Now she was back in position, resting against the wall, trying to look bored.

She was anything but. She had access to a Knight Radiant, perhaps two if the Sibling could locate Lift. "That is well," she whispered, the Sibling transferring her words to Kaladin. "For now, I am reluctantly working with our captors. They have me and my scholars locked away in the eastern basement study room, near the gemstone pillar."

Do you know what's wrong with the Radiants? he asked.

"To an extent, yes," she whispered. "The details are somewhat technical, but the tower had ancient protections to defend it from enemies who were using Voidlight. A Fused scholar inverted this; it now suppresses those who would use Stormlight. She did not complete the tower's corruption, however. I narrowly prevented her from doing so by erecting a barrier around the pillar. Unfortunately, that same barrier prevents me from undoing the work she did there."

So . . . what do we do?

"I don't know," Navani admitted. Dalinar would have probably told her to act strong, to pretend she had a plan when she didn't—but she wasn't a general. Pretending never worked with her scholars; they appreciated honesty. "I've barely had time to plan, and I'm still dragging from yesterday."

I know that feeling, Kaladin said.

"The enemy has made the Oathgates work somehow," Navani said, a plan forming in her mind. "My first goal is to continue protecting the Sibling, the spren of the tower. My second goal is to get word to my husband and the other monarchs. If we could figure out how the enemy is making the Oathgates work, I might be able to get my spanreeds functioning and send warning."

That sounds like a pretty good start, Brightness, Kaladin said. *I'm glad to have a direction to work toward. So you want me to find out how they're operating the Oathgates?*

"Exactly. My only guess is that they are powering them with Voidlight somehow—but I tried to make fabrials use Voidlight in the past, and failed. I know for a fact, however, that the enemy has functional spanreeds. I haven't been able to get a good look at one of those—but if you could find out how they're using the Oathgates, or other fabrials, that would give me something to work with."

I'd need to get close to the Oathgates to do that, Kaladin said. *And not be seen doing so.*

"Yes. Can you manage that? I know you said your powers aren't functioning completely."

I . . . I'll find a way, Brightness. I suspect the enemy won't be using the Oathgates until nighttime. I think they're trying to keep up a front of nothing being wrong with the tower, in case Dalinar sends scouts. They have some humans wearing Alethi uniforms patrolling outside. At night, even distant Windrunners trying to watch would be visible in the darkness. I suspect they'd find this a safer time to use the Oathgates.

Curious indeed. How long did Raboniel realistically think she could keep up such a subterfuge? Surely Dalinar would withdraw from the battlefield in Azir and focus everything on discovering what was wrong with Urithiru. Unless there were aspects to this that Navani wasn't considering.

The implications of that frightened her. She was blind, locked away in this basement.

"Highmarshal," she said to Kaladin, "I'll try to contact you again tomorrow around the same time. Until then, be warned. The enemy will be seeking a way to disrupt the shield I erected. There are three nodes hidden in the tower, large gemstones infused with Stormlight that are maintaining the barrier, but the Sibling won't say where they are.

"These nodes are direct channels to the heart of the tower, and as such are great points of vulnerability. If you find one, tell me. And be aware, if the enemy gains access to it, they can complete the tower's corruption."

Yes, sir. Er. Brightness.

"I need to go. Lift is awake somewhere too, so it would be worth keeping an eye out for her. At any rate, take care, Highmarshal. If the task proves too dangerous, retreat. We are too few right now to take unwise risks."

Understood. After a moment's pause, the Sibling's voice continued, *He has gone back to unpacking his supplies. You should be careful though, how you ask after fabrials. Do not forget that I consider what you have done to be a high crime.*

"I've not forgotten," Navani said. "But surely you don't oppose the Oathgates."

I do not, the Sibling said, sounding reluctant. *Those spren have gone willingly to their transformations.*

"Do you know why it works? Powering the Oathgates with Voidlight?"

No. The Oathgates are not part of me. I will leave you now. Our talking is suspicious.

Navani didn't press the matter, instead making another circuit around her scholars. She wasn't certain whether she trusted what the Sibling said. Could spren lie? She didn't think she'd ever asked the Radiants' spren. A foolish oversight.

At any rate, in Kaladin she at least had a connection to the rest of the tower. A lifeline. That was one step forward in finding a way out of this mess.

When in such a state, detachment is enviable. I have learned that my greatest discoveries come when I abandon lesser connections.

—From *Rhythm of War,* page 3 undertext

T wo days after defeating Taravangian's traitors, Dalinar stood in the war tent, helping prepare for the larger offensive against the singers in Emul. Just behind him stood Szeth in disguise. Nobody gave the man a second glance; Dalinar often had members of the Cobalt Guard with him.

Dalinar surveyed the war table with its maps and lists of troop numbers. So many different pieces, representing the state of their fighting across many different battlefronts. When he'd been younger, these types of abstractions had frustrated him. He'd wanted to be *on* the battlefield, Blade in hand, smashing his way through enemy lines and making such maps obsolete.

Then he'd begun to see the armies behind the little squares on the sheets of paper. Begun to truly grasp how the movement of troops—supplies, logistics, large-scale tactics—was more important than winning a given battle in person. And it had excited him.

Somehow he'd moved beyond that now. War—and all its facets—no longer excited him. It was important, and it was a thing he would do. But he had discovered a greater duty.

How do we win? Truly win, *not merely gain an advantage for a time?*

He mused on these thoughts as his generals and head scribes presented their final conclusions on the Veden betrayal.

"Our troops in southern Alethkar were successfully supported by the Thaylen ships, as you advised," Teshav said. "Our generals along the coast were able to retreat through a series of fortresses as you directed. They have regrouped at Karanak—which we control. Because none of our battalions were completely surrounded by Vedens, we suffered virtually no losses."

"Our navy locked the Veden ships into their ports," said Kmakl, the aging Thaylen prince consort. "They won't break our blockade anytime soon, unless the Fused and Skybreakers give them heavy air support."

"We destroyed almost all the Vedens who betrayed us here," said Omal, a short Azish general who wore a brightly colored patterned sash across his uniform coat. "Your leadership on the battlefield was excellent, Blackthorn—not to mention the timeliness of your warnings before the battle. Instead of burning our supply dumps and rescuing their king, they were nearly eliminated."

Dalinar looked across the table at the Mink, who was smiling with a gap-toothed sense of satisfaction.

"This was very well handled, Uncle," Jasnah said to him, surveying the war table map. "You averted a catastrophe."

Noura conferred with the Azish emperor, who sat on a throne near the side of the battle tent, then walked over. "We regret the loss of such an important ally in Taravangian," she said. "This betrayal will be felt—and prosecuted—by the Azish for generations. That said, we too approve of your handling of the situation. You did well to remain suspicious of him all these months, and we were unwise to think his treachery was all in the past."

Dalinar leaned over the table, which was lit with spheres. Though he missed the large illusory map he could create with Shallan, there was something about the tangible feeling of *this* map, the paper marked up with the thoughts of his best generals, that spoke to him. As he stared, everything but the map seemed to fade from his view.

Something was still wrong. Taravangian had been so *subtle* for so many months. Yet now he let himself be captured?

His armies in Jah Keved seem not to care much about him, Dalinar thought, reading the displayed battle reports and figures as if they were whispered explanations in his ears. *The Veden highprinces will be happy to put their own men in charge. And they seem quick to side with the singers, as the Iriali were.*

Kharbranth, led by Taravangian's daughter Savrahalidem, had disavowed their former ruler and proclaimed themselves neutral in the conflict—with their surgeons willing to continue serving whichever side petitioned their aid. Dalinar would have his ships blockade them just in case—but he wasn't about to land troops there and fight a costly battle for such a relatively unimportant target. They likely knew that.

The real prize was Taravangian himself. Someone Dalinar already held captive. After the elderly king's careful posturing over the years, how had he let his empire collapse practically overnight?

Why? Why risk it now?

"What news of Urithiru?" Dalinar asked.

"Windrunners should return soon with their latest visual on the tower," Teshav said from the dim perimeter of the table. "But Brightness Navani's most recent spanreed letter indicates that our people there are managing well."

Navani continued to send soldiers hiking along the outside of the mountain faces to deliver messages. Each new bit told them a little more. Some of Taravangian's scholars had activated a device like the one Highmarshal Kaladin had found. A separate collapse of the tunnels below—likely the work of saboteurs—made getting in and out that way impossible.

The device was hidden, and Navani hadn't been able to find and deactivate it. She worried the search would take weeks. Unfortunately, Dalinar's scouts had proven the device's effectiveness. If they drew too close, they not only lost their powers, but dropped unconscious.

For now though, it seemed that everyone was safe—though inconvenienced. If Dalinar hadn't been anticipating the betrayal, things could have gone very differently. He could imagine a version of events where Taravangian's betrayal threw the coalition into chaos, allowing the singer military to surge forward and push Dalinar's troops all the way back to Azimir. There, without proper resupply and support, they could have been crushed.

Perhaps that's it, he thought. *Perhaps that was what Taravangian was intending—why he risked so much.* The king, so far, had remained silent during interrogations. Perhaps Dalinar could speak to him directly and get more information. But he worried that somehow all of this was according to Taravangian's plans, and Dalinar was second-guessing himself at every point.

"Monarchs," Dalinar said to the group, "I suggest we continue our battle for Emul until we have more information about Urithiru."

"Agreed," the Azish emperor said immediately.

"I will seek approval from the guilds of Thaylenah and the queen," Prince Kmakl said, scanning through naval reports. "But for now, I have no problem with continuing to let the Alethi generals lead. However, Brightlord Dalinar, you realize this betrayal is going to make recovering your homeland even more difficult."

"I do," Dalinar said. "I still believe that the best thing we can do for Alethkar's eventual recovery is to first secure the West."

Each of those words was a knife stabbing at his heart. It meant giving Alethkar up for years. Perhaps longer. With Jah Keved as a staging area, he'd been able to entertain dreams of striking right for Kholinar. No longer.

Storming Taravangian. Damnation take you.

With Kmakl and the Azish weighing in, the sole monarch who hadn't spoken up was Jasnah. She inspected the maps, Wit—as ever—standing at her shoulder.

"I assume, Uncle," she said, "that you will be letting the Mink prosecute this campaign?"

"This is a larger conflict than one man can direct on his own," Dalinar said. "But after his handling of the battle two days ago, I think he's proven his worth. One of the reasons I worked so hard to recruit him was to have his particular genius directing our strategy."

"At the will of the monarchs," the Mink said, "I'll do this—but remember your promises. I won't have you escape them. Once we inevitably liberate Alethkar, my kingdom is next."

Jasnah nodded. "I would like to see your battle plans, General Dieno. I give my initial approval to our continued offensive into Emul, but I will want details. Losing access to the Oathgates is going to prove disruptive."

With that, Dalinar called an end to the meeting. People began to uncover spheres around the perimeter of the war pavilion—revealing how enormous it truly was. It had to be large enough to accommodate everyone's entourages, and so the map table looked small once everyone started retreating to their sections of the tent.

Kmakl made his way over to the Thaylen scribes, where they used spanreeds to send minutes of the meeting home to Fen and the Thaylen guildmasters. Dalinar shook his head. He agreed with Fen's decision to stay behind, and wished that Jasnah had made the same choice. Too many monarchs in one location made him nervous.

It also bothered him that so much of what Queen Fen did was subject to the whims of a bunch of merchants and guildmasters. If they did win this war, he'd see if he could find a way to help her wrest control of her kingdom from those eels.

The Azish and Emuli contingents began to vacate the war tent, letting in some fresh air. Dalinar used a handkerchief to mop at the sweat on the back of his neck—this region of Roshar wasn't as muggy as the parts around the Reshi Isles, but the summer weather here was still too hot for his taste. He almost wanted to have one of the Windrunners fly him up to a higher altitude where he could get some proper cold air and think clearly.

He settled for stepping outside the tent and surveying the camp. They'd commandeered a small town named Laqqi, just inside the Emuli border, not too far from Azimir. That placed it about a three-day march from the battlefront, where their lines—soon to be reinforced—held against the enemy forces to the south.

Little more than a village, Laqqi had been overrun by troops setting up supply stations and command tents. Workers reinforced the eastern approach to block storms, and Windrunners soared through the air. This position made for an excellent command center, close enough to the battlefront to be reached by short flight, but far enough away to be protected from ground assault.

Dalinar took some time out here, after checking that little Gav was playing happily with his governess, to think about Evi. Storms, he'd been so proud at Adolin's birth. How had he let himself miss so much of his son's childhood?

He turned those memories over in his head. At first, he'd found being able to remember Evi to be novel—but the more the memories settled with him, the more they felt comfortable, like a familiar seat by the fire. He was ashamed of so much of what he'd remembered about himself, but he would not trade these memories again. He needed them. Needed her.

He enjoyed the fresh air for a time, breathing deeply, before he returned to the tent to get something to drink. Szeth followed with his hand on his oversized sword—the silver sheath and black hilt were masked by a disguise. Szeth didn't say anything, but Dalinar knew that he considered his defeat by Nale to be shameful. In Dalinar's estimation, it spoke more of the Herald's skill than anything else. Why was it Nale so often stayed out of battles, overseeing his Skybreakers from afar?

Jasnah joined Dalinar as he poured himself some wine in the tent, by the bar. She knew what Szeth really was, but she was too politic to give him so much as a glance.

"You're stepping away from the fight, Uncle," she noted quietly. "I expected you to lead the war effort here personally."

"I have found someone more capable to do the job."

"Pardon, Uncle, but you should find a better lie. You *never* let go of something you're interested in doing yourself. It's one of your more consistent behaviors."

He stilled himself, then glanced about the room. She shouldn't have confronted him here, where representatives of the other monarchs might hear. Knowing Jasnah, that was part of the reason she had done so. With her, every conversation was a little contest, and she always considered the terrain.

"I'm beginning to realize something," he said softly, stepping her over to the side, away from the bar. Szeth stayed close, as did Wit. Others gave them space. "My powers as a Bondsmith are more valuable than we have known. I told you about how, in the battle, I touched Nalan and saw his past."

"A feat you've been unable to replicate with Shalash or Talenelat."

"Yes, because I don't know what I'm doing!" Dalinar said. "I am a weapon we haven't fully investigated. I need to learn how to use these powers—use them for more than merely renewing spheres and opening the perpendicularity."

"I appreciate someone wanting to learn, Uncle," Jasnah said. "But you are *already* a powerful weapon. You are one of our greatest military minds."

"I need to become something more," Dalinar said. "I'm worried that this war is going to be an endless give-and-take. We seize Emul, but lose Jah Keved. Back and forth, back and forth. How do we *win*, Jasnah? What is our end goal?"

She nodded slowly. "We need to push Odium to an accord. You think learning about your powers can help you achieve this?"

Over a year had passed since Odium had agreed to a contest by champions—but since then, Dalinar hadn't seen the being. No visits. No visions. Not even a messenger.

"Rayse—Odium—is not one to be pushed into anything," Wit said from over Jasnah's shoulder. "He might have agreed to a contest in theory, Blackthorn, but he never set terms. And he won't, as long as he thinks he's winning this war. You need to frighten him, convince him that he might lose. Only then will he proceed with a contest of champions—as long as the terms limit his losses."

"I would rather a complete victory than something that allows Odium to hedge his bets," Dalinar said.

"Ah, delightful," Wit replied, holding up his palm and mimicking writing something down. "I'll just make a note that you'd like to win. Yes, how *foolish* of me not to realize that, Blackthorn. Total victory. Over a god. Who is currently holding your homeland, and recently gained the allegiance of one of the strongest militaries on the planet. Shall I also have him bake you something sweet as an apology for this whole 'end of the world' mess?"

"That will do, Wit," Dalinar said with a sigh.

"The baking thing is an actual tradition," Wit added. "I once visited a place where—if you lose a battle—your mother has to bake the other fellow something tasty. I rather liked those people."

"Pity you didn't remain with them longer," Dalinar said.

"Ha! Well, I didn't think it wise to stay around. After all, they were cannibals."

Dalinar shook his head, focusing back on the task at hand. "Wit says we have to somehow persuade Odium we're a threat. But *I* think the enemy is manipulating us. This entire trick with Taravangian has me unsettled. We're dealing with a god, but we aren't using all the tools at our disposal."

He held up his palm. "With this, I can touch his world, the Spiritual Realm. And when I was fighting Nalan, I felt something, saw something. What if I could reforge the Oathpact? If the Fused stopped being reborn, would that not give us—at last—an edge over Odium? Something to *force* him to negotiate on our terms?"

Jasnah folded her arms, pensive. Wit, however, leaned in. "You know," Wit whispered, "I think he might be right. I feel ashamed to admit it, but the Blackthorn has seen further than we have, Jasnah. He is more valuable as a Bondsmith than as a general—or even a king."

"You make a good argument, Uncle," Jasnah admitted. "I'm simply worried. If your powers are so incredible, it feels dangerous to experiment with them. My own first forays into Soulcasting were deadly at times. What will your greater abilities do, by accident, in similar situations?"

It was a valid point, one that left them solemn as they picked up cups of wine and drank in silence, thinking. As they stood there, Prince Kmakl passed by on his way out of the tent, listening as a scribe read him a draft of a letter to the merchant lords of Thaylen City.

"Another topic, Uncle," Jasnah noted. "Lately, I see your eyes narrow when you look at Prince Kmakl. I thought you liked Fen and her husband."

"I do like them," he said. "I just don't like how much bureaucracy Fen has to go through before anything gets done. The Azish are even worse. Why name your ruler an 'emperor' if he has to get approval from a dozen different functionaries to do his job?"

"One is a constitutional monarchy, the other a scholarly republic," Jasnah said, sounding amused. "What did you expect?"

"A king to be a king," he muttered, drinking the rest of his wine in one gulp.

"Both of their governments go back centuries," Jasnah said. "They've had generations to refine their processes. We'd do well to learn from them." She eyed him, thoughtful. "The days of absolute power in one person's hands will likely soon pass us by. I wouldn't be surprised if I'm the last true Alethi monarch."

"What would your father say, hearing you talk like that?"

"I suspect I could make him understand," she said. "He was interested in his legacy. Building something that would span generations. His goals were laudable, but his methods . . . well, our kingdom has been difficult to maintain. A king ruling by the gauntlet and sword can easily see it slip away when he weakens. Compare this to the Azish system, where a bad Prime is unable to single-handedly ruin their government."

"And a good one is unable to accomplish much," Dalinar said, then held his hand up to forestall further argument. "I see what you're saying. But I find nobility in the traditional way of rule."

"Having read the histories, I believe the nobility you imagine is created from stories *about* the inhabitants of ancient days, but rarely possessed by said inhabitants. Those kings tended to live short, brutal lives. No matter. Once we win this war, I expect to have decades to persuade you."

Kelek help him. Dalinar poured himself more orange wine.

"I will think on what you said about your powers," Jasnah said, "and I will see if I can offer any advice on how to proceed. For now, Uncle, know that I trust your judgment in this, and will help support the Mink if you take a smaller role in war planning. You are right, and I was wrong to question."

"One is never wrong to question," Dalinar said. "You taught me that."

She patted his arm fondly, then walked off to turn her attention to the maps the Mink was marking up on the war table.

Wit lingered, smiling at Dalinar. "I agree with her," he whispered. "And on the topic of monarchs, I will have you know that *I* find you to be an endearing despot. You're so pleasant, I *almost* don't find it horrifying that I'm living among a people willing to trust a single man with near-absolute power over the lives of hundreds of thousands—while completely ignoring proper checks and balances upon his potential greed, jealousy, or ambition."

"Did you really have to come with us, Wit?" Dalinar asked. "I . . ." He trailed off. Then shook his head.

"What?" Wit asked.

"Never mind. Saying anything would provide you with more rocks to throw at me."

"And you're supposed to be the dumb one," Wit said, grinning. "When have I ever mocked you, though?"

"All the time, Wit. You mock everyone."

"Do I? Do I really? Hmmm . . ." He tapped his chin. "I'm gainfully employed as Queen's Wit, and she expects me to provide only the best of mockery on her behalf. I need to be careful about simply giving it away. Who is going to buy the cow, and all that."

Dalinar frowned. "What is a cow?"

"Big, juicy, delicious. Wish I could still eat them. You don't seem to have them around here, which I find amazing, as I'm sure there was one somewhere in Sadeas's lineage. Paternal grandfather perhaps. Watch the highprinces. There's almost certainly going to be a show." He sauntered off to take his customary position near Jasnah.

Watch the highprinces? What did that mean? For the most part, they were becoming a useful lot. Aladar kept reinforcing Dalinar's trust in him, and Dalinar had sent him to oversee the withdrawal in Alethkar. Hatham had fallen into line, and Dalinar had him watching the supply chain from Azimir. Bethab was proving quite useful as an ambassador stationed in Thaylen City—or, well, his wife was the useful one, but they were both proving helpful. Roion was dead with honors, his son carefully chosen to not make things difficult. Even *Sebarial* was relevant these days.

One highprince was currently with Dalinar in Emul. Ruthar. Dalinar focused on the brawny, bearded man. He was the worst of those left; he fancied himself a soldier, but had never worn a proper uniform in his life. Today he hovered near the far end of the bar, by the strong wines. At least he'd learned to stop contradicting Dalinar in front of the other monarchs.

Dalinar narrowed his eyes toward Jasnah, who was making a display of going over the battle plans with the Mink. *She's putting on a show,* he thought, noting how she specifically called out details on the maps, suggesting troop arrangements. She did a fair job, though she was no general.

The Mink listened to her suggestions, but likely wouldn't take many of them. He seemed to find her fascinating. Well, Jasnah was a rare gemstone for certain. Was her show for the Mink? No . . . this had to do with Ruthar, didn't it?

Further musings were interrupted as a figure in blue entered the tent. Lyn the Windrunner wore her hair in a braid, though wisps had pulled free during her flight. She'd led the most recent scouting of Urithiru.

Dalinar waved her over, and noted Jasnah at the map table quieting and turning to listen as Lyn gave her report.

"We met with the soldier the queen sent," the Windrunner explained, saluting. "I myself tried to step through the invisible barrier and approach. I dropped to the snow like I'd taken a hit straight to the jaw. The soldier had to drag me out to the others."

"Did you see my wife?"

"No, sir," Lyn said. "But that hike . . . it looks brutal. Radiants can't get within hundreds of yards of the tower, so this soldier has to march all the way back and forth along the ridges for hours to get to where he can send messages."

Dalinar rubbed his chin in thought. Navani's messages seemed trustworthy, and she cautioned patience. But passcodes were not foolproof, and something about this just felt wrong. "What can you see from a distance? Anything?"

"We had to use spyglasses," Lyn said. "There weren't as many people out as usual, but there were some Windrunners on the roof, and I think I made out Teft up there, and Isom the Lightweaver. They held up a big sign, with glyphs that we *think* read 'patience' and 'progress.'"

Dalinar nodded. "Thank you, Radiant. Go give a full report, with details, to Brightness Teshav, then get something to eat."

"Thank you, sir," she said. She started toward the exit.

Something nagged at Dalinar, however. That weight hadn't *completely* eased. "Lyn?" he called.

"Sir?"

"The enemy has Lightweavers. Or at least something similar."

"Yes, sir," she said. "Though the only confirmed report we have of them is that incursion at the Thaylen vault a year ago."

He resisted shooting a glance at Szeth—so quiet, so easy to forget—standing nearby, wearing the face of an Alethi man.

"Ask Companylord Sigzil to send another team of scouts later tonight," Dalinar said. "I'll infuse the traveling gemstones for another run. Have this new team watch the tower from a distance, hidden, then report anything suspicious they might see."

"Wise suggestion, sir," Lyn said, then bowed and retreated.

Jasnah nodded to him, then returned to her exaggerated discussion of the maps. Yes, she *was* acting a role here.

Dalinar glanced at Ruthar, whose face was steadily growing redder. Perhaps he'd had a few drinks too many while waiting for the monarchs to finish their planning, but plainly he did *not* like how Jasnah was blatantly interjecting herself into the war plans. It was a masculine art, and Ruthar had been forbidden from participating in the planning today.

Looking at him, it was hard not to agree with what Jasnah had said about Alethkar. Gavilar's grand unification of the kingdom hadn't lasted ten years past his death before essentially breaking into civil war. Alethi squabbling had ended up favoring men like Ruthar. Oily, belligerent, aggressive. The last representation of old Alethkar.

Jasnah was making herself into bait. And Ruthar bit. Hard.

"Am I the only one seeing this?" Ruthar asked a little too loudly to his attendants. "I didn't say anything when she was made queen. Other nations have queens. But are any of *them* in this room interrogating a general?"

One of his companions tried to calm him, but he brushed her off, shouting, "It's a disgrace! Dalinar writing? He might as well put on a havah and start painting. We *deserve* the judgments of the Almighty, after giving the throne to a godless wh—" He stopped himself just in time, perhaps realizing how still the tent had grown.

Dalinar stepped forward to berate the man. There was nothing for it now but to—

"Wit," Jasnah said, her voice cold.

Wit strode forward, his hands spread to the sides, as if stepping out from behind curtains to face an adoring crowd. "I see you're envious of those more skilled in the masculine arts than you, Ruthar," Wit said. "I agree, you could use lessons on how to be a man—but those in this room would teach lessons far too advanced. Let me call in a eunuch to instruct you, and once you've reached his level, we'll talk further."

"Harsher," Jasnah said.

"You speak of honor, Ruthar, though you've never known it," Wit said, his voice rising. "You'll never find it though. You see, I hid your honor in a place you could never find it: in the arms of someone who truly loves you."

"Wit," Jasnah said. "*Harsher.*"

"I've been speaking to your children, Ruthar," Wit said. "No, this part isn't a joke. Relis, Ivanar. Yes, I know them. I know a lot of things. Would you like to explain to the queen where Ivanar's broken arm last month *truly* came from? Tell me, do you beat your children because you're a sadist, or because you're a coward and they are the only ones who won't dare fight back? Or . . . oh, silly Wit. It's both, isn't it?"

"How *dare* you!" Ruthar roared, shoving away the attendant who tried to control him. Angerspren rose around his feet, like pools of bubbling blood. "I demand trial by swords! Me versus you, stupid fool. Or me against your champion, if you're too much of a coward to face me!"

"Trial by combat accepted," Wit said lightly, undoing his belt and sliding free his sheathed sword. "Shall we?"

"Fine!" Ruthar said, drawing his sword, causing many of the women and attendants to scatter to the sides of the large tent.

"This is idiocy," Dalinar said, stepping between them. "Ruthar, you've been baited. Killing a Queen's Wit is punishable by exile and forfeit of title. You *know* this."

Ruthar grunted, the words sinking in.

"Besides," Dalinar said, glancing over his shoulder, "that man is no simple Wit. I'm not sure if you *can* kill him."

"You tell me I'd forfeit my title," Ruthar growled. "What title? What *lands* do I hold? And exile? We are *in* exile, Blackthorn. Maybe I should challenge you. You've lost our kingdom, and now you expect me to waste my time in foreign lands? Protecting those we should have conquered? We *would* have, if your nephew had been half the man his father was."

"Ruthar," Wit said, "you don't need to fight him. Or me. I accept your challenge, but I exercise my right to choose a champion. You won't risk losing your lands by killing a Wit."

"Excellent," Ruthar said. "I accept. Stop trying to interfere, Blackthorn."

Dalinar reluctantly stepped to the side. He felt a mounting dread, but there was nothing illegal here. And he doubted any action he could take would prevent this trap from springing.

"So," Ruthar said, brandishing his sword. "Wit. You call *me* coward, then wiggle out of a challenge? So be it! Who do you want me to kill, then?"

"Your Majesty?" Wit said. "If you don't mind?" He cocked his sheathed sword to the side, hilt out, as Jasnah brushed past and drew the weapon—a thin, silvery blade that Dalinar didn't think he'd ever seen unsheathed.

Dalinar's dread deepened as Jasnah stepped into striking range, batting aside Ruthar's sword. He recovered from his shock and blocked her next strike. She was better than Dalinar might have expected, but her stance was uncertain, and she overreached. At best, she was equal to a promising student.

She had two distinct advantages though. She was Radiant. And Ruthar was an idiot.

"I refuse this," he said, tossing his sword aside. "I will not face a woman in combat. It is demeaning."

And so, Jasnah stabbed him straight through the throat.

This lunge was better than the previous one, but it was not her skill that won the fight—it was the fact that Ruthar underestimated how far she would go. Indeed, Ruthar's eyes bulged as shockspren shattered around him as yellow glass. He stumbled back, gushing lifeblood across his beautiful doublet.

"Renarin!" Jasnah called.

Dalinar's younger son scrambled into the tent from outside, and the full level of her preparation became manifest. The twisting feeling in Dalinar's stomach began to release. He'd been preparing to lock down the tent, send guards for Ruthar's next of kin, and institute martial law.

Renarin scurried forward and used his powers as a Truthwatcher to heal Ruthar, sealing up the wound in the man's neck before he bled out. Still, Dalinar caught the eye of Fisk, the current captain of the Cobalt Guard. He was a solid fellow, bearer of the Blade Loremaker. Fisk nodded in understanding, and covertly signaled his soldiers to create a perimeter around the tent—nobody in or out—until Dalinar was ready to let news of this incident spread.

Jasnah held Wit's sword out to her side, and he took it, clicking his tongue. "Not willing to wipe the blood off first, Brightness? I suppose this is the sword's first kill. Adonalsium knows, I could never give her that myself. Still." He wiped the weapon clean with a white handkerchief, glancing at Ruthar. "I'll be billing you for a new handkerchief."

Both Wit and Jasnah pointedly ignored the horrified expressions of the room's attendants. The standout exception was the Mink, who was grinning at the show. Dalinar almost expected him to begin applauding.

Dalinar felt no such mirth. Although she hadn't gone all the way, he didn't like Jasnah's statement. Duels of passion were—if not common—an accepted part of Alethi culture. He himself had killed more than one man at a feast or other gathering. It was reminiscent, however, of their barbaric days as broken princedoms. Times that the Alethi tried to pretend had never happened. These days, this sort of thing was supposed to be handled in a more civilized way, with formal challenges and duels in arenas days later.

"Ruthar," Jasnah said, standing above him. "You have insulted me thrice tonight. First, by implying a queen should not take concern for the welfare of her own armies. Second, by threatening to assault my Wit, a man who is an extension of the royal will. Third and worst of all, by judging me unfit to defend myself, despite my calling as a Knight Radiant.

"As you have died tonight, and I have bested you legally in combat, I name you forfeit of your title. It will pass to your eldest son, who has been speaking quite frankly with Wit recently. It seems he will make a far more fitting highprince."

"That bastard!" Ruthar croaked. "That traitorous bastard!"

"Not yours then, is he?" Wit said. "That explains why I like him."

"What you do from here is your choice," Jasnah said. "Unfortunately, by the time you leave this tent, you will find that your princedom has quite thoroughly moved on. You'll be barred entrance to your own camp, should you try to return. I suggest you join the military as a new recruit. Alternatively, you may take up the queen's charity at the Beggars' Feasts and poorhouses."

She left him gaping on the floor and touching his healed neck—still wet with blood. Renarin awkwardly hurried after Jasnah as she moved over to the map table.

Wit dropped his bloody handkerchief before Ruthar. "How remarkable," he said. "If you spend your life knocking people down, you eventually find they won't stand up for you. There's poetry in that, don't you think, you storming personification of a cancerous anal discharge?"

Dalinar marched up beside Jasnah at the table. Szeth stayed close behind him, carefully watching Ruthar, silent but making certain Dalinar's back was guarded. Renarin stood with his hands in his pockets and refused to meet Dalinar's gaze. The boy likely felt guilty for keeping this little plan quiet, though Dalinar wasn't angry at him. Denying Jasnah was next to impossible in situations like this.

"Don't glare at me, Uncle," Jasnah said softly. "It was a lesson I had to give. Ruthar was a mouthpiece for many other discontented grumblings."

"I had assumed," he said, "that you of all people would wish to teach your lessons *without* a sword."

"I would much prefer it," she said. "But you cannot tame a feral axehound with kind words. You use raw meat."

She eyed the still-stunned people in the tent. They were all quite deliberately staying away from Ruthar. Dalinar met Fisk's eyes, then nodded again. The lockdown could be eased. Ruthar's closest allies were fickle, and would see his fallen state as a disease to be avoided. Jasnah had already secured the loyalty of those who could have been dangerous—his family and military advisors.

"You should know," Dalinar said, "that I found this entire experience distasteful. And not only because you didn't warn me it was going to happen."

"That is *why* I didn't warn you," Jasnah said. "Here. This may calm you." She tapped a paper she'd set onto the map table, which the Mink picked up and began reading with great interest. He looked like he hadn't been so entertained in years.

"A draft of a new law," the short man said. "Forbidding trial by sword. How unexciting."

Jasnah plucked the paper from his fingers. "I will use my own *unfortunate* experience today as an example of why this is a terrible tradition. Ruthar's blood will be the last such spilled. And as we leave this era of barbarism, each and every attendant at court will know that Alethkar's first queen is a woman unafraid of doing what needs to be done. Herself."

She was firm, so Dalinar tucked away his anger, then turned to leave. A part of him understood her move, and it *was* likely to be effective. Yet at the same time, it displayed that Jasnah Kholin—brilliant, determined—was not perfect. There were things about her that unnerved even the callous soldier that lived deep inside him.

As he walked away, Renarin hurried over. "Sorry," the boy whispered. "I didn't know she hadn't told you."

"It's all right, son," Dalinar said. "I suspect that without you, she'd have gone through with the plan anyway—then left him to bleed out on the floor."

Renarin ducked his head. "Father. I've . . . had an episode."

Dalinar stopped. "Anything urgent?"

"No."

"Can I find you later today, maybe tomorrow?" Dalinar asked. "I want to help contain the fallout from this stunt."

Renarin nodded quickly, then slipped out of the tent. Ruthar had stumbled to his feet, holding his neck, his gaudy yellow outfit now ruined. He searched around the room as if for succor, but his former friends and attendants were quietly slipping away—leaving only soldiers and the queen, who stood with her back to him. As if Ruthar were no longer worth attention.

Wit stood in his jet-black suit, one hand on the map table, leaning at a nearly impossible angle. Dalinar often found Wit with a grin on his face, but not today. Today the man looked cold, emotionless. His eyes were deep voids, their color invisible in the dim light.

They maneuvered Ruthar expertly, Dalinar thought. *Forced him to make all the wrong moves. Could . . . I do something similar in facing Odium?* Anger the god somehow, forcing him to accept a reckless agreement?

How did one intimidate a creature as powerful as Odium? What, on all of Roshar, could a god possibly fear or hate so much? He'd have to bring up the matter with Jasnah and Wit. Though . . . not today.

Today he'd had enough of their machinations.

*This song—this tone, this rhythm—sounds so familiar, in ways I
cannot explain or express.*

—From *Rhythm of War*, page 5

Only the femalens among your staff read?" Raboniel asked to
Craving as they stood in the hallway outside the room with the
crystal pillar. "I would have thought better of your instruction,
Venli, considering how capable you are in other areas. Your staff shouldn't
follow foolish human customs."

Venli's staff of singers—the ones carefully recruited in Kholinar over
the last year—had arrived in Urithiru via the Oathgate transfers early
this morning. Raboniel had immediately put them to work. Nearby, the
femalens were sorting through the boxes of notes and equipment
the human queen had moved out into the hallway. Young human scribes
were adding to that, repositioning boxes, making a general scene of
chaos.

Venli's staff, at Raboniel's order, were doing their best to make sense
of it—and to read through the pages and pages of notes to try to find
important points to bring to Raboniel's attention. They would soon take
scholarform to help, but the task was still difficult. Venli had instructed
them to do their best.

Today, Raboniel stood with her back to the blue shield, watching the
confusion in the hallway and humming to herself.

Venli hummed to Indifference. "Ancient One," she said, "my staff are
good—but they are culturally Alethi. My own people, the listeners, would

have happily taught them a better way—but the listeners were taken by Odium, in his wisdom."

"Do you question Odium, Venli?" Raboniel said to Craving.

"I have been taught that Passion does a person credit, Ancient One," Venli said. "And to wonder, to question, is a Passion."

"Indeed. Yet there are many among the Fused who think such Passions should be denied to everyone but themselves. You might find Odium shockingly like one of us in this regard. Or perhaps instead we are like him." She nodded toward the mess of human scribes and Venli's staff, working in near-perpetual motion like a pile of cremlings feasting after the rain. "What do you think of this?"

"If I had to guess, the human queen seems to be *trying* to make a mess."

"She's creating ways to stall that won't appear like purposeful interference," Raboniel said to Ridicule, though she seemed more amused than angry. "She complains that she doesn't have enough space, and constantly reshuffles these boxes to buy time. Also, I suspect she's trying to establish a presence outside the room—even if just in this hallway—so that she has a better chance of putting her people where they can overhear what we're saying. She seems to be getting more information than I expected; some of her people might be able to speak my language."

"I find that difficult to believe, Lady of Wishes. From what I've been led to understand, it wasn't but a year ago that they finally figured out how to read the Dawnchant."

"Yes, curious," Raboniel said, smiling and speaking to Craving. "Tell me, Venli. Why is it you serve so eagerly after knowing what Odium did to your people?"

Timbre pulsed in worry, but Venli had already prepared an answer. "I knew that only the very best among us would earn his favor and reward. Most were simply not worthy."

Raboniel hummed softly, then nodded. She returned to her own work, studying the shield around the pillar. "I'm waiting on reports of the Pursuer's sweep of the upper floors of the first tier. As well as news of his search for Radiants."

"I will go immediately and ask, Ancient One," Venli said, stepping away.

"Venli," Raboniel said. "Many mortals in the past sought elevation to stand among the Fused. You should know that, after our initial elevation, he never again granted such a lofty gift to a mortal."

"I . . . Thank you, Ancient One." She hummed to Tribute and withdrew, picking her way through the increasingly cluttered hallway. Within her, Timbre pulsed to Amusement. She knew that Venli had no aspirations of becoming a Fused.

"Do not be so quick to laud me," Venli whispered to the spren. "The person I was not so long ago would have been *thrilled* by the possibility of becoming immortal."

Timbre's pulses seemed skeptical. But she hadn't known Venli during that time—and as well she hadn't.

As Venli reached the end of the hallway, she was joined by Dul, the tall stormsetter who was in Venli's inner group of singers. The ones she'd been promising, over the last year, that she would help escape the Fused.

Today Dul wore mediationform, with an open face and smooth, beautiful carapace. He had a mostly red skin pattern with tiny hints of black, like submerged rocks in a deep red sea. He fell into stride with Venli as they walked out into the chamber with the stairs. As far as she knew, this large open room—in the shape of a cylinder—was the sole way up from the basement. They marched up the stairs that wound around the outside, passing over a section of hastily rebuilt steps, until they were far enough from others that no one would be able to overhear them.

She quickly checked Shadesmar. That place was strange, with glowing light suffusing everything, but best she could tell, no Voidspren were watching them. Here, isolated on the steps, she felt reasonably safe chatting.

"Report," she whispered.

"As you hoped," he replied as they walked, "we have been able to arrange the supply dumps from Kholinar to our benefit. Alavah and Ron are covertly making packs of supplies that will be easy to grab and take if we need them."

"Excellent," Venli said.

"I don't know how we'll escape without being spotted," Dul said. "Everyone is on edge in this place, and they have guards watching carefully outside for Alethi scouts."

"Something is going to happen, Dul," Venli said to Determination. "The humans will try to revolt, or an attack will come, or perhaps that captive queen will find a way to turn fabrials against the Fused.

"When that happens, whatever it is, we're going to be ready to run. I was led here through the mountains, and I memorized the route. We can sneak through those valleys, hiding from the Heavenly Ones in the tree cover. There *has* to be some out-of-the-way location up here in these wilds where a few dozen people can lose themselves to the world."

Dul paused on the steps, and hummed to Hope. He nearly seemed to have tears in his eyes.

"Are you all right?" Venli asked, stopping beside him.

He hummed a little louder. "After all this time, I can taste it, Venli. An escape. A way out."

"Be careful," she said. "We will need some kind of ploy to convince everyone we died, so they don't search for us. And we have to be very careful not to draw suspicion before that."

"Understood," he said, then hummed to Tension. "We've had a problem with Shumin, the new recruit."

She hummed to Reprimand.

"She tried recruiting others," Dul explained. "She's been implying she knows someone planning to start a rebellion against the Fused."

Venli hummed to Derision. She didn't normally use Odium's rhythms with her friends, but it fit the situation too well.

Dul sighed like a human. "It's the same old problem, Venli. The people willing to listen to us *are* going to be a little unreliable—if they were fully capable or smart, they wouldn't dare keep secrets from the Fused."

"So what does that say about you and me?" Venli asked.

"Pretty sure that was clearly implied," Dul said with a grin, speaking to Amusement.

"Isolate Shumin," Venli said. "We don't dare return her to Kholinar without supervision, but see if you can get her assigned to some kind of menial task without much time to interact with others. And emphasize to her *again* that she's not to recruit."

"Understood," he said softly to Consolation. He glanced upward, along the wide set of winding steps. "I hear the humans almost won here on these steps. No Radiants, and they stood against Fused and Regals."

"Briefly," Venli said. "But . . . yes, it was a sight. I almost wanted them to win."

"Is there a path for us there, Venli?" he asked to Pleading. "Go to them, help them, and get help in return?"

"You know far more about humans than I do," Venli said. "What do your instincts say?"

He glanced away. "They don't see us as people. Before, they wouldn't let me and Mazish marry. One of the only times I spoke to my master was to make that request—a single word, with as much passion as I could muster. He was angry that I *dared* talk to him. One storming word . . ."

He attracted an angerspren that prowled up the steps below him, like sparking lightning. Timbre pulsed morosely. Her kind had been treated similarly. Yet Venli found herself thinking about the fight on these steps. They were valiant, these humans. Though you obviously had to be careful not to let them get too much power over you.

"When you get back to the others," Venli said, continuing to climb, "put a few of our people on the crews that are gathering and caring for the unconscious Knights Radiant. We should watch them for an opportunity, just in case."

She had originally hoped they would be able to train her in her powers—but that seemed impossible now. She still didn't know if she'd be able to use them here without being detected, and was trying to think of a way to find the answer to that.

"Understood, Brightness." He nodded to her as they reached the top of the steps, then parted ways.

Venli hummed to Longing. She hoped she wasn't causing Dul to sing hopeless songs; though she spoke to Confidence, she didn't know whether there would be a chance for them to escape in the coming weeks. And the more time she spent with Raboniel, the more she worried. That Fused saw things she shouldn't be able to, piercing plots with keen eyes.

Each day Venli's people lived in secret was another chance for them to be exposed, taken quietly in the night, and either executed or forced to become hosts for the Fused. They needed what she'd promised: to live on their own, as their own nation. Could she really provide that though? Venli, who had never touched anything in her life without making a storm of it. She had gotten one people destroyed already.

Timbre pulsed consoling ideas as Venli made her way through the corridors.

"I wish I could believe, Timbre," she said softly. "I really wish I could. But you don't know what you're working with in me. You don't understand."

Timbre pulsed, inquisitive. She wanted to know. Venli had long remained silent about the more difficult parts of her past.

The time to share them, however, was long overdue. "The worst of it began," Venli whispered, "when the humans visited us the second time. . . ."

52

A PATH TOWARD SAVING

EIGHT AND A HALF YEARS AGO

A delicate touch . . .'" Jaxlim said. "'To . . . To . . .'"

Venli froze. She looked up from her place by the wall, where she was using some paper—a gift from the humans—to play with letters and beats. Representations of sounds in a possible written language, like the humans used.

Her mother stood by the window, doing her daily recitations. The same calming songs, performed by the same beautiful voice that had been Venli's guide all her days. The foundation upon which she'd built her life.

"'A delicate touch . . .'" Jaxlim began again. But again she faltered.

"'Nimbleform has a delicate touch,'" Venli prompted. "'Gave the gods this form to many . . .'"

But her mother didn't continue singing. She stared out the window, silent, not even humming. It was the second time this week she'd completely forgotten a stanza.

Venli rose, setting aside her work and taking her mother's hand. She attuned Praise, but didn't know what to say.

"I'm merely tired," Jaxlim said. "From the stress of these strange days and their stranger visitors." The humans had promised to return, and since their departure months ago, the family had been abuzz with different ideas of what to do about the strange creatures.

"Go," Jaxlim said. "Find your sister. She said she'd come listen to a recitation, and at least learn the Song of Listing. I will get some sleep. That's what I need."

Venli helped her mother to the bed. Jaxlim had always seemed so strong, and indeed her body was fit and powerful. Yet she wobbled as she lay down, shaken. Not on the outside, but deep within.

Until recently, Jaxlim had *never* forgotten songs. To even suggest it would have been unthinkable.

Once her mother was situated, Venli attuned Determination and stepped out of their home—not into a forest clearing, but into a city. One of the ten ancient ones, surrounded by a broken wall and populated by the remnants of buildings.

Finding the humans had emboldened Venli's family. Bearing newly bestowed weapons, they'd marched to the Shattered Plains and claimed a place among the ten, defeating the family who had held it before them. Once, Venli would have walked tall and proud at that victory.

Today, she was too unsettled. She went searching, ignoring cries to Joy in greeting. Where was Eshonai? Surely she hadn't gone off again, not without telling her sibling and mother. . . .

Fortunately, Venli found her at a scouting tower, built up along the broken wall near the front gates of the city. Eshonai stood on the very top, watching out to the northwest, the direction the humans had come from.

"Venli!" she said, grabbing her arm and pulling her to the front of the flimsy wooden scout tower. "Look! That seems like smoke in the distance. From their campfires perhaps?"

Venli looked down at the wobbly tower. Was this safe?

"I've been thinking about what we can learn from them," Eshonai said to Excitement. "Oh, it will feel so good to show them to the rest of the families! That will stop everyone from doubting our word, won't it? Seeing the humans themselves!"

"That will feel good," Venli admitted. She knelt, holding to the wooden floor while Eshonai stood up on her toes. Storms! It looked like she was about to climb onto the railing.

"What must their cities be like?" Eshonai said. "I think I will leave with them this time. Travel the world. See it all!"

"Eshonai, no!" Venli said. And the true panic in her rhythm made Eshonai finally pause.

"Sister?" she asked.

Venli searched for the right words. To talk to Eshonai about their mother. About what . . . seemed to be happening. But she couldn't confront it. It was as if by voicing her fears, she'd make them real. She wanted to pretend it was nothing. As long as she could.

"You were supposed to come today," Venli said, "and listen to one of the songs. Maybe learn one again."

"We have you and Mother for that," Eshonai said, looking toward the horizon. "I haven't the mind for it."

But I need you with me, Venli thought. *With us. Together.*
I need my sister.

"I'm going to lead a scout group to go investigate that smoke," Eshonai said, moving toward the ladder. "Tell Mother for me, will you?"

She was gone before Venli could say anything. A day later, Eshonai came back triumphant. The humans had indeed returned.

∴

It didn't take long for Venli to find the humans tedious.

Though they'd barely noticed her on the first visit, this time they wouldn't leave her alone. They wanted to hear the songs over and over. It was so frustrating! They couldn't replicate the songs if they *did* memorize them—they couldn't hear the rhythms.

Worse, when she performed, the humans kept interrupting and asking for more information, more explanations, more accurate translations. *Infuriating,* she thought, attuned to Irritation. She'd started to learn their language because Jaxlim insisted, but it didn't seem a good use of her time or her talents. The humans should learn *her* language.

When they finally let her go for the day, she stepped out of the building and welcomed the sunlight. Sitting outside were three of those dull-minded, stupid "parshmen" who didn't have songs. Seeing them made Venli uncomfortable.

Was that what the humans thought *she* was like? Some simpleton? Some of her family tried to talk to the parshmen, but Venli stayed away. She didn't like how they made her feel. They weren't her people, any more than the humans were.

She scanned the bustling city, noting the crowds of listeners nearby. The humans drew so many gawkers. Listeners from many families—even lowly ones who didn't have a city—came to catch a glimpse. Lines of people of all varieties of skin patterns stuffed the streets, meaning that Venli was crowded as she pushed through them.

"They probably won't come out for a while yet," she said to Reprimand to a group of listeners she didn't recognize.

"You are the apprentice keeper of songs," one of them said, "of the family who discovered the humans." He said it to Awe, which made Venli pause. So he knew of her, did he?

"I am no apprentice," she said. "I am simply waiting, as is respectful, upon my mother's word before I take my place."

She glanced back toward the building she'd left. Like many in the city, it was made of ancient walls covered in crem, with a roof of carapace. The humans had been allowed to make camp here, *inside* the walls, with their tents and their strange wooden vehicles that could withstand a storm. It seemed unfair that their *moving* structures should last better than the buildings the listeners built.

"I've spent many hours with them so far," Venli said to Consideration. "What would you know of them? I can tell you."

"Do they really lack souls?" asked a female in mateform. Silly things. Venli intended to never adopt that form.

"That's one theory," Venli said. "They can't hear the rhythms, and they seem dull of speech and mind. Makes me wonder why they were so difficult for our ancestors to fight."

"They work metal as if it were wax," another said. "Look at that armor."

"Far less practical than carapace would be," Venli said.

"We don't have carapace armor anymore," another said.

That was true, of course; their current forms *didn't* have much carapace. Most of what they knew about grander forms such as warform came from the songs. And Venli, infuriatingly, hadn't made progress in discovering that one.

Still, wouldn't growing your own armor be much better than what the humans did? Well, she answered a few more questions, though she wished for the listeners to notice how tired she was from reciting songs all day. Couldn't they at least have fetched her something to drink?

Eventually she moved on, and tried to push through her bad mood. She should probably enjoy reciting songs for the humans—she did enjoy the music. But she didn't miss that Jaxlim always had them come to Venli. Her mother didn't want to be seen making a mistake by anyone, particularly not these humans.

Deep down, that was probably the real source of Venli's irritation. The knot of worry that festered in her gut, making her feel helpless. And alone.

Nearby, on the street, listeners changed their rhythms. Venli suspected what it was before she turned and saw Eshonai striding down the street. Everyone knew her, of course. The one who had discovered the humans.

Venli almost went to her. But why? There was never any comfort to be found in her presence. Only more talk of the human world, their cities and their mystery. And no talk of the real problems at home Eshonai continued to ignore.

So instead, Venli slipped between two small buildings and emerged onto a street on the other side. Maybe she could go to the fields and see Demid. She started that way . . . then stopped. No, they had decided not to show the humans how they used Stormlight to grow plants. The songs cautioned that this secret should not be shared. So they weren't working the fields, and Demid wouldn't be there.

Instead Venli made her way down to the plateaus, where she could be alone. Just her and the lifespren. She attuned Peace to check the time, then settled down and stared over the broken plateaus, trying to soothe her worry about her mother. Worry that she would have to take over being keeper of songs, as she'd claimed she was to those listeners—a boast that now seemed far too puffed up.

Venli didn't want to replace Jaxlim. She wanted to go back to the way things had been before the humans arrived.

The moment she thought that, she saw a human female leave the city above and come walking in her direction. Venli sighed. Couldn't they leave her for one movement? Well, they all assumed she couldn't speak their language, and so she could play dumb. And . . . it wouldn't require much pretending. Their rhythmless dead language was hard to understand.

The female gestured for permission, then sat next to Venli. She was the one with the rings on her exposed hand. Some kind of surgeon, Venli had been told. She didn't seem important. Most everyone ignored her—she was basically one of the servants.

"It's quite impressive, isn't it?" the human said *in the listener tongue,* looking over the Shattered Plains. "Something terrible must have happened here. Doesn't seem like those plateaus could have formed naturally."

Venli attuned Anxiety. The woman spoke the words without a rhythm, yes, but they were perfectly understandable.

"How . . ." Venli said, then hummed to Betrayal.

"Oh, I've always been good with languages," the female said. "My name is Axindweth. Though few here know me by that name, I give it to you."

"Why?"

"Because I think we're going to be friends, Venli," she said. "I've been sent to search out someone like you. Someone who remembers what your people used to be. Someone who wants to restore the glory that you've lost."

"We *are* glorious," Venli said, attuning Irritation and standing.

"Glorious?" Axindweth said. "Living in crem huts? Making stone tools because you've forgotten how to forge metal? Living all your lives in two forms, when you used to have dozens?"

"What do *you* know about any of this?" Venli said, turning to leave. Her mother would be very interested to hear one of the humans had been hiding the ability to speak their language.

"I know much about too many things," the woman said. "Would you like to learn how to obtain a form of power, Venli?"

Venli looked back. "We abandoned those. They are dangerous. They let the old gods control our ancestors."

"Isn't it odd," Axindweth said, "how much stock you put in what your ancestors said? A dusty old group of people that you've never met? If you gathered a collection of listeners from the other families, would you let *them* decide your future? That's all they were, your ancient ancestors. A random group of people."

"Not random," Venli said to Praise. "They had strength. They left their gods to find freedom."

"Yes," Axindweth said. "I suppose they did."

Venli continued on her way. Stupid human.

"There were forms of power that could heal someone, you know," the human said idly.

Venli froze in place. Then she spun, attuning Betrayal again. How did she know about Venli's mother?

"Yes," Axindweth said, toying with one of her rings, staring out away from Venli. "Great things were once possible for your people. Your ancestors, the ones you revere, might have been brave. But have you ever asked yourself about the things they didn't leave you in songs? Have you seen the holes in their stories? You bear the pain of their actions, living without forms for generations. Exiled. Shouldn't *you* have the choices they did, weighing forms of power against your current life?"

"How do you know all these things?" Venli demanded, walking back. "How do you know about forms of power? Who *are* you?"

The woman removed something from within her covered sleeve. A single glowing gemstone. Blood red.

"Take that into a storm," the woman said. "And break it. Inside, you will find a path toward saving those you love."

The woman stood and left the gem sitting on the rock.

...be made of polished bronze metal, but moves as smoothly as flesh. The faint grooves that lace their surface are unique to each individual.

Their pupils dilate, despite appearing to be holes poked in bronze orbs.

They have no eyelashes. When they have eyebrows, they are shaped of the same bronze substance as their skin.

Most Reachers maintain a form that closely matches human physiognomy, but on occasion there are unique variations.

The muscularity of their form does not appear to correlate directly with their relative strength. They do not require exercise or nutrition.

Their clothing choices are quite eclectic. From Azish wraps and patterns to Thaylen sailor garb, there seems to be no cohesive style to what they wear.

They appear in the Physical Realm as a small ball of white fire that pulses, emitting little rings of light in bursts. When they move they leave behind a glowing trail like that of a comet.

I am led to wonder, from experiences such as this, if we have been wrong. We call humans alien to Roshar, yet they have lived here for thousands of years now. Perhaps it is time to acknowledge there are no aliens or interlopers. Only cousins.

—From *Rhythm of War*, page 5 undertext

Timbre was uncharacteristically silent as Venli finished her account. Venli had taken the long way up to the sixth floor to gather reports for Raboniel, and had spent the time explaining about that day— the day she'd made her first choice down this path. The day she'd taken that gemstone, and hidden it from her mother and her sister.

Venli could tell herself all she wanted that her motives had been noble. She knew the truth. She'd kept that secret because she'd been afraid of losing the glory of discovering a new form to her sister.

Instead, the reverse had happened; Venli lived her sister's destiny. *Venli* had ended up with Timbre. *Venli* had become Radiant. Venli had *lived*. These were proof that the cosmere made mistakes.

Venli entered the refreshingly cool sixth-floor balcony room where scouting operations had been set up. Raboniel thought the humans had deliberately destroyed maps of the tower, so this group was making their own. Ruling this place was going to be a huge chore, one Venli was glad she didn't have to organize.

The singers here hummed to Praise as Venli entered, showing her respect. Even the two relayform Regals gave deference to a Voice such as Venli. She asked for, and was given, a wide range of reports on the activities up here.

Everything from the seventh floor up was unoccupied. Consequently, they were setting up checkpoints at each stairwell on the sixth floor, worried that panicked humans might try to hide on the many upper floors once confinement to quarters was relaxed. And confinement to quarters *would* need to be relaxed soon. The humans were running out of food and water. Venli suspected Raboniel would give the word for normal operations to recommence by the end of the day.

They'd found a large number of unconscious Radiants, many of whom had been in the homes of people trying to protect or hide them. Venli hummed to Derision as she scanned the list. The foolish people were lucky; Raboniel was more lenient than some Fused. She had ordered that anyone found keeping Radiants would be punished, and the Radiants executed— but that any Radiants revealed willingly would be spared.

It had been a wise move: many Radiants had been offered up after her announcement. The few found *later* had been executed, along with one member of each family hiding them. A stern but just application of the law. Timbre found it horrifying. Venli found it amazing Raboniel hadn't executed them all.

She wants these Radiants for something, she thought. *Something to do with her plans, her experiments.* Venli had not forgotten what had earned the Lady of Wishes her terrible reputation: an attempt long ago to create a disease that would end the war by exterminating all of humankind.

Well, Venli might have her own use for these Radiants. She listened with half an ear to the reports, until the relayform said something that drew her full attention.

"Wait," Venli said. "Repeat that?"

"A human surgeon killed one of our number during the investigations the other night," the malen said.

"I haven't heard of this," Venli said.

"We reported it at the time, and a Fused took charge immediately, so we assumed it had gotten back to Raboniel. This human took an unconscious Windrunner with him when he fled."

"Which Fused did you report this to?"

"The Pursuer."

Timbre pulsed worryingly.

"Do we have a description of this human surgeon?" Venli asked.

"Tall male," the Regal said. "Shoulder-length wavy hair. Slave brands. The soldier who witnessed the event claimed the human was glowing with Stormlight, but we suspect our soldier was merely rattled. He proved to be a coward, and has been assigned to waste detail."

Venli hummed to Thoughtfulness, though she felt a mounting dread. Kaladin Stormblessed was in the tower; he hadn't gone with the main bulk of his kind to the war in Emul. And he was . . . somehow still conscious? Leshwi would want to know that. She had asked Venli to watch over Raboniel specifically, but surely this was a matter deserving of her true master's attention.

"I see," Venli said to Thoughtfulness. "Has this human been found?"

"He fled to the upper floors," the Regal explained to Spite. "We searched and found nothing—even the Pursuer, who was certain the human was close, was unable to locate him."

"The Lady of Wishes will find this interesting," Venli said. "Send me word if anything more is discovered."

The Regal hummed to Command in acknowledgment, then gave Venli a list with descriptions of all the other Radiants surrendered to this group. Raboniel wanted them kept all in one room, being watched. Venli would have to put her people to work looking for a suitable location.

One conscious Windrunner, when all the others remained unconscious. Yes, she'd find a way to send a note about this to Leshwi. "The singer who saw the human kill our soldier," Venli said, moving to leave. "Give me his name and station. The Lady of Wishes may want me to interrogate him."

The Regal hummed to Derision. "The coward won't be able to tell you much. If the Lady of Wishes is truly interested in this murderous human, she should wait until this evening for another report."

"Why?"

"By then the Pursuer will have interrogated the human's family," the Regal said. "And will have exacted revenge for the death of our soldier."

The rhythms went silent. Timbre, hidden deep within Venli's gemheart, seemed to be holding her breath.

"We captured them, then?" Venli said.

"They're locked in the clinic a short way from here," the Regal said to Craving. "A surgeon, his wife, one child. We only now discovered they are the murderous human's family. It's a pity the Lady of Wishes has ordered us to be so tame during this occupation, but at least we'll get a little blood tonight."

Venli tried to hum to Conceit as she left, but found nothing. No rhythms at all—it was unnerving. She shoved the list of descriptions in her pocket, and as soon as she was a short way from the scout post she hissed, "What are you doing?"

Timbre pulsed, and the rhythms slowly returned. Venli relaxed. For a moment she'd worried something was wrong.

Timbre pulsed morosely. To her, something *was* wrong.

"I agree that it's unfortunate about the Windrunner's family," Venli said. "But at the same time, their son *was* involved in killing one of our troops."

Timbre pulsed again.

"I suppose they *aren't* our troops," Venli agreed. "But why do you care so much? Don't you hate humans?"

That drew a sharp rebuke. Just because Timbre and the other Reachers had decided not to bond humans any longer, it didn't mean she *hated* them. And killing someone's family because they resisted? That *was* terrible. Many Fused wouldn't take that step, but the Pursuer—and his troops . . . well, she'd heard the bloodthirst in that relayform's rhythms.

Venli walked in silence, troubled. She had her own business to see to, her own problems. Yet Timbre continued to pulse softly, urging her. Venli had seen the Blackthorn once in a vision. The Bondsmith. He'd shown her kindness. And so many of the humans of this tower, they were just people trying to live their lives.

Eshonai would have done something.

"I'm a fraud, Timbre," Venli whispered. "A fake Radiant. I don't know what I'm doing."

Timbre pulsed. The meaning was clear.

I do.

It was enough. Venli turned and started down the steps, picking up speed as she went. There wasn't much Venli could do directly to help the family. Her authority as Voice certainly wouldn't extend to countering the will of the Pursuer.

Instead she made her way to the majestic atrium of the tower. This enormous opening far within the tower reminded her of the shaft that led to the basement—a circular breach in the stone. Only this was on a far grander scale, over a hundred feet wide. It stretched tall, high into the darkness above, and seemed to reach all the way to the very top.

Lifts ran up and down the inside of the atrium, though they needed Voidlight to work now. The far wall—pointed directly east—was not stone, but instead a flat glass window. Amazingly large, it showed snow-covered peaks and provided natural light to the entire atrium.

The lifts were barely in use, as the singers were focused on establishing control of the lower floors. To avoid alerting human Windrunner scouts, the *shanay-im* were forbidden from soaring around outside. They'd taken up residence here instead, within this grand hall, hovering in the open air. Venli used her authority to commandeer a lift, then made her way up to the fifteenth floor. Here she found Leshwi meditating with her long clothing drifting beneath her, with only two servants to see to her needs. She'd donated the others to Raboniel.

Leshwi noticed Venli immediately, cracking an eye. Venli sent the two servants away and hummed to Craving, standing patiently and waiting for her mistress to formally acknowledge her. Leshwi drifted over to the balcony and rested one hand on the railing.

Venli approached quickly, humming to Tribute.

"Why have you not approached in secret, as I explained?" Leshwi demanded.

Leshwi had set up a method for Venli to clandestinely deliver notes about Raboniel. Venli found the whole thing a baffling part of Fused politics. Raboniel knew that Venli was spying, and Leshwi knew that Raboniel knew, yet they both pretended the subterfuge was unknown.

"The Windrunner you wish to defeat is here in the tower," Venli said, "and I have reason to believe he did not fall unconscious. In fact, he still has access to his powers."

Leshwi hummed abruptly to Exultation. A telling choice.

"Where?" Leshwi said.

"He killed a soldier who was trying to collect the unconscious Radiants," Venli said, "then escaped into the tower. He rescued one other Windrunner."

"Honor propels him," Leshwi said, "even now. Even after his god's death. This is excellent news, Venli. You did well to break protocol to bring me this. Does the Pursuer know?"

"Yes, unfortunately."

"Raboniel will let him ignore my prior claim," Leshwi said. "He won't even be reprimanded for it, so long as it is in service of hunting a fugitive. Poor Stormblessed. He has given them the spear by which to impale him. If I wish to fight him myself, I will need to locate him first."

"And *do* you wish to fight him, Ancient One?" Venli asked. "Is that truly why you want to find him? To kill him?"

"Why would you ask this?" Leshwi asked to Craving.

Venli would have let it die at that, feeling foolish. But Timbre pulsed, nudging her.

"You seem to respect him," Venli said.

Leshwi hummed softly, but Venli did not catch the rhythm. Odd. Her powers normally let her understand anything her mistress said or implied. There *was* something familiar about that rhythm though.

"It is rare to find a human who can fight in the skies well enough to be a challenge for me," Leshwi said. "And his spren . . . I hear she is ancient. . . . But never mind that. You will not raise this matter with me again."

Timbre pulsed, indicating Venli should *tell* her mistress. About them. About being *Radiant*.

Stupidity. Venli immediately shied back at the idea. Leshwi would kill her.

"Is there something else?" Leshwi said to Command.

"Stormblessed's family is being held by the Pursuer's guards," Venli said. "They are on the sixth floor, in a clinic at the perimeter, near the main corridor. The Pursuer plans to interrogate them, and I fear it will turn ugly. Many of his troops are angry they were forbidden to kill during the incursion. They are . . . excitable."

"Violent and bloodthirsty, you mean."

"Yes, Ancient One. The . . . the family of the Windrunner would be an excellent resource for us, mistress. If you wish to find him before the Pursuer, then perhaps holding them would give us an advantage."

Leshwi hummed to Thoughtfulness. "You are merciful, Venli. Do not reveal this Passion to others. Wait here."

Leshwi pushed off and soared downward, doing a loop and turning gracefully into the lit central corridor on the sixth floor. Venli waited, Timbre pulsing in concern.

It took a good hour for Leshwi to finally return, soaring upward from the direction of the large market on the ground floor.

"What did you do?" Venli asked.

"I took the Windrunner's family into my custody," Leshwi said. "My position gives me authority over the Pursuer."

"You didn't hurt them, did you?" Venli asked to Pleading.

Leshwi stared at her, and only after a moment did Venli realize she'd slipped and used one of the old rhythms. Pleading was one of Roshar's rhythms, not Odium's.

"I did not," Leshwi said. "And now that I've moved—and extended myself in this way—the Pursuer won't dare harm them. At least not unless the power dynamic shifts in the tower. I placed the family in a safe location and told them to remain hidden. We might need them, as you indicated."

Venli hummed to Subservience.

"Find a place where we can watch them, then send me a note. I will consider if there is a way to use them to find Stormblessed, and for now will spread a rumor that I have disposed of them. Even if the Pursuer finds the truth, though, they should be safe for the time being. That said, I give warning again: You must *not* let others see your compassion for humans. It will be misconstrued, particularly with you being the child of traitors."

"Yes, Ancient One."

"Go," she said. "I consider what I have done here today a favor to you. Do not forget it."

Venli hummed to Subservience and left quickly. Timbre pulsed encouragingly.

"I *am* a false Radiant," Venli said. "You know this."

Timbre pulsed again. Perhaps. But today had been a step in the right direction.

*It would have been so easy if Voidlight and Stormlight destroyed
one another. Such a simple answer.*

—From *Rhythm of War*, page 6

"Grampa," little Gavinor asked. "Was my daddy brave when he
died?"

Dalinar settled down on the floor of the small room, setting
aside the wooden sword he'd been using to play at a greatshell hunt. Had
Adolin ever been this small?

He was determined not to miss so much of Gav's life as he had his
sons'. He wanted to love and cherish this solemn child with dark hair and
pure yellow eyes.

"He was very brave," Dalinar said, waving for the child to come sit
in his lap. "So very brave. He went almost alone to our home, to try to
save it."

"To save me," Gav said softly. "He died because of me."

"No!" Dalinar said. "He died because of evil people."

"Evil people . . . like Mommy?"

Storms. This poor child.

"Your mother," Dalinar said, "was also brave. She didn't do those terrible things; it was the enemy, who had taken over her mind. Do you
understand? Your mother loved you."

Gav nodded, serious beyond his years. He did like playing at greatshell
hunts, though he didn't laugh during them like other children would. He
treated even play as a somber occasion.

Dalinar tried to restart the pretend hunt, but the boy's mind seemed overshadowed by these dark thoughts. After just another few minutes, Gav complained that he was tired. So Dalinar let his nursemaid take him to rest. Then Dalinar lingered at the doorway, watching her tuck him into bed.

What five-year-old *wanted* to go to bed? Though Dalinar had not been the most dutiful parent, he did remember lengthy complaints from both Adolin and Renarin on evenings like this, when they insisted they *were* old enough to stay up and they did *not* feel tired. Gav instead clutched his little wooden sword, which he kept with him at all times, and drifted off.

Dalinar left the small home, nodding to the guards outside. The Azish thought it strange that the Alethi officers brought families to war, but how else were children to learn proper military protocol?

It was the evening following Jasnah's stunt with Ruthar, and Dalinar had spent most of the day—before visiting Gav—speaking via spanreed to highlords and highladies, smoothing over their concerns about the near execution. He'd made certain the legality of Jasnah's actions would not be questioned. And he'd personally talked to Relis, Ruthar's son.

The young man had lost a bout to Adolin back in the warcamps, and Dalinar had worried about his motivations now. However, it seemed that Relis was eager to prove he could be a loyalist. Dalinar had made certain that his father was taken to Azimir and given a small house there, where he could be watched. Regardless of what Jasnah said, Dalinar wouldn't have a former highprince begging for scraps.

Finally—after smoothing things over with the Azish, who did *not* appreciate Alethi trials by sword—he was feeling he had the situation under control. He stopped in the middle of the camp, thoughtful. He'd almost forgotten Renarin's talk of his episode the day before.

Dalinar turned and strode through the warcamp—a bustling illustration of organized chaos. Messengers ran this way and that, mostly wearing the patterned livery of the various Azish scribe orders. Alethi captains had their soldiers hauling supplies or marking the stone ground with painted lines to indicate directions.

A trail of wagons snaked in from the northwest, a lifeline to populated lands and fertile hills untouched by war. Fearing that this camp was already a big target, Dalinar had posted many of his Soulcasters in Azimir.

The landscape was different from what he knew. More trees, less grass, and strange fields of shrubs with interlocking branches that created vast snarls. Despite that, the signs he saw in this village were all too familiar. A bit of cloth trapped in the hardened crem beside the roadway. Burnt-out buildings, torched either out of a sadistic amusement, or to deny beds and stormshutters to the army that had moved in next. Those fires had been fed by homes with too many possessions left behind.

Engineers had continued to shore up the eastern stormwall, where a natural windbreak created a cleft. Normally this shoring process would have taken weeks. Today Shardbearers cut out stone blocks, which Windrunners made light enough to push into position with ease. The ever-present Azish functionaries were supervising.

Dalinar turned toward the Windrunner camp, troubled. Jasnah's stunt had overshadowed their conversation about monarchs and monarchies—but now that he dwelled on it, he found it as disturbing as the duel. The way Jasnah had talked . . . She had seemed *proud* of the idea that she might be Alethkar's last queen. She intended to see Alethkar left with some version of a neutered monarchy, like in Thaylenah or Azir.

How would the country function without a proper monarch? The Alethi weren't like these persnickety Azish. The Alethi liked real leaders, soldiers who were accustomed to making decisions. A country was like an army. Someone strong needed to be in charge. And barring that, someone *decisive* needed to be in charge.

The thoughts persisted as he neared the Windrunner camp and smelled something delicious on the air. The Windrunners continued a tradition begun in the bridge crews: a large communal stew available to anyone. Dalinar had originally tried to regulate the thing. However, while he usually found the Windrunners agreeable to proper military decorum, they had absolutely refused to follow proper quartermaster requisition and mess requirements for their evening stews.

Eventually Dalinar had done what any good commander did when faced by such persistent mass insubordination: He backed down. When good men disobeyed, it was time to look at your orders.

Today he found the Windrunners visited by an unusual number of Thaylens. The stews tended to attract whichever soldiers felt most out of place, and Dalinar suspected the Thaylens were feeling that way, being so far from the oceans. Companylord Sigzil was taking a turn at storytelling. Renarin was there too in his Bridge Four uniform, watching Sigzil with rapt attention. Regardless of war or storm, the boy tried to find his way to this fire every evening.

Dalinar approached, and only then did he realize the stir he was causing. Soldiers nudged one another, and someone ran to get him a stool. Sigzil paused in his story, saluting smartly.

They think I've come to approve of the tradition, Dalinar realized. They seemed to have been waiting for it, judging by how eagerly one of the Windrunner squires brought him a bowl. Dalinar accepted the food and took a bite, then nodded approvingly. That inspired applause. After that, there was nothing to do but settle down and keep eating, indicating that the rest of them could go on with their ritual.

When he glanced over at his son, Renarin was smiling. A reserved grin; you rarely saw teeth from Renarin. However, the lad didn't have his box out, the one he often used to occupy his hands. He was relaxed here among these people.

"That was good of you, Father," Renarin whispered, moving closer. "They've been waiting for you to stop by."

"It's good stew," Dalinar noted.

"Secret Horneater recipe," Renarin said. "Apparently it has only two lines of instructions. 'Take everything you have, and put him in pot. Don't let anyone airsick touch seasonings.'" Renarin said it fondly, but he hadn't finished his bowl. He seemed distracted. Though . . . he always seemed distracted. "I assume you're here to talk about . . . what I told you? The episode?"

Dalinar nodded.

Renarin tapped his spoon against the side of his bowl, a rhythmic click. He stared at the cookfire flamespren. "Does it strike you as cruel of fate, Father? My blood sickness gets healed, so I can finally be a soldier like I always wanted. But that same healing has given me another kind of fit. More dangerous than the other by far."

"What did you see this time?"

"I'm not sure I should say. I know I told you to come talk to me, but . . . I vacillate. The things I see, they're of him, right? I think *he* shows me what he wants. That's why I saw you becoming his champion." He glanced down at his bowl. "Glys isn't convinced the visions are bad. He says we're something new, and he doesn't think the visions are specifically from Odium—though perhaps his desires taint what we see."

"Any information—even if you suspect your enemy is feeding it to you—is useful, son. More wars are lost to lack of information than are lost to lack of courage."

Renarin set his bowl beside his seat. It was easy to fall into the habit of underestimating Renarin. He always moved in this deliberate, careful way. It made him seem fragile.

Don't forget, part of Dalinar thought. *When you were broken on the floor, consumed by your past, this boy held you. Don't forget who was strong, when you—the Blackthorn—were weak.*

The youth stood up, then gestured for Dalinar to follow. They left the circle of firelight, waving farewell to the others. Lopen called out, asking Renarin to "look into the future and find out if I beat Huio at cards tomorrow." It seemed a little crass to Dalinar, bringing up his son's strange disorder, but Renarin took it with a chuckle.

The sky had grown dim, though the sun wasn't fully set yet. These western lands were warmer than Dalinar liked—particularly at night. They didn't cool off as was proper.

The Windrunner camp was near the edge of the village, so they strolled out into the wilderness near some snarls of bushes and a few tall trees—with broad canopies—that had grown out of the center, perhaps somehow using the bushes for extra strength. This area was relatively quiet, and soon the two of them were alone.

"Renarin?" Dalinar asked. "Are you going to tell me what you saw?"

His son slowed. His eyes caught the light of the now-distant campfire. "Yes," he said. "But I want to get it right, Father. So I need to summon it again."

"You can *summon* it?" Dalinar said. "I thought it came upon you unexpectedly."

"It did," Renarin said. "And it will again. But right now, it simply is." He turned forward and stepped into the darkness.

∴

As Renarin stepped forward, the ground beneath his feet became dark glass, spreading from the heel of his boot. It cracked in a web of lines, a purposeful pattern, black on black.

Glys, who preferred to hide within Renarin, grew excited. He'd captured this vision as it came, so they could study it. Renarin wasn't quite so enthusiastic. It would be so much easier if he were like other Radiants.

Stained glass spread out around him, engulfing the landscape, a phantom light shimmering and glowing from behind in the darkness. As he walked, each of his footsteps made the ground pulse red, light shining up through the cracks. His father wouldn't be able to see what he did. But hopefully Renarin could describe it properly.

"I see you in this vision," Renarin said to his father. "You're in a lot of them. In this one you stand tall, formed as if from stained glass, and you wear Shardplate. Stark white Shardplate, though you are pierced with a black arrow."

"Do you know what it means?" Dalinar said, a shadow barely visible from behind the glass window depicting him.

"I think it might be a symbol of you, who you were, who you become. The more important part is the enemy. He makes up the bulk of this image. A window of yellow-white light breaking into smaller and smaller pieces, into infinity.

"He is like the sun, Father. He controls and dominates everything—and although your figure raises a sword high, it's facing the wrong direction. You're fighting and you're fighting, but not him. I think I understand the meaning: you want a deal, you want a contest of champions, but you're going to keep fighting, and fighting, and fighting distractions. Because why would the enemy agree to a contest that he can theoretically lose?"

"He already agreed," Dalinar said.

"Were terms set?" Renarin asked. "A date picked? I don't know if this vision is what he wants us to see. But either way . . . I don't think he's worried enough to agree to terms. He can wait, keep you fighting, keep *us* fighting. Forever. He can make this war so it never ends."

Dalinar stepped forward, passing through the stained glass that represented him—though he wouldn't know he had done so.

It seemed to Renarin as if his father never aged. Even in his earliest memories, Renarin remembered him looking like this—so powerful, so unchanging, so strong. Some of that was from the things his mother had told Renarin, building an image in his head of the perfect Alethi officer.

It was a tragedy that she hadn't lived to see Dalinar become the man she'd imagined him to be. A shame that Odium had seen her killed. That was the way Renarin *had* to present it to himself. Better to turn his pain against the enemy than to lose his father along with his mother.

"I have stared Odium in the eyes," Dalinar said. "I have faced him. He expected me to break. By refusing, I've upended his plans. It means he can be defeated—and equally important, it means he doesn't know everything or see everything."

"Yes," Renarin said, walking across broken glass to look up at the enormous depiction of Odium. "I don't think he's omnipresent, Father. Well, part of him is everywhere, but he can't access that information— any more than the Stormfather knows everything the wind touches. I think . . . Odium might see like I do. Not events, or the world itself, but *possibilities.*

"This war is dangerous for us, Father. In the past, the Heralds would organize our forces, fight with us for a time—but would then return to lock away the souls of the Fused in Damnation, preventing their rebirths. That way, each Fused we killed was an actual casualty. But the Oathpact is broken now, and the Fused cannot be locked away."

"Yes . . ." Dalinar said, moving to stand beside Renarin. "I've been thinking about this myself. Trying to determine if there was a way to restore the Oathpact, or to somehow otherwise make the enemy fear. This is new ground, for both us and Odium. There must be something about this new reality that unnerves him. Is there anything else you see?"

See the blackness that will be, Renarin? Glys said.

"Friction between the two of you," Renarin said, pointing up at the stained glass. "And a blackness interfering, marring the beauty of the window. Like a sickness infecting both of you, at the edges."

"Curious," Dalinar said, looking where Renarin had pointed, though he'd see only empty air. "I wonder if we'll ever know what that represents."

"Oh, that one's easy, Father," Renarin said. "That's me."

"Renarin, I don't think you should see yourself as—"

"You needn't try to protect my ego, Father. When Glys and I bonded, we became . . . something new. We see the future. At first I was confused at my place—but I've come to understand. What I see interferes with Odium's ability. Because I can see possibilities of the future, my knowledge changes what I will do. Therefore, his ability to see my future is obscured. Anyone close to me is difficult for him to read."

"I find that comforting," Dalinar said, putting his arm around Renarin's shoulders. "Whatever you are, son, it's a blessing. You might be a different kind of Radiant, but you're Radiant all the same. You shouldn't feel you need to hide this or your spren."

Renarin ducked his head, embarrassed. His father knew not to touch him too quickly, too unexpectedly, so it wasn't the arm around his shoulders. It was just that . . . well, Dalinar was so accustomed to being able to do whatever he wanted. He had written a storming *book*.

Renarin held no illusions that he would be similarly accepted. He and his father might be of similar rank, from the same family, but Renarin had never been able to navigate society like Dalinar did. True, his father at times "navigated" society like a chull marching through a crowd, but people got out of the way all the same.

Not for Renarin. The people of both Alethkar and Azir had *thousands* of years training them to fear and condemn anyone who claimed to be able to see the future. They weren't going to put that aside easily, and particularly not for Renarin.

We will be careful, Glys thought. *We will be safe.*

We will try, Renarin thought to him.

Out loud, he merely said, "Thank you. It means a lot to me that you believe that, Father."

You will ask him? Glys said. *So my siblings can be?*

"Glys wants me to note," Renarin said, "that there are others like him. Other spren that Sja-anat has touched, changed, made into . . . whatever it is we are."

"What she does is not right. Corrupting spren?"

"If I'm a blessing, Father, how can we reject the others? How can we condemn the one who made them? Sja-anat isn't human, and doesn't think like one, but I believe she *is* trying to find a path toward peace between singers and humans. In her own way."

"Still . . . I've felt the touch of one of the Unmade, Renarin."

And by one, you judge the others? Renarin didn't say it though. People too often said things as soon as they popped into their heads. Instead he waited.

"How many corrupted spren are we talking about?" Dalinar finally asked.

"Only a handful," Renarin said. "She won't change intelligent spren without their consent."

"Well, that's valuable to know. I'll consider it. Are you . . . in contact with her?"

"Not in months. Glys is worried at how silent she's become, though he thinks she is somewhere near right now."

She creates in us a faction loved by neither men nor Odium, Glys agreed. *No home. No allies. She might be destroyed by either. We will need more. Like you and like me. Together.*

Around Renarin, the stained glass windows began to crumble. It took Stormlight and effort by Glys to re-create them—and he was plainly getting tired. Gradually, Renarin's world became normal.

"Let me know if she contacts you," Dalinar said. "And if any of these episodes come upon you, bring them to me. I know a little of what it is like, son. You aren't as alone as you probably think."

He knows you, Glys said, thrilled by the idea. *He does and will.*

Renarin supposed that maybe he did. How unusual, and how comforting. Renarin—tense at first—leaned against his father, then accepted the offered strength as he watched the future become dust around him.

We need more, Glys said. *We need more like us, who will be. Who?*

I can think of one, Renarin said, *who would be a perfect choice. . . .*

55

KINSHIP WITH
THE OPEN SKY

We must not let our desires for a specific result cloud our perceptions.

—From Rhythm of War, page 6 undertext

With Stormlight, Kaladin had been able to investigate his little hideout, finding it slightly larger than he'd pictured. A stone shelf along one wall gave him a place to put Teft. He'd washed the man, then dressed him in the loose robe, with bedpan in place. One of the sacks Kaladin had taken from the monastery—stuffed with clothing—made a makeshift pillow. He'd need to find blankets, but for now his friend seemed as comfortable as Kaladin could make him.

Teft was still willing to take water, sucking it from the large metal syringe Kaladin brought back. Indeed, Teft lapped up the contents eagerly. He seemed so close to coming awake, Kaladin expected him to start cursing at any moment, demanding to know where his uniform had gone.

Syl watched, uncharacteristically solemn. "What will we do if he dies?" she asked softly.

"Don't think about that," Kaladin said.

"What if I can't help thinking about it?"

"Find something to distract you."

She sat on the stone shelf, hands in her lap. "Is that how you stand it? Knowing everyone is going to die? You just . . . don't think about it?"

"Basically," Kaladin said, refilling his syringe from the wooden water jug, then putting the tip into Teft's mouth and slowly emptying it. "Everyone dies eventually."

"I won't," she said. "Spren are immortal, even if you kill them. Someday I'll have to watch you die."

"What brought this on?" Kaladin asked. "This isn't like you."

"Yup. Right. Of course. Not like me." She plastered a smile on her face. "Sorry."

"I didn't mean it that way, Syl," Kaladin said. "You don't have to pretend."

"I'm not."

"I've used enough fake smiles to not be fooled by one. You were doing this earlier too, before the problems in the tower started. What happened?"

She looked down. "I've . . . been remembering what it was like when Relador, my old knight, died. How it made me sleep for so many years, straight through the Recreance. I keep wondering, will that happen to me again?"

"Do you feel a darkness?" Kaladin asked. "A whisper that everything will always turn out for the worst? And at the same time a crippling—and baffling—impulse pushing you to give up and do nothing to change it?"

"No," she said, shaking her head. "Nothing like that. Just a worry in the back of my mind that I keep circling around to. Like . . . I have a present I want to open, and I get excited for a little while—only to remember I already opened it and there was nothing inside."

"Sounds like how I used to feel when I remembered Tien was dead," Kaladin said. "I'd get used to living life as normal, feeling good—only to be reminded by seeing a rock in the rain, or by seeing a wooden carving like the ones he used to do. Then my whole day would come crashing down."

"Like that! But it doesn't crash my day down. Just makes me settle back and think and wish I could see him again. It still hurts. Is something wrong with me?"

"That sounds normal to me. Healthy. You're dealing with the loss when you never really did so before. Now that you're coming fully back to yourself, you're finally confronting things you've been ignoring."

"You just told me not to think about it though," Syl said. "Will that actually help?"

Kaladin winced. No, it wouldn't. He'd tried. "Distractions *can* be helpful. Doing something, reminding yourself there's a lot out there that's wonderful. But . . . you do have to think about these things eventually, I guess." He filled the syringe again. "You shouldn't ask me about this sort of problem. I'm . . . not the best at dealing with them myself."

"I feel like I shouldn't *have* to deal with them," Syl said. "I'm a spren, not a human. If I'm thinking like this, doesn't it mean I'm broken?"

"It means you're alive," Kaladin said. "I'd be more worried if you *didn't* feel loss."

"Maybe it's because you humans created us."

"Or it's because you're a little piece of divinity, like you always say." Kaladin shrugged. "If there *is* a god, then I think we could find him in the way we care about one another. Humans thinking about the wind, and honor, might have given you shape from formless power—but you're your own person now. As I'm my own person, though my parents gave me shape."

She smiled at that, and walked across the shelf wearing the form of a woman in a havah. "A person," she said. "I like thinking like that. Being like that. A lot of the other honorspren, they talk about what we were *made* to be, what we *must* do. I talked like that once. I was wrong."

"A lot of humans are the same," he said, leaning down so he was eye level with her. "I guess we both need to remember that whatever's happening in our heads, whatever it was that created us, we get to choose. That's what makes us people, Syl."

She smiled, then her havah bled from a light white-blue to a deeper blue color, striking and distinct, like it was made of real cloth.

"You're getting better at that," he said. "The colors are more vibrant this time."

She held up her arms. "I think the closer I get to your world, the more I can become, the more I can change."

She seemed to like that idea and sat, making her dress fade from one shade of blue to another, and then to a green. Kaladin finished giving Teft the syringe of water, then held it up. The sides of the metal had fingerprints in them, sunken into the surface. This device had been Soulcast into metal after first being formed from wax—the fingerprints were a telltale sign.

"You can become more things," he said. "Like a syringe maybe? We talked about you becoming other tools."

"I think I could do it," she said. "If I could manifest as a Blade right now, I could change shape to be like that. I think . . . you imagining it, me believing it, we could do even more. It—"

She cut off as a faint scraping sounded outside, from near the doorway. Immediately Kaladin reached for his scalpel. Syl came alert, zipping up into the air around him as a ribbon of light. Kaladin crept toward the door. He'd covered up the gemstone in the wall on this side with a piece of cloth. He didn't know if his light would shine out or not, but wasn't taking any chances.

But he could hear. Someone *was* out there, their boots scraping stone. Were they inspecting the door?

He made a snap decision, slipping his hand under the cloth and pressing it against the stone, commanding it to open. The rocks began to split. Kaladin prepared to leap out and attack the singer on the other side.

But it wasn't a singer.

It was Dabbid.

The unassuming bridgeman wore street clothing, and he stepped away from the door as it opened. He saw Kaladin and nodded to him, as if this were all completely expected.

"Dabbid?" Kaladin said. Other than Rlain, Dabbid was the only original bridgeman who hadn't manifested Windrunner powers. So it made sense he was awake. But how had he found his way here?

Dabbid held up a pot with something liquid inside. Kaladin gave it a sniff. "Broth?" he asked. "How did you know?"

Dabbid pointed at the line of crystal on the wall, where the tower spren's light began to twinkle. Surprising; along with being mute, the man didn't often volunteer information.

Holding the pot awkwardly, Dabbid tapped his wrists together. *Bridge Four.*

"I am *so* glad to see you," Kaladin said, leading him into the room. "How did you get broth? Never mind. Here, come sit by Teft." Dabbid was one of the first men Kaladin had saved when he'd started administering medical aid to the bridgemen. While Dabbid's physical wounds had healed, his battle shock was the strongest Kaladin had ever seen.

Regardless, he was a *wonderful* sight. Kaladin had been worrying about leaving Teft. If Kaladin died on a mission, that would be a death sentence for Teft too. Unless someone else knew about him.

He got Dabbid situated, then showed him the use of the syringe and had him start feeding Teft. Kaladin felt bad, putting the mute bridgeman to work as soon as he arrived, but—by Syl's internal clock—night would soon arrive. Kaladin needed to get moving.

"I'll explain more when I return," Kaladin promised. "Dabbid, can you get this door open? In case you need to fetch more food and water."

Dabbid walked over and put his hand on the door's gemstone; it opened for him as easily as it did for Kaladin. That was somewhat worrisome. Kaladin touched the wall garnet. "Tower spren?" he asked.

Yes.

"Is there a way I can lock these doors, so they can't be opened by just anyone?"

It was once possible to attune them to individuals. These days, I must simply leave a given door so it can be opened by anyone, or lock it so none can open it.

Well, it was good to know that—in a pinch—he should be able to ask the Sibling to lock the door. For now, it was enough that Dabbid could get in and out.

Kaladin nodded to Syl, left one gemstone to give Dabbid light, then slipped out.

⁂

Navani had asked Kaladin to observe the Oathgates up close as they were activated. To see if he could figure out why they functioned when other fabrials did not.

Unfortunately, Kaladin doubted he'd be able to get all the way down to the Oathgate plateau by sneaking through the hallways of the tower. He had made it to an out-of-the-way monastery on the fourth floor, yes, but that was a long way from the highly populated first two floors. Even if humans weren't confined to quarters, Kaladin couldn't saunter along without getting stopped. Kaladin Stormblessed drew attention.

Instead, he wanted to try climbing along the outside of the tower. Before he'd learned to fly, he'd stuck rocks to the chasm wall and climbed them. He figured he could do something similar now. The enemy had plainly ordered the Heavenly Ones to stay inside, and few people went out on the balconies.

So he made his way onto a balcony on the tenth floor right as dusk was arriving. He'd tied a sack to his belt, and in it he'd stuffed the four scrub brushes he'd gotten from the monastery. Earlier, he'd cut the bristles free with his scalpel, leaving them flat on the front but with a curved handle for holding.

Kaladin couldn't paint his hands with a Full Lashing to stick them to things. Lopen kept sticking his clothing or hair to the floor, but a Radiant's skin seemed immune to the power. Perhaps Kaladin could have rigged some gloves that worked, but the brush handholds seemed sturdier.

He leaned out of the balcony and checked to see if anyone was watching. It was growing dark already. He doubted anyone would be able to see him in the gloom, so long as he didn't draw in too much Stormlight. By keeping it mostly in the brushes attached to the wall, he wouldn't glow so much that he risked being spotted. At least, the risk of that felt far less than the risk of sneaking through the occupied floors.

Best to try it first in a way that wasn't dangerous. Kaladin took out one of the brushes and infused it with Stormlight, then pressed the flat side against a pillar on the balcony. With it affixed in place, he was able to hang his entire weight on it—dangling free—without it pulling off or the handle breaking.

"Good enough," he said, recovering the Stormlight from the Lashing. He took off his socks, but replaced his boots. He scanned the air for Heavenly Ones one last time, then stepped over the side of the balcony and balanced on the little ledge outside. He looked down toward the stones far below, but they were lost in the evening darkness. He felt as if he were standing on the edge of eternity.

He'd always liked being up high. Even before becoming Radiant, he'd felt a certain kinship with the open sky. Standing here, part of him wanted to jump, to feel the rushing wind. It wasn't some suicidal tendency, not this time. It was the call of something beautiful.

"Are you scared?" Syl said.

"No," Kaladin said. "The opposite. I've gotten so accustomed to leaping from high places that I'm not nearly as worried about this as I probably should be."

He infused two of the brushes, then moved to the far left side of the balcony. Here the stone wall made a straight "path" toward the ground between balconies. Kaladin took a deep breath and swung out and slammed one brush against the stone, then the other.

He found footholds on the stone, but they were slippery. Once, there had been a great deal of ornamentation on the rock out here—but years of highstorms had smoothed some of that out. Perhaps Lift could have climbed it without help, but Kaladin was glad he had Stormlight. He infused the toes of his boots through his feet, then stuck them to the wall too.

He started toward the ground, unsticking one limb, moving it, then sticking it back. Syl walked through the air beside him, as if striding down invisible steps. Kaladin found the descent more difficult than he'd anticipated. He had to rely a great deal on his upper-body strength, as it was difficult to get the boots to stick right, with just the toes.

He'd release one brush from the wall, then slide it into place while holding on with only one hand, then move his feet before moving the other. Though Radiant, he was sweating from exertion by the time he reached the fifth floor. He decided to take a break, and—after having Syl check to make sure it was empty—he moved over and swung onto a balcony. He settled down, breathing deeply, a few spiky coldspren moving across the balcony rail toward him, like friendly cremlings.

Syl darted into the hallway to make sure nobody was near. Fortunately, the increasingly cold tower—and the desire for subterfuge—seemed to have convinced most of the invading singers to take quarters far inward. So long as he stayed away from patrols, he should be safe.

He sat with his back to the balcony railing, feeling his muscles burn. As a soldier, then a bridgeman, he'd grown accustomed to the sensation of overexerted muscles. He almost felt cheated these days, because Stormlight's healing made the feeling rare. Indeed, after he sat for a minute, the sensation was completely gone.

Once Syl returned, he resumed his climb. As he did, a couple of wind-spren drew near: little lines of light that looped about him. As he descended toward the fourth floor, they would occasionally show faces at him—or the outlines of figures—before giggling and flitting off.

Syl watched them with fondness. He wanted to ask her what she was thinking, but didn't dare speak, lest someone inside hear voices coming in through a window. He took care to press his handholds into place quietly.

Kaladin hit a snag as he reached the fourth floor. Syl noticed first, be-coming a ribbon and making the glyph for "stop" in the air beside him. He froze, then heard it. Voices.

He nodded to Syl, who went to investigate. He felt her concern through the bond; when Syl was a Blade, they had a direct mental connection—but when she was not in that shape, the connection was softer. They'd been practicing on sending words to one another, but they tended to be vague impressions.

This time, he got a sense of some distinct words. . . . *singers . . . with spyglasses . . . third-floor balcony . . . looking up . . .*

Kaladin hung in place, silent as he could be. He could hear them below and to the left, on a balcony. They had spyglasses? Why?

To watch the sky, he thought, trying to project the idea to Syl. *For Wind-runner scouts. They won't want to use the Oathgate until they're certain nobody is watching.*

Syl returned, and Kaladin started to feel his muscles burning again. He wiped his sweaty brow on his sleeve, then carefully—his teeth gritted—drew in Stormlight to release one of his brush handholds. His skin started to release luminescent smoke, but before the light became too obvious, he re-Lashed the brush and stretched out, attaching it to the rock as far to his right as he could reach.

He moved to the side, away from the occupied balcony. He could climb across the next balcony over. As he moved, he heard the singers chatting in Alethi—femalen voices he thought, though some singer forms made gender difficult to distinguish from the voice. Judging by the conversation, they were indeed watching for Windrunners. They did Oathgate transfers at night deliberately—when flying Radiants would be starkly visible, glow-ing in the night sky.

Kaladin crossed over two balconies to his right, then continued down another open flat corridor of stone. He was on the northern part of the tower, and had moved west to get away from the scouts. Syl kept check-ing the nearby balconies as Kaladin continued his methodical pace. Unfortunately, soon after he'd passed the third floor, a dark light flashed from the Oathgates. It was tinged violet like Voidlight, but was brighter than a Voidlight sphere.

Kaladin took a moment to rest, hanging on but not moving. "Syl," he whispered. "Go check on those scouts on the balcony. Tell me if they're still watching the sky."

She zipped off, then returned a moment later.

"They're packing up their things," she whispered. "Looks like they're leaving."

That was what he'd feared. The enemy would use the Oathgates as infrequently as possible, as moving singer troops in and out of the tower would expose them to spying eyes. If the scouts were packing up, it was a fairly solid indication that the Oathgates wouldn't be used again tonight. Kaladin had been too slow.

But the gate had flashed with Voidlight. So he knew they'd done *something* to the fabrial. He'd have to try again tomorrow; he'd moved slower than he'd intended today, but he felt good about the process. A little more practice, and he could probably get down fast enough. But would getting close to the Oathgates tell him anything about what had been done to them? He didn't feel he knew enough about fabrials.

For now, he started climbing back up to see how much more difficult it was. This was slower, but the footholds with his boots were more helpful. As he ascended, he found a fierce pride in the effort. The changes to the tower had tried to keep him confined to the ground, but the sky was *his*. He'd found a way to scale her again, if in a less impressive way. If he . . .

Kaladin paused, hanging from his handholds, as something struck him. Something that he felt profoundly stupid for having not seen immediately.

"The scouts on the balcony," he whispered to Syl as she darted in to see why he'd stopped. "What would they have done if they'd spotted Windrunners in the sky?"

"They'd have told the others to stop the transfer," Syl said, "so the fact that the Oathgate glowed the wrong color wouldn't give away the truth."

"How?" Kaladin asked. "*How* did they contact the Oathgate operators? Did you see flags or anything?"

"No," Syl said. "They were just sitting there writing in the dark. They must have been using . . . a *spanreed*."

One that worked in the tower. Navani was trying to figure out how the enemy was operating fabrials. What if he could hand her one? Surely that would lead to more valuable information than he would get by observing the Oathgates.

Syl zipped over to the balcony the scouts had been using. "I can see them!" she said. "They've packed up, and they're leaving, but they're just ahead."

Follow, Kaladin sent her mentally, then moved as quickly as he could in that direction. He might have missed the night's transfer, but there was still a way he could help.

And it involved stealing that spanreed.

But how can we not, in searching, wish for a specific result? What scientist goes into a project without a hope for what they will find?

—From *Rhythm of War*, page 6 undertext

Venli inspected the large model of the tower. Such an intricate construction, a masterwork of sculpting, bathed in violet moonlight through the window. What had it been used for by the Radiants of old, all those years ago? Was this a forgotten art piece, or something more? She'd heard several Voidspren saying that perhaps it was a scale model for the spren to live in, but—for all its intricacy—it didn't have things like furniture or doors.

She walked around it, passing through the middle, where it was split to show a cross section. For some reason, seeing it in miniature highlighted how impossibly vast the tower was. Even reconstructed like this, it was twice Venli's height.

She shook her head and left the model behind, moving among the fallen Radiants, each of whom lay silent on the floor of this large chamber. According to Raboniel's request, Venli had found a place to keep them all together. She'd wanted them on the ground floor, close enough to the basement rooms to be sent for, but that region of the tower was quite well occupied. So rather than go to the trouble of kicking people out of a chamber to use, Venli had appropriated this newly discovered—and empty—one. It had only one entrance, so it was easy to guard, and the window provided natural light.

There were around fifty of them in total. Perhaps with such low numbers, Raboniel's forces could have taken this place even if the Radiants had fought. Perhaps not. There was something about these modern Radiants. The Fused seemed to be constantly surprised by them. Everyone had expected impotence, inexperience. Roshar had gone centuries without the Radiant bond. These had no masters to train them; they had to discover everything on their own. How did they do so well?

Timbre pulsed her thoughts on the matter. Sometimes ignorance was an advantage, as you weren't limited by the expectations of the past. Perhaps that was it. Or perhaps it was something else. New, younger spren, enthusiastic—pitted against weary old Fused souls.

Venli lingered near the body of a young woman. The Radiants were each lying on a blanket and draped with a sheet, corpselike, leaving only their faces exposed. This Radiant, however, was stirring. Her eyes were closed, but her face twitched, as if she were in the grip of a terrible nightmare. She might be. Odium had invaded Venli's mind in the past; who knew how far his corrupting touch could reach?

Windrunner, Venli thought, reading the markings on the floor next to the woman. They listed whatever Venli's team had been able to learn about the individual Radiants from interrogating the tower's humans. She glanced down the row toward another Radiant whose face was making similar expressions. Also a Windrunner.

She finished her inspection and met up with Dul. It had turned out to be simple for Venli to put her most trusted people in charge of the fallen Radiants, as Raboniel thought it a good use for them.

"The other Windrunners," Venli said softly. "Do they all seem . . ."

"Closer to waking?" Dul asked to Awe. "Yeah. They do. Any time one of the Radiants stirs, it's always a Windrunner. We've caught some of them muttering in their sleep."

"Raboniel asked me specifically to check on this," Venli said to Anxiety. "She seemed to have anticipated it."

"Not hard to guess," Dul said. "The Radiant who is awake—supposedly roaming the tower—is a Windrunner, right?"

Venli nodded, looking along the rows of bodies. Venli's loyalists moved among them, administering broth and changing soiled blankets.

"This was a good maneuver, putting us here," Dul whispered. "Caring for the humans gives us an excuse to collect blankets and clothing for when we leave. I've begun putting away broth paste that should keep."

"Good," Venli said to Anxiety. "When only our people are around, test those Windrunners and see if you can wake one up."

"And if we succeed?" Dul asked to Skepticism. "I think that's a terrible idea."

Venli's first instinct—even still—was to slap him. How dare he question her? She pushed away that instinct, though it warned her that she was the same selfish person, despite it all. A few Words didn't suddenly make her something better.

"Their powers would be suppressed," Venli explained to him. "So they shouldn't be a danger to you. And if they are violent, get away and let it be assumed they woke up spontaneously. That will keep us from being implicated."

"Fine, but why risk it?"

"Escaping and hiding will be far easier with the help of one like these," Venli said. "At the very least, we'll need a distraction to get out. The Windrunners waking and suddenly fighting would provide that."

She glanced at Dul, who still hummed to Skepticism.

"Look," Venli said as they completed a walk around the room, "I don't like humans any more than you do. But if we truly want to escape, we'll need to make use of every advantage we can find." She swept her hand across the room of unconscious Radiants. "This could be a very large one."

Finally, Dul hummed to Reconciliation. "I suppose you're right. It's worth trying, though I'm not sure how to wake these up. What we need is a surgeon. Could probably use one anyway; some of these seem to be getting sores and drawing rotspren. Others won't take any broth, though they have hungerspren buzzing around them."

Venli attuned Peace as an idea occurred to her. "I'm sure I could get you surgeons. In fact, I know of one who might be willing to help our cause. A human. He's in hiding, because of certain matters we shouldn't spread. But I think we could place him here, to help."

Dul nodded, humming to Appreciation. Venli left, stepping out onto the floor of the atrium—with the long vertical shaft running up toward the top of the tower. She passed several Regals standing guard at the door to the room with the model. Leshwi had told her to put the surgeon and his family someplace safe; well, this made sense.

Curfew was nearing, so here on the floor of the atrium, people were hurrying about their last-minute activities. The humans—no longer confined to quarters—had crept from their shells like vines after a storm. Many of them lived around the atrium, and they had pulled out carts, making temporary shops here near the large window. Like spren to the Passions, the humans sought out the sunlight.

Tonight, they walked timidly and kept their distance from Venli, as if they couldn't believe that they were supposed to continue on as if nothing had happened. Venli found a stairwell and hurried up, causing a few human women to pull to one side and gasp softly, drawing wormlike fearspren. Sometimes Venli forgot how fearsome her Regal form looked. She'd grown comfortable with it, and more and more it felt like her natural state—even if there was a Voidspren trapped in her gemheart.

On the second floor, Venli made her way toward a meeting point near the atrium balcony. She was supposed to give service to a team of Fused tonight, in case they needed an interpreter. Many Fused had trouble speaking to modern singers. That made sense, considering how short a time they'd been back. Venli found it odder that some—like Raboniel—had already learned to speak modern Alethi.

Venli arrived at the meeting place, surprised to find several Deepest Ones: the strange Fused with limber bodies and milky-white eyes glowing red from behind. They enjoyed spending their time sunken in rock as much as the Heavenly Ones liked to soar. She had occasionally walked into a room to find one or two of them lingering there, sunken into the floor, revealing only their faces, eyes closed.

Tonight four stood in a clump, attended by a few ordinary singers carrying equipment. The Fused were arguing among themselves in their language.

"I did not think the sand would work," one of the Deepest Ones said to Spite. Their rhythms sounded off. Muted. "I was right in this. You should acknowledge it."

"There are too many different fabrials in the tower," said another. "And too many spren. The device we hunt doesn't leave a strong enough impression to be noticeable, hidden as it is."

"You're searching for the fabrial that is creating the shield around the crystal pillar," Venli guessed. Raboniel had mentioned the field was created by a fabrial—which she theorized would have several gemstones, called nodes, maintaining it, hidden somewhere in the tower.

The Deepest Ones did not directly reprimand her for speaking without first being addressed. As Raboniel's Voice, Venli had a certain amount of authority, even with these. Not to command, but certainly to speak.

"Why not use secretspren?" she asked. "They can find fabrials as easily as they find Radiants, can't they?"

"The entire tower is a fabrial," one of the Deepest Ones said. "The secretspren are useless here; they spin in circles, confused. Asking them to find a specific use of Light in here is like asking them to find a specific patch of water in an ocean."

"Useless spren," another said. "Have you seen the chaosspren?"

Venli had. Those types of Voidspren—normally invisible to anyone but the ones they appeared to—left sparks in the air now, as if somehow responding to the dampening field. In this place, even someone who couldn't look into Shadesmar could know whether they were being watched or not.

As Venli thought on that, she attuned Excitement. No invisible spren . . . and the secretspren were useless. That meant a Radiant in the tower would be free to use their powers without being noticed.

She could use her powers without being noticed.

The implications of it made Timbre begin to thrum to Excitement as well, in time with Venli's attunement. Finally. They could practice.

Dared she, though?

"Voice," one of the Deepest Ones said, waving her over. It was a femalen with pale white skin, swirled with the faintest lines of red. "We need to find these nodes. But without secretspren, we might have to search the entire tower. You will begin interrogating humans, asking if they've seen a large gemstone that seems unattached from any visible fabrial."

"As you wish, Ancient One," Venli said to Abashment. "But if I may say, this seems an inelegant solution. Are the nodes not likely to be hidden?"

"Yes," another said, "but they will also need to be accessible. Their purpose is to let Radiants charge the shield with Stormlight."

"Be that as it may, Ancient One, I am skeptical," Venli said. "Assuming humans answered me truthfully, I suspect they would not know anything. They have not finished mapping all the floors of the tower, let alone its secret places. Do you truly wish us to spend months talking to each human, asking them if they've seen something as vague as a random gemstone?"

The Deepest Ones hummed to Destruction, but otherwise did not contradict her. As with many of the Fused, they did not object out of hand to being challenged, not if the argument was a good one. Venli could learn from them in that regard.

"This is as I said," one said to the others. "We could search this place for *years* and discover nothing."

"Won't the nodes be connected to the crystal pillar?" Venli asked.

"Yes," said one of the Deepest Ones. "By veins of crystal, for transporting Stormlight."

"Then we could follow those," Venli said. "You could sink into the rock and find them, then trace them outward."

"No," said another to Derision. "We cannot see while embedded. We can hear, and we can sing, and the tones of Roshar guide us. But this fabrial is made to be silent to us. To trace the lines, we would need to break apart the stone—and sever all the connections to the pillar. That might destroy the tower's protections entirely, letting the Radiants awaken and defeating our purpose."

"So if you did find a gemstone in the tower," Venli said, "you couldn't know whether it was tied to the protective field. You might break the gemstone and find it was tied to something else entirely."

The Fused hummed at her in Derision. Venli was pushing the boundaries of the interference they would accept. "No, foolish one," the femalen said. "This fabrial of protection is *new*. Added to the tower *after* its creation. There will be few other gemstones like it. The rest of the tower works as a single entity, which is why Raboniel was able to engage its protections by infusing it with Voidlight."

That . . . didn't really explain as much as they seemed to think, but Venli hummed to Subservience to indicate she appreciated the information and the correction. Her mind, however, was still daunted by the implications of what she'd learned earlier. She'd spent all these months being timid about her powers, telling herself she didn't dare use them. Why was she so worried now, though?

Timbre pulsed. Indicating it was all right to be afraid of trying something new. It was natural.

But that wasn't it, not entirely. It seemed that most of Venli's life, she'd been afraid of the wrong things. Her curiosity had led to her people's downfall. And now she played with powers she didn't understand, gathering an entire group of hopefuls who depended on her.

If she made a wrong move, Dul and the others were doomed.

The Deepest Ones conferred. The femalen continued to watch Venli, however. The other three seemed to regard her as their foremost, for they quieted when she spoke.

"You are mortal," she said to Venli. "You are the Last Listener. Few Regals earn a true title, and I find it odd to see the child of traitors developing one. Tell me, where would *you* place these nodes, if you were to do so?"

"I . . ." Venli attuned Agony. "I have no knowledge of the tower. I couldn't say."

"Guess," the Fused prompted. "Try."

"I suppose," Venli said, "I would put it someplace easy to give it Stormlight, but a place no one would search. Or . . ." A thought occurred to her, but she quieted it. She didn't want to help them. The longer it took to fully corrupt the tower, the better it seemed for her people. "No, never mind. I am foolish, Ancient One, and ignorant."

"Perhaps, but you are also mortal—and think like one," the Fused considered. "Mortals are busy. They live short lives, always stuffed with so many things to do. Yet they are also lazy. They want to do none of what they should. Would you not say this is true?"

"I . . . Yes, of course," Venli said. This was not a Fused wanting someone to object.

"Yes," said another Deepest One. "Would they not put the gemstone nodes, at least one of them, where Stormlight could renew it *naturally*?"

"Storms reach this high only occasionally," another said, "but they *do* come up here. So it would make sense to put one in reach of the occasional free infusion of power."

Timbre pulsed to Sorrow inside Venli. This was exactly the idea she'd chosen not to share. Where was the best place for a node? Outside somewhere—but not on the balconies, where it could be spotted. She looked across the atrium toward the large window. The Deepest Ones had come to the same conclusion apparently, for they flowed away toward the far wall, to look for signs of a gemstone embedded outside.

Timbre pulsed to Disappointment.

"I didn't *try* to help," Venli whispered. "Besides, they mostly figured it out on their own."

Timbre pulsed again. Hopefully it would turn out to be nothing. It was just a guess, after all.

The Fused had left her with no instructions, so she remained with the servants—until she spotted a familiar figure hurrying through the corridor. Mazish, Dul's wife, one of Venli's inner circle.

She stepped forward quickly, intercepting the squat workform—who was humming to Anxiety.

"What?" Venli asked.

"Venli," she said. "Venli, they . . . they've found *another*."

"Another Radiant?" Venli asked to Confusion.

"No. No, not that. I mean." She seized Venli by the arm. "Another one of you. Another *listener*."

57

CHILD OF ODIUM

EIGHT AND A HALF YEARS AGO

Eshonai found the humans endlessly fascinating.

Between their first and second visits, Eshonai had organized several trips to try to find their homeland. Suddenly, everyone had wanted to join her, and she'd led large expeditions. Those had been all song, and no crescendo, unfortunately—the only thing she'd been able to locate was a solitary human outpost to the west.

They'd told her to expect a second visit soon, but now that visit seemed to be drawing to a close. So Eshonai took every remaining opportunity to watch the humans. She loved the way they walked, the way they talked, even the way they *looked* at her. Or sometimes didn't.

Like today, as she strolled through Gavilar Kholin's camp. His servants barely glanced at her as they packed. She stepped up beside one worker, who was unstringing a large metal bow. The man *must* have seen her standing there—but when he stood up a few minutes later, he jumped to find her beside him.

Such strange behavior. Sometimes she thought she could read the rhythms in the human motions—like that man with the bow would be attuned to Anxiety. Yet they still didn't seem to grasp that listeners could hear something they could not. What would it be like to go about all the time without a rhythm in your head? It must be painful. Or lonely. So empty.

The various humans continued their packing, storing everything in wagons for the day's storm. The humans were good at judging the arrival of those—though they were often wrong on the hour, they were usually right on the day. This, however, was no routine pre-storm packing job.

They would soon leave; she could read this in the way they talked to each other, the way they double-checked bindings and folded tents with more precision than usual. They weren't planning to unpack any of it for a while.

She wished they would stay longer—their first interaction had been so short, and now this second visit was over almost before it began. Perhaps she could go with them, as she'd told Venli. She'd asked how far beyond the hills their home was, but they didn't answer, and refused to share their maps.

Eshonai moved to slip out of camp, but stopped as she noticed one man standing off from the rest. Dalinar Kholin looked out, eastward, toward the Origin of Storms.

Curious, Eshonai walked up to him, noting that he had his Shardblade out. He held it lightly before him, the tip sunken into the stone. He seemed to be searching for something, but before him stretched only the Plains—an empty expanse.

Unlike the others, he noticed her approach immediately, turning as she made the slightest scrape on the stones while walking. She froze beneath his gaze, which always seemed to be the stare of a greatshell.

"You're one of the interpreters," he said.

"Yes."

"What was your name?"

"Eshonai," she said, though she had little doubt he'd forget again. The humans didn't seem to be able to distinguish very well between different listeners.

"Have you been out there?" he asked, nodding toward the Plains. "To the center?"

"No," she said. "I'd like to go, but the old bridges . . . they do not stand. It would take work, much work, to put them back. Most of my people don't like . . . what is the word? Going where it is difficult to go?"

"Exploring, perhaps," he said.

"Yes. Exploring. We once exploring. But now, very little exploring." *Until recently.*

He grunted. "You're good with our language."

"I like it," she said. "Speaking new ways. Thinking new ways. They are same, yes?"

"Yes, perhaps they are." He turned and looked over his shoulder toward the west. Toward his homeland. "Perhaps your people are afraid to return to where they once lived."

"Why fear that?" Eshonai asked, attuning Confusion.

"Places have power over us, parshwoman," he said. "Places have memories. Sometimes when you go to a place you've never been, it can be wonderful . . . because it lets you be someone else. No expectations. No storming memories."

"I like new places," she said. "Because . . . they are new." She attuned Irritation. That hadn't come out as she'd wanted it to; she felt stupid, speaking their language. It was difficult to express anything deep while speaking it, because the rhythms didn't match the sounds.

"Wise words," Dalinar said.

Wise words? Was he being patronizing? Humans seemed to not expect much from her people, and were surprised whenever a complex conversation happened. As if they were amused that the listeners were not as dull-minded as parshmen.

"I would like to go to see places where you live," Eshonai said. "I would visit you, and have you visit us, more."

Dalinar dismissed his Blade, sending it away with a puff of white fog. She attuned Confusion.

"My brother has taken an interest in you," Dalinar said softly. "This . . . Well, be more cautious with your invitations, parshwoman. Our attention can be dangerous."

"I do not understand," she said. It sounded as if he were warning her against his own.

"I have grown tired of pushing people around," Dalinar said. "In my wake, I've left too many smoldering holes where cities used to be. You are something special, something we've never seen before. And I know my brother—I know that look in his eyes, that excitement.

"His interest could benefit you, but it could have an equal cost. Do not be so quick to share your stormshelter with men you just barely met. Don't offend, but also don't be too quick to bend. Any new recruit needs to learn both lessons. In this case, I'd suggest politeness—but care. Do not let him back you into a corner. He will respect you if you stand up for yourselves. And whatever you do, *don't* give him any reason to decide he wants what you have."

Be forceful, stand up for themselves, but don't offend their king? How did that make any sense? Yet looking at him—listening to his calm but firm voice—she thought she did understand. His intent, as if given to her by a rhythm.

Be careful with us was what he was saying. *We are far more dangerous than you think.*

He had mentioned . . . burning cities.

"How many cities do your people live in?" she asked.

"Hundreds," he said. "The number of humans in our realm would stagger you. It is many times the number of parshmen I've seen here living with you."

Impossible. That . . . was impossible, wasn't it?

We know so little.

"Thank you," she said to Appreciation. She got it to click, the way of speaking his language but putting a rhythm to it. It *could* work.

He nodded to her. "We are leaving. I realize this visit was short, but my brother needs to return to his lands. You will . . . certainly meet us again. We will send a more permanent envoy. I promise you this."

He turned, moving with the momentum of a shifting boulder, and walked toward his stormwagon.

∴

Venli felt as if the bright red gemstone would burn its way through her clothing. She huddled in one of the stormshelters: a group of wide slits in the ground near the city, which they'd covered over with animal carapace and crem. Each was in the top of a hill, so the sides could drain.

Venli's immediate family gathered together in this one to chat and feast, as was their habit during storm days. The others seemed so cheerful, speaking to Joy or Appreciation while they ate beside the fire, listening as Venli's mother sang songs by the light of uncut gemhearts.

Those could be organic, lumpish things. While they took in Stormlight, none were nearly as bright as the strange gemstone in her pocket. The one the human had given her. Venli felt as if it should be on fire, though it was as cold as a normal gemstone. She attuned Anxiety and glanced at the others, worrying they'd see that too-red glow.

I'm supposed to go out into the storm, she thought, listening to the rain pound distant stone. *Does this count? I can see the storm out there, flashing and making its own rhythm, too frantic. Too wild.*

No, she wasn't close enough. Hiding in one of these shelters wouldn't allow her to adopt mateform, which was the sole transformation they did regularly. No one wanted to go back to dullform, after all.

There *were* other forms to be found. She'd been close to warform. And now . . . this gemstone . . .

She'd carried it for weeks, terrified of what might happen. She glanced at her mother, and the close family members who sat and listened. Enraptured by the beautiful songs. Even Venli, who had heard them hundreds of times, found herself wanting to drift back and sit at her mother's feet.

None of them knew what was happening. To Jaxlim. Mother hid it well. Was it true, that other forms could help her? The humans were leaving now, so this was the last chance Venli would have to try the gemstone, then—if it didn't work—get answers from the human who had given it to her.

Venli attuned Determination and rose from her place, walking toward the end of the shelter, where they'd tied their gemstones to be renewed—close enough to the storm to be given light by the Rider's touch. Several of the others whispered behind her, their voices attuned to Amusement. They thought she had decided to adopt mateform, which she'd always been adamant she would never do.

Her mother had smiled when she'd asked, explaining that few ever *intended* to adopt mateform. She acted as if it was simply something that happened, that an urge overtook you, or you sat too close to the exit during a storm—then poof, the next thing you knew, you'd become a silly idiot looking to breed. It was embarrassing to think others assumed Venli was doing that now.

She reached the wet stone at the edge of the shelter, where rainspren clustered with eyes pointed upward and grasping claws below. The wind and thunder were louder here, like the war calls of a rival family, trying to frighten her away.

Perhaps it would be best just to give the gemstone to her mother, and let *her* go try to find the new form. Wasn't that what this was about?

No, Venli thought, trembling. *No. It's not.*

Months spent trying to find new forms had gotten her nowhere—while Eshonai gained more and more acclaim. Even their mother, who had called her explorations foolish, now spoke of Eshonai with respect. The person who had found the humans. The person who had changed the world.

Venli had done what she was supposed to. She'd remained with her mother, she'd spent endless days memorizing songs, dutiful. But Eshonai got the praise.

Before her nerves betrayed her, Venli stepped out onto the hillside, entering the storm. The force of the wind made her stumble and slide down the slick rock. In an eyeblink she went from sheltered, song-filled warmth to icy chaos. A tempest with sounds like instruments breaking and songs failing. She tried to hold to the Rhythm of Resolve, but it was the Rhythm of Winds by the time she scrambled behind a large boulder and pressed her back against the stone.

From there, her mind devolved to the Rhythm of Pleading, bordering on panic. What was she doing? This was *insanity.* She'd often *mocked* those who went out in the storms without shields or other protections.

She wanted to return to the shelter, but she was too frightened to move. Something large crushed the ground nearby, causing her to jump, but a moment of darkness in the howling tempest prevented her from seeing how close the impact had been. As if the lightning, the wind, and the rain all conspired against her.

She reached into her pocket and took out the gemstone. What had seemed so bright before now seemed frail. The red light barely illuminated her hand.

Break it. She was supposed to break it. With fingers already numb from the cold, she searched around, eventually finding a large stone. The ground was shattered here in a circle the size of a listener. She retreated to the relative shelter of the boulder, shivering as she held the gemstone in one hand, the rock in the other.

Then silence.

It was so sudden, so unexpected, that she gasped. The rhythms in her mind became as one, a single steady beat. She looked upward into pure blackness. The ground around her seemed dry all of a sudden. She slowly turned around, then huddled down again. There was something in the sky, something like a face made from clouds and natural light. The impression of something vast and unknowable.

You wish to take this step? a not-voice said, vibrating through her like a rhythm.

"I . . ." This was him, the spren of highstorms—the Rider of Storms. The songs called him a traitor.

You have spent so long as children of no god, the rhythm said to her. You would make this choice for all of your people?

Venli felt both a thrill and a terror at those words. So there *was* something in the gemstone?

"My . . . my people need forms!" she shouted up toward the vast entity.

This is more than forms. This power changes mortals.

Power?

"You served our enemies!" she called to the sky. "How can I trust what you say?"

Yet you trust the gift of one of those enemies? Regardless, I serve no one. Not man or singer. I simply am. Farewell, child of the Plains.

Child of Odium.

The vision ended as abruptly as it had begun, and Venli was again in the storm. She nearly dropped her burdens in shock, but then—huddling against the gleeful wind—she set the glowing gemstone on the ground. She gripped the rock in her hand, slick with rain. She wavered.

Should she take more care?

What greatness was achieved by being careful, though?

Eshonai hadn't been careful, and she'd discovered a new world. Venli slammed the stone downward and crushed the gem. Light escaped in a puff, and she winced in the pelting rain, bracing herself for a wondrous transformation.

"Finally!" a voice said to the Rhythm of Irritation. "*That* was unpleasant." The red light turned into a tiny human male, standing with hands on hips, glowing faintly in the storm.

Venli pulled her arms in tight, shivering, blinking rainwater out of her eyes. "Spren," she hissed. "I have summoned you to grant me one of the ancient forms."

"You?" he asked. "How old are you? Are there any others I could talk to?"

"Show me this secret first," she said. "Then we will give your form to others. It can heal them, right? That is what I was told."

He didn't reply.

"You will not deny me this!" Venli said, though her words were lost in a sudden peal of thunder. "I've suffered long to accomplish this goal."

"Well, you're certainly *dramatic*," the little spren said, tapping his foot. "Guess we use the tools we find in the shed, even if they've got a little rust on them. Here's the deal. I'm going to take up residence inside of you, and together we're going to do some incredible things."

"We will bring useful forms to my people?" Venli asked, her teeth chattering.

"Well, yes. And also no. For a while, we'll need you to appear as if you are still in workform. I need to scout out how things are on old Roshar these days. It's been a while. You think you can get into Shadesmar, if we need to?"

"Sh-Shadesmar?" she asked.

"Yes, we need to get to the storm there. The newer one in the south? Where I entered that gemstone . . . You have no idea what I'm talking about. Delightful. Right, then. Get ready, we've got *a lot* of work to do. . . ."

⁘

Eshonai attuned Anxiety as she stood by the mouth of the shelter, searching for her sister. She couldn't make out much in the tempest. The flashes of lightning, though brilliant, were too brief to give her a real picture of the landscape.

"She really did it, did she?" Thude asked to Amusement as he stepped up beside her, chewing on some fruit. "After all that complaining, she sauntered out to become a mate."

"I doubt it," Eshonai said. "She's been trying to find warform for months now. She's not looking to become a mate. She's too young, anyway." The humans had been surprised at how young Eshonai and Venli were—apparently, humans aged more slowly? But Venli was still months away from official adulthood.

"Younger ones have made the decision," Thude said, rubbing at his beard. "I've thought about it, you know? There's a certain bond to once-
694   mates."

"You just think it sounds fun," Eshonai said to Reprimand.

He laughed. "I do at that." Thunder shook the enclosure, silencing both of them for a time as they listened to it, both attuning the Rhythm of Winds out of deference. There was something wondrous—if dangerous—about feeling the very vibrations of the storm.

"This isn't the time to be distracted by something silly like mateform," Eshonai said. "The humans are leaving again once this storm ends. We should be talking about sending someone with them."

"You're too responsible for your own good sometimes, Eshonai," Thude replied, his arm up against the top of the enclosure as he leaned forward, letting the rain hit his face.

"Me? Responsible?" she said. "Mother might have words for you on *that* topic."

"And each one would remind me how alike the two of you are," Thude said, attuned to Joy and grinning at the storm like a fool. "I'm going to do it one of these days, Eshonai. I'm going to see if Bila will go with me. Life is meant to be more than working the fields or chopping wood."

With that, Eshonai could agree. And she supposed she could understand someone wanting to do something different with their life. None of them would exist if their parents hadn't decided to become mates.

The idea still made her want to attune Anxiety. She disliked how much that form changed the way people thought. She wanted to be herself, with her own desires and passions, not let some form override her. Of course, there was an argument that she was even now influenced by workform. . . .

She attuned Determination and put that out of her mind. Venli. Where was she? Eshonai knew she shouldn't fear for her sister. Listeners went into the storms all the time, and while it was never strictly safe, she didn't need to hum to Anxiety like the humans did when they talked of storms. Storms were a natural part of life, a gift from Roshar to the listeners.

Though a little piece of Eshonai . . . a part she hated to acknowledge . . . noted how much easier life would be without Venli around, complaining all the time. Without her jealousy. Everything Eshonai did—every conversation, or plan, or outing—was made harder when Venli decided to be involved. Complications would materialize out of calm air.

It was weakness in Eshonai that she should feel this way. She was supposed to love her sister. And she didn't really *want* harm to come to Venli, but it was difficult not to remember how peaceful it had been to explore on her own, without any of Venli's drama. . . .

A figure appeared out of the storm, slick with rain, backlit by lightning. Eshonai felt guilty again, and attuned Joy by force upon seeing it was Venli. She stepped out into the storm and helped her sister the rest of the way.

Venli remained in workform. A wet, shivering femalen in workform.

"Didn't work, eh?" Thude asked her.

Venli looked at him, as mute as a human, her mouth opening a little. Then, unnervingly, she grinned. A frantic, uncharacteristic grin.

"No, Thude," Venli said. "It didn't work. I will have to try many, many more times to find warform."

He hummed to Reconciliation, eyeing Eshonai. She'd been right—it hadn't been about mateform after all.

"I should like to sit by the fire," Venli said, "and warm myself."

"Venli?" Eshonai said. "Your words . . . where are their rhythms?"

Venli paused. Then she—as if it were a struggle—began humming to Amusement. It took her a few tries.

"Don't be silly," Venli said. "You just weren't listening." She strode toward the fire, walking with a swagger that seemed even more confident than normal. The high-headed stroll of a femalen who thought that the storms began and ended upon her whims.

58

SPANREEDS

I find this experience so odd. I work with a scholar from the ancient days, before modern scientific theory was developed. I keep forgetting all the thousands of years of tradition you completely missed.

—From *Rhythm of War*, page 6 undertext

K aladin landed on the balcony with a muted thump. Syl was a glowing ribbon of light farther into the building. He couldn't see the scouts who had packed up and left with the spanreeds, but he trusted Syl was watching them.

He followed into the darkness, putting his Stormlight into a sphere so he didn't glow. He had failed to spy on the Oathgates, but if he could somehow steal one of those Voidlight spanreeds, he could still help Navani.

He crept as quickly as he dared in the darkness, one hand on the wall. He soon neared a hallway with lanterns along the wall; as this was the third floor of the tower, much of it was occupied and lit. The lanterns revealed two femalen singers ahead, wearing havahs and chatting quietly. Syl carefully darted into side tunnels and nooks behind them.

Kaladin trailed far behind, relying on Syl to point out turns, as the two singers were often out of his direct line of sight. This section of the tower was a large laundry facility, where darkeyes could come to use public water and soap. He passed several large rooms without doors where the floor was shaped into a sequence of basins.

It was nearly empty now. The tower's pumps hadn't been changed to work on Voidlight, it seemed. He did have to avoid several water-carrying teams—humans pulling carts, with singer guards—moving through the tunnels. Syl soon came zipping back, so he ducked into a darkened alcove near an empty room full of baskets for laundry. The place smelled of soap.

"Guard post ahead," she whispered. "They went through it. What do you want to do?"

"Any Fused nearby?" Kaladin asked.

"Not that I saw. Only ordinary singers."

"Theoretically, regular guards shouldn't be able to see you unless you let them. Follow those singers with the spanreeds. Hopefully their rooms are nearby. If they split up, pick the one with the blue havah—the embroidery indicates she's the more important. Once you know where her room is, come back, then we can sneak in another way and steal the spanreed."

"Right. If they get too far away from you though, I'll lose myself. . . ."

"Return if you start to feel that," he said. "We can try another night."

Syl soared off without another word, leaving Kaladin hiding inside the room with the baskets. Unfortunately, he soon heard voices—and peeked to see a pair of singers with baskets walking down the hallway. Even an occupying force of ancient evil soldiers needed to do laundry, it seemed. Kaladin closed the door, shutting himself in darkness, then—realizing there was a chance they were coming to dump their baskets in this very room—he grabbed a broom and lashed it across the door.

Since he'd infused the broom on either end, no Stormlight should show through the door. A moment later it rattled as they tried to push it inward. Annoyed voices outside complained in Azish as they tried the door again. He gripped his knife, darkness weighing upon him. The horror of the nightmares, and a fatigue that went far deeper than the earlier strain to his muscles. A tiredness that had been with him so long, he'd accepted it as normal.

When the door rattled again, he was *certain* it was a dark force come to claim him. He heard the sounds of bowstrings, and of Gaz yelling for the bridgemen to run. Screams of men dying, and . . . And . . .

He blinked. The door had fallen still. When . . . when had that happened? He gave it a few minutes, wiping the sweat from his forehead, then un-Lashed the broom and cracked the door. Two abandoned baskets sat nearby, no singers in sight. He let out a long breath, then pried his fingers off his scalpel and tucked it away.

Eventually Syl returned. "They weren't going to their rooms," she said, animatedly dancing around in patterns as a ribbon of light. "They dropped off their spanreed in a room ahead where there are *dozens* of spanreeds, watched over by a couple of senior femalens."

Kaladin nodded, breathing deeply, fighting back the tiredness.

"You . . . all right?" Syl asked.

"I'm fine," Kaladin said. "That's a spanreed hub you found. Makes sense they'd set one up in the tower." Maintaining hundreds of spanreeds could grow unwieldy, so many highlords and highladies would set up hubs. Disparate locations—like guard posts around the tower—could send reports to a central room, where the hub attendants sifted for important information and sent it to those in power.

The singers were keeping their reeds in central locations to be checked out, used, and returned. The reeds wouldn't go home with individual scribes. This wasn't going to be as easy as sneaking into a bedroom to grab one, but the hub might offer other opportunities.

"We need to get past that guard post," Kaladin whispered, burying his fatigue.

"There's something else, Kaladin," Syl said. "Look out the door, down the tunnel."

Frowning, he did as she requested, peeking out and watching down the tunnel. He was confused, until he saw something pass in the air—like rippling red lightning.

"That's a new kind of Voidspren," he said. The ones he'd seen in the past that looked like lightning moved along the ground.

"It's not, though," Syl said. "That spren should be invisible to people, but something is off about its aura. It is leaving a trail that I noted the guards watching."

Curious. So the tower was interfering with spren invisibility? "Did the guards look at you when you passed?"

"No, but they might just not have noticed me."

Kaladin nodded, watching a little longer. That spren in the distance didn't pass again. "It's worth the risk," he decided, "in proceeding. At least we'll know if we're being spied upon."

"But what about that guard post?" she asked.

"I doubt we'll be able to sneak around it," he said. "They'll have all directions guarded for something valuable like a spanreed hub. But a lot of these rooms have small tunnels at the tops for ventilation. Perhaps we can sneak through one of those?"

Syl led him carefully to an intersection. He peered right, to where four guards blocked the way, two at either side of the hallway. Spears at the crooks of their arms, they wore Alethi-style uniforms with knots on the shoulders. Kaladin was able to spot one of the ventilation holes nearby, but this one was far too small for him to squeeze into.

He'd stood on guard duty himself like that on a number of occasions. If these four were well trained, there would be no luring them away with simple distractions. If you wanted a path well protected, you often posted four. Two to investigate any disturbances, two to remain vigilant.

With the hallway this narrow, and with those guards looking as alert as they were . . . Well, he'd been there. The only times when he'd been drawn away, it had involved someone with proper authority commandeering him for another task.

"Syl," he whispered, "you're getting better at changing colors. Do you think you could change your coloring to appear like a Voidspren?"

She cocked her head, standing beside him in the air, then scrunched up her face in a look of concentration. Her dress changed to red, but not her "skin," even though it was simply another part of her. Strange.

"I think this is all I can manage," she said.

"Then make the dress cover your hands with gloves and put on a mask."

She cocked her head, then changed her clothing so she was wrapped in phantom cloth. That bled to a deep red, making her entire form glow with that color.

She inspected her arms. "Do you think it will fool them?"

"It might," Kaladin said. He pulled a length of rope from his sack, then Lashed it to the wall. "Go order all four of them to come with you, then pull them over here to look at this."

"But . . . doesn't that rope risk causing a bigger disturbance? Like, what if they go for backup?"

"We need something reasonable enough to have caused a Voidspren to get riled up. I know guard duty though, and those are common warforms. Regular soldiers. I'm guessing that so long as there's no danger, they'll just make a report on it."

He hid down a side hallway, waiting as Syl flew off toward the guard post. She didn't look exactly like a Voidspren, but it was a reasonable approximation.

She drew near to the post, then spoke loudly enough that he heard her easily. "You there! I am super annoyed! Super, super annoyed! How can you stand there? Didn't you see?"

"Brightness?" one of them said, in Alethi. "Er, Ancient One? We are to—"

"Come on, come on! No, all of you. Come see this! Right now. I'm really annoyed! Can't you tell?"

Kaladin waited, tense. Would it work? Even when acting angry, there was a certain perkiness to Syl's voice. She sounded too . . . lively to be a Voidspren.

The guards followed though—and as he'd hoped, the glowing length of rope on the wall caught their attention entirely. Kaladin was able to sneak out behind them, passing the post.

At the end of this hallway was the door Syl said led into the spanreed room. Kaladin didn't dare slip through it; he'd step directly into the middle of a hub of activity. Instead he prowled into a smaller hallway to the right—and here he finally caught a break. High up on the wall, near the ceiling, a dark cleft indicated a large ventilation shaft in the stone. Maybe big enough for him to squeeze through.

Syl returned—once again white-blue, and likely invisible. "They're sending one of their number to make a report," she said. "Like you said." She peeked into the shaft in the rock Kaladin had found. "What is this?"

Ventilation? he thought, trying to send the idea to her so he wouldn't have to make noise.

It worked. "Seems too big for that," she said. "This place is so strange."

With two of his brushes, Kaladin was able to haul himself up and inspect the cleft in the stone. Syl flew into the darkened shaft toward some light at the other end. He heard the guards talking as they came back, but he was around the corner from them now, out of sight.

This ventilation shaft looked like it turned toward the spanreed room just to the left. It *was* big enough. Maybe.

Syl waved, excited. So he squeezed in. It was more than wide enough to the right and left, but it was barely high enough. He had to move using his brush handholds to pull himself along. He worried the scraping sounds he made would give him away—but he was rewarded when the shaft opened up to the left, revealing a small, well-lit room. The shaft he'd entered ran through the middle of the large thick wall between this room and whatever was on the other side.

That meant Kaladin was able to peek in—hidden mostly behind the stone—at the room from the top of the wall. Spanreeds stood poised on many pieces of paper, waiting for reports. There was no sign of the two singer women from earlier—they'd delivered their spanreed and gone off duty. However, two other femalens in rich dresses maintained the reeds, checking for blinking lights and moving reeds between actively writing on boards and inactive piles on the tables.

Syl entered, and none of them glanced at her, so she seemed to actually be invisible. So, she began reading the reports that were coming in. The door opened and one of the guards entered, requesting a report be sent to his superior. They'd found what appeared to be the sign of a Radiant—something the Pursuer had told everyone to watch for.

Kaladin might not have much time before the creature himself arrived. Best to move quickly. As the guard left, Kaladin quietly maneuvered in the tight quarters, reaching to his waist and pulling out some of his rope. Directly beneath him was a table with a number of spanreeds, including a leather case that had a few nibs sticking out of it.

He needed to wait for the perfect moment. Fortunately, several spanreeds started blinking at once—and they must have been important ones, for the two femalens quickly turned to these and stopped working on the soldier's report. Kaladin Lashed his rope to one of his brushes, then infused the flat of the brush with a Reverse Lashing—commanding it to attract certain objects only. In this instance, that leather case.

The femalens were so preoccupied that Kaladin felt his chance had come. He lowered the brush on the rope toward the table. As the brush drew near, the leather case moved of its own volition, pulled over so it stuck to the brush.

Heart thumping, certain he was about to be caught, Kaladin drew it up, the case sticking to the end, the spanreeds inside clinking softly. Nobody noticed, and he pulled it into the shaft.

Inside the case, he found an entire group of spanreeds—at least twenty. Perhaps they'd just been delivered, as they were still wrapped in pairs, with twine around them. Judging by the way the rubies glowed with Voidlight, he was hopeful that they would work in the tower.

He tucked the large pouch away in his sack. He then spared a thought for all the important information that was likely being relayed through this room. Could he steal some of it?

No. He'd already risked enough today. He sent a quick thought to Syl, who came zipping up to him as he wiggled backward through the ventilation shaft. She flitted on ahead of him, then called from behind, "Hallway is empty."

He eased out of the hole, catching the edge with his fingers and hanging a moment before quietly dropping the last few feet to the floor of the corridor. He peeked back out toward the guard post.

"Now what?" Syl said. "Want me to imitate a Voidspren again?"

He nodded. Part of him wanted to try another path, as he worried that these soldiers might grow suspicious at the same ruse. But he also knew they'd fallen for it once, and he knew a direct way to the perimeter using this path. Safer this way.

As Syl was getting ready, however, Kaladin spotted something farther down this hallway, away from the guards. A flashing light. He held up his hand to stop Syl, then pointed.

"What is that?" she said, zipping off toward the light. He followed more cautiously, stepping up to a blinking garnet light. Frowning, Kaladin pressed his hand against it.

"Brightness Navani?" he asked.

No, a voice said. It had a middling pitch, not necessarily male or female. *I need you, Radiant. Please. They've found me.*

"You?"

One of the nodes! That protect me. Please. Please, you have to defend it. Please.

"How do you know? Have you told Brightness Navani?"

Please.

"Where?" he said.

Second level, near the central atrium. I will lead you. They realized that one of the nodes would be open to the air, to be renewed by Stormlight. They've sent for her. The Lady of Pains. She'll take my mind. Please, Radiant. Protect me.

Syl hovered beside him. "What?" she asked.

He lowered his hand. He was so tired.

But today, he couldn't afford to be tired. He had to be Kaladin Stormblessed. Kaladin Stormblessed fought anyway.

"We're going to need to find me a better weapon," he said. "Quickly."

59

THE LATTICE OF A GROWING CRYSTAL

This point regarding the Rhythm of War's emotional influence will be of particular interest to El.

—From *Rhythm of War*, page 10

K aladin knew there was a chance he was making a huge mistake. He didn't understand the nature of the tower or what was going on with it and Navani. He was risking a great deal by revealing himself.

However, that garnet light had rescued him from the Pursuer's clutches. And right now, he'd heard something in the spren's voice. A genuine fright. Terror, combined with a plea for protection, was not something Kaladin could ignore.

He was fatigued mentally and physically. As he ran, he drew a field of exhaustionspren, like jets of dust. Worse, a part of him panicked these days every time he went to pick up a weapon. He'd trained himself these last months to function despite those things. He leaned on the spike of energy that coursed through him, even before he drew in Stormlight. He let that control him, instead of the fatigue.

It would catch up to him eventually. But for now, he could pretend to be strong. Pretend to be a soldier again.

The four guards were facing in the other direction, so Kaladin—running at full speed—nearly reached them before the first guard spun around. Kaladin took the chance to burst alight with power, earning him another fraction of a second as the guard panicked, his eyes going wide with fright.

He shouted as Kaladin drew close, hands out before him, waiting for the thrust of the spear. A lot of men were afraid of something sharp coming at them, but as long as his Stormlight held, Kaladin's only real danger was getting outnumbered and overwhelmed.

Kaladin caught the spear as the singer thrust it. He then yanked, throwing the enemy off balance. He'd been taught that maneuver by Hav, who said it was necessary to learn, but almost impossible to execute. Kaladin added his own twist by infusing the shaft with a Full Lashing, making it stick to the guard's hands. Then he shoved the weapon to the side, sticking it to a second guard's spear as he spun.

Kaladin grabbed that spear, infusing it as well, then left both guards stuck to their weapons. As they shouted in surprise, Kaladin held the shafts of the crossed spears—one in each hand—and shoved them upward so the tips struck the ceiling. Then he smoothly ducked through the peaked opening, leaving the two men crying out and struggling as they tried unsuccessfully to free their weapons and hands.

Kaladin slammed his shoulder into the third guard, infusing the singer's coat with a slap to the back. He shoved this guard into the fourth. They fell in a lump, entangled and stuck together. Kaladin danced on his toes, awaiting the next attack. It didn't come. The singers stayed where he'd put them, shouting and railing as they struggled to move.

He kicked a spear up and seized it out of the air. *Hello, old friend. I keep finding my way back to you, don't I?* Perhaps it wasn't *Teft's* addiction he needed to worry about. There was always an excuse for why Kaladin needed the spear again, wasn't there?

This was what he'd been afraid of. This was what made him tremble. The worry that he would never be able to put it down.

He tucked the spear under his arm and took off through the tunnel. A twinkling garnet light appeared on the floor in front of him, moving along one of the strata, leading the way toward a stairwell ahead.

"No," Kaladin said, hoping the tower's spren could hear him. "There will be a guard post at the bottom. I can already hear them responding to those shouts. To reach the second floor, we go out a perimeter balcony, down the outside, and then head inward. That will lose any tails we pick up."

The spren seemed to have heard, for they sent a light moving along the wall next to him—opposite Syl's blue-white ribbon on his other side. They reached the balcony in a few short minutes, a fraction of the time it had taken to sneak inward. They were at the rim of the tower, but the central atrium was far at the eastern side. All the way inward. He'd have to cross the entire second floor to reach it.

He heard shouts behind him, so he'd been right about picking up tails. He stuck his spear to his back by infusing part of it and slapping it against his shirt, then he unwound the rope around his waist. A quick infusion on the end let him stick it to the railing as he stepped up in a fluid motion and leaped off, sticking the other end to his shirt in case he slipped, then holding tight.

He swung out and around, then onto the balcony below. This one, unfortunately, was occupied. So after he recovered his rope, he charged through a family's room—leaping and sliding across their dinner table. He was out the door a moment later, spear in hand. He heard a distant shout of anger from outside the balcony, as the singers above realized he'd gone a way they couldn't follow.

The tower's spren found him here and began guiding him. The strata and lines of crystal didn't always run directly down the corridors, so sometimes the light would spiral around him, following the grain of the stone. Other times the light would vanish when there was no direct path for it, but it would always appear ahead of him again, glowing on the floor or wall, urging him onward.

He drew attention, naturally. The late hour meant that he didn't encounter crowds to slow him, but it also meant there wasn't much else to distract the guard patrols. He infused and tossed his spear at a pair of guards who stumbled into the hallway ahead of him—then stole one of their dropped weapons as they struggled and cursed, trying to get his old weapon to stop sticking to their fingers.

The next set weren't so easily defeated. He found them organizing hastily at an intersection—one he had to pass through, or endure a long detour. Kaladin slowed in the corridor, watching them form up with nets in hand. His first instinct was to take to the walls and disorient them. But of course he didn't have access to that ability—he suspected it would be a long time before he internalized that gravitational Lashings didn't work.

He took his spear in a one-handed grip, the butt tucked under his arm, then nodded to Syl. Together, they rushed the blockade. A few soldiers had crossbows, so he infused the wall with his free hand. When those loosed, the bolts swerved toward the stone.

The group with the nets hung back behind singers with axes. The weapons reminded him of the Parshendi, but the singers were dressed like the Azish, with colorful coats, no gemstones woven into the malens' beards.

They knew how to fight Radiants. The axe wielders came in quickly, forcing him to engage, and then the nets started flying. Kaladin swiped one away with his spear, but that exposed him, and an axe bit him in the side—the kind of wound that would spell death for an ordinary soldier.

Kaladin pulled himself free of the axe, the biting pain fading as his Stormlight healed him, but another net came soaring overhead. They wouldn't mind if they caught some of their number in it, so long as they tangled Kaladin long enough for them to start hacking at him.

Feeling his solitude more than ever, Kaladin dodged the net by retreating. He wanted to infuse one of the nets and stick it to the floor so it couldn't be recovered, but he couldn't bend over to touch it.

Maybe I should remove my boots, he thought. That idea flew counter to all of his training, but he didn't fight like he once had. These days, a stubbed toe would be healed instantly—while being able to infuse the ground he walked on would be a huge advantage.

He kept the singers at bay with some careful lunges, then backed up before a net could catch him. Unfortunately, this group was probably meant to stall him while Regals and Fused could be mustered. It was working perfectly. Without a Shardblade, Kaladin was far from unstoppable. He was forced away until he reached another intersection.

"Kaladin," Syl said, hovering beside his head as a ribbon of light. "To your left."

He spared a glance to see a flashing garnet light on the wall farther down the left-hand corridor. Well, he certainly wasn't going to push through these soldiers anytime soon. He took off in a dash toward the light, and the soldiers—rightly timid when facing a Radiant—followed more cautiously. That gave Kaladin time to kick open a door, following the light, and enter an upscale glassmaker's shop.

It seemed like a dead end until he spotted the hint of a gemstone set into the wall behind the counter. He leaped over it and infused the stone, and was rewarded as the wall parted. He slipped through the opening, then set the thing closing behind him.

This put him in a second, larger shop, filled with half-finished dressing dummies. He startled a late-night worker, a human with a Thaylen naval mustache and curled eyebrows. He dropped his adze and leaped to his feet, then clapped his hands.

"Brightlord Stormblessed!" he exclaimed.

"Quietly," Kaladin said, crossing the room and cracking the door to peek out. "You need to hide. When they come asking, you didn't see me."

The hallway outside was clear, and Kaladin was pretty sure he knew where he was. This shortcut had completely circumvented the blockade. Hopefully that would confuse the soldiers as they tried to track him. Kaladin moved to sneak out the door, but the woodworker caught him by the arm.

"Radiant," he said. "How? How do you still fight?"

"The same way you do," Kaladin said. "One day at a time, always taking the next step." He took the man's wrist with his hand. "Don't get yourself killed. But also don't give up hope."

The man nodded.

"Hide," Kaladin said. "They'll come searching for me."

He pulled free and joined Syl. After about ten minutes of jogging, he heard shouting to his right, but nobody came running—and he realized where they thought he was heading: to a set of stairs that led directly toward the larger stairwell, which in turn led to the basement. They thought he was trying to rescue the queen, or maybe reach the crystal pillar.

Their error let him follow some back pathways without meeting any patrols, until he finally drew near the atrium. He'd managed to cross the entire floor, but he was now so deeply embedded within the tower that he was essentially surrounded.

The light led him around to the northern side of the tower, through some residential hallways, with lights under the doors. Rooms near the atrium and its grand window were popular—here, people could still see sunlight, but the atrium was generally warmer than the perimeter, with easy access to lifts.

The area was unnaturally silent, perhaps under curfew. He was used to the atrium region being alive with the sound of people talking all hours of the day, the lifts clanking faintly as they moved. Tonight it was hushed. He crept along the tower spren's path, wondering when he'd find resistance. Surely someone would have put together what he was doing. Surely they would . . .

He stopped in the hallway as he saw bright light ahead. He could have sworn he'd reached the furthermost edge of the tower, the place near the enormous glass window that looked out to the east. There shouldn't be any more rooms here, but ahead and to his right, moonlight spilled through an opening.

He inched up to find the area strewn with rubble. A secret door in the wall had been broken open; when he peeked through, he saw a short tunnel that ended at open air. This *was* the eastern wall of the tower, the flat side of Urithiru. The secret tunnel here was old, not newly cut, and had been created open to the air of the mountains.

The Pursuer was here, standing with another Fused and inspecting a strange device at the end of the short tunnel, right where it ended and opened to the air. A glowing sapphire, easily as large as a chasmfiend's gemheart, had been set into a built-in stand rising from the floor. The entire mechanism was covered over in crem, so it had been here a while, and the Fused had needed to break off a crem crust to reach the gemstone.

The implication struck Kaladin immediately. As the Sibling had hinted, a node to defend the tower had been placed where it could draw in Stormlight naturally from the storms, when they reached this high. The unfamiliar Fused was a tall femalen with a topknot of red-orange hair. She wore practical battle gear, leather and cloth, and stood with her hands clasped behind her back as she inspected the sapphire.

The other was, as he'd noted earlier, the Pursuer. A hulking mountain of chitin and dark brown cloth, with eyes glowing a deep red. All of the spheres had been removed from the lanterns in the hallway behind Kaladin, so the only light came from the sapphire.

"See?" the femalen said in Alethi as they spotted Kaladin. "I told you he'd come. I keep my promises, Pursuer. He's yours."

The red eyes focused on Kaladin, then went dark as a ribbon of crimson light burst from the center of the Pursuer's mass. The body—a discarded husk—collapsed to the floor. Kaladin raised his spear, gauging where the Pursuer would land. He thrust on instinct, hoping to catch the Fused as he materialized.

This time, however, the Pursuer's ribbon jogged and looped a few times, disorienting Kaladin. He thrust again, missing the mark as the Pursuer coalesced to the side of Kaladin's spear. The creature lunged for Kaladin, who danced backward into the darkened hallway outside the tunnel.

The creature stepped into the broken doorway. So, Kaladin infused his spear and tossed it at the Pursuer—who reflexively caught it. That stuck his hands to the spear, and Kaladin leaped forward and shoved himself against the Fused, getting him to step backward. The two ends of the spear stuck to the walls on either side of the opening.

Kaladin leaped away, leaving the creature partially immobilized, awkwardly trying to move with both hands locked into place. Then, of course, the Pursuer just dropped that body as a husk and launched out as a ribbon of light. Kaladin cursed. He was too unpracticed with this kind of fighting—and this kind of opponent. What had worked on the soldiers was a foolish move here. He lunged to grab his spear, but it fell beneath the collapsing husk.

The Pursuer materialized directly behind Kaladin, grabbing him with powerful hands, preventing him from reaching the spear. It was a poor weapon for this fight anyway. The Pursuer obviously excelled at getting in close.

Kaladin twisted, trying to wrench free, but the Pursuer gripped him in a precise hold, executed perfectly, immobilizing both of Kaladin's arms. The creature then pushed, using his superior weight to knock Kaladin to his knees.

The Pursuer didn't try to choke Kaladin. The creature didn't even release him with one hand to grab a knife, as he had during their previous fight. All the Pursuer had to do was hold Kaladin still until his Stormlight ran out. They were deep within the tower, surrounded by other singers and Fused. The longer this fight lasted, the worse it would go for Kaladin.

He struggled, trying to pull free. In response, the Pursuer leaned in and spoke with a thick accent. "I will kill you. It is my right. I have killed every person—human or singer—who has ever killed me."

Kaladin tried to roll them both to the side, but the Pursuer held them stable.

"No one has ever defeated me twice," the creature whispered. "But if you somehow managed such a feat, I would keep coming. We are no longer confined to Braize at the end of the war, and I am immortal. I can follow you forever. *I* am the spren of *vengeance*."

Kaladin tried to infuse his opponent, as he might have with a gravitational Lashing. The Light resisted, but that wasn't surprising. Fused had powers of their own, and for some reason that made them difficult to infuse.

So he instead stretched and brushed the floor with one hand, infusing the stone. It trapped the Pursuer's feet, but it also stuck to Kaladin's boots, locking them together.

"Let go now," the Pursuer said. "Die, as is *your* right. You will never be able to sleep soundly again, little Radiant. I will always come, always hunt you. As sure as the storms. I will—"

"Put him down!" a stern voice said as a red spren strode across the floor. "Right now! We need him. You can kill him after!"

The Pursuer relaxed his grip, perhaps stunned to be given an order by a Voidspren. Kaladin elbowed the Pursuer in the chin—which hurt like a hammer to the elbow—forcing the creature to let go. That let Kaladin lunge forward and recover some Stormlight by brushing the floor, which in turn set his feet free. He scrambled away, leaving enough Stormlight infused in the floor to keep the Pursuer planted in place.

The creature focused on Syl. "You lie well, for an honorspren," he said. His body crumbled, his ribbon vanishing around a corner. As before, he seemed to need a break after abandoning a third body.

Kaladin suspected that if the Pursuer made a fourth body, he wouldn't have enough Voidlight left to escape it. That might be how you killed him: trap him in the fourth body. Either that, or catch him by surprise and kill him before he could eject, which was what Kaladin had done before.

"Thanks," Kaladin said as Syl turned blue again. He grabbed his spear, then glanced over his shoulder and saw some humans peeking out of their rooms, watching the fight. He waved for them to close their doors, then hopped through the rubble and dashed toward the Fused at the end of the secret tunnel.

As he approached, he spotted a glass globe, perhaps six inches in diameter, set into a small alcove in the wall near the gemstone. At first he thought it was some kind of lighting fixture, but it was wrapped in metal wires like a fabrial. What on Roshar?

He didn't have time to inspect it further, for the Fused was pressing her hand against the sapphire. The gemstone's light had started to fade.

She's corrupting the pillar, Kaladin thought, *using this as a conduit to touch it.* He leveled his spear at her.

She stopped and turned to regard him. "The Pursuer isn't lying," she said in accented Alethi. "He *will* hunt you forever. To the abandonment of all reason and duty."

"Step away from the gemstone," Kaladin said.

"He'll return shortly," she noted. "You should flee. He has placed Void-light gemstones in stashes nearby, so he can reinfuse himself and make new bodies."

"I said *step away.*"

"You're a Windrunner," she said. "You won't hurt me if I'm not a threat."

"Touching that gemstone makes you a threat. Step away."

She did, which meant walking toward him, clasping her hands behind her. "What is it, do you suppose, that makes you able to continue using your powers? I'll admit, I *had* worried about the Windrunners. They say your Surges are closest to Honor."

Kaladin gripped his spear, uncertain what to do. Stab her? He had to protect the gemstone.

Or destroy it, he thought. Storms, that would weaken the shield Navani had set up—and if the enemy had found *this* one so quickly, how long would it be until they discovered the others? He glanced to Syl on his shoulder, and she shook her head. She didn't know what to do either.

"Ah," the Fused said. "He's back. On with you, then."

Kaladin risked looking over his shoulder, cursing as he saw a distinctly bloodred ribbon of light approaching. Making a snap decision, Kaladin dropped his spear and pulled out his scalpel. Then he quickly sliced the laces on his boots.

The Pursuer appeared inside the tunnel and grabbed for him, but Kaladin bent—dodging the grip—and infused the floor with a Full Lashing. Then he leaped forward around the Pursuer, leaving his shoes stuck to the stone. The Pursuer couldn't help but land on that floor, trapping him in place.

Kaladin held out his scalpel, barefoot as he backed up into the rubble of the broken wall that had been opened. The Pursuer eyed him, remaining rooted on the ground. Then he grinned and left his body, shooting toward Kaladin.

Kaladin retreated through the opening into the outer corridor, infusing the floor again, using up a large amount of his Stormlight. He was able to roll away from the Pursuer's next attack, which again left the creature rooted. But Kaladin couldn't step forward and reclaim the Light he'd used, not without getting within the Pursuer's reach.

His Stormlight was almost gone, something the Pursuer had clearly figured out. The creature left his second body, the first already starting to crumble. When Kaladin leaped forward to try to retrieve his Stormlight, the Pursuer darted at him as a ribbon of light—like a snapping eel—and Kaladin retreated.

The two watched one another in the dark corridor. The Pursuer could only form one more body before he'd need to renew his Voidlight, or risk fighting in his fourth body and perhaps being killed. But Kaladin's Light was low—and he didn't have a quick way to get more.

Storms. The other Fused—the femalen—had returned to the gemstone and was working on it again.

"We have to destroy it, Kaladin," Syl whispered.

She was right. He couldn't defend this place on his own. He'd simply have to hope that the other nodes were better hidden. Though . . . how could something be better hidden than in the *middle* of a *wall*?

Kaladin took a deep breath, then dashed forward to force the Pursuer to materialize. He did so—but only after zipping back into the center of the second pool of Light Kaladin had made. That let the creature materialize standing on the remnants of his second husk, which was stuck to the Light.

The Fused crouched low, hands out and ready to grab Kaladin if he tried to run past. Kaladin was forced to shy back.

I can't afford to fight him the way he wants, Kaladin thought. *If he gets me into his grip, I'll end up pinned.*

When he'd killed the creature before, Kaladin had used the Pursuer's assumptions against him. This time he wasn't making the same mistake, but he was still so very confident.

Use that. *Let him defeat himself.*

Kaladin turned and started running in the opposite direction.

Behind, the Pursuer began laughing. "That's right, human! Flee! You see it now! Run and be pursued."

Syl zipped up alongside Kaladin. "What's the plan?"

"He's called the Pursuer," Kaladin said. "He loves the chase. When we were doing what humans shouldn't do—trying to fight him—he was deliberate and careful. Now we're fleeing prey. He might get sloppy. But he won't leave that third body until we're far enough away that he's sure we won't just double back and attack that other Fused. Go warn me when he does."

"Right." She darted off to watch.

Kaladin took a few turns in the corridor, then said, "Tower spren, I need you!" A garnet light ahead started flashing quickly as if anxious.

Kaladin jogged to it, and Syl came darting back. "The Pursuer is recharging—but he's not leaving the fabrial unwatched! He's getting Voidlight from the other Fused."

Kaladin nodded as he pressed his hand to the wall. The tower spren spoke in his mind.

SheiskillingmeSheiskillingmeSheiskillingme. Stopitstopit.

"I'm trying," Kaladin said. He dug out some of his gemstones, then infused his Stormlight into them to preserve what he had left. "I'm not convinced I can beat that monster again. Not without a team on a battlefield. He fights too well one-on-one. So, I need another hidden room. One with only a single exit—and with a door that will open and close fast."

You're going to hide? the Sibling said, hysterical. *You can't—*

"I won't abandon you, but you need to do this for me. We don't have much time. Please."

"Kaladin!" Syl said. "He's coming!"

Kaladin cursed, leaving the Sibling and dashing for an intersection in the dark corridors ahead.

"Duck!" Syl said.

Kaladin ducked, narrowly avoiding the Pursuer's grip as he materialized. As Kaladin darted a different direction, the creature tried again, dropping a husk and shooting ahead of Kaladin.

Trying to play the part of panicked prey, Kaladin turned and ran the other way—though he hated putting his back to the creature like that. He could almost feel him, forming with arms grabbing at Kaladin's neck. . . .

As he dashed through the corridor, people who had been watching snapped their doors shut. Behind him, the Pursuer laughed. Yes, he understood *this* kind of fight. He enjoyed it. "Run!" he shouted. "Run, little human!"

Ahead, garnet light flashed, then began moving down a side hallway. Kaladin scrambled that direction as Syl warned him the Pursuer was coming. The garnet light, fortunately, moved up a wall straight ahead, then flashed, revealing a gemstone hidden in the rock. Kaladin drew in the Light of one of his spheres and infused the gemstone, making the door begin to open. It was faster than previous ones, as he'd asked.

Syl cried, "He's almost here!"

"As soon as I walk in," Kaladin whispered to the tower's spren, "start closing the door. Then lock it."

He glanced back, and saw the red light rapidly approaching. So, taking a deep breath, Kaladin ducked through the once-hidden doorway. As he'd asked, it immediately began to grind closed. Kaladin turned to face outward, anxious as he pulled free his scalpel. He made it look like he intended to stand and fight.

Go for my back again, like you've done before. Please.

The ribbon danced in over his head. Kaladin leaped forward, squeezing through the tight doorway as it closed, right as the Pursuer appeared in the room behind him.

Kaladin fell forward and scrambled across the ground. Behind him, the door thumped closed. He waited, his heart thundering in his chest, as he turned and watched the doorway. Would the Pursuer's ribbon be small enough to squeeze through? These hidden doors sealed so tightly they were almost impossible to see from the outside, and Syl had physical form as a ribbon. He assumed the same rules applied to the Pursuer.

Syl flitted down beside him, taking the shape of a young woman in a Bridge Four uniform. She colored it a dark blue.

Quiet. Followed by a yell of rage, muffled to near silence by the intervening stone. Kaladin grinned, picking himself up. He thought he heard the Pursuer yell, "Coward!"

He gave the closed door a salute, then turned to jog back the way he had come. Again he had to hiss at people to close their doors and stay out of sight. Where was their sense of self-preservation?

Their eyes were hopeful when they saw him. And in those expressions, he understood why they had to look, regardless of the danger. They thought everyone had been conquered and controlled, but here was a Radiant. Their hopes pressed on him as he finally reached the hidden tunnel. The femalen Fused with the topknot stood in a posture of concentration, her hand pressed against the sapphire.

She didn't *seem* to be corrupting it. Indeed, she had brought out a large diamond and was holding it up to the sapphire—drawing light from it. Stormlight, it seemed, although it was tinged faintly the wrong color.

Kaladin scooped a piece of broken rubble from the floor. The sides of the rubble were smoothly cut. The work of a Shardblade.

Kaladin leaped forward and shoved the Fused back, trying to knock her off the cliff. That caused her to exclaim and fall out of her trance, though she grabbed a protruding rock and prevented herself from falling.

Before she could stop him, Kaladin slammed his rubble into the gemstone, cracking it. That was enough—cracked gemstones couldn't hold Stormlight—but he slammed it a few more times to be certain, breaking the sapphire free of its housing and sending it tumbling into the void outside.

It vanished into darkness, plummeting hundreds upon hundreds of feet down the sheer cliff toward the rocks far below. Kaladin felt something when it broke free. A faint sense that the darkness in the tower had grown stronger—or perhaps Kaladin was only now recognizing the results of the Fused's recent attempt at corrupting the tower.

He puffed out, the deed done, and backed away. In that moment though—his Stormlight running low, his energy deflating, the darkness growing stronger—he flagged. He reached out for the wall as his vision wavered, and the fatigue seemed to be almost too much.

A shadow moved in front of him, and he forced himself alert—but not before the Fused in the topknot managed to ram a knife into his chest. He felt an immediate spike of pain and pulled out his scalpel, but the Fused jumped back before he could strike.

Painspren wriggled up from the stone as Kaladin stumbled, bleeding. He drew in the last of his Stormlight and pressed his hand to the wound. Storms. His mind . . . was fuzzy. And the darkness seemed so strong.

The Fused, however, didn't seem interested in striking again. She tucked away her knife and laced her fingers before herself, watching him. Oddly, he noticed that the glass sphere that had been in the little stone alcove was gone. Where had the Fused put it?

"You continue to heal," she noted. "And I saw the use of Adhesion earlier. I assume from the way you move, confined to the ground, that Gravitation has abandoned you. Does your hybrid power work? The one your kind often uses to direct arrows in flight?"

Kaladin didn't respond. He gripped his scalpel, waiting to heal. The pain lingered. Was healing slower than usual? "What did you to do me?" he demanded, hoarse. "Was that blade poisoned?"

"No," she said. "I merely wanted to inspect your healing. It seems to be lethargic, does it not? Hmmm . . ."

He didn't like how she looked at him, so discerning and interested—like a surgeon inspecting a corpse before a dissection. She didn't seem to care that he had destroyed her chance at corrupting the tower—perhaps because Kaladin's attack had furthered her eventual goal of reaching the crystal pillar.

He raised his scalpel, waiting for his storming wound to heal. It continued to do so. Languidly.

"If you kill me," the Fused noted, "I will simply be reborn. I will choose the most innocent among the singers of the tower. A mother perhaps, with a child precisely old enough to understand the pain of loss—but not old enough to understand why her mother now rejects her."

Kaladin growled despite himself, stepping forward.

"Yes," the femalen said. "A true Windrunner, all the way to your gemheart. Fascinating. You had no continuity of spren or traditions from the old ones, I'm led to believe. Yet the same attitudes, the same structures, arise naturally—like the lattice of a growing crystal."

Kaladin growled again, sliding to the side toward his discarded spear and shoes.

"You should go," the Fused said. "If you've killed the Pursuer again, it will make for quite the stir among my kind. I don't believe that's ever been accomplished. Regardless, I have Fused and Regals on their way to join us and finish his work. You might escape them, if you leave now."

Kaladin hesitated, uncertain. His instincts said he should do the opposite of whatever this femalen said, out of principle. But he thought better of it and fled into the corridors—his side aching—trusting in the tower spren and Syl to guide him out of danger and to a safe hiding place.

60

ESSAI

Who is this person? You used no title, so I assume they are not a Fused. Who, then, is El?

—From *Rhythm of War*, page 10 undertext

Venli felt all rhythms freeze when she saw Rlain in the cell. Like the silence following a crescendo.

In that silence, Venli finally believed what Mazish had told her. In that silence, all of Roshar changed. Venli was no longer the last. And in that silence, Venli thought she could hear something distant beyond the rhythms. A pure tone.

Rlain looked up through the bars, then sneered at her.

The moment of peace vanished. He'd picked up some human expressions, it seemed. Did he recognize her in this form? Her skin patterns were the same, but she and Rlain had never been close. He likely saw only an unfamiliar Regal.

Venli retreated down the hallway, passing several empty cells with bars on the doors. It was the day after the incident with Stormblessed and the destruction of the node. Venli had been on her way to visit Rlain when the event had occurred, drawing her away to attend her master.

Curiously, though Venli had assumed that Raboniel would be furious, instead she'd taken it in stride. She'd almost seemed *amused* at what had occurred. She was hiding something about her motivations. She seemed to not *want* the corruption to happen too quickly.

At any rate, dealing with the aftermath of the incident had involved Venli interpreting late into the night for various Fused. It hadn't been until this morning that she'd been able to break away and come check on what Mazish had told her.

Rlain. Alive.

Near the door, Venli met with the head jailer: a direform Regal with a crest of spikes beginning on his head and running down his neck.

"I didn't realize we *had* a prison," she said to him—softly, and to Indifference.

"The humans built it," he replied, also to Indifference. "I interviewed several of the workers here. They claim they were keeping the assassin in here."

"*The* assassin?"

"Indeed. He vanished right before we arrived."

"He should have fallen unconscious."

"Well, he didn't, and nobody has seen anything of him."

"You should have told me of this earlier," Venli said. "The Lady thinks that certain Radiants might still be able to function in the tower. It's possible this one is out there somewhere, preparing to kill."

The direform hummed to Abashment. "Well, we've been prepping this place in case we need to lock up a Regal with proper comforts. We've got a larger brig for human prisoners. Figured this would be a good place for your friend there, until official word arrived."

Venli glanced along the hall of empty cells, lit by topaz lanterns hanging from the ceiling. They gave the chamber a soft brown warmth, the color of cremstone.

"Why did you lock him away?" she asked.

"He's an essai," the direform said to Derision, using an ancient word they'd picked up from the Fused. It meant something along the lines of "human lover," though her form told her it technically meant "hairy."

"He was a spy my people sent to watch them."

"Then he betrayed you," the direform said. "He claims he'd been held by the humans against his will, but it didn't take much asking around to find the truth. He was friendly with the Radiants—was their servant or something. Could have left at any time, but stayed. Wanted to keep being a slave, I guess." He changed to the Rhythm of Executions—a rarely used rhythm.

"I will speak with him," Venli said. "Alone."

The direform studied her, humming to Destruction in challenge. She hummed it back—she outranked this one, so long as she was Raboniel's Voice.

"I will send again to the Lady of Wishes," he finally said, "to inform her that you have done this."

"As you will," Venli said, then waited pointedly until he stepped out and shut the door. Venli glanced into Shadesmar, as she'd grown into the habit of doing, though she'd learned Voidspren couldn't hide in the tower. It was instinct by now. And she—

Wait. There *was* a Voidspren here.

It was hiding in the body of a cremling. Most spren could enter bodies, if they couldn't pass through other solid objects. She wasn't terribly familiar with all the varieties of Voidspren, but this one must have realized that it couldn't hide in the tower as it once had, so used this method to remain unseen.

She attuned Anxiety, and Timbre agreed. Was it watching her, or Rlain? Or was it simply here to patrol? Had she done anything recently that would give her away?

She maintained her composure, pretending to think as she strolled in the prison chamber. Then she pretended to notice the cremling for the first time, then shooed it away. The thing scuttled down the wall and out under the door. She glanced into Shadesmar, and saw the Voidspren—through the hundreds of shimmering colors that made up the tower—retreating into the distance alongside the tiny speck of light that represented the cremling.

That left her nervous enough that she paced a few times—and checked again—before finally she forced herself to return to the cell. "*Rlain.*"

He looked up at her. Then he frowned and stood.

"It's me," she said to Peace, speaking in the listener language for an extra measure of privacy. "Venli."

He stepped closer to the bars, and his eyes flickered to her face. He hummed to Remembrance. "I was under the impression they had killed all of the listeners."

"Only most of us. What are you *doing* here, Rlain? Last we knew, the humans had discovered you in the warcamps and executed you!"

"I . . . wasn't discovered," he said. He spoke to Curiosity, but his body language—he had indeed picked up some human attitudes—betrayed his true emotions. He obviously didn't trust her. "I was made an example, used as an experiment. They put me in the bridge crews. I don't think anyone ever suspected I was a spy. They just thought I was too smart for a parshman."

"You've been living among them all this time? That guard says you're an ess—a human sympathizer. I can't believe you're alive, and I'm not the . . . I mean . . ." Language failed her, and she ended up standing there, humming the Rhythm of the Lost and feeling like an idiot. Timbre chimed in, giving the same rhythm—and that helped somehow.

Rlain studied her. He'd probably heard that forms of power changed a person's personality—storms . . . they'd always known that. Known they were dangerous.

"Rlain," she said, her voice soft, "I'm me. *Truly* me. This form doesn't . . . change me like stormform did for the others."

Timbre pulsed. Tell him the truth. Show him what you are.

She locked up. *No.* She couldn't.

"The others?" he asked, hopeful. "Remala? Eshonai? She fought Adolin, we think, in battle. Do you know . . . if she is . . ."

"I saw my sister's corpse myself at the bottom of the chasms," she said to Pain. "There aren't any others left but me. He . . . Odium took them, made them into Fused. He saved me because he wanted me to tell stories about our people, use them to inspire the newly freed singers. But I think he was afraid of us, as a group. So he destroyed us."

She hummed to the Rhythm of the Lost again. Rlain eventually joined her and stepped forward until he was right beside the bars.

"I'm sorry, Venli," he eventually said. "That must have been awful."

He doesn't know, she realized, *that I caused all this. How could he? He was among the humans. To him, I'm simply . . . another survivor.*

She found that idea daunting.

"You need to free me," Rlain said. "I hoped they'd accept my story, but I'm too well known in the tower. You stand out when you're the only 'parshman' anyone knows."

"I'll see what I can do," Venli said to Reconciliation. "The guard doesn't trust me—a lot of them don't—and talking to you will make that worse. If I do get you out, what are you going to do? You won't get me into trouble, will you?"

He frowned at her, then hummed to Irritation.

"You *are* a human sympathizer," Venli said.

"They're my friends," he said. "My family, now. They aren't perfect, Venli, but if we want to defeat Odium we're going to need them. We're going to need this tower."

"Do we want to defeat Odium?" Venli asked. "A lot of people like the way things are going, Rlain. We have a nation of our own—not a few shacks in a backwater countryside, but a *real* nation with cities, roads, infrastructure. Things—I might add—that were largely built by the efforts of enslaved singers. The humans don't deserve our loyalty or even an alliance. Not after what they did."

Rlain didn't object immediately. Instead he hummed to Tension. "We find ourselves caught, literally, between two storms," he finally said. "But if I'm going to pick one to walk through, Venli, I'll pick the highstorm. That was once our storm. The spren were our allies. And yes, the humans tried to exploit the listeners, then tried to destroy us—but the Fused are the ones who *succeeded.* Odium chose to destroy our people. I'm not going to serve him. I . . ."

He trailed off, perhaps realizing what he was saying. He'd tried to start the conversation noncommittal, plainly worried she was an agent for

Odium. Now he'd confirmed where he stood. He looked to her, and his humming fell silent. Waiting.

"I don't know if any good can be done by fighting him, Rlain," she whispered. "But I . . . keep secrets from Odium myself. I've been trying to build something separate from his rule, a people I could . . . I don't know, use to start a new group of listeners."

Trying, in her own pitiful way, to undo what she'd done.

"How many?" Rlain asked, to Excitement.

"A dozen so far," Venli said. "I have them watching over the fallen Radiants. I have some authority in the tower, but I don't know how far it will extend. It's complicated. The various Fused have different motivations, and I'm wrapped up in the threads of it all. I helped save some humans who were going to be executed—but I'm not interested in allying with them in general."

"Who did you save? The queen?"

"No, someone far less important," Venli said. "A surgeon and his wife, who were—"

"Lirin and Hesina?" he asked to Excitement. "The child too, I hope."

"Yes. How did you—"

"You *need* to get me *out*, Venli," Rlain said. "And get me to Hesina. I have something useful I could show her—and you, if you want to help."

"I've been trying to tell you," Venli whispered, glancing over her shoulder at the door. "I have *some* authority, but there are many who distrust me. I don't know if I can get you free. It might draw too much attention to me."

"Venli," he said to Confidence, "look at me."

She met his gaze. Had he always been this intense? Eshonai had known him better than she had.

"You need to do this," Rlain said to her. "You need to use whatever influence you have and *get me out*."

"I don't know if—"

"Stop being so insufferably selfish! Do something *against* your own self-interest, for the greater good, for once in your *storming* life, Venli."

She hummed to Betrayal. She didn't deserve that. She'd just told him how she was trying to rebuild the listeners. But he hummed louder to Confidence, so she aligned her rhythm to his.

"I'll try," she said.

⁘

Though Raboniel often spent her time down near the crystal pillar—or with the human scholars in the chambers nearby—the Lady of Wishes had indicated she would be about other duties today. By asking around, Venli found that she was for some reason at the Blackthorn's former rooms.

Venli stepped inside, where an unusual number of Fused had gathered and were systematically going through the warlord's belongings—cataloguing them, making notations about them, and packing them away. Venli passed through and saw one crate contained socks: each pair recorded and carefully stored.

They were putting all of his things into storage, but why had they dedicated Fused to such a mundane job? What was more, these were important Fused, none of the more erratic or crazy represented. Leshwi herself had been pressed into the work, and that all together whispered something meaningful: Someone very high up in the singer hierarchy was interested in this man. To the point of wanting to dissect and understand his each and every possession, no matter how ordinary.

Venli moved around the perimeter of the room, careful to stay away from the broad doors or windows leading to the balcony. Those had been draped off, but the rules were strict during daylight hours. No singers were to show themselves outside, lest they accidentally reveal the truth to Windrunner scouts.

She found two humans she didn't recognize at the doorway into the bedroom, watching what occurred inside. There, Raboniel was speaking to a third human. The tall male was dressed in a coat and trousers that seemed elegant to Venli's eyes—though she knew little of their fashion. More striking was the strange creature on his shoulder, an odd thing unlike any Venli had ever seen. It stood on two legs like a person, though its face ended in a beak and it had brightly colored scales that looked *soft*, of all things. When she entered, it turned and stared at her, and she was unnerved by how bright and intelligent its eyes seemed.

The Lady of Wishes sat in a chair by the bed, her face passive, with stacks of papers and books beside her.

Who was this man, and why would Raboniel pause her research to give him an audience? The Lady normally ignored requests from humans, going so far as to have several "important" ones flogged when they demanded audiences. More curious, as Venli edged around the side of the room, she saw that the man's face was scarred in several places, bespeaking a roughness in contrast to his fine clothing.

"The only thing I find remarkable," Raboniel said to Derision, "is how audacious you are, human. Do you not understand how easily I could have you beaten or killed?"

"That would be to throw away a useful opportunity," the man said, loud and bold—a human version of the Rhythm of Determination. "And you are not one who throws away something useful, are you, Ancient One?"

"Use is relative," Raboniel replied. "I will throw away an opportunity I'll never have time to exploit if it is preventing me from something better."

"What is better than free riches?" he said.

"I have Urithiru," she said. "What need have I of spheres?"

"Not that kind of riches," the man said, with a smile. He stepped forward and respectfully handed her a large pouch. Raboniel took it, and it made a soft clink. Raboniel undid the top, and stared inside. She sat there for a long moment, and when she next spoke, her voice was *devoid* of rhythms. "How? Where did you get this?"

"I bring a gift," was all the man said. "To encourage you to meet with my *babsk* to negotiate terms. I had thought to wait until the current . . . turmoil subsided, but my *babsk* is determined. We will have a deal for use of the Oathgates. And we will pay."

"It is . . . a fine gift," Raboniel finally said.

"That is not the gift," he said. "That is a mere advance on our future payments. This is the gift."

He gestured to the side, and the strange creature on his shoulder whistled. The two men that Venli had seen outside entered, carrying something between them—a large cloth-covered box. It barely fit through the door, and was heavy, judging by the *thump* it made when they set it down.

The lead human whipped the cloth off, revealing a small teenage human girl in a box with bars on the sides. The dirty creature growled as she huddled in the center, shadowed. The man gestured dramatically, then bowed and began to walk away.

"Human?" Raboniel said. "I did not dismiss you. What is this? I need no slaves."

"This is no slave," the man said. "But if your master does happen to ever locate Cultivation, suggest that he ask her precisely *why* she made an Edgedancer who is fueled by Lifelight and not Stormlight." He bowed again—a formal military bow—then withdrew.

Venli waited, expecting Raboniel to demand he be executed, or at least flogged. Instead she started humming to Conceit. She even smiled.

"I am confused, Ancient One," Venli said, looking after the man.

"You needn't be," Raboniel said, "for this has nothing to do with you. He *is* dramatic, as I was warned. Hopefully he thinks I was put onto the back foot by his little stunt. Did he *really* deliver me a Radiant who is awake despite the tower's protections?" She peered in at the caged child, who stared back defiantly and growled. "Barely seems tame."

She clapped, and several servants entered. "Take this one to a secure place and do not let her go. Be careful. She might be dangerous." As they took the cage, she turned to Venli and spoke to Craving. "So, was it really another of your people, as the reports say?"

"Yes," Venli said. "I know him. His name is Rlain. A listener."

"A child of traitors," Raboniel said.

"As am I," Venli said, then paused. She took a deep breath and changed her rhythm to Conceit. "I would have him released to my care. I haven't any other kin to speak of. He is precious to me."

"Odium specifically made your kin extinct," Raboniel said. "You are the last. A distinction that you should appreciate, for the way it makes you unique."

"I do not wish uniqueness," Venli said. "I wish to keep this malen alive and enjoy his company. I have served well in several capacities, to multiple Fused. I demand this compensation."

Raboniel hummed to Derision. Venli panicked, and nearly lost her will—but Timbre, always watching, pulsed to *Conceit*. A rhythm of Odium, but the best counterpart to Resolve. The rhythm Venli needed to continue to express now. She did so, humming it, as she didn't trust herself to speak.

"Very well," Raboniel said, picking up her papers to begin reading again. "Your Passion does you credit. He is yours. Be certain he doesn't cause problems, for I will lay them at your charge."

Venli hummed to Tribute, then quickly retreated. Inside, Timbre pulsed to one of the normal rhythms. She seemed in pain, as if using one of the wrong rhythms had been hard for her. But they'd done it. Like she'd freed the Windrunner's family.

Timbre pulsed. Freedom. That was to be her next oath, Venli realized. To free those who had been taken unjustly. She almost said a new oath out loud, right there, but Timbre pulsed in warning.

So she returned to her rooms before going to Rlain. She shut the door to her quarters, then whispered the words.

"I will seek freedom for those in bondage," she said, then waited. Nothing happened. Had it worked?

A distant sensation struck her, a femalen voice, so very far away—but thrumming with the pure rhythm of Roshar.

These words, it said, *are not accepted.*

Not accepted? Venli sank down into a chair. Timbre pulsed to the Rhythm of Confusion. But in her gemheart, Venli realized she knew the reason. She'd just watched a child trapped in a cage be hauled off by Raboniel's servants. It seemed obvious, now that she considered.

She couldn't honestly speak those words. Not when she was concerned with freeing Rlain primarily because she wanted another listener to confide in. Not when she was willing to ignore the need of a child locked in a cage.

If she wanted to honestly progress as a Radiant, she'd need to do as Rlain had said and start thinking about someone other than herself. And it was beyond time for her to begin treating her powers with the respect they deserved.

Singer folios focus on how fashion augments singer forms and skin patterns.
Specifically, this plate illustrates how a Fused might dress their envoyform
Voice in a way that demands attention in a crowded gathering.

61

OIL AND WATER

In other circumstances, I would be fascinated by this sand to the point of abandoning all other rational pursuits. What is it? Where did it come from?

—From *Rhythm of War*, page 13

Finally, at long last, Navani heard Kaladin's voice.

I'm sorry, Brightness, he said, his voice transmitted via the Sibling to Navani. *I collapsed when I got back last night, and fell asleep. I didn't intentionally keep you waiting.*

Upon arriving at the chamber of scholars in the morning, Navani had discovered—via the Sibling—that she had slept through what had nearly been the end of their resistance. She had then waited several interminable hours to hear from the Windrunner.

"Don't apologize," Navani whispered, standing in her now customary place, her hands behind her, touching the line of crystal on the wall as she surveyed her working scholars. Guards stood at the door, and the strange insane Fused sat in her place by the far wall, but no one interfered directly with Navani. "You did what you had to—and you did well."

I failed, Kaladin said.

"No," Navani said softly, but firmly. "Highmarshal, your job is not to save the tower. Your job is to buy me time enough to reverse what has been done. You didn't fail. You accomplished something incredible, and because of it we can still fight."

His reply was long in coming. *Thank you,* he said, his voice bolstered. *I needed to hear those words.*

"They are true," Navani said. "Given enough time, I'm confident I can flush the tower of the enemy's Light, then instead prime it with the proper kind."

It came down to the nature of Stormlight, Voidlight, and the way the Sibling worked. Navani needed to take a crash course in Light, and figure out exactly what had gone wrong.

Breaking the node seems to have made things worse, Kaladin said. *Healing takes longer now. A Fused hit me with a knife, and it took a good ten minutes before my Stormlight fully healed the wound.*

"I doubt that was due to the breaking of the node," Navani said. "Raboniel was able to corrupt the Sibling further before you stopped her."

Understood. I do feel bad I couldn't protect the node, but Brightness, I think doing so would be impossible. If the others get discovered, we'll have to destroy them too.

"I agree," she said. "Do what you have to in order to give me more time. Anything else to report?"

Oh, right! Kaladin said. *I couldn't get to the Oathgates in time. I thought I'd be able to easily climb down to the ground floor, but it was a longer process than I imagined.*

"You didn't fly?"

Those Lashings don't work, Brightness. I need to use Adhesion to make handholds. I'll need to practice more—or find another way up and down—if you want me to try to reach the Oathgates. Regardless, I did snatch some spanreeds for you. Full sets, it turns out, twelve of them.

Syl has been inspecting them, and she thinks she knows the reason they work. Brightness, the spren inside have been corrupted, like Renarin's spren. The rubies work on Voidlight now, as you suspected, and these spren must be the reason.

Navani let out a long breath. This had been one of her guesses; she hadn't wanted it proven. If she needed to acquire corrupted spren, she was unlikely to be able to get any fabrials working without Raboniel knowing.

"Rest," she told Kaladin, "and keep your strength up. I will figure out a path to reverse what is happening here."

We need to warn Dalinar, Kaladin said. *Maybe we could get half of one of these spanreeds to him.*

"I don't know how we'd accomplish that," Navani said.

Well, I guess it depends on how far down the tower's defenses go. It's possible I could leap off a ledge, fall far enough to get outside the suppression, then activate my Lashings. But that would leave you without access to a Radiant. Honestly, I'm loath to suggest it. I don't know if I could leave, considering how things are.

"Agreed," Navani said. "For now, it's more important that I have you here with me. Keep watch for Lift; the Sibling has lost track of her, but she was awake like you are."

Understood, he said.

"Are you otherwise well? Do you have food?"

Yeah. I have another of my men helping me. He's not a Radiant, but he's a good man.

"The mute?" Navani guessed.

You know Dabbid?

"We've met. Give him my best."

Will do, Brightness. Really though, I don't think I can rest. I need to practice climbing the outside of the tower—but even with practice, I'm worried I won't be fast enough. What if a node is discovered on the fortieth floor? It would take me hours to climb that high.

"A valid worry," she said. "I'll see if I can find a solution. Let's talk tomorrow around this time."

Understood.

She pushed off the wall and strolled through the room. She didn't want to be seen talking to herself; surely the singers knew to watch for signs that someone was Radiant. She conversed softly with Rushu, explaining her plans for the next phase of time-wasting.

Rushu approved, but Navani felt annoyed as she moved on. *I need to do more than waste time,* Navani thought. *I need to work toward our freedom.*

She'd been formulating her plan. Step one was to continue making certain they didn't lose ground, and Kaladin would have to handle that. Step two was getting word to Dalinar. Now that she had spanreeds, perhaps she could find a way.

It was the third step that currently concerned her. In talking to the Sibling, Navani had confirmed a number of things she'd previously suspected. The tower regulated pressure and heat for those living inside—and it had once done a far better job of this, along with performing a host of other vital functions.

Most of that, including the tower's protections against Fused, had ended around the Recreance. The time when the Radiants had abandoned their oaths—and the time when the ancient singers had been transformed into parshmen, their songs and forms stolen. The actions of those ancient Radiants had somehow broken the tower—and Raboniel, by filling the tower with Voidlight, was starting to repair it in a twisted way.

Navani felt smothered by it all. She needed to fix a problem using mechanisms she didn't understand—and indeed had learned about only days ago. She paced, massaging her temples. She needed a smaller problem she could work on first, to give her brain some time away from the bigger problem.

What was a smaller problem she could fix? Helping Kaladin move faster up and down through the tower? Was there a hidden lift that she could . . .

Wait.

A way for one person to quickly get up and down, she thought. *Storms.* She turned on her heel and walked to the other side of the room, suppressing—as best she could—visible signs of her excitement.

The junior engineer Tomor had survived the initial assault. Navani had him recalculating the math on certain schematics. She leaned down beside the young ardent and pointed at his current project, but whispered something else.

"That glove you made," she said. "The one that you wanted to use as a single-person lift. Where is it?"

"Brightness?" he asked, surprised. "In the boxes out in the hallway."

"I need you to sneak it out," she whispered, "when you leave today."

The singers let her lesser scholars move more freely than Navani. What else could they do? Force three dozen people to sleep in this room, without facilities? A few of the key scholars—Navani, Rushu, Falilar—were always escorted, but the subordinates weren't paid as much attention.

"Brightness?" Tomor said. "What if I get caught?"

"You might be killed," she whispered. "But it is a risk we must take. A Radiant still fights, Tomor, and he needs your device to climb between floors."

Tomor's eyes lit up. "My device . . . Stormblessed needs it?"

"You know he's the one?"

"Everyone's talking about him," Tomor said. "I thought it was a fanciful rumor."

"Bring such rumors to me, fanciful or not," Navani said. "For now, I need you to sneak that glove out and leave it hidden somewhere it won't be discovered, but where Kaladin can reasonably retrieve it."

"I'll try, Brightness," Tomor said, nervous. "But fabrials don't work anymore."

"Leave that to me," she said. "Include a quick sketch of a map to the location of the weights on the twentieth floor, as he'll need to visit those too."

With the conjoined rubies Kaladin had stolen in those spanreeds, they could hopefully make the device function. She'd have to coach Kaladin through installing it all. And the rubies would be smaller than the ones Tomor had built into the device; would they be able to handle the weight? She'd need to do some calculations, but assuming Tomor had used the newer cages that didn't stress the rubies as much, it should work.

She rose to go speak to some of the others in the same manner and posture, to hide the importance of her conversation with Tomor. During the second such conference, however, she noticed someone at the doorway.

Raboniel. Navani took a deep breath, composing herself and smothering her spike of anxiety. Raboniel would likely be unhappy about what had happened last night. Hopefully she didn't suspect Navani's part in it.

Unfortunately, a guard soon walked into the room, then made straight for Navani. Raboniel didn't fetch an inferior personally. Navani couldn't banish the anxietyspren that trailed her as she joined the Fused at the doorway.

Raboniel wore a gown today, though of no cut Navani recognized. Loose and formless, it felt like what an Alethi woman would wear to bed. Though the Fused wore it well with her tall figure, it was strangely off-putting to see her in something that seemed more regal than martial.

The Fused didn't speak as Navani arrived. Instead she turned and walked out of the chamber with a relaxed gait. Navani followed, and they entered the hallway with the murals. Down to the left, the shield surrounding the crystal pillar glowed a soft blue.

"Your scholars," Raboniel finally noted, "do not seem to be making much progress. They were to deliver up to my people fabrials to test."

"My scholars are frightened and unnerved, Ancient One," Navani said. "It might take weeks before they feel up to true studies again."

"Yes, and longer, if you continue having them repeat work in an effort to not make progress."

She figured that out faster than I anticipated, Navani thought as the two strolled along the hallway toward the shield. Here a common singer soldier in warform was working under the direction of several Fused. With a Shardblade.

They'd known the singers had claimed some Blades from the humans they'd fought—but Navani recognized this one. It had belonged to her son. Elhokar's Blade, Sunraiser.

Navani kept her face impassive only with great effort, though the anxietyspren faded and an agonyspren arrived instead: an upside-down face carved from stone pressing out from the wall nearby. It betrayed her true emotions. That loss ran deep.

Raboniel glanced at it, but said nothing. Navani kept her eyes forward. Watching that horrible Blade in that awful creature's hand. The warform held the weapon at the ready. It held no gemstone at its pommel; it seemed that the warform didn't have it bonded. Or perhaps the summoning mechanism didn't work in the tower, with the protections in place.

The warform attacked the shield—and contrary to Navani's expectation, the Blade bit into the blue light. The warform carved off a chunk, which evaporated to nothing before it hit the floor—and the shield restored itself just as quickly. The warform tried again, attempting to dig faster. After a few minutes of watching, Navani could tell the effort was futile. The bubble regrew too quickly.

"Fascinating behavior, wouldn't you say?" Raboniel asked Navani.

Navani turned toward Raboniel, steeling herself against the memories brought forth by the sight of the sword. She could cry for her child again tonight, as she had done many nights in the past. For now, she would *not* show these creatures her pain.

"I've never seen anything like that shield, Lady of Wishes," she said. "I couldn't *begin* to understand how it was created."

"We could unravel its secrets, if we tried together," Raboniel said, "instead of wasting our time watching one another for hidden motives."

"This is true, Ancient One," Navani said. "But if you want my cooperation and goodwill, perhaps you shouldn't flaunt in front of me the Blade taken from the corpse of my son."

Raboniel stiffened. She glanced at the warform with the weapon. "I did not know."

Didn't she? Or was this another game?

Raboniel turned, nodding for Navani to follow as they walked away from the shield.

"If I might ask, Ancient One," Navani said, "why do you give the Blades you capture to common soldiers, and not keep them yourselves?"

Raboniel hummed to one of her rhythms, but Navani could never tell them apart. Singers seemed to be able to distinguish one rhythm from another after hearing a short word or a couple of seconds of humming.

"Some Fused do keep the Blades we capture," Raboniel said. "The ones who enjoy the pain. Now, I fear I must make some changes in how you and your scholars operate. You are distracted, naturally, by preventing them from giving me too much information. I have unconsciously put you in a position where your obvious talents are wasted by foolish politicking.

"These are the new arrangements: You will work by yourself at my desk in a separate room from the other scholars. Twice a day, you may give them written directions, which I will personally vet. That should give you more time for worthwhile pursuits, and less for deceit."

Navani drew her lips to a line. "I think that is unwise, Ancient One," she said. "I am accustomed to working directly with my scholars. They are far more efficient when I am personally directing their efforts."

"I find it difficult to imagine them being *less* efficient than they are currently, Navani," Raboniel said. "We will work this way from now on. It is not a matter I care to debate."

Raboniel had a long stride, and used it purposely to force Navani to hurry to match her. Upon reaching the scholars' chambers, Raboniel turned left instead of right—entering the room Navani's scholars had been using as a library.

Raboniel's desk in this chamber had once belonged to Navani. The Fused gestured, and Navani sat as instructed. This was going to be inconvenient—but that was Raboniel's intent.

The Fused went down on one knee, then picked through a box on the floor here. She set something on the desk. A glass globe? Yes, like the one that had been near the first node Navani had activated.

"When we discovered the node operating the field, this was connected to it," Raboniel said. "Look closely. What do you see?"

Navani hesitantly picked up the globe, which was heavier than it appeared. Though it was made of solid glass, she spotted an unusual construction inside. Something she hadn't noticed, or understood, the first time she'd seen one of these. The globe had a pillar rising through the center. . . .

"It's a reproduction of the crystal pillar room," Navani said, her eyes widening. "You don't suppose . . ."

"That's how the field is created," Raboniel said, tapping the globe with an orange carapace fingernail. "It's a type of Soulcasting. The fabrial is persuading the air in a sphere around the pillar to think it is solid glass. That's why cutting off a piece accomplishes nothing."

"That's incredible," Navani said. "An application of the Surge I never *anticipated*. It's not a full transformation, but a half state somehow. Kept in perpetual stasis, using this globe as a model to mimic . . ."

"There must be similar globes at the other nodes."

"Clearly," Navani said. "After this one was detached, did it make the shield seem weaker than before?"

"Not that we can tell," Raboniel said. "One node must be enough to perpetuate the transformation."

"Fascinating . . ."

Don't get taken in, Navani. She wants you to think like a scholar, not like a queen. She wants you working for her, not against her.

That focus was even more difficult to maintain as Raboniel set something else on the table. A small diamond the size of Navani's thumb, full of Stormlight. But . . . was the hue faintly off? Navani held it up, frowning, turning it over in her fingers. She couldn't tell without a Stormlight sphere to compare it to, but it did seem this color was faintly teal.

"It's not Stormlight, is it?" she asked. "Nor Voidlight?"

Raboniel hummed a rhythm. Then, realizing Navani wouldn't understand, said, "No."

"The third Light. I *knew* it. The moment I learned about Voidlight, I wondered. Three gods. Three types of Light."

"Ah," Raboniel said, "but this isn't the third Light. We call that Lifelight.

Cultivation's power, distilled. This is something different. Something unique. It is the reason I came to this tower. It is a *mixing* of two. Stormlight and Lifelight. Like . . ."

"Like the Sibling is a child of both Honor and Cultivation," Navani said.

Storms. That was what the Sibling had meant by *their* Light no longer working. They hadn't been able to make the tower function any longer because something had happened to the tower's Light.

"It came out in barely a trickle," Raboniel said. "Something is wrong with the tower, preventing it from flowing." Her rhythm grew more energetic. "But this is proof. I have long suspected that there must be a way to mix and change the various forms of Light. These three energies are the means by which all Surges work, and yet we know so little about them.

"What could we do with this power if we *truly* understood it? This Towerlight is proof that Stormlight and Lifelight can mix and create something new. Can the same be done with Stormlight and Voidlight? Or will that prove impossible, since the two are opposites?"

"Are they, though?" Navani asked.

"Yes. Like night and day or oil and water. But perhaps we can find a way to put them together. If so, it could be a . . . model, perhaps, of our peoples. A way toward unity instead of strife. Proof that we, although opposites, can coexist."

Navani stared at the Towerlight sphere, and she felt compelled to correct one thing. "Oil and water aren't opposites."

"Of course they are," Raboniel said. "This is a central tenet of philosophy. They cannot mix, but must remain ever separated."

"Just because something doesn't mix doesn't make them opposites," Navani said. "Sand and water don't mix either, and you wouldn't call *them* opposites. That's beside the point. Oil and water can mix, if you have an emulsifier."

"I do not know this word."

"It's a kind of binding agent, Ancient One," Navani said, standing. If her things were still in here . . . yes, over at the side of the room, she found a crate holding simple materials for experiments.

She made up a vial with some oil and water, adding some stumpweight sap extract as a simple emulsifier. She shook the resulting solution and handed it to Raboniel. The Fused took it and held it up, waiting for the oil and water to separate. But of course they didn't.

"Oil and water mix in nature all the time," Navani said. "Sow's milk has fat suspended in it, for example."

"I . . . have accepted ancient philosophy as fact for too long, I see," Raboniel said. "I call myself a scholar, but today I feel a fool."

"Everyone has holes in their knowledge. There is no shame in ignorance. In any case, oil and water aren't opposites. I'm not certain what the opposite of water would be, if the word even has meaning when applied to an element."

"The various forms of Light *do* have opposites," Raboniel said. "I am certain of it. Yet I must think on what you've shown me." She reached over and tapped the sphere full of Towerlight. "For now, experiment with this Light. To keep you focused, I must insist you remain in this room until finished each day, except when accompanied to use the chamber."

"Very well," Navani said. "Though if you want my scholars to actually develop something for you, this idea of them drawing plans and you testing them is foolish. It won't work, at least not well. Instead, Ancient One, I suggest you deliver to us gemstones that can power fabrials that work in the tower."

Raboniel hummed for a moment, regarding the emulsion. "I will send such gems to your people as proof of my willingness to work together." She turned to go. "If you intend to use ciphers to give hidden instructions to your scholars, kindly make them difficult ones. The spren I will use to unravel your true messages do like a challenge. It gives them more variety in existence."

Raboniel set a guard at the door, but didn't restrict Navani's access within the room. It was otherwise unoccupied: it held only bookshelves, crates, and the occasional sphere lantern. There were no other exits, but near the rear of the room Navani found a vein of crystal hidden among the strata.

"Are you there?" she asked, touching it.

Yes, the Sibling replied. *I am closer to death than ever. Surrounded by evils on all sides. Men and singers alike seeking to abuse me.*

"Don't create a false equivalency," Navani said. "My kind might not understand the harm we've done to spren, but the enemy *certainly* knows the harm they cause in corrupting them."

Regardless. I will soon die. Only two nodes remain, and the previous one was discovered so rapidly.

"More proof that you should be helping us, not them," Navani whispered, peeking through the stacks to see that she hadn't aroused the guard's attention. "I need to understand more about how these various forms of Light work."

I don't think I can explain much, the Sibling said. *For me, it all simply worked. Like a human child can breathe, so I used to make and use Light. And then . . . the tones went away . . . and the Light left me.*

"All right," Navani said. "We can talk on that more later. For now, you need to tell me where the other nodes are."

No. Defend them once they are found.

"Sibling," Navani said, "if Kaladin Stormblessed can't protect a node, no one can. Our goal should be to *distract* and *mislead*, to prevent the Fused from ever finding them. To do this, I'll need to know where the nodes are."

You talk so well, the Sibling said. *So frustratingly well. You humans always sound so reasonable. It's only later, after the pain, that the truth comes out.*

"Hide it if you wish," Navani said. "But you have to know, after watching Kaladin fight for you, that we are severely outmatched. Our sole hope is to prevent the nodes from being located. If I knew where at least *one* of them was, I could come up with plots to deflect the enemy's attention."

Come up with those plots first, the Sibling said. *Then talk to me again.*

"Fine," Navani said. She slipped a few books off the shelf to hide what she'd been doing, then walked to her seat. There, she began writing down everything she knew about light.

EIGHT YEARS AGO

Eshonai turned the topaz over in her fingers and attuned Tension. A topaz *should* glow with a calm, deep brown—but this one gave off a wicked orange light, like the bright color along the back of a sigs cremling warning that it was poisonous.

Looking closely, Eshonai thought she could make out the spren trapped in it. A painspren, frantically moving around. Though . . . perhaps she imagined the frantic part. The spren was mostly formless when inside the gemstone, having reverted to the misty Stormlight that created all of their kind. Still, it couldn't be *happy* in there. How would she feel if she were locked into a room, unable to explore?

"You learned this from the humans?" Eshonai said.

"Yes," Venli said. She sat comfortably between two of the elders in the small council room, which was furnished with woven mats and painted banners.

Venli wasn't one of the Five—the head elders—but she seemed to think she belonged among them. Something had happened to her these last few months. Where she'd once been self-indulgent, she now radiated egotism and confidence. She hummed to Victory as Eshonai passed the gemstone to one of the elders.

"Why did you not bring this to us earlier, Venli?" Klade asked. The reserved elder took the gemstone next. "The humans have been gone for months now."

"I thought I might be wrong," Venli said to Confidence. "I decided to see if I could trap a spren on my own. Surely you wouldn't have wanted to be bothered by my fancies, should I have been wrong."

"I hadn't heard of this thing they can do," Klade said to Reconciliation. "Do you think you could trap a lifespren? If so, we could better choose when we adopt mateform. That would be convenient."

"Try this stone," Venli said, taking it, then handing it to Varnali next. "I think it might be the secret to warform."

"A dangerous form," Varnali said. "But useful."

"It is not a form of power," Klade said. "It is within our rights to claim it."

"The humans make overtures," Gangnah—foremost among them—said to Annoyance, a rhythm used to elicit sympathy for a frustrating situation. "They act as if we are a nation united, not a group of squabbling families. I wish we could present to them a stronger face. They have accomplished so much during our centuries apart, while we remember so little."

"Pardon, elders," Eshonai said to Reconciliation. "But they have advantages we do not. A much larger population, ancient devices to create metals, a land more sheltered from the storms."

She'd recently returned from her latest exploration efforts—which the elders now fully supported. She'd sought to circumvent the human trading post, then find their home. She'd attuned Disappointment more than once; every place she *thought* she'd find the humans had been empty. They'd found packs of wild chulls, and even spotted a distant and rare group of Ryshadium.

No humans. Not until she'd returned to their trading post, which had been transformed into a small fort—built from stone and staffed by soldiers and two scribes. The humans had a message for her there. The human king wished to "formalize relations" with her people, whom they referred to as "Parshendi."

She'd returned with the message to find this: Venli sitting among the elders. Venli, so *sure* of herself. Venli replicating human techniques that Eshonai—despite spending the most time with them—hadn't heard them discuss.

"Thank you, Eshonai," Gangnah said to Appreciation. "You have done well on your expedition." Workform had carapace only along the backs of the hands in small ridges, and Gangnah's was beginning to whiten at the edges. A sign of her age. She turned to the others and continued. "We will need to respond to this offer. The humans expect us to be a nation. Should we form a government like they have?"

"The other families would never follow us," Klade said. "They already resent how the humans paid more attention to us."

"I find the idea of a king distasteful," added Husal, to Anxiety. "We should not follow them in this."

Eshonai hummed to Pleading, indicating she wished to speak again.

"Elders," she said, "I think I should visit the other families and show them my maps."

"What would that accomplish?" Venli asked to Skepticism.

"If I show them how much there is to the world, they will understand that we are smaller as a people than we thought. They will want to unite."

Venli hummed to Amusement. "You think they'd simply join with us? Because they saw maps? Eshonai, you are a *delight*."

"We will consider your proposal," Gangnah said, then hummed to Appreciation—as a dismissal.

Eshonai retreated out into the sunlight as the elders asked Venli additional questions about creating gemstones with trapped spren. Eshonai attuned Annoyance. Then, by force, she changed her rhythm to Peace instead. She *always* felt anxious after an extended trip. She wasn't annoyed with her sister, just the general situation.

She let herself rove outward to the cracked wall that surrounded the city. She liked this place; it was old, and old things seemed . . . thoughtful to her. She walked along the base of the once-wall, passing listeners tending chulls, carrying in grain from the fields, hauling water. Many raised a hand or called to a rhythm when they saw her. She was famous now, unfortunately. She had to stop and chat with several listeners who wanted to ask about her expedition.

She suffered the attention with patience. Eshonai had spent years trying to inspire this kind of interest about the outside world. She wouldn't throw away this goodwill now.

She managed to extract herself, and climbed up a watchpost along the wall. From it, she could see listeners from other families moving about on the Plains, or driving their hogs past the perimeter of the city.

There are more of them about than usual, she thought. One of the other families might be preparing an assault on the city. Would they be so bold? So soon after the humans had come and changed the world?

Yes, they would be. Eshonai's own family had been that bold, after all. The others might assume Eshonai's people were getting secrets, or special trade goods, from the humans. They would want to put themselves into a position to receive the humans' blessings instead.

Eshonai needed to go to them and explain. Why fight, when there was so much more out there to experience? Why squabble over these old, broken-down cities? They could be building new ones as the humans did. She attuned Determination.

Then she attuned right back to Anxiety as she saw a figure walking distractedly along the base of the wall. Eshonai's mother wore a loose brown robe, dull against the femalen's gorgeous red and black skin patterns.

Eshonai climbed down and ran over. "Mother?"

"Ah," her mother said to Anxiety. "I know you. Can you perhaps help me? I seem to find myself in an odd situation."

Eshonai took her mother by the arm. "Mother."

"Yes. Yes, I'm your mother. You are Eshonai." The femalen looked around, then she leaned in. "Can you tell me how I arrived here, Eshonai? I don't seem to remember."

"You were going to wait for me to get home," Eshonai said. "With food."

"I was? Why didn't I do that, then?"

"You must have lost track of time," Eshonai said, to Consolation. "Let's get you home."

Jaxlim hummed to Determination and refused to be budged, seeming to become more conscious, more herself by the second. "Eshonai," she said, "we have to confront this. This is not simply me feeling tired. This is something worse."

"Maybe not, Mother," Eshonai said. "Maybe it . . ."

Her mother hummed to the Rhythm of the Lost. Eshonai trailed off.

"I must make certain your sister knows the songs," Jaxlim said. "We may have reached the riddens of my life, Eshonai."

"Please, come and rest," Eshonai said to Peace.

"Rest is for those with time to spare, dear," her mother said, but let herself be led in the direction of their home. She pulled her robe tight. "I can face this. Our ancestors took weakness upon themselves to bring our people into existence. They faced frailty of body and mind. I can face this with grace. I must."

Eshonai settled her at home with something to eat. Then, Eshonai considered getting out her new maps to show her mother, but hesitated. Jaxlim never did like hearing about Eshonai's travels. It was best not to upset her.

Why did it have to happen like this? Eshonai finally got what she wanted out of life. But progress, change, couldn't happen without the passing of storms and the movement of years. Each day forward meant another day of regression for her mother.

Time. It was a sadistic master. It made adults of children—then gleefully, relentlessly, stole away everything it had given.

They were still eating when Venli returned. She always had a hidden smile these days, as if attuning Amusement in secret. She set her gemstone—the one with the spren—on the table.

"They're going to try it," Venli said. "They are taking volunteers now. I'm to provide a handful of these gemstones."

"How did you learn to cut them as humans do?" Eshonai asked.

"It wasn't hard," Venli said. "It merely took a little practice."

Their mother stared at the gemstone. She wiped her hands with a cloth, then picked it up. "Venli. I need you to return to practice. I don't know how much longer I will be suited to being our keeper of songs."

"Because your mind is giving out," Venli said. "Mother, why do you think I've been working so hard to find these new forms? This can help."

Eshonai attuned Surprise, glancing at their mother.

"Help?" Jaxlim said.

"Each form has a different way of thinking," Venli said. "That is preserved in the songs. And some were stronger, more resilient to diseases, both physical and mental. So if you were to change to this new form . . ."

Her mother attuned Consideration.

"I . . . hadn't realized this," Eshonai said. "Mother, you must volunteer! This could be our answer!"

"I've been trying to get the elders to see," Venli said. "They want young listeners to try the change first."

"They will listen to me," Jaxlim said to Determination. "It is, after all, my job to speak for them to hear. I will try this form, Venli. And if you have truly accomplished this goal of yours . . . well, I once thought that being our new keeper of songs would be your highest calling. I hadn't considered that you might *invent* a calling with even more honor. Keeper of forms."

Eshonai settled back, listening to her sister humming to Joy. Only . . . the beat was off somehow. Faster. More violent?

You're imagining things, she told herself. *Don't let jealousy consume you, Eshonai. It could easily destroy your family.*

I am told that it is not the sand itself, but something that grows upon it, that exhibits the strange properties. One can make more, with proper materials and a seed of the original.

—From *Rhythm of War*, page 13 undertext

K aladin thrashed, sweating and trembling, his mind filled with visions of his friends dying. Of Rock frozen in the Peaks, of Lopen slain on a distant battlefield, of Teft dying alone, shriveled to bones, his eyes glazed over from repeated use of firemoss.

"No," Kaladin screamed. "No!"

"Kaladin!" Syl said. She zipped around his head, filling his eyes with streaks of blue-white light. "You're awake. You're all right. Kaladin?"

He breathed in and out, taking deep lungfuls. The nightmares felt so *real*, and they *lingered*. Like the scent of blood on your clothing after a battle.

He forced himself to his feet, and was surprised to find a small bag of glowing gemstones on the room's stone ledge.

"From Dabbid," Syl said. "He left them a little earlier, along with some broth, then grabbed the jug to go get water."

"How did he . . ." Maybe he'd gotten them from the ardent at the monastery? Or maybe he'd quietly taken them from somewhere else. Dabbid could move around the tower in ways that Kaladin couldn't—people always looked at Kaladin, remembered him. It was the height, he guessed. Or maybe it was the way he held himself. He'd never learned to keep his head down properly, even when he'd been a slave.

Kaladin shook his head, then did his morning routine: stretches, exercises, then washing as best he could with a cloth and some water. After that he saw to Teft, washing him, then shifting the way the man was lying to help prevent bedsores. That all done, Kaladin knelt beside Teft's bench with the syringe and broth, trying to find solace from his own mind through the calming act of feeding his friend.

Syl settled onto the stone bench beside Teft as Kaladin worked, wearing her girlish dress, sitting with her knees pulled up against her chest and her arms wrapped around them. Neither of them spoke for a long while as Kaladin worked.

"I wish he were awake," Syl finally whispered. "There's something happy about the way Teft is angry."

Kaladin nodded.

"I went to Dalinar," she said, "before he left. I asked him if he could make me feel like humans do. Sad sometimes."

"What?" Kaladin asked. "Why in the Almighty's tenth name would you do something like that?"

"I wanted to feel what you feel," she said.

"*Nobody* should have to feel like I do."

"I'm my own person, Kaladin. I can make decisions for myself." She stared sightlessly past Teft and Kaladin. "It was in talking to him that I started remembering my old knight, like I told you. I think Dalinar did something. I wanted him to Connect me to you. He refused. But I think he somehow Connected me to who I was. Made me able to remember, and hurt again . . ."

Kaladin felt helpless. He had never been able to struggle through his *own* feelings of darkness. How did he help someone else?

Tien could do it, he thought. *Tien would know what to say.*

Storms, he missed his brother. Even after all these years.

"I think," Syl said, "that we spren have a problem. We think we don't change. You'll hear us say it sometimes. 'Men change. Singers change. Spren don't.' We think that because pieces of us are eternal, we are as well. But pieces of humans are eternal too.

"If we can choose, we can change. If we can't change, then choice means nothing. I'm *glad* I feel this way, to remind me that I haven't always felt the same. Been the same. It means that in coming here to find another Knight Radiant, I was *deciding*. Not simply doing what I was made to, but doing what I *wanted* to."

Kaladin cocked his head, the syringe full of broth halfway to Teft's lips. "When I'm at my worst, I feel like I *can't* change. Like I've *never* changed. That I've always felt this way, and always will."

"When you get like that," Syl said, "let me know, all right? Maybe it will help to talk to me about it."

"Yeah. All right."

"And Kal?" she said. "Do the same for me."

He nodded, and the two of them fell silent. Kaladin wanted to say more. He *should* have said more. But he felt so tired. Exhaustionspren swirled in the room, though he'd slept half the day.

He could see the signs. Or rather, he couldn't ignore them anymore. He was deeply within the grip of battle shock, and the tower being under occupation didn't magically fix that. It made things worse. More fighting. More time alone. More people depending on him.

Killing, loneliness, and stress. An unholy triumvirate, working together with spears and knives to corner him. Then they just. Kept. Stabbing.

"Kaladin?" Syl said.

He realized he'd been sitting there, not moving, for . . . how long? Storms. He quickly refilled the syringe and lifted it to Teft's lips. The man was stirring again, muttering, and Kaladin could almost make out what he was saying. Something about his parents?

Soon the door opened and Dabbid entered. He gave Kaladin a quick salute, then hurried over to the bench near Teft and put something down on the stone. He gestured urgently.

"What's this?" Kaladin asked, then unwrapped the cloth to reveal some kind of fabrial. It looked like a leather bracer, the type Dalinar and Navani wore to tell the time. Only the construction was different. It had long leather straps on it, and a metal portion—like a handle—that came up and went across the palm. Turning it over, Kaladin found ten rubies in the bracer portion, though they were dun.

"What on Roshar?" Kaladin asked.

Dabbid shrugged.

"The Sibling led you to this, I assume?"

Dabbid nodded.

"Navani must have sent it," Kaladin said. "Syl, what time is it?"

"About a half hour before your meeting with the queen," she said, looking upward toward the sky, occluded behind many feet of stone.

"Next highstorm?" Kaladin asked.

"Not sure, a few days at least. Why?"

"We'll want to restore the dun gemstones I used in that fight with the Pursuer. Thanks for the new ones, by the way, Dabbid. We'll need to find a way to hide the others outside to recharge though."

Dabbid patted his chest. He'd do it.

"You seem to be doing better these days," Kaladin said, settling down to finish feeding Teft.

Dabbid shrugged.

"Want to share your secret?" Kaladin asked.

Dabbid sat on the floor and put his hands in his lap. So Kaladin went back to his work. It proved surprisingly tiring—as he had to forcibly keep his attention from wandering to his nightmares. He was glad when, upon finishing, Syl told him the time had arrived for his check-in with Navani.

He walked to the side of the room, pressed his hand against the crystal vein, and waited for her to speak in his mind.

Highmarshal? she said a few minutes later.

"Here," he replied. "But, since I was on my way to becoming a full-time surgeon, I'm not sure I still have that rank."

I'm reinstating you. I managed to have one of my engineers sneak out a fabrial you might find useful. The Sibling should be able to guide you to it.

"I've got it already," Kaladin said. "Though I have no idea what it's supposed to do."

It's a personal lift, meant to levitate you up and down long distances. To help you travel the height of the tower.

"Interesting," he said, glancing at the device laid out on the stone bench. "Though, I'm not one for technology, Brightness. Pardon, but I barely know how to turn on a heating fabrial."

You'll need to learn quickly then, Navani said. *As you'll need to replace the rubies in the fabrial with the Voidspren ones from the spanreeds you stole. We'll need all twelve pairs. Do you see a map in with the device?*

"Just a moment," he said, digging in the sack and pulling out a small folded map. It led to a place on the twentieth floor, judging by the glyphs. "I've got it. I should be able to reach this place. The enemy isn't guarding the upper floors."

Excellent. There are weights in a shaft up there where you'll need to install the other halves of those rubies. A mechanism on the fabrial bracer will drop one of those weights, and that force will transfer through the bracer. You'll be pulled in whatever direction you've pointed the device.

"By my arm?" Kaladin asked. "That doesn't sound comfortable."

It isn't. My engineer has been trying to fix that. There is a strap that winds around your arm and braces against your shoulder, which he thinks might help.

"All right . . ." he said. It was something to do, at least.

But fabrials? He'd always considered them toys for rich people. Though he supposed that was becoming less and less the case. Breeding projects were creating livestock with larger and larger ruby gemhearts, and fabrial creation methods were spreading. It seemed every third room had a heating fabrial these days, and spanreeds were cheap enough that even the enlisted men could afford to pay to send messages via one.

Navani coached him through replacing the rubies. Fortunately, the case of spanreeds he'd stolen included a few small tools for undoing casings. It wasn't any more difficult than replacing the buckles on a leather jerkin.

Once it was done, he and Syl ventured out, sneaking up nine floors. He didn't use any Stormlight; he didn't have enough to waste. Besides, it felt good to work his body.

On the twentieth floor, the garnet light led him to the location the map had described. Inside he found the weights and the shaft, and Navani walked him through installing the matching rubies. He began to grasp how the device worked. The big weights were more than heavy enough to lift a man. Five of the rubies in his fabrial were connected to these weights, binding them together.

The other seven rubies were used to activate and control the weights. The intricate system of pulleys and mechanisms was far more complex than he could understand, but essentially it allowed him to switch to a different weight when one had dropped all the way. He could also slow the weight's fall or stop it completely, modulating how quickly he was being pulled.

Each weight should be able to pull you hundreds of feet before running out, Navani said via a garnet vein on the wall. *These shafts plunge all the way down to the aquifers at the base of the mountain. That means you should be able to soar all the way up from the ground floor to the top of the tower using one weight.*

The bad news is that once all five weights have fallen, the device will be useless until you rewind them. There is a winch in the corner; it's an arduous process, I'm afraid.

"That's annoying," Kaladin said.

Yes, it is mildly inconvenient that we have to wind a crank to experience the wonder of making a human being safely levitate hundreds of feet in the air.

"Pardon, Brightness, but I can usually do it with far less trouble."

Which is meaningless right now, isn't it?

"I suppose it is," he said. He looked at the fabrial, now attached to his left arm, with the straps winding around all the way to his shoulder. It was a little constrictive, but otherwise fit quite well. "So, I point it where I want to go, activate it, and I'll get pulled that way?"

Yes. But we made the device so that it won't move if you let go—it was too dangerous otherwise. See the pressure spring across your palm? Ease off that, and the brake on the line will activate. Do you see?

"Yes," Kaladin said, making a fist around the bar. It had a separate metal portion wrapped around it on one side, with a spring underneath. So the harder he squeezed, the faster the device would pull him. If he let go completely, he'd stop in place.

There are two steps to the fabrial's use. First, you have to turn the device on—conjoining the rubies. The switch you can move with your thumb? That's for this purpose. Once you flip it, your arm will be locked into its current orientation, and won't be able to move the bracer in any direction except forward.

The second step is to start dropping a weight. If a weight falls all the way, swap to the next one using the dial on the back of your wrist. You see it?

"I do," he said.

Once you stop, you'll remain hanging until you disengage the device. But so long as you have another weight that hasn't run out, you can turn the dial to that one, then continue moving upward. Or if you're bold enough, you can disengage the device and fall for a second while you point it another direction, then engage it again and set it to pull you that way instead.

"That sounds dangerous," Kaladin said. "If I'm up high in the air, and need to get over to a balcony or something, I have to drop into free fall for a bit to reset the direction of the device so it can pull me laterally instead of up and down?"

Yes, unfortunately. The engineer who created this has grand and lofty ideas— but not much practical sense. But it's better than nothing, Highmarshal. And it's the best I can do for you right now.

Kaladin took a deep breath. "Understood. I'm sorry if I sounded ungrateful, Brightness. It's been a rough few days. I'm glad for the help. I'll familiarize myself with it."

Excellent. You shouldn't have to worry about the Voidlight in the gemstones running out through practice—conjoined rubies don't use much energy to maintain their connection. But they will run out naturally, over time. We'll have to figure out what to do about that when it happens.

For now, I'm hoping the Sibling will soon trust me enough to tell me where to find the remaining nodes. Once I have that information, I can devise a plan to protect them, perhaps by distracting the enemy's search toward a different region of the tower. It's vital that you keep that shield in place as long as possible, to give me time to figure out what is wrong with the Light in the tower and its defenses.

"Any movement there?" Kaladin asked.

No, but I'm currently focused on filling holes in my understanding. Once I have the proper fundamentals on Stormlight and Voidlight, I hope I'll make more rapid progress.

"Understood," Kaladin said. "I'll contact you again in a few hours, if you can make time, to discuss my experience with this device."

Thank you.

He stepped away from the wall. Syl stood in the air beside him, inspecting the fabrial.

"So?" Kaladin asked her. "What do you think?"

"I think you're going to look *extremely* silly using it. I can't wait."

He walked out to a nearby hallway. Up here on the twentieth floor, he should be safe practicing in the open—assuming he stayed away from the atrium. He walked the length of the hallway, setting out amethysts to light the way. Then he stood at one end, looking down the line of lights. The fabrial left his fingers free, but that bar in the center of his hand would interfere with fighting. He'd have to one-hand his spear, as if he were fighting with a shield.

"We're going to try it here?" Syl asked, darting over to him. "Isn't it for getting up and down?"

"Brightness Navani told me it pulls you in whatever direction you point it," he said. "New Windrunners always want to go up with their Lashings—but the more experience you have, the more you realize you can accomplish far more if you think in three dimensions."

He pointed his left hand down the hallway and opened his palm. Then, thinking it wise, he took in a little Stormlight. Finally, he used his thumb to flip the little lever and engage the mechanism. Nothing happened.

So far so good, he thought, trying to move his hand right or left. It resisted, held in place. Good.

He eased his hand into a fist, squeezing the bar across his palm, and was immediately pulled through the corridor. He skidded on his heels, and wasn't able to slow himself at all. Those weights really *were* heavy.

Kaladin opened his hand, stopping in place. Because the device was still active, when he lifted his feet off the ground, he stayed in the air. However, this also put an incredible amount of stress on his arm, especially the elbow.

Yes, the device in its current state might be too dangerous for anyone without Stormlight to use. He put his feet back down and tapped the toggle with his thumb to disengage the device, and his arm immediately dropped free. The weight—when he went to check on it—was hanging a little further down into the shaft. As soon as he'd disengaged the device, the brakes had locked, holding the weight in place.

He went out into the hallway, engaged the device, and gripped the bar firmly. That sent him soaring forward. He tucked up his feet, straining—with effort—to keep himself otherwise upright. In that moment, difficult though the exercise was, he felt something come alive in him again. The wind in his hair. His body soaring, claiming the sky, albeit in an imperfect way. He found the experience familiar. Even intuitive.

That lasted right up until the moment when he noticed the quickly approaching far wall. He reacted a little too slowly, first trying to Lash himself backward by instinct. He slammed into the wall hand-first and felt his knuckles *crunch.* The device continued trying to go forward, crushing his mangled hand further, forcing it to keep the bar compressed. The device held him affixed to the wall until he managed to reach over with his other hand and flip the thumb switch, releasing the mechanism and setting him free.

He gasped in pain, sucking the Stormlight from a nearby amethyst on the floor. The healing happened slowly, as it had the other day. The pain was acute; he gritted his teeth while he waited—and split skin, broken by bones, made him bleed on the device, staining its leather.

Syl scowled at the painspren crawling around the floor. "Um, I was wrong. That wasn't particularly funny."

"Sorry," Kaladin said, eyes watering from the pain.

"What happened?"

"Bad instincts," he said. "Not the device's fault. I just forgot what I was doing."

He sat to wait, and he *heard* the joints popping and the bones grinding as the Stormlight reknit him. He'd come to rely on his near-instantaneous healing; this was agony.

It was a good five minutes before he shook out his healed hand and stretched it, good as new, other than some lingering phantom pain. "Right," he said. "I'll want to be more careful. I'm playing with some incredible forces in those weights."

"At least you didn't break the fabrial," Syl said. "Strange as it is to say, it's a lot easier to get you a new hand than a new device."

"True," he said, standing. He launched himself down the hallway back the way he had come, this time maintaining a careful speed, and slowed himself as he neared the other end.

Over the next half hour or so he crashed a few more times, though never as spectacularly as that first one. He needed to be very careful to point his hand straight down the center of the hallway, or else he'd drift to the side and end up scraping across the wall. He also had to be acutely aware of the device, as it was remarkably easy to flip the activation switch accidentally by brushing his hand against something.

He kept practicing, and was able to go back and forth for quite a while before the device stopped working. He lurched to a halt midflight, hanging in the center of the hallway.

He rested his feet on the ground and deactivated the device. The weight he'd been using had hit the bottom. That had lasted him quite a long time—though much of that time had been resetting and moving around. In actual free fall, he probably wouldn't have longer than a few minutes of flight. But if he controlled the weight, using it in short bursts, he could make good use of those minutes.

He wouldn't be soaring about fighting Heavenly Ones in swooping battles with this. But he *could* get an extra burst of speed in a fight, and maybe move in an unexpected direction. Navani intended him to use it as a lift. It would work for that, certainly. And he intended to practice going up and down outside once it was dark.

But Kaladin also saw martial applications. And all in all, the device worked better than he'd expected. So he walked to the end of the hallway to set up again.

"More?" Syl asked.

"You have an appointment or something?" Kaladin asked.

"Just a little bored."

"I could crash into another wall, if you like."

"Only if you promise to be amusing when you do it."

"What? You want me to break more fingers?"

"No." She zipped around him as a ribbon of light. "Breaking your hands isn't very funny. Try a different body part. A funny one."

"I'm going to stop trying to imagine how to manage that," he said, "and get back to work."

"And how long are we going to be doing this decidedly unfunny crashing?"

"Until we don't crash, obviously," Kaladin said. "I had months to train with my Lashings, and longer to prepare for my first fight as a spearman. Judging by how quickly the Fused found the first node, I suspect I'll have only a few days to train on this device before I need to use it."

When the time came—assuming Navani or the Sibling could give him warning—he wanted to be ready. He knew of at least one way to quiet the nightmares, the mounting pressure, and the mental exhaustion. He couldn't do much about his situation, or the cracks that were ever widening inside him.

But he *could* stay busy, and in so doing, not let those cracks define him.

64

PERSONAL REMINDER

The sand originated offworld. It is only one of such amazing wonders that come from other lands—I have recently obtained a chain from the lands of the dead, said to be able to anchor a person through Cognitive anomalies. I fail to see what use it could be to me, as I am unable to leave the Rosharan system. But it is a priceless object nonetheless.

—From *Rhythm of War*, page 13 undertext

Jasnah had never gone to war. Oh, she'd been *near* to war. She'd stayed behind in mobile warcamps. She'd walked battlefields. She'd fought and killed, and had been part of the Battle of Thaylen Field. But she'd never *gone to war.*

The other monarchs were baffled. Even the soldiers seemed confused as they parted, letting her stride forward among them in her Shardplate. Dalinar, though, had understood. *Until you stand in those lines, holding your sword and facing down the enemy force, you'll never understand. No book could prepare you, Jasnah. So yes, I think you should go.*

A thousand quotes from noted scholars leaped to her mind. Accounts of what it was like to be in war. She'd read hundreds; some so detailed, she'd been able to smell the blood in the air. Yet they all fled like shadows before sunlight as she reached the front of the coalition armies and looked out at the enemy.

Their numbers seemed endless. A fungus on the land ahead, black and white and red, weapons glistening in the sun.

Reports said there were about forty thousand singers here. That was a number she could comprehend, could analyze. But her eyes didn't see forty thousand, they saw *endless* ranks. Numbers on a page became meaningless. She hadn't come to fight forty thousand. She'd come to fight a *tide*.

On paper, this place was the Drunmu Basin in Emul. It was a vast ocean of shivering grass and towering pile-vines. In meetings, the Mink had insisted that a battle here favored the coalition side. If they let the enemy retreat to cities and forts, they could hunker down and make for tough shells to crack. Instead he'd pushed them to a place where they'd feel confident standing in a full battle, as they had a slight advantage in high ground and the sun to their backs. Here they would stand, and the Mink could leverage the coalition's greater numbers and skill to victory.

So logically she understood that this was a battle that her forces wanted. In person, she felt overwhelmed by the distance to the enemy—distance she, with the others, would have to cross under a barrage of enemy arrows and spears. It was hard not to feel small, even in her Plate.

The horns sounded, ordering the advance, and she noted two Edgedancers keeping close to her—likely at her uncle's request. Though she'd always imagined battles beginning with a grand charge, her force moved mechanically. Shields up, in formation, at a solid march that the veteran troops maintained as arrows started falling. Running would break the lines, not to mention leave the soldiers winded when they arrived.

She winced as the first arrows struck. They fell with an arrhythmic series of *snaps*, metal on wood, like hail. One bounced off her shoulder and another skimmed her helm. Fortunately, the arrows were soon interrupted as Azish light cavalry executed a raid on the enemy archers. She heard the hooves, saw the Windrunners soaring overhead, guarding the horsemen from the air. The enemy kept misjudging cavalry, which hadn't been available in significant numbers thousands of years ago.

Through it all, the Alethi troops kept marching forward, shields up. It took an excruciatingly long time, but since Jasnah's side was the aggressor, the enemy had no impetus to meet them. They maintained their position atop their shallow incline. She could see why the enemy would think it wise to stand here, as Jasnah's forces had to make their assault up this hillside.

The enemy resolved into a block of figures in carapace and steel armor, holding large shields and sprouting with pikes several lines deep. These singers did not fight like the Parshendi on the Shattered Plains; these were drilled troops, and the Fused had adapted quickly to modern warfare. They had a slight myopia when it came to cavalry, true, but they knew far better how to most effectively employ their Surgebinders.

By the time Jasnah's block of troops was in position, she felt exhausted from staying at a heightened level of alert during the march. She stopped with the others, grass retreating in a wave before her—as if it could sense the coming fight like it sensed a storm. She had ordered her Plate to intentionally dull its light, so it looked like that of an ordinary Shardbearer. The enemy would still single her out, but not recognize her as the queen. She would be safer this way.

The horns rang out. Jasnah started up the last part of the incline at not quite a run. It was too shallow to be called a hill, and if she'd been out on a walk, she wouldn't have remarked much on the slope. But now she felt it with each step. Her Plate urged her to move, as did the Stormlight she breathed in, but if she ran too far ahead of her block of troops she could be surrounded. The enemy would have Fused and Regals hiding among their ranks, waiting to ambush her. Other than the Heavenly Ones, few Fused chose to meet Shardbearers in direct combat.

Jasnah summoned Ivory as a Blade, the weapon falling into her waiting gauntlets. *Ready?* she asked.

Yes.

She charged the last few feet to the pike block and swept with Ivory. Her job was to break their lines; a full Shardbearer could cause entire formations to crumble around her.

To their credit, this singer formation did not break. It buckled backward, pikes scraping her armor as she tried to get in close and attack, but it held. Her honor guard—along with those two Edgedancers—came in behind to keep her from being surrounded. Nearby, another block of five thousand soldiers hit the enemy. Grunts and crunches sounded in the air.

Holding her Blade in a two-handed grip, Jasnah swept back and forth, cutting free pike heads and trying to strike inward at the enemy. They moved with unexpected flexibility, singers dancing away, staying out of the range of her sword.

This is less effective, Ivory said to her. *Our other powers are. Use them?*

No. I want to know the real feeling of war, Jasnah thought. *Or as close to it as I can allow myself, in Plate with Blade.*

Ever the scholar, Ivory said with a long-suffering tone as Jasnah shouldered past some pikes—which were practically useless against her—and managed to ram her Blade into the chest of a singer. The singer's eyes burned as she fell, and Jasnah ripped the sword around, causing others to curse and shy back.

It wasn't only academics that drove her. If she was going to order soldiers into battle, she needed more than descriptions from books. She needed to *feel* what they felt. And yes, she could use her powers. Soulcasting had proven useful to her in fights before, but without Dalinar, she had limited Stormlight and wanted to conserve it.

She *would* escape to Shadesmar if things went poorly. She wasn't foolish. Yet this knowledge nagged at her as she swept through the formation, keeping the enemy busy. She couldn't ever *truly* feel what it was like to be an unfortunate spearman on the front lines.

She could hear them shouting as the two forces crashed together. The formations seemed so deliberate, and on the grand scale they were careful things. Positioned with a kind of terrible momentum that forced the men at the front to fight. So while the block remained firm, the front lines ground against one another, screaming like steel being bent.

That was a feeling Jasnah would never experience. The weight of a block of soldiers on each side crushing you between them—with no possible escape. Still, she wanted to know what she could. She swept around, forcing more singers back—but others began prodding her with pikes and spears, shoving her to the side, threatening to trip her.

She'd underestimated the effectiveness of those pikes; yes, they were useless for breaking her armor, but they *could* maneuver her like a chull being prodded with poles. She stumbled and felt her first true spike of fear.

Control it. Instead of trying to right herself, she turned her shoulder toward the enemy, turning her off-balance stumble into a rush, crashing out of the enemy ranks near her soldiers. She hadn't killed many of the enemy, but she didn't need to. Their ranks rippled and bowed from her efforts, and her soldiers exploited this. On either side of her, they matched pikes and spears with the enemy—the front row of her soldiers rotating to the back line of the block every ten minutes under the careful orders of the rank commander.

Engulfed by the sounds of war, Jasnah turned toward the enemy, and her honor guard formed up behind her. Then—sweat trickling down her brow—she charged in again. This time when the enemy parted around her, they revealed a hulking creature hidden in their ranks. A Fused with carapace that grew into large axelike protrusions around his hands: one of the Magnified Ones. Fused with the Surge of Progression, which let them grow carapace with extreme precision and speed.

The regular soldiers on both sides kept their distance, forming a pocket of space around the two. Jasnah resisted using her powers. With her Shards, she should be evenly matched against this creature—and her powers would quickly reveal who she was, as there were no other Surgebinders in the coalition army who had their own Plate.

There is another reason you fight, Ivory said, challenging her.

Yes, there was. Instead of confronting that, Jasnah threw herself into the duel, Stormlight raging in her veins. She sheared free one of the Fused's axe-hands, but the other slammed into her and sent her sprawling. She shook her head, resummoning her Blade and sweeping upward as the Fused rammed its hand down. She cut off the axe, but the trunk of the creature's arm slammed against her chest. Carapace grew over her like the roots of a tree, pinning her to the ground.

The Fused stepped away, snapping the carapace free at its elbow, leaving her immobilized. Then he turned as her honor guard distracted him.

Ah, we're getting so much wonderful experience, Ivory said to her. *Delightful.*

Other soldiers came in at Jasnah and began ramming thin pikes through her faceplate. One pierced her eye, making her scream. Stormlight healed her though, and her helm sealed the slit to prevent further attacks. With Stormlight, she didn't need it to breathe anyway. But this, like her quick summoning of her Blade, was a concession. It risked revealing what she was.

She ripped her hand free of the constricting carapace, then used Ivory as a dagger to cut her way out. She rolled free, tripping singers and kicking at their legs to send them sprawling. But as she came out of her roll, that storming Fused lunged in, slamming two axe-hands at her head, cracking the Plate. The helm howled in pain and annoyance, then lapped up her Stormlight to repair itself.

Such fun is, Ivory said. *But of course, Jasnah mustn't use her powers. She wants to play soldier.*

Jasnah growled, going to one knee and punching her fist at the Fused's knee—but it overgrew with carapace right before she connected. Her punch didn't even move the creature. Ivory became a short sword in her hand as she slashed at the Fused—but this exposed her to another hit in the helm, which laid her flat. She groaned, putting one hand against the rock.

Steady stone, a part of her mind thought. *Happy and pleased with its life on the plains.* No, it would resist her requests to change.

Ivory formed as a shield on her arm as the enemy began smashing. Blood on her cheek mixed with sweat; though her eye had healed, the regular soldiers were trying to get at her again, her honor guard doing their best to hold them back.

Fine.

She reached out to the air, which was stagnant and morose today. Draining Stormlight from the gemstones at her waist, she gave it a single command. *Change.* No begging, as she'd tried when younger. Only firmness.

The bored air accepted, and formed into oil all around them. It rained from the sky in a splash, and even appeared in the mouths of fighting soldiers. Her honor guard knew to withdraw at that sign, coughing and stumbling as they stepped back from the fight around her in a ten-yard circle. The enemy soldiers remained in place, cursing and coughing.

Jasnah slammed her fists together—one affixed with steel, the other with flint. Sparks erupted in front of her, and the entire section of the battlefield came alight.

The Magnified One stumbled in shock, and Jasnah leaped at him, forming Ivory into a needle-like Blade that she rammed directly into his chest. Her lunge was on target, and pierced the enemy's gemheart. The Fused toppled backward, eyes burning like the fires around her.

She finished off as many of the enemy soldiers as she could find in the flames. Her helm—transparent as glass from the inside—started to get covered in soot, and soon she had to retreat out of the fire.

Her vision was clear enough to see the horror of the nearby singers as they witnessed a burning Shardbearer explode from the fires, as if from the center of Damnation itself. That fear stunned them as she hit their line like a boulder, working death upon the collapsing ranks. Their corpses fell among the gleeful spren that writhed on the battlefield, exulting in the powerful emotions. Fearspren, painspren, anticipationspren.

She fought like a butcher. Hacking. Kicking. Throwing bodies into the lines to panic the others. Making waves that her soldiers exploited. At one point, something slammed into her from behind, and she assumed she'd have to face another Fused—but it was a dead Windrunner, dropped from the skies above by a passing Heavenly One.

She left the dead man on the bloody ground and returned to the battle. She didn't think of strategy. Strategy was for stuffy tents and calm conversations over wine. She simply killed. Striking until her arms were sluggish despite both armor and Stormlight. Though her troops rotated, she didn't give herself that luxury. How could she? They were struggling and bleeding in a foreign land, for stakes she promised them were important. If she rested, more of them died.

After what seemed like an eternity, she found herself gasping, wiping blood from her helm to see. The helm opened vents on the side, bringing in cool fresh air, and she stumbled, standing alone on the battlefield. Wondering why she'd started breathing again.

Running out of Stormlight, she thought, numb. She looked down at her gauntleted palm, which was stained with orange singer blood. How had she gotten so much on her? She vaguely remembered fighting another Fused, and some Regals, and . . .

And her block of troops was marching up toward the center of the battle, on trumpeted orders that echoed in her head. Horn blasts that meant . . . that meant . . .

Jasnah, Ivory said. *To the side, see what is.*

One of the Edgedancers moved among the fallen, searching for those they could heal. The second stepped up to Jasnah and pressed a large topaz into her hand. He then gestured toward the rear lines.

"I need to do more," Jasnah said.

"Continue in this state," the Edgedancer said, "and you will do more harm than good. More soldiers will die to protect you than you will cost the enemy. Do you want that, Your Majesty?"

That cut through the numbness, and she turned to where he pointed. Reserves formed up there, among standards proclaiming battle commanders and field medic stations.

"You need to rest," the Edgedancer said. "Go."

She nodded, accepting the wisdom and stumbling away from the battlefield. Her honor guard—reduced to half its former size—followed her in an exhausted clot. Shoulders slumped. Faces ashen. How long had it been? She checked the sun.

That can't be, she thought. Not even two hours?

The battle had moved away from this region, leaving corpses like fallen branches behind a storm. As she approached, a figure in black broke off from the reserves and hastened through the mess to meet her. What was Wit doing here?

He was trailed by a small group of servants. As they reached her, he snapped his fingers, and the servants rushed forward to towel down Jasnah's armor. She dismissed her helm, opening her face to the air—which felt cold, despite Emul's heat. She left the rest of her armor in place. She didn't dare remove it, in case enemies came hunting her.

Wit proffered a bowl of fruit.

"What is this?" she asked.

"Valet service."

"On the battlefield?"

"A place without much Wit, I agree. Or, I should say, a place that only exists when Wit has failed. Still, I should think I would be welcome. To offer a little perspective."

She sighed, but didn't object further. Most Shardbearers had crews to help keep them fighting. She did need a drink and some more Stormlight. She found herself staring, however. At . . . well, all of it.

Wit remained quiet. He was expert at knowing when to do that, though admittedly he rarely employed the knowledge.

"I've read about it, you know," she eventually said. "The feeling you get out there. The focus that you need to adopt to cope with it, to keep moving. Simply doing your job. I don't have their training, Wit. I kept getting distracted, or frightened, or confused."

He tapped her hand. The closed left gauntlet, where she held the Edgedancer's topaz. She stared at it, then drew in the Light. That made her feel better, but not all of her fatigue was physical.

"I'm not the unstoppable force I imagined myself to be," she said. "They know how to deal with Shardbearers; I couldn't bring down a Fused in a fair fight."

"There are no fair fights, Jasnah," Wit said. "There's never been such a thing. The term is a lie used to impose imaginary order on something chaotic. Two men of the same height, age, and weapon will not fight one another fairly, for one will always have the advantage in training, talent, or simple luck."

She grunted. Dalinar wouldn't think much of that statement.

"I know you feel you need to show the soldiers you can fight," Wit said softly. "Prove to them, maybe to yourself, that you are as capable on a battlefield as Dalinar is becoming with a book. This is good, it breaks down barriers—and there will be those wrongheaded men who would not follow you otherwise.

"But take care, Jasnah. Talented or not, you cannot conjure for yourself a lifetime of experienced butchery through force of will. There is no shame in using the powers you have developed. It is not unfair—or rather, it is no more unfair when the most skilled swordsman on the battlefield falls to a stray arrow. Use what you have."

He was right. She sighed, then took a piece of fruit—gripping it delicately between two gauntleted fingers—and took a bite. The cool sweetness shocked her. It belonged to another world. It washed away the taste of ash, renewing her mouth and awakening her hunger. She'd grown that numb after just two hours of fighting? Her uncle had, on campaign, fought for hours on end—day after day.

And he bore those scars, she supposed.

"How goes the battle?" she asked.

"Not sure," Wit said. "But the generals were right; the enemy is determined to stand here. They must think they can win, and so let us perpetuate this pitched battle, rather than forcing us into temperamental skirmishes."

"So why do you sneer?"

"It's not a sneer," he said. "Merely my natural charisma coming through." He nodded to the side, to where a distant hill—small but steep-sided— flashed with light. Thunder cracked the air despite the open sky. Men tried to rush the position, and died by the dozens.

"I think we're coming to the end of traditional battlefield formations," Wit said.

"They served us well today."

"And perhaps will for a time yet," Wit said. "But not forever. Once upon a time, military tactics could depend on breaking enemy positions with enough work. Enough lives. But what do you do when no rush—no number of brave charges—will claim the position you need?"

"I don't know," she said. "But the infantry block has been a stable part of warfare for millennia, Wit. It has adapted with each advance in technology. I don't see it becoming obsolete any time soon."

"We will see. You think your powers are unfair because you slay dozens, and they cannot resist? What happens when a single individual can kill *tens of thousands* in moments—assuming the enemy will kindly bunch up in a neat little pike block. Things will change rapidly when such powers become common."

"They're hardly common."

"I didn't say they were," he said. "Yet."

She took a drink, and finally thought to order her honor guard to rest. Their captain would send in fresh men.

Wit offered to massage her sword hand, but she shook her head. She instead ate another piece of fruit, then some ration sticks he gave her to balance the meal. She accepted a few pouches of spheres as well. But as soon as her fresh honor guard arrived, she marched out in search of a field commander who would know where to best position her.

※

Seven hours later, Jasnah tromped across a quiet battlefield, searching for Wit. He'd visited her several times during the fighting, but it had been hours since their last encounter.

She hiked through the remnants of the battle, feeling an odd solitude. As darkness smothered the land, she could almost pretend the scattered lumps were rockbuds, not bodies. The scents, unfortunately, did not go away with the light. And they remained a signal, defiant as any banner, of what had happened here. Blood. The stench of burning bodies.

In the end, loss and victory smelled the same.

They sounded different though. Cheers drifted on the wind. Human voices, with an edge to them. These weren't cheers of joy, more cheers of relief.

She made for a particular beacon of light, the tent with an illuminated set of coalition flags flying at the same height, one for each kingdom. Inside, she'd be welcomed as a hero. When she arrived, however, she didn't feel like entering. So she settled down on a stone outside within sight of the guards, who were wise enough not to run and fetch anyone. She sat for some time and stared out at the battlefield, figuring Wit would locate her eventually.

"Daunting, isn't it?" a voice asked from the darkness.

She narrowed her eyes, and searched around until she found the source: a small man sitting nearby, throwing sparks from his Herdazian spark-flicker in the night. Each burst of light illuminated the Mink's fingers and face.

"Yes," Jasnah said. "'Daunting' is the right word. More so than I'd anticipated."

"You made a wise choice, going out there," the Mink said. "Regardless of what the others said. It's too easy to forget the cost. Not only to the boys who die, but to the ones who live. Every commander should be reminded periodically."

"How did we do?"

"We broke the core of their strength," he said. "Which is what we wanted—though it wasn't a rout. We'll need another battle or two on nearly this scale before I can tell you if we've really won or not. But today was a step forward. Do that often enough, and you'll inevitably cross the finish line."

"Casualties?"

"Never take casualty reports on the night of the battle, Brightness," he said. "Give yourself a little time to enjoy the meal before you look at the bill."

"*You* don't seem to be enjoying yourself."

"Ah, but I am," he said. "I am staring at the open sky, and wearing no chains." He stood up, a shadow against the darkness. "I'll tell the others I've seen you, and that you are well, if you'd rather retreat to your tent. Your Wit is there, and unless I misunderstand, something has disturbed him."

She gave the Mink her thanks and stood. Wit was disturbed? The implications of that harried her as she marched through the frontline warcamp to her tent. Inside, Wit sat at her travel table, scribbling furiously. So far, she'd caught him writing in what she thought were five different alien scripts, though he didn't often answer questions about where they had originated.

Today, he snapped his notebook closed and plastered a smile on his face.

She trusted him, mostly. And he her, mostly. Other aspects of their relationship were more complicated.

"What is it, Wit?" she said.

"My dear, you should rest before—"

"*Wit.*"

He sighed, then leaned back in his seat. He was immaculate, as always, with his perfectly styled hair and sharp black suit. For all his talk of frivolity, he knew exactly how to present himself. It was something they'd bonded over.

"I have failed you," he said. "I thought I'd taken all necessary precautions, but I found a pen in my writing case that did not work."

"So . . . what? Is this a trick, Wit?"

"One played on me, I'm afraid," he said. "The pen was *not* a pen, but a creature designed to appear like a pen. A cremling, you'd call it, cleverly grown to the shape of something innocent."

She grew cold, and stepped forward, her Plate clinking. "One of the Sleepless?"

He nodded.

"How much do you think it heard?"

"I'm uncertain. I don't know when it replaced my real pen, and I'm baffled how my protections—which are supposed to warn me of entities like this—were circumvented."

"Then we have to assume they know everything," Jasnah said. "All of our secrets."

"Unfortunately," Wit said. He sighed, then pushed his notebook toward her. "I'm writing warnings to those I communicated with. The bright side is that I don't *think* any of the Sleepless are working with Odium."

Jasnah had only recently learned that the Sleepless were anything other than a myth. It had taken meeting a friendly one—seeing with her own eyes that an entity could somehow be made up of thousands of cremlings working in concert—for her to accept their existence.

"If it's not working for the enemy, then who?" she asked.

"Well, I've written to my contacts among them, to ask if it is one of theirs keeping a friendly eye on amiable allies. But . . . Jasnah, I know at least one of them has thrown their lot in with the Ghostbloods."

"Damnation."

"I believe it is time," Wit said, "that I told you about Thaidakar."

"I know of him," Jasnah said.

"Oh, you think you do," he said. "But I've *met* him, several times. On other planets, Jasnah. The Ghostbloods are not a Rosharan organization, and I don't think you appreciate the danger they present. . . ."

65

HYPOTHESIS

As we dig further into this project, I am left questioning the very nature of God. How can a God exist in all things, yet have a substance that can be destroyed?

—From *Rhythm of War*, page 21

L ight was far more interesting than Navani had realized.

It constantly surrounded them, flooding in through windows and beaming from gemstones. A second ocean, white and pure, so omnipresent it became invisible.

Navani was able to order texts brought from Kholinar, ones she'd presumed lost to the conquest. She was able to get others from around the tower, and there were even a few with relevant chapters already here in the library room. All were collected at Raboniel's order and delivered, without question, to Navani for study.

She consumed the words. Locked away as she was, she couldn't do much else. Each day she wrote mundane instructions to her scholars—and hid ciphered messages within them that equated to nonsense. Rushu would know what she was doing from context, but the Fused? Well, let them waste their time trying to figure out a reason to the figgldygrak she wrote. Their confusion might help her slip through important messages later.

That didn't take much time, and she spent the rest of her days studying light. Surely there could be no *harm* in her learning, as Raboniel wanted. And the topic was so fascinating.

What *was* light? Not just Stormlight, but all light. Some of the ancient scholars claimed you could measure it. They said it had a *weight* to it. Others disagreed, saying instead that it was the *force* by which light moved that one could measure.

Both ideas fascinated her. She'd never thought of light as a thing. It simply . . . was.

Excited, she performed an old experiment from her books: splitting apart light into a rainbow of colors. All you had to do was put a candle in a box, use a hole to focus the light, then direct it through a prism. Then, curious, she extrapolated and—after several attempts—was able to use *another* prism to recombine the component colors into a beam of pure white light.

Next, she used a diamond infused with Stormlight instead of a candle. It worked the same, splitting into components of light, but with a larger band of blue. Voidlight did the same, though the band of violet was enormous, and the other colors mere blips. That was strange, as her research indicated different colors of light should only make bands brighter or weaker, not increase their size.

The most interesting result happened when she tried the experiment on the Towerlight Raboniel had collected. It wasn't Stormlight *or* Lifelight, but a combination of the two. When she tried the prism experiment with this light, *two separate* rainbows of colors—distinct from one another— split out of the prism.

She couldn't recombine them. When she tried sending the colors through another prism, she ended up with one beam of white-blue light and a separate beam of white-green light, overlapping but not combined as Towerlight was.

She sat at the table, staring at the two dots of light on the white paper. That green one. Could it be Lifelight? She likely couldn't have told the difference between it and Stormlight, without the two to compare—it was only next to one another that Stormlight looked faintly blue, and Lifelight faintly green.

She stood up and dug through the trunk of personal articles she'd had Raboniel's people fetch for her, looking for her journals. The day of Gavilar's death was still painful to remember, fraught with a dozen different conflicting emotions. She'd recorded her impressions of that day's events six separate times, in differing emotional states. Sometimes she missed him. At least the man he had once been, when they'd all schemed together as youths, planning to conquer the world.

That was the face he'd continued to show most everyone else after he'd started to change. And so, for the good of the kingdom, Navani had played along. She'd created a grand charade after his death, writing about Gavilar the king, the unifier, the mighty—but just—man. The ideal monarch. She'd given him exactly what he'd wanted, exactly what she'd threatened to withhold. She'd given him a legacy.

Navani closed the journal around her finger to hold her place, then took a few deep breaths. She couldn't afford to become distracted by that tangled mess of emotions. She reopened the journal and turned to the account she'd made of her encounter with Gavilar in her study on the day of his death.

He had spheres on the table, she had written. *Some twenty or thirty of them. He'd been showing them to his uncommon visitors—most of whom have vanished, never to be seen again.*

There was something off about those spheres. My eyes were drawn to several distinctive ones: spheres that glowed with a distinctly alien light, almost negative. Both violet and black, somehow shining, yet feeling like they should extinguish illumination instead of promote it.

Navani reread the passages, then inspected the pale green light she had split out of the Towerlight. Lifelight, the Light of Cultivation. Could Gavilar have had this Light too? Could she have mistaken Lifelight diamonds for emeralds? Or, would Lifelight in a gemstone appear identical to a Stormlight one at a casual glance?

"Why wouldn't you *talk* to me, Gavilar?" she whispered. "Why wasn't I worth trusting. . . ." She braced herself, then read further in her account—right up to the point where Gavilar plunged the knife in the deepest.

You aren't worthy. That's why, she read. *You claim to be a scholar, but where are your discoveries? You study light, but you are its opposite. A thing that destroys light. You spend your time wallowing in the muck of the kitchens and obsessing about whether or not some lighteyes recognizes the correct lines on a map.*

Storms. That was so painful.

She forced herself to linger on his words. *You are its opposite. A thing that destroys light . . .*

Gavilar had spoken of the same concept as Raboniel, of light and its opposite. Coincidence? Did it have to do with that sphere that bent the air?

The guard at her door began humming, then stepped to the side. Navani could guess what that meant. Indeed, Raboniel soon entered, followed by that other Fused who was so often nearby. The femalen with a similar topknot and skin pattern, but a blank stare. Raboniel seemed to like to keep her near, though Navani wasn't certain if it was for protection or for some other reason. The second Fused was one of the more . . . unhinged that Navani had seen. Perhaps the more sane ones purposely kept an eye on specific insane ones, to prevent them from hurting themselves or others.

The insane Fused walked over to the wall and stared at it. Raboniel walked toward the desk, so Navani rose and bowed to her. "Ancient One. Is something wrong?"

"Merely checking on your progress," Raboniel said. Navani made room so Raboniel could bend down, the orange-red hair of her topknot brushing the table as she inspected Navani's experiment: a box letting out the illumination from a Towerlight gemstone, which was split through a prism, then recombined through another into two separate streams of light.

"Incredible," Raboniel said. "This is what you do when you experiment, instead of fighting against me? Look, Stormlight *and* Lifelight. As I said."

"Yes, Ancient One," Navani said. "I've been reading about light. The illumination that comes from the sun or candles cannot be stored in gemstones, but Stormlight can. So what *is* Stormlight? It is not simply illumination, as it gives *off* illumination."

"It's as if Stormlight is at times a liquid. It behaves like one when you draw it from a full gemstone into an empty one, mimicking osmosis. While captured, the illumination given off by Stormlight behaves like sunlight: it can be split by a prism, and diffuses the farther it gets from its source. But the Stormlight must be different from the illumination it radiates. Otherwise, how could we hold it in a gemstone?"

"Can you combine them?" Raboniel asked. "Stormlight and Voidlight, can they be mixed?"

"To prove that humans and singers can be unified," Navani said.

"Yes, of course. For that reason."

She's lying, Navani thought. She couldn't be certain, as singers often acted in strange ways, but Navani suspected more here.

The strange insane Fused began saying something in their language. She stared up at the wall, then said it louder.

Raboniel glanced at her, hummed softly, then looked at Navani. "Have you discovered anything more?"

"That's about it," Navani said. "I couldn't get Lifelight and Stormlight to recombine, but I don't know if this counts as truly splitting them apart—as I've only split their radiation, not the pooled Light itself."

"I've thought about your mixing of oil and water, and I am intrigued. We need to know. Can Stormlight and Voidlight be mixed? What would happen if they were combined?"

"You are quite focused on that idea, Ancient One," Navani said, thoughtfully leaning back. "Why?"

"It's why I came here," Raboniel said.

"Not to conquer? You talk of peace between us. What would that alliance be like, to you, if we could achieve it?"

Raboniel hummed a rhythm and opened Navani's box, taking out the sphere of Towerlight. "The war has stretched so long, I've seen this kind of tactic play out dozens of times. We have never held the tower before, true, but we've seized Oathgates, taken command posts, and held the capital of

Alethela a couple of times. All part of an eternal, endless slog of a war. I want to end it. I *need* to find the tools to *truly* end it, for all of our . . . sanity."

"End how?" Navani pressed. "If we work together like you want, what happens to my people?"

Raboniel turned the Towerlight sphere over in her fingers, ignoring the question. "We've known about this new Light ever since the tower was created—but I am the one who theorized it was Stormlight and Lifelight combined. You have confirmed this. This *is* proof. Proof that what I want to do is possible."

"Have you ever heard of spheres that *warp* the air around them?" Navani asked. "Like they were extremely hot?"

Raboniel's rhythm cut off. She turned toward Navani. "Where did you hear of such a thing?"

"I remembered a conversation about it," Navani lied, "from long ago— with someone who claimed to have seen one."

"There are theories," Raboniel said. "Matter has its opposite: negative axi that destroy positive axi when combined. This is known, and confirmed by the Shards Odium *and* Honor. So some have thought . . . is there a negative to light? An anti-light? I had discarded this idea. After all, I assumed that if there was an opposite to Stormlight, it would be Voidlight."

"Except," Navani said, "we have no reason to believe that Stormlight and Voidlight are opposites. Tell me, what would happen if this theoretical negative light were to combine with its positive?"

"Destruction," Raboniel said. "Instantaneous annihilation."

Navani felt cold. She'd told her scholars—the ones to whom she'd entrusted Szeth's strange sphere—to experiment with the air-warping light. To move it to different gemstones, to try using it in fabrials. Could it be that . . . they'd somehow mixed that sphere's contents with ordinary Voidlight?

"Continue your experiments," Raboniel said, putting down the sphere. "Anything you need for your science shall be yours. If you can combine Voidlight and Stormlight without destroying them—therefore proving they are *not* opposites . . . well, I should like to know this. It will require me to discard years upon years of theories."

"I have no idea where to begin," Navani protested. "If you let me have my team back . . ."

"Write them instructions and put them to work," Raboniel said. "You have them still."

"Fine," Navani said, "but I have *no idea* what I'm doing. If I were trying to do this with liquids, I'd use an emulsifier—but what kind of emulsifier does one use on *light*? It defies reason."

"Try anyway," Raboniel said. "Do this, and I'll free your tower. I'll take my troops and walk away. This knowledge is worth more than any one location, no matter how strategic."

I'm sure, Navani thought. She didn't believe for a single heartbeat that Raboniel would do so—but at the same time, this knowledge would obviously give Navani an edge. Why did Raboniel want to prove, or disprove, that the two Lights were opposites? What *was* her game here?

She wants a weapon, perhaps? That explosion I inadvertently caused? Is that what Raboniel is hunting?

The Fused by the wall started talking again, louder this time. Again Raboniel hummed and glanced over.

"What does she say?" Navani asked.

"She . . . asks if anyone has seen her mother. She's trying to get the wall to talk."

"Her mother?" Navani thought, cocking her head. She hadn't thought that the Fused would have parents—but of course they did. The creatures had been born mortal, thousands of years ago. "What happened to her mother?"

"She's right here," Raboniel said softly, gesturing to herself. "That was another hypothesis of mine that was disproven. Long ago. The thought that a mother and daughter, serving together, might help one another retain their sanity."

Raboniel walked to her daughter and turned her to steer her out the door. And while singers tended not to show emotion on their faces, Navani thought for sure she could read pain in Raboniel's expression—a wince—as the daughter continued to ask for her mother. All the while staring unseeingly past her.

66

BEARER OF AGONIES

I am not convinced any of the gods can be destroyed, so perhaps I misspoke. They can change state however, like a spren—or like the various Lights. This is what we seek.

—From *Rhythm of War*, page 21 undertext

Dalinar touched his finger to the young soldier's forehead, then closed his eyes and concentrated.

He could see something extending from the soldier, radiating into the darkness. Pure white lines, thin as a hair. Some moved, though one end remained affixed to the central point: the place where Dalinar's finger touched the soldier's skin.

"I see them," he whispered. "Finally."

The Stormfather rumbled in the back of his mind. *I was not certain it could be done,* he said. *The power of Bondsmiths was tempered by Honor, for the good of all. Ever since the destruction of Ashyn.*

"How did you know about this ability?" Dalinar said, eyes still closed.

I heard it described before I fully lived. Melishi saw these lines.

"The last Bondsmith," Dalinar said. "Before the Recreance."

The same. Honor was dying, possibly mad.

"What can I do with these?" Dalinar asked.

I don't know. You see the Connections all people have: to others, to spren, to time and reality itself. Everything is Connected, Dalinar, by a vast web of interactions, passions, thoughts, fates.

The more Dalinar watched the quivering white lines, the more details he could pick out. Some were brighter than others, for example. He reached out and tried to touch one, but his fingers went through it.

Spren have these too, the Stormfather said. *And the bond that makes Radiants is similar, but far stronger. I don't think these little ones are particularly useful.*

"Surely these mean something," Dalinar said.

Yes, the Stormfather said. *But that doesn't mean they can be exploited. I heard Melishi say something once. Imagine you had two pieces of cloth, one red, one yellow. Before you and your brother parted, you each reached into a bag and selected one—but kept it hidden, putting it away in a box, unseen.*

You parted, traveling to distant quarters of the land. Then, by agreement, let us say that on the same day at the same time you each opened your box and took out your cloth. Upon finding the red one, you'd instantly know your brother had found the yellow one. You shared something, that bond of knowledge—the Connection exists, but isn't something that can necessarily be exploited. At least not by most people. A Bondsmith though . . .

Dalinar removed his finger and opened his eyes, then thanked the young soldier—who seemed nervous as he returned to his place near the front of the building, joining the still-disguised Szeth. Dalinar checked his arm fabrial. Jasnah and the others should be returning from the front lines soon. The battle won, the celebrations completed. All without Dalinar.

It felt so strange. Here he was, worried about Navani and the tower—but unable to do anything until he had more information. Worried about Adolin off in Shadesmar—separated from him, like the two brothers in the Stormfather's story. Shared destinies, shared fates, yet Dalinar felt powerless to help either his son or his wife.

You do have a part in this, he told himself firmly. *A duty. Master these powers. Best Odium. Think on a scale bigger than one battle, or even one war.* It was difficult, with how slowly his skills seemed to be progressing. So much time wasted. Was this what Jasnah had experienced all those years, chasing secrets when nobody else had believed her?

He had another duty today, in addition to his practice. He'd been putting it off, but he knew he should delay no longer. So, he collected Szeth and walked through the camp, turning his path toward the prison.

He needed to talk to Taravangian in person.

The building that housed the former king was not a true prison. They hadn't planned for one of those in the temporary warcamp here in Emul. A stockade, yes. But military discipline was by necessity quick. Anything demanding more than a week or two in confinement usually resulted in a discharge or—for more serious infractions—an execution.

Taravangian required something more permanent and more delicate. So they'd blocked off the windows on a sturdy home, reinforced the door, and set guards from among Dalinar's best soldiers. As Dalinar approached, he noted how the upper-floor windows were now filled with stark crem bricks, mortared into place. It had felt wrong to give Taravangian a home instead of a cell—but seeing those windows, it also felt wrong to leave him without sunlight.

Dalinar nodded to the salutes at the door, then waited for the guards to undo the locks and pull the door open for him. Nobody worried about his safety or made a comment about his single guard. They all thought the precautions were to prevent Taravangian from being rescued, and would never have wondered whether the Blackthorn could handle himself against an elderly statesman.

They didn't have any inkling, even now, how dangerous Taravangian was. He sat on a stool near the far wall of the main room. He'd put a ruby into the corner and was staring at it. He turned when Dalinar entered, and actually smiled. Storming man.

Dalinar waved for Szeth to remain right inside the door as the guards closed and locked it behind them. Then Dalinar approached the corner, wary. He'd charged into many a battle with less trepidation than he now felt.

"I had wondered if you would come," Taravangian said. "It has been nearly two weeks since my betrayal."

"I wanted to be certain I wasn't somehow being manipulated," Dalinar said, honestly. "So I waited until certain tasks were accomplished before coming to you, and risking letting you influence me."

Though, deep down, Dalinar admitted that was mostly an excuse. Seeing this man was painful. Perhaps he should have let Jasnah interrogate Taravangian, as she'd suggested. But that seemed the coward's route.

"Ah, certain tasks are accomplished, then?" the old man asked. "By now you've surely recovered from the betrayal of the Veden armies. You've clashed with Odium's forces in Emul? I warned Odium that we should have moved earlier, but he was adamant, you see. This was the way he wanted it to happen."

The frankness of it felt like a boot directly to Dalinar's gut. He steeled himself. "That stool is too uncomfortable for a man of your years. You should be given a chair. I thought they'd left the building furnished. Do you have a bed? And surely they gave you more than a single sphere for light."

"Dalinar, Dalinar," Taravangian whispered. "If you wish me to have comfort, don't ask after the chair or the light. Answer my questions and talk to me. I need that more than—"

"Why?" Dalinar interrupted. He held Taravangian's gaze, and was shocked at how much asking the question *hurt*. He'd known the betrayal was coming. He'd known what this man was. Nevertheless, the words were *agonizing* as they slipped from his lips again. "Why? *Why* did you do it?"

"Because, Dalinar, you're going to lose. I'm sorry, my friend. It is unavoidable."

"You can't know that."

"Yet I do." He sagged in his seat, turning toward the corner and the glowing sphere. "Such a poor imitation of our comfortable sitting room in Urithiru. Even that was a poor imitation of a real hearth, crackling with true flames, alive and beautiful. An imitation of an imitation.

"That's what we are, Dalinar. A painting made from another painting of something great. Perhaps the ancient Radiants could have won this fight, when Honor lived. They didn't. They barely *survived*. Now we face a god. Alone. There is no victory awaiting us."

Dalinar felt . . . cold. Not shocked. Not surprised. He supposed he could have figured out Taravangian's reasoning; they'd talked often about what it meant to be a king. The discussions had grown more intense, more meaningful, once Dalinar had realized what Taravangian had done to acquire the throne of Jah Keved. Once he'd known that—instead of chatting with a kindly old man with strange ideals—he had been talking to another murderer. A man like Dalinar himself.

Now he felt disappointed. Because in the end, Taravangian had let that side of him rule. No longer on the edge. His friend—yes, they were friends—had stepped off the cliff.

"We *can* defeat him, Taravangian," Dalinar said. "You are not nearly so smart as you think."

"I agree. I was once, though." He clarified, perhaps noticing Dalinar's confusion. "I visited the Old Magic, Dalinar. I saw her. Not just the Nightwatcher, I suspect, but the other one. The one you saw."

"Cultivation," he said. "There *is* one who can face Odium. There were *three* gods."

"She won't fight him," Taravangian said. "She knows. How do you think I found out we'd lose?"

"She told you that?" Dalinar strode forward, squatting down beside Taravangian, coming to eye level with the aged man. "She *said* Odium would win?"

"I asked her for the capacity to stop what was coming," Taravangian said. "And she made me brilliant, Dalinar. Transcendently brilliant, but just once. For a day. I vary, you know. Some days I'm smart, but my emotions seem stunted—I don't feel anything but annoyance. Other days I'm stupid, but the tiniest bit of sentimentality sends me into tears. Most days I'm like I am today. Some shade of average.

"Only one day of brilliance. One *single* day. I've often wished I'd get another, but I guess that was all that Cultivation wanted me to have. She wanted me to see for myself. There *was* no way to save Roshar."

"You saw no possible out?" Dalinar said. "Tell me honestly. Was there absolutely no way to win?"

Taravangian fell silent.

"Nobody can see the future perfectly," Dalinar said. "Not even Odium. I find it impossible to believe that you, no matter how smart, could have been *absolutely* certain there was no path to victory."

"Let's say you were in my place," Taravangian said. "You saw a shadow of the future, the best anyone has ever seen it. Better, in fact, than any mortal could achieve. And you saw a path to saving Alethkar—everyone you love, everything you know. You saw a very plausible, very reasonable opportunity to accomplish this goal.

"But you also saw that to do more—to save the world itself—you would have to rely on such wild bets as to be ludicrous. And if you failed at those very, very, *very* long odds, you'd lose everything. Tell *me* honestly, Dalinar. Would you not consider doing what I did, taking the rational choice of saving the few?" Taravangian's eyes glistened. "Isn't that the way of the soldier? Accept your losses, and do what you can?"

"So you sold us out? You helped *hasten* our destruction?"

"For a price, Dalinar," Taravangian said, staring again at the ruby that was the room's hearth. "I *did* preserve Kharbranth. I tried, I promise you, to protect more. But it is as the Radiants say. Life before death. I saved the lives of as many as I could—"

"Don't use that phrase," Dalinar said. "Don't sully it, Taravangian, with your crass justifications."

"Still standing on your high tower, Dalinar?" Taravangian asked. "Proud of how far you can see, when you won't look past your own feet? Yes, you're very noble. How *wonderful* you are, fighting until the end, dragging every human to death with you. They can all die knowing you never compromised."

"I made an oath," Dalinar said, "to protect the people of Alethkar. It was my oath as a highprince. After that, a greater oath—the oath of a Radiant."

"And is that how you protected the Alethi years ago, Dalinar? When you burned them alive in their cities?"

Dalinar drew in a sharp breath, but refused to rise to that barb. "I'm not that man any longer. I changed. I take the next step, Taravangian."

"I suppose that is true, and my statement was a useless gibe. I wish you *were* that man who would burn one city to preserve the kingdom. I could work with that man, Dalinar. Make him see."

"See that I should turn traitor?"

"Yes. As you live now, *protecting* people isn't your true ideal. If that were the case, you'd surrender. No, your *true* ideal is never giving up. No matter the cost. You realize the pride in that sentiment?"

"I refuse to accept that we've lost," Dalinar said. "That's the problem with *your* worldview, Taravangian. You gave up before the battle started. You think you're smart enough to know the future, but I repeat: *Nobody* knows for certain what will happen."

Strangely, the older man nodded. "Yes, yes perhaps. I could be wrong. That would be wonderful, wouldn't it, Dalinar? I'd die happy, knowing I was wrong."

"Would you?" Dalinar said.

Taravangian considered. Then he turned abruptly—a motion that caused Szeth to jump, stepping forward, hand on his sword. Taravangian, however, was just turning to point at a nearby stool for Dalinar to sit.

Taravangian glanced at Szeth briefly and hesitated. Dalinar thought he caught a narrowing of the man's eyes. Damnation. He'd figured it out.

The moment was over in a second. "That stool," Taravangian said, pointing again. "I carried it down from upstairs. In case you visited. Would you join me here, sitting as we once did? For old times' sake?"

Dalinar frowned. He didn't want to take the seat out of principle, but that *was* prideful. He would sit with this man one last time. Taravangian was one of the few people who truly understood what it felt like to make the choices that Dalinar had. Dalinar pulled over the stool and settled down.

"I *would* die happily," Taravangian said, "if I could see that I was wrong. If you won."

"I don't think you would. I don't think you could stand not being the one who saved us."

"How little you know me, despite it all."

"You didn't come to me, or any of us," Dalinar said. "You say you were extremely smart? You figured out what was going to happen? What was your response? It wasn't to form a coalition; it wasn't to refound the Radiants. It was to send out an assassin, then seize the throne of Jah Keved."

"So I would be in a position to negotiate with Odium."

"That argument is crem, Taravangian. You didn't need to murder people—you didn't need to be king of Jah Keved—to accomplish any of this. You *wanted* to be an emperor. You made a play for Alethkar too. You sent Szeth to kill me, instead of talking to me."

"Pardon, Blackthorn, but please remember the man you were when I began this. He would not have listened to me."

"You're so smart you can predict who will win a war before it begins, but you couldn't see that I was changing? You couldn't see that I'd be more valuable as an ally than as a corpse?"

"I thought you would fall, Dalinar. I predicted you would join Odium, if left alive. Either that or you would fight my every step. Odium thought the same."

"And you were both wrong," Dalinar said. "So your grand plan, your masterful 'vision' of the future was simply *wrong*."

"I . . . I . . ." Taravangian rubbed his brow. "I don't have the intelligence right now to explain it to you. Odium will arrange things so that no matter what choice you make, he will win. Knowing that, I made the difficult decision to save at least one city."

"I think you saw a chance to be an emperor, and you took it," Dalinar said. "You wanted power, Taravangian—so you could give it up. You wanted to be the glorious king who sacrificed himself to protect everyone else. You have always seen yourself as the man who must bear the *burden* of leading."

"Because it's true."

"Because you like it."

"If so, why did I let go? Why am I captured here?"

"Because you want to be known as the one who saved us."

"No," Taravangian said. "It's because I knew my friends and family could escape if I let you take me. I knew that your wrath would come upon me, not Kharbranth. And as I'm sure you've discovered, those who knew what I was doing are no longer involved in the city's government. If you were to attack Kharbranth, you would attack innocents."

"I'd never do that."

"Because you have me. Admit it."

Storm him, it was true—and it made Dalinar angry enough to draw a single boiling angerspren at his feet. He had no interest in retribution against Kharbranth. They, like the Vedens—like Dalinar himself—had all been pawns in Taravangian's schemes.

"I know it is difficult to accept," Taravangian said. "But my goal has never been power. It has always *only* been about saving whomever I could save."

"I can't debate that, as I don't know your heart, Taravangian," Dalinar said. "So instead I'll tell you something I know for certain. It *could* have gone differently. You could have truly joined with us. Storms . . . I can imagine a world where you said the oaths. I imagine you as a better leader than I ever could have been. I feel like you were so close."

"No, my friend," Taravangian said. "A monarch cannot make such oaths and expect to be able to keep them. He must realize that a greater need might arise at any time."

"If so, it's impossible for a king to be a moral man."

"Or perhaps you can be moral and still break oaths."

"No," Dalinar said. "No, oaths are part of what *define* morality, Taravangian. A good man must strive to accomplish the things he's committed to do."

"Spoken like a true son of Tanavast," Taravangian said, clasping his hands. "And I believe you, Dalinar. I believe you think exactly what you say. You *are* a man of Honor, raised to it through a life of his religion—which you might be upending, but it retains its grip on your mind.

"I wish I could commend that. Perhaps there *was* another way out of this. Perhaps there *was* another solution. But it wouldn't be found in your oaths, my friend. And it would not involve a coalition of noble leaders. It would involve the sort of business with which you were once so familiar."

"No," Dalinar said. "There is a *just* way to victory. The methods must match the ideal to be obtained."

Taravangian nodded, as if this were the inevitable response. Dalinar sat back on his seat, and they sat in silence together for a time, watching the tiny ruby. He hated how this had gone, how the argument forced him into the most dogmatic version of his beliefs. He knew there was nuance in every position, yet . . .

Aligning his methods and his goals was at the very soul of what he'd learned. What he was trying to become. He had to believe there was a way to lead while still being moral.

He stared at that ruby, that glimmer of red light, reminiscent of an Everstorm's lightning. Dalinar had come here expecting a fight, but was surprised to realize he felt more sorrow than he did anger. He felt Taravangian's pain, his regret for what had occurred. What they had both lost.

Dalinar finally stood up. "You always said that to be a king was to accept pain."

"To accept that you must do what others cannot," Taravangian agreed. "To bear the agonies of the decisions you *had* to make, so that others may live pure lives. You should know that I have said my goodbyes and intentionally made myself worthless to Odium and my former compatriots. You will not be able to use my life to bargain with anyone."

"Why tell me this?" Dalinar said. "You would make it worthless to keep you prisoner. Do you *want* to be executed?"

"I simply want to be clear with you," Taravangian said. "There is no further reason for me to try to manipulate you, Dalinar. I have achieved what I wanted. You may kill me."

"No, Taravangian," Dalinar said. "You have lived your convictions, however misguided they may be. Now I'm going to live mine. And at the end, when I face Odium and win, you will be there. I'll give you this gift."

"The pain of knowing I was wrong?"

"You told me earlier that you *wished* to be proven wrong. If you're sincere—and this was never about being right or about gaining power—then on that day we can embrace, knowing it is all over. Old friend."

Taravangian looked at him, and there were tears in his eyes. "To that day, then," he whispered. "And to that embrace."

Dalinar nodded and withdrew, collecting Szeth at the door. He paused briefly to tell the guards to bring Taravangian some more light and a comfortable chair.

As they walked away, Szeth spoke from behind him. "Do not trust his lies. He pretends to be done plotting, but there is more to him. There is *always* more to that one."

Dalinar glanced at the stoic bodyguard. Szeth so rarely offered opinions.

"I don't trust him," Dalinar said. "I can't walk away from any conversation with that man, no matter how innocent, without going over and over what he said. That's part of why I was so hesitant to go in there."

"You are wise," Szeth said, and seemed to consider the conversation finished.

*Do not mourn for what has happened. This notebook was a dream
we shared, which is itself a beautiful thing. Proof of the truth of my
intent, even if the project was ultimately doomed.*

—From *Rhythm of War*, page 27

Venli scrambled through the hallways of Urithiru. She shoved
past a group of humans who were too slow to get out of the way,
then pulled to a halt, breathing heavily as she looked out onto
the balcony.

That song . . . That song reminded her of her mother's voice.

But it wasn't her, of course. The femalen who sat by the balcony—
weaving a mat and singing to Peace—was not Jaxlim. Her red skin pattern was wrong, her hairstrands too short. Venli leaned against the stone
doorway as others on the balcony noticed her, and the femalen's voice cut
off. She glanced toward Venli and began to hum to Anxiety.

Venli turned and walked away, attuning Disappointment. Hopefully
she hadn't frightened the people. A Regal looking so wild must have given
them a scare.

Timbre pulsed inside her.

"I keep hearing her songs," Venli said. "In the voices of people I pass.
I keep remembering those days when I sang with her. I miss those days,
Timbre. Life was so simple then."

Timbre pulsed to the Lost.

"She didn't have much sense left when my betrayal came," Venli explained to the spren's question. "Part of me thinks that a mercy, as she

never knew. About me . . . Anyway it was the storms that eventually killed her. She was with the group that escaped, but they fled into the chasms. And then . . . we did what we did. The flood that came upon the Plains that day . . . Timbre, she drowned down there. Dead by my hand as surely as if I'd stabbed her."

The little spren pulsed again, consoling. She felt Venli couldn't *completely* be blamed for what she'd done, as the forms had influenced her mind. But Venli had *chosen* those forms.

She often thought back to those early days, after releasing Ulim. Yes, her emotions had changed. She'd pursued her ambition more and more. But at the same time, she hadn't responded like Eshonai, who had seemed to become a different person entirely when adopting a form of power. Venli seemed more resistant somehow. More herself, regardless of form.

That should have made her attune Joy, for she could only guess this had helped her escape Odium's grip. But it also made her responsible for what she'd done. She couldn't blame it on spren or forms. She'd been there, giving those orders.

Timbre pulsed. *I helped.* And . . . yes, she had. When she'd first appeared, Venli had grown stronger, more able to resist.

"Thank you," Venli said. "For that, and for what you continue to do. I'm not worthy of your faith. But thank you."

Timbre pulsed. Today was the day. Raboniel was spending all her time with Navani, and seemed to be thoroughly enjoying the difficulty of manipulating the former queen. That left Venli free. She'd secured a small sack of gemstones, some with Voidlight, some with Stormlight.

Today she was going to see what it *really* meant to be on this path of Radiance.

She'd already selected an area in which to practice. During morning reports, Venli had learned the Pursuer's scouts were carefully combing the fifteenth floor. The majority of Raboniel's soldiers were busy watching the humans, and didn't often venture to the higher floors. So Venli had chosen a place on the eighth floor—a place that the Pursuer had already searched, but that was far from population centers.

The tower up here was silent, and oddly reminded her of the chasms in the Shattered Plains. Those stone pits had also been a place where the sun was difficult to remember—and also a place resplendent with beautiful stone.

She ran her fingers across a wall, expecting to feel bumps from the vibrant strata lines, but it was smooth. Like the walls of the chasms, actually. Her mother had died in those pits. Likely terrified, unable to understand what was happening as the water rushed in and . . .

Venli attuned the Lost and put down her small sack of spheres. She took out a Stormlight one first, then glimpsed into Shadesmar. She hadn't again seen the Voidspren she'd spotted near Rlain's cell, though she'd watched carefully these last few days. She'd eventually put Rlain together with the surgeon and his wife, and delivered all three of them to help care for the fallen Radiants.

Shadesmar revealed no Voidspren hiding in cremlings, so she hesitantly returned her vision to the Physical Realm and drew in a breath of Stormlight. That she could do, as she'd practiced it together with Timbre over the months.

Stormlight didn't work like Voidlight did. Rather than going into her gemheart, it infused her entire body. She could feel it raging—an odd feeling more than an unpleasant one.

She pressed her hand to the stone wall. "Do you remember how we did this last time?" she asked Timbre.

The little spren pulsed uncertainly. That had been many months ago, and had drawn the attention of secretspren, so they had stopped quickly. It seemed, though, that all Venli had needed to do was press her hand against the wall, and her powers had started activating.

Timbre pulsed. She wasn't convinced it would work with Stormlight, not with the tower's defenses in place. Indeed, as Venli tried to do . . . well, anything with the Stormlight, she felt as if there were some invisible wall blocking her.

She couldn't push the Stormlight into her gemheart to store it there—not with the Voidspren trapped inside. So Venli let the Light burn off on its own, breathing out to hasten the process. Then she took out a Voidlight sphere. She could get these without too much trouble—but she didn't dare sing the Song of Prayer to create them herself. She worried about drawing Odium's attention; he seemed to be ignoring her these days, and she'd rather it remain that way.

Timbre pulsed encouragingly.

"You sure?" Venli said. "It doesn't seem right, for some reason, to use his power to fuel our abilities."

Timbre's pulsed reply was pragmatic. Indeed, they used Voidlight every day—a little of it, stored in their gemheart—to power Venli's translation abilities. She wasn't certain if her ability to use Voidlight for Radiant powers came from the fact that she was Regal, or if any singer who managed a bond would be able to do the same.

Today, she drew the Voidlight in like Stormlight, and it infused her gemheart fully. The Voidlight didn't push her to move or act, like the Stormlight had. Instead it enflamed her emotions, in this case making her more paranoid, so she checked Shadesmar again. Still nothing there to be alarmed about.

She pressed her hand to the wall again, and tried to feel the stone. Not with her fingers. With her soul.

The stone responded. It seemed to stir like a person awaking from a deep slumber. *Hello,* it said, though the sounds were drawn out. She didn't hear the word so much as feel it. *You are . . . familiar.*

"I am Venli," she said. "Of the listeners."

The stones trembled. They spoke with one voice, but she felt as if it was also many voices overlapping. Not the voice of the tower, but the voices of the many different sections of stones around her. The walls, the ceiling, the floor.

Radiant, the stones said. *We have . . . missed your touch, Radiant. But what is this? What is that sound, that tone?*

"Voidlight," Venli admitted.

That sound is familiar, the stones said. *A child of the ancient ones. Our friend, you have returned to sing our song again?*

"What song?" Venli asked.

The stone near her hand began to undulate, like ripples on the surface of a pond. A tone surged through her, then it began to pulse with the song of a rhythm she'd never heard, but somehow always known. A profound, sonorous rhythm, ancient as the core of Roshar.

The entire wall followed suit, then the ceiling and the floor, surrounding her with a beautiful rhythm set to a pure tone. Timbre, with glee, joined in—and so Venli's body aligned with the rhythm, and she felt it humming through her, vibrating her from carapace to bones.

She gasped, then pressed her other hand to the rock, aching to feel the song against her skin. There was a rightness about this, a perfection.

Oh, storms, she thought. *Oh, rhythms ancient and new. I belong here.*

She *belonged* here.

So far, everything she'd done with Timbre had been accidental. There had been a momentum to it. She'd made choices along the way, but it had never felt like something she deserved. Rather, it was a path she had fallen into, and then taken because it was better than her other options.

But here . . . she *belonged* here.

Remember, the stones said. The ground in front of her stopped rippling and formed shapes. Little homes made of stone, with figures standing beside them. Shaping them. She heard them humming.

She *saw* them. Ancient people, the Dawnsingers, working the stone. Creating cities, tools. They didn't need Soulcasting or forges. They'd dip lengths of wood into the stone, and come out with axes. They'd shape bowls with their fingers. All the while, the stone would sing to them.

Feel me, shaper. Create from me. We are one. The stone shapes your life as you shape the stone.

Welcome home, child of the ancients.

"How?" Venli asked. "Radiants didn't exist then. Spren didn't bond us . . . did they?"

Things are new, the stones hummed, *but new things are made from old things, and old peoples give birth to new ones. Old stones remember.*

The vibrations quieted, falling from powerful thrummings, to tiny ripples, to stillness. The homes and the people melted back to ordinary stone floor, though the strata of this place had changed. As if to echo the former vibrations.

Venli knelt. After several minutes, breathing in gasps, she realized she was completely out of Voidlight. She searched her sack, and found all of her spheres drained save for a single mark. She'd gone through those spheres with frightening speed. But that moment of song, that moment of connection, had certainly been worth the cost.

She drew in this mark, then hesitantly placed her hand to the wall again. She felt the stone, willing and pliable, encouraging her and calling her "shaper." She drew out the Voidlight and it infused her hand, making it glow violet-on-black. When she pressed her thumb into the stone, the rock molded beneath her touch, as if it had become crem clay.

Venli pressed her entire hand into the stone, making a print there and feeling the soft—but still present—rhythm. Then she pulled off a piece of the rock and molded it in her fingers. She rolled it into a ball, and the viscosity seemed to match what she needed—for when she held her hand forward and imagined it doing so, the stone ball melted into a puddle. She dropped it then, and it clicked when it hit the ground—hard, but imprinted by her fingers.

She picked it up and pressed it back into the wall, where it melded with the stone there as if it had never been removed.

Once she was done, she considered. "I want this, Timbre," she whispered, wiping her eyes. "I *need* this."

Timbre thrummed excitedly.

"What do you mean, 'them'?" Venli asked. She looked up, noticing lights in the hallway. She attuned Anxiety, but then the lights drew closer. The three little spren were like Timbre: in the shape of comets with rings of light pulsing around them.

"This is dangerous," Venli hissed to Reprimand. "They shouldn't be here. If they're seen, the Voidspren will destroy them."

Timbre pulsed that spren couldn't be destroyed. Cut them with a Shardblade, and they'd re-form. Venli, however, wasn't so confident. Surely the Fused could do something. Trap them in a jar? Lock them away?

Timbre insisted they'd simply fade into Shadesmar in that case, and be free. Well, it was risky, no matter what she said. These spren seemed more . . . awake than she'd expected though. They hovered around her, curious.

"Didn't you say spren like you need a bond to be aware in the Physical Realm? An anchor?"

Timbre's explanation was slightly ashamed. These were eager to bond Venli's friends, her squires. That had given these spren access to thoughts and stability in the Physical Realm. Venli *was* the anchor.

She nodded. "Tell them to get out of the tower for now. If my friends start suddenly manifesting Radiant powers—and the stone starts singing in a place others could see—we could find ourselves in serious trouble."

Timbre pulsed, defiant. How long?

"Until I find a way out of this mess," Venli said. She pressed her hand to the wall, listening to the soft, contented hum of the stones. "I'm like a baby taking her first steps. But this might be the answer we need. If I can sculpt us an exit through the collapsed tunnels below, I should be able to sneak us out. Maybe we can even make it seem like we died in a further cave-in, covering our escape."

Timbre pulsed encouragingly.

"You're correct," Venli said. "*We* can do this. But we need to take it slowly, carefully. I rushed to find new forms, and that proved a disaster. This time we'll do things the right way."

68

ONE FAMILY

EIGHT YEARS AGO

Eshonai accompanied her mother into the storm.

Together they struck out into the electric darkness, Eshonai carrying a large wooden shield to buffer the wind for her mother, who cradled the bright orange glowing gemstone. Powerful gusts tried to rip the shield out of Eshonai's hand, and windspren soared past, giggling.

Eshonai and her mother passed others, notable for the similar gemstones they carried. Little bursts of light in the tempest. Like the souls of the dead said to wander the storms, searching for gemhearts to inhabit.

Eshonai attuned the Rhythm of the Terrors: sharp, each beat puncturing her mind. She wasn't afraid for herself, but her mother had been so frail lately.

Though many of the others stood out in the open, Eshonai led her mother to the hollow she'd picked out earlier. Even here, the pelting rain felt like it was trying to burrow through her skin. Rainspren along the top of the ridge seemed to dance as they waved along with the furious tempest.

Eshonai huddled down beside her mother, unable to hear the rhythm the femalen was humming. The light of the gemstone, however, revealed a grin on Jaxlim's face.

A grin?

"Reminds me of when your father and I came out together!" Jaxlim shouted at Eshonai over the stormwinds. "We'd decided not to leave it to fate, where one of us might be taken and the other not! I still remember the strange feelings of passion when I first changed. You're too afraid of that, Eshonai! I do want grandchildren, you realize."

"Do we have to talk about this now?" Eshonai asked. "Hold that stone. Adopt the new form! Think about it, *not* mateform."

Wouldn't *that* be an embarrassment.

"The lifespren aren't interested in someone my age," her mother said. "It simply feels nice to be out here again! I'd been beginning to think I would waste away!"

Together they huddled against the rock, Eshonai using her shield as an improvised roof to block the rain. She wasn't certain how long it would take the transformation to begin. Eshonai herself had only adopted a new form once, as a child—when her father had helped her adopt workform, since the time of changes had come to her.

Children needed no form, and were vibrant without one—but if they didn't adopt a form upon puberty in their seventh or eighth year, they would be trapped in dullform instead. That form was, essentially, an inferior version of mateform.

Today, the storm stretched long, and Eshonai's arm began to ache from holding the shield in place. "Anything?" she asked of her mother.

"Not yet! I don't know the proper mindset."

"Attune a bold rhythm!" Eshonai said. That was what Venli had told them. "Confidence or Excitement!"

"I'm trying! I—"

Whatever else her mother said was lost in the sound of thunder washing across them, vibrating the very stones, making Eshonai's teeth chatter. Or perhaps that was the cold. Normally chill weather didn't bother her—workform was well suited to it—but the icy rainwater had leaked through her oiled coat, sneaking down along her spine.

She attuned Resolve, keeping the shield in place. She *would* protect her mother. Jaxlim often complained that Eshonai was unreliable, prone to fancy, but that wasn't true. Her exploration was difficult work. It was *valuable* work. She *wasn't* unreliable or lazy.

Let her mother see this. Eshonai holding her shield in defiance of the rain—in defiance of the Rider of Storms himself. Holding her mother close, warming her. Not weak. Solid. Dependable. *Determined.*

The gemstone in her mother's hands began to glow brighter. *Finally,* Eshonai thought, shifting to give her mother more space to enact the transformation, the recasting of her soul, the ultimate connection between listener and Roshar itself.

Eshonai shouldn't have been surprised when the light burst from the gemstone and was absorbed—like water rushing to fill an empty vessel—into her *own* gemheart. Yet she was. Eshonai gasped, the rhythms disrupting and vanishing—all but one, an overwhelming sound she'd never heard before. A stately, steady tone. Not a rhythm. A pure note.

Proud, louder than the thunder. The sound became everything to her as her previous spren—a tiny gravitationspren—was ejected from her gemheart.

The pure tone of Honor pounding in her ears, she dropped the shield—which flew away into the dark sky. She wasn't supposed to have been taken, but in the moment she didn't care. This transformation was wonderful. In it, a vital piece of the listeners returned to her.

They needed more than they had. They needed *this*.

This . . . this was *right*. She embraced the change.

While it happened, it seemed to her that all of Roshar paused to sing Honor's long-lost note.

∴

Eshonai came to, lying in a puddle of rainwater cloudy with crem. A single rainspren undulated beside her, its form rippling and its eye staring straight upward toward the clouds, little feet curling and uncurling.

She sat up and surveyed her tattered clothing. Her mother had left Eshonai at some point during the storm, shouting that she needed to get under cover. Eshonai had been too absorbed by the tone and the new transformation to go with her.

She held up her hand and found the fingers thick, meaty, with carapace as grand as human armor along the back of the hand and up the arm. It covered her entire body, from her feet up to her head. No hairstrands. Simply a solid piece of carapace.

The change had shredded her shirt and coat, leaving only her skirt—and that had snapped at the waist, so it barely hung on her body. She stood up, and even that simple act felt different than it had before. She was *propelled* to her feet by unexpected strength. She stumbled, then gasped, attuning Awe.

"Eshonai!" an unfamiliar voice said.

She frowned as a monstrous figure in reddish-orange carapace stepped over some rubble from the highstorm. He had tied his wrap on awkwardly, plainly having suffered a similar disrobing. She attuned Amusement, though it didn't look silly. It seemed impossible that such a dynamic, muscular figure could *ever* look silly. She wished there were a rhythm more majestic than Awe. Was that what *she* looked like too?

"Eshonai," the malen said with his deep voice. "Can you believe this? I feel like I could leap up and touch the clouds!"

She didn't recognize the voice . . . but that pattern of marbled skin *was* familiar. And the features, though now covered by a carapace skullcap, were reminiscent of . . .

"Thude?" she said, then gasped again. "My voice!"

"I know," he said. "If you've ever wished to sing the low tones, Eshonai, it seems we've found the perfect form for it!"

She searched around to see several other listeners in powerful armor standing and attuning Awe. There were a good dozen of them. Though Venli had provided around two dozen gemstones, it seemed not all of the volunteers had taken to the new form. Unsurprising. It would take them time and practice to determine the proper mindset.

"Were you overwhelmed too?" Dianil said, striding over. Her voice was as deep as Eshonai's now, but that curl of black marbling along her brow was distinctive. "I felt an overpowering need to stand in the storm basking in the tone."

"There are songs of those who first adopted workform," Eshonai said. "I believe they mention a similar experience: an outpouring of power, an amazing tone that belonged purely to Cultivation."

"The tones of Roshar," Thude said, "welcoming us home."

The twelve of them gathered, and though she knew some better than others, there seemed to be an instant . . . connection between them. A comradery. They took turns jumping, seeing who could get the highest, singing to Joy, as silly as a bunch of children with a new toy. Eshonai hefted a rock and hurled it, then watched it soar an incredible distance. She even drew a gloryspren—with flowing tails and long wings.

As the others selected their own rocks to try beating her throw, she heard an incongruous sound. The drums? Yes, those *were* the battle drums. A raid was happening at the city.

The others gathered around her, humming to Confusion. An attack by one of the other families? *Now?*

Eshonai wanted to laugh.

"Are they *insane?*" Thude asked.

"They don't know what we've done," Eshonai said, looking around at the flat expanse of rock outside the city where they'd engaged the highstorm. Many listeners were only now making their way out of the sheltered cracks in the ground.

Their best warriors, however, would have stayed at the city in the small, strong structures built there. More than one family had claimed a city right after a storm. It was one of the best times to attack, assuming you could muster your numbers quickly enough.

"This is going to be fun," Melu said to Excitement.

"I don't know if that's the correct way to think of it," Eshonai said, though she felt the same eagerness. A desire to charge in. "Though . . . if we can arrive before the boasts are done . . ."

The others began attuning Amusement or Excitement, grinning. Eshonai led the way, ignoring the calls of those leaving the stormshelter. There was a more urgent matter to attend to.

As they approached the city, she could see the rival family mustered outside the gateway, lifting spears and making challenges and taunts. They wore white, of course. It was how one knew an attack was happening, rather than a request for trade or other interaction.

As long as the boasts were continuing, the actual battle hadn't yet begun. She'd participated in several fights for cities during her family's years trying to claim one, and they'd always been nasty affairs—the worst one leaving over a *dozen* people dead on each side.

Well, today they'd see about . . .

She stopped, holding up her hand to make the others pause. They did so—though a part of Eshonai wondered why she had decided to take charge. It simply felt natural.

They'd been approaching a fissure in the wall surrounding the city. That wall might once have been grand, but mere hints of its former majesty remained. Most of it had worn low, split by large gaps.

Here, a figure moved in the shadows. It looked ominous, dangerous— but then Venli emerged into the light, waving them forward. How had she gotten to the city so quickly?

Eshonai approached, and Venli looked her up and down with a slow, deliberate gaze. The drums beat in the background, urging Eshonai forward. Yet that look in her sister's eyes . . .

"So it worked," Venli said. "Praise the ancient storms for that. You look good, sister. All bulked up and ready to serve."

"This isn't who I am," Eshonai said, gesturing to the form. "But there is a certain . . . thrill to holding it."

"Go visit Sharefel," Venli said. "He's waiting for you."

"The drums . . ." Eshonai said.

"The enemy will continue howling insults for a little while yet," Venli said. "Visit Sharefel."

Sharefel. The family's Shardbearer. Upon obtaining this city, by tradition the defeated family had given up the city's Shards for her family to protect and keep.

"Venli," Eshonai said. "We do *not* use Shards upon other listeners. Those are for hunts alone."

"Oh, sister," Venli said to Amusement, walking around her, then inspecting Thude and the others. "If we're going to *ever* stand a hope of resisting the humans—when they inevitably turn against us—we must be ready to bear the weapons with which we were blessed."

Eshonai wanted to attune Reprimand at the suggestion, but she remembered the things Dalinar Kholin had said to her. If the listeners weren't unified, they *would* be easy pickings.

"I want to get to the fight," Melu said to Excitement, an anticipation-spren—like a long streamer connected to a round sphere below—bouncing around behind her.

"I think it's worth trying not to kill anyone," Thude said to Consideration. "With this form . . . I feel it would be unfair."

"Bear the Shards," Venli urged. "Show them the dangers of approaching us to demand battle."

Eshonai pushed past her sister, and the others followed. Venli trailed along behind as well. Eshonai didn't intend to use the Shards against her people, but perhaps there *was* a purpose to visiting Sharefel. She wound through the city, passing crem-filled puddles and vines stretching out from rockbuds to lap up the moisture.

The Shardbearer's hut was by the front wall, near the drums. It was one of the strongest structures in the city, one they always kept well-maintained. Today the door was open, welcoming. Eshonai stepped into the doorway.

"Ah . . ." a soft voice said to the Rhythm of the Lost. "So it is true. We have warriors once more."

Eshonai stepped forward, finding the elderly listener sitting in his seat, light from the doorway illuminating his pattern of mostly black skin. Feeling it appropriate, even if she didn't quite know why, she knelt before him.

"I have long sung the old songs," Sharefel said, "dreaming of this day. I always thought I would be the one to find it. How? What spren?"

"Painspren," Eshonai said.

"They flee during storms."

"We captured them," Eshonai said as a couple of others entered the chamber, striking dangerous silhouettes. "Using a human method."

"Ahh . . ." he said. "I shall try it myself then, at the next storm. But this is a new era, and deserves a new Shardbearer. Which of you will take my Shards? Which of you can bear this burden, and this glory?"

The group became still. Not all families had Shardbearers; there were only eight sets among all the listeners. Those who held the proper eight cities were blessed with them, to be wielded only in hunts against greatshells. Those were rare events, where many families would band together to harvest a gemheart for growing crops, then feast upon the slain beast.

That . . . did not seem the future of their Shards anymore. *If the humans discover we have these,* Eshonai thought, *it* will *be war.*

"Give the Shards to me," Melu said to Excitement. She stepped forward, though Thude put his hand upon her breastplate as if to restrain her.

She hummed to Betrayal, and he hummed to Irritation. A challenge from both.

This could get ugly *very* quickly.

"No!" Eshonai said. "No, none of us will take them. None of us are ready." She looked to the elderly Shardbearer. "You keep them. With Plate, you are as firm as any warrior, Sharefel. I merely ask that you stand with us today."

The drums stopped sounding.

"I will not lift the Blade against other listeners," Sharefel said to Skepticism.

"You will not need to," Eshonai said. "Our goal today will not be to win a battle, but to promise a new beginning."

．．．

A short time later, they stepped out of the city. Once, gates had likely stood in this opening, but the listeners could not create wooden marvels on that scale. Not yet.

The battle had already started, though it hadn't moved to close combat yet. Her family's warriors would step forward and throw their spears, and the other family would dodge. Then the attacking family would return spears. If someone was hit, one side might withdraw and give up the battle. If not, eventually one side might rush the other.

Spren of all varieties had been drawn to the event, and spun or hovered around the perimeters. Eshonai's family's archers hung back, their numbers a show of strength, though they wouldn't use their weapons here. Bows were too deadly—and too accurate—to be used in harming others.

There . . . *had* been times, unfortunately, when in the heat of fighting, traditions had been broken. Normal battles had become horrific massacres. Eshonai had never been part of one of those, but she'd seen the aftereffects during her childhood, when passing a failed assault on another city.

Today, both sides stopped as the warforms emerged—accompanied by a full Shardbearer in glistening Plate. Eshonai's family parted, humming to Awe or Excitement.

Eshonai picked up a spear, as did several of the others. They came to a halt in the center of the field. The opposing family scrambled back, their warriors brandishing spears. Their postures—and the few sounds of humming Eshonai could make out—were terrified.

"We have found warform," Eshonai shouted to Joy. An inviting rhythm, not an angry one. "Come, join us. Enter our city, live with us. We will share our knowledge with you."

The others shied away further. One of them shouted, to Reprimand, "You'll consume us! Make us slaves. We won't be our own family any longer."

"We are all *one* family!" Eshonai said. "You fear being made slaves? Did you see the poor slaveforms the humans had? Did you see the armor of the humans, their weapons? Did you see the fineness of their clothing, the wagons they created?

"You cannot fight that. I cannot fight that. But together, *we* could fight that. There are tens of thousands of listeners around the Plains. When the humans return, let us show them a united *nation,* not a bunch of squabbling tribes." She gestured to the other warforms, then let her gaze linger on Sharefel in his Shardplate.

"We won't fight you today," Eshonai said, turning back to the enemy family. "*None* of this family will fight you today. But if any of you persist, you will *personally* discover the true might of this form. We are going to approach the Living-Songs family next. You may choose to be the first to join with our new nation, and be recognized for your wisdom for generations. Or you can be left until the end, to come groveling for membership, once our union is nearly complete."

She hefted her spear and threw it—shocking herself with the power behind that throw. It soared over the enemy family and disappeared far into the distance. She heard more than one of them humming to the Rhythm of the Terrors.

She nodded to the others, and they joined her, marching into the city. A few seemed annoyed. They wanted a battle to test their abilities. She'd never known listeners to be bloodthirsty, and she didn't feel this form had changed her that much—but she did admit she felt a certain eagerness.

"We should train," she said to the others. "Work out some of our aggression."

"That sounds wonderful," Thude said.

"As long as we can do it in front of everyone else," Melu said to Irritation. "I'd like them to understand how easily I could have cracked their skulls." She looked to Eshonai. "But . . . that was well done. I guess I'm glad I didn't have to rip anyone apart."

"How did you learn to give speeches?" one of the others asked from behind. "Did you learn that talking to those trees, out in the wilderness?"

"I'm not a hermit, Dolimid," she said to Irritation. "I just like the idea of being free. Of not being locked into one location. As long as we don't know what is out there, we're likely to be surprised. Tell me, would we be scrambling now to get our people in order if we'd simply *explored* our surroundings? We could have been preparing to face the humans for generations, if we hadn't been so afraid."

The others hummed to Consolation, understanding. Why had Eshonai had so much trouble persuading people before? Was her present ease because of the connection she felt with these listeners, the first warforms?

There was so much to learn from this form, so much to experiment with. She felt a spring in her step. Perhaps this would be a better form for exploration—she could leap obstacles, run faster. There was so much *possibility*.

They entered the city, her family's warriors—those who had been throwing their spears outside—trotting in with them, immediately accepting the authority of the warforms. As they passed Sharefel's hut, she saw Venli again, lurking in the shadows. This was *her* victory, after a fashion.

Eshonai probably should have gone to congratulate her, but couldn't bring herself to do it. Venli didn't need more songs praising her. She already had a big enough ego.

Instead, Eshonai led the group to the stormshelter, where the rest of their family was emerging. Each and every one deserved to see the new form up close.

69

PURE TONES
OF ROSHAR

I leave you now to your own company.

—From *Rhythm of War*, page 27

Navani hit the tuning fork and touched it to a glowing diamond. When she pulled it away from the gemstone, a tiny line of Stormlight followed behind it—and when she touched the fork to an empty diamond, the Stormlight flowed into it. The transfer would continue as long as the fork made the second diamond vibrate.

Sometimes I think of it like a gas, she thought, taking notes on the speed of the flow. *And sometimes a liquid. I keep wavering between the two, trying to define it, but it must be neither one. Stormlight is something else, with some of the properties of both a liquid and a gas.*

After completing this control experiment—and timing how quickly the Stormlight flowed—she set up the real experiment. She did this inside a large steel box her scholars had created for dangerous experiments, Soulcast into shape with a thick glass window at one end. She'd forced the enemy to drag it in from the hallway outside, then place it on top of her desk.

She wasn't certain if this would save her from a potential explosion, but since the box didn't have a top, the force of the destruction *should* go upward—and as long as she stayed low and watched through the window, it should shield her.

It was the best she could do in these difficult circumstances. She told the singers she was taking normal precautions, and tried not to indicate to them that she expected an explosion. And indeed she didn't—the sphere that had killed her scholars had *not* been Voidlight, but something else. Something Navani didn't yet understand. She was convinced that mixing Voidlight and Stormlight wouldn't create an explosion, but a new kind of Light. Like Towerlight.

She began this next experiment the same way as the previous one, drawing out Stormlight and sending it toward another diamond. Then she reached into the box with tongs and placed a Voidlight diamond in the center of the flow, between the Stormlight diamond and the tuning fork.

The Stormlight didn't react to the Voidlight diamond at all. It simply streamed around the dark gemstone and continued to the vessel diamond. As the tuning fork's tone quieted, the stream weakened. When the fork fell silent, the Stormlight hanging in the air between the two diamonds puffed away and vanished.

Well, she hadn't expected that to do anything. Now for a better test. She'd spent several days working under a singular hypothesis: that if Stormlight reacted to a tone, Voidlight and Towerlight would as well. She'd needed to take a crash course in music theory to properly test the idea.

The Alethi traditionally used a ten-note scale—though it was more accurately two five-note quintaves. This was right and orderly, and the greatest and most famous compositions were all in this scale. However, it wasn't the *only* scale in use around the world. There were dozens. The Thaylens, for example, preferred a twelve-note scale. A strange number, but the twelve steps *were* mathematically pleasing.

In researching the tone the tuning fork created, she'd discovered something incredible. Anciently, people had used a *three-note* scale, and a few of the compositions remained. The tone that drew Stormlight was the first of the three notes from this ancient scale. With some effort—it had required sending Fused to Kholinar through the Oathgate to raid the royal music conservatory—she'd obtained tuning forks for the other two notes in this scale. To her delight, Voidlight responded to the third of the three notes.

She hadn't been able to find any indication in her reading that people had once known these three notes correlated to the three ancient gods. No Alethi scholars seemed to know that one of these tones could prompt a reaction in Stormlight, though Raboniel had—upon questioning—said she'd known. Indeed, she'd been surprised to learn that Navani had only recently discovered the "pure tones of Roshar," as she called them.

Navani had tried singing the proper tones, but hadn't been able to make the light respond. Perhaps she couldn't match the pitch well enough, because Raboniel had been able to do it—singing and touching one gemstone, then moving her finger to another while holding the note. The Stormlight had followed her finger just as it did a tuning fork.

Today Raboniel was off tending to other tasks, but Navani could use the tuning forks to replicate her singing ability. Three tones: a note for

Honor, a note for Odium, and a note for Cultivation. Yet Vorinism only worshipped the Almighty. Honor.

Theology would have to wait for another time. For now, she set up her next experiment. She created streams of Stormlight and Voidlight—drawing each out from a diamond in a corner of her box—and crossed the streams at the center. The two lights pushed upon one another and swirled as they met, but then separated and streamed to their separate forks.

"All right," Navani said, writing in her notebook. "What about this?" She picked up the partially empty Voidlight diamond and then brought out a fresh Stormlight diamond, fully infused.

In fabrial science, you captured a spren by creating a gemstone with a kind of vacuum in it—you drew out the Stormlight, leaving a sphere with a void or suction inside. It would then pull in a nearby spren, which was made of Light. It was like any pressure differential.

She hoped to be able to refill the Voidlight sphere with Stormlight, now that a portion of the Voidlight had been removed. She hit the tuning fork, started the Stormlight streaming out of its diamond, then tried to get it to go into the Voidlight diamond by making it vibrate to the fork's tone.

Unfortunately, when she touched the tuning fork to the Voidlight diamond, it immediately stopped vibrating and the tone died. Extinguished like a candle doused with water. She was able to get the Stormlight to bunch up against the Voidlight diamond, by putting the fork next to it, but when she got the Voidlight to stream out toward the side of the table—theoretically creating an active pressure differential in that diamond—she couldn't get it to suck Stormlight in. Only once all of the Voidlight was out could she infuse the diamond with Stormlight.

"Like oil and water indeed," she said, making notes. Yet the way the streams didn't repel one another when touching felt like proof they weren't opposites.

She rose and—after noting the results of this experiment—went to talk to the Sibling. Navani could easily fool the guards into thinking she was simply strolling among the bookshelves to read a passage or two, as she often did this. Today, she began picking through the books on the back shelf while resting her hand on the Sibling's vein in the wall.

"Are we being watched?" Navani asked.

I've told you, the Sibling said. *Voidspren can't be invisible in the tower. That protection is different from the one suppressing enemy Surgebinders, and Raboniel hasn't corrupted it yet.*

"You also told me you could sense if a Voidspren was near."

Yes.

"So . . . are any near?"

No, the Sibling said. *You do not trust my word?*

"Let's just call it a healthy paranoia on my part," Navani said. "Tell me again of—"

You continue to experiment with fabrials, the Sibling interrupted. *We need to talk more about that. I do not like what you've been doing.*

"I haven't captured any more spren," Navani whispered. "I've been working with Stormlight and Voidlight."

Dangerous work. The man who forges weapons can claim he's never killed, but he still prepares for the slaughter.

"If we're going to restore your abilities, I need to understand how Light works. So unless you have a better idea for me to do this, I'm going to have to continue to use gemstones and—yes—fabrials."

The Sibling fell silent.

"Tell me again about Towerlight," Navani said.

This is growing tedious.

"Do you want to be saved, or not?"

. . . Fine. Towerlight is my *Light, the Light I could create.*

"Did you need a Bondsmith to make it?"

No. I could make it on my own. And my Bondsmith could create it, through their bond with me.

"And that Light, in turn, powered the tower's defenses."

Not only the defenses. Everything.

"Why does it no longer work?"

I already explained that!

"This is a common investigative method," Navani said calmly, flipping through her book with her left hand. "My goal is to make you restate facts in different ways, leading you to explain things differently—or to remember details you forgot."

I haven't forgotten anything. The defenses no longer work because I don't have the Light for them. I lost most of my strength when I lost the ability to hear the two pure tones of Roshar. I can make only a tiny amount of Light, enough to power a few of the tower's basic fabrials.

"Two tones of Roshar?" Navani said. "There are three."

No, there are two. One from my mother, one from my father. The tone of Odium is an interloper. False.

"Could part of the reason you lost your abilities relate to that tone *becoming* a pure tone of Roshar? Odium truly becoming one of the three gods?"

I . . . don't know, the Sibling admitted.

Navani noted this hypothesis.

We need to find a way to restore my Towerlight, the Sibling said, *and remove the Voidlight from my system.*

"And that," Navani said, "is exactly what I'm working on." If she could figure out how to combine two Lights, then it would be the first step toward creating Towerlight.

She clearly needed an emulsifier, a facilitator. What kind of emulsifier could "stick" to Stormlight and make it mix with Voidlight? She shook her head, taking her hand off the vein on the wall. She'd been here too long, so she took a book and strolled to the front of the room, lost in thought. However, as she reached her desk, she found a small box waiting for her.

She glanced at the guard by the door, who nodded. Raboniel had sent it. Navani opened the box, breathless, and found a brightly glowing diamond. At first glance, it seemed to be another Stormlight sphere. But as she held it up and placed it next to a true one, she could see the green tinge to the one Raboniel had sent.

Lifelight. She'd promised to get some for Navani.

"Did she say how she acquired this?" Navani asked.

The guard shook his head.

Navani had a guess. The Sibling had lost sight of Lift, but had explained something was odd about that girl. Something Navani held as a hope that might get them out of this.

Hands steady—though anticipationspren shot up around her—Navani used the middle tuning fork on this new diamond. And it worked: she was able to draw Lifelight out and send it streaming into a gemstone.

Towerlight was Lifelight and Stormlight combined. So perhaps Lifelight—the Light of Cultivation—had some property that allowed it to mix with other Lights. Holding her breath, Navani repeated her earlier experiments, except with Lifelight instead of Voidlight.

She failed.

She couldn't get Stormlight and Lifelight to mix. No use of tuning forks, no touching of the streams or clever use of gemstone differentials, worked.

She tried mixing Voidlight and Lifelight. She tried mixing all three. She tried every experiment she'd listed in her brainstorming sessions earlier. Then she did them all again, until—because each experiment allowed a little Lifelight to vanish into the air—she'd used it all up.

Shooing away exhaustionspren, she stood, frustrated. Another dead end. This was as bad as the morning's experiments, when she'd tried everything she could think of—including using two tuning forks at once—to make Towerlight move from its gemstone. She'd failed at that as well.

She gathered all the used diamonds and deposited them by the door guard to be picked up and reinfused—there was a highstorm coming today. After that, she paced, frustrated. She knew she shouldn't let the lack of results bother her. Real scientists understood that experiments like this weren't failures; they were necessary steps on the way to discovery. In fact, it would have been remarkable—and completely unconventional—to find a good result so early in the process.

The problem was, scientists didn't have to work under such terrible deadlines or pressures. She was isolated, each moment ticking them closer to disaster. The only lead she had was in trying to mix the Lights, in the hope that she could eventually create more Towerlight to help the Sibling.

She wandered the room, pretending to inspect the spines of books on the shelves. *If I make my discovery, Raboniel will know, since a guard is always watching. She'll force the answer out of me, and so even in these attempts to escape, I'm furthering her goals—whatever those are.*

Navani was on the cusp of something important. The revelations she'd been given about Stormlight fundamentally changed their understanding of it and the world at large. Three types of power. The possibility they could be blended. And . . . possibly something else, judging by that strange sphere that warped the air around it.

Her instincts said that this knowledge would come out eventually. And the ones who controlled it, exploited it, would be the ones who won the war.

I need another plan, she decided. If she did discover how to make Towerlight, and if the shield did fall, Navani needed a way to isolate the crystal pillar for a short time. To defend it, perhaps to work on it.

Navani gripped her notebook in her safehand, to appear as if she were writing down the titles of books. Instead she quickly took notes on an idea. She'd been told she could have anything she needed, so long as it was relevant to her experiments. They also let her store equipment out in the hallway.

So, what if she created some fabrial weapons, then stored them in the hallway? Innocent-looking fabrials that, once activated, could be used to immobilize guards or Fused coming to stop her from working on the pillar? She sketched out some ideas: traps she could create using seemingly innocent fabrial parts. Painrials to administer agony and cause the muscles to lock up. Heating fabrials to burn and scald.

Yes . . . she could create a series of defenses in the form of failed experiments, then store them "haphazardly" in crates along the hallway. She could even arm them by using Voidspren gems, as she could demand those for use in her experiments.

These plans soothed her; this was something meaningful she could do. However, the experiments, and their potential, still itched at her. What was Raboniel's true goal? Was it to make a weapon herself—like the one that had destroyed the room and Navani's two scientists?

A few hours had passed, so it wouldn't look strange if she went to the back of the stacks again. She picked up a book and settled down in a chair she'd placed nearby. Although she wasn't directly visible to the guard, she pretended to read as she reached her hand to the wall and touched the vein.

"Any spren nearby?" Navani asked.

I cannot feel any, the Sibling said with a resigned tone.

"Good. Tell me, do you know anything of the explosion that happened on the day of the invasion? It involved two of my scientists in a room on the fifth floor."

I felt it. But I do not know what caused it.

"Have you ever heard of a sphere, or a Light, that *warps* the air around it? One that appears to be Voidlight unless you look at it long enough to notice the warping effect?"

No, the Sibling said. *I've never heard or seen anything like that—though it sounds dangerous.*

Navani considered, tapping her finger against the wall. "I haven't been able to get any of the Lights to mix. Do you know of any potential binding agent that could make them stick together? Do you know how Towerlight is mixed from Stormlight and Lifelight?"

They don't mix, the Sibling said. *They come together, as one. Like I am a product of my mother and father, so Towerlight is a product of me. And stop asking me the same questions. I don't care about your "investigative methods." I've told you what I know. Stop making me repeat myself.*

Navani took a deep breath, calming herself with effort. "Fine. Have you been able to eavesdrop on Raboniel at all?"

Not much. I can only hear things near a few people that are relevant. I can see the Windrunner. I think the Edgedancer has been surrounded by ralkalest, which is why she's invisible. Also, I can see one particular Regal.

"Any ideas on why that is?"

No. Regals weren't often in the tower in the past, and never this variety. She can speak all languages; perhaps this is why I can see near her. Though she vanishes sometimes, so I cannot see all she does. I can also see near the crystal pillar, but with the field set up, I hear mere echoes of what is happening outside.

"Tell me those, then."

It's nothing relevant. Raboniel is trying her own experiments with the Light—and she hasn't gotten as far as you have. This seems to frustrate her.

Curious. That did a little for Navani's self-esteem. "She really wants this hybrid Light. I wonder . . . maybe fabrials made with a hybrid Stormlight-Voidlight would work in the tower, even if the protections were turned against her again. Maybe that is why she wants it."

You are foolish to presume to know what one of the Fused wants. She is thousands of years old. You can't outthink her.

"You'd better hope that I can." Navani flipped a few pages in her notebook. "I've been thinking of other ways out of this. What if we found you someone to bond, to make them Radiant? We could—"

No. Never again.

"Hear me out," Navani said. "You've said you'll never bond a human again, because of the things we do to spren. But what about a singer? Could you theoretically bond one of them?"

We are talking of resisting them, and now you suggest I bond one? That seems insane.

"Maybe not," Navani said. "There's a Parshendi in Bridge Four. I've met him, and Kaladin has vouched for him. He claims that his people rejected the Fused long ago. What about him? Not a human. Not someone who has ever created a fabrial—someone who knows the rhythms of Roshar."

The Sibling was silent, and Navani wondered if the conversation was over. "Sibling?" she asked.

I had not considered this, they said. *A singer who does not serve Odium? I will need to think. It would certainly surprise Raboniel, who thinks that I am dead or sleeping.*

In any case, I cannot form a bond now, with the protections up. I would need him to touch my pillar.

"What if I had him here?" Navani said. "Ready to try when the shield falls? And with some distractions in place to give you time to talk to him."

I cannot form a bond with just anyone, the Sibling said. *In the past I spent years evaluating Bondsmith squires to select one who fit me exactly. Even they eventually betrayed me, though not as badly as other humans.*

"Can we really afford pickiness right now?"

It's not pickiness. It is the nature of spren and the bond. The person must be willing to swear the correct oaths, to unite instead of divide. They must mean it, and the oaths must be accepted. It is not simply a matter of throwing the first person you find at me.

Beyond that, since I cannot create Towerlight, they will not be able to either. A bond would do nothing unless we solve the problems with my powers. It would be better if you focused on that problem instead.

"Fine," Navani said, sensing an opening. "But I need time to research all of this. It is difficult to work while feeling I have a knife to my neck. If I knew the nodes were being defended, that would take the pressure off me. Tell me where one of them is. I have a list here of plans to protect it. I can read them off to you."

The Sibling was silent, so Navani continued.

"We can have Kaladin start searching—loudly and obviously—on a different level, leading the enemy on a chase in the wrong direction. In the meantime, while they're distracted, we could sneak up to the node and reinforce its defenses.

"We have some crem that hasn't hardened yet, kept wet in the tower stores. We could seal up the node location entirely. Maybe run the crem through with some training sheaths for Shardblades, so it would be extra difficult to cut. That could earn us hours to get troops in to defend it, if it does get discovered.

"Or, if I knew where one of the nodes was, I might be able to have Kaladin begin infusing it with more Stormlight. That might counteract the Voidlight that Raboniel has used on you. If she can corrupt you through a node, could we not perhaps cleanse you through one? I think it's worth trying, because my efforts to create Towerlight are stalled."

She waited, gripping her pad tightly. Her other ideas were sketchier than those. She wouldn't use them unless these arguments didn't work.

So good with words. Humans are like persuasionspren. I can't speak with one of you without being changed.

Navani continued to wait. Silence was best now.

Fine, the Sibling said. *One of the two remaining nodes is in the well at the center of the place you call the Breakaway market. It is near other fabrials there. One hidden among many.*

"On the first floor?" Navani asked. "That's such a populated area!"

All of the nodes are down low. There was talk of installing others farther away, but my Bondsmith did not have the resources—my falling-out with the humans was driving them away. The project wasn't completed. Only the four on the first few floors were completed.

Navani frowned—though the well was a clever place to hide a fabrial. Many of the workings of the tower remained mysterious to modern scholars, so a cluster of gemstones working as pumps might indeed camouflage another fabrial. In fact, Navani had studied drawings of those pumps herself. Had this mechanism been there, unnoticed, all along?

This is a good node for your agent to visit, the Sibling said. *Because it can be reached from the back ways. Have your Windrunner visit it through the aquifers, and we will see if—by infusing it with Stormlight—he can counteract the corruption. It might not work, as I am not simply of Honor or of Cultivation. But . . . it could help.*

"And the final node?" Navani asked.

Is mine alone, the Sibling replied. *Show me that your work on this one helps, human, and then we can speak further.*

"A fair compromise," Navani said. "I *am* willing to listen, Sibling."

She left the wall and grabbed some books to read, to cover what she'd been doing. And she did need to study more, after all. She'd have loved to have more books on music theory, but this archive didn't have anything more specific on the topic. She did have Kalami's notes about the gemstones they'd discovered that used certain buzzing vibrations as substitutes for letters. Perhaps those would help.

She was browsing through those notes, walking idly among the stacks, when she saw the Sibling's light flashing. She hurried over, nervous about how bright the light was. She glanced at the guard, hoping he hadn't seen, and put her hand to the wall.

"You need to—"

They've found the node in the well. We're too late.

"What? *Already?*"

I am as good as dead.

"Contact Kaladin."

They already have the node, and he's too far away. We—

"Contact Kaladin," Navani said. "*Now.* I'll find a way to distract Raboniel."

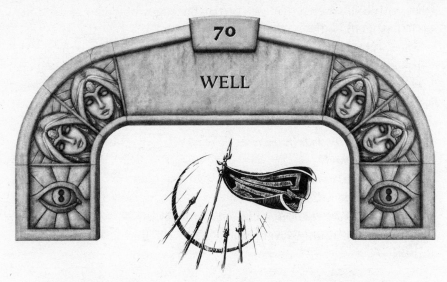

70

WELL

Opposites. Opposites of sounds. Sound has no opposite. It's merely overlapped vibration, the same sound, but sound has meaning. This sound does, at least. These sounds. The voices of gods.

—From *Rhythm of War*, final page

Kaladin awoke to something dark attacking him.

He screamed, struggling against the clinging shadows. They'd been assaulting him for an eternity, wrapping around him, constricting him. Voices that never relented, fingers of shadow that drilled into his brain.

He was in a dark place full of red light, and the shadows laughed and danced around him. They tormented him, flayed him, stabbed him again and again and wouldn't let him die. He fought back the hands that gripped, then he crawled across the floor, pulling up against the wall and breathing shallowly. The rushing sounds of his own blood in his ears drowned out the laughter.

One shadow continued watching him. One terrible shadow. It stared at him, then turned and took something from beside the wall before vanishing. Vanishing . . . out the door.

Kaladin blinked, and the shadows melted from his mind. The terrible laughter, the phantom pain, the whispers. His mind always interpreted those as Moash's voice.

A nightmare. Another nightmare.

"Kaladin?" Syl asked. She sat on the floor in front of him. He blinked, glancing sharply one way, then the other. The room seemed to settle into place. Teft sleeping on the stone bench. A few chips set out for light. Fear-spren, like globs of goo, undulating in the corners.

"I . . ." He swallowed, his mouth dry. "I had a nightmare."

"I know."

He carefully relaxed his posture, embarrassed at how he must appear huddled up by the wall. Like a child frightened of the dark. He couldn't afford to be a child. Too much depended on him. He stood up, his clothing sweaty. "What time is it?"

"Midday," she said.

"My schedule is completely off." He tried to pull himself together as he stepped over to get a drink, but he stumbled and caught himself on the ledge. He had to grip it tightly as the nightmare threatened to resurface. Storm-father. This was the most oppressive one yet.

"Kaladin . . ." Syl said.

He took a long drink, then froze.

His spear was gone from beside the door.

"What happened?" he demanded, slamming the tin cup down harder than he'd intended. "Where is my spear!"

"The Sibling contacted us," she said, still sitting on the floor. "That's why Dabbid tried to wake you. Another node has been found—*inside* the well in the market. The enemy is there already."

"Storms!" Kaladin said. "We need to go." He reached for Navani's fabrial and his pouch of gems. He found the latter, but the fabrial was gone.

"Dabbid?" Kaladin demanded.

"You were huddled there muttering," Syl said, finally lifting into the air. "And you didn't seem to be able to see me. The Sibling is terrified. I could hear them while sitting on Dabbid's shoulder. And so . . ."

Kaladin grabbed the bag of gems and dashed out of the room, Syl following as a ribbon of light. He caught up with Dabbid at the first stairwell—just two hallways over. The shorter bridgeman stood with the spear and fabrial held close to his chest, staring down with a panicked expression.

He jumped as he saw Kaladin, then let out a loud relieved sigh. Kaladin took the fabrial.

"You were going to go try to stop the Fused," Kaladin said. "Because I didn't get up."

Dabbid nodded.

"Dabbid, you barely know how to use a spear," Kaladin said, quickly strapping on the fabrial. He'd had only four days of practice with the device. It would have to be enough.

Dabbid didn't respond, of course. He helped Kaladin strap the fabrial on, then held out the spear.

Kaladin took it, then gave the Bridge Four salute.

Dabbid returned it. Then, remarkably, said something, in a voice soft and gravelly. "Life. Before. Death."

Storms. Those were the first words Kaladin had ever heard from the man. He grinned, gripping Dabbid by the shoulder. "Life before death, Dabbid."

Dabbid nodded. There wasn't time for more; Kaladin turned away from the stairwell and began running again. Screams from the nightmare echoed in his head, but he didn't have time for weakness. He had to stop the corruption of that gemstone—and barring that, he had to destroy the node. That was the only way to buy Navani the time she needed.

He had to get there quickly, which meant he couldn't use the stairs. He'd have to go straight down through the atrium.

⁖

"I need to see the Lady of Wishes immediately!" Navani proclaimed to the guard. "I've made a discovery of incalculable value! It cannot wait for—"

The guard—a Regal stormform—simply started walking and gestured for her to follow. He didn't even need the full explanation.

"Excellent," Navani said, joining him in the hallway. "I'm glad you see the urgency."

The guard walked her to the large stairwell that led up to the ground floor. A Deepest One stood here, her fingers laced before her. "What is it?" she asked in heavily accented Alethi. "A sudden illness?"

"No," Navani said, taken aback. "A discovery. I think I've found what the Lady of Wishes was searching for."

"But of course you can't share it with anyone but Raboniel herself," the Fused said, a faintly amused rhythm to her voice.

"Well, I mean . . ." Navani trailed off.

"I'll see if I can reach her via spanreed," the Fused said. "I'll tell her it is *most* urgent."

Storms. They were *expecting* an attempted distraction from Navani. That thought was reinforced as the Fused glided to a cabinet that had been set up by the wall. She carefully, but slowly, selected a spanreed from the collection stored there.

It was a reverse distraction. They'd *known* Navani would attempt something like this. But how had they known that *she* would know that . . .

She stepped back, her eyes widening as the terrible implications struck her. Kaladin was in serious danger.

Barefoot and armed with a spear, Kaladin burst out onto the walkway around the atrium, then hurled himself out into the open space eleven stories in the air. Full of Stormlight—hoping it would save him in case this didn't work—he pointed his hand directly beneath him and engaged Navani's fabrial.

As soon as it was activated, he lurched to a halt in the air, hovering—his muscles straining as he was basically doing a handstand with one hand. But as long as the counterweight in the distant shaft was held motionless, Kaladin would be as well.

He gripped the bar across his left hand and began to fall downward, almost as if he were Lashed. In fact, he was counting on it seeming like nothing was wrong with his powers—that he was a full Windrunner ready for battle. He wouldn't be able to keep up such a facade for long, but perhaps it would gain him an advantage.

His descent—at a speed a notch below insane—gave him a view out the enormous atrium window, running all the way up the wall to his right. Strangely, it was dark outside, though Syl had said it was midday. He didn't have to ask for clarification, as a flash of lightning bespoke the truth. A highstorm. He still found it incredible that he could be so deep within a tower that one could be going on without him realizing it. Even in the best stormshelters, you usually felt the rumbles of thunder or the anger of the wind.

His fall certainly drew attention. Heavenly Ones dressed in long robes turned from their midair meditations. Shouts rose from Regals or singers along the various levels. He wasn't certain if Leshwi was among them or not, as he passed too quickly.

Using the fabrial, he slowed himself before he hit the ground, then deactivated the device entirely and fell the last five feet or so. Stormlight absorbed that drop, and he startled dozens of people—many of them human—who hadn't heard the disturbance above. Commerce was now allowed and encouraged by the Fused, and the atrium floor had become a secondary market—though a more transient one than the Breakaway a short distance off. That was where he would find the well.

Kaladin's luminescence would be starkly visible against the dark window, lit in flashes. The shouts of alarm above were swallowed in the voluminous atrium as Kaladin oriented himself, then ran for a stack of crates. He took a few steps up them to launch into the air some ten feet high, then he pointed his left hand and engaged Navani's device.

He flew like a Windrunner, his body upright, left arm held at chest height, elbow bent. It *might* look like he was using Lashings. Though Windrunners sometimes dove and flew headfirst like they were swimming, just as often they would fly "standing" up straight—like he did now.

He did tuck his legs up as he went soaring over the heads of the people, who ducked. Syl zipped along beside him, imitating a stormcloud. People cried out, surprised—but also excited—and Kaladin worried about what he was showing them. He didn't want to inspire a revolt that would get hundreds killed.

The best he could hope for was to get in, destroy the fabrial, and get out alive. That goal whispered of a much larger problem. Navani had said there were four nodes. Today, he'd try to destroy the third. At this rate, the last one would fall in a few days, and then what?

He pushed that thought out of his mind as he flew along the top of a corridor, inches from the textured stone ceiling. He didn't have time for second-guessing, or for dwelling on the crippling darkness and anxiety that continued to scratch at his mind. He had to ignore that, then deal with the effects later. Exactly as he'd been doing far too long now.

"Watch for an ambush," he told Syl as they burst from the corridor and into the Breakaway market. This large room, truly cavernous, was four stories high and packed with shops along the ground. Many were along roadways that Navani—reluctantly adapting to the will of the people—had laid out in the way they wanted. Other parts were snarls of tents and semipermanent wooden structures.

Central to the layout was the enormous well. Kaladin wasn't high enough to see over the buildings and make it out, but he knew the location. The Edgedancer clinic was nearby, though it was now staffed by ordinary surgeons. He hoped his parents and little brother had made it safely there, where the other surgeons would hide them. They'd checked a few days back and found his father's clinic empty.

Storms. If he lost his family . . .

"The Pursuer!" Syl said. "He was waiting by the other entrance."

Kaladin reacted just in time, deactivating the fabrial and dropping to the ground, where he tucked and rolled. The relentless Fused appeared from his ribbon of light and dropped to the ground too, but Kaladin rolled to his feet out of the creature's reach.

"Your death," the creature growled, crouched among terrified marketgoers, "is growing tedious, Windrunner. How is it you recovered all of your Lashings?"

Kaladin launched himself into the air, activating the device and shooting upward. It jerked his arm painfully, but he'd grown used to that—and Stormlight worked to heal the soreness. He'd also practiced his old one-handed spear grips. Hopefully that training would serve him today.

He wasn't nearly as maneuverable with this device as he was with Lashings. Indeed, as the Pursuer gave chase as a ribbon, Kaladin's only real recourse was to cut the device and drop past him. Near the ground, Kaladin pointed his hand to the side and reengaged the device, then went shooting out across the crowd in the general direction of the well. Maybe—

He lurched to a stop as the first of the device's weights bottomed out. A heartbeat later the Pursuer slammed into him, grabbing him around the neck and hanging on.

"Kaladin!" Syl shouted. "Heavenly Ones! Over a dozen of them! They're streaming in through the tunnels."

"Good," Kaladin said with a grunt, dropping his spear and grappling against the Pursuer with the hand he could move.

"*Good?*" she asked.

He couldn't both grapple and twist the dial on his fabrial—the one that would activate the second weight. But he *could* deactivate the device using one hand, so he did that, dropping them ten feet to the ground. The Pursuer hit first with a grunt. He hung on though, rolling Kaladin to try to pin him.

"Turn . . . the dial," Kaladin said to Syl, using both hands to struggle with the Pursuer.

"When you die," the creature said in his ear, "I will find the next Radiant your spren bonds and kill *them* too. As payment for the trouble you have given me."

Syl zipped down to his left wrist and took the shape of an eel, pushing against the raised section at the center of the dial. She could turn a page, lift a leaf. Would she be strong enough to—

Click.

Kaladin twisted in the Pursuer's grip, barely managing to press his left hand to the creature's armored chest. Activating the device sent them both moving upward—but slowly. Storms, Kaladin hadn't thought this through. He'd only be able to lift as much as the counterweight. Apparently he and the Pursuer together were about that heavy.

Fortunately, rather than taking advantage of the slow movement, the Pursuer paused and glanced at Kaladin's hand, trying to figure out what was happening. So, as they inched upward, Kaladin was able to rip his right hand free. He reached for the scalpel he'd affixed in a makeshift sheath at his belt, then brought it up and rammed it into the Pursuer's wrist, slicing the tendons there.

The creature immediately let go, vanishing, leaving a husk behind. Once that dropped off of Kaladin, he immediately went darting up into the sky, pulled by his hand in an awkward motion that nearly ripped his arm from its socket.

"This . . . isn't that effective, is it?" Syl asked.

"No," Kaladin said, slowing himself by relaxing his grip. He went to draw in more Stormlight, but realized he still had plenty raging in his veins. That was one advantage of the fabrial; he didn't use up Light nearly as quickly.

The Heavenly Ones circled him in the air, but kept their distance. Kaladin searched for the Pursuer—the creature had used two bodies. He had a third one to waste before the fight became dangerous for him, so he wouldn't retreat yet.

There, Kaladin thought, noting the red ribbon weaving between Heavenly Ones. The motions looked timid, uncommitted, and Kaladin took a moment to figure out why. The Pursuer was trying to delay Kaladin; each moment wasted was another one that might lead to the Sibling being corrupted.

Below, the market streets were quickly emptying of people. Kaladin's fears about them revolting weren't being realized, fortunately—but he couldn't spend forever in a standoff with the Pursuer. So he disengaged the device and started falling.

This finally made the Pursuer dart for him, and Kaladin quickly re-engaged the device—lurching to a halt. He twisted—though he couldn't move his left arm—and prepared his knife. This sudden motion made the Pursuer back off, however. Could the creature . . . be afraid? That seemed implausible.

Kaladin didn't have time to reflect, as he needed to engage the Pursuer a third time for his plan to work. So he turned away, inviting the attack—and receiving it as the Pursuer committed, darting in and forming a body that grabbed for Kaladin. Despite trying to speed away, Kaladin wasn't quite able to evade the creature's grip.

Kaladin was forced to let the Pursuer grab him around the neck as he stabbed the creature in the arm between two plates of carapace, trying to sever the tendons. The monster grunted, his arm around Kaladin's throat. They continued to soar about thirty feet off the ground. Kaladin ignored the tight grip and maneuvered the scalpel. Perhaps if he could force the Pursuer to waste Voidlight healing . . .

Yes. Cut enough times to be worried, the Pursuer let go and flew away, seeking a place to recover. Panting, Kaladin used the device to drop to the ground. He landed on an empty street between two tents. People huddled inside both, crowding them.

Kaladin forced himself to jog to where he'd dropped his spear. Heavenly Ones circled above, preparing to attack. Syl moved up beside him, watching them. Two dozen now. Kaladin searched them, hoping . . .

There. He raised his spear toward Leshwi, who hovered apart from the others, wearing clothing too long for practical battle—even in the air. This event had caught her unaware.

Please, he thought. *Accept the fight.*

That was his best hope. He couldn't fight them all at once; he could barely face the Pursuer. If he wanted any chance of getting to the node, he'd need to fight a single opponent—one who wasn't as relentless as the Pursuer.

He worried he'd already wasted too much time. But if he could get Leshwi to agree to a duel . . .

She raised her spear toward him.

"Syl," he said, "go to the well and find the fabrial of the node. It's probably a sapphire, and should have a glass sphere nearby like the one we saw before."

"Right," she said. "It will probably be underwater. That's what the Sibling said. Near the pump mechanisms. Can . . . can you swim?"

"Won't need to, with Stormlight to sustain me and the fabrial to move me," Kaladin said, lifting his hand and rising into the air above the market. "But the well is likely under heavy guard. Our best chance to destroy the fabrial will be for me to break from this fight and fly straight down to it, then hit the device in one blow before anyone realizes what I'm doing. I'll need you to guide me."

"Sounds good." She hesitated, looking toward him.

"I'll be all right," he promised.

She flew off to do as he requested. He might be too late already. He could feel something changing. A greater oppression, a heaviness, was settling upon him. He could only assume it was the result of the Fused corrupting the Sibling.

Well, he couldn't move in that direction until Syl had the way prepared for him, so this would have to do. He leveled out in the air opposite Leshwi, his hand still held upward above him. The pose made him look overly dramatic, but he tried to appear confident anyway.

Leshwi wore the same body as last time, muscular, tall, wrapped in flowing black and white clothing. Her lance was shorter than normal, perhaps intended for indoor fighting.

Right. Well, he hoped to give a good showing in this fight, long enough to give Syl time to scout for him. So he cut the fabrial and dropped in the air, spinning and giving himself a few seconds of free fall. He felt almost like a real Windrunner—which was dangerous, as he almost tried to sculpt his fall with his hands in the wind. Fortunately, he remembered to engage the device as he neared the rooftops.

He lurched to a stop with a painful *jolt,* his arm bent, his elbow held close to his side. He had the most stability this way, his muscles keeping him as if he were standing upright with his left arm tucked in to keep his center of gravity close and tight.

He gripped the device's bar and his left hand tugged him forward, zooming over the roofs of the shops. It made for a pitiful approximation of a true Windrunner maneuver, but Leshwi dove after him anyway, echoing their previous contests.

Eyes watering from the pain in his arm, Kaladin dropped to a rooftop and spun to raise his spear toward Leshwi, gripping it firmly in his right hand—a classic formation grip, with the spear up beside his head. *Heal!* he thought at his arm as Leshwi slowed above, holding her lance in one hand and hovering.

She was plainly cautious, so Kaladin infused a patch of the rooftop with a Reverse Lashing, picturing it pulling on tassels of clothing. Leshwi's robes rippled and were pulled toward Kaladin, but she took a knife from her belt and cut them, dropping her train and much of the excess clothing to flutter down to affix itself to the rooftop.

Kaladin raised himself into the air again, wincing at the pain in his shoulder.

"What is wrong, Windrunner?" Leshwi asked in heavily accented Alethi, coming closer. "Your powers fail you."

"Fight me anyway," Kaladin called up at her. As he did, he caught a glimpse of the Pursuer's bloodred ribbon weaving out of a building below.

Leshwi followed his gaze and seemed to understand, for she raised her lance toward him in an attack posture. Kaladin took a deep breath and returned his spear to the overhand grip, weapon up by his head, his elbow cocked. He'd been trained in this grip for shield and spear combat. It was best with a group of friends each with shields up—but what combat wasn't?

He waited for her to get close, then stabbed at her, causing her to dodge away. The Pursuer's ribbon fluttered around nearby, weaving between watching Heavenly Ones.

Leshwi made a few more token attempts to engage him, and for a moment the fight seemed almost fair. Then Leshwi rose into the air and passed overhead, while Kaladin was left to twist—then disengage his device and drop a few feet before lurching into a hanging position, facing her. She cocked her head, then flew to the side and attacked him from that direction.

He tried to deflect, but he was too immobile. Her spear bit him in the left arm, causing him to grunt in pain. Blood spread from the wound, and—as before—it didn't heal immediately. In fact, his Stormlight seemed to be responding slower than it had earlier in this fight.

Storms, this had been a mistake. He couldn't duel Leshwi like this. He'd be better off on the ground; he'd be outmatched against opponents with the high ground, but at least he wouldn't be frozen in place. If Navani ever wanted these devices to be useful in aerial combat, she had a lot of work to do.

So he fled, engaging the device and sending himself flying between a couple of Heavenly Ones who moved dutifully to the sides to let Leshwi follow. Even the Pursuer seemed to respect the duel, as his ribbon stopped following and vanished below.

At least that part of Kaladin's plan had worked. Unfortunately, Leshwi had clearly put together that he couldn't veer to either side—and that his acceleration was limited to a single Lashing, the maximum from one falling weight. So while he crossed the vast room in seconds, the moment he slowed to prevent himself from hitting the wall, she slammed into him from behind. The force of the hit made him grip the speed-control bar by accident, and he was rammed into the wall by his own fist, Leshwi pressing him from behind.

She put a knife to his neck. "This is a sham, Stormblessed," she said in his ear. "This is no contest."

He squeezed his eyes shut, fighting off the pain of the hit and the cut to his arm—though that finally appeared to be healing. Slowly, but at least it was happening.

"We could drop to the ground," he said through gritted teeth. "Fight a duel without Surges."

"Would you actually do that?" Leshwi said. "I think you cannot spare the time. You're here to interfere with whatever the Lady of Wishes is doing."

Kaladin grunted his reply, not wanting to waste Stormlight by speaking.

Leshwi, however, pulled away in the air, leaving him to turn around awkwardly as he'd done before, with a dropping lurch. She drifted down to eye level with him. Past her, he spotted Syl rising into the air and coming toward him. She made a quick glyph in the air. *Ready.*

As Leshwi started talking, he fixed his attention on her so she wouldn't think anything was amiss.

"Surrender," she said. "If you give your weapon to me now, I might be able to get the Lady of Wishes to turn aside the Pursuer. Together we could start to work toward a true government and peace for Roshar."

"A true government and peace?" Kaladin demanded. "Your people are in the middle of *conquering* mine!"

"And did your leader not conquer his way to the throne?" she asked, sounding genuinely confused. "This is the way of your people as well as mine. Besides, you must admit my people govern better. The humans under our control have not been treated unfairly. Certainly they live better than the singers fared under your domination."

"And your god?" Kaladin asked. "You can promise me that once human-kind has been subdued, he won't have us exterminated?"

Leshwi didn't respond, though she hummed to a rhythm he couldn't distinguish.

"I know the kind of men who follow Odium," Kaladin said softly. "I've known them all my life. I bear their brands on my forehead, Leshwi. I could almost trust you for the honor you've shown me—if it didn't mean trusting him as well."

She nodded, and seemed to accept this as a valid argument. She began lowering, perhaps to engage in that fight he'd suggested, without powers.

"Leshwi," he called after she had lowered partway. "I feel the need to point out that I didn't *agree* to fight you below. I simply noted it was an option."

"What is the distinction?" she called up.

"I'd rather you not see this as a broken oath," he said, then disengaged the fabrial and pointed it right at Syl before launching himself that direction—straight over Leshwi's head.

He didn't wait to see if she gave chase. Syl streaked ahead of him, leading him straight across the room toward the blue pool of water at the center. Guards were there, pushing people into buildings, but the way was open. The other Heavenly Ones kept their distance from him, assuming he was still dueling with Leshwi.

He cut the fabrial right as he passed over the well, then pointed his hand down and engaged it. His aim was true, and he sucked in more Stormlight as he splashed into the water. It *hurt* to hit, far more than he'd expected from something soft like water. His arm kept pulling him downward though, despite the resistance.

It quickly grew dark, and a part of him panicked at never having been this far beneath water before. His ears reacted oddly, painfully. Fortunately, his Stormlight sustained him in the chill depth. It also gave him light to see a figure below, swimming beside a group of glowing gemstones on the wall, secured here deep beneath the surface.

The figure turned toward him, her topknot swirling in the water—lit from the side by a variety of gemstone hues. It was her, the one who had been so fascinated with him last time. This time she seemed surprised, drawing a dagger from her belt and swinging it at him.

However, Kaladin found that Navani's fabrial worked far better in this environment. He could easily disengage it and swing it in another direction without dropping or lurching—and the added pull meant he easily outmaneuvered this Fused.

He spun around her and moved lower in the water. The well's shaft was only about ten feet wide, so when she pushed off a wall, she could reach him—but behind her, Syl highlighted the correct gemstone.

He engaged his own fabrial, which towed him past the Fused, letting her get a clean cut across his chest with her dagger. Blood clouded the water, but Kaladin connected his fist against the sapphire, knocking it free. He spun his spear in the water and jabbed it at the wires of the fabrial cage, then pried loose the glass sphere. That should do it.

Now to get out. He looked upward through the red water, and began to feel dizzy. Healing was coming so slowly.

Syl soared ahead of him as he used the fabrial to rise up, leaving the annoyed Fused behind. Syl's light was encouraging, as it seemed to be getting darker in here.

My Stormlight is running out. Storms. How was he going to get away? Dozens of Fused awaited him above. He . . . he might have to surrender, as Leshwi had insisted. Would they let him, now?

What was that rumbling? He saw light shimmering above, but it was *shrinking.* Syl made it out, but she didn't seem to have realized he was lagging behind her. And the light was vanishing.

A lid, he realized with panic. *They're putting a lid over the top of the well.* As he neared, in the last sliver of light he saw the hulking form of the Pursuer. Smiling.

The lid thumped in place right before Kaladin arrived. He burst into the small section of air between the top of the well's water level and the lid, gasping for breath.

But he was trapped. He slammed against the wood, trying to use the power of Navani's device to lift it—but he heard thumping as weights, likely stones, were set on top of it. More and more of them.

The Pursuer had been ready for this. He knew that even if Kaladin's gravitational Lashings worked, enough weight would keep the lid in place. In fact, it felt like the weights were alive. People, dozens of them, climbing on top of the lid. Of course. Why use stone when humans were heavy enough and far easier to move?

Kaladin pounded on the wood as he felt Syl panicking, unable to reach him. His Stormlight was fading, and it seemed the walls and the lid were closing in on him. He'd die in here, and it wouldn't take long. All the Pursuer had to do was wait. They could seal it above, denying him fresh air. . . .

In that moment of pure terror, Kaladin was in one of his nightmares again.

Blackness.

Encircled by hateful shadows.

Trapped.

Anxiety mounted inside him, and he began to thrash in the water, screaming, letting out the rest of his Stormlight. In that moment of panic, he didn't care. But as he fell hoarse from shouting, he heard—strangely enough—Hav's voice. Kaladin's old sergeant, from his days as a recruit.

Panic on the battlefield kills more men than enemy spears. Never run. Always retreat.

This water came from somewhere. There was another way out.

Kaladin took a deep breath and dove beneath the black water, feeling it surround him. His panic returned. He didn't know which way was up and which way was down. How could you forget which way the *sky* was? But all was blackness. He fished in his pouch, finally managing to think clearly. He got out a glowing gemstone, but it slipped from his fingers.

And sank.

That way.

He pointed his fist toward the falling light and engaged Navani's device. He was in no state for delicacy, so he squeezed as tight as he could and lurched, towed by his arm farther into the darkness. He plunged past the fabrials and the Fused—she was swimming upward, and didn't seem concerned with him.

His ears screamed with a strange pain the deeper he went. He started to breathe in more Stormlight, but stopped himself. Underwater, he risked getting a lungful of liquid. But . . . he had no idea how to get Light when submerged. How had they never thought about this?

It was good that the device kept pulling him, because he might not have had the presence of mind to keep moving on his own. That was proven as he reached the gemstone he'd dropped, a garnet, and found it sitting on the bottom of the tube. A bright sapphire glowed here too, the one he'd knocked free. He grabbed it and disengaged the gauntlet fabrial, but it took him precious seconds to think and search around.

The tunnel turned level here. He moved in that direction, engaging the device, letting it pull him.

His lungs started to burn. He was still surviving on the breath he'd taken above, and didn't know how to get more Stormlight. He was still trailing blood as well.

Was that light ahead, or was his vision getting so bad that he was seeing stars?

He chose to believe it was light. When he reached it—more fabrial pumps—he shut off his fabrial, pointed his hand upward, and engaged the device again. Nightmares chased him, manifestations of his anxiety, and it was as if the world were crushing him. Everything became blackness once more.

The only thing he felt was Syl, so distant now, terrified. He thought that would be his last sensation.

Then he broke out of the water into the air. He gasped—a raw and primal action. A physiological response rather than conscious choice. Indeed, he must have blacked out anyway, for when he blinked and his senses returned, he found himself hanging by his aching arm from the ceiling in a reservoir beneath the tower.

He shook his head, and looked at his hand. He'd dropped the sapphire, and when he tried to breathe in Stormlight, nothing came. His pouch was empty of it. He must have fed off it while drifting in and out of consciousness. He was tempted to let himself sleep again. . . .

No! They'll be coming for you!

He forced his eyes open. If the enemy had explored the tower enough to know about this reservoir, they would come looking to be certain he was dead.

He disengaged the fabrial and dropped into the water. The cold shocked him awake, and he was able to use the fabrial to tug himself to the side of the reservoir. He crawled out onto dry stone. Amusingly, he was enough a surgeon to worry about how he'd contaminated this drinking water. Of all the things to think about right now . . .

He wanted to sleep, but could see blood dripping from his chest and arm, the wounds there not fully healed. So he stumbled to the side of the chamber and sucked the Stormlight from the two lamps there. Yes, the enemy knew about this place. If he hadn't been so addled, he'd have put together earlier that the light meant someone was changing the gemstones.

He stumbled, sodden and exhausted, down the hallway. There would be an exit. He vaguely remembered news of Navani's scouts finding this reservoir. They'd only known about it by having Thaylen free divers inspect the fabrials in the well.

Keep thinking. Keep walking. Don't drift off.

Where was Syl? How far was he from her now? He'd traveled quite a way in the darkness of that water.

He reached steps, but couldn't force himself to climb them. He just stood, numb, staring at them. So he used the fabrial. Slow, easy climbs with it tugging him up at one angle, then another. Back and forth. Again and again.

He knew he was close when he heard rumbling. The highstorm. It was still blowing, so he hadn't been in that blackness for an eternity. He let it call to him as he continued half-flying, half-trudging upward.

Finally he staggered out of a room on the ground floor of the tower. He emerged right into the middle of a group of singer troops shouting for people to go to their quarters.

The storm rumbled in the near distance. Several of the soldiers turned toward him. Kaladin had a moment of profound disconnect, as if he couldn't believe he was still alive. As if he'd thought that trudge up the stairwell had been his climb to the Tranquiline Halls.

Then one of the guards leveled a spear at him, and Kaladin's body knew what to do. Exhausted, wounded, nerves worn all the way to Damnation, Kaladin grabbed that spear and twisted it out of the man's hands, then swept the legs of the next soldier.

A few Regals not far off shouted, and he caught sight of a Heavenly One—not Leshwi—rising into the air and pointing a lance at him. They weren't through with him yet.

He turned and ran, holding that stolen spear, drawing in Stormlight from lanterns—but feeling it do nothing at all to heal him. Even the slow healing from before had apparently stopped working. Either he'd further undermined his powers somehow by destroying the fabrial, or—more likely—the Sibling was too far gone toward corruption.

Chased by dozens of soldiers, Kaladin ran for the storm. Though it was dangerous outside, at least the enemy would have difficulty finding him in the tempest. He couldn't fight them—the only way to escape was to do something truly desperate.

He reached the front entryway of the tower, where winds coursed in through a portal that might once have held a wooden gate. They'd never taken the time to put in a new one. Why would they? The storms rarely reached this high.

Today they had.

Today, Kaladin reached the winds.

And like everything else today, they tried their best to kill him.

Voice of Lights. Voice for Lights. If I speak for the Lights, then I must express their desires. If Light is Investiture, and all Investiture is deity, and deity has Intent, then Light must have Intent.

—From *Rhythm of War*, final page

Dalinar no longer feared highstorms.

It had been some time now since he'd worried that he was mad. Yet—as a poorly treated horse learned to flinch at the mere sound of a whip—something had persisted inside of Dalinar. A learned response that a storm meant losing control.

So it was with a deep and satisfying sense of relief that today, Dalinar realized he didn't fear the storm. Indeed, when Elthebar listed the time of today's storm, Dalinar felt a little surge of *excitement*. He realized he felt more awake on highstorm days. More capable.

Is that you? he asked of the Stormfather.

It is us, the Stormfather replied. *Me and you. I enjoy passing over the continent, as it gives me much to see—but it also tires me as it energizes you.*

Dalinar stepped away from the table and dismissed his attendants and scribes, who had finished briefing him on the latest intelligence regarding Urithiru. He could barely control his mounting concern about Navani and the tower. Something was wrong. He could feel it in his bones.

So he'd begun looking for options. The current plan was for him to lead an expedition into Shadesmar, sail to the tower, then open up a perpendicularity to let spies in. Unfortunately, they didn't know if it would work. Would he even be able to activate a perpendicularity in the area?

He had to try *something*. The latest letters from Navani, although they did contain her passcodes, felt unlike her. Too many delays, too many assurances she was fine. He'd ordered a team of workers to begin clearing the rubble that prevented his scouts from entering through the basement. That would reportedly take weeks, and Shardblades couldn't be summoned in the region, being suppressed like fabrials and Radiant powers.

He pressed his palm flat against the table, gritting his teeth. He ignored the stack of reports from the front lines. Jasnah and the others were handling the war, and he could see their victory approaching. It wasn't inevitable, but it was highly likely.

He should be focusing on his Bondsmith training. But how could he? He wanted to find a set of Plate, borrow a Blade, and go march to the battlefront and find someone to attack. The idea was so tempting, he had to acknowledge how much he'd come to depend on emotional support from the Thrill of battle. Storms, sometimes he longed so *powerfully* for the way he'd felt alive when killing. Such emotions were remarkably similar to what he'd felt upon giving up the drink. A quiet, anxious yearning that struck at unexpected moments—seeking the pleasure, the *reward*.

He couldn't blame everything he'd done on the Thrill. That had been Dalinar in those boots, holding that weapon and glorying in destruction. That had been Dalinar lusting to kill. If he let himself go out and fight again, he knew he'd realize a part of him still loved it.

And so, he had to remain here. Find other ways of solving his problems. He stepped out of his personal dwelling, another small stone hut in Laqqi, their command city.

He took a deep breath, hoping the fresh air would clear his mind. The village was now fully fortified against both storms and attacks, with high-flying scout posts watching the land all around and Windrunners darting in to deliver reports.

I must get better with my powers, Dalinar thought. *If I had access to the map I could make with Shallan, we might be able to see exactly what is happening at Urithiru.*

It would not help, the Stormfather said in his mind, a sound like distant thunder. *I cannot see the tower. Whatever weakens the Windrunners when they draw close weakens me too, so the map would not reveal the location. However, I could show it to you. Perhaps you can see better than I.*

"Show me?" Dalinar asked, causing Szeth—his omnipresent shadow—to glance at him. "How?"

You can ride the storm with me, the Stormfather said. *I have given others this privilege on occasion.*

"Ride the storm with you?" Dalinar said.

It is like the visions that Honor instructed me to grant, only it is now. Come. See.

"Martra," Dalinar said, looking to the scribe who had been assigned to him today. "I might act odd for a short time. Nothing is wrong, but if I am not myself when my next appointment begins, please make them wait."

"Um . . . yes, Brightlord," she said, hugging her ledger, eyes wide. "Should I, um, get you a chair?"

"That would be a good idea," Dalinar said. He didn't feel like being closed up inside. He liked the scent of the air, even if it was too muggy here, and the sight of the open sky.

Martra returned with a chair and Dalinar settled himself, facing eastward. Toward the Origin, toward the storms—though his view was blocked by the large stone stormbreak.

"Stormfather," he said. "I'm—"

He became the storm.

Dalinar soared along the front of the stormwall, like a piece of debris. No . . . like a gust of wind blowing with the advent of the storm. He could see—comprehend—far more than when he'd flown under Windrunner power.

It was a great deal to take in. He surged across rolling hills with plants growing in the valleys between them. From up high it looked like a network of brown islands surrounded by greenery—each and every lowland portion filled to the brim with a snarl of underbrush. He'd never seen anything quite like it, the plants unfamiliar to him, though their density did faintly remind him of the Valley where he had met Cultivation.

He didn't have a body, but he turned and saw that he towed a long shadow. The storm itself.

When the Windrunner flew on my winds, he zipped about, the Stormfather said, and Dalinar felt the sounds all around him. *You simply think. You complain about meetings, but you are well suited to them.*

"I grow," Dalinar said. "I change. It is the mark of humanity, Stormfather, to change. A prime tenet of our religion. When I was Kaladin's age, I suspect I would have acted as he."

We approach the mountains, the Stormfather said. *Urithiru will come soon. Be ready to watch.*

A mountain range started to grow up to Dalinar's right, and he realized where they must be—blowing through Triax or Tu Fallia, countries with which he had little experience. These weren't the mountains where he'd find Urithiru, not yet. So he experimented with motion, soaring closer to the overgrown valleys.

Yes . . . this landscape was alien to him, the way the underbrush snarled together so *green*. Full of grass, broad leaves, and other stalks, all woven together with vines and bobbing with lifespren. The vines were a netting tying it all together, tight against storms.

He saw curious animals with long tentacles for arms and leathery skin instead of chitin. Malleable, they easily squeezed through holes in the underbrush and found tight pockets in which to hide as the stormwall hit. Strange that everything would be so different when it wasn't that far from Alethkar. Only a little trip across the Tarat Sea.

He tried to hang back to inspect one of the animals.

No, the Stormfather said. *Forward. Ever forward.*

Dalinar let himself be encouraged onward, sweeping across the hills until he reached a place where the underbrush had been hollowed out to build homes. These valleys weren't so narrow or deep that flooding would be a danger, and the buildings were built on stilts a few feet high anyway. They were grown over by the same vine netting, the edges of the buildings melding with the underbrush to borrow its strength.

Once, this village had likely been in an enviable location—protected by the surrounding plants. Unfortunately, as he blew past, he noted multiple burned-out buildings, the rest of the village in shambles.

The Everstorm. Dalinar's people had adapted to it; large cities already had walls on all sides, and small villages had been able to rely upon their government's stockpiles to help them survive this change in climate. But small, isolated villages like this had taken the brunt of the new storm with nobody to help. How many such places existed on Roshar, hovering on the edge of extinction?

Dalinar was past the place in a few heartbeats, but the memory lingered. Over the last two years, what cities and towns hadn't been broken by the sudden departure of the parshmen had been relentlessly attacked by storm or battle. If they won—*when* they won—the war, they would have a great deal of work to do in rebuilding the world.

As he continued his flight, he saw something else discouraging: a pair of foragers trapped while making their way back toward their home. The ragged men huddled together in a too-shallow ravine. They wore clothing of thick woven fibers that looked like the rug material that came out of Marat, and their spears weren't even metal.

"Take mercy upon them," Dalinar said. "Temper your fury, Stormfather."

It is not fury. It is me.

"Then protect them," Dalinar said as the stormwall hit, plunging the ill-fated men into darkness.

Should I protect all who venture out into me?

"Yes."

Then do I stop being a storm, stop being me?

"You can be a storm with mercy."

That defies the definition and soul of a storm, the Stormfather said. *I must blow. I make this land exist. I carry seeds; I birth plants; I make the landscape permanent with crem. I provide Light. Without me, Roshar withers.*

"I'm not asking you to abandon Roshar, but to protect those men. Right here. Right now."

I . . . the Stormfather rumbled. *It is too late. They did not survive the stormwall. A large boulder crushed them soon after we began speaking.*

Dalinar cursed, an action that translated as crackling lightning in the nearby air. "How can a being so close to divinity be so *utterly* lacking in honor?"

I am a storm. I cannot—

You are not merely a storm! Dalinar bellowed, his voice changing to rumbles of thunder. *You are capable of choice! You hide from that, and in so doing, you are a COWARD!*

The Stormfather did not respond. Dalinar felt him there, subdued—like a petulant child scolded for their foolishness. Good. Both Dalinar and the Stormfather were different from what they once had been. They had to be better. The world *demanded* that they be better.

Dalinar soared up higher, no longer wanting to see specifics—in case he was to witness more of the Stormfather's unthinking brutality. Eventually they reached snow-dusted mountains, and Dalinar soared to the very top of the storm. Lately the storms had been creeping higher and higher in the sky—something people wouldn't normally notice, but which was quite obvious in Urithiru.

It is natural, the Stormfather said. *A cycle. I will go higher and higher until I am taller than the tower, then the next few storms will lower. The highstorm did this before the tower existed.*

There seemed to be a timidity to the words, uncharacteristic of the Stormfather. Perhaps Dalinar had rattled him.

Soon he saw the tower approaching.

You can see it? the Stormfather said. *The details?*

"Yes," Dalinar said.

Look quickly. We will pass rapidly.

Dalinar steered himself as a gust of wind, fixating upon Urithiru. Nothing seemed overtly wrong with it. There wasn't anyone up on the Cloudwalk level, but with the storms growing higher, that wouldn't be advisable anyway.

"Can we go inside?" Dalinar asked as they approached.

You may, the Stormfather said. *I cannot go inside, just as I cannot infuse spheres indoors. When a piece splits off, it is no longer me. You will need to quickly rejoin, or the vision will end.*

Dalinar picked the lowest accessible balcony in the tower's east-jutting lobes, up on the fourth tier, and lowered himself until he was right on target. As the storm passed, he soared in through the open balcony into the quiet hallway beyond.

It was over too swiftly. A rush through a dark hallway until he found the southern diagonal corridor, where he tried to reach the ground floor, but Dalinar was suddenly pulled out another balcony without having seen any signs of life. The stormwall passed by to crest the mountains and continue on toward Azir and his body.

"No," Dalinar said. "We need to look again."

You must continue forward. Momentum, Dalinar.

"Momentum kept me doing terrible things, Stormfather. Momentum *alone* is not a virtue."

We cannot do what you ask.

"Stop making excuses and *try* for once!" Dalinar said, provoking lightning around him. He resisted the push to continue at the front and—though it caused the Stormfather to groan with fits of thunder—Dalinar moved into the inner portions of the storm. The black chaos behind the stormwall.

He was wind blowing against wind, a man swimming against a tide, but he pushed all the way back to Urithiru. The Stormfather grumbled, but Dalinar didn't sense pain from the spren. Just . . . surprise. As if the Stormfather were genuinely curious about what Dalinar had managed to do.

It was difficult to stay in place, but he hovered outside the first tier, searching for anything alarming. The fury of the wind tugged at him. The Stormfather rumbled, and lightning flashed.

There. Dalinar felt something. A . . . faint Connection, like when he learned someone's language. His Surgebinding, his powers, drew him through the wind around the outside base of the tower—until he found something remarkable. A single figure, almost invisible in the darkness, clinging to the outside of the tower on the eighth level.

Kaladin Stormblessed.

Dalinar could not fathom what had brought the Windrunner to expose himself like this in a storm, but here he was. Holding on tightly to a ledge. His clothing was ragged, and he was wounded—bleeding from numerous cuts.

"Blood of my fathers," Dalinar whispered. "Stormfather, do you see him?"

I . . . feel him, the Stormfather said. *Through you. He seems to be waiting for the center of the storm, where his spheres and Stormlight will renew.*

Dalinar drew close to the young man, who had buried his head into his shoulder for protection. He was soaked through, a piece of his shirt slapping against the stone over and over.

"Kaladin?" Dalinar shouted. "Kaladin, what has happened?"

The young man didn't move. Dalinar calmed himself, resisting the furious winds, and drew power from the soul of the storm.

KALADIN, he said.

Kaladin shifted, turning his head. His skin had gone pale, his hair matted and whipped into rain-drenched knots. Storms . . . he looked like a dead man.

WHAT HAS HAPPENED? Dalinar demanded as the storm.

"Singer invasion," Kaladin whispered into the wind. "Navani captured. The tower on lockdown. Other Radiants are all unconscious."

I WILL FIND HELP.

"Radiant powers don't work. Except mine. Maybe those of a Bondsmith. I'm fighting. I'm . . . trying."

LIFE BEFORE DEATH.

"Life . . ." Kaladin whispered. "Life . . . before . . ." The man's eyes fluttered closed. He sagged, going limp, and dropped off the wall, unconscious.

NO. Dalinar gathered the winds, and with a surge of strength, used them to hurl Kaladin up and over the ledge of the balcony, onto the eighth floor of the tower.

That strained his abilities, and at last the tide grabbed Dalinar and *forced* him toward the front of the storm. As it happened, he was ejected from the vision and found himself in Emul, sitting in his chair. An honor guard of soldiers had arrived, forming a circle around him so people couldn't gawk. Though it had been a long time since Dalinar had been taken involuntarily in a vision, he appreciated the gesture.

He shook himself, rising to stand. Nearby, Martra held up her notebook. "I wrote down everything you said and did! Like Brightness Navani used to. Did I do it right?"

"Thank you," Dalinar said, scanning what she'd written. It seemed he had spoken out loud, like when in one of the old visions. Only, Martra hadn't heard the parts where he'd spoken as the storm.

One of the guards coughed, and Dalinar noticed one of the others gawking at him. The youth turned away immediately, blushing.

Because I was reading, Dalinar thought, handing back the notebook. He looked at the sky, expecting to see stormclouds—though here the highstorm would still be hours away from this region.

Stormfather, he thought. *The tower was invaded. Our worst fears are confirmed. The enemy controls Urithiru.* Storms, that felt painful to acknowledge. First Alethkar, then the tower? And Navani captured?

Now he knew why the enemy had thrown away Taravangian. Maybe even the entire army here in Emul. They'd been sacrificed to keep Dalinar occupied.

"Go to Teshav," Dalinar said to Martra. "Have her gather the monarchs and my highlords. I need to call an emergency meeting. Cancel everything else I was to do today."

The young woman yelped, perhaps at being given such an important task. She ran on his orders immediately. The soldiers parted at Dalinar's request, and he looked toward the sky again.

Stormfather, did you hear me?

You have hurt me, Dalinar. This is the second time you have done so. You push against our bond, forcing me to do things that are not right.

I push you to stretch, Dalinar said. *That is always painful. Did you hear what Stormblessed told me?*

Yes, he said. *But he is wrong. Your powers will not work at Urithiru. It seems . . . they have turned the tower's protections against us. If that is true, you would need to be orders of magnitude stronger, more experienced than you are, to open a perpendicularity there. You'd have to be strong enough to overwhelm the Sibling.*

I need to say more oaths, Dalinar said. *I need to better understand what I can do. My training goes too slowly. We need to find a way to speed it up.*

I cannot help you. Honor is dead. He was the only one who knew what you could do, in full. He was the only one that could have trained you.

Dalinar growled in frustration. He began to pace the unworked stone in front of his warcamp house.

Kaladin, Shallan, Jasnah, Lift . . . all of them picked up on their powers naturally, Dalinar said. *But here I am, many months after our Bonding, and I have barely progressed.*

You are something different from them, the Stormfather replied. *Something greater, more dangerous. But also more complicated. There has never been another like you.*

Distant thunder. Drawing closer.

Except . . . the Stormfather said.

Dalinar looked up as a thought struck him. Likely the same one that had occurred to the Stormfather.

There was another Bondsmith.

⁂

A short time later, an out-of-breath Dalinar arrived at a small building in the far northern part of the camp. People raced about, preparing for the imminent storm, but he ignored them. Instead he burst into the small building, surprising a woman tending to a hulking man seated on the floor, bent forward, muttering to himself.

The woman leaped to her feet, reaching for the sword she wore at her side. She was of a difficult race to distinguish—maybe Azish, with that dark skin tone. But her eyes were wrong—like a Shin person. These two were beings trapped outside of time. Creatures almost as ancient as Roshar. The Heralds Shalash and Talenelat.

Dalinar ignored the woman's threatening pose and strode forward, seizing her by the shoulders. "There were ten of you. Ten Heralds. All were members of an order of Knights Radiant."

"No," Shalash said. "We were before the Radiants. They were modeled upon us, but we were not in their ranks. Except for Nale."

"But there was one of you who was a Bondsmith," Dalinar said. "Ishi, Herald of Luck, Herald of Mysteries, Binder of Gods."

"Creator of the Oathpact," Shalash said, forcing herself out of Dalinar's grip. "Yes, yes. We all have names like that. Useless names. You should stop talking about us. Stop worshipping us. Stop *painting* us."

"He's still alive," Dalinar said. "He was unchained by the oaths. He would understand what I can learn to do."

"I'm sure," Shalash said. "If any—except me—are still sane, it would be him."

"He's near here," Dalinar said, in awe. "In Tukar. Not more than a short flight southeast of this very town."

"Isn't there an army in the way?" Shalash said. "Isn't pushing the enemy back—crushing them into Ishar's army—our *main* goal right now?"

"That's what Jasnah and our army are doing," Dalinar said. "But I have another task. I need to find a way to speak to the god-priest, then convince him to help me rescue Urithiru."

72

OUTMATCHED

Intent matters. Intent is king. You cannot do what I attempt by ac-cident. You must mean it. This seems a much greater law than we've ever before understood.

—From *Rhythm of War*, endnotes

Navani sat quietly in her cell of a library room, waiting. Hours passed. She requested food and was given it, but neither the guard nor the Deepest One watching her answered when she asked questions. So she waited. Too nervous to study. Too sick to her stomach to dare try speaking to the Sibling.

After all her assurances and promises, Navani had proven untrustworthy after all.

Raboniel finally arrived, wearing a simple outfit of trousers, a blouse, and a Thaylen vest. She'd previously said she found their designs fascinating. She'd chosen traditionally male clothing, but likely didn't mind the distinction.

The Lady of Wishes observed Navani from the doorway, then shooed the guards away. Navani gritted her teeth, then stood up and bowed. She'd been hurt, outmatched, and defeated. But she couldn't let anger and humiliation rule. She *needed* information.

"You didn't persist in trying to contact me," Raboniel said. "I assume you realized what had happened."

"How long were you listening in on my conversations with the Sibling, Ancient One?" Navani said.

"Always," Raboniel said. "When I could not be listening in, I had another Fused doing it."

Navani closed her eyes. *I gave them the secret to the third node. I pried it out of the Sibling, walking directly into the enemy's plan.*

"You shouldn't be too hard on yourself," Raboniel said. "The Sibling is truly to blame—they always *have* been so innocent. And unaware of their own naiveness. When I touched the pillar, I knew the Sibling was awake—but pretending to be dead. So I let the ruse continue, and I listened. I couldn't know that decision would bear fruit, but that is why you nurture nine seeds and watch for the one that begins growing."

"The Sibling told me . . ." Navani said. "They said we couldn't outthink you."

"Yes, I heard that," Raboniel said. "It made me worry that you'd spotted my surveillance. It seemed too obvious a line said to distract me."

"How?" Navani asked, opening her eyes. "How did you do it, Ancient One? Surely the Sibling would have known if their communication could be compromised."

Raboniel hummed a rhythm, then walked over and tapped Navani's stacks of notes. "Study. Find us answers about Light, Navani. Stop trying to fight me; help me end this war instead. That was *always* your purpose here."

Navani felt nausea stirring her insides. She'd thrown up once already from the sick feeling of what she'd done. What she'd cost the Sibling. She forced it down this time, and as Raboniel left, she managed to ask one more question.

"Kaladin," she said. "The Windrunner. Did you kill him, Ancient One?"

"I didn't," she said. "Though I did land a fine cut on him. You have likely realized that he succeeded in destroying the node, as the shield is still up. However, when the Windrunner was spotted fleeing the tower a good half hour after, his wound hadn't healed—so I think the Sibling's transformation is almost complete. This makes your Windrunner's powers quite unreliable. I find it unlikely he survived after running out into the storm."

"Into the *storm*?" Navani asked.

"Yes. A pity. Perhaps the Sibling can tell you if he is dead or not—if so, I should very much like to study his corpse."

Raboniel left. Navani pushed through her sickness to write, then burn, a prayer of protection for Kaladin. It was all she could do.

Then she rested her head on the table to think about the profound scope of her failure.

THE END OF
Part Three

INTERLUDES

SZETH • CHIRI-CHIRI • TARAVANGIAN

Highspren are enigmatic beings in the best of circumstances. In Shadesmar, their forms are as solid as any of the other spren, although they appear as human-shaped holes in reality, spaces that look out onto unfamiliar starry skies

Distinguishing individual highspren is incredibly difficult, unless they happen to have a distinct silhouette. However, highspren seem to have no difficulty in identifying one another.

When they move, the stars do not move with them. Watching these beings walk is like looking through a moving window onto an alternate reality.

In the Physical Realm, they appear as a tear or hole, hanging in the air.

SZETH

Szeth-son-Honor tried to slouch.

Dalinar said that slouching a little would help him imitate an ordinary soldier on a boring guard duty. Dalinar said Szeth prowled when he walked, and was too intense when standing at watch. Like a fire burning high when it should be smoldering.

How did one *stop* being intense? Szeth tried to understand this as he forced himself to lean against a tree, folding his arms as Dalinar had suggested. In front of him, the Blackthorn played with his grandnephew, the child of Elhokar. Szeth carefully checked the perimeter of the small clearing. Watching for shadows. Or for people suspiciously lingering in the nearby camp—visible through the trees.

He saw nothing, which troubled him. But he tried to relax anyway.

The cloudy sky and muggy weather today were reminiscent of the coast of Shinovar, where Szeth's father had worked as a shepherd in his youth. With this thick grass, Szeth could almost imagine he was home. Near the beautiful white cliffs, listening to lambs bleat as he carried water.

He heard his father's gentle words. *The best and truest duty of a person is to add to the world. To create, and not destroy.*

But no. Szeth was not home. He was standing on profane stone in a forest clearing outside a small town in Emul. Dalinar knelt down, showing Gavinor—a child not yet five—how to hold his practice sword.

It had been a few minutes, so Szeth left the tree and made a circuit of the clearing, inspecting a few suspicious bundles of vines. "Do you see anything dangerous, sword-nimi?" he asked softly.

Nope, the sword said. *I think you should draw me. I can see better when I'm drawn.*

"When you are drawn, sword-nimi, you attempt to drain my life."

Nonsense. I like you. I wouldn't try to kill you.

The weapon projected its pleasant voice into Szeth's mind. Dalinar didn't like the sensation, so the sword now spoke only to Szeth.

"I see nothing dangerous," Szeth said, returning to his place beside the tree, then tried to at least *appear* relaxed. It was difficult, requiring vigilance and dedication, but he did not want to be chastised by Dalinar again.

That's good, right? Nothing dangerous?

"No, sword-nimi," Szeth said. "It is not good. It is concerning. Dalinar has so many enemies; they will be sending assassins, spies. If I do not see them, perhaps I am too lax or too unskilled."

Or maybe they aren't here to find, the sword said. *Vasher was always paranoid too. And he could* sense *if people were near. I told him to stop worrying so much. Like you. Worry, worry, worry.*

"I have been given a duty," Szeth said. "I will do it well."

Dalinar laughed as the young boy held his toy sword high and proclaimed himself a Windrunner. The child had been through a horrifying experience back in Kholinar, and he was quiet much of the time. Haunted. He'd been tortured by Voidspren, manipulated by the Unmade, neglected by his mother. Though Szeth's sufferings had been different, he couldn't help but feel a kinship with the child.

Dalinar clearly enjoyed seeing the child become more expressive and enthusiastic as they played. Szeth was reminded again of his own childhood spent playing with the sheep. A simple time, before his family had been given to the Honorblades. Before his gentle father had been taught to kill. To subtract.

His father was still alive, in Shinovar. Bearer of a different sword, a different burden. Szeth's entire family was there. His sister, his mother. It had been long since he'd considered them. He let himself do so now because he'd decided he wasn't Truthless. Before, he hadn't wanted to sully their images with his mind.

Time to make another round of the clearing. The child's laughter grew louder, but Szeth found it *painful* to hear. He winced as the boy jumped up on a rock, then leaped for his granduncle to catch him. And Szeth . . . if Szeth moved too quickly, he could catch sight of his own frail soul, attached incorrectly to his body, trailing his motions like a glowing afterimage.

Why do you hurt? the sword asked.

"I am afraid for the child," Szeth whispered. "He begins to laugh happily. That will eventually be stolen from him again."

I like to try to understand laughter, the sword said. *I think I can feel it. Happy. Ha! HA! Vivenna always liked my jokes. Even the bad ones.*

"The boy's laughter frightens me," Szeth said. "Because I am near. And I am . . . not well."

He should not guard this child, but he could not bring himself to tell Dalinar, for fear the Blackthorn would send him away. Szeth had found purpose here in following an Ideal. In trusting Dalinar Kholin. He could not afford to have that Ideal shaken. He could not.

Except . . . Dalinar spoke uncertainly sometimes. Concerned that he wasn't doing the right thing. Szeth wished he didn't hear Dalinar's weakness, his worries. The Blackthorn needed to be a moral rock, unshakable, always certain.

Dalinar was better than most. He *was* confident. Most of the time. Szeth had only ever met *one* man more confident than Dalinar in his own morality. Taravangian. The tyrant. The destroyer. The man who had followed Szeth here to this remote part of the world. Szeth was certain that, when he'd been visiting Taravangian with Dalinar the other day, the old man had seen through his illusory disguise.

The man would not let go. Szeth could feel him . . . *feel* him . . . plotting.

When Szeth returned to his tree, the air split, showing a blackness speckled faintly with stars beyond. Szeth immediately set down his sword by the trunk of the tree.

"Watch," he said, "and shout for me if danger comes."

Oh! All right! the sword said. *I can do that. Yes, I can. You might want to leave me drawn though. You know, so that if someone bad comes along, I can really get 'em.*

Szeth walked around the rear of the tree, following the rift in the air. It was as if someone had pried back the fabric of reality, like splitting skin to look at the flesh underneath.

He knelt before the highspren.

"You do well, my acolyte," the spren said, its tone formal. "You are vigilant and dedicated."

"I am," Szeth said.

"We need to discuss your crusade. You are a year into your current oath, and I am pleased and impressed with your dedication. You are among the most vigilant and worthy of men. I would have you earn your Plate. You still wish to cleanse your homeland?"

Szeth nodded. Behind, Dalinar laughed. He didn't seem to have noticed Szeth's momentary departure.

"Tell me more of this proposed crusade," the highspren said. It had not blessed Szeth with its name, though Szeth was its bonded Radiant.

"Long ago, my people rejected my warnings," Szeth said. "They did not believe me when I said the enemy would soon return. They cast me out, deemed me Truthless."

"I find inconsistencies to the stories you tell of those days, Szeth," the highspren said. "I fear that your memory, like those of many mortals, is incomplete or corrupted by the passage of time. I will accompany you on your crusade to judge the truth."

"Thank you," Szeth said softly.

"You may need to fight and destroy those who have broken their own laws. Can you do this?"

"I . . . would need to ask Dalinar. He is my Ideal."

"If you progress as a Skybreaker," the highspren said, "you will need to *become* the law. To reach your ultimate potential, you must know the truth yourself, rather than relying on the crutch presented by the Third Ideal. Be aware of this."

"I will."

"Continue your duty for now. But remember, the time will soon come when you must abandon it for something greater."

Szeth stood as the spren made itself invisible again. It was always nearby, watching and judging his worthiness. He entered the clearing and found Dalinar chatting quietly with a woman in a messenger uniform.

Immediately Szeth came alert, seizing the sword and striding over to stand behind Dalinar, prepared to protect him.

I hope it's all right that I didn't call for you! the sword said. *I could sense her, although I couldn't see her, and she seemed to be not evil. Even if she didn't come over to pick me up. Isn't that rude? But rude people can be not evil, right?*

Szeth watched the woman carefully. If someone wanted to kill Dalinar, they'd surely send an assassin who seemed innocent.

"I'm not sure about some of the things on this list," she was saying. "A pen and paper? For a man?"

"Taravangian has long since abandoned the pretense of being unable to read," Dalinar said.

"Then paper will let him plot against us."

"Perhaps," Dalinar said. "It could also simply be a mercy, giving him the companionship of words. Fulfill that request. What else?"

"He wishes to be given fresh food more often," she said. "And more light."

"I asked for the light already," Dalinar said. "Why hasn't the order been fulfilled?"

Szeth watched keenly. Taravangian was making demands? They should give him nothing. He was *dangerous*. He . . .

Szeth froze as the little boy, Gavinor, stepped up to him. He raised a wooden sword hilt-first toward Szeth. The boy should fear him, yet instead he smiled and waggled the sword.

Szeth took it, hesitant.

"The stone is the oddest request," the messenger woman said. "Why would he have need of a perfectly round, smooth stone? And why would he specify one with a vein of quartz?"

Szeth's heart nearly stopped. A round stone. With quartz inclusions?

"An odd request indeed," Dalinar said, thoughtful. "Ask him why he wants this before fulfilling the request."

A round stone.

With quartz inclusions.

An Oathstone.

For years, Szeth had obeyed the law of the Oathstone. The centuries-old tradition among his people dictated the way to treat someone who was Truthless. An object, no longer a man. Something to own.

Taravangian wanted an Oathstone. Why?

WHY?

As the messenger trotted away, Dalinar asked if Szeth would like to join sword practice, but he could barely mumble an excuse. Szeth returned to his spot by the tree, clutching the little wooden sword.

He *had* to know what Taravangian was planning.

He had to stop the man. Before he killed Dalinar.

CHIRI-CHIRI

Chiri-Chiri tried to hide in her grass. Unfortunately, she was growing too big. She wasn't like a regular cremling, those that scuttled around, tiny and insignificant. She was something grander. She could think. She could grow. And she could fly.

None of that helped as she tumbled out of the grass of the pot onto the desktop. She rolled over and clicked in annoyance, then looked toward Rysn, who sat making noises with another soft one. Chiri-Chiri did not always understand the mouth noises of the soft ones. They did not click, and there was no rhythm to them. So the sounds were sometimes just noises.

Sometimes they were not. There *was* a pattern to them that she was growing better at understanding. And there was a *mood* at times to their tones, almost like a rhythm. She crawled closer along the desk, trying to listen.

It was difficult. Chiri-Chiri did not like listening. She liked to do what felt right. Sleeping felt right. Eating felt right. Saying she was happy, or hungry, or sad felt right.

Communication should be about moods, desires, needs. Not all these flapping, flapping, sloppy wet noises.

Like the ones Rysn made now, talking to the old soft one who was like a parent. Chiri-Chiri crawled over the desk and into her box. It didn't smell as alive as the grass, but it was nice, stuffed with soft things and covered over with some vines. She clicked for it. Contentment. Contentment felt right.

"I do not understand half of what you explain, Rysn," the old soft one said as the two sat in chairs beside the table. Chiri-Chiri understood some of the words. And his hushed tone, yet tense. Confused. That was confusion. Like when you are bitten on the tail by one you thought was happy. "You're saying these things . . . these Sleepless . . . are all around us? Moving among us? But they aren't . . . human?"

"They are as far from human as a being can get, I should guess," Rysn said, sipping her tea. Chiri-Chiri understood her better. Rysn wasn't confused. More thoughtful. She'd been that way ever since . . . the event at the homeland.

"This is not what I thought I was preparing you for," the old soft one said, "with your training in negotiation."

"Well, you always liked to travel paths others thought too difficult," Rysn said. "And you relished trading with people ignored by your competition. You saw opportunity in what others discarded. This is somewhat the same."

"Pardon, Rysn—dear child—but this feels *very* different."

The two fell silent, but it wasn't the contented silence of having just eaten. Chiri-Chiri turned to snuggle back into her blankets, but felt a vibration coming up through the ground. A kind of call, a kind of warning. One of the rhythms of Roshar.

It reminded her of the carapace of the dead ones she had seen in the homeland. Their hollow skull chitin, their gaping emptiness, so still and noiseless. A silence of having eaten all, and having then been consumed.

Chiri-Chiri could not hide. The rhythm whispered that she could not do only easy things. Dark times were coming, the hollow skulls warned. And the vibrations of that place. Encouraging. Demanding. *Be better. You must be better.*

And so, Chiri-Chiri climbed out of her box and crawled up onto the arm of Rysn's chair. Rysn scooped her up, assuming she wanted scratches at the part along her head where carapace met skin. And it did feel nice. Nice enough that Chiri-Chiri forgot about hollow skulls and warning rhythms.

"Why do I feel," the old soft one said, "that you shouldn't have told me about any of this? The more people who know what you've done, Rysn, the more dangerous it will be for you."

"I realize this," she said. "But . . . Babsk . . . I had to tell *someone*. I need your wisdom, now more than ever."

"My wisdom does not extend to the dealings of gods, Rysn," he said. "I am just an old man who thought himself clever . . . until his self-indulgences nearly destroyed the life and career of his most promising apprentice."

Rysn sat up sharply, causing Chiri-Chiri to start and nip at her fingers. Why did she stop scratching?

Oh. Emotions. Chiri-Chiri could nearly feel them thrumming through Rysn, like rhythms. She was sad? Why sad? They had enough to eat. It was warm and safe.

Was it about the hollowness? The danger?

"Babsk," Rysn said. "You *still* blame yourself for my foolishness? My follies were *mine* alone."

"Ah, but I knew of your brashness," he said. "And it was my duty to check it." He took her hands, so Chiri-Chiri nipped at them a little—until Rysn glared at her. They didn't taste good anyway.

The two soft ones shared something. Almost like they *could* project emotions with a vibration or a buzz, instead of flapping their lips and squishing their too-melty faces. Those really were odd. Why didn't all their skin flop off, without carapace to hold it in? Why didn't they hurt themselves on everything they bumped?

But yes, they shared thoughts. And finally the old one nodded, standing. "I will help you bear this, Rysn. Yes, I should not complain about my own deficiencies. You have come to me, and show me great honor in doing so."

"But you mustn't tell anyone," she said to him. "Not even the queen. I'm sorry."

"I understand," he said. "I will ponder what you've told me, then see what advice—if any—I can have on this unique situation." He took his hat and moved to leave, but hesitated and said a single word. "Dawnshards." He imbued it with meaning somehow. Disbelief and wonder.

After he'd left, a few nips got Rysn to start scratching again. But she felt distracted, and soon Chiri-Chiri was unable to enjoy the scratches. Not with the hollow eyes speaking to her. Warning her.

To enjoy easy days, sometimes you had to first do difficult things. Rysn activated her chair—which flew a few inches off the ground, though it didn't have any wings. Chiri-Chiri jumped off onto the desk.

"I need something to eat," Rysn said. And Chiri-Chiri concentrated on the sounds, not the tired cadence.

Eat. Food.

"Eeeaaat." Chiri-Chiri tried to get her mandibles to click the sounds, blowing through her throat and making her carapace vibrate.

Rysn smiled. "I'm too tired. That almost sounded . . ."

"Rrrrrizzznn," Chiri-Chiri said. "Eeeeaat. Voood." Yes, that seemed right. Those were good mouth noises. At least, Rysn dropped her cup of tea and made a shocked vibration.

Perhaps doing it this way *would* be better. Not just because of the hollow skulls. But because, if the soft ones could be made to understand, it would be far easier to get scratches when they were required.

THE SWORD

Taravangian awoke hurting. Lately, each morning was a bitter contest. Did it hurt more to move or to stay in bed? Moving meant more pain. Staying in bed meant more anguish. Eventually he chose pain.

After dressing himself with some difficulty, he rested at the edge of the bed, exhausted. He glanced at the notes scratched on the side of an open drawer. Should he hide that? He should. The words appeared jumbled to him today. He had to stare at them a long time to get them to make sense.

Dumb. How dumb was he? Too . . . too dumb. He recognized the sensation, his thoughts moving as if through thick syrup. He stood. Was that light? Yes, sunlight.

He shuffled into the main room of his prison. Sunlight, through an open window. Strange. He hadn't left a window open.

Windows were all boarded up, he thought. *Someone broke one. Maybe a storm?*

No. He slowly realized that Dalinar must have ordered one opened. Kindly Dalinar. He liked that man.

Taravangian made his way to the sunlight. Guards outside. Yes, they would watch. They knew he was a murderer. He smiled at them anyway, then opened the small bundle on the windowsill. A notebook, a pen, and some ink. Had he asked for that? He tried to remember.

Storms. He wanted to sleep. But he couldn't sleep through another day. He'd done that too often.

He returned to his room and sat—then realized he had forgotten what he'd intended to do. He retraced his steps, looked down at the pen and paper again, and only then remembered. He went back into his bedroom. Unhooked the drawer with the instructions. Slowly read them.

Then again.

He laboriously copied them into the notebook. They were a list of things he needed to say if he could meet Szeth alone. Several times, the words "Don't talk to Dalinar" were underlined. In his current state, Taravangian was uncertain about that. Why not talk to him?

Smarter him was convinced they needed to do this themselves. Dalinar Kholin could *not* be entrusted with Taravangian's plans. For Dalinar Kholin would do what was right. Not what was needed.

Taravangian forced himself to get food. He had some in the other room, bread that had gone stale. He should have asked for better food. Only after chewing on it did he think to go look at the table right inside his door where they delivered his meals. Today was the day new food came. And there it was. Fresh bread. Dried meat. No jam.

He felt like a fool. Why not look for fresh food *before* forcing yourself to choke down the old stuff? It was difficult to live like this. Making easy mistakes. Forgetting what he was doing and why.

At least he was alone. Before he'd gotten good staff, people had always been so angry at him when he was stupid. And since he got emotional when stupid, he often cried. Didn't they understand? He made their lives difficult. But he *lived* the difficulty. He wasn't trying to be a problem.

People took their minds for granted. They thought themselves wonderful because of how they'd been born.

"Traitor!" a voice called into the room. "You have a visitor!"

Taravangian felt a spike of alarm, his fingers shaking as he closed and gripped the notebook. A visitor? Szeth had come? Taravangian's planted seed bore fruit?

He breathed in and out, trying to sort through his thoughts. They were a jumble, and the shouting guard made him jump, then scramble toward the sound. He prepared himself for the sight of Szeth. That haunted stare. Those dead eyes. Instead, at the window, Taravangian saw a young man with black hair peppered blond. The Blackthorn's son Renarin.

Taravangian hesitated, though the guards waved for Taravangian to come speak to the youth.

He hadn't prepared for this. Renarin. Their quiet salvation. Why had he come? Taravangian hadn't prepared responses in his notebook for *this* meeting.

Taravangian stepped up to the window, and the guards retreated to give them privacy. Here Taravangian waited, expecting Renarin to speak first. Yet the boy stood silent, keeping his distance from the window—as if he thought Taravangian would reach out and grab him.

Taravangian's hands were cold. His stomach churned.

"Something changed," Renarin finally said, looking away as he spoke. He avoided meeting people's eyes. Why? "About you. Recently. Why?"

"I do not know, Brightlord," Taravangian said—though he felt sweat on his brow at the lie.

"You've hurt my father," Renarin said. "I believe he thought, up until recently, that he could change you. I don't know that I've seen him as morose as when he speaks of you."

"I would . . ." Taravangian tried to think. Words. What words? "I would that he had changed me, Brightlord. I would that I could have been changed."

"I believe that is true," Renarin said. "I see your future, Taravangian. It is dark. Not like anything I've seen before. Except there's a point of light flickering in the darkness. I worry what it will mean if that goes out."

"I would worry too."

"I can be wrong," Renarin said. He hesitated, then closed his eyes—as if carefully thinking through his next words. "You are in darkness, Taravangian, and my father thinks you are lost. I lived through his return, and it taught me that no man is ever so far lost that he cannot find his way back. You are not alone."

The young man opened his eyes, stepped forward, then lifted his hand and presented it toward Taravangian. The gesture felt awkward. As if Renarin wasn't quite sure what he was doing.

He wants me to take his hand.

Taravangian didn't. Seeing it made him want to break into tears, but he contained himself.

Renarin withdrew his hand and nodded. "I'll let you know if I see something that could help you decide." With that the boy left, accompanied by one of the guards—the man who had yelled at Taravangian earlier.

That left one other guard: a short, nondescript Alethi man who walked up to the window to eye Taravangian. Taravangian watched Renarin walking away, wishing he had the courage to call after the boy.

Foolish emotions. Taravangian was not lost in darkness. He had chosen this path, and he knew precisely where he was going. Didn't he?

"He is wrong," the guard said. "We can't all return from the dark. There are some acts that, once committed, will always taint a man."

Taravangian frowned. That guard had a strange accent. He must have lived in Shinovar.

"Why did you ask for an Oathstone?" the guard demanded. "What is your purpose? Do you wish to tempt or trick me?"

"I don't even know you."

The man stared at him with unblinking eyes. Eyes like one of the dead . . . and Taravangian finally understood what on any other day he would have seen immediately. The guard wore a different illusion today.

"Szeth," Taravangian whispered.

"Why? Why do you seek an Oathstone? I will *not* follow your orders again. I am becoming my own man."

"Do you have the sword?" Taravangian asked. He reached out, foolish though it was, and tried to grab Szeth. The man stepped away in an easy motion, leaving Taravangian grasping at air. "The sword. *Did you bring it?*"

"I *will not serve you*," Szeth said.

"Listen to me," Taravangian said. "You have to . . . the sword . . . Wait a moment." He furiously began flipping through the notebook for the words he'd copied from the desk drawer.

"'The sword,'" he read, "'is something we didn't anticipate. It was nowhere in the Diagram. But Odium fears it. Do you understand? He *fears* it. I think it might be able to harm him. We attack him with it.'"

"I will not serve you," Szeth said. "I will not be manipulated by you again. My stone . . . was always only a stone. . . . My father said . . ."

"Your father is dead, Szeth," Taravangian said. "Listen to me. Listen." He read from the notebook. "'Fortunately, I believe his ability to see us here is limited. Therefore, we may talk freely. I doubt you can harm Odium directly unless you are in one of his visions. You must get into one of those visions. Can you do this?'"

There were more notes in the book about how to manipulate Szeth. Taravangian read them, and the words made him hurt. Hadn't this man been through enough?

He rejected those manipulations and looked up at Szeth. "Please," Taravangian whispered. "Please help me."

Szeth didn't appear to have heard. He turned to go.

No! "Listen," Taravangian said, going off script, ignoring the orders of his smarter self. "Give *Dalinar* the sword. Dalinar is taken to Odium's vision sometimes. It should travel with him. Do you understand? Odium thinks the sword is in Urithiru. He *doesn't realize you're here.* He can't see it because of Renarin."

Smarter Taravangian claimed he didn't want to work with Dalinar because it was too dangerous, or because Dalinar wouldn't believe. Those lies made dumb Taravangian want to pound his fists at his own face out of shame. But the truth was more shameful.

Szeth did not care which Taravangian he was speaking to. "I don't understand your manipulations," the man said as he walked away. "I should have realized I wouldn't be able to understand the way your mind works. All I can do is refuse."

He left, sending the other guard back to watch Taravangian—who stood gripping his little notebook, crying.

PART

FOUR

A Knowledge

ADOLIN • SHALLAN • NAVANI •
VENLI • ESHONAI • BRIDGE FOUR

The Calligraphic Phonemes

A	I	M	SH		
B	F	N	T		
V	P	O	TH		
CH	G	U	Y		
K	H	R	J		
D	L	S	Z		
E					

The Hybrid Phonemes (below) have gained popularity recently and incorporate shortcut experienced calligraphers have used for decades. In a hundred years, I suspect this set will supersede the others and be the basis for a more streamlined Alethi glyph system.

A	I	M	SH		
B	F	N	T		
V	P	O	TH		
CH	G	U	Y		
K	H	R	J		
D	L	S	Z		
E					

Now, on to different things! (Finally.) You know my tendency towards boredom, and I suspect your giving me this latest errand was less to collect information and more for your own amusement, to see if you could interest me in something other than smuggling artifacts, covertly collecting strange weapons, and drawing in those secret sketchbooks you've endlessly chided me about since you discovered them. (For the record, I also enjoy learning rude phrases in other languages, thank you very much. I'm not entirely uncultured.)

I regret to inform you that your clever scheme to make a scholar of me might have, unfortunately, worked. For, while I hope to never return to the Calligraphers Guild, I did discover something intriguing.

The instructors in the guild, especially the self-proclaimed calligro-cartographer Isasik Shulin, have repeatedly told us it is futile to pick apart the phonemes from old glyphs. Nobody tells me what not to do (except for you, though I don't always listen), so picking apart old glyphs is exactly what I've done, dissecting them like little biology projects. My rebellion yielded very little until I teased out some bits from the ancient glyph for Roshar, which oddly looks a lot like the ancient symbol for the Knights Radiant, but the phonemes in the glyph don't say "Roshar." If you separate out its components, this emerges:

Glyph for "Roshar"

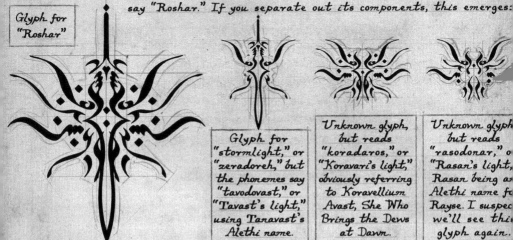

Glyph for "stormlight," or "zeradoreh," but the phonemes say "tavodovast," or "Tavast's light," using Tanavast's Alethi name.

Unknown glyph, but reads "koradaros," or "Koravari's light," obviously referring to Koravellium Avast, She Who Brings the Dews at Dawn.

Unknown glyph but reads "rasodonar," o "Rasan's light, Rasan being a Alethi name fo Rayse. I suspec we'll see thi glyph again.

Then again, I also dissected the glyph for "love" and discovered the principle phonemes for "friendly cremling," so I could be, as they say, seeing shades in the mist, unless we're looking for a new name for our little organization.

Next page: How to swear like a Horneater. Oo'kali'laa'e

73

WHICH MASTER
TO FOLLOW

EIGHT YEARS AGO

Venli could hear new rhythms. She tried to hide this fact, attuning the old, boring rhythms around others. It was so *difficult*. The new rhythms were her majesty, the proof that she was special. She wanted to shout them, *flaunt* them.

Quiet, Ulim said from her gemheart. *Quiet for now, Venli. There will be time enough later to enjoy the Rhythm of Praise.*

She attuned Exultation, but did not hum it as she walked through the room where her scholars worked. Ulim had given her hints about finding another form, nimbleform. He wouldn't tell her the exact process yet, so she'd gathered these scholars and set them to work.

Over time, she intended to use them as an excuse to reveal many important discoveries. Including ones that Ulim had promised her. Greater forms than these. Power.

You are special, Ulim whispered as she idled near a pair of her scholars who were trying to trap a windspren that had flown in to tease them. *I could sense you from far away, Venli. You were chosen by our god, the true god of all singers. He sent me to explain how wonderful you are.*

The words comforted her. Yes. That was right. She *would* wear forms of power. Only . . . hadn't she once wanted those . . . for her mother? Wasn't that the point?

You will be great, he said within her gemheart. *Everyone will recognize your majesty.*

"Well, I want nimbleform soon," she whispered to Ulim, stepping out of the chamber. "It has been too long since warform. My sister and her sycophants get to tromp around the cities on display like heroes."

Let them. Those are your grunts, who will be sent to die fighting the humans once our plot is accomplished. You should take time "finding" nimbleform. It will be too suspicious for you to find another so soon.

She folded her arms, listening to the new rhythm praise her. The city buzzed with activity, thousands of listeners from a dozen families passing by. Eshonai and the others had made great strides toward true unity, and the elders of the various families were talking to one another.

Who would get the glory for that? Venli had orchestrated this grand convergence, but everyone *ignored* her.

Perhaps she should have taken warform. Ulim had urged her to be one of the first, but she'd hesitated. She hadn't been frightened, no, but she'd assumed she could manipulate better without taking the form.

That had been a mistake, and this was her reward: Eshonai taking all the credit. Next time, Venli would do it herself.

"Ulim," she whispered, "when will the other Voidspren be ready?"

Can't say for certain, he replied. *That stupid Herald is still standing strong all these years later. We have to work around him.*

"The new storm," Venli whispered.

Yes. It's been building in Shadesmar for centuries. We need to get our agents close enough to it on this side—a place that is out in the ocean, mind you—so they can use gemstones to pull my brothers and sisters across. Then those stones have to be physically transported here. You have no idea how much of a pain it all is.

"I'm well acquainted by now," she said to Derision. "You never shut up about it."

Hey, you're the only one I get to talk to. And I like to talk. So . . .

"Nimbleform. When?"

We have bigger problems. Your people aren't ready to accept forms of power. At all. They're far too timid. And the way they fight . . .

"What's wrong with the way we fight?" Venli asked to Conceit. "Our warriors are powerful and intimidating."

Please, Ulim replied. *The humans have remembered how to make good steel all these centuries, and even figured out some things we never learned. Meanwhile, your people throw spears at each other like primitives. They yell and dance more than they fight. It's embarrassing.*

"Maybe you should have gone to the humans then."

Don't be childish, Ulim said. *You need to know what you're facing. Imagine a hundred thousand men in glistening armor, moving in coordinated blocks, lifting a wall of interlocking shields—broken only by the spears coming out to bite your flesh.*

Imagine thousands upon thousands of archers loosing waves of arrows that sweep in a deadly rain. Imagine men on horseback charging—thunder without lightning—and riding down anyone in their path. You think you can face that with a few semicoherent boasts?

Venli's confidence wavered. She looked out toward the Shattered Plains, where their warforms trained on a nearby plateau. She'd nudged them toward that, following Ulim's suggestions. He knew a lot about manipulating people; with his help she could get the others to do pretty much anything.

A part of her thought she should be concerned about that. But when she tried to think along those lines, her mind grew fuzzy. And she ended up circling back to whatever she'd been thinking about before.

"Eshonai guesses that the humans are bluffing about how many cities they have," she said. "But if they have dozens like they told us, then our numbers would be roughly equal. If we can get all the families to listen to us."

Roughly equal? Ulim said, then started laughing. An outrageous sound, uproarious. It made her gemheart vibrate. *You and them? Even? Oh, you blessed little idiot.*

Venli felt herself attune Agony. She *hated* the way he made her feel sometimes. He'd whisper about how great she was, but then they'd get deep into a conversation and he'd speak more freely. More derogatorily.

"Well," she said, "maybe we don't have to fight them. Maybe we can find another way."

Kid, you're not gonna have a choice on that one, Ulim said. *They will make sure of it. You know what they've done to all the other singers in the world? They're slaves.*

"Yes," Venli said. "Proof that my ancestors were wise in leaving."

Yeah, please don't say that around any of my friends, Ulim said. *You'll make me look bad. Your ancestors were traitors. And no matter what you do, the humans will make you fight. Trust me. It's what they always do.*

Your primitive little paradise here is doomed. Best you can do is train some soldiers, practice using the terrain to your advantage, and prepare to get some actual forms. You don't get to choose to be free, Venli. Just which master to follow.

Venli pushed off from the wall and began walking through the city. Something was wrong about Ulim. About her. About the way she thought now . . .

You have no idea the power that awaits you, Venli, Ulim said to the Rhythm of Craving. *In the old days, forms of power were reserved for the most special. The most valuable. They were strong, capable of amazing feats.*

"Then how did we ever lose?" she asked.

Bah, it was a fluke. We couldn't break the last Herald, and the humans found some way to pin the whole Oathpact on him. So we got stuck on Braize. Eventually the Unmade decided to start a war without us. That turned out to be exceedingly stupid. In the past, Odium granted forms of power, but Ba-Ado-Mishram thought she could do it. Ended up handing out forms of power as easily as Fused give each other titles, Connected herself to the entire singer species. Became a little god. Too little.

"I . . . don't understand."

I'll bet you don't. Basically, everyone relied way too much on an oversized spren. Trouble is, spren can get stuck in gemstones, and the humans figured this out. End result: Ba-Ado-Mishram got a really cramped prison, and everyone's souls got seriously messed up.

It will take something big to restore the minds of the singers around the world. So we're going to prime the pump, so to speak, with your people. Get them into stormform and pull the big storm over from Shadesmar. Odium thinks it will work, and considering he's anything but a little *god, we are going to do what he says. It's better than the alternative, which generally involves a lot of pain and the occasional flavorful dismemberment.*

Venli nodded to some listeners passing by. Members of another family; she could tell by the colors of the bands on their braids and the type of gemstone bits in the men's beards. Venli deliberately hummed one of the weak old rhythms for them to hear, but these newcomers didn't give her a second glance despite her importance.

Patience, Ulim said. *Once the Return arrives, you will be proclaimed as the one who initiated it—and you will be given everything you deserve as the most important of all listeners.*

"You say my ancestors were traitors," Venli whispered. "But you need us. If they hadn't split off, you wouldn't have us to use in your plot. You should bless what they did."

They got lucky. Doesn't mean they weren't traitors.

"Perhaps they knew what Ba-Ado-Mishram was going to do, and so they attuned Wisdom, not Betrayal, in their actions."

She knew the name, of course. As a keeper of songs, she knew the names of all nine Unmade—who were among the gods her people swore to never follow again. But the more she talked with Ulim, the less regard she gave the songs. The old listeners had memorized the wrong things. How could they retain the names of the Unmade, but forget something as simple as how to adopt workform?

Anyway, who cares what your ancestors did? Ulim said. *We need to prepare your people for forms of power, then get them to summon Odium's storm. Everything will take care of itself after that.*

"That might be harder than you think, spren," Venli said to Derision. She quieted her voice as another group of listeners passed. The city was so packed these days, you could barely find any peace to think.

Forms of power, Venli. The ability to reshape the world. Strength beyond anything you've ever dreamed of having.

She stuffed her hands into the pockets of her robe as she reached the heart of the city. She hadn't realized she was coming this way, to her family's home. She stepped inside, and found her mother picking apart a rug she had woven. Jaxlim glanced up at Venli, jumping.

"It's only me," Venli said to Peace.

"I got it wrong again," Jaxlim said, huddling over her rug. "Wrong every time . . ."

Venli tried to attune Indifference, one of the new rhythms, but she couldn't find it. Not here, not with her mother. She instead settled down on the floor, cross-legged, like she'd sat as a child when learning the songs.

"Mother?" Venli asked to Praise. "Everyone makes mistakes."

"Why can't I do anything *right* anymore?"

"Mother, can you tell me the first song?" Venli whispered.

Jaxlim kept picking at the rug.

"You know it," Venli said. "Days we sing. Days we once knew? Days of—"

"Days of pain," Jaxlim said, to the Rhythm of Memories. "Days of loss. Days of glory."

Venli nodded as Jaxlim continued. This song was more of a chant, the original recitation of her people leaving the war. Leaving their gods. Striking out on their own.

This is painful to hear, Ulim noted. *Your people had* no idea *what they were doing.*

Venli ignored him, listening, feeling the Rhythm of Memories. Feeling . . . like herself. This *had* all been about finding a way to help her mother, hadn't it? At the start?

No, she admitted. *That's what you told yourself. But you want more. You've always wanted more.*

She knew forms changed the way a person thought. But was she in a new form now? Ulim had been dodgy in explaining it. Evidently she had a normal spren in her gemheart to give her workform—but Ulim was there too, crowding in. And he could speak to her, even hear what she was thinking.

You single-handedly delivered warform to your people, Ulim whispered. *Once you give them additional forms, they will revere you. Worship you.*

She wanted that respect. She wanted it so *badly.* But she forced herself to listen to what her ancestors had done, four hundred of them striking out alone, wearing dullform.

The fools were inbred, then, Ulim said. *No wonder . . .*

"These people created us," she whispered. Her mother continued singing, and didn't seem to have heard the interruption. "They were *not* fools. They were heroes. Their *primary* teaching, preserved in everything we do, is to *never* let our gods rule us again. To never take up forms of power. To never serve Odium."

Then don't serve him, Ulim said. *Deal with him. You have something he needs—you can approach him from a place of power. Your ancestors were lowly things; that was why they wanted to leave. If they'd been at the top, like your people will be, they'd have never wanted such a thing.*

Venli nodded. But she was more persuaded by other arguments. War *was* coming with the humans. She could feel it in the way their soldiers eyed her people's weapons. They had enslaved those parshmen. They'd do the same to Venli's people.

The ancient songs had become irrelevant the moment Eshonai had led the humans to the Shattered Plains. The listeners could no longer hide. Conflict *would* find them. It was no longer a choice between their gods or freedom. It was a choice between their gods and human slaving brands.

How do we proceed? Ulim asked.

Venli closed her eyes, listening to her mother's words. Her ancestors had been desperate. "We will need to be equally desperate," Venli whispered. "My people need to see what I have seen: that we can no longer remain as we have been."

The humans will *destroy them.*

"Yes. Help me prove it."

I am your servant in this, Ulim said to Subservience. *What do you propose?*

Venli listened. Jaxlim's voice cracked and she trailed off. Jaxlim had forgotten the song again. The older femalen turned away and cried softly.

It broke Venli's heart.

"You have agents among the humans, Ulim?" Venli whispered.

We do.

"Can you communicate with them?"

I have ways of doing so.

"Have your agents influence those at the palace," Venli said. "Get the Alethi to invite us to visit. Their king spoke of it before he left; he's considering it already. We must bring our people there, then show them how powerful the humans are. We must overwhelm my people with our own insignificance."

She stood up, then went to comfort her mother.

We must make them afraid, Ulim, Venli thought. *We must make them sing to the Terrors long into the night. Only then will they listen to our promises.*

It shall be done, he replied.

Words.
I used to be good with words.
I used to be good at a lot of things.

Venli tried to attune the Rhythm of Conceit as she walked the halls of Urithiru. She kept finding the Rhythm of Anxiety instead. It was difficult to attune an emotion she didn't feel; doing so felt like a worse kind of lie than she normally told. Not a lie to others, or to herself. A lie to Roshar.

Timbre pulsed comfortingly. These were dangerous times, requiring dangerous choices.

"That sounds an awful lot like the things Ulim told me," Venli whispered.

Timbre pulsed again. The little spren was of the opinion that Venli couldn't be blamed for what she'd done, that the Voidspren had manipulated her mind, her emotions, her goals.

Timbre, for all her wisdom, was wrong in this. Ulim had heightened Venli's ambitions, her arrogance, but *she'd* given him the tools to work with. A part of her continued to feel some of those things. Worse, Ulim had occasionally left her gemheart during those days, and she'd still gone through with those plans, without his influence.

She might not bear *full* blame for what had happened. But she'd been a willing part of it. Now she had to do her best to make up for it. So she kept her head high, walking as if she owned the tower, trailed by Rlain, who carried the large crate as if on her orders. Everyone needed to see her treating him as a servant; hopefully that would quash some of the rumors about the two of them.

He hurried closer as they entered a less populated section of the tower. "The tower *does* feel darker now, Venli," he said to the Rhythm of Anxiety—which didn't help her own mood. "Ever since . . ."

"Hush," she said. She knew what he'd been about to say: Ever since the fight in the market.

The whole tower knew by now that Kaladin Stormblessed, Windrunner and champion, fought. That his powers still functioned. The Fused had worked hard to spread a different narrative—that he'd been faking Radiant powers with fabrials, that he'd been killed during a cruel attack on innocent singer civilians in the market.

Venli found that story far-fetched, and she knew Stormblessed only by reputation. She doubted the propaganda would fool many humans. If Raboniel had been behind it, the message would have been more subtle. Unfortunately, the Lady of Wishes spent most of her time with her research, and instead let the Pursuer lead.

His personal troops dominated the tower. Already there had been a half dozen instances of singers beating humans near to death. This place was a simmering cauldron, waiting for the added bit of fuel that would bring it to a boil. Venli needed to be ready to get her people out when that happened. Hopefully the crate Rlain carried would help with that.

Head high. Hum to Conceit. Walk slowly but deliberately.

By the time they reached the Radiant infirmary, Venli's nerves were so tight she could have played a rhythm on them. She shut the door after Rlain—they'd recently had it installed by some human workers—and finally attuned Joy.

Inside the infirmary, the human surgeon and his wife cared for the comatose Radiants. They did a far better job of it than Venli's staff; the surgeon knew how to minimize the formation of sores on the humans' bodies and how to spot signs of dehydration.

When Venli and Rlain entered, the surgeon's wife—Hesina—hurried over. "Is this them?" she asked Rlain, helping him with the crate.

"Nah, it's my laundry," he said to Amusement. "Figured Venli here is so mighty and important, she might be able to get someone to wash it for me."

Joking? *Now?* How could he act so indifferent? If they were discovered, it would mean their executions—or worse.

The human woman laughed. They carried the box to the back of the room, away from the door. Hesina's son put down the shoestrings he'd been playing with and toddled over. Rlain ruffled his hair, then opened the crate. He moved the decoy papers on top, revealing a group of map cases.

Hesina breathed out in a human approximation of the Rhythm of Awe.

"After Kal and I parted," Rlain explained, "and the queen surrendered, I realized I could go anywhere in the tower. A little black ash mixed with water covered my tattoo, blending it into my pattern. Humans were confined to quarters, and so long as I looked like I was doing something important, the singers ignored me.

"So I thought to myself, 'What can I do to best undermine the occupation?' I figured I had a day at most before the singers got organized and people started asking who I was. I thought about sabotaging the wells, but realized that would hurt too many innocents. I settled on this."

He waved his hand over the round tubes filling the crate. Hesina took one out and unrolled the map inside. It depicted the thirty-seventh floor of the tower, meticulously mapped.

"So far as I know," Rlain said, "guard posts and master-servant quarters just contain maps of the lower floors. The upper-level maps were kept in two places: the queen's information vault and the map room. I stopped by the map room and found it burned out, likely at the queen's order. The vault was on the ground floor, far from where her troops could have reached. I figured it might still be intact."

Rlain shrugged a human shrug. "It was shockingly easy to get in," he continued to Resolve. "The human guards had been killed or removed, but the singers didn't know the value of the place yet. I walked right through a checkpoint, stuffed everything I could into a sack, and wandered out. I said I was on a search detail sent to collect any form of human writing."

"It was brave," Lirin the surgeon said, stepping over and folding his arms. "But I don't know how useful it will be, Rlain. There's not much they'd want on the upper floors."

"It might help Kaladin stay hidden," Rlain said.

"Maybe," Lirin said. "I worry you put yourself through an awful lot of effort and danger to accomplish what might add up to a mild inconvenience for the occupation."

The man was a pragmatist, which Venli appreciated. She, however, was interested in other matters. "The tunnel complex," she said. "Is there a map here of the tunnels under the tower?"

Rlain dug for a moment, then pulled out a map. "Here," he said. "Why?"

Venli took it reverently. "It's one of the few paths of escape, Rlain. I came in through those tunnels—they're a complicated maze. Raboniel knew her way through, but I doubt I could get us out on my own. But with this . . ."

"Didn't the enemy collapse those tunnels?" Lirin asked.

"Yes," Venli said. "But I might have a way around that."

"Even if you do," Lirin said, "we'd have to travel through the most heavily guarded section of the tower—where the Fused are doing their research on the tower fabrials."

Yes, but could she use her powers to form a tunnel through the stone? One that bypassed Raboniel's workstation and the shield, then intersected with these caverns below?

Perhaps. Though there was still the greater problem. Before they could run, she had to ensure the Fused wouldn't give chase. Escaping the tower only to die by a Heavenly One's hand in the mountains would accomplish nothing.

"Rlain," Hesina said. "These are wonderful. You did more than anyone could have expected of you."

"I might have been able to do more, if I hadn't messed up," Rlain said to Reconciliation. "I was stopped in the hallway, asked to give the name of the Fused I was operating under. I should have played dumb instead of using the name of one I'd heard earlier in the day. Turns out that Fused doesn't *keep* a staff. She's one of the lost ones."

"You could have locked yourself in a cell the moment the tower fell," Lirin said, "and pretended to be a prisoner. That way, the Fused could have liberated you, and no one would be suspicious."

"Every human in the tower knows about me, Lirin," Rlain said. "The 'tame' Parshendi your son 'keeps.' If I'd tried a ploy like that, the singers would have found me eventually, and I'd have ended up in a cell for real." He shrugged again. "Did anyway though."

He and Hesina began digging through the maps, Rlain chatting with them as they did. He seemed to like these humans, and looked more comfortable around them than he was with her. Beyond that, the way he used human mannerisms to exaggerate his emotions—the way the rhythms were a subtle accent to his words, rather than the driving power behind them—it all seemed a little . . . pathetic.

Lirin returned to his work tending the unconscious. Venli strolled over to him, attuning Curiosity. "You don't like what they're doing," Venli said, nodding toward the other two.

"I'm undecided," Lirin said. "My gut says that stealing a few maps won't hurt the occupation. But perhaps if we turned the maps *in* and claimed we found them in a forgotten room, there's a good chance it would earn us favor with the Fused. Perhaps it would prove Hesina and I aren't malcontents, so we could come out of hiding."

"It isn't the hiding that protects you," Venli said, "it is Lady Leshwi's favor. Without it, the Pursuer would kill you, no matter what you did to prove yourself. He'd kill other Fused, if he thought it would let him fulfill his tradition. And the others would applaud him."

Lirin grunted—a human version of Derision, she thought—as he knelt beside a Radiant and lifted her eyelids to check her eyes. "Nice to know your government has its idiocies too."

"You really don't want to resist, do you?" Venli said to Awe. "You truly want to live with the occupation."

"I resist by controlling my situation," Lirin said. "And by working with those in power, rather than giving them reason to hurt me and mine. It's a lesson I learned very painfully. Fetch me some water."

Venli was halfway to the water station before she realized she'd done what he said, despite telling him—*several* times—that he needed to show her more respect. What a strange man. His attitude was so commanding and in charge, but he used it to reinforce his own subservience.

Timbre thrummed as Venli returned to him with the water. She needed to practice her powers some more—particularly if she might be required to tunnel them down through many feet of rock to reach an exit. She took the tunnel map and gave it to Jial, one of her loyalists. Jial folded it and placed it into her pocket as a knock sounded at the door.

Venli glanced toward Rlain and Hesina, but they'd apparently heard, for they covered up the crate of maps. It still looked suspicious to Venli, but she went to the door anyway. Fused wouldn't knock.

Accordingly, she opened the door and let in a group of humans who bore water jugs on poles across their shoulders. Six workers—the same ones as always. That was good, for although Venli had permission from Raboniel to bring a human surgeon in to care for the fallen Radiants, she had lied in saying she'd gone to the clinic to recruit him.

Eventually, Lirin and Hesina would be recognized—but best to limit their exposure to as few people as possible. The water carriers delivered their burdens to the room's large troughs, then helped with the daily watering of the patients. It demanded near-constant work to give broth and drink to so many unconscious people.

Venli checked the time by the Rhythm of Peace. She needed to visit Raboniel for translation duty soon—there were books in Thaylen that the Lady of Wishes wanted read to her.

She doesn't care about anything other than her research, Venli thought. *What could be so important?*

"You there," Lirin said. "What is that on your head?"

Venli turned to find the surgeon confronting one of the water bearers. Lirin pushed back the hair on the man's head and pointed. She hummed to Irritation—the surgeon was generally calm, but once in a while something set him off. She strode over to settle the situation, to find that the water bearer—a short man with far too much hair on his body—had painted his forehead with some kind of ink.

"What is that?" Venli asked.

"Nothing, Brightness," the man said, pulling out of Lirin's grip. "Just a little reminder." He moved on, but one of the other water carriers—a female this time—had a similar marking on her forehead.

"It's a *shash* glyph," Lirin said.

As soon as Venli knew it was writing, her powers interpreted it. "Dangerous? Why do they think they're dangerous?"

"They don't," Lirin said—wearing his upset emotions on his face. "They're fools."

He turned to go, but Venli caught him by the arm and hummed to Craving. Which of course he couldn't understand. So she asked, "What does it *mean?*"

"It's the brand on . . . on the forehead of Kaladin Stormblessed."

Ah . . . "He gives them hope."

"That hope is going to get them killed," Lirin said, lowering his voice. "This isn't the way to fight, not with how brutal the Regals in the tower have started acting. My son may have gotten himself killed resisting them. Heralds send it isn't true, but his example *is* going to cause trouble. Some of these might get the terrible idea of following in his steps, and that will inevitably provoke a massacre."

"Maybe," Venli said, letting him go. Timbre pulsed to an unfamiliar rhythm that echoed in her mind. What *was* it? She could swear she'd never heard it before. "Or maybe they simply need something to keep them going, surgeon. A symbol they can trust when they can't trust their own hearts."

The surgeon shook his head and turned away from the water carriers, instead focusing on his patients.

like many other spren in Shadesmar,
peakspren wear human clothing.

Peakspren fashion,
and to some degree
their textures, remind
me of the Unkalaki

The cracks in their skin
don't appear to affect
them in any way.

Some of these
cracks almost
seem to form
glyphs or symbols.

There is as much variety in color and texture to their stone
forms as could be imagined by any geologist. They can be as
smooth as polished marble or as rough as porous basalt.

In the Physical Realm, peakspren can disappear into
stone to stay hidden. To reappear, they break out of
other nearby stone, even if it's as small as a pebble.

*There was a time when others would approach me for help with a
problem. A time when I was decisive. Capable. Even authoritative.*

I t was a crystalline day in Shadesmar as Adolin—guarded as always by
two honorspren soldiers—climbed to the top of the walls of Lasting
Integrity. During his weeks incarcerated in the fortress, he'd discovered that there *were* weather patterns in Shadesmar. They just weren't the
same type as in the Physical Realm.

When he reached the top of the wall, he could see a faint shimmer
in the air. It was only visible if you could look a long distance. A kind of
violet-pink haze. Crystalline, they called it. On days like these, plants in
Shadesmar grew quickly enough to see the change with your eyes.

Other types of "weather" involved spren feeling invigorated or dreary,
or certain types of smaller spren getting more agitated. It was never about
temperature or precipitation.

From the top of the wall, he could really get a sense of the fortress's
size. Lasting Integrity was enormous, several hundred feet tall. It was also
hollow, and had no roof. Rectangular and resting on the small side, all
four of its walls were perfectly sheer, without windows. No human city
would ever have been built this way; even Urithiru needed fields at its base
and windows to keep the people from going mad.

But Lasting Integrity didn't follow normal laws of nature. You could walk
on the interior walls. Indeed, to reach the top, Adolin had strolled vertically up the inside of the fortress wall. His body thought he had been
walking on the ground. However, at the end of the path, he'd reached the

battlements. Getting onto them had required stepping off what seemed to be the edge of the ground.

As he'd done so, gravity had caught his foot, then propelled him over so he was now standing at the very top of the fortress. He felt vertigo as he glanced *down* along a wall he'd recently treated as the ground. In fact, he could see all the way to the floor hundreds of feet below.

Thinking about it gave him a headache. So he looked outward across the landscape. And the view . . . the view was spectacular. Lasting Integrity overlooked a sea of churning beads lit by the cold sun so they shimmered and sparkled, an entire ocean of captured stars. Huge swells washed through the bay and broke into crashing falls of tumbling beads.

It was mesmerizing, made all the more interesting by the lights that congregated and moved in the near distance. Tukar and the people who lived there, reflected in the Cognitive Realm.

The other direction had its own less dramatic charms. Rocky obsidian shores gave way to growing forests of glass, lifespren bobbing among the trees. Lifespren were larger here, though still small enough that he wouldn't have been able to see them save for the bright green glow they gave off.

These lights blinked off and on, a behavior that seemed unique to this region of Shadesmar. Watching, Adolin could swear there was a coordination to their glows. They'd blink in rippling waves, synchronized. As if to a beat.

He took it in for a moment. The view wasn't why he'd come, however. Not fully. Once he'd spent time drinking in the beauty, he scanned the nearby coast.

Their camp was still there, tucked away a short walk into the highlands, nearer the trees. Godeke, Felt, and Malli waited for the results of his trial. With some persuasion, the honorspren had allowed Godeke to come in, given him a little Stormlight, and let him heal Adolin's wound. The honorspren had expelled Godeke soon after, but permitted Adolin to communicate with his team via letters.

They'd traded—with his permission—a few of his swords to a passing caravan of Reachers for more food and water. Non-manifested weapons were worth a lot in Shadesmar. The Stump, Zu, and the rest of Adolin's soldiers had left to bring word to his father. Though Adolin had initially anticipated a quick and dramatic end to his incarceration, the honorspren hadn't wanted an immediate trial. He should have realized the punctilious spren would want time to prepare.

Though aspects of the delay were frustrating, the wait favored him. The longer he spent among the honorspren, the more chance he had to persuade them. Theoretically. So far, the spren of this fortress seemed about as easy to persuade as rocks.

One other oddity was visible from this high perch. Gathering on the coast nearby was an unusual group of spren. It had begun about two weeks ago as a few scattered individuals, but those numbers grew each day. At this point, there had to be two hundred of them. They stood on the coast all hours of the day, motionless, speechless.

Deadeyes.

"Storms," said Vaiu. "There are so many."

Vaiu was Adolin's primary jailer for excursions like this. He was a shorter honorspren and wore a full beard, squared like that of an ardent. Unlike many others, Vaiu preferred to go about bare-chested, wearing only an old-style skirt a little like an Alethi takama. With his winged spear, he seemed like a depiction of a Herald from some ancient painting.

"What happened to the ones you let in?" Adolin asked.

"We put them with the others," Vaiu explained. "Everything about them seems normal, for deadeyes. Though we don't have space left for more. We never expected . . ." He shook his head. There were no lights of souls near those deadeyes; this wasn't a gathering of Shardbearers in the Physical Realm. The deadeyes were moving of their own accord, coming up from the depths to stand out here. Silent. Watching.

The fortress had quarters for deadeyes. Though Adolin had little love for these honorspren and their stubbornness, he had to admit there *was* honor in the way they treated fallen spren. The honorspren had dedicated themselves to finding and caring for as many as they could. Though they'd taken Maya and put her in with the others, they let Adolin visit her each morning to do their exercises together. While they wouldn't let her wander free, she was treated quite well.

But what would they do with so many? The honorspren had taken in the first group, but as more and more deadeyes arrived, the fortress had reluctantly shut its gates to them.

"It doesn't make any sense," Vaiu said. "They should all be wandering the oceans, not congregating here. What provoked this behavior?"

"Has anyone tried asking them?" Adolin asked.

"Deadeyes can't talk."

Adolin leaned forward. Around his hands on the railing, pink crystal fuzz began to grow: the Shadesmar version of moss, spreading because of the crystalline day.

The distance was too great for him to distinguish one scratched-out face from another. However, he did notice when one vanished into mist. Those spren were Shardblades—hundreds of them, more than he'd known existed. When their owners summoned them, their bodies evaporated from

Shadesmar. Why were they here? Deadeyes usually tried to keep close to their owners, wandering through the ocean of beads.

"There is a Connection happening," Vaiu said. "Deadeyes cannot think, but they are still spren—bound to the spiritweb of Roshar herself. They can feel what is happening in this keep, that justice will finally be administered."

"If you can call it justice," Adolin said, "to punish a man for what his ancestors did."

"*You* are the one who suggested this course, human," Vaiu said. "You took their sins upon you. This trial cannot possibly make remediation for the thousands murdered, but the deadeyes sense what is happening here."

Adolin glanced at his other guard, Alvettaren. She wore a breastplate and a steel cap—both formed from her substance, of course—above close-cropped hair. As usual she stared forward, her lips closed. She rarely had anything to add.

"It is time for today's legal training," Vaiu said. "You have very little time until the High Judge returns and your trial begins. You had best spend it studying instead of staring at the deadeyes. Let's go."

⁖

Veil was really starting to hate this fortress. Lasting Integrity was built like a storming monolith, a stupid brick of a building with *no windows*. It was impossible to feel anything other than *trapped* while inside these walls.

But that wasn't the worst of it. The worst was how honorspren had no respect whatsoever for the laws of nature. Veil opened the door from the small building she shared with Adolin, looking out at what seemed to be an ordinary street. A walkway of worked stone led from her front door and passed by several other small buildings before dead-ending at a wall.

However, as soon as she stepped out, her brain started to panic. Another flat surface of stone hung in the air *above* her, instead of the sky. It was clustered with its own buildings—and people, mostly honorspren, walked along its pathways. To her left and right were two other surfaces, much the same.

The actual sky was *behind* her. She was walking on the inside surface of one of the walls of the fortress. It squeezed her mind, making her tremble. *Shallan*, Veil thought, *you should be leading. You'd like the way this place looks.*

Shallan did not respond. She huddled deep within, refusing to emerge. Ever since they'd discovered that Pattern had been lying to them, probably for years, she had become increasingly reclusive. Veil was able to coax her out now and then, but lately something . . . dangerous had come with her. Something they were calling Formless.

Veil wasn't certain it was a new persona. If it wasn't, would that be even worse?

Veil let Radiant take over. Radiant wasn't so bothered by the strange geometry, and she took off down the path without feeling vertigo—though even she had trouble sometimes. The worst parts were the strange halfway zones at the corners where each plane met, where you had to step from one wall to another. The honorspren did it easily, but Radiant's stomach did somersaults every time she had to.

Shallan, Radiant thought, *you should sketch this place. We should carry drawings with us when we leave.*

Nothing.

Honorspren liked to keep the hour exactly, so the bells told Radiant she was on time as she turned up the side of the wall toward the sky, passing various groups of spren going about their business. This wall of the fortress—the southern plane—was the most beautified, with gardens of crystalline plants of a hundred different varieties.

Fountains somehow flowed here, the only free water Radiant had seen in Shadesmar. She passed one fountain that surged and fell in powerful spouts; if a spray got beyond about fifteen feet high, the water would suddenly break off the top and stream down toward the *actual* ground rather than back toward the wall plane. Storms, this place didn't make any kind of sense.

Radiant turned away from the fountain and tried to focus on the people she was passing. She hadn't expected to find anyone other than honorspren in here, considering how strict the fortress was, but apparently its xenophobic policy had only been instituted a year ago. Any other people then living inside the fortress were allowed to stay, though they'd be forbidden reentry if they left.

That meant ambassadorial delegations from the other spren nations—as well as some tradespeople and random wanderers—had been grandfathered into the honorspren lockdown. Most importantly, seventeen humans lived here.

Without direction from Shallan, and with the honorspren taking their time preparing their trial, Radiant and Veil had reached a compromise. They'd find Restares, the person Mraize had sent them to locate. They wouldn't take any actions against him unless they could get Shallan to decide, but Radiant was perfectly willing to locate him. This man, the phantom leader of the Sons of Honor, was a key part of this entire puzzle—and she was intensely curious why Mraize wanted him so badly.

Restares was, according to Mraize, a human male. Radiant carried a description of the man in her pocket, though none of the honorspren Veil had asked knew the name. And unfortunately, the description was rather vague. A shorter human with thinning hair. Mraize said Restares was a secretive type, and would likely be using an alias and perhaps a disguise.

He was supposedly paranoid, which made perfect sense to Radiant. Restares led a group of people who had worked to restore the singers and the Fused. The coming of the Everstorm had led to the fall of multiple kingdoms, the deaths of thousands, and the enslavement of millions. The Sons of Honor were deplorable for seeking these things. True, it wasn't clear their efforts had in fact influenced the Return, but she could understand why they wanted to hide.

Upon first entering the fortress, she'd asked to be introduced to the other humans residing in the place. In response, the honorspren had given her the full list of all humans living here. With limited locations to search, she'd assumed her task would be easy. Indeed, it had started out that way. She'd started with the largest group of people: a caravan of traders from a kingdom called Nalthis, a place out in the darkness beyond the edges of the map. Veil had chatted with them at length, discovering that Azure—who had moved on from the fortress by now—was from the same land.

Radiant had trouble conceptualizing what it meant for there to be kingdoms out away from the continent. Did Azure's people live on islands in the ocean?

No, Veil thought. *We're avoiding the truth, Radiant. It means something else. Like Mraize told us. Those people came from another land. Another world.*

Radiant's mind reeled at the thought. She took a deep breath, slowing near a group of trees—real ones from the Physical Realm, kept alive with Stormlight instead of sunlight—that were the centerpieces of this park. The tops were so high that when leaves fell off, they drifted down toward the real ground, through the middle of the fortress.

Shallan, Radiant thought. *You could come and talk to people from other worlds. This is too big for Veil and me.*

Shallan stirred, but as she did, that darkness moved with her. She quickly retreated.

Let's focus on today's mission, Radiant, Veil said.

Radiant agreed, and forced Veil to emerge. She could handle the strange geography; she had to. She put her head down and continued. None of the travelers from Nalthis looked like Restares, or seemed likely to be him in disguise. The next handful on her list had been Horneaters; apparently there was a clan of them who lived in Shadesmar. She'd doubted any were Restares, but she'd interviewed each of them just in case.

That done, Veil had been left with five people. Four turned out to be wanderers. None had been open about their pasts, but over the weeks she'd met with them one by one. After conversing with each, she had reported on them to Mraize. He had eliminated each of those as possibilities.

Now, only a single name remained on her list. This person was the most reclusive of them all—but was male, and the descriptions of him from the honorspren indicated that he was probably her quarry. Today she would finally catch a glimpse of him. With the subject confirmed she could call Mraize, find out what message she was supposed to deliver to Restares, then be done with this mission.

The target called himself "Sixteen." He supposedly came out of his home once every sixteen days exactly—the regularity of it amused the honorspren, who suffered the odd fellow because of the novelty. No one knew how he survived without food, and no one reported a terrible stench or anything like that from him—though he didn't ever seem to bathe or empty a chamber pot. Indeed, the more she'd learned about him, the more Veil was certain this mysterious man was her target.

His home was a small box built near the statue garden. Veil had made a habit of visiting this garden, where she tried to coax Shallan out by drawing. It worked occasionally, though Shallan usually retreated after a half hour or so of sketching.

Today, Veil curled up on a bench with a sketchpad, coat enveloping her, hat shading her eyes. Today was the day that Sixteen would emerge, assuming he followed his pattern. All she had to do was wait and not act suspicious.

Shallan, Veil said, opening the sketchbook. *See? It's time to draw.*

Shallan started to emerge. Unfortunately, a faint humming sound made her panic and Veil was thrust back into control. She sighed, glancing to the side—to where Pattern walked among the statues, which she'd been told were of honorspren killed in the Recreance. Tall men and women with heroic builds and clothing that—though made of stone—seemed to ripple in the wind. How odd that they'd made these; after all, the real individuals were still around, though deadeyed.

Pattern bobbed over to her. He was easy to tell from other Cryptics; he had an excitable spring to his step, while others slunk or crept, more furtive.

"I thought you were watching the Nalthians today," Veil said.

"I was!" he said, plopping down on the bench beside her. "But Veil, I do not think any of them are Restares. They do not look like him at all. They do not even look like people from Roshar. Why do you think Azure appeared so much like an Alethi, when these have the wrong features?"

"Don't know," Veil said, pretending to sketch. "But this Restares could be using something like Lightweaving. I need you to watch them carefully."

"I am sorry," Pattern said, his pattern slowing, like a wilting plant. "I miss being with you."

You're worried you'll miss something important, traitor, Shallan thought. *And want an excuse to keep spying on me.*

Veil sighed again. She reached over and put her hand on Pattern's. He hummed softly.

We need to confront him, Radiant thought. *We need to find out exactly why he is lying.*

Veil wasn't so certain. It was all growing so messy. Pattern, Shallan's past, the mission they were on. She needed Shallan to remember. That would solve so much.

Wait, Radiant thought. *Veil, what do you know? What do you remember that I do not?*

"Veil?" Pattern asked. "Can I talk to Shallan?"

"I can't force her to emerge, Pattern," Veil said. Stormwinds; she suddenly felt so tired. "We can try later, if you want. For now, Sixteen is going to come out of that house in a few minutes. I need to be ready to intercept him in a way that reveals his face, but doesn't make him suspicious of me."

Pattern hummed. "Do you remember," he said softly, "when we first met on the boat? With Jasnah? Mmm . . . You jumped in the water. She was so shocked."

"Nothing shocks Jasnah."

"That did. I barely remember—I was so new to your realm."

"That wasn't the first time we met though," Radiant said, sitting up straighter. "Shallan had spoken oaths before, after all. She had a Shardblade."

"Yes." If he had been human, his posture would have been described as unnaturally still. Hands clasped, seated primly. His pattern moved, expanding, contracting, rotating upon itself. Like an explosion.

"I think," he finally said, "we have been doing this wrong, Radiant. I once tried to help Shallan remember, and that was painful for her. Too painful. So I started to think it was good for her not to remember. And the lies *were* delicious. Nothing is better than a lie with so much truth."

"The holes in her past," Radiant said. "Shallan doesn't want to remember them."

"She can't. At least not yet."

"When Shallan summoned you as a Blade," Radiant said, "and killed her mother, were you surprised? Did you know she was going to do something that drastic?"

"I . . . don't remember," Pattern said.

"How can you not remember?" Radiant pressed.

He remained quiet. Radiant frowned, considering the lies she'd caught him in during the last few weeks.

"Why did you want to bond a human, Pattern?" Radiant found herself asking. "In the past, you've seemed so certain that Shallan would kill you. Yet you bonded her anyway. Why?"

This is a dangerous line of questioning, Radiant, Veil warned. *Be careful.*

"Mmm . . ." Pattern said, humming to himself. "Why. So many answers to a why. You want the truest one, but any such truth is also a lie, as it pretends to be the only answer." He tipped his head to the right, looking toward the sky—though so far as she knew, he didn't "see" forward, as he didn't have eyes. He seemed to sense all around him.

She glanced in the same direction. Colors shimmered in the sky. It was a crystalline day.

"You and the others," Pattern said, "refer to Shadesmar as the world of the spren, and the Physical Realm as 'your' world. Or the 'real' world. That is not true. We are not two worlds, but one. And we are not two peoples, but one. Humans. Spren. Two halves. Neither complete.

"I wanted to be in the other realm. See that part of our world. And I knew danger was coming. All spren could sense it. The Oathpact was no longer working correctly. Voidspren were sneaking onto Roshar, using some kind of back door. Two halves cannot fight this enemy. We need to be whole."

"And if Shallan killed you?"

"Mmm. I was sure you would. But together, we Cryptics thought we needed to try. And I volunteered. I thought, maybe even if I die it will be the step other spren need. You cannot reach the end of a proof without many steps in the middle, Shallan. I was to be the middle step." He turned toward her. "I no longer believe you will kill me. Or perhaps I wish to no longer believe you will kill me. Ha ha."

Radiant wanted to believe. She wanted to know.

This will lead to pain, Veil warned.

"Can I trust you, Pattern?" Radiant asked.

"Any answer will be a lie," he said. "I cannot see the future like our friend Renarin. Ha ha."

"Pattern, have you lied to us?"

His pattern wilted. ". . . Yes."

Radiant took a deep breath. "And have you been spying on us? Have you been using the cube Mraize gave us, in secret?"

"I'm sorry, Radiant," he said softly. "I couldn't think of another way."

"Please answer the questions."

"I have," he said, his pattern growing even smaller.

There, Radiant thought. *Was that so hard? We should have asked him right away, Veil.*

It was only then that she noticed, deep inside, that Shallan was seething. Twisting about herself, trembling, fuming, alternating between terror and anger.

That . . . didn't seem good.

Pattern's pattern swirled small and tight. "I try to be worthy of trust. That is not a lie. But I have brought someone for Shallan to meet. I think it is important."

He stood with a smooth inhuman motion, then gestured behind him with one long-fingered hand. Radiant frowned and glanced over her shoulder. Leaves from the trees farther up the plane lazily drifted down the central corridor. A faint shimmer dusted the air, and a small crystal tree started to grow in miniature on the bench beside her hand.

Standing near a statue behind them was a dark figure wearing a stiff robe. Like Pattern's, but dustier. And a head trapped in shadow. Twisted and wrong.

Damnation, Veil thought.

Shallan emerged. She grabbed Radiant, shoved her away someplace dark and small, and slammed the door shut.

Shallan . . . Veil thought, then her voice crumpled. She should remain sectioned away. In the past, they hadn't talked to one another this way. They'd simply taken turns being in control, as they were needed.

Shallan was in control. The other two became whispers. "No," she said to Pattern. "We are not doing this."

"But—" he said.

"*NO,*" she said. "I want *nothing* from you, Pattern. You are a traitor and a liar. You have betrayed my trust."

He wilted, flopping onto the bench. Shallan saw movement from the corner of her eye and spun, her heart thundering in her ears. The small building she'd come here to watch—Sixteen's home—had opened, and a furtive figure had emerged. Hunched over, face hidden in the cowl of a cloak, the figure hurried through the statue park.

Excellent. It was time to fulfill Mraize's mission.

Shallan . . . Veil whispered.

She ignored the voice and settled down on the bench, acting nonchalant as she opened her notebook. Veil's plan had included wandering through the statue park, idly flipping through her notebook, then bumping into Sixteen—hopefully getting a good look at his face.

Unfortunately, Shallan wasn't in position yet to do that. She'd been distracted by Pattern and his lies. She stood and meandered toward the statue garden, trying to appear nonthreatening. She needed to determine for certain that Sixteen was her target. Then . . .

Then what.

Kill him.

What are you doing? Veil thought. Such a distant, annoying voice. Couldn't she quiet it entirely?

You were the one who wanted to go forward with Mraize's plan, Shallan thought. *Well, I agree. So two of us have decided.*

I wanted to gather information, Veil thought. *I wanted to use it against him. Why are you suddenly so aggressive?*

Because this was exactly who Shallan was. Who she'd always been. She stalked toward the statue garden. Radiant was, of course, screaming and railing at her—but she was outvoted.

Shallan had been watching and learning these last months, and she'd picked up some things from Veil. She knew to get into Sixteen's blind spot, then stop and appear like she was sketching a statue—so when he turned to glance around, she seemed unremarkable.

She knew to glide forward when he turned away. She knew to step carefully, putting the heel of her foot down first and rolling toward the toe. She knew to walk on the sides of her feet as much as possible, not letting the flats slap.

She got right up behind Sixteen as he hunched over, fiddling with some notes. She grabbed him by the shoulder, then spun him around. His hood fell, revealing his face.

He was Shin; there was no mistaking that pale, almost sickly skin and those childlike eyes. Restares was a short Alethi man with wispy hair. This man was short, yes, but completely bald, and was not Alethi. So unless Mraize was wrong and Restares was a Lightweaver, this was not her man.

He shouted and said something to her in a language she didn't recognize. She released him, and he fled toward his home. Her heart thumping in her chest, she pulled her hand out of the satchel. She hadn't even realized she'd reached into that, for a weapon.

She didn't need it. This wasn't him.

Pattern walked up, having recovered some of his characteristic perkiness. There was no sign of the other spren he'd wanted her to meet.

"Well!" he said. "That was exciting. But this is not him, is it?"

"No," Shallan said. "It's not."

"Shallan, I need to explain to you. What I've been doing."

"No," Shallan said, covering her pain. "It is done. Let's move forward instead."

"Mmm . . ." Pattern said. "I . . . What has happened to you? Something has changed. Are you . . . Veil?"

"No," Shallan said. "I'm me. And I've finally made a difficult decision that was a long time coming. Come on, we need to report to Mraize. His intel was wrong—Restares is not in this fortress."

76

HARMONY

*Such skills, like my honor itself, are now lost to time. Weathered
away, crushed to dust, and scattered to the ends of the cosmere. I
am a barren tree of a human being. I am the hollow that once was a
mighty peak.*

The Sibling refused to speak to Navani.

She lowered her hand and stared at the garnet vein in the wall.
Such a wonderful secret. In plain sight, surrounding her all this
time. So common your eyes passed over it, and if you noticed it at all,
you remarked only briefly. Simply another pattern in the strata.

The soul of Urithiru had been watching her all along. Perhaps if Navani
had discovered it sooner, they could have achieved a different result.

She replaced her hand on the vein. "I'm sorry," she whispered. "Please
know that I'm sorry. Truly."

For the briefest moment, she thought the Sibling would respond this
time. Navani felt something, faint as the movement of a shadow deep
within the ocean. No words came.

With a sigh, Navani left the crystal vein and wound her way through
the shelves of the small library to reach her desk beside the door. Today,
in addition to the guard, Raboniel's daughter—with the topknot and the
vacant eyes—sat on the floor right inside.

Navani settled onto her seat, trying to ignore the insane Fused. Notes
and half-finished experiments cluttered her desk. She didn't have the least
bit of interest in continuing them. Why would she? Everything she'd attempted so far had been a sham. She wrote out her daily instructions to the

scholars—she was having them perform tests on Voidspren fabrials, which Raboniel had delivered before everything went wrong. She gave this to a messenger, then sat there staring.

Eventually Raboniel herself made an appearance, wearing an Alethi havah that fit her surprisingly well. Clearly a good dressmaker had tailored it to the Fused's taller, more broad-shouldered frame. One might have thought her form would make her unfeminine, particularly with the unpronounced bust common to most singer femalens. Instead—with the excellent cut and the confidence of her stride—Raboniel wore the dress as if it had always been designed to accentuate someone of height, power, and poise. She had made this fashion her own. Adolin would have approved.

At least he was safe. Adolin, Renarin, Jasnah, Dalinar, and little Gav. Her entire family safe from the invasion and the mess Navani had made. It was one small blessing she could thank the Almighty for sending her.

Raboniel had brought a stool—a low one, so that when she sat on it, she was at eye level with Navani. The Fused set a basket on the floor, then pulled out a bottle of burgundy wine. A Shin vintage, sweeter than traditional Alethi wines, known as an *amosztha*—a Shin wine made from grapes.

"Your journals," Raboniel said, "indicate you are fond of this vintage."

"You read my journals?" Navani said.

"Of course," Raboniel said, setting out two glasses. "You would have wisely done the same in my position." She uncorked the bottle and poured half a cup for Navani.

She didn't drink. Raboniel didn't force her, instead inspecting the wine with an expert eye, then taking a sip. "Ah, yes," she said. "*That* is a taste infused with *memory*. Grapes. Your ancestors never could get them to live outside Shinovar. Too cold, I believe. Or perhaps it was the lack of soil. I found that explanation odd, as grapevines seem similar to many of our native plants.

"I wasn't there when your kind came to our world. My grandmother, however, always mentioned the smoke. At first she thought you had strange skin patterns—but that was because so many human faces had been burned or marked by soot from the destruction of the world they left behind.

"She talked about the way your livestock moaned and cried from their burns. The result of humans Surgebinding without oaths, without checks. Of course, that was before *any* of us understood the Surges. Before the spren left us for you, before the war started."

Navani felt the hair go up on the back of her neck as she listened. Storms. This creature . . . she had lived during the shadowdays, the time before history. They had no primary accounts of those days. Yet one sat before her, drinking wine from Navani's secret stash, musing about the origins of humanity.

"So long ago," Raboniel said, with a soft, almost indistinguishable cadence to her words. "So very, very long ago. What has it been? Seven *thousand* years? I don't think you can comprehend how tired I am of this war, Navani. How tired all of us are. Your Heralds too."

"Then let's end it," Navani said. "Declare peace. Withdraw from the tower and I will convince Dalinar to engage in talks."

Raboniel turned her wine cup around, as if trying to see the liquid within from different angles. "You think talks haven't been tried? We are born to fight one another, Navani. Opposites. At least so I thought. I always assumed that if Stormlight and Voidlight could be forced to truly mix, then . . . poof, they'd annihilate one another. Much as we're doing to one another in this endless war . . ."

"Is that what this is all about?" Navani asked. "Why you want me to combine the Lights so badly?"

"I need to know if you're right," Raboniel said. "If you are, then so much of what I've planned will collapse. I wonder . . . whether sometimes I can't see clearly anymore. Whether I assume what I *want* to be true *is* true. You live long enough, Navani, and you forget to be careful. You forget to question."

Raboniel nodded toward Navani's desk. "No luck today?"

"No interest," Navani said. "I think it is time for me to accept your initial offer and start carrying water."

"Why waste yourself like that?" Raboniel asked, her rhythm becoming intense. "Navani, you *can* still defeat me. If it wasn't possible for humans to outthink the Fused, you'd have fallen during the first few Returns. The first few Desolations, as you call them.

"Instead you always pushed us back. You fought with *stones,* and you beat us. My kind pretends we know so much, but during many Returns, we'd find ourselves struggling to *catch up* to your kind. That is our terrible secret. We hear the rhythms, we understand Roshar and the spren. But the rhythms don't change. The spren don't change.

"If you and I discover this secret together, you'll be able to use it better than I will. Watch and see. At the very least, prove me wrong. *Show* me that our two Lights can meld and mix as you theorize."

Navani considered it, though storms, she knew she shouldn't have. It was another trick—another catalyst added to the system to push the reaction forward. Yet Navani couldn't lie to herself. She *did* want to know. As always, questions teased her. Questions were disorder awaiting organization. The more you understood, the more the world aligned. The more the chaos made sense, as all things should.

"I've run into a problem," Navani said, finally taking a sip from her cup. "I can make the two Lights intersect—I can get them to pool around the same gemstone, swirling out like smoke caught in a current of air. But they won't mix."

"Opposites," Raboniel said, leaning forward to look at the diagrams and notes Navani had made on each failed attempt.

"No, merely inert substances," Navani said. "The vast majority of elements, when combined, produce no reaction. I'd have long ago named these two things immiscible if I hadn't seen Towerlight."

"It is what gave me the original idea," Raboniel said. "I decided if there was a hybrid between Honor's Light and Cultivation's, there must be a *reason* no one had mixed Odium's Light with either."

"Questions are the soul of science," Navani said, sipping her wine. "But assumptions must be proven, Ancient One. From my research I believe these two aren't opposites, but it isn't *proven* to me yet."

"And to prove it?"

"We need an emulsifier," Navani said. "Something that causes them to mix. Unfortunately, I can't fathom what such an emulsifier would be, though it might be related to sound. I only recently learned that Stormlight responds to tones."

"Yes," Raboniel said, taking a sphere off the desk. "The sounds of Roshar."

"Can you hear the Light?" Navani asked.

Raboniel hummed—then thought to nod—her response. She held up a diamond, crystalline and pure, filled with Stormlight from the highstorm the day before. "You have to concentrate, and know what you're seeking, to hear it from a sphere. A pure tone, extremely soft."

Navani hit the proper tuning fork, letting the tone ring in the room. Raboniel nodded. "Yes, that is it. Exactly the same. Only . . ."

Navani sat up. "Only?"

"The sphere's tone has a rhythm to it," Raboniel explained, eyes closed as she held the sphere. "Each Light has a rhythm. Honor's is stately. Cultivation's is stark and staccato, but builds."

"And Odium's?"

"Chaos," she said, "but with a certain strange logic to it. The longer you listen, the more sense it makes."

Navani sat back, sipping her wine, wishing she had access to Rushu and the other scholars. Raboniel had forbidden her from drawing on their expertise in this matter, giving the problem to Navani alone. Navani, who wasn't a scholar.

What would Jasnah do in this situation? Well, other than find a way to
kill Raboniel?

Navani felt the answers were right in front of her. So often, that was the case with science. The ancient humans had fought with stone weapons, but the secrets to metallurgy had been within their grasp. . . .

"Does Towerlight have a tone?" Navani asked.

"Two tones," Raboniel said, opening her eyes and setting down the Stormlight sphere. "But they aren't simply the tones of Cultivation and of Honor. They are . . . different, changed so that they are in harmony with one another."

"Curious," Navani said. "And is there a rhythm to it?"

"Yes," Raboniel said. "Both tones adopt it, harmonizing as they play the same rhythm. A symphony combining Honor's control and Cultivation's ever-building majesty."

Their Towerlight spheres had all run out by now, and Raboniel had no way to restore them, so there was nothing for them to check.

"Plants grow by Stormlight," Navani said, "if you beat the proper rhythm in their presence."

"An old agricultural trick," Raboniel said. "It works better with Lifelight, if you can find some."

"*Why*, though?" Navani asked. "Why does Light respond to tones? Why is there a rhythm that makes plants grow?" Navani dug in her materials and began setting up an experiment.

"I have asked myself this question many times," Raboniel said. "But it seems like asking why gravity pulls. Must we not accept some fundamentals of science as baselines? That some things in this world simply work?"

"No, we don't have to," Navani said. "Even gravity has a mechanism driving it. There are proofs to show why the most basic addition problems work. Everything has an explanation."

"I have heard," Raboniel said, "that the Lights respond to sound because it is reminiscent of the voice of the Shards commanding them to obey."

Navani hit the tuning forks, touched them to their respective gemstones, then put them in place. A thin stream of Stormlight ran from one gemstone, a thin stream of Voidlight from the other. They met together at the center—swirling around an empty gemstone. Neither Light entered it.

"Voidlight and Stormlight," Navani said. "The voices of gods." Or perhaps something older than that. The reason the beings called gods spoke the way they did.

Raboniel came in close, shoulder-to-shoulder with Navani as they observed the streams of Light.

"You said that Stormlight and Lifelight make a rhythm together when they mix," she said. "So, if you could imagine a rhythm that mixed Stormlight and *Voidlight*, what would it be like?"

"Those two?" Raboniel said. "It wouldn't work, Navani. They are opposites. One orderly, organized. The other . . ."

Her words drifted off, and her eyes narrowed.

". . . the other chaotic," Raboniel whispered, "but with a *logic* to it. An understandable logic. Could we perhaps contrast it? Chaos always seems more powerful when displayed against an organized background. . . ." Finally she pursed her lips. "No, I cannot imagine it."

Navani tapped the rim of her cup, inspecting the failed experiment.

"If you could hear the rhythms," Raboniel said, "you'd understand. But that is beyond humans."

"Sing one for me," Navani said. "Honor's tone and rhythm."

Raboniel complied, singing a pure, vibrant note—the tone of Stormlight, the same as made by the tuning fork. Then she made the tone waver, vibrate, pulse in a stately rhythm. Navani hummed along, matching the tone, trying to affix it into her mind. Raboniel was obviously overemphasizing the rhythm, making it easier for her to recognize.

"Change now," Navani said, "to Odium's rhythm."

Raboniel did so, singing a discordant tone with a violent, chaotic rhythm. Navani tried to match it with Honor's tone. She had vocal training, like any lighteyed woman of her dahn. However, it hadn't been an area of express study for her. Though she tried to hold the tone against Raboniel's forceful rhythm, she quickly lost the note.

Raboniel cut off, then softly hummed a different rhythm. "That was a fine attempt," Raboniel said. "Better than I've heard from other humans, but we must admit you simply aren't built for this kind of work."

Navani took a drink, then swirled the wine in her cup.

"Why did you want me to sing those rhythms?" Raboniel asked. "What were you hoping to accomplish?"

"I thought that perhaps if we melded the two songs, we could find the proper harmony that would come from a combination of Stormlight and Voidlight."

"It won't be that easy," Raboniel said. "The tones would need to change to find a harmony. I've tried this many times, Navani, and always failed. The songs of Honor and Odium do not mesh."

"Have you tried it with a human before?" Navani asked.

"Of course not. Humans—as we just proved—can't hold to a tone or rhythm."

"We proved nothing," Navani said. "We had a single failed experiment." She set her cup on the table, then crossed the room and dug through her things. She emerged with one of her arm sheaths, in which she'd embedded a clock and other devices. Like other Stormlight fabrials in the tower, it didn't work any longer. But it *was* rigged to hold a long sequence of gemstones.

Navani ripped off the interior leather of the sheath, then settled at the table and fiddled with the screws and set new gemstones—full of Stormlight—into it.

"What is this?" Raboniel said.

"You can hear the songs and rhythms of Roshar," Navani said. "Perhaps it's merely because you have better hearing."

Raboniel hummed a skeptical rhythm, but Navani continued setting the gemstones.

"We can hear them because we are the children of Roshar," Raboniel said. "You are not."

"I've lived here all my life," Navani said. "I'm as much a child of this planet as you are."

"Your ancestors were from another realm."

"I'm not speaking of my ancestors," Navani said, strapping the sheath on so the flats of the gemstones touched her arm. "I'm speaking of myself." She reset her experiment on the table, sending new lines of Stormlight and Void-light out of gemstones, making them swirl at the center around an empty one.

"Sing Honor's tone and rhythm again, Ancient One," Navani asked.

Raboniel sat back on her stool, but complied. Navani closed her eyes, tightening her arm sheath. It had been built as a fabrial, but she wasn't interested in that function. All she wanted was something that would hold large gemstones and press them against her skin.

She could feel them now, cool but warming to her touch. Infused gemstones always had a tempest inside. Was there a sound to them too? A vibration . . .

Could she hear it in there? The tone, the rhythm? With Raboniel singing, she thought she could. She matched that tone, and felt something on her arm. The gemstones reacting—or rather the Stormlight inside reacting.

There *was* a beat to it. One that Raboniel's rhythm only hinted at. Navani could sing the tone and feel the gemstones respond. It was like having a stronger singer beside her—she could adapt her voice to match. The Stormlight itself guided her—providing a control, with a beat and rhythm.

Navani added that rhythm to her tone, tapping her foot, concentrating. She imagined a phantom song to give it structure.

"Yes!" Raboniel said, cutting off. "Yes, that's it!"

"Odium's rhythm now," Navani said to Honor's tone and beat.

Raboniel did so, and it struck Navani like a wave, making her tone falter. She almost lost it, but the gemstones were her guide. Navani sang louder, trying to hold that tone.

In turn, Raboniel sang more forcefully.

No, Navani thought, taking a breath then continuing to sing. *No, we can't fight.* She took Raboniel's hand, singing the tone, but softer. Raboniel quieted as well. Holding the Fused's hand, Navani felt as if she were reaching for something. Her tone changed slightly.

Raboniel responded, their two tones moving toward one another, step by step, until . . .

Harmony.

The rhythms snapped into alignment, a burst of chaotic notes from Raboniel—bounded by a regular, orderly pulse from Navani.

Heartbeats. Drumbeats. Signals. *Together.*

Navani reached over and placed their clasped hands on the empty gemstone at the center of the experiment, holding them there as they sang for an extended moment in concert. In tandem, a pure harmony where neither took control.

The two of them looked at each other, then fell silent. Carefully, they removed their hands to reveal a diamond glowing a vibrant black-blue. An impossible color.

Raboniel trembled as she picked the gemstone out of its place, then held it up, humming a reverential rhythm. "They did not annihilate one another, as I assumed. Indeed, as part of me hoped. You were right, Navani. Remarkably, I have been proven wrong." She turned the gemstone in her fingers. "I can name this rhythm: the Rhythm of War. Odium and Honor mixed together. I had not known it before today, but I recognize its name; I know this as surely as I know my own. Each rhythm carries with it an understanding of its meaning."

The sphere they had created was different from Szeth's—blue instead of violet, and lacking the strange distortion. Navani couldn't be certain, but it seemed to her *that* was what Raboniel had been seeking.

"Ancient One," Navani said. "Something confuses me. Why would you have preferred that these two annihilate one another?" Navani had an inkling why. But she wanted to see what she could prompt the Fused to reveal.

Raboniel sat for a long time, humming softly to herself as she inspected the gemstone. She seemed fascinated by the motion within, the Stormlight and the Voidlight mixed to form something that surged in brilliant raging storms, then fell still—peaceful and quiet—between.

"Do you know," the Fused finally asked, "how Honor was killed?"

"I . . . am not certain I accept that he was."

"Oh, he was. At least the being you call the Almighty—the being who controlled the Shard of power that was Honor—is dead. Long dead. Do you know *how?*"

"No."

"Neither do I," Raboniel said. "But I wonder."

Navani sat back in her seat. "Surely, *if* it is true—and my husband says it is, so I accept the possibility—then the mechanisms of the deaths of gods are far beyond the understanding of humans and Fused alike."

"And did you not tell me earlier that *everything* has a mechanism? The gods give us powers. What are those powers? Gravitation, Division, Transformation . . . the fundamental Surges that govern all things. You said that nothing simply *is*. I accept that, and your wisdom. But by that same logic, the gods—the Shards—must work not by mystery, but by knowledge."

She turned the gemstone in her fingers, then met Navani's eyes. "Honor was killed using some process we do not yet understand. I assume, from things I have been told, that some *opposite* was used to tear his power apart. I thought if I could discover this opposite Light, then we would have power over the gods themselves. Would that not be the power to end a war?"

Storms. *That* was what he'd wanted. *That* was what Gavilar had been doing.

Gemstones. Voidlight. A strange sphere that *exploded* when affixed to a fabrial . . . when mixed with another Light . . .

Gavilar Kholin—king, husband, occasional monster—had been searching for a way to kill a god.

Suddenly, the extent of his arrogance—and his magnificent planning—snapped together for Navani. She knew something Raboniel did not. There *was* an opposite to Voidlight. It wasn't Stormlight. Nor was it this new mixed Light they'd created. But Navani *had* seen it. Held it. Her husband had given it to Szeth, who had given it to her.

By the holiest name of the Almighty . . . she thought. *It makes sense.* But like all great revelations, it led to a multitude of new questions. Why? How?

Raboniel stood up, completely oblivious to Navani's epiphany. The Fused tucked away the gemstone, and Navani forced herself to focus on this moment. This discovery.

"I thought for certain it was something about the nature of Odium's power contrasting Honor's power that led to the destruction," Raboniel said. "I was wrong, and you have proven exceedingly helpful in leading me to this proof. Now, I must abandon this line of reasoning and focus on my actual duty—the securing of the tower."

"And your promise that you would leave if I helped you find this Light?"

"I'm sorry," Raboniel said. "Next time, try not to be so trusting."

"In the end," Navani whispered, "you are his, and I am Honor's."

"Unfortunately," Raboniel said. "You may remain here and continue whatever other research you wish. You have earned that, and my gratitude. If you would like to seek a simple job in the tower instead, I will arrange it. Consider your options, then tell me your wishes." Raboniel hesitated. "It is rare for a Fused to be in the debt of a human."

With that, she left. Navani, in turn, downed the rest of the cup of wine, her head abuzz with implications.

77

THE PROPER LEGALITY

Venli ducked out of the way of a patrol of human guards. As she hid in the doorway, she attuned Peace in an attempt to calm her emotions. She'd come with her people to sign the treaty, but that—and the feast to mark the occasion—was still hours away. While her people prepared, Venli crept through forbidden hallways in their palace.

The pair of guards, chatting in the Alethi tongue, continued on their patrol. She breathed quietly, trying hard not to let the majesty of this human building overwhelm her. Ulim assured her that her people had built equally grand structures once, and they would again. They would build such amazing creations, this palace of Kholinar would look like a hut by comparison.

Would that she could skip this middle part, where she was required to be in such danger. Planning with Ulim, that she liked. Being famous for revealing warform, that she loved. This creeping about though . . . She'd expressly disobeyed human rules, slipping into forbidden sections of the palace. If she were caught . . .

She closed her eyes and listened to the Rhythm of Peace. *Only a little longer,* she thought. *Just until Ulim's companions reach us. Then this will all be over.*

However, she found herself questioning more now that Ulim had left her gemheart. Ulim spoke of a hidden storm and a coming war, with figures of legend returning to fight. That talk spun in her head—and things that seemed so rational a day ago now confused her. Was this really the best way to convince her people to explore forms of power? Wasn't she toying with war and destruction? Why *was* Ulim so eager?

As soon as they'd reached the palace, he'd insisted that she help him gather a bag of gemstones left by his agent here. More spren, like him, ready to be delivered to Venli's scholars. That hadn't been part of the original plan. She'd merely wanted to show her people how dangerous the humans were.

But what was she to do? She'd started this boulder rolling down the cliff. If she tried to stop it now, she'd be crushed. So she continued doing as he said. Even if, without him in her gemheart, she felt old and dull. Without him, she couldn't hear the new rhythms. She craved them. The world made more sense when she listened to those.

"There you are," Ulim said, zipping down the hallway. He moved like lightning, crawling along the top of the stone—and he could vanish, making only certain people able to see him. "Why are you cringing like a child? Come on. We must be moving."

She glanced around the corner. The guards had long since moved on. "I shouldn't have to do this," Venli hissed at him. "I shouldn't have to expose myself."

"Someone needs to carry the gemstones," Ulim said. "So unless you want me to find someone *else* to be the greatest among your people, do what I say."

Fine. She crept after him, though she'd lately found Ulim's tone increasingly annoying. She disliked his crass, dismissive attitude. He'd better not abandon her again. He had claimed he needed to scout the way, but she was half convinced he wanted her to be discovered.

He led her up a stairwell. The Rhythm of Fortune blessed her, and she emerged onto the top floor without meeting any humans—though she did have to hide in the stairwell as more guards passed.

"Why must we come all the way up here!" she hissed after they passed. "Couldn't your friend have brought the gemstones into the basement, where all the other listeners are?"

"I . . . lost contact with her," Ulim admitted.

"You *what*?" Venli said.

He whirled on the floor, then the lightning rose up to form his little humanlike figure. "I haven't heard from Axindweth in a few days. I'm certain it's all right. We have a meeting point where she leaves things for me. The gemstones will be there."

Venli hummed to Betrayal. How could he leave out such an important detail? She was sneaking through the human palace—jeopardizing the treaty—based on flawed information? Before she could demand more answers, however, Ulim turned back into a patch of energy on the floor and shot forward.

She had no choice but to scramble after him across the hallway, feeling terribly exposed. They should have brought Demid. She liked how he listened to what she said, and he always had a ready compliment. He'd enjoy sneaking about, and she'd feel braver with him along.

She wove through the hallways, certain she'd be discovered at any moment. Yet by some miracle, Ulim got her through to a small room with chamber pots scattered across the floor. She pulled out a gemstone and noted a hole in the floor on one side of the room—it looked like they dumped waste in here, pouring it into some foul cesspit several stories below.

This was her goal? A privy? She gagged, and was forced to start breathing through her mouth.

"Here," Ulim said, crackling on the side of one of the chamber pots.

"So help me," Venli said to Skepticism, "if I find human waste inside . . ."

She removed the lid. Fortunately, the interior was clean and empty save for a folded piece of paper.

Ulim pulsed to Exultation. He'd been worried, it seemed. Venli unfolded the paper, and knew the Alethi script well enough to figure out it was a list of cleaning instructions.

"It's ciphered," Ulim said. "Do you think we'd be so stupid as to leave notes in the open where anyone could read them? Let me interpret. . . ."

He formed into the shape of a human, standing on a table full of pots. She hated that he took a human form rather than that of a listener. He leaned forward, his eyes narrow.

"Bother," he said.

"What?"

"Let me think, femalen," he snapped.

"What does it say?"

"Axindweth says she's been discovered," he said. "She's a very specific and rare kind of specialist—the details need not concern you—but there is apparently another of her kind in the palace. An agent for someone else. They found her and turned the human king against her. She's decided to pull out."

". . . Pull out?" Venli said. "I don't understand that phrasing."

"She's leaving! Or left. Perhaps days ago."

"Left the palace?"

"The *planet*, you idiot."

Ulim blurred, carapace-like barbs breaking his skin and jabbing out, then retracting. It seemed to happen to the beat of one of the new rhythms, perhaps Fury.

Ulim told her so little. Venli knew there was a way to travel from this world to the place the humans called Damnation. The land of the Voidspren. Many thousands of spren waited there to help her people, but they couldn't get free without some Surge or power. Something to . . . pull them across the void between worlds.

So what did this mean? Had his agent returned to the world Ulim had come from? Or had she gone someplace else? Was she gone for good? How were they going to transfer spren across to this land, to build power for the storm?

Most importantly, did Venli *want* that to happen? He'd promised her forms of power, but she'd assumed that she'd bring this to the Five after frightening them with how powerful the humans were. Everything was moving so quickly, slipping out of her control. She almost demanded answers, but the way those spikes broke Ulim's skin—the way he pulsed— made her remain quiet. He was a force of nature come alive. And the particular force he exhibited now was destructive.

Eventually his pulsing subsided. The spikes settled beneath his skin. He remained standing on the table, staring at the sheet of paper with the offending words.

"What do we do?" Venli finally asked.

"I don't know. There is nothing here for us. I . . . I have to leave, see if I can find answers elsewhere."

"Leave?" Venli said. "What about your promises? What about our plans?"

"We *have no plans*!" Ulim said, spinning on her. "You said coming here would *intimidate* your people. Is that happening? Because from what *I've* seen, they seem to be enjoying themselves! Planning to feast and laugh, maybe get into storming bed with the humans!"

Venli attuned Determination, and then it faded to Reconciliation. She had to admit it; her people *weren't* intimidated, not like she was. Even Eshonai had grown more relaxed—not more worried—as they'd interacted with the humans. These days, Venli's sister didn't even wear warform.

Venli wanted to blame her alone, but the problems with the listeners were far bigger than Eshonai. No one else seemed to see what Venli did. They should have been terrified by all the parshmen—the enslaved singers—in the palace. Instead, Venli's people seemed *curious*.

No one saw the threat Venli did. She didn't understand, or believe, some of the things Ulim said. But in coming here, Venli realized for herself that the humans could not be trusted. If she didn't do anything, it would be her people—her *mother*—enslaved to the humans.

Ulim formed into crackling lightning and zipped down the table leg and along the floor. She took a step after him, attuning the Terrors—but he was gone, out under the door. By the time she looked into the hall, he'd vanished.

She closed the door and found herself breathing heavily. She was alone in the enemy's stronghold, having snuck into forbidden hallways. What should she do? What *could* she do?

Wait. Ulim would come back.

He didn't though. And each moment she stood there attuned to the Terrors was more excruciating than the last. She had to strike out on her own. Perhaps she could sneak back the way she'd come? She ripped up the note, then dumped it out the shaft with the waste. She attuned Determination and slipped from the room.

"You there!"

She cringed, attuning Mourning. One hallway. She hadn't been able to cross even *one hallway*.

A human soldier in a glistening breastplate marched up, a long, wicked weapon in his hand—a spear, but with an axe's head.

"Why are you here?" he asked her in the Alethi tongue.

She played dumb, speaking in her own language. She pointed toward the steps. Perhaps if he thought she couldn't speak Alethi, he'd simply let her go?

Instead he took her roughly by the arm and marched her along the hallway. Each time she tried to pull away he yanked harder, leading her down the steps and through this maze of a palace. He eventually deposited her in a room where several women were writing with spanreeds—Venli still wished her people knew how to make those. A gruff older soldier with a proper beard took reports.

"Found this one on the top floor," the guard said, pushing Venli into a seat. "She was poking around in a suspicious way."

"Does she speak Alethi?" asked the man with the beard.

"No, sir," the man said. He saluted, then returned to his post.

Venli sat quietly, trying not to attune rhythms with too much dread. Surely this wouldn't look *too* bad. She could complain she got lost. And wandered up several flights of stairs . . . And snuck past guards . . . When they'd been told several times to stay away . . .

When I find Ulim again, she thought, attuning Betrayal, *I will* . . . What? What could she do to a spren? What was she without him and his promises? She suddenly felt very, very small. She *hated* that feeling.

"You look like one of their scholars," the older man said, his arms folded. "You really can't speak Alethi? Or were you playing dumb?"

"I . . . was playing dumb." She immediately regretted speaking. Why had she exposed herself?

The man grunted. Their version of attuning Amusement, she thought. "And what were you doing?"

"Looking for the privy."

Dead flat stare. The human version of attuning Skepticism.

"I found it," she said to Reconciliation. "Eventually. Room with all the pots."

"I'm going to note this," he said, nodding to one of the scribes, who began writing. "Your name?"

"Venli," she said.

"If you were a human, I'd lock you up until someone came for you—or I'd give you to someone who could get me answers. But that treaty is being signed tonight. I don't want to cause any incidents. Do you?"

"No, sir," she said.

"Then how about this? You sit here, in this room with us, for the next four hours. Once the feast happens and the treaty is signed, we'll see. Everything happens without a problem, and you can go in for the after-feast. Something goes wrong . . . well, then we'll have another conversation, won't we?"

Venli attuned Disappointment, but nothing was going to happen. She'd probably suffer nothing more than a talking-to from her sister. Part of her would rather be locked up.

She nodded anyway. In truth, she found the man's actions surprisingly rational. Keeping her close would stop anything she might have planned—and if she truly was a lost guest, he wouldn't be in any real trouble for holding her for a few hours.

She contemplated insisting she was too important for this. She discarded that idea. Caught so quickly after being abandoned by Ulim . . . Well, it was hard to keep pretending she was strong. The feeling of smallness persisted.

The soldier left her to go talk quietly to the women, and Venli made out some of their conversation. He had them report to other guard stations in the palace, informing them he'd picked up a wandering "Parshendi" and asking if anyone else had seen individuals entering forbidden or suspicious locations.

Venli found herself attuning *Praise* unexpectedly. It was . . . nice to be alone. Lately, Ulim had always been around. She began thinking about how she could clean this up. Go talk to the Five. Maybe—despite how much it hurt to admit it—go ask Eshonai for advice.

Unfortunately, Ulim soon zipped in through the open door as a trail of red lightning. She hummed Confusion, then Betrayal, as he moved up her chair leg and formed into a person on her armrest.

"We have a big problem," Ulim said to her.

She hummed a little louder.

"Oh, get over yourself, girl," he said. "Listen, there are *Heralds* in the palace tonight."

"Heralds?" she whispered. "Here? They're dead!"

"Hush!" he said, glancing over his shoulder at the humans. "They're not dead. You have no idea how royally, colossally, *incredibly* ruined we are. I saw Shalash first and followed her—then ran across not only Kalak, but *Nale*. I think he saw me. He shouldn't have been able to, but—"

A figure darkened the doorway to the guard post. The bearded soldier looked up. Venli turned slowly, attuning Anxiety. The newcomer was an imposing figure with deep brown skin and a pale mark on his cheek, almost like a listener might have as part of their skin pattern. He was in uniform, though it wasn't of the cut the Alethi wore.

He looked at Venli, then pointedly at Ulim—who groaned. Then the man finally looked over at the soldier.

"Ambassador?" the guardsman asked. "What do you need?"

"I heard a report that you are holding one of the thinking parshmen here," the newcomer said. "Is this her?"

"Yes," the guardsman said. "But—"

"I request," the man said, "to have this prisoner released into my care."

"I don't think I can do that, Ambassador," the guardsman said, glancing at the scribes for confirmation. "You . . . I mean, that is a *very* unusual request."

"This femalen is important to this night's activities," the man said. He stepped forward, placing something on the nearest scribe's desk. "This is a seal of deputation. I have legal jurisdiction in this land, as granted by your king. You will authenticate it."

"I'm not sure . . ." the scribe woman said.

"You will authenticate it," the man repeated. Perfectly void of emotion or rhythm. He made Venli feel cold. Particularly as he turned toward her.

Behind him, the scribes began scribbling with their spanreeds. The newcomer blocked most of Venli's view of them.

"Hello, Ulim," the man said in a soft, steady voice.

"Um . . . hello, Nale," the spren said. "I . . . um. I didn't expect to see you here. Um, today. Anytime, actually . . . Ever . . . How is, ah, Shalash?"

"Small talk is unnecessary, Ulim," Nale said. "We are not friends. You persist only because I cannot destroy spren." The strange man affixed his unblinking gaze on Venli. "Listener. Do you know what this is?"

"Just another spren," she said.

"You are wise," Nale said. "He *is* just another spren, isn't he? How long have you known him?"

Venli didn't reply—and she saw Ulim pulse to Satisfaction. He did not want her speaking.

"Brightlord," one of the scribes called. "It appears you are correct. You may requisition this prisoner. We were simply going to hold her until—"

"Thank you," Nale said, taking his seal from the scribe, then walked out into the hall. "Follow, listener."

Ulim hopped onto her shoulder and grabbed hold of her hair. "Go ahead," he whispered. "But don't tell him anything. I am in so much trouble. . . ."

Venli followed the strange man from the guard room. She'd never seen a human that shade before, though it wasn't a true onyx like a listener pattern. This was more the color of a rockbud shell.

"How many are there?" Nale asked her. "Spren like him? How many have returned?"

"We—" Ulim began.

"I would hear the listener," Nale said.

She'd rarely known Ulim to be quiet, and he rarely did as she asked. At *this* man's rebuke, however, Ulim fell immediately silent. Ulim was *frightened* of this being. So did that mean the songs about them were true?

A Herald. Alive.

Ulim was right. The Return had begun. The humans would soon be marching to destroy her people. It was the only conclusion she could come to, based on her knowledge of the songs. And based on meeting this man.

Storms. Her people *needed* forms of power.

And to get them, she somehow had to navigate this conversation without being murdered by this creature.

"Answer my question," the Herald said. "How many spren like him are there? How many Voidspren have returned?"

"I have seen only this one," Venli said.

"It is impossible that he has remained on Roshar all these years," Nale said. "It has been . . . a long time, I believe. Generations perhaps, since the last true Desolation?"

How could this creature not remember how long it had been since the Returns ended? Perhaps he was so far above mortals that he didn't measure time the same way.

"I thought it impossible for them to cross the distance between worlds," Nale said. "Could it have been . . . No. Impossible. I've been vigilant. I've been careful. You must tell me! How did you accomplish his return?"

So cold. A voice with no rhythms, and no human emotions. Yet those words . . . He was raving. Perhaps it wasn't that he measured time differently, but that he was addled? Though she'd been considering telling him the truth, that instinct retreated before his dead words.

She might not trust Ulim completely, but she *certainly* couldn't turn to this Herald instead.

"We didn't do anything to return them," she said, taking a gamble based on what he'd said earlier. "It was what *you* did."

"Impossible," Nale repeated. "Ishar said only a Connection between the worlds could cause a bridge to open. And Taln has not given in. I would know if he had. . . ."

"Do not blame us," Venli said, "for your failure."

Nale kept his eyes forward. "So, Gavilar's plan is working. The fool. He will destroy us all." Nale sneered, a sudden and unexpected burst of emotion. "That foolish idiot of a man. He lures us with promises, then breaks them by seeking that which I *told* him was forbidden! Yes. I heard it tonight. The proof I need. I know. I know. . . ."

Storms, Venli thought. *He really is mad.*

"I have been vigilant," the man ranted. "But not vigilant enough. I must take care. If the bonds start forming again . . . if we let the pathway open . . ." He suddenly stopped in the hallway, making her halt beside him. His face became flat again. Emotionless. "I believe I must offer you a service, listener. The king is planning to betray your people."

"What?" she said.

"You can prevent disaster," Nale said. "There is a man here in the city tonight. I have been tracking him due to his unusual circumstances. He possesses an artifact that belonged to a friend of mine. I have sworn not to touch said artifact, for . . . reasons that are unimportant to you."

Confusion thrummed in Venli's ears. But on her shoulder, Ulim had perked up.

"I have legal jurisdiction here to act on behalf of the king," Nale said. "I cannot, however, take specific action *against* him. Tonight I found reason to have him killed, but it will take me months of planning to achieve the proper legality.

"Fortunately, I have read your treaty. There is a provision allowing one party to legally break it and attack the other—should they have proof the other is conspiring against them. I know for a fact that Gavilar is planning to use this very provision to assault your people in the near future. I give you this knowledge, sworn by a Herald of the Almighty. You have proof that he is conspiring against you, and may act.

"The man who can help you is a slave for sale in the market. The person who owns him is hoping some of the king's wealthy visitors will want to pick up new servants before the feast. You have little time remaining. The slave you want is the sole Shin man among the crowd. The gemstones your people wear as ornaments will be enough to buy him."

"I don't understand," Venli said.

Nale looked at Ulim on her shoulder. "This Shin man bears Jezrien's Blade. And he is expertly trained in its employ." He looked back to Venli. "I judge you innocent of any crime, using provision eighty-seven of the Alethi code—pardon of a criminal who has a more vital task to perform for the good of the whole."

He then strode away, leaving them in the hall.

"That was . . ." Ulim said. "Wow. He's far gone. As bad as some of the

Fused. But that was well done, Venli. I'm trying not to sound too surprised. I think you may have fooled someone who is basically a god."

"It's an old trick, Ulim," she said. "Everyone—humans, listeners, and apparently gods—deep down suspects that every failure is their own. If you reflect blame on them, most people will assume they are responsible."

"Maybe I gave up on you too easily," he said. "Old Jezrien's Blade is here, is it? Curious . . ."

"What does that mean?"

"Let's say," Ulim told her, "your people were to start a war with the humans. Would that lead your people to the desperation we want? Would they take the forms we offer?"

"Attack the humans?" Venli said to Confusion. They stood alone in the hallway, but she still hushed her voice. "Why would we do what that Herald said? We're not here to *start* a war, Ulim. I merely want to get my people ready to face one, should the humans try to destroy us!"

Ulim crackled with lightning, then moved up her arm, toward her gemheart. She hesitated to let him in. He worked in strange ways, not according to the rules. He could move in and out of her without a highstorm to facilitate the transformation.

He began to vibrate energy through her. *You were so clever, Venli, tricking Nale. This is going to work. You and me. This bond.*

"But . . . a war?"

I don't care why Nale thought we should attack the king, Ulim said. *It has given me a seed of an idea. It's not his plan, but* your *plan we're following. We came here to make your people see how dangerous the humans are. But they are foolish, and you are wise. You can see how much of a threat they are. You need to show them.*

"Yes," Venli said. That *was* her plan.

Ulim slipped into her gemheart.

The humans are planning to betray you, Ulim said. *A Herald confirmed it. We* must *strike at them first.*

"And in so doing, make our people desperate," Venli said. "When the humans retaliate, it will threaten our destruction. Yes . . . Then I could persuade the listeners they need forms of power. They must accept our help, or be annihilated."

Exactly.

"A war would . . . likely mean the deaths of thousands," Venli said, attuning Anxiety. The rhythm felt small and weak. Distant. "On both sides."

Your people will be restored to their true place as rulers of this entire land,

Ulim said. *Yes, blood will spill first. But in the end you will rule, Venli. Can you pay this small price now, for untold glories in the future?*

If it meant being strong enough to never again be weak? Never again feeling as small as she had today?

"Yes," she said, attuning Destruction. "What do we do?"

Inkspren weapons may or may not be
sheathed, and sometimes hang in the air
at their sides or backs, not needing to
be attached physically to remain with them.

They do not wear armor.
Instead, the armor is a part of
their form and sometimes defies
human concepts of anatomy

It reminds me less of steel
and more of shell or carapace

Each surface has an
iridescent sheen, a
rainbow shimmer that
moves independently of
the surrounding lights

In the Physical Realm,
inkspren can change their
size, but not their shape.
They can be as large as a human,
or as small as a speck of
dust, but they will always
look like themselves.

78

THE HIGH JUDGE

So, words. Why words, now? Why do I write?

Shallan hurried into the room she shared with Adolin, putting the strange experience with Sixteen behind her. No need to think about . . . that other spren. The Cryptic deadeye. *Stay focused, and don't let Radiant slip out again.*

Pattern shadowed her, closing the door with a click. "Aren't you supposed to be meeting with Adolin right now?"

"Yes," Shallan said, kneeling beside the bed and pulling out her trunk. "That makes this the best time to contact Mraize, as we don't risk Adolin walking in on us."

"He will wonder where you are."

"I'll make it up to him later," Shallan said, unlocking the trunk and looking in.

"Veil?" Pattern said, walking up.

"No, I'm Shallan."

"Are you? You feel wrong, Shallan. Mmm. You must listen. I did use the cube. I have a copy of the key to your trunk. Wit helped me."

"It's no matter," Shallan said. "Done. Over. Don't care. Let's move on and—"

Pattern took her hands, kneeling beside her. His pattern, once so alien to her eyes, was now familiar. She felt as if by staring at its shifting lines, she could see secrets about how the world worked. Maybe even about how she worked.

"Please," Pattern said. "Let me tell you. We don't have to talk about your past; I was wrong to try to force you. Yes, I did take the cube. To talk to Wit. He has a cube like it too, Shallan! He told me.

"I was so worried about you. I didn't know what to do. So I went to him, and he said we could talk with the cube, if I was worried. Mmm . . . About what was happening with you. He said I was very funny! But when I talked to him last, he warned me. He's been spied on by the Ghostbloods. The things I told him, another heard. That was how Mraize knew things."

"You talked to Wit," Shallan whispered. "And a spy overheard? That . . . That means . . ."

"None of your friends are traitors," Pattern said. "Except me! Only a little though! I am sorry."

No spy. And Pattern . . .

Was this another lie? Was she getting so wrapped up in them that she couldn't see what was true? She gripped his too-long hands. She wanted so badly to trust again.

Your trust kills, Shallan, the dark part of her thought. The part she named Formless. Except it wasn't formless. She knew exactly what it was.

For now, she retreated—and released Veil and Radiant. Veil immediately took control and gasped, putting her hand to her head. "Storms," she whispered. "That was a . . . strange experience."

"I have made things worse," Pattern said. "I am very foolish."

"You tried to help," Veil said. "But you should have come to me. I'm Veil, by the way. I could have helped you."

Pattern hummed softly. Veil got the sense that he didn't trust her completely. Well, she wasn't certain she trusted her own mind completely, so there was that.

"There's a lot to think about in what you said," Veil said. "For now, please don't keep anything more from us. All right?"

Pattern's pattern slowed, then quickened, and he nodded.

"Great." Veil took a deep breath. Well, that was over.

Who killed Ialai? Shallan whispered from inside.

Veil hesitated.

Perhaps Pattern was *the one who moved the cube all those times,* Shallan said. *And he's the reason Mraize knew about the seed we planted about the corrupted spren. But someone killed Ialai. Who was it?*

Storms. There was more to this mess. A lot more. Veil, however, needed time to digest it. So for now, she put all of that aside and picked up the communication cube. She repeated the incantation. "Deliver to me Mraize, cube, and transfer my voice to him."

It took longer this time than others; she didn't know what the difference was. She sat there some ten minutes before Mraize finally spoke.

"I trust you have only good news to report, little knife," his voice said.

"It's bad news—but you're getting it anyway," she said. "This is Veil, with Pattern here. We've eliminated the final human in Lasting Integrity from consideration. Either Restares has learned to disguise himself beyond my ability to spot him, or he's not here."

"How certain are you of this?" Mraize said, calm. She'd never seen him get upset at bad news.

"Depends," she said. "Like I said, he *could* have disguised himself. Or maybe your intel is wrong."

"It's possible," Mraize admitted. "Communication between realms is difficult, and information travels slowly. Have you asked if any humans left the fortress recently?"

"They claim the last human who left was five months ago," she said. "But that was Azure, not Restares. I know her. I've described our quarry to several honorspren, but they say the description is too vague, and that many humans look alike to them. I'm inclined to think they're telling the truth. They completely neglected to mention that Sixteen—the person I've spent the last few days planning to intercept—was Shin."

"Troubling," Mraize said.

"You've been vague in your answers to me," Veil said. "Let me ask clearly. Could Restares have become a Lightweaver? Cryptics have different requirements for bonding than most Radiants."

"I highly doubt Restares would have joined any Radiant order," Mraize said. "It's not in his nature. I suppose, however, that we can't discount the possibility. There are variations on Lightweaving in the cosmere that do not require a spren—plus the Honorblades exist and are poorly tracked these days, even by our agents."

"I thought they were all in Shinovar, except the one Moash wields."

"They were." Mraize said it simply, directly, with an implication: She wasn't getting any more information on that topic. Not unless she finished this mission, whereupon he had promised to answer all her questions.

"You should equip yourself with Stormlight," Mraize suggested. "If you have not found Restares, there is a chance he knows you are there—and that could be dangerous. He is not the type to fight unless cornered, but once pushed, there are few beings as dangerous on this planet."

"Great, wonderful," Veil said. "Nice to know I have to start sleeping with one eye open. You could have warned me."

"Considering your paranoia, would you have done anything differently?" Mraize sounded amused.

"You're probably right about the Stormlight," Veil said. "The honorspren do have a store of it; they let us use it to heal Adolin. Makes me wonder where they obtained all the perfect gemstones to hold it for so long."

"They've had millennia to gather them, little knife," Mraize said. "And they love gemstones, perhaps for the same reason we admire swords. During the days of the Radiants, some even believed the stories of the Stone of Ten Dawns, and spent lifetimes hunting it. How will you obtain Stormlight from these honorspren?"

"I'll begin working on a plan," she said.

"Excellent. And how is your . . . stability, little knife?"

She thought about Shallan taking control, locking Veil and Radiant away somehow. "Could be better," she admitted.

"Answers will help free you," Mraize said. "Once you've earned them."

"Perhaps," Veil said. "Or perhaps you'll be surprised at what I already know." The trouble wasn't getting answers. It was finding the presence of mind to accept them.

Now, was there a way she could confirm what Pattern had said? About Wit, and the Ghostbloods spying on him? She toyed with the idea, but decided not to say anything. She didn't want to tell Mraize too much.

Her musings were interrupted by the sound of people shouting. That was uncommon here in honorspren territory.

"I need to go," she told Mraize. "Something's happening."

<hr />

The honorspren had a multitude of reasons for delaying Adolin's trial. Their first and most obvious excuse was the need to wait for the "High Judge," a spren who was out on patrol. Adolin had spent weeks assuming this was the Stormfather, because of things they'd said. Yet when he'd mentioned that the other day, the honorspren had laughed.

So now he had no idea who or what the High Judge was, and their answers to him were strange. The High Judge was some kind of spren, that seemed clear. But not an honorspren. The judge was of a variety that was very rare.

In any case, waiting for the High Judge to return gave the honorspren time to prepare documentation, notes, and testimonies. Had that all been ready, though, they wouldn't have allowed the trial to proceed yet. Because Adolin, they explained, was an idiot.

Well, they didn't say it in so many words. Still, he couldn't help but suspect that was how they felt. He was woefully ignorant of what they considered proper trial procedure. Thus he found himself in today's meeting. Every two days he had an appointment for instruction. The honorspren were quite clear: His offer, worded as it had been, let them condemn him as a traitor and murderer. Though that hadn't completely been his intent, this trial would let them pin the sins of the ancient Radiants on him. Before they did so, they wanted him to understand proper trial procedure. What strange beings.

He stepped softly through the library, a long flat building on the northern plane of Lasting Integrity. Honorspren liked their books, judging by the extensive collection—but he rarely saw them in here. They seemed to enjoy owning the books, treating them like relics to be hoarded.

His tutor, on the other hand, was a different story. She stood on a step stool, counting through books on an upper shelf. Her clothing, made of her substance, was reminiscent of a Thaylen tradeswoman's attire: a knee-length skirt with blouse and shawl. Unlike an honorspren, her coloring was an ebony black, with a certain sheen in the right light. Like the variegated colors oil made on a sword blade.

She was an inkspren; Jasnah had bonded one, though Adolin had never seen him. This one called herself Blended—a name that felt peculiar to him.

"Ah, Highprince," she said, noting him. "You *are*."

"I am," he said. During their weeks talking together, he'd grown mostly accustomed to her distinctive style of speaking.

"Good, good," she said, climbing down the steps. "Our time nearly is not. Come, we must talk."

"Our time nearly is not?" Adolin said, hurrying alongside her. She was shorter than most honorspren, and wore her hair—pure black like the rest of her—pinned up in something that wasn't quite a braid. Though her skin was mostly monochrome black, faint variations outlined her features, making her round face and small nose more visible.

"Yes," she said. "The honorspren have set the date for your trial. It is."

"When?"

"Three days."

"The High Judge is here, then?" Adolin asked as they reached their study table.

"He must be returning soon," she said. "Perhaps he already *is* in this place. So, we must make decisions." She sat without ceasing her torrent of words. "You are not ready. Your progress is not, Highprince Adolin. I do not say this to be insulting. It simply is."

"I know," he said, sitting down. "Honorspren law is . . . complex. I wish you could speak for me."

"It is not their way."

"It seems designed to be frustrating."

"Yes," she agreed. "This is unsurprising, as it was devised by a stuck-up bunch of prim, overly polished buttons."

There was no love lost between inkspren and honorspren. And Blended was supposedly among the more diplomatic of her type—she was the official inkspren emissary to Lasting Integrity.

"I know an honorspren in my realm," Adolin said. "She can be . . . interesting at times, but I wouldn't call her prim."

"The Ancient Daughter?" Blended asked. "She's not the only one whose personality *is* as you speak. Many honorspren used to be like that. Others still are. But Lasting Integrity, and those who here are, have had a strong effect on many honorspren. They preach isolation. Others listen."

"It's so extreme," Adolin said. "They must see there is a better way of dealing with their anger at humans."

"Agreed. A better solution is. I would simply kill you."

Adolin started. ". . . Excuse me?"

"If a human tries to bond me," Blended said, flipping through the books in her stack, "I will attack him and kill him. This better solution is."

"I don't think Radiants *force* bonds," Adolin said.

"They would coerce. I would strike first. Your kind are not trustworthy." She set aside one of her books, shaking her head. "Regardless, I am worried about your training. It is weak, through no fault of yours. The honorspren will use the intricacies of their laws against you, to your detriment. You will be as a child trying to fight a duel. I believe trials among your kind are more direct?"

"Basically, you go before the lighteyes in charge and plead your case," Adolin said. "He listens, maybe confers with witnesses or experts, then renders judgment."

"Brief, simple," she said. "Very flawed, but simple. The honorspren of this region like their rules. But perhaps a better solution is." She held up one of the books she'd been looking through when he arrived. "We can motion for a trial by witness. A variety more akin to what you know already."

"That sounds great," Adolin said, relaxing. If he had to listen to one more lecture including terms like "exculpatory evidence" and "compensatory restitution," he would ask them to execute him and be done with it.

Blended took notes as she spoke. "It is well I spent these weeks training you in basics. This will prepare you for your best hope of victory, which is this format. Therefore, before I explain, recite to me your general trial strategy."

They'd gone over this dozens of times, to the point that Adolin could have said it backward. He didn't mind; you drilled your soldiers in battle formations until they could do maneuvers in their sleep. And this trial would be like a battle; Blended had repeatedly warned him to be wary of verbal ambushes.

"I need to persuade them that I cannot be held accountable for the actions of the ancient Radiants," Adolin said. "That they cannot shun me or my father because of things done by ancient humans. In order to accomplish this, I will prove my character, I will prove that the modern Radiants are unconnected to the old orders, and I will prove that our actions in the face of the current crisis are proof of the honor men display."

Blended nodded. "We will choose a trial by witness. Assuming your motion is accepted, the trial will happen in three phases over three days. The first day, the High Judge is presented with three testimonies against your cause. The next day, you give your testimony. The final day, accusers are allowed one rebuttal, then judgment is requested. This format is not often chosen, because it allows so much weight of testimony against you. However, factoring in how weak your grasp of legal systems is, well . . . this choice is best."

Adolin felt a tremble deep inside. He wished for a fight he could face with sword in hand—but that was the trouble. Any given Radiant could do better than he at such a fight, so his expertise with the sword was effectively obsolete. He could not train himself to the level of a Radiant; they could heal from wounds and strike with supernatural grace and strength. The world had entered an era where simply being good at swordplay was not enough.

That left him to find a new place. Father always complained about being unsuited for diplomacy; Adolin was determined not to make the same complaint. "If I may plead my case on the second day," he said, "then I'm for it. The other methods you suggested would require me to understand too much of their law."

"Yes," Blended said. "Though I worry that in giving testimony, you will incriminate yourself. Worse, you risk asking questions of the audience, presenting an opening for their condemnations. You could end up one man facing a crowd of experts in the law and rhetoric."

"I *have* to speak for myself though," Adolin said. "I fail to see how I can achieve what I want without talking to them. I need to prove myself and appeal to their honor."

Blended flipped through pages of notes. He'd noticed that when she wouldn't look at him, it meant she had something difficult to say.

"What?" Adolin asked her.

"You believe much in their honor, Prince Adolin. Your sense of justice . . . is."

"They are honorspren," he said. "Don't they basically *have* to be honorable?"

"A conundrum is in this thing," Blended said. "Yes, they *are* honorspren. But honor . . . isn't something that . . . that *is*."

"What do you mean?"

"Men define honor," Blended said. "And no god can enforce it, no longer. Beyond that, spren like us are not mindless things. Our will is strong. Our perceptions mold our definitions of concepts such as honor and right and wrong. Just as with humans."

"You're saying that what they perceive as honorable might not be what I perceive as honorable. Syl warned me as much."

"Yes," she said. "What they *are* defines honor to them. *Whatever* they are."

"That's . . . frightening," Adolin admitted. "But there is goodness to them. They care for the deadeyes, even Maya, with great concern and attention."

"Hmmm, yes," Blended said. "That one. Did another spren tell you her name?"

"No, she told me herself."

"Deadeyes don't speak. This is."

"You all keep saying that, but you're wrong," Adolin said. "I heard her in my mind. Only once, true, but she said her name. Mayalaran. She's my friend."

Blended cocked her head. "Curious. Very curious . . ."

"Deep down, the honorspren must want to help. Surely they'll listen to me. Surely I can make them see."

"I will give you the best chance I can," she said. "But please understand. Spren—all spren—fear you with *good* reason. In order to prove you wrong, they need only prove that bonding men *is* a risk. That past failings of men *justify* wariness."

"Everything is a risk," Adolin said.

"Yes. Which is why this trial . . . is not strong for you. This truth *is*, Prince Adolin."

"To hear you say it like that," he said, trying to laugh about it, "it sounds like I have no chance!"

She closed her book. And did not respond.

He took a deep breath. "All right. How do we proceed?" he asked.

"I suspect the best thing is to discover if the High Judge's return is." Blended stood up, leaving the books on the table as she strode toward the doors. Adolin was expected to keep up. She claimed to hate the honorspren because of an ancient rivalry, but she sure did act like them. Neither gave much deference to human titles, for example. Adolin didn't consider himself stuck-up, but couldn't they treat him with a little more respect?

Outside, as always, he had that moment of jarring disconnect—his brain trying to reconcile that down wasn't down and up wasn't up. That people walked along all four faces inside the rectangular tower.

He doubted he could ever feel at ease in this place. The spren claimed it was not Surgebinding that let them walk on the walls here; the long-standing presence of the honorspren instead allowed the tower to choose a different type of natural law. Perhaps that sort of talk made sense to Shallan. Where was she anyway? She was often late to these tutoring meetings, but she usually showed up.

Blended led him across to the corner where the northern plane met the western plane; most of the official buildings were on the western one.

Adolin always found this part curious; he had to step out and put one leg on the wall. He followed that by leaning back as he lifted his other leg, feeling like he was about to fall. Instead everything seemed to rotate, and he found himself standing on another plane.

"You do that better than most humans," Blended noted. "They often seem nauseated by the process."

He shrugged, then followed as she walked him toward a row of short buildings clustered near the base of the tower. Most buildings in Lasting Integrity were only one story. He wasn't certain what happened if they got too tall; were you in danger of falling off?

They passed groups of honorspren, and he thought about what Blended had said regarding their natures. Not simply of honor—of honor as defined by the spren themselves. Well, maybe they weren't all as stuffy as they seemed. He'd catch laughter or a hint of a mischievous grin. Then an older uniformed honorspren would walk past—and everyone would grow solemn again. These creatures seemed trapped between an instinct for playfulness and their natures as the spren of oaths.

He anticipated another tedious discussion with the honorspren who managed his case—but before Adolin and Blended entered the building of justice, she stopped and cocked her head. She waved for him to follow in another direction, and he soon saw why. A disturbance was occurring on the ground plane, near the gates into the city. A moment of panic made him wonder if his friends had decided to rescue him against his wishes— followed by a deeper worry that all those deadeyes outside had snapped and decided to rush the fortress.

It was neither. A group of spren crowded around a newly arrived figure. "The High Judge?" Adolin guessed.

"Yes," Blended said. "Excellent. You can make your petition to him." She walked that direction, down along the face of the western plane.

Adolin followed until he saw the details of the figure everyone was making such a fuss over.

The High Judge, it appeared, was human.

❖❖

"Human?" Veil said, stopping in place. "That's impossible."

She squinted at the figure below, and didn't need to get close to see what her gut was already telling her. A short Alethi man with thinning hair. That was him, the one she'd been hunting. The High Judge was Restares.

"Mmm..." Pattern said. "They *did* say the High Judge was a spren. Perhaps the honorspren lied? Mmm..."

Veil stepped up to a small crowd of honorspren who had gathered on the southern plane to gawk at the newcomer. One was Lusintia, the honor-spren assigned to show Veil around on her first day in the fortress. She was a shorter spren, with hair kept about level with the point of her chin. She didn't wear a uniform, but the stiff jacket and trousers she preferred might as well have been one.

Veil elbowed her way over to Lusintia, earning shocked glances from the honorspren, who generally didn't crowd in such a way. Pattern followed in her wake.

"That can't be the High Judge," Veil said, pointing. "I *specifically* asked if the High Judge was human."

"He's not," Lusintia said.

"But—"

"He might have the form of a man," Lusintia said. "But he is an eternal and immortal spren who blesses us with his presence. That is Kalak, called Kelek'Elin among your people. Herald of the Almighty. He commanded us not to tell people he was here—and ordered us specifically to not speak of him to humans, so we were not allowed to answer your questions until you saw him for yourself."

One of the Heralds. Damnation.

The man Mraize had sent her to find—and, she suspected, the man he wanted her to kill—was one of the *Heralds*.

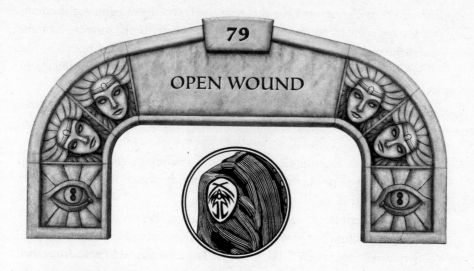

Jezrien is gone. Despite being all the way out here in Lasting Integrity, I felt him being ripped away. The Oathpact was broken already, but the Connection remained. Each of us can sense the others, to an extent. And with further investigation, I know the truth of what happened to him. It felt like death at first, and I think that is what it ultimately became.

Rlain stepped into the laundry room, and felt every single *storming* head in the place turn to look at him. The singer guards at the door perked up, one nudging the other and humming to Curiosity. Human women working the large tubs of sudsy water turned as they scrubbed. Men who were toiling at bleaching vats—with long poles to move the cloth inside—stopped and wiped brows. Chatter became whispers.

Rlain. Traitor. Reject. Oddity.

He kept his head high—he hadn't lived through Bridge Four to be intimidated by a quiet room and staring eyes—but he couldn't help feeling like he was the one gemstone in the pile that didn't glow. Somehow, with the singers invading Urithiru, he'd become *more* of an outsider.

He strode past the vats and tubs to the drying station. Some of the tower's original fabrials—the lifts, the main wells, the air vents—had been altered to work with Voidlight. That meant the workers here could set out large racks for drying in this room where the vents blew a little stronger. There was talk that the Fused would get other fabrials in the tower working soon, but Rlain wasn't privy to their timelines.

Near the drying racks he found a small cart waiting for him, filled with clean bedding. He counted the sheets as the foreman—a lighteyed human who always seemed to be standing around when Rlain visited—leaned against the wall nearby, folding his arms.

"So," he said to Rlain, "what's it like? Roaming the tower. Ruling the place. Pretty good, eh?"

"I don't rule anything," Rlain said.

"Sure, sure. Must feel good though, being in charge of all those people who used to own you."

"I'm a listener," Rlain said to Irritation. "I was never an Alethi slave, just a spy pretending to be one." Well, except for Bridge Four. That had felt like *true* slavery.

"But your people are in charge now," the man prodded, completely unable to take a hint.

"They aren't my people," Rlain said. "I'm a listener—I come from an *entirely* different country. I'm as much one of them as *you* are an Iriali."

The man scratched his head at that. Rlain sighed and wheeled the cart over to pick up some pillows. The women there didn't usually talk to him, so he was able to pile up the pillows without getting more than a few scowls.

He *could* hear their whispers, unfortunately. Better than they probably thought he could.

". . . Don't speak too loudly," one was saying. "He'll report you to them."

"He was here all along," another hissed. "Watching the Windrunners, planning when best to strike. He's the one who poisoned them."

"Hovers over them like a vengeful spren," a third said. "Watching to kill any who wake up. Any who—"

She squealed as Rlain spun toward the three women. Their eyes opened wide and they drew back. Rlain could *feel* their tension as he walked up to them.

"I like cards," he said.

The three stared at him in horror.

"Cards," Rlain said to Longing. "I'm best at towers, but I like runaround too. I'm pretty good, you know. Bisig says it's because I'm good at bluffing. I find it fun. I *like* it."

The three women exchanged looks, obviously confused.

"I thought you should know something about me," Rlain said. "I figured maybe if you did, you would stop making things up." He nodded to them, then forcibly attuned Peace as he went back to tie the pillows into place on the top of his cart. As he began wheeling it away, the whispers started again.

"You heard him," the first woman hissed. "He's a gambler! Of course.

Those kind can see the *future*, you know. Foul powers of the Void. He likes to take advantage of those unwise enough to bet against him. . . ."

Rlain sighed, but kept going. At the door, he knew to step to the side as one of the singer guards tried to trip him. They hadn't tired of that same old terrible trick—no matter how many times he visited. He shoved his way out the door quickly, but not before one of them called, "See you tomorrow, traitor!" to the Rhythm of Reprimand.

Rlain pushed the cart through the halls of Urithiru. There were a lot of people out, both human and singer. Bringing water from the wells was a full-time duty for many hundreds of workers. A lot of the population had moved away from the perimeter, which was growing too cold. Instead they crowded together into these interior rooms.

Humans gave way for him. Most of the singers didn't glance at him, but those who did usually noticed his tattoo. Their rhythms changed, and their eyes followed him. Some hated him for the treason of his ancestors. Others had been told the listeners were a brave frontrunner group who had prepared for Odium's return. These treated Rlain with reverence.

In the face of it all—the frightened humans, the mistrusting Regals, the occasionally awed ordinary singers—he wished he could simply be *Rlain*. He hated that to every one of them, he was some kind of representation of an entire people. He wanted to be seen as a person, not a symbol.

The closest he'd come had been among the men of Bridge Four. Even though they'd named him "Shen," of all things. That was like naming one of their children "Human." But for all their faults, they had succeeded in giving him a home. Because they'd been willing to try to see him for himself.

As he pushed his cart, he caught sight of that cremling again. The nondescript brown one that would scuttle along walls near the ceiling, blending in with the stonework. They were still watching him.

Venli had warned him about this. Voidspren invisibility didn't work properly in the tower. So it appeared that, to keep an eye on someone here, they'd begun entering an animal's gemheart. He tried to pretend he hadn't seen it. Eventually, it turned and scuttled down a different hallway. Voidspren weren't fully able to control the animals they bonded; though apparently the dumber the animal, the easier they were to influence. So there was no way of telling if the Voidspren had decided it had seen enough for the day, or if its host was merely distracted.

Rlain eventually reached the atrium, and like many people, he briefly basked in the light coming through the large eastern window. There was always a lot of traffic in here these days. Though only the privileged among the singers were allowed to use the lifts, people of both species came here for light.

He crossed the atrium with his cart, then pushed it through into the Radiant infirmary. He still couldn't relax—as a surprising number of humans moved through the room among the unconscious Radiants.

Ostensibly they all had a reason to be there. Water carriers, people to change the bedpans, others recruited to help feed broth to the Radiants. There were always new volunteers—the men and women of the tower were turning coming here into some kind of pilgrimage. Look in on the Radiants. Care for them. Then go burn prayers for them to recover. None of the people working in here seemed bothered by the fact that—not two years ago—they would have cursed by the Lost Radiants.

Eyes chased Rlain as he—forcing himself to walk to the beat of the Rhythm of Peace—delivered the cart of freshly laundered sheets and pillows to those changing them. A man with one arm and haunted eyes was overseeing this work today. Like most of the others in the room, he'd painted his forehead with the *shash* glyph. That baffled Rlain.

A few days ago, Lezian the Pursuer had ordered his men to beat those who wore the forehead mark—though only a day later, that order had been reversed by Raboniel. Still seemed strange that so many humans would wear the thing. They had to realize they were singling themselves out.

Though he'd been forced to rein in his men, and there had been fewer incidents recently, the Pursuer continued to push for more brutality in the tower. Unnervingly, he'd placed a few guards here in the infirmary: two stormform Regals currently, on rotation with several other Regals, who stood watch at all hours.

Rlain felt their stares on him as he walked to the back of the room where Lirin and Hesina had used hanging sheets to section off a part as a kind of office and living quarters for themselves. Rlain forced himself to attune Confidence until he could step between the sheets.

Inside he found Lirin peeking out at the stormforms. A small surgery station was set up behind him, where Lirin could see patients—because of course he needed to do that. Kaladin had spoken of his father, and Rlain felt he knew Lirin and Hesina, though he'd interacted with them in person for only a few weeks.

"Well?" Rlain asked.

"The stormforms have seen me and Hesina," Lirin whispered. "We couldn't stay hidden all the time. But I don't think it matters. By this point, *someone* must have recognized us. I wouldn't be surprised if those Regals were sent here in the first place because this 'Pursuer' discovered we were here."

"Maybe you should remain quiet," Rlain said, searching the ceiling for cremlings. "Or maybe we should get you out."

"We've been watching for cremlings," Lirin said. "And haven't seen any.

Nothing so far. As for the Pursuer, Venli says that we should be safe from him, so long as that Heavenly One, Leshwi, protects us."

"I don't know how much I trust any of them, Lirin," Rlain said. "Particularly Fused."

"Agreed," Lirin said. "What games are they playing? Leshwi didn't even ask after my son. Do you have any idea why they are acting this way?"

"Sorry," Rlain said. "I'm baffled. Our songs barely mention the Fused except to say to avoid them."

Lirin grunted. Like the others, he seemed to expect Rlain to understand the Fused and Regals more than he did—but to the surgeon's credit, he and Hesina had accepted Rlain without suspicion, despite his race. For all that Lirin complained about Kaladin, it seemed he considered someone his son called a friend to be worthy of trust.

"And Venli?" Lirin asked. "She wears a Regal form. Can we trust her?"

"Venli could have left me in prison," Rlain said. "I think she's proven herself."

"Unless it's a long con of some sort," Lirin said, his eyes narrowing.

Rlain hummed to Reconciliation. "I'm surprised to hear of your suspicion. Kaladin said you always saw the best in people."

"My son doesn't know me nearly as well as he presumes," Lirin said. He continued standing by the drapes.

Rlain made his way past the surgery table to where Hesina had set out one of his stolen maps on the floor. There, he hummed to Anxiety. "Maybe we shouldn't have these out," he whispered. "With those Regals around."

"We can't live our lives terrified of enemies at every corner, Rlain," Hesina said. "If they wanted to take us, they'd have done it already. We have to assume we're safe, for now."

Rlain hummed to Anxiety. But . . . there was wisdom in her words. He forced himself to calm. He had seen that cremling, yes, but didn't *know* it had a Voidspren. Perhaps he *was* jumping at shadows. Likely, he was just on edge because of the way everyone treated him during his trips through the tower.

"I keep thinking," Hesina said, looking over the map, "that if we could get this to Kal, it might help."

Rlain glanced at Lirin, humming to Curiosity. Hesina wouldn't catch the rhythm, but she clearly understood his body language.

"Lirin's dispute is not mine," Hesina said. "He can play the stoic pacifist all he wants—and I'll love him for it. But I'm not going to leave Kal out there alone with no help. You think if he had exact maps of the tower, he might have a better chance?"

"Couldn't hurt," Rlain said, kneeling beside her. They'd all heard about what Kaladin had done the other day—appearing spectacularly in the Breakaway market, engaging the Fused, fighting in the air.

The Fused were obviously frightened. They had immediately started publicizing that they'd killed him. Too quickly, and too forcefully, without a body to show. The people of the tower weren't buying it, and neither was Rlain. He'd joined Bridge Four later than most, but he'd been there for Kaladin's most dramatic transformations. Stormblessed was alive in the tower somewhere, planning his next move.

Hesina continued to pore over the map of the tower's sixth floor—but Rlain noticed something else. Hesina had set another map aside, one of the Shattered Plains. Rlain unrolled it fully and found himself attuning the Rhythm of the Lost. He'd never seen a full map, this detailed, of the entire Plains.

The immensity didn't surprise him. He'd been out there as both listener and bridgeman. He'd flown with the Windrunners. He understood the scope of the Shattered Plains, and was prepared for Narak to seem diminutive when compared to the expanse of plateaus stretching in all directions. But he wasn't prepared for how *symmetrical* it all was, now that he could see it all at once.

Yes, the Plains had most definitely been broken in a pattern. He hummed to Curiosity as he peered closer, and he picked out some cramped writing on the far eastern side of the Plains—where the plateaus were worn smaller by the winds. That was the direction the chasmfiends migrated after breeding or pupating. A dangerous area full of greatshells, herd animals, and predators as large as buildings.

"Hesina?" Rlain said, turning the map in her direction. "Can you read this part to me?"

She leaned over. "Scout report," she said. "They found a camp out there, it seems. Some kind of large caravan or nomadic group. Maybe they're Natans? A lot of this area is unexplored, Rlain."

He hummed to himself, wondering if he should learn to read. Sigzil was always talking about how useful it was, though Rlain didn't like the idea of relying on written words that had no life, instead of on songs. A piece of paper could be burned, lost, destroyed in a storm—but an entire people and their songs could not be so easily . . .

He trailed off. An entire people. It struck him anew that he was alone.

No, Venli is here, he thought. There were two of them. He'd never particularly liked Venli, but at least he wasn't the sole listener. It made him wonder. Should they . . . try to rebuild? The idea nauseated him for multiple reasons. For one, the times he'd tried mateform himself, things hadn't gone the way he—or anyone really—had expected.

Lirin abruptly pulled back from the curtains. His motion was so sudden that Hesina took it as a warning and immediately grabbed a sheet and pulled it over the maps. Then she laid out some bandages—to appear as if she'd spread the sheet onto the floor to keep the bandages clean as she rolled them. It was an excellent cover-up—one Rlain ruined by belatedly moving to tuck away his map of the Shattered Plains.

"It's not that," Lirin said, grabbing Rlain by the shoulder. "Come look. I think I recognize one of the workers."

Lirin pointed out through the drapes, directing Rlain toward a short man. He had a mark on his forehead, but it wasn't an inked *shash* glyph. It was a Bridge Four tattoo like Rlain's own. Dabbid kept his eyes down, walking with his characteristic sense of mute subservience.

"I think that man was one of Kaladin's friends," Lirin said. "Am I right?"

Rlain nodded, then hummed softly to Anxiety and stepped out into the main room. He and Dabbid had often been set to work together as the only two members of Bridge Four who hadn't gained Windrunner abilities. Seeing him opened that wound again for Rlain, and he hummed forcibly to Peace.

It wasn't his fault that spren were as racist as humans. Or as singers. As people.

He quietly took Dabbid by the arm, steering him away from the Regals. "Storms, I'm glad to see you," Rlain whispered. "I was worried about you, Dabbid. Where have you been? Were you frightened? Here, come help me bring some water to the others. Like the work we used to do, remember?"

He could imagine the poor mute hiding in a corner, crying as enemies flooded the tower. Dabbid had become kind of a mascot for Bridge Four. One of the first men Kaladin had saved. Dabbid represented what had been done to them, and the fact that they'd survived it. Wounded, but still alive.

Dabbid resisted as Rlain tugged him toward the water trough. The shorter bridgeman leaned in, then—remarkably—*spoke*.

"Rlain," Dabbid said. "Please help. Kaladin is asleep, and he won't wake up. I think . . . I think he's dying."

80

THE DOG
AND THE DRAGON

The singers first put Jezrien into a gemstone. They think they are clever, discovering they can trap us in those. It only took them seven thousand years.

Kaladin existed in a place where the wind hated him.

He remembered fighting in the market, then swimming through the well. He vaguely remembered running out into the storm—wanting to let go and drop away.

But no, he couldn't give up. He'd climbed the outside of the tower. Because he'd known that if he fled, he'd leave Dabbid and Teft alone. If he fled, he'd leave Syl—maybe forever. So he'd climbed and . . .

And the Stormfather's voice?

No, *Dalinar's* voice.

That had been . . . days ago? Weeks? He didn't know what had happened to him. He walked a place of constant winds. The faces of those he loved appeared in haunting shadows, each one begging for help. Flashes of light burned his skin, blinded him. The light was *angry*. And though Kaladin longed to escape the darkness, each new flash trained him to be more afraid of the light.

The worst part was the wind. The wind that hated him. It flayed him, slamming him against the rocks as he tried to find a hiding place to escape it.

Hate, it whispered. *Hate. Hate hate.*

Each time the wind spoke, it broke something inside Kal. Ever since he could remember—since childhood—he had loved the wind. The feel of it on his skin meant he was free. Meant he was alive. It brought new scents, clean and fresh. The wind had always been there, his friend, his companion, his ally. Until one day it had come to life and started talking to him.

Its hatred crushed him. Left him trembling. He screamed for Syl, then remembered that he'd abandoned her. He couldn't remember how he'd come to this terrible place, but he remembered *that*. Plain as a dagger in his chest.

He'd left Syl alone, to lose herself because he'd gotten too far away. He'd abandoned the wind.

The wind crashed into him, pressing him against something hard. A rock formation? He was . . . somewhere barren. No sign of rockbuds or vines in the flashes of terrifying light. Only endless windswept, rocky crags. It reminded him of the Shattered Plains, but with far more variation to the elevations. Peaks and precipices, red and grey.

So many holes and tunnels. Surely there was a place to hide. *Please. Just let me rest. For a minute.*

He pushed forward, holding to the rock wall, trying not to stumble. He had to fight the wind. The terrible wind.

Hate. Hate. Hate.

Lightning flashed, blinding him. He huddled beside the rock as the wind blew stronger. When he started moving, he could see a bit better. Sometimes it was pure darkness. Sometimes he could see a little, though there was no light source he could locate. Merely a persistent directionless illumination. Like . . . like another place he couldn't remember.

Hide. He had to hide.

Kal pushed off the wall, struggling against the wind. Figures appeared. Teft begging to know why Kal hadn't rescued him. Moash pleading for help protecting his grandparents. Lirin dying as Roshone executed him.

Kal tried to ignore them, but if he squeezed his eyes shut, their cries became louder. So he forced himself forward, searching for shelter. He struggled up a short incline—but as soon as he reached the top, the wind reversed and blew him from behind, casting him down the other side. He landed on his shoulder, scraping up his arm as he slid across the stone.

Hate. Hate. Hate.

Kal forced himself to his knees. He . . . he didn't give up. He . . . wasn't a person who was allowed to give up. Was that right? It was hard . . . hard to remember.

He got to his feet, his arm hanging limp at his side, and kept walking. Against the wind again. *Keep moving. Don't let it stop you. Find a place. A place to hide.*

He staggered forward, exhausted. How long had it been since he'd slept? Truly slept? For years, Kal had stumbled from one nightmare to another.

He lived on willpower alone. But what would happen when he ran out of strength? What would happen when he simply . . . couldn't?

"Syl?" he croaked. "Syl?"

The wind slammed into him and knocked him off balance, shoving him right up to the rim of a chasm. He teetered on the edge, terrified of the darkness below—but the wind didn't give him a choice. It pushed him straight into the void.

He tumbled and fell, slamming into rocks along the chasm wall, denied peace even while falling. He hit the bottom with a solid *crack* to his head and a flash of light.

Hate. Hate. Hate.

He lay there. Letting it rail. Letting it pummel him. Was it time? Time to finally let go?

He forced himself to look up. And there—in the distance along the bottom of the chasm—he saw something beautiful. A pure white light. A longing warmth. The sight of it made him weep and cry out, reaching for it.

Something real. Something that didn't hate him.

He *needed* to get to that light.

The fall had broken him. One arm didn't work, and his legs were a mess of agony. He began crawling, dragging himself along with his working arm.

The wind redoubled its efforts, trying to force him back, but now that Kaladin had seen the light, he *had* to keep going. He gritted his teeth against the pain and hauled himself forward. Inch after inch. Defying the screaming wind, ignoring the shadows of dying friends.

Keep. Moving.

The light drew closer, and he longed to enter it. That place of warmth, that place of peace. He heard . . . a sound. A serene tone that wasn't spiteful wind or whispered accusations.

Closer. Closer.

A little . . . farther . . .

He was just ten feet away. He could . . .

Suddenly, Kaladin began to *sink*. He felt the ground change, becoming *liquid*. Crem. The rock had somehow become crem, and it was sucking him down, collapsing beneath him.

He shouted, stretching his good arm toward the glowing pool of light. There was nothing to climb on, nothing to hold on to. He panicked, sinking deeper. The crem covered him, filling his mouth as he screamed—begging—reaching a trembling hand toward the light.

Until he slipped under the surface and was again in the suffocating

darkness. As he sank away, Kal realized that the light had never been there for him to reach. It had been a lie, meant to give him a moment of hope in this awful, *horrible* place. So that hope could be taken. So that he could finally.

Be.

Broken.

A glowing arm plunged into the crem, burning it away like vapor. A hand seized Kaladin by the front of his vest, then heaved him up out of the pool. A glowing white figure pulled him close, sheltering him from the wind as it hauled him the last few feet toward the light.

Kaladin clung to the figure, feeling cloth, warmth, living breath. Another person among the shadows and lies. Was this . . . was this Honor? The Almighty himself?

The figure pulled him into the light, and the rest of the crem vanished, leaving a hint of a taste in Kaladin's mouth. The figure deposited Kaladin on a small rock situated like a seat. As it stepped back, the figure drew in color, the light fading away, revealing . . .

Wit.

Kaladin blinked, glancing around. He was at the bottom of a chasm, yes, but inside a bubble of light. Outside, the wind still raged—but it couldn't affect this place, this moment of peace.

He put a hand to his head, realizing he didn't hurt any longer. In fact, he could see now that he was in a nightmare. He was *asleep*. He must have fallen unconscious after fleeing into the tempest.

Storms . . . What kind of fever did he have to prompt such terrible dreams? And why could he see it all so clearly now?

Wit looked up at the tumultuous sky far above, beyond the chasm rims. "This isn't playing fair. Not fair at all . . ."

"Wit?" Kaladin asked. "How are you here?"

"I'm not," Wit said. "And neither are you. This is another planet, or it looks like one—and not a pleasant one, mind you. The kind without lights. No Stormlight ones, gaseous ones, or even electric ones. Damn place barely has an atmosphere."

He glanced at Kaladin, then smiled. "You're asleep. The enemy is sending you a vision, similar to those the Stormfather sent Dalinar. I'm not certain how Odium isolated you though. It's hard for Shards to invade minds like this except in a specific set of circumstances."

He shook his head, hands on his hips, as if he were regarding a sloppy painting. Then he settled down on a stool beside a fire that Kaladin only now saw. A warm, inviting fire that completely banished the chill, radiating straight through Kaladin's bones to his soul. A pot of simmering stew sat on top, and Wit stirred it, sending spiced fragrances into the air.

"Rock's stew," Kaladin said.

"Old Horneater recipe."

"Take everything you have, and put him in pot," Kaladin said, smiling as Wit handed him a bowl of steaming stew. "But it's not real. You just told me."

"Nothing is real," Wit said. "At least by one measure of philosophy. So enjoy what you seem to be able to eat and don't complain."

Kaladin did so, taking the most wonderful bite of stew he'd ever tasted. It was hard to avoid glancing out past the glowing barrier of light at the storm outside.

"How long can I stay with you?" Kaladin asked.

"Not long, I fear," Wit said, serving himself a bowl of stew. "Twenty minutes or so."

"I have to go back out into that?"

Wit nodded. "I'm afraid it's going to get worse, Kaladin. I'm sorry."

"Worse than this?"

"Unfortunately."

"I'm not strong enough, Wit," Kaladin whispered. "It has all been a lie. I've never been strong enough."

Wit took a bite of his stew, then nodded.

"You . . . agree?" Kaladin asked.

"You know better than I what your limits are," Wit said. "It's not such a terrible thing, to be too weak. Makes us need one another. I should never complain if someone recognizes their failings, though it might put me out of a job if too many share your wisdom, young bridgeman."

"And if all of this is too much for me?" Kaladin asked. "If I can't keep fighting? If I just . . . stop? Give up?"

"Are you close to that?"

"Yes," Kaladin whispered.

"Then best eat your stew," Wit said, pointing with his spoon. "A man shouldn't lie down and die on an empty stomach."

Kaladin waited for more, some insight or encouragement. Wit merely ate, and so Kaladin tried to do the same. Though the stew was perfect, he couldn't enjoy it. Not while knowing that the storm awaited him. That he wasn't free of it, that it *was* going to get worse.

"Wit?" Kaladin finally said. "Do you . . . maybe have a story you could tell me?"

Wit froze, spoon in his mouth. He stared at Kaladin, lowering his hand, leaving the spoon between his lips—before eventually opening his mouth to stare slack-jawed, the spoon falling into his waiting hand.

"What?" Kaladin asked. "Why are you so surprised?"

"Well," Wit said, recovering. "It's simply that . . . I've been waiting for
someone to actually *ask*. They never seem to." He grinned, then leaned

forward and lowered his voice. "There is an inn," he whispered, "that you cannot find on your own. You must stumble across it on a misty street, late at night, lost and uncertain in a strange city.

"The door has a wheel on it, but the sign bears no name. If you find the place and wander inside, you'll meet a young man behind the bar. He has no name. He cannot tell it to you, should he want to—it's been taken from him. But he'll know you, as he knows everyone who enters the inn. He'll listen to everything you want to tell him—and you *will* want to talk to him. And if you ask him for a story, he'll share one. Like he shared with me. I will now share it with you."

"All right . . ." Kaladin said.

"Hush. This isn't the part where you talk," Wit said. He settled in, then turned his hand to the side with a curt gesture, palm up. A Cryptic appeared beside him, forming as if from mist. This one wore a stiff robe like they did in Shadesmar, the head a lacy and intricate pattern somehow more . . . fine and graceful than that of Shallan's Pattern.

The Cryptic waved eagerly. Kaladin had heard that Wit was a Light-weaver now, but he hadn't been surprised. He felt he'd seen Wit Lightweave long ago. Regardless, he didn't act like he was in one of the Radiant orders. He was just . . . well, Wit.

"This story," Wit said, "is a meaningless one. You must not search for a moral. It isn't *that* kind of story, you see. It's the *other* kind of story."

The Cryptic held up a flute, and Kaladin recognized it. "Your flute!" he said. "You found it?"

"This is a dream, idiot," Wit said. "It's not real."

"Oh," Kaladin said. "Right."

"I'm real!" the Cryptic said with a musical, feminine voice. "Not imaginary at all! Unfortunately, I *am* irrational! Ha ha!" She began to play the flute, moving her fingers along it—and while soft music came out, Kaladin wasn't certain what she was doing to produce the sounds. She didn't have lips.

"This story," Wit said, "is called 'The Dog and the Dragon.'"

"The . . . what and the what?" Kaladin said. "Or is this not the part where I speak yet?"

"You people," Wit said. "A dog is a hound, like an axehound." He held up his palm, and a creature appeared in it, four-legged and furry, like a mink—only larger, and with a different face shape.

"It is funny, you can't realize," Wit said. "Humans will selectively breed for the same traits regardless of the planet they're on. But you can't be amazed at the convergent examples of domestication across the cosmere. You can't know any of this, because you live on a giant ball of rock full of slime where everything is wet and cold all the time. This is a dog,

Kaladin. They're fluffy and loyal and wonderful. This, on the other hand, is a dragon."

A large beast appeared in his other hand, like a chasmfiend—except with enormous outstretched wings and only four legs. It was a brilliant pearlescent color, with silver running along the contours of its body. It also had smaller chitinous bits than a chasmfiend—in fact, its body was covered with little pieces of carapace that looked smooth to the touch. It stood proud, with a prominent chest and a regal bearing.

"I know of just one on Roshar," Wit noted, "and she prefers to hide her true form. This story isn't about her, however, or any of the dragons I've met. In fact, the dragon is barely in the story, and I'd kindly ask you not to complain about that part, because there's really nothing I can do about it and you'll only annoy Design."

The Cryptic waved again. "I get annoyed easily!" she said. "It's endearing."

"No it's not," Wit said.

"It's endearing!" Design said. "To everyone but him! I drew up a proof of it!" The music continued playing as she spoke, and the way she moved her fingers on the flute seemed completely random.

"One day, the dog saw the dragon flying overhead," Wit continued, sending the illusory dragon soaring above his hand.

Kaladin was glad for the story. Anything to keep his attention off the hateful wind, which he could faintly hear outside, howling as if eager to rush into the bubble of light and assault him.

"The dog marveled," Wit said, "as one might expect. He had never *seen* anything so majestic or grand. The dragon soared in the sky, shimmering with iridescent colors in the sunlight. When it curved around and passed above the dog, it called out a mighty challenge, demanding in the human tongue that all acknowledge its beauty.

"The dog watched this from atop a hill. Now, he wasn't particularly large, even for a dog. He was white, with brown spots and floppy ears. Not of any specific breed or lineage, and small enough that the other dogs often mocked him. He was a common variety of a common species of a common animal that most people would rightfully ignore.

"But when this dog stared at the dragon and heard the mighty boast, he came to a realization. Today, he had encountered something he'd always wished for but never known. Today he'd seen perfection, and had been presented with a goal. From today, nothing else mattered.

"He was going to become a dragon."

"Hint," Design whispered to Kaladin, "that's impossible. A dog can't become a dragon."

"Design!" Wit said, turning on her. "What did I *tell* you about spoiling the ending of stories!"

"Something stupid, so I forgot it!" she said, her pattern bursting outward like a blooming flower.

"Don't *spoil stories!*" Wit said.

"That's stupid. The story is really long. He needs to hear the ending so he'll know it's worth listening all the way."

"That's *not* how this works," Wit said. "It needs drama. Suspense. *Surprise.*"

"Surprises are dumb," she said. "He should be informed if a product is good or not before being asked to commit. Would you like a similar surprise at the market? Oh, you can't buy a *specific* food. You have to carry a sack home, cut it open, *then* find out what you bought. Drama. Suspense!"

Wit gave Kaladin a beleaguered look. "I have bonded," he said, "a *literal* monster." He made a flourish, and a Lightweaving appeared between them again, showing the dog on a hilltop covered in grass that looked dead, since it didn't move. The dog was staring upward at the dragon, which was growing smaller and smaller as it flew away.

"The dog," Wit continued, "sat upon that hilltop through an entire night and day, staring. Thinking. Dreaming. Finally, he returned to the farm where he lived among others of his kind. These farm dogs all had jobs, chasing livestock or guarding the perimeter, but he—as the smallest—was seldom given any duty. Perhaps to another this would be liberating. To him it had always been humiliating.

"As any problem to overcome is merely a set of *smaller* problems to overcome in a sequence, he divided his goal of becoming a dragon into three steps. First, he would find a way to have colorful scales like the dragon. Second, he would learn to speak the language of men like the dragon. Third, he would learn to *fly* like the dragon."

Wit made the scene unfold in front of Kaladin. A colorful land, with thick green grass that wasn't dead after all—it simply didn't move except in the wind. Creatures unlike any Kaladin had ever seen, furry and strange. Exotic.

The little dog walked into a wooden structure—a barn, though it hadn't been built with stone on the east side to withstand storms. It barely looked waterproof. How would they keep the grain from spoiling? Kaladin cocked his head at this oddity as the dog encountered a tall man in work clothing sorting through bags of seeds.

"The dog chose the scales first," Wit continued, accompanied by the quiet flute music, "as it seemed the easiest, and he wanted to begin his transformation with an early victory. He knew the farmer owned many seeds in a variety of colors, and they were the shape of little scales. Because he was not a thief, the dog did not take these—but he asked the other animals where the farmer obtained new ones.

"It turns out, the farmer could *make* seeds by putting them in the ground, waiting for plants to grow, then taking more seeds from the stalks. Knowing this, the dog borrowed some seeds and did the same, accompanying the farmer's eldest son on his daily work. As the youth worked, the dog moved alongside him, digging holes for seeds with his paws and planting them carefully with his mouth."

It was an amusing scene, watching the dog work. Not only because the animal did all this with feet and snout—but because the ground *parted* when the dog pawed at it. It wasn't made of stone, but something else.

"This is in Shinovar, isn't it?" Kaladin asked. "Sigzil told me about ground like that."

"Hush," Wit said. "This isn't the part where you talk. The farmer's eldest son found the dog's actions quite amusing—then incredible as the dog went out each day, gripping a watering can in his teeth. The little dog watered each seed, just as the farmer did. He learned to weed and fertilize. And eventually the dog was rewarded with his own small crop of colorful seeds.

"After replacing what he'd borrowed from the farmer, the dog got himself wet and rolled in his seeds, sticking them all over his body. He then presented himself to the other dogs.

"'Do you admire my wonderful new scales?' he asked his fellow animals. 'Do I not look like a dragon?'

"They, in turn, laughed at him. 'Those are not scales!' they said. 'You look stupid and silly. Go back to being a dog.'"

Kaladin put a spoonful of stew into his mouth, staring at the illusion. The way the colors worked was mesmerizing, though he had to admit the dog did look silly covered in seeds.

"The dog slunk away, feeling foolish and hurt. He had failed at his first task, to have scales like a dragon. The dog, however, was not daunted. Surely if he could *speak* with the grand voice of a dragon, they would all see. And so, the dog spent his free time watching the children of the farmer. There were three. The eldest son, who helped in the fields. The middle daughter, who helped with the animals, and the toddler—who was too young to help, but was learning to speak."

Wit made the family appear, working in the yard—the farmer's wife, who was taller than the farmer. A youth, lanky and assiduous. A daughter who would someday share her mother's height. A baby who toddled around the yard, tended by them all as they did their chores.

"This," Wit noted, "is almost too easy."

"Too easy?" Kaladin asked, absently taking another bite of stew.

"For years, I've had to make do with *hints* of illusions. *Suggesting* scenes. Leaving most to the imagination. Now, having the power to do more, I find it less satisfying.

"Anyway, the dog figured that the best way to learn the language of men was to study their youngest child. So the dog played with the baby, stayed with him, and listened as he began to form words. The dog played with the daughter too, helped her with yard work. He soon found he could understand her, if he tried hard. But he couldn't form words.

"He tried *so hard* to speak as they did, but his mouth could not make that kind of speech. His tongue did not work like a human tongue. Eventually, while watching the tall and serious daughter, he noticed she could make the words of humans on paper.

"The dog was overjoyed by this. It was a way to speak without having a human tongue! The dog joined her at the table where she studied, inspecting the letters as she made them. He failed many times, but eventually learned to scratch the letters in the dirt himself.

"The farmer and his family thought this an amazing trick. The dog was sure he had found a way to prove he was becoming a dragon. He returned to the other dogs in the field and showed them his writing ability by writing their names in the dirt.

"They, however, could not read the words. When the dog explained what writing was, they laughed. 'This is not the loud and majestic voice of a dragon!' the dogs said. 'This is speaking so quietly, nobody can hear it! You look silly and stupid. Go back to being a dog.'

"They left the dog to stare at his writing as rain began to fall, washing the words away. He realized they were correct. He had failed to speak with the proud and powerful voice of the dragon."

The image of the dog in the rain felt far too familiar to Kaladin. Far too *personal*.

"But there was still hope," Wit said. "If the dog could just *fly*. If he could achieve this feat, the dogs would *have* to acknowledge his transformation.

"This task seemed even harder than the previous two. However, the dog had seen a curious device in the barn. The farmer would tie bales of hay with a rope, then raise or lower them using a pulley in the rafters.

"This was essentially flying, was it not? The bales of hay soared in the air. And so, the dog practiced pulling on the rope himself, and learned the mechanics of the device. He found that the pulley could be balanced with a weight on the other side, which made the bales of hay lower slowly and safely.

"The dog took his leash and tied it around him to make a harness, like the ones that wrapped up the hay. Then he tied a sack slightly lighter than he was to the rope, creating a weight to balance him. After using his mouth to tie the rope to his harness, he climbed to the top of the barn's loft, and called for the other dogs to come in. When they arrived, he leaped gracefully off the loft.

"It worked! The dog lowered down slowly, striking a magnificent pose in the air. He was *flying*! He soared like the dragon had! He felt the air around him, and knew the sensation of being up high, with everything below him. When he landed, he felt so proud and so free.

"Then the other dogs laughed the loudest they had ever laughed. 'That is not flying like a dragon!' they said. 'You fell slowly. You looked so stupid and silly. Go back to being a dog.'

"This, at long last, crushed the dog's hopes. He realized the truth. A dog like him simply could not become a dragon. He was too small, too quiet, too silly."

Frankly, the sight of the dog being lowered on the rope *had* looked a bit silly. "They were right," Kaladin said. "That wasn't flying."

Wit nodded.

"Oh, is this the place where I talk?" Kaladin said.

"If you wish."

"I don't wish. Get on with the story."

Wit grinned, then leaned forward, waving in the air and making the sounds of shouting come from a distant part of the illusion, not yet visible. "What was that? The dog looked up, confused. He heard noises. Sudden shouting? Yells of panic?

"The dog raced out of the barn to find the farmer and his family huddled around the small farmyard well, which was barely wide enough for the bucket. The dog put his paws up on the edge of the well and looked down. Far below, in the deep darkness of the hole, he heard crying and splashing."

Kaladin leaned forward, staring into the darkness. A pitiful, gurgling cry was barely audible over the splashing.

"The littlest child of the farmer and his wife had fallen into the well," Wit whispered, "and was *drowning*. The family screamed and wept. There was nothing to be done. Or . . . was there?

"In a flash, the dog knew what to do. He bit the bucket off the well's rope, then had the eldest son tie the rope to his harness. He wrote 'lower me' in the dirt, then hopped up onto the rim of the well. Finally, he threw himself into the well as the farmer grabbed the crank.

"Lowered down on this rope, the dog 'flew' into the darkness. He found the baby all the way underwater, but shoved his snout in and took hold of the baby's clothing with his teeth. A short time later, when the family pulled him back up, the dog appeared holding the littlest child: wet, crying, but very much alive.

"That night, the family set a place for the little dog at their table and gave him a sweater to keep him warm, his name written across the front with letters he could read. They served a feast with food the dog had helped grow. They gave him some of the cake celebrating the birthday of the child whose life he had saved.

"That night, it rained on the other dogs, who slept outside in the cold barn, which leaked. But the little dog snuggled into a warm bed beside the fire, hugged by the farmer's children, his belly full. And as he did, the dog sadly thought to himself, 'I could not become a dragon. I am an utter and complete failure.'

"The end."

Wit clapped his hands, and the images vanished. He gave a seated bow. Design lowered her flute and flared out her pattern again, as if to give her own bow.

Then Wit picked up his bowl of stew and continued eating.

"Wait," Kaladin said, standing. "That's *it*?"

"Did you miss 'the end' at the end?" Design said. "It indicates that is the end."

"What kind of ending is that?" Kaladin said. "The dog decides he's a failure?"

"Endings are an art," Wit said loftily. "A precise and *unquestionable* art, bridgeman. Yes, that is the ending."

"Why did you tell me this?" Kaladin demanded.

"You asked for a story."

"I wanted a *useful* story!" he said, waving his hand. "Like the story of the emperor on the island, or of Fleet who kept running."

"You didn't specify that," Wit said. "You said you wanted a story. I provided one. That is all."

"That's the wrong ending," Kaladin said. "That dog was *incredible*. He learned to write. How many animals can write, on any world?"

"Not many, I should say," Wit noted.

"He learned to farm and to use tools," Kaladin said. "He saved a child's *life*. That dog is a storming hero."

"The story wasn't about him trying to be a hero," Wit said. "It was about him trying to be a dragon. In which, pointedly, he *failed*."

"I told you!" Design said happily. "Dogs can't be dragons!"

"Who cares?" Kaladin said, stalking back and forth. "By looking up at the dragon, and by trying to become better, he outgrew the other dogs. He achieved something truly special." Kaladin stopped, then narrowed his eyes at Wit, feeling his anger turn to annoyance. "This story is about me, isn't it? I said I'm not good enough. You think I have impossible goals, and I'm *intentionally* ignoring the things I've accomplished."

Wit pointed with his spoon. "I *told* you this story has no meaning. You promised not to assign it one."

"As a matter of fact," Design said, "you didn't give him a chance to promise! You simply kept talking."

Wit glared at her.

"Blah blah blah blah blah!" she said, rocking her pattern head back and forth at each word.

"Your stories always have a point," Kaladin said.

"I am an *artist,*" Wit said. "I should thank you not to demean me by insisting my art must be trying to *accomplish* something. In fact, you shouldn't enjoy art. You should simply admit that it exists, then move on. Anything else is patronizing."

Kaladin folded his arms, then sat. Wit, playing games again. Couldn't he ever be clear? Couldn't he ever say what he meant?

"Any meaning," Wit said softly, "is for you to assign, Kaladin. I merely tell the stories. Have you finished your stew?"

Kaladin realized he had—he'd eaten the entire bowl while listening.

"I can't keep this bubble up much longer, I'm afraid," Wit said. "He'll notice if I do—and then he'll destroy me. I have violated our agreement, which exposes me to his direct action. I'd rather not be killed, as I have seven more people I wanted to insult today."

Kaladin nodded, standing up again. He realized that somehow, the story fired him up. He felt stronger, less for the words and more for how annoyed he'd grown at Wit.

A little light, a little warmth, a little *fire* and he felt ready to walk out into the winds again. Yet he knew the darkness would return. It always did.

"Can you tell me the real ending?" Kaladin asked, his voice small. "Before I go back out?"

Wit stood and stepped over, then put his hand on Kaladin's back and leaned in. "That night," he said, "the little dog snuggled into a warm bed beside the fire, hugged by the farmer's children, his belly full. And as he did, the dog thought to himself, 'I doubt any dragon ever had it so good anyway.'"

He smiled and met Kaladin's eyes.

"It won't be like that for me," Kaladin said. "You told me it would get worse."

"It will," Wit said, "but then it will *get better.* Then it will get worse again. Then better. This is life, and I will not lie by saying every day will be sunshine. But there will be sunshine again, and that is a very different thing to say. That is truth. I promise you, Kaladin: *You will be warm again.*"

Kaladin nodded in thanks, then turned to the hateful winds. He felt a push against his back as Wit sent him forward—then the light vanished, along with all it contained.

SEVEN YEARS AGO

Eshonai tipped her head back, feeling water stream off her carapace skullplate. Returning to warform after so long in workform felt like revisiting a familiar clearing hidden in the trees, rarely encountered but always waiting for her. She *did* like this form. She would *not* see it as a prison.

She met Thude and Rlain as they emerged from hollows in the stone where they too had returned to this form. Many of her friends had never left it. Warform was convenient for many reasons, though Eshonai didn't like it quite as well as workform. There was something about the aggression this form provoked in her. She worried she would seek excuses to fight.

Thude stretched, humming to Joy. "Feels good," he said. "I feel alive in this form."

"Too alive," Rlain said. "Do the rhythms sound louder to you?"

"Not to me," Thude said.

Eshonai shook her head. She didn't hear the rhythms any differently. Indeed, she'd been wondering if—upon adopting this form again—she'd hear the pure tone of Roshar as she did the first time. She hadn't.

"Shall we?" she asked, gesturing toward the spreading plateaus. Rlain started toward one of the bridges, but Thude sang loudly to Amusement and charged the nearby chasm, leaping and soaring over it with an incredible bound.

Eshonai dashed after him to do the same. Each form brought with it a certain level of instinctual understanding. When she reached the edge, her body knew what to do. She sprang in a powerful leap, the air whistling through the grooves in her carapace and flapping the loose robe she'd worn into the storm.

She landed with a solid crunch, her feet grinding stone as she slid to a stop. The Rhythm of Confidence thrummed in her ears, and she found herself grinning. She *had* missed that. Rlain landed next to her, a hulking figure with black and red skin patterns forming an intricate marbling. He hummed to Confidence as well.

"Come on!" Thude shouted from nearby. He leaped another chasm.

Attuning Joy, Eshonai ran after him. Together the three of them chased and dashed, climbed and soared—spanning chasms, climbing up and over rock formations, sprinting across plateaus. The Shattered Plains felt like a playground.

This must be what islands and oceans are like, she thought as she surveyed the Plains from up high. She'd heard about them in songs, and she'd always imagined an ocean as a huge network of streams moving between sections of land.

But no, she'd seen Gavilar's map. In that painting, the bodies of water had seemed as wide as countries. Water . . . with nothing to see but more water. She attuned Anxiety. And Awe. Complementary emotions, in her experience.

She dropped from the rock formation and landed on the plateau, then bounded after Thude. How far would she have to travel to find those oceans? Judging by the map, only a few weeks to the east. Once such a distance would have been daunting, but now she'd made the trek all the way to Kholinar and back. The trip to the Alethi capital had been one of the sweetest and most exhilarating experiences of her life. So many new places. So many wonderful people. So many strange plants, strange sights, strange foods to taste.

When they'd fled, the same wonders had become threats overnight. The entire trip home had been a blur of marching, sleeping, and foraging in human fields.

Eshonai reached another chasm and leaped, trying to recapture her excitement. She increased her pace, coming up even with Thude and eventually passing him—before the two of them pulled to a halt to wait for Rlain, who had slowed a few plateaus back. He had always been a careful one, and he seemed better able to control the inclinations of the new form.

Her heart racing, Eshonai reached out of habit to wipe her brow—but this form didn't have sweat on her forehead to drip into her eyes. Instead, the carapace armor trapped air from her forward motion, then pushed it up underneath to cool her skin.

The awesome energy of the form meant she could probably have kept running for hours before feeling any real strain. Perhaps longer. Indeed, the warforms during their flight from Alethkar had carried food for the others and *still* moved faster than the workforms.

At the same time, Eshonai was getting hungry. She remembered well how much food this form required at each meal.

Thude leaned against a high rock formation as they waited, watching some windspren play in the air. Eshonai wished she'd brought her book for drawing maps of the Plains. She'd found it in the human market of Kholinar—such a small, simple thing. It had been expensive by Alethi standards, but oh so cheap by her standards. An entire book of papers? All for a few little bits of emerald?

She'd seen steel weapons there too. Sitting in the market. *For sale.* The listeners protected, polished, and revered each weapon they'd found on the Plains—keeping them for generations, passed down from parent to child. The humans had entire stalls of them.

"This is going to go poorly for us, isn't it?" Thude asked.

Eshonai realized she'd been humming to the Lost. She stopped, but met his eyes and knew that he knew. Together they walked around the stone formation and looked westward, toward the cities that had for centuries been listener homes. Dark smoke filled the air—the Alethi burning wood as they set up enormous cookfires and settled into their camps.

They'd arrived in force. Tens of thousands of them. Swarms of soldiers, with dozens of Shardbearers. Come to exterminate her people.

"Maybe not," Eshonai said. "In warform, we're stronger than they are. They have equipment and skill, but we have strength and endurance. If we *have* to fight them, this terrain will heavily favor us."

"Did you really have to do it though?" Thude asked to Pleading. "Did you *need* to have him killed?"

She'd answered this before, but she didn't avoid the responsibility. She *had* voted for Gavilar to die. And she'd been the reason for the vote in the first place.

"He was going to bring them back, Thude," Eshonai said to Reprimand. "Our ancient gods. I *heard* him say it. He thought I'd be happy to hear of it."

"So you killed him?" Thude asked, to Agony. "Now they'll kill *us*, Eshonai. How is this any better?"

She attuned Tension. Thude, in turn, attuned Reconciliation. He seemed to recognize that bringing this up again and again was accomplishing nothing.

"It is done," Eshonai said. "So now, we need to hold out. We might not even have to fight them. We can harvest gemstones from the greatshells and speed crop growth. The humans can't leap these chasms, and so they'll have trouble ever getting to us. We'll be safe."

"We'll be trapped," Thude said. "In the center of these Plains. For months, perhaps years. You're fine with that, Eshonai?"

Rlain finally caught up to them, jogging over and humming to Amusement—perhaps he thought the two of them silly for speeding ahead.

Eshonai looked away from Thude and stared out across the Plains—not toward the humans, but toward the ocean, the Origin. Places she could have gone. Places she'd *planned* to go. Thude knew her too well. He understood how much it hurt to be trapped here.

They will strike inward, she thought. *The humans won't come all this way to turn around because of a few chasms. They have resources we can only imagine, and there are so many of them. They'll find a way to get to us.*

Escaping out the other side of the Plains wasn't an option either. If the chasmfiends there didn't get them, the humans eventually would. To flee would be to abandon the natural fortification of the Plains.

"I'll do what I have to, Thude," Eshonai said to Determination. "I'll do what is right whatever the cost. To us. To me."

"They have fought wars," Thude said. "They have generals. Great military thinkers. We've had warform for only a year."

"We'll learn," Eshonai said, "and create our own generals. Our ancestors paid with their very minds to bring us freedom. If the humans find a way to come for us in here, we *will* fight. Until we persuade the humans that the cost is too high. Until they realize we won't go meekly to slavery, like the poor beings they use as servants. Until they learn they cannot have us, our Blades, or our souls. We are a *free* people. Forever."

⁂

Venli gathered her friends around, humming softly to Craving as she revealed the gemstones in her hands. Voidspren. Five of them, trapped as Ulim had been when first brought to her.

Inside her gemheart, he hummed words of encouragement. Ever since the events at the human city, he'd treated her with far more respect. And he'd never again abandoned her. The longer he remained, the better she could hear the new rhythms. The rhythms of power.

She had claimed this section of Narak—the city at the center of the Plains—for her scholars. Friends who she and Ulim had determined, after careful discussion, shared her hunger for a better world. Trustworthy enough, she hoped. Once they had Voidspren in their gemhearts, she'd be far more confident in their discretion.

"What are they?" Demid asked, his hand resting on Venli's shoulder. He'd been the first and most eager to listen. He didn't know everything, naturally, but she was glad to have him. She felt stronger when he was around. Braver than Eshonai. After all, could Eshonai have ever taken *this* step?

"These hold spren," Venli explained. "When you accept one into your gemheart, they'll hold your current spren with them, keeping you in your current form—but you'll have a secret companion to help you. Guide you. Together, we're going to solve the greatest challenge our people have ever known."

"Which is?" Tusa asked to Skepticism.

"Our world is connected to another," Venli explained, handing one gemstone to each of her friends. "A place called Shadesmar. *Hundreds* of spren exist there who can grant us the ability to harness the power of the storms. They've traveled a long way, as part of a great storm. They've gone as far as they can on their own, however. Getting gemstones like these to our side takes enormous effort, and is impossible on a large scale.

"So we need another way to bring those spren across. We're going to figure it out, then we're going to persuade the rest of the listeners to join with us in adopting forms of power. We'll be smart; we won't be ruled by the spren this time around. We'll rule them.

"Eshonai and the others have foolishly thrown everyone into an unwanted war. So *we* have to take this step. We will be remembered as the ones who saved our people."

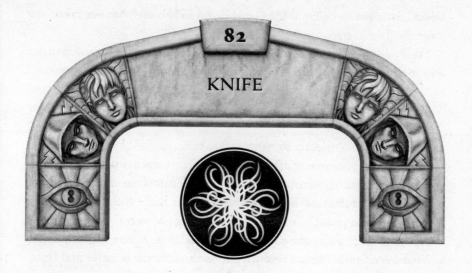

Oh . . . Father . . . Seven thousand years.

"H ow could you not tell me this?" Radiant demanded as she knelt and shouted at the cube on the floor. "Restares is not only the honorspren's High Judge, he's one of the *storming* Heralds!"

"You didn't require the information at that time," Mraize's voice said. "Be Veil. She will understand."

"Veil is even *more* angry at you, Mraize," Radiant said, standing up. "You sent us into a dangerous situation without proper preparation! Withholding this information wasted *weeks* while the three of us searched the fortress like an idiot."

"We didn't want you asking after a Herald," Mraize said, his voice frustratingly calm. "That might have alerted him. So far as we're aware, he hasn't figured out that we know his true identity. Gavilar may have known, but no others in the Sons of Honor had an inkling that they served one of the very beings they were seeking—in their naive ignorance—to restore to Roshar. The irony is quite poetic."

"Mmm . . ." Pattern said from beside the door, where he was watching for Adolin.

"What?" Radiant asked him. "You like irony now too?"

"Irony tastes good. Like sausage."

"And have you ever tasted sausage?"

"I don't believe I have a sense of taste," Pattern said. "So irony tastes like what I imagine sausage would taste like when I'm imagining tastes."

Radiant rubbed her forehead, looking back at the cube. So unfair. She was accustomed to being able to stare down her troops, but one could not properly glare at a man who talked to you out of a box.

"You told us we'd know what to do when we found Restares," Radiant told Mraize. "Well, we are here now and we have *no* idea how to proceed."

"What did you do the moment you found out?" Mraize said.

"Cursed your name."

"Then?"

"Contacted you directly to curse at you some more."

"Which was the correct choice. See, you knew exactly what to do."

Radiant folded her arms, warm with anger. Frustration. And . . . admittedly . . . embarrassment. She bled into being Veil, and the anger returned.

"The time has come," she said, "for us to deal, Mraize."

"Deal? The deal has already been set. You do as I have requested, and you will receive the offered reward—in addition to the practice and training you are receiving under my hand."

"That is interesting," Veil said. "Because I see this differently. I have come all this way, through great hardship. Because of Adolin's sacrifice, I've gained access to one of the most remote fortresses on Roshar. I have succeeded where you explicitly told me your other agents have failed.

"Now that I'm here, instead of receiving 'training' or 'practice' as you say, I find that you've been withholding vital information from me. From my perspective, there is no incentive to continue this arrangement, as the promised reward is of little interest to me. Even Shallan is questioning its value.

"Your refusal to give me important information makes me question what else you held back. Now I'm questioning if what I'm to do here is possibly against my interests, and the interests of those I love. So let me ask plainly. Why am I really here? Why are you so interested in Kelek? And why—explicitly—should I continue on this path?"

Mraize did not respond immediately. "Hello, Veil," he finally said. "I'm glad you came out to speak with me."

"Answer my questions, Mraize."

"First, it is time to open the cube," Mraize said.

Veil frowned. "The communication cube? I thought you said that would ruin the thing."

"If you break into it, you *will* ruin it. Pick it up. Heft it. Listen for the side where my voice is weakest as I hum."

She knelt beside the cube again and picked it up, listening to Mraize's humming voice. Yes . . . the sound was weaker from one direction.

"I've found it," she said.

"Good," Mraize said. "Put your hand on that plane of the cube and twist it to the right."

She felt it click as she touched it. She suspected Mraize had done something to unlock the device from wherever he was. When she twisted that plane of the cube, it turned easily and came off, revealing a small compartment that contained an intricate metal dagger with a gemstone on the end of the grip.

"So you *do* want me to kill him," she said.

"One cannot kill a Herald," Mraize said. "They are immortal. Do not think of Kelek as a person. He is an ageless, eternal spren formed of Honor's substance and will. He is as gravity or light. Force, not man."

"And you want me to stab that force with this knife," Veil said, undoing the straps and prying it out from the cube. The cavity was only a small part of the hollow portion in the cube, and a layer of steel sectioned off the rest. Mraize's voice came from the sealed portion. How had he weighted the cube such that she didn't feel one end was heavier than the other?

"I want you," he said, "to collect the soul of Kelek, also known as Restares. The knife will trap his essence in that gemstone."

"That seems overly cruel," Veil said, looking over the knife.

"Cruel like the spanreeds you so eagerly use, despite the spren trapped inside? It is no different. The being called Kelek is a receptacle of incredible knowledge. Gemstone imprisonment will not hurt him, and we will be able to communicate with him."

"We have *two* other Heralds in the tower," Veil said. "I could ask them anything you want to know."

"You think they'd answer? How useful have they been, talking to Jasnah? Talenelat is completely insane, and Shalash is deceptively reticent. They talk of their Oathpact, yes, and fighting the Fused—but rarely reveal anything practical."

"This isn't very persuasive," Veil said. "Yes, I know what you want me to do—but I suspected it from the beginning. If you want me to do this, I need to know *why*. What *specifically* do you expect to learn from him?"

"Our master, Thaidakar, has an . . . affliction similar to that of the Heralds. He needs access to a Herald to learn more about his state so he might save himself from the worst of its effects."

"That's not good enough," Veil said. "Radiant and Shallan won't let me do your dirty work for such a petty reason." She put the dagger back in the cube. "I came here to report on Restares's location. Shallan specifically told you we wouldn't kill him—and yes, I count stabbing him with this device as the same thing."

"Little knife," Mraize said, his voice growing softer, "why did Sadeas need to die?"

She hesitated, her hand still on the dagger, which she was trying to reattach to the straps in the cube.

"This being," Mraize continued, "that they call Kelek is a monster.

He, along with the other eight, abandoned their Oathpact and stranded Talenelat—the Bearer of Agonies—alone in Damnation, to withstand torture for thousands of years. The enemy has returned, but have the Heralds come to help? No. At best they hide. At worst, their madness leads them to hasten the world's destruction.

"Kelek has become indecisive to the point of madness. And like most of them, he is afraid. He wants to escape his duties. He worked with Gavilar knowing full well that doing so would cause the return of the Fused and the end of our peace, because he hoped to find a way to escape this world. A way to abandon us as he had already abandoned his oaths and his friends.

"He possesses knowledge essential to our fight against the invaders. However, he will not share it willingly. He hides himself away in the world's most remote fortress and tries to pretend there is no war, that he is not culpable. He *is*. The only way to make him do his duty is to bring him back by force—and the best and easiest way to do that is to trap his soul."

Storms. That was a longer speech than she usually got out of Mraize. There was passion, conviction to his voice. Veil almost felt persuaded.

"I can't move against him," she said. "He is set to judge Adolin in this trial. If Kelek vanished, that would throw all kinds of suspicion on us—and Adolin would most certainly be imprisoned. I can't risk it."

"Hmm . . ." Mraize said. "If only there were a way that someone—having locked away Kelek's soul—could take his place. Wear his face. Pass judgment, vindicating your husband and commanding the honorspren to join the war again. If *only* we had sent a person capable of single-handedly turning the tide of this war through the use of a targeted illusion."

In that moment, Veil lost control to Shallan. Because what Mraize said here . . . it made too much sense.

Oh storms, Shallan thought, growing cold. *Stormfather above and Nightwatcher below . . . He's right. That is a solution to this problem. A way to let Adolin win. A way to bring the honorspren back.*

So this was how he manipulated her this time. She wanted to buck him for that reason alone. If only what he said weren't so logical. It would be easy to replace Kelek, assuming she could get some Stormlight. . . .

No, Veil warned. *It's not that easy. We'd have a difficult time impersonating a Herald.*

We'd do the replacement at the last moment, Shallan thought. *On the final day of the trial—to reduce the amount of time we need to pretend, and to give us a few days to scout out his personality.*

"Killing Sadeas saved thousands of lives," Mraize continued in his soft, oily voice. "Delivering Kelek to us, sending the honorspren to bond Windrunners, could save *millions*."

"Veil isn't certain we could imitate a Herald," Shallan said.

"The Herald is erratic," Mraize said. "All of them are now. With a few pointers, you could escape notice. Honorspren are not good at noticing subterfuge—or at distinguishing what is odd behavior for humans, or those who were once human. You can accomplish this. And after the trial, 'Kelek' could insist he has to visit Urithiru himself, leaving the spren completely ignorant of what you've done."

"It would be wrong, Mraize. It *feels* wrong."

"Earlier, Veil demanded a deal. Though I normally reject this sort of talk, I find it encouraging that she did not demand money, or power. She wanted information, to know why she was doing what she did. You three are worthy hunters.

"So I will revise the deal as requested. Perform as I ask here, and I will release you from your apprenticeship. You will become a full member of our organization—you will not only have access to the knowledge you seek, but also have a say in what we are doing. Our grand plans."

Inside, Veil perked up at this. But Shallan was surprised by how much *she* responded to that offer. A full Ghostblood? That was the way . . . The way to . . .

"Strike at a Herald," she said. "It sounds wrong, Mraize. Very wrong."

"You are weak," he said. "You know it."

She bowed her head.

"But part of you is not," he continued. "A part that *can be* that strong. Let that side of you do what needs to be done. Save your husband, your kingdom, and your world all at once. Become that hunter, Shallan.

"Become the knife."

⁘

The honorspren surrounding the High Judge made room for Adolin as he approached, Blended following behind. He didn't miss the glares that many of them gave her. No, there was no love lost between the two varieties of spren.

He should probably feel reverence for the High Judge. This was Kelek, though the spren called him Kalak for some reason. Either way, he was one of the Heralds—so Blended had explained. Many people back home thought of him as the Stormfather, and though that had never been true, he *was* one of the most ancient beings in all of creation. A god to many. An immortal soldier for justice and Honor.

He was also short, with thinning hair. He felt like the type of man you'd find administering some minor city in the backwater of Alethkar. And if he was anything like Ash or Taln, the two Heralds who now resided at Urithiru . . .

Well, his acquaintance with those two caused Adolin to lower his expectations in this particular case.

Kelek spoke with several honorspren leaders as they strolled up the lower portion of the western plane, entering a stone pathway made up of a multitude of colored cobblestones vaguely in the pattern of a gust of wind. The group paused as they saw Adolin ahead.

He removed his hand from his sword out of respect, then bowed to the Herald.

"Hmm? A human?" Kelek said. "Why is he here? He looks dangerous, Sekeir."

"He is," said the honorspren beside Kelek. Sekeir was a leader of the fortress, and appeared as an ancient honorspren with a long blue-white beard. "This is Adolin Kholin, son of Dalinar Kholin."

"The Bondsmith?" Kelek said, and *shied away* from Adolin. "Good heavens! Why have you let him in here?"

"I have come, great one," Adolin said, "to petition the honorspren for their aid in our current battle."

"Your current battle? Against Odium?" Kelek laughed. "Boy, you're doomed. You realize that, right? Tanavast is *dead*. Like, completely dead. The Oathpact is broken somehow. The only thing left is to try to get off the ship before it sinks."

"Holy Lord," Sekeir said, "we let this one in because he offered to stand trial in the stead of the humans, for the pain they have caused our people."

"You're going to try him for the *Recreance*?" Kelek asked, looking around uncertainly at the others near him. "Isn't that a bit extreme?"

"He offered, Holy Lord."

"Not a smart one, is he?" Kelek looked to Adolin, who hesitantly pulled up from his bow. "Huh. You've gotten yourself in deep, boy. They take this kind of thing *very* seriously around here."

"I hope to show them, great one, that we are not their enemies. That the best course forward is for them to join us in our fight. It is, one might say, the *honorable* choice."

"Honor is dead," Kelek snapped. "Aren't you paying attention? This world belongs to Odium now. He has his own storm, for heaven's sake."

Blended nudged Adolin. Right. He was so distracted by Kelek that he'd forgotten the purpose of meeting with him.

"Great one," Adolin said, "I've decided to petition for a trial by witness. Would you be willing to grant me this?"

"Trial by witness?" Kelek said. "Well, that would make this mess end faster. What do you think, Sekeir?"

"I don't think this would be a wise—"

"Hold on; I don't care what you think," Kelek said. "Here I am, years after joining you, and you *still* don't have a way for me to get off this cursed world. Fine, boy, trial by witness it is. We can start it . . . um, the day after tomorrow? Is that acceptable for everyone?"

No one objected.

"Great," Kelek said. "Day after tomorrow. Okay then. Um . . . let's have it at the forum, shall we? I guess everyone will want to watch, and that has the most seats."

"Object to this," Blended whispered to Adolin. "Do not let it be. You don't want to have to persuade the audience as well as the judge."

"Great one," Adolin said, "I had hoped this to be an intimate, personal discussion of—"

"Tough," Kelek said. "You should have thought of that before coming in here to create a storm. Everyone knows how this trial will end, so we might as well make a good time of it for them."

Adolin felt a sinking sensation as Kelek led the group of honorspren around him. Though few lighteyed judges were ever truly impartial, there was an expectation that they'd try to act with honor before the eyes of the Almighty. But this Herald basically told him the trial would be a sham. The man had made his judgment before hearing any arguments.

How on Roshar was that *ever considered a deity?* Adolin thought, in a daze. The Heralds had fallen so far.

Either that, or . . . perhaps these ten people had *always* been only that. People. After all, crowning a man a king or highprince didn't necessarily make him anything grander than he'd been. Adolin knew that firsthand.

"That could have gone better," Blended said, "but at least a trial by witness is. Come. I have one day, it seems, to prepare you to be thrown into the angerspren's den. . . ."

83

THE GAMES OF MEN AND SINGERS

I remember so few of those centuries. I am a blur. A smear on the page. A gaunt stretch of ink, made all the more insubstantial with each passing day.

Venli knelt on the floor of a secluded hallway on the fifteenth floor of Urithiru. The stones whispered to her that the place had once been called Ur. The word meant "original" in the Dawnchant. An ancient place, with ancient stones.

There was a spren that lived here. Not dead, as Raboniel had once proclaimed. This spren was the veins of the tower, its inner metal and crystal running through walls, ceilings, floors.

The stones had not been created by that spren, though a grand project had reshaped them. Reshaped Ur, the original mountain that had been here before. The stones *remembered* being that mountain. They remembered so many things, which they expressed to Venli. Not with words. Rather as impressions, like those a hand left in crem before it dried.

Or the impression Venli's hands left in the floor as they sank into the eager stone. *Remember,* the stones whispered. *Remember what you have forgotten.*

She remembered sitting at her mother's feet as a child, listening to the songs. The music had flowed like water, etching patterns in her brain—memories—like the passage of time etched canals in stone.

Listeners were not like humans, who grew slow as trees. Listeners grew like vines, quick and eager. By age three, she'd been singing with her mother. By age ten, she'd been considered an adult. Venli remembered those years—looking up to Eshonai, who seemed so big, although just a year older than Venli. She had vague memories of holding her father's finger as he sang with her mother.

She remembered love. Family. Grandparents, cousins. How had she forgotten? As a child, ambition and love had been like two sides of her face, each with its own vibrant pattern. To the sound of Odium's rhythms, one side had shone, while the other withered. She had become a person who wanted only to achieve her goals—not because those goals would help others, but because of the goals themselves.

It was in that moment that Venli saw for herself the depth of his lies. He claimed to be of all Passions, and yet where was the love she'd once felt? The love for her mother? Her sister? Her friends? For a while, she'd even forgotten her love for Demid, though it had helped to awaken her.

It felt wrong to be using his Light to practice her Surgebinding, but the stones whispered that it was well. Odium and his tone had become part of Roshar, as Cultivation and Honor—who had not been created alongside the planet—had become part of it. His power was natural, and no more wrong or right than any other part of nature.

Venli searched for something else. The tone of Cultivation. Odium's song could suffuse her, fueling her powers and enflaming her emotions, but that tone . . . that tone had belonged to her people long before he'd arrived. While she searched for it, she listened to her mother's songs in her mind. Like chains, spiked into the stone so they'd remain strong during storms, they reached backward through time. Through generations.

To her people, leaving the battlefield. Walking away rather than continuing to squabble over the same ground over and over. They hadn't merely rejected the singer gods, they'd rejected the *conflict*. Holding to family, singing to Love despite their dull forms, they'd left the war and gone a new way.

The tone snapped into her mind, Cultivation and Odium mixing into a harmony, and it thrummed through Venli. She opened her eyes as power spread from her through the stones. They began to shake and vibrate to the sound of her rhythm, liquid, forming peaks and valleys in time with the music. The floor, ceiling, and walls before her rippled, and a trail of people formed from the stone. Moving, alive again, as they strode away from pain, and war, and killing.

Freedom. The stones whispered to her of freedom. Rock seemed so stable, so unchangeable, but if you saw it on the timescale of spren, it was always changing. *Deliberately.* Over centuries. She had never known her ancestors, but she knew their songs. She could sing those and imitate their courage. Their love. Their wisdom.

The power slipped from her, as it always did. The tone faded, and her control over the stone ended. She needed more practice and more Light. Still, she didn't need Timbre's encouraging thrum to keep her spirits high as she stood. For she had in front of her, in miniature, a sculpture of her ancestors striking out toward the unknown.

More, she had their songs. Because of her mother's diligent and insistent teaching, the songs had not died with the listeners.

⁘

An hour later, Venli walked the hallways much lower in the tower, waiting for Leshwi.

She met with the Heavenly One almost every day. Raboniel knew the meetings were happening, of course. And Leshwi knew that Raboniel knew. Still, Venli and Leshwi met in secret; it was all part of the dance of politics between the Fused.

They met as if by happenstance. Leshwi hovered solemnly through a corridor at the right time, her long black train rustling against the stone. Venli fell into step beside her mistress.

"The Pursuer has found the Windrunner's parents, Ancient One," Venli said. "I'm certain of it. He posted two nightform Regals at the Radiant infirmary."

"Which ones?"

"Urialin and Nistar."

"'Light' and 'mystery,'" Leshwi said, translating their names from the ancient language. Like many of the Regals, they had taken new names for themselves upon their awakening. "Yes, this is a signal. But the Pursuer is not that subtle; if you look, I suspect that Raboniel is the one who suggested those two."

"What do we do?" Venli said to Anxiety.

"Nothing, for now. My authority extends far enough to protect them. This is merely a warning."

"Raboniel threatens to let the Pursuer have the humans," Venli said. "That is why she posted those two guards. To lord her advantage over us."

"Perhaps," Leshwi said, floating with her hands behind her back. "Perhaps not. Raboniel does not think like other Fused, Venli. She hears a much grander song. A skewed and twisted one, but one she seeks to sing without traditional regard for Odium's plans or those of Honor, now dead."

"She makes her own side then," Venli said. "She seeks to play both armies against one another and profit herself."

"Do not transpose your mortal ambitions upon Raboniel," Leshwi said to Ridicule. "You think too small, Venli, to understand her. *I* think too small to understand her. Regardless, you did well in bringing this to me. Watch for other signs like this."

They reached the atrium, the hallway they'd been following merging with it like a river flowing into a sea. Here, Heavenly Ones soared up and down, delivering supplies to the scouts and Masked Ones on the upper floors. Those continued to keep watch for Windrunners. The charade was wearing thin at this point; Raboniel was certain Dalinar Kholin had seen through it and knew something very wrong was happening at the tower.

The supplies to the upper floors could have been delivered via the lifts. However, Raboniel had put the Heavenly Ones to work, making it very clear that she had both the authority and the inclination to keep them busy.

This had driven off many of them, who preferred their sanctuaries in Kholinar. Perhaps that had been the point. Leshwi instead did as she was asked. She floated up and over the railing, her long train slipping over and then falling to drift in the open air beneath her. Another Heavenly One soared upward past them, trailing cloth of gold and red.

"Ancient One," Venli said to Craving, stepping up to the railing. "What are we watching Raboniel for, if not to understand how she's trying to gain advantage over us? What is the purpose of my spying?"

"We watch," Leshwi said, floating down to eye level with Venli, "because we are frightened. To Raboniel, the games of men and singers are petty things—but so are their *lives*. We watch her, Venli, because we want a world to remain when she is finished with her plots."

Venli felt a chill, attuning the Terrors. As Leshwi flew off, Venli took a lift, haunted by those words. *The games of men and singers are petty things . . . but so are their lives. . . .*

The ominous words pulled Venli down from her earlier optimism. After stepping off the lift, she decided to stop and check on Rlain and the others. She couldn't help attuning Agony at the idea of those Regals in the infirmary. At least the surgeon and his wife had the good sense to mostly stay out of sight.

Venli slipped into the draped-off section of the room, where Hesina was keeping watch today. She nodded as Venli entered, then grimaced and glanced toward the others inside. There was a new human here, one Venli didn't recognize, who stood with his eyes down, not speaking.

A tension in the room was coming entirely from Lirin and Rlain, who faced off at the rear, Rlain humming softly to Betrayal. What on Roshar?

"I can't believe I'm hearing this," Rlain said. "I *can't* believe it. He's your *son*."

"My son is long dead, bridgeman," Lirin said, quickly packing a small bag full of surgical implements. "Kaladin kept trying to explain this, and

I only recently started understanding. He doesn't want to be my son anymore. If that's the case, it's difficult for me to see him as anything other than a killer and an agitator. Someone who recklessly endangered not just my family, but the lives of every human in the tower, while pursuing a vengeful grudge."

"So you're going to leave him to die?" Rlain demanded.

"I didn't say that," Lirin snapped. "Do *not* put words in my mouth. I'll go as I would for anyone wounded."

"And afterward?" he demanded. "You said—"

"I *said* we'd see," Lirin said. "It's possible I'll need to bring him down here to give him long-term care."

"You would give him up for execution!"

"If that's what is required, then so be it. I'll do my job as a surgeon, then let Kaladin deal with the consequences of his actions. I'm finished being a pawn in games of death. For *either* side."

Rlain threw up his hands. "What is the point of trying to save him if you're intending to have him killed!"

"Quiet!" Venli hissed, glancing out the flimsy drapes toward the others in the room outside. "What is going on here?"

Lirin glared at Rlain, who again hummed to Betrayal.

"Our son survived the events of the other day," Hesina said to Venli. "This is one of his friends. He says Kaladin's powers aren't working properly, and his wounds aren't healing. He's in a coma and is slowly dying of what sounds like internal bleeding."

"That or an infection," Lirin said, stuffing a few more things into his bag. "Can't tell from the description."

"We're not taking you to him," Rlain said, "unless you *promise* not to give him and Teft up to the enemy." He looked to the other man in the room, the newcomer, who nodded in agreement.

"Then he'll die for certain," Lirin snapped. "Blood on *your* hands."

The two glared at each other, and Venli attuned Irritation. As if she didn't have enough to worry about.

"I'll go," Hesina said, walking over and taking the surgery bag off the table.

"Hesina—"

"He's my son too," she said. "Let's be on with this, Rlain. I can show you how to treat the fever and give him some anti-inflammatories, along with something to fight the infection."

"And if it *is* internal bleeding?" Lirin asked. "He will need surgery. You can't perform an operation like that in the field, Hesina."

He sounded angry, but those were *fearspren* at his feet. Not angerspren. The surgeon turned away and pretended to arrange his instruments. But humans were so full of emotion, it spilled out of them. He couldn't hide what he was feeling from Venli. Frustration. Worry.

He could say what he wanted. But he loved his son.

"He needs to be brought here," Lirin said, his voice laden with pain as plain as any rhythm. "I will go with you to help him. Then . . . I want you to listen to my suggestion. If he's in a coma, he *will* need long-term care. We can put him in this room and pretend he's unconscious like the others. It's the best way."

"He'd rather die," the newcomer whispered. There was something odd about his voice that Venli couldn't place. He slurred his words.

The chamber fell silent. Save for one thing.

Timbre vibrated with excitement inside Venli. The little spren was at it so loudly, Venli was certain the others would hear. How could they not?

"It was going to catch up to Kal eventually," Lirin said, his tone morose. "Most soldiers don't die on the battlefield, you know. Far more die from wounds days later. My son taught you about triage, didn't he? What did he say about people with wounds like his?"

The two former bridgemen glanced at each other.

"Make them comfortable," the human with the slurred words said. "Give them drink. Pain medication, if you can spare it. So they are peaceful when they . . . when they die."

Again the room grew quiet. All save for Timbre, practically bursting with sound.

It's time. It's time. It's time!

When Venli spoke, she almost believed it was Timbre saying the words and not her.

"What if," she said, "I knew about an Edgedancer whose powers still seem to work? One who I think we can rescue?"

⋄⋄

It didn't take much time to explain the plan. Venli had been thinking about this for days now; she'd only needed some practice with her powers, and a little help from Rlain.

The Edgedancer was kept in the same cell Rlain had occupied not long ago. Venli could get through that wall with ease; she was in control of her powers enough for that. The real trick would be pulling off the rescue without revealing or implicating herself.

Timbre pulsed in annoyance as Venli and Rlain hurried toward the cell. The human, Dabbid, was taking another route. Venli didn't want to be seen walking with him.

"How did you get a Shardblade?" Rlain asked softly, to Curiosity. "And how do they not know you have one?"

"It's a long story," Venli said. Mostly because she hadn't thought of a proper lie yet.

"It's Eshonai's, isn't it? Do you know what happened to her? I know you said she's dead . . . but how?"

She died controlled by a Voidspren, Venli thought, *because I tricked her into inviting one into her gemheart. She fell into a chasm after fighting a human Shardbearer, then drowned. Alone. I found her corpse, and—under the direction of a Voidspren—desecrated it by stealing her Shards. But I don't have them.*

There was a lot she *could* say. "No. I got it from a dead human. I bonded it while traveling to Kholinar, before the Fused found me and the others."

"That was when they . . . they . . ." Rlain attuned the Rhythm of the Lost.

"Yes," Venli said to the same rhythm. "When they took the rest of our friends. They left me because Odium wanted me to travel around, telling lies about our people to 'inspire' the newly awakened singers."

"I'm sorry," Rlain said. "That must have been difficult for you, Venli."

"I survived," Venli said. "But if we're going to save this Radiant, we *need* to be certain the Fused can't trace this break-in to us. You can't intervene, Rlain. The human has to manage the distraction himself."

Rlain hummed to Consideration.

"What?" Venli asked.

"Dabbid isn't the person I'd put in charge of something like this," he said. "Until today, I thought he was completely mute."

"Is he trustworthy?"

"Absolutely," Rlain said. "He's Bridge Four. But . . . well, I'd like to know why he spent so long without talking. The bridge runs hit him hard, I know, but there's something else." He hummed to Determination. "I won't intervene unless something goes wrong."

"If you do, we *all* have to go into hiding," Venli said to Skepticism. "So make *sure* before you do anything."

He nodded, still humming to Determination, and they split up at the next intersection. Venli found her way to a particular quiet section of hallway, lit only by her held sphere. Most humans stayed away from this area; the Pursuer's troops were housed nearby. Raboniel's occasional orders for peace to be maintained in the tower were barely enough to restrain those soldiers.

She attuned Peace—sometimes used by listeners for measuring time. Beyond this wall was the cell. As the fourth movement of the rhythm approached, Venli pressed her hand against the stone and drew in Voidlight, requisitioned just earlier to replace what she'd used. Storms, she hoped news of her taking so much didn't reach Raboniel.

Timbre pulsed reassuringly. This stone, like the one earlier today, responded to Venli's touch. It shivered and rippled, as if it were getting a good back-scratching.

The stone whispered to her. *Move to the side.* It guided her to the correct spot to breach the cell. Timbre's rhythms pulsed through the rock, making it vibrate with the Rhythm of Hope. The fourth movement of Peace arrived— the moment when Rlain would signal Dabbid to go in to the guards, bringing food for their lunch. Merely another servant doing his job. Nothing unusual, even if lunch came early today.

Timbre exulted in the Rhythm of Hope as Venli pushed her hand into the stone. It felt good, warm and enveloping. Unlike what happened with the Deepest Ones, Venli displaced the rock. It became as crem in her fingers, soft to the touch.

She wasn't expert enough to get it to move on its own into the shapes she wanted. It usually did what it wanted in those cases, such as forming the tiny statues on the floor above. So for now, she simply pushed her hand forward until it hit air on the other side. Then she pressed with her other hand and pulled the two apart, forming an opening straight through the stone—the normally hard rock curling and bunching up before her touch.

A surprised set of human eyes appeared at the other end of the foot-long hole, looking through at her.

"I'm going to get you out," Venli whispered to the Rhythm of Pleading, "but you have to *promise* you won't tell anyone what I've done. You won't tell them about the powers I'm using. Not even other Radiants. They think I'm cutting you out with a Shardblade."

"What are you?" the human whispered in Alethi.

"Promise me."

"Fine, promised. Done. Hurry. The guards are eating, and they didn't even share none of it."

Venli continued shoving aside the stone. It took a ton of Light, and Timbre pulsed to Consolation—apparently she thought Venli's efforts crude, lacking finesse and skill.

Well, it did the job. She managed to form a hole big enough for the human girl. When Venli let go of the stone, it hardened instantly—she had to shake a few chips of it free of her fingers. The girl poked it, then hopped through.

Hopefully the guards would assume a human Stoneward had survived and saved the girl. Venli gestured for the Edgedancer to follow her—but the girl wavered. She seemed as if she was going to bolt away in another direction.

"Please," Venli said. "We need you. To save a life. If you run now, he'll die."

"Who?"

"Stormblessed," Venli said. "Please, hurry with me."

"You're one of them," the girl said. "How'd you get Radiant powers?"

"I . . . am not Radiant," Venli said. "I have powers from the Fused that are like Radiant powers. I'm a friend of Rlain. The listener who was a bridgeman? Please. I wouldn't free you only to put you in danger, but we *need* to go, now!"

The girl cocked her head, then nodded for Venli to go first. The Edge-dancer followed on silent feet, sticking to the shadows.

Eshonai used to walk like that, Venli thought. *Quietly in the wilderness, to not disturb the wildlife.* This girl didn't have that same air about her though.

Timbre was pulsing contentedly to Hope. Venli couldn't feel the same yet, not until she was certain Rlain and Dabbid hadn't been caught. She led the little Radiant girl to a room nearby to wait.

"You're a traitor to them, then?" the girl asked her.

"I don't know what I am," Venli said. "Other than someone who didn't want to see a child kept in a cage."

Venli jumped almost to the ceiling when Rlain finally strode in with Dabbid. The quiet bridgeman ran over and hugged the human girl, who grinned.

"Eh, moolie," she said. "Strange friends ya got these days. You seen a chicken around here? Big red one? I lost 'im when I was running away."

Dabbid shook his head, then knelt before the girl. "Healing. It works?"

"Eh!" she said. "You can talk!"

He nodded.

"Say 'buttress,'" she told him. "It's my favorite word."

"Healing?" he asked.

"Yeah, I can still heal," she said. "I think. I should be able to help him."

He took her hand, insistent.

"I'll go with you," Rlain said. He glanced at Venli and she hummed to Skepticism, indicating she wouldn't go. She had to attend Raboniel.

"I won't stay away too long," Rlain promised her. "I don't want to draw suspicion." The other two left, but he lingered, then hummed to Appreciation. "I'm sorry about what I said when you first saw me in the cell. You're not selfish, Venli."

"I am," she said. "A lot of things are confusing to me these days—but of that fact I'm certain."

"No," he said. "Today you're a hero. I know you've been through rough times, but today . . ." He grinned and hummed to Appreciation again, then ducked out after the others.

If only he knew the whole story. Still, she felt upbeat as she headed toward the scholar rooms below.

"Can I say the words now?" she asked Timbre.

The pulse indicated the negative. Not yet.

"When?" Venli asked.

A simple, straightforward pulse was her answer.

You'll know.

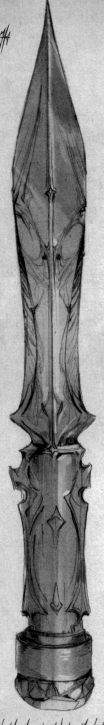

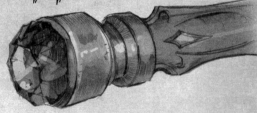

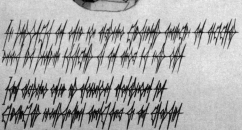

Midius once told me ... told me we could use Investiture ... to enhance our minds, our memories, so we wouldn't forget so much.

Raboniel made good on her promise to leave Navani to her own designs. The Fused studied the shield that protected the Sibling—but without Navani to accidentally act as a spy, Raboniel's progress wasn't nearly as rapid as before. Occasionally—when pacing so she could glance out past the guard—Navani would catch Raboniel sitting on the floor beside the blue shield, holding up the sphere full of Warlight and staring at it.

Navani found herself in a curious situation. Forbidden to take part in the administration of the tower, forbidden direct contact with her scholars, she had only her research to occupy her. In a way, she had been given the gift she'd always wished for: a chance to *truly* see if she could become a scholar.

Something had always prevented her from full dedication. After Gavilar's death, she'd been too busy guiding Elhokar and then Aesudan. Perhaps Navani could have focused on scholarship when she'd first come to the Shattered Plains—but there had been a Blackthorn to seduce and then a new kingdom to forge. For all she complained about politics and the distractions of administering a kingdom, she certainly did find her way into the middle of both with frightful regularity.

Perhaps Navani *should* go do menial labor. At least that way she'd be among the people. And wouldn't risk doing any more damage. Except ... Raboniel would certainly never let her go around unsupervised. Plus, the lure of unknown secrets called to Navani. She had information Raboniel did not. Navani had *seen* a sphere that warped air, filled with what seemed to be some kind of anti-Voidlight. She knew about the explosion.

The thing Raboniel wanted to create was possible. So . . . why not try to find out how to make it? Why not see what she could *actually* do? *The power to destroy a god. Negative Light. Can I crack the secret?*

What if Navani was thinking too small in trying to save the tower? What if there was a way to end the war once and for all? What if Navani really *could* find a way to destroy Odium?

She needed to try. But how to even start? Well . . . the best way to encourage discoveries from her scholars was usually to cultivate the proper environment and attitude. Keep them studying, keep them experimenting. Oftentimes the greatest discoveries came not because a woman was looking for them, but because she was so engrossed in some other topic that she started making connections she never would have otherwise.

So, over the next few days, Navani tried to replicate this state in herself. She ordered parts, supplies, fabrial mechanisms—some all the way from Kholinar—and they were delivered without a word of complaint. That included, most importantly, many gemstones bearing corrupted spren to power fabrials.

To warm up, she spent time creating weapons that wouldn't look like weapons. Traps she could use, if she grew truly desperate, to defend her room or the pillar room. She wasn't certain how she would deploy them—or if she would need to. For now, it was something scholarly to do, something familiar, and she threw herself wholeheartedly into the work.

She hid painrials inside other fabrials, constructed to appear innocuous. She made alarms to distract, using technology they'd discovered from the gemstones left by the old Radiants in Urithiru. She used conjoined rubies to make spring traps that would release spikes.

She put Voidlight spheres in her fabrial traps, then set them to be armed by a simple trick. A magnet against the side of the cube, in precisely the right place, would move a metal lever and arm the traps. This way they wouldn't activate until she needed them. She had these boxes stored out in the hallway, as if they were half-completed experiments she intended to return to in a few days. The space was already lined with boxes from the other scholars, so Navani's additions didn't feel out of place.

Afterward, she had Raboniel help her make more Warlight for experiments. Navani couldn't create it by herself, unfortunately. No combination of tuning forks or instruments replicated Raboniel's presence—but so far as Navani could tell, the Fused also couldn't create it without a human's help.

Navani got better at humming the tone, mastering the rhythm. In those moments, she felt as if she could hear the very soul of Roshar speaking to her. She'd never been particularly interested in music, but—like her growing obsession with Light—she found it increasingly fascinating. Waves, sounds, and what they meant for science.

Underlying all the work she did was a singular question: How would one make the *opposite* of Voidlight? What had been in that sphere of Gavilar's?

In Vorinism, pure things were said to be symmetrical. And all things had an opposite. It was easy to see why Raboniel had assumed the dark Light of the Void would be the opposite of Stormlight, but darkness *wasn't* truly an opposite of light. It was simply the absence of light.

She needed some way to measure Investiture, the power in a gemstone. And she needed some kind of model, a form of energy that she knew had an opposite. What things in nature had a *provable*, measurable opposite?

"Magnets," she said, pushing aside her chair and standing up from her notes. She walked up to the guard at her chamber door. "I need more magnets. Stronger ones this time. We kept some in the chemical supplies storehouse on the second floor."

The guard hummed a tone, and accompanied it with a long-suffering sigh for Navani's benefit. He glanced around for support, but the only other singer nearby was Raboniel's daughter, who sat outside the room with her back to the wall, holding a sword across her lap and staring off into the distance while humming. It wasn't a rhythm, Navani realized, but a tune she recognized—a human one sung sometimes at taverns. How did the Fused know it?

"I suppose I can see it done," the guard said to Navani. "Though some of our people are growing annoyed by your persistent demands."

"Take it up with Raboniel," Navani said, walking to her seat. "Oh, and the Fused use some kind of weapon that draws Stormlight out of Radiants they stab. Get me some of that metal."

"I'll need the Lady of Wishes to approve *that*," the guard said.

"Then ask her. Go on. I'm not going to run off. Where do you think I'd go?"

The guard—a stormform Regal—grumbled and moved off to do as she asked. Navani had teased out a few things about him during her incarceration. He'd been a parshman slave in the palace at Kholinar. He thought she should recognize him, and . . . well, perhaps she should. Parshmen had always been so invisible though.

She tried a different experiment while she waited. She had two halves of a conjoined ruby on the desk. That meant a split gemstone—and a split spren, divided right through the center. She was trying to see if she could use the tuning fork method to draw out the halves of the spren and rejoin them in a larger ruby. She thought that might please the Sibling, who still wouldn't talk to her.

She put a magnifying lens on one half of the gemstone and watched as the spren within reacted to the tuning fork. This was a corrupted flamespren; that shouldn't change the nature of the experiment, or so she hoped.

It *was* moving in there, trying to reach the sound. It pressed against the wall of the gemstone, but couldn't escape. *Stormlight can leak through microholes in the structure,* Navani thought. *But the spren is too large.*

A short time later, someone stepped up to the doorway; Navani noticed the darkening light of someone moving in front of the lamp. "My magnets?" Navani asked, holding out her hand while still peering at the spren. "Bring them here."

"Not the magnets," Raboniel said.

"Lady of Wishes," Navani said, turning and bowing from her seat. "I apologize for not recognizing you."

Raboniel hummed a rhythm Navani couldn't distinguish, then walked over to inspect the experiment.

"I'm trying to rejoin a split spren," Navani explained. "Past experience shows that breaking a gemstone in half lets the flamespren go—but in that case, the two halves grow into separate flamespren. I'm trying to see if I can merge them back together."

Raboniel placed something on the desk—a small dagger, ornate, with an intricately carved wooden handle and a large ruby set at the base. Navani picked it up, noting that the center of the blade—running like a vein from tip to hilt—was a different kind of metal than the rest.

"We use these for collecting the souls of Heralds," Raboniel noted. "Or that was the plan. We've taken a single one so far, and . . . there have been complications with that capture. I had hoped to harvest the two you reportedly had here, but they left with your expeditionary force."

Navani flipped the weapon over, feeling cold.

"We've used this metal for several Returns to drain Stormlight from Radiants," Raboniel said. "It conducts Investiture, drawing it from a source and pulling it inward. We used it to fill gemstones, but didn't realize until the fall of Ba-Ado-Mishram that capturing spren in gemstones was possible. It was then that one of us—She Who Dreams—realized it might be possible to trap a Herald's soul in the same way."

Navani licked her lips. So it was true. Shalash had told them Jezerezeh'Elin had fallen. They hadn't realized how. This was better than absolute destruction though. Could he be recovered this way?

"What will you do with their souls?" Navani asked. "Once you have them?"

"Same thing you've done with the soul of Nergaoul," Raboniel said. "Put them somewhere safe, so they can never be released again. Why did you want this metal? The guard told me you'd asked after it."

"I thought," Navani said, "this might be a better way to conduct Storm-light and Voidlight—to transfer it out of gemstones."

"It would work," Raboniel said. "But it isn't terribly practical. Raysium is exceptionally difficult to obtain." She nodded to the dagger she'd given Navani. "That specific weapon, you should know, contains only a small amount of the metal—not enough to harvest a Herald's soul. It would not, therefore, be of any danger to me—should you consider trying such an act."

"Understood, Ancient One," Navani said. "I want it only for my experiments. Thank you." She touched the tip of the dagger—with the white-gold metal—to one half of the divided ruby. Nothing happened.

"Generally, you need to stab someone with it for it to work," Raboniel said. "You need to touch the soul."

Navani nodded absently, resetting her equipment with the tuning fork and the magnifying lens, then watching the spren inside move to the sound. She set the tip of the dagger against it again, watching for any different behavior.

"You seem to be enjoying yourself," Raboniel noted.

"I would enjoy myself more if my people were free, Lady of Wishes," Navani said. "But I intend to use this time to some advantage."

Their defense of the tower, frail though it was, had utterly collapsed. She couldn't reach Kaladin, hear the Sibling, or plan with her scholars. There was only one node left to protect the heart of the tower from corruption.

Navani had a solitary hope remaining: that she could imitate a scholar well enough to build a new weapon. A weapon to kill a god.

In her experiment, nothing happened. The spren couldn't get out of the ruby, even with the tone calling it. The spren was vivid blue, as it was corrupted, and appeared as *half* a spren: one arm, one leg. Why continue to manifest that way? Flamespren often changed forms—and they were in-famous for noticing they were being watched. Navani had read some very interesting essays on the topic.

She picked up a small jeweler's hammer. Carefully, she cracked the half ruby, letting the spren escape. It sprang free, but was immediately captured by the dagger. Light traveled along the blade, then the ruby at the base began to glow. Navani confirmed that the half spren was inside.

Interesting, Navani thought. *So, what if I break the other half of the ruby and capture that half in the same gemstone?* Excited, she reached to grab the other half of the ruby—but when she moved it, the dagger skidded across the table.

Navani froze. The two halves of the spren were still conjoined? She'd expected that to end once the original imprisonment did. Curious, she moved the dagger. The other half of the ruby flew out several feet toward the center of the room.

Too far. *Much* too far. She'd moved the dagger half a foot, while the paired ruby had moved three times as far. Navani stared at the hovering ruby, her eyes wide.

Raboniel hummed a loud rhythm, looking just as startled. "How?" she asked. "Is it because the spren is corrupted?"

"Possibly," Navani said. "Though I've been experimenting with conjoined spren, and corrupted ones seem to generally behave the same as uncorrupted ones." She eyed the dagger. "The gemstone on the dagger is larger than the one it was in before. Always before, you had to split a gemstone in two equal halves to conjoin them. Perhaps by moving one half to a larger gemstone, I have created something new. . . ."

"Force multiplication?" Raboniel asked. "Move a large gemstone a short distance, and cause the small gemstone to go a very long one?"

"Energy will be conserved, if our understanding of fabrial laws is correct," Navani said. "Greater Light will be required, and moving the larger gemstone will be more difficult in equivalency to the work done by the smaller gemstone. But storms . . . the implications . . ."

"Write this down," Raboniel said. "Record your observations. I will do the same."

"Why?" Navani asked.

"The Rhythm of War, Navani," Raboniel said as an explanation—though it didn't seem one to Navani. "Do it. And continue your experiments."

"I will," she said. "But Lady of Wishes, I'm running into another problem. I need a way to measure the strength of Stormlight in a gemstone."

Raboniel didn't press for details. "There is sand that does this," she said.

"Sand?"

"It is black naturally, but turns white in the presence of Stormlight. It can, therefore, be used to measure the strength of Investiture—the more powerful the source of power nearby, the quicker the sand changes. I will get some for you." She hummed loudly. "This is amazing, Navani. I don't think I've known a scholar so capable, not in many Returns."

"I'm not a . . ." Navani trailed off. "Thank you," she said instead.

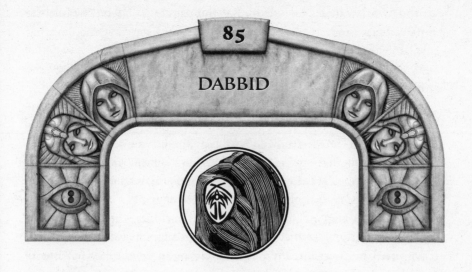

85

DABBID

Why would I want to remember?

D abbid had been different all his life.

That was the word his mother had used. "Different." He liked that word. It didn't try to pretend. Something *was* different about him. He had been six when he started talking. He still couldn't do adding in his head. He could follow instructions, but he forgot steps if they were too long.

He was different.

The surgeons hadn't been able to say the reason. They said some people are just different. He was always going to be like this. The midwife, when she heard about him later, said the cord was wrapped around his neck when he was born. Maybe that was why.

When he'd been young, Dabbid had tried putting a rope around his neck to see how it felt. He hadn't jumped off a ledge. He hadn't tied the other end to anything. He hadn't tried to die. He'd just tightened it a little, so he could know what baby Dabbid had felt.

When someone saw, everyone had panicked. They called him stupid. They took ropes away from him for years. They thought he was too dumb to know it would hurt him. He often got into trouble like that. Doing things others wouldn't do. Not understanding it would make people panic. He had to be very careful not to make regular people frightened. They liked to be scared of him. He did not know why. He was different. But not scary different.

It had gotten worse when his mother died. People had become meaner on that day. It wasn't his fault. He hadn't even been there. But suddenly, everyone was meaner. He ended up at war, serving a lighteyes. Washing his clothing.

When a darkeyed baby was born to the man's wife, everyone had gotten angry at Dabbid. He'd explained that they were wrong. Everybody was wrong sometimes.

It hadn't been until much later that he'd realized the brightlady had lied. To punish someone other than her secret lover. He *could* understand things, if he had time to think about them. Sometimes.

He'd ended up running bridges. Dabbid didn't remember much from that time. He'd lost track of the days. He'd barely spoken back then. He had been confused. He had been frightened. He had been angry. But he didn't let people know he was angry. People got scared and hurt him when he was angry.

He'd done his job, terrified more each day, certain he would die. In fact, he'd figured he must already be dead. So when a horse—from one of Sadeas's own soldiers—had all but trampled him, shoving him and hurling him to the ground, his arm broken, he'd curled up and waited to die.

Then . . . Kaladin. Kaladin Stormblessed. He hadn't cared that Dabbid was different. He hadn't cared that Dabbid had given up. Kaladin hauled him out of Damnation and gave him another family.

Dabbid couldn't quite recall when he'd started to come out of his battle shock. He hadn't ever *really* lost it. Who could? People clapping sounded like bowstrings snapping. Footfalls sounded like hooves. Or he'd hear singing, like the Parshendi, and he was there again. Dying.

Still, he had started to feel better. Somewhere along the way, he'd started to feel like his old self. Except he'd had a new family. He'd had *friends*.

And none of them had known he was different.

Well, they thought he was another kind of different. They thought he had been hurt by the battle, like all of them. He was *one* of them. They hadn't known about his mind. How he'd been born.

He didn't like it when people used the word "stupid" for the way he was. People called one another stupid when they made mistakes. Dabbid wasn't a mistake. He could *make* mistakes. Then he was stupid. But not always. He couldn't think fast like others. But that made him different, not stupid. Stupid was a choice.

In the past, his speech had told people he was different. He'd figured that out when he was moving from job to job after his mother died. When he'd spoken, they'd known. So . . . with Bridge Four . . . he'd just kept on not speaking.

That way they wouldn't know. That way they wouldn't realize he was Dabbid different. He could just be Bridge Four different.

Then everyone had started getting spren. Except him. And then the tower had started talking to him. And . . . he still wasn't certain if he'd done something stupid or not. But going to Rlain, that *hadn't* been stupid. He was certain of it.

So today, he tried not to think about his mistakes. He tried not to think about how if he'd been stronger, he could have helped Kaladin fight. He tried not to think about how he'd lied to the others by pretending he couldn't speak. He tried to focus on what he could do to help.

He led Rlain up through the tunnels. They met singers a couple of times. Rlain talked, his voice calm with rhythms, and the singers let them go. They went up and up, and Dabbid showed him a hidden stairwell. They snuck past the guard patrols on the sixth floor.

Up and up. Dabbid's heart thumped. Worrying. Would Lift meet them, like she'd promised? Lift knew the tower better than they did. She said she could make it on her own. But would she run away?

When they reached the meeting place on the tenth floor, they found her waiting. She sat on the ground, eating some curry and bread.

"Where did you get *that*?" Rlain asked.

"Fused," she said, gesturing. "Funny. They need to eat. Suppose that means they poop, right?"

"I suppose," Rlain said, sounding disapproving.

"Ain't that a kick in the bits?" Lift asked. "You get made immortal; you can live through the centuries. You can fly, or walk through rock, or something like that. But you still gotta piss like everyone else."

"I don't see the point of this conversation," Rlain said. "Hurry. We need to get to Kaladin."

Lift rolled her eyes in an exaggerated way, then stood up and handed Dabbid some flatbread. He nodded in thanks and tucked it away for later.

"When didya start talkin'?" Lift asked him.

"I was six," he said. "Mom said."

"No, I mean . . ." She gestured at him.

Dabbid felt himself blush, and he looked at his feet. "I could for a long time. Just didn't."

"Didn't want to talk? I've *never* felt like that. Except this once, when I ate the queen's dinner, but it had been sitting *out*, see, and she didn't put it away like she should have. It's her fault, I told her, because it's like leavin' a sword out where a baby could step on it and cut up her foot or somethin'."

"Can we please keep moving?" Rlain demanded.

Dabbid led them the rest of the way. He felt more anxious now. Was he too late? Had Kaladin died while he was gone? Was he too slow to help? Too different to have realized earlier what he should have done?

Dabbid led them to the place on the eleventh floor, but the door had stopped working. It had been too long since Kaladin infused it. They had Lift though, and when she pressed her hand to the gemstone, the door opened.

It smelled of sweat and blood in there. Dabbid hurried past the place where Teft lay unconscious, reaching Kaladin. On the floor, wrapped in blankets. Thrashing. Still alive.

Still alive.

"Storms," Lift said, stepping over. Kaladin's face was coated in sweat. His teeth were gritted, his eyes squeezed shut. He flailed in his blankets, growling softly. Dabbid had cut off his shirt to look for wounds. While there were scabs all along Kaladin's side, the worst part was the infection. It spread across the skin from the cut. A violent redness. Hateful, covered in little rotspren.

Lift stepped back, wrapping her arms around herself. "Storms."

"I've . . . never seen a fever like that," Rlain said, towering over the two of them. Did he know how large he was in warform? "Have you?"

Lift shook her head.

"Please," Dabbid said. "Please help."

Lift held out her hand, palm forward, and burst alight with power. Stormlight rose from her skin like white smoke, and she knelt. She shied away as Kaladin thrashed again, then she lunged forward and pressed her hand to his chest.

The redness immediately retreated, and the rotspren fled, as if they couldn't stand the presence of her touch. Kaladin's back arched. He was hurting!

Then he collapsed into the blankets. Lift pressed her other hand against his side, and the wound continued to heal, the redness fleeing. She furrowed her brow and bit her lip. Dabbid did the same. Maybe it would help.

She pushed so much Stormlight into Kaladin he started glowing himself. When she sat back, the scabs flaked off his side, leaving smooth new skin.

"That . . . was hard," she whispered. "Even harder than when I saved Gawx." She wiped her brow. "I'm sweating."

"Thank you," Dabbid said, taking her hand.

"Ew," she said. Oh. It was the hand she'd just used to wipe her head.

"*Thank you*," he said.

She shrugged. "My awesomeness—the slippery part—doesn't work anymore. But this does. Wonder why."

Rlain went to close the door. Dabbid tried to make Kaladin comfortable, bunching up a blanket to make a pillow. His friend was still unconscious, but sleeping peacefully now.

"I have a lot of questions, Dabbid," Rlain said. "First off, why have you been keeping quiet when you could speak?"

"I . . ."

"He don't gotta say nothin' if he don't wanna," Lift said. She'd found their rations already, and was eating. Wow.

"He's Bridge Four," Rlain said. "We're family. Family doesn't lie to one another."

"I'm sorry," Dabbid said softly. "I just . . . didn't want you to know I'm . . . different."

"We're all different," Rlain said, folding his arms. Storms, he was so frightening in carapace armor.

"I'm more different," Dabbid said. "I . . . I was born different."

"You mean born . . . you know . . . an idiot?" Rlain said.

Dabbid winced. He hated that word, though Rlain didn't use it hatefully. It was just a word to him.

"Touched," Lift said. "I've known lotsa kids like him on the street. They don't think the same way as everyone else. It happens."

"It happens," Dabbid agreed. "It happened to me. But you didn't know. So you couldn't treat me like I was . . . wrong. You know about being extra different, right Rlain?"

"I guess I do," he said. "You shouldn't feel that you have to hide what you are though."

"I will be fixed," Dabbid said, "when I get a spren. Becoming Radiant will heal me, because my brain isn't supposed to be like this. I was hurt after I was born. The tower said so."

"The tower?" Rlain asked.

"The tower can talk," Lift said. "It's a spren."

"And it promised to heal you, Dabbid?"

He nodded. Though it hadn't said that in so many words. He wondered now if it had been lying.

The queen hadn't been pleased by how he'd snuck around, doing tasks for the Sibling. Maybe he should be more suspicious. Even of spren.

But someday . . . when he was Radiant . . .

Rlain dug out a new set of blankets for Kaladin from the pile. Dabbid had washed those earlier, as he'd wanted something to do. They got Kaladin untangled from the sweaty ones, then wrapped him in—

"What in storming Damnation are you fools doing?" a gruff voice said from behind them.

Dabbid froze. Then turned around slowly. Lift was perched on the end of Teft's shelf, absently munching on a ration bar—Soulcast grain, cooked and pressed. She was pulling her hand back from Teft's exposed foot, Stormlight curling off her body.

Teft, in turn, was pushing himself up to sit.

Teft was *awake*.

Dabbid let out a whoop and leaped up. Rlain just started humming like he did sometimes.

"What?" Lift said. "Wasn't I supposed to heal the stinky one too?"

"Stinky?" Teft said, looking under his blanket. "Where in Damnation are my clothes? What happened to me? We were at the tavern, right? Storms, my *head*."

"You can wake the Radiants?" Rlain asked, rushing over and seizing Lift by the arms. "Why didn't you say something?"

"Huh?" she said. "Look, shellhead, I've been in a stormin' *cage*. My spren vanished, said he was going to try to get help, and I ain't heard from him since. Bet he joined the Voidbringers, storming traitor. I don't know what's been goin' on in the tower. What's wrong with the others?"

"In a cage?" Teft said. "Why? And where are my *storming* clothes?"

"There's a lot to explain, Teft," Rlain said. "The tower is occupied by the enemy and . . ." He stopped, then frowned, glancing toward Kaladin.

Kaladin . . . Kaladin was *stirring*. They all hushed. Even Teft. Kaladin blinked and *opened his eyes*. He grew tense, then saw Rlain and Dabbid and relaxed, taking a deep breath.

"Is this a dream?" he whispered. "Or am I finally awake?"

"You're awake, Kal," Rlain said, kneeling to take Kaladin by the shoulder. "Thank the purest tones. You're awake. It worked."

Dabbid stepped back as Teft said something, causing Kaladin to sit up—then laugh in joy. It had worked.

Dabbid wasn't Radiant. He wasn't brave. He wasn't smart. But today he hadn't been stupid either.

Once, Kaladin had pulled Dabbid out of Damnation itself. It felt good to return that act of heroism with a small one of his own.

86

THE SONG OF MORNINGS

ONE AND A HALF YEARS AGO

A s the war with the humans progressed, Venli became increasingly certain she'd made the correct decision.

How could her people, after generations of stagnation, hope to stand by themselves in the world? If recent reports were true, the humans had *Surgebinders* again, like those spoken of in the songs. Ulim was right. A bigger war than this was coming. Venli's people needed to be prepared.

Venli stood with folded arms, attuned to Confidence as she watched a listener warband return from a raid. Eshonai and her soldiers had won the day, and they brought a large gemheart with them. Eshonai herself delivered it up to Denshil, their head of farming.

Her warriors didn't look like victors. Bloody, wounded, their ancient weapons sagging in their grips as if weighted by groundspren. More than a few of the soldiers walked alone. Warpairs who had lost a member.

Venli watched with hidden glee. Surely they were close to breaking. If she could bring them a form of power . . . would they accept it? Venli remembered her hesitance, and weakness, when she'd started along this path years ago. She'd been technically a youth then, though fully grown. Now she was an adult. She saw as an adult did.

She turned and cut through a side street of the ancient city, passing large crem-covered walls like tall ridges of natural stone. You'd have to cut deep with a Shardblade to find the worked stone at the heart.

This was the more direct way, so she was waiting as Denshil walked past with the gemstone. He was scrawny even when wearing workform, and had a pattern of black and red skin that looked like true marblework, all rough and coarse. He jumped as he saw Venli.

"What are you doing," he hissed to Anxiety as she walked along beside him.

"Acting naturally," she said. "I'm head of our scholars. It's normal for me to visit our farmers and see how their work is progressing."

He still acted nervous, but at least he attuned Peace as they walked. It didn't matter. They passed few listeners on the streets. All who weren't absolutely needed as farmers, caretakers, or other essential workers had joined Eshonai.

In a perfect bit of poetry, this ensured that the bravest of the listeners—those most likely to resist Venli when she brought them stormform—fought on the front lines each day, dying. Each corpse brought Venli one step closer to her goal.

She'd stopped pretending this was *only* about protecting her people. As she'd grown into herself and become more confident, she'd decided what she truly wanted. True freedom—with the power to make certain she'd never have to be dependent upon anyone else, listener or spren. True freedom couldn't exist while someone else had power over you.

So yes, her work was about helping her people, in part. But deep within her—where the rhythms began—Venli promised herself that *she* would be the one who obtained the most freedom.

"How goes your work?" Venli asked to Confidence.

Denshil's rhythm slipped to Anxiety again. Foolish farmer. He'd better not give them away.

"The others believe me," he said softly, "and they should. I'm not saying anything that's a *lie*, really. If we cut these gemhearts like the humans do, they hold more Stormlight. But I don't mention the extra bits I cut off before delivering the faceted stone to the fields. . . ."

"How much have you saved?"

"Several hundred gemstones."

"I need more," Venli said.

He blatantly attuned Irritation. "More? What crazy rhythm are you listening to?"

"We need one for every listener in the city."

"I can't," he said. "If you—"

"You *can*," Venli said to Reprimand. "And you will. Cut the gemstones smaller. Give less to the fields."

"And if we end up starving because of it? Gemstones break, you know, when you sing to them. We *will* run out."

"We won't live long enough to starve, Denshil. Not if the humans get here. Not if they find your children and take away their songs . . ."

The malen attuned Longing immediately. The listeners had few children these days. Most had stopped taking mateform years ago, and they had never been as fecund a people as the humans apparently were.

"Think how you could improve," Venli said. "For them, Denshil. For your daughter."

"We should bring this to the Five," he said.

"We will. You can watch me bring the proposal to them. This will be done properly—you and I are simply preparing the way."

He nodded, and Venli let him rush on ahead to the ancient building where he practiced gem cutting—an art Ulim had taught him.

Say a name on the breeze and it will return, she thought, noting a red light glowing from within an old abandoned building. They'd had to cut the window out to get to the structure inside. She strolled over, and Ulim stepped out onto the windowsill—invisible to everyone but those he chose.

"You've learned to lie very well," he said to Subservience.

"I have," she said. "Are we ready?"

"Close," he said. "I feel the storm on the other side. I think it's nearly here."

"You think?" Venli demanded.

"I can't see into Shadesmar," he snapped to Derision.

She didn't quite understand his explanations of what was happening. But she knew a storm was mounting in Shadesmar. In fact, the storm had been building for generations—growing in fury, intensity. It barred the way to Damnation.

That storm was where Ulim had originally come from. There were also thousands of another kind of spren in the storm: stormspren. Mindless things like windspren or flamespren.

Venli had to find a way to pull those stormspren across and capture them. To that end, a large portion of the roiling storm had been broken off by the god of gods, the ancient one called Odium. This storm was his strength, his essence. Over painful months, he'd moved the storm across the landscape—unseen—until it arrived here. Kind of. Almost.

"What will happen," Venli asked to Curiosity, "when my storm comes to this world?"

"Your storm?"

"I am the one who summons it, spren," she said. "It is *mine*."

"Sure, sure," he said. A little too quickly, and with too many hand gestures. He had grown obsequious over the last few years—and liked to pretend that his betrayal of her in the Kholinar palace had never happened.

"When this storm comes, you *will* serve me," Venli said.

"I serve you now."

"Barely. Promise it. You'll serve me."

"I will serve," he said. "I promise it, Venli. But we have to *bring* the stormspren to this side first. And persuade the listeners to take the forms."

"The second will not be a problem."

"You're too certain about that," he said. "Remember, they killed the Alethi king to *prevent* this from happening. Traitors."

He got hung up on that idea. Though he'd been the one to whisper about the location of the slave with the Honorblade—and he'd agreed to help start a war to make her people desperate—he *could not* get over the reasoning her people had used. Ulim hadn't found out about Eshonai's experience with King Gavilar until weeks later, and he'd been livid. How dare the listeners do exactly what he wanted, but for the wrong reason!

Foolish little spren. Venli attuned Skepticism—and *almost* felt something different, something more. A better rhythm. Right outside her reach.

"Focus less on that," Venli said. "And more on your duties."

"Yes, Venli," he said, voice cooing as he spoke to Subservience. "You're going to be amazed by the power you get from stormform. And the massive storm you'll bring through? It will be unlike *anything* the world has ever seen. Odium's raw power, blowing across the world in the wrong direction. It will devastate the humans, leave them broken and easily conquered. Ripe for your domination, Venli."

"Enough," she said. "Don't sell it so hard, Ulim. I'm not the child you found when you first arrived here. Do your job, and get the storm into position. I'll capture the stormspren."

"How, though?"

How. "They are the spren of storms, right?"

"Well, *a* storm," Ulim said. "In the past, they mostly spent their time inside gemhearts. Odium would directly bless the singer, making them a kind of royalty. They didn't really wander about much."

Royalty? She liked the sound of that. She smiled, imagining how Eshonai would act toward her *then*.

"My scholars are confident," Venli said. "From what you've told them, and the experiments we've done with other kinds of spren, we think if we can gather a small collection of stormspren in gemstones, others will get pulled through more easily."

"But we need that initial seed!" Ulim said. "How?"

She nodded to the sky, where her imaginings had brought forth a gloryspren. An enormous brilliant sphere, with wings along the sides. "Those pop in when we think the proper thoughts. Feel the right things. So, what brings stormspren?"

"A storm . . ." Ulim said. "It might work. Worth trying."

They'd have to experiment. Even with his help, it had taken several tries to figure out nimbleform—and that was a relatively easy form. Still, she was pleased with their progress. Yes, it had taken far, far longer than she'd anticipated. But over those many years, she'd become the person she was now. Confident, like her younger self had never been.

She turned to make her way toward where her scholars studied the songs, written in the script she'd devised. Unfortunately, she soon spotted a tall, armored figure heading her direction. Venli immediately turned down a side road, but Eshonai called to her. Venli attuned Irritation. Eshonai would follow her if she hurried on, so she slowed and turned.

Venli's sister looked so strange in Shardplate. It . . . well, it *fit* her. It supernaturally molded to her form, making space for her carapace, shaping itself to her figure, but it was more than that. To Venli, some of the warforms seemed like they were playing pretend—their faces didn't match their new shape. Not Eshonai. Eshonai *looked* like a soldier, with a wider neck, powerful jaw and head, and enormous hands.

Venli regretted encouraging Eshonai to visit the former Shardbearer. She hadn't expected that years later, she'd feel dwarfed by her sister. Though much about Venli's life was enviable now—she had position, friends, and responsibility—there was a part of her that wished she'd been able to obtain this without Eshonai *also* gaining high station.

"What?" Venli asked to Irritation. "I have work to do today, Eshonai, and—"

"It's Mother," Eshonai said.

Venli immediately attuned the Terrors. "What about her? What's wrong?"

Eshonai attuned Resolve and led Venli quietly to their mother's home on the outskirts of town. A small structure, but solitary, with plenty of room for gardening projects.

Their mother wasn't in the garden, working on her shalebark. She was inside lying on a hard cot, her head wrapped in a bandage. One of Venli's scholars—Mikaim, who was their surgeon—stepped away from the cot. "It's not bad," she said. "Head wounds can be frightful, but it was little more than a scrape. The bigger worry is how afraid she was. I gave her something to help her sleep."

Venli hummed to Appreciation and Mikaim withdrew. Eshonai stood opposite Venli over the cot, her helmet under her arm, and for a time the two of them hummed together to the Lost. A rare moment when they both heard the same rhythm.

"Do you know what happened?" Venli finally asked.

"She was found wandering one of the outer plateaus. Frightened, acting like a little child. She didn't respond to her own name at first, though by the time she got here she had recovered enough to begin answering questions about her childhood. She didn't remember how she hurt herself."

Venli breathed deeply, and listened to the haunting Rhythm of the Lost, a violent beat with staccato notes.

"We might need to confine her to her house," Eshonai said.

"No!" Venli said. "Never. We can't do that to her, Eshonai. Imprisonment *on top* of her ailment?"

Eshonai attuned Reconciliation, settling down on the floor, her Shardplate scraping softly. "You're right, of course. She must be allowed to see the sky, look to the horizon. We can get her a servant perhaps. Someone to keep watch over her."

"An acceptable accommodation," Venli said, lingering beside the cot. She really should check on her scholars.

Eshonai leaned—gingerly, because her Plate was so heavy—against the wall. She closed her eyes, humming to Peace. It was forced, a little loud. She was trying to override other rhythms.

She looks more like herself sitting like that, Venli thought idly, remembering Eshonai as a child. The sister who would pick Venli up when she scraped her knee, or who would chase cremlings with her. Eshonai had always seemed so vibrant—so alive. As if she'd been trying to burst out, her soul straining against the confines of a flawed body.

"You always led me toward the horizon," Venli found herself saying. "Even as children. Always running to the next hill to see what was on the other side . . ."

"Would that we could return," Eshonai said to the Lost.

"To those ignorant days?"

"To that joy. That innocence."

"Innocence is more false a god than the ones in our songs," Venli said, sitting beside her sister. "People who chase it will find themselves enslaved."

Venli felt tired, she realized. She'd been spending far too many nights thinking of plans. And it would only get worse, as she needed to start going out into storms to trap stormspren.

"I'm sorry I brought us to this," Eshonai whispered to Reconciliation. "We've lost so many. How far will it go? All because I made a snap decision in a moment of tension."

"That sphere," Venli said. "The one King Gavilar gave you . . ." They'd all seen it, though it had faded several months later.

"Yes. A dark power. And he claimed to be seeking to return our gods."

Ulim had been nervous about Gavilar's sphere. The little spren said Gavilar hadn't been working with him, or any of Odium's agents—indeed, he'd been hostile to them. So Ulim had no idea how he'd obtained Odium's Light.

"Maybe," Venli said, "if the humans are seeking to contact our gods, perhaps we should explore the option too. Perhaps the things from our songs are—"

"Stop," Eshonai said to Reprimand. "Venli, what are you saying? You better than most should know the foolishness of what you say."

I'm always a fool to you, aren't I? Venli attuned Irritation. Unfortunately, this was the Eshonai she'd come to know. Not the child who encouraged her. The adult who held her back, ridiculed her.

"Sing the song with me," Eshonai said. "'Terrible and great they were, but—'"

"Please don't turn this into another lecture, Eshonai," Venli said. "Just . . . stop, all right?"

Eshonai trailed off, then hummed to Reconciliation. The two of them sat for a time, the light outside dimming as the sun drifted toward the horizon. Venli found herself humming to Reconciliation as well. She explored the rhythm, finding a complementary tone to Eshonai's, seeking again—for a brief moment—to be in tune with her sister.

Eshonai quietly changed to Longing, and Venli followed. And then, cautiously, Venli switched to Joy. Eshonai followed her this time. Together they made a song, and Venli began singing. It had been . . . well, years since she'd practiced the songs. She'd long ago stopped thinking of herself as the apprentice song keeper; they had plenty of others to uphold their traditions, now that they'd united the families.

She still remembered the songs though. This was the Song of Mornings. A teaching song, meant to train a young child for more complex rhythms and songs. There was something satisfying about a simple song you could sing well. You could add your own complexity. And you could sing the song's soul—rather than struggle with missed lyrics or failed notes.

She let her voice drift off at the end, and Eshonai's humming quieted. Dusk fell outside. The perfectly wrong time for the Song of Mornings. She loved that it had worked so well anyway.

"Thank you, Venli," Eshonai said. "For all that you do. You don't get enough credit for having brought us these forms. Without warform, we wouldn't stand a chance of resisting the humans. We'd probably be their slaves."

"I . . ." Venli tried to attune Confidence, but it slipped away from her. "As long as you and Demid know what I did, I suppose it doesn't sting so much when others pass me over."

"Do you think you could find me a different form?" Eshonai said. "A form that would let me talk better, more diplomatically? I could go to the humans and explain what happened. Maybe I could speak with Dalinar Kholin. I feel like . . . like he might listen, if I could find him. If I could make my tongue work. They don't hear the rhythms, and it's so difficult to explain to them. . . ."

"I can try," Venli said, Pleading sounding in her ears. Why Pleading? She hadn't attuned that.

"Then maybe I could talk to you," Eshonai said quietly, drooping from fatigue. "Without sounding like I'm trying to lecture. You'd know how I really feel. Mother would understand that I don't try to run away. I just want to see . . ."

"You'll see it someday," Venli promised. "You'll see the whole world. Every vibrant color. Every singing wind. Every land and people."

Eshonai didn't respond.

"I . . . I've been doing things you might not like," Venli whispered. "I should tell you. You'll explain that what I'm doing is wrong though, and you're always right. That's part of what I hate about you."

But her sister had already drifted off. The stiff Shardplate kept her in a seated position, slumped against the wall, breathing softly. Venli climbed to her feet and left.

That night, she went into the storm to hunt stormspren for the first time.

87

TRIAL BY WITNESS

Maybe if I remembered my life, I'd be capable of being confident like I once was. Maybe I'd stop vacillating when even the most simple of decisions is presented to me.

The weather turned energetic by the time Adolin's trial arrived. The honorspren he passed chatted more, and seemed to have more of a spring to their steps as they flowed toward the forum on the southern plane of Lasting Integrity.

He couldn't feel the weather, though Blended said it was like a faint drumming in the back of her mind, upbeat and peppy. Indeed, the inkspren seemed chattier.

He felt more nervous than at his first ranked duel—and far less prepared. Legal terms, strategies, even the details of his political training all seemed distant as he walked down the steps to the amphitheater floor. As Blended had feared, the place was packed with honorspren. Many wore uniforms or other formal attire, though some wore loose, flowing outfits that trailed behind them as they walked. These seemed more free-spirited. Perhaps their presence would help the crowd turn to his side.

Blended said that was important. The High Judge—being who he was—would likely listen to the mood of the crowd and judge accordingly. Adolin wished someone had explained to him earlier how fickle his judge would be. That might favor Adolin, fortunately: he could depend on some level of erratic behavior from Kelek, whereas the honorspren were basically all against him from the start.

They didn't boo as he reached the floor of the forum; they had too much decorum. They hushed instead. He found Shallan seated next to Pattern over on the left side. She pumped her fist toward him, and he had the impression she was Radiant at the moment.

Kelek sat upon a thronelike seat with a bench before it, both built in among the forum's tiers. The Herald seemed imposing, and Adolin was reminded that—despite the man's odd behavior—Kelek was thousands of years old. Perhaps he would listen.

"All right, all right," Kelek said. "Human, get over there on the podium and stand there until this show finishes and we can execute you."

"Holy One," an honorspren said from his side. "We do *not* execute people."

"What else are you going to do?" Kelek said. "You don't have prisons, and I doubt he'll care if you exile him. Hell, half the people in this place would regard escaping your presence to be a *reward*."

"We are building a proper holding cell," the honorspren said, looking toward Adolin. "So he can be kept healthy and on display for years to come."

Wonderful, Adolin thought, stepping into the place indicated. The consequences of failure, however, had always been far bigger than his own life. The war needed Radiants, and Radiants needed spren. If Adolin failed, it meant leaving thousands of troops to die without proper support.

He needed to stand here, tall and confident, and *win* this challenge. Somehow.

He turned to face the crowd. According to Blended, today would be the worst of the days. Three witnesses against him. Tomorrow he'd get to have his say.

"Very well," Kelek said. "I suppose you need to give trial terms, Sekeir?"

The bearded honorspren stood up. "Indeed, Honored One."

"Make it fast," Kelek said.

Adolin took a moment of enjoyment from the affronted way Sekeir received that injunction. The honorspren had likely planned a lengthy speech.

"As you wish, Honored One," Sekeir said. "Today, we enter a trial as demanded by this human, Adolin Kholin, to determine if he can bear the sins of the Recreance—where men killed their spren. Since this event happened, which no one disputes, then we must simply prove that we are wise to stay away from all humans as a result."

"Right, then," Kelek said. "Human, this works for you?"

"Not exactly, Honored One," Adolin said, using the opening statement Blended had helped him prepare. "I did not agree to be tried for my ancestors. I agreed to be tried for myself. I told the honorspren I personally bear no blame for what humans did in the past. Because of that, I contend that the honorspren are acting dishonorably by ignoring my people's pleas for help."

Kelek rubbed his forehead. "So we're arguing over even the definitions? This doesn't bode well."

"There is no argument," Sekeir said. "Honored One, he says he wishes to bear no sins of his ancestors, and we should instead prove why he specifically can't be trusted. But the Recreance is a large portion of why we cannot trust his kind! We set the terms when he entered: He would have to stand trial for all humankind. He can dissemble if he wishes, but he *did* enter our fortress, and therefore agreed to our terms."

Kelek grunted. "That makes sense. Human, you're going to have to stand trial as he wishes. That said, I'll keep your arguments in mind when I finally judge."

"I suppose I must agree," Adolin said. Blended had warned him not to push too hard here.

"So . . . trial by witness, right?" Kelek said. "I'm to listen to the arguments presented, then decide. Either the honorspren are being selfish, denying honor, and I should command them to go to the battlefield. Or I decide they've been wise, that humans are not worthy of trust—and we throw this man in a prison as an example?"

"Yes, Honored One," Sekeir said.

"Great," Kelek said. "I assume you had no lack of volunteers, Sekeir. Who is first?"

"Amuna," said the honorspren. "Come, and bear your witness."

The audience whispered quietly as a female spren rose from her spot on the front row. She wore a warrior's pleated skirt and a stiff shirt. She was slender and willowy, and when she stepped she was as graceful as a leaf in the wind. Adolin recognized her; this was the spren to whom he'd been forced to surrender Maya on their first day in Lasting Integrity. He'd occasionally seen Amuna again during his daily visits to Maya.

The two honorspren sitting beside her bore ragged clothing and scratched-out eyes like Maya's. On a glowing honorspren's face, the scratches made a stark contrast.

"You all know me," said the spren in the pleated skirt, "so I will speak for the benefit of Highprince Adolin. I am Amuna, and my duty is to care for the deadeyes in Lasting Integrity. We take their care very seriously."

"And the ones watching outside?" Adolin asked. He was allowed to talk during testimonies, though Blended had warned him to be careful. If he was too belligerent, the High Judge could order him gagged. And he had to be careful not to address the audience in a way that invited them to interrogate him.

"We . . . cannot accept them all in, unfortunately," Amuna said. "We had not thought to see so many. We *have* tried to invite in all of the honorspren deadeyes."

"Are there many?" Adolin asked.

"In total? We have some twenty deadeyed honorspren in the fortress now, though there were some *two thousand* honorspren alive at the time of your betrayal. A single one survived."

"Syl," Adolin said.

"The Ancient Daughter was in a catatonic state," Amuna said, "and was spared. But every other honorspren—every *single* one—had answered the call of the Radiants during the False Desolation. Can you understand the magnitude of that tragedy, Highprince Adolin? The murder of an entire species, all in one day? Absolute extermination, performed by the most intimate of friends?

"We often encounter deadeyes wandering aimlessly in the barrens, or standing in the shallows of the ocean. We bring them here, give them Stormlight, care for them the best we can. Frequently, we can do only a little before they are summoned away to your world—where their corpses are used to continue your brutal murders!"

She turned, gesturing toward the two deadeyes on the bench—and though she faced Adolin, her words were obviously for the crowd. They, not the High Judge, were the true adjudicators.

"This is what you'd have us return to?" she demanded. "You say you aren't the same people who lived so long ago, but do you honestly think you're any better than them? I'd contend you are worse! You pillage, and murder, and burn. You spare no expense nor effort when given an opportunity to ruin another man's life. If the ancient Radiants were not trustworthy, then how can you *possibly* say that you are?"

Murmurs of assent washed through the crowd. They didn't jeer or call as a human audience might—he'd suffered that during many a dueling bout. Blended had warned him not to say too much by way of defense today, but they seemed to want *something* from him.

"Every man fails his own ideals," Adolin said. "You are right. I am not the honorable man I wish that I were. But my father is. Can you deny that the Stormfather himself was willing to take a chance upon a man from this epoch?"

"This is a good point," Kelek said, leaning forward. "The Stormfather is all we have left of old Tanavast. I would not have thought to find his Bondsmith again, no indeed."

Amuna spun toward Adolin. "Do you know what would happen, Prince Adolin, if the Stormfather were to be killed?"

Adolin paused, then shook his head.

"A wise answer," she said. "As no one knows. We were fortunate that no Bondsmiths existed at the time of the Recreance, though how the Sibling knew to end their bond early is a matter of dispute. I can only imagine the catastrophe that awaits us when your father kills his spren."

"He won't," Adolin said. "My father is no common man."

"Such could be said of all the Radiants in times past," Amuna said, stepping toward him. "But now, *I* am the one who cares for the betrayed. I hear their voiceless sorrow; I see their sightless pain. I would have Lasting Integrity pulled down, stone by stone, before I agree to send a single honorspren to suffer a similar fate."

She bowed to Kelek, then turned and sat between the two deadeyes. They continued to sit, faces forward, motionless.

Adolin ground his teeth and glanced to Shallan for support. At least there was one friendly face out in that crowd. He forced himself to remain standing, hands clasped behind him in the posture his father used when he wanted to appear commanding. He'd worn his best coat. For all it mattered. Storms, he felt exposed here on the floor, surrounded by all the glowing figures. This was worse than when he'd been alone in the dueling arena facing four Shardbearers. At least then he'd had his Blade in hand and Plate on his back.

They waited for Kelek to call the next witness. The High Judge, instead, spent a good twenty minutes writing in his notebook. He was a divine being, like a kind of ardent, if magnified a thousand times. It wasn't surprising to see him writing. Adolin just hoped the notes he was taking related to the testimony. He half expected that the Herald was solving word puzzles like the ones Jasnah enjoyed.

Eventually, the Herald dug something out of his pocket—fruit it seemed, though it was bright green and it crunched when Kelek took a bite.

"Looks good," Kelek said. "Nothing too unexpected, though I have to say he *does* have a good point. An unchained Bondsmith is dangerous, but the Stormfather *did* choose one anyway. . . ."

"You know how erratic the Stormfather has been lately," said an elderly female honorspren at Kelek's side. "His wisdom is no longer something to trust."

"Valid, valid," Kelek said. "Well then, next witness."

"Next to speak will be Blended," Sekeir said. "Inkspren emissary to Lasting Integrity."

What? Adolin thought as his tutor stood up from the crowd and walked to the floor of the arena. The watching honorspren murmured together quietly at the sight.

"Wait," Adolin said. "What is this?"

"They asked me to witness against you," she said. "So a spren who is not an honorspren would have a chance to weigh in on this proceeding."

"But . . . you're my tutor. Didn't you volunteer to train me?"

"I wanted you well-trained," she said, "so the trial could be as fair as possible. This thing is. But my hatred of what your kind did also is." She turned to Kelek. "Honored One, I was alive when men betrayed us. Unlike the honorspren, my kind were not so foolish as to assign *all* as Radiant spren. We lost over half our numbers, but some of us watched from outside."

She eyed Adolin. "We knew men as they were and are. Untrustworthy. Changeable. Spren find it difficult to break a bond. Some say it is impossible for us. Men, however, barely last a day without betraying some Ideal.

"Why should we beings of innate honor have been surprised when the event happened? It is not the fault of men that they are as fickle as the falling rain. This thing is. They should not be trusted, and the shame of doing so is our fault. Never again should spren and men bond. It is unnatural."

"Unnatural?" Adolin said. "Spren and skyeels bond to fly. Spren and greatshells bond to grow. Spren and singers bond to create new forms. This is as natural as the changing seasons."

And thank you, Shallan, he thought, glancing at her, *for your interest in all this.*

"Humans are not from this land," Blended said. "You are invaders, and bonds with you are *not* natural. Be careful what you say—you will encourage us to return to the singers. They betrayed us long ago, but never on the scale of the humans. Perhaps the highspren have the correct idea in joining with the armies of the Fused."

"You'd side with them?" Adolin said. "Our *enemies*?"

"Why not?" she said, strolling across the stage. "They are the rightful heirs of this land. They have been pushed to desperation by your kind, but they are no less reasonable or logical. Perhaps your kind would do better to acknowledge their rule."

"They serve Odium," Adolin said, noticing many of the honorspren shifting in their seats, uncomfortable. "Men might be changeable, yes. We might be corrupt at times, and weak always. But I know evil when I see it. Odium is *evil*. I will never serve him."

Blended eyed the crowd, who nodded at Adolin's words. She gave him a little nod herself, as if in acknowledgment of a point earned.

"This tangent is irrelevant," she said, turning to Kelek. "I can say, with some ease, that a good relationship between honorspren and inkspren is not. Any would acknowledge this. My testimony's value is, then, of extra import.

"I *lived through* the pain and chaos of the Recreance. I saw my siblings, beloved, dead. I saw families ripped apart, and pain flowing like blood. We might be enemies, but in one thing unification *is*. Men should *never again* be trusted with our bonds. If this one wishes to accept punishment for the thousands who escaped it, I say let him. Lock him away. Be done with him and any who, like him, wish to repeat the massacre of the past." She looked directly at Adolin. "This truth is."

Adolin felt at a loss to say anything. What defense could he offer? "We are not the same as the ones before," he said.

"Can you promise you will be different," she demanded. "Absolutely promise it? Promise that *no* further spren will be killed from bonds, if allowed to be?"

"Of course not," Adolin said.

"Well, I *can* promise that none will die so long as no more bonds are made. The solution *is* easy."

She turned and walked back to her place.

Adolin looked to Kelek. "There are no promises in life. Nothing is sure. She says spren won't die without bonds, but can you say what will happen if Odium reigns?"

"I find it most curious she'd prefer that possibility, young man," Kelek said. He started writing in his notebook again. "But it is seriously damning of you that an inkspren would be willing to testify alongside an honorspren. Damning indeed . . ." Kelek took another bite of his fruit, leaving only the core, which he absently set on the table in front of him.

Frustrated, Adolin forced himself to calm. The trial was proceeding well on at least one axis. The honorspren weren't trying to force the actual sins of the Recreance on him; they were taking a more honorable approach of proving that men hadn't changed, and bonds were too risky.

Blended and he had decided this tactic was safer for Adolin; Kelek could very well decide that there was no reason to imprison him for things the ancients did. At the same time, Adolin was losing the hearts of the watching spren. What would it matter if he "won" the trial if the spren were even more strongly convinced they shouldn't help in the conflict?

He searched the crowd, but found mostly resentful expressions. Storms. Did he really think he could prove anything to them? Which of the ten fools *was* he for starting all this?

No, I'm not a fool, he told himself. *Just an optimist. How can they not see? How can they sit here and judge me, when men are dying and other spren fight?*

The same way, he realized, that the highprinces had spent so long playing games with the lives of soldiers on the Shattered Plains. The same way any man could turn his back on an atrocity if he could persuade himself it wasn't his business.

Men and spren were not different. Blended had tried to tell him this, and now he saw it firsthand.

"The third and final witness," the honorspren officiator said, "is Notum, once captain of the ship *Honor's Path*."

Adolin felt his stomach turn as Notum—looking much improved from the last time Adolin had seen him—emerged from the top of the forum, where a group of standing honorspren had obscured him from Adolin's view. Still, Adolin was shocked. Notum had been forbidden to enter Lasting Integrity despite his wounds, and had stayed with the others outside the walls—though the honorspren of the tower had delivered him some Stormlight to aid in his healing. Messages from Godeke had indicated that Notum had eventually returned to patrol.

Now he was here—and in uniform, which was telling. He also wouldn't meet Adolin's eyes as he stepped down onto the floor of the forum. Spren might claim the moral high ground; they claimed to be made of honor. But they also *defined* honor for themselves. As men did.

"Offered to end your exile, did they, Notum?" Adolin asked softly. "In exchange for a little backstabbing?"

Notum continued to avoid his gaze, instead bowing to Kelek, then unfolding a sheet of paper from his pocket. He began to read. "I have been asked," he said, "to relate the erratic behavior I witnessed in this man and his companions. As many of you know, I first encountered this group when they fled the Fused in Celebrant over one year ago. They used subterfuge to . . ."

Notum trailed off and looked toward Adolin.

Give him Father's stare, Adolin thought. *The stern one that made you want to shrivel up inside, thinking of everything you'd done wrong. A general's stare.*

Adolin had never been good at that stare.

"Go ahead," he said instead. "We got you in trouble, Notum. It's only fair that you get a chance to tell your side. I can't ask anything of you other than honesty."

"I . . ." Notum met his eyes.

"Go on."

Notum lowered his sheet, then said in a loud voice, "Honor is not dead so long as he lives in the hearts of men!"

Adolin had never heard the statement before, but it seemed a trigger to the honorspren crowd, who began standing up and shouting in outrage—or even in support. Adolin stepped back, amazed by the sudden burst of emotion from the normally stoic spren.

Several officials rushed the floor of the forum, pulling Notum away as he bellowed the words. "Honor is not dead so long as he lives in the hearts of men! Honor is not—"

They dragged him out of the forum, but the commotion continued. Adolin put his hand on his sword, uncertain. Would this turn ugly?

Kelek shrank down in his seat, looking panicked as he put his hands to his ears. He let out a low whine, pathetic and piteous, and began to shake. The honorspren near him called for order among the crowd, shouting that they were causing pain to the Holy One.

Many seemed outraged at Notum's words, but a sizable number took up his cry—and these were pushed physically out of the forum. There was a tension to this society Adolin hadn't seen before. The honorspren were no monolith; disagreement and tension swam in deep waters here—far below the surface, but still powerful.

The officiators cleared the forum—even Shallan and Pattern were forced out. Everyone basically ignored Adolin. As the place finally settled down, and only a few officials remained, Adolin walked up the few forum steps to the High Judge's seat. Kelek lounged in his seat, ignoring the fact that he'd been curled up on the floor trembling mere moments earlier.

"What was that?" Adolin asked him.

"Hmmm?" Kelek said. "Oh, nothing of note. An old spren argument. Your coming has opened centuries-old wounds, young man. Amusing, isn't it?"

"Amusing? That's all?"

Kelek started whistling as he wrote in his notebook.

They're all insane, Adolin thought. *Ash said so. This is what thousands of years of torture does to a mind.*

Perhaps it was best not to push on the raw wound.

"That went well for me today, wouldn't you say?" Adolin asked him.

"Hmm?" Kelek said.

"One witness could not refute my point about my father," Adolin said. "Another made my argument for me by pointing out that siding against the Radiants is practically serving Odium. Then Notum put his honor before his own well-being. It went well for me."

"Does it matter?" Kelek asked.

"Of course it does. That's why I'm here."

"I see," Kelek said. "Did the ancient Radiants betray their spren, killing them?"

"Well, yes," Adolin said. "But that's not the question. The question is whether modern humans can be blamed."

Kelek continued writing.

"Honored One?" Adolin asked.

"Do you know how old I am, young man?" Kelek looked up and met Adolin's eyes, and there was *something* in them. A depth that made him, for the first time, seem distinctly inhuman. Those eyes seemed like eternal holes. Bored through time.

"I," Kelek said softly, "have known many, *many* men. I've known some of the best who ever lived. They are now broken or dead. The best of us inevitably cracked. Storms . . . I ran when the Return came this time, because I knew what it meant. Even Taln . . . Even Taln . . ."

"He didn't break," Adolin said.

"The enemy is here, so he did," Kelek said firmly. He waved toward the honorspren. "They deserve better than you, son. They deserve better than *me*. I could never judge them for refusing to bond men. How could I? I could *never* order them back into that war, back into that hole. To do so would be to . . . to abandon what little honor I have left. . . ."

Adolin took a deep breath. Then he nodded.

"I just told you that your cause is hopeless," Kelek said, turning to his writing. "You do not seem concerned."

"Well, Honored One," Adolin said. "I agreed to this trial—even with Sekeir's insistence I be blamed for what my ancestors did—because it was the only way to get a chance to talk to the honorspren. Maybe you will judge against me—but so long as I get a chance to have my say, then that will be enough. If I persuade even one or two to join the battle, I'll have won."

"Optimism," Kelek said. "Hope. I remember those things. But I don't think you understand the stakes of this trial, child—nor do you understand what you've stumbled into. The things that inkspren said—about joining Odium's side—are on the minds of many spren. Including many in this very fortress."

That hit Adolin like a gut punch. "Honorspren would *join* the enemy?" Adolin said. "That would make them no better than the highspren!"

"Indeed; I suspect their dislike of highspren is part of why they hesitate. The honorspren in favor of joining the enemy worried how such a suggestion would be received. But here you are, giving them a chance to make their arguments, acting as a magnet for all of their frustration and hatred.

"Many are listening. If honorspren start joining the enemy . . . well, many other varieties of spren would soon follow. I dare think they'd go in large numbers." Kelek didn't look up. "You came here to recruit. But I suspect you will end up tipping these finely balanced scales, and not in the direction you desire."

⁜

About an hour after the first stage of the trial—an hour she'd spent consoling Adolin in his sudden terror that he would accidentally cause a mass defection of spren to the side of the enemy—Shallan climbed a tree.

She stretched high, clinging to a branch near the top. It was a normal tree, one of the real ones the honorspren managed to grow here. It felt good to feel bark beneath her fingers.

She reached with one arm into the open space above the tree, but couldn't feel anything different. Had she hit the barrier yet? Maybe a little farther . . .

She shimmied a little higher, then reached out, and thought she felt an oddity as she got exactly high enough. An invisible tugging on the tips of her fingers.

Then her foot slipped.

In a second she was tumbling through the air. She didn't fall all the way to the base of the structure, merely to the floor of her plane. She hit with a loud *crack,* then lay dazed before letting out a loud groan.

Lusintia the honorspren was at her side a moment later.

As I suspected . . . Veil thought. *She always seems to be nearby.* She'd clearly been assigned to watch Shallan.

"Human!" she said, her short hair hanging along the sides of her white-blue face. "Human, are you hurt?"

Shallan groaned, blinking.

"Mmm . . ." Pattern said, stepping over. "Rapid eye blinks. This is serious. She could die."

"Die?" Lusintia said. "I had no idea they were so *fragile!*"

"That was a long fall," Pattern said. "Ah, and she hit her head when she landed on the stones here. Not good, not good."

Other honorspren were gathering, muttering to themselves. Shallan groaned again, then tried to focus on Pattern and Lusintia, but let her eyes slip shut.

"We must act quickly," Pattern said. "Quickly!"

"What do we do!" Lusintia said.

"You have no hospital here?"

"Of course we don't have a hospital!" Lusintia said. "There are only a couple dozen humans here."

"Mmm . . . but you won't let them come back in if they leave, so they are basically caged here. You should feel bad. Very bad. Yes."

Storms, Veil thought. *Is that the best he can do? How did we ever let him fool us?*

"Tell me what to do!" Lusintia said. "Do we carry her out to that Edgedancer?"

"It will take too long. She will die. Poor human whom I love very much. It will be tragic for her to die here, in the center of honorspren power and protection. Unless, of course, she were to be given Stormlight."

"Wait . . . Stormlight?"

"Yes, she *is* Radiant," Pattern said. "It would heal her."

Shallan suppressed a smile. Pattern *was* a tad transparent, but the honorspren here plainly had little experience with humans. They swallowed the bait without question, and soon Shallan was being carried by a team of four. She tucked away the piece of cloth-wrapped stone she'd used to smack the ground as she landed, giving the impression that she'd hit her head.

In reality, her arm *did* ache. She had undoubtedly bruised it when she hit, though this wasn't the worst self-inflicted wound she'd sustained in the name of science. At least this time her scheme hadn't involved deliberately embarrassing herself in front of several attractive men.

She made sure to groan occasionally, and Pattern kept exclaiming how worried he was. That kept Lusintia and the other honorspren motivated as they hauled Shallan to a specific building, their footfalls echoing against enclosing stone.

They had a hushed but urgent conversation with a guard. Shallan made a particularly poignant whimper of pain at exactly the right moment, and then she was in. Light surrounded her as she was brought someplace brilliant. They hadn't let her in here last time, when they retrieved Stormlight for Adolin's healing.

She let her eyes flutter open and found that most of the Stormlight was contained in a large construction at the center of the room. A kind of vat, or tall jar. This was technology Shallan hadn't heard of before coming to Shadesmar, and apparently not even the honorspren knew how it worked. They could be purchased from a group of strange traveling merchants called the Eyree.

Shelves nearby held a collection of loose gemstones, each glowing brightly. The wealth of Lasting Integrity: gemstones—gathered over millennia—so flawless, so perfect, that they didn't leak. She'd been told a gemstone like this could, with repeated exposures to storms, absorb far more Stormlight than its size should be able to contain.

She tested this, reaching out with a weak hand toward one of them and sucking in a breath of Stormlight—which streamed to her as a glowing, misty white light.

She immediately felt better: invigorated, alert. Storms, how she'd missed that. Simply *holding* Stormlight was stimulating. She grinned—not part of the act—then decided to leap to her feet. The ache in her arm vanished; she felt like dancing with joy.

Instead she let Veil take over. This next part needed her—Shallan remained the better actress, but Veil was better at most other espionage skills.

Veil made a show of touching her head where she'd been "wounded." "What happened?" she asked. "I don't remember. I was trying to see if I could reach the barrier where the gravity of the plane ran out."

"You were very foolish, human," Lusintia said. "You are so fragile! How could you endanger yourself in such a manner? Do you not realize that mortals die if broken?"

"It was in the name of science," Veil said, reaching to her waist where she'd secured her notebook before climbing. She yanked it out and dropped it in a flurry. At the same time she swept her safehand to the side and dropped a dun emerald in place of a brightly glowing one.

The sleight of hand—performed hundreds of times beneath Tyn's watch, then perfected on her own—was covered as she stumbled and brushed the shelf, disturbing the many gems and shaking their light. She was able to slip the stolen emerald into her black leather glove.

This all happened in the moment the honorspren focused on her falling notebook. Veil quickly snatched it off the ground and held it to her chest, grinning sheepishly.

"Thank you," she said. "You saved my life."

"We would not have you die," Lusintia said. "Death is a terrible thing, and we . . ." She trailed off, looking at the shelf and the dun emerald it now contained. "Storms alight! You ate the *entire thing*? Human, how . . ."

Another spren, an angry male in uniform, began shoving Shallan out. "That was *years'* worth of stored Stormlight!" he exclaimed. "Get out! Go, before you eat anything more! If you fall again, I will have you turned away!"

Veil smothered her grin, apologizing as she stumbled out and met Pattern outside. An embarrassed Lusintia was forced to stay behind and fill out a report on the incident.

"Mmm . . ." Pattern said. "Thank you for letting me lie. Did it work?"

Veil nodded.

"Mmm. They are stupid."

"Stupidity and ignorance are not the same thing," Veil said. "They're just unaccustomed to both humans and subterfuge. Come on. Let's make ourselves scarce before someone thinks to search me."

88

FALLING STAR

A YEAR AND A HALF AGO

A banging came on the door, and Eshonai pulled it open and stared out into a tempest. Grand lightning flashes shattered the blackness in brief emotional bouts, revealing Venli, her eyes wide, grinning and soaked, clutching something in two hands before her.

She stumbled into the room, trailing water—which caused their mother to chide her. Jaxlim was in one of her . . . episodes where she saw the two of them as children.

Venli—seemingly oblivious to anything other than the gemstone—wandered past their mother. She rubbed her thumb on the gemstone, which was about a third the size of her fist.

"Storms," Eshonai said, pushing the door closed. "You did it?" She set the beam in place, then left it rattling in the wind as she stepped over to Venli.

But . . . no, the gemstone wasn't glowing. Was it? Eshonai leaned closer. It *was* glowing, but barely.

"It worked," Venli whispered to Awe, clutching the stone. "It *finally* worked. The secret *is* lightning, Eshonai! It pulls them through. When I drew close enough right after a strike, I found *hundreds* of them. I snagged this one before the others returned to the other side. . . ."

"The other side?" Eshonai asked.

Venli didn't respond. She seemed like a different person lately, always exhausted from working long nights—and from her insistence on going out in each and every storm to try to capture a stormspren. And now this. Venli cradled the gemstone, ignoring the water streaming from her clothing.

"Venli?" Eshonai said. "If you want my help in bringing this to the Five, you will need to let me see what you've done."

Venli stared at her, quiet, no rhythm at all. Then she stood tall and hummed to Confidence, proffering the gemstone. Eshonai attuned Curiosity and took it. Yes . . . it did have a spren inside, though it glowed with an odd light. Too dark, almost dusty. Smoky. It was difficult to tell its color through the green of the emerald, but it seemed shadowed, like lightning deep within the clouds.

"This spren is unlike any I've ever seen," Eshonai said.

"Stormform," Venli whispered. "Power."

"Dangerous power. This could destroy the listeners."

"Eshonai," Venli said to Reprimand, "our people are already *being* destroyed. Don't you think that this time, instead of making a snap decision based on songs from thousands of years ago, we should at least *try* a different solution?"

Rumbling thunder outside seemed to agree with Venli's words. Eshonai handed the gemstone back, then hummed to Betrayal to indicate what she thought of Venli's argument. But the rhythm didn't express how deeply the words cut.

Turning her back on her sister, Eshonai walked to the door again and threw aside the bar. Ignoring both Venli and her mother as they cried objections, Eshonai stepped out into the storm.

The wind hit her hard, but in warform's armor she barely felt the icy raindrops. She stood in the light spilling from the door until Venli pushed it closed, plunging Eshonai into darkness.

She attuned the Rhythm of Winds and started walking. Humans feared the storms. They always hid indoors. Eshonai respected the storms, and usually preferred to meet them with a stormshield. But she did not fear them.

She walked away from her mother's house, eastward into the wind. These days, her life had constantly been against the wind. It blew so hard, she barely felt she was making progress. Maybe she'd have been better off letting it steer her.

If she hadn't fought so much—if she hadn't spent so much time thinking about her explorations or her dreams—would she have settled into her role as general faster? If she'd doubled down on her raids at the start, would she have been able to shove the humans out of the warcamps before they got a foothold?

Like a rockbud, humans were. Soft at first, but capable of gripping onto the stone and growing into something practically immovable. In this—despite their lack of rhythms—they belonged to Roshar better than the listeners did. If she could truly travel the world, would she find them growing in every crevice?

She neared the edge of the plateau that made up the central heart of Narak, the city of exile. She walked carefully, letting flashes of lightning guide her way. She stepped right up to the edge of the chasm, facing into the wind.

"What do you want from us?" she shouted. "Answer me, Rider! Spren of the storm! You're a traitor like us, aren't you? Is that why you sent Venli those little spren?"

The wind blasted her, as if to push her off balance. Debris spun and sputtered in the wind, spiraling around her—the lightning making each piece seem frozen in the moment. A quick sequence of bolts struck nearby, and the thunder vibrated and rattled her carapace. Absolute darkness followed.

At first she thought maybe the Rider of Storms had chosen to appear to her. However, this darkness was ordinary. She could still feel the wind, rain, and debris.

"What kind of choice is this?" she demanded. "Either we let the humans destroy us, or we turn away from the *one* thing that defines us? The one value that matters?"

Darkness. Rain. Wind. But no reply.

What had she expected? An actual answer? Was this a prayer, then? Didn't make a lot of sense, considering that the very thing she resisted was a return to her people's old gods.

Those gods had never deserved reverence. What was a god who only made demands? Nothing but a tyrant with a different name.

"Everything I've done," she said into the wind, "has been to ensure we remain our own people. That's all I want. I gave up my dreams. But I will not give up our minds."

Brave words. Useless words. They would have to take Venli's discovery to the Five, and they would have to let her test it. Eshonai knew that as well as she knew the Rhythm of Peace. They couldn't reject a potential new form now.

She turned to go, then heard something. Rock scraping on rock? Was the plateau cracking? Though she could barely hear it, the noise must be quite loud to reach her over the din of the tempest.

Eshonai stepped backward—but her footing seemed unsteady, and she didn't want to move without a flash of lightning to guide her. What if—

Branching light flashed in the heavens far to the east. It lit the sky white, highlighting debris, illuminating the land around her. Everything except for an enormous shadow silhouetted in front of her.

Eshonai's breath caught. The rhythms froze in her head. That shape . . .

sinuous, yet massive. Claws as thick as her body gripping the rim of the chasm mere feet in front of her. It couldn't be—

Lightning flashed again, and she saw its face. A chasmfiend snout, with jagged swords for teeth, head cocked to the side to watch her.

She didn't run. If it wanted her, she was already dead. Prey ran, and the beasts were known to play with things that acted like prey, even if they weren't hungry. Still, standing there in pitch-darkness—not daring to attune a rhythm—was the hardest thing she'd ever done.

When the lightning next flashed, the chasmfiend had lowered its incredible head toward her, its eye close enough that she could have stabbed it without needing to lunge.

Darkness fell. Then a small burst of light appeared directly ahead of her. A small spren made of white fire. It zipped forward, trailing an afterimage. Like a falling star. It moved closer, then spun around her.

By its light, she could see the chasmfiend slowly retreat into the chasm, its spikelike claws leaving scores on the stone. Her heart beating like thunder, Eshonai attuned Anxiety and hurried home. The strange little spren followed her.

89

VOICE OF LIGHTS

Instead I think, if I were to remember my life in detail, I would be-come even worse. Paralyzed by my terrible actions. I should not like to remember all those I have failed.

D ays passed. Navani barely noticed.

For the first time in her life, she let go completely. No wor-ries about Dalinar or Jasnah. No worries about the tower. No thoughts about the million other things she should be doing.

This was what she should be doing.

Or so she allowed herself to believe. She let herself be free. In her lit-tle room of a laboratory, everything fit together. She'd met scholars who claimed they needed chaos to function. Perhaps that was true for some, but in her experience, good science wasn't about sloppy inspiration. It was about meticulous incrementalization.

With no distractions, she was able to draw up precise experiments—charts, careful measurements, *lines.* Science was all about lines, about im-posing order on chaos. Navani reveled in her careful preparations, without anyone to tease her for keeping her charts so neat or for refusing to skip any steps.

Sometimes Raboniel visited and joined in the research, writing her own musings alongside Navani's in their notebook. Two opposing forces in harmony, focused on a single goal.

Raboniel gave her the strange black sand, explaining the difference be-tween static and kinetic Investiture. Navani observed and measured, learn-ing for herself. The sand slowly turned white when exposed to Stormlight or Voidlight. However, if a fabrial was *using* the Light, the sand changed faster.

You could wet the sand to reset it to black, though it had to be dry again before it could turn white. It was a useful way to measure how much Light a given fabrial was using. She noticed that it also changed colors in the presence of spren. This was a slow change too, but she *could* measure it.

Anything you could measure was useful to science. But for these few blessed days, it seemed like time was *not* properly measurable—for hours passed like minutes. And Navani, despite the circumstances, found herself *loving* the experience.

⁘

"I don't know exactly where the sand comes from," Raboniel said, settled on her stool beside the wall, flipping through Navani's latest set of charts. "Offworld somewhere."

"Offworld?" Navani asked, looking up from the fabrial she'd been housing. "As in . . . another . . . planet?"

Raboniel hummed absently. A confirmation? Navani felt she could tell what this rhythm meant.

"I wanted to go, for years," Raboniel said. "Visit the place myself. Unfortunately, I learned it wasn't possible. I'm trapped in this system, my soul bound to Braize—you call it Damnation—a planet farther out in orbit around the sun."

To hear her speak of such things so casually amazed Navani. Other worlds. The best telescopes couldn't do more than confirm the existence of other celestial bodies, but here she was, speaking to someone who had *visited* one of them.

We came from another, Navani reminded herself. *Humans, migrating to Roshar.* It was so strange for her to think about, to align the mythos of the Tranquiline Halls with an actual location.

"Could . . . I visit them?" Navani asked. "These other worlds?"

"Likely—though I'd stay away from Braize. You'd have to get through the storm to travel there anyway."

"The Everstorm?"

Raboniel hummed to an amused rhythm. "No, no, Navani. You can't travel to Braize in the Physical Realm. That would take . . . well, I have no idea how long. Plus there's no air in the space between planets. We sent Heavenly Ones to try it once. No air, and worse, the strange pressures required them to carry a large supply of Voidlight for healing. Even so prepared, they died within hours.

"One instead travels to other worlds through Shadesmar. But again, stay away from Braize. Even if you could get through the barrier storm, the place is barren, devoid of life. Merely a dark sky, endless windswept crags, and a broken landscape. And a lot of souls. A lot of not particularly sane souls."

"I'll . . . remember that."

Other worlds. It seemed too vast a concept for her to grasp right now—and that was saying something, as she was presently contemplating the death of a god. She turned to her experiment. "Ready."

"Excellent," Raboniel said, closing the book. "Mizthla?"

Navani's stormform guard entered the room, seeming somewhat annoyed. Though that was common for him. "Mizthla" was his singer name; he said the Alethi had called him Dah. A simple glyph instead of a true name, because it was easier to remember. Perhaps if she had lived her entire life called something because of its utility, Navani would have shared his disposition.

She presented him with the fabrial, which was . . . well, not a true fabrial. The housing was a mere coil of copper wires around some gemstones. Raboniel knew a method of *changing* the polarity of a magnet, a process involving the lightning channeled from a stormform. Captive lightning seemed to have boundless potential applications, but Navani kept herself focused—maybe the polarity-swapping process would also work on gemstones filled with Voidlight.

Navani and Raboniel left the room, as the lightning could be unpredictable. "Remember," Navani said on her way out, "only a *tiny* release of energy. Don't melt the coils this time."

"I'm not an idiot," the Regal said to her. "Anymore."

Outside, Navani glanced down the hallway—lined with boxes of equipment, some hiding her traps—toward the shield around the Sibling. It seemed darker inside than before.

She and Raboniel avoided the topic. Working closely together did not make them allies, and both recognized it. In fact, Navani had been trying to find a way to hide future discoveries from Raboniel, if she made any.

Lightning flashed in the room, then Mizthla called for them. They hurried in as he set the coiled-up fabrial on the desk. It was likely still hot to the touch, so Navani gave it a few minutes, despite wanting to rip the gemstones out immediately to inspect the result.

"I have noticed something in your journals," Raboniel said as the two of them waited. "You often remark that you are not a scholar. Why?"

"I've always been too busy to engage in true scholarship, Ancient One," Navani said. "Plus, I don't know that I have the mind for it; I'm not the genius my daughter is. So I've always seen it as my duty to grant patronage to true scholars, to publicize their creations and see them properly encouraged."

Raboniel hummed a rhythm, then picked up the fabrial with the copper coiling it. The metal burned her fingers, but she healed from it. "If you are not a scholar, Navani," she said, "then I have never met one."

"I admit that I have trouble accepting that, Ancient One. Though I'm pleased to have fooled you."

"Humility," Raboniel said. "It's not a Passion my kind often promote. Would it help you believe if I told you that you no longer have to use titles when speaking to me? Your discoveries so far are enough to recommend you as my equal."

This seemed an uncommon privilege. "It does help, Raboniel," Navani said. "Thank you."

"Thanks need not be provided for something self-evident," Raboniel said, holding up the fabrial. "Are you ready?"

Navani nodded. Raboniel pulled the gemstones out from within the coil, then inspected them. "The Voidlight seems unchanged to me," she said.

Navani hadn't expressly told Raboniel she was hunting for anti-Voidlight. She shrouded her quest in many different kinds of experiments—like this one, where she explained she simply wanted to see if Light responded to exposure to lightning. She suspected that Raboniel suspected, however, that Navani was at least still intrigued by the idea of anti-Light.

Navani sprinkled some of the black sand on the tabletop, then placed the gemstone in the center, measuring the strength of the Investiture inside. But because the air didn't warp around this gemstone, she secretly knew her experiment had failed. This was not anti-Voidlight. She made a note in her log. Another failed experiment.

Raboniel hummed a rhythm. A regretful one? Yes, that was what it seemed to be. "I should return to my duties," she said, and Navani could pick out the same rhythm in her voice. "The Deepest Ones are close to finding the final node."

"How?" Navani asked.

"You know I can't tell you that, Navani." Though she had spoken of leaving, she remained sitting. "I'm so tired of this war. So tired of capturing, killing, losing, dying."

"We should end it then."

"Not while Odium lives."

"You'd actually kill him?" Navani asked. "If you had the chance?"

Raboniel hummed, but looked away. *That humming is . . . embarrassment?* Navani thought. *She recognizes she's lied to me, at least by implication. She doesn't truly want to kill Odium.*

"When you were hunting the opposite of Voidlight, you didn't want to use it against him," Navani guessed. "You teased me with the idea, but you have another purpose."

"You learn to read rhythms," Raboniel said, standing up.

"Or I simply understand logic." Navani stood, and took Raboniel's hands. The Fused allowed it. "You don't have to kill the Sibling. Let's find another path."

"I'm not killing the Sibling," Raboniel said. "I'm . . . doing something worse. I'm unmaking the Sibling."

"Then let's *find another path.*"

"You think I haven't searched for one already?" She removed her hands from Navani's, then picked up and proffered their notebook, the one where they logged their experiments. *Rhythm of War,* they called it. Odium and Honor working together, if only for a short time.

"I've run some experiments on the conjoined rubies you created—the ones of different sizes," Raboniel said. "I think you'll like the implications of what I've discovered; I wrote them in here earlier. This might make moving your enormous sky platforms easier."

"Raboniel," Navani said, taking the notebook. "Negotiate with me, help me. Let's join forces. Let's make a treaty, you and I, ignoring Odium."

"I'm sorry," the Fused said. "But the best chance we have of ending this war—barring a discovery between us—is for my kind to control Urithiru. I *will* finish my work with the Sibling. Ultimately, we are still enemies. And I would not be where I am—able to contemplate a different solution—if I were not fully willing to do what has been asked of me. Regardless of the cost, and regardless of the pain it causes."

Navani steeled herself. "I had not thought otherwise, Lady of Wishes. Though it leaves me sorrowful." On a whim, she tried humming to the Rhythm of War. It didn't work—the rhythm required two people in concert with one another.

In return, however, Raboniel smiled. "I would give you something," she said, then left.

Confused, Navani sat at the table, feeling tired. These days of furious study were catching up to her. Had it been selfish to spend so much time pretending to be a scholar? Didn't Urithiru beg for a queen? Yes, it would be wonderful to find a power to use against Odium, but . . . did she really think *she* could solve such a complex problem?

Navani tried to return to her experiments. After an hour, she conceded that the spark wasn't there. For all her talk of control and organization, she now found herself subject to the whims of emotion. She couldn't work because she didn't "feel" it. She would have called that nonsense—though of course not to their face—if one of her scholars had told her something similar.

She stood abruptly, her chair clattering to the ground. She'd picked up a habit of pacing from Dalinar, and found herself prowling back and forth in the small chamber. Eventually Raboniel appeared in the doorway, accompanied by two nimbleform singers.

The Fused waved, and the femalens hurried into the room. They carried odd equipment, including two thin metal plates perhaps a foot and a half square and a fraction of an inch thick, with some odd ridges and crenellations cut into them. The nimbleforms attached them to Navani's desk with clamps, so the metal plates spread flat, one on each side—like additions to the desk's workspace.

"This is an ancient form of music among my kind," Raboniel said. "A way to revel in the rhythms. As a gift, I have decided to share the songs with you."

She gestured and hummed to the two young singers, who jumped to obey, each pulling out a long bow—like one might use on a stringed instrument. They drew these along the sides of the metal plates, and the metal began to vibrate with deep tones, though they had a *rougher* texture to them. Full and resonant.

Those are Honor's and Odium's tones, Navani thought. Only these were the shifted versions that worked in harmony with one another.

Raboniel stepped up beside Navani. In accompaniment to the two tones, she played a loud rhythm with two sticks on a small drum. The sequence of beats grew loud and stately, then soft and fast, alternating. It wasn't exactly the Rhythm of War, but it was as close as music could likely get. It vibrated through Navani, loud and triumphant.

They continued at it for an extended time, before Raboniel called a stop and the two young singers—sweating from the work of vigorously making the tones—quickly gathered the plates, unclamping them from the sides of the desk.

"Did you like it?" Raboniel asked her.

"I did," Navani said. "The tones were a terrible cacophony when combined, but somehow beautiful at the same time."

"Like the two of us?" Raboniel asked.

"Like the two of us."

"By this music," Raboniel said, "I give you the title Voice of Lights, Navani Kholin. As is my right."

Raboniel hummed curtly, then *bowed* to Navani. With no other words, she waved for the singers to take their equipment and go. Raboniel retreated with them.

Feeling overwhelmed, Navani walked up to the open notebook on her desk. Inside, Raboniel had written about their experiments in the women's script—and her handwriting was growing quite practiced.

Navani understood the honor in what she'd just been given. At the same time, she found it difficult to feel proud. What did a title, or the respect of one of the Fused, mean if the tower was still being corrupted, her people still dominated?

This is why I worked so hard these last few days, Navani admitted to herself, sitting at the desk. *To prove myself to her.* But . . . what good was that if it didn't lead to peace?

The Rhythm of War vibrated through her, proof that there *could* be harmony. At the same time, the nearly clashing tones told another story. Harmony could be reached, but it was exceedingly difficult.

What kind of emulsifier could you use with people, to make *them* mix? She closed the notebook, then made her way to the back of the room and rested her hand on the Sibling's crystal vein.

"I have tried to find a way to merge spren who were split by fabrial creation," she whispered. "I thought it might please you."

No response came.

"Please," Navani said, closing her eyes and resting her forehead against the wall. "Please forgive me. We need you."

I . . . The voice came into her mind, making Navani look up. She couldn't see the spark of the Sibling's light in the vein, however. Either it wasn't there, or . . . or it had grown too dim to see in the light of the room.

"Sibling?" she asked.

I am cold, the voice said, small, almost imperceptible. *They are killing . . . killing me.*

"Raboniel said she is . . . unmaking you."

If that is true I . . . I will . . . I will die.

"Spren can't die," Navani said.

Gods can die . . . Fused can . . . can die . . . Spren can . . . die. If I am made into someone else, that is death. It is dark. The singer you promised me though . . . I can see him sometimes. I like watching him. He is with the Radiants. He would have made . . . a good . . . a good bond. . . .

"Then bond him!" Navani said.

Can't. Can't see. Can't act through the barrier.

"What if I brought you Stormlight?" Navani said. "Infused you the same way they've been infusing you with Voidlight? Would that slow the process?"

Cold. They listen. I'm afraid, Navani.

"Sibling?"

I don't . . . want . . . to die. . . .

And then silence. Navani was left with that haunting word, *die,* echoing in her mind. At the moment, the Sibling's fear seemed far more powerful than the Rhythm of War.

Navani had to do *something.* Something more than sitting around daydreaming. She stalked back to her desk to write down ideas—any ideas, no matter how silly—about what she could do to help. But as she sat, she noticed something. Her previous experiment rested there, mostly forgotten. A gemstone amid sand. When the singers had set up their plates, they hadn't disturbed Navani's work.

The music of the plates had caused the entire desktop to vibrate. And that had made the sand vibrate—and it had therefore made patterns on her desktop. One pattern on the right, a different on the left, and a third where the two mixed.

Stormlight and Voidlight weren't merely types of illumination. They weren't merely strange kinds of fluid. They were *sounds. Vibrations.*

And in vibration, she'd find their opposites.

Regardless, I write now. Because I know they are coming for me. They got Jezrien. They'll inevitably claim me, even here in the honorspren stronghold.

Adolin stepped onto his podium at the honorspren forum. The circular disc had been pulled out to the center of the arena. Today, he would have the stage all to himself.

He'd arrived early, so he wouldn't have to push his way through the crowd. He wanted to appear in control, awaiting their scorn rather than taking the long walk down the steps with everyone watching. One felt like the action of a man who had orchestrated his situation. The other felt like a prisoner being led to execution.

Shallan and Pattern seated themselves as others began to arrive. The forum could hold a couple hundred spren, and as the honorspren—all glowing faintly white-blue—settled, he noted that far more of them wore uniforms today. The ones who had seemed sympathetic to Notum's proclamation were conspicuously absent from the seats. Adolin found that frustrating, though he did notice some spren from yesterday crowding around the top, where they could stand and watch.

The honorspren seemed determined to seed the seated positions with those who were predisposed against him. *No reason to sweat,* Adolin thought, standing with his hands clasped behind his back. *It's just your one chance to speak for yourself. Your one chance to turn all this around.*

Ideally, this would be the day that went best for him. He could explain his case and answer questions from the audience. Kelek's words from the day before weighed heavily upon him; this wasn't merely about the honorspren and whether some would join the Windrunners. It was a much larger argument.

Was humankind worth fighting for? Adolin somehow had to make that argument today. Blended had warned him he'd need to fend off questions and keep the argument on topic. He couldn't afford to engage the crowd too directly, couldn't afford to let them control the conversation.

That done, the trial would convene for one final meeting, where the honorspren could present a single last witness, whom Adolin could question, to rebut his arguments.

He bowed to Kelek as the Herald arrived. He'd changed into official-looking violet robes, a marked difference from yesterday. Did that mean he was taking this more seriously?

Adolin waited respectfully for the High Judge to seat himself among the group of honorspren officials. Adolin had learned that six of them were among the "ten honored by storms." The ten oldest existing honorspren, other than Syl. Hierarchy was important to this group.

"All right," Kelek said. "Let's get this over with. You may speak."

"Thank you, Honored One," Adolin said, then turned toward the crowd. "I don't think my words today will surprise anyone. Yet I've staked my future on the opportunity to say them to you. In person. To look you in the eyes, and ask you if you *truly* think this is justice.

"Men hold grudges. It is one of our greatest failings. Sometimes families will continue a cycle of hatred for generations, all for some slight that no one remembers. While I won't compare your very real pain and betrayal to something so insignificant, I hope to find in you—immortal pieces of Honor—a more perfect way of—"

"Did you know," a spren in the front row interrupted, "that your father almost killed the Stormfather?"

Adolin stumbled in his speech. "I will answer questions at the end," he said. "As I was saying, I had hoped to find—"

"Did you know about it?" the honorspren demanded, shouting. "Did you know he *almost killed the Stormfather*?"

"I find that difficult to believe," Adolin said. He glanced up at the top of the forum, where the standing spren were shuffling and whispering to one another. The audience fell quiet, waiting for Adolin. A question had been asked, but he didn't have to answer it, not yet. He controlled the floor.

So he remained focused as Blended had taught him, then purposefully continued his statement. "In *you*," Adolin said to the crowd, "I had hoped to find *honor*. Ancient spren bonded with us because they believed that together, we became something stronger, something *better* than we were alone.

"I admit to human weakness. I will not hide it. But I have not seen you admit to *your* weakness. You claim to be creations of honor. That you are better than men. Yet you refuse to prove it, to show it.

"I know of spren who do. Brave spren, who have come to the battle to join with men. In so doing, they have become *stronger*. They grow, like the people who bond them. Why do we need Radiants? Because they represent our best selves. We are of Honor and Cultivation. Honor, for an ideal. Cultivation, for the power to reach *toward* that ideal.

"The Stormfather himself agrees that this is the correct choice. People may not be perfect, but they're worth helping strive *for* perfection. And *you* are worth more than you can ever be sitting alone and refusing to grow."

That went over well. The honorspren liked a good speech, he'd learned—and those at the top in particular seemed swayed. He took a breath, preparing to move to his next point. Unfortunately, in the pause, that same honorspren from before leaped to his feet.

"The Stormfather made his choice," the spren said loudly, "and in so doing, put himself in danger—he nearly died. Did you *know about this*?"

Kelek leaned forward in his judge's seat. That was dangerously close to a statement, which the audience was not allowed to make. Trial by witness allowed Adolin to make declarations, but the audience could only question.

"I did not know of this event," Adolin told the spren. "So I cannot offer insight into why it happened, or what the circumstances were."

"How could you not know?" a different spren, in the second row, demanded. "If you've come to persuade us to become Radiant spren, shouldn't you know the cost of what you're asking? I think—"

"Enough of that," Kelek snapped. "Do you want to be ejected, Veratorim?"

The spren quieted immediately.

"Proceed, human," Kelek said, settling back and lacing his fingers before himself.

"My second argument," Adolin said, "is to show to you that the kingdoms of the world have put aside their differences to unite together to face this challenge. I brought a letter from my cousin, Jasnah, which was torn up. Fortunately, I can quote parts to you. She proves that the modern kingdoms are—"

"Has she tried to kill *her* spren?" the spren in the first row asked.

"She proves," Adolin continued, "that our modern kingdoms are united in ways that—"

"Yes, but has she tried to kill her spren?"

"Look," Adolin snapped, "do you want me to talk or not? Do you want to hear my testimony, like you've offered, or do you just want to take shots at me?"

The spren smiled. And Adolin realized what he'd done. By asking a question, Adolin had invited an answer.

"I think," the spren said, standing up, "that the most relevant question is if these new Radiants can be trusted. *That's* what you need to prove. The Stormfather *told* us that Dalinar Kholin forced him to physically manifest. Dalinar Kholin, your father, using the *Stormfather's essence* to work one of the Oathgates!"

"That's against his oath!" another one exclaimed. "Did you know about your father's actions?"

"I'm sure he had good reasons," Adolin said. "If you would—"

"Good reasons?" the standing honorspren said. "He was *running away*. Does this seem like the kind of behavior we should trust in a Bondsmith? From the man *you* said was ideal, that *you* promised would never betray us. How do you respond to this?"

Adolin looked to Kelek. "Can I please continue my witness?"

"You invited this discussion, son," Kelek said. "You need to engage him now." Kelek nodded toward the crowd at the top of the forum. Those who had joined with Notum yesterday waited quietly, wanting answers.

Adolin sighed, glancing to Shallan for strength before continuing. "I cannot speak for my father. You'll have to ask him. I trust him; the Stormfather trusts him; that should be enough."

"He is a walking disaster," the spren said. "He is a murderer by his own testimony. This is *no* Bondsmith."

Adolin ignored that, as it wasn't a question. And theoretically, he could let this subject die and continue.

"Jasnah's letter," he began, "is—"

"Kaladin Stormblessed almost killed *his* spren too," a completely different honorspren said. "The Ancient Daughter, most precious of children. Did you know that?"

Adolin ground his teeth. "I do know what happened between Kaladin and Syl. It was a difficult time for all of us, a point of transition. Kaladin didn't know he was breaking his oaths—he was merely having a difficult time navigating conflicting loyalties."

"So you're ignorant *and* dangerous," the spren in the second row said. "Your Radiants barely know what they're doing! You could kill your spren by accident!"

Kelek waved, and the spren was grabbed by attendants and carried up and out of the forum. But Adolin saw this for what it was. A coordinated attack, and the ejection a calculated risk to get the words out.

"We're *not* killing our spren," Adolin said to the crowd. "These incidents are isolated, and we don't have proper context to discuss them."

"Is that so?" yet another honorspren said. "You can *swear* that none of your Radiants have killed their spren?"

"Yes! None of them have. They . . ." He trailed off.

Damnation. He'd met one, hadn't he? Killed recently—that Cryptic in the market.

"They what?" the spren demanded.

If he answered the question truthfully, it could be the end. Adolin took a deep breath, and did what Blended had warned him against. He engaged the audience. "I could answer, but you don't care, do you? You obviously planned together how to attack me today. This is an ambush. You don't care about honor, and you don't care what I have to say. You simply want to throw things at me."

He stepped forward and lifted his hands to the sides. "All right. Go ahead! But know this! You say that spren don't lie, that spren are not changeable like men? Next time you try to pretend that is true, remember this day! Remember how you lied when you said I'd have a fair trial. Remember how you treated the man who came to you in good faith!"

The crowd fell silent. Even his most vocal challengers sat.

"You were warned about this trial multiple times, human," Kelek said from behind. "They have made their choice."

"Not all of them," Adolin said. "I *thought* I'd find rational people inside these gates. Honorable spren. But you know what? I'm happy I didn't. Because now I know you for what you are. You're people, like any of us. Some of you are scared. It makes you afraid to commit. It makes you consider things you would once have thought irrational.

"I understand that. I am *glad* to find you are like humans, because I know what it means. It means you question—that you're afraid, you're uncertain. Believe me, I feel these things too. But you can't sit here and pretend that all humans are the same, that all humans deserve to be thrown away, when you yourselves are as flawed as we are. This trial proves it. Your hearts prove it."

He stared out at them. Daring them. Challenging them.

Finally, looking uncomfortable, the spren in the first row cleared his throat and stood. "Did you know—"

"Oh, cut the act," Adolin said to him. "You want to continue this farce? Fine. Do what you're going to do. I'll make it legal and ask—what is it you've *obviously* planned next to try to discredit me?"

The spren searched about the audience, uncertain. "I . . . Well, did you know about this?" He waved toward the top of the forum. The spren there parted, and everyone turned, looking up at someone being led down the steps by Amuna, the limber honorspren who kept the deadeyes. Today she led a Cryptic—one with a broken pattern, the head wilted.

Damnation. It was as he'd feared.

"Do you know this Cryptic?" Amuna demanded from the steps.

"If it's the same one I saw when I first landed on these shores," Adolin said, "then no. I just saw them once, in the market where the caravans cross."

"You know her story?"

"I . . . Yes, I was told it by a shopkeeper."

"She was killed only a few years ago," Amuna said. "This is proof of your lies. Modern Radiants cannot be trusted."

"There is no evidence that a Radiant did this," Adolin said. "We encountered humans—who have nothing to do with my people—who attacked Notum. Perhaps *they* attacked her."

"That kind of attack leaves a spren who can eventually be healed, with enough Stormlight," Amuna said. "The only *true* death for a spren— the only way to create a deadeye—is through broken Radiant oaths." Amuna gestured toward the deadeye. "This Cryptic didn't fall during the days of the Recreance. She was killed less than a decade ago. By one of your Radiants."

"Likely someone new, untested," Adolin said. "Someone we don't know about. Not one of ours; a poor new Radiant who didn't understand what they were doing. If you'd simply . . ."

But he knew he'd lost them. The crowds shifted, pulling away from the Cryptic, scooting in their seats. Another spren from the first row stood up and shouted questions at Adolin, joined by a dozen others, their words piling atop one another. How many spren would have to die before he admitted Radiants were a bad idea? Did he know the old Radiants had killed their spren because they worried about something *more* dangerous?

Adolin lowered his arms before the assault. Blended had tried to prepare him as best she could, but Adolin was no expert in legal defenses. He'd let himself be maneuvered, like being backed into unfavorable footing in a duel.

The reveal of the Cryptic overshadowed anything else he might say, any other arguments he could make. He looked to Kelek, who nodded, then gestured for him to go. Angry questions battered Adolin as he walked up the steps with as much dignity as he could manage. He knew when a duel was rigged. They'd been *telling* him from the beginning that it would be. And still he'd believed he could convince them.

Idiot.

⁜

Some hours after Adolin's second day of trial, Shallan closed her eyes, resting her head against his bare chest, listening to his heartbeat.

She would never have thought she'd find that sound so comforting. For most of her life, she'd never considered what it would mean to be this close to someone. It would have been alien for her to imagine the blissful warmth of skin against skin, her safehand reaching alongside his face, fingers curled into his hair. How could she possibly have anticipated the wonderful intimacy of feeling his breath on her hair, of listening to his heartbeat, louder to her than her own. The rhythm of his life.

Lying there, everything seemed—for a moment—perfect.

Adolin rested his arm across her bare back. The room was dark, their drapes drawn closed. She wasn't accustomed to darkness; usually you had a chip sitting out to give at least a little light. But here they had no spheres.

Except what she had hidden in the trunk. Sequestered with the cube that spoke between realms. And a very special knife.

"I love you," Adolin whispered in the dark. "What did I do to deserve you?"

"Blaspheme, perhaps," she said. "Or play pranks on your brother. I'm not sure what a person might do to make the Almighty curse them with me. Perhaps you were simply too slow to run away."

He trailed his hand up her bare spine, making her shiver as he finally rested it on the back of her head. "You're brilliant," he whispered. "Determined. Funny."

"Sometimes."

"Sometimes," he admitted, and she could hear the smile on his lips. "But always beautiful."

He thought that. He actually did. She tried to believe she deserved it, but it was difficult. She was so wrapped up in lies, she literally didn't know who she was anymore.

What if he found out? What if he knew what she *really* was?

"Your terrible taste in women," Shallan whispered, "is one of the things I love most about you." She pressed her head to his chest again, feeling the blond hairs tickle her cheek. "And I do love you. That's the only thing I've figured out about my life."

"After today, I have to agree with you on this trial idea of mine. It was a terrible plan."

"I'd be the world's biggest hypocrite if I couldn't love you despite your occasional stupid idea."

He rubbed the back of her head through her hair. "They're going to imprison me," he said. "They're already building the cell. I will be a symbol to them, a display for other spren to come and see."

"I'll break you out," Shallan said.

"How?"

"I stole some Stormlight," she said. "I'll grab my agents and Godeke, and we'll stage a rescue. I doubt the honorspren will give chase; they're too paranoid for that."

Adolin breathed out in the darkness.

"Not going to forbid me?" Shallan asked.

"I . . . don't know," he said. "There are some here who want to listen to me, Shallan. Some I can persuade. But they're afraid of dying, and I find myself uncertain. Not everyone is suited to war, and that's what I'm recruiting them for. I can't truthfully promise them they'll live, that their Radiants won't betray them. Maybe it's not right to demand they join us."

"Kelek told you their leaders were considering going to the enemy's side," Shallan said. "If that happens, those spren will end up bonding people anyway, regardless of what they think now. And the people they'll bond aren't the type to worry about the safety of their spren."

"True," Adolin said. "Storms, I wish I could get through to everyone here. Maybe tomorrow. I have a chance to rebut their witness, ask my own questions. . . ."

"Adolin? You said this is a terrible plan. Will the last day change that?"

"Maybe not," he said. "But at least it's a terrible plan that lets me engage with them. It lets them see a human trying to be honorable. Even if he's terrible at it."

"You're not terrible at being honorable."

He grimaced. "Someone smarter could have won this," he said softly. "Jasnah could have made them see. Instead it's just me. I wish . . . I wish I *knew*, Shallan. What to do. How to make them see."

She squeezed her eyes shut, attempting to return to that earlier moment of perfection. She couldn't. There was too much pain in his voice. His heartbeat had sped up. His breathing no longer felt serene to her, but frustrated.

It tore her apart to hear him like this. This was the man who had kept them all together when Kholinar fell, the man who was normally so optimistic. He'd come here determined to prove to his father—and maybe to himself—that he was still valuable. This stupid trial was going to take that from him.

Unless.

No, Radiant thought. *We can't fulfill Mraize's plan. He's manipulating you.*

We do what two of us agree to, Shallan said. *And I agree it is time to do as Mraize wants. We will take Kelek's soul, and we will imitate him at the trial. Veil and I will—*

No, Veil thought.

Shallan's breath caught. What?

I change my mind, Veil said. *I side with Radiant. I will* not *go kill Kelek. Two against one, Shallan.*

Something stirred deep inside of Shallan.

"I . . ." Adolin whispered. "I wish I could find out who killed that poor Cryptic. That's what ruined it today. Ruined it all."

It is time.

"This trial is not ruined," Formless said to Adolin. "You know, the more I contemplate it, the more I think maybe this trial *wasn't* such a bad idea. You're right. At least you're getting a chance to show them what an honorable man looks like."

"For all the good it's doing," Adolin said.

"I don't know," Formless said. "The High Judge *is* one of the Heralds. Maybe he'll end up surprising you. . . ."

And so, I'll die.

Yes, die. If you're reading this and wondering what went wrong—why my soul evaporated soon after being claimed by the gemstone in your knife—then I name you idiot for playing with powers you only presume to understand.

Teft felt like a wet sack of socks that had been left out in a storm. The honest-by-Kelek's-own-breath truth was that he'd figured he'd done it again. When he'd woken up naked and sickly, he'd assumed he'd gone back to the moss. In that moment, he'd hated himself.

Then he'd seen Dabbid and Rlain. When he saw their joy—more heard it in Rlain's case—Teft knew he couldn't truly hate himself. This was where the oaths had brought him. His self-loathing was, day by day, fading away. Sometimes it surged again. But he was stronger than it was.

The others loved him. So, whatever he'd done, he would get up and make it right. That was the oath he'd taken, and by the Almighty's tenth name, he would keep it.

For them.

Then he'd found out the truth. He *hadn't* broken. He *hadn't* taken up the moss. It *wasn't* his fault. For once in his storming excuse for a life, he had been kicked to the gutter and woken up with a headache—and it *hadn't* been due to his own weakness.

A few days of healing later, he still found it remarkable. His streak held strong. Almost seven months with no moss. Damnation. He had an urge for some moss now, honestly. It would take the edge off his pounding headache.

But *Damnation. Seven months.* That was the longest he'd gone without touching the stuff since . . . well, since joining the army. Thirty years.

Never count those years, Teft, he told himself as Dabbid brought him some soup. *Count the ones you've been with friends.*

The soup had some meat in it, finally. What did they think would happen if he ate something proper? He'd been out for a few days, not a few years. That wasn't enough time to turn into some kind of invalid.

In fact, he seemed to have weathered it better than Kaladin. Stormblessed sat on the floor—refused to take the bench because it was "Teft's." Had a haunted look to him and was a little shrunken, like he'd been hollowed out with a spoon. Whatever he'd seen when suffering those fevers, it hadn't done him any good.

Teft had felt that way before. Right now he was mostly aches, but he'd felt that way too.

"And we were supposed to be off storming duty," Teft grumbled, eating the cold soup. "Civvies. This is how we end up? Fate can be a bastard, eh, Kal?"

"I'm just glad to hear your voice," Kaladin said, taking a bowl of soup from Dabbid. "Wish I could hear hers . . ."

His spren. He'd lost her somehow, in the fighting when he'd gotten wounded.

Teft glanced to the side, to where Phendorana sat primly on the edge of his bench. He'd needed to reach to summon her, and she said she didn't remember anything that had happened since he went unconscious. She'd been . . . sort of unconscious herself.

Phendorana manifested as an older human woman, with mature features and no-nonsense Thaylen-style clothing, a skirt and a blouse. Her hair blew free as if in a phantom wind. Unlike Syl or some of the other honorspren, Phendorana preferred to manifest at the same size as a human.

She glanced at Teft, and he nodded toward Kaladin. Phendorana drew in a breath and sighed pointedly. Then—judging by how Kaladin's spoon paused halfway to his mouth—she let the others in the room see her.

"Your Surgebinding still works?" Phendorana asked Kaladin.

"Not as well as it did before the last fight," Kaladin said. "But I can draw in Stormlight, stick things together."

It was the same for Teft, but they'd found that if Lift didn't show up and do her little Regrowth thing to him every ten hours or so, he'd start to slip back into a coma. Something was *definitely* strange about that kid.

"If you can Surgebind," Phendorana said, "your bond is intact. The Ancient Daughter might have lost herself through separation—it is difficult for us to exist fully in this realm. However, I suspect she will stay close by instinct. If you can get to where you lost her, you should be fine."

"Should be," Kaladin said softly, then started eating again. He nodded in thanks as Dabbid brought him a drink.

They hadn't pushed Dabbid too hard on the fact that he could talk. It wasn't a lie, keeping quiet like he had. Not a betrayal. They each fought their own personal Voidbringers, and they each chose their own weapons. When it had come time to face the storm, Dabbid had done right by Teft and Kaladin. That was what mattered. That was what it meant to be Bridge Four.

A man could choose not to talk if he didn't want to. Wasn't no law against it. Teft knew a handful of people who should maybe try a similar tactic.

They continued eating in silence. After their initial joy at reuniting, their enthusiasm had dampened. Each thing Teft heard about their situation seemed worse than the one before. Fused in the tower. The queen captive. Radiants fallen. The tower spren slowly being corrupted, to the point that it was almost dead. Kaladin couldn't get it to talk to him anymore, and neither could Dabbid.

Grim days he'd awakened to. Almost wished they'd left him in a storming coma. What good was he at fixing any of this?

Phendorana glanced at him, sensing his emotions. He pointed his spoon at her and winked in thanks. No, he wasn't going to be down on himself. He'd sworn an Ideal.

Regardless. Grim days. Grim storming days.

The door opened a short time later, and Rlain entered with Lift, who scuttled forward and sniffed at the pot of soup. She wrinkled her nose.

"Be glad we have anything," Kaladin said. "That ardent in the monastery deserves credit. More than we gave him when we visited, Teft."

"Most people want to be helpful," Teft said. "Even if they need a nudge now and then. Kelek knows I do."

Lift hopped up onto his bench and stepped around Phendorana, then touched Teft, infusing him with Stormlight. He took a deep breath. And storm him, the air felt a little warmer. At least now he wouldn't fall asleep in his soup.

Rlain closed the door, then settled on the ground in the tight confines, his back to the stone wall, bits of his carapace scraping the stone.

"No news from the queen," Rlain said. "Lift managed to talk to one of the scholars, and she says Navani has been isolated for over two weeks now. She's imprisoned, forced to sleep in the scholars' rooms by herself."

"We're all basically imprisoned," Teft said. "Every storming one of us."

"No," Kaladin said. "We five are free."

"So what do we do?" Rlain asked. "We don't know where the last node is, the one keeping that shield up on the Sibling. If we did, it's not like we could protect it."

Kaladin had told them, in disheartening detail, about how difficult it had been to get in and destroy the previous two. Protecting one against the entire might of Odium's forces? Impossible. Teft agreed on that.

"If we break this last one," Teft said, "that's it. Tower's finished. But if we wait, the Fused will find a way to break it themselves. Tower's finished."

"We can't fight an entire army on our own," Kaladin said. "Teft and I have barely recovered, and our powers are temperamental at best. Two of us have lost our spren."

"The girl can wake the other Radiants," Teft said.

"The other Radiants are guarded," Kaladin said.

"Guards can be distracted or dealt with," Rlain said. "We did something similar to get Lift out. Venli is on our side. Or at least she's not on the other side—and she's Voice to the head Fused leading the occupation. We have resources."

Kaladin tipped his head back, his eyes closed.

"Lad?" Teft asked.

"I don't want any of you to take this the wrong way," Kaladin said, not opening his eyes. "I'm not giving up. I'm not broken. No more than usual. But I'm tired. Extremely tired. And I have to wonder. I *have* to ask myself. Should we keep fighting? What do we want to accomplish?"

"We want to win," Rlain said. "Free the tower. Restore the Radiants."

"And if we can't plausibly do that?" Kaladin leaned his head forward and opened his eyes. They'd gone dark again, of course, now that he'd been days without his Blade. The longer you kept your spren bonded, the more slowly the color faded. "I have to at least ask. Is it possible my father is correct? I'm starting to worry about what we might cause people to do if we keep fighting."

They grew quiet. And storm Teft if it wasn't a valid question. One not enough soldiers asked themselves. Right here, right now, should I be fighting? Is there a better way?

Teft took a spoonful of soup. "Did Sigzil ever explain to you boys how I got my father killed?"

The other occupants of the room turned to stare at him with slack jaws. He knew the rumors of what he'd done had moved through Bridge Four—and in the past he'd snapped at people who'd asked him about it. Storming fools.

"What?" Teft said. "It happened a long time ago. I'm over it, mostly. And a man shouldn't hide from what he's done. Gotta air things like this." He dug into his soup, but found his appetite waning. He set the bowl aside, and Phendorana put her hand on his.

"You were . . . young, weren't you?" Kaladin asked, carefully.

"I was eight when my father died," Teft said. "But the problems all started far earlier. It was some travelers, I think, who introduced the idea to the people of my hometown. Not quite a city. You might know it. Talinar? No? Nice place. Smells like flowers. Least in my memory it does. Anyway, the people of the town started meeting secretly. Talking about things they shouldn't have. The return of the Lost Radiants."

"How do you think they knew?" Kaladin asked. "You gave me Stormlight when I was dying, all the way back when *I* didn't know what I was doing. You recognized that it would heal me."

"Teft and I used to think," Phendorana said, "that the group who visited Teft's hometown—the Envisagers, they called themselves—were servants of some important lighteyes in Kholinar. Maybe they overheard what people like Amaram were planning, and ran with it. Only . . ."

". . . Only that was forty-five years ago," Teft said. "And when I asked Brightness Shallan about the group Amaram was part of, everything *she'd* found indicated they'd started less than ten years ago. But that's beside the point. I mean, I only met the leaders once, when my parents brought me to the initiation ceremony."

He shivered, remembering. The blasphemous things they'd chanted—shrouded in dark robes, with spheres affixed to masks to represent glowing eyes—had terrified the boy he'd been. But that hadn't been the worst. The worst had been what they'd done to try to become Radiants. The things they'd pushed their members to do. His mother had been one of those. . . .

"It turned dark," Teft said. "The things my people—my family—did . . . Well, I was around eight when I went to the citylord. I told him, thinking he'd run the worst of the troublemakers out of town. I didn't realize . . ."

"What nahn was your family?" Kaladin asked.

"Sixth," Teft said. "Should have been high enough to avoid execution. My mother was already dead by then, and my father . . ." He glanced up at the rest of them, and felt their sympathy. Well, he didn't want any storming sympathy. "Don't look at me like that. It was a long time ago, like I said. I eventually joined the military to get away from that town.

"It haunted me for a long time. But ultimately, you know what? You know Kelek's own *storming* truth? Because of what my parents did and taught me, I was able to save *you*, Kal. They won in the end. They were *right* in the end." He picked up his soup and forced himself to begin eating it. "We can't storming see the future, like Renarin can. We've gotta do what we think is best, and be fine with that. It's all a man can do."

"You think we should keep fighting?" Rlain said.

"I think," Teft said, "that we need to rescue those Radiants. Maybe we don't need to fight, but we've *got* to get *them* out. I don't like the smell of what you've been telling me. Lined up like that, watched over? The enemy is planning something for our friends."

"I can wake them," Lift said. "But they ain't gonna be in fightin' shape. And I'll need a whole bunch of food. Like . . . an entire chull's worth."

"If we can wake them," Rlain said, "we don't need to fight. We can have them run. Escape."

"How?" Kaladin asked. "We can't possibly hope to get all the way to the Oathgates."

"There's a window," Rlain said. "In the infirmary room. We can break it maybe, and escape out that way."

"To fall hundreds of feet," Kaladin said.

"That might take the Windrunners out of the influence of the tower," Teft said with a grunt. He thought about dropping hundreds of feet, not knowing if his powers would reactivate before he hit bottom. "I'd try it, and prove it can be done. The rest of you could watch and see if I fly up in the distance. If I do, you could follow."

Kaladin rubbed his forehead. "Assuming we could break the glass. Assuming we could get enough Stormlight to infuse the Windrunners. Assuming they're strong enough, after being incapacitated for so long, to try something that insane. Look, I like that we're exploring ideas . . . but we need to take time to consider all our options."

Teft nodded. "You're the officer. I leave the decision to you."

"I'm not an officer any longer, Teft," Kaladin said.

Teft let the objection slide, though it was completely wrong. One thing a good sergeant knew was when to let the officer be wrong. And Kaladin *was* an officer. He'd acted like one even when he'd been a slave. Like he'd been raised by a bunch of lighteyes or something. His official status or rank couldn't change what he was.

"For now," Kaladin said, "we wait. If we have to, we will break in and rescue the Radiants. But first we need to recover, we need to plan, and we need to find a way to contact the queen. I'd like her input."

"I might be able to get in to see her," Rlain said. "They have servants cart food and water to her and her scholars. Venli's people are often assigned that detail, and I could hide my tattoo and substitute for one of them."

"Good," Kaladin said. "That would be great. And while we wait, we don't do anything too rash. Agreed?"

The others nodded, even Lift and Dabbid. Teft too, though this wasn't the sort of situation where you had luxuries like time to come up with the perfect plan. Teft determined he'd just have to be ready to act. Take that next storming step. You couldn't change the past, only the future.

He ate his soup as the conversation turned to lighter topics, and found himself smiling. Smiling because they were still together. Smiling because he'd made the right decision to stay in the tower when Kal needed him. Smiling because he had survived so long without moss or drink, and was able to wake up and see color to the world.

Smiling because, for how bad everything could be, some things were still good.

He shifted as Phendorana poked him. He looked over and caught her grinning as well.

"Fine," he muttered. "You were storming right. You have always been right."

Teft *was* worth saving.

92

A GIFT

The bond is what keeps us alive. You sever that, and we will slowly decompose into ordinary souls—with no valid Connection to the Physical or Spiritual Realms. Capture one of us with your knives, and you won't be left with a spren in a jar, foolish ones. You'll be left with a being that eventually fades away into the Beyond.

Venli stood dutifully beside Raboniel, acting as her Voice as daily reports were delivered. Mostly Venli was here to interpret. While Raboniel had learned Alethi quite well—she claimed to have always been talented at languages—many of their current group of Regals spoke Azish, having been parshmen in that region.

Today Raboniel took the reports while sitting on a throne at the mouth of the hallway with the murals. This meant they were at the bottom of the stairwell leading upward to the ground floor. Venli couldn't help but be reminded of the humans who had died in the last hopeless push to reach the crystal pillar. Those memories were laced with the scents of burning flesh and the sounds of bodies hitting the ground.

Venli glanced at the freshly built portion of steps, hastily constructed with scaffolding underneath to replace the part broken during the fighting. Then she attuned Indifference—a rhythm of Odium. She had to be certain those rhythms continued to punctuate her words, though lately they made her mouth feel coated in oil.

"The Lady of Wishes hears your report," Venli said to the current Regal, who stood bowed before them. "And commends you on your Passion for the search—but you are wrong, she says. The Windrunner *is* alive. You are to redouble your efforts."

The Regal—wearing a sleek form known as relayform, often worn by scouts—bowed lower. Then she retreated up the steps.

"I believe that is the last of them, Ancient One," Venli said to Raboniel.

Raboniel nodded and rose from her throne, then walked into the hallway leading to the two scholar rooms. Her specially tailored Alethi-style dress fluttered as she walked, accentuating the lean, thin pieces of carapace armor along her arms and chest.

Venli followed; the Fused hadn't indicated she should withdraw. Though Raboniel had a workstation and desk set up at the end of the hallway, she always preferred to take reports out near the stairwell. It was as if Raboniel lived two separate lives here. The commander-general of the singer armies seemed so different from the scholar who cared nothing for the war. The second Raboniel was the truer one, Venli thought.

"Last Listener," Raboniel mused. "Last no more. Your people were the only group of singers to successfully reject Fused rule and make their own kingdom."

"Were there . . . unsuccessful attempts?" Venli dared ask, to Craving.

"Many," Raboniel said. She hummed to Ridicule. "Do not make the same mistake as the humans, assuming that the singers have always been of one mind. Yes, forms change our thinking at times, but they merely enhance what's inside. They bring out different aspects of our personalities.

"Humans have always tried to claim that we are nothing but drones controlled by Odium. They like that lie because it makes them feel better about killing us. I wonder if it assuaged their guilt on the day they stole the minds of those they enslaved."

Raboniel's desk was nestled right up against the shield—which, once a bright blue, had grown dark and violet.

Raboniel sat and began looking through her notes. "Do you regret what you personally did, Last Listener?" she asked to Spite. "Do you hate yourself for your betrayal of your people?"

Timbre pulsed. Venli should have lied.

Instead she said, "Yes, Ancient One."

"That is well," Raboniel said. "We all pay dearly for our choices, and the pain lingers, when one is immortal. I suspect you still crave the chance to become a Fused. But I have found in you a second soul, a regretful soul.

"I am pleased to discover it. Not because I admire one who regrets their service—and you should know Odium does not look favorably upon second-guessing. Nevertheless, I had thought you to be like so many others. Abject in your cravings, ambitious to a fault."

"I was that femalen," Venli whispered. "Once."

Raboniel glanced at her sharply, and Venli realized her mistake. She'd said it to the Lost. One of the old rhythms that Regals weren't supposed to be able to hear.

Raboniel narrowed her eyes and hummed to Spite. "And what are you now?"

"Confused," Venli said, also to Spite. "Ashamed. I used to know what I wanted, and it seemed so simple. And then . . ."

"Then?"

"They all died, Ancient One. People I . . . loved dearly, without realizing the depth of my feelings. My sister. My once-mate. My mother. All just . . . gone. Because of me."

Timbre pulsed reassuringly. But Venli didn't want reassurance or forgiveness at that moment.

"I understand," Raboniel said.

Venli stepped closer, then knelt beside the table. "Why do we fight?" she asked to Craving. "Ancient One, if it costs so much, *why* fight? Why suffer so much to secure a land we will not be able to enjoy, because all those we love will be gone?"

"It is not for *us* that we fight," Raboniel said. "It is not for *our* comfort that we destroy, but for the comfort of those who come after. We sing rhythms of Pain so they may know rhythms of Peace."

"And will he ever let *us* sing to Peace?"

Raboniel did not respond. She shuffled through a few papers on her table. "You have served me well," she said. "A little distractedly, perhaps. I ascribe that to your true allegiance being to Leshwi, and your reports to her interfering with your duties to me."

"I am sorry, Ancient One."

Raboniel hummed to Indifference. "I should have arranged for a regular meeting for you to give her your spy reports. Maybe I could have written them for you, to save time. At any rate, I cannot fault you for loyalty to her."

"She . . . doesn't like you very much, Ancient One."

"She is afraid of me because she is shortsighted," Raboniel said. "But Leshwi is among the best we have, for she has managed to not only remember why we fight, but to *feel* it. I am fond of Leshwi. She makes me think that once we win, there will be some Fused who can rule effectively. Even if she is too softhearted for the brutalities we now must perpetuate."

Raboniel selected a paper off the desk and handed it to Venli. "Here. Payment for your services. My time in the tower runs short; I will finish unmaking the Sibling, and then will be on to other tasks. So I will now dismiss you. If you survive what comes next, there is a chance you may find some peace of your own, Venli."

Venli took the paper, humming to Craving. "Ancient One," she said, "I am a weak servant. Because I am so confused about what I want, I do not deserve your praise."

"In part, this is true," Raboniel said. "But I like confusion. Too often we belittle it as a lesser Passion. But confusion leads a scholar to study further and push for secrets. No great discovery was ever made by a femalen or malen who was confident they knew everything.

"Confusion can mean you have realized your weaknesses. I forget its value sometimes. Yes, it can lead to paralysis, but also to truth and better Passions. We imagine that great people were always great, never questioning. I think they would hum to Ridicule at that idea. Regardless, take that gift and be off with you. I have much to do in the coming hours."

Venli nodded, scanning the paper as she rose. She expected a writ of authority—given by Fused to favored servants, granting them extra privileges or requisitions. Indeed, there was exactly that on the front. But on the back was a hastily sketched map. What was this?

"I had hoped to find good maps of the tower," Raboniel noted to Fury. "But Navani had some burned, and disposed of the others—though she feigns ignorance. This, however, is a report from a human scout who was flying along the eastern rim of the Shattered Plains."

Upon closer inspection, the page read in the human femalen writing system, *it appears the group we assumed were Natan migrants are instead Parshendi. A group of a few thousand, with a large number of children.*

Venli read it again.

"Did some of your kind leave?" Raboniel asked absently. "Before the coming of the Everstorm?"

"Yes. Rebels who did not want the new forms, along with the children and the elderly. They . . . escaped into the chasms. Shortly before the storms met, and the floodwaters came. They . . . they should have been completely destroyed. . . ."

"Should have. What a hateful phrase. It has caused me more grief than you could know." She began writing in one of her notebooks. "Perhaps it has treated you with kindness."

Venli clutched the paper and ran, not giving Raboniel a proper farewell.

93

STRONG ENOUGH

I felt it happen to Jezrien. You think you captured him, but our god is Splintered, our Oathpact severed. He faded over the weeks, and is gone now. Beyond your touch at long last.

I should welcome the same. I do not. I fear you.

Formless awoke early on the day of Adolin's final judgment. It was time. She slipped from the bed and began dressing. Unfortunately, she'd moved a little too quickly, as Adolin stirred and yawned.

"Veil's clothing," he noted.

Formless didn't respond, still dressing.

"Thank you," Adolin said, "for Shallan's support last night. I needed her."

"There are some things only she can do," Formless said. Would that be a problem, now that Shallan no longer existed?

"What's wrong, Veil?" Adolin said, sitting up in bed. "You seem different."

Formless pulled on her coat. "Nothing's different. I'm the same old Veil."

Don't you use my name, Veil thought deep inside. *Don't you dare lie to him like that.*

Formless stopped. She'd thought Veil locked away.

"No," Adolin said. "Something *is* different. Become Shallan for a moment. I could use her optimism today."

"Shallan is too weak," Formless said.

"Is she?"

"You know how troubled her emotions are. She suffers *every day* from a traitorous mind." She put on her hat.

"I knew a one-armed swordsman once," Adolin said, yawning. "He had trouble in duels because he couldn't hold a shield, or two-hand a sword."

"Obviously," Formless said, turning and rummaging in her trunk.

"But I tell you," Adolin said, "no one could arm-wrestle like Dorolin. *No one.*"

"What is your point?"

"Who do you think is stronger?" Adolin asked. "The man who has walked easily his entire life, or the man with no legs? The man who must pull himself by his arms?"

She didn't reply, fiddling with the communication cube, then tucking Mraize's knife into her pocket along with her gemstone of Stormlight.

"We don't always see strength the right way," Adolin said. "Like, who is the better swimmer? The sailor who drowns—giving in at long last to the current after hours of fighting—or the scribe who has never stepped into the water?"

"Do you have a point with these questions?" Formless snapped, slamming her trunk closed. "Because I don't see one."

"I know. I'm sorry." Adolin grimaced. "I'm not explaining it well. I just . . . I don't think Shallan is as weak as you say. Weakness doesn't make someone weak, you see. It's the opposite."

"That is foolishness," she said. "Return to sleep. Your trial is in a couple hours, and you shouldn't be fatigued for it."

Formless stalked out into the living room. There she hid by the side of the door and waited to see if Adolin followed. Pattern perked up from where he'd been sitting at the desk, and Formless quieted him with a glare.

Adolin didn't come out. She heard him sigh loudly, but he remained in bed.

Good. She had to act quickly. Formless needed to give him this last gift, the gift of winning here in Lasting Integrity. She owed the memory of Shallan that much.

I know what you're doing, Veil whispered. *I've finally figured it out.*

Formless froze. She checked on Radiant—tucked into the prison of her mind, trying to break free but unable to speak. So why could Veil?

Well, she could ignore a voice or two. Formless sat at the desk and sketched the layout of the judge's home. They'd paced it off yesterday, and peeked in windows. With her talent for spatial awareness, this floor plan should be accurate.

You aren't a new persona, Veil thought. *If you were, you couldn't draw like that. You can lie to yourself, but not me.*

Formless froze again. Was this what she wanted? What she *really* wanted? She wasn't sure of anything anymore.

There were so many questions. Why was Veil able to talk? Who had killed Ialai? How would she extricate herself from Adolin, from the Radiants? Was that the life she desired?

Formless steeled herself, quieting the questions. She placed a hand on her forehead, breathing deeply.

Pattern stepped over, so Formless closed the sketchbook and slid it into her satchel.

". . . Veil?" Pattern asked. "What are you doing?"

"It has to happen today," Formless said. She checked the clock. "Soon. Before the judge leaves his quarters." She gripped the gemstone she'd hidden in her pocket.

"Veil," Pattern said. "This is not a good idea."

He is right, Veil thought. *He is right, Shallan.*

I am Formless, she thought back.

No you're not, Shallan.

"I wouldn't be so quick to tell me what is right and wrong, Pattern," Formless said to him. "We still haven't dealt with your betrayal and your lies. Perhaps you aren't the best judge of morality, and should leave that to me."

His pattern slowed and his shoulders slumped, and he stepped backward as if he wanted to vanish into the shadows.

Formless drew out a little Stormlight, savoring the sensation of it inside her veins. Then she performed a Lightweaving.

It worked. Formless was a composite of the three—a single person with Shallan's drawing and Lightweaving abilities, Radiant's determination and ability to get things done, and Veil's ability to push aside the pain. Veil's ability to see the *truth.*

The best of all three of them.

Lies, Shallan, Veil thought. *Storms. I should have seen this. I should have known. . . .*

She glanced at herself in the mirror, and found the Lightweaving to be perfect. She looked exactly like Lusintia, the honorspren woman. She even gave off the same faint glow. This was going to be so easy.

Formless packed her drawing tools in case she needed to quickly sketch a new face. A Lightweaving disguised her satchel as a cloth bag like the ones the honorspren used.

Bells from below announced that it was about an hour until the trial. She crossed the room, passing Pattern, who had withdrawn to the corner. He stood in the shadows, his pattern moving lethargically.

"What's happening?" he said. "Something is very wrong with you, Shallan. I have handled this so poorly. I talked to Wit yesterday, and he—"

"You're *still* doing that?" Formless said. "You're still *disobeying* me?"

Pattern pulled away further.

"I've had enough of you," Formless hissed. "Stay here and cover for me with Adolin. We'll talk about this at length after the trial."

She took a deep breath and peeked out to make sure no one was watching—they might wonder why Lusintia had been in Shallan's house—then slipped out and began crossing the southern plane. The fortress was quiet. Spren didn't sleep, but they did have less active periods. They would congregate at "night" in the homes of friends, leaving the walkways of the fortress relatively unwatched.

A few leaves fluttered through the open air between the four sides. Formless tried not to look at the other three planes, three cities making an impossible box around her. She wasn't good at—

"Veil," a voice said behind her. "I need to explain. I must tell you the truth. Mmm . . ."

She groaned and turned. Pattern was following her like a barely weaned axehound pup.

"You'll give away my disguise!" she snapped at him.

He stopped, his pattern slowing.

"You must know what Wit said," Pattern replied. "He is so wise. He seems to like you and hate everyone else. Ha ha. He made fun of me. It was very funny. I am like a chicken. Ha ha."

Formless closed her eyes and sighed.

"He said to tell you that we trust you," Pattern said. "And love you. He said I should tell you that you deserve trust and love. And you do. I'm sorry I've been lying. For a very long time. I'm so sorry. I didn't think you could handle it."

"Shallan couldn't," she said. "Go to the room and wait. I'll deal with you *later*."

She strode away, and fortunately he didn't follow. It was time to become the woman she'd been building toward ever since she left her home to steal from Jasnah. Formless could finally join the Ghostbloods. She didn't care about Shallan's past. Let it sleep. She could be like Veil, who didn't have to worry about such things.

You're pretending to be like me, Veil thought. *But Wit is right. You deserve to be loved, Shallan. You do.*

The High Judge's quarters were all the way at the top of the plane, near the battlements. It was difficult to ignore the strange geometry up here, past the parks and the trees, because the sky was so close. She wanted to spend time drawing it, but of course she wasn't like that anymore. She needed to find all this disorienting and strange. Like Veil.

It helped to focus on the target: a small building near the corner of the wall. She passed several honorspren, but not many. She waved to those who waved to her, but mostly strode forward with a sense of purpose.

Once Formless arrived, she loitered near the house, glancing around until she could be reasonably certain no one was looking. That was difficult, with multiple planes to watch. At least the plan was simple. Step up to the door. Soulcast the doorknob into smoke to get past the lock. Sneak in and make her way to the back room, which was the High Judge's study. Knife him before he could react, then take his place for the trial.

This was her last step. This was the end.

I . . . Radiant said, her voice distant. *I killed Ialai.*

Formless froze in place.

I saw . . . Radiant whispered, *that you were about to do it. That you had poison secreted in your satchel. So I stepped in. To protect you. So you . . . didn't have to do it. To prevent . . . what is happening to you now . . . Shallan . . .*

She squeezed her eyes shut. No. No, she wouldn't back down. She *had* to do this. To end it. To end the wavering.

She opened her eyes, strode up to the door, and grabbed the knob with her freehand. It vanished beneath her touch. Soulcasting really *was* easier on this side. The knob barely cared that she asked it to change.

She pushed open the door. The room inside was packed. Pieces of furniture stacked atop one another. Rolled tapestries. Knickknacks and mementos, like a small glass chicken on the windowsill and a pile of dusty letters on a table.

Formless shut the door with a quiet motion. The windows provided enough light to see by, and she could see the glow of candlelight beneath the room's other door, the one that led into the High Judge's study. Kelek was here. She revealed Mraize's knife, then stepped forward.

As she did so, she felt a coldness—like a sharp breeze. Stormlight left her in a rush. Formless paused, then glanced over her shoulder.

Veil stood behind her.

"I know why you're doing this, Shallan," Veil said. "There's no fourth persona. Not yet. You've given yourself another name, so you can tuck away the pain. You take that step though, and it will be real."

"This is who I want to be," Formless said. "Let me go."

"You're running again," Veil said. "You think you don't deserve Adolin, or your place as a Radiant. You're terrified that if your friends knew what you truly were, they'd turn away from you. Leave you. So you're going to leave them first.

"That's why you kept spending time with the Ghostbloods. That's why you're here. You see this as an out from your life. You figure if you *become* the despicable person the darkness whispers that you have been, then it will all be decided. No going back. Decision's made."

Formless . . . Formless . . .

Was just Shallan.

And Shallan wanted to do this. She wanted to show them what she truly was. So it would be over.

"I can't be Shallan," she whispered. "Shallan is weak."

Shallan put her hands to her eyes and trembled. Veil felt her emotions in a sudden wave of pain, frustration, shame, and confusion. It made her shake as well.

"Who is a better swimmer?" Veil whispered. "It's the sailor who has swum his entire life, even if he encounters rough seas that challenge him. Who is the stronger man? It *is* the man who must pull himself by his arms. And that swordsman with one arm . . . He was probably the best in raw skill. He couldn't win because of his disadvantages, but he wasn't weaker than the others."

Shallan stilled.

"Adolin is right," Veil said. "He's always been right about you. Tell me. Who is the strongest of mind? The woman whose emotions are always on her side? Or the woman whose own thoughts betray her? You have fought this fight every day of your life, Shallan. And *you are not weak.*"

"Aren't I?" Shallan demanded, spinning. "I killed my own father! I strangled him with my own hands!"

The words cut deep, like a spike through the heart. Veil winced visibly. But that cut to the heart somehow let warmth bleed out, flowing through her. "You have borne that truth for a year and a half, Shallan," Veil said, stepping forward. "You kept going. You *were* strong enough. You made the oath."

"And Mother?" Shallan snapped. "Do you remember the feel of the Blade forming in our hands for the first time, Veil? I do. Do you remember the *horror* I felt at the strike, which I never meant to make?"

Her mother, with stark red hair—a length of metal in her chest as her beautiful green eyes turned to coal. Burning out of her face. Shallan's voice, screaming at what she'd done. Screaming, *begging* to take it back. Wishing she were dead. Wishing . . . Wishing . . .

Another spike to the heart. More warmth bleeding out, blood flowing with thunderous heartbeats. Veil always felt so cold, but today she felt warm. Warm with pain. Warm with life.

"You can bear it," Veil whispered. She stepped forward, eye-to-eye with Shallan. "You can remember it. Our weakness doesn't make us weak. Our weakness makes us strong. For we had to carry it all these years."

"No," Shallan said, her voice growing soft. "No. I can't . . ."

"You can," Veil whispered. "I've protected you all these years, but it's time for me to leave. It's time for me to be done."

"I can't," Shallan said. "I'm *too weak!*"

"I don't think you are. Take the memories." Veil reached out her hand. "Take them back, Shallan."

Shallan wavered. Formless had vanished like a puff of smoke, revealing all her lies. And there was Veil's hand. Inviting. Offering to *prove* that Shallan was strong.

Shallan took her hand.

Memories flooded her. Playing in the gardens as a child, meeting a Cryptic. A beautiful, spiraling spren that dimpled the stone. Wonderful times, spent hidden among the foliage in their special place. The Cryptic encouraged her to become strong enough to help her family, to stand against the terrible darkness spreading through it.

Such a blessed time, full of hope, and joy, and truths spoken easily with the solemnity and wonder of a child. That companion had been a true friend to an isolated child, a girl who suffered parents who constantly fought over her future.

Her spren. A spren who could talk. A spren she could confide in. A companion.

And that companion had not been Pattern. It had been a different Cryptic. One who . . . One who . . .

Shallan fell to her knees, arms wrapped around herself, trembling. "Oh storms . . . Oh, God of Oaths . . ."

She felt a hand on her shoulder. "It's all right, Shallan," Veil whispered. "It's all right."

"I know what you are," Shallan whispered. "You're the blankness upon my memories. The part of me that looks away. The part of my mind that protects me from my past."

"Of course I am," Veil said. "I'm your *veil,* Shallan." She squeezed Shallan's shoulder, then turned toward the closed door. Had Kelek heard them talking . . . or . . . had they even spoken out loud?

Shallan surged to her feet. No. It hurt *too much.* Didn't it make more sense to become what Mraize wanted? Adolin would hate her for what she did. Dalinar would hate her. Shallan represented the very thing they all said they would never do. The thing they blamed for all of their problems. The thing that had doomed humankind.

She . . . she was worthless. She reached for the doorknob.

You can bear it, Radiant whispered.

No. She could become Formless and join the Ghostbloods wholeheartedly. Become the woman she'd created for herself, the strong spy who lived a double life without it bothering her. She could be confident and collected and painless and perfect.

Strength before weakness, Radiant said.

Not a woman who had . . . who had . . .

Be strong.

Shallan turned, breathing out, and Stormlight exploded from her like her life's own blood. It painted the room before her, coloring it, changing it to a lush garden. Covered in bright green vines and shalebark of pink and red.

Within it, a hidden place where a girl cried. The girl wept, then screamed, then said the terrible words.

"I don't *want* you! I hate you! I'm done! You never existed. You are nothing. And I am *finished*!"

Shallan didn't turn away. She *wouldn't.* She felt the ripping sensation again. The terrible pain, and the awful horror.

She hadn't known what she was doing, not truly. But she *had* done it.

"I killed her," Shallan whispered. "I killed my spren. My wonderful, beautiful, kindly spren. I broke my oaths, and I killed her."

Veil stood with her hands clasped before her. "It's going to hurt," Veil warned. "I'm sorry for the pain, Shallan. I did what I could—but I did it for too long."

"I know," Shallan said.

"But I have no strength that you do not, Shallan," Veil said. "You are me. We are me."

Veil became Stormlight, glowing brightly. The color faded from her, becoming pure white. Her memories integrated into Shallan's. Her skills became Shallan's. And Shallan recognized everything she had done.

She remembered preparing the needle hidden in her satchel to kill Ialai. She saw her past, and her growing worry in all its self-destructive horror. Saw herself growing into the lie that she could never belong with Adolin and the Radiants, so she began searching for another escape.

But that escape wasn't strength. *This* was strength. She closed her eyes, bearing the burden of those memories. Not only of what she'd done recently, but what she'd done in the garden that day. Terrible memories.

Her memories.

As there was nothing left for Veil to protect Shallan from feeling, she began to fade. But as she faded, one last question surfaced: *Did I do well?*

"Yes," Shallan whispered. "Thank you. Thank you *so* much."

And then, like any other illusion that was no longer needed, Veil puffed away.

Shallan took a deep breath, her pain settling in. Storms . . . Pattern was here. Not her new Pattern, the first one. The deadeye. Shallan needed to find her.

Later. For now, she had a job to do. As she gathered herself, the door to the study clicked open, and light spilled around a figure. An Alethi man with wispy hair and weary eyes. Shallan knew that expression well.

"I see," Kelek said. "So you are the one sent to kill me?"

"I was sent for that purpose," she said, holding up the knife. She set it on a nearby table. "Sent by someone who didn't realize I'd be strong enough to say no. You're safe from me, Kelek."

He walked over and picked up the knife in timid fingers. "So this is like the one they used on Jezrien?"

"I don't know," Shallan said honestly. "A group called the Ghostbloods wanted me to use that on you."

"Old Thaidakar has always wanted my secrets," Kelek said. "I thought it would be the man, your husband, who came for me. I wonder if he knows I've had trouble fighting these days. It's so hard to decide. To do anything really . . ."

"Is that why you've been so hard on Adolin?" Shallan asked. "At the trial?"

Kelek shook his head. "You two stumbled into a little war of ideologies. The older honorspren—they're so frightened of what happened to their predecessors. But the young ones want to go fight."

"I can tell you about the people who sent me," Shallan said. "We can share information. But first I have a request. You're about to convict my husband in this sham of a trial. I'd like you to reconsider."

Kelek wiped his brow with a handkerchief from his pocket. "So many questions," he said, as if he hadn't heard her request. "Who else knows I'm here? I feel like I'm close to finding a way offworld. Maybe . . . Maybe I should wait. . . ."

"I have information that could help you," Shallan said. "But I want to trade. There isn't much time for us to—"

She was interrupted as the door slammed open, revealing several honorspren—including Lusintia, the one Shallan had impersonated. She gestured aggressively at Shallan, who stepped back, reaching into her pocket for her gemstone.

It was dun. Somehow, in what she'd done with Veil, she'd used it all up.

"Attempting to influence the course of the trial?" Lusintia demanded. "Colluding with the judge?"

"She was . . . doing nothing of the sort," Kelek said, stepping up beside Shallan. "She was bringing me news from the Physical Realm. And I'd have you *not* barge into my quarters, thank you very much."

Lusintia stopped, but then looked over her shoulder toward a bearded male honorspren. Shallan recognized him as Sekeir, the one who had acted as prosecutor against Adolin on the first day of the trial. An important spren, perhaps the most important in the fortress. And one of the oldest ones.

"I think, Honored One," Sekeir said softly, "that you might be having another bout of your weakness. We shall have to sequester you, I'm afraid. For your own good . . ."

Nevertheless, I'm writing answers for you here, because something glimmers deep within me. A fragment of a memory of what I once was.

I was there when Ba-Ado-Mishram was captured. I know the truth of the Radiants, the Recreance, and the Nahel spren.

Adolin made no effort to arrive early to the last day of the trial. Indeed, each footstep felt leaden as he trudged toward the forum. He could see from a distance that the place was crowded—with even more spren gathered at the top of the steps than yesterday. Nearly every honorspren in the fortress had come to watch him be judged.

Though he didn't relish facing them, he also couldn't give up this opportunity. It was his last chance to speak for himself, for his people. He had to believe that some of them were listening.

And if he lost? If he was condemned to imprisonment? Would he let Shallan rescue him, as she'd offered?

If I did, he thought, *I would prove what the leaders of the honorspren have been saying all along: Men aren't worthy of trust.* What if the only way to win here was to accept their judgment? To spend years in a cell?

After all, what else are you good for, Adolin? The world needed Radiants, not princes—particularly not ones who had refused the throne. Perhaps the best thing he could do for humanity was become a living testimony of their honor.

That thought troubled him as he reached the crowd. They parted for him, nudging one another, falling silent as he descended.

Storms, I wasn't built for problems like this, Adolin thought. He hadn't slept well—and he worried about the way Shallan had been acting lately. She wasn't sitting in her spot, and neither was Pattern. Was she going to skip this most important day of the trial?

He was about halfway down the steps when he noticed another oddity: Kelek wasn't there. Sekeir—the aged honorspren with the long beard—had taken his place. He waved for Adolin to continue.

Adolin reached the floor of the forum and walked over to the judge's seat. "Where is Kelek?"

"The Holy One is indisposed," Sekeir said. "Your wife went to him in secret and tried to influence the course of the trial."

Adolin felt a spike of joy. So *that* was what she'd been up to.

"Do not smile," Sekeir said. "We discovered a weapon of curious design, perhaps used to intimidate the Holy One. Your wife is being held, and the Holy One is . . . suffering from his long time as a Herald.

"We have relieved him as High Judge, and I will sit in his place. You will find the documentation on your seat, to be read to you if you wish. The trial will continue under my direction. I am a far lesser being, but I will not be as . . . lax as he was."

Great, Adolin thought. *Wonderful.* He tried to find a way to use this to his advantage. Could he stall? Make some kind of plea? He looked at the audience and saw trouble, division. Perhaps he was a fool, but it seemed like some of them *wanted* to listen. *Wanted* to believe him. Those felt fewer than yesterday; so many others watched him with outright hostility.

So how could Adolin reach them?

Sekeir started the trial by calling for silence, something Kelek had never bothered to do. Apparently the hush that fell over the crowd wasn't enough, for Sekeir had three different spren ejected for whispering to one another.

That done, the overstuffed spren stood up and read off a prepared speech. And storms, did it go on. Windy passages about how Adolin had brought this upon himself, about how it was good that humans finally had a chance to pay for their sins.

"Do we need this?" Adolin interrupted as Sekeir paused for effect. "We all know what you're going to do. Be on with it."

The new High Judge waved to the side. A spren stepped up beside Adolin, a white cloth in her hands. A gag. She pulled it tight between her hands, as if *itching* for a chance.

"You may speak during the questioning of the witness," Sekeir said. "The defendant is not allowed to interrupt the judge."

Fine. Adolin settled into parade rest. He didn't have an enlisted man's experience with standing at attention, but Zahel had forced him to learn this stance anyway. He could hold it. Let them see him bear their lashes without complaint.

His determination in that regard lasted until Sekeir, at long last, finished his speech and called for the final witness to be revealed.

It was Maya.

Amuna led her by the hand, forcing back the watching honorspren. Though Adolin had gone to see Maya each morning—and they'd let him do his exercises with her—bars had separated them. They hadn't otherwise allowed him to interact with her, claiming deadeyes did best when it was quiet.

If so, why were they dragging her into the middle of a crowd? Adolin stepped forward, but the honorspren at his side snapped the gag in warning. He forced himself back into parade rest and clenched his jaw. Maya didn't *seem* any worse for the attention. She walked with that customary sightless stare, completely oblivious to the whispering crowd.

Sekeir didn't hush them this time. The bearded honorspren smiled as he regarded the stir Amuna and Maya made. They placed Maya on her podium, and she turned and seemed to notice Adolin, for she cocked her head. Then, as if only now aware of it, she regarded the crowded audience. She shrank down, hunching her shoulders, and glanced around with quick, jerky motions.

He tried to catch her gaze and reassure her with a smile, but she was too distracted. Damnation. Adolin hadn't hated the honorspren, despite their tricks, but this started him seething. How *dare* they use Maya as part of their spectacle?

Not all of them, he reminded himself, reading the mood of the crowd. Some sat quietly, others whispered. And more than a few near the top wore stormy expressions. No, they didn't care for this move either.

"You may speak now, prisoner," Sekeir said to Adolin. "Do you recognize this deadeye?"

"Why are you questioning me?" Adolin said. "She is supposed to give witness, and I'm supposed to question her. Yet you've chosen a witness who cannot answer your questions."

"I will guide this discussion," Sekeir said. "As is my right as judge in the case of a witness too young or otherwise incapable of a traditional examination."

Adolin sought out Blended, a single black figure in a sea of glowing white ones. She nodded. This was legal. There were so many laws she hadn't had time to explain—but it wasn't her fault. He suspected he couldn't have understood every detail of the law even with years of preparation.

"Now," Sekeir said, "do you know this spren?"

"You know I do," Adolin snapped. "That is Mayalaran. She is my friend."

"Your 'friend,' you say?" Sekeir asked. "And what does this friendship entail? Do you perhaps have dinner together? Participate in friendly chats around the campfire?"

"We exercise together."

"Exercise?" Sekeir said, standing from his seat behind the judge's table. "You made a weapon of her. She is not your friend, but a convenient tool. A weapon by which you slay other men. Your kind never asks permission of Shardblades; you take them as prizes won in battle, then apply them as you wish. She is not your friend, Adolin Kholin. She is your *slave*."

"Yes," Adolin admitted. He looked to Maya, then turned away. "*Yes*, storm you. We didn't know they were spren at first, but even now that we do . . . we use them. We need to."

"Because you *need* to *kill*," Sekeir said, walking up to Adolin. "Humans are monsters, with a lust for death that can never be sated. You thrive upon the terrible emotions of the Unmade. You don't fight Odium. You *are* Odium."

"Your point is made," Adolin said more softly. "Let Maya go. Pass your judgment."

Sekeir stepped up to him, meeting his eyes.

"Look at her," Adolin said, gesturing. "She's terrified."

Indeed, Maya had shrunk down further and was twisting about, as if to try to watch all the members of the audience at once. She turned so violently, in fact, that Amuna and another honorspren stepped up to take her arms, perhaps to prevent her from fleeing.

"You want this to be easy, do you?" Sekeir asked Adolin, speaking in a softer voice. "You don't *deserve* easy. I had this fortress working in an orderly, organized manner before you arrived. You have no idea the frustration you have caused me, human." The honorspren stepped away from Adolin and faced the crowd, thrusting his hand toward Maya.

"Behold this spren!" Sekeir commanded. "See what was done to her by humans. This Kholin asks us to offer ourselves for bonds again. He asks us to trust again. It is vital, then, that we examine carefully the results of our last time trusting men!"

Maya began to thrash, a low growl rising in her throat. She did *not* like being constrained.

"This is a trial by witness!" Adolin shouted at Sekeir. "You are interfering, and go too far."

Blended nodded, and other honorspren in the crowd had stood up at the objection. They agreed. Whatever the law was, Sekeir was stretching it here.

"This witness," Sekeir said, pointing at Maya again, "lost her voice because of what *your people* did. I must speak for her."

"She doesn't want you to speak for her!" Adolin shouted. "She doesn't want to *be* here!"

Maya continued to push against her captors, increasingly violent. Some of the crowd responded with jeers toward Adolin. Others muttered and gestured toward Maya.

"Does it make you uncomfortable?" Sekeir demanded of Adolin. "Convenient, now, for you to care about what she wants. Well, *I* can read her emotions. That thrashing? It is the pain of someone who remembers what was done to her. She condemns you, Adolin Kholin."

Maya's cries grew louder. Frantic, guttural, they weren't proper shouts. They were the pained anguish of someone who had forgotten how to speak, but still needed to give voice to her agony.

"This poor creature," Sekeir shouted over the increasing din, "condemns you with each groan. She is our final witness, for hers is the pain we must never forget. Listen to her demand your punishment, Adolin Kholin! She was innocent, and your kind murdered her. Listen to her cry for blood!"

Maya's shouts grew louder and more *raw*. Some honorspren in the crowd pulled back, and others covered their ears, wincing. Adolin had heard that scream before, the time he'd tried to summon her as a Blade while in Shadesmar.

"She's in pain!" Adolin shouted, lunging forward. The spren watching him, however, had been waiting for this. They grabbed him and held him tight. "Let her go, you bastard! Your point is made!"

"My point cannot be made strongly enough," Sekeir shouted. "It must be repeated over and over. You will not be the only traitor who comes with a smile, begging to exploit us. My people must stay firm, must remember this moment, for their own good. They need to *see* what humans did!"

Maya's voice grew louder, gasping breaths punctuated by ragged howls. And in that moment, Adolin . . . *felt* her pain somehow. A deep agony. And . . . anger?

Anger at the honorspren.

"They trusted you," Sekeir said, "and you murdered them!"

She clawed at the hands, trying to free herself, her teeth flashing as she twisted her scratched-out eyes one way, then the other. Yes, Adolin could feel that agony as if it were his own. He didn't know how, but he *could*.

"Listen to her!" Sekeir said. "Accept her condemnation!"

"LET HER GO!" Adolin shouted. He struggled, then went limp. "Storms. Just let her go."

"I refuse judgment!" Sekeir said. "I don't need to give it. In the end, her testimony is the only one needed. Her *condemnation* is all we ever needed. Listen to her shouts; remember them as you rot, Adolin Kholin. Remember what your kind did to her. Her screams *are* your judgment!"

Maya's howls came to a crescendo of anguish, then she fell silent, gasping for breath. Weak. Too weak.

Take it, Adolin thought to her. *Take some of my strength.*

She looked right at him, and despite her scratched-out eyes, she *saw* him. Adolin felt something, a warmth deep within him. Maya drew in air, filling her lungs. Her expression livid as she gathered all of her strength, she prepared to shout again. Adolin braced himself for the screech. Her mouth opened.

And she spoke.

"*We! CHOSE!*"

The two words rang through the forum, silencing the agitated honorspren. Sekeir, standing with his back to her, hesitated. He turned to see who had interrupted his dramatic speech.

Panting, hunched forward in the grip of her captors, Maya managed to repeat her words. "We . . . We chose. . . ."

Sekeir stumbled away. The hands holding Adolin went slack as the honorspren stared in shock.

Adolin pulled free and crossed the stage. He shoved aside the startled Amuna and supported Maya, putting her arm across his shoulder to hold her up as he would a wounded soldier. She clung to him, stumbling as she struggled to remain upright.

Even as she did, however, she whispered it again. "We chose," she said, her voice ragged as if she had been shouting for hours. "Adolin, we *chose.*"

"Blood of my fathers . . ." Adolin whispered.

"What is this?" Sekeir said. "What have you done to her? The sight of you has caused her to rave in madness and—"

He cut off as Maya pointed at him and released a terrifying screech, her jaw lowering farther than it should. Sekeir put his hand to his chest, eyes wide as her screech transformed into words.

"You. Cannot. Have. My. *SACRIFICE!*" she shouted. "Mine. My sacrifice. Not yours." She pointed at the crowd. "Not theirs." She pointed at Adolin. "Not his. Mine. *MY SACRIFICE.*"

"You knew what was going to happen when the Radiants broke their oaths," Adolin said. "They didn't murder you. You decided together."

She nodded vigorously.

"All this time," Adolin said, his voice louder—for the audience. "Everyone *assumed* you were victims. We didn't accept that you were partners with the Radiants."

"We chose," she hissed. Then, belting it loud as an anthem, "*WE CHOSE.*"

Adolin helped her step over to the first row of benches, and the honorspren sitting there scrambled out of the way. She sat, trembling, but her grip on his arm was fierce. He didn't pull away; she seemed to need the reassurance.

He looked around at the crowd. Then toward Sekeir and the other eldest honorspren seated near the judge's bench.

Adolin didn't speak, but he *dared* them to continue condemning him. He dared them to ignore the testimony of the witness they'd chosen, the one they'd pretended to give the power of judgment. He let them mull it over. He let them think.

Then they began to trail away. Haunted, perhaps confused, the honorspren began to leave. The elders gathered around Sekeir, who remained standing, dumbfounded, staring at Maya. They pulled him away, speaking in hushed, concerned tones.

They didn't touch Adolin. They stayed far from him, from Maya. Until eventually a single person remained in the stands. A female spren in a black suit, her skin faintly tinged with an oily rainbow. Blended stood up, then picked her way down the steps.

"I should like to take credit," she said, "for your victory in what everyone assumed was an unwinnable trial. But it was not my tutelage, or your boldness, that won this day."

Maya finally let go of Adolin's arm. She seemed stronger than before, though her eyes were still scratched out. He could feel her curiosity, her . . . awareness. She looked up at him and nodded.

He nodded back. "Thank you."

"Stren . . ." she whispered. "Stren. Be . . ."

"Strength before weakness."

She nodded again, then turned her scratched-out gaze toward the ground, exhausted.

"I don't intend to forget that you testified against me," Adolin said to Blended. "You played both sides of this game."

"It was the best way for me to win," she said, inspecting Maya. "But you should know that I suggested to the honorspren elders that they use your deadeye as a witness. They were unaware of the legal provision that allowed them to speak for her."

"Then her pain is *your* fault?" Adolin demanded.

"I did not suggest they treat her with such callousness," Blended said. "Their act *is* their own, as *is* their shame. But admittedly, I knew how they might act. I wanted to know if a truth exists—the one you said to me."

Adolin frowned, trying to remember.

"That she spoke," Blended reminded him. "To you. That friendship *exists* between you. I sought proof, and found that her name—recorded in old documents of spren treaties—*is* as you said. A curious fact to find. Indeed."

Blended strolled around Adolin and studied Maya's face. "Still scratched out . . ." she said. "Though a bond between you *is*."

"I'm . . . no Radiant," Adolin said.

"No. That is certain." Maya met Blended's gaze. "But something *is* happening. I must leave this place at last and return to the inkspren. If the words this deadeye spoke *are* . . ."

"If what she said is true," Adolin said, "then you have no further excuse for refusing humankind the bonds they need."

"Don't we?" Blended asked. "For centuries, my kind told ourselves an easy lie, yes. That humans had been selfish. That humans had murdered. But easy answers often *are*, so we can be excused.

"This truth, though, means a greater problem is. Thousands of spren *chose* death instead of letting the Radiants continue. Does this not worry you more? They truly believed that—as humans claimed at the time—Surgebinding would destroy the world. That the solution was to end the orders of Radiants. Suddenly, at the cost of many lives."

"Did you know the full cost, Maya?" Adolin asked, the question suddenly occurring to him. "Did you and your Radiants know that you would become deadeyes?"

Adolin felt Maya searching deep, pushing through her exhaustion, seeking . . . memories that were difficult for her to access. Eventually, she shook her head and whispered, "Pain. Yes. Death? No. Maybe."

Adolin sat beside her, letting her lean against him. "Why, Maya? Why were you willing to do it?"

"To save . . . save . . ." She sagged and shook her head.

"To save us from something worse," Adolin said, then looked to Blended. "What does it mean?"

"It means we've had all of this terribly wrong for much time, Highprince Adolin," she said. "And my own stupidity is. I have always thought myself smart." She shook her head as she stood before them, arms folded. "What an effective test. Very effective."

"This?" Adolin said, waving to the empty forum. "This was a complete and utter farce."

"I meant a different test," Blended said. "The *true* trial—the one you've been engaging in for the last few years: the test for this spren's loyalty. She was the only judge who ever mattered, and today was her chance to offer judgment." Blended leaned forward. "You passed."

With that she turned to go and strode up the steps—her stark onyx coloring making her seem a shadow with no accompanying body. "Easy answers no longer are," she said. "But if deadeyes can begin to return . . . this is grand news. Important news. I will convey this to my people.

"I do not know if making new Radiants is a good idea—but I must admit that your ancestors were not traitors. Something *did* frighten them enormously, to cause humans and spren to destroy their bonds. And if the spren did not know they would die . . . then pieces of this puzzle are still missing. The questions are more complicated, and more dangerous, than we ever knew."

With that, Blended left. Adolin let Maya rest for a few minutes. When he finally stood up, she joined him. She followed him as she normally did, expressionless and mild, but he could feel that she was not as insensate as she'd been. She was conserving energy.

She wasn't healed, but she was better. And when he had needed her, she had been willing to struggle through death itself to speak for him.

No, he thought. *She spoke for herself. Don't make the same mistake again.*

He needed to find Shallan and head to the Oathgate so they could share what he'd learned. Maybe the honorspren would swallow their pride and help. Maybe they would, as Blended said, find other reasons to fear.

Either way, he suspected the Radiant relationship would never be the same again.

FOURTEEN MONTHS AGO

Venli scrambled through a nightmare of her own making.

Beneath a blackened sky, humans and listeners fought with steel and lightning. She heard screams more often than commands, and beneath it all, a new song. A song of summoning, joined by thousands of voices. The Everstorm was coming, building to a crescendo as the listeners called it.

She'd imagined this day as an organized effort by the listeners—led by her. Instead there was chaos, war, and death.

She did not join in the singing. She splashed through deep puddles, seeking to escape. The Weeping rains streamed down, soft but persistent. She passed listeners she recognized, all standing in a line, their eyes glowing red as they sang.

"Faridai," she said to one of them. "We have to get away. The humans are sweeping in this direction."

He glanced at her, but continued singing. The whole line seemed completely oblivious to the rain, and mostly oblivious to her words. She attuned Panic. They were overwhelmed by the new form, consumed by it.

She felt that same impulse, but was able to resist. Perhaps because of her long association with Ulim? She wasn't certain. Venli hurried away, looking over her shoulder. She couldn't make out much of what was happening on the battlefield. It stretched across multiple plateaus, veiled in mist and rain, shadowed by pitch-black clouds. Occasional bursts of red lightning showed that many of the new stormforms *were* fighting.

Hopefully they could control their powers better than Venli could. When she had released the energy of stormform—expecting grand attacks that smote her foes—the lightning had gone in wild directions, unpredictable. She didn't think she had hurt a single human, and now she felt limp, the glorious energy expended—and slow to renew.

She hid by a large lump of rock that might have been a building long ago. Behind her, humans attacked the line of listeners she'd left; she heard screams, felt a *crack* as lightning was released.

Their song did not start again, but she heard humans cursing and talking in their crude tongue, voices echoing over the sound of the rain. More dead. The storm was building, yes—nearly upon them. But how many listeners would be slaughtered before it arrived?

Surely the other battlefronts are doing better, she thought, squeezing her eyes closed and listening to the Rhythm of Panic. *Surely the listeners are winning.*

What of Ulim's promises? What of Venli's throne? She breathed in cold air, water streaming along the sides of her face, leaving her skin numb and her carapace chilled. She pressed against the rocks, trembling. It was all wrong. She wasn't supposed to be here. She was supposed to be safe.

The sound of boots scraping stone made her open her eyes in time to see a spear coming at her. She lunged to the side, but the weapon struck across the ridges on her cheek and nose, cutting only a thin slice in her skin— mostly deflecting off the carapace mask stormform had given her face.

She fell to the ground in a puddle and tried to pull away, one hand out and pleading. The human loomed over her, a terrible figure with his features completely lost in the shadow of his helm. He raised his spear.

"No, no," Venli said to Subservience in his language. "Please, no. I'm scholar. No weapon. Please, no."

He brandished his spear, but as she cringed—turning aside her face—no blow came. The man stepped away, then jogged off, joining some of his fellows who were forming up against an approaching group with glowing red eyes.

Venli felt at the scrape the spear had caused, amazed at how little it had wounded her. Then she felt at her skin, her clothing. He'd . . . he'd just left her alone. As she'd asked. She stared after the man, attuning Derision. The fool didn't know how important a listener he'd spared. He should have killed her.

Derision seemed to fade though, as she considered. Was . . . was that the proper rhythm, the proper feeling, she should feel upon being saved? What had happened to her these last few years? What had she let happen to her?

For a moment she heard the Rhythm of Appreciation instead. Part of her, it seemed, didn't want to bask in the glory of the new form. Part of her longed for the comforts of the familiar. When she'd been weak.

And this is strength? she thought as she picked herself up off the ground, listening to the thunder.

The new storm was approaching. It would save them, exterminating the humans and elevating the listeners who survived. She simply had to make certain she was one of them. She scurried away to search out a stronger group of listeners to protect her. She entered an open section of plateau, slick with water, near one of the chasms.

Bands of humans and listeners roamed along the edge of the chasm here, trying to get an upper hand against one another. If anything, the fighting in this area was more horrifying. She forcibly attuned Conceit and moved along the perimeter. Conceit. A good rhythm, a counterpart to Determination or Confidence—only grander. Conceit was a proud, strong rhythm with a surging fanfare of quick, complex, and bold beats.

That was how she needed to feel. This was her battlefield. She'd crafted this, she'd brought it all together. There was nothing to fear here. This was her victory celebration.

She passed one of the humans' dead horses, a Ryshadium by the size. It had been killed by lightning, so at least some of her people were capable of controlling their new abilities. Ahead—illuminated by scattered light through a patch of clouds—she saw two brilliant figures fighting along the edge of the chasm. Shardbearers.

Venli didn't know the human, but the listener was Eshonai. She was the last of their Shardbearers. The Plate was distinctive, even if the new form had . . . changed her. It was hard to associate the terrible warlord Eshonai had become with the thoughtful femalen who had tried so hard to find a way out of the war.

Venli stopped beside a broken spire of rock and hunkered down, watching through the rain as the two clashed. Eshonai—particularly the enhanced Eshonai—could handle a duel on her own. Venli would just be in the way.

She was able to tell herself this, and believe it, right up until Eshonai was shoved off the rim of the chasm. One moment she was holding her own against the human. The next she was gone. Plunged into the abyss.

Venli watched her go with a feeling of disconnect. In Shardplate, Eshonai could survive that fall. Probably. Venli was the one in danger, with the human Shardbearer nearby. The new rhythms thrummed through her, whispering of power. Heightening her emotions. She was herself, not overly influenced by the form. In control. Not a slave.

Yet she felt . . . nothing. For a form that seemed so vibrant with emotions, that was wrong. Could the old Venli have watched her sister take a potentially deadly fall without so much as a sorrowful rhythm? Strange. Why no concern? What was happening to her?

Venli withdrew. She . . . she'd go find Eshonai later. Help get her out of the chasm. They could attune Amusement together as they thought of Venli—a simple scholar—doing *anything* to help in a fight between two Shardbearers.

The battlefield decayed further as Venli sought refuge. Screams. Lightning blasts. She saw in it something more terrible than just a clash over the future of their peoples. She saw something that *enjoyed* the killing. A force that seemed to be growing with the new storm, a force that loved passion, anger—any emotion, but especially those that came when people struggled.

Emotion was never stronger than when someone died. This force sought it, *craved* it. Venli felt its presence like a building miasma, more oppressive than the rainclouds or the storm. She crept among some large rock formations. Lumps that had been buildings, now blanketed by thick crem. She wasn't certain where she was in relation to the center of Narak.

Fortunately, she found a narrow fissure between the ancient buildings. She squeezed in, wet and overwhelmed by the building sensation. Something was coming, something incredible. Something terrible.

The new storm was here.

Venli allowed herself to attune the rhythm of her true emotions—the wild, frenetic beat of the Rhythm of Panic. A more virulent version of the Rhythm of the Terrors. Everything went black, the last few hints of sunlight consumed by the *weight* of this new storm. Then, red lightning. It electrified the sky, and Venli crouched. No. She was still too exposed.

She knew with a sudden, inexplicable confidence that if the storm saw her, it *would* destroy her.

Between bolts of lightning, she pushed out of the cavity of rock and felt her way along the side of the stone building. The winds began to howl. Something else . . . something else was coming. A highstorm too?

Panic almost overwhelmed her. Then—to her incredible relief—her fingers felt something. A hole cut into one of the crem-covered buildings. This was fresh, the cuts unnaturally smooth; a Shardbearer had been here.

She eagerly sought refuge inside, trying to banish the Rhythm of Panic, replace it with something else. Outside, the winds began to clash. She pressed against the rear wall of the small empty chamber, lit by the increasingly violent flashes of light outside. First red. Then white. Then the two tangled like fighting greatshells, crushing the land around them as they grappled.

Debris began to whip past the opening, lit by the rapid flashes, and the rhythms in her head went crazy. Breaking apart, movements of one melding with another. The ground trembled and groaned, and Venli sought to hide deeper in the building, away from the violence. As she passed a doorway, however, the floor undulated and she was cast to the ground.

With a sound so loud her whole body vibrated, an entire section of the stone building was ripped free—including the room she'd just left.

She was pelted by rain, exposed to the howling winds through the broken wall. This was the end. The end of the world. Tiny, terrified, she pressed herself between two solid-seeming chunks of rock and closed her eyes, unable to hear the rhythms over the sound of the tempest.

She knew what rhythm she'd hear if she could, though. For there, pressed between stones, Venli was forced to admit what she really was. The truth that had always been there, covered over, encrusted with crem. Exposed only when the winds cut her to her soul.

She was no genius forging a new path for her people. Everything she'd "discovered" had been given or hinted at by Ulim.

She was no queen deserving of rule. She cared nothing for her people. Just for her own self.

She wasn't powerful. The winds and the storms reminded her that no matter what she did—no matter how hard she tried, no matter how much she pretended—she would always be small.

She had pretended she was those things, and would likely pretend them again as soon as she could lie to herself. As soon as she was safe. But here—with everything else flayed away and her soul stripped bare—Venli was forced to admit what she truly was. What she'd always been.

A coward.

I tell you; I write it. You must release the captive Unmade. She will not fade as I will. If you leave her as she is, she will remain imprisoned for eternity.

Rlain found her crying.

Venli could count on her fingers the number of times she could remember crying. Not merely attuning Mourning, but actually *crying*. Today she couldn't help herself. She knelt in the sectioned-off part of the infirmary room, overlooking the large map of the Shattered Plains that Rlain had stolen. She was alone. Lirin and Hesina were in the main room, seeing to the patients.

A note on the map hinted at what Raboniel had said: a group of nomads in the hills. Her people. They had *survived*.

She turned to Rlain, who—shocked—was humming to Awe at finding her like this.

"We're not the last," Venli whispered. "They are alive, Rlain. Thousands of them."

"Who?" He knelt. "What are you talking about?"

Venli wiped her eyes—she wouldn't have her tears destroying this glorious map. Venli handed him the note Raboniel had given her, but of course he couldn't read. So she read it out loud for him.

"You mean . . ." he said, attuning Awe. "Thousands of them?"

"It was Thude," Venli said. "He refused stormform. So did most of Eshonai's closest friends. I . . . I wasn't thinking back then. . . . I would have had them killed, but Eshonai separated them off and *let* them escape. Part of her fought, so she gave them a chance, and . . . And then . . ."

Storms, she was a mess. She wiped her eyes again.

"You would have had them *killed*?" Rlain asked. "Venli, I don't understand. What is it you're not telling me?"

"Everything," she whispered to Pleading. "A thousand lies, Rlain."

"Venli," he said, taking her hand. "Kaladin is awake. Teft is too. We have a plan. The start of one, at least. I came to explain it to Lirin and Hesina. We're going to try to wake the Radiants, but we need to get those stormforms out of the room. If you know something that might help, now would be a good time to talk."

"Help?" Venli whispered. "Nothing I do helps. It only hurts."

Rlain hummed to Confusion. At a gentle prompting from Timbre, Venli started talking. She began with the strange human woman who had given her the sphere, and went all the way up to when Thude and the others left.

She didn't hide her part in it. She didn't coat it with the Rhythm of Consolation. She gave it to him raw. The whole terrible story.

As she spoke, he pulled farther and farther away from her. His expression changed, his eyes widening, his rhythms moving from shocked to angry. As she might have expected. As she wanted.

When she finished, they sat in silence.

"You are a monster," he finally said. "*You* did this. You are responsible."

She hummed to Consolation.

"I suppose the enemy would have found another way," he said, "without your help. Regardless, Venli. You . . . I mean . . ."

"I need to find them," she said, rolling up the map. "There are daily transfers to Kholinar. Raboniel has released me from my duties here, and given me a writ allowing me to requisition whatever I need. I should be able to procure a spot in the next transfer, and from there go with some Heavenly Ones on a scouting mission out to the Shattered Plains."

"And in so doing, you'd lead the enemy directly to our people," Rlain said. "Venli, Raboniel obviously *wants* you to do this. She knows you're going to run to them. You're playing into whatever plot she has."

She'd considered that. She wasn't exactly in the most rational state of mind, however. "I have to do something, Rlain," she whispered. "I need to see them with my own eyes, even if I have to *walk* there."

"I agree, we should do that as soon as it's reasonable," Rlain said. He glanced toward the curtains, then spoke more quietly. "But now isn't the time. We have to save the Radiants."

"Do you *really* want me there when you do, Rlain? Do you want me around?"

He fell silent, then hummed to Betrayal.

"Smart," she said.

"I don't want you around right now, Venli," he said. "But storm me, we *need* you. And I think you're trustworthy. You told me this, after all. And who knows how much of what you did was influenced by your forms or those Voidspren?

"For now, let's work on saving the Radiants. If you're truly sorry for what you did, then this is the best way to prove it. After that, we can seek out our people *without* leading the Fused to them."

She looked away, then hummed to Betrayal herself. "No. This isn't my fight, Rlain. It never was. I have to go see if this map is true. I have to."

"Fine," he snapped. He stood to leave, then paused. "You know, all those months running bridges—then training with Kal and the others—I wondered. I wondered deep down if I was a traitor. I now realize I didn't have the first *notes* of understanding what it meant to be a traitor."

He ducked out between the curtains. Venli quietly tucked the map of the Shattered Plains into its case, then put it under her arm. It was time for her to go.

She found both Dul and Mazish caring for the fallen Radiants. Venli pulled them aside, and whispered, "The time has come. Are we ready to leave?"

"Finally," Dul said to Excitement. "We've siphoned away rations, canteens of water, blankets, and some extra clothing from what we were given to care for the Radiants. Harel has it all ready in packs, hidden among the other supplies in the storage room we were given."

"The people are ready," Mazish said. "Eager. We think we can survive in the cold up here for months."

"We'll need those supplies," Venli said, "but we might not have to survive in the mountains. Look." She showed them the writ of authority Raboniel had given her. "With this, we can get through the Oathgates, no questions asked."

"Maybe," Dul said to Appreciation. "So we go to Kholinar, but then what? We're back where we began."

"We take the supplies, and we use this writ to leave the city," Venli explained. "We hike out to the east and disappear into the wilderness to the east of Alethkar, like my ancestors did so many generations ago."

Then we make our way to the Shattered Plains, she thought. But . . . that would take too long. Could Venli find a way to scout ahead, using the aid of the Heavenly Ones? Perhaps get dropped off nearer the Unclaimed Hills, without revealing what she was truly seeking?

It seemed a lot to demand of this one writ. Plus, Raboniel knew about the listeners who had survived. Surely she'd eventually tell the other Fused.

For the moment, Venli didn't care. "Gather the others," she whispered. "The humans are going to attempt to rescue the Radiants here soon. The chaos should cover our escape. I want us to leave in the next day or two."

The other two attuned Resolve; they trusted her. More than she trusted herself. Venli doubted she would find redemption among the listeners who had escaped the Fused. In fact, she expected accusation, condemnation.

But . . . Venli *had* to try to reach them. For when they'd escaped, they'd taken her mother with them. Jaxlim might be dead—and if not, her mind would still be lost to age.

But she was also the last person—the *only* person—who might still love Venli, despite it all.

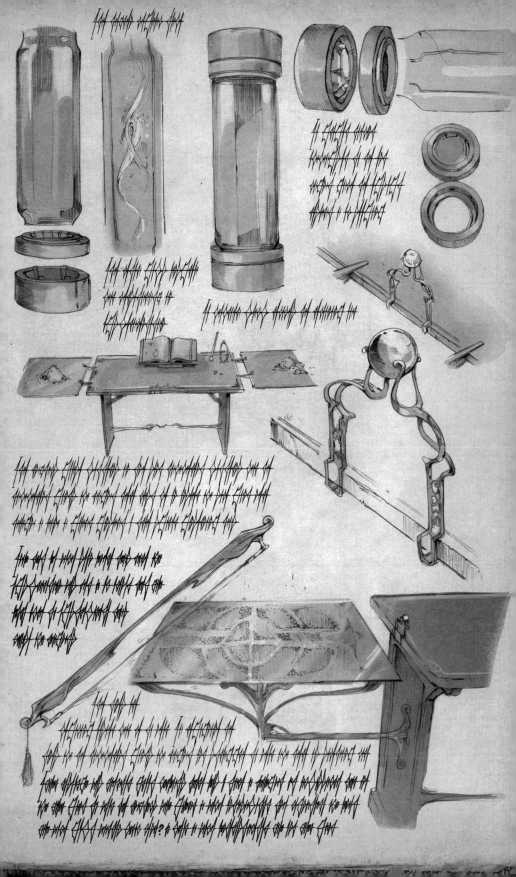

As one who has suffered for so many centuries . . . as one whom it broke . . . please find Mishram and release her. Not just for her own good. For the good of all spren.

For I believe that in confining her, we have caused a greater wound to Roshar than any ever realized.

Navani entered a feverish kind of study—a frantic near madness—as the work consumed her. Before, she had organized. Now she merely fed the beast. She barely slept.

The answer was here. The answer *meant* something. She couldn't explain why, but she *needed* this secret.

Food became a distraction. Time stopped mattering. She put her clocks away so they wouldn't remind her of human constructs like minutes and hours. She was searching for something deeper. More important.

These actions horrified a part of her. She *was* still herself, the type of woman who put her socks in the drawer so they all faced the same direction. She loved patterns, she loved order. But in this quest for meaning, she found she could appreciate something else entirely. The raw, *dis*organized chaos of a brain making connections paired with the single-minded order of a quest for one all-consuming answer.

Could she find the opposite to Voidlight?

Stormlight and Voidlight had their own kind of polarity. They were attracted to tones like iron shavings to a magnet. Therefore, she needed a tone that would push light *away*. She needed an opposite sound.

She wanted fluid tones, so she had a slide whistle delivered, along with a brass horn with a movable tube. However, she liked the sound of the plates best. They were difficult to increment, but she could order new ones cut and crafted quickly.

Her study morphed from music theory—where some philosophers said that the true opposite of sound was silence—to mathematics. Mathematics taught that there were numbers associated with tones—frequencies, wavelengths.

Music, at its most fundamental level, *was math*.

She played the tone that represented the sound of Voidlight again and again, embedding it into her mind. She dreamed it when she slept. She played it first thing when she arose, watching the patterns of sand it made on a metal plate. Dancing grains, bouncing up and down, settling into peaks and troughs.

The opposite of most numbers was a negative number. Could a tone be negative? Could there be a negative wavelength? Many such ideas couldn't exist in the real world, like negative numbers were an artificial construct. But those peaks and troughs . . . could she make a tone that produced the *opposite pattern*? Peaks where there were troughs, troughs where there were peaks?

During her feverish study into sound theory, she discovered the answer to this. A wave could be negated, its opposite created and presented in a way that *nullified* the original. Canceling it out. They called it destructive interference. Strangely, the theories said that a sound and its opposite *sounded exactly the same*.

This stumped her. She played the plates she'd created, indulging in their resonant tones. She put Voidlight spheres into her arm sheath and listened until she could hum that tone. She was delighted when—after hours of concerted practice—she could draw Voidlight out with a touch, like the Fused could do.

Humans *could* sing the correct tones. Humans *could* hear the music of Roshar. Her ancestors might have been aliens to this world, but she *was* its child.

That didn't solve the question though. If a tone and its destructive interference sounded the same, how could she sing one and not the other?

She played the tone on a plate, humming along. She next played a tuning fork, listened to the tones of the gemstones, then came back to the plate. It was wrong. *Barely* off. Even though the tones matched.

She asked for, and was given, a file. She tried to measure the notes the plate made, but eventually had to rely on her own ear. She worked on the plate, filing off small sections of the metal and then pulling the bow across it, getting the plate closer and closer.

She could *hear* the tone she wanted, she thought. Or was it madness? This desire to create an anti-sound?

It took hours. Maybe days. When it finally happened, she knelt bleary-eyed on the stone floor at some unholy hour. Holding a bow, testing her newest version of the plate. When she played this particular tone—bow on steel—something happened. Voidlight was shoved *out* of the sphere attached to the plate. It was pushed *away* from the source of the sound.

She tested it again, then a third time to be sure. Though she should have wanted to shout for joy, she simply sat there staring. She ran her hand through her hair, which she hadn't put up today. Then she laughed.

It worked.

.·.

The next day—washed and feeling *slightly* less insane—Navani incremented. She tested how loud the tone needed to be to produce the desired effect. She measured the tone on different sizes of gemstones and on a stream of Voidlight leaving a sphere to flow toward a tuning fork.

She did all of this in a way that—best she could—hid what she was doing from her watching guard. Hunched over her workspace, she was relatively certain the Regal there wouldn't be able to tell she'd made a breakthrough. The one last night hadn't watched keenly; he'd been dozing through much of it.

Confident that her tone worked, she began training herself to *hum* the tone the plate made. It did sound the same, but somehow it *wasn't* the same. As when measuring spren—which reacted to your thoughts about them—this tone needed *Intent* to be created. You had to know what you were trying to do.

Incredibly, it mattered that she *wanted* to hum the opposite tone to Odium's song. It sounded crazy, but it worked. It was repeatable and quantifiable. Inside the madness of these last few days, science still worked.

She had found Voidlight's opposite tone. But how could she create Light that expressed this tone? For answers, she looked to nature. A magnet could be made to change its polarity with some captive lightning, and another magnet could realign the pole. But Raboniel had mentioned they could *magnetize* an ordinary piece of metal that way too.

So were they really changing the polarity of the magnet? Or were they *blanking* the existing polarity—then rewriting it with something new? The idea intrigued her, and she made a few key requests of her jailers—some objects that would have to be fetched from one of the labs near the top of the tower.

Soon after, Raboniel came to check on her. Navani braced herself. She'd been planning for this.

"Navani?" the Fused asked. "This latest request is quite odd. I don't know what to make of it."

"It's just some esoteric lab equipment," Navani said from the desk. "Nothing of any real note, though it would be fun to use in some experiments. No bother if you can't find it."

"I authorized the request," Raboniel said. "If it is there, you shall have it."

That was a rhythm to express curiosity. She made a note in her book; she was trying to list them all.

"What are you working on?" Raboniel asked. "The guard tells me of a terrible sound you have been making, something discordant."

Damnation. The new tone *didn't* sound the same to a Regal. Could she explain it away? "I'm testing how atonal sounds influence Voidlight, if at all."

Raboniel lingered, looking over Navani's shoulder. Then she glanced at the floor, where a bucket of icy water, with snow from outside, held a submerged gemstone. It was an attempt to see if temperature could blank the tone of Voidlight.

"What are you not telling me?" Raboniel said to a musing rhythm. "I find your behavior . . . intriguing." She glanced to the side as her daughter trailed into the room.

The younger Fused was drooling today. Raboniel had a servant periodically put a cloth against the side of her daughter's mouth. It wasn't that her face was paralyzed; more that she didn't seem to notice or care that she was drooling.

"You write about something called 'axi' in our notebook," Navani said, trying to distract Raboniel. "What are these?"

"An axon is the smallest division of matter," Raboniel said. "Odium can see them. Theoretically, with a microscope powerful enough, we could see little balls of matter making up everything."

Navani had read many theories about such a smallest division of matter. It spoke to her state of mind that she barely considered it a curiosity to have such theories confirmed by a divine source.

"Do these axi have a polarity?" Navani asked, as she monitored the temperature of her experiment.

"They must," Raboniel said. "We theorize that axial interconnection is what holds things together. Certain Surges influence this. The forces between axi are fundamental to the way the cosmere works."

Navani grunted, writing another notation from the thermometer.

"What are you *doing*?" Raboniel asked.

"Seeing if a colder temperature changes the vibrations in a gemstone," Navani admitted. "Would you hold this one and tell me if the rhythm changes—or grows louder—as it warms up?"

"I can do that," Raboniel said, settling down on the floor beside the desk. Behind, her daughter mimicked her. The attendant—a singer in workform—knelt to dab at the daughter's lips.

Navani took the gemstone out with a pair of tongs and gave it to Raboniel. Though Navani could faintly hear the tones of gemstones if she pressed a lot of them to her skin, her skill wasn't fine-tuned enough to detect small changes in volume. She needed a singer to finish this experiment. But how to keep Raboniel from figuring out what she'd discovered?

Raboniel took the sphere and waited, her eyes closed. Finally she shook her head. "I can sense no change in the tone. Why does it matter?"

"I'm trying to determine if anything alters the tone," Navani said. "Creating Warlight requires a slight alteration of Odium's and Honor's tones, in order to put them into harmony. If I can find other things that alter Voidlight's tone, I might be able to create other hybrids."

It was a plausible enough explanation. It should explain her requests for plates and other devices, even the ice.

"A novel line of reasoning," Raboniel said to her curiosity rhythm.

"I had not thought you would take notice," Navani said. "I assumed you were busy with your . . . work." Unmaking the Sibling.

"I still need to bring down the final node," Raboniel said. "Last time I touched the Sibling, I thought I could sense it. Somewhere nearby . . . but it is very, very small. Smaller than the others . . ." She rose from the floor. "Let me know if you require further equipment."

"Thank you," Navani said from her desk. Raboniel lingered as Navani recorded her notes about the ice water experiment.

Navani managed to appear unconcerned right until she heard the plates being shifted. She turned to see Raboniel pulling out the new one, the one she'd hidden beneath several others. Damnation. How had she picked out that one? Perhaps it showed the most use.

Raboniel looked to Navani, who forced herself to turn away as if it were nothing. Then Raboniel played it.

Navani breathed out quietly, closing her eyes. She'd racked her mind for ways to hide what she was doing, taking every precaution she could . . . but she should have known. She was at such a severe disadvantage, watched at all times, with Raboniel always nearby. Navani opened her eyes and found Raboniel staring wide-eyed at the plate. She placed a sphere of Voidlight and played again, watching the Light eject from the sphere.

Raboniel spoke to a reverential rhythm. "A tone that *forces out* Voidlight?"

Navani kept her face impassive. Well, that answered one question. She'd wondered if the person playing the note needed the proper Intent to eject the Voidlight, but it seemed that creating the plate to align to her hummed tones was enough.

"Navani," Raboniel said, lowering the bow, "this is remarkable. And *dangerous*. I felt the Voidlight in my gemheart respond. It wasn't ejected, but my very *soul* cringed at the sound. I'm shocked. And . . . and *befuddled*. How did you create this?"

"Math," Navani admitted. "And inspiration."

"This could lead to . . ." Raboniel hummed to herself, then glanced at the bucket of ice water. "You're trying to find a way to dampen the vibrations of the Voidlight so you can rewrite it with a different tone. A different polarity. That's why you asked about axi." She hummed to an excited rhythm. And Damnation if a part of Navani wasn't caught up in that sound. In the thrill of discovery. Of being *so close*.

Careful, Navani, she reminded herself. She had to do her best to keep this knowledge from the enemy. There was a way, a plan she'd been making should Raboniel intrude as she had. A possible path to maintaining the secrets of anti-Voidlight.

For now, she needed to seem amenable. "Yes," Navani said. "I think what you wanted all along is possible, Raboniel. I have reason to believe there *is* an opposite Light to Voidlight."

"Have you written this down?"

"No, I've merely been toying with random ideas."

"A lie you must tell," Raboniel said. "I do not begrudge you it, Navani. But know that I *will* rip this room apart to find your notes, if I must."

Navani remained quiet, meeting Raboniel's gaze.

"Still you do not believe me," Raboniel said. "That we are so much stronger when working together."

"How could I trust your word, Raboniel?" Navani said. "You've already broken promises to me, and each time I've asked to negotiate for the benefit of my people or the Sibling, you've refused."

"Yes, but haven't I led you to a weapon?" she asked. "Haven't I given you the secrets you needed to make it this far? Within reach of something that could *kill a god*? All because we worked together. Let's take this last step as one."

Navani debated. She knew that Raboniel wasn't lying; the Fused *would* rip this room apart to find Navani's notes. Beyond that, she'd likely take away Navani's ability to requisition supplies—halting her progress.

And she was *so* close.

With a sigh, Navani crossed the room and took her notebook—the one they'd named *Rhythm of War*—from a hidden spot under one of the shelves. Perhaps Navani *should* have kept all of her discoveries in her head, but she'd been unable to resist writing them down. She'd needed to see her ideas on the page, to use notes, to get as far as she had.

Raboniel settled in to read, to learn what Navani had discovered about this new tone—humming a rhythm of curiosity to herself. A short time later, a servant arrived at the door carrying a large wooden box.

"At last." Navani stepped over, taking the box from the servant. Inside was a glass tube a little less than a foot in diameter, though it was several feet long, with thick metal caps on the ends.

"And that is?" Raboniel asked.

"A Thaylen vacuum tube," Navani said. "From the Royal Institute of Barometric Studies. We had this device near the top floor of the tower, where we were doing weather experiments."

She set the device down and took the notebook back from Raboniel, making a few notations to start her next experiment. The metal caps could be unscrewed to reveal chambers that, with the seals in place, wouldn't disturb the vacuum in the central glass chamber. She opened one end, then affixed an empty diamond into it. Next she used her jeweler's hammer to crack a gem full of Voidlight—which made it start to leak. She quickly affixed it into the berth on the other side of the vacuum tube. She redid the ends, then used a fabrial pump to remove the air from the side chambers.

Finally, she undid the clasps that sealed the side berths, opening them to the central vacuum. If she'd done everything correctly, little to no air would enter the central glass chamber—and she now had a gemstone on either end.

Raboniel loomed over Navani as she observed the Voidlight floating out into the vacuum. It didn't act as air would have—it wasn't pulled out, for example. Whatever Voidlight was, it didn't seem to be made up of axi. It was an energy, a power.

"What are we doing?" Raboniel asked softly.

"I believe this is the only way to completely separate Voidlight from the songs of Roshar," Navani explained. "There can be no sound in a vacuum, as there is no air to transfer the waves. So as this gemstone ejects Voidlight, I'm hoping the Light will not be able to 'hear' Odium's rhythm—for the first time in its existence."

"You think it doesn't emit the rhythm itself," Raboniel said, "but *echoes* it. Picks it up."

"Like spren pick up mannerisms from humans," Navani said. "Or how a piece of metal can be magnetized by touching a magnet over a long period of time."

"Ingenious," Raboniel whispered.

"We'll see," Navani said. She grabbed her bow, then pressed the plate against the side of the vacuum chamber and began playing her anti-Voidlight tone.

Raboniel winced at the sound. "The Light won't be able to hear," she said. "It's in a vacuum, as you said."

"Yes, but it's moving across, and will soon touch the empty diamond at the other side," Navani said. "I want this to be the first thing it hears when it touches matter."

They had to wait a good while as the Voidlight drifted in the vacuum, but Navani kept playing. In a way, this was the culmination of her days of fervor. The climax to the symphony of madness she'd been composing.

Voidlight eventually touched the empty diamond and was pulled inside. She waited until a good measure of it had been drawn in, then had Raboniel undo the clasp separating the diamond's enclosure from the vacuum. Navani opened this to a little *pop* of sound, then plucked out the diamond. It glowed faintly violet-black. She stared at it, looking closer, until . . .

Yes. A faint warping of the air around it. She felt a thrill as she handed it to Raboniel—who screamed.

Navani caught the diamond as Raboniel dropped it. The Fused pulled her hand to her breast, humming violently.

"I take it the sound wasn't pleasant," Navani said.

"It was like the tone that plate makes," Raboniel said, "but a thousand times worse. This is a *wrongness*. A vibration that *should not exist*."

"It sounds exactly the same as the tone of Odium to me," Navani said. She set the gemstone on her desk beside the dagger Raboniel had given her. The one that could channel and move Light.

Navani sat in the chair beside it. Raboniel joined her, moving a stool from beside the wall. Together, both of them stared at the little gemstone that seemed so wrong.

"Navani," Raboniel said. "This . . . This changes the world."

"I know," Navani said. She rubbed her forehead, sighing.

"You look exhausted," Raboniel noted.

"I've barely slept for days," Navani admitted. "Honestly, this is all so overwhelming. I need a break, Raboniel. To walk, to think, to gather my wits and get my blood moving again."

"Go ahead," Raboniel said. "I'll wait." She waved for the guard to go with Navani, though the Fused herself continued staring at the gemstone. In fact, Raboniel was so fixated on the diamond that she didn't notice Navani take *Rhythm of War* as she stepped out with the guard into the hallway.

She braced herself. Expecting . . .

An explosion.

It shook the corridor, striking with such physical force that Navani's guard jumped in shock. They both spun around to see smoke spewing from the room they'd left. The guard rushed back—grabbing Navani by the arm and hauling her along.

They found chaos. The desk had exploded, and Raboniel lay on the floor. The Fused's face was a mask of pain, and her front had been *shredded*—her havah ripped apart, the carapace scored and broken, the skin at her joints stuck with pieces of glass. Or diamond? She hadn't taken much shrapnel to the head, fortunately for her, though orange blood seeped from a thousand little wounds on her arms and chest.

At any rate, Raboniel was still alive, and Navani's scheme had failed. Navani had assumed that, in her absence, Raboniel would take the next step—to try mixing Voidlight with the new Light. Raboniel kept saying she expected the Lights to puff away when mixed, vanishing. She didn't expect the explosion.

Navani had hoped that if she died, it would delay Raboniel's corruption of the tower long enough for Navani to properly weaponize this new Light. That was not to be. The explosion had been smaller than the one that had destroyed the room with the scholars, and Raboniel was far tougher than a human.

A treasonous part of Navani was glad the Fused had not died. Raboniel sat up, then surveyed the room. Several of the bookshelves had collapsed, spilling their contents. Raboniel's daughter was still sitting where she'd been, as if she hadn't even noticed what had happened, despite the fact that she bore cuts on her face. Her attendant appeared to be dead, lying slumped on the ground, facedown. Navani felt a spike of legitimate sorrow for that.

"What did you do?" Navani said. "Lady of Wishes, what happened?"

Raboniel blinked as she stood. "I . . . put the diamond we created into the hilt of the dagger, then used the tip to draw Voidlight from another gemstone, to mix them. It seemed the best way to see if the two Lights would cancel one another out. I thought . . . I thought the reaction would be calm, like hot and cold water mixing. . . ."

"Hot and cold water don't immediately annihilate one another when they meet," Navani said. "Besides, heat under pressure—like Light in a gemstone—is another matter."

"Yes," Raboniel said, blinking several times, seeming dazed. "If you use the lightning of a stormform to ignite something under pressure, it always explodes. Perhaps if Voidlight and anti-Voidlight meet in open air, you'd get no more than a pop. But these were inside a gemstone. I have acted with supreme stupidity."

Other Fused—Deepest Ones—melded in through the walls to see what had happened. Raboniel waved them all off as her cuts healed under the power of her internal Voidlight. The Deepest Ones took the servant, who fortunately stirred as they carried him.

The desk was broken, the wall marked by a black scar. Navani smelled smoke—bits of desk still burned. So the explosion had involved heat, not pressure alone. Raboniel shooed away the guard and the other Fused, then picked through the rubble of the desk.

"No remnants of the dagger," Raboniel said. "Another embarrassment I must suffer, losing such a valuable weapon. I have others, but I'll need to eventually move you out of this room and have it scrubbed for every scrap of raysium. We might be able to melt it down and reforge the dagger."

Navani nodded.

"For now," Raboniel said, "I would like you to make me another gemstone filled with that anti-Voidlight."

"Now?" Navani asked.

"If you please."

"Don't you want to change?" Navani asked. "Have someone pick the shards of glass out of your skin . . ."

"No," Raboniel said. "I wish to see this process again. If you please, Navani."

It was said to a rhythm that indicated it would happen, regardless of what Navani "pleased." So she prepared the vacuum chamber—it had been behind Raboniel, sheltered from the brunt of the blast, fortunately. As Navani worked, Raboniel sent someone for another Herald-killing dagger. Why did she need that? Surely they weren't going to mix the Lights after what had happened.

Feeling an ominous cloud hanging over her, Navani repeated her experiment, this time filling the gemstone a little less—just in case—before removing it and holding it up.

Raboniel took it, and though she didn't drop it this time, she did flinch. "So strange," she said. She fitted it into her second dagger. Then she undid a screw and slipped out the piece of metal running through the center. She flipped it around—it had points on both ends, and a hole for the screw—before replacing it.

"To make the anti-Voidlight flow out of the gemstone along the blade?" Navani asked. "Instead of drawing in what it touches?"

"Indeed," Raboniel said. "You may wish to take cover." Then she turned, walked across the room, and stabbed her daughter in the chest.

Navani was too stunned to move. She stood there amid the rubble, gaping as Raboniel loomed over the other Fused, pushing the weapon in deeper. The younger Fused began to spasm, and Raboniel held her, ruthless as she pressed the weapon into her daughter's flesh.

There was no explosion. The Voidlight inside the Fused wasn't under pressure as it was in a gemstone, perhaps. There was a stench of burning flesh, and the skin blistered around the wound. The younger Fused trembled and screamed, clutching at her mother's arm with a clawed hand.

Then her eyes turned milky, like white marble. She went limp, and Navani thought she saw something escape her lips. Smoke? As if her entire insides had been burned away.

Raboniel pulled the dagger out, then tossed it away like a piece of rubbish. She cradled her daughter's body, pressing her forehead against that of the corpse, holding it close and rocking back and forth.

Navani walked over, listening to Raboniel's sorrowful rhythm. Though Raboniel's topknot of hair spilled around her face, Navani saw tears slipping down her red-and-black cheeks.

Navani wasn't certain she'd ever seen a singer cry before. This was not ruthlessness at all. This was something else.

"You killed her," Navani whispered.

Raboniel continued to rock the corpse, holding it tighter, shaking as she hummed.

"Elithanathile," Navani said, whispering the tenth name of the Almighty. "You killed her forever, didn't you?"

"No more rebirth," Raboniel whispered. "No more Returns. Free at last, my baby. *Free.*"

Navani pulled her hand up to her chest. That pain . . . she knew that pain. It was how she'd felt hearing of Elhokar's death at the hands of the bridgeman traitor.

Raboniel had done *this* killing though. Performed it herself! But . . . had the actual death happened long ago? Centuries ago? What had it been like, living with a child whose body constantly returned to life long after her mind had left her?

"This is why," Navani said, kneeling beside the two. "Your god hinted that anti-Voidlight was possible, and you suspected what it would do. You captured the tower, you imprisoned and pushed me, and possibly delayed the corruption of the Sibling. Because you hoped to find this anti-Voidlight. Not because you wanted a weapon against Odium. Because you wanted to show a mercy to your daughter."

"We could never create enough of this anti-Light to threaten Odium," Raboniel whispered. "That was another lie, Navani. I'm sorry. But you took my dream and you fulfilled it. After I had given up on it, you persisted.

One might think the immortal being would be the one to continue pursuing an idea to its end, but it was you."

Navani knelt with her hands in her lap, feeling like she'd witnessed something too intimate. So she gave Raboniel time to grieve.

Fused grieved. The immortal destroyers, the mythical enemies of all life, grieved. Raboniel's grief looked identical to that of a human mother who had lost her child.

Eventually, Raboniel rested the body on the ground, then covered up the wound with a cloth from her pocket. She wiped her eyes and stood, calling for the guard to bring her some servants.

"What now?" Navani asked her.

"Now I make sure this death was truly permanent," Raboniel said, "by communicating with the souls on Braize. If Essu has indeed died a final death, then we'll know you and I have achieved our goal. And . . ." She trailed off, then hummed a rhythm.

"What?" Navani asked.

"Our notebook." Raboniel looked toward where it sat on the floor. Navani had placed it there while creating the second anti-Voidlight gemstone.

Raboniel hummed a different rhythm as servants entered, and she gave terse orders. She sent some to burn her daughter's corpse and send honors and the ashes to the family that had donated the body to her daughter. She had others gather the vacuum tube and metal plates from Navani's experiments.

Navani stepped forward to stop them, but Raboniel prevented her with a calm—but firm—hand. The Fused took the notebook from Navani's fingers.

"I will have a copy made for you," she promised Navani. "For now, I need this one to reconstruct your work."

"You saw how I did this, Raboniel."

"Yes, but I need to create a new plate, a new tone. For Stormlight."

Navani tried to pull free, but Raboniel's hold was firm. She hummed a dangerous rhythm, making Navani meet her eyes. Eyes that had been weeping were now firm and unyielding.

"So much for your words about working together," Navani said. "And you *dared* imply I was wrong to keep trying to hide things from you."

"I *will* end the war," Raboniel said. "That is the promise I will keep, for today we have discovered the means. Finally. A way to make certain that the Radiants can no longer fight. They function as Fused do, you see. If we kill the human, another Radiant will be born. The fight becomes eternal, both sides immortal. Today we end that. I have preserved the

Radiants in the tower for a reason. Anti-Stormlight will need subjects for testing."

"You can't be implying . . ." Navani said. "You don't mean . . ."

"Today is a momentous day," Raboniel said, letting go and walking after the servants carrying Navani's equipment. "Today is the day we discovered a way to destroy Radiant spren. I will let you know the results of the test."

THE END OF

Part Four

İNTERLUDES

◆

HESINA • ADIN • TARAVANGIAN

HESINA

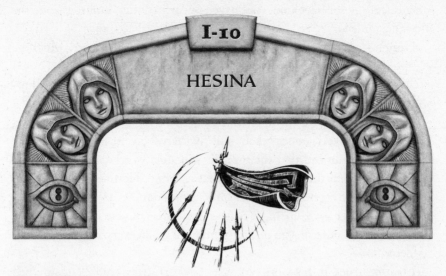

Hesina made a small notation in her notebook, kneeling above a map she'd rolled out on the floor. The cache Rlain had brought included five maps of Alethkar focused on different princedoms. Sadeas's was included, with notes about singer troop placements in certain cities and whatever else the scouts had seen while doing reconnaissance of the area.

It had taken her until now to realize she could check on Tomat. The city had several long paragraphs of attached observations, written by Kara the Windrunner. The singers had the city wall under repair, which was incredible on its own. That had been broken since . . . what, her *grandfather's* days? The infamous Gap would be gone if she ever visited again.

She couldn't find specifics about the people who had lived in the city, but that wasn't surprising. The Windrunners hadn't been able to get too close, after all. At least there were no reports of burnt-out houses, as in some other cities. It seemed the city had given in without too much of a fight, which boded well for local survival rates.

She wrote each detail in her notebook, then glanced up as Lirin slipped into their sectioned-off surgery chamber. He let the draped sheets fall closed, fabric rustling. He'd been studying the large model of Urithiru that was at the back of the infirmary room.

"You found Tomat?" he asked, adjusting his spectacles and leaning down beside her. "Huh. Anything useful?"

"Not much," she said. "Similar notes to other cities."

"Well, we'd probably know if your father died," Lirin said, straightening to gather some bandages from the counter.

"And how is that?"

"He'd be haunting me, obviously," Lirin said. "Living as a shade in the storms, calling for my blood. As I haven't heard a thing, I must assume the old monster is alive."

Hesina rolled up the map and gave her husband a flat glare, which he accepted with a smile and a twinkle to his eye.

"It's been twenty-five years," Hesina said. "He might have softened toward you by now."

"Stone doesn't soften with time, dear," Lirin replied. "It merely grows brittle. I think we'd sooner see a chull fly than see your father grow *soft*." He must have noticed that the topic legitimately worried her, because he turned away from the gibes. "I'd bet that he's fine, Hesina. Some men are too ornery to be bothered by something as mundane as an invasion."

"He wouldn't give up his business easily, Lirin. He's stubborn as a lighteyes—he'd order his guards to fight, even when everyone else had surrendered."

Lirin returned to his work, and after a short delay, said, "I'm sure he's fine."

"You are thinking that if he lifted a sword," Hesina said, "he deserved whatever he got."

And her father *would* use a sword. Under a special writ of forbearance from the citylord, who—even three decades ago—had been accustomed to doing whatever her father bullied him into doing. She'd met only one man who dared defy him.

"I'm thinking," Lirin said, "that my wife needs a supportive husband, not a self-righteous one."

"And our son?" she asked. "Which version of you does he deserve?"

Lirin stiffened, bandages held in front of him. She turned away, trying to contain her emotions. She hadn't planned to snap at him, but . . . well, she supposed she hadn't forgiven him for driving Kaladin away.

Lirin quietly stepped over, then settled down on the floor beside her, putting aside the bandages. Then he held up his hands. "What do you want of me, Hesina? Do you want me to abandon my convictions?"

"I want you," she said, "to appreciate your incredible son."

"He was supposed to be better than this. He was supposed to be better than . . . than I am."

"Lirin," she said softly. "You can't keep blaming yourself for Tien's death."

"Would he be dead if I hadn't spent all those years defying Roshone? If I hadn't picked a fight?"

"We can't change the past. But if you continue like this, you'll lose another son."

He looked up, then shifted his eyes away immediately at Hesina's cold glare. "I wouldn't have let him die," Lirin said. "If they hadn't decided to go get that Edgedancer, I'd have gone to Kaladin like they asked."

"I know that. But would you have insisted on bringing him here?"

"Maybe. He could have needed extended care, Hesina. Isn't it better to bring him here, where I can watch him? Better than letting him go on fighting an impossible battle, getting himself and others killed in this foolish war."

"And would you have done that to another soldier?" she pressed. "Say it wasn't your son who was wounded. Would you have brought *that* boy here and risked him being imprisoned, maybe executed? You've healed soldiers before, sending them back out to fight. That's always been your conviction. Treat anyone, no strings attached, no matter the circumstances."

"Maybe I need to rethink that policy," he said. "Besides, Kaladin has told me many times that he's not my son any longer."

"Great. I'm glad we could chat so I could persuade you to be *more* stubborn. I see that your thoughts and feelings are evolving on this topic—and because you're you, they're going the absolute *wrong* direction."

Lirin sighed. He stood and grabbed the stack of bandages, then turned to leave their little draped-off chamber.

Storm it, she wasn't done with him yet. Hesina rose, surprised at the depth of her frustration. "Don't you leave," she snapped, causing him to stop by the drapes.

"Hesina," he said, sounding tired. "What do you *want* from me?"

She stalked over to him, pointing. "I left everything for you, Lirin. Do you know why?"

"Because you believed in me?"

"Because I *loved* you. And I *still* love you."

"Love can't change the realities of our situation."

"No, but it *can* change people." She seized his hand, less a comforting gesture and more a demand that he remain there with her, so they could face this together. "I know how stressed you feel. I feel it too—feel like I'm going to get *crushed* by it. But I'm not going to let you continue to pretend Kaladin isn't your son."

"The son I raised would *never* have committed murder in my surgery room."

"Your *son* is a *soldier*, Lirin. A soldier who inherited his father's determination, skill, and compassion. You tell me honestly. Who would you rather have out there fighting? Some crazed killer who enjoys it, or the boy you trained to *care*?"

He hesitated, then opened his mouth.

"Before you say you don't want *anyone* fighting," Hesina interrupted, "know that I'll recognize that as a lie. We both know you've admitted that people need to fight sometimes. You simply don't want it to be your son, despite the fact that he's probably the *best* person we could have chosen."

"You obviously know the responses you want from me," Lirin said. "So why should I bother speaking?"

Hesina groaned, tipping her head back. "You can be so *storming frustrating.*"

In return, he squeezed her hand gently. "I'm sorry," he said, his voice softer. "I'll try to listen better, Hesina. I promise."

"Don't just listen better," she said, pulling him out of the draped-off section and waving toward the larger room. "See better. Look. What do you see?"

The place was busy with humans who wanted to care for the Radiants. Hesina had instituted a rotation so that everyone got a chance. Beneath the gaze of two watching stormform Regals, people of all ethnicities— and wearing all kinds of clothing—moved among the comatose Radiants. Administering water, changing sheets, brushing hair.

Hesina and Lirin used a more carefully cultivated group—mostly ardents—to handle delicate matters like bathing the patients, but today's caregivers were common inhabitants of the tower. Darkeyes made up the majority of these, but each and every one wore a *shash* glyph like Kaladin's painted on their forehead.

"What do you see?" Hesina whispered again to Lirin.

"Honestly?" he asked.

"Yes."

"I see fools," he said, "refusing to accept the truth. Resisting, when they'll just get crushed."

She heard the words he left off: *Like I was.*

She towed him by his arm to one side of the room, where a man with only one arm sat on a stool, painting the glyph on a young girl's head. She ran off to her duty as Lirin and Hesina arrived. The man stood respectfully. Bearded, wearing a buttoned shirt and trousers, he had three moles on his cheek. He nodded to Hesina and Lirin. Almost a bow. As far as he could go without provoking a reaction from the watching Fused, who didn't like such signs of respect shown to other humans.

"I know you," Lirin said, narrowing his eyes at the man. "You're one of the refugees who came to Hearthstone."

"I'm Noril, sir," the man said. "You sent me to the ardents, on suicide watch. Thank you for trying to help."

"Well," Lirin said, "you seem to be doing better."

"Depends on the day, sir," Noril said. "But I'd say I'm better than I was

when you met me."

Lirin glanced at Hesina, who squeezed his hand and gestured her chin toward Noril's forehead and the glyph.

"Why do you wear that glyph?" Lirin asked.

"To honor Stormblessed, who still fights." Noril nodded, as if to himself. "I'll be ready when he calls for me, sir."

"Don't you see the irony in that?" Lirin asked. "It was fighting in your homeland that made you flee, and therefore get into all the trouble you've faced. Fighting lost you everything. If people would stop with this nonsense, *I* would have to see far fewer men with battle shock like yours."

Noril settled down on his stool and used his hand to stir his cup of black paint, which he placed between his knees. "Suppose you're right, sir. Can't argue with a surgeon about the nonsense we do. But sir, do you know why I get up each day?"

Lirin shook his head.

"It's hard sometimes," Noril said, stirring. "Coming awake means leaving the nothingness, you know? Remembering the pain. But then I think, 'Well, *he* gets up.'"

"You mean Kaladin?" Lirin asked.

"Yes, sir," Noril said. "He's got the emptiness, bad as I do. I can see it in him. We all can. But he gets up anyway. We're trapped in here, and we all want to do something to help. We can't, but somehow he can.

"And you know, I've listened to ardents talk. I've been poked and prodded. I've been stuck in the dark. None of that worked as well as knowing this one thing, sir. He still gets up. He still fights. So I figure . . . I figure I can too."

Hesina squeezed Lirin's hand again, pulling him away as she thanked Noril with a smile.

"You want me to acknowledge," Lirin whispered, "that what Kaladin's doing is helping that man, while my surgeon's treatments could have done nothing."

"You said you'd listen," she said. "You asked what I *want* of you? I want you to talk to them, Lirin. The people in this room. Don't challenge them. Don't argue with them. Simply ask them why they wear that glyph. And *see* them, Lirin. Please."

She left him standing there and returned to her maps. Trusting in him, and the man she knew he was.

ADIN

Adin was going to be a Windrunner someday.

He had it all figured out. Yes, he was just a potter's son, and spent his days learning how to turn crem into plates. But the highmarshal himself had once been a darkeyed boy from an unknown village. The spren didn't *just* pick kings and queens. They watched everyone, looking for warriors.

So, as he followed his father through the halls of Urithiru, Adin found opportunities to glare at the invaders. Many might have said that at thirteen, he was too young to become a Radiant. But he knew for a fact there was a girl who had been chosen when she was younger than him. He had seen her leaving food out for old Gavam, the widow who sometimes forgot to collect her rations.

You had to be brave, even when you thought nobody was watching. That was what the spren wanted. They didn't care how old you were, if your eyes were dark, or if the bowls you made were lopsided. They wanted you to be *brave*.

Glaring at singers wasn't much. He knew he could—and would have to—do more. When the time was right. And he couldn't let the enemy catch him being unruly. So for now, he stepped to the side of the corridor with his father and let the large group of warforms pass. He dutifully stood there, his father's hand on his shoulder, their heads bowed.

But as soon as the warforms had passed, Adin looked up. And he glared after them, angry as he could be.

He wasn't the only one. He caught Shar, the seamstress's daughter, glaring too. Well, her uncle was a Windrunner, so maybe she figured she had a better chance than most—but surely the spren were more discerning than that. Shar was so bossy, you'd think she was lighteyed.

Doesn't matter, Adin reminded himself. *The spren don't care if you're bossy. They just want you to be brave.* Well, he could handle a little competition from Shar. And when he got his spren first, maybe he could give her a few tips.

Adin's father caught him glaring, unfortunately, and squeezed his shoulder. "Eyes down," he hissed.

Adin obeyed reluctantly, as another group of soldiers marched past—all heading for the atrium. Had there been some kind of disturbance? Adin had better not have missed another appearance by Stormblessed. He couldn't *believe* he'd spent the last fight napping.

He hoped the spren would look at people's parents when choosing their Radiants. Because Adin's father was extremely brave. Oh, he didn't glare at passing soldiers, but he didn't need to. Adin's father spent many afternoons tending the fallen Radiants. Directly beneath the gaze of the *Fused*. And every night he went out in secret, doing *something*.

Once the soldiers passed, everyone else continued on their way. Adin's ankle hurt a little, but it mostly felt better from when he'd hurt it. So he didn't even limp anymore. He didn't want a spren to see him acting weak.

What *was* going on? He went up on his toes, trying to look over the crowd, but his father didn't let him linger. Together they entered the market, then turned toward Master Liganor's shop. It felt strange to keep following their normal routine. How could they continue making pottery at a time like this? How could Master Liganor open the shop for business like nothing was happening? Well, that was part of their bravery. Adin had figured it out.

They entered the back of the shop and set up in the workroom. Adin got busy, knowing that they had to act normal—so the enemy wouldn't figure out something was up. You had to get them to feel secure, comfortable. Today, Adin did that by heaving out his bucket of crem, pouring off the water on top, and mixing it until it was a paste. Then he mashed it for his father until it was just the right consistency—a little more squishy than dough.

He worked the lump aggressively, showing those spren—who were undoubtedly watching him by now—that he had good strong arms. Windrunners needed strong arms, because they didn't use their legs much, on account of them flying around everywhere.

As he worked the crem—his arms starting to burn, the earthy scent of wet rock filling the air—he heard the front door shut. Master Liganor had arrived. The old man was nice, for a lighteyes. Once upon a time, he'd done all the glaze work on the pottery himself, but now it was all completed by Gub, the other journeyman besides Adin's father.

Adin mashed the crem to the proper consistency, then handed a chunk to his father, who had been cleaning and setting the wheel. Adin's father hefted it, pushed one finger in, then nodded approvingly. "Make another batch," he said, putting the chunk onto his wheel. "We'll practice your plates."

"I won't need to be able to make plates once I can fly," Adin said.

"And what if it takes you until your twenties to become a Windrunner?" his father asked. "You'll need to do something with your time until then. Might as well make plates."

"Spren don't care about plates."

"They must," his father said, spinning up the wheel by pumping his foot on the pedal. "Their Radiants have to eat, after all." He started shaping the crem. "Never underestimate the value of a job well done, Adin. You want a spren to notice you? Take pride in every job you do. Men who make sloppy plates will be sloppy fighting Fused."

Adin narrowed his eyes. How did his father know that? Was it merely another piece of wisdom drawn from his never-ending well of fatherly quips, or . . . was it from personal experience? Regardless, Adin dragged out another bucket of crem. They were running low. Where would they get more, now that traders weren't coming in from the Plains?

He was halfway through mixing the new batch when Master Liganor entered, wringing his hands. Short, bald, and tubby, he looked like a vase—the kind that had been made with too short a neck to really be useful. But he was nice.

"Something's happening, Alalan," the master said. "Something in the atrium. I don't like it. I think I'll close the shop today. Just in case."

Adin's father nodded calmly, still shaping his current pot. When he was on a pot, nothing could shake him. He kept sculpting, wetting his fingers absently.

"What do you think?" Master Liganor asked.

"A good idea," Adin's father replied. "Put out the glyph for lunch, and maybe we can reopen later."

"Good, good," the master said, bustling out of the workshop into the attached showroom. "I think . . . I think I'll head to my room for a while. You'll keep working? We're low on water pots. As always."

Master Liganor closed and latched the wooden windows at the front of the small shop, then locked the door. Then he went upstairs to his rooms.

As soon as he was gone, Adin's father stood up, leaving a pot *half-finished* on the wheel. "Watch the shop, son," he said, washing his hands, then walked toward the back door.

Short, with curly hair and a quiet way about him, he was not the type someone would pick out of a crowd as a hero. Yet Adin knew exactly where he was going. Adin stood up, hands coated in crem. "You're going to go see what's happening, aren't you? In the atrium?"

His father hesitated, his hand on the doorknob. "Stay here and watch the shop."

"You're going to paint your head with the glyph," Adin said, "and go watch over the Radiants. Just in case. I want to go with you."

"Your ankle—"

"Is fine now," Adin said. "If something *does* go wrong, you'll need me to run home and tell Mother. Plus, if there's trouble, there could be looting here in the market. I'll be safer with you."

Adin's father debated, then sighed and waved him forward. Adin felt his heart thundering in his chest as he hurried to obey. He could feel it, an energy in the air. It would happen *today*.

Today, he'd pick up a spear and earn his spren.

VULNERABLE

Taravangian had given up on being smart.

It seemed that the longer he lived, the less his intelligence varied each day. And when it did vary, it seemed to move steadily downward. Toward stupidity. Toward sentimentality. His "smart" days lately would have been average just months ago.

He needed to act anyway.

He could not afford to wait upon intelligence. The *world* could not afford to wait upon the whims of his situation. Unfortunately, Taravangian had no idea how to proceed. He'd failed to recruit Szeth; Taravangian was too stupid to manipulate that man now. He'd started a dozen letters to Dalinar, and ripped them all up.

The right words. Dalinar would only respond to the *right* words. Plus, whatever Taravangian wrote seemed too much a risk to Kharbranth. He couldn't sacrifice his home. He *couldn't*.

Worse, each day he found time slipping away faster and faster. He'd wake from a nap in his chair and the entire day had passed. Usually it was the pain that woke him.

He wasn't simply old. He wasn't simply feeble. This was worse.

Today, Taravangian forced himself to move to keep from drifting off again. He hobbled through his prison of a house. Trying so hard to *think*. There had to be a solution!

Go to Dalinar, a part of him urged. *Don't write him. Talk to him.* Was Taravangian actually waiting on the right words, or was there another reason he delayed? A willing disregard for the truth. The slightly smarter version of him didn't want to give this up to the Blackthorn.

He shuffled toward the small bathroom on the main floor, leafing through his notebook, looking over hundreds of crossed-out notes and ideas. The answer was here. He *felt* it. It was so frustrating, knowing how smart he *could* be, yet living below that capacity so much of the time. Other people didn't understand intelligence and stupidity. They assumed people who were stupid were somehow less human—less capable of making decisions or plans.

That wasn't it at all. He could plan, he merely needed time. He could remember things, given a chance to drill them into his brain. Part of being smart, in his experience, was about *speed* more than *capacity*. That and the ability to memorize. When he'd created problems to test his daily intelligence, they had taken these dynamics into account, measuring how quickly he could do problems and how well he could remember the equations and principles needed to do so.

He had none of that ability now, but he needed none of it. The answer *was* here, in the notebook. He settled down on the stool in his bathroom—too tired to move the seat elsewhere—as he flipped through the pages.

Taravangian had a huge advantage over almost everyone else. Others, stupid or smart, tended to overestimate their abilities. Not Taravangian. He knew exactly how it felt to be both smart and stupid. He could use that.

He *had* to. He needed to use every advantage he had. He had to create a plan as daring as the Diagram—and do so without the gifts Cultivation had given him.

The plan of a man, not a god.

He racked his brain for anything in the Diagram relating to Nightblood, the sword. But there was nothing. They hadn't anticipated the sword. Still, he had been given a report by agents he'd sent to research it by interviewing one of its former bearers. Taravangian pulled tidbits from that report from the recesses of his mind, then wrote them on a fresh page of his notebook.

The sword feeds on the essence that makes up all things, he wrote, scribbling by the light of a single ruby sphere. *It will draw out Stormlight eagerly, feasting. But if there is no Stormlight, it will feed on one's own soul.* The agent had noted that Nightblood worked like a larkin, the beasts that could feed on Investiture.

What else did he know? What other clues could he give himself?

Odium has greatly expanded intelligence, he wrote. *He can be in many places at once and can command the elements. But he* feels *the same way a man does. He can be tricked. And he seems to have a central . . . self, a core person.*

Szeth had refused to listen to Taravangian. However, the man *had* come when Taravangian seeded the proper incentive out into the world. So maybe he didn't need to make Szeth do anything other than arrive in the same place as Odium. The Shin assassin was reckless and unstable. Surely Szeth would strike out against Odium if he saw the god manifesting.

But how? How can I possibly make the timing work?

Taravangian sighed, his head thumping with pain. He looked across at the small hand mirror he'd set up on the counter. The ruby sphere he was using for light reflected in the mirror.

But his face did not reflect.

Instead he saw a shadowy figure, female, with long flowing black hair. The entire figure was a shadow, the eyes like white holes into nothingness. Taravangian blinked very slowly, then began to tremble with fear. Storms.

Storms.

He attempted to gather his wits and control his emotions. He probably would have run to hide if he had the strength. In this case, his weakening body served him, as it forced him to sit there until he could control himself.

"H . . . hello, Sja-anat," he finally managed to say. "I had not realized any of the Un . . . Unmade were here."

What is wrong with you? a voice said in his mind, warped and distorted, like a dozen voices overlapping. *What has happened to you?*

"This is how I am sometimes. It is . . . the Nightwatcher's fault."

No, the other one. The god. She touched three that I know. The child. The general. And you. The Old Magic . . . the Nightwatcher . . . I begin to wonder if it was all a cover, these many centuries. A way for her to secretly bring in people she wanted to touch. She has been playing a far more subtle game than Odium realized.

Why did you go to her? What did you ask?

"For the capacity to stop what was coming," he said. He was too frightened to lie. Even the smart him hadn't wanted to face one of these things.

She sows many seeds, Sja-anat said. *Can you do it? Can you stop what is coming?*

"I don't know," Taravangian whispered. "*Can* it be stopped? Can . . . *he* be stopped?"

I am uncertain. The power behind him is strong, but his mind is exposed. The mind and the power seek different goals. This leaves him . . . not weak, but vulnerable.

"I have wondered," Taravangian said, glancing down at his notebook, "if he is merely playing with me. I assume he looks over my shoulder at everything I write."

No. He is not everywhere. His power is, but he is not. There are limits, and his Voidspren eyes fear coming too close to a Bondsmith.

Something itched at Taravangian through the fear and confusion. Sja-anat . . . she spoke like she *wanted* Odium to fall. Wasn't there something in the Diagram about this? He tried to remember.

Storms. Was she tricking him into confessing? Should he stay quiet and not say anything?

No. He had to try.

"I need a way to lure Odium to me," Taravangian said. "At the right time."

I will arrange for you to be given gemstones with two of my children inside, she said. *Odium searches for them. He watches me, certain I will make a mistake and reveal my true intentions. We are Connected, so my children appearing will draw his attention.*

Good luck, human, when he does come. You are not protected from him as many on this world are. You have made deals that exempt you from such safety.

She faded from the mirror, and Taravangian hunched over, trembling as he continued to write.

PART
FÍVE

Knowing a Home of Songs,
Called Our Burden

THE KNIGHTS RADIANT · NAVANI ·
BRIDGE FOUR · TARAVANGIAN ·
VYRE · LEZIAN · WIT

I look forward to ruling the humans.

—Musings of El, on the first of the Final Ten Days

To Dalinar, the scent of smoke was inexorably tied to that of blood. He would have trouble counting how many times he'd performed this same long hike across a fresh battlefield. It had become a habit to perform a kind of autopsy of the fighting as he surveyed its aftermath. One could read the movements of troops by the way the dead had fallen.

Swaths of singers there indicated a line had broken and chaos had ruled. Human corpses bunched up against the wide river showed the enemy had used the waters—sluggish, since it had been a few days since the last storm—to push an entire company onto poor footing. Bodies stuck with arrows in the front indicated the first beats of the battle—and arrows in the back indicated the last ones, as soldiers broke and fled. He passed many corpses stuck with arrows bearing white "goosefeathers," a kind of fletching the Horneaters had delivered in batches to aid the war effort.

Blood flowed across the field, seeking little rifts in the stone, places where rainwater had left its mark. The blood here was more orange than red, but the two mixed to make an unwholesome shade, the off-red of a rotting methi fruit.

The smoke hung heavy in the air. On a battlefield this far afield, you burned the dead right here—sending only the officers home, already made into statues by the Soulcasters. Singer and human bodies smelled the same when they burned, a scent that would always bother him because of a specific battlefield. A specific city. A burned-out scar that was the mark of his greatest failure, and his greatest shame.

Charnel groups moved through the dead today, solemnly cutting patches from uniforms, as each was supposed to have the man's name inked on the back by the quartermaster scribe. Sometimes that didn't happen. Or sometimes the writing was ruined in the fighting. Those families would go without closure for the rest of their lives. Knowing, but wondering anyway.

Hoping.

Walking among the dead, he couldn't help but hear Taravangian's terrible—yet hauntingly logical—voice. There was a way to see the war ended. All Dalinar had to do was stop fighting. He wasn't ready yet, but the time might come. Every general knew there was a time to turn your sword point down and deliver it to your enemy with head bowed. Surrender was a valid tactic when your goal was the preservation of your people—at some point, continuing to fight worked contrary to that goal.

He could trust that the Fused were not intent on extinction. Odium, however . . . he could not trust. Something told Dalinar the ancient god of humankind, long abandoned, would not view this battlefield with the same regret Dalinar did.

He finished his grim survey, Szeth at his side as always. Several Azish generals, each newly decorated for their valor in this battle, also accompanied him. Along with two Emuli leaders, who were archers. Remarkably, the highest calling among the Emuli army was seen as *archery*. Dalinar knew his way around a bow, though he'd never considered it a particularly regal weapon, but here it was revered.

Dalinar walked a careful line for the local generals. He did not want them to see how much he reviled the deaths. A commander could not afford to revile the work in which he engaged. It did not make them bad men to be proud of their victory, or to enjoy tactics and strategy. Dalinar's forces would not get far employing pacifists as field generals.

But storms . . . ever since he'd conquered the Thrill and sent it to be sunk deep in the ocean, he'd found himself loathing these smells, these sights. That was becoming his deepest secret: the Blackthorn had finally become what men had been accusing him of for years. A soldier who had lost the will to kill.

He looped around, leaving the dead behind, instead passing victorious companies feasting in the very shadow of their butchery. He congratulated them, acted like the figurehead he'd made of himself. Of all those he saw, only the Mink seemed to notice the truth. That there was a reason Dalinar had worked so hard to find his replacement.

The short Herdazian man fell in behind Dalinar. "The war in Emul is done as of this battle," the Mink said. "The rest is cleanup. Unless the enemy infuses his troops here with serious resources—which would be incredibly wasteful at this point—we'll own Emul within the month."

"The enemy threw it away," Dalinar said.

"That's a stronger term than I'd use," the Mink said. "They fought. They wanted to hold. At the same time, they knew they couldn't move resources away from Jah Keved right now. That would risk destabilizing there, and perhaps lead us to claim it in the coming months.

"It is well the enemy wants to occupy and rule, not just destroy. They *could* have thrown enough at us here to end us on this front—but that would have left the rest of their war efforts in ruin. As it is, they knew exactly how many troops to put in Emul to lure us in with a large enough force—but they also knew to cut their losses if the battle turned against them."

"You've been extremely helpful," Dalinar said.

"Just remember your promise. Alethkar next, then Herdaz."

"Urithiru before both," Dalinar said. "But you have my word. No operations against the Iriali, no attempt to seize Jah Keved, until your people are free."

He likely didn't need the promise—the Mink was a wily man, and had easily recognized that if Dalinar were ever to recover Alethkar, it would be the best thing that could happen for an eventual recovery of the Mink's homeland. Once Jah Keved had gone to the enemy, Herdaz's tactical importance had soared.

The Mink departed to go enjoy the post-battle celebration with his personal unit of Herdazian freedom fighters. Dalinar ended up in the small battlefield command tent beside a goblet full of rubies. Couldn't they have been a different color?

Storms. It had been a long time since a battle had affected him like this.

It's like I'm drifting in the ocean, he thought. *We won today, but Navani is still trapped.* If he couldn't retake Urithiru, everything collapsed. Losing it was a huge setback in his *true* goal: pushing Odium to be frightened enough to make a deal.

So he sprang to his feet with relief when Sigzil the Windrunner entered, along with two of his team and Stargyle the Lightweaver—a handsome man with a soldier's build and a ready smile. The name was a little much; Dalinar doubted he'd had that one since birth, but he had a reputation for friendliness, and the lighteyed women of the court certainly seemed to think highly of him.

Like the other Lightweavers, the man refused to wear a uniform. Something about not feeling right wearing it again. Indeed, he bowed to Dalinar instead of saluting.

"Tell me good news, Radiant Sigzil," Dalinar said. "Please."

"Stargyle?" Sigzil asked.

"Sure thing," Stargyle said, breathing in Stormlight from a pouch at his belt. He began to paint with his fingers in the air. Each of them did it differently—Shallan had explained that they each needed some kind of focus to make their Surgebinding work. Hers was drawings. Stargyle appeared to have a different method, something more akin to painting.

The Lightweaving created a view from above, surveying a shoreline landscape. An army camped along the shore, though it didn't have much discipline. Large groups of men around campfires, no real uniforms. A variety of weapons. Ishar's troops seemed to have good numbers, however, and they were well-equipped. Their success on the battlefields in this region made Dalinar careful not to underestimate them. They might not have proper uniforms, but these were battle-hardened veterans.

"Here, Brightlord," Stargyle said—and the image began moving, as if in real life. "I can keep it all in my head, so long as I focus on the colors."

"The colors?" Dalinar said.

"I was a pigmenter's son growing up, Brightlord. I've always seen the world by its colors. Squint your eyes a little, and everything is really just color and shapes."

Dalinar inspected the moving illusion. It depicted the entire camp of people, and most interestingly a large pavilion at the center. It was colored in ringed patterns, like the bracelets he'd seen Tukari wear. He thought they had religious significance, though he didn't know much about the region. The Tukari were renowned for their mercenaries, their perfumes, and he believed their jewelry.

The illusion rippled as Dalinar walked closer. A single person stood in front of the pavilion. He wasn't wearing the same clothing as the soldiers, and wasn't holding a weapon.

"We get down closer in a second, sir," Sigzil said. "You should notice the person out front."

"I see him," Dalinar said, leaning forward.

Indeed, the image soon drew closer to the pavilion, and the figure became more distinct. An older man. Didn't seem Tukari, or Alethi. Yes . . . he was probably Shin, which was what Wit had said Ishar would appear to be. An older Shin man with a white beard and pale skin. Tukar was named after Tuk, their word for the Herald Talenelat—but it wasn't Taln who ruled them. Not now. It was a different Herald.

Ishar wore simple robes, deep blue. He spread his hands out to the sides, frost crystallizing on the stone around him, forming lines.

A glyph. The symbol for mystery, a question.

It seemed directed at Dalinar specifically. This was absolutely the right man. Dalinar didn't need to consult the drawings that Wit had provided.

He heard a hiss from beside him, and glanced with surprise to see that

Szeth had left his post by the entrance to the tent. He'd joined Dalinar, standing very close to the illusion.

"One of my . . ." Szeth stopped himself, likely remembering that he wore the image of an Alethi man. "Blood of my fathers," he said instead, "that man is Shin?"

"Rather," Dalinar said, "he is from the people who long ago settled Shinovar and became the Shin. The Heralds existed before our nationalities were formed."

Szeth seemed transfixed, as if he'd never considered that one of the Heralds might be Shin. Dalinar understood; he'd seen many depictions of all ten Heralds, and they were usually all painted as Alethi. You had to search the masterworks of earlier ages to find depictions of the Heralds representing all the peoples of Roshar.

The illusion moved on from Ishar as the Windrunners finished their sweep of the area, bringing Stargyle higher, safely out of bowshot. The Lightweaving disintegrated.

"That's all we saw, Brightlord," Stargyle said. "I could show it again, if you want."

"No need," Dalinar said. "We've found him . . . and he's waiting for me."

"Waiting for you, sir?" Sigzil asked, glancing toward Lyn and Leyten.

"Yes," Dalinar said. "Do another scouting mission, and report back on what you find. I want to consult with Jasnah first—but we're going to go meet that man, Radiant Sigzil, and find out what he knows."

I had my title and my rhythms stripped from me for daring insist they should not be killed, but should instead be reconditioned. Repurposed.

—Musings of El, on the first of the Final Ten Days

Jasnah leaned back in her chair, lit by spherelight. The spanreed report had just arrived; today's conflict with the enemy armies had ended. The coalition forces had won. Emul was, essentially, now theirs.

She still ached from her part in earlier battles, though she'd sat this one out—Dalinar had been there, and they didn't want to put both of them on the same battlefield at once. Regardless, this particular offensive being finished checked one thing off her list, but there was so much to do, still, with Urithiru in enemy hands.

Her house here in their command camp was far nicer than the one Dalinar had picked for himself. She'd chosen it not for the luxury, or for the space, but because it had a second floor. Locked away in a central room on the second level—sharing no walls with the outside, alone save for Wit's company—she could finally let herself relax. If a Shardbearer broke in, or if a Skybreaker came through one of the upper windows, her fabrial traps would go off—sounding the alarm and giving her time to fight or escape into Shadesmar before she could be killed.

She had a boat waiting on the other side, as close to analogous to this location as Shadesmar would allow. She kept stores of Stormlight in the pockets of her dressing gown, which she now wore. She would never again be caught unaware. She would never again be left struggling in Shadesmar without proper resources, forced to spend weeks hunting a perpendicularity. It was only with these preparations that Jasnah felt safe enough to let herself become frustrated.

In her lifetime studying history, Jasnah had been guided by two principles. First, that she must cut through the biases of the historians in order to understand the past. Second, that only in understanding the past could she properly prepare for the future. She'd dedicated so much to this study. But a life's work could be shaken when history got up and started talking to you.

She leafed through papers more valuable than the purest emerald, filled with her interviews with the Heralds Ash and Taln. Living history. People who had *seen* the events she'd read about. In essence, years of her life had been wasted. What good were her theories now? They were halfway-reliable re-creations of what *might* have happened, pieced together from fragments of different manuscripts.

Well, now she could simply ask. The Challenge of Stormhold? Oh, Ash had been there. King Iyalid had been drunk. The treaty of four nights? A delaying tactic intended to position the enemy for a betrayal. All those debates, and Jochi was right while Jasnah was wrong. Settled as easily as that.

Of course, there were things the Heralds didn't know, things they wouldn't say, or—in Taln's case—things they *couldn't* say. Jasnah flipped through the pages, trying to piece together anything from her more recent interviews that would help with the situation at Urithiru. Even the Heralds knew little of this Sibling, the secretive tower spren.

She needed to present this to the other Veristitalians, see what they could tease from it all. Yet the words of the Heralds cast doubt on her second guiding principle—that the past was the best gauge of the future. There was another way. The enemy could see what would happen in the future. That terrified her. In relying on the past, Jasnah saw the future through occluded glass from within a chasm, if at all. Odium had a prime spot atop the watchtower.

She sighed, and Wit unfolded himself from the chair snug in the corner on the other side of the room. He stretched, then wandered over and knelt beside her before taking her unclothed safehand and kissing the tip of the index finger.

At that, Jasnah felt a little thrill of mystery. She'd come to realize, early in her youth, that she didn't approach relationships the same way everyone else seemed to. Her partners in the past had always complained that she was too cold, so academic. That had frustrated her. How was she to learn what others felt if she couldn't ask them?

She didn't have that problem with Wit. He presented an entire world of other problems, but he never was bothered by her questions. Even if he often dodged them.

"My dear," he said, "you pay me no heed. Be careful not to give undue attention only to the ravings of the mad. I warn you, without proper affection, your Wit will wilt."

She removed her hand from his grip and studied him. Keen eyes. A nose that was perhaps a bit too sharp. Most women, she suspected, would find him physically attractive. And indeed she appreciated his statuesque quality, with such interesting proportions and such an intense face. The nose humanized him, in her opinion, made him feel more real.

Curiously, he wasn't Alethi, but he had transformed himself to look like one. She'd been able to tease that much from him. He was something more ancient. He'd laughed when she'd asked, and said the Alethi hadn't *existed* when he'd been born, so he couldn't have been credited the honor of being one of her gifted people.

She found the way he spoke fascinating. After all this time—and all her worries—here was one who was her intellectual equal. Perhaps her *superior.* She didn't trust him, of course. But that was part of what intrigued her.

"How do we beat him, Wit?" she asked softly. "If he can truly see the future, then what possible chance do we have?"

"I once knew a man," Wit said, "who was the finest gambler in all his realm. Where he lived, you make your cards walk themselves around the table by breathing life into them. He was the best. Intelligent, skilled with the Breath of life, a shrewd gambler—he knew exactly how to bet and when. Everyone was *waiting* for the day when he lost. And eventually he did."

"That's different, Wit," Jasnah said. "He couldn't literally see the future."

"Ah, but you see, I was *rigging* the games. So I did know the future—as much as Odium does, anyway. I *shouldn't* have been able to lose. Yet I did."

"How?"

"Someone *else* rigged the game so that no matter what move I made, I could not win. The game was a tie, something I hadn't anticipated. I'd focused my cheating on making certain I didn't lose, but I'd bet on myself winning. And I bet it all, you see—if I'd have been more clever, I'd have let less be lost."

"So," she said, "how do we set it up so Odium doesn't win, even if he can't lose?"

Wit unfolded a paper from his pocket, still kneeling beside her. He seemed to genuinely like her, and she found his companionship invigorating. Full of questions, delights, and surprises. She could provide the intimacy he desired, though she knew he found her lack of excitement on that axis odd, perhaps unsatisfying. That was not a new experience for her;

she'd always found it curious how others put their physical urges ahead of the more powerful emotions of bonding, relating, and engaging.

The chance to scheme, to *connect* with a being like Wit—*that* was exciting. She was curious how the relationship would develop, and that invigorated her. After so many failures, this was something new and interesting.

She cupped his face with her hand. She wished she could, deep down, truly trust him. He was something she, and this world, had never before known. That was electrifying. It was also so *extremely* dangerous.

Wit smiled at her, then smoothed out the paper on her writing desk. It was scribed in his own hand, of course. He came from a land where men had been encouraged to write, the same as women. He shot her a glance, then his smile became a grin. Yes, he *did* seem genuinely fond of their relationship, as much as she was. Indeed, he said it had taken him by surprise as it had her.

"A contract," she said, turning from him and reading the paper. "For Dalinar's contest with Odium." Wit had undoubtedly sculpted each word with precision. "If Dalinar wins, Odium retreats to Damnation for a thousand years. If Odium wins, he must remain in the system, but gets Roshar to do with as he pleases. The monarchs will submit to his rule—as will the Radiants who follow Dalinar."

"Perfect," Wit said. "Wouldn't you say?"

Jasnah sat back. "Perfect for you. If this is agreed to, you win no matter what. Odium remains contained in the Rosharan system either way."

Wit spread his hands before himself. "I've learned a few things since that challenge with the cards so many years ago. But Jasnah, this *is* for the best. If Dalinar wins, well, your people get what they want. But if Dalinar loses, Odium is contained. We're limiting our losses—making certain that at the boundaries of this planet, hell and hate must halt."

"It puts everything on this one contest of champions," Jasnah said. "I hate that tradition even when played for lower stakes."

"Says the woman who used me in a ploy to manipulate that very tradition not two weeks ago."

"Lower stakes," Jasnah repeated, "involving a meaningless loss such as your death."

"Jasnah!"

"Wit, you're immortal," she said. "You told me yourself."

"And you believed me?" he asked, aghast.

She paused and studied him.

He grinned, then kissed her hand again. He seemed to think that sort of thing would eventually spark passion in her. When in truth, physical stimulation was so inferior to mental stimulation.

"I told you I haven't died when killed—yet," he said. "Doesn't mean someone won't find a way someday, and I'd rather not give them an opportunity. Besides, even for me, being killed can confound."

"Don't distract me," she said. "Can we really risk the fate of the world on a simple *duel*?"

"Ah, but it's not a duel, Jasnah. That's the thing. It's not about the *contest*, but what *leads up* to the contest. I know Rayse. He is arrogant and enjoys being worshipped. He never does anything without delighting in how he can show off.

"He's also careful. Subtle. So to win, we need to make him certain he can't utterly lose. This contract does that. If his fail state is that he has to wait a thousand years to try again, well, that won't bother him. He has been here for thousands of years already. So he'll see another thousand as an acceptable loss. But to you and the budding Radiants, a thousand years is a *long* time. Long as a soulless star slumbers."

"A soulless star."

"Yes."

"Slumbers."

"As they do."

She stared at him flatly.

"Long as a rat rends rust?" he asked.

"Long as seasons see stories?"

"Oh, that's *delightful*, Jasnah. Pretend I was the one who could somehow stress said symphonion sounds."

She cocked an eyebrow at him.

"It means beautiful," he said.

"No it doesn't." She again studied the contract. "Sometimes I feel you aren't taking this as *seriously* as you should, Wit."

"It's a personal failing," he said. "The more serious something becomes, the more I find myself inappropriately involved. Indeedy."

Jasnah sighed.

"I'll stop," he said with a grin. "I promise. But look, Jasnah, Rayse— Odium—*is* someone we can defeat. If he has one great failing it's that he thinks he's smarter than he is. He tried exceptionally hard to make Dalinar into his champion. Why? Because he doesn't merely want to win, he wants to win in a way that *says* something. To everyone watching.

"He was so certain he could turn the Blackthorn that he bet almost everything on that singular gamble. Now he must be scared. While he pretends he has a dozen other plans, he's scrambling to locate a champion who can legitimately win. Because he knows—same as I'm telling you— that the contest *won't* only be about who can stab the hardest with their spear."

"What will it be about then?"

"Same thing it's always about, Jasnah," Wit said. "The hearts of men and women. Do you trust the hearts of those who fight on your side?"

She paused, and hoped he didn't read too much into it. Staring at the contract, she couldn't help but feel outmatched by all of this. She, who had been preparing for nearly two *decades* for these exact events, felt uncertain. Did she trust her *own* heart, when confronted with ancient troubles that had surely defeated better women than her?

"A wise answer," Wit whispered.

"I didn't give one."

"A wise answer." He squeezed her hand. "If you give Odium this contract—and get me the *assurance* that he *cannot* break free of this planetary system no matter what happens—then you won't have to trust the hearts of mortals, Jasnah. Because you'll have me. And everything I can give you."

"You've told me he would destroy you if he found you."

"We'll add a line to the contract," Wit said, "naming me as a contractual liaison for Honor—whom Dalinar represents. This will protect me from Odium's direct attacks for the life of the contract. He will *have* to abide by those terms, as they are part of the promise Rayse made by taking up the Shard of Odium. To fail that promise would give others an opening against him, and said failures have killed gods before. Odium knows it. So do this, and I can help you openly. As myself."

"And who is that, Wit?" she asked. "Who are you *really*?"

"Someone," he said, "who wisely turned down the power the others all took—and in so doing, gained freedoms they can never again have. I, Jasnah, am someone who *is not bound*."

She met his eyes—the eyes of something that wasn't a man. A thing that was eternal as a spren. Or, if he was to be believed, something even *older*.

"I feel," she said, "like I should be terrified by that statement."

"That's why I'm so fond of you," he said. "You are poised, you are smart, and you are always ready with a ploy; but when each of those things fails you, Jasnah, you are—above all else—*paranoid*."

100

WATCHERS
AT THE RIM

*Humans are weapons. We singers revere Passion, do we not? How
can we throw away such an excellent channeling of it?*

—Musings of El, on the first of the Final Ten Days

K aladin woke with a start, ready to fight.

He struggled, his heart racing as he found his hands bound.
Why? What was happening? He grunted, thrashing in the darkness, and . . .

He started to remember.

He'd tied his hands together on purpose, to prevent him from punching
someone who woke him, like he'd done to Dabbid yesterday. He gasped,
fighting the terror as he huddled against the wall. Kaladin told himself
the visions were only nightmares, but he still wanted to claw at his own
skull. Burrow into it, pull out all the terrible thoughts, the overwhelming
darkness. Storms. He was . . . he was . . .

He was so *tired*.

Eventually he managed to calm himself enough to free his hands. He
searched around the black chamber, but saw nothing. They hadn't left out
any lights. Teft, however, was snoring softly.

Everything was all right. Kaladin was . . . was all right. . . .

He fumbled around his mat, looking for the canteen he'd placed there
when going to sleep. What had awakened him? He remembered a . . . a
song. A distant song.

He found the canteen, but then saw a light on the wall. Faint, almost
invisible even in the darkness. Hesitant, he wiped the sweat from his brow,

then reached out and touched the garnet. A voice, so very quiet, spoke in his mind.

. . . help . . . please . . .

Storms. The tower spren sounded frail.

"What is wrong? They found the last node?"

Yes . . . at . . . the model . . .

The model? Kaladin frowned, then remembered the large model of the tower in the infirmary room. In *there?* Near the Radiants?

Storms. That was where his parents were.

There is something else . . . so . . . much . . . worse. . . .

"What?" Kaladin demanded. "What could be worse?"

They will . . . soon kill . . . all the Radiants. . . .

"The Radiants?" Kaladin said. "The captive ones?"

. . . Please . . . send . . . me Rlain. . . .

The voice faded along with the light. Kaladin took a deep breath, trembling. Could he do this again? He took out a sphere, then woke Teft.

The other bridgeman came awake, grabbing Kaladin by the arm reflexively. His grip was weak. Despite what he said, the time in a coma had left him enervated.

I have to fight, Kaladin thought. *I'm the only one who can.*

"What is it?" Teft said.

"Something's happening," Kaladin said. "The tower's spren woke me, saying the final node has been located. The Sibling told me the Radiants are in danger, and asked me to send Rlain. I think they meant to send Rlain to Navani, like we'd been planning. Our hand seems to have been forced. We need to try to rescue the Radiants."

Teft nodded, groaning as he sat up.

"You don't seem surprised," Kaladin said.

"I'm not," Teft said, heaving himself to his feet. "This was coming, lad, no matter what we did. I'm sorry. Doesn't seem we have time to do it your father's way."

"Watchers at the rim," Kaladin said softly. "We'll need to move quickly. You get Lift ready to sneak in to the Radiants, so she can begin waking them up. I'll make a fuss outside to lure out the guards and distract the Pursuer. If the guards don't come out though, you'll have to neutralize them."

"All right then. Good enough." Teft pointed to the side, to where something lay folded on the ground. Bridge Four uniforms. Kaladin had asked Dabbid to get them changes of clothing. That was what he'd found? As they began to dress, Dabbid returned, frantic. He came up and grabbed Kaladin's arm.

"The tower spren talked to you too?" Kaladin asked.

Dabbid nodded. "They sounded so weak."

"Do you know where Rlain is?" Kaladin asked.

"I'm going to meet him," Dabbid said. "Fourth floor. Something's happened with Venli that has him really shaken. He didn't want to talk in the infirmary."

"Tell him the plan is a go," Kaladin said. "Someone needs to inform the queen. Do you think you two can get to her?"

"Rlain thinks he can," Dabbid said. "I will go with him. People ignore me."

"Go then," Kaladin said. "Tell her what we're doing, and that we're going to have to get the Radiants out. Then you two take up hiding in this room, and don't make any storms. We'll escape with the Radiants, get Dalinar, and return for you."

Dabbid wrung his hands, but nodded. "Bridge Four," he whispered.

"Bridge Four," Kaladin said. "I don't want to leave you two alone, Dabbid, but we *need* to move now—and I want the queen to be contacted. Plus . . . the Sibling said something. About sending Rlain to them."

"They said it to me too," Dabbid said. He gave the salute, which Kaladin returned, then moved off at a run.

"If something goes wrong," Kaladin said to Teft, continuing to dress in his uniform, "get out that window."

They'd practiced Kaladin's trick of infusing objects and his boots to climb down walls. In an emergency, someone might have to jump out the window and hope to regain their powers before they hit the ground—but that was an absolute last resort. The current plan was for the Windrunners to climb down the outside, each with another Radiant strapped to their backs.

It was far from a perfect plan, but it was better than letting the Fused murder the Radiants while they were in comas.

"Even if you only get yourself out," Kaladin said, "do it, rather than staying and making a hopeless stand. Take your spren and get to Dalinar."

"And you?" Teft said. "You'll follow, right?"

Kaladin hesitated.

"If I run, you run," Teft said. "Look, what happened the last two times a node was discovered?"

"The Pursuer was waiting for me," Kaladin admitted.

"He will be again," Teft said. "This is a trap, plain and simple. What the enemy *doesn't* know is that we don't care about the node. We're trying to free the Radiants. So distract him a little, yes, but then run and let them have their storming fabrial."

"I could try that."

"Give me an oath, lad. We can't do anything more in this tower. We need to reach Dalinar. I'm going to head that way with as many Radiants as I can rescue. You've got my back, right?"

"Always," Kaladin said, nodding. "I swear it. Get as many of the Radiants out as you can, and then run. Once you do, I'll follow."

101

UNDERTEXT

I love their art. The way they depict us is divine, all red shades and black lines. We appear demonic and fearsome; they project all fear and terror upon us.

—Musings of El, on the first of the Final Ten Days

Dalinar stepped into the Prime's warcamp home, and immediately felt as if he'd entered the wrong building. Surely this was a storage room where they were keeping extra furniture gathered from the surrounding abandoned towns.

But no, Dalinar was merely accustomed to austerity. It was an Alethi wartime virtue for a commander to eschew comfort. Dalinar had perhaps taken this idea too far on occasion—but he'd become comfortable with simple furniture, bare walls. Even his rooms in Urithiru had grown too cluttered for his taste.

Young Yanagawn came from a different tradition. This entry room was so full of rich furniture—painted bronze on every surface that wasn't of some plush material—that it created a maze Dalinar had to wind through to reach the other side. Adding to the difficulty, the room was *also* packed with a battalion's worth of servants. Twice Dalinar encountered someone in bright Azish patterns who had to physically climb onto a couch to let him pass.

Where had they found all of this? And those tapestries draping every visible space on the walls. Had they carried them all this way? He knew the Azish were more accustomed to long supply chains—they didn't have access to the number of food-making Soulcasters that the Alethi did—but this was excessive, wasn't it?

Though, he noted, turning back across the room as he reached the other side, *this would certainly slow an assassin or a force who tried to break in here and attack the Prime.*

In the next room he found an even greater oddity. The Prime—Yanagawn the First, Emperor of Makabak—sat in a throne at the head of a long table. Nobody else ate at the table, but it was stuffed with lit candelabras and plates of food. Yanagawn was finishing his breakfast, mostly pre-cut fruit. He wore a mantle of heavy cloth and an ornate headdress. He ate primly, spearing each bite of fruit with a long skewer, then raising it to his lips. He barely seemed to move, with one hand held crossed before his chest as he manipulated the skewer with the other.

A large rank of people stood to either side of him. They mostly seemed to be camp followers. Washwomen. Wheelwrights. Reshi chull keepers. Seamstresses. Dalinar picked out only a few uniforms.

Jasnah had already arrived for the meeting. She stood among the groups of people, and a servant ushered Dalinar in that direction as well, so he joined the bizarre display. Standing and watching the emperor eat his fruit one delicate bite at a time.

Dalinar liked the Azish—and they'd proven to be good allies with a shockingly effective military. But storms above and Damnation beyond, were they strange. Although curiously, he found their excess to be less nauseating than when an Alethi highprince indulged. In Alethkar this would be an expression of arrogance and a lack of self-restraint.

Here, there was a certain . . . cohesion to the display. Alethi servants of the highest order wore simple black and white, but the Azish ones were dressed almost as richly as the emperor. The overflowing table didn't seem to be *for* Yanagawn. He was merely another ornament. This was about the position of Prime, and the empire itself, more than an elevation of the individual man.

From what Dalinar had heard, they'd had trouble appointing this most recent Prime. The reason for that was, of course, standing directly behind Dalinar: Szeth, the Assassin in White, had killed the last two Primes. At the same time, Dalinar couldn't imagine *anyone* wanting to be Prime. They had to deal with all this pomp, always on display. Maybe *that* was why their "scholarly republic" worked in a way Jasnah liked so much. They had accidentally made the position of emperor so awful, no sane person would want it—so they'd needed to find other ways to rule the country.

Dalinar had learned enough social grace to remain quiet until the display was complete. Each of the onlookers was then given a bronze plate full of food, which they accepted after bowing to the emperor. As they left one by one, other servants quickly made space at the table for Jasnah and

Dalinar, though the clock he wore in his arm bracer told him he was still a few minutes early for the meeting.

Damnation's own device, that was. Had him hopping about like the Prime. Though admittedly, Dalinar was realizing how much less of his time was wasted now that everyone knew precisely when to meet together. Without ever saying a word, Navani was bringing order to his life.

Be safe. Please. My life's light, my gemheart.

He sent Szeth out, as neither of the other two monarchs had guards in the room. As they settled—the last of the observers leaving—Noura bowed to the Prime, then took a seat at the table deliberately positioned to be lower than the three of them. Some in the empire considered it a scandal that Dalinar, Jasnah, and Fen were always seated at the same height as the Prime, but Yanagawn had insisted.

"Dalinar, Jasnah," the youth said, relaxing as he removed his headdress and set it onto the table. Noura gave him a glance at that, but Dalinar smiled. She obviously thought the Prime should maintain decorum, but Dalinar liked seeing the youth grow more comfortable with his position and his fellow monarchs. "I'm sorry we didn't have plates of food for you as well," Yanagawn continued in Azish. "I should have known you'd both arrive early."

"It would have made a fine memento, Majesty," Jasnah said, laying out some papers on the table. "But we were not of the chosen today, so it wouldn't feel right to be so favored."

The boy looked to Noura. "I told you she understood."

"Your wisdom grows, Imperial Majesty," the older woman said. She was an Azish vizier—a high-level civil servant. Her own outfit had less gold on it than the Prime's, but it was nevertheless fantastically colored, with a cap and contrasting coat of a multitude of patterns and hues. Her long hair was greying and wound into a braid that emerged from her cap on one side.

"All right, Jasnah," Yanagawn said, leaning forward to inspect Jasnah's papers—though as far as Dalinar knew, he couldn't read Alethi. "Tell it to me straight."

Dalinar braced himself.

"We have practically no chance of recovering Urithiru," Jasnah said in Azish, her voice barely accented. "Our scouts confirm that fabrials don't work near it. That means if we were to re-create a smaller version of my mother's flying machine to deliver troops, it would drop the moment it drew too close.

"They've also blocked off the caverns. My uncle delivered a small force to the bottom, and that action seems to have informed the enemy that we know their ruse is up. They are no longer sending fake messages via spanreed, and we've seen singer troops on the balconies.

"With a Shardblade—which we discovered can be delivered into the protected area so long as it is not bound—our troops can cut through the blockage at the bottom. But while doing that the force would be exposed to archers on higher ground. And if we made it through that rubble, fighting all the way up through a contested tunnel system would be a nightmare.

"A march by soldiers along the tops of the mountains is impossible for a multitude of reasons. But if we *did* reach the tower, we'd lose. Our battlefields are a careful balance of Radiant against Fused, Shardbearer against Regal, soldier against soldier. At Urithiru, we'd have no Radiants—and the entire strategy would topple."

"We'd have Kaladin," Dalinar said. "His powers still work. The Stormfather thinks it's because he's far enough along in his oaths."

"With all due respect to him," Jasnah said, "Kaladin is just one man—and one you *relieved of duty* before we left."

She was correct, of course. Common sense dictated that one man was nothing against an army of Fused. Yet Dalinar wondered. Once, in the warcamps, he'd argued with Kaladin's soldiers who had set up a vigil for the young Windrunner—then presumed dead. Dalinar had been proven wrong that time. Now, he found himself possessing some of the same faith as those soldiers.

Beaten down, broken, surrounded by enemies, Kaladin continued to fight. He knew how to take the next step. They couldn't leave him to take it alone.

"Our best chance," Dalinar said to the others, "is to deliver me and a force through Shadesmar to the tower. I might be able to open a perpendicularity there, and we could surprise the enemy with an attack."

"You *might* be able to open one there, Uncle," Jasnah said. "What does the Stormfather think?"

"He isn't certain I am far enough along in my oaths or my skills to manage it yet," Dalinar admitted.

Jasnah tapped her notes. "An assault through Shadesmar would require a large number of ships—something we don't have on that side, and which I see no way of obtaining."

"We *need* to find a way to support Kaladin, Navani, and whatever resistance they are building," Dalinar said. "We might not need a large force of ships. A small group of trained soldiers might be able to sneak in, then disable the fabrial the enemy is using to stop Radiants."

"Undoubtedly," Jasnah said, "that is the method the enemy used to get *into* the tower. They will be guarding against this same tactic."

"So what?" Yanagawn said, chewing on some nuts he had hidden in a pocket of his oversized robes. "Jasnah, you argue against every point Dalinar makes. Are you saying we should give up *Urithiru* to the enemy?"

"Our entire war effort falls apart without it," Noura said. "It was the means by which we connected our disparate forces!"

"Not necessarily," Jasnah said, showing some small maps to the Prime. "As long as we have a stronger navy—and proper air support—we can control the southern half of Roshar. It will necessitate weeks or months of travel—but we can coordinate our battlefields as long as we have span-reeds."

"Still," Yanagawn said, glancing at Noura. The older woman nodded in agreement.

"This is a major blow," Dalinar said. "Jasnah, we *can't* simply abandon Urithiru. You yourself spent *years* trying to locate it."

"I'm not suggesting we do, Uncle," she said, her voice cold. "I'm merely presenting facts. For now, I think we need to act as if we will not soon retake the tower—which might mean moving against Ishar's forces in Tukar, so we can secure those positions. At any rate, we should be planning how to support our forces in southern Alethkar against the Vedens."

They were all valid points, the core of a cohesive and well-reasoned battle strategy. She was trying hard, and mostly succeeding, at learning to be a capable tactical commander. He couldn't blame her for feeling she had something to prove there; her entire life had been a series of people demanding she prove herself to them.

However, her quickness to abandon Urithiru smelled too similar to what Taravangian had done in abandoning Roshar. Give up quickly, once you think you're beaten.

"Jasnah," he said, "we *need* to try harder to liberate Urithiru."

"I'm not saying we shouldn't, only that such an action is going to be very difficult and costly. I'm trying to outline those costs so we're aware of them."

"The way you talk lacks hope."

"'Hope,'" she said, spreading her papers out on the table. "Have I ever told you how much I dislike that word? Think of what it means, what it implies. You have hope when you're outnumbered. You have hope when you lack options. Hope is always irrational, Uncle."

"Fortunately, we are not entirely rational beings."

"Nor should we want to be," she agreed. "At the same time, how often has 'hope' been the reason someone refuses to move on and accept a realistic attitude? How often has 'hope' caused more pain or delayed healing? How often has 'hope' prevented someone from standing up and doing what needs to be done, because they cling to a wish for everything to be different?"

"I would say," Yanagawn said, leaning forward, "that hope defines us, Jasnah. Without it, we are not human."

"Perhaps you are correct," Jasnah said, a phrase she often used when she wasn't convinced—but also didn't want to continue an argument. "Very well then, let us discuss Urithiru."

"Your powers will work," Dalinar said, "at least partially. You have said the Fourth Ideal."

"Yes," she said. "I have—though the Stormfather is uncertain whether the fourth oath will truly allow a Radiant to withstand the suppression. Am I correct?"

"You are," Dalinar said. "But if the enemy is resupplying via the Oathgates, there is only *one* way we can realistically do anything about this situation. We must destroy their suppression fabrial. And so my suggestion of a small team makes the most sense."

"And you are to lead it?" Jasnah said.

"Yes," Dalinar said.

"You are still far from mastering your powers. What if you *can't* open a perpendicularity at Urithiru?"

"I've been experimenting, practicing," Dalinar said. "But yes, I've a long way to go. So I've been considering another solution." He selected one of Jasnah's maps, then turned it for the others to see. "We came here to Emul to use a hammer-and-anvil tactic, shoving our enemy against an army here. The army of Ishar, the being the Azish call Tashi."

"Yes, and?" Jasnah asked.

"I have scouts surveying his position," Dalinar said, "and have visual confirmation—shown to me via Lightweaving—that the man himself is there. Wit's drawings confirm it. I have spoken with the Stormfather, and the two of us think this is our best solution. Ishar is a master with the Bondsmithing art. If I can recruit him, he could be the secret to saving Urithiru."

"Pardon," Noura said. "But haven't we determined that the Heralds are all . . . insane?" It was hard for her to say; their religion viewed the Heralds as deities. The Makabaki people worshipped *them*, and not the Almighty.

"Yes," Dalinar said, "but Ash indicates Ishar might have escaped with less damage than others. She trusts him."

"We've had letters from Ishar, Uncle," Jasnah said. "That are not encouraging."

"I want to try speaking with him anyway," Dalinar said. "We've been mostly ignoring his armies, other than to use them as our anvil. But if I were to approach with a flag of peace and parley, Ishar—"

"Wait," Yanagawn said. "You're going to go personally?"

"Yes," Dalinar said. "I need to see Ishar, ask him questions."

"Send your Radiants," Noura said. "Take this being captive. Bring him here. Then talk to him."

"I would rather go myself," Dalinar said.

"But . . ." Yanagawn said, sounding utterly baffled. "You're a king. This is even worse than when Jasnah went out in Plate and fought the enemy!"

"It's an old family tradition, Majesty," Jasnah said. "We are prone to putting ourselves into the thick of things. I blame long-standing Alethi conditioning that says the best general is the one who leads the charge."

"I suppose," Yanagawn said, "that a history of having excessive numbers of Shards might create a feeling of invincibility. But Dalinar, why do you raise this point now? To get our advice?"

"More to warn you," he said. "I've deliberately put the Mink in command of our military so I can step away to see to more . . . spiritual matters. Jasnah and Wit are preparing a contract for me to present to Odium, once we have pushed him to come speak to me again.

"Until we can make that work, I need to do something to help. I need to bring Ishar to our side—then see if he can teach me how to restore the Oathpact and help me rescue Urithiru."

"Well," Yanagawn said, looking to Noura. "Being allies with the Alethi is . . . interesting. Go with Yaezir's own speed then, I suppose."

Yaezir is dead, Dalinar thought, though he didn't say it.

Jasnah took the reins of the conversation next, explaining the contract she was preparing for Odium. She and Dalinar had already talked to Queen Fen earlier, via spanreed. Dalinar offered some explanations, but mostly let Jasnah do the persuading. She had an uphill battle, as getting the monarchs to agree to this contest would take some doing.

Jasnah could manage it; he was confident in her. His job, he was increasingly certain, involved his Bondsmithing, the Oathpact, and the Heralds.

Eventually the meeting came to an end. They agreed to meet again to talk over more points in the contract, but for now Yanagawn had to attend some religious ceremonies for his people. Dalinar needed to prepare for his trip to Tukar; he intended to go as soon as was reasonable.

As they rose to leave, Yanagawn replaced his headdress. "Dalinar," the youth said, "do we know anything of Lift? We left her at the tower."

"Kaladin said the other Radiants were unconscious," Dalinar said. "That probably includes her."

"Maybe," Yanagawn said. "She often does what she isn't supposed to. If you hear word, send to me, please?"

Dalinar nodded, joining Jasnah and withdrawing from Yanagawn's palace. The exterior might look as ordinary as every other building in the village, but a palace it was.

He collected Szeth, who was holding something for him. Dalinar took the large book—intimidating in size, though he knew it to be shorter than it appeared. The paper inside was covered with his own bulky letter-lines, larger and thicker than was proper, drawn deliberately with his fat fingers.

He held the book toward Jasnah. He'd allowed early drafts and portions of it to be shared—and they'd gotten out all over the coalition by now. However, he hadn't considered the book finished until he'd made some last changes earlier this week.

"*Oathbringer?*" she said, taking it eagerly. "It's complete?"

"No, but my part is done," Dalinar said. "This is the original, though the scribes have made copies following my last round of alterations. I wanted you to have the one I wrote."

"You should feel proud, Uncle. You make history with this volume."

"I fear you'll find it to be mostly religious drivel."

"Ideas are not useless simply because they involve religious thinking," Jasnah said. "Nearly all of the ancient scholars I revere were religious, and I appreciate how their faith shaped them, even if I do not appreciate the faith itself."

"The things you said about hope in the meeting," Dalinar said. "They bothered me, Jasnah. But perhaps in a good way. Who in the world would dispute an idea as fundamental as hope? Yet because we all accept it as vital, we don't think about it. What it really means. You do."

"I try," she said, glancing back toward the Prime's palace. "Tell me. Am I pushing too hard to establish myself as a military leader? I feel it's an important precedent, as your book here is, but . . . I hit the target a little too squarely, didn't I?"

Dalinar smiled, then put his hand on hers, which held up the book. "We are revealing a new world, Jasnah, and the way before us is dark until we bring it light. We will be forgiven if we stumble on unseen ground now and then." He squeezed her hand. "I would like you to do something for me. All of the great philosophical texts I've read have an undertext."

"Yes, about that . . ." He wasn't the only man who had been shaken to discover that for centuries, the women in their lives had been leaving commentaries for one another. Something dictated by a man would often have his wife's or scribe's thoughts underneath, never shared aloud. An entire world, hidden from those who thought they were ruling it.

"I would like you to write the undertext for *Oathbringer*," Dalinar said. "Openly. To be read and discovered by any who would like to read it."

"Uncle?" Jasnah said. "I'm not certain the tradition should continue. It was questionable to begin with."

"I find the insights offered in the undertexts to be essential," Dalinar said. "They change how I read. History is written by the victors, as many are fond of saying—but at least we have contrary insights by those who watched. I would like to know what you think of what I've said."

"I will not hold back, Uncle," Jasnah said. "If much of this *is* religious, I will be compelled to be honest. I will point out your confirmation biases, your fallacies. Perhaps it would be better if you gave the undertext task to my mother."

"I considered that," he said. "But I promised to unite instead of divide. I don't do that by giving my book only to those who agree with me.

"If we're revealing a new world, Jasnah, should we not do it together? Arguments and all? I feel like . . . like we are never going to agree on the details, you and I. This book though—it could show that we agree on the more important matters. After all, if an avowed atheist and a man starting his own religion can unite, then who can object that *their* personal differences are too large to surmount?"

"That's what you're doing, then?" she asked. "Creating a religion?"

"Revising the old one, at the very least," Dalinar said. "When the full text of this is released . . . I suspect it will create a larger schism among Vorinism."

"Me being involved won't help that."

"I want your thoughts nonetheless. If you are willing to give them."

She pulled the book close. "I consider it among the greatest honors I have ever been offered, Uncle. Be warned, however, I am not known for my brevity. This could take me years. I will be thorough, I will offer counterpoints, and I may undermine your entire argument. But I *will* be respectful."

"Whatever you need, Jasnah." He smiled. "I hope that in your additions, we will create something greater than I could have alone."

She smiled back. "Don't say it that way. You make it sound like the odds are against it being possible, where I should say that is the most reasonable outcome. Thank you, Uncle. For your trust."

To humans, our very visages become symbols. You find echoes of it even in the art from centuries before this Return.

—Musings of El, on the first of the Final Ten Days

There was a long line at the Oathgates today, but that was nothing new. Raboniel was certain the human kingdoms knew of the occupation by now, and so had authorized the Oathgates to be opened more frequently, allowing singer troops and servants occupying the tower to rotate out.

Venli's group of fifteen friends huddled behind her, holding their supplies—hopefully appearing to be merely another batch of workers given a chance to return to Kholinar for a break. Venli pulled her coat tight against the wind. Listeners didn't get as cold as humans seemed to, but she could still feel the bite of the wind—particularly since this form had carapace only as ornamentation, not true armor.

She wasn't completely certain what to do after reaching Kholinar. Raboniel's writ would certainly get her people out of the city, and even out of Alethkar. But Venli couldn't wait the weeks or months it would take for them to walk to the Shattered Plains. She *had* to find out if her mother was still alive.

How far would the power of the writ go? Raboniel was feared, respected. Could Venli get her entire team of fifteen flown to that scout post via Heavenly One? Her mind spun with lies about a secret mission from Raboniel at the Shattered Plains. Indeed, it wasn't too far from the truth. Raboniel had all but commanded her to go investigate the listener remnants.

And what then? Venli thought. *Raboniel knows about them. She knows I'm going. She's manipulating me. For what end?*

It didn't matter. Venli had to go. It was time.

Timbre pulsed softly as she stood in the line, map case over her shoulder, trying to ignore the wind.

"Are you disappointed in me?" Venli whispered to Conceit. "For leaving Rlain and the humans?"

Timbre pulsed. Yes, she was. The little spren was never afraid to be straight with Venli.

"What do you expect me to do?" she whispered, turning her head away from Dul so he wouldn't hear her talking. "Help with their insane plan? He'll get all those Radiants killed. Besides, you think I'd be any help to them?"

Timbre pulsed. Venli was doing well. Learning. She could help.

If I weren't a coward, Venli thought. "What if we got you a different host? A singer who cares, like Rlain."

Timbre pulsed.

"What do you mean?" Venli demanded. "You can't *want* me. I'm an accident. A mistake."

Another pulse.

"Mistakes can't be wonderful, Timbre. That's what *defines* them as mistakes."

She pulsed, more confident. How could she be *more* confident with each complaint? Stupid spren. And why wasn't this line moving? The transfers should be quick; they needed to exchange people and supplies before the highstorm arrived.

Venli told her people to wait, then stepped out of line. She marched to the front, where a couple of singers—formerly Azish, by their clothing—were arguing.

"What is it?" Venli demanded to Craving.

The two took in her Regal form, then the femalen answered. "We have to wait to perform the exchange, Chosen," she said, using an old formal singer term. "The human who works the Oathgates for us has run off."

"No one else has a living Blade, which is needed to operate the fabrial now," the other explained. "If you could find the one they call Vyre, and ask when he will return . . ."

Venli glanced toward the sky. She could feel the wind picking up. "The highstorm is nearly here. We should move everyone inside."

The two argued at first, but Venli spoke more firmly. Soon they started herding the frustrated singers toward the tower. Venli walked along the plateau, Timbre pulsing excitedly. She saw this as an opportunity.

"Why do you believe in me?" Venli whispered. "I've given you no reason. I've ruined everything I've touched. I'm a selfish, impotent, sorry excuse for a listener."

Timbre pulsed. Venli had saved her. Venli had saved Lift.

"Yes, but I had to be coaxed into both," Venli said. "I'm not a hero. I'm an accident."

Timbre was firm. Some people charged toward the goal, running for all they had. Others stumbled. But it wasn't the speed that mattered.

It was the direction they were going.

Venli lingered at the entrance to Urithiru. She hesitated, glancing over her shoulder. The previous highstorm had reached all the way past the sixth tier. This one would likely envelop nearly the entire tower, a rare occurrence, their scholars thought. She felt as if she could sense the power of it, the fury bearing down on them.

"What if," she whispered to Timbre, "I offered to use this writ to smuggle Stormblessed or his family out of Urithiru?"

Timbre pulsed uncertainly. Would the writ's authority extend that far? Venli thought perhaps it would. She wouldn't be able to get any of the unconscious Radiants out; they were too closely watched, and someone would send to Raboniel for confirmation. But a few "random" humans? That might work.

She found Dul and the others inside the front doors. Venli gathered them around, away from prying ears, and quickly handed her writ to Mazish. "Take this," Venli said. "If I don't return, you should be able to use it to get away."

"Without you?" Mazish said. "Venli . . ."

"I'll almost certainly return," Venli said. "But just in case, take the map too. You'll need it to find your way to the other listeners in secret."

"Where are you going?" Dul asked.

Venli hummed to the Lost. "I think we should offer to bring the surgeon and his family—including their son, the Windrunner—out with us. Help them escape the tower, take them to their own people at the Shattered Plains."

She watched them, expecting fear, perhaps condemnation. This would jeopardize their safety.

Instead, as a group, they hummed to Consideration.

"Having a Windrunner on our side could be useful," Mazish said. "He could certainly help us get to the Shattered Plains quicker."

"Yes!" said Shumin, the new recruit—still a little too eager for Venli's taste. "This is a *great* idea!"

"Would he help us though?" Dul asked.

"He treated Rlain well," Mazish said. "Even when he thought Rlain was only another parshman. I don't like what the humans did, but if we put this one in our debt, my gut says he won't betray us."

Venli scanned the other faces. Singers with a variety of skin patterns, now humming a variety of rhythms. None of them hummed to Betrayal, and they gave her encouraging nods.

"Very well," Venli said, "wait for me until the storm has passed. If I've not returned by then, take the next Oathgate transfer to Kholinar. I'll find you there."

They hummed at her words, so Venli started toward the atrium, hoping she'd be quick enough to stop Rlain from trying his desperate plan. She didn't know for certain if he'd take her offer. But this *was* the direction she should be moving.

．．

Navani knelt on the floor of her office. It still smelled of smoke from the explosion the day before.

Despite Raboniel saying she wanted to scrape the chamber for broken pieces of the dagger, no one arrived to do that. They hadn't taken her to her rooms above. They hadn't brought her meals. They'd simply left her alone.

To contemplate her utter failure.

She felt numb. After her previous failure—when she'd exposed the node to her enemies—she'd picked herself up and moved on. This time she felt stuck. Worn. Like an old banner left too long exposed to the elements. Ripped by storms. Bleached by the sun. Now hanging in tatters, waiting to slip off the pole.

We can kill Radiant spren.

In the end, all Raboniel's talk of working together had been a lie. Of course it had. Navani had *known* it would be. She'd planned for it, and tried to hide what she knew. But had she really expected that to work? She'd repeatedly confirmed to herself that she couldn't outthink the Fused. They were ancient, capable beyond mortal understanding, beings outside of time and . . . And . . .

And she kept staring at the place where Raboniel's daughter had died. Where Raboniel had wept, holding the corpse of her child. Such a *human* moment.

Navani curled up on her pallet, though sleep had eluded her all night. She had spent the hours listening to the Fused in the hallway playing notes on metal plates and demanding new ones—until one final sound had echoed against the stone hallways. A chilling, *awful* sound that was wrong in all the right ways. Raboniel had found the tone.

The tone that could kill spren.

Should Navani feel pride? Even in that time of near madness, her research had been so meticulous and well annotated that Raboniel was able to follow it. What had taken Navani days, the Fused replicated in hours, breaking open a mystery that had stood for thousands of years. Evidence that Navani was a true scholar after all?

No, she thought, staring at the ceiling. *No, don't you dare take that distinction for yourself.* If she'd been a scholar, she'd have understood the implications of her work.

She was a child playing dress-up again. A farmer could stumble across a new plant in the wilderness. Did that make him a botanist?

She eventually forced herself up to do the only thing she was certain she couldn't ruin. She found ink and paper in the wreckage of the room, then knelt and began to paint prayers. It was partially for the comfort of familiarity. But storm her, she still *believed.* Perhaps that was as foolish as thinking herself a scholar. Who did she think was listening? Was she only praying because she was afraid?

Yes, she thought, continuing to paint. *I'm afraid. And I have to hope that someone, somewhere, is listening. That someone has a plan. That it all matters somehow.*

Jasnah took *comfort* in the idea that there was no plan, that everything was random. She said that a chaotic universe meant the only actions of actual importance were the ones they decided were important. That gave people autonomy.

Navani loved her daughter, but couldn't see it the same way. Organization and order existed in the very way the world worked. From the patterns on leaves to the system of compounds and chemical reactions. It all whispered to her.

Someone had known anti-Voidlight was possible.

Someone had known Navani would create it first.

Someone had seen all this, planned for it, and put her here. She had to believe that. She had to believe, therefore, that there was a way out.

Please, she prayed, painting the glyph for divine direction. *Please. I'm trying so hard to do what is right. Please guide me. What do I do?*

A voice sounded outside the room, and in her sleep-deprived state, she first mistook it for a voice speaking to her in answer. And then . . . then she heard what it was saying.

"The best way to distract the Bondsmith is to kill his wife," the voice said. Rough, cold. "I am therefore here to perform the act that you have so far refused to do."

Navani stood and walked to the door. Her femalen guard was someone new, but she didn't forbid Navani from peering down the hall toward Raboniel's workstation beside the Sibling's shield.

A man in a black uniform stood before Raboniel. Neat, close-cropped black hair, a narrow hawkish face with a prominent nose and sunken cheeks. Moash. The murderer.

"I continue to have use for the queen," Raboniel said.

"My orders are from Odium himself," Moash said. If a Fused's voice was overly ornamented with rhythms and meaning, his voice was the opposite. Dead. A voice like slate.

"He ordered you to come to me, Vyre," Raboniel said. "And I requested for you to be sent. So today, I need you to deal with my problems first. There is a worm in the tower. Eating his way through walls. He is increasingly an issue."

"I warned you about Stormblessed," Moash said. "I warned all of you. And you did not listen."

"You will kill him," Raboniel said.

"No enemy can kill Kaladin Stormblessed," Moash said.

"You promised that—"

"*No enemy* can kill Stormblessed," Moash said. "He is a force like the storms, and you cannot kill the storms, Fused."

Raboniel handed Moash something. A small dagger. "You speak foolishness. A man is merely a man, no matter how skilled. That dagger can destroy his spren. Spread that sand, and it will turn faintly white when an invisible spren flies overhead. Use it to locate his honorspren, then strike at it, depriving him of power."

"I can't kill him," Moash repeated a third time, tucking the dagger away. "But I promise something better. We make this a covenant, Fused: I ruin Stormblessed, leave him unable to interfere, and you deliver me the queen. Accepted?"

Navani felt herself grow cold. Raboniel didn't even glance in her direction. "Accepted," Raboniel said. "But do another thing for me. The Pursuer has been sent to destroy the final node, but I think he is delaying to encourage Stormblessed to show up and fight him for it. Break the node for me."

Moash nodded and accepted what seemed to be a small diagram explaining the location of the node. He turned on his heel with military precision and marched up the hallway. If he saw her, he made no comment, passing like a cold wind.

"Monster," Navani said, angerspren at her feet. "Traitor! You would attack your own friend?"

He stopped short. Staring straight ahead, he spoke. "Where were you, lighteyes, when your son condemned innocents to death?" He turned, affixing Navani with those lifeless eyes. "Where were you, *Queen*, when your son sent *Roshone* to Kaladin's hometown? A political outcast, a known murderer, exiled to a small village. Where he couldn't do any damage, right?

"Roshone killed Kaladin's brother. You could have stopped it. If any of you cared. You were never my queen; you are nothing to me. You are nothing to anyone. So don't speak to me of treason or friendship. You have no *idea* what this day will cost me."

He continued forward, bearing no visible weapon save the dagger tucked into his belt. A dagger designed to kill a spren. A dagger that Navani had, essentially, created. He reached the end of the hallway, burst alight with Stormlight—which somehow worked for him—and streaked into the air, rising through the open stairwell toward the ground floor.

Navani slumped in the doorway, objections withering in her throat. She knew he was wrong, but she couldn't find her voice. Something about that man unnerved her to the point of panic. He wasn't human. He was a Voidbringer. If that word had ever applied to any, it was Moash.

"What do you need?" her guard asked. "Have you been fed?"

"I . . ." Navani licked her lips. "I need a candle, please. For burning prayers."

Remarkably, she fetched it. Taking the candle, shivering, Navani cupped the flame and walked to her pallet. There, she knelt and began burning her glyphwards one at a time.

If there was a God, if the Almighty was still out there somewhere, had he created Moash? Why? Why bring such a thing into the world?

Please, she thought, begging as a ward shriveled, her prayers casting smoke into the air. *Please. Tell me what to do. Show me something. Let me know you're there.*

As the last prayer drifted toward the Tranquiline Halls, she sat back on her heels, numb, wanting to huddle down and forget about her problems. When she moved to do so, however, in the candlelight she caught sight of something glittering amid the wreckage of her desk. As if in a trance, Navani rose and walked over. The guard wasn't looking.

Navani brushed aside ash to find a metal dagger with a diamond affixed to the pommel. She stared at it, confused. It had exploded, hadn't it?

No, this is the second one. The one Raboniel used to kill her daughter. She tossed it aside, as if hating it, once the deed was done.

A precious, priceless weapon, and the Fused had discarded it. How long had Raboniel been awake? Did she feel like Navani, exhausted, pushed to the limit? Forgetting important details?

For there, glimmering violet-black in the gemstone, was a soft glow. Not completely used up in the previous killing.

A small charge of anti-Voidlight.

∴

Kaladin took the steps down one at a time. Unhurried as he walked toward the trap.

A certain momentum pushed him forward. As if his next actions were Soulcast into stone, already unchangeable. A mountain seemed to fill in behind him, blocking his retreat.

Forward. Only forward. One step after another.

He emerged from the stairwell onto the ground floor. Two direform Regals had been guarding the path, but they backed off—hands on swords, humming frantically. Kaladin ignored them, turning toward the atrium. He set his spear to his shoulder and strode through this central corridor.

No more hiding. He was too tired to hide. Too wrung-out for tactics and strategy. The Pursuer wanted him? Well, he would have Kaladin, presented as he had always been seen. Dressed in his uniform, striding to the fight, his head high.

Humans and singers alike scattered before him. Kaladin saw many of the humans wearing the markings Rlain had described—*shash* glyphs drawn on their foreheads. Storm them, they believed in him. They wore the symbol of his shame, his failure, and his imprisonment. And they made it something better.

He couldn't help feeling that this was it. The last time he'd wear the uniform, his final act as a member of Bridge Four. One way or another, he had to move on from the life he'd been clinging to and the simple squad of soldiers who had formed the heart of that life.

All these people believed in a version of him who had already died. Highmarshal Kaladin Stormblessed. The valiant soldier, leader of the Windrunners, stalwart and unwavering. Like Kal the innocent youth, Squadleader Kaladin the soldier in Amaram's army, and Kaladin the slave . . . Highmarshal Stormblessed had passed. Kaladin had become someone new, someone who could not measure up to the legend.

But with all these people believing in him—falling in behind him, whispering with hope and anticipation—perhaps he could resurrect Stormblessed for one last battle.

He didn't worry about exposing himself. There was nowhere to run. Regals and singer soldiers gathered in bunches, tailing him and whispering harshly, but they would let a Fused deal with a Radiant.

Other Fused would know, though. Kaladin had been claimed already. He was Pursued.

As Kaladin drew near to the Breakaway—the hallway to his right would merge with the large open marketplace—he finally felt her. He stopped fast, looking that direction. The dozens of people following him hushed as he stared intently and raised his right hand in the direction of the market.

Syl, he thought. *I'm here. Find me.*

A line of light, barely visible, bounced around in the distance. It turned and spun toward him, picking up speed—its path growing straighter. She grew brighter, and awareness of her blossomed in his mind. They were not whole, either one, without the other.

She recovered herself with a gasp, then landed on his hand, wearing her girlish dress.

"Are you all right?" he whispered.

"No," she said. "No, not at all. That felt . . . felt like it did when I nearly died. Like it did when I drifted for centuries. I feel sad, Kaladin. And cold."

"I understand those feelings," he replied. "But the enemy, Syl . . . they're going to execute the Radiants. And they might have my parents."

She peered up at him. Then her shape fuzzed, and she was instantly in a uniform like his, colored Kholin blue.

Kaladin nodded, then turned and continued, shadowed by the hopes and prayers of hundreds. Shadowed by his own reputation. A man who would never cry in the night, huddled against the wall, terrified. A man he was determined to pretend to be. One last time.

He checked Navani's flying gauntlet, which he'd attached to his belt—easy to unhook, if needed—at his right side so it pointed behind him. Kaladin and Dabbid had reset its conjoined weights the other night. It hadn't worked so well for him in the previous fight, but now he understood its limitations. It was a device designed by engineers, not soldiers. He couldn't wear it on his hand, where it would interfere with his ability to hold a spear. But perhaps it could offer him an edge in another capacity.

With Syl flying as a ribbon of light beside his head, he strode into the atrium—with that endless wall of glass rising as a window in front of him. An equally endless hollow shaft in the stone rose up toward the pinnacle of the tower, surrounded by balconies on most levels. Heavenly Ones hovered in the air, though he didn't have time to search for Leshwi.

Syl moved out in front of him, then paused, hovering, seeming curious. "What?" he asked.

Highstorm coming, she said in his head.

Of course there was. It was that kind of day.

People in the atrium began to scatter as they saw him, accompanied by anticipationspren. As the place emptied, he picked out a hulking figure standing in the dead center of the chamber, blocking the way to the room on the other side—the infirmary.

Kaladin brandished his spear in challenge. But the Pursuer cared nothing for honor. He was here for the kill, and he came streaking at Kaladin to claim it.

Watch them struggle. Witness their writhing, their refusal to sur-
render. Humans cling to the rocks with the vigor of any Rosharan
vine.

—Musings of El, on the first of the Final Ten Days

There he is," Teft said, ducking and moving with the crowd of
people in the atrium. With a cloak over his uniform, he didn't draw
attention. He'd found that was often the case. Kaladin turned heads,
even if he was dressed in rags. He was that kind of man.

But Teft? He looked forgettable. In this cloak he was simply another
worker, walking with his daughter through the atrium. Hopefully Lift
would keep her head down so the hood of her own cloak obscured her
features—otherwise someone might wonder why his "daughter" looked
an awful lot like a certain bothersome Radiant who was always making
trouble in the tower.

"What took him so long?" Lift whispered as the two of them sidled over
along the wall of the atrium, acting frightened of the sudden rush of people
who made way for Kaladin and the Pursuer.

"Boy likes to grandstand," Teft said. But storms, it was hard not to feel
inspired at the sight of Kaladin framed in the entryway like that in a sharp
blue uniform, his hair free, his scars bold and stark on his forehead. Eyes
intense enough to pierce the darkest storm.

You did good with that one, Teft, he thought—giving himself permission
to feel a little pride. *You ruined your own life something fierce, but you did good*
with that one.

Phendorana whispered comfort in his ear. She'd shrunk, at his request, and rode on his shoulder. He nodded at the words. If his family hadn't gotten involved with the Envisagers, he wouldn't have known how to help Kaladin when he'd needed it. And then the Blackthorn probably would have died, and they wouldn't have found this tower. So . . . maybe it was time to let go of what he'd done.

Together, they inched along the wall toward the infirmary. Storm him if having his own personal spren wasn't the best thing that had happened to him, other than Bridge Four. She could be a little crusty at times, which made them a good match. She also refused to accept his excuses. Which made them an even better match.

Kaladin started fighting, and Teft couldn't spare him much more than a wish of goodwill. The lad would be fine. Teft simply had to do his part.

They waited to see if the guards in the infirmary came out at the ruckus, and blessedly they did. Unfortunately, one remained at the door, gaping at the battle but apparently determined to remain at his post.

Stormform Regal too, which was just Teft's luck. Still, he and Lift were able to work the press of the crowd to their advantage, pretending they were confused civilians. Maybe that stormform would let them "hide" in the infirmary.

Instead, the Regal at the door showed them an indifferent palm, gesturing for them to flee in another direction. He turned aside a number of other people who saw the infirmary as a convenient escape, so Teft and Lift didn't draw undue attention.

People in the atrium cried out as Kaladin and the Pursuer clashed. Heavenly Ones floated down to watch the battle, their long trains descending like curtains, adding to the surreal sight. In fact, *everybody's* eyes were fixed on the contest between Kaladin and the Pursuer. So, Teft took the Regal guard by the arm. These Regals had that captive lightning running through them, so touching the singer gave Teft a shock. He cried out and shook his hand, backing away as the stormform turned toward him in annoyance.

"Please, Brightlord," Teft said. "What is happening?"

As the Regal focused on him, Lift slipped around behind and cracked the door open.

"Be on with you," the Regal said. "Don't bother—"

Teft rushed the singer, tackling him around the waist and throwing him backward through the open door. The Regal's powers sent another shock through Teft, but in the confusion, Teft was able to get him to the ground and put him in a deadman's hold.

Lift shut the door with a click. She waited, anxious, as Teft struggled to keep pressure on the creature's throat. He pulled in all the Stormlight he had, but felt the stormform's power growing—the creature's skin crackling with red lightning.

"Healing!" Teft said.

Lift leapt over and pressed her hand against his leg as the stormform released a bolt of power straight through Teft into the floor. The *crack* it made was incredible. Teft felt a burning pain, like someone had decided to use his stomach as a convenient place to build their firepit.

But he held on, and Lift healed him. He even managed to roll to the side and use Stormlight to stick the Regal to the ground. That let him keep the pressure on and resist the shocks that followed—less powerful than the first.

Finally the Regal went limp, unconscious. Teft huffed and stood, though he first had to unstick his clothing from the floor. Storming Stormlight. He looked down and found the front of his shirt had been burned clean through.

He glanced to Phendorana, who had grown to full size. She folded her arms thoughtfully.

"What?" he asked.

"Your hair is standing up," she said, then grinned. She looked like a little kid when she did that, and he couldn't help returning the expression.

"Move!" she said to him. "Seal the door!"

"Right, right." He stepped over and infused the doorframe with Stormlight. Someone would have heard that lightning bolt. "Lift," he shouted as he worked, "get to it! I want these Radiants up and taking orders faster than an arrow falls." He glanced to Phendorana, standing beside him and meeting his eyes. "We *can* do this. Get them up, grab Kal's family, get out."

"Through the window?" she asked.

Outside the east-facing window was a sheer drop of hundreds of feet. He felt moderately good about his ability to climb down it. How far would everyone have to get before their Radiant powers returned? He feared the Heavenly Ones would find out before then and come after them.

Well, he'd see what the others said, once they were awake. Teft turned from the now-sealed door to inspect the room and Lift's progress. Where was that surgeon and his—

Lift screamed.

She leaped back as one of the bodies on the floor nearby emerged from beneath the sheet. The figure—dressed all in black—swung a *Shardblade* at her. She nearly managed to get away, but the Blade caught her in the thighs, cutting with the grace of an eel through the air.

Lift collapsed, her legs ruined by the Blade.

The figure in the black uniform turned from Lift and—blazing with Stormlight—focused on Teft. Sunken cheeks, prominent nose, glowing eyes.

Moash.

⁜

Kaladin didn't run.

He knew what the Pursuer would do.

Indeed, the creature acted as he had each time before—dropping a husk and streaking toward Kaladin to grapple him. That was one husk spent. The Pursuer had two others before he would be trapped in his form and had to either flee, or face Kaladin and risk dying.

Kaladin stepped directly into the Pursuer's path and dropped his spear, willingly entering the grapple. Turning at the last moment, he caught the Pursuer's hands as they reached for him. Thrumming with Stormlight, Kaladin held the Pursuer's wrists. Storms, the creature was stronger than he was. But Kaladin wouldn't run or hide. Not this time. This time he only had to give Teft and Lift enough space to work.

And Kaladin had discovered something during their last fight. This creature was *not* a soldier.

"Give in, little man," the Pursuer said. "I am as unavoidable as the coming storm. I will chase you forever."

"Good," Kaladin said.

"Bravado!" the Pursuer said, laughing. He managed to hook Kaladin's foot, then used his superior strength to shove Kaladin to the ground. Best Kaladin could do was hang on and pull him down as well. The Pursuer kneed Kaladin in the gut, then twisted to get him in a hold. "So foolish!"

Kaladin writhed, barely able to keep from being immobilized. Syl flitted around them. As the Pursuer tried for a lock, Kaladin twisted around and met the Pursuer's eyes, then smiled.

The Pursuer growled and repositioned to press Kaladin against the ground by his shoulders.

"I'm not afraid of you," Kaladin said. "But you're going to be afraid of me."

"Madness," the Pursuer said. "Your inevitable fate has caused madness in your frail mind."

Kaladin grunted, back to the cold stone, using both hands to push the Pursuer's right hand away. He kept his eyes locked on to the Pursuer's.

"I killed you," Kaladin said. "And I'll kill you now. Then every time you return for me, I'll kill you *again*."

"I'm immortal," the Pursuer growled. But his rhythm had changed. Not so confident.

"Doesn't matter," Kaladin said. "I've heard what people say about you. Your life isn't the blood in your veins, but the legend you live. Each death kills that legend a little more. Each time I defeat you, it will rip you apart. Until you're no longer known as the Pursuer. You'll be known as the Defeated. The creature who, no matter how hard he tries, *can't ever beat ME.*"

Kaladin reached down and activated Navani's device at his belt, then pressed the grip that dropped the weight. It was as if someone had suddenly tied a rope to his waist, and then pulled him out of the Pursuer's grip, sliding him across the floor of the atrium.

He deactivated the device, then rolled to his feet, looking across the short distance at his enemy. Syl fell in beside him, glaring at the Pursuer in a perfect mimic of his posture. Then, together, they smiled as Kaladin pulled out his scalpel.

⁖

Moash kicked Lift toward the wall, sending her limp and tumbling. She lay still and didn't move after that. Moash floated forward, blade out, attention affixed solely on Teft.

Teft cursed himself for a fool. He'd focused on taking care of the Regal at the door; he should have known to check for irregularities. Now that he looked, he could see Kal's parents and brother bound and gagged, visible through a gap in the cloth of the draped-off section at the rear.

The real trap wasn't outside with the Pursuer. It was in here, with a much deadlier foe: a man who had been trained for war by Kaladin himself.

"Hello, Teft," Moash said softly, landing in front of the rows of unconscious people on the floor. "How are the men?"

"Safe from you," Teft said, pushing aside his cloak and unsheathing the long knife he had hidden underneath. Couldn't move through a crowd unseen with a spear, unfortunately.

"Not all of them, Teft," Moash said. There was a shadow on his face, despite the room's many lit spheres.

Moash lunged forward and Teft danced back, stepping carefully over the body of the unconscious Regal. He had space here in front of the door with no fallen Radiants to upset his footing. All Moash did at first was open a sack and throw something out across the floor nearby. Black sand? What on Roshar?

Teft held out his weapon, Phendorana at his side, but the knife seemed tiny compared to Moash's weapon: the assassin's Honorblade. The one that had killed old Gavilar.

It looked wicked in Moash's hand, shorter than most Blades—but in a lithe, deliberate way. This wasn't a weapon for slaying great monsters of stone.

It was a weapon for killing men.

Humans are a poem. A song.

—Musings of El, on the first of the Final Ten Days

H ey," someone said to the Rhythm of Reprimand, "what are you doing?"

Rlain turned, shifting the barrel of water from one shoulder to the other. Dabbid pulled in close to him, frightened at the challenge. The two of them were in a nondescript passage of Urithiru, close to the steps down to the basement. This was the last guard post, and Rlain thought they had made it past.

"We're delivering water," Rlain said to Consolation, tapping his small water barrel. He wore makeup covering his tattoo, blending it into his skin pattern. "To the scholars."

"Why are you doing it?" the singer said. Not a Fused or Regal, merely an ordinary guard. She walked over and put a hand on Rlain's shoulder. "Let the human do that kind of work, friend. You are meant for greater things."

He glanced at Dabbid—who looked at the ground—and attuned Irritation. This wasn't the kind of resistance he'd anticipated.

"It's my job," Rlain said to the guard.

"Who assigned axehounds' work to a singer?" she demanded. "Come with me. You strike an imposing figure in warform. I'll teach you the sword. We're recruiting for our squad."

"I . . . I would rather do what I'm supposed to," he said to Consolation. He pulled free, and thankfully she let him go. He and Dabbid continued along the hallway.

"Can you believe it?" she said from behind. "How can so many keep on thinking like slaves? It's sad."

"Yeah," one of the other guards said. "I wouldn't expect it of that one most of all, considering."

Rlain attuned Anxiety.

"That one?" the femalen said, her voice echoing in the hallway.

"Yeah, he's that listener, isn't he? The one that was in prison until Raboniel's Voice pulled him out?"

Damnation. Rlain walked a little quicker, but it was no use, as he soon heard boots chasing him. The guard grabbed him by the elbow.

"Wait now," she said. "You're the listener?"

"I am," Rlain said to Consolation.

"Delivering water. You. A traitor?"

"We're not . . ." He attuned Determination and turned around. "We're not traitors. Venli is Raboniel's *Voice*."

"Yeah," the femalen said. "Well, you're not going down where the human queen is, not until I get confirmation that you're allowed. Come with me."

Dabbid pulled in closer to Rlain, trembling. Rlain looked toward the singer guards. Four of them.

No. He wasn't going to fight them. And not only because of the numbers. "Fine," he said. "Let's ask your superior, so I can get on with my duty."

They pulled him away, and Dabbid followed, whimpering softly as they were led—step by step—farther from their goal. Well, if the Sibling wanted him down there for some reason, they'd have to find a way to get him out of this.

⁘

The Pursuer lunged for Kaladin. Kaladin, however, was ready. He activated Navani's device, which was still attached to his belt. That tugged Kaladin backward faster than a man could leap, and so he stayed out of the Pursuer's grip.

By this point, the singers had cleared most of the atrium of civilians. They'd lined the walls with soldiers—but not the flat side of the room with the window—though crowds continued to watch from the hallways and the balconies. Trusting in Kaladin.

Heavenly Ones hovered above the circular chamber, as if to judge the contest. In effect it was an arena. Kaladin projected as much strength and confidence as he could. He almost started to feel it, the worn-out, weathered fatigue retreating.

He needed the Pursuer to believe. To understand. That he had far more to lose from this contest than Kaladin did.

And he seemed to. For as Kaladin reached the other side of the room and disengaged Navani's device, the creature ejected his second body and shot toward Kaladin as a ribbon. He wanted to end this battle quickly.

The window had darkened from the approaching stormwall, which announced the highstorm. It hit with a fury that Kaladin could barely hear, and spheres became the room's only source of light.

Kaladin seized the Fused out of the air as he formed, and they clashed again. That was the Pursuer's third body. If he ejected this time, he'd have to go recharge, or risk forming a fourth body—and being killed.

They went to ground again, rolling as they wrestled, Kaladin trying to maneuver his knife. The Pursuer could heal with Voidlight, but the more of that he lost, the more likely he'd have to retreat.

This time the creature offered no taunts as he tried to get a grip on Kaladin's head. Likely to smash it into the ground, as he knew Kaladin's healing wasn't working properly. That gave Kaladin a chance to stab upward, forcing the Pursuer to grab his arm instead.

"You're no soldier," Kaladin said loudly, his voice echoing to all of those listening. "That's what I realized about you, Defeated One. You've never faced death."

"Silence," the Pursuer growled, twisting Kaladin's wrist.

Kaladin grunted, then rolled them both to the side, narrowly protecting his wrist from serious damage. He dropped the knife. Fortunately, he had found others.

"I've faced it every day of my life!" Kaladin shouted, rolling on top of the Fused. "You wonder why I don't fear you? I've *lived* with the knowledge that death is hounding me. You're nothing new."

"Be. *QUIET!*"

"But I'm something you *have never* known," Kaladin shouted, slamming the Pursuer down by his shoulders. "Thousands of years of life can't prepare you for something you've never met before, Defeated One! It can't prepare you for someone who *does not fear* you!"

Kaladin pulled out his boot knife and raised it. The Pursuer, seeing that coming, didn't do what he should have. He didn't try to grapple or knee Kaladin's stomach. He panicked and shot away as a ribbon of light, fleeing.

He materialized a short distance away in front of the watching soldiers. His fourth body. His last one. The one he was vulnerable in. He turned to look back at Kaladin, now standing atop his husk.

"I am death itself, Defeated One," Kaladin said. "And I've finally caught up to you."

Venli found a mob of people blocking the central corridor as she tried to reach the atrium. She attuned Anxiety and pushed through the press. Since she was a Regal, people did make way. Eventually she reached the front of the crowd, where a group of warforms stood in a line, blocking the way forward.

She suspected she knew what was happening. Rlain and his friends had already begun their rescue plan. She was too late.

"Make room," Venli demanded to Derision. "What is happening?"

One of the warforms turned. Venli didn't know him personally, but he was one of the Pursuer's soldiers. "Our master is fighting Stormblessed," he said. "We're to keep a perimeter, prevent people from interfering."

Venli craned her neck, tall enough to see that the room was being guarded by about a hundred of the Pursuer's troops, though she also saw some of Raboniel's personal guard—which she'd picked up from Leshwi.

Venli attuned the Terrors. What now? Could she help? She found, as she searched, that she genuinely *wanted* to. Not because Timbre was pushing her, and not because this was merely the path she was on. But because of the songs of the stones. And the whispers of those who had come before her.

"I'm the Voice of the Lady of Wishes," Venli said. "You think that your blockade applies to me? Step aside."

Reluctantly, the soldiers made way for her. And once she had a clear view, she couldn't help but pause. There *was* something about the way Stormblessed fought. Even grappling with the Pursuer, rolling across the ground, there was a certain determination to him. He freed himself from the grapple, then somehow leaped back twenty feet, though his powers shouldn't have been working that well.

The Pursuer became a ribbon and chased him, but Stormblessed didn't run. He reached out and *seized* the Pursuer right as he appeared. Fascinating. She could see why Leshwi found the human so interesting.

There was nothing Venli could do about this battle. She had to think about Rlain, and Lirin and his family. She searched the air and located Leshwi hovering nearby.

Venli made her way over to Leshwi as Stormblessed stood tall atop the Pursuer's husk. The lady floated down. She would not interfere in a duel such as this.

"This looks bad for Stormblessed," Venli whispered.

"No," Leshwi said to Exultation. "The Pursuer has used all of his husks. He will need to flee and renew."

"Why doesn't he?" Venli asked.

"Look," Leshwi said, and pointed at the silent atrium. A perimeter of soldiers with humans crowded behind them, peeking through. Fused in the air. All staring at the two combatants.

An incredible soldier, who seemed immortal and impervious, completely in control.

And a Fused, who somehow looked small by comparison.

.•.

Teft dodged through the infirmary. He didn't dare engage Moash directly; instead he tried to stay out of reach. Buying time. For what though?

Moash drifted closer to them, eyes glowing.

"Stormblessed isn't going to come in and help, is he?" Phendorana asked softly, floating beside Teft.

"Kaladin can't be everywhere at once," Teft said. "He's just one man, though he often forgets that." He jumped backward over a body. Lift had stirred, and was quietly pulling herself across the ground toward one of the nearby Radiants, her legs dragging behind.

Good girl, Teft thought. He needed to keep Moash's attention.

"Never known a man to turn traitor as hard as you did," Teft called to Moash. "What was it that got you? What made you willing to kill your own?"

"Peace," Moash said, halting in the middle of the room. "It was peace, Teft."

"This is peace?" Teft said, gesturing. "Fighting your friends?"

"We're not fighting. You run like a coward."

"Every good sergeant is a coward! And proud of it! Someone needs to talk sense to the officers!"

Moash hovered in place, a black stain in the air. Before he could look and see Lift, Phendorana appeared to him, standing a short distance away. Moash glanced toward her sharply. Good, good. Distraction.

Moash, however, casually turned and slashed his Shardblade through the face of a Radiant beneath him. The unconscious woman's eyes burned and Lift cried out in horror, heaving herself forward to reach the body—as if she could do anything.

Moash glanced at Teft, then raised his Blade toward Lift.

"Fine!" Teft said, striding forward. "Bastard! You want me? Fine! Fight me! I'll show you who the better man is!"

Moash landed beside the body and walked straight toward Teft. "We both know who the better warrior is, Teft."

"I didn't say better warrior, you idiot," Teft said, lunging in with his knife. The stab was a feint, but Moash knew it. He sidestepped at precisely the right time, and tripped Teft as he tried to turn and swing again.

Teft went down with a grunt. He tried to roll, but Moash landed and kicked him in the side, hard. Something *crunched* in Teft's chest. A wound that blossomed with pain and didn't heal, despite his Stormlight.

Moash loomed overhead and raised his Blade, then swung it down without further comment. Teft dropped his knife—useless against a Blade—and raised his hands. He felt something from Phendorana. A harmony between them.

Teft was forgiven. Teft was *forgiven* and he was *close*.

Moash's Shardblade met something in the air—a phantom spear shaft, barely coalescing between Teft's hands—and *stopped*. It threw sparks, but it *stopped*. Teft gritted his teeth and held on as Moash finally showed an emotion. Surprise. He stumbled back, his eyes wide.

Teft let go, and Phendorana appeared beside him on the ground, puffing from exertion. He felt sweat trickling down his brow. Manifesting her like that—even a little—had been like trying to push an axehound through a keyhole. He wasn't certain he, or she, could do it a second time.

Best to try something else. Teft held his side, grimacing as he forced himself into a kneeling position. "All right, lad. I'm done. You got me. I surrender. Let's wait for Kaladin to show up, and you can continue this conversation with him."

"I'm not here for Kaladin, Teft," Moash said softly. "And I'm not here for your surrender."

Teft steeled himself. *Grapple him*, he thought. *Make that Blade a liability, too big to use.* His best hope.

Because Teft *did* have hope. That was what he'd recovered, these years in Bridge Four. The moss might take him again, but if it did . . . well, he would fight back again. The past could rot.

Teft, Windrunner, had *hope*.

He managed to get to his feet, prepared for Moash to lunge at him—but when Moash moved, it wasn't toward Teft. It was toward Phendorana.

What? Teft stood stunned as Moash pulled a strange dagger from his belt and slammed it down—right where Phendorana was kneeling.

She looked up with surprise and took the knife straight in the forehead. Then she screamed.

Teft leaped for her, howling, watching in horror as she *shrank*, writhing as Moash's dagger pinned her to the floor. Her essence *burned*, flaring outward like an explosion.

Something ripped inside Teft. Something deeper than his own heart. A part of his soul, his being, was torn away. He collapsed immediately, falling near the white spot in the sand that was all that remained of Phendorana.

No. No . . .

It hurt so much. Agony like a sudden terrible stillness. Nothingness. *Emptiness.*

It . . . it can't be. . . .

Moash tucked the dagger away methodically. "I can't feel sorrow anymore, Teft. For that I am grateful."

Moash turned Teft over with his foot. His broken ribs screamed, but felt like such an insignificant pain now.

"But you know what?" Moash said, standing over him. "There was *always* a part of me that resented how you were so eager to follow him. Right from the start, his little axehound. Licking his feet. He loves you. I thought I'd have to use his father. But I am . . . satisfied to have found something better."

"You are a monster," Teft whispered.

Moash took Teft calmly by the front of his burned shirt and hoisted him up. "I am no monster. I am merely silence. The quiet that eventually takes all men."

"Tell yourself that lie, Moash," Teft growled, gripping the hand that held him, his own hand clawlike from the horrible pain. "But know this. You can kill me, but you can't have what I have. You can *never* have it. Because *I* die knowing I'm loved."

Moash grunted and dropped him to the ground. Then he stabbed Teft directly through the neck with his Shardblade.

Confident, and somehow still full of hope, Teft died.

For ones so soft, they are somehow strong.

—Musings of El, on the first of the Final Ten Days

The highstorm blowing outside the enormous window presented a view that Kaladin often saw, but others rarely knew. Flashing lightning, a swirling tempest, power raw and unchained.

Kaladin stepped off the Pursuer's decaying husk and walked forward. *Toward* the enemy.

The Pursuer searched around, likely realizing how large his audience was. Hundreds watching. He lived by lore, by reputation. He always killed anyone who killed him. He won each conflict eventually.

Now he saw that crumbling. Kaladin could hear it in the increasingly panicked rhythm the Pursuer hummed. Saw it in his eyes.

"Run," Kaladin told him. "Flee. I'll chase you. I will *never* stop. I am eternal. I am the storm."

The Pursuer stumbled back, but then encountered his soldiers holding the perimeter, humming an encouraging rhythm. Behind them humans gawked, their foreheads painted.

"Has it been long enough, do you think?" Syl whispered. "Are the others free?"

"Hopefully," Kaladin said. "But I don't think they'll be able to escape into that highstorm."

"Then they'll have to come out here, and we'll have to push for the crystal pillar room," she said, looking toward the infirmary. "Why haven't they appeared yet?"

"Once we defeat the Pursuer—when he breaks and runs—we'll find out," Kaladin said, unhooking Navani's device from his waist.

"Something's wrong," she said softly. "Something dark . . ."

Kaladin stepped to the very center of the atrium, marked by a swirling pattern of strata. He pointed his knife at the Pursuer. "Last body," Kaladin called. "Come fight, and we'll see who dies. We'll see if your reputation survives the hour."

The Pursuer, to his credit, came charging in. As he arrived, grabbing Kaladin, Kaladin pressed Navani's device against the Pursuer's chest and Lashed the bar down, binding it in place.

It launched backward, carrying the Pursuer with it. He slammed into the glass of the window, and his carapace cracked as he struck. He shook himself, recovering quickly—but didn't heal. He'd used up his Voidlight.

With effort, the Pursuer struggled to move the device, and managed to extricate himself from it—leaving it pressed to the window, which was smeared with his orange blood. More blood dripped from the cracked carapace at his chest.

Kaladin stalked toward him, holding the knife. "Flee."

The Pursuer's eyes widened and he stepped to the side, toward his soldiers.

"Flee!" Kaladin said.

The creature fell silent, no humming, no speaking.

"RUN FROM ME!" Kaladin demanded.

He did, dripping blood and shoving his way past the singer soldiers. He'd retreated from previous battles, but this time they both knew it meant something different.

This creature was no longer the Pursuer. He knew it. The singers knew it. And the humans watching behind knew it. They began to chant, gloryspren bursting in the air.

Stormblessed.

Stormblessed.

Stormblessed.

Trembling, Kaladin retrieved and deactivated Navani's device, then returned to the center of the room. He could feel their energy propelling him. A counter to the darkness.

He turned toward the infirmary. The door had been opened. When had that happened? He stepped toward it, but could see the Radiants in their lines on the floor, covered in sheets. Why weren't they up and awake? Were they feigning? That could work, pretending they were still asleep.

Something dropped from above. A body hit the ground in front of Kaladin with a callous *smack* of skull on stone. It rolled, and Kaladin saw burned-out eyes. A terribly familiar bearded face. A face that had smiled at him countless times, cursed at him an equal number, but had always been there when everything else went dark.

Teft.

Teft was dead.

⁘

Moash landed a short distance from where Kaladin knelt over Teft's body. Several of the watching soldiers stepped toward the Windrunner, but Moash raised his hand and stopped them.

"No," he said softly as Heavenly Ones hovered down around him. "Leave him be. This is how we win."

Moash knew exactly what Kaladin was feeling. That crushing sense of despair, that knowledge that nothing would be the same. Nothing could *ever* be the same. Light had left the world, and could never be rekindled.

Kaladin cradled Teft's corpse, letting out a low, piteous whine. He began to tremble and shake—becoming as insensate as he had when King Elhokar had died. As he had after Moash had killed Roshone. And if Kaladin responded that way to the deaths of his enemies . . .

Well, Teft dying would be worse. Far, far worse. Kaladin had been unraveling for years.

"That," Moash said to the Fused, "is how you break a storm. He'll be useless from here on out. Make sure nobody touches him. I have something to do."

He walked into the infirmary room. At the rear was the model of the tower, intricate in its detail, cut into a cross section with one half on either side. He knelt and peered at a copy of the room with the crystal pillar.

Beside it, produced in miniature, were a small crystal globe and gemstone. The fabrial glowed with a tiny light, barely visible. The final node of the tower's defenses, placed where anyone who looked would see it, but think nothing of it.

Raboniel had known though. How long? He suspected she'd figured it out days ago, and was stalling to continue her research here. That one was trouble. He summoned his Blade and used the tip to destroy the tiny fabrial.

Then he walked over to the sectioned-off portion of the room. The child Edgedancer lay here, tied up and unconscious, next to Kaladin's parents and brother. Odium was interested in the Edgedancer, and Moash had been forbidden to kill her. Hopefully he hadn't struck her head too hard. He didn't always control that as he should.

For now, he grabbed Lirin by his bound hands and dragged him—

screaming through his gag—out of the infirmary. There Moash waited until the Pursuer came flying back as a shameful ribbon of light.

The Pursuer formed a body, and Moash pushed Lirin into the creature's hands. "This is Stormblessed's father," Moash whispered. "No! Don't say it loudly. Don't draw Kaladin's attention. His father is insurance; Kaladin has huge issues with the man. If Kaladin somehow regains his senses, *immediately* kill his father in front of him."

"This is nonsense," the Pursuer growled. "I could kill Stormblessed now."

"No," Moash said, grabbing the Pursuer and pointing at his face. "You know I have our master's blessing. You know I speak to Command. You *will not* touch Stormblessed. You can't hurt him; you can't kill him."

"He's . . . just a man. . . ."

"*Don't touch him,*" Moash said. "If you interfere, it will awaken him to vengeance. We don't want that yet. There are two paths open to him. One is to take the route I did, and give up his pain. The other is the route he *should* have taken long ago. The path where he raises the only hand that can kill Kaladin Stormblessed. His own."

The Pursuer didn't like it, judging by the rhythm he hummed. But he accepted Kaladin's bound and gagged father and seemed willing to stay put.

The guards had quieted the rowdy humans, and the atrium was falling still. Kaladin knelt before the storm, clinging to a dead man, shaking. Moash hesitated, searching inside himself. And . . . he felt nothing. Just coldness.

Good. He had reached his potential.

"Don't ruin this," he told the gathered Fused. "I need to go kill a queen."

◆◆

Navani waited for her chance.

She had tried talking to the Sibling, but had heard only whimpers. So she had returned to the front of her room to wait for her chance to arrive.

It came when her door guard suddenly shouted, putting her hands to her head in disbelief. She ran down the hallway. When Navani peeked out, she saw what had caused the commotion: the field around the crystal pillar was gone. Someone had destroyed the final node. The Sibling was exposed.

Navani almost ran over to attack with the anti-Voidlight dagger. She hesitated though, eyeing her traps in the hallway.

A magnet. I need a magnet.

She'd seen one earlier, near the wreckage of her desk. She scrambled over and picked it up out of the rubble. Outside, she heard Raboniel's order echo with a clear voice.

"Run," she said to the guard. "Tell the Word of Deeds and the Night Known to attend me. We have work to do."

The guard dashed away. When Navani peeked out again, Raboniel was stepping into the chamber with the crystal pillar, alone.

A chance. Navani slipped into the hallway and moved quietly toward Raboniel. After passing the crates with her carefully prepared traps, she touched the magnet to a corner of the last crate and heard a *click*. She only dared take the time to arm one: a painrial that filled anyone who crossed this point in the hallway with immense agony.

That done, she moved to the end of the corridor. The room with the crystal pillar seemed darker than she remembered it. The Sibling had been almost fully corrupted.

Raboniel stood with her hand pressed against the pillar to finish the job. Navani forced herself forward, dagger held in a tight grip.

"You should run, Navani," Raboniel said to a calm rhythm, her voice echoing in the room. "There is a copy of our notebook on my desk in the hallway, along with your anti-Voidlight plate. Take them and make your escape."

Navani froze in place, holding the dagger's hilt so tightly, she thought she might never be able to uncurl her fingers.

She knows I'm here. She knows what she did in sending the guard away. Logic, Navani. What does it mean?

"You're letting me go on purpose?" she said.

"Since the final node has been destroyed," Raboniel said, "Vyre will soon return to claim his promised compensation. However, if you have escaped on your own . . . well, then I have not defaulted on my covenant with him."

"I can't leave the Sibling to you."

"What do you think to do?" Raboniel asked. "Fight me?" She turned, so calm and composed. Her eyes flickered to the dagger, then she hummed softly to a confused rhythm. She'd forgotten about it. She wasn't as in control as she pretended.

"Is this how you wish to end our association?" Raboniel asked. "Struggling like brutes in the wilderness? Scholars such as we, reduced to the exploitation of common blades? Run, Navani. You cannot defeat a Fused in battle."

She was right on that count. "I can't abandon the Sibling," Navani said. "My honor won't allow it."

"We're all children of Odium in the end," Raboniel said. "Children of our Passions."

"You just said we were scholars," Navani said. "Others might be controlled by their passions. We are something more. Something better." She took a deep breath, then turned the dagger in her hand, hilt out. "I'll give you this, then you and I can go back to my room to wait together. If Vyre *does* defeat Stormblessed, I will submit to him. If not, you will agree to leave the Sibling."

"A foolish gamble," Raboniel said.

"No, a compromise. We can discuss as we wait, and if we come to a more perfect accommodation, all the better." She proffered the dagger.

"Very well," Raboniel said. She took the dagger with a quick snap of her hand, showing that she didn't completely trust Navani. As well she shouldn't.

Raboniel strode down the hallway, Navani following several paces behind.

"Let's get to this quickly, Navani," Raboniel said. "I should think that the two of us—"

Then Raboniel stepped directly into Navani's fabrial trap.

106

A HUNDRED DISCORDANT RHYTHMS

For ones so varied, they are somehow intense.

—Musings of El, on the first of the Final Ten Days

K aladin clung to Teft's limp form and felt it all crumbling. The flimsy facade of confidence he had built to let himself fight. The way he pretended he was fine.

Syl landed on his shoulder, arms wrapped around herself, and said nothing. What was there to say?

It was over.

It was all just . . . over. What was there to life if he couldn't protect the people he loved?

Long ago, he'd promised himself he'd try one last time. He'd try to save the men of Bridge Four. And he'd failed.

Teft had been so vibrant, so alive. So sturdy and so constant. He'd finally defeated his own monsters, had really come into his own, claiming his Radiance. He had been a wonderful, loving, *amazing* man.

He'd depended on Kaladin. Like Tien. Like a hundred others. But he couldn't save them. He *couldn't* protect them.

Syl whimpered, shrinking in on herself. Kaladin wished he could shrink as well. Maybe if he'd lived as his father wanted, he could have avoided this. He said he fought to protect, but he didn't end up protecting anything, did he? He just destroyed. Killed.

Kaladin Stormblessed wasn't dead. He'd never existed.

Kaladin Stormblessed was a lie. He always had been.

The numbness claimed him. That hollow darkness that was so much worse than pain. He couldn't think. Didn't want to think. Didn't want anything.

This time, Adolin wasn't there to pull him out of it. To force him to keep walking. This time, Kaladin was given exactly what he deserved.

Nothing. And nothingness.

Navani froze in place. Raboniel—suddenly struck with incredible pain from Navani's trap—collapsed, dropping the dagger. Steeling herself, Navani went down on her hands and knees, then lunged forward to grab it.

The pain was excruciating. But Navani had tested these devices upon herself, and she knew what they did. She lost control of her legs, but managed to crawl forward and plunge the dagger into Raboniel's chest. She kept her weight on the weapon, pressing it down, smelling burned flesh.

Raboniel screamed, writhing, clawing at Navani. The painrial did its job however, and prevented her from fighting back effectively.

"I'm sorry," Navani said through gritted teeth. "I'm . . . sorry. But next time . . . try . . . not . . . to be . . . *so trusting.*"

The painrial soon ran out. Navani had set it up days ago, with a small Voidlight gemstone for power. It hadn't been intended to work for very long. She was pleased by the range though. She'd specifically worked on that feature.

Navani sat up, then wrapped her arms around herself, trying to fight off the phantom effects of the pain. Finally she looked toward Raboniel's corpse.

And found the Fused's eyes quivering, not glassy and white like her daughter's had been. Navani scrambled away.

Raboniel moved her arms limply, then turned her head toward Navani.

"How?" Navani demanded. "Why are you alive?"

"Not . . . enough . . . Light . . ." Raboniel croaked. She gripped the knife in her chest and pulled it free, letting out a sigh. "It hurts. I'm . . . I'm . . . not . . ." She closed her eyes, though she continued to breathe.

Navani inched forward, wary.

"You must take . . . the notebook . . ." Raboniel said. "And you must . . . run. Vyre . . . returns."

"You tell me to run, after I tried to kill you?"

"Not . . . tried . . ." Raboniel said. "I . . . cannot hear rhythms. . . . My soul . . . dying . . ." She pried open her eyes and fixed them on Navani. "You . . . tricked me well, Navani. Clever, clever. Well . . . done."

"How can you say that?" Navani said, glancing toward the desk and the papers on it.

"Live . . . as long as I . . . and you can appreciate . . . anything . . . that still surprises you. . . . Go, Navani. Run . . . The war must . . . end."

Navani felt sick, now that she'd gone through with it. An unexpected pain pricked her at the betrayal. Nevertheless, she moved to the desk and picked up the notebook.

I need to get this out of the tower, she realized. *It is perhaps even more important than the Sibling. A way to kill Fused permanently. A way to . . .*

To end the war. If both Radiant spren and Fused could die for good, it *could* stop, couldn't it?

"Stormfather," she whispered. "That's what it was all about." Raboniel wanted to end the war, one way or another. The notebook Navani held was a copy, and Navani realized that the original notebook would be in Kholinar, delivered to the leaders of the singer military—likely along with the vacuum chamber and the metal plates.

Navani walked over to Raboniel. "You wanted a way to end it," she said. "You don't care who wins."

"I care," Raboniel whispered. "I want . . . the singers to win. But your side . . . winning . . . is better than . . . than . . ."

"Than the war continuing forever," Navani said.

Raboniel nodded, her eyes closed. "Go. Run. Vyre will—"

Navani looked up as a blur flashed in the hallway, reflecting light. A *thump* hit her chest, and she grunted at the impact, stunned—briefly—before pain began to wash through her body. Sharp and alarming.

A knife, she thought, befuddled to see the hilt of a throwing knife sticking from the side of her torso, next to her right breast. When she took a breath, the pain sharpened with a sudden spike.

She looked up, pressing her hand to the wound, feeling warm blood spill out. At the far end of the hallway, a figure in a black uniform walked slowly forward. A Shardblade appeared in his hand. The assassin's Blade.

Moash had returned.

Highmarshal Kaladin was dead.

⁘

Venli watched the human, so consumed by his grief that he knelt there, motionless, for minutes on end. And they all watched. Silent Heavenly Ones. Solemn guards. Disbelieving humans. No one seemed to want to speak, or even breathe.

That was how Venli should have felt upon losing her sister. Why didn't she have the emotions of a normal person? She'd been sad, but she didn't think she'd *ever* been so overcome by grief that she acted like Stormblessed.

Timbre pulsed comfortingly inside her. Everyone was different. And Venli *was* on the right path.

Except . . . there wasn't really a point in returning to help now, was there? It was over. Beside her, Leshwi descended until her feet touched the ground, then she bowed her head.

Show her, Timbre pulsed. *What you are.*

"What? Now?"

Show her.

Reveal what she was, in front of everyone? Venli shrank at the thought, attuning the Terrors.

One by one the other Heavenly Ones touched down, as if in respect. For an enemy.

"This is stupidity," the Pursuer said, shoving Lirin into Leshwi's hands. "I can't believe we're all just standing here."

Leshwi looked up from her vigil, humming to Spite. Then, amazingly, she pulled out a knife and cut Lirin's hands free.

"I have not forgotten how you tried to turn the Nine against me," the Pursuer said, pointing at Leshwi. "You seek to destroy my legacy."

"Your legacy is dead, Defeated One," Leshwi said. "It died when you ran from him."

"My legacy is untouched!" the Pursuer roared, causing Venli to stumble back, afraid. "And this is complete madness! I will prove myself and continue my tradition!"

"No!" Leshwi said, passing the still-gagged human to one of the other Heavenly Ones. She grabbed the Pursuer, but he left a husk in her hand, exploding out as a ribbon of light to cross the atrium floor.

"No . . ." Venli whispered.

The Pursuer appeared above Stormblessed. The Fused yanked a sharpened carapace spur off his arm, then—holding it like a dagger—he grabbed the kneeling man by one shoulder.

Kaladin Stormblessed looked up and let loose a howl that seemed to vibrate with a hundred discordant rhythms. Venli attuned the Lost in return.

The Pursuer stabbed, but Stormblessed grabbed his arm and turned, becoming a blur of motion. He somehow twisted around so he was behind the Pursuer, then found a knife somewhere on his person—moving with such speed that Venli had trouble tracking him. Stormblessed slammed the knife at the Pursuer's neck, who barely ejected from the husk in time.

He re-formed and tried to grab Stormblessed again. But there was no contest now. Kaladin moved like the wind, fast and flowing as he rammed his dagger through the Pursuer's arm, causing him to shout in pain. A knife toward the face followed, and the Pursuer ejected yet again. No one chanted or shouted this time, but when Stormblessed turned around, Venli saw his face—and she immediately attuned the Terrors.

His eyes were glowing like a Radiant's, his face a mask of pain and anguish, but the eyes . . . she *swore* the light had a yellowish-red cast to it. Like . . . like . . .

The Pursuer appeared near the soldiers at the perimeter by the wall. "Go!" he shouted to his men. "Attack him! Kill him, and then kill the other Radiants! Your orders are chaos and death!"

The Pursuer charged forward. The soldiers followed, then shied away. They wouldn't face Stormblessed and those eyes of his, so the Pursuer was left with no choice but to engage. Venli didn't know if he realized, but he was on his final body. Perhaps he knew he couldn't run this time, not and salvage any kind of reputation.

Stormblessed dashed to him, and they met near the vast window, flashing with lightning. The Pursuer tried to grab him, and Kaladin welcomed it, folding into the deadly embrace—then expertly slamming them both up against the window. Kaladin pressed the Pursuer to the glass—the storm outside flashed, shaking the tower, vibrating it and splashing it with light.

In that moment, Kaladin did something to the window. As he stepped back, he left the Pursuer stuck to the glass, immobilized and lacking the Voidlight to eject his soul. Kaladin didn't attack. Instead he reached down and infused the ground, but with power that didn't glow as strong as she thought it should.

The Pursuer's head . . . it was pulling forward against his neck, his eyes bulging. He groaned, and Venli realized that Stormblessed had infused the ground, then made it *pull* on the Pursuer's head. But his body was stuck to the wall.

Kaladin turned and strode toward the watching Heavenly Ones as the Pursuer's head *ripped* from his body and slammed to the floor with a crunch.

"Stormblessed," Leshwi said, stepping out to meet him. "You have fought and won. Your loss is powerful, I know, as mortals are—"

Kaladin shoved her aside. He was coming for Venli, she was sure of it. She braced herself, but he stalked past her, leaving her trembling to the Terrors. Instead Kaladin strode for the Heavenly One who was holding his father. Of course.

That Heavenly One panicked as any would. She shot off into the air, carrying the man. Two other Heavenly Ones followed.

Stormblessed looked up, then launched into the air using the strange fabrial that mimicked the Lashings.

Venli slumped to the ground, feeling worn out, though she hadn't done anything. At least it seemed to be over.

But not for the soldiers from the Pursuer's personal army, who gathered around his corpse. Dead a second time, to the same man. His reputation might be in shambles, but he *was* still Fused. He would return.

The soldiers turned toward the infirmary, remembering his last orders. They couldn't kill Stormblessed.

But they could finish off the invalid Radiants.

⁖

Kaladin could barely see straight. He had only a vague memory of killing the Pursuer. He knew he'd done it, but remembering was hard. Thinking was hard.

He soared upward, chasing the creatures who had taken his father. He heard Lirin's shouts echoing from above, so he'd gotten his gag off. Each sound condemned Kaladin.

He didn't actually believe he could save his father. It was as if Lirin was already dead, and was screaming at Kaladin from Damnation. Kaladin wasn't exactly certain why he followed, but he had to get up high. Perhaps . . . perhaps he could see better from up high. . . .

Syl streaked ahead of him, entering the shafts that let lifts reach the final tiers of the tower. She landed on the topmost level of Urithiru. Kaladin arrived after activating a second weight halfway through the flight, then swung himself over the railing and deactivated the device in one move. He landed facing a Heavenly One who tried to block his path.

Kaladin . . .

He left that Heavenly One broken and dying, then tore through the upper chambers. Where?

The roof. They'd make for the roof to escape. Indeed, he found another Fused blocking the stairwell up, and Kaladin slammed Navani's device into the Fused's chest and locked it in place, sending him flying away, up through the stairwell and off into the sky.

Kaladin . . . I've forgotten. . . . Syl's voice. She was zipping around him, but he could barely hear her.

Kaladin burst out onto the top of the tower. The storm spread out around them, almost to the pinnacle, a dark ocean of black clouds rumbling with discontent.

The last of the Heavenly Ones was here, holding Kaladin's father. The Fused backed away, shouting something Kaladin couldn't understand.

Kaladin . . . I've forgotten . . . the Words. . . .

He advanced on the Heavenly One, and in a panic she threw his father. Out. Into the blackness. Kaladin saw Lirin's face for a brief moment before he vanished. Into the pit. The swirling storm and tempest.

Kaladin scrambled to the edge of the tower and looked down. Suddenly he knew why he'd come this high. He knew where he was going. He'd stood on this ledge before. Long ago in the rain.

This time he jumped.

107

UNITING

For ones so lost, they are somehow determined.

—Musings of El, on the first of the Final Ten Days

Navani managed to get to her feet, but after a few steps—fleeing toward the pillar, away from Moash—she was light-headed and woozy. Each breath was agony, and she was losing so much blood. She stumbled and pressed up against the wall—smearing blood across a mural of a comet-shaped spren—to keep from falling.

She glanced over her shoulder. Moash continued walking, an inevitable motion. Not rushed. His sword—with its elegant curve—held to the side so it left a small cut in the floor beside him.

"Lighteyes," Moash said. "Lying eyes. Rulers who fail to rule. Your son was a coward at the end, Queen. He begged me for his life, crying. Appropriate that he should die as he lived."

She saved her breath, not daring to respond despite her fury, and pressed on down the hallway, trailing blood.

"I killed a friend today," Moash said, his terrible voice growing softer. "I thought surely *that* would hurt. Remarkably, it didn't. I have become my best self. Free. No more pain. I bring you silence, Navani. Payment for what you've done. How you've lived. The way you—"

Navani hazarded a glance over her shoulder as he cut off suddenly. Moash had stopped above Raboniel's body. The Fused had latched on to his foot with one hand. He cocked his head, seeming baffled.

Raboniel *launched* herself at him, clawing up his body. Her legs didn't work, but she gripped Moash with talonlike fingers, snarling, and stabbed him repeatedly with the dagger Navani had left.

The knife had no anti-Voidlight remaining—but it *was* draining his Stormlight. Raboniel had reversed the blade. Moash flinched at the attack, distracted, trying to maneuver his Shardblade to fight off the crazed Fused who grappled with him.

Move! Navani thought to herself. Raboniel was trying to buy time.

Even with renewed vigor, Navani didn't get far before the pain became too much. She stumbled into the room with the crystal pillar, abandoning thoughts of trying to escape into the tunnels beneath Urithiru.

Instead she forced herself forward to the pillar, then fell against it. "Sibling," she whispered, tasting blood on her lips. "Sibling?"

She expected to hear whimpering or weeping—the only response she'd received over the last few days. This time she heard a strange tone, both harmonious and discordant at once.

The Rhythm of War.

· ·

Dalinar flew through the air, Lashed by Lyn the Windrunner, on his way to find the Herald Ishar.

He felt something . . . rumbling. A distant storm. Everything was light around him up here, the sun shining, making it difficult to believe that somewhere it was dark and tempestuous. Somewhere, someone was lost in that blackness.

The Stormfather appeared beside him, moving in the air alongside Dalinar—a rare occurrence. The Stormfather never had features. Merely a vague impression of a figure the same size as Dalinar, yet extending into infinity.

Something was wrong.

"What?" Dalinar said.

The Son of Tanavast has entered the storm for the last time, the Stormfather said. *I feel him.*

"Kaladin?" Dalinar said, eager. "He's escaped?"

No. This is something far worse.

"Show me."

· ·

Kaladin fell.

The wind tossed him and whipped at him. He was just rags. Just . . . rags for a person.

I've forgotten the Words, Kaladin, Syl said, weeping. *I see only darkness.* He felt something in his hand, her fingers somehow gripping his as they fell in the storm.

He couldn't save Teft.

He couldn't save his father.

He couldn't save himself.

He'd pushed too hard, used a grindstone on his soul until it had become paper thin. He'd failed anyway.

Those were the only Words that mattered. The only true Words.

"I'm not strong enough," he whispered to the angry winds, and closed his eyes, letting go of her hand.

※

Dalinar was the storm around Kaladin. And at the same time he wasn't. The Stormfather didn't give Dalinar as much control as he had before, likely fearing that Dalinar would want to push him again. He was right.

Dalinar watched Kaladin tumble. Lost. No Stormlight. Eyes closed. It wasn't the bearing of a man who was fighting. Nor was it the bearing of someone who rode the winds.

It was the bearing of someone who had given up.

What do we do? Dalinar asked the Stormfather.

We witness. It is our duty.

We must help.

There is no help, Dalinar. He is too close to the tower's interference to use his powers, and you cannot blow him free of this.

Dalinar watched, pained, the rain his tears. There had to be something. *The moment between,* Dalinar said. *When you infuse spheres. You can stop time.*

Slow it greatly, the Stormfather said, *through Investiture and Connection to the Spiritual. But just briefly.*

Do it, Dalinar said. *Give him more time.*

※

Venli hummed to Agony as the slaughter began.

Not of the Radiants, not yet. Of the *civilians.* As soon as the Pursuer's soldiers started toward the helpless Radiants, the watching crowd of humans went insane. Led by a few determined souls—including a gruff-looking man with one arm—the humans started fighting. A full-on rebellion.

Of unarmed people against trained soldiers in warform.

Venli turned away as the killing began. The humans didn't give up though. They flooded the space between the warforms and the room with the Radiants, blocking the way with their own bodies.

"Can we prevent this?" Venli asked Leshwi, who had settled beside her after being pushed aside by Stormblessed.

"I will need the authority of Raboniel to countermand this particular order," Leshwi said to Abashment. "The Pursuer has command of law in the tower. I have already sent another of the Heavenly Ones to ask Raboniel."

Venli winced at the screams. "But Raboniel said these Radiants were to be preserved!"

"No longer," Leshwi said. "Something happened in the night. Raboniel had needed the Radiants for tests she intended to perform, but she had one of them brought to her, and afterward she said she needed no further tests. The rest are now a liability, possibly a danger, should they wake." She looked toward the dying humans, then shied away as some warforms ran past with bloody axes.

"It is . . . unfortunate," Leshwi said. "I do not sing to Joy in this type of conflict. But we have done it before, and will do it again, in the name of reclaiming our world."

"Can't we be better?" Venli begged to Disappointment. "Isn't there a way?"

Leshwi looked at her, cocking her head. Venli had again used one of the wrong rhythms.

Venli searched the room, past the angerspren and fearspren. Some of the singer troops weren't joining in the killing. She picked out Rothan and Malal, Leshwi's soldiers. They hesitated and did not join in. Leshwi picked better people than that.

Show her, Timbre pulsed. *Showhershowhershowher.*

Venli braced herself. Then she drew in Stormlight from the spheres in her pocket, and let herself begin glowing.

Leshwi hummed immediately to Destruction and grabbed Venli by the face in a powerful grip.

"What?" she said. *"What have you done?"*

⁘

Kaladin entered the place between moments.

He'd met the Stormfather here on that first horrible night when he'd been strung up in the storm. The night when Syl had fought so hard to protect him.

This time he drifted in the darkness. No wind tossed him, and the air became impossibly calm, impossibly quiet. As if he were floating alone in the ocean.

Why won't you say the Words? the Stormfather asked.

"I've forgotten them," Kaladin whispered.

You have not.

"Will they mean anything if I don't feel them, Stormfather? Can I *lie* to swear an Ideal?"

Silence. Pure, incriminating silence.

"He wants me, as he wanted Moash," Kaladin said. "If he keeps pushing, he'll have me. So I have to go."

That is a lie, the Stormfather said. It is his ultimate lie, Son of Honor. The lie that says you have no choice. The lie that there is no more journey worth taking.

He was right. A tiny part of Kaladin—a part that could not lie to himself—knew it was true.

"What if I'm too tired?" Kaladin whispered. "What if there's nothing left to give? What if *that* is why I cannot say your Words, Stormfather? What if it's just too much?"

You would consign my daughter to misery again?

Kaladin winced, but it was true. Could he do that to Syl?

He gritted his teeth as he began to struggle. Began to fight through the nothingness. Through the inability to think. He fought through the pain, the agony—still raw—of losing his friend.

He screamed, trembled, then sank inward.

"Too weak," he whispered.

There simply wasn't anything left for him to give.

⁘

It's not enough, Dalinar said. He couldn't see in this endless darkness, yet he could *feel* someone inside it. Two someones. Kaladin and his spren.

Storms. They hurt.

We need to give them more time, Dalinar said.

We cannot, the Stormfather said. *Respect his frailty, and don't force me on this, Dalinar! You could break things you do not understand, the consequences of which could be catastrophic.*

Have you no compassion? Dalinar demanded. *Have you no heart?*

I am a storm, the Stormfather said. *I chose the ways of a storm.*

Choose better, then! Dalinar searched in the darkness, the infinity. He was full of Stormlight in a place where that didn't matter.

In a place where all things Connected. A place beyond Shadesmar. A place beyond time. A place where . . .

What is that? Dalinar asked. *That warmth.*

I feel nothing.

Dalinar drew the warmth close, and understood. *This place is where you make the visions happen, isn't it?* Dalinar asked. *Time sometimes moved oddly in those.*

Yes, the Stormfather said. *But you must have Connection for a vision. You must have a reason for it. A meaning. It cannot be just anything.*

GOOD, Dalinar said, forging a bond.

What are you doing?

CONNECTING HIM, Dalinar said. UNITING HIM.

The Stormfather rumbled. *With what?*

For ones so confused, they are somehow brilliant.

—Musings of El, on the first of the Final Ten Days

Kaladin jolted, opening his eyes in confusion. He was in a small tent. What on Roshar?

He blinked and sat up, finding himself beside a boy, maybe eleven or twelve years old, in an antiquated uniform. Leather skirt and cap? Kaladin was dressed similarly.

"What do you think, Dem?" the boy asked him. "Should we run?"

Kaladin scanned the small tent, baffled. Then he heard sounds outside. A battlefield? Yes, men yelling and dying. He stood up and stepped out into the light, blinking against it. A . . . hillside, with some stumpweight trees on it. This wasn't the Shattered Plains.

I know this place, Kaladin thought. *Amaram's colors. Men in leather armor.*

Storms, he was on a battlefield from his youth. The exhaustion had taken a toll on him. He was hallucinating. The surgeon in him was worried at that.

A young squadleader walked up, haggard. Storms, he couldn't be older than seventeen or eighteen. That seemed so young to Kaladin now, though he wasn't that much older. The squadleader was arguing with a shorter soldier beside him.

"We can't hold," the squadleader said. "It's impossible. Storms, they're gathering for another advance."

"The orders are clear," the other man said—barely out of his teens himself. "Brightlord Sheler says we're to hold here. No retreat."

"To Damnation with that man," the squadleader said, wiping his sweaty hair, surrounded by jets of exhaustionspren. Kaladin immediately felt a kinship with the poor fool. Given impossible orders and not enough resources? Looking along the ragged battle line, Kaladin guessed the man was in over his head, with all the higher-ranked soldiers dead. There were barely enough men to form three squads, and half of those were wounded.

"This is Amaram's fault," Kaladin said. "Playing with the lives of half-trained men in outdated equipment, all to make himself look good so he'll get moved to the Shattered Plains."

The young squadleader glanced at Kaladin, frowning. "You shouldn't talk like that, kid," the man said, running his hand through his hair again. "It could get you strung up, if the highmarshal hears." The man took a deep breath. "Form up the wounded men on that flank. Tell everyone to get ready to hold. And . . . you, messenger boy, grab your friend and get some spears. Gor, put them in front."

"In front?" the other man asked. "You certain, Varth?"

"You work with what you have . . ." the man said, hiking back the way he had come.

Work with what you have.

Everything spun around Kaladin, and he suddenly remembered this exact battlefield. He knew where he was. He knew that squadleader's face. How had he not seen it immediately?

Kaladin *had* been here. Rushing through the lines, searching for . . . Searching for . . .

He spun on his heel and found a young man—too young—approaching Varth. He had an open, inviting face and too much spring in his step as he approached the squadleader. "I'll go with them, sir," Tien said.

"Fine. Go."

Tien picked up a spear. He gathered the other messenger boy from the tent and started toward the place where he'd been told to stand.

"No, Tien," Kaladin said. "I can't watch this. Not again."

Tien came and took Kaladin's hand, then walked him forward. "It's all right," he said. "I know you're frightened. But here we can stand together, all of us. Three are stronger than one, right?" He held out his spear, and the other boy—who was crying—did the same.

"Tien," Kaladin said. "Why did you do it? You should have stayed safe."

Tien turned to him, then smiled. "They would have been alone. They needed someone to help them feel brave."

"They were slaughtered," Kaladin said. "So were you."

"So it was good someone was there, to help them not feel so alone as it happened."

"You were terrified. I saw your eyes."

"Of course I was." Tien looked at him as the charge began, and the enemy advanced up the hillside. "Who wouldn't be afraid? Doesn't change that I needed to be here. For them."

Kaladin remembered getting stabbed on this battlefield . . . killing a man. Then being forced to watch Tien die. He cringed, anticipating that death, but all went dark. The forest, the tent, the figures all vanished.

Except for Tien.

Kaladin fell to his knees. Then Tien, poor little Tien, wrapped his arms around Kaladin and held him. "It's all right," he whispered. "I'm here. To help you feel brave."

"I'm not the child you see," Kaladin whispered.

"I know who you are, Kal."

Kaladin looked up at his brother. Who somehow, in that moment, was full grown. And Kaladin was a child, clinging to him. Holding to him as the tears started to fall, as he let himself weep at Teft's death.

"This is wrong," Kaladin said. "I'm supposed to hold *you*. Protect *you*."

"And you did. As I helped you." He pulled Kaladin tight. "Why do we fight, Kal? Why do we keep going?"

"I don't know," Kaladin whispered. "I've forgotten."

"It's so we can be with each other."

"They all die, Tien. Everyone dies."

"So they do, don't they?"

"That means it doesn't matter," Kaladin said. "None of it *matters*."

"See, that's the wrong way of looking at it." Tien held him tighter. "Since we all go to the same place in the end, the moments we spent with each other are the only things that *do* matter. The times we helped each other."

Kaladin trembled.

"Look at it, Kal," Tien said softly. "See the colors. If you think letting Teft die is a failure—but all the times you supported him are meaningless—then *no wonder* it always hurts. Instead, if you think of how lucky you both were to be able to help each other when you *were* together, well, it looks a lot nicer, doesn't it?"

"I'm not strong enough," Kaladin whispered.

"You're strong enough for me."

"I'm not good enough."

"You're good enough *for me*."

"I wasn't there."

Tien smiled. "You *are* here *for me*, Kal. You're here for all of us."

"And . . ." Kaladin said, tears on his cheeks, "if I fail again?"

"You can't. So long as you understand." He pulled Kaladin tight. Kaladin rested his head against Tien's chest, blotting his tears with the cloth of his shirt. "Teft believes in you. The enemy thinks he's won. But *I* want to see his face when he realizes the truth. Don't you? It's going to be *delight-ful.*"

Kaladin found himself smiling.

"If he kills us," Tien said, "he's simply dropped us off at a place we were going anyway. We shouldn't hasten it, and it *is* sad. But see, he *can't* take our moments, our Connection, Kaladin. And those are things that *really* matter."

Kaladin closed his eyes, letting himself enjoy *this* moment. "Is it real?" he finally asked. "Are *you* real? Or is this something made by the Stormfather, or Wit, or someone else?"

Tien smiled, then pressed something into Kaladin's hand. A small wooden horse. "Try to keep track of him this time, Kal. I worked hard on that."

Then Kaladin dropped suddenly, the wooden horse evaporating in his hand as he fell.

He searched around in the endless blackness. "Syl?" he called.

A pinprick of light, weaving around him. But that wasn't her.

"SYL!"

Another pinprick. And another.

But those weren't her. *That* was. He reached into the darkness and seized her hand, pulling her to him. She grabbed him, physical in this place and his own size.

She held to him, and shook as she spoke. "I've forgotten the Words. I'm supposed to help you, but I can't. I . . ."

"You are helping," Kaladin said, "by being here." He closed his eyes, feeling the storm as they broke through the moment between and entered the real world.

"Besides," he whispered, "I know the Words."

Say them, Tien whispered.

"I have always known these Words."

Say it, lad! Do it!

"I accept it, Stormfather! *I accept that there will be those I cannot protect!*"

The storm rumbled, and he felt warmth surrounding him, Light infusing him. He heard Syl gasp, and a familiar voice, not the Stormfather's.

THESE WORDS ARE ACCEPTED.

"We couldn't save Teft, Syl," Kaladin whispered. "We couldn't save Tien. But we *can* save my father."

And when he opened his eyes, the sky exploded with a thousand pure lights.

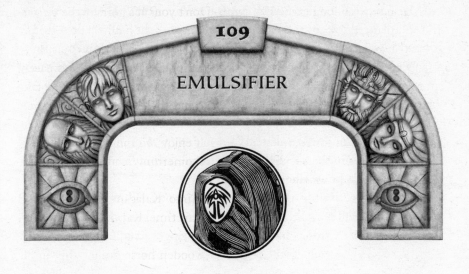

109

EMULSIFIER

For ones so tarnished, they are somehow bright.

—Musings of El, on the first of the Final Ten Days

Leshwi fell to her knees before Venli, not flying, not hovering. On her *knees*. Venli knelt as well, as Leshwi still held to her face—but the grip softened.

A cool, beautiful light flooded in through the window behind. Like a frozen lightning bolt, brighter than any sphere. Bright as the sun.

"What have you done, Venli?" Leshwi said. "What have you *done*?"

"I . . . I swore the First Ideal of the Radiants," Venli said. "I'm sorry."

"Sorry . . ." Leshwi said. A joyspren burst around her, beautiful, like a blue storm. "*Sorry?* Venli, they've *come back* to us! They've *forgiven us.*"

What?

"Please," Leshwi said to Longing, "ask your spren. Do they know of an honorspren named Riah? She was my friend once. Precious to me."

Leshwi . . . had friends? Among the spren?

Storms. Leshwi had lived *before* the war, when men and singers had been allies. Honor had been the god of the Dawnsingers.

Timbre pulsed.

"She . . . doesn't know Riah," Venli said. "But she doesn't know a lot of honorspren. She . . . doesn't think any of the old ones survived the human betrayal."

Leshwi nodded, humming softly to . . . to one of the old rhythms.

"My spren though," Venli said. "She . . . has friends, who are willing to maybe try again. With us."

"My soul is too long owned by someone else for that," Leshwi said.

Venli glanced toward the fighting. The sudden light hadn't halted them. If anything, it had made the Pursuer's soldiers more determined as they attacked. They seemed to enjoy the company of the angerspren and painspren. Some of the humans had wrestled away weapons, but most of them fought unarmed, trying desperately to keep the Radiants safe.

"I don't know what to do," Venli whispered. "I keep wavering between two worlds. I'm too weak, mistress."

Leshwi rose into the air, then ripped her side sword from its sheath. "It's all right, Voice. I know the answer."

She flew directly into the fight and began pulling away the soldiers, shouting for them to halt. When they didn't, Leshwi started swinging. And in seconds her troops had joined her, as singer fought singer.

⁘

"Sibling," Navani whispered, clinging to the pillar. "What is happening? Why do you make that rhythm?"

Navani? The voice that responded was soft as a baby's breath on her skin. Almost imperceptible. *I hear this rhythm. I hear it in the darkness. Why?*

"Where is it coming from?"

There.

Navani was given an impression, a vision that overlaid her senses. A place in the tower . . . the atrium, dark from a storm blowing outside? Down here, deep within the basement, she hadn't realized one was going on.

Fighting. People were fighting, struggling, dying. Navani squinted at the vision. Her pain was fading—though a part of her felt that was a bad sign. But she could see . . . a Fused, flying a foot off the ground, fighting beside someone infused with Voidlight. A Regal? And those were humans with them, standing together. Side by side.

"What are they doing?" Navani asked.

Fighting other singers. I think. It's so dark. Why do they fight each other?

"What's in that room they defend?" Navani whispered.

That is where they put the fallen Radiants.

"Emulsifier," Navani whispered.

What?

"A joined purpose. Humans and singers. Honor and Odium. They're fighting to protect the helpless, Sibling."

The vision faded, but before it did, Navani spotted Rlain—the singer who worked with Bridge Four.

"He's there," Navani said, then found herself coughing. Each convulsion made the pain flare up again. "Sibling, he's there!"

Too far, they whispered. *Too late . . .*

Outside in the hallway, Moash hacked at Raboniel's left arm—making it fall limp. She clawed at him with her remaining arm, hissing, as the hand with the dagger dropped its weapon and dangled uselessly.

"Take me," Navani whispered to the Sibling. "Bond me."

No, the Sibling said, voice faint.

"Why?"

You aren't worthy, Navani.

⁎

Rlain heard the shouting long before they reached the atrium. The guards holding him attuned Anxiety and hurried him and Dabbid faster, though Rlain remained optimistic. That noise had to be from Kaladin's fight with the Pursuer.

Rlain was, therefore, utterly shocked when they walked into the atrium to find a full-on civil war. Singers fought against singers, and a group of humans stood side by side with one of the forces.

Rlain's guards went running—perhaps to find some kind of authority figure to sort out this nonsense—leaving him and Dabbid. But the fray ended quickly, and the side with the humans won. Few of the singers seemed to want to fight Fused, and so the troops fled, leaving the dead behind them.

"What?" Dabbid asked softly, the two of them hanging back in one of the side corridors where some human civilians—brave enough to watch, but not skilled enough to join—clustered.

Rlain made a quick assessment, then attuned the Rhythm of Hope. Five of the Heavenly Ones—and about twenty Regals under their command—had turned upon the soldiers of the Pursuer. The other Heavenly Ones seemed to have refused to join either side, and had retreated up higher into the atrium.

That was Leshwi, hovering near the front of the side that had won—holding a sword coated in orange singer blood. She seemed to be in charge.

A good number of people, both human and singer, were down and bleeding. It was a mess. "They need field surgeons," Rlain said. "Come on."

He and Dabbid raced in and—as Kaladin had trained them—started a quick triage. People began helping, and in minutes Rlain had them all binding wounds for both singers and humans, regardless of which side they'd fought on.

Lirin had supplies in the infirmary, fortunately—and when Dabbid returned with them, he brought Hesina, who seemed rattled by the fighting. It was a few minutes before Rlain got an explanation. Lirin had been taken? Kaladin had given chase?

Rlain attuned the Lost. No wonder Hesina looked like she'd been through a storm. Still, she seemed eager to have something to do, and took over leading the triage.

That let Rlain step away for a breather and wipe his hands. Some humans who had seen it all gave him scattered explanations. The Pursuer had ordered the slaughter of helpless Radiants, and both humans and singers had resisted his army. Before Rlain could go demand answers from Venli, several gruff human men approached him. He recognized them from the sessions Kaladin had been doing, helping them with trauma. They'd been forced to pick up weapons again, the poor cremlings.

"Yes?" Rlain asked.

They led him to a body placed reverently beside the wall, the eyes burned out. Teft.

Rlain fell to his knees as Dabbid joined him, letting out a quiet whimper, anguishspren surrounding them. They knelt together, heads bowed. Rlain sang the Song of the Fallen, a song for a dead hero. It seemed the plan hadn't gone off too well for them either.

"Lift?" he asked.

"She's in the infirmary," Dabbid whispered. "Unconscious. Legs dead from a Blade. Looks like someone hit her hard on the head. She . . . is bleeding. I tried to give her Stormlight. Nothing happened."

Rlain attuned Mourning. Lift could heal others, but—like with Kaladin and Teft—her internal healing wasn't working. So much for waking the Radiants. He bowed his head for Teft, then left him there. Let the dead rest. It was their way, and he wished to be able to give the man a proper sky burial. Teft had been a good person. One of the best.

Behind him, other matters drew Rlain's attention. The humans and singers were already squabbling.

"You need to submit," Leshwi was saying, hovering above them in her imperious Fused way. "I will explain to Raboniel that the soldiers were uncontrolled and didn't obey my orders."

"And you think she'll let us walk?" one of the human women shouted. "We need to get out of here *right now*."

"If I let you go," Leshwi said, "it will seem that I am in rebellion. We can contain this if you submit."

"You're not in rebellion?" one of the men demanded. "What was *that* then?"

"We ain't obeying one of *you* again," another bellowed. "Ever!"

Shouts from both sides rose as singers ordered the people not to argue with one of the Fused. Rlain turned from one group to the other, then attuned Determination and wiped the makeup from his tattoo. He strode out between the groups. Field medicine wasn't the only thing Bridge Four had taught.

"Listen up!" he shouted to Confidence. "All of you!"

Remarkably, they fell silent. Rlain did his best Teft impersonation as he turned to the humans. "You all, you know me. I'm Bridge Four. I know you don't like me, but are you willing to trust me?"

The humans grumbled, but most of them nodded, prompted by Noril. Rlain turned toward the singers. "You all," he barked to Confidence, "*absolutely* committed treason. You acted against Odium's wishes, and he will seek retribution for that. You're as good as dead—and you Fused, you're in for an eternity of torture. Fortunately, you have *two people* here who can guide you—listeners from a people who escaped his control. So if you want to survive, you're going to *listen to me.*"

Leshwi folded her arms. But then muttered, "Fine." The other Heavenly Ones seemed willing to follow her lead.

Venli rushed over, and she was infused with the deep violet light of Voidlight. Far more so than an ordinary Regal. She glowed more, in fact, than a Fused.

"What are *you*?" Rlain demanded.

"A Radiant," she said to Consolation. "Kind of. I can use Voidlight to power my abilities, so they work in the tower."

"Figures," Rlain grumbled. "Kelek's breath . . . I wait years, then *you* of all people grab a spren first." Maybe that was too much Teft. "Anyway, it explains how you got Lift out. We need to get moving. Odium won't stand for a rebellion among his own. So you singers are going to come with us. We're going to grab the Radiants and we're going to carry them out onto the plateau, where we'll escape via the Oathgates to the Shattered Plains."

"That puts us in the humans' power," Leshwi said.

"I'll get you out of it," Rlain said. "*After* we're all safe. Understood? Gather up our wounded, grab those Radiants, and let's *get going*. Before Raboniel knows there was a rebellion, I want all involved parties—human and singer—out of this tower. Go!"

They started moving, trusting that he knew what he was saying. Which . . . he wasn't certain he did. Transporting a bunch of unconscious people would be slow, and there was a highstorm outside.

"Rlain," Venli said to Awe. "You gave orders to a *Fused*."

He shrugged. "It's all about an air of authority."

"It's more than that," she said. "How?"

"I had good teachers," Rlain said, though he was a little surprised himself. He was a spy, used to staying back, letting others lead while he watched. Today, though, there hadn't been anyone else. And having been rejected by both sides, he figured he was an outsider—and therefore as close to a neutral party as there could be in this conflict.

Everyone worked together to move the unconscious Radiants and the wounded. Even Leshwi and the five other Heavenly Ones each carried a wounded soldier. Rlain spent the time checking the balconies up above. The dozens of Heavenly Ones who hadn't joined the battle had now vanished. Carrying word to Raboniel, undoubtedly. Or marshaling their personal forces to stop this rebellion.

Once everyone was together, Rlain waved for them to follow as he started the hike out. Venli hurried up beside him.

"How are we going to work the Oathgate?" she whispered.

"I know the mechanism," Rlain said. "I assume we can use your Blade to figure it out."

Venli hurried at his side as they entered a corridor. "My *Blade*?"

"You told me you cut Lift out of her cell with a Shardblade. I wondered why they let you have one instead of giving it to a Fused, but now I can piece it together. Yours is a living Radiant Blade—which can work the Oathgates. I guess your Voidlight lets you summon it?"

Venli hummed to Anxiety. "I don't have a Blade, Rlain."

"But—"

"I was lying! I used my powers to get her out. Timbre says I'm a long way from earning my own Blade!"

Damnation. "We'll figure something out," he said. "Right now, we need to keep moving."

110

REBORN

Radiant.

—Musings of El, on the first of the Final Ten Days

A black storm.
Black wind.
Black rain.
Then, piercing the blackness like a spear, a lance of light.
Kaladin Stormblessed.
Reborn.

Kaladin exploded through the darkness, surrounded by a thousand joyful windspren, swirling like a vortex. "Go!" he shouted. "Find him!"

Though it felt like he'd been falling for hours, he had spent most of that time in the place between moments. If he was still falling through the sky, mere seconds had passed, and his father was falling somewhere below him.

Still alive.

Kaladin pointed downward, reaching out, preparing himself as hundreds of windspren met the storm and blew it back, creating an open path. A tunnel of light leading toward a single figure tumbling in the air, distant.

Still alive.

Kaladin's Lashings piled atop one another as Syl spun around him, laughing. Storms, how he'd missed her laughter. With his hand outstretched, Kaladin watched as a windspren slammed into it and flashed, outlining his hand with a glowing transparent gauntlet.

A dozen others slammed into him, joyful, exultant. Lines of light exploded around him as the spren transformed—being pulled into this realm and choosing to Connect to him.

He watched that tiny tumbling figure as it drew closer and closer. The ground, so near. They'd fallen the length of the tower and hundreds of feet below it in the storms.

The ground rose up to meet them.

Almost. *Almost.* Kaladin stretched out his hand, and—

⁘

Not worthy.

The words echoed against Navani's soul, and for the moment she forgot Moash. She forgot the tower. She was someplace else.

Not good enough.

Not a scholar.

Not a creator.

You have no fame, accomplishment, or capacity of your own. Everything that is distinctive about you came from someone else.

"Lies," she whispered. And they were.

They truly were.

She pressed her hand to the pillar. "Take me as your Bondsmith. I *am* worthy, Sibling. I say the Words. Life before death."

No. So soft. *We are . . . too different. . . . You capture spren.*

"Who better to work together than two who believe differently?" she said. "Strength before weakness. We can compromise. Isn't that the soul of building bonds? Of *uniting*?"

Moash kicked Raboniel away and she hit the wall, limp as a doll.

"We can find the answers!" Navani said, blood dribbling from her lips. "Together."

You . . . just want . . . to live.

"Don't you?"

The Sibling's voice grew too soft to hear. Moash looked down the hallway toward Navani.

So she closed her eyes and tried to hum. She tried to find Stormlight's tone, pure and vibrant. But she faltered. Navani couldn't hear that tone, not right now. Not with everything falling apart, not with her life seeping away.

She found herself humming a different tone instead. The one Raboniel had always given her, with its chaotic rhythm. Yes, this close to death, Navani could only hear that. His tone. Eager to claim her.

The Sibling whimpered.

And Navani inverted the tone.

All it took was Intent. Odium gave her the song, but she twisted it back upon him. She hummed the song of anti-Voidlight, her hand pressed to the pillar.

Navani! the Sibling said, voice growing stronger. *The darkness retreats ever so slightly. What are you doing?*

"I . . . created this for you . . ." Navani said. "I tried to . . ."

Navani? the Sibling said. *Navani, it's not enough. The song isn't loud enough. It seems to be hurting that man though. He has frozen in place. Navani?*

Her voice faltered. Her bloody hand slipped down to her side, leaving marks on the pillar.

I can hear my mother's tone, the Sibling said. *But not my tone. I think it's because my father is dead.*

"Honor . . ." Navani whispered. "Honor is not . . . dead. He lives inside the hearts . . . of his children. . . ."

Does he? Truly? It seemed a plea, not a challenge.

Does he? Navani searched deep. Was what she'd been doing honorable? Creating fabrials? Imprisoning spren? Could she really say that? Odium's tone rang in her ears, though she'd stopped humming its inverse.

Then, a pure song. Rising up from within her. Orderly, powerful. Had she done harm without realizing it? Possibly. Had she made mistakes? Certainly. But she'd been trying to help. That was *her* journey. A journey to discover, learn, and make the world better.

Honor's song welled up inside her, and she sang it. The pillar began to vibrate as the Sibling sang Cultivation's song. The pure sound of Lifelight. The sound began to shift, and Navani modulated her tone, inching it closer and closer to . . .

The two snapped into harmony. The boundless energy of Cultivation, always growing and changing, and the calm solidity of Honor—organized, structured. They vibrated together. Structure and nature. Knowledge and wonder. Mixing.

The song of science itself.

That is it, the Sibling whispered to the Rhythm of the Tower. *My song.*

"Our emulsifier," Navani whispered to the Rhythm of the Tower.

The common ground, the Sibling said. *Between humans and spren. That is . . . that is why I was created, so long ago. . . .*

A rough hand grabbed Navani and spun her around, then pressed her against the pillar. Moash raised his Blade.

Navani, the Sibling said. *I accept your Words.*

Power flooded Navani. Infused her, making her pain evaporate like water on a hotplate. Together, she and the Sibling *created* Light. The energy surged through her so fully, she felt it bursting from her eyes and mouth as she looked up at Moash and spoke.

"Journey before destination, you bastard."

.·.

Lirin hung in the air, his eyes squeezed closed, trembling. He remembered falling, and the awful tempest. Darkness.

It had all vanished. Something had yanked on his arm—slowing him carefully enough to not rip his arm off, but jarringly enough that it ached.

Stillness. In a storm. Was he dead?

He opened his eyes and searched upward to find a column of radiant light stretching hundreds of feet in the air, holding back the storm. Windspren? Thousands upon thousands of them.

Lirin dangled from the gauntleted fist of a Shardbearer in resplendent Shardplate. Armor that seemed *alive* as it glowed a vibrant blue at the seams, Bridge Four glyphs emblazoned across the chest.

A flying Shardbearer. Storms. It was him.

Kaladin proved it by rotating so that they were right-side up—then hoisting Lirin into a tight embrace. Remarkably, as Lirin touched the Plate, he couldn't feel it. It became completely transparent—barely visible, in fact, as a faint outline around Kaladin.

"I'm sorry, Father," Kaladin said.

"Sorry? For . . . for what?"

"I thought your way might be correct," Kaladin said. "And that I'd been wrong. But I don't think it's that simple. I think we're both correct. For us."

"I think perhaps I can accept that," Lirin said.

Kaladin leaned back—still holding him as they dangled barely twenty feet above the rocks. Storms. Was that how close they'd come? "Cutting it a little tight, don't you think, son?"

"A surgeon must be timely and precise."

"This is timely?" Lirin said.

"Well, you do hate it when people waste time," Kaladin said, grinning. Then he paused, letting go of Lirin with one arm—which was somewhat disconcerting, though Lirin now seemed to be floating on his own. Kaladin touched Lirin's forehead with fingers that felt normal, despite being faintly outlined by the gauntlet.

"What is this?" Kaladin asked.

Lirin remembered, with some embarrassment, what he'd finally let that one-armed fool Noril do to him. A painted *shash* glyph on Lirin's forehead.

"I figured," Lirin said, "that if an entire tower was going to show faith in my son, I could maybe try to do the same. I'm sorry, son. For my part." He reached up and brushed aside Kaladin's hair to see the brand there.

But as he did, he found scabs flaking away, the brands falling off to the stones below like a shell outgrown, discarded. Clean, smooth skin was left behind.

Kaladin reached to his forehead in shock. He prodded at the skin, as if amazed. Then he laughed, grabbing Lirin in a tighter embrace.

"Careful, son," Lirin said. "I'm not a Radiant. We mortals break."

"Radiants break too," Kaladin whispered. "But then, fortunately, we fill the cracks with something stronger. Come on. We need to protect the people in that tower. You in your way. Me in mine."

III

UNCHAINED

And so I am not at all dissatisfied with recent events.

—Musings of El, on the first of the Final Ten Days

Dalinar returned from the Stormfather's vision and found himself still flying with the Windrunners—face mask in place, wrapped in several layers of protective clothing.

He felt clunky and slow after being the winds moments ago. But he reveled in what he'd heard and felt. What he'd said.

These Words are accepted.

Whatever was happening at Urithiru, Kaladin would face it standing up straight. God Beyond bless it to be enough, and that the Windrunner could reach Navani. For now, Dalinar had to focus on his current task.

He urged his speed to increase, but of course that did nothing. He had no control over this lesser flight; in it, Dalinar was little more than an arrow propelled through the air by someone else's power—buffeted by the jealous winds, which did not want him invading their sky.

A part of him acknowledged the puerile nature of these complaints. He was *flying.* Covering a hundred miles in less than half an hour. His current travel was a wonder, an incredible achievement. But for a brief time he'd known something better.

At least this particular flight was nearly finished. It was a relatively quick jump from the battlefields of Emul down to the border of Tukar, where Ishar's camp had been spotted. The main bulk of the god-priest's armies had repositioned during the coalition's campaign, fortifying positions in case the singers or Dalinar's army tried to advance into Tukar.

So as Dalinar's team reached the coast, they found several depopulated camps, marked by large bonfire scars on the stone. The region had been denuded—trees chopped for lumber, hills stripped of anything edible. An army could forage and hunt to stay alive here in the West, where plants grew more readily. In the Unclaimed Hills, that had never been possible.

Sigzil slowed their group of five Windrunners, Dalinar, and Szeth into a hovering position. Beneath them, Ishar's large pavilion remained, and some hundred soldiers stood in a ring in front. These wore similar clothing: hogshide battle leathers with hardened cuirasses painted a dark blue, closer to black than the Kholin shade. Not a true uniform, but in a theme at least. Considering their lack of Soulcasters and the prevalence of herdsmen in the area, the equipment made sense. They were armed mostly with spears, though some had steel swords.

"They're ready for us all right," the Azish Windrunner said, steadying Dalinar in the air so he didn't drift away. "Brightlord, I don't like this."

"We're all Radiant," Dalinar said, "with plenty of gemstones and a Bondsmith to renew our spheres. We're as prepared as anyone could be for whatever will happen below."

The companylord glanced toward Szeth, who had been ostensibly flown by Sigzil, but had actually used his own Stormlight. Dalinar had let Sigzil in on the secret, naturally—he wouldn't leave an officer ignorant of his team's capabilities.

"Let me at least send someone else down first," Sigzil said. "To talk, find out what they want."

Dalinar took a deep breath, then nodded. He was impatient, but one did not build good officers by ignoring their legitimate suggestions. "That would be wise."

Sigzil conferred with his Windrunners, then swooped toward the ground. Apparently "someone else" had meant him. Sigzil landed and was met by Ishar himself, who emerged from the pavilion. Dalinar could identify the Herald immediately. There was a bond between them. A Connection.

Sigzil was not attacked by the soldiers in the large ring. Talking to Shalash these last few days, Dalinar thought he had a good picture of the old Herald. He had always imagined Ishi as a wise, careful man, thoughtful. Really, Dalinar's image of him had always been similar to that of Nohadon, the author of *The Way of Kings*.

Shalash had disabused him of these notions. She presented Ishar as a confident, eager man. Energetic, more a battlefield commander than a wise old scholar. He was the man who had discovered how to travel between worlds, leading humans to Roshar in the first place.

One word that Shalash had never used was "crafty." Ishar was a bold thinker, a man who pulled others after him on seemingly crazed ideas that worked. But he was not a subtle man. Or at least he hadn't been. Shalash warned that all of them had changed over the millennia, their . . . personal quirks growing more and more pronounced.

Dalinar was not surprised that Sigzil was able to speak to the man, then fly back up safely. Ishar did not seem the type to plan an ambush.

"Sir," Sigzil said, floating up beside Dalinar. "I . . . don't think he's altogether sane, despite what Shalash says."

"That was expected," Dalinar said. "What did he say?"

"He claims to be the Almighty," Sigzil said. "God, born again, after being shattered. He says he's waiting for Odium's champion to come and fight him for the end of the world. I think he means you, sir."

Chilling words. "But he's willing to talk?"

"Yes, sir," Sigzil said. "Though I must warn you I don't like this entire situation."

"Understood. Take us down."

Sigzil gave the orders, and they made their way to the ground and landed in the center of the ring of soldiers. A few Windrunners summoned Shardblades; the others, not yet of the Third Ideal, carried spears. They surrounded Dalinar in a circular formation, but he patted Sigzil on the shoulder and made them part.

He walked toward Ishar, Szeth shadowing him on one side, Sigzil on the other. Dalinar had not expected the old Herald to look so strong. Dalinar was used to the frailty of men like Taravangian, but the person before him was a warrior. Though he was outfitted in robes and wearing an ardent's beard, his forearms and stance clearly indicated he was accustomed to holding a weapon.

"Champion of Odium," Ishar said in a loud, deep voice, speaking Azish. "It has been a long wait."

"I am not Odium's champion," Dalinar said. "I wish to be your ally in facing him, however."

"Your lies cannot fool me. I am Tezim, first man, aspect of the Almighty. I alone prepare for the end of the worlds. I should not have ignored your previous messages to me; I see now what you are. What you must be. Only a servant of my enemy could have captured Urithiru, my holy seat."

"Ishar," Dalinar said softly. "I know what you are."

"I am that man no longer," Ishar said. "I am Herald of Heralds, sole bearer of the Oathpact. I am more than I once was and I will become yet more. I shall absorb your power, Odium, and become a god among gods, Adonalsium reborn."

Dalinar took a tentative step forward, waving for the others to stay back.

"I spoke to Ash," Dalinar said calmly. "She said to tell you that Taln has returned. He's hurt, and she pleads for your help in restoring him."

"Taln . . ." Ishar said. He adopted a far-off look. "Our sin. Bearer of our agonies . . ."

"Jezrien is dead, Ishar," Dalinar said. "Truly dead. You felt it. Ash felt it. He was captured, but his soul faded away after that. Her *father*, Ishar. She lost her father. She needs your counsel. Taln's madness terrifies her. She needs you."

"I prepared myself for your lies, champion of Odium," Ishar said. "I had not realized they would be so . . . reasonable. Yet you have already done too much to prove who you are. Taking my holy city. Summoning your evil storm. Sending your minions to torment my people. You have corrupted the spren to your side, so you can have false Radiants, but I have discovered your secrets." He held his hands as if to summon a Blade. "The time for the end is upon us. Let us begin the battle."

A weapon appeared from mist in his hands. A sinuous Shardblade lined with glyphs Dalinar did not recognize—though the Blade itself was vaguely familiar. Had he seen it before?

Szeth hissed loudly. "That Blade," he said. "The Bondsmith Honorblade. My *father's* sword. Where did you get it? What have you done to my father?"

Ishar stepped forward to strike at Dalinar.

.·.

While some humans left Rlain's band of rebels—returning to their rooms, hoping they hadn't been recognized—most of them stayed. Indeed, the numbers increased as many of the resisters fetched their families. Because Rlain had to let them go fetch families. What else could they do? Leave them to the Pursuer, who was known to target the loved ones of people he hunted?

All of this ate away at their time. They were also slowed by the need to carry both the wounded and the unconscious Radiants. Rlain did what he could to keep the main group moving, taking them through the Breakaway, avoiding the central corridor—where they'd be too easily exposed to Heavenly Ones from above.

However, he found himself attuning Despair. They were being watched—that cremling that harbored a Voidspren was following them along the wall. Rlain's band wasn't quite halfway through the market—still a fair distance from the front of the tower—when *cracks* broke the air, causing gawking marketgoers to flee. Stormform lightning strikes, used as a signal to empty the streets.

Rlain backed his haggard group against the wall of the large cavern and put their soldiers up front, the Heavenly Ones flying above. Deepest Ones began to emerge from the floor in front of them, and dozens of stormforms approached.

"You're right, listener," Leshwi said, lowering down beside him. "I couldn't have talked us out of this. *He* knows what we did. Those who approach are humming the Rhythm of Executions."

"Maybe we should have tried to reach the crystal pillar room," Rlain said. "And escaped through the tunnels beneath, as Venli suggested."

"No," Leshwi said. "Those tunnels are blocked. Our best hope was to escape out the front entrance of the tower, and perhaps cross the mountains. Unfortunately, judging by those rhythms, these who come aren't being sent by Raboniel. Odium wants me to know. I will be tortured like the Heralds once I return to Braize." She saluted Rlain. "So first, we fight."

Rlain nodded, then gripped his spear. "We fight," he said, then turned to Venli, who had stepped up by his side. "Are there any other spren like the one who bonded you? Would some want other willing singers? Someone like me?"

"Yes," Venli said to Mourning, "but I sent them away. The Fused would have seen them, hunted them." She paused, then her rhythm changed to Confusion. "And Timbre says . . . she says you're spoken for?"

"What?" he said. "By that honorspren who said he'd take me? I turned him down. I . . ."

The room went dark.

Then it shone as crystals grew out from his feet like . . . like stained glass windows, covering the floor. They showed a figure rising in blue-glowing Shardplate, and a tower coming alight.

Keep fighting, a voice said in his head. *Salvation will be, Rlain, listener. Bridger of Minds. I have been sent to you by my mother, at the request of Renarin, Son of Thorns. I have watched you and seen your worthiness.*

Speak the Words, and do not despair.

⁘

Sigzil blocked Ishar's attack using his Shardblade. The other Windrunners swarmed forward to protect Dalinar. Szeth, however, stumbled away. The sight of that Honorblade had plainly upset him.

The watching Tukari soldiers started to close their circle, but Ishar ordered them back. Then he danced away from Sigzil, shouting at Dalinar. "Fight me, champion! Face me alone!"

"I brought no weapon, Ishar," Dalinar said. "The time for the contest of champions has not yet come."

Ishar fought brilliantly as the other Windrunners tried to gang up on him. He was a blur with a flashing Blade, parrying, dodging, skepping his Blade—making it vanish for a brief moment to pass through a weapon trying to block it. The Windrunners had only recently started practicing the technique; Ishar performed the complex move with the grace of long familiarity.

He is a duelist, Dalinar thought. *Storms, and a good one.*

What did you expect? the Stormfather rumbled in his mind. *He defended mankind for millennia. The Heralds were not all warriors when they began, but all were by the end. Existing for three thousand years in a state of near-constant war changes men. Among the Heralds, Ishar was average in skill.*

Ishar faced all five Windrunners at once, and it seemed *easy* for him. He blocked one, then another, stepping away as a third tried to spear down from above, then swept around with his Blade, slicing the heads off two non-Shard spears.

Sigzil's Shardblade became a long dueling sword designed for lunges. He struck when Ishar's back was turned, but the Herald casually twisted and caught the Blade with one finger—touching it along the unsharpened side—and guided it past him. Sigzil stumbled as he drew too close, and Ishar lifted that same hand and slammed it against Sigzil's chest, sending him sprawling backward to the stones.

Ishar then turned and raised his Shardblade in one hand to deflect one of Lyn's strikes. Leyten came in, trying to flank, but he looked clumsy compared to the old Herald. Fortunately for the five, Ishar merely defended himself.

Despite earnestly trying, none could land a blow. It was as if . . . as if they were trying to hit where Ishar *was*, while he was able to move in anticipation of where they *would be*.

He is average among them? Dalinar asked. *Then . . . who was the best?*

Taln.

The one who sits in my camp? Dalinar thought. *Unable to do more than mumble?*

Yes, the Stormfather said. *There was no dispute. But take care; Ishar's skill as a duelist is a lesser danger. He has recovered his Honorblade. He is a Bondsmith unchained.*

Ishar suddenly dashed forward, rushing into one of Sigzil's attacks. The old man ducked the strike, then came up and touched Sigzil on the chest. When Ishar's hand withdrew, he trailed a line of Stormlight behind him. He touched his hand to the ground, and Sigzil stumbled, gasping as his glow started to fade. Ishar had apparently tethered Sigzil to the stones with some kind of glowing rope that drained the Stormlight out and into the ground.

The other four followed, almost faster than Dalinar could track. One after another, tethered to the stone. Not bound, not frozen, but their Light draining away—and all of them stumbled, slowing, as if their lives were being drained with it.

Dalinar glanced at Szeth, but the Shin man had fallen to his knees, wide eyed. Storms. Dalinar should have known better than to depend on the assassin as a bodyguard. Navani had warned him; Szeth was nearly as unstable as the Heralds.

Dalinar didn't want to see what happened when his troops ran out of Stormlight. He braced himself and thrust his hands between realms, then slammed them together as closed fists, knuckles meeting. In this, he united the three realms, opening a flash of power that washed away all color and infused the Radiants with Light.

Within the well of Light, Dalinar was nearly blinded—figures were mere lines, all shadows banished. Ishar, however, was distinct. Pale, eyes wide, whitened clothing rippling. He dropped his Blade and it turned to mist. Transfixed, he stepped toward Dalinar.

"How?" Ishar asked. The word sounded clear, an incongruity against the soundless rush of power surrounding them. "You . . . you open Honor's path. . . ."

"I have bonded the Stormfather," Dalinar said. "I need you, Ishar. I don't need the legend, the Herald of Mysteries. I need the man Ash says you once were. A man willing to risk his life, his work, and his very soul to save mankind."

Ishar strode closer. Holding the portal open was difficult, but Dalinar kept his hands pressed together. For the moment only he and Ishar existed here, in this place painted white. Ishar stopped a step or two from Dalinar. Yes, seeing another Bondsmith had shaken him.

I can reach him, Dalinar thought.

"I need a teacher," Dalinar said. "I don't know my true capabilities. Odium controls Urithiru, but I think with your help we could restore the Radiants there. Please."

"I see," Ishar said softly. He met Dalinar's eyes. "So. The enemy has corrupted the Stormfather too. I had hoped . . ."

He shook his head, then reached out and pressed his hand to Dalinar's chest. With the strain of keeping the perpendicularity open, Dalinar wasn't able to move away in time. He tried to drop the perpendicularity, but when he pulled his hands apart, it remained open—power roaring through.

Ishar touched his hand to his own chest, creating a line of light between him and Dalinar. "I will take this bond to the Stormfather. I will bear it myself. I sense . . . something odd in you. A Connection to Odium. He sees you as . . . as the one who will fight *against* him. This cannot be right. I will take that Connection as well."

Dalinar gasped, falling to his knees as something was torn from him—it felt as if his very soul was being ripped out. The Stormfather screamed: a terrifying, agonized sound, like lightning that warped and broke.

No, Dalinar thought. *No. Please . . .*

A shadow appeared on the field of whiteness. A shape—the shape of a black sword. This single line of darkness swiped through the line connecting Dalinar to Ishar.

The white cord exploded and frayed, trailing wisps of darkness. Ishar was cast away, hitting the stone. The perpendicularity remained open, but its light dimmed to reveal Szeth standing between Dalinar and Ishar, brandishing his strange black Shardblade. His illusion melted off like paint in the rain, breaking into Light—which was sucked into the sword and consumed.

"Where," Szeth said to Ishar, his voice quiet, "did you get that Blade you bear?"

The Herald seemed not to have heard him. He was staring at Szeth's sword as it dripped black liquid smoke. Around it, the white light of the perpendicularity warped and was consumed, like water down a drain.

Szeth spun and stabbed the sword into the heart of the perpendicularity. The Stormfather shouted in anger as the perpendicularity collapsed, folding in upon itself.

In a flash, the world was full of color again. All five Windrunners lay on the ground, but they were stirring. Ishar scrambled to his feet before Szeth—who stood with one arm wreathed in black tendrils, gripping the sword that dripped nightmares and bled destruction.

"Answer me!" Szeth screamed. "Did you kill the man who held that Blade before you?"

"Of course not, foolish man," Ishar said, summoning his Blade. "The Shin serve the Heralds. They held my sword *for me.* They returned it when I revealed myself."

Dalinar wiped his brow, pulling himself to his feet. He felt numb, but at the same time . . . warm. Relieved. Whatever the Herald had begun, he had not been able to finish.

Are you all right? he asked the Stormfather.

Yes. He tried to steal our bond. It should not be possible, but Honor no longer lives to enforce his laws. . . .

The perpendicularity. Did Szeth . . . destroy it?

Don't be foolish, the Stormfather said. *No creation of mortal hands could* destroy *the power of a Shard of Adonalsium. He merely collapsed it. You could summon it again.*

Dalinar was not convinced that the thing Szeth bore was a simple "creation of mortal hands." But he said nothing as he forced himself to check on the Windrunners, whose Connections to the ground had vanished. Leyten had found his feet first and was helping Sigzil, who sat on the ground with a hand to his head.

"I think your worries about this meeting were well advised," Dalinar said, kneeling beside the Azish man. "Can you get us into the air?"

"Damnation," Sigzil whispered. "I feel like I spent last night drinking Horneater white." He burst alight with Stormlight, drawing it from the pouch at his belt. "*Storms.* The Light isn't washing away the pain."

"Yeah," Lyn said. The other three Windrunners were sitting up. "My head is pounding like a Parshendi drum, sir, but we should be able to Lash."

Dalinar glanced at Szeth, who was alight with Stormlight—though it was being drawn at a ferocious rate into his weapon. "My people," Szeth shouted, "were *not* going to return your weapons to you. We kept your secrets, but you lie if you say my father gave you that Blade!"

"Your father was barely a man when I found him," Ishar said. "The Shin had accepted the Unmade. Tried to make gods of them. *I* saved them. And your father *did* give me this Blade. He thanked me for letting him die."

Szeth screamed, charging Ishar—who raised his Blade to casually block him, as he had with the Windrunners. However, the meeting of the two Blades caused a burst of power, and the shock wave sent both men sprawling backward.

Ishar hit hard, dropping his Blade—and Dalinar was in position to see the length of the Honorblade as it hit and bounced, then came to a rest half stuck into the ground. There was a *chip* in its unearthly steel where it had met the black sword.

Dalinar, in all his life, had never seen a Shardblade marred in such a way, let alone one of the *Honorblades.*

Ishar looked up at Szeth, dazed, then grabbed his Blade and shouted an order. His soldiers—who had watched all this in silence—broke their circle, moving into a formation. Sigzil put his hand on Dalinar's shoulder, infusing him, preparing to Lash him.

"Wait," Dalinar said as Ishar stood and slammed his fists together. A perpendicularity opened, as it had before, releasing a powerful explosion of light.

Impossible . . . the Stormfather said in Dalinar's mind. *I didn't feel it happen. How does he do this?*

You're the one who warned me he was dangerous, Dalinar thought. *Who knows what he's capable of?*

Across the stone field, Szeth sheathed his sword just before it began feasting on his soul. Dalinar pointed Leyten that way. "Grab him. Get into the air. We're leaving. Sigzil, Lash me."

"Right, sir."

"Dalinar. Dalinar Kholin."

That . . . that was Ishar's voice.

"I can see clearly," the voice said from within the perpendicularity. "I do not know why. Has a Bondsmith been sworn? We have a Connection, all of us. . . . Nevertheless, I feel my sanity slipping. My mind is broken, and I do not know if it can be healed.

"Perhaps you can restore me for a short time after an Ideal is spoken near me. Everyone sees a little more clearly when a Radiant touches the Spiritual Realm. For now, listen well. I have the *answer*, a way to fix the problems that beset us. Come to me in Shinovar. I can reset the Oathpact, though I must be sane to do it. I must . . . have help . . . to . . ."

The voice stumbled, as if warping.

". . . to defeat you, champion of Odium! We will clash again, and I am ready for your wiles this time! You will not defeat me when next we meet, though you bear a corrupted Honorblade that bleeds black smoke! I *am ALMIGHTY.*"

Dalinar lurched, rising into the air as the Lashing took effect. The Windrunners darted up after him, including Leyten, who grabbed Szeth. As they left the column of light, Dalinar could see Ishar's soldiers stepping into the perpendicularity.

A short time later it vanished. The Herald, his men, and the Honorblade were gone. Transported into Shadesmar.

⁘

Together, Navani and the Sibling could *create* Light.

Light that drove the monster Moash back along the corridor, holding his arm before his eyes. Light that drove the knife from Navani's side as it healed her wound. Light that brought fabrials to life, Light that sang with the tones of Honor and Cultivation in tandem.

But her spren . . . The Sibling was so weak.

Navani grasped the pillar, pouring her power into it, but there was so much chaos muddying the system, like crem in a cistern of pure water. The Voidlight Raboniel had injected.

Navani couldn't destroy it, but maybe she could vent it somehow. She saw the tower now as an *entity*, with lines of garnet very like veins and arteries. And she *inhabited* that entity. It became her body. She saw thousands of closed doors the scouts had missed in mapping the tower. She saw brilliant mechanisms for controlling pressure, heat—

No, stay focused.

I think we need to vent the Voidlight, Navani said to the Sibling.

I . . . the Sibling said. *How?*

I can sing the proper tone, Navani said. *We fill the system with as much Tower-light as will fit, then we stop and vibrate these systems here, here, and here with the anti-Voidlight tone.*

I suppose, the Sibling said. *But how can we create the vibration?*

There's a plate on Raboniel's desk. I'll have my scholars play that. I'll need a model to sing it, but with that, I should be able to transfer the vibration through the system. That should force the enemy's corruption out through these broken gemstones in the pump mechanism. What do you think?

. . . Yes? the Sibling said softly. *I think . . . yes, that might work.*

With that done, we will need to restart the tower's protections, Navani said. *These are complex fabrials . . . made of the essence of spren. Of* your *essence?*

Yes, the Sibling said, their voice growing stronger. *But they are complicated, and took many years of—*

Pressure fabrial here, Navani said, inspecting it with her mind. *Ah, I see. A network of attractors to bring in air and create a bubble of pressure. Quite ingenious.*

Yes!

And the heating fabrials . . . not important now . . . but you've made housings for them out of metals—you manifested physically as metal and crystal, like Shardblades manifest from smaller spren.

YES!

As she began working, Navani noticed an oddity. What was that moving through the tower? Highmarshal Kaladin? Flying quickly, his powers restored, wrapped in spren as armor. He had achieved his Fourth Ideal.

And he was going the wrong direction.

She could easily see his mistake. He'd decided the best way to protect the tower was to come here, to the pillar, and rescue Navani. But no, he was needed elsewhere.

She drew his attention with flashing lights on the wall.

Sibling? Kaladin's voice soon sounded through the system as he touched the crystal vein.

Yes and no, Highmarshal, Navani said. *The pillar is secure. Get to the Breakaway market. Tell the enemies you find there that they'd best retreat quickly.*

He obeyed immediately, changing the direction of his flight.

Navani, full of incredible awareness, got to work.

.•.

Dalinar persuaded the Windrunners to linger in the sky above Ishar's camp, rather than flying immediately back to the Emuli warcamp.

He worried about them though. The Radiants drooped like soldiers who had completed a full-day, double-time march. Ordinarily Stormlight would have perked them up, but they complained of headaches their powers couldn't heal.

The effects shouldn't be permanent, the Stormfather said. *But I cannot say for certain. Ishar Connected them to the ground. Essentially, their powers saw the stones as part of their body—and so tried to fill the ground with Stormlight as it fills their veins.*

I can barely make sense of what you said, Dalinar replied, hanging in the sky far above Ishar's camp. *How are such things possible?*

The powers of a Bondsmith are the powers of creation, the Stormfather said. *The powers of gods, including the ability to link souls. Always before, Honor was here to guard this power, to limit it. It seems that Ishar knows how to make full use of his new freedom.*

The Stormfather paused, then rumbled more softly. *I never liked him. Though I was only a wind then—and not completely conscious—I remember him. Ishar was ambitious even before madness took him. He cannot bear sole blame for the destruction of Ashyn, humankind's first home, but he was the one Odium first tricked into experimenting with the Surges.*

You don't particularly like anyone, Dalinar noted.

Not true. There was a human who made me laugh once, long ago. I was somewhat fond of him.

It felt like a rare attempt at levity. Dared Dalinar hope it was progress in the ancient spren?

Below, Ishar's large pavilion waited, flapping in the gentle wind. Dalinar had seen no sign of servants or soldiers peeking out.

"Sir?" Sigzil said, floating over to Dalinar. "My troops need to rest."

"A few minutes longer," Dalinar said, narrowing his eyes.

"What are we waiting for, sir?"

"To see if Ishar returns. He fled to Shadesmar. He could return at any moment. If he does, we're leaving at speed. But if he doesn't . . ." Ishar hadn't been expecting to run. Szeth, and that strange Blade, had driven him away. "This could be a rare opportunity, Companylord. He was a scholar among Heralds; he might have written notes that give hints to applications of Bondsmith powers."

"Understood, sir," Sigzil said.

Dalinar glanced toward Szeth, who floated on his own away from the others, Lashed into the sky by his own power. Dalinar nodded toward him, and Sigzil—catching the meaning—gave Dalinar a brief Lashing that sent him over beside the assassin.

Szeth was muttering to himself. "How did he know? How did the old fool *know?*"

"Know what?" Dalinar said as he drifted near Szeth. "Ishar? How did he know about your people?"

Szeth blinked, then focused on Dalinar. It was odd to see him look-ing like himself with that too-pale skin and those wide eyes. Dalinar had grown accustomed to his Alethi illusions.

"I must begin preparing myself," Szeth said. "My next Ideal is my quest, my pilgrimage. I must return to my people, Blackthorn. I must face them."

"As you wish," Dalinar said. He wasn't certain he wanted to unleash this man upon anyone, least of all the one neutral kingdom of note in this conflict. But Jasnah had indicated it would happen, and besides, he doubted he could stop Szeth from doing anything he truly wanted to. "Your people. They have all of the Honorblades?"

"All but three," Szeth said. "The Blade of the Windrunners was mine for years. The Blade of the Skybreakers was reclaimed by Nin long ago. And of course the Blade of the Stonewards was never ours to protect. So there were seven, but if Ishar has his Blade . . ."

You don't need those other swords, a perky voice said in Dalinar's mind. *I am as good as ten swords. Did you see how great I was?*

"I saw," Dalinar said to the sword. "You . . . chipped a Shardblade. An *Honorblade.*"

I did? Wow. I am a great sword. We destroyed a lot of evil, right?

"You promised not to speak into the minds of others, sword-nimi," Szeth said softly. "Do you not remember?"

I remember. I just forgot.

"I will send a team with you to Shinovar," Dalinar said. "As soon as we return to our camp."

"No," Szeth said. "No. I must go alone, but not yet. I must prepare. I have . . . something important to do. He knew. He should not have known. . . ."

Storms. Dalinar wasn't certain who was more insane: Szeth or the sword. The combination was particularly unnerving.

Without them, you would be dead, the Stormfather said, *and I'd be bonded against my will. This Shin man is dangerous, but I fear Ishar more.*

"Sigzil," Dalinar called. "I don't think he's going to return anytime soon. Take us down. Let's see if he left anything of value in that tent."

⋅⋅

Adin raised the spear he'd found in the atrium. People were crying, sur-rounded by fearspren, as the group of beleaguered humans and singers together made a circle around their wounded. They pushed the elderly and the children to the center, but Adin didn't go with those. The spren watch-ing would see that he wasn't the type to hide. Even women had picked up weapons, including the surgeon's wife, who had given her son to one of the young girls at the center to hold. War was a masculine art, but when you started attacking women, you'd stopped engaging in war. You deserved anything that happened to you after that point.

Adin's father was among the wounded. Alive, bless the Heralds, but bleeding badly. He'd fought for the Radiants, when Adin . . . Adin had hidden in the hallway.

Storm him, he wasn't going to be a coward again. He . . . he wasn't. Adin fell into line beside a fearsome parshman in incredible carapace armor, then tried to position himself with his spear out, in that parshman's same posture.

The stormforms marched in, singing a terrible song. Adin found himself trembling, his hands slick on his spear.

Oh, storms.

In that moment, he didn't want to earn a spren. He didn't want to fight. He wanted to be home making plates, listening to his father hum. He didn't want to be standing here, knowing that they were all . . . all going to . . .

A hand took Adin by the shoulder and moved him backward. Not all the way back, but enough for the figure to stand in front of him. It was the quiet bridgeman, Dabbid. Adin didn't complain, not after seeing those stormforms. Felt good to have someone in front of him, though the bridgeman's spear shook. He was acting afraid to fool the enemy, right?

The stormforms didn't release lightning, which was good. The others had thought they might not, because of the marketplace. Their powers were too wild. Regardless, there seemed to be . . . be *hundreds* of them. A call came from somewhere behind, and they came charging in—rippling with red lightning that flashed when they touched something.

In seconds, everything was chaos. Adin screamed, squeezing his eyes shut, holding out his spear and shaking.

No, he had to fight. He had to—

Something knocked into him from behind, throwing him forward. The strike dazed him, and he lost his spear. When he rolled over, a Voidbringer with red eyes stood above him. The creature casually speared downward.

Adin didn't even have time to scream before—

Clink.

Clink?

The stormform cocked his head, humming an odd song. He stabbed at Adin's chest, but the spear stopped short again. Adin looked at his body as he lay prone on the floor.

His torso was surrounded by glittering blue armor. He raised his hands, and found them covered in gauntlets.

He was in Shardplate.

He was in SHARDPLATE.

"Ha!" he shouted, and kicked at the stormform. The creature went *flying,* soaring twenty feet and slamming into a wall. Adin had barely felt any resistance. It was like he'd always imagined. It . . .

The Shardplate vanished off him and turned into a group of *windspren,* which soared over to Dabbid, who was about to take an axe to the head.

Clink.

Both combatants—the human now shrouded in Shardplate, and the enemy who had hit him—froze in place, stunned. The enemy backed away, and the Plate flew off *again,* this time surrounding the lead Heavenly One. She'd been spearing at a stormform who released a flash of lightning that enveloped her.

When Adin's eyes cleared, he saw her floating in Shardplate, staring at her hands in obvious wonder. Confused, the stormforms began calling out, disengaging and re-forming into ranks.

The armor burst apart, forming those strange windspren who flew into the air overhead before latching on to a figure hovering above the buildings.

The Plate had fit everyone, but him it *matched.* A brilliant Knight Radiant in glowing armor, holding aloft an intricate Shardspear. He left the helmet off so they could all see. Kaladin Stormblessed, bright as the sun.

"I bring word from the Sibling!" he shouted. "They don't remember inviting you in. And considering that they aren't merely the master of this house, they literally are this house, your actions are quite the insult."

Brilliant lights suddenly began running up the walls, making the very core of the stones glow as if molten in the center. Similar lights burst to life in the ceiling.

The ground trembled, as if the entire mountain were shaking. Clanking sounds rang in the hallways, like distant machines, and *wind* began to blow in the vast chamber—which now was as bright as day. Most amazing, the lightning on the stormforms went *out.*

Deepest Ones, who had been clawing out of the ground and grabbing at the feet of soldiers, began screaming and going limp, trapped in the stone. The Heavenly Ones who had been helping dropped to the ground suddenly, then collapsed, unconscious.

Groans sounded from behind. The Radiants on the floor at the center of the circle began stirring. They were *awake!*

"You may turn in your weapons," Stormblessed said to the enemy. "And return to your kind unharmed, so long as you promise me one thing."

He smiled. "Tell *him* that I'm *particularly* going to enjoy hearing what he looked like when he found out what happened here today."

∴

A strange, unpleasant stench struck Dalinar as he stepped into Ishar's pavilion.

The odor was chemically harsh, and he felt a faint burning in his eyes. He blinked in the dim light, finding a large chamber filled with slab tables and sheets shrouding something atop them. Bodies? The Windrunners had gone in first, of course, but they were busy inspecting the recesses of the tent to check for an ambush.

Dalinar walked up to one of the slabs and yanked off the shroud. He simply found a body underneath, an incision in its abdomen made with clean surgical precision. Male, with the clothing cut off and lying beside the body. Very pale skin and stark white hair—in death, the hair and skin seemed almost the same color. That skin had a blue cast to it; probably a Natan person.

So Ishar was a butcher, a mad surgeon as well as a crazed theocrat. For some reason, that relieved Dalinar. It was disgusting, but this was an ordinary kind of evil. He'd expected something worse.

"Sir?" Mela the Windrunner called from across the room. "You should see this."

Dalinar walked over to Mela, who stood beside one of the other slabs. Szeth remained in the doorway to the pavilion, seated on the ground, holding his sheathed sword across his lap. He seemed not to care about the investigation.

Another corpse—half revealed by a drawn-back sheet—was on the slab in front of Mela, though this one was far stranger. The elongated body had a black shell covering most of it, from neck to feet. That had been cut free to open up the chest. Dalinar couldn't make sense of the shell. It looked like clothing, kind of, but was hard like singer carapace—and had apparently been attached to the skin.

The head was a soggy mass of black flesh, soft like intestines, with no visible eyes or features.

"What on Roshar . . ." Dalinar said. "The hands seem human, if too long, but the rest of it . . ."

"I have no idea," Mela said. She glanced away and shivered. "It's not human, sir. I don't know what it is."

In the back of Dalinar's mind, the Stormfather rumbled.

This . . . the spren said. *This is not possible.*

What? Dalinar asked.

That is a Cryptic, he said. *The Lightweaver spren. Only they don't have bodies in this realm. They can't.*

"Sir," Lyn said from a nearby slab. The corpse she'd uncovered was a pile of vines vaguely shaped like a person.

Cultivationspren . . . the Stormfather said. *Return to that first body you saw. Now.*

Dalinar did not object and walked toward the front of the pavilion. What he'd first dismissed as an ordinary body now seemed anything but. The white-blue hair, the pieces of clothing that were—he now recognized— the exact same color as the body. The Stormfather's thunder grew distant.

I knew him, the Stormfather said. *I could not see it at first. I did not want to see it. This is Vespan. Honorspren.*

"So they're not . . . some kind of attempt at making men into mimicries of spren," Dalinar said. "These are *actual* spren *corpses?*"

Spren don't have corpses, the Stormfather said. *Spren do not die like men. They are power that cannot be destroyed. They . . . This is* IMPOSSIBLE.

Dalinar searched through the chamber, where more and more drawn-back sheets revealed different strange corpses. Several just skeletons, others piles of rock.

This place is evil, the Stormfather said. *Beyond evil. What has been done here is an abomination.*

Sigzil jogged over, holding some ledgers he'd found in the rear. Dalinar couldn't make sense of them, but Sigzil pointed at the Azish glyphs, reading them.

"This is a list of experiments, I think," the companylord said. "The first column is the name of a spren, the second column a date. The third is a time . . . maybe how long they lived? None seem to have survived longer than a few minutes."

"Blood of my fathers," Dalinar said, his hands trembling. "And this last column?"

"Notes, sir," Sigzil said. "Here, the last entry. 'Our first honorspren lived nearly fifteen minutes. A new record, and orders of magnitude longer than all previous attempts. Honorspren seem to have the most humanlike essences. When transferred, the organs and muscles form most naturally. We must capture more of them.

"'Cryptics and ashspren are impossible to bring over properly with our current knowledge. The process of creating bodies for them results in a physical form that collapses upon itself immediately. It appears their physiology works against the fundamental laws of the Physical Realm.'"

"Storms," Leyten said, running a hand through his short hair. "What does it mean?"

Leave this place immediately, the Stormfather said. *We must warn my children.*

"Agreed," Dalinar said. "Grab anything you think might be useful and meet me outside. We're leaving."

⬦

Moash fled through the tower, using Lashing after Lashing, as he felt the structure rumble. Felt it come alive. Felt light begin to surround him.

Her light. The queen's light.

And before that, a terrible sound. It had pushed away his Connection to Odium, forcing Moash to feel pain for the things he'd done—pain he didn't want. Pain he'd given away.

That pain seethed and spread inside him. He'd killed Teft.

He'd. Killed. *TEFT.*

Get out, get out, get out! he thought as he tore through a hallway, uncaring whether he hit people with his Shardblade as he passed over their heads. He needed it ready. In case Kaladin found him. In case he hadn't broken.

The walls were glowing, and the light seemed *brighter* to Moash than it should have. He wasn't supposed to feel afraid! He'd given that away! He couldn't be the man he *needed* to be if he was afraid, or . . . Or.

The pain, the shame, the anger at himself was worse than the fear.

Get out. Go. Go!

The suffocating light surrounded him, burned him as he burst out the front gates of the tower. He *felt* more than saw what happened behind. Each level of the tower came alive, one at a time. The air warped with sudden warmth and pressure. So much light.

So much light!

Moash Lashed himself into the sky, darting out away from the tower. Soon after, however, he slammed into a hard surface. He dropped into something soft but cold, pained as his Stormlight kept him alive—barely. It ran out before it could fully heal him, so he lay there in the cold. Waiting for the numbness.

He wasn't supposed to have to *feel* anymore. That was what he'd been *promised.*

He couldn't blink. He didn't seem to have eyelids anymore. He couldn't see either—his vision had been burned away. He listened to distant cheers, distant sounds of exultation and joy, as he lay in the cold on the mountainside. The snow numbed his skin.

But not his soul. Not his wretched soul.

"Teft, I . . ." He couldn't say it. The words wouldn't form. He *wasn't* sorry for what he'd done. He was only sorry for how his actions made him feel.

He didn't want this pain. He deserved it, yes, but he didn't *want* it.

He should have died, but they found him. A few Heavenly Ones who had been in the air when the tower was restored. They'd awoken, it seemed, after falling from the sky and leaving the tower's protections. They gave him Stormlight, then lifted him, carrying him away.

Odium's gift returned, and Moash breathed easier. Blissfully without his guilt. His spine healed. He could walk by the time they dropped him among a camp of a few others who had managed to flee the tower.

But he couldn't see them. No matter how much Stormlight he was given, his eyes didn't recover. He was blind.

112

TERMS

Roshar will be united in its service of the greater war.

—Musings of El, on the first of the Final Ten Days

Exhausted and confused, Dalinar and the Windrunners eventually landed back at their Emuli warcamp, mere minutes before a high-storm was scheduled to arrive. He felt the weight of failure pulling him down, strong as gravity. He sagged as he dismissed the Windrunners to go rest.

He'd gone all that way for nothing. He was no closer to understanding his powers. No closer to doing something about the capture of Urithiru. No closer to rescuing Navani.

He probably should have gone to Jasnah to explain what they'd found, but he was so tired. He plodded through the camp, towing his failure like a cart behind him, populated by swirling exhaustionspren.

And that was when they found him: women running up with spanreeds to the tower that were suddenly working again. Messengers surrounded by gloryspren, bringing amazing news. Navani in contact, the tower and Oathgates functioning. Dalinar listened to it in a daze.

Good news. Finally, good news.

He wanted to immediately get flown to Azimir so he could go see Navani, but he recognized the foolishness in that. He needed at least a short rest before enduring another lengthy flight, and there was that imminent highstorm to worry about. He ordered a message sent to his wife, promising to come to her before the day was out. Then he asked Jasnah and the Prime if he could meet with them after the storm.

After that, they left him to at last approach the small building he made his base. It felt like coming home. Of course, he'd lived enough of his life out on campaign that "home" had acquired a loose definition. Any place with a soft bed usually counted.

Urithiru really is safe now, Dalinar, the Stormfather said in his mind. *I was so distracted by the dead spren that I didn't notice at first. The Sibling has fully awakened. Another Bondsmith? The implications of this . . .*

Dalinar was still trying to deal with those himself. Navani bonding a spren? That was wonderful, but he was so emotionally worn at the moment, he just wanted to sit and *think.* He pushed open the door to his house, stumbled through, and entered a vast golden field.

The ground shimmered as if infused with Stormlight. Dalinar pulled to a halt and turned around. The doorway was gone, the doorknob having vanished from his hand. The sky was a deep reddish orange, like a sunset.

He was in a vision. But he hadn't heard the highstorm hit.

And . . . no. This wasn't a highstorm vision. This was something else. He turned with trepidation, looking across the glimmering field to where a figure—clad in golden robes—stood on a nearby hilltop, facing away from Dalinar and staring out at the horizon.

Odium. *Storms within,* Dalinar thought, flagging. *Not now. I can't face him right now.*

Well, a soldier couldn't always pick his battlefield. This was the first time Odium had appeared to him in a year. Dalinar needed to use this.

He took a deep breath and pushed through his fatigue. He hiked up the hillside and eventually stopped beside the figure in gold. Odium held a small scepter like a cane, his hand resting on the ball at the top.

He appeared different from when Dalinar had last seen him. He still resembled a wise old man with a grey beard cut to medium length. A paternal air. Sagacious, knowing, understanding. Only now his skin was glowing in places, as if it had grown thin and a light inside was seeking to escape. The god's eyes had gone completely golden, as if they were chunks of metal set into a statue's face.

When Odium spoke, there was a harsh edge to his tone, his words clipped. Barely holding in his anger.

"Our Connection grows, Dalinar," Odium said. "Stronger by the day. I can reach you now as if you were one of my own. You should be."

"I will ever and always be *my* own," Dalinar said.

"I know you went to see Ishar. What did he tell you?"

Dalinar clasped his hands behind him and used the old commander's trick of remaining silent and staring in thought. Stiff back. Strong posture. Outwardly in control, even if you're one step from collapsing.

"You *were* supposed to be my champion, Dalinar," Odium said. "Now I see how you resisted me. You've been working with Ishar all along, haven't you? Is that how you learned to bind the realms?"

"You find it inconvenient, don't you?" Dalinar said. "That you cannot see my future. How does it feel to be human, Odium?"

"You think I fear humanity?" Odium said. "Humanity is *mine*, Dalinar. All emotions belong to me. This land, this realm, this people. They live for me. They always have. They always will."

And yet you come to me, Dalinar thought. *To berate me? You stayed away all these months. Why now?*

The answer struck him like the light of a rising sun. Odium had lost the tower—Urithiru was safe and there was another Bondsmith. He'd failed again. And now he thought Dalinar had been working with Ishar.

Cultivation's gift, though it had bled Dalinar, had given him the strength to defy Odium. All this time, he'd been asking what a god could possibly fear, but the answer was obvious. Odium feared men who would not obey him.

He feared Dalinar.

"Ishar told me some curious things this latest visit," Dalinar said. "He gave me a book with secrets in it. He is not as mad as I feared, Odium. He showed me my Connection to you, and explained how limited you are. Then he proved to me that a Bondsmith unchained is capable of incredible feats." He looked at the ancient being. "You are a god. You hold vast powers, yet they bind you as much as they free you. Tell me, what do you think of a human bearing the weight of a god's powers, but without that god's restrictions?"

"The power will bind you eventually, as it has me," Odium said. "You don't understand a fraction of the things you pretend to, Dalinar."

Yet you're afraid *of me*, Dalinar thought. *Of the idea that I might fully come into my power. That you're losing control of your plans.*

Perhaps Dalinar's errand to Tukar hadn't been a failure. He hadn't gained Ishar's wisdom, but so long as Odium *thought* he had . . .

Bless you, Renarin, Dalinar thought. *For making my life unpredictable to this being. For letting me bluff.*

"We made an agreement," Odium said. "A contest of champions. We never set terms."

"I have terms," Dalinar said. "On my desk. A single sheet of paper."

Odium waved his hand and the words began appearing—written as if in glowing golden ink—in the sky before them. Enormous, intimidating.

"You didn't write this," Odium said, his eyes narrowing. "Nor did that Elsecaller." The light grew more vibrant beneath Odium's skin, and Dalinar could feel its heat—like that of a sun—rising. Making his skin burn.

Anger. Deep anger, white hot. It was consuming Odium. His control was slipping.

"Cephandrius," Odium spat. "Ever the rat. No matter where I go, there he is, scratching in the wall. Burrowing into my strongholds. He could have been a god, yet he insists on living in the dirt."

"Do you accept these terms?" Dalinar asked.

"By this, if my champion wins," Odium said, "then Roshar is mine? Completely and utterly. And if yours wins, I withdraw for a millennium?"

"Yes. But what if you break your word? You've delayed longer than you should have. What if you refuse to send a champion?"

"I cannot break my word," Odium said, the heat increasing. "I basically am incapable of it."

"Basically?" Dalinar pressed. "What happens, Odium, if you *break your word*."

"Then the contract is void, and I am in your power. Same, but reversed, if *you* break the contract. You would be in my power, and the restrictions Honor placed upon me—chaining me to the Rosharan system and preventing me from using my powers on most individuals—would be void. But that is not going to happen, and I am not going to break my word. Because if I *did*, it would create a hole in my soul—which would let Cultivation kill me.

"I am no fool, and you are a man of honor. We will both approach this contest in *good faith*, Dalinar. This isn't some deal with a Voidbringer from your myths, where one tricks the other with some silly twist of language. A willing champion from each of us and a fight to the death. They will meet on the top of Urithiru. No tricks, no lies."

"Very well," Dalinar said. "But as the terms state, if your champion is defeated, it isn't only you who must withdraw for a thousand years. The Fused must go with you, locked away again, as well as the spren that make Regals. No more forms of power. No more Voidspren."

The light pulsed inside Odium and he turned his eyes back toward the horizon. "I . . . cannot agree to this."

"The terms are simple," Dalinar said. "If you—"

"I said I *cannot* agree," Odium said. "The Everstorm has changed everything, and Cephandrius should have realized this. Singers can adopt Regal forms powered by the Everstorm. The Fused are free now; they can be reborn without my intervention. The Oathpact could have imprisoned them, but it is now defunct. I am *literally* unable to do as you ask, not without destroying myself in the process."

"Then we cannot have an accommodation," Dalinar said. "Because I'm certainly not going to agree to anything less."

"And if I agreed to less?"

Dalinar frowned, uncertain, his mind muddled from fatigue. The creature was going to try to trick him. He was certain of it. So, he did what he thought best. He said nothing.

Odium chuckled softly, rotating his scepter beneath his hand so the butt ground against the golden stone at their feet. "Do you know why I make men fight, Dalinar? Why I created the Thrill? Why I encourage the wars?"

"To destroy us."

"Why would I want to destroy you? I am your *god*, Dalinar." Odium shook his head, staring into the infinite golden distance. "I need soldiers. For the true battle that is coming, not for one people or one miserable windswept continent. A battle of the gods. A battle for *everything*.

"Roshar is a training ground. The time will come that I unleash you upon the others who are not nearly as well trained. Not nearly as *hardened* as I have made you."

"Curious," Dalinar said. "I don't know if you've noticed, but your 'hardening' tactic has resulted in Fused who are going mad from the stress."

The light grew stronger inside Odium, seeming as if it might explode from his skin.

"If your champion wins, I will step away for a thousand years," he said. "I will retreat to Braize, and I will no longer speak to, contact, or influence the Fused or Voidspren. But I cannot contain them. And you will have to pray that your descendants are as lucky as you are, as I will be less . . . lenient when I return."

Dalinar started to speak, but Odium interrupted.

"Let me finish," he said. "In exchange for you giving up one thing you wanted, I will give up one in turn. If I win, I will give up my grand plans for Roshar. I will leave this planet for a thousand years, and abandon all I've worked for here. I give you and the singers freedom to make your own peace. Freedom for you, and freedom for me.

"This is all I ask for my victory: As you represent Honor, you can relax his prohibitions on me. No matter what happens in the contest, you never have to worry about me again. All I want is *away from this miserable system*."

Of course it wouldn't be as easy as Wit had promised. Dalinar wavered. Wit looked out for himself, as he'd always said he would. The contract reinforced that idea. Odium offered a different, tempting prospect. To be rid of him, to fight this war as an ordinary war . . .

Two forces pulled at him. Which did he trust? He doubted that any mortal—Jasnah included—could construct a contract good enough to hold a god. But to simply give Wit what he desired?

Who do you trust more? Wit, or the god of anger?

It wasn't really in question. He didn't trust Wit much, but he didn't trust

Odium at all. Besides, if Honor had died to trap this god here on Roshar, Dalinar had to believe the Almighty had done so for good reason.

So he turned to go. "Send me back, Odium," Dalinar said. "There will be no agreement today."

A flare of *heat* washed over him from behind. Dalinar spun, finding Odium glowing with a bright red-gold light, his eyes wide, his teeth clenched.

Stand firm, Dalinar thought to himself. *Wit says he can't hurt you. Not without breaking his word . . . not without inviting his own death . . .*

Wit hadn't included that last part. But Dalinar stood his ground, sweating, his heart racing. Until at last the power abated, the heat and light retreating.

"I would prefer," Odium said, "to make an agreement."

Why so eager? Dalinar thought. *It's the power, isn't it? It's ripping you apart for delaying. It wants out.*

"I've offered you an agreement," Dalinar said.

"I've told you that I *cannot* keep to these terms. I can seal myself away, but not my minions. I can demand that the Fused and the Unmade retreat—but not all currently obey my will. And I can do *nothing* about the Regals."

Dalinar took a deep breath. "Fine," he said, "but *I* cannot entertain an agreement that frees you from this world. So we should focus on our conflict, you and me. If I win, you are exiled to Damnation and withdraw from the conflict entirely. If you win, *I* will go into exile, and my people will have to fight without my aid."

"You offer a mortal life for that of a *god*?" Odium demanded. "No, Dalinar. If I win, I want the Knights Radiant. The forces of Alethkar and Urithiru will surrender to my Fused, and your Radiants will end this war. The other foolish kingdoms of men can keep fighting if they wish, but your people and mine will begin preparing for the *true* war: the one that will begin when the gods of other worlds discover the strength of Surgebinding. Your heirs will be bound to this, as you are."

"I cannot negotiate for people who are not yet born," Dalinar said. "Nor can I promise my Radiants will follow you, as you cannot promise the Fused will obey you. As I said, this must be between you and me. But . . . if you win, *I* will agree to order my armies to stand down and stop the fighting. I will give up the war, and those who wish to join you will be allowed to do so."

"Not good enough, Dalinar. Not nearly good enough." Odium took a long, suffering breath. That light pulsed inside of him, and Dalinar felt a kind of kinship to the ancient god then. Sensing *his* fatigue, which somehow mirrored Dalinar's own. "I want so much more than Roshar, so much more than one planet, one people. But my people . . . tire. I've worn them thin with this eternal battle. They seek endings, terrible endings. The entire war has changed, based on what your wife has done. You realize this."

"I do," Dalinar said.

"It is time for a true accommodation. A true ending. Do you not agree?"

"I . . . Yes. I realize it. What do you propose?"

Odium waved dismissively at the contract Wit had drawn up. "No more talk of *delays,* of sending me away. Of half measures. We have a contest of champions on the tenth of next month," Odium said. "At the tenth hour."

"So soon? The month ends tomorrow."

"Why delay?" Odium asked. "I know my champion. Do you know yours?"

"I do," Dalinar said.

"Then let us stop dancing and commit. On the tenth, our champions meet. If you win, I will withdraw to the kingdoms I currently hold—and I enforce an end to the war. I will even give up to you Alethkar, and restore your homeland to you."

"I must have Herdaz too."

"What?" Odium said. "That meaningless little plot of land? What are they to you?"

"It's the matter of an oath, Odium," Dalinar said. "You will restore to me Herdaz and Alethkar. Keep whatever other lands you've taken; they mostly followed you freely anyway. I can accept this, so long as you are still trapped on Roshar, as Honor wished."

"I will," Odium said, "though I will be able to focus my attentions on sending agents to the rest of the cosmere, using what I've conquered here as enough for now. However, if *I* win the contest of champions, I keep everything I've conquered—Herdaz and Alethkar included. And I want one other small thing. I want you, Dalinar."

"My life? Odium, I intend to be my own champion. I'll have died if you win."

"Yes," Odium said, eyes shining golden. "You will have. And you will give your soul to me. You, Dalinar, will join the Fused. You will become immortal, and will *personally* serve me. Bound by your oaths. *You* will be the one I send to the stars to serve my interests in the cosmere."

A cold shock ran through Dalinar. Like he'd felt the first time he'd been stabbed. Surprise, disbelief, terror.

You will join the Fused.

"Are we agreed?" Odium said, his skin now glowing so brightly that his features were difficult to make out. "You have gotten from me more than I ever thought I would give up. Either way, the war ends and you will have secured the safety of your allies. At the cost of gambling your own soul. How far does your honor extend, Blackthorn?"

Dalinar wavered. Stopping now, with Azir and Thaylenah safe—with a good portion of Roshar protected, and with a chance for more in Alethkar and Herdaz if he won—was truly more than he ever thought possible. A true end to the war.

Jasnah spoke of the need for councils. Groups of leaders. She thought putting too much power in the hands of one individual was dangerous. He could finally see her point, as he stood there on that field of golden light. This new deal would be good for his allies—they'd celebrate it, most likely. But he couldn't know for certain. He had to make a decision.

Dared he do that? Dared he risk his own soul?

I have to contain him, Dalinar thought. His people were celebrating their victory in Emul, but he knew—deep down—the enemy had given it away. He had preferred to secure his power elsewhere. The Mink had said it himself: If Odium had wanted to crush Azir, he could have. Instead, he'd secured what he had. Odium knew that in controlling Jah Keved, Alethkar, and Iri, he owned the strongest portion of Roshar.

Without this deal, Dalinar saw years of fighting ahead. Decades. Against an enemy whose Fused were constantly reborn. From years spent defending Alethkar, he knew exactly how difficult it would be to retake. Dalinar saw his people dying by the thousands, unsuccessfully trying to seize lands he himself had fortified.

Dalinar would lose this war in the long run. Honor had all but confirmed it. Renarin said victory in a traditional sense was nearly impossible as long as Odium drove his forces. And Taravangian, whom Dalinar didn't trust but *did* believe, had foreseen the same fact. The enemy *would* win, wearing them down over centuries if need be.

Their best chance was for Dalinar's champion to defeat Odium's. If that champion failed, then Dalinar's only reasonable option would be surrender anyway. He knew that, deep in his gut. Most importantly, this seemed his only *real* chance to free Alethkar.

He had to do it. He hadn't achieved what he had through indecision. He either trusted his instincts, and the promises of his god, or he had nothing.

He took a deep breath. "Final terms are these: A contest of champions to the death. On the tenth day of the month Palah, tenth hour. We each send a willing champion, allowed to meet at the top of Urithiru, otherwise unharmed by either side's forces. If I win that contest, you will remain bound to the system—but you will return Alethkar and Herdaz to me, with all of their occupants intact. You will vow to cease hostilities and maintain the peace, not working against my allies or our kingdoms in any way."

"Agreed," Odium said. "But if I win, I keep everything I've won—including your homeland. I still remain bound to this system, and will still cease hostilities as you said above. But I will have your soul. To serve me, immortal. Will you do this? Because I agree to these terms."

"And I," Dalinar whispered. "I agree to these terms."

"It is done."

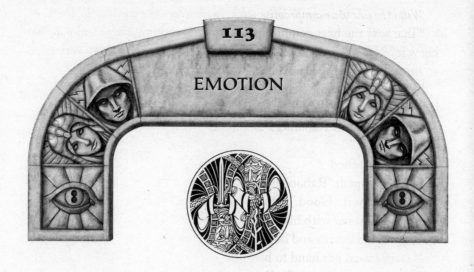

113

EMOTION

And I will march proudly at the head of a human legion.

—Musings of El, on the first of the Final Ten Days

Disconnecting from the powers of the Sibling left Navani feeling small. Was this really what life had been like before? Before she'd blended her essence with the Sibling's—and gained awareness of the intricate motions of the thousands of fabrials that made up the Sibling's physical form?

She now felt so normal. Almost. She retained a hint of awareness in the back of her mind. A sense for the veins of crystal that permeated the tower; if she rested her hand against a wall she could sense its workings.

Heat. Pressure. Light. *Life.*

I swore I would never do this again, the Sibling said in her mind. *I swore I was done with humans.*

"Then it's good that spren, like humans, can change their minds," Navani said. She was a little surprised to find her body as she remembered it. With a cut in her havah, bloodstained where the knife had taken her.

Our bond is unusual, the Sibling said. *I still do not know what I think of what we've done.*

"If we meant our words, and keep them, does it matter?"

What of fabrials? the Sibling asked. *You did not promise to stop capturing spren.*

"We will find a compromise," Navani said, picking her way out of the room with the crystal pillar. "We will work together to find an acceptable path forward."

Will it be like your compromise with Raboniel, where you tricked her?

"That was the best compromise she and I could come to, and we both knew it," Navani said. "You and I can do better."

I wish to believe you, the Sibling said. *But as of yet, I do not. I am sorry.*

"Merely another problem to solve," Navani said, "through application of logic and hope, in equal measure."

She approached Raboniel's fallen body in the hallway, then knelt over it. "Thank you."

The eyes opened.

Navani gasped. "Raboniel?"

"You . . . lived. Good." One of her hands twitched; it seemed that Moash had cut her with his Blade low enough that it hadn't burned out her eyes, though one arm and both legs were obviously dead.

Navani raised her hand to her lips.

"Do . . . not . . . weep," Raboniel whispered. "I . . . would have killed . . . you . . . to accomplish . . . my goal."

"Instead, you saved me."

Raboniel breathed in a shallow breath, but said nothing.

"We'll meet again," Navani said. "You will be reborn."

"No. If I . . . die . . . I will return . . . mad. My soul . . . is burned . . . almost all away. . . . Do not . . . Please . . . Please . . ."

"What, then?" Navani said.

"This new Light . . . works. My daughter . . . is truly gone. So I made . . . more . . . anti . . . anti . . ."

"Anti-Voidlight. Where?"

Raboniel rocked her head to the side, toward her desk, situated in the hallway near the opening to the crystal pillar room. Navani rose and searched through the drawers, finding a black sack containing a diamond filled with the precious, terrible Light.

She returned and affixed the diamond to the dagger, which was wet with Moash's blood. After cleaning it and reversing the metal strip, she knelt beside Raboniel.

"Are you sure?" Navani asked.

Raboniel nodded. Her hand twitched, and Navani reached over and held it, which made the Fused relax.

"I . . . have done . . . what I wished. Odium . . . is worried. He may . . . allow . . . an ending. . . ."

"Thank you," Navani said softly.

"I never . . . thought . . . I would be sane . . . at the end. . . ."

Navani raised the dagger. And for the first time, she wondered if she was strong enough for this.

"I do wish . . ." Raboniel said, "I could hear . . . rhythms . . . again. . . ."

"Then sing with me," Navani said, and began to sing Honor's tone.

The Fused smiled, then managed a weak hum to Odium's tone. Navani modulated her tone, lowering her voice, until the two snapped together in harmony one last time.

Navani positioned the dagger above the wound in Raboniel's breast.

"End it . . . Navani . . ." Raboniel whispered, letting the song cease. "Make *sure* they let it all . . . end."

"I will," she whispered back, then—humming her best, holding the hand of a former immortal—Navani thrust the dagger in deep. Raboniel's nerves had mostly been severed, so she didn't spasm as her daughter had. Her eyes went a glassy marble white, and a breath escaped her lips—black smoke as her insides burned away. Navani kept humming until the smoke dissipated.

You have performed a kindness, the Sibling said in her head.

"I feel awful."

That is part of the kindness.

"I am sorry," Navani said, "for discovering this Light. It will let spren be killed."

It was coming to us, the Sibling said. *Consequences once chased only humans. With the Recreance, the consequences became ours as well. You have simply sealed that truth as eternal.*

Navani pressed her forehead against Raboniel's as the Fused had done for her daughter. Then she rose, surrounded by exhaustionspren. Storms. Without the Towerlight infusing her, her fatigue returned. How long had it been since she'd slept?

Too long. But today, she needed to be a queen. She tucked the dagger away—it was too valuable to simply leave lying around—and took her copy of *Rhythm of War* under her arm.

She left a note on Raboniel's corpse, just in case. *Do not dispose of this hero's body without first consulting the queen.*

Then she went to create order from the chaos of a tower suddenly set free.

∴

Taravangian awoke late in the day. He barely remembered falling asleep. He barely . . . could . . .

Could barely . . . think.

He was stupid. Stupider than he'd ever been before.

That made him weep. Stupid weeping. He cried and cried, overwhelmed by emotion and shamespren. A sense of failure. Of anger at himself. He lay there until hunger drove him to stand.

His thoughts were like crem. Thick. Slow. He stumbled down to the window, where they had left his basket of food. Trembling, he clutched it, weeping at his hunger. It seemed so *strong*. And storms, he drew so many spren when stupid.

He sat beside his fake hearth, and couldn't help wishing that Dalinar could be there with him. How grand that had been. To have a friend. A real *friend* who understood him. He trembled at the idea, then began digging in the basket.

He stopped as he found a note. Written by Renarin Kholin, sealed by his signet. Taravangian sounded out each glyph. It took forever—drawing a fleet of concentrationspren like ripples in the air—for him to figure out what it said.

Two words. *I'm sorry*. Two gemstones, glowing brightly, were included with the note. What were these?

I'm sorry. Why say that? What had the boy seen? He knew his future wasn't to be trusted. Other spren fled, and only fearspren attended him as he read those words. He needed to hide! He climbed off his chair and crawled to the corner.

He quivered there until he felt too hungry. He crawled over and began eating the flatbread in the basket. Then some kind of purple Azish vegetable mash, which he ate with his fingers. It tasted *so good*. Had he ever eaten anything so wonderful? He cried over it.

The gemstones continued to glow. Large ones. With something moving in them. Hadn't . . . hadn't he been told to watch for something like that?

Thunder crackled in the sky, and Taravangian looked up. Was that the Everstorm? No. No, it was a highstorm. He hadn't realized it would come today. Thunder rattled the shutters, and he dropped the bread. He hid again in the corner with globs of trembling fearspren.

The thunder sounded angry.

He knows, Taravangian thought. *The enemy knows what I've done.* No. No, wrong storm.

He needed a way to *summon* Odium. Those gems. That was what they were for!

It would happen today.

Today he died.

Today it ended.

The door to his hut slammed open, broken at the hinges. Outside, guards scrambled away from a figure silhouetted against a darkening sky. The storm was almost here.

And Szeth had come with it.

Taravangian gasped, terrified, as this was not the death he had foreseen. He'd waited so long for a transcendent day when he would be supremely intelligent again. He'd never wondered about the opposite. A day when he was all emotion. A day when thoughts didn't move in his brain, and spren swarmed him, feeding gluttonously upon his passions.

Szeth stood quietly, his illusion gone, his bald head—freshly shaved—reflecting the light of the spheres that had spilled from the basket.

"How did you know?" the Shin finally asked. "And how long have you known?"

"Kn-known?" Taravangian forced out, crawling to the side through the fearspren.

"My father," Szeth said.

Taravangian blinked. He could barely understand the words, he was so stupid. Emotions fought inside him. Terror. *Relief* that it would soon be over.

"How did you know my father was dead?" Szeth demanded, striding into the room. "How did you know that Ishar reclaimed his sword? *How?*"

Szeth no longer wore white—he'd changed to an Alethi uniform. Why? Oh, disguise. Yes.

He wore the terrible sword at his side. It was too big. The tip of the sheath dragged against the wooden floor.

Taravangian hunched to the wall, trying to find the right words. "Szeth. The sword. You must . . ."

"I must do nothing," Szeth said, approaching steadily. "I ignore you as I ignore the voices in the shadows. You know the voices, Taravangian? The ones you gave me."

Taravangian huddled down, closing his eyes. Waiting, too overcome with emotion to do anything else.

"What are these?" Szeth said.

Taravangian opened his eyes. The gemstones. Szeth picked them up, frowning. He hadn't drawn that terrible sword.

Say something. What should he say? Szeth couldn't harm those. Taravangian needed them!

"Please," he cried, "don't break them."

Szeth scowled, then threw them—one after the other—at the stone wall, shattering them. Strange spren escaped, transparent windspren that trailed red light. They laughed, spinning around Szeth.

"Please," Taravangian said through the tears. "Your sword. Odium. You—"

"Ever you manipulate me," Szeth interrupted, watching the windspren. "Ever you seek to stain my hands with the blood of those *you* would kill. You brought all this upon us, Taravangian. The world would have been able to stand against the enemy if you hadn't made me murder half their monarchs."

"No!" Taravangian said. He stood up with effort, scattering the spren around him, his heart thundering in his chest. His vision immediately began to swim. He'd stood up too quickly. "We killed to *save* the world."

"Murders done to save lives," Szeth said softly, tracking Taravangian with eyes dark and shadowed from the room's poor light, now that the spheres were gone. "Idiocy. But I wasn't ever to object. I was Truthless. I simply followed orders. Tell me. Do you think that absolves a man?"

"No," Taravangian said, trembling with the weight of his guilt, shamespren bursting around him and floating, as petals of rockbud blossoms, to the ground.

"A good answer. You are wise for one so stupid."

Taravangian tried to dash away past Szeth. But of course his legs gave out. He got tripped and collapsed in a heap. He groaned, his heart thumping, his vision swimming.

A moment later, strong hands lifted him and slammed him back against the wall amid swarming exhaustionspren. Something *snapped* in Taravangian's shoulder, and pain spiked through his body.

He drooped in Szeth's grip, breathing out in wheezes.

The room started to grow golden.

"All this time," Szeth said, "I wanted to keep my honor. I tried *so hard*. You took advantage of that. You broke me, Taravangian."

Light. That golden light.

"Szeth," Taravangian said, feeling blood on his lips. Storms. "Szeth . . . He is here. . . ."

"I decide now," Szeth said, reaching toward his waist—not for the terrible sword, but for the small knife he was wearing beside it. "I *finally* decide. Me. No one else compelling me. Taravangian, know that in killing you, I make it *my choice*."

Rumbling thunder. A brilliant, terrible golden light. Odium appeared. When he did, his face was distorted, his eyes shining with angry power. Thunder broke the landscape, and Szeth began to fade.

You should not tempt me today, Taravangian! Odium thundered. *I have lost my champion* AGAIN, *and now I am bound by an agreement I do not want. How do they know how to move against me?* HAVE YOU BETRAYED ME, TARAVANGIAN? *Have you been speaking to Sja-anat?* WHAT HAVE YOU DONE?

The awe of that force—that transcendent power—left Taravangian quivering, spren of a dozen varieties swirling around him, fighting for his attention. So many *emotions*. He barely noticed Szeth pulling the knife free, for he was so overwhelmed—awed, frightened, excited all at once.

Fear won.

Taravangian cried out, his shoulder afire with pain, his body broken.

His plans had been silly. How had he thought to outthink a god when stupid? He couldn't do that when smart. No wonder he'd failed.

Did you fail?

The sword is here.

Odium is here.

Cold steel bit Taravangian's skin as Szeth stabbed him right in the chest. At the same moment, Taravangian felt something pushing through his fear, his pain. An emotion he'd never thought to feel himself. Bravery.

Bravery surged through him, so powerfully he could not help but move. It was the dying courage of a man on the front lines charging an enemy army. The glory of a woman fighting for her child. The feeling of an old man on his last day of life stepping into darkness.

Bravery.

The Physical Realm faded as Odium pulled Taravangian into the place between worlds. Taravangian's body was not as weak here. This form was a manifestation of his mind and soul. And those were strong.

The sword at Szeth's waist—that strange, terrible sword—manifested here, in this realm where Odium brought Taravangian. The god looked down and saw the curling black darkness, and seemed surprised.

Taravangian seized the sword and pulled it free of its scabbard, hearing it scream for pleasure. He turned and thrust it upward—black smoke curling around his hands.

"Destroy!" the sword bellowed. "DESTROY!"

Taravangian *rammed* it up into Odium's chest.

The sword drank greedily of the god's essence, and as it did, Taravangian felt a *snap*. His body dying. Szeth finishing the job. He knew it immediately. Taravangian was dead. Anger rose in him like he had never known.

Szeth had *killed* him!

Odium screamed, and the golden place shattered, turning to darkness. The sword undulated in Taravangian's grip, pulling power from the god it had stabbed.

The figure that contained Odium's power—the *person* who controlled it—evaporated, taken by the sword. That alone was so much Investiture that Taravangian felt the sword grow dull in his fingers. Full, lethargic. As when a hot brand was shoved into a barrel of water, there was an initial hiss—but this power was too vast for the sword to drink.

It killed the person holding that power, however, which left a hole. A *need*. A . . . vacuum, like a gemstone suddenly without Stormlight. It reached out, and Taravangian felt a distinct *Connection* to it.

Passion. Hatred. Today, Taravangian was *only* passion. Hatred, fear, anger, shame, awe. Bravery. The power loved these things, and it surged around him, enveloping him.

His soul vibrated.

Take me, the power pled, speaking not in words, but in emotion. *You are perfect. I am yours.*

Taravangian hesitated briefly, then thrust his hands into the well of power.

And Ascended to godhood, becoming Odium.

114

BROKEN GODS

They should not be discarded, but helped to their potential. Their final Passions.

—Musings of El, on the first of the Final Ten Days

Rlain walked with Venli and his new friends—Dul, Mazish, and the others Venli had recruited—to the Oathgate, where Kaladin waited to transfer them to the Shattered Plains.

Rlain felt in a stupor, despite a day having passed since his revelation. Since speaking his first Words as a Truthwatcher.

The spren had been watching him, from the heart of a cremling. Rlain and Venli had mistaken Tumi for a Voidspren, but he wasn't exactly the same thing. Once an ordinary mistspren, Tumi had let Sja-anat touch him, and in so doing make him into something new. A spren of both Honor and Odium.

Tumi pulsed to a new rhythm. The Rhythm of War. Something he had learned recently. Something important for his siblings to hear.

Renarin knows? Rlain thought.

He suggested you, Tumi said. *And told our mother about you. He was right. Our bond will be strong, and you will be wondrous. We are awed by you, Rlain. The Bridger of Minds. We are honored.*

Honored. That felt good. To be chosen because of what *he'd* done.

Kaladin waited for them at the transfer room. He made the transfer with the Sylblade. The air of the Shattered Plains was wetter, and felt . . . familiar to Rlain as they stepped onto a platform outside Narak.

There they met with Leshwi and the other four Fused who, upon being transferred here earlier, had regained consciousness. Leshwi hovered over and tipped her head toward Kaladin in respect.

"You could stay here at Narak," Kaladin said to her. "We'd welcome your aid."

"We fought against our own to preserve lives," Leshwi said. "We do not wish that to continue. We will find a third option, outside this war. The path of the listeners."

"We'll find our way out here," Venli said to Confidence. "Somehow."

"Well, go with honor then," Kaladin said. "And with the queen's promise. If you change your minds, or if you and yours need refuge, we'll take you in."

The Heavenly Ones took to the air, humming to Praise. They began lowering the new listeners—and their supplies—down into the chasm for the hike eastward. With the highstorm passed, and with Fused to watch for chasmfiends from above, they should be able to make their way to the eastern flats where the other listeners had gone.

Rlain gave Venli a hug and hummed to Praise.

"I don't deserve any of this," she whispered to him. "I was weak, Rlain."

"Then start doing better," he told her, pulling back. "That is the path of Radiance, Venli. We're both on it now. Write me via spanreed once you find the others, and give my best to Thude and Harvo, if they made it."

She hummed to Appreciation. "You will come to us soon?"

"Soon," he promised, then watched her go.

Kaladin stepped up beside Rlain and rested a hand on his shoulder. Rlain couldn't feel the Plate, though it was apparently *always there*—invisible, but ready when needed. Like a Shardblade, but made up of many spren.

Kaladin didn't ask if Rlain wanted to leave with the others. Rlain had established that he needed to stay, at least until Renarin returned. Beyond that . . . well, there was something Rlain had started to fear. Something nebulous but—once it occurred to him—persistent. If the humans had a chance to win this war, but at the expense of taking the minds of all the singers as they'd done in the past, would they take it? Would they enslave an entire people again, if given the opportunity?

The thought disturbed him. He trusted Kaladin and his friends. But humankind? That was asking a lot. Someone needed to remain close, in order to watch and be certain.

He would visit the listeners. But he was a Radiant and he was Bridge Four. Urithiru was his home.

"Come on," Kaladin said. "It's time to go give Teft a proper send-off. Among friends."

Taravangian's vision expanded, his mind expanded, his *essence* expanded. Time started to lose meaning. How long had he been like this?

He became the power. With it, he began to understand the cosmere on a fundamental level. He saw that his predecessor had been sliding toward oblivion for a long, long time. Weakened by his battles in the past, then deeply wounded by Honor, this being had been enslaved by the power. Failing to claim Dalinar, then losing the tower and Stormblessed, had left the being frail. Vulnerable.

But the *power* was anything but frail. It was the power of life and death, of creation and destruction. The power of gods. In his specific case, the power of emotion, passion, and—most deeply—the power of raw, untamed *fury*. Of hatred unbound.

In this new role, Taravangian had two sides. On one was his knowledge: ideas, understandings, truths, lies . . . Thousands upon thousands of possible futures opened up to him. Millions of potentials. So numerous that even his expanded godly mind was daunted by their variety.

On the other side was his fury. The terrible fury, like an unbridled storm, churned and burned within him. It too was so overwhelming he could barely control it.

He was aware of what he'd left behind in the mortal realm. Szeth had long since climbed to his feet and sheathed Nightblood. Beside him, the assassin had found a burned-out corpse, mostly eaten by the sword's attack. That was Rayse, Taravangian's predecessor, but Szeth wasn't able to tell. The sword had consumed clothing and most of the flesh, leaving bits of stone-grey bone.

They think that's me, Taravangian thought, reading the possible futures. *Szeth didn't see what happened to me spiritually. He doesn't know Odium was here.*

Almost all possible futures agreed. Szeth would confess that he'd gone to kill Taravangian, but somehow Taravangian had drawn Nightblood—and the weapon had consumed him.

They thought him dead. He was free. . . .

Free to destroy! To burn! To wreak havoc and terror upon those who had doubted him!

No. No, free to plan. To devise a way to save the world from itself. He could see so far! See so much! He needed to think.

To burn!

No, to plot!

To . . . To . . .

Taravangian was startled as he became aware of something else. A growing power nearby, visible only to one such as him. A godly power, infinite and verdant.

He was not alone.

$\bullet \atop \bullet \bullet$

They gave Teft a king's funeral, Soulcasting him to stone. A sculptor would be commissioned to create a depiction of Phendorana to erect next to him. The Sibling said there was a room, locked away, where the ancient Radiants stood forever as stone sentries. It would feel good to see Teft among them, in uniform and looking at them all with a scowl, despite the embalmer's best efforts.

It felt right.

All of Bridge Four came, except for Rock. Skar and Drehy had relayed the news after returning to the Shattered Plains—it seemed Kaladin wouldn't be seeing Rock again.

Together, the men and women of Bridge Four praised Teft, drank to him, and burned prayers for him in turn. Afterward, they sought a tavern to continue celebrating in a way Teft would have loved, even if he wouldn't have let himself participate.

Kaladin waited as they drifted away. They kept checking on him, of course, worried for his health. Worried about the darkness. He appreciated each and every one of them for it, but he didn't need that type of help today.

He was kind of all right. A good night's sleep, and finding peace restored to the tower, had helped. So he sat there, looking at the statue created from Teft's body. The others finally seemed to sense he needed to be alone. So they left him.

Syl landed beside him fully sized, in a Bridge Four uniform. He could faintly feel her when she rested her head on his shoulder.

"We won't stop missing him, will we?" she asked softly.

"No. But that's all right. So long as we cling to the moments we had."

"I can't believe you're taking this better than I am."

"I thought you said you were recovering."

"I am," she said. "This still hurts though." Once the tower had been restored, she'd mostly returned to herself. Some of what she'd felt had been gloom from what Raboniel had done.

Some of it wasn't.

"We could ask Dalinar," Kaladin said. "If maybe there's something wrong with you. A bond or something unnatural."

"He won't find one. I'm merely . . . alive. And this is part of being alive. So I'm grateful, even if part of it stinks."

He nodded.

"Really stinks," she added. Then for good measure, "Stinks like a human after . . . how long has it been since you had a bath?"

He smiled, and the two of them remained there, looking up at Teft. Kaladin didn't know if he believed in the Almighty, or in the Tranquiline Halls, or whether people lived after they died. Yes, he'd seen something in a vision. But Dalinar had seen many dead people in his visions, and that didn't mean they still lived somewhere. He didn't know why Tien had given the wooden horse to him, as if to prove the vision was real, only for it to immediately vanish.

That seemed to indicate Kaladin's mind had fabricated the meeting. He didn't let it prevent him from feeling that he'd accomplished something important. He'd laid down a heavy burden. The pain didn't go away, but most of the shame . . . that he let fall behind him.

Eventually, he stood up and embraced Teft's statue. Then he wiped his eyes and nodded to Syl.

They needed to keep moving forward. And that involved deciding what he was going to do with himself, now that the crisis had ended.

⁘

Taravangian grew more capable by the moment.

The power molded him as he bridled it. He stepped to the edge of infinity, studying endless possibilities as if they were a million rising suns and he were standing on the bank of an eternal ocean. It was beautiful.

A woman stepped up beside him. He recognized her full hair, black and tightly curled, along with her vibrant round face and dark skin. She had another shape as well. Many of them, but one deeper and truer than the others.

"Do you understand now?" she asked him.

"You needed someone who could tempt the power," Taravangian said, his light gleaming like gold. "But also someone who could control it. I asked for the capacity to save the world. I thought it was the intelligence, but later wondered if it was the ability to feel. In the end, it was both. You were preparing me for this."

"Odium's power is the most dangerous of the sixteen," she said. "It ruled Rayse, driving him to destroy. It will rule you too, if you let it."

"They showed you this possibility, I assume," Taravangian said, looking at infinity. "But this isn't nearly as . . . certain as I imagined it. It shows you things that can happen, but not the hearts of those who act. How did you *dare* try something like this? How did you know I'd be up to the challenge?"

"I didn't," she said. "I couldn't. You were heading this direction—all

I could do was hope that if you succeeded, my gift would work. That I had changed you into someone who could bear this power with honor."

Such power. Such *incredible* power. Taravangian peered into infinity. He'd wanted to save his city, and had succeeded. After that, he'd wanted to save Roshar. He could do that now. He could end this war. Storms, Dalinar and Odium's contract—which bound Taravangian just as soundly—would do that already.

But . . . beyond that, what of the entire cosmere? He couldn't see that far yet. Perhaps he would eventually be able to. But he did know his predecessor's plans, and had access to some of his knowledge. So Taravangian knew the cosmere was in chaos. Ruled by fools. Presided over by broken gods.

There was so much to do. He sorted through Odium's previous plans and saw all their flaws. How had he let himself be maneuvered into this particular deal with Dalinar? How had he let himself rely so much upon a contest of champions? Didn't he know? The way to win was to make sure that, no matter the outcome, you were satisfied. Odium should never have entered a deal he could not absolutely control.

It can still be done, Taravangian realized, seeing the possibilities—so subtle—that his predecessor had missed. *Yes . . . Dalinar has set himself up . . . to fail. I* can *beat him.*

"Taravangian," Cultivation said, holding her hand out to him. "Come. Let me teach you about what you've been given. I realize the power is overwhelming, but you *can* control it. You can do better than Rayse ever did."

He smiled and took her hand. Inside, he exulted.

Oh, you wonderful creature, he thought. *You have no idea what you have done.*

He was finally free of the frailties of body and position that had always controlled and defined him. He *finally* had the freedom to do what he'd desired.

And now, Taravangian was going to save them all.

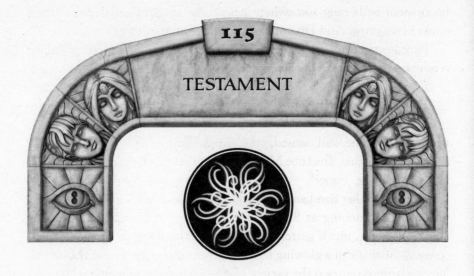

115

TESTAMENT

Yes, I look forward to ruling the humans.

—Musings of El, on the first of the Final Ten Days

Shallan sat by candlelight, writing quietly in her notebook. Adolin pulled his chair up beside her. "She looks better," he said, "than she did when I saw her in the market. But I don't know, Shallan."

Shallan put down the pen, then took his hands, glancing to the side where—in their little chamber in Lasting Integrity—her first spren sat on a chair, Pattern standing beside her and humming. Had the limp fibers of her head pattern straightened?

In talking with Pattern, they'd decided upon an Alethi name for Shallan's previous Cryptic. One that fit, best they could tell, with the meaning of her individual pattern.

"Testament does seem better, Adolin," Shallan said. "Thank you for speaking with her."

Maya sat on the floor, cross-legged, in a kind of warrior's pose. She hadn't recovered completely, but she *was* improved. And though she still didn't say much, Shallan doubted many beings—human or spren—had ever spoken words quite so valuable as Maya had at the trial. One might say, by simple economics, that Maya was one of the best orators who ever existed. If you aren't going to say much, then you might as well make what you *do* say mean something.

It gave them hope that whatever Shallan had done to Testament could also be repaired.

"I'll try to explain everything Maya and I have done," Adolin said as honorspren bells rang somewhere near. "But the truth is, I don't think either of us know. And I'm not exactly an expert on all this."

"Recent events considered? I think you're the *only* expert." Shallan reached up and cupped his face. "Thank you, Adolin."

"For?"

"Being you. I'm sorry for the secrets."

"You did tell me," he said. "Eventually." He nodded toward the knife with the gemstone, still unused, which rested beside her open notebook on one side of the table. The cube Mraize had sent rested on the other side. "The bells are ringing. Time?"

She removed her hand and situated herself at the desk. Adolin fell silent, waiting and watching as Shallan lifted the top of Mraize's cube. With help from Kelek, they'd gotten it open without harming the thing inside: a spren in the shape of a glowing ball of light, a strange symbol at the center. No one here recognized the variety of spren, but Wit called it a seon.

"Are you well, Ala?" Shallan asked. It was said like *A-lay*.

"Yes," the spren whispered.

"You can come out of the cube. You don't need to live in there anymore."

"I'm . . . supposed to stay. I'm not supposed to talk. To you. To anyone."

Shallan glanced at Adolin. The odd spren resisted attempts to get it free. It acted . . . like an abused child.

Another in the list of Mraize's crimes, Radiant thought.

Agreed, Shallan replied.

Radiant remained. They agreed that once they found the right path, she would eventually be absorbed as Veil had been. For now, Shallan's wounds were still fresh. Practically bleeding. But what she'd done would finally let her begin to heal. And she knew why Pattern had always been so certain she would kill him. And why he'd acted like a newly bonded spren when she'd begun noticing him on the ship with Jasnah. The simple answer was the true one. He *had* been newly bonded.

And Shallan had not one Shardblade, but two.

She still had questions. Things about her past didn't completely align yet, though her memory was no longer full of holes. There was much they didn't understand. For example, she was certain that, during the years between killing Testament and finding Pattern, her powers had still functioned in some small ways.

Some of this, Kelek said, had to do with the nature of deadeyes. Before the Recreance, they had never existed. Kelek said he thought this was why Mraize was hunting him. Something to do with the fall of the singers, and the Knights Radiant, so long ago—and the imprisoning of a specific spren.

"Contact Mraize please, spren," she whispered to the ball of light. "It is time."

The ball floated into the air, and the next part took barely a moment. The globe of light shifted to make a version of his face speaking to her. "Little knife," the face said in Mraize's voice. "I trust the deed has been done?"

"I did it," Shallan said. "It hurt so much. But she is gone."

"Excellent. That . . . *She*, little knife?"

"Veil and I are one now, Mraize," Shallan said, resting her hand on her notebook—which contained the fascinating things Kelek had told her about other worlds, other planets. Places he desperately wished to see.

Like the other Heralds, Kelek wasn't entirely stable. He was unable to commit to ideas or plans. However, to one thing he *had* committed: He wanted off Roshar. He was convinced that Odium would soon take over the world completely and restart torturing all the Heralds. Kelek would do practically anything to escape that fate.

There was a long pause from Mraize. "Shallan," he finally said, "we do *not* move against other Ghostbloods."

"I'm not one of the Ghostbloods," Shallan said. "None of us ever were, not fully. And now we are stepping away."

"Don't do this. Think of the cost."

"My brothers? Is that what you're referencing? You must know by now that they are no longer in the tower, Mraize. Pattern and Wit got them out before the occupation even occurred. Thank you for this seon, by the way. Wit says that unbound ones are difficult to come by—but they make for extremely handy communication across realms."

"You will never have your answers, Shallan."

"I have what I need, thank you very much," she said as Adolin put a comforting hand on hers. "I've been speaking to Kelek, the Herald. He seems to think the reason you're hunting him is because of an Unmade. Ba-Ado-Mishram? The one who Connected to the singers long ago, giving them forms of power? The one who, when trapped, stole the singers' minds and made them into parshmen?

"Why do you want the gemstone that holds Ba-Ado-Mishram, Mraize? What are you intending to do with it? What power do the Ghostbloods seek with a thing that can bind the minds of an entire people?"

Mraize didn't respond. The seon, imitating his face, hovered in place. Expressionless.

"I'll be returning to the tower soon," Shallan said. "Along with those honorspren who have decided—in light of recent revelations—to bond with humans. When I do, I expect to find you and yours gone. Perhaps if you cover yourself well, I won't be able to track you down. Either way, I *am* going to find that gemstone before you do. And if you get in my way . . . well, it will be a fun hunt. Wouldn't you say?"

"This will not end well for you, Shallan," Mraize said. "You make an enemy of the most powerful organization in all the cosmere."

"I think we can handle you."

"Perhaps. Can you handle my master? Can you handle *her* master?"

"Thaidakar?" Shallan guessed.

"Ah, so you've heard of him?"

"The Lord of Scars, Wit calls him. Well, when you next meet this Lord of Scars, give him a message from me."

"He comes here in avatar only," Mraize said. "We are too far beneath his level to be worthy of more."

"Then tell his *avatar* something for me. Tell him . . . we're done with his meddling. His influence over my people is finished." She hesitated, then sighed. Wit *had* asked nicely. "Also, Wit says to tell him, 'Deal with your own stupid planet, you idiot. Don't make me come over there and slap you around again.'"

"So it must be," Mraize said. "Know that in doing this, you have moved against the Ghostbloods in the most offensive of ways. We are now at war, Shallan."

"You've always been at war," Shallan said. "*I've* finally picked a side. Goodbye, Mraize. End contact."

The floating spren molded into a globe instead of Mraize's face. Shallan sat back, trying not to feel overwhelmed.

"Whoever they are," Adolin said, "we *can* handle them."

Ever optimistic. Well, he had good reason. With the leaders of the honorspren in disgrace, and Lasting Integrity open again to all who would visit, he had accomplished his mission. He'd been correct all along, both about the honorspren and about Shallan herself.

Shallan reached forward and flipped to the next page in her notebook, where she'd done a drawing using Kelek's descriptions. It showed a pattern of stars in the sky, and listed the many worlds among them.

Shallan had kept her head down too long. It was time to soar.

◆◆

The listeners raised bows toward Venli as she walked up to their camp, alone, after insisting that the others stay back a few hundred feet.

She didn't blame the listeners for turning weapons against her. They assumed she had come to finish the job she'd started. So she raised her hands and hummed to Peace, waiting.

And waiting.

And waiting.

Finally, Thude himself emerged from behind their fortification of piled rocks. Storms, it was good to see him. By the counts they'd done from the air, almost all of them must have made it through the narrows and out this side. A thousand listener adults, along with many children.

Thude approached, wearing warform, but he stopped short of striking range. Venli continued to stand and hum, feeling a hundred bows focused on her. This eastern plain beyond the hills was a strange place—so open, and full of a surprising amount of grass.

"Storms. *Venli?*" Thude turned to dash back behind the fortifications.

She realized he must have just now seen her patterns. She was wearing a form he'd never known, so of course he hadn't recognized her from a distance. "Thude!" she called out, taking in enough Stormlight to glow in the daylight. "Thude, please!"

He stopped, seeing her Light.

"Did my mother make it?" she asked to Longing. "Is she alive?"

"She is," he called. "But her mind is gone."

"I think I might have a way to heal her."

"Traitor," he shouted. "You think I believe you? You would have had us killed!"

"I understand," she said softly to Consolation. "I deserve everything you can call me, and more. But I'm trying as I never did before. Please, listen to what I have to say."

He wavered, then crossed the stone to meet her. "Do the others know where we are? Does the enemy know?"

"I'm not sure," Venli said. "The humans found you. One Fused knew of you, but she is dead now. I don't know who she told."

"What is a Fused?"

"There's a lot you don't know," Venli said. "Our gods have returned, terrible as warned. I was largely responsible for this, even if Rlain says he's certain they would have found their way back anyway."

Thude perked up at Rlain's name.

"We're going to have to do something to protect ourselves," Venli said. "Something to make everyone leave us alone." She held out her hand, and a little spren in the shape of a comet flew up from the grass and started circling it. "She's new to this realm and a little confused. But she's seeking someone to bond and make into a Radiant. Like me and my friends."

"You came to us last time with a spren who wanted a bond," Thude said to Reprimand. "And what happened?"

"This will be different," Venli said, alight with Stormlight. "I've changed. I promise you all the time you need to test my words. To decide without being pushed. For now, please let me see my mother."

He hummed to Winds at last, a sign for her to follow, as he started walking back to camp. Venli attuned Joy.

"There are more of these spren that will make listeners into Radiants?" he asked.

"Yes," she said.

"How many?"

"Hundreds," she said.

The Rhythm of Joy grew loud inside Venli as she entered the camp—though many who saw her hummed to Anxiety. She cared for only one sight. An old singer woman sitting by a tent made from woven reeds.

Venli's heart leaped, and the rhythms sounded more pure. More vibrant. Jaxlim really was alive. Venli rushed forward, collapsing to her knees before Jaxlim, feeling as if she were again a child. In the good way.

"Mother?" she asked.

Jaxlim looked up at her. There was no recognition in the old listener's eyes.

"Without her," Thude said, stepping up beside Venli, "we're losing the songs. Nobody else who knew them escaped. . . ."

"It's all right," Venli said, wiping her tears. "It's going to be all right." Timbre, within Venli, let out a glorious song.

Venli held out her hand, and the little lightspren inched into the air, then began spinning around Venli's mother. The Reachers were searching for people who exemplified their Ideal: freedom. And the listeners were the perfect representation.

However, a Radiant bond required volition, and her mother couldn't speak Ideals—though the Reachers indicated that the start of the bonding process didn't require that. They also thought becoming Radiant would heal her mother, though they couldn't say for certain. Mental wounds were difficult, they explained, and healing depended greatly on the individual.

Jaxlim *could* still want this, couldn't she? She could still choose? "Listen, Mother," Venli pled to Peace. "Hear me. Please." Venli began singing the Song of Mornings. The first song she'd learned. Her mother's favorite. As she sang, listeners gathered around, lowering their weapons. They started humming rhythms to match hers.

When she finished, Thude knelt beside her. The little spren had slipped into Jaxlim's body to seek her gemheart, but no change had happened yet. Venli took out a Stormlight sphere, but her mother did not drink it in.

"It was beautiful," Thude said. "It's been too long since I heard one of the songs."

"I will restore them to you," Venli whispered, "if you'll have me. I understand completely if you won't—but I've brought other Radiants with me, my friends. Along with some of the enemy who have chosen to defect and become listeners."

Thude hummed to Skepticism.

"Again, if you turn me aside, that is understandable," Venli said. "But at least listen to my friends. You're going to need allies to survive in this new world, a world of Surgebinders. We can't go alone as we did before."

"We're not alone," Thude said. "I think you'll find that things have changed for us, as they have for you."

Venli hummed to Consideration. Then she heard a scraping sound, like rock on rock. Or . . . claws on rock?

A shadow fell over Venli, and she started, staring up at a powerful long neck with a wicked arrowhead face on the end. A chasmfiend. Here. And no one was panicking.

Storms. "That's . . ." she whispered. "That's how you got out of the chasms that night, during the storm?"

Thude hummed Confidence.

Before she could demand answers, something else interrupted her. A voice.

"Venli? Venli, is that you?"

Venli looked down to see that her mother's eyes had focused, *seeing* her.

Your Words, Venli, a distant femalen voice said in her mind, *are now accepted.*

116

MERCY

Nearly as much as I look forward to serving you, newest Odium.
Who was so recently one of them. You understand. And you are the
one I've been waiting to worship.

—Musings of El, on the first of the Final Ten Days

Around four hours after Teft's funeral, Kaladin went looking for Dalinar. The Blackthorn had returned the previous night, but Kaladin had been too exhausted that evening to do more than salute him, then find his bed.

So, he excused himself from the party at Jor's winehouse and soared up toward the top of the tower. It felt good to fly up all on his own. Here, as reported by the messenger who'd brought him the news, Kaladin and Syl found the Bondsmith . . . er, the Stormfather's Bondsmith . . . taking reports with Navani. The other Bondsmith. That was going to take some getting used to.

Kaladin and Syl intended to linger outside the small council room until Dalinar finished his current meeting, but as soon as he saw them, he broke it off and came trotting over.

"Kaladin," he said. "I've been meaning to speak with you."

"You've been busy, sir," Kaladin said. He glanced down at his uniform. "Maybe I shouldn't be wearing this."

Dalinar actually *blushed*. What a remarkable sight. "About that," he said. "I should have known I couldn't—and shouldn't—try to relieve someone like you from—"

"Sir," Kaladin interrupted. He glanced at Syl, who nodded. He turned back to Dalinar. "Sir, you were right. I have a lot of healing to do before I should be in command again."

"Even still?" Dalinar asked, glancing at Kaladin's forehead—and the missing brands. "After what you have accomplished? After swearing the Fourth Ideal?"

"The Ideals don't fix us, sir," Kaladin said. "You know that. We have to fix ourselves. Perhaps with a little help." He saluted. "We were on the correct path with me, sir. I *need* to take time away from the battle. Maybe so much time that I never return to full command. I have work to do, helping men like me and Dabbid. I'd like your permission to continue."

"Granted," Dalinar said. "You've grown, soldier. Few men have the wisdom to realize when they need help. Fewer still have the strength to go get it. Well done. Very well done."

"Thank you, sir," Kaladin said.

Dalinar hesitated—something seemed to be troubling him. He put his hands behind his back, watching Kaladin. Everyone else was celebrating. Not Dalinar.

"What is it, sir?" Kaladin asked.

"I haven't made it public knowledge yet, but Odium and I have set a time for our contest of champions."

"That's excellent," Kaladin said. "How long?"

"Ten days."

"Ten . . . *days*?"

Dalinar nodded.

Syl gasped, and Kaladin felt a spike of alarm. He'd always kind of thought . . . He'd spent this year assuming that . . .

"Sir," Kaladin said. "I can't . . ."

"I know, son," Dalinar said quietly. "You weren't right for the champion job anyway. This is the sort of thing a man must do himself."

Kaladin felt cold. Ten days. "The war . . . Does this mean . . . it will be over?"

"One way or another, it will end," Dalinar said. "The terms will enforce a treaty in ten days, following the contest. The contest will decide the fate of Alethkar, among . . . other items. Regardless, the hostilities will continue until that day, and so we must remain vigilant. I expect the enemy to make a play to capture what he can, before the treaty finalizes borders. I perhaps made a miscalculation there.

"Regardless, an end *is* in sight. But I'm going to need help from someone before this contest arrives. The fight won't simply be a swordfight— I can't explain what it *will* be. I don't know that I understand yet either, but I'm increasingly confident I need to master what I can of my powers."

"I don't know if I can help with that, sir," Kaladin said. "Though we share a Surge, our abilities seem very different."

"Yes, but there is one who *can* help me. Unfortunately, he's insane. And so, Kaladin, I do not need you as a soldier right now. I need you as a surgeon. You are of the few who personally understand what it means to have your own mind betray you. Would you be willing to go on a mission to recover this individual and find a way to help him, so he can help me?"

"Of course, sir," Kaladin said. "Who is it?"

"The Herald Ishi," Dalinar said. "Creator of the Oathpact, Herald of Truth, and original binder of the Fused."

Syl whistled softly.

"Sir," Kaladin said, feeling unnerved. "Ten days isn't enough to help someone with *ordinary* battle shock. It will take years, if we can even find proper methods. To help a Herald . . . Well, sir, their problems seem far beyond mine."

"I know, soldier," Dalinar said. "But I think Ishar's malady is supernatural in nature, and he gave me clues to help him recover. All I need from you now is an agreement to help. And a willingness to travel to Shinovar in somewhat . . . odd company."

"Sir?" Kaladin asked.

"I'll explain later," Dalinar said. "I need time to think this over, decide what I really want to do."

Kaladin nodded, but glanced at Syl, who whistled again. "Ten days?" she said. "I guess it's happening. . . ."

Dalinar started back toward his meeting—then paused and reached for something on a nearby table. A flute?

Wit's flute.

"Lift had this," Dalinar said, handing it toward Kaladin. "She said that Dabbid recognized it as yours."

"It is," Kaladin said with awe. "How is Lift, by the way?"

"My lunch is gone," Dalinar said. "So I'd say she's doing fine. We found her spren once the tower was restored, and they have—for some reason—decided to begin carrying around a bright red chicken." He sighed. "Anyway, she said she found that flute in a merchant's bin down in the Breakaway. One who sells salvage from the Shattered Plains. There might be other things your men were forced to abandon there."

Huh. "Did she say which merchant?" Kaladin asked.

⁘

The Pursuer drew in a deep, angry breath as he woke.

Then he screamed in rage.

It felt good to have lungs again. It felt good to shout his frustration. He would continue to scream it. Killed. A second time. By that Windrunner. That insolent mortal, who thought his victory was due to his *skill* and not raw luck!

The Pursuer screamed again, glad for the sound to accompany his fury. His voice echoed; he was someplace dark, but enclosed. That made him pause. Shouldn't he . . . be out in the storm?

"Are you quite done, Defeated One?" a voice said in their language, but with no rhythm.

The Pursuer sat up, twisting to look around. "Who dares call me—" He cut off as he saw who stood on the other side of the room, lit only by a Voidlight sphere held casually in his hand: a sleek figure looking out a dark window, his back to the Pursuer. The figure had twisting horns on his head and carapace that reflected the light wrong. He always ripped off his natural carapace formations at each rebirth, then replaced them with metal inclusions. They were incorporated into his body by Voidlight healing and his own special talents.

El. The one with no title.

The Pursuer silenced himself. He didn't fear this Fused. He feared no one. But . . . to El, he did not complain.

"Where am I?" the Pursuer asked instead. "Why have I been reborn so quickly? I was on Braize for barely a day before I felt the pull."

"We didn't want to wait," El said softly, still facing away from the Pursuer. No rhythms. El was forbidden rhythms. "So we had it done the old way. The way before the storms."

"I thought Odium wasn't doing that any longer."

"Our new god made an exception, Defeated One."

The Pursuer grunted, picking himself up off the ground. "They gave your title to another, you know. A human."

"I've heard."

"Disrespectful," the Pursuer said to Derision. "It should have remained unused. Give me that Voidlight. I need to recharge myself, to earn back my legacy."

"Earn back?"

The Pursuer forced himself to keep his tone respectful, to not shout. The one with no title could be . . . difficult. "I will hunt the mortal who killed me," the Pursuer said. "I will kill him, and then anyone he ever loved. I will murder mortal after mortal until my vengeance is recognized, my atonement made. I assume you all know this, if you couldn't wait for me to be reborn. So give me that *damn* Voidlight."

El turned, smiling in the shadows. "It is for you, Lezian."

"Excellent," the Pursuer said, stalking forward.

"But you mistook me," El said. "When we said we did not want to have to wait for your rebirth, it was not your convenience that troubled us, but mine. I am very curious, you see, and you were the sole appropriate subject."

"Subject for what?" the Pursuer asked, reaching the window and looking out over Kholinar at night.

"Oh, to see if this really works." El raised the Voidlight sphere . . . and the Pursuer saw it was attached to a knife. Did the Light look wrong somehow? Warping the air around the gemstone?

"I think this might hurt," El said, then grabbed the Pursuer by the front of his beard. "Enjoy this final Passion, Defeated One."

He plunged the knife down as the Pursuer struggled.

And his soul ripped itself apart.

❖

Kaladin walked the now-bright streets of the Breakaway, bathed in cool steady light from above. The transformation the tower had undergone already was amazing. The air had become as warm as it was in Azir, an envelope of temperate weather that extended out to the fields.

People breathed more easily now. The entire tower was not only properly ventilated, it had water running through hidden pipes into many rooms, like they had in rich cities such as Kharbranth. And that was just the beginning. While some rooms in the tower had once held normal wooden doors, many others had stone doors that opened to the touch. They hadn't realized how many rooms they'd missed while exploring because they'd been closed when the tower had last shut down. The place was truly a wonder.

He finally found the merchant shop Lift had told Dalinar about. Though the hour was growing late, the market was busy with people celebrating, so a lot of the shops were open, this one included. Kaladin was directed to a bin of salvage, and he began rifling through it, Syl on his shoulder. He found Rock's razor. And some of Sigzil's brushpens. And . . .

He held up a miniature wooden horse, carved in exacting detail.

Syl breathed out an awed sound.

"I lost this before coming to the Shattered Plains," Kaladin said. "I lost this in *Alethkar*. Tien gave it to me the day we were recruited into the army, and it was taken with my other things when I became a slave. How . . ."

He clutched the horse close to his chest. He was so amazed that he walked off, and had to come running back to pay for what he'd taken. After that, he trotted back toward the tavern. He'd promised earlier that he would meet Dabbid, Noril, and the others he'd rescued from the monastery sick rooms, to decompress from yesterday's events.

Kaladin would do as Dalinar asked, and go to save the Herald Ishi. That was for tomorrow, however. Today, Kaladin had another promise to keep. After all, he'd told Teft he would join these meetings and start taking care of himself.

.·.

Dalinar felt energized as he smelled the crisp cool air of the mountains. He stood at the very top of the tower, drinking it in while holding Navani, her warmth pressed against him. The sun had set, and he'd had enough of reports for the day. He wanted time with his wife and to look at the stars.

"I should have known you'd find a way out of it on your own," he whispered to Navani as Nomon bathed them in light. "I should have seen your potential."

She squeezed his arms. "I didn't see it either. I spent a long time refusing to do so."

Dalinar heard a rumbling in his mind. Not angry rumbling though. More . . . contemplative.

"The Stormfather doesn't know what to make of this," Dalinar said. "I think he finds it strange. Apparently, his Bondsmith and the Nightwatcher's Bondsmith sometimes had relationships, but the Sibling's Bondsmith was always apart."

"The Sibling is . . . curious that way," Navani said. "I'll introduce you, once they are ready. It might take them time."

"As long as it's within ten days," Dalinar said. "I can't guarantee what will happen after then."

"That deal you made . . ." she said.

"I'm sorry. I had to make an agreement while I had him. It isn't everything we wanted, but—"

"It's a good deal, Dalinar," Navani said. "Inspired, even. We will have peace, even if we have to give up Alethkar. I think we've all been coming to realize that was a probability. Instead, this gives us a chance. I just wish . . . That last bit you agreed to. That worries me."

He nodded. "Yes," he whispered. "I know."

This was his job though. To sacrifice himself, if need be, for everyone else. In that . . . In that Taravangian was right.

It still felt so wrong for Taravangian to be dead. Dalinar would never have a chance to prove to Taravangian that Dalinar's way was correct. Gone. Without a farewell. Burned away in another stupid plot to manipulate Szeth.

"At least we can stop the bloodshed," Navani said. "Tell our troops to hold position and wait for the contest."

"Yes," Dalinar said.

Unless . . . Should Dalinar have insisted the contest happen *sooner*? He didn't feel ready. But would he ever?

Something feels wrong, he thought. *Something has changed. We need to be ready for these next ten days.* He felt that truth like a twisting in his stomach.

"I feel your tension," Navani said.

"I'm second-guessing what I've done," Dalinar said.

"The best information we have indicates this contest is our most reasonable hope of success," Navani said. "And I doubt anyone the enemy presents can best Stormblessed."

"I'm . . . not going to pick Kaladin, gemheart."

"Why?" Navani asked. "He's our best warrior."

"No," Dalinar said. "He's our best soldier. But even if he were in peak fighting shape, I don't think he'd be our best warrior. Or our best killer.

"Wit says the enemy can't violate our agreement, and isn't likely to try to misinterpret it—not intentionally. In fact, Wit seems to think the victory is already ours, but he got what he wanted. Odium will remain trapped either way. I'm worried though. There's more I'm missing; I'm sure of it. At the very least, I think I left Odium too much room to continue fighting in the coming ten days."

"We'll find the answers, Dalinar," Navani said. "We have a goal now. If you can win this contest, that will be enough. We will find a way to live in this new world, with the singers in their lands, and humans in ours."

Navani squeezed his arm again, and he took a deep breath, intent on enjoying this moment. Storms, it felt good to be holding her. Beneath them, the tower's lights shone brightly in the night—and down in the corridors, it was positively *warm*. He'd had to come all the way up here to smell mountain air.

"I should have known," Dalinar repeated. "About you."

"I don't think so," Navani said. "It was a remarkable stroke of luck that I figured it all out."

"Not luck," Dalinar said. "Conviction. Brilliance. I was scared for you, but should have remembered when I was scared *of* you—and realized how much danger the Fused were in by trying to take your fabrials from you. You are incredible. You've *always* been incredible."

She breathed out a long, contented sigh.

"What?" he said.

"It's good to hear someone say that."

He held her for an extended moment of peace. But eventually, their crowns came calling. People came looking for Navani to settle something regarding the tower, and she was forced to leave.

Dalinar lingered on the top of the tower. He settled down on the edge, putting his legs over the side—the place where Kaladin had reportedly leapt into the darkness of the storm.

You were wise to give the Windrunner more time during his fall, the Stormfather said, approaching Dalinar. *You were wise to show . . . mercy.*

"It's an important concept to learn," Dalinar said to him. "The more you study it, the more human you will become."

I do not wish to become human, the Stormfather said. *But perhaps I can learn. Perhaps I can change.*

"That's all it takes," Dalinar said. "A willingness."

You are wrong though. I do understand mercy. I have expressed it, on occasion.

"Really?" Dalinar said, curious. "When?"

117

ONE FINAL GIFT

FOURTEEN MONTHS AGO

Eshonai hit the ground of the chasm in a furious splash. Above, the battle for Narak continued, and the rest of the listeners summoned the Everstorm.

She should be leading them! She was foremost among them! She leaped to her feet and shouted to a dozen horrible rhythms in a row, her voice echoing in the chasm. It did no good. She had been defeated by the human Shardbearer, sent tumbling into the chasms.

She needed to get out of here and find the fight again. She started trudging forward. Though the water came up to her waist, the flow was not swift. It was merely a constant, steady stream from the Weeping—and in Shardplate she was able to walk against the current. Her greaves flooded with chill water.

Which way was which? The lack of light confused her, but after a moment of thinking, she realized she was being silly. She didn't need to go either direction. She needed to go *up*. The fall must have dazed her more than she'd realized.

She picked a rough-feeling section of wall and began clawing her way up. She managed to get halfway to the top—using the awesome gripping strength of Shardplate, the Rhythm of Conceit pounding in her ears. But then the way the chasm wall bulged presented a problem. In the darkness, she couldn't find a proper handhold, and the flashes of lightning above were too brief to help.

Lightning. Was that lightning too frequent, too bright, to be coming from other stormforms? Her own powers had been ruined by the water, naturally. She could barely feel any energy in her; it flooded out the moment it started to build.

What *was* happening? That was the Everstorm coming, wasn't it? Yes, she could feel its power, its energy, its *beauty*. But there was something else.

Listening to the howling wind, she realized what it was. A second storm. A highstorm was coming as well.

She attuned the Rhythm of Panic.

The two storms clashed, making the very ground tremble.

Clinging to the wall within the chasm, Eshonai felt the wind howling above. The lightning made her feel like she was blinking her eyes quickly, light and darkness alternating.

Then she heard a roar. The terrible sound of water surging through the chasm, becoming an incredible wave. She braced herself, but when the water hit, it ripped her off the wall.

It was here, within these highstorm rainwaters, that Eshonai's first battle began: the fight for survival.

She slammed into a rock, her helmet cracking. Escaping Stormlight lit the dark waters as they filled her helmet, suffocating her. She thrashed in the current and managed to grab something hard—an enormous boulder lodged into the center of the chasm.

With a heave, she pulled herself out of the water. A few precious moments later her helmet emptied, letting her gasp for air.

I'm going to die, she thought, the Rhythm of Destruction pounding in her ears. Water thundered around her, splashing her armor, and lightning spasmed in the sky above. *I'm going to die . . . as a slave.*

No.

An ember within Eshonai came alive. The part of herself she'd reserved, the part that would not be contained. The part that made her let Thude and the others escape. It was the core of who she was: a person who had insisted on leaving the camps to explore, a person who had always longed to see what was over the next hill.

A person who would *not be held captive.*

That was when her second battle began.

Eshonai screamed, trying to banish the Rhythm of Destruction. If she was to die here, she would die as herself! It was a highstorm. In highstorms, transformations came upon all people, listeners and humans alike. Within a highstorm, death walked hand in hand with salvation, singing a harmony.

Eshonai began summoning her Blade—but in a rumbling flash, her boulder shifted and she lost her grip. The Rhythm of Panic ruled her briefly as she was again submerged. Lightning flashing above made the water seem to glow as she was smashed into one chasm wall, then another.

Not Panic. Not your rhythms.

I reject you.
My life. My death.
I WILL BE FREE.

Sunken deep in the water, Eshonai summoned her Blade and rammed it into the chasm wall. For some reason, she thought she could hear its voice, far away. Screaming?

She clung to it anyway—holding steady before the current. She banished all rhythms, but she could not breathe. Darkness began to close in upon her. Her lungs stopped burning. As if . . . as if everything was going to be all right . . .

There. A tone. The strange, haunting one she'd heard when taking warform. It seemed . . . one of the pure tones of Roshar. It began a stately rhythm. Then a second tone, chaotic and angry, appeared beside it. The two drew closer, closer, then snapped together.

They melded into harmony, making a song of Honor and Odium both. A song for a singer who could fight, but also for a soldier who wanted to lay down her sword. She found this tone as, in the blackness, a small spren—shaped like a shooting star—appeared ahead of her.

Eshonai strained, reaching, clawing.

Her head came above water, and then her helm blessedly emptied. The rush of the river was slowing. She gasped sweet air, but then her hand slipped from her sword, and she slipped back under the water and was towed away—though with less force than before.

She attuned the rhythm. The Rhythm of War, the rhythm of victories and losses. The rhythm of a life at its end. To its beats, she resummoned her Blade and rammed it into the ground, holding it tightly as the waters slowed further.

She would not die. She would *live*. She *was* strong enough. Her journey was not at an end. *Not. Yet.*

She held on, belligerent, until the water slowed. Until the weight of her Plate was enough to resist the current without her effort, and she slumped against the bottom of the chasm, her back to the wall, water streaming over her.

She felt at her side, where the Plate had broken—as had her body. She bled from a deep gash here, her carapace ripped away. Each breath came as a ragged, sodden mess, and she tasted blood.

But in her mind, she cycled through the rhythms of her childhood. Awe. Confidence. Mourning. Determination. Then Peace.

She had lost the first battle.

But she had *won* the second.

And so, to the Rhythm of Victory, she closed her eyes. And found herself drifting in a place full of light.

What is this? Eshonai thought.

You were highly Invested when you died, a voice said. It rumbled with the sound of a thousand storms, echoing through her. So you persist. For a short time.

Invested? Eshonai thought.

You were Radiant when you died. You couldn't say the Words, under the water, but I accepted them anyway. How do you think You survived that long without breathing?

She floated. *So . . . this is my soul?*

Some would call it that, said the Rider of Storms. Some would say it is a spren formed by the power you left, imprinted with your memories. Either way, this is the end. You will pass into eternity soon, and even I cannot see what is beyond.

How long? Eshonai asked.

Minutes. Not hours.

She had no eyes to close, but she relaxed in the light. Floating. She could hear the rhythms. All of them at once, with accompanying songs.

What did it mean, then? she asked as she waited. *Life.*

Meaning is a thing of mortals, the Rider said. It is not a thing of storms.

That's sad.

Is it? he asked. I should think it encouraging. Mortals search for meaning, so it is proper they should create it. You get to decide what it meant, Eshonai. What you meant.

If I decide, then I failed, she thought. *I gave my people to the enemy. I died alone, defeated. I betrayed the gift of my ancestors. I am a shame to all previous listeners.*

I would think the opposite, the Rider said. In the end, you made the same choice as your ancestors. You gave away power for freedom. You know those ancient listeners as few ever have, or ever will.

That gave her peace as she felt her essence begin to stretch. As if it were moving toward something distant.

Thank you, she said to the Rider.

I did nothing. I watched you fall and did not stop it.

The rain cannot stop the bloodshed, she said, fading. *But it washes the world afterward anyway. Thank you.*

I could have done more, the Rider replied. Perhaps I should have.

It . . . is enough. . . .

No, he said. I can give you one final gift.

Eshonai stopped stretching, and instead found herself pulled toward something powerful. She had no eyes, but she suddenly had an awareness—

the storm. She had become *the storm*. She felt every rumble of thunder as her heartbeat.

WATCH, the Rider said. YOU WANTED TO KNOW WHAT WAS BEYOND THE NEXT HILL. SEE THEM ALL.

She soared with him, enveloping the land, flying above it. Her rain bathed each and every hill, and the Rider let her see the world with the eyes of a god. Everywhere the wind blew, she was. Everything the rain touched, she felt. Everything the lightning revealed, she knew.

She flew for what felt like an eternity, sustained by the Rider's own essence. She saw humans in infinite variety. She saw the captive parshmen— but saw the hope for their freedom. She saw creatures, plants, chasms, mountains, snows . . . she passed it *all*. Everything.

The entire world. She *saw* it. Every little piece was a part of the rhythms. The world *was* the rhythms. And Eshonai, during that transcendent ride, understood how it fit together.

It was wonderful.

When the Rider finished his passage—exhausted and limping as he passed into the ocean beyond Shinovar—she felt him let go. She faded, but this time she felt her soul *vibrating*. She understood the rhythms as no one ever could without having seen the world as she had.

FAREWELL, ESHONAI, the Rider of Storms said. FAREWELL, RADIANT.

Bursting with songs, Eshonai let herself pass into the eternities, excited to discover what lay on the other side.

DIRTY TRICKS

W it strolled the hallways of Elhokar's old palace on the Shattered Plains, searching for an audience. He flipped a coin in the air, then caught it before snapping his hand forward and spreading his fingers to show that the coin had vanished. But of course it was secretly in his other hand, palmed, hidden from sight.

"Storytelling," he said to the hallway, "is essentially about cheating."

He tucked the coin into his belt with a quick gesture, keeping up the flourishes of his other hand as a distraction. In a moment he could present both hands empty before him. He added to the theatrics by pushing back his sleeves.

"The challenge," he said, "is to make everyone believe you've lived a thousand lives. Make them *feel* the pain you have not felt, make them *see* the sights you have not seen, and make them *know* the truths that you have made up."

The coin appeared in his hand, though he'd simply slipped it out of his belt again. He rolled it across his knuckles, then made it split into two— because it had always been two coins stuck together. He tossed those up, caught them, and then made them appear to be four after adding the two he'd been palming in his other hand.

"You use the same dirty tricks for storytelling," Wit said, "as you do for fighting in an alley. Get someone looking the wrong direction so you can clock them across the face. Get them to anticipate a punch and brace themselves, so you can reposition. Always hit them where they aren't prepared."

With a flourish, he presented both hands forward, empty again. On his coat, Design made a peppy humming sound. "I found one!" she said. "In your belt!"

"Hush," Wit said. "Let the audience be amazed."

"The audience?"

Wit nodded to the side, where a few odd spren were following in the air. Almost invisible, and trailing red light. Windspren—but the wrong color. She was expanding her influence, that old one was. He was curious where it would lead. Also horrified. But the two emotions were not mutually exclusive.

"I don't think they care about your tricks," Design said.

"*Everyone* cares about my tricks."

"But you can make the coins vanish with Lightweaving," she said. "So it doesn't matter how many you hide in your belt. And if you do something amazing, everyone will assume it was done with Surgebinding!"

Wit sighed, tossing four coins in the air, then catching them and presenting one solitary coin.

"They don't even use those for money here," Design added. "So you'll only distract them. Use spheres."

"Spheres glow," Wit said. "And they're tough to palm."

"Excuses."

"My life is *only* excuses." He wound the coin across his knuckles. "The illusion without Lightweaving is superior, Design."

"Because it's fake?"

"Because the audience *knows* it's fake," Wit said. "When they watch and let themselves be amazed, they are *joining in* the illusion. They're giving you something vital. Something powerful. Something *essential.* Their belief.

"When you and the audience both start a performance knowing that a lie is going to be presented, their willing energy vibrates in tune with yours. It propels you. And when they walk away at the end, amazed but knowing they've been lied to—with their permission—the performance lingers in their minds. Because the lie was real somehow. Because they know that if they were to rip it apart, they could know how it was done. They realize there must have been flaws they could have caught. Signs. Secrets."

"So . . . it's better . . ." Design said, "because it's worse than an illusion using real magic?"

"Exactly."

"That's stupid."

Wit sighed. He bounced his coin off the ground with a metallic *pling,* then caught it. "Would you go bother someone else for a while?"

"Okay!" Design said excitedly. She moved off his coat and to the floor, then zipped away. His audience of corrupted windspren trailed after her. Traitors.

Wit started down a side hallway, but then felt something. A tingling that made his Breaths go wild.

Ah . . . he thought. He'd been expecting this; it was why he had left the tower, after all. Odium couldn't find him there.

He hiked to Elhokar's former sitting room and made himself available—visible, easy to reach. Then, when the *presence* entered the nondescript stone chamber, Wit bowed.

"Welcome, Rayse!" Wit said. "It's been not nearly long enough."

I noticed your touch on the contract, a dramatic voice said in his head.

"You've always been a clever one," Wit said. "Was it my diction that clued you in, my keen bargaining abilities, or the fact that I included my *name* in the text?"

What game do you play here?

"A game of sense."

. . . What?

"Sense, Odium. The only kind I have is nonsense. Well, and some cents, but cents are nonsense here too—so we can ignore them. Scents are mine aplenty, and you never cared for the ones I present. So instead, the sense that matters is the sense Dalinar sensibly sent you."

I hate you.

"Rayse, dear," Wit said, "you're supposed to be an idiot. Say intelligent things like that too much, and I'll need to reevaluate. I know you adjusted the contract, trying for an advantage. How does it feel to know that Dalinar bested you?"

I shall have my vengeance, Odium said. *Even if it takes an eternity, Cephandrius, I* will *destroy you.*

"Enjoy that!" Wit said, striding toward the door. "Let me know how the brooding treats you. I spent a century doing it once, and I think it improved my complexion."

So interesting, Odium said. *How did I never see you there, in all my planning . . . Tell me, whom would you pick as champion? If you were in my place?*

"Why does it matter?" Wit asked.

Humor me.

Wit cocked his head. There was something odd about this change in tone from Odium. Asking whom Wit would choose? Rayse wouldn't care to know.

Never mind, Odium said quickly. *It matters not. Whomever I pick, they will destroy Dalinar's champion! Then I will use him, and my minions on this planet, to finally do whatever I wish!*

"Yes, but where will you find that many willing horses . . ." Wit said, continuing on his way out the door. He started whistling as Odium's presence remained behind. That had gone *exactly* as he'd imagined. Except that last part. He slowed, turning the words over in his mind.

Was Rayse growing more thoughtful? Wit didn't need to worry, did he?

After all this, Odium would be safely imprisoned, no matter what happened. There was no way out. . . .

Unless . . .

Wit's breath caught, but then he forced himself to keep whistling and walking.

A power *slammed* into him from behind. A golden energy, infinite and deadly. Wit's eyes went wide, and he gasped, sensing something horribly *wrong* about that power.

I have made an error, I see, the power said, soft and thoughtful. *I am new to this. I should not have pushed for information. It's all about giving you what you expect. Even a being thousands of years old can be tricked. I know this from personal experience now.*

"Who are you?" Wit whispered.

Odium, the power said. *Let me see . . . I cannot harm you. But here, you have used this other Investiture to store your memories, haven't you? Because you've lived longer than a mortal should, you need to put the excess memories somewhere. I can't see your mind, but I can see these, can't I?*

For the first time in a long, long while, Wit felt true terror. If Odium destroyed the Breaths that held his memories . . .

I don't believe this will cause you actual harm . . . Odium said. *Yes, it seems my predecessor's agreements will allow me to—*

Wit stopped in the hallways of Elhokar's old palace on the Shattered Plains. He searched around, then cocked his head. Had he heard something?

He shook his head and continued forward, looking for an audience. He flipped a coin in the air, then caught it before snapping his hand forward and spreading his fingers to show that the coin had vanished. But of course it was secretly in his other hand, palmed, hidden from sight.

"Storytelling," he said to the empty hallway, "is essentially about cheating."

He tucked the coin into his belt with a quick gesture, keeping up the flourishes of his other hand as a distraction. Then he heard a *pling* as something slipped free of his belt. He stopped and found one of his fake coins on the ground, the ones that could be stuck together to appear as one.

But just one half? That should have been safely tucked away in the little pocket hidden in his shirt. He picked it up, glanced around to see that no one had noticed the mistake.

"Pretend you didn't see that, Design," he said.

But she wasn't there on his coat. Storming spren. Had she slipped away when he hadn't been looking? He put a hand to his head, feeling an odd disorientation.

Something was wrong. But what?

"The challenge . . ." he said, tucking away the fake coin, "is to make everyone believe you've lived a thousand lives. . . . Make them *feel* the pain, the sights, the truths . . ."

Damn. It was wrong somehow. "You use the same dirty tricks for storytelling," Wit whispered, "as you do for fighting in an alley. Always be ready to hit them where they aren't prepared."

But no one was listening. Hadn't there been a couple of Sja-anat's minions following him earlier? He vaguely remembered . . . Design chasing them away?

Wit stared around himself, but then felt something. A tingling that made his Breaths go wild.

Ah . . . he thought. He'd been expecting this; it was why he had left the tower. Odium couldn't find him there.

He hiked the short distance to Elhokar's former sitting room and made himself available—visible, easy to reach. Then, when the *presence* entered the nondescript stone chamber, Wit bowed.

"Welcome, Rayse!" Wit said. "It's been not nearly long enough."

I noticed your touch on the contract, a dramatic voice said in his head.

"You've always been a clever one," Wit said. "Was it my brilliant prose that clued you in, my keen bargaining abilities, or the fact that I included my *name* right there for you to read?"

What game do you play here?

"A game of sense."

. . . What?

"Sense, Odium. The only kind I have is nonsense. Well, and some cents . . ." He glanced down at the coin he still held in his hand, then cocked his head.

I hate you.

"Rayse," Wit said, looking up, "you're supposed to be an idiot. Say intelligent things like that too much, and I'll need to reevaluate. . . . Anyway, I know you adjusted the contract, trying for an advantage. How does it feel to know that Dalinar Kholin, a simple mortal, has gotten the better of you?"

I shall have my vengeance, Odium said. *Even if it takes an eternity, Cephandrius, I will destroy you.*

"Enjoy that!" Wit said, striding toward the door. "Let me know how you enjoy the time with yourself. The Beyond knows, no one *else* can stand your company."

It doesn't matter! Odium roared. *My champion will destroy Dalinar's, and then I will use him and my other minions here to do whatever I wish!*

"Yes, well," Wit said from the door, "once you're done, at least try to remember to wash your hands." He slammed the door, then spun and continued on his way. He tried to find a tune to whistle, but each one sounded wrong. Something was fiddling with his perfect pitch.

Odium's presence had remained behind. Was . . . something wrong?

Don't trouble yourself, he thought. *This is working.*

After all, Wit's first face-to-face meeting with Odium in over a thousand years had gone *exactly* as he had imagined.

THE END OF

Book Four of

THE STORMLIGHT ARCHIVE

ENDNOTE

Burdens, Our Calling.
Songs of Home, a knowledge:
Knowing a Home of Songs, called our burden.

—Ketek written by El, Fused scholar of human art forms,
to commemorate the restoration of the Sibling

Poem is curious in its intentional weighting of the last line, where Alethi poets traditionally weight the center word and build the poem around it. Singers, it can be seen, have a different interpretation of the art form.

ARS ARCANUM

THE TEN ESSENCES AND THEIR HISTORICAL ASSOCIATIONS

NUMBER	GEMSTONE	ESSENCE	BODY FOCUS	SOULCASTING PROPERTIES	PRIMARY / SECONDARY DIVINE ATTRIBUTES
1 Jes	Sapphire	Zephyr	Inhalation	Translucent gas, air	Protecting / Leading
2 Nan	Smokestone	Vapor	Exhalation	Opaque gas, smoke, fog	Just / Confident
3 Chach	Ruby	Spark	The Soul	Fire	Brave / Obedient
4 Vev	Diamond	Lucentia	The Eyes	Quartz, glass, crystal	Loving / Healing
5 Palah	Emerald	Pulp	The Hair	Wood, plants, moss	Learned / Giving
6 Shash	Garnet	Blood	The Blood	Blood, all non-oil liquid	Creative / Honest
7 Betab	Zircon	Tallow	Oil	All kinds of oil	Wise / Careful
8 Kak	Amethyst	Foil	The Nails	Metal	Resolute / Builder
9 Tanat	Topaz	Talus	The Bone	Rock and stone	Dependable / Resourceful
10 Ishi	Heliodor	Sinew	Flesh	Meats, flesh	Pious / Guiding

The preceding list is an imperfect gathering of traditional Vorin symbolism associated with the Ten Essences. Bound together, these form the Double Eye of the Almighty, an eye with two pupils representing the creation of plants and creatures. This is also the basis for the hourglass shape that was often associated with the Knights Radiant.

Ancient scholars also placed the ten orders of Knights Radiant on this list, alongside the Heralds themselves, who each had a classical association with one of the numbers and Essences.

I'm not certain yet how the ten levels of Voidbinding or its cousin the Old Magic fit into this paradigm, if indeed they can. My research suggests that, indeed, there should be another series of abilities that is even more esoteric than the Voidbindings. Perhaps the Old Magic fits into those, though I am beginning to suspect that it is something entirely different.

Note that I currently believe the concept of the "Body Focus" to be more a matter of philosophical interpretation than an actual attribute of this Investiture and its manifestations.

THE TEN SURGES

As a complement to the Essences, the classical elements celebrated on Roshar, are found the Ten Surges. These, thought to be the fundamental forces by which the world operates, are more accurately a representation of the ten basic abilities offered to the Heralds, and then the Knights Radiant, by their bonds.

> **Adhesion:** The Surge of Pressure and Vacuum
> **Gravitation:** The Surge of Gravity
> **Division:** The Surge of Destruction and Decay
> **Abrasion:** The Surge of Friction
> **Progression:** The Surge of Growth and Healing, or Regrowth
> **Illumination:** The Surge of Light, Sound, and Various Waveforms
> **Transformation:** The Surge of Soulcasting
> **Transportation:** The Surge of Motion and Realmatic Transition
> **Cohesion:** The Surge of Strong Axial Interconnection
> **Tension:** The Surge of Soft Axial Interconnection

ON THE CREATION OF FABRIALS

Five groupings of fabrial have been discovered so far. The methods of their creation are carefully guarded by the artifabrian community, but they appear to be the work of dedicated scientists, as opposed to the more mystical Surgebindings once performed by the Knights Radiant. I am more and more convinced that the creation of these devices requires forced enslavement of transformative cognitive entities, known as "spren" to the local communities.

ALTERING FABRIALS

Augmenters: These fabrials are crafted to enhance something. They can create heat, pain, or even a calm wind, for instance. They are powered—like all fabrials—by Stormlight. They seem to work best with forces, emotions, or sensations.

The so-called half-shards of Jah Keved are created with this type of fabrial attached to a sheet of metal, enhancing its durability. I have seen fabrials of this type crafted using many different kinds of gemstone; I am guessing that any one of the ten Polestones will work.

Diminishers: These fabrials do the opposite of what augmenters do, and generally seem to fall under the same restrictions as their cousins. Those artifabrians who have taken me into confidence seem to believe that even greater fabrials are possible than what have been created so far, particularly in regard to augmenters and diminishers.

PAIRING FABRIALS

Conjoiners: By infusing a ruby and using methodology that has not been revealed to me (though I have my suspicions), you can create a conjoined pair of gemstones. The process requires splitting the original ruby. The two halves will then create parallel reactions across a distance. Spanreeds are one of the most common forms of this type of fabrial.

Conservation of force is maintained; for instance, if one is attached to a heavy stone, you will need the same strength to lift the conjoined fabrial that you would need to lift the stone itself. There appears to be some sort of process used during the creation of the fabrial that influences how far apart the two halves can go and still produce an effect.

Reversers: Using an amethyst instead of a ruby also creates conjoined halves of a gemstone, but these two work in creating *opposite* reactions. Raise one, and the other will be pressed downward, for instance.

These fabrials have only just been discovered, and already the possibilities for exploitation are being conjectured. There appear to be some unexpected limitations to this form of fabrial, though I have not been able to discover what they are.

WARNING FABRIALS

There is only one type of fabrial in this set, informally known as the Alerter. An Alerter can warn one of a nearby object, feeling, sensation, or phenomenon. These fabrials use a heliodor stone as their focus. I do not know whether this is the only type of gemstone that will work, or if there is another reason heliodor is used.

In the case of this kind of fabrial, the amount of Stormlight you can infuse into it affects its range. Hence the size of gemstone used is very important.

WINDRUNNING AND LASHINGS

Reports of the Assassin in White's odd abilities have led me to some sources of information that, I believe, are generally unknown. The Windrunners were an order of the Knights Radiant, and they made use of two primary types of Surgebinding. The effects of these Surgebindings were known—colloquially among the members of the order—as the Three Lashings.

BASIC LASHING: GRAVITATIONAL CHANGE

This type of Lashing was one of the most commonly used Lashings among the order, though it was not the easiest to use. (That distinction belongs to the Full Lashing below.) A Basic Lashing involved revoking a being's or object's spiritual gravitational bond to the planet below, instead temporarily linking that being or object to a different object or direction.

Effectively, this creates a change in gravitational pull, twisting the energies of the planet itself. A Basic Lashing allowed a Windrunner to run up walls, to send objects or people flying off into the air, or to create similar effects. Advanced uses of this type of Lashing would allow a Windrunner to make himself or herself lighter by binding part of his or her mass upward. (Mathematically, binding a quarter of one's mass upward would halve a person's effective weight. Binding half of one's mass upward would create weightlessness.)

Multiple Basic Lashings could also pull an object or a person's body downward at double, triple, or other multiples of its weight.

FULL LASHING: BINDING OBJECTS TOGETHER

A Full Lashing might seem very similar to a Basic Lashing, but they worked on very different principles. While one had to do with gravitation, the other had to do with the force (or Surge, as the Radiants called them) of Adhesion—binding objects together as if they were one. I believe this Surge may have had something to do with atmospheric pressure.

To create a Full Lashing, a Windrunner would infuse an object with Stormlight, then press another object to it. The two objects would become bound together with an extremely powerful bond, nearly impossible to break. In fact, most materials would themselves break before the bond holding them together would.

REVERSE LASHING: GIVING AN OBJECT A GRAVITATIONAL PULL

I believe this may actually be a specialized version of the Basic Lashing. This type of Lashing required the least amount of Stormlight of any of the three Lashings. The Windrunner would infuse something, give a mental command, and create a *pull* to the object that yanked other objects toward it.

At its heart, this Lashing created a bubble around the object that imitated its spiritual link to the ground beneath it. As such, it was much harder for the Lashing to affect objects touching the ground, where their link to the planet was strongest. Objects falling or in flight were the easiest to influence. Other objects could be affected, but the Stormlight and skill required were much more substantial.

LIGHTWEAVING

A second form of Surgebinding involves the manipulation of light and sound in illusory tactics common throughout the cosmere. Unlike the variations present on Sel, however, this method has a powerful Spiritual element, requiring not just a full mental picture of the intended creation, but some level of Connection to it as well. The illusion is based not simply upon what the Lightweaver imagines, but upon what they *desire* to create.

In many ways, this is the most similar ability to the original Yolish variant, which excites me. I wish to delve more into this ability, with the hope to gain a full understanding of how it relates to cognitive and spiritual attributes.

SOULCASTING

Essential to the economy of Roshar is the art of Soulcasting, in which one form of matter is directly transformed into another by changing its spiritual nature. This is performed on Roshar via the use of devices known as Soulcasters, and these devices (the majority of which appear to be focused on turning stone into grain or flesh) are used to provide mobile supply for armies or to augment local urban food stores. This has allowed kingdoms on Roshar—where fresh water is rarely an issue, because of highstorm rains—to field armies in ways that would be unthinkable elsewhere.

What intrigues me most about Soulcasting, however, are the things we can infer about the world and Investiture from it. For example, certain gemstones are requisite in producing certain results—if you wish to produce grain, your Soulcaster must both be attuned to that transformation *and* have an emerald (not a different gemstone) attached. This creates an economy based on the relative values of what the gemstones can create, not upon their rarity. Indeed, as the chemical structures are identical for several of these gemstone varieties, aside from trace impurities, the *color* is the most important part—not their actual axial makeup. I'm certain you will find this relevance of hue quite intriguing, particularly in its relationship to other forms of Investiture.

This relationship must have been essential in the local creation of the table I've included above, which lacks some scientific merit, but is intrinsically tied to the folklore surrounding Soulcasting. An emerald can be used to create food—and thus is traditionally associated with a similar Essence. Indeed, on Roshar there are considered to be ten elements; not the traditional four or sixteen, depending upon local tradition.

Curiously, these gemstones seem tied to the original abilities of the Soulcasters who were an order of Knights Radiant—but they don't seem *essential* to the actual operation of the Investiture when performed by a living Radiant. I do not know the connection here, though it implies something valuable.

Soulcasters, the devices, were created to *imitate* the abilities of the Surge of Soulcasting (or Transformation). This is yet *another* mechanical imitation of something once available only to a select few within the bounds of an Invested Art. The Honorblades on Roshar, indeed, may be the very first example of this—from thousands of years ago. I believe this has relevance to the discoveries being made on Scadrial, and the commoditization of Allomancy and Feruchemy.

STONESHAPING

As I've had further occasion to study the use of Investiture on Roshar, and the curious manifestation of it known as Surgebinding, I've found occasion to ruminate further on the nature of Intent and Connection.

The power known as Stoneshaping, as practiced by the orders of Stonewards and Willshapers, is an excellent example of this. This ability manipulates the Surge of Cohesion, and is in many ways a cousin to the axial manipulation known as microkinesis—as both grant the ability to manipulate the forces that bind individual axi together. Fortunately, in my explorations, it appears that Stoneshaping is far less . . . explosive of a power, bounded by the rules that Honor placed upon it to protect from the mistakes that happened on Yolen.

Nevertheless, a practiced Stoneward or Willshaper can mold stone as if it were clay, weakening the bonds between axi. (Indeed, this can be done to other materials as well, I'm led to believe, but stone is the easiest and most common application.) This is not simply a chemical process. Normally, one might expect heat to be involved to excite the axi, but this is not the case. Indeed, it is the Intent of the user that is relevant here.

The stone senses the desire of the Stoneward, and the practitioner is able to shape it through desire as much as through physical force. I don't believe I properly understood the way Investiture responds to the conscious Intent of the user until I read of the interactions of spren and sapient beings on Roshar. There is so much to learn here and so much to explore.

I have sent my best agent to embed among the Stonewards. His research has been most illuminating. It suggests there are three ways we can look at the nature of Intent as it relates to Stoneshaping.

Willingness: Stone seems to be uniformly willing to obey the commands of a Surgebinder attuned to Cohesion. This is curious, as stone is often among the most difficult of materials to work with in Soulcasting—even more difficult than living beings, depending on those beings' emotional, mental, and spiritual states.

Why is stone so eager to change for a Stoneward or Willshaper? What about it makes it so likely to respond to their desires, to incorporate them, and to enjoy the result? Like a willing audience at a comedy, the stone lets the Surgebinder guide it.

Connection: The stone can sense the Intent of the Surgebinder, and even their past. I have reliable reports of stone reaching back through generations of Connection to display events, feelings, emotions, and ideas from long ago. It will shape the faces of Stonewards long dead. It will create pictures of events long forgotten. What I initially dismissed as an inferior form of microkinesis is, indeed, much more focused and—in some ways—more remarkable. There is a divining property to Stoneshaping I had not thought to find.

Command: The Stoneshaper must often make a Command, mental or verbal, to truly control the stone. This is much like many other arcana around the cosmere, and is in itself not that novel. However, I find electrifying the news out of the mountains of Ur, that their current queen seems to have been able to Command the creation of an anti-Investiture. Long theorized, this will be my first true evidence it is possible—and can only be created through Intent.

I think that perhaps Foil, deep within his ocean, would find this information supports my theories over his. And he'd do well to listen to me on this matter if he ever wishes to achieve control over the aethers, as he has insisted is his goal.